PRAISE FOR *AMAZING JOURNEYS*

"...a unique and impressive red, white, and blue-collar collection of refreshing translations of Verne that gives new life to some of the old storyteller's most famous tales."

— *Science Fiction Studies*

"...this new version emphasizes the wit, theatricality, and brilliance captured by the writer in these remarkable tales. Here is a classic series of adventures that, in spite of technological advances, will still enthrall the reader, and should be part of every young person's library."

— *San Francisco Book Review*

AMAZING JOURNEYS

Five Visionary Classics

Jules Verne
(1828–1905)

JULES VERNE

AMAZING JOURNEYS

Five Visionary Classics

In New, Complete Translations by
FREDERICK PAUL WALTER

JOURNEY TO THE CENTER OF THE EARTH
FROM THE EARTH TO THE MOON
CIRCLING THE MOON
20,000 LEAGUES UNDER THE SEAS
AROUND THE WORLD IN 80 DAYS

excelsior editions

AN IMPRINT OF STATE UNIVERSITY OF NEW YORK PRESS

Published by
State University of New York Press, Albany

Translations and critical materials
© 2010 by Frederick Paul Walter

For information, contact
State University of New York Press, Albany, NY
www.sunypress.edu

Production, Laurie Searl
Marketing, Fran Keneston

Library of Congress Cataloging-in-Publication Data

Verne, Jules, 1828–1905.
[Novels. English. Selections]
Amazing journeys : five visionary classics /
in new, complete translations by Frederick Paul Walter.
p. cm.
Includes bibliographical references.
ISBN 978-1-4384-3238-0 (pbk. : alk. paper) 1. Verne, Jules, 1828–1905—Translations into English.
2. Science fiction, French—Translations into English. I. Walter, Frederick Paul. II. Verne, Jules,
1828–1905. Voyage au centre de la terre. English III. Verne, Jules, 1828–1905. De la terre à la lune.
English IV. Verne, Jules, 1828–1905. Autour de la lune. English V. Verne, Jules, 1828–1905.
Vingt mille lieues sous les mers. English VI. Verne, Jules, 1828–1905.
Tour du monde en quatre-vingts jours. English VII. Title.
PQ2469.A2 2010
843'.8—dc22
2009040087

10 9 8 7 6 5 4 3 2 1

Lifelong thanks to

WALTER JAMES MILLER

poet, teacher,
mentor, friend, and
father of Verne studies
in North America

CONTENTS

SCIENCE AND SHOWBIZ:
Going Places with Jules Verne

Frederick Paul Walter

True or not, a favorite Jules Verne anecdote has the famous Frenchman visiting a Paris government official in the 1880s. By then Verne was an international celebrity, and his novels had taken countless readers where nobody had gone before: the ocean depths, the earth's core, the moon, the whole solar system. When Verne entered the official's chambers, the man pushed him into a chair and plumped pillows around him. "Make yourself comfortable, Monsieur Verne," the official urged. "You must be exhausted after all that traveling!"

From his childhood Verne had been fascinated by faraway places. He grew up in the medium-sized French metropolis of Nantes on the Loire River, some thirty miles upstream from a major Atlantic seaport. Shipping and transportation were the leading industrial concerns, long-distance travel was in full swing, steam-powered locomotives and ocean liners were available to the general public. Air travel wasn't so available, but the many well-advertised flights by gas balloon were definitely in the public eye. All of these developments tantalized Jules Verne's young imagination.

BOY AUTHOR

He wrote from his boyhood on, a sample of his poetry surviving from his fourteenth year, half of a novel from his eighteenth (Lottman, 13, 17). By his early twenties Verne was already being paid for his writing, though not munificently. During the 1840s and 1850s, he penned over twenty plays (Margot, 14–16), mostly knockabout farces and the books and lyrics for musical comedies. His first staged work, *The Broken Straws*, enjoyed a professional Paris run of a dozen or so performances in 1850. Over the following decade he kept up the scriptwriting and in addition managed to publish several pieces of short fiction, some of them hinting at his interest in science and its future possibilities.

Another couple decades would go by before Verne turned into a best-selling author, but those early tales already gave off glimmers of the famous novels to come. The science of aeronautics drives his short story "A Journey by Balloon" (1851), likewise one of those death-craving monomaniacs who keep reappearing in his mature fiction. The novelette "Wintering in the Ice" (1855) features a search for a lost sea captain in the subarctic seas, foreshadowing the polar quests in several later works. Another novelette, "Master Zacharius" (1854), unveils the demented, power-hungry side of science, a perspective he would return to in books throughout his career. A third novelette, "The First Ships in the Mexican Navy" (1851), shows young Verne exploiting his source materials as shrewdly as his later self: with just a map and somebody's travel memoirs, he convincingly sketches an inland journey through regions he'd never personally visited (or ever would).

Along with these early yarns, Verne completed about fourteen new scripts (Butcher, 110). A musical comedy, *The Comrades of the Mint Leaf* (1852), had a performance run just shy of a month: a rustic sex farce with a nitwit plotline, its effect is difficult to judge without the music. But an unproduced script that he wrote the following year makes for enjoyable reading and has plenty of recognizable Verne shenanigans: *A Foster Son* (1853) is a racy sitcom full of running gags, nonstop wordplay, bawdy double meanings, and shameless plot twists . . . the piece is hopelessly lightweight, but many of its jokes still work; Verne may not have been a major dramatist, but he *was* a first-rate gag writer and vaudevillian.

Yet another theater piece foreshadows his great novels as clearly as the first short stories: *Mr. Chimpanzee* (1857). Staged in Paris the year after its writing (Jules-Verne, 37), it's a slapstick comedy set to music. However its offbeat setting is a natural history museum, it boasts a speculative science angle that's typical Verne, prehistoric monsters such as the ichthyosaurus and megatherium are among the museum exhibits, and there are allusions to the Count de Buffon, the great French naturalist who would be a frequent source for the masterpieces ahead.[*]

Meanwhile Verne also did some book-length work during those early days: a chatty UK travelogue that he finished in 1860 but never published in his lifetime (today it's available as *Backwards to Britain*). Even so, whether he was generating theater pieces, short fiction, or book-size nonfiction, he had little genuine success till he finally hit on this winning combination: stories of science and exploration . . . that were highly theatrical.

BREAKTHROUGH

When he published his first novel, Verne was already a seasoned pro. He'd been writing for twenty years, and his output had been onstage and in print for over half that time. Then, in 1862, he took a manuscript to an interview with Pierre-Jules Hetzel (1814–1886), described by the author's grandson (Jules-Verne, 54) as "one the greatest publishers France has ever known." Hetzel's stable of writers was a who's who of 19th century French literature: Balzac, Hugo, Zola, Baudelaire, George Sand—and Jules Verne would become his biggest moneymaker.

Verne's manuscript was about balloon travel over Africa and it tackled the crux of the matter. As his grandson wrote a century later (Jules-Verne, 57), "aeronautics was in its infancy. No satisfactory solution had yet been found for steering a balloon." So Verne's book imagined "a balloon that could climb or descend at will to take advantage of the different wind directions at different altitudes." Revised and refined, the tale came out in 1863 as *Five Weeks in a Balloon*. An instant hit, it enjoyed a big print run and was soon turned into actuality by real-life balloonists.

The next year Hetzel had major plans for Verne: he launched one of history's first family magazines, a fortnightly periodical named the *Magasin d'éducation et de récréation* . . . a moniker that today's media whizzes might be tempted to translate as *Facts and Fun*. It grew into one of the century's publishing phenomena (Lottman, 95–96), and Verne could take much of the credit. Hetzel wanted intriguing stories to serialize in his publication, and Verne supplied him with a sequence of adventure novels that were both educational and entertaining, combining up-to-the-minute scientific fact and dramatic exploits spiced with humor. After their serialization Verne's visionary yarns were published in deluxe hardcover editions, and over the years he produced some sixty books in this fashion. Hetzel marketed the whole line under the enticing rubric of *Voyages extraordinaires*, and the English wording *Amazing Journeys* captures both the sense and verve of the French.

---

[*] American Vernian Frank Morlock has created English acting versions of these and other scripts by Jules Verne. They're online at http://jv.gilead.org.il/works.html#plays (accessed November 3, 2009).

At last the ideas in Verne's early short fiction came to full bloom. "Wintering in the Ice," a search for a lost mariner in the North Sea, led to full-scale polar quests in *The Adventures of Captain Hatteras* (1866), *20,000 Leagues Under the Seas* (1870), and *The Fur Country* (1873), not to mention the mighty three-volume search for another missing seaman in *Captain Grant's Children* (1868). As for the aeronautics in his short story "A Journey by Balloon," they supplied ingredients not only for his breakthrough book *Five Weeks in a Balloon* but also for important later novels, including his desert-island masterwork *The Mysterious Island* (1875), his interplanetary comedy *Hector Servadac* (1877), and his tale of aerial warfare *Robur the Conqueror* (1886). Finally his spooky novelette "Master Zacharius," dealing with science's dark, sinister potential, raised concerns he would revisit in novels throughout his career: *20,000 Leagues*, *The Begum's Millions* (1879), *Facing the Flag* (1896), and *Master of the World* (1904). In short, the seeds were there from the start.

FABULOUS FIRST DECADE

For the rest of his life, Verne stayed under contract to the Hetzel publishing house, but his best-remembered books appeared during their first decade together: the five "visionary classics" in this volume. His instincts and skills fully developed, Verne shot like a comet into public view, and he took that public on some staggering first-time journeys: into the earth, to the ocean floor, to the moon, around the globe in record time. His later novels, splendid as many of them are, come off as variations on a theme: in the *The Black Indies* (1877) Verne goes back underground, in *Hector Servadac* back into outer space, in *The Steam House* (1880) and *The Robinson Crusoe School* (1882) back to locales on Phileas Fogg's 80-day itinerary. In that fabulous first decade of 1863–1872, Verne's powers were on full display.

What *were* those powers? Consider this: by some estimates Jules Verne is the "most translated writer in the world," the "most read" of all authors (Butcher, xix). What magic had he mastered to account for this phenomenal standing?

Verne's virtuosity as a storyteller isn't well understood in America and England. A good deal of nonsense has been recycled about him by critics who apparently haven't read his works or studied his life; no need to name names—the bunkum that follows can be found in many reference works and blanket surveys. Several, for instance, describe Verne as a cockeyed optimist whose yarns look on science's bright side, darkening only late in his career. Wildly inaccurate: even the fiction from Verne's youth is jittery about science's potential, as are two of the early novels in this volume. Others, meanwhile, call Verne a stay-at-home, an armchair recluse who journeyed only in his head. Equally untrue: he was an energetic tourist and yachtsman, visiting America and traveling repeatedly around the UK, mainland Europe, and the Mediterranean. Still another contingent claims his fiction is incurably conventional and wedded to bourgeois values. Hopelessly wrong: Verne's heroes are innovators, oddballs, outcasts, rebels, and anti-imperialists.

Finally, and least justified of all, they rate him a stodgy writer, lacking in color, finesse, or talent for characterization. This is more than wrong, it's loony: in their original French these novels bubble with jokes, pranks, theatrics, scientific thrills, and bigger-than-life characters. It's their raddled old Victorian translations that are stodgy—and it's the scholarship relying on them that's lacking. Consequently, before moving on to this volume's accurate *new* translations, this essay intends to celebrate that storytelling virtuosity mentioned above.

Though Verne had no in-depth scientific training, he clearly had a knack for giving the sciences popular appeal. It helped that he also had a knack for legwork and research, and his grandson (Jules-Verne, 58) describes how the famed novels came into being: "A mass of facts are skillfully incorporated into the narrative—facts that by themselves would have remained unattractive or even inaccessible to the general readers that Verne had in mind. In this respect alone, Verne shows himself to be a consummate storyteller." And just how dependable were those vaunted facts? His grandson again: they were "scrupulously accurate and up to date. . . . [He] kept a "respect for accuracy throughout his life. Indeed, on many occasions Hetzel used his influence to get Verne introduced to specialists whose brains he wished to pick."

As a consequence his novels have often been praised for their farseeing science. Walter James Miller, spearheading Verne scholarship in America (Miller, viii), once commented that the Frenchman's two moon novels "anticipated every stage of the actual space effort of the 1960s." And while their nomenclature may be in continual flux, the extinct life forms in *Journey to the Center of the Earth* (1864) or the marine fauna in *20,000 Leagues* can still be found in today's databases and textbooks. Apparently he was a man who never forgot a fact, and his personal library housed thousands of books, clippings, and memoranda. One day the English crime novelist Marie A. Belloc paid both Verne and his library a visit. "The room is lined with bookcases, and in the middle a large table groans under a carefully sorted mass of newspapers, reviews, and scientific reports," she writes (Belloc, 209). "A number of cardboard pigeonholes . . . contain the twenty-odd thousand notes garnered by the author during his long life."

THEATRICAL FLAIR

A zest for science is only part of Verne's magic, the rest is his theatricality. This kicks in immediately, at the research stage. He has a flair for sifting through his subject matter and cherry-picking its most dramatic aspects, its angles that have storytelling and attention-getting potential. He has particular fun with the mores and folkways of far-off cultures: Icelandic cuisine with its 20-year-old butter sauces in *Journey to the Center of the Earth* . . . the Yankee willingness to smoke cigars around high explosives in *From the Earth to the Moon* (1865) . . . the goofy product lines (false teeth and hairpieces) of his traveling salespeople in *Claudius Bombarnac* (1892).

Similarly, when his objectives are educational or he's laying factual groundwork, he can dramatize and sugarcoat with the best of them, adding color with an anecdote, a joke, a parable. In *From the Earth to the Moon*, for instance, you can duplicate the moon's movements (p. 150) simply by strolling around your dinner table . . . or, in Chapter 6 of *Circling the Moon* (1869), a train engineer can illustrate the effect of heat on motion just by applying the brakes. Nor does Verne balk at exaggerating for effect, at overdoing things in a good cause: *20,000 Leagues* is loaded with outsized marine life—25-foot reef sharks, 60-foot narwhals, 185-foot rorquals, even "giant lobsters" and "titanic crabs." As for the prehistoric reptiles in *Journey to the Center of the Earth*, they're familiar to paleontologists, but their sizes ("forty feet wide," "at least a hundred feet long") are heftier than any known fossils.

The astounding punch line to Chapter 36 in the latter book is an example of an additional Verne specialty: the eye-popping plot twist. Others include the switcheroo at the halfway point of *The Mighty Orinoco* (1898) . . . the reverse-English endings of *Around the World in 80 Days* (1872) and *Michael Strogoff*

(1876) . . . the windup of his low comedy *Keraban the Pigheaded* (1883), where Verne paints his title character into the tightest possible corner, then extricates him with a cheeky surprise gimmick. On the other hand he also knows how to get serious with his theatrics: three of the yarns in this volume feature vicious storms at sea, events actually expressive of his characters' inner turmoil. The tempests in *Journey to the Center of the Earth* (pp. 102–4), *20,000 Leagues* (524–25), and *Around the World in 80 Days* (602–4) are among the most horrific in literature—their gale speeds "are four times that of a locomotive shooting along at full throttle," they unleash "lightning bolts like broods of snakes running loose in the sky," they fill the air with "complex noises made up of crashing breakers, howling winds, claps of thunder."

And Verne's terrifying set pieces are sometimes more than just good theater (Walter 2008, 2): they can "strike us at a visceral level, assail our animal essence, prey on our most primitive fears." Among these harrowing episodes: the crisis in *20,000 Leagues* where the submarine runs short of oxygen . . . and the narrator's near-death experience in Chapters 26–28 of *Journey to the Center of the Earth.* If Verne seems flamboyant and prankish elsewhere, in these instances he's all ruthless economy and specificity (Walter 2008, 3): "He doesn't pussyfoot, sentimentalize, or parade strings of adjectives. No, he narrows his narrative to the tightest, leanest, most disquieting details."

ARCHETYPAL CHARACTERS

Two other facets of Verne's theatricality are central to his storytelling power: his large-scale characters and his versatile comedy.

As for the first, he's rarely given credit for his feats of characterization, though Captain Nemo and Phileas Fogg are household words and many of his other creations are now stock figures. In fact his engineers, astronomers, and geologists are true originals for one simple reason: unlike such earlier savants as Faustus, Frankenstein, and Coppelius, Verne's researchers are engaged in recognizable scientific pursuits. Some, such as the naturalist Aronnax in *20,000 Leagues Under the Seas* or Dr. Clawbonny in *The Adventures of Captain Hatteras*, are rational, capable professionals. Others are the original versions of two familiar archetypes, science's yin and yang: the absent-minded professor and the mad inventor.

Earliest of Verne's "nutty professors" is the high-strung Lidenbrock in *Journey to the Center of the Earth:* heart of gold, stressful to live with. His immediate successors include the disoriented Paganel in *Captain Grant's Children* and the oblivious Thomas Black in *The Fur Country*, resident funny men, Verne's designated sources of comic relief. As for the mad inventors and explorers, the maniacs bent on destruction, domination, or some other grim objective, Verne's initial attempt—and a genuinely scary one—is the nameless skyjacker in his short story "A Journey by Balloon." Next comes the pole-seeking Captain Hatteras, who *does* go certifiably mad, then Verne's most complex creation, the multilayered, ambivalent, darkly elusive Captain Nemo. A later figure, the aeronaut Robur, is a Nemo variant: beneficial in *Robur the Conquerer*, bad news in *Master of the World*.

There's more to be said about Captain Nemo, but first a quick look at the obsessives and compulsives who pack Verne's pages. Generally they're played for laughs: the chatterbox Frenchman Ardan . . . the diehard manhunter Inspector Fix . . . and even more extreme, the warmongering J. T. Maston, who tends to go off the deep end in the most literal sense—he nearly topples into a 900-foot well, barely avoids "a nasty fall" off a stage, almost tumbles down the 280-foot tube of a giant telescope, then at last personally brains himself and collapses in a heap. As for female characters, women and wooing scenes are common in Verne's plays but scarce in his fiction: Hetzel's contracts restricted him to adventure writing for a family audience. Yet when women do show up in the novels, they're assertive and independent: the efficient Grauben in *Journey to the Center of the Earth* . . . the tough explorers Paulina Barnett in *The Fur Country* and the titular heroine of *Mrs. Branican* (1891) . . . even the voluptuous Aouda in *Around the World in 80 Days*.

And in one case, finally, a character assumes mythic stature: Captain Nemo is the result of special circumstances, of a character not turning out as planned. At first he was simply one man against the world—though, unlike Dumas's Count of Monte Cristo, a man bent on political rather than private revenge. But the original Captain Nemo had a detailed history, nationality, cause, and antagonist. The published novel specifies *none* of these things and the book's aura and effect are different from nearly anything else in Verne.

 Some of this may have been a lucky accident, but in any event Verne's publisher Pierre-Jules Hetzel was to blame. Like many an editor since, Hetzel could be invasive and tyrannical; today's scholars roast him regularly, not only for his trigger-happy interfering with Verne's texts but also for his profiteering and hard financial bargains. Yet good things sometimes came from his meddling: the political particulars in Verne's first drafts of *20,000 Leagues* worried Hetzel, and Verne ended up steering the book down a new path, a path he hadn't taken since his eerie novelette "Master Zacharius." Clearly it was meant to be. Though far from its author's first intentions, the novel's revamped version became colossally successful and today is often regarded as Verne's magnum opus. Nemo is shadowy, mystifying, numinous, his drives and objectives taking vague shape only near the end. Yet we experience enough of him to see him as human—his sardonic humor, his impressive IQ, his flickers of temper—so when he hates, lashes out, and inflicts fearful suffering, he's the Verne hero who approaches tragic stature. Unlike Fogg, who also has mysterious antecedents, Nemo is never comic material.

But he rises even above tragedy to the otherworldly: his nebulous background gives him a mythic, almost preternatural presence. At the end Captain Nemo grows "astoundingly" in the narrator's mind, evolves into "the Man of the Waters, the Spirit of the Seas," and takes on "superhuman proportions." Ultimately he himself becomes that "shrouded human figure" the narrator recalls from Poe.

NOSE-THUMBING HUMOR

The first English-speaking scholar to look closely at Verne's comedy, Arthur B. Evans (2005, 96–99) calls his novels "humorous, witty, theatrical," repeatedly lauds them for their "humor and wordplay," and finds that "they're teeming with double entendres, authorial 'winks' and self-referential parody." He concludes that "anglophone readers have never been able to savor Verne's wit."

Sad but true. This major aspect of Verne is often missed entirely in his English translations, likewise in their English commentaries. Unfortunately some types of jokes don't carry over from language to language: puns, for instance, with their dependence on soundalikes and multiple meanings. And Verne was a chronic punster, whether he's mauling a maxim of the zoologist Linnaeus (approximated on p. 324), or mingling the sports of knitting and hitting (p. 648 substitutes a different sort of joke). In any case nose-thumbing humor is Verne's bodyguard, and he uses it not only for itself but to lubricate a wide range of snags and bottlenecks: plot slowdowns, dreary technical details, far-fetched developments, even utterly insoluble problems such as the takeoff acceleration in *From the Earth to the Moon*. And as Evans notes (1988, 144), Verne's gag writing covers the waterfront: "slapstick, situation comedy, witticisms, exaggerations, social satire, understatement, ethnic humor, absurdities, black humor, and so on." If the translator has the spunk to look for decent English equivalents, much of this humor *can* cross the Atlantic.

Understatement? A Verne trademark is the deadpan wisecrack. Here's the stoic guide in *Journey to the Center of the Earth:* "He carried economy of motion to the point of stinginess." Or Barbicane after bypassing Texas as the site for his moon shot: "his unpopularity in Texas was on a par with General Santa Anna's." Or the Frenchman Ardan's role aboard the space capsule: "In this miniature cosmos he stood for Gallic impulsiveness and talkativeness, and believe me, these attributes were adequately represented." Self-referential parody? Verne will sometimes kid his own scholarly apparatus, as with his two impish footnotes in *The Mysterious Island* (Walter 1999, 9): "Footnote 1 refers us to Footnote 2, which refers us right back to Footnote 1." Nor, conversely, is there any shortage of humor at the service of graver purposes. Miller (162) calls *From the Earth to the Moon* an "all-out satire on militarism. . . . no writer—not even Aristophanes, Voltaire, or Joseph Heller—has conceived of better ways to satirize war and the military mind."

JULES VERNE'S LEGACY

As stated, the five "visionary classics" in this volume appeared during the incandescent first decade of Verne's collaboration with Hetzel. They're a staggering legacy: *Journey to the Center of the Earth*, the first time-travel novel . . . *From the Earth to the Moon* and *Circling the Moon*, the first hard-science tales of space exploration . . . *20,000 Leagues Under the Seas*, the first novel of a vendetta that's global rather than personal . . . and as for *Around the World in 80 Days*, it remains one of the planet's favorite thrillers to this moment.

The first four are regularly regarded as milestones of science fiction, but Verne also wrote a large number of straight adventure stories, yarns where the sciences are simply geography and sociology. His other achievements in that first decade included *The Adventures of Captain Hatteras*, a fictional conquest of the North Pole forty years before Peary, and one of Verne's most massive works, a tripledecker rescue mission entitled *Captain Grant's Children*. From then on, as previously noted, his novels tended to be variations on a theme. Most were geographic adventures, but aside from the spy thriller *Michael Strogoff* and the desert-island epic *The Mysterious Island*, it's his occasional sorties into scientific speculation that provoke the most interest today: his interplanetary journey *Hector Servadac*, his high-tech gothic novel *Castle in the Carpathians* (1892), his mad-inventor sagas *Facing the Flag* and *Master of the World*, the grisly dystopia he unveils in *The Begum's Millions*.

During much of the 20th century, it was traditional to call Verne "The Father of Science Fiction." This has come under noisy reassessment in recent decades: SF has grown increasingly respectable in many graduate schools, and new approaches are needed for master's theses, doctoral dissertations, and career-building papers. Many who write about Verne have had to duck the conventional wisdom and find new tacks. Unfortunately some of this rethinking has verged on the silly. Certain UK scholars, for instance, insist that Verne had no actual interest in science—somehow forgetting his hundreds of pages on the topics of chemistry, biology, astronomy, geology, paleontology, and meteorology, not to mention nautical and aeronautical engineering. And speaking of the latter, one American critic even claims that Verne's futuristic vehicles were already technically feasible when he wrote about them—ignoring, of course, the famous ones such as the space capsule in the moon novels, the supersub in *20,000 Leagues*, the giant helicopter in *Robur the Conquerer*, the all-terrain walker in *The Steam House*, the mobile landmass in *Propeller Island* (1895), etc.

Even so, the old labeling of Verne as "Father of Science Fiction" has come in for backtalk. Of course the legitimacy of this title has always relied on what one means by "father" and "science fiction": for example, a good case can be made for the genre's springing up in antiquity, in assorted creation myths or Plato's utopias. Once again it depends on how you define SF, both the science part and the fiction part.* To illustrate: if the science has to be a recognizable discipline, if the fiction has to be genuine narrative prose, and if both have to deal with some visionary or speculative development, then a plausible candidate for first SF novel might be Verne's *Journey to the Center of the Earth* with its prehistoric monsters and time-travel motif. Or, if we raise the bar and the science has to be rigorously pragmatic and provable, then the palm might go to Verne's *From the Earth to the Moon*, the pioneering specimen of "hard" SF. But either way there's still a hitch. What about unknown competitors? Earlier works by obscure authors? Stories that fell through the cracks? Citing only French authors, Evans asserts (1988, 2) that there "were many writers of this brand of narrative who preceded [Verne] . . . and remain all but forgotten today."

Finally, and pertinent to the above, it has become trendy in recent years (Mann, 8) to classify Mary Shelley's horror classic *Frankenstein* (1818) as "the first true SF novel." This has been tempting for some Anglophile critics (Wolfe, xix): they can leave Verne out altogether and bookend the form's genesis with two Brits, Shelley and H. G. Wells, "the first real science fiction writers." The snag is that *Frankenstein* itself flatly disagrees with this classification. Shelley's unique novel has been cherished for its seminal insights on human duality and the creator-creation relationship: there's virtually *no recognizable science* onstage in the body of the story, certainly not in the brief "workshop" sequence where Victor Franken-stein fabricates his humanoid creature. Chapter 4 candidly refuses to tell the reader how he manages this: "that cannot be," the text insists, and a leading British literary critic (Sutherland, 29) calls Shelley's writing here "a piece of magnificent Gothic fuzz." Does Victor employ the arts of sorcery, alchemy, or surgery? There isn't a single specific. And that's because Shelley had minimal thematic interest in Victor's labwork; her novel would have proceeded along the same lines had he simply waved a magic wand.

This notion of *Frankenstein* as SF was first proposed by British novelist Brian Aldiss, who claims Shelley imbued her book (Aldiss, 23) with "new scientific ideas" but doesn't say where those ideas actually are in the story. This hasn't kept others from likewise calling the novel true SF. How so? Because (Clute and Nicholls, 1099) Victor builds a "mechanically sound body and shocks it into life." Or because (Mann, 8) Shelley contributes "the added dimension of science" and the monster is "literally shocked into existence by electricity."

The only problem is that nobody seems to have *read* Shelley's novel, at least not recently or carefully. They're confusing the story on the page with the story at the cinema. In the novel the monster is emphatically *not* shocked into life by elec-

---

* The web page http://scifi.about.com/od/scififantasy101/a/SCIFI_defs.htm offers over fifty definitions by critics and practitioners. Most insist on a dash of bona fide science (accessed November 3, 2009).

tricity—that tidbit is from the 1931 Boris Karloff movie! So these folks are fixated on the films, Aldiss, for instance, repeatedly calling Victor "Baron Frankenstein," even though the word "baron" doesn't occur even once in Shelley's text. As for Wolfe's skipping everybody between *Frankenstein* and H. G. Wells, he seems ignorant not just of Shelley but of several SF pioneers—not only Jules Verne but the Americans Poe and Perce, the Russian Mikhailov, the Rosny brothers in France, the time-traveling Twain, even the Britishers Rider Haggard and Conan Doyle, all of whom penned varieties of science fiction before Wells.

Sadly, all scholarship suffers when some participants play fast and loose, and you wonder if this instance is simply nationalistic vanity. Not content with claiming Shakespeare, Austen, and Chaucer, do some Brits also need to claim a first in science fiction? There are precedents for such obfuscating: in 1911–12 when the Norwegian Amundsen raced the Britisher Scott to the South Pole, Amundsen was the first to reach it by over a month. Yet, as a later historian noted (Huntford, 513), the "most astonishing manipulations of facts were performed in order to prove that the British had not been worsted. . . . English schoolchildren were taught that Scott discovered the South Pole." If you can't win playing by the rules, rewrite the rules.

VERNE FOR AMERICANS

Whether or not Verne "fathered" the genre of science fiction, clearly he was the writer who first brought the form to world notice, the writer who first lionized science's achievements and possibilities, and—most crucially—the writer who first produced a *body* of science fiction. Alone among those early authors, he was more than a one-shot wonder, he was an actual career professional: in his lifetime he wrote eighteen SF novels, including half a dozen of the genre's best-known titles. As for their literary standing, one of his major modern successors (Asimov, xii) called Verne's science fiction "the first truly successful tales of this type." And like Asimov himself, the Frenchman also produced a huge amount of engrossing and entertaining work in other genres: adventure, mystery, intrigue, even nonfiction.

Since Verne's era science fiction has come a good way. Yet in some respects science *fact* still hasn't caught up with him. Of the journeys in this volume, only Phileas Fogg's is realistic for today's readers—assuming they can budget the travel dollars. Two others, the moon shot and the *Nautilus*'s underwater voyage, are theoretically possible but well out of reach for civilians. As for a trip to the earth's core, not in this lifetime. What's more, Verne raised other burning questions that have yet to be resolved: one biggie (p. 193) is the issue of "whether life exists on other worlds." Astronomers haven't a definitive answer today any more than they had in 1865. Fiction, of course, has given thousands of answers . . . science none.

To read Jules Verne, then, is to go back to the basics, back to first causes, back to the sparkling source. It isn't surprising that he remains enormously popular around the globe, and even in our English-speaking world new translations and annotated editions of his books keep appearing, some of them titles never previously available in our language. New film versions keep premiering as well. His best-known books continue to thrive on high school reading lists.

Even so, his books can be a consumer challenge. Here in America Verne is for sale in so many adaptations and condensations: decent English renderings of the full-length originals are often tricky to come by. Why? In the 19th century (Taves and Micheluk, xi), "Verne's stories were rushed into publication—poorly translated, extensively abridged, and even censored for American and British readers." Though improved translations have since entered the U.S. and UK markets, truncated and error-ridden versions of his most famous titles are still rampant.

The book in your hands is an effort to solve the problem. It's a handy omnibus volume of Verne's best-loved novels in new, accurate, communicative translations. These five classics are more than household words, they're joyous parts of our American heritage, from their films and Saturday morning cartoons to their connections with the U.S.S. *Nautilus*, the NASA space missions, and our other technological triumphs. And the USA itself is crucial to these novels: two have major American sequences, one divides its time between America and outer space, and still another takes place entirely in the U.S. So this volume is targeted to the American public: these are reader-friendly translations, translations complete down to the smallest substantive detail, translations that aim to convey the humor, theatricality, and scientific excitement this essay has been honoring.

For American purchasers, then, the texts convert metric figures to feet, miles, pounds, and other U.S. equivalents. The Americana, too, will be convincing for U.S. readers, sparing you the eye-rolling moments that can occur with overseas translators. In addition these new translations benefit not only from current Verne scholarship but from today's worldwide access to academic, institutional, and educational databases: it's possible to compare and cross-check multiple versions of the original French, and it's possible, too, to render the marine biology in *20,000 Leagues*, the surface features in *Circling the Moon*, and the obscure locales on Phileas Fogg's itinerary with unprecedented clarity and accuracy.

Finally these translations work to suggest Verne's style and tone—the stealthy wit, irreverent prankishness, tale-spinning virtuosity, and showbiz flamboyance of one of literature's leading humorists and satirists. This is a Verne almost completely unknown to Americans . . . yet a Verne who has an uncannily American mindset.

Specialists, educators, and students are encouraged to consult the Textual Notes starting on p. 657: these pinpoint the policies, priorities, and textual decisions underlying the translations. In preparing this volume I've run up unpayable debts to a host of kindly individuals: my wife Barbara Ann Bryant for her boundless patience and support; leading SF novelist Jane Lindskold for her invaluable mentoring; Dr. Gary Dunham, SUNY Press's Executive Director, for his dedication to Jules Verne and good books in general; Laurie Searl, Senior Production Editor, for her gifts of ingenuity and diplomacy; Dr. Alan Hale, President of the Earthrise Institute, for help with the cosmology in *From the Earth to the Moon;* and Verne specialists Dr. William Butcher, Dr. Arthur B. Evans, Dennis Kytasaari, Dr. Julia Mastro, Andrew Rogulich, and Dr. Peter Schulman for help with matters too numerous to record. This volume wouldn't have been possible without their benevolent assistance, however all errors and shortcomings are my own.

REFERENCES

Aldiss, Brian. 1973. *Billion year spree: The true history of science fiction.* New York: Doubleday.

Asimov, Isaac. 1966. Introduction. In *A journey to the center of the earth* by Jules Verne. New York: Heritage.

Belloc, Marie A. 1895. Jules Verne at home. *Strand Magazine* 9 (February): 206–213. Full text online at http://jv.gilead.org.il/belloc/

Butcher, William. 2006. *Jules Verne: The definitive biography*. New York: Thunder's Mouth.

Clute, John, and Peter Nicholls, eds. 1993. *The encyclopedia of science fiction*. New York: St. Martin's.

Evans, Arthur B. 1988. *Jules Verne rediscovered: Didacticism and the scientific novel*. New York: Greenwood.

———. 2005. Jules Verne's English translations. *Science Fiction Studies* 32 I (March) 80–104.

Huntford, Roland. 1986. *The last place on earth*. New York: Atheneum.

Jules-Verne, Jean. 1976. *Jules Verne: A biography*. Translated and adapted by Roger Greaves. New York: Taplinger.

Lottman, Herbert R. 1996. *Jules Verne: An exploratory biography*. New York: St. Martins.

Mann, George, ed. 2001. *The mammoth encyclopedia of science fiction*. New York: Carroll & Graf.

Margot, Jean-Michel. 2005. Jules Verne: The successful, wealthy playwright. *Extraordinary Voyages* 12 (October): 10–16.

Miller, Walter James. 1995. *The annotated Jules Verne: From the earth to the moon*. 2nd ed. New York: Gramercy.

Sutherland, John. 2000. *The literary detective: 100 puzzles in classic fiction*. New York: Oxford.

Taves, Brian, and Stephen Michaluk, Jr. 1996. *The Jules Verne encyclopedia*. Lanham, MD: Scarecrow.

Walter, Frederick Paul. 1999. Chronological disorder in The Mysterious Island. *Extraordinary Voyages* 5 (July), 8–9

———. 2008. Jules Verne faces death. *Extraordinary Voyages* 15 (Sept.), 1–5.

Wolfe, Gene. 2007. Introduction: Speak science fiction like an earthling. In *Brave new worlds: The Oxford dictionary of science fiction*, ed. Jeff Prucher. New York: Oxford.

AMAZING JOURNEYS

Five Visionary Classics

Journey to the Center of the Earth

First published in 1864

This astonishing book is the world's first time-travel novel. It also has claims to two other literary firsts: use of monsters from the Age of Dinosaurs . . . and premiere appearance of the "nutty professor" archetype.

As the earliest novel of time travel, *Journey to the Center of the Earth* ushers in one of the three standard ploys that activate this SF subgenre: finding another era hidden in today's universe—an approach reworked by such successors as Doyle's *The Lost World* (1912) and Burroughs's *The Land that Time Forgot* (1918). The other two standard ploys also made their debuts in the 19th century, but distinctly later: the dream or hallucination gambit, unveiled in Twain's *A Connecticut Yankee in King Arthur's Court* (1889), and the futuristic technology tactic, introduced in Wells's *The Time Machine* (1895).

In Verne's pioneering novel his explorers penetrate the innards of our globe by literally descending the ladder of time. The science here is geology, subdivision paleontology, and for the 1860s it's sometimes surprisingly good science. For instance one of the prehistoric reptiles we meet is the seagoing ichthyosaurus, given a lizard's tail in many early restorations. Yet a few ichthyosaur fossils from Holzmaden, Germany included carbonized outlines of the creature's soft tissue, showing that the monster had a *fishlike* tail, and Verne, unlike many contemporaries, was paying attention: "its vertical tail fins stick out of the waves," he accurately notes in Chapter 33.

Otherwise the taut, swift writing is a marvel: the opening paragraph where something's afoot immediately . . . the sassy realism of the novel's early stages, softening us up to accept its staggering revelations later on . . . the use of a present-tense ship's log (Chapters 32–35) to put over the more phantasmagoric bits, including that shuddery, much-imitated detail of the "bite marks" in Chapter 33 . . . and all oiled by Verne's trademark humor and gag writing, much of it accessible to American readers if only the translator has the knack and will take the time.

Chief source of fun is Hamburg geologist Otto Lidenbrock, the original nutty professor, cantankerous, maniacal, and so impatient that he potted flowers in his parlor, then "tugged on their leaves to make them grow quicker." He also perpetrates one of Verne's most outlandish flimflam acts: by juggling commonplace facts about tides, lunar gravity, and earthquakes in Chapter 6, he somehow wheedles us into actually suspending our disbelief in the whole "hollow earth" idea—a conjuring trick Wells may have remembered while writing Chapter 19 of *The Invisible Man* (1897).

Professor Lidenbrock's wild-eyed exploits are recounted by his young nephew Axel, maybe the first of those wisecracking narrators who keep their feet on the ground while describing genius at work—U.S. readers will recall Archie Goodwin sparring with Nero Wolfe in Rex Stout's detective novels. Accordingly some commentators claim that *Journey to the Center of the Earth* is Axel's coming-of-age story; it's easy to agree—he's the voice of sanity, the continually amused observer, the one who ultimately gets the science right.

But not everything is amusing, and in Chapters 26–28 Axel has a near-death experience. It takes place in four stages and amounts to one of Verne's most harrowing and viscerally disturbing feats of storytelling—yet the whole unsettling episode is also a bridge to the trailblazing final third of this little masterwork, its time-traveling payoff that arguably marks the true birth of science fiction. *Translator.*

1

ON SUNDAY, May 24, 1863, Professor Lidenbrock, my uncle, came rushing back to his little house at 19 Königstrasse,[1] one of the most venerable streets in Hamburg's historical district.

Old Martha must have figured she was running well behind schedule, because our Sunday dinner had barely started to sizzle on the kitchen stove.

"Oh good," I said to myself. "My uncle's the most impatient man alive—if he's hungry, he'll howl in anguish."

"Professor Lidenbrock already?" old Martha exclaimed in astonishment, half opening the dining room door.

"Yes, Martha. But dinner has every right not to be fixed, because it isn't two o'clock yet. The bells at St. Michael's just rang half past one."

"Then why is Professor Lidenbrock back so soon?"

"Most likely he'll tell us."

"There he is! I'm staying out of it, Mr. Axel, you reason with him."

And old Martha retreated to her culinary laboratory.

I was on my own. But reasoning with the world's most cantankerous professor wasn't an option for my less than decisive personality. Accordingly I was about to retire discreetly to my little bedroom upstairs, when the front door squealed on its hinges; wooden stairs creaked under big feet, and the master of the house shot through the dining room, rushing instantly into his study.

But during this speedy crossing, he'd tossed into a corner his cane with the nutcracker head, on the table his wide shaggy hat, and at his nephew these booming words:

"Axel, follow me!"

Before I had time to move a muscle, the professor was already calling me with a sharp note of impatience:

"Well, what's taking you so long?"

I scooted into the study of my daunting overseer.

Otto Lidenbrock had no malice in him, I freely admit; but unless he experiences some unlikely personality changes, he'll go to his grave a dreadful eccentric.

He was a professor at the Johanneum, Hamburg's renowned prep school, and he taught a course in mineralogy during which he lost his temper once or twice like clockwork. It wasn't that he was concerned with having diligent pupils in his classes, or how closely they paid attention to him, or how successful they were later in life; these details didn't bother him in the least. To use an expression from German philosophy, he taught "subjectively," for his own benefit rather than for the benefit of others. He was a self-centered scholar, a well of scientific knowledge whose pulley groaned when you tried to draw something out of it: in short, he was stingy with his learning.

There are a few professors of this type in Germany.

Unfortunately my uncle's pronunciation wasn't tremendously adept, not a problem in private but definitely one when he talked in front of an audience, and this is a regrettable flaw in a public speaker. In essence, during his presentations at the Johanneum, the professor would often stop short and do battle with some recalcitrant word that wouldn't pass through his lips, one of those words that fought back, swelled up, and finally popped out in the unscientific form of a cussword. Ergo his noisy losses of temper.

Now then, mineralogy has many half-Greek, half-Latin terms that are difficult to pronounce, scientific names so harsh sounding that they would scald a poet's lips. I don't want to be critical of this science, far from it. But when one is faced with expressions like rhombohedral crystallization, retinasphalt resin, ghelenite, fangasite, lead molybdate, manganese tungstate, and zircon titanate, the most agile tongue can be excused for stumbling.

So folks around town knew about this forgivable defect of my uncle's, took advantage of him, laid in wait for the trouble spots, and laughed when he flew into a rage, which

---

[1] *Translator's note.* German: "King St."

is bad manners even for a German. And if there were always huge floods of attendees in a Lidenbrock class, how many of these diligent listeners were there mainly to be entertained by the professor's colorful temper!

Be that as it may, I can't say too often that my uncle was a true scientist. Though he sometimes broke his specimens due to the overly rough way he tested them, he had both a geologist's soul and a mineralogist's eye. Wielding his hammer, his steel pry bar, his magnetic needle, his blowtorch, and his flask of nitric acid, he was a man to reckon with. By the way that it fractured, its appearance, its hardness, its melting point, its sound, smell, and taste, he could classify any mineral without hesitation, putting it in its rightful place among the 600 varieties science has tallied to date.

Accordingly the name Lidenbrock was resoundingly honored in the schools and national societies. Famous scientists such as Messrs. Humboldt and Humphry Davy or Captains Franklin and Sabine never neglected to pay him a visit when they passed through Hamburg. Messrs. Ebelmen, Becquerel, Brewster, Jean-Baptiste Dumas, Milne-Edwards, and Henri Sainte-Claire Deville consulted him enthusiastically on the most enthralling matters of chemistry. This science was indebted to him for some pretty splendid discoveries, and in 1853 there appeared in Leipzig a *Treatise on Transcendental Crystallography* by Professor Otto Lidenbrock, a huge folio volume with plates, which, however, didn't sell enough to break even.

In addition my uncle was curator of the mineralogical museum owned by Mr. Struve the Russian ambassador, an invaluable collection known throughout Europe.

So this was the individual who was badgering me with such impatience. Picture a tall lean man with an iron constitution and with boyish blond hair that subtracted a solid ten years from the fifty he'd accumulated. His big eyes continually rolled around behind his good-sized glasses; his long thin nose looked like a sharpened blade; mischief-makers even claimed that it was magnetic and attracted iron filings. Unadulterated slander: the only thing his nose attracted was snuff, and plenty of it in all honesty.

When I add that my uncle took mathematically perfect three-foot strides, that he walked with his fists tightly clenched (the sign of a hotheaded personality), you'll know enough not to start longing for his companionship.

He lived in his little house on Königstrasse, a dwelling that was half wood, half brick, and broken up by a gable; it overlooked one of those winding canals that cross right through the oldest section of Hamburg, which, luckily, the fire of 1842 had respectfully avoided.

True, the old house leaned a bit, shoving its belly in the way of pedestrians; it wore its roof pulled down over one ear, like the peaked hat of a student in the Tugendbund;[2] the verticality of its lines left something to be desired; but in the main it stood firm, thanks to an old elm that was forcefully embedded in the front of it and that poked its flowering buds through the window panes in the springtime.

For a professor in Germany, my uncle was almost wealthy. The house belonged entirely to him, both container and contents. The contents included his godchild Grauben, a girl of seventeen from Virland,[3] along with old Martha and myself. In my twofold capacity as nephew and orphan, I became his lab assistant during his experiments.

I'll admit I had a ravenous passion for the geological sciences; the blood of a mineralogist coursed through my veins, and I was never bored in the presence of my precious pebbles.

All in all one could lead a happy life in that little house on Königstrasse, despite its owner's lack of patience—because, though his manner tended to be a little rude, he was nevertheless fond of me. But that man couldn't wait for anything and he was in a bigger rush than nature herself.

---

[2] *Translator's note.* German: "Circle of Excellence." Prussian secret society and youth movement.

[3] *Translator's note.* Today northeast Estonia.

In April, after he'd planted mignonette and morning glory cuttings in the clay pots in his parlor, every morning like clockwork he went and tugged on their leaves to make them grow quicker.

With an eccentric of that caliber, I had no choice but to obey. So I rushed into his study.

2

THIS STUDY was an honest-to-goodness museum. Every specimen in the mineral kingdom was there, labeled and organized to absolute perfection according to the three major divisions: flammable, metallic, and lithoid minerals.

How I knew them, these knickknacks from the science of mineralogy! Instead of frittering the time away with boys my own age, how often I'd had fun dusting these samples of graphite, anthracite, soft coal, brown coal, and peat! And those bits of bitumen, resin, and organic salt had to be protected from the tiniest mote of dust! And likewise these metals ranging from iron to gold, whose comparative market values meant nothing since all scientific specimens are created equal! Plus all those stones, which were plentiful enough to rebuild the whole house on Königstrasse, even to add on a nice extra room—which would have suited me just fine!

But as I went into the study, I didn't pay any attention to these wonders. My thoughts focused strictly on my uncle. He was sunk in his wide easy chair, which was upholstered in Utrecht velvet, and he held in his hands a book he was examining with the deepest wonderment.

"What a book!" he kept crowing.

This exclamation reminded me that Professor Lidenbrock was also a madcap bibliophile in his weak moments; but an old tome had value in his eyes only if it was hard to find, or at least hard to read.

"Well," he said to me, "can't you see what I've got here? I came across it this morning while rummaging around in that shop owned by Hevelius the Jew. Why, it's an incalculable treasure!"

"Magnificent," I responded with sham enthusiasm.

In actuality it was just an old quarto volume whose spine and boards seemed to be covered in heavy calfskin, a yellowish tome with a faded page marker hanging out of it— why make such a fuss?

Even so, the professor kept uttering cries of wonderment.

"Look at it," he said, answering his own questions. "Is it tolerably pleasing to the eye? Yes, it's wondrous, and what a binding! Is it a book that opens easily? Yes, because it stays open no matter which page you're on! But does it close firmly? Yes, because the cover and leaves are a perfect fit with no separations or gaps anywhere! And its spine hasn't developed a single crack after 700 years of use! Ah, even such master binders as Bozerian, Closs, or Purgold would be proud to call it their handiwork!"

While speaking in this way, my uncle consecutively opened and closed the old tome. At the very least I felt I should ask him what the book was about, though I couldn't have cared less.

"And what's the title of this wondrous volume?" I inquired with an eagerness too energetic to be sincere.

"This work," my uncle replied excitedly, "is the *Heimskringla*[4] by Snorre Sturluson, the famed Icelandic author from the 12th century! It's a chronicle of the Norwegian aristocrats who ruled over Iceland!"

"Really!" I exclaimed, going all out. "And of course it's a translation into our own German language?"

"That's rich!" the professor instantly shot back. "A translation? And what would I want with a translation? Who gives a fig for your translation? This is the original work in the Icelandic language, a magnificent dialect that's both simple and elaborate, that features the widest variety of grammatical combinations and many ways of transforming words!"

"Just like German," I got in with some aptness.

---

[4] *Translator's note.* Icelandic: "Cycles of the World."

"Right," my uncle replied, shrugging his shoulders, "not to mention that the Icelandic language features three genders like Greek and declines proper nouns like Latin!"

"Hmm," I put in, my disinterest starting to crumble. "And what about the book's type—is it attractive?"

"Type? Axel you wretch, who told you this was set in type? You *did* say type, didn't you? Aha, you mistook this for a printed book! Why, you foolish boy, it's a manuscript, a runic manuscript."

"Runic?"

"Yes! Are you going to ask me to explain that word too?"

"I don't need any help," I remarked in the tone of a man whose pride has just been pricked.

But my uncle continued in high style, forcing me to sit through a lecture on things I had absolutely no desire to learn.

"Runes," he went on, "used to be the handwritten letters of the Icelandic alphabet, and tradition has it that they were devised by Odin himself. Therefore, you irreverent youth, behold and marvel at these symbols that sprang from the brow of a god!"

I'd run out of comebacks and I swear I was all set to bow down (which is the sort of response that's bound to placate gods and kings alike, since it never takes any effort on their part), when an incident occurred that shifted the course of our conversation.

This was the appearance of a dirty scrap of parchment, which slid out of the ancient tome and fell to the ground.

My uncle rushed at this goody with an eagerness easy to understand. An old document cooped up since time immemorial in an old book—this couldn't fail to have great value in his eyes.

"What's this?" he exclaimed.

And at the same time he carefully flattened out the piece of parchment on his tabletop; it measured five inches long by three wide and was covered with crosswise rows of arcane letters.

Here's exactly how it looked. I've chosen to make these peculiar symbols public, because they led Professor Lidenbrock and

his nephew to undertake the 19th century's strangest expedition:

$$\text{ᛉ.ᛄᛕᚺᛋᛅ ᚠᛚᛄᛅᛏᛆᛏᛋ ᚺᛅᛅᚱᛁᛒᛏ}$$
$$\text{ᛒᛚᛏᛅᛅᛁᚠ ᚾᛚᛅᛅᛁᛁᚠ ᛕᛁᛏᛒᚫᛕᛅ}$$
$$\text{ᚾᛏᛅᛁᛁᛕ ᛁᛏᛕᛁᛏᛅᛅ ᛕᚾ ᚱᛒᚫᛅᚫ}$$
$$\text{ᛏᛦᛏᛕᛅᛏᛁ ᛕᚾᛁᛏᛕᚱᛏ ᚫᚫᛁᚾᛅᛁ}$$
$$\text{ᛁᛏᚾᛁᛁᚫ .ᛕᚺᛕᚱᚫᛕ ᛁᛏᛁᛁᛒᛕ}$$
$$\text{ᚱᛕᛒᚫᛦᛁ ᛏᛏᚾᛏᚾᛏ ᚠᚫᛁᛕᛏᚾ}$$
$$\text{ᛒᛏᛁᛁᛁᛕ ᚴᛕᛏᛁᛒᚴ ᚠᛏᛒᛁᛁI}$$

For a few seconds the professor pondered this sequence of letters; then, lifting up his eyeglasses, he said:

"It's runic; these characters are absolutely identical to those in Snorre Sturluson's manuscript. But . . . what could they mean?"

Since runes struck me as simply an invention by scholars to bamboozle the man in the street, I wasn't sorry to see my uncle in a fog. At least that's how it seemed to me from the movements of his fingers, which were starting to twitch dreadfully.

"Nevertheless it's old Icelandic," he mumbled between clenched teeth.

And Professor Lidenbrock had to know what he was talking about, because he was regarded as a genuine polyglot. Not that he could chat fluently in all 2,000 languages and 4,000 dialects used on the surface of the globe, but he definitely knew his fair share.

So, after running into this obstacle, he was about to give in completely to the hotheaded side of his personality, and I saw a furious scene in the offing, when the little wall clock over the fireplace chimed the hour of two.

At once old Martha opened the study door and said:

"Mealtime."

"The meal can go to blazes!" my uncle roared. "Along with the person who cooked it and the people who eat it!"

Martha fled. I flew after her and ended up in my usual seat in the dining room, I'm not sure how.

I waited a few seconds. The professor didn't come. To my knowledge this was the first time he'd missed the sacred ritual of Sunday dinner. And what a dinner it was! Parsley soup, a ham omelet seasoned with sorrel and nutmeg, loin of veal with plum sauce, and candied shrimp for dessert, all of it washed down with a delightful bottle of Moselle.

That's what my uncle was going to miss because of an old scrap of paper. I swear to you, I felt it was my duty—in my capacity as dedicated nephew—to eat enough for the two of us. Which I conscientiously did.

"I've never seen anything like it," old Martha said. "Professor Lidenbrock isn't at the table!"

"It's hard to believe."

"This is a sign of some earth-shattering development!" the old servant went on, shaking her head.

In my view it wasn't a sign of anything at all, other than a frightful scene when my uncle found that his dinner had been eaten.

I was down to my last shrimp when a booming voice snatched me from the delights of dessert. I made it from the dining room to the study in a single bound.

3

"IT'S CLEARLY RUNIC," the professor said, knitting his brow. "But there's a secret here, and I'll discover it, or else . . ."

He finished his thought with a vehement gesture.

"Sit right there," he added, thumping one side of the table with his fist, "and take this down."

In a second I was ready.

"Now, I'm going to dictate to you every letter in our alphabet that corresponds to each of these Icelandic symbols. We'll see what that gives us. But by St. Michael, be very careful you don't make any mistakes!"

His dictation started. I gave it my best effort. He called out each letter one after the other, which formed the following unintelligible sequence of words:

mm.rnlls	*esreuel*	*seecJde*
sgtssmf	*unteief*	*niedrke*
kt,samn	*atrateS*	*Saodrrn*
emtnael	*nuaect*	*rrilSa*
Atvaar	*.nscrc*	*ieaabs*
ccdrmi	*eeutul*	*frantu*
dt,iac	*oseibo*	*KediiY*

When I'd finished this task, my uncle instantly took the sheet I'd just been writing on and examined it carefully for a good while.

"What's it supposed to mean?" he kept saying mechanically.

Believe me, I couldn't have informed him. Anyhow he didn't ask my opinion and went on talking to himself:

"This is what's known as a cryptogram," he said, "in which the sense is hidden by deliberately mixing up the letters, which will form an understandable sentence if they're put in the right order. Just think—maybe this explains or indicates some major discovery!"

For my part I seriously doubted that it did any such thing; but I wisely kept my views to myself.

The professor took the book and the parchment, then compared them to each other.

"These two pieces of writing aren't by the same hand," he said. "The cryptogram came later than the book—right off I see conclusive proof of this. In essence the first letter is a *double m*, which you won't find in Sturluson's book because it was only added to the Icelandic alphabet in the 14th century. Hence there are at least 200 years between the manuscript and the document."

This, I admit, struck me as pretty reasonable.

"So I'm led to believe," my uncle went on, "that one of the book's owners must have scrawled these mysterious letters. But who in blazes *was* this owner? Wouldn't he have put his name somewhere in the manuscript?"

My uncle lifted up his eyeglasses, took a strong magnifying lens, and gave the first pages of the book a careful inspection. On the second leaf, on the back of the half-title page, he found a sort of stain that looked superficially like an ink blotch. But after studying it closely, he made out a few half-erased letters. My uncle realized he was on to something; he slaved over that blotch with the help of his huge magnifying lens and he ended up identifying the following symbols, runic letters that he read off without hesitation:

ᚧᛚᛏᛂ ᛋᛁᚵᚴᛐᛋᛆᛏᚷ

"Arne Saknussemm!" he shouted in a triumphant tone. "Why, that's a name indeed, and an Icelandic name to boot—he was a scientist in the 16th century, a famous alchemist!"

I looked at my uncle in definite wonderment.

"Those alchemists," he went on, "included such men as Avicenna, Roger Bacon, Ramon Llull, and Paracelsus. They were the only real scientists of their day. They made discoveries that rightly amaze us. Why couldn't this Saknussemm have buried some startling new idea inside this unintelligible cryptogram? It must be so. It *is* so."

This theory fired the professor's imagination.

"No doubt," I ventured to reply. "But what was the scientist's motive for hiding his wonderful discovery in such a way?"

"Why? Heavens, how would I know! Didn't Galileo use wordplay to conceal his findings about Saturn? Anyhow we'll soon see: I intend to learn the secret of this document and I won't eat or sleep till I've figured it out."

Oh Lord, I thought.

"Nor will you, Axel," he continued.

"Holy smoke," I said to myself, "it's a good thing I ate enough dinner for two!"

"And first," my uncle put in, "we need to find the language of this 'code.' That shouldn't be hard."

I looked up quickly at these words. My uncle went on with his monologue:

"Nothing could be easier. There are 132 letters in this document, consisting of 79 consonants versus 53 vowels. Now then, that's pretty close to the average breakdown of words in southerly languages, while dialects up north are infinitely richer in consonants. Consequently we're dealing with a southern language."

These inferences seemed perfectly sound.

"But which language is it?"

Here I expected him to flaunt his learn-ing, but instead he began an in-depth analysis.

"This Saknussemm," he went on, "was an educated man; now then, whenever he didn't write in his mother tongue, he must have opted for the language used by all cultured minds in the 16th century: I mean Latin. If I'm mistaken, I can still try Spanish, French, Italian, Greek, and Hebrew. But scientists in the 16th century normally wrote in Latin. Consequently I'm entitled to say *a priori:*[5] this is in Latin."

I shot forward in my chair. Remembering my Latin lessons, I rebelled against the claim that this sequence of outlandish words could belong to the gentle language of Virgil.

"Yes, it's in Latin," my uncle went on, "but mixed-up Latin."

Nice work, I thought. If you can unmix it, uncle, you're the best.

"Let's examine it carefully," he said, picking up the sheet of paper I'd been writing on. "Here's a sequence of 132 letters apparently laid out in the wrong order. There are words where we find only consonants, such as *mm.rnlls* at the outset, and on the other hand, some where vowels are abundant—for instance the fifth item, *unteief*, or the second-last one, *oseibo*. Now then, this is obviously a random arrangement: it has occurred *mathematically* due to some unknown principle that's determining the sequence of these letters. I haven't the slightest doubt that the original sentence was written down correctly, then turned inside out according to some rule that we need to discover. Anybody who has the key to this 'code' will read it easily. But what's the key? Axel, do you know it?"

I didn't reply to this question and for good reason. My eyes were glued to a delightful portrait hanging on the wall, Grauben's portrait. Just then my uncle's ward was staying with a relative in Altona, and her absence left me quite gloomy—because I can now admit it, the pretty Virlander and the professor's nephew loved each other with a patience and serenity that were thoroughly German. We'd gotten engaged without my uncle's knowl-

---

[5] *Translator's note.* Latin: "before the fact."

edge, since he was too wrapped up in his geology to understand feelings like ours. Grauben was a blue-eyed blonde, a delightful girl though her nature was a little stern and serious minded; but she loved me all the same. For my part I adored her, if there *is* such a verb in the Teutonic tongue! So the picture of my little Virlander had instantly transferred me from the real world into the realm of memories and dreams.

I saw her again in my mind's eye, the loyal companion of my work and play. Every day she helped me get my uncle's precious stones in order; we labeled them together. She was a thoroughly seasoned mineralogist, our Miss Grauben! She could have put more than one expert to shame. She loved to delve into knotty scientific problems. What delicious hours we spent together doing research! And how many times I envied the fate of those unfeeling stones she touched with her delightful hands!

Then, when it was time to relax, the two of us would head outside, take the tree-lined walk along Alster Lake, and make our way together to the old tar-spattered mill that looks so picturesque at the lake's far end; we held hands and chatted as we went. I told her sweet nothings and she did her best to smile. In this fashion we reached the banks of the Elbe, and after bidding good evening to the swans that glided among the big white water lilies, we would ride the steam barge back to the pier.

Now then, I'd gotten to this point in my daydream, when my uncle banged his fist on the table and snapped me forcefully back to reality.

"Let's see," he said. "To mix up the letters in a sentence, it strikes me that the first idea that should spring to mind is to jot down the words vertically instead of writing them horizontally."

Oho, I thought.

"We'll have to see what comes of it. Axel, dash off any sentence you like on this slip of paper; but instead of laying out the letters in sequence one after the other, put them consecutively in vertical columns, so as to arrange them in groups of five or six."

I saw what he was getting at and immediately wrote from top to bottom:

H	o	u	i	G	e
o	v	,	t	r	n
w	e	m	t	a	!
I	y	y	l	u	
l	o	l	e	b	

"Good," the professor said without reading it. "Now lay out these words on a horizontal line."

I did so and got the following sentence:

HouiGe ov,trn wemta! Iyylu loleb

"Perfect!" my uncle put in, snatching the paper out of my hands. "This already has the appearance of the old document: the vowel groupings are as hopelessly out of order as the consonants; there are even capital letters in the middle of words, also a comma—the same as with Saknussemm's parchment!"

These comments were extremely shrewd, I had to admit.

"Now then," my uncle continued to my face, "in order to read the sentence you've just written, and which I don't know, all I have to do is consecutively take the first letter of each word, then the second, the third, and so on."

And much to his amazement, and even more to mine, my uncle read:

How I love you, my little Grauben!

"Huh?" the professor put in.

Yes, bumbling lover that I was, I'd unwittingly scribbled this incriminating sentence!

"So you're in love with Grauben, are you?" my uncle resumed in a proper guardian's voice.

"Yes . . . no . . ." I stammered.

"So you're in love with Grauben," he went on mechanically. "All right, let's apply my procedure to the document in question."

Lapsing back into his all-consuming thoughts, my uncle had already forgotten my rash words. I say rash though a scientist's head can't understand matters of the heart.

But luckily the major business of the document had the upper hand.

From the instant he started his crucial experiment, Professor Lidenbrock's eyes flickered like lightning behind his glasses. His fingers trembled as he picked up the old parchment. He was seriously on edge. Finally he gave a loud cough; in a solemn voice, consecutively calling out the first letter of each word, then the second, he dictated the following sequence to me:

*mmessunkaSenrA.icefdoK.segnittamurtn
ecertserrette,rotaivsadua,ednecsedsadne
lacartniiiluJsiratracSarbmutabiledmek
meretarcsilucoYsleffenSnI.*

I admit it, by the end I was excited; called out one by one, these letters hadn't made the slightest sense to me; so I was waiting for the professor to let some magnificent Latin sentence roll imposingly from his lips.

But who could have seen it coming? A ferocious smack of the fist made the table shudder. Ink spurted into the air, the pen leaped out of my hand.

"That's not it!" my uncle shouted. "It makes no sense at all!"

Then he shot through the study like a cannonball, went down the stairs like an avalanche, rushed onto Königstrasse, and ran off at top speed.

4

"HE'S GONE?" Martha exclaimed, hurrying out at the sound of the front door slamming—which it did with such force, the whole house shook.

"Yes," I replied, "far gone."

"Well, I'll be! And what about his dinner?" the old servant put in.

"He'll be skipping dinner."

"And what about his supper?"

"He'll be skipping supper."

"Excuse me?" Martha said, clasping her hands.

"No, my good Martha, he won't be eating another thing, nor will the rest of the house! Uncle Lidenbrock has put us all on a starva-tion diet till the moment he solves some old gibberish that's utterly insoluble."

"Dear God, so we'll just die of hunger!"

I didn't dare admit it, but with a man as stiff-necked as my uncle, that was sure to be our fate.

Seriously alarmed, the old servant went whimpering back to her kitchen.

Once I was on my own, the thought occurred to me of going and telling Grauben everything. But how could I leave the house? The professor might return at any moment. And what if he called me? And what if he wanted to get back to decoding his word puzzle, which was hard enough to stump old Oedipus? And if I didn't come when he called, what would happen?

The wisest course was to stay put. As it happened, a mineralogist in Besançon had just sent us an assortment of silica geodes that needed classifying. I got to work. These hollow stones are full of little crystals inside, and I sorted, labeled, and arranged them all in their display case.

But this activity didn't distract me. That business of the old document kept nagging at me in the strangest manner. I felt lightheaded and in the grip of a vague uneasiness. I had a hunch that a catastrophe was on the way.

At the end of an hour, my geodes were on the right shelves. Then, arms dangling, head thrown back, I dropped into the big easy chair upholstered in Utrecht velvet. I lit my pipe, which had a long curving stem and a carved bowl that depicted a water nymph stretching out lackadaisically; then I had fun watching its wood charring, a process that was gradually turning my nymph into a full-fledged Negress. Now and then I listened for footsteps clattering on the stairs. Not a one. Where could my uncle have been at that moment? I pictured him running under the lovely trees along the road to Altona, thrashing around, taking swipes at the wall with his cane, his arm vehemently striking the weeds, beheading the thistles, and rousing isolated storks from their sleep.

Would he come back in triumph or despair? Which of them would prevail, the professor or the secret? While asking myself these questions, my fingers mechanically picked up the piece of paper covered with that unintelligible sequence of letters I'd scribbled. I asked myself over and over:

"What could they mean?"

I tried to group these letters so they formed words. Not possible! When I assembled them into twos, threes, fives, or sixes, all I got was utter nonsense. Admittedly the 14th, 15th, and 16th letters made the English word *ice*. The 84th, 85th, and 86th formed the word *sir*. Finally, in the body of the document, in its second and third lines, I also noted the Latin words *rota*, *nec*, *ira*, *atra*, and *mutabile*.

Holy smoke, I thought, these last words would seem to bear out my uncle's thinking as to the document's language! And furthermore, in the fourth line I also spotted the word *luco*, which can be translated as *sacred wood*. It's true that in the third line you could read the word *tabiled*, which has a thoroughgoing Hebrew ring to it, and in the last line the terms *mer*, *arc*, and *mère*, which are pure French.

It was crazy making! Four different dialects in this ridiculous sentence! What relationship could exist between the words *ice*, *sir*, *temper*, *cruel*, *sacred wood*, *changing*, *mother*, *arch*, or *sea?* Only the first and last went together with any ease: given a document written in Iceland, it didn't amaze me that a *sea of ice* was in the picture. But forging ahead and figuring out the rest of the cryptogram was another story.

I was wrestling, then, with an insoluble difficulty; my brain was overheating; when I looked at that piece of paper, I kept having to close my eyes; the 132 letters seemed to flit around me like those silver spots that swirl through the air when you get an intense rush of blood to your head.

I was in the grip of some sort of hallucination; I was suffocating; I needed air. I mechanically fanned myself with the piece of paper, whose back and front flashed consecutively in front of my eyes.

To my surprise, just as the back was toward me during one of these quick about-faces, I thought I caught sight of some perfectly readable words, the Latin words *craterem* and *terrestre* among others!

Suddenly a light went on in my brain; all by themselves these clues had given me a glimpse of the truth; I'd discovered the rule governing the code. To understand this document, it wasn't even necessary to read it through the other side of the paper. Not at all. It was just as easy to spell it out just as it was, just as it had been dictated to me. All the professor's clever explanations were confirmed. He was right about the arrangement of the letters, right about the language of the document! A "mere nothing" was all he'd lacked to be able to read this Latin sentence from start to finish, and sheer luck had just put this "mere nothing" in my hands.

You can imagine how excited I felt! My vision blurred. I couldn't help it. I spread out the piece of paper on the table. To grasp its secret, all I needed was a single glance.

Finally I managed to calm my agitation. To settle my nerves, I made a point of walking two laps around the room, then I went back and sank into the huge easy chair.

"Now read it," I snapped, after recharging my lungs with an ample supply of air.

I bent over the table; I put my finger consecutively on each letter, and without stopping, without hesitating for a second, I spoke the whole sentence out loud.

Then what astonishment, what terror swept over me! I stood still at first, as if stunned by a sudden blow. What! This deed I'd just learned about had actually been done? A human being had been daring enough to reach . . . ?

"Oh no!" I exclaimed, jumping up. "Absolutely not! My uncle mustn't find out about this! The last thing I need is for him to hear of such a journey! He would want a crack at it himself! Nothing could hold him back! He's such a die-hard geologist! He would make this trip no matter what, in the face of anything and everything! And he would take me along with him, and we would never return! Never! Never!"

I can't describe how worked up I was.

"No, It's not going to happen!" I said firmly. "I can keep this notion from getting into his tyrannical brain—and I *will!* If he turns this document over and over, he could get lucky and find the key! It's got to be destroyed."

The last vestiges of a fire were in the hearth. I grabbed not only the sheet of paper but Saknussemm's parchment; my feverish hands were all set to throw the whole works onto the coals and wipe out this threatening secret, when the study door opened. My uncle appeared.

5

I HAD JUST ENOUGH time to put the ill-omened document back on the table.

Professor Lidenbrock seemed deeply preoccupied. The thoughts obsessing him hadn't given him a moment's peace; obviously he'd investigated and analyzed the business, dedicating all his intellectual resources to the task during his stroll, and he'd come back ready to try out some new explanation.

Sure enough, he sat in his easy chair, took up his pen, and started putting down formulas like those in an algebraic calculation.

I kept an eye on his trembling hand; I hung on his every movement. So what unexpected result would he accidentally come up with? I was trembling too, and for no good reason, since the true explanation, the "only answer," had already been found, and it was automatically pointless to look any farther.

For three long hours my uncle toiled away without speaking, without looking up, erasing, continuing, crossing out, making a thousand fresh starts.

I was well aware that if he managed to arrange these letters into every position they could occupy relative to each other, the sentence would turn up. But I was also aware that a mere 20 letters could be put together in 2 quintillion, 432 quadrillion, 902 trillion, 8 billion, 176 million, 640 thousand different ways. Now then, there were 132 letters in the sentence, and these 132 letters gave any number of different sentences consisting of at least 133 characters, an almost uncountable number and utterly impractical to work with.

This way of solving the problem called for such a heroic effort, I felt sure I was safe.

But time went by; night fell; noises from the street died down; still bending over his work, my uncle saw nothing, not even old Martha half opening the door; and he heard nothing, not even the good woman's voice saying:

"Will master be eating supper this evening?"

Accordingly Martha had to go off unanswered. As for me, after holding out for a few hours, I fell into an uncontrollable doze and slept away at one end of the sofa while Uncle Lidenbrock kept figuring and erasing.

When I woke up the next morning, that tireless workhorse was still on the job. His red eyes, his pallid color, his hair twined around his feverish fingers, and his flushed cheekbones were pretty clear signs of his dreadful struggle with the impossible, of the cerebral exertions and mental exhaustion that must have marked the hours he'd spent at it.

I honestly pitied him. Despite all the complaints I felt justified in registering with him, I was starting to feel for him a little. The poor man was so fixated on this one idea, he'd forgotten to lose his temper. He was exerting every living ounce of his strength against one single pressure point, and since he hadn't blown off steam in his usual way, you had grounds for fearing a pent-up explosion any second now.

With a snap of the fingers, with a single word, I could have unclamped that iron vise squeezing his skull. Yet I didn't do a thing

But I'm a good-hearted fellow. Why did I keep quiet at such a time? In my uncle's best interests, that's why.

"No, no," I told myself over and over. "I won't bring it up! He would try to go there, I know it; nothing could hold him back. He has a volcanic intellect and he would risk his life to do something no other geologist has done. I won't say a word; by sheer luck I'm privy to this secret and I'll *keep* it a secret! If Professor Lidenbrock discovers it, it'll be the death of him! Let him guess it if he can. I don't want to be responsible for leading him down the road to perdition."

My mind made up, I folded my arms and waited. But I hadn't reckoned on an incident that occurred a few hours later.

When old Martha tried to leave the house and go to the market, she found that the door wouldn't open. The big key was missing from the lock. Who had removed it? My uncle obviously, when he came back the night before from his breakneck excursion.

Was this on purpose? Or by accident? Did he intend to subject us to the hardships of hunger? This struck me as a bit much. What! Were Martha and I to be the scapegoats in a situation that hadn't the tiniest thing to do with us? Undoubtedly we were, and I recalled a distressing enough precedent. In essence, while my uncle was working a few years back on his great classification system for minerals, he went forty-eight hours without eating, and the whole house had to adhere to this scientific regimen. For my part I came down with a severe bellyache, not much fun for a hungry growing boy.

Now then, it struck me that breakfast was about to go the way of last night's supper. Even so, I was determined to play the hero and not give in to any twinges of hunger. Martha took it quite seriously and was devastated, the dear woman. For my part, the impossibility of leaving the house worried me more, for good reason. And you know what that reason was.

My uncle kept on working, his intellect lost in the realm of explanations; he was far from this world, truly beyond any worldly needs.

Toward noontime my hunger was goading me in earnest. The night before, Martha had quite innocently used up all the supplies in the larder; there wasn't a thing left in the house. Yet I stood my ground. I made it a sort of point of honor.

Two o'clock sounded. This was getting silly, unbearable even. The scales fell from my eyes. I started to tell myself that I was making too much of the document's importance; that my uncle wouldn't give it any credence; that he would see it as simply a hoax; that if worst came to worst and he wanted to attempt the adventure, we could restrain him against his will; finally, that he himself might discover the key to the "code," so my going without food was pointless.

These struck me as excellent arguments, though I would have rejected them in exasperation the night before; thus I felt it was perfectly ridiculous of me to wait this long and I decided to tell him everything.

Consequently I was looking for a lead-in to the topic, one that wasn't too abrupt, when the professor stood up, put on his hat, and got set to go out.

What was this? Was he leaving the house with us still locked in? No way.

"Uncle!" I said.

He didn't seem to hear me.

"Uncle Lidenbrock!" I repeated, raising my voice.

"Huh?" he put in like a man suddenly waking up.

"Well, what about the key?"

"Which key? The front door key?"

"No, no," I snapped, "the key to the document!"

The professor peered at me over his eyeglasses; undoubtedly he noted something odd in my facial expression, because he instantly grabbed my arm and queried me with his eyes as if he couldn't speak. Even so, no question had ever been put more plainly.

My head moved up and down.

He shook his in a pitying sort of way, as if dealing with a madman.

I nodded more forcefully.

A sharp flash glittered in his eyes; his grip got threatening.

Given the circumstances, this wordless conversation would have intrigued the most disinterested onlooker. And I'd honestly reached the point of no longer daring to speak, because I was so afraid my uncle would instantly smother me to death in joyous embraces. But he clutched me so tightly, a response was mandatory.

"Yes, the key to the code! By sheer luck . . . !"

"What do you mean?" he snapped with indescribable excitement.

"Here," I said, offering him the sheet of paper I'd written on. "Read that."

"But it doesn't make any sense!" he replied, crumpling the sheet up.

"It doesn't if you read it from front to back, but in reverse . . ."

27

I hadn't finished my sentence before the professor let out a shout—no, more than a shout, a genuine bellow! The truth had just dawned in his mind. He was transformed.

"Oh, Saknussemm, you clever rascal!" he exclaimed. "So first you wrote your sentence backward?"

Rushing to the piece of paper, vision impaired and voice choked with emotion, he read the whole document, proceeding from the last letter to the first.

It ran as follows:

In Sneffels Yoculis craterem kem
delibat umbra Scartaris Julii intra
calendas descende, audas viator,
et terrestre centrum attinges . . .
Kod feci. Arne Saknussemm.

Which is bastardized Latin that can be translated in this way:

Go down into the crater of Snaefells
Jökull, which Scartaris's shadow
caresses just before the calends[6] of
July, O daring traveler, and you'll
make it to the center of the earth.
I've done so. Arne Saknussemm.

Reading this, my uncle jumped as if he'd gotten a shock from accidentally touching a Leyden jar. His delight, daring, and conviction were magnificent. He paced back and forth; he held his head in both hands; he rearranged the chairs; he stacked his books; he did an unbelievable juggling act with his precious geodes; he threw a punch this way, a slap that way. Finally his nerves settled down, and like a man drained by far too much exertion, he collapsed into his easy chair.

"So what time is it?" he asked after a few seconds of silence.

"Three o'clock," I answered.

"Heavens, my last meal must be completely digested! I'm dying of hunger. Let's eat. Then afterward . . ."

"Afterward?"

---

[6] *Translators note.* First day of the month in the ancient Roman calendar.

"Pack my trunk."

"Huh?" I exclaimed.

"Yours too!" responded the pitiless professor, going into the dining room.

6

At these words I shivered all over. But I got a grip on myself. I was even determined to put a good face on things. Only scientific logic could stop Professor Lidenbrock. Now then, there were arguments—and good ones—that disputed the possibility of any such journey. Go to the center of the earth? What lunacy! But I kept my dialectic ammunition ready for a timely moment and I got busy with my meal.

There's no need to describe how my uncle had stood cursing in front of the empty table. Reasons were given. Old Martha was set free. She ran off to the market and was so efficient, within an hour I'd appeased my hunger and gotten back to assessing the situation.

During the meal my uncle was almost jolly, though the jokes he cracked were the sort that are too erudite to ever cause much trouble. After dessert he motioned me to follow him into his study.

I did so. He sat at one end of his worktable, I sat at the other.

"Axel," he said in a tolerably gentle voice, "you're a very clever boy; you did me a great service when I was tired of struggling and ready to stop looking for the explanation. What would have become of me? Who knows! I'll never forget this, my boy, and you'll have your share in the glory we're about to earn."

Good, I thought, he's in a pleasant mood—it's time for a discussion about that glory!

"First of all," my uncle went on, "I'm swearing you to the most absolute secrecy, is that clear? The scientific world isn't short of men who envy me, and quite a few would willingly undertake this journey, but they mustn't have a clue till we're back."

"You honestly think," I said, "there are that many who would dare such a thing?"

"Definitely! Who would hesitate to win this kind of renown? If the document were made public, a whole army of geologists would be hot on Arne Saknussemm's heels!"

"That's where I'm not convinced, uncle, because we haven't a shred of proof that this document is authentic."

"Excuse me? And what about the book we found it in?"

"Fine, I admit this Saknussemm wrote these lines, but does it follow that he actually went through with such a journey, that this old parchment couldn't be part of a hoax?"

This last word was on the risky side, and I almost regretted having spoken it. The professor's heavy eyebrows lowered, and I was afraid I'd jeopardized the rest of the discussion. Luckily nothing came of it. The ghost of a smile appeared on the lips of my stern conversation partner, and he replied:

"We'll see about that."

"Wait!" I put in, a little irked. "Just let me get out all the objections that relate to this document."

"Go ahead, my boy, don't pull any punches. Feel perfectly free to express your views. You're no longer my nephew, you're my colleague. Please proceed."

"All right, first off I'll ask you about this Snaefells, this Jökull, and this Scartaris—I've never heard of them, what are they?"

"Nothing could be simpler. The other day, as it happens, I received a map from my friend August Petermann in Leipzig; it couldn't have come at a better time. Take down the third atlas in the second subdivision of the main bookcase, section Z, row 4."

I got up, and thanks to these meticulous directions, I quickly found the desired atlas. My uncle opened it and said:

"Here's one of the best maps of Iceland, Ebenezer Henderson's, and I believe it will give us the solution to all your difficulties."

I leaned over the map.

"See how this island is made up of volcanoes," the professor said, "and note that they're all given the name *Jökull*. This word is Icelandic for *glacier*, and at Iceland's high latitude, most eruptions see daylight after coming through layers of ice. Ergo this term *Jökull*, which is applied to every volcanic peak on the island."

"Fine," I replied, "but what does Snaefells mean?"

I hoped this was a question without an answer. I was mistaken. My uncle went on:

"Follow me along Iceland's west coast. You notice Reykjavik, the capital? Right. Fine. Go up through these countless fjords the sea has gnawed into the coastline, then halt a little below latitude 65°. What do you see there?"

"A sort of peninsula that looks like a bare bone with an enormous joint at the end."

"An apt comparison, my boy; now, do you notice anything above that joint?"

"Yes, a mountain seems to have sprung up in the sea."

"Good, that's Snaefells!"

"*The* Snaefells?"

"The very same, a mountain 5,000 feet high, one of the most notable on the island—and sure to be the most famous in the entire world, if its crater leads to the center of the globe."

"But that's impossible!" I snapped, shrugging my shoulders and rebelling against any such notion.

"Impossible?" Professor Lidenbrock replied in a stern tone. "And why is that?"

"Because this crater is obviously clogged with lava and burning rocks, which means—"

"And what if it's an extinct crater?"

"Extinct?"

"Yes. The number of active volcanoes on the surface of the globe is currently around 300; but there's a far larger population of extinct volcanoes. Now then, Snaefells ranks among the latter and since antiquity it has erupted only once, back in 1219; from that day to this, its rumblings have gotten quieter and quieter and it's no longer considered an active volcano."

I had absolutely no comeback to these clear-cut assertions; so I retreated to other puzzling aspects of the document.

"What's the meaning of this word Scartaris," I asked, "and how do the calends of July fit in?"

My uncle thought this over for a short

while. At that moment I had hope, but it was a fleeting moment because he soon answered me as follows:

"What you find puzzling is quite clear to me. This shows the clever pains Saknussemm took to leave exact directions to his discovery. Snaefells consists of several craters, so it was necessary to indicate which one of them leads to the center of the globe. What did our Icelandic scholar do? He'd noted that as the calends of July drew near, in other words, toward the last days of the month of June, one of the mountain peaks, Scartaris, cast its shadow right on the opening of the crater in question, and he recorded that fact in his document. How could he have come up with a more explicit indication, and once we've arrived at the summit of Snaefells, how could we possibly hesitate over which route to take?"

No doubt about it, my uncle had an answer for everything. It was quite clear to me that he was unstoppable when it came to the words in this old parchment. Therefore I quit pestering him on this aspect, and since it was absolutely essential to talk him out of the business, I moved on to the scientific objections, which to my thinking were serious enough by themselves.

"Very well," I said, "I have to admit that Saknussemm's sentence is clear and doesn't leave any room for doubt in a person's mind. I even agree that the document looks perfectly genuine. That old scientist did go down into Snaefells; he did see Scartaris's shadow caress the edge of the crater before the calends of July; thanks to the legendary tales of his day, he'd even heard about that crater ending up at the center of the earth; but as for getting there himself, as for making that journey and coming back from it—did he undertake any such trip? I say no, a thousand times no!"

"And what's your reason?" my uncle said with a conspicuous sneer in his tone.

"Every supposition in science indicates that such an undertaking is out of the question!"

"Does every supposition say *that?*" the professor replied, putting on a wide-eyed expression. "Oh, those dastardly suppositions! They're going to be such a hindrance, those wretched suppositions!"

I could see that he was poking fun at me, but I kept on going nevertheless:

"Yes, it's universally known that the temperature gets over 1.8° hotter for every 70 feet you go below the surface of the globe; now then, assuming this ratio stays constant, and given that the earth's radius is around 3,900 miles, the temperature at its center exceeds 360,000° Fahrenheit. So any matter existing at the heart of the globe is in a white-hot, gaseous state, because neither the hardest rocks nor the metals gold and platinum can withstand that much heat. Consequently I'm justified in asking if it's possible to go into such an environment."

"Thus, Axel, it's the heat that baffles you?"

"Certainly. If we reach a depth of only twenty-five miles, we'll have made it to the inner edge of the earth's crust, because the temperature will already be about 2,400° Fahrenheit."

"And you're afraid you'll start to liquefy?"

"I'll let *you* answer that question," I replied in exasperation.

"Here's what I conclude," Professor Lidenbrock remarked, getting on his high horse. "Inasmuch as we're acquainted with barely 1/12,000 of the earth's radius, neither you nor anybody else knows for a certainty what's going on inside our globe; science is on a noble quest for perfection, and every supposition is regularly demolished by new suppositions. Till Joseph Fourier came along, didn't we believe that temperatures in outer space were continually decreasing, and don't we know today that the coldest temperatures in the celestial regions range from -40° to -60° Fahrenheit? Why wouldn't it be this way with the earth's internal heat? Instead of getting hot enough to liquefy the world's toughest minerals, why wouldn't it just reach a maximum temperature at a particular depth?"

My uncle had taken the issue into the realm of sheer conjecture, so there was nothing I could say.

"Well then," he continued, "I'll have you

know that qualified scientists, Poisson among others, have proven that if a temperature of 360,000° Fahrenheit exists at the heart of the globe, the white-hot gases coming from the melted matter would acquire such expansive power, the earth's crust couldn't withstand them and would blow up like the walls of a boiler from too much steam pressure."

"Those are Poisson's views, uncle, nothing more."

"Agreed, but other noteworthy geologists hold the same views, insisting that our globe's interior isn't made up of gas, water, or even the heaviest rocks known to us, because if such were the case, the earth would weigh only 50% of what it actually does."

"Bosh, you can make figures prove anything you want!"

"And is it the same, my boy, with facts? Hasn't it been established that the number of volcanoes has shrunk considerably since the first days of the world? And if this central heat does exist, can't we then conclude that it's getting weaker?"

"If you keep wandering off into guesswork, uncle, I see no point in this discussion."

"But I do, and I'll mention that my views have been seconded by highly capable people. Do you remember when the famous English chemist Sir Humphry Davy paid me a visit in 1825?"

"Hardly, since I didn't enter the world till nineteen years later."

"Well, Humphry Davy came to see me on his way through Hamburg. We had a lengthy discussion covering, among other matters, the theory that the earth's inner nucleus was liquid. The two of us agreed that such a liquid state wasn't possible, on grounds that science has never been able to refute."

"What grounds?" I said, a little surprised.

"Namely that this mass of liquid, like the oceans, would be controlled by the moon's gravitational pull, and as a consequence it would cause internal tides twice a day, which would lift up the earth's crust and give rise to earthquakes at regular intervals!"

"But even so, it's obvious that the surface of the globe has been subject to combustion, and it's naturally assumed that the outer crust cooled off first while the heat retreated to the center."

"A fallacy," my uncle replied. "The earth heated up through combustion on its surface and no other way. Its surface consisted of a large number of metals such as potassium and sodium, which have the property of igniting at the merest contact with air and water; when the steam in the sky turned into rain and fell on the ground, these metals caught on fire; and little by little, when the water got down into the crevices in the earth's crust, it started new fires complete with explosions and eruptions. Ergo the many volcanoes in the first days of the world."

"Now *that's* a clever theory!" I exclaimed, almost forgetting myself.

"And one that Humphry Davy made me aware of by a very simple experiment in my own home. Using chiefly the metals I've just mentioned, he molded a shiny ball that represented our globe to perfection; when you sprinkled water lightly over its surface, a blister swelled up on it, oxidized, and formed a tiny mountain; a crater popped open on top; an eruption took place and filled the entire ball with so much heat, it became impossible to hold the thing in your hand."

To tell the truth, I was starting to be swayed by the professor's arguments; besides, he made the most of them with his usual zeal and enthusiasm.

"You see, Axel," he added, "the character of that central nucleus has given rise to a variety of theories among geologists; there are only the flimsiest proofs for this concept of internal heat; my feeling is that it doesn't exist and can't exist; besides, we'll see for ourselves, and as Arne Saknussemm did, we'll find out just where we stand on this major question."

"All right, fine!" I replied, won over by his enthusiasm. "Yes, we'll see for ourselves—if down there we *can* see!"

"And why not? Can't we rely on electrical phenomena to light us, and even on atmospheric pressure, since it can turn the air luminous as we get closer to the center?"

"True," I said, "that's always a possibility."

"It's a certainty," my uncle replied triumphantly. "But not a word, do you hear? Not a word on this whole matter, so nobody gets any notions of discovering the center of the earth before we do."

7

THAT'S HOW THIS unforgettable session ended. This conversation left me feverish. I went out of my uncle's study with my wits spinning, and there wasn't enough air in the streets of Hamburg to clear my head. So I walked as far as the banks of the Elbe, on the side where the steam ferry connects the town with the Harburg railway line.

Was I convinced by what I'd just learned? Had I simply been overcome by Professor Lidenbrock's domineering personality? Should I take him seriously when he vowed to visit the center of the earth's bedrock? Had I been listening to the deranged speculations of a madman or the scientific inferences of a great genius? Where did the truth end in all this and the fallacies start?

I was drifting in the midst of a thousand contradictory theories, unable to get a good grip on any of them.

Yet I recalled how convinced I'd felt, though my enthusiasm was starting to simmer down; but I would have been willing to leave immediately, before I had any time for second thoughts. Yes, right then I didn't lack the courage to buckle up my suitcase.

Even so, I must admit that in another hour this high excitement had died away; I'd steadied my nerves and climbed from the earth's far-off depths back to its surface.

"It's ridiculous!" I exclaimed. "It's an insult to common sense! No right-thinking fellow would ever take such a proposition seriously. There isn't a thing that's real in the whole business! I've dozed off and had a bad dream."

Meanwhile I'd walked along the bank of the Elbe and gone around the town. After heading up past the harbor, I arrived at the road to Altona. I went that way because I had a hunch—a hunch that paid off, because I soon spotted my little Grauben walking with a brisk step, coming fearlessly back to Hamburg.

"Grauben!" I yelled from a good way off.

The girl stopped, a bit concerned, I imagine, at hearing somebody call her this way on a major thoroughfare. With ten more steps I was at her side.

"Axel!" she put in, surprised. "Oh, so you've come to meet me? That was kind of you, sir."

But when she looked me over, Grauben couldn't miss my attitude of uneasiness and confusion.

"What is it?" she said, reaching a hand toward me.

"It's this, Grauben!" I exclaimed.

In two seconds and three sentences, my pretty Virlander was up to date on the situation. For a short while she kept silent. Were our hearts pounding with the same intensity? I don't know, but her hand didn't tremble in mine. We took a hundred steps without speaking.

"Axel!" she finally said to me.

"My dear Grauben!"

"It will be a splendid journey!"

I jumped a foot at these words.

"Yes, Axel, a journey worthy of a scientist's nephew. It's good for a man to earn distinction through some major undertaking."

"What's this, Grauben? You're not going to talk me out of such an expedition?"

"No, dear Axel, and I would gladly travel along with you and your uncle, except a poor girl is bound to be a hindrance to you."

"You're serious?"

"I'm serious."

O women young and old, your female hearts are beyond all comprehension! You're either the most timid or the most courageous of creatures! Logic doesn't figure in your lives. What! The girl was encouraging me to take part in this expedition? She wouldn't have been afraid to attempt the adventure herself? Though I was the man she loved, she was spurring me on?

I felt flustered and—I may as well admit it—ashamed.

"Grauben," I went on, "let's see if you say the same thing tomorrow."

"Tomorrow, dear Axel, I'll say what I've said today."

Holding hands, Grauben and I continued on our way in total silence. I was a broken man from the day's excitements.

After all, I thought, the calends of July are still far off—before that time quite a few developments could arise that might cure my uncle of his mania for traveling underground.

Night had fallen when we arrived at the house on Königstrasse. I expected to find the place quiet, my uncle in bed as was his custom, and old Martha giving the dining room its final nightly flick of the feather duster.

But I hadn't reckoned on the professor's impatience. I found him storming around, all aquiver in the midst of a band of deliverymen who were dumping sundry articles in the driveway; our old servant didn't know what to make of it.

"Come on, Axel, hurry up, you wretch!" my uncle shouted from afar when he spotted me. "Your trunk isn't packed, my papers aren't in order, I can't find the key to my travel bag, and my gaiters haven't arrived!"

I stood dumbfounded. My voice gave out. My lips were barely able to enunciate these words:

"We're really going, then?"

"Yes, you miserable youth! You went for a stroll when you should have been here!"

"We're really going?" I repeated in a feeble voice.

"Yes, the day after tomorrow at the crack of dawn."

I couldn't listen to another word and I fled to my little bedroom.

There were no more grounds for doubt. My uncle had just spent the afternoon rounding up a good number of the articles and implements he needed for his journey; the driveway was clogged with enough rope ladders, knotted ropes, torches, flasks, grappling irons, picks, alpenstocks, and mattocks to overload at least ten men.

I had a ghastly night. The next morning, bright and early, I heard my name being called. I'd sworn I wouldn't open my door.

But there was no way I could resist the sweet voice that spoke these words: "Axel, my dear!"

I emerged from my bedroom. I figured my weary expression, pallor, and red, sleepless eyes would have an effect on Grauben and get her to change her mind.

"Ah, my dear Axel," she told me, "I see you're feeling better! A good night's rest has calmed you down."

"Calmed me down?" I exclaimed.

I rushed over to my mirror. Well, I'll be! I didn't look as bad as I thought. It was hard to believe.

"Axel," Grauben told me, "I've had a long talk with my guardian. He's a bold scientist, a man of great courage, and you mustn't forget that his blood flows in your own veins. He has described his plans to me, his expectations, why and how he hopes to reach his destination. He'll manage it, I haven't the slightest doubt. Oh, dear Axel, it's splendid to devote yourself this way to science! What glory lies in store for Professor Lidenbrock, and it will reflect on his companion! When you come back, Axel, you'll be a man, his equal, free to speak, free to take action, free at last to . . ."

Blushing, the girl didn't finish. Her words poured life into me. Yet I still didn't believe we were going. I dragged Grauben into the professor's study.

"Uncle," I said, "is it absolutely settled that we're going?"

"What! You question it?"

"No," I said, to avoid contradicting him. "I just want to know why we're in such a rush."

"Because time is running out! And time lost can never be regained!"

"But it's only May 26, and till the end of June . . ."

"Huh? Oh, you blockhead, do you think Iceland is that easy to get to? If you hadn't left here like a maniac, I would have taken you to the Copenhagen counter at Liffender & Co., and you would have seen that a boat runs from Copenhagen to Reykjavik only on the 22nd of each month."

"And so?"

"And so if we wait till June 22, we'll arrive too late to see Scartaris's shadow caress the crater of Snaefells! So we need to reach Copenhagen as fast as we can, then hunt for some other means of transportation. Go pack your trunk!"

There wasn't a word I could say. I went up to my bedroom. Grauben followed me. She took care of the items I needed for the trip, organizing them in a little suitcase. She was no more concerned than if I were going on an outing to Lübeck or Helgoland. Her little hands went back and forth unhurriedly. She chatted calmly. She gave me the most practical reasons in favor of our expedition. She bewitched me, and I felt thoroughly angry with her. Sometimes I had an urge to flare up, but she handled me with care and methodically kept on with her tranquil chores.

Finally the last strap on the suitcase got buckled. I headed down to the first floor.

All day long more and more tradesmen were arriving with electrical devices, weapons, and instruments of physical measurement. Old Martha was utterly at a loss.

"Is master insane?" she said to me.

I signaled yes.

"And he's taking you with him?"

Yes again.

"Where to?" she said.

My finger pointed toward the center of the earth.

"To the cellar?" the old servant exclaimed.

"No," I said after a beat, "lower down."

Evening came. I have no idea where the time went.

"Tomorrow morning," my uncle said, "we leave at six o'clock on the dot."

At ten o'clock I fell on my bed like a dead weight.

During the wee hours my night terrors took over again.

I spent those hours dreaming of chasms. I was in the grip of hallucinations. I felt the professor's sinewy hand grab me, drag me, pull me down, yank me under. I was dropping into the depths of a bottomless pit, going faster and faster like an object released in space. My life was nothing more than one never-ending fall.

I woke up at five o'clock, a broken man from exhaustion and agitation. I went down to the dining room. My uncle was at the table. He was wolfing down his food. I looked at him with a feeling of horror. But Grauben was there. I didn't say a thing. I couldn't eat.

At 5:30 there was a rumbling sound out in the street. A bulky carriage had arrived to take us to the train station in Altona. Soon it was chock full of my uncle's luggage.

"What about your trunk?" he said to me.

"It's ready," I replied, weak in the knees.

"Then hurry and fetch it down or you'll make us miss the train!"

Dodging my destiny struck me as impossible by that point. I went back up to my bedroom, let my suitcase slide down the stair steps, and dashed after it.

Just then my uncle was solemnly handing over "the house's reins" to Grauben. My pretty Virlander maintained her usual calm. She hugged her guardian, but she couldn't keep back a tear while brushing my cheek with her gentle lips.

"Grauben!" I exclaimed.

"Go, my dear Axel, go," she told me. "You're leaving a fiancée behind, but you'll come back to find a wife."

After holding Grauben in my arms, I took my seat in the carriage. Standing on the doorstep, Martha and the girl waved a last goodbye to us. Then, urged on by the driver's whistle, the two horses dashed off at a gallop down the road to Altona.

8

IN REALITY A SUBURB of Hamburg, Altona is the end of the line for the railway from Kiel, which was to take us to the shores of the Belt region.[7] In less than twenty minutes we would be entering the province of Holstein.

By 6:30 the carriage had pulled up in front of the terminal; along with his voluminous travel gear, my uncle's many packages were unloaded, transferred weighed, tagged, then reloaded into the baggage car, and by

---

[7] *Translator's note.* Straits off Denmark leading to the Baltic Sea.

seven o'clock we sat face to face in the same compartment. With a blast of steam the locomotive moved out. We were on our way.

Was I resigned to my fate? Not yet. But I was distracted from my major woes by the fresh morning air and the wayside features that were changing with such swiftness as the train raced past them.

As for the professor's thoughts, obviously they were running ahead of the train, which moved too slowly for the liking of his impatient nature. We were alone in the passenger car but didn't talk. My uncle went back through his pockets and his travel bag with painstaking care. I could plainly see that he had all the required paperwork for putting his plans into execution.

Among others, one neatly folded sheet of letterhead came from the Danish chancellery and bore the signature of Mr. Christensen, consul in Hamburg and a friend of the professor's. In Copenhagen this would make it quite easy for us to get letters of introduction to Iceland's governor.

I also spotted the notorious document, lovingly nestled in the most secret compartment of his wallet. I cursed it from the bottom of my heart, then went back to inspecting the countryside. This was a huge sequence of muddy, fertile-looking plains, monotonous and unremarkable: quite a convenient landscape for laying train tracks and nicely conducive to those direct routes so dear to railway companies.

But this monotony didn't last long enough to tire me out, because within three hours of our departure, the train came to a halt in Kiel, a hop, skip, and jump from the sea.

Since our baggage was booked through to Copenhagen, there was no cause for concern. But the professor kept an anxious eye on it during its transference to the steamboat. There it vanished deep into the hold.

In his hurry my uncle had overestimated the time for connections between the railway and the boat, so we were left with a whole workday to ourselves. The steamer *Ellenora* didn't leave till nighttime. Ergo we had nine feverish hours during which our cantankerous traveler consigned to eternal damnation the railways, shipping firms, and governments that tolerated such inefficiency. I was expected to echo his sentiments when he tackled the *Ellenora*'s captain on this topic. He tried to make the man get up steam without wasting another second. The latter showed him the door.

In Kiel, like anywhere else, a day has to run its course. By strolling along the green banks of the bay above the little town, by striding through the shaggy woods that make this village look like a nest in a cluster of branches, by marveling at the country homes all equipped with their little cold-shower bathhouses, in short, by much gadding and grumbling about, we made it to ten o'clock in the evening.

Swirls of smoke from the *Ellenora* filled the sky; its deck quivered from the boiler's vibrations; we went on board and cornered both the upper and lower berths in the only stateroom on the boat.

At 10:15 the steamer loosed its moorings and ran swiftly over the dark waters of the Great Belt.

It was a black night; the breeze was favorable, the sea running high; a few shore lights were visible in the darkness; later on the beam from a lighthouse—I didn't know its location—flickered above the waves; which is all that sticks in my memory of this first crossing.

By seven o'clock in the morning, we'd docked at Korsør, a small town situated on the west coast of Zealand. There, jumping ship and boarding another train, we rode through a landscape just as flat as the countryside of Holstein.

We traveled for three more hours before reaching Denmark's capital. My uncle didn't close his eyes the whole night. In his impatience I swear he was trying to push our passenger car along with his feet.

At last he spotted a patch of sea.

"The Sound!" he exclaimed.

On our left was a huge building that looked like a hospital.

"It's an insane asylum," said one of our fellow travelers.

Oh good, I thought. That's where we're due to end our days—in an institution! And as big as this hospital was, it still would have been too small to hold the sum total of Professor Lidenbrock's insanity!

Finally, at ten o'clock in the morning, we set foot in Copenhagen; loaded into a carriage, our baggage went with us to the Phoenix Hotel in Bredgade. This was the work of a good half an hour, because the railway terminal is located outside town. Then, after hurriedly washing up, my uncle dragged me along behind him. The hotel porter spoke German and English; but in his capacity as prize polyglot, the professor questioned him in proper Danish, and it was in proper Danish that this individual gave him directions to the Museum of Northern Antiquities.

The wonders gathered in this unusual establishment allow visitors to reconstruct the country's past through its old stone weapons, goblets, and jewels; the museum's curator was Professor Thomson, scholar and friend of the Danish consul in Hamburg.

My uncle had a heartfelt letter of introduction for him. Generally scholars aren't very accepting of each other. But here things were quite different. Professor Thomson was an accommodating man and he gave Otto Lidenbrock a cordial reception, likewise his nephew. I need hardly mention that my uncle didn't share his secret with the museum's excellent curator. Quite simply, we wanted to visit Iceland as casual tourists.

Professor Thomson put himself completely at our disposal, and we wandered the wharves looking for an outbound ship.

I was hoping for a total absence of any means of transportation, but it wasn't to be. The *Valkyrie*, a little Danish schooner, was due to set sail for Reykjavik on June 2. The captain, Mr. Bjarne, was on board. His future passenger was so gleeful, he squeezed the man's hand hard enough to crush it. This high-powered handshake caught the decent fellow a little by surprise. He viewed going to Iceland as a simple matter, just doing his job. My uncle thought it a noble calling. Given this enthusiasm for traveling aboard his craft, the good captain took advantage of it and doubled the ticket price. But we weren't being persnickety.

"Be on board Tuesday by seven o'clock in the morning," Captain Bjarne said, after pocketing a respectable number of specie dollars.[8]

Then we thanked Professor Thomson for his kind assistance and went back to the Phoenix Hotel.

"Things are looking up!" my uncle kept saying. "What a stroke of luck that we found a craft ready to leave! Now let's have lunch and go tour the town."

We made our way to Kongens Nytorv, an odd-shaped public square where a pair of leveled cannons are mounted that are too innocuous to frighten a child. Nearby at No. 5 was a made-over French restaurant run by a cook named Vincent; we had an ample lunch there for the reasonable price of four marks (about 55¢) per person.

Then I took a boyish pleasure in roaming through the town; my uncle let me stroll as I pleased; but his eyes saw nothing, neither the modest royal palace, nor the pretty 17th century bridge straddling the canal in front of the antiquities museum, nor that immense memorial to the sculptor Thorvaldsen, all decorated with ugly mural paintings and containing statues of his inside, nor snug little Rosenborg Castle in a park of some beauty, nor the wonderful renaissance edifice housing the stock exchange, nor its steeple consisting of the intertwined tails of four bronze dragons, nor the big windmills on the ramparts, their huge arms inflating like a ship's sails in a sea breeze.

What delectable strolls we would have taken, my pretty Virlander and I—toward the harbor where double-deckers and frigates slept placidly below red roofs, along the green banks of the strait, through that shadowy thicket with the fortress hidden deep inside, its cannons poking their blackish muzzles between the branches of elderberry bushes and willow trees.

But alas, my poor Grauben was far away—and could I ever hope to see her again?

However, though my uncle paid no attention to these beguiling locales, he was terrifi-

---

[8] *Translator's note.* Scandinavian currency, at the time worth about 5¢ more than a U.S. dollar.

cally taken with the appearance of a certain steeple situated on the island of Amager, which makes up the southeast quadrant of Copenhagen.

I had orders to start walking that way; I boarded a little steamboat that ran up and down the canals, and in a few seconds it pulled alongside the wharf at the Royal Dockyard.

We traveled down a few narrow streets where some convicts, dressed in pants that were half yellow and half gray, were toiling away under the eyes of cops with billy clubs; then we arrived in front of Vor Frelsers Kirke.[9] This church wasn't a notable tourist attraction. But here's why its tallish steeple had caught the professor's attention: rising from a platform overhead, an outside staircase wound around the spire, unrolling its coils high into the air.

"Let's go up it," my uncle said.

"But what if we get dizzy?" I remarked.

"All the more reason for going; we need to get used to it."

"Even so . . ."

"Come on, I tell you—quit wasting time."

I had to obey. A custodian who lived across the street handed us a key, and we started our climb.

My uncle led the way, stepping smartly. I followed him with some trepidation, because my head could start spinning with disgraceful ease. The iron nerve and soaring confidence of an eagle weren't among my virtues.

So long as we were confined to the winding stairs inside the tower, everything was all right; but 150 steps later the wind abruptly hit me in the face—we'd made it to the platform below the steeple. There the open-air staircase started upward, protected by a frail handrail; getting narrower and narrower, its steps seemed to rise into infinity.

"I'll never make it!" I exclaimed.

"You're not planning on being a coward, are you?" the professor replied mercilessly. "Up you go!"

All I could do was follow him, hanging on tight. The outside air made me giddy; I felt

the steeple swaying in the gusts of wind; my legs gave out on me; soon I was crawling on my knees, then on my belly; I shut my eyes; I felt airsick.

Finally my uncle dragged me by the collar, and I arrived just underneath the ball on top.

"Look," he told me, "and look well! You need to get *an education in depth!*"

I opened my eyes. In the midst of the gray smog below, I saw houses flattened out as if they'd fallen and collapsed. Disheveled clouds were going past overhead—and by an optical illusion in reverse, they seemed to be standing still while the steeple, the ball, and I all were being swept along at fantastic speed. Far off in one direction stretched the green countryside, in the other glittered the sea under the sun's rays. Looking like seagull wings, a few white sails were in the Sound, which rolled up to the headland of Elsinore, while the shores of Sweden undulated in the east, scarcely blurred by the mists. This whole immense panorama whirled around me as I looked.

Nevertheless I had to get up, stand straight, and keep looking. This first session of my education in dizziness lasted an hour. When it was finally all right for me to go back down and set foot on the solidly paved streets, I was stiff all over.

"We'll start again tomorrow," my instructor said.

And for the next five days, in fact, I continued this dizzying exercise, and in spite of myself I made noticeable progress in the art of "looking down from on high."

9

THE DAY OF OUR departure arrived. The previous day our obliging Professor Thomson had brought us compelling letters of introduction to Baron Trampe, Iceland's governor, Reverend Pictursson, the auxiliary bishop, and Mr. Finsen, Reykjavik's mayor. In return my uncle awarded him the heartiest of handshakes.

By six o'clock in the morning on the 2nd, our precious baggage was safe aboard

---

[9] *Translator's note.* Danish: "Church of Our Savior."

the *Valkyrie*. The captain showed us to our cabins, which were rather cramped and located under a sort of deckhouse.

"Do we have a good wind?" my uncle asked.

"Excellent," Captain Bjarne replied. "It's out of the southeast. We'll leave the Sound with the wind on our quarter and all sails set."

Its foresail, spanker sail, topsail, and topgallant sail unfurled, the schooner got going in a few seconds and stood into the strait under full canvas. An hour later Denmark's capital seemed to sink beneath the far-off waves, and the *Valkyrie* skimmed the coast of Elsinore. In my jittery frame of mind, I half expected to see Hamlet's ghost wandering over this fabled embankment.

"O magnificent madman!" I said. "Surely you would have approved of us! Maybe you would have gone with us to the center of the globe, looking for a way to resolve your perpetual doubts!"

But nothing was visible on the ancient walls. Anyhow the castle's a good deal younger than the valiant prince of Denmark. It now functions as a luxurious lodge for the official who watches over the Sound, a strait that 15,000 ships of all nations go through annually.

Kronborg Castle soon vanished into the mist, likewise the tower of Helsingborg built on the Swedish side, while the schooner listed a little under breezes out of Kattegat Strait.

The *Valkyrie* was a top-notch sailing ship, but with sailpower you never really know what to expect. It was carrying a cargo to Reykjavik of coal, housewares, crockery, woolens, and a load of wheat. A five-man crew, all Danish, was sufficient to run the vessel.

"How long a trip is this?" my uncle asked the captain.

"About ten days," the latter replied, "if we don't hit too many northwest squalls abreast of the Faroe Islands."

"But in general you won't have to face any major delays?"

"No, Professor Lidenbrock. We'll make it, rest assured."

Toward evening the schooner doubled the Skaw, a cape at the northern tip of Denmark, then went through Skagerrak Strait during the night, hugged the lower end of Norway abreast of Cape Lindesnes, and stood into the North Sea.

Two days later we'd raised the shores of Scotland level with Peterhead, then the *Valkyrie* steered toward the Faroe Islands, passing between the Orkneys and the Shetlands.

Soon our schooner was taking a beating from the waves of the Atlantic; it needed to tack into the north wind and had some trouble reaching the Faroes. On the 8th the captain spotted Mykines Island, the westernmost of this group, and from then on he made straight for Cape Portland,[10] located on Iceland's southerly coast.

The crossing wasn't especially eventful. I handled this oceangoing ordeal pretty well; my uncle, much to his annoyance and even more to his shame, was seasick the whole time.

So he wasn't able to converse with Captain Bjarne on the topic of Snaefells, the ways of traveling to it, the forms of transportation available; he had to wait for answers till after his arrival and he spent the whole time lying in his cabin, whose bulkheads made cracking sounds whenever the boat gave a sharp pitch. You must admit, his fate wasn't exactly undeserved.

By the 11th we'd sighted Cape Portland. We could make out Mýrdals Jökull towering over it, because the weather was clear just then. The cape is a big, steeply sloping mountain that has the whole seashore to itself.

The *Valkyrie* stayed a sensible distance off the coastline, sailing westward along it amid sundry congregations of whales and sharks. Soon an immense rock came in sight, pierced clear through by an opening from which the foaming sea spilled furiously. The Westman Islands seemed to sprout from the ocean's liquid plains like a harvest of rocks. From then on the schooner stayed out in the open, to give itself decent room for rounding

---

[10] *Translator's note.* Today known as Dyrhólaey.

Cape Reykjanes, which forms the westerly corner of Iceland.

The sea was really running high, and this kept my uncle from climbing on deck to marvel at these coastlines so slashed and pummeled by winds out of the southwest.

Forty-eight hours later we emerged from a storm that had forced the schooner to run with all its canvas taken in, then to the east we sighted the beacon on Skagen Point, where perilous rocks extend a good way out under the waves. An Icelandic pilot came on board, and three hours later the *Valkyrie* dropped anchor in front of Reykjavik in Faxa Bay.

The professor finally came out of his cabin, a little pale, a little bedraggled, but still enthusiastic and with a smug look in his eyes.

Townspeople had gathered on the wharf, exceptionally interested in the arrival of a ship that was bringing something for everybody.

My uncle wasted no time vacating his aquatic prison—or, more accurately, his sea-going sick bay. But before leaving the schooner's deck, he dragged me to the bow and there his finger guided me toward the northerly part of the bay, to a lofty mountain with two crests, a pair of volcanic cones covered with perpetual snow.

"That's Snaefells!" he exclaimed.

Then, after swearing me with a gesture to absolute silence, he got down into the dinghy waiting for him. I did likewise, and soon we set foot on the soil of Iceland.

The first person to appear was a fine-looking man in the uniform of a general. Which wasn't his rank, however—he was just a magistrate, the island's governor, none other than Baron Trampe. The professor realized who he was dealing with. He handed the governor his letters from Copenhagen and struck up a brief conversation with the man in Danish, a conversation where I remained completely extraneous for obvious reasons. But the outcome of this first exchange was that Baron Trampe put himself completely at Professor Lidenbrock's disposal.

My uncle got a thoroughly friendly welcome from the mayor, Mr. Finsen, whose uniform was no less warlike than the governor's but whose personality and job description were just as amicable.

As for the auxiliary bishop, Reverend Pictursson, he was currently making his diocesan rounds in the district up north; for the moment we had to do without the pleasure of his acquaintance. But Mr. Fridriksson, instructor in the natural sciences at the Reykjavik academy, was a delightful man whose assistance proved quite valuable to us. This unpretentious scholar spoke only Icelandic and Latin; he came and offered me his services in the language of Horace, and I felt we had an automatic understanding. In fact, during my whole stay in Iceland, he was the only local I could have a conversation with.

His house consisted of three rooms, and this fine man placed two of them at our disposal; soon we'd taken up residence along with our baggage, whose magnitude rather astonished the good people of Reykjavik.

"Well, Axel," my uncle told me, "we're making progress and the hardest part is over."

"The hardest part? You're serious?" I exclaimed.

"Absolutely—it's literally all downhill from here!"

"If you look at it that way, you're right. But ultimately what goes down must come up, correct?"

"Oh, that doesn't worry me in the least! See here, we have no time to lose! I'm going to head over to the library. Maybe I'll find one of Saknussemm's manuscripts there and I'll be more than happy to consult it."

"In the meantime I'll explore the town. Wouldn't you like to do that as well?"

"Oh, it's of middling interest to me. What's notable in this nation of Iceland isn't above but below."

I went out and wandered casually around.

It would take some doing to get lost on Reykjavik's two streets. So I didn't feel compelled to ask directions, which offers plenty of potential for misunderstanding when your language is pantomime.

The town extends over some rather low,

marshy ground between two hills. An immense lava flow covers the soil on one side and slopes down toward the sea in a fairly gentle manner. On the other side, bounded to the north by the enormous glacier of Snaefells, there stretched the vastness of Faxa Bay, where only the *Valkyrie* currently lay at anchor. Ordinarily fishing wardens from England and France stay moored farther out; but just then they were patrolling the island's easterly shores.

The longer of Reykjavik's two streets runs parallel to the beach; here the merchants and traders live in wooden huts built from red beams laid out horizontally; located more to the west, the other street leads toward a little lake between the houses of the bishop and other individuals not engaged in commerce.

I'd soon gone up and down these bleak, dreary lanes; at times I glimpsed a patch of faded grass that looked like an old overused carpet with no pile left, or something vaguely resembling a garden whose scanty vegetables—potatoes, cabbage, lettuce—wouldn't have been out of place on a table in Lilliput; there were also a few wilted wallflowers trying to catch a little sunshine.

About halfway down the residential street, I found the public cemetery, encircled by an earthen wall and offering plenty of room. With a few strides I then arrived at the governor's mansion, a shanty compared to our city hall in Hamburg, a palace next to the hovels of the Icelandic populace.

Between the little lake and the town stood the church, built in the Protestant style and constructed from charred stones that the volcanoes themselves had gone to the trouble of excavating; in a good west wind, its red roof tiles were clearly destined to fly off in all directions, much to the dismay of the faithful.

On a nearby overlook I spotted the national academy, where, as our host later informed me, you could master Hebrew, English, French, and Danish—four languages I don't know a syllable of, I'm ashamed to say. I would have ranked at the bottom of the forty students enrolled in this little college—

and wouldn't have been deemed worthy of sharing one of those double-bedded cupboards they sleep in, which must suffocate the sicklier ones their very first night.

In three hours I'd inspected not only the town but its surroundings. The overall appearance of the place was exceptionally dismal. No trees, no vegetation worth mentioning. Sharp crests of volcanic rock everywhere. Icelandic shanties are made of earth and peat, their walls slanting inward. They look like roofs sitting on the ground. Except that these roofs are comparatively fertile meadows. Thanks to the heat inside these dwellings, grass grows on them to near perfection, and they're carefully mowed at haymaking time, otherwise farm animals will come and graze on these lawn-covered lodgings.

I ran into few residents during my excursion. Going back down the commercial street, I found most of the populace busy with the drying, salting, and shipping of codfish, their chief export item. The men looked hardy but on the heavy side, blond Germanic types with brooding eyes, vaguely sensing they were apart from the rest of humanity, poor exiles banished to this icy land where nature might as well have made them Eskimos, since she'd condemned them to live on the edge of the polar circle! I tried in vain to catch a smile on their faces; sometimes they laughed with a sort of automatic muscle contraction, but they never smiled.

Their clothing consisted of a rough pea jacket made of black wool (a material going by the name *vadmel* in Scandinavian countries), a wide-brimmed hat, pants with red trim, and a doubled-over piece of leather by way of footwear.

The women looked downcast and resigned, their faces pleasant enough but never showing any emotion, and they were dressed in a blouse and skirt of dark *vadmel:* girls wore a little brown knitted cap over their wreaths of braided hair; wives wrapped a colored handkerchief around their heads, topping it with a crest of white linen.

Reentering Mr. Fridriksson's house after a hearty stroll, I found my uncle already in our host's company.

10

DINNER WAS ON the table; Professor Liden- brock eagerly wolfed it down, his enforced abstinence at sea having turned his belly into a bottomless pit. More Danish than Icelandic, the meal was nothing notable in itself; but our host, more Icelandic than Danish, re- minded me of the hospitable heroes of yore. He made it clear that this was our home even more than his.

The conversation proceeded in the local language, which my uncle interspersed with German and Mr. Fridriksson with Latin so that I could keep up. It ran to scientific mat- ters, as is appropriate for scholars; but Pro- fessor Lidenbrock took the greatest pains not to give anything away, and with every sen- tence his eyes swore me to utter silence on the subject of our future plans.

First of all Mr. Fridriksson asked my un- cle how his research at the library had panned out.

"Library!" the latter exclaimed. "It's noth- ing more than a few odd books on shelves that are almost empty!"

"Excuse me?" Mr. Fridriksson responded. "We own 8,000 volumes, quite a few of them rare and valuable—works in the old Scandi- navian language as well as all the current bestsellers, which we order from Copenhagen every year."

"How do you figure 8,000 volumes? By my count—"

"Oh, Professor Lidenbrock, they circu- late all around the country! Book learn- ing is popular in our icy old island! Every farmer, every fisherman, knows how to read and does read. We believe that books shouldn't mildew behind iron bars where interested people can't see them; instead they're meant to live out their days under the eyes of readers. Accordingly these volumes pass from hand to hand, are pored over, are read and reread, and often return to their shelves only after being gone for a year or two."

"And meanwhile," my uncle replied in some annoyance, "foreign visitors—"

"What do you want? Foreigners have their own libraries back home, and more than anything else our farmers need to be edu- cated. I say to you again, a love for book learning runs in every Icelander's blood. Accordingly, in 1816 we formed the Ice- landic Literary Society, and it's still going strong; foreign scholars consider it a privi- lege to participate; it publishes books meant to instruct our countrymen and genuinely benefit the nation. If you would like to be one of our corresponding members, Pro- fessor Lidenbrock, you'll do us the greatest honor."

My uncle belonged to a hundred or so scientific societies already, but he accepted with a good grace that pleased Mr. Frid- riksson.

"Now," the latter continued, "kindly let me know what books you hoped to locate in our library, and maybe I can give you some information on them."

I looked at my uncle. He was hesitant to answer. This related directly to his plans. However, after thinking it over, he decided to speak his mind.

"Mr. Fridriksson," he said, "I wanted to find out if, among your older holdings, you owned the writings of Arne Saknus- semm?"

"Arne Saknussemm!" replied the Reykja- vik educator. "You mean that 16th century scholar who was also a great naturalist, al- chemist, and explorer?"

"Exactly."

"One of the glories of Icelandic science and literature?"

"That's correct."

"A man of worldwide fame?"

"I won't argue with you."

"An individual with as much daring as genius?"

"I see you're quite familiar with him."

My uncle was basking in bliss at hearing his hero spoken of this way. He devoured Mr. Fridriksson with his eyes.

"Well then," he asked, "where are his writings?"

"Ah, his writings—we don't have any."

"What! Nowhere in Iceland?"

"Neither in Iceland nor anywhere else."

"And why not?"

"Because Arne Saknussemm was persecuted on grounds of heresy, and in 1573 his writings were burned in Copenhagen by the executioner's own hands."

"Very good! Perfect!" my uncle exclaimed, much to the consternation of our instructor in the natural sciences.

"Huh?" the latter put in.

"Yes, everything's clear, everything connects, everything's explained! Saknussemm had been put on the Index[11] and he was forced to hide the fruits of his genius, so I understand why he needed to bury his secret in an unintelligible cryptogram . . ."

"What secret?" Mr. Fridriksson instantly asked.

"A secret that . . . uh . . ." my uncle replied, stammering.

"Is this some special document you happen to have?" our host went on.

"No . . . I was indulging in pure speculation."

"Fine," replied Mr. Fridriksson, who had the decency to not press the matter, seeing that his conversation partner looked uncomfortable. "I hope," he added, "that you won't leave our island without delving into its mineralogical treasures."

"Certainly not," my uncle replied. "But I'm a Johnny-come-lately—haven't other experts already passed this way?"

"That's right, Professor Lidenbrock. The work that Messrs. Olafsen and Povelsen carried out at the king's command, Troïl's investigations, the scientific mission undertaken by Messrs. Gaimard and Robert aboard the *Search*, a French sloop of war,[12] and the recent findings of scientists sailing on the frigate *Queen Hortense* all have contributed powerfully to our knowledge of Iceland. But believe me, there's still plenty to do."

"You think so?" my uncle asked in a hearty voice, trying to subdue the gleam in his eyes.

"Yes. There are so many little-known mountains, glaciers, and volcanoes to study! And trust me, you needn't go far—look at that mountain rearing up on the horizon. That's Snaefells."

"Oh?" my uncle put in. "Snaefells?"

"Yes, one of our most interesting volcanoes, and people rarely go inside its crater."

"It's extinct?"

"Heavens yes. It's been extinct for over 500 years."

"Well then," my uncle replied, hurriedly crossing his legs to keep from leaping into the air, "I have a hankering to start my geological research near that Sefells . . . Fesells . . . what was the name?"

"Snaefells," good old Mr. Fridriksson said again.

This part of the conversation took place in Latin; I understood it perfectly and I could barely keep a straight face as I watched my uncle suppress the elation exuding from every part of him; he tried to put on an expression of childlike innocence, which made him look like a scowling old devil.

"Yes," he put in, "your words settle it for me! We'll attempt to scale that Snaefells, maybe even examine its crater!"

"I'm so sorry," Mr. Fridriksson replied, "that my workload won't let me take time off; it would be both pleasant and profitable for me to go with you."

"Oh no, no, no!" my uncle instantly replied. "We wouldn't dream of inconveniencing anybody, Mr. Fridriksson; I thank you with all my heart. The presence of such an expert as yourself would be highly beneficial, but the obligations of your profession . . ."

I prefer to think that our host, in the innocence of his Icelandic soul, wasn't aware of my uncle's blatant manipulations.

"I fully approve of your starting with that volcano, Professor Lidenbrock," he said. "You'll reap a rich harvest of unusual discoveries. But, tell me, how do you expect to reach the Snaefells peninsula?"

"By water—we'll row across the bay. That's the quickest route."

---

[11] *Translator's note.* List of banned books issued by the Inquisition.

[12] The *Search* was sent out in 1835 by Admiral Louis-Isidore Duperrey to look for traces of a missing expedition, the Baron de Blosseville's on the *Lillois*, whose fate is still unlearned.

"Surely. But it's impossible to go that way."

"Why?"

"Because we don't have a single rowboat in Reykjavik."

"Great Lucifer!"

"You'll need to travel by land, following the coastline. It'll be longer but more interesting."

"Fine. I'll see about hiring a guide."

"I've got just the man for you."

"Somebody who's smart and reliable?"

"Yes, a resident of the peninsula. He hunts eider ducks for their down, he's very capable, and you'll be pleased with him. He speaks perfect Danish."

"And when can I meet him?"

"Tomorrow if you like."

"Why not today?"

"He doesn't get here till tomorrow."

"Tomorrow, then," my uncle replied with a sigh

This significant conversation ended a few seconds later with the German educator giving warm thanks to the Icelandic one. During this dinner my uncle had just learned some significant things, including Saknussemm's biography and why the document was so secretive, along with the news that our host wouldn't be going with him on his expedition, and that as early as tomorrow a guide would be at his service.

11

THAT EVENING I took a short stroll along Reykjavik's shoreline, came back early, lay down, and fell sound asleep on my hardboard bed.

When I awoke I heard my uncle talking a mile a minute in the next room. I got up at once, dressed quickly, and joined him.

He was chatting in Danish with a tall man of muscular build. This strapping fellow must have been unusually strong. His eyes were set in a very solid, forthright cranium and looked shrewd to me. They were a pensive blue. Long hair, which would have qualified as red even in England, fell over his athletic shoulders. This islander was supple in his movements, but his arm motions were minimal, as if he was a man who didn't know or care about body language. His whole being suggested a personality that was utterly serene, not lazy but tranquil. You sensed that he was completely self-reliant, that he worked at his own pace, and that nothing in the world could surprise or disturb his philosophical outlook.

I detected these shadings of character in the way this Icelander was listening to the frenzied torrent of words coming from his conversation partner. He stood with his arms folded, motionless in the midst of my uncle's speeded-up gestures; to say no, his head shifted from left to right; to say yes, it lowered—and these moves were so negligible, his long hair scarcely quivered. He carried economy of motion to the point of stinginess.

Honestly, I never would have guessed from the look of him that this fellow was a hunter by trade; he wasn't about to scare the game away, that was certain, but how did he ever manage to catch anything?

Mr. Fridriksson cleared matters up when he informed me that this serene individual was just "an eider hunter"—he dealt with a duck whose fluffy feathers ranked as the island's most precious treasure. In essence these fluffy feathers are known as eiderdown, and gathering it doesn't call for any great outlay of activity.

During the first days of summer, the female eider, a lovely breed of duck, goes and builds her nest among the rocks in those fjords that edge the whole coastline.[13] Her nest built, she upholsters it with the delicate feathers she plucks from her own belly. The hunter—or, more accurately, the gatherer—arrives soon after, steals the nest, and the female starts her work all over again. She continues in this vein so long as she has any down left. When she's completely stripped, it's the male's turn to despoil himself. Only, since the latter's tough, heavy covering hasn't any market value, the hunter doesn't bother to swipe the babies' latest cradle; so the nest is done; the

---

[13] In Scandinavian countries a narrow bay is called a fjord.

female lays her eggs; the little ones hatch, and a year later the eiderdown harvest starts again.

Now then, since an eider duck doesn't elect to build her nests on steep rocks but rather on flat, convenient boulders near the water's edge, the Icelandic hunter can practice his calling without going to a lot of trouble. He's a farmer who doesn't have to sow or reap his crops, just gather them.

This solemn, stoic, silent individual was named Hans Bjelke; he came recommended by Mr. Fridriksson. He was our future guide. His manner and my uncle's were in striking contrast.

Yet they easily reached an understanding. Neither of them worried about wages, the one ready to take whatever was offered, the other ready to give whatever was asked. No bargain was ever more easily struck.

Now then, as the result of its terms, Hans agreed to guide us to the village of Stapi, located on the southerly coast of the Snaefells peninsula at the very foot of the volcano. This would total about twenty-two miles overland, a two-day journey to my uncle's thinking.

But when he learned it was an issue of Danish miles, which are 24,000 feet each, he had to redo his calculations and budget seven or eight days for the trip, in view of the inadequate roads.

Four horses were to be put at our disposal, two for carrying my uncle and me, another two assigned to our baggage. As was his custom, Hans would go on foot. He knew this part of the coast perfectly and he promised to take the shortest route.

His agreement with my uncle didn't conclude with our arrival in Stapi; he was to remain in the professor's employ over the whole period of time required by the latter's scientific excursions, and his wage was to be three riksdalers per week (about $3.50). Only it was expressly stipulated that this sum would be paid our guide every Saturday evening, a condition that was a *sine qua non* [14] for his agreeing.

---

[14] *Translator's note*. Latin: an "absolute essential."

Our departure was scheduled for June 16. My uncle wanted to hand our hunter a down payment on the trip, but the latter gave him a one-word refusal:

"*Efter*," he put in.

"After," the professor told me for my edification.

The treaty signed, Hans took his leave as cool as a cucumber.

"He's quite a man!" my uncle exclaimed. "But he hasn't any inkling of the marvelous role that the future has in store for him to play."

"Then he's coming along with us to the . . . "

"Yes, Axel, to the center of the earth."

We had forty-eight hours still to go; much to my regret I had to spend them on our travel preparations; it took all our shrewdness to organize everything in the most advantageous way, instruments on one side, weapons on another, tools in this bundle, provisions in that one. There were four categories in all.

The instruments consisted of:

1) An Eigel thermometer with gradations as high as 300° Fahrenheit, which struck me as either too much or not enough. Too much, if the atmospheric heat should indeed get this high, in which case we would cook to death. Not enough, if it came to measuring the temperature of hot springs or any other entities in a molten state.

2) A pressure gauge running on compressed air, which was designed to register atmospheric pressures higher than those at sea level. In essence an ordinary barometer wouldn't have been adequate, since the atmosphere's pressure was supposed to increase proportionally as we went down below the surface of the earth.

3) A chronometer made by the younger Boissonnas in Geneva, which was meticulously synchronized with the meridian of Hamburg.

4) Two compasses, one measuring inclination and the other declination.

5) A spyglass for nighttime use.

6) Two Ruhmkorff devices, which, with the help of an electric current, provided a

light source that's very reliable, very portable, and not a bit cumbersome.[15]

Our weapons included two Colt revolvers plus two rifles manufactured by Purdey and Moore & Co. Why the firearms? Presumably we had neither savages nor wild animals to fear. But my uncle seemed to value his arsenal as much as his instruments—especially his substantial supply of guncotton, which isn't affected by moisture and has greater explosive power than regular gunpowder.

The tools included two picks, two mattocks, a silk rope ladder, three alpenstocks, an ax, a hammer, a dozen iron wedges and pegs, plus some long knotted ropes. This couldn't help amounting to a mighty bundle, because the ladder by itself was 300 feet in length.

Finally there were the provisions; though not huge, it was a reassuring package because I knew it held a six-month supply of meat concentrate and dried biscuit. Gin was all the liquid we took, water was totally absent; but we carried flasks, and my uncle figured there would be springs for filling them; nothing came of the objections I managed to raise as to the quality, the temperature, or even the nonexistence of such springs.

To finish off this detailed laundry list of our travel gear, I'll make note of our portable medicine chest, which contained blunt-tipped scissors, splints for fractures, a strip of raw linen tape, bandages, compresses, sticking plasters, a bleeding cup—fearful things all; in addition there was a row of vials filled with dextrin, rubbing alcohol, solution of lead acetate, ether, vinegar, and ammonia, all drugs whose functions were less than reassuring; finally there were the ingredients needed for the Ruhmkorff devices.

My uncle was careful to not forget a supply of tobacco, gunpowder for hunting, and a tinderbox, plus he girded his loins with a leather money belt containing prudent reserves of gold, silver, and paper currency. Six pairs of sturdy boots, waterproofed by a coating of tar and rubber cement, were located in the tool category.

"Dressed, shod, and equipped like this," my uncle told me, "there's no reason we won't go far."

We spent the whole day of the 14th in organizing these various items. That evening we dined at the home of Baron Trampe, along with the mayor of Reykjavik and Dr. Hyaltalin, the country's foremost physician. Mr. Fridriksson wasn't on the guest list; I found out later that he and the governor had quarreled over some administrative issue and didn't fraternize. So I wasn't in a position to understand a single word spoken during this semiformal dinner. All I noticed was that my uncle talked the whole time.

By the next day, the 15th, we'd finished our preparations. Our host filled the professor with noticeable pleasure by handing him a map of Iceland incomparably more accurate than Henderson's—a map based on the geodetic surveys of Messrs. Scheel and Frisak plus the topographical investigations of Mr. Björn Gunnlaugsson. Drafted by Mr. Olaf Nikolas Olsen on a scale of 1:480,000 and published by the Icelandic Literary Society, it was an invaluable document for a mineralogist.

We spent our last evening in close conversation with Mr. Fridriksson, whom I

---

[15] Mr. Ruhmkorff's device consists of a Bunsen battery that's activated with the help of potassium dichromate, which is odorless; an induction coil puts the electricity generated by the battery in contact with a specially designed lantern; inside this lantern there's a glass spiral in which a vacuum has been created and only a slight residue of nitrogen or carbon dioxide gas remains. When the device is turned on, this gas becomes luminous and produces a continual whitish light. The battery and coil are placed in a leather bag with a strap, which the traveler slings over his shoulder. Placed outside, the lantern gives more than enough light even in utter darkness; it lets you venture among the most flammable gases without any fear of an explosion, and it won't die out even in the heart of the deepest rivers. Mr. Ruhmkorff is a skilled and knowledgeable physicist. His major discovery is the induction coil, which lets you generate high-voltage electricity. Recently, in 1864, he won the $10,000 prize that France awards every five years for the most inventive application of electricity.

found deeply congenial; our chat was followed by a rather restless night, on my part at least.

At five o'clock in the morning, I woke up to the neighing and prancing of four horses under my window. I got dressed in a hurry and went down to the street. There Hans had finishing loading up our baggage, barely moving a muscle so to speak. Yet he did his work with unusual skill. My uncle contributed more noise than help, and our guide seemed to be paying very little attention to his recommendations.

By six o'clock everything was ready. Mr. Fridriksson shook hands with us. My uncle thanked him in wholehearted Icelandic for his kind hospitality. As for me, I put together a cordial tribute in my best Latin; then we climbed into our saddles, and along with his last farewell Mr. Fridriksson tossed me a line by Virgil that seemed to have been written just for us, we travelers who weren't sure of our way:

Et quacumque viam dederit
fortuna sequamur.[16]

12

WE HEADED OFF beneath a sky that was overcast but calm. No tiring heat to dread, no disastrous downpours. Perfect tourist weather.

At the outset of the undertaking, the pleasure of riding on horseback through unknown country put me in a relaxed frame of mind. I was all caught up in the delights of sightseeing, following my inclinations, enjoying my freedom. I was starting to go along with this business.

"Besides," I said to myself, "what's there to worry about? We'll travel through some extremely interesting country! We'll scale a most distinctive mountain! If worst comes to worst, we'll go down inside an extinct crater! It's quite clear that's all this Saknussemm actually did. As for the presence of some hall-

---

[16] *Translator's note.* Latin: "And we'll take whatever path fate provides."

way leading to the center of the globe—sheer fantasy, sheer impossibility! So let's quit quibbling and have all the fun we can on this expedition."

I'd reached these conclusions by the time we were outside Reykjavik.

Hans led the way at a quick, rhythmic, steady pace. The two horses carrying our baggage followed him without needing to be guided. My uncle and I brought up the rear and we actually didn't cut too poor a figure on our small but hardy steeds.

Iceland is one of the biggest islands in Europe. Its surface area measures 40,000 square miles and it has only 60,000 residents. Geographers have divided it into four quadrants, and we had to cross the sector known as the Southwest Quarter *(Sudvestr Fjordùngr)* pretty much at an angle.

Leaving Reykjavik behind, Hans immediately took to the seacoast. We crossed some scanty meadows that had a hard time looking green; yellow fared better. On the horizon were masses of trachyte, their craggy summits looking like a blur in the fog to the east; now and then a few patches of snow caught the diffuse light, gleaming on the slopes of far-off pinnacles; certain peaks stood up straighter, punctured the gray clouds, reappeared above the shifting mists, and looked like reefs emerging into the open air.

Often these chains of barren rocks formed a headland near the sea and bit into the meadows; but they always left enough space to get past. Besides, our horses instinctively picked the most promising locales without ever relaxing their pace. My uncle didn't even have the consolation of urging his steed onward with voice or whip; he had no reason to be impatient. I couldn't help grinning at the sight of that tall figure on his little horse—his long limbs brushed the ground and he looked like a centaur with six legs.

"A fine beast!" he said. "You'll see, Axel, that there's no shrewder animal than an Icelandic horse. Snowfalls, rainstorms, unmanageable trails, boulders, glaciers—nothing stops him. He's gallant, modest, and dependable. Never stumbles, never shies. When there's a river or fjord to cross (and there'll be some), you'll see him turn into an amphibian, charge across the water without hesitation, and get right to the opposite bank! But don't hurry him, let him be—and with him doing the carrying, we'll cover our ten land leagues per day."

"No doubt we will," I replied. "But what about our guide?"

"Oh, he doesn't worry me! Men like him don't even notice they're walking. This fellow moves so few muscles, I bet he never gets tired. Anyhow I'll let him have my steed in a pinch. If I don't stretch my limbs, I'll soon get a charley horse. The arms will be fine, but the legs need looking after."

Meanwhile we were heading forward at a good clip. The countryside was nearly a wilderness already. Here and there a lonely farmhouse—some freestanding *boër*[17] built with wood, earth, and pieces of lava—loomed like a beggar at the edge of a sunken road. These dilapidated shanties looked as if they were asking alms from passersby, and you were half inclined to make a charitable contribution. In this region roads and even trails were totally lacking, and though the vegetation grew slowly, it was quick to cover any traces left by the few travelers who came this way.

Even so, this corner of the province is located just a hop, skip, and jump from the capital, so it's ranked among the populated, sophisticated parts of Iceland. So where did that leave those regions even wilder than this wilderness? After clearing half a mile, we still hadn't run into a single farmer standing in his cottage doorway, nor a single uncivilized shepherd grazing a flock more civilized than himself; just a few cows and sheep left on their own. What were we to expect, then, from those tortuous districts turned upside down by eruptive phenomena, those localities created by volcanic explosions and underground convulsions?

We were to make their acquaintance before much longer; but after checking Olsen's map, I saw that one could bypass them by going along the winding shoreline. In essence the major volcanic activity is concentrated largely inland; there beds of

rock (known as "traprock" in Scandinavian speech) sit on top of each other in horizontal layers—bands of trachyte, outpourings of basalt, that igneous gravel known as tuff, all sorts of volcanic conglomerates, lava flows, and streams of molten porphyry have made this region so ugly that it's uncanny. I had no idea at this point what a sight was waiting for us on the Snaefells peninsula, where the fiery character of this volcanic waste has wreaked fearsome havoc.

Two hours after we'd left Reykjavik, we arrived at the village of Gufunes, known as an *aoalkirkja*, or church headquarters. It had nothing notable to offer. Only a few houses. Barely enough to rate as a hamlet in Germany.

Hans halted there for half an hour; he doled out our frugal breakfast, answered yes or no to my uncle's questions about the nature of the route, and when we asked him the locality where he figured to spend the night:

"Garðar," he merely said.

I checked the map to find out where Garðar was.[18] I spotted a village with this name on the banks of the Hvalfjord, four Danish miles from Reykjavik. I showed it to my uncle.

"Only four Danish miles!" he said. "Eighteen statute miles out of a hundred! There's a pleasant stroll for you."

He tried to make a comment to our guide —who didn't answer him, went out in front of the horses, and took to the trail again.

Three hours later, still trampling the faded grass of these meadows, we had to go around the Kollafjord, a detour that was easier and less time-consuming than crossing this bay. Soon we entered a *pingstaoer*, or county seat, named Ejulberg, whose bell tower would have rung twelve noon if Icelandic churches had been wealthy enough to own clocks; but they're in the same boat as their parishioners, who haven't any pocket watches and get along just fine.

There we freshened up the horses; afterward they took us down a narrow beach between a chain of hills and the sea, bringing us

---

[17] Dwelling for Icelandic peasants.

[18] *Translator's note.* Today it's known as Innrihólmur.

at one go to the *aoalkirkja* of Brantär, then, a mile farther on, to the *annexia* of Saurbaer, a church annex located on the southerly bank of the Hvalfjord.

By then it was four o'clock in the afternoon; we'd cleared four Danish miles, or slightly more than eighteen statute miles.[19]

At this location the fjord was well over two statute miles across; the breakers dashed noisily against the sharp boulders; this bay was spread out between walls of rock—they were like sheer inclines 3,000 feet high and were notable for their layers of brown between the reddish hues of their beds of tuff. As shrewd as our horses were, I didn't quite foresee us crossing a full-fledged inlet while riding on the back of a quadruped.

"If they *are* shrewd," I said, "they won't even try to cross over. Anyhow it's my job to be shrewd for them."

But my uncle didn't want to wait. He spurred his horse toward the shore. As soon as his steed got wind of waves undulating against a coastline, the beast came to a halt. My uncle had instincts of his own and urged it on again. Once more the creature refused, shaking its head. Next came cusswords and cracks of the whip, then kicks from the animal, which was now trying to unseat its rider. Finally the little horse bent its knees, withdrew from between the professor's legs, and left him standing on two stones at the water's edge like the Colossus of Rhodes.

"Oh, that damned animal!" shouted the horseman, suddenly transformed into a pedestrian and as mortified as a cavalry officer demoted to foot soldier.

"*Färja,*" our guide put in, tapping him on the shoulder.

"What! A ferry?"

"*Der,*" Hans replied, indicating a boat.

"Yes!" I exclaimed. "There's a ferry."

"Then you should have told me! All right, let's get going!"

"*Tidvatten,*" our guide went on.

"What's he saying?"

"He's saying tide," my uncle replied, translating the Danish word for me.

"No doubt we have to wait for the tide?"

"*Förbida?*" my uncle asked.

"*Ja,*" Hans replied.

My uncle stamped his foot, while the horses headed toward the ferry.

I fully appreciated why we had to hold off crossing this fjord and needed to wait till the tide was at a certain point—the moment when the sea reaches its highest level and goes slack. At this juncture the ebb and flow have no noticeable effect, and the ferry runs no risk of being dragged to the far end of the bay or out to the open sea.

The favorable moment didn't arrive till six o'clock in the evening; two ferrymen, the four horses, our guide, my uncle, and I took our places on a sort of flat, flimsy-looking barge. I was used to our steam ferries on the Elbe and found the boatmen's oars a dismal propulsion unit. It took over an hour to finally cross this fjord; but we arrived undamaged at the other side.

Thirty minutes later we reached the *aoalkirkja* (church headquarters) of Garðar.

13

NIGHT SHOULD HAVE fallen, but below the 65th parallel, the nocturnal brightness of these polar regions needn't have surprised me; during the months of June and July in Iceland, the sun doesn't set.

Nevertheless the temperature had dropped. I was cold and above all hungry. Thank heavens for the *boër* that opened hospitably to take us in.

It was the home of a peasant, but in matters of hospitality it was as good as a king's. On our arrival, the master of the house came out, shook our hands, and without any further ado motioned us to follow him.

And follow is what we did, because walking abreast would have been impossible. A long, dark, narrow passageway provided access to this dwelling, which was built from roughly squared beams, and this hallway led you to each of its rooms; there were four of these: the kitchen, a workroom for weaving, the *badstofa* or family dormitory, and best of all, the guest bedroom. My uncle's height hadn't been taken into account when the

---

[19] Nearly eight geographic leagues.

house was built, and he didn't neglect to bang his head three or four times against the roof rafters.

We were ushered into our bedroom, a sort of large parlor with a floor of packed earth and lit by a window whose panes consisted of sheep membranes that weren't awfully transparent. The bedding amounted to some dry straw tossed into two wooden frames that were painted red and decorated with Icelandic proverbs. I hadn't expected to be this comfortable; throughout the house, however, there reigned a strong odor of dried fish, cured meat, and sour milk that my nostrils found pretty rank.

After we'd set aside our wayfarer's trappings, we heard our host's voice inviting us to come into the kitchen, which, even in the bitterest cold, was the only room where a fire burned.

My uncle was quick to obey this friendly decree. I followed suit.

The kitchen fireplace was of the old-fashioned variety; a solitary stone in the middle of the room provided the hearth; a hole in the roof let the smoke out. This kitchen also functioned as a dining room.

When we went in, our host acted as if he'd never seen us before and greeted us with the word "*Saellvertu*," which means "be happy," then he came and kissed us on the cheek.

After that his wife spoke the same words and followed them with the same ritual; then the couple put their right hands over their hearts and gave a deep bow.

I need to mention right away that this Icelandic lady was the mother of nineteen children—and all of them, big or little, were milling around helter-skelter inside the swirls of smoke pouring out of the hearth and all over the room. Every second I saw a small blonde head and pouty face emerge from the fog. You would have sworn they were a choir of half-washed angels.

My uncle and I greeted the whole brood very warmly; soon there were three or four of the brats on our shoulders, just as many on our knees, and the rest between our legs. The ones who could talk kept saying "*Saellvertu*" in every tone imaginable. The ones

who couldn't talk hollered even louder.

This choral concert was interrupted by the announcement of mealtime. Just then the hunter came back inside, having gone and seen to the feeding of his horses—in other words, he'd thriftily turned them loose out in the fields; the poor beasts had to be content with munching the skimpy moss on the rocks and some not-very-filling seaweed; tomorrow they would dependably come back on their own and resume the previous day's labors.

"*Saellvertu*," Hans put in.

Then serenely, mechanically, without one kiss being any more energetic than another, he greeted his host, hostess, and their nineteen children.

The ceremony over, we sat down at the table—twenty-four of us in all, hence one on top of the other in the most literal sense. The luckiest of us had only two brats on our knees.

But this miniature world fell silent when the soup arrived—Icelanders are naturally closemouthed, even the youngsters, and this inclination resurfaced and held sway. Our host served us some lichen soup that wasn't at all unpleasant, then an enormous piece of dried fish swimming in sour butter that had been aged for twenty years—and therefore was vastly preferable to fresh butter, according to Icelandic notions of good eating. Along with this came some *skyr*, a sort of cottage cheese with a biscuit on the side and the tangy juice of juniper berries adding flavor; finally, our drink was a mixture of whey and water that's known in this country as *blanda*. As for the nutritional value of this unusual food, I couldn't pass judgment. My dessert was a thick buckwheat mush, and I was so hungry, I swallowed it to the last mouthful.

Mealtime over, the children vanished; the adults gathered around the hearth, which had been stoked with peat, heather, cow pies, and dried fish bones. Then, after "feeling the heat," the various contingents retired to their respective bedrooms. As was the custom, our hostess offered to tug off our socks and trousers; but when we politely declined, she didn't insist and I was finally able to curl up in my bed of straw.

At five o'clock the next morning, we said good-bye to our Icelandic peasant; my uncle had much trouble making him accept a reasonable payment for his kindness, then Hans gave the signal to start off.

A hundred steps from Garðar, the terrain started to change character; the ground turned marshy and was harder to travel over. On our right the mountain chain stretched into infinity like an immense system of natural battlements, so we went along its outer slopes; often there were streams to cross, and we needed to ford them without getting our baggage too wet.

The wilderness got more and more desolate; but at times the shadows of human beings seemed to dart off into the distance; when the windings of our path unexpectedly brought us closer to one of these wraiths, I was suddenly filled with loathing at the sight of its swollen head, gleaming skin, lack of hair, and the repulsive sores that were showing through tears in its wretched rags.

The unfortunate creature didn't come and hold out its deformed hand; instead it ran off, but not so quickly that Hans couldn't call out his usual "*Saellvertu*" by way of greeting.

"*Spetelsk*," he said.

"A leper!" my uncle echoed.

And the mere word had its repellent effect. The horrifying disease of leprosy is fairly common in Iceland; it isn't contagious but hereditary; accordingly these wretched people aren't allowed to marry.

These apparitions hardly helped to cheer up the countryside, which was getting extremely dreary; the last tufts of grass had just now died away under our feet. There were no trees, aside from a few clumps of dwarf birches that looked like brushwood. Nor any animals, except a few horses whose owner couldn't feed them and let them wander over these dismal plains. Sometimes a falcon soared through the gray clouds, flying down south in a big hurry; this primitive, melancholy expanse was affecting me, and my memories kept taking me back to my homeland.

Soon we had to go over several unimportant little fjords, then finally an honest-to-goodness gulf; it was slack tide at the time,

allowing us to cross immediately and reach the hamlet of Álftanes, which was located 4½ statute miles farther on.

That evening, after fording the Álftá and the Hítará, two rivers well supplied with trout and pike, we were forced to spend the night in an abandoned shack worthy of being haunted by every gremlin in Scandinavian mythology; Jack Frost was definitely on the premises and he strutted his stuff all night long.

The following day wasn't especially eventful. Still the same marshy ground, the same unchanging view, the same dreary features. By evening we'd covered half the distance we had to travel and we bedded down in the *annexia*, or church annex, of Krösolbt.

On June 19 a lava field stretched underfoot for about 4½ statute miles; this type of geological formation is called *hraun* in these parts; the ridges of lava on its surface were shaped like pieces of cable, sometimes unwound, sometimes coiled up; an immense lava flow had come down from the mountain range nearby—its craters are extinct today, but this volcanic waste testified to their potency in the past. Meanwhile a few wisps of steam were seeping from hot springs here and there.

We didn't have time to investigate these phenomena; it was essential to keep on going. Beneath the hooves of our steeds, the marshy ground soon reappeared; little lakes cut across it. By then we were heading west; as big as it was, we'd actually worked our way around Faxa Bay, and Snaefells's two white peaks soared into the clouds some twenty statute miles away.

Our horses made good time; difficult terrain didn't stop them; as for me, I was starting to get very tired; my uncle still sat as straight and tall as on our first day out. I couldn't help marveling at him—just as I marveled at our hunter, who treated the expedition like a short stroll.

On Saturday, June 20, at six o'clock in the evening, we reached Búðir, a village located on the seacoast, and our guide asked for his agreed-upon wages. My uncle paid up. This time it was Hans's very own family—in other words, his uncles and first cousins—who of-

51

fered us their hospitality; we were warmly welcomed, and without abusing their good nature, I would gladly have stayed with these decent folks and recuperated from the stresses of our journey. But my uncle had nothing to recuperate from and wouldn't hear of it; the next day he ordered me out to my faithful steed and I was back in the saddle again.

The ground was affected by the closeness of our mountain, whose granite roots were coming out of the earth like those of an old oak. We were going around the volcano's immense base. The professor didn't take his eyes off it; he shook his fist, he seemed to be issuing it a challenge, and he said: "There's the giant I'm going to overcome!" Finally, after a four-hour trek, the horses halted on their own at the rectory door in Stapi.

14

SITTING IN THE SUNLIGHT that reflected off the volcano, Stapi is a village made up of some thirty shanties and built smack in the middle of the lava. It lies at the far end of a small fjord that's enclosed by basaltic walls of the strangest character.

As you know, basalt is a brown rock of igneous origin. It takes on orderly shapes that fall into startling patterns. Here nature proceeds geometrically and operates as men do, as if she were working with a square, a pair of compasses, and a plumb line. Everywhere else she practices her craft by flinging down big disorganized masses, her rough-hewn cones, her flawed pyramids, the peculiar sequences of her lines; but here it's as if she wanted to provide a model of orderliness—prior to the architects of olden times, she created a stark symmetry that the splendors of Babylon and the wonders of Greece have never surpassed.

I'd heard of the Giant's Causeway in Ireland and Fingal's Cave on one of the Hebrides Islands, but a basaltic support structure was a sight that hadn't yet been offered to my eyes.

Now then, outside Stapi this phenomenon was on view in all its glory.

Like the whole coast of the peninsula, the wall around the fjord consisted of a series of vertical pillars thirty feet high. These were straight, rigorously proportioned, and supported a section of molding made of horizontal pillars that formed a half arch overhanging the sea. At periodic intervals under this natural rain trough, a person's eyes detected some openings that were marvelously designed—they looked like pointed arches, and waves came rushing and foaming through them from far out. Torn loose by the ocean's fury, a few sections of basalt lay on the ground like the rubble of some bygone temple, ancient ruins that stayed forever young, that hadn't been eroded by the passing centuries.

This was the last stage of our journey above ground. Hans had guided us shrewdly, and it cheered me a little to think that he would continue on with us.

When we reached the door of the pastor's house—just a lowly shack, no better looking or more comfortable than its neighbors—I saw a man busy shoeing a horse, hammer in hand, leather apron around his midriff.

"*Saellvertu*," the hunter said to him.

"*God dag*," the horseshoer replied in flawless Danish.

"*Kyrkoherde*," Hans put in, turning to my uncle.

"The pastor!" echoed the latter. "It seems, Axel, that this gallant fellow is the pastor."

In the meantime our guide was bringing the *kyrkoherde* up to date on things; the man interrupted his work, gave the kind of shout no doubt in standard use between horses and horse traders, and at once a huge old harridan came out of the shack. If she didn't stand six feet off the ground, she was as close as makes no difference.

I was in dread that she'd come to plant Icelandic kisses on us travelers; but she did nothing of the sort and wasn't even very courteous when she ushered us into her home.

The guest bedroom struck me as the worst room in the rectory—cramped, dirty, and smelly. But we had to put up with it. Our pastor didn't seem to practice the hospitality of yore. Far from it. Before the day was out, I saw that we were dealing with a blacksmith, a fisherman, a hunter, and a carpenter, not at all with a minister of the Lord. True, it was a weekday. Maybe he made up for it on Sunday.

I don't want to be critical of these poor clergymen, who, after all, are quite hard up; the salary they earn from the Danish government is laughable, and they net only a quarter of the parish tithe, which amounts to less than sixty marks (about $18) in today's money. Ergo their need to work for a living; but when you fish, hunt, and shoe horses, you end up taking on the traits, attitudes, and morals of hunters, fishermen, and other less than polished people; that same evening I noticed that our host didn't include sobriety on his list of virtues.

My uncle quickly realized what sort of man he was dealing with; instead of a decent, deserving scholar, he found a plodding, boorish peasant. Consequently he decided to set out right away on his great expedition and leave this barely hospitable vicarage. Paying no attention to his exhaustion, he decided to go spend a few days in the mountains.

So the day after our arrival in Stapi, we started getting ready for our departure. Hans secured the services of three Icelanders to take over from the horses and carry our baggage; but once we'd reached the floor of the crater, these locals were to retrace their footsteps and leave us to fend for ourselves. This point was an absolute given.

At this juncture my uncle had to inform the hunter that he intended to carry out a scouting expedition into the farthest reaches of the volcano.

Hans was content to nod his head. Going there or elsewhere, delving into the bowels of his island or traveling on its surface, it was all the same to him. As for me, till then I'd been entertained by the incidents of our journey and I'd given little thought to the future—but now my old feelings came back stronger than ever. What was I to do? The only place I would have been tempted to oppose Professor Lidenbrock was back in Hamburg, not at the foot of Snaefells.

One idea above all others had me terrifically bothered, an idea that was frightening enough to rattle nerves less skittish than mine.

"Look here," I said to myself. "We're going to scale Snaefells. Fine. We're going to inspect its crater. Good. Others have done it and didn't die in the attempt. But that's not all. If we find a path down into the bowels of the earth, if that ill-fated Saknussemm told the truth, we'll get lost among the volcano's underground hallways. Now then, there's no guarantee that Snaefells is really extinct. Where's the proof that another eruption isn't in the works? Just because the monster has been asleep since 1219, does it follow that he can't wake up again? And if he *does* wake up, what'll happen to us?"

This called for serious thought and that's what I gave it. I couldn't sleep without dreaming about eruptions. Now then, if I were to play a part in such a volcanic drama, a piece of slag wasn't my idea of a congenial role.

I'd finally had it; I decided to lay the matter before my uncle in the most cunning way I could—in the form of a theory that was completely unworkable.

I went and found him. I shared my fears with him, then backed off so he could explode at will.

"That's been concerning me," he merely replied.

What was the meaning of these words? Was he ready to listen to reason? Was he thinking of tabling his plans? It seemed too good to be true.

After a few seconds of silence during which I didn't dare question him, he went on, saying:

"That's been concerning me. Ever since we reached Stapi, I've been worried about this major issue you've just brought up, because we mustn't do anything rash."

"Definitely not," I replied with energy.

"For 600 years Snaefells has been silent, but it can still speak. Now then, eruptions are always preceded by universally recognized phenomena. Therefore I've questioned the residents of this region, I've examined the terrain, and I can say to you, Axel, that there won't be any eruptions."

I was stunned by this statement and hadn't a single comeback.

"You doubt my words?" my uncle said. "Very well, come with me."

I obeyed mechanically. Leaving the rectory, the professor took a path that led right through a gap in the basaltic wall and away from the sea. Soon we were in the open countryside, if you can give such a name to an immense pile of volcanic waste. It looked like the whole landscape had been pummeled by a shower of enormous stones—traprock, basalt, granite, and all sorts of pyroxenic rocks.[20]

Here and there I saw curls of steam rising into the air; these white fumes are known as *reykir* in Icelandic speech and they came from hot springs, their intensity indicating the volcanic activity underground. My fears seemed to be justified. Accordingly I fell off my high horse when my uncle told me:

"You see all this smoke, Axel? Well, it proves we have nothing to fear from the volcano's wrath."

"By thunder!" I exclaimed.

"Get this into your head," the professor went on. "When an eruption's coming, these curls of steam grow twice as intense, then vanish completely during the entire time of the phenomenon, because this elastic fluid loses its vital pressure and exits through the crater instead of escaping through crevices in the earth. So if these fumes stay in their normal state, if their strength doesn't increase, if you round out this information with the fact that the wind and rain aren't being replaced by air that's quiet and sultry, then you can conclude there won't be an eruption in the near future."

"But—"

"Enough. When science has spoken, it behooves you to hold your tongue."

I went back to the vicarage, tail between my legs. My uncle had thrashed me soundly using scientific arguments. Even so, I still had one hope left, namely that when we reached the floor of the crater, there wouldn't be any hallway, and despite all the Saknussemms on earth, it would be impossible to go deeper.

---

[20] *Translator's note*. Rocks composed of silica.

I spent the wee hours afterward in one long nightmare that took place inside a volcano, and I saw myself launched from the underground depths to interplanetary space in the form of a lava rock.

The next day, June 23, Hans was waiting for us, his companions loaded down with provisions, tools, and instruments. Two alpenstocks, two rifles, and two cartridge belts had been set aside for my uncle and me. Hans, a man of foresight, had filled a goatskin water bag and added it to our baggage—which, along with our flasks, guaranteed us a week's supply of water.

It was nine o'clock in the morning. Our pastor and his tall old harridan were waiting for us in front of their door. No doubt the hosts wanted to bid the travelers a final farewell. But that farewell took the unexpected form of a fearsome bill itemized down to the parsonage air we'd breathed—polluted air, I daresay. This fine pair swindled us like a Swiss innkeeper and charged a pretty penny for their overrated hospitality.

My uncle paid up without haggling. A man leaving for the center of the earth doesn't worry about a few riksdalers.

This issue settled, Hans gave the signal to start off, and in a few seconds we'd left Stapi behind.

15

SNAEFELLS IS 5,000 feet high. Its two volcanic cones are the end of a stretch of trachyte that stands out from the island's mountain system. From our starting point you couldn't make out the silhouette of either peak against the grayish background of the sky. All I saw was an enormous snowcap riding low on the giant's forehead.

We walked single file, our hunter in the lead; the latter went up such narrow paths, two people couldn't have gone abreast. So it became almost impossible to hold a conversation.

Beyond the basaltic walls around the fjord by Stapi, the soil at first was a fibrous, herbaceous peat, the residue of bygone vegetation from the marshlands of this peninsula; this mass of still-untapped fuel would have been enough to heat Iceland's whole populace for a century; judging from the depth of certain ravines, this huge peat bog often went as deep as seventy feet down and featured consecutive layers of charred rubble separated by sheets of pumice mixed with that igneous gravel known as tuff.

Despite my anxieties I was a true nephew of Professor Lidenbrock and I took a studious interest in the mineralogical curiosities on display in this huge showroom of the natural sciences; at the same time I relived Iceland's entire geological history in my head.

Apparently this highly unusual island emerged from the depths of the waters at a comparatively recent time. What's more, it may still be rising at a rate that's barely noticeable. If this is so, we can attribute its origin to the action of underground fires. In which case, then, Sir Humphry Davy's thinking, Saknussemm's document, and my uncle's ambitions all go up in smoke. This theory led me to carefully examine the character of the soil, and I soon worked out the sequence of phenomena that had presided over its formation.

Utterly lacking in sedimentary rock, Iceland is made up of nothing but volcanic tuff, in other words, clusters of stones and rocks that are porous in texture. Before its volcanoes came into existence, this island consisted of a mountainous mass of traprock that slowly rose above the waves under pressure from forces in the earth's center. The inner fires hadn't yet burst out into the open.

Later, though, a wide crack cut across the island on a diagonal from the southwest to the northeast, and from this crevice a sort of trachyte batter gradually poured out to the last drop. So it wasn't a violent phenomenon that took place; this crevice was an enormous outlet, and after the molten matter had been discharged from the bowels of our globe, it spread serenely in wide sheets or bosomy masses. Crystalline rocks such as feldspars, syenites, and porphyries appeared at this time.

But thanks to this outpouring, the island increased considerably in density, and as a result its powers of resistance increased as

well. After its trachyte crust had cooled, the reader can imagine how much elastic fluid was stored in its bosom when it no longer had any outlet. So there came a time when the mechanical force of these gases was so great, they heaved up the cumbersome crust and gouged out tall chimneys for themselves. Ergo the volcano's upheaval from that crust, followed by a crater suddenly puncturing the volcano's summit.

Then the eruptive phenomena led to volcanic phenomena. Basaltic waste was the first substance to escape from those newly formed openings, and the plain we were crossing just then offered the most marvelous specimens to our eyes. We walked over these heavy, dark-gray rocks, which, as they cooled, had been molded into prisms with hexagonal bases. In the distance we saw a large number of flattened cones that used to be fire-breathing mouths.

Then, after the basaltic eruption had run its course and its craters had gone extinct, the volcano gained in strength, providing a way out for lava and this tuff that was composed of ash and slag, and I noticed that their long streams had spread over the mountainside like luxuriant tresses.

This was the sequence of phenomena that put Iceland on the map; everything had come from the action of the inner fires, and it was insane to imagine that this internal mass could ever be anything but a white-hot liquid. It was especially insane to plan on reaching the center of the globe!

So as we moved toward our assault on Snaefells, I felt encouraged about the outcome of our undertaking.

The path got harder and harder; the terrain was rising; shards of rock would break loose, and we had to exercise scrupulous care to keep from taking dangerous tumbles.

Hans went forward as serenely as if he were on level ground; sometimes he vanished behind big boulders and we lost sight of him for a moment; then a high-pitched whistle would escape from his lips and tell us which direction to take. What's more, he often halted, gathered some of the rocky rubble, arranged it in an identifiable manner, and thus set up cairns that were meant to show the way on our return trip. A sound precaution in theory, but future developments made it irrelevant.

Three exhausting hours on the trail had brought us only to the base of the mountain. There Hans gave the signal to halt, and we all shared a nominal lunch. My uncle ate two mouthfuls at a time, hoping to set out again more quickly. But this nutrition break was also a rest break, and he had to wait for the good pleasure of our guide, who gave the signal to start off an hour later. The three Icelanders ate in moderation and didn't say a single word, being just as closemouthed as their comrade the hunter.

We now began scaling the slopes of Snaefells. Due to an optical illusion common in the mountains, its snowy summit seemed quite near, yet how many long hours we took to reach it! And above all how tired we got! The stones weren't cemented to the ground or bound together by weeds—they slid away underfoot and vanished down onto the plain with the speed of an avalanche.

In certain localities the mountainside formed at least a 36° angle with the horizon; it was impossible to scale, and we had to work our way around these steep, stony trails, not an easy task. At such times we assisted each other with the help of our alpenstocks.

I must say that my uncle kept as close to me as possible; he never lost sight of me, and on many occasions his arms gave me solid backing. No doubt he himself had an instinctive sense of balance, because he never faltered. Though carrying loads, the Icelanders clambered up that peak with the agility of mountaineers.

Seeing how high the top of Snaefells was, it struck me as hopelessly out of reach from this side, unless its slopes started slanting at a gentler angle. Luckily, after an hour of exertion and athletic achievement, a sort of staircase showed up unexpectedly in the middle of a huge carpet of snow spreading over the volcano's rump, and it simplified our ascent. It had formed from one of those streams of stones that shoot out during eruptions and that Icelanders call *stinâ*. If this falling stream hadn't been halted by the layout of these mountainsides, it would have gone rushing into the sea to form new islands.

As it was, these stairs did us a real favor. The slope got steeper, but these stone steps let us scale it with ease—and quickly too, so that when I stayed to the rear for a moment while my companions kept climbing, I saw them already shrinking to microscopic size in the distance.

By seven o'clock in the evening, we'd gone up the 2,000 steps of this staircase and were overlooking a bulge in the terrain—the base of the mountain's crater, a sort of foundation that supported the cone proper.

The sea lay 3,200 feet down. We'd gone past the snow line, rather a bit lower in Iceland due to the climate's year-round humidity. It was fiercely cold. The wind was blowing hard. I was exhausted. The professor soon saw that my legs flatly refused to do my bidding, and despite his impatience he decided to call a halt. So he signaled to the hunter, who shook his head, saying:

"*Ofvanför.*"

"Apparently we need to go higher," my uncle said.

Then he asked Hans his reason for this answer.

"*Mistour,*" our guide replied.

"*Ja, mistour,*" one of the Icelanders repeated in a rather apprehensive tone.

"What does this word mean?" I asked nervously.

"Look," my uncle said.

My eyes flew to the plain. Spinning like a tornado, an immense column of ground-up pumice, sand, and dust had risen into the air; the wind backed it against the side of Snaefells where we were clinging; this murky curtain stretched in front of the sun and cast a huge shadow over the mountain. If that tornado went lower, we were sure to be entwined in its eddies. This phenomenon, which occurs fairly often when winds blow off the glaciers, goes by the name of *mistour* in Icelandic speech.

"*Hastigt, hastigt!*" our guide shouted.

I didn't have to know Danish to understand that we needed to follow Hans as fast as we could. The latter started to work his way around the cone of the crater, but he went at an angle so that the going would be easier. Soon the tornado swooped down, and the mountain shuddered at the impact; caught in its whirlwinds, stones fell in showers just as if it were an eruption. Luckily we were on the opposite gradient and protected from any danger. If our guide hadn't taken this precaution, our bodies would have been hacked to pieces, reduced to powder, and scattered far and wide like the remains of some mysterious meteor.

Even so, Hans didn't deem it wise to spend the night on the side of the cone. We kept zigzagging upward; we had 1,500 feet left to cover and the job took five hours; the detouring, going at angles, and backtracking must have added up to at least 7½ miles. I'd reached my limit; I was collapsing from hunger and cold. The air was getting thinner and wasn't sufficient for the full play of my lungs.

Finally, by eleven o'clock in the dead of night, we'd made it to the top of Snaefells, and before taking shelter inside its crater, I had time to see "the midnight sun" at the lowest point in its progression, casting its pale rays over that island sleeping at my feet.

16

OUR LITTLE BAND quickly gobbled up supper, then did its best to settle in for the night. At 5,000 feet above sea level, our mattresses were hard, our shelter less than secure, our circumstances plenty difficult. Yet I enjoyed an especially peaceful sleep that night, one of the best I'd spent in a good while. I didn't even have any dreams.

The air was very brisk the next morning, and we awoke half frozen but under radiant sunlight. I got up from my granite mattress, went and enjoyed the magnificent sight unfolding beneath my eyes.

I was standing on the summit of one of Snaefells's two peaks, the southern one. From there I commanded a view of most of the island. As is usual at all high elevations, the perspective made the shorelines stand out while the central portions seemed to recede. It was as if one of Helbesmer's relief maps had been spread out at my feet. I saw deep valleys crisscrossing every which way, cliff sides cut down to the size of quarries, lakes turned into ponds, rivers demoted to creeks. Heading off to my right were countless glaciers and peak after peak, some of them lightly wreathed in smoke. Their layers of snow looked like foam, and those endless, undulating mountains called to mind the surface of a choppy sea. If I turned to the west, the majestic expanse of the ocean unfolded like an extension of those wool-covered summits. My eyes could barely make out where the land stopped and the waves started.

So I was deep in that exalted trance a lofty mountaintop can induce—and this time I didn't feel dizzy because I was finally getting used to looking down from afar. My dazzled eyes were bathing in the sunlight's translucent radiance. I forgot who I was, where I was, and led the airborne life of a sprite or a sylph, those fantastic denizens of Scandinavian folklore. I was getting tipsy from the sensual pleasure of being up so high—without a thought for the depths into which my fate would soon plunge me. But I was snapped back into contact with reality by the arrival of the professor and Hans, who joined me on the mountaintop.

Turning to the west, my uncle pointed to a pale mist, a haze, a suggestion of land looming above the line of the waves.

"Greenland!" he said.

"Greenland?" I exclaimed.

"Yes, we're about eighty-five miles away, and during a thaw ice floes from up north carry polar bears as far as Iceland. But that doesn't concern us. We're on top of Snaefells and here are two peaks, one to the north, the other to the south. Hans will tell us what name the Icelanders have given the one that's now supporting us."

Asked this question, the hunter replied: "Scartaris."

My uncle shot me a triumphant glance.

"Head for the crater!" he said.

The crater of Snaefells formed an upside-down cone whose opening could well have been over a mile across. As for its depth, I put it at about 2,000 feet. You can imagine what this container must have been like when it was full of fire and thunder. The floor of this funnel didn't measure any more than 500 feet around, so its fairly gentle slopes made it easy to get all the way down. I couldn't help comparing this crater to an enormous wide-mouthed musket, and the comparison terrified me.

We're going down into a musket, I thought, when maybe it's loaded and the tiniest bump could jar it into going off—this is a job for a madman!

But I didn't back out. Looking unconcerned, Hans resumed the lead in our little band. I followed him without saying a word.

To make our descent easier, Hans took a very extended elliptical path around the inside of the cone. We had to walk in the midst of rocks dumped by eruptions, pieces of which would break loose, then rush and rebound all the way down into the depths. As they fell, the air reverberated with echoes that were unusually resonant.

Glaciers had formed inside some parts of the cone. Then Hans proceeded with the greatest caution, probing the ground with his alpenstock to spot crevasses. At certain dubious junctures we needed to rope ourselves together with a long line, so if one man were to stumble without warning, his companions could keep him from falling. This mutual supportiveness was a prudent policy, but risks still remained.

Yet, despite the difficulties of going down slopes our guide didn't know, we managed the trip without any accidents—except for dropping a bundle of rope, which escaped from the hands of one of the Icelanders and took a shortcut to the bottom of the pit.

By noon we'd made it too. I looked up and saw the mouth of the cone overhead, framing a patch of sky that was nearly a perfect circle, though now significantly smaller. The pinnacle of Scartaris intruded at just one point, standing out against the vastness.

In the floor of the crater opened three chimneys, which had expelled lava and steam from the central furnace when Snaefells was active. Each of these chimneys was over thirty yards across. They were gaping right at our feet. I didn't have the nerve to look down into them. As for Professor Lidenbrock, he conducted a high-speed examination of their layouts; he puffed and panted; he ran from one to the other, waving his arms and throwing out unintelligible remarks. Sitting on chunks of lava, Hans and his companions watched him in action; clearly they took him for a madman.

All at once my uncle gave a yell. I thought he'd suddenly slipped and fallen into one of the three chasms. He hadn't. I could see him—his arms were outstretched, his legs wide apart, and he stood facing a hunk of granite set in the crater's center, like an enormous pedestal built for a statue of Pluto. His posture was that of a man thoroughly astonished, but whose astonishment would soon change into maniacal glee.

"Axel! Axel!" he shouted. "Come here, come here!"

I ran. Neither Hans nor the Icelanders moved a muscle.

"Look!" the professor said to me.

Then, sharing his astonishment if not his glee, I peered at the boulder's western face, saw some runic letters the years had half eroded, and read this name I cursed a thousand times over:

"Arne Saknussemm!" my uncle exclaimed. "Can you still have any doubts?"

I didn't answer and went back in dismay to my lava bench. The evidence was overwhelming.

I have no idea how long I sat there, deep in thought. All I know is that when I looked up, I saw only my uncle and Hans on the floor of the crater. The Icelanders had been paid off and were now heading down the outside slopes of Snaefells on their way back to Stapi.

At the foot of a rock, Hans dozed off serenely on a lava flow where he'd fixed himself a makeshift bed; but my uncle paced around the floor of the crater like a wild animal in a pit dug by some trapper. I hadn't the strength or desire to stand up, so I took our guide as my model, fell into an uneasy slumber, and thought I was hearing noises or feeling tremors inside the mountain's walls.

That's how we spent our first night on the floor of the crater.

The next morning a dull, gray, cloudy sky had settled over the top of the cone. What made me most aware of it wasn't the darkness filling the chasm but the anger consuming my uncle

I knew the underlying reason, and a remnant of hope sprang back to life in my heart. Here's why.

Three routes opened at our feet, but Saknussemm had taken only one of them. According to that Icelandic scholar, we were to identify it from the characteristic he'd reported in his cryptogram—namely, Scartaris's shadow would come and caress its rim during the last days of the month of June.

In essence you could think of that sharp peak as the indicator of an immense sundial, whose shadow on a given day pointed the way to the center of the globe.

Now then, if there's a shortage of sunlight, there's no shadow. Consequently there's no signpost. It was June 25. If the heavens stayed overcast for the next six days, we would need to put off our skywatching for another year.

I won't even try to describe the impotent rage seething in Professor Lidenbrock. The day wore on, but no shadow came and stretched out on the floor of the crater. Hans didn't stir from his perch; yet he must have been wondering what we were waiting for, if he wondered about anything. My uncle didn't make a single remark to me. He kept his eyes perpetually on the sky, lost in its foggy gray hue.

On the 26th, still nothing. A mixture of rain and snow fell all day long. Hans built a shanty out of pieces of lava. I had fun watching thousands of makeshift waterfalls tumble down the insides of the cone, every stone contributing to the raucous background noise.

My uncle couldn't contain himself any longer. It was enough to infuriate the most patient man, because he truly was sinking in sight of shore.

But Heaven always mingles great sorrow with great joy, and there were pleasures in store for Professor Lidenbrock that made up for these heartbreaking aggravations.

The sky was still overcast the next day; but on Sunday, June 28, the third-last day of the month, the change of the moon brought a change in the weather. Old Sol flooded the crater with light. Every knoll, every rock, every stone, and every jagged edge got its share of the sun's wholesome aura and immediately cast its shadow on the ground. The sharp-edged silhouette of Scartaris stood out above them all, shifting inch by inch as the golden orb moved over its arc.

My uncle shifted along with it.

At noon, when this shadow was shortest, it came and gently licked the rim of the middle chimney.

"There it is!" the professor yelled. "There it is!" Then he added in Danish: "This way to the center of the globe!"

I looked at Hans.

"*Forüt!*" our guide put in serenely.

"Forward!" my uncle echoed.

It was 1:13 in the afternoon.

17

THE REAL JOURNEY started. Till this point our exertions had won out over our difficulties; now the latter would be cropping up literally at every step.

I still hadn't looked into this bottomless pit that was waiting to swallow me. The time had come. I still could participate in the undertaking or refuse to attempt it. But I was ashamed to back out in front of the hunter. Hans had gone along with this venture so serenely, with such lack of concern, such utter nonchalance in the face of all danger, that I blushed at the thought of being less courageous. If I'd been on my own, I would have brought up a whole series of weighty arguments; but in the presence of our guide, I held my tongue; I recalled my pretty Virlander and I headed over to the middle chimney.

As I said, it measured some thirty yards across, or a hundred yards around. I held onto an overhanging rock, leaned out, and looked down. My hair stood on end. I was conscious of a great void, an awareness that took hold of my entire being. I felt my center of gravity shifting inside me, my head starting to spin like a drunk's. Nothing is more intoxicating than this lure of the depths. I was on the verge of falling. A hand restrained me. It belonged to Hans. No doubt about it, my education at the Frelsers Kirke in Copenhagen hadn't gone "deep enough into the subject."

Though I'd risked only a brief glance down this shaft, I'd determined how it was laid out. Its walls were nearly vertical but featured many ledges that were sure to make our descent easier. However, though steps weren't lacking, a handrail was. A rope tied to the rim would have given us adequate support, but how could we untie it once we'd gotten to its lower end?

My uncle used a very simple procedure to do away with this difficulty. He uncoiled a rope as thick as your thumb and 400 feet long; first he payed out half of it, looped it around a jutting chunk of lava, then tossed the other half into the chimney. At that point each of us could descend by holding both halves together in one hand, which would keep the rope from unwinding; once we'd gone 200 feet down, nothing could be simpler than to gather the rope back in by letting go of one end and hauling in the other. Then we would repeat the process *ad infinitum*.

"Now," my uncle said after finishing up these preparations, "let's see to our baggage; we'll divide it into three bundles and each man will strap one of them on his back; I'm talking about just the breakable items."

Apparently the daredevil professor didn't include our persons in this last category.

"Hans," he went on, "will look after the tools and some of the provisions, you, Axel, another third of the provisions plus the weapons, and I myself the rest of the provisions along with the delicate instruments."

"But," I said, "who'll look after carrying down our clothes and all these ladders and ropes?"

"They'll go down by themselves."

"How?" I asked.

"You'll see."

My uncle was partial to extreme measures and resorted to them without hesitation.

Under his direction Hans combined all the unbreakable items into one package, tied it tightly, and simply dropped it into the chasm.

I heard the noisy whoosh that comes from layers of air being thrust aside. Leaning out and looking into the depths, my uncle watched the descent of his baggage with approving eyes, straightening up only after it was out of sight.

"Good," he put in. "Now for us."

I ask you as a right-thinking person— could anybody hear such words without getting the shivers?

The professor strapped the package of instruments on his back; Hans took the one with the tools, I the one with the weapons. Our descent got under way in the following order: Hans, my uncle, and I. It took place in absolute silence, broken only by bits of rocky rubble rushing down into the depths.

I went with the flow, so to speak, intently grasping the two ropes with one hand, the other adding support with the help of my alpenstock. One single idea consumed me: I was in dread that our lifeline would give way. This rope struck me as too weak to bear the weight of three people. I relied on it as little as possible, performing miraculous balancing acts on these lava ledges, which my feet tried to clutch like hands.

If Hans stood on one of these slippery steps and it turned shaky, he said in his serene voice:

"*Gif akt!*"

"Watch out!" my uncle echoed.

Half an hour later we'd made it to the top of a boulder, which was stuck firmly in the rock face of the chimney.

Hans pulled on one end of the rope; the other end shot into the air; after flying past the crag overhead, it fell toward us, scraping loose an ultra dangerous shower—or hailstorm, rather—of stones and lava fragments.

Leaning out and looking down from our cramped plateau, I noted that the bottom of this hole was still invisible.

We resumed our operations with the rope, and half an hour later we'd gone another 200 feet down.

During such a descent I'm not sure that even the most fanatical geologist would have tried to study the character of the rocks in the area. For my part I rarely bothered with them; whether they were Pliocene, Miocene, Eocene, Cretaceous, Jurassic, Triassic, Permian, Carboniferous, Devonian, Silurian, or earlier still, it was of little concern to me. But no doubt the professor did his usual investigating and note taking, because during one of our rest breaks he told me:

"The farther down I go, the more confident I feel. The organization of these volcanic rocks bears out Davy's thinking completely. We're deep in primeval terrain, a terrain that witnessed the chemical process of metals igniting after contact with air and water. I completely reject the concept of a central heat source. Anyhow we'll soon see."

Always the same conclusion. You can appreciate that I was in no mood to argue. He took my silence to mean consent, and we started on down again.

After three more hours I still hadn't glimpsed the bottom of the chimney. When I looked up I saw that its mouth was shrinking noticeably. Due to their gentle slope, the walls were drawing closer together. Little by little it was getting darker.

But we kept descending; it struck me that the stones breaking loose from the walls made a duller sound as they were pulled down, that they must be reaching the floor of the chasm very quickly.

Since I'd been careful to keep accurate track of our operations with the rope, I could accurately work out how deep we'd gone and how long we'd taken.

By that point we'd repeated the whole process fourteen times, each repetition lasting half an hour. So this made 7 hours, plus fourteen quarter-hour rest breaks amounting to 3½ hours. Total: 10½ hours. We'd gotten started at one o'clock, so just then it had to be eleven o'clock.

As for how deep we were, we'd done the whole process fourteen times and on each occasion went 200 feet down the rope, which made a total of 2,800 feet.

Just then Hans's voice rang out.

"*Halt!*" he said.

I pulled up short just as I was about to stomp on my uncle's head.

"Here we are," said the latter.

"Where?" I asked, skidding down next to him.

"At the bottom of this vertical chimney."

"So is there any other way out?"

"There is. I can make out a sort of corridor angling off to the right. We'll look into it tomorrow. First let's eat supper, then get some sleep."

It still wasn't completely dark. We opened the provision bag; after eating, each of us did his best to bed down on a mattress of stones and lava rubble.

And when I opened my eyes while lying on my back, I saw a speck of light at the upper end of this 3,000-foot tube, now transformed into a gigantic spyglass.

It was a star that didn't twinkle anymore, and according to my calculations, it had to be Beta in Ursa Minor.

Then I fell sound asleep.

18

AT EIGHT O'CLOCK in the morning, a ray of sunshine came and woke us. The thousand facets of the lava on the walls gathered it up as it went past and scattered it about like a shower of sparks.

This beam of light was bright enough for us to see things around us.

"All right, Axel, what do you say now?" my uncle exclaimed, rubbing his hands. "Did you ever spend a more peaceful night in our house on Königstrasse? No more buggies rumbling, no more vendors calling, no more boatmen hollering!"

"It's definitely very quiet at the bottom of this shaft, but there's something frightening about all this stillness."

"Come now!" my uncle exclaimed. "If you're frightened already, what will you feel like later on? We still haven't gone a single inch into the bowels of the earth."

"What do you mean?"

"I mean we've made it only to the ground floor of the island. This long vertical tube, which leads down from Snaefells's crater, stops at around sea level."

"You're sure of this?"

"Quite sure. Check our barometer."

In essence, while we'd been busy descending, the mercury had gradually risen in the instrument and stopped at twenty-nine inches.

"As you can see," the professor went on, "we still have just our normal atmospheric tension, so I can't wait till it's time for a pressure gauge to replace this barometer."

In essence this instrument would become unusable once the air's weight had exceeded the pressure that the device registers at sea level.

"But," I said, "isn't there a danger this continually increasing pressure will be too much for us?"

"Not really. We'll descend slowly and our lungs will get used to breathing the heavier atmosphere. Balloonists end up running short of air when they rise into the higher strata, and we ourselves will maybe get an overdose. But that's preferable in my opinion. Let's not waste another second. Where's the package that went ahead of us into the interior of this mountain?"

I remembered that we'd failed to find it the night before. My uncle questioned Hans, who looked around carefully with his hunter's eyes and replied:

"*Der huppe!*"

"Up there."

In fact the package had gotten caught on a jutting piece of rock about a hundred feet over our heads. Like a cat, the agile Icelander instantly clambered up to it, and in a few minutes the package had rejoined us.

"Now," my uncle said, "let's eat breakfast, but let's eat it like men who could have a long road ahead."

We ate some dried meat and biscuit, washing it down with a few sips of water mixed with gin.

Breakfast over, my uncle reached into his pocket and pulled out a notebook he used for recording his findings; he took up his various instruments one after the other, then jotted down the following data:

Monday, July 1

Chronometer—8:17 in the morning.
Barometer—29.6 inches.
Thermometer—43° Fahrenheit.
Heading—east-southeast.

This last reading referred to the dark hallway and was the compass indication.

"Now, Axel," the professor exclaimed in an exultant voice, "we're truly going to plunge into the bowels of our globe. So this is the actual moment when our journey starts."

With that my uncle reached up and clutched the Ruhmkorff device hanging from his neck; with his other hand he put the electric current in contact with the glass spiral inside the lantern, and a tolerably bright light dispelled the shadows in the hallway.

Hans carried our second Ruhmkorff device, which he activated as well. This inventive use of electricity let us travel a good while by creating an artificial daytime even in the midst of the most flammable gases.

"Off we go!" my uncle put in.

Each of us shouldered his burden. Hans was in charge of pushing the package of rope and clothing ahead of him; with me in third place, we went into the hallway.

Just as this dark corridor was swallowing me up, I looked overhead and saw for the last time, framed in the field of that immense tube, those skies of Iceland I would "never again set eyes on."

During the most recent eruption in 1219, lava had fought its way through this tunnel. It had lined the insides with a thick, shiny coat of plaster; the reflections made our electric light a hundred times brighter.

The only difficulty with this route lay in our not sliding too fast down a slope that slanted at about a 45° angle; luckily some worn-down areas and periodic bumps took the place of steps, and we descended by simply letting our baggage run ahead of us while tied to a long rope.

But the formations that served as steps underfoot had turned into stalactites on other surfaces. Porous in some localities, the lava featured little round blisters: adorned with transparent specks of glass, milky quartz crystals hung from the domed ceiling like chandeliers and seemed to switch on as we went past. It was as if the spirits of the underworld were lighting up their palace to welcome visitors from the land above.

"It's magnificent!" I exclaimed in spite of myself. "What a sight, uncle! Look at the lava changing color, see how it goes from reddish brown to brilliant yellow, and in such subtle stages—don't you marvel at it? And how about those crystals that shine like ceiling globes?"

"Aha, you're catching on, Axel!" my uncle replied. "So, my boy, you think this is splendid, do you? You'll be seeing quite a bit more, I expect. Just keep on walking!"

It would have been more appropriate if he'd said "keep on sliding," because that was our leisurely method on these steep slopes. As Virgil says, *facilis descensus Averni.*[21] I often checked our compass, and it gave our direction as southeast with unruffled consistency. This lava flow didn't angle off to one side or the other. It was as rigid as a straight line.

Yet it wasn't getting noticeably warmer. This bore out Davy's suppositions, and more than once I was astonished when I checked our thermometer. Two hours after we'd started off, it still read only 50° Fahrenheit, in other words, an increase of 7°. I felt justified in thinking that our descent was more sideways than straight down. As for accurately determining how deep we'd gone, nothing could be easier. The professor had kept accurate track of just how much our route had swerved or slanted, though he didn't share his ultimate findings.

Near eight o'clock in the evening, he gave the signal to halt. Hans promptly sat down. We hung the lamps from a jutting piece of lava. We were in a sort of cavern, and it wasn't short of air. On the contrary. A distinct breeze wafted over us. What was creating it? What atmospheric disturbance was

---

[21] *Translator's note.* Latin: "Easy is the descent to the underworld."

responsible for its presence? It was a problem I didn't try to solve just then. I was so tired and hungry, I couldn't think straight. It takes a huge expenditure of energy to climb downward for seven consecutive hours. I was exhausted. Therefore the word "halt" was music to my ears. Hans spread some food out on a chunk of lava, and we all ate heartily. But one thing worried me: we'd used up half of our water supply. My uncle had counted on replenishing it from underground springs, but so far they'd been utterly lacking. I couldn't help calling his attention to the matter.

"You're surprised there haven't been any springs?" he said.

"Certainly, worried even. Our water won't last more than five days."

"Don't worry, Axel. My answer to you is that we *will* find water, and more than we could want."

"When?"

"When we've left this casing of lava behind us. How could springs spurt out of walls like these?"

"But maybe this lava flow continues to a great depth. It seems to me we still haven't covered much of a distance vertically."

"What makes you assume that?"

"Because if we'd gone a lot farther inside the earth's crust, the heat would be more intense."

"According to your way of thinking," my uncle replied. "What does our thermometer show?"

"Barely 59° Fahrenheit, meaning an increase of only 16° since we started off."

"All right, and your conclusion is . . . ?"

"Here's what I conclude. According to science's most detailed findings, the temperature gets 1.8° hotter for every 100 feet you go into our globe's interior. But some regional conditions can change this figure. Consequently, near Yakutsk in Siberia people have noted that it increases this much every 36 feet. Apparently this difference comes from the ability of the rock to conduct heat. I would likewise add that in the vicinity of an extinct volcano, and in deposits of gneiss, people have noted that this temperature rise of 1.8° occurs only every 125 feet. Therefore, since this last theory is the most promising, let's use it as the basis for our calculations."

"Calculate away, my boy."

"Nothing to it," I said, running the numbers in my notebook. "9 times 125 feet gives us a depth of 1,125 feet."

"Nothing could be more correct."

"Well then?"

"Well then, according to *my* findings, we've reached a depth of 10,000 feet below sea level."

"It can't be!"

"If it isn't, numbers have stopped being numbers."

The professor's calculations were the correct ones. We'd already gone 6,000 feet below the greatest depths reached by man, the coal mines of Kitzbühel in Tirol and Wuttemberg in Bohemia.

The temperature should have been nearly 178° Fahrenheit in this locality, but it was barely 59°. Which was significant food for thought.

19

AT SIX O'CLOCK the next morning, Tuesday, June 30, our descent resumed.

We kept following the lava hallway, actually a natural gradient that sloped as gently as those ramps that still replace staircases in old houses. We continued in this way till 12:17, the exact instant when we caught up with Hans, who had just halted.

"Aha!" my uncle exclaimed. "We've made it to the end of the chimney."

I looked around me. We were standing in an intersection, a fork in the road with two paths heading off, both dark and narrow. Which one was the right way? There lay the problem.

But my uncle didn't want to look indecisive in front of our guide and me; he picked the eastern tunnel, and soon all three of us were deep inside it.

Besides, any indecision in front of that divided roadway could have dragged on indefinitely, because there weren't any clues that might have led us to choose one route over the other; all we could do was take a chance.

The slope of this new hallway was barely noticeable, its subdivisions quite erratic. Now and then a sequence of arches would unfold in front of our steps like the outer naves of a Gothic cathedral. Here the artists of the Middle Ages could have studied every form of religious architecture originating in the pointed arch. A mile farther along we bowed our heads under low-slung archways in the Romanesque style, their stout pillars implanted in the mass of stone and groaning beneath the springing of their vaults. In certain localities this state of affairs gave way to squat support structures that looked like something a beaver had built, and we slithered on our bellies through these tight intestinal passages.

The temperature stayed at a bearable level. I automatically thought about how hot it had been when lava spewed out of Snaefells and rushed along this route that was now so tranquil. I pictured those fiery torrents in my mind, dashing against the corners of this hallway, building up supercharged steam in this cramped space.

Here's hoping, I thought, that this venerable volcano doesn't backslide into his old ways!

These were bright ideas I definitely didn't share with Uncle Lidenbrock; he wouldn't have understood. The only thing he thought about was forging ahead. He walked, he slid, he even tumbled, and with praiseworthy conviction all in all.

By six o'clock in the evening, after a stroll that barely strained us, we'd gone five miles farther south but scarcely a quarter of a mile deeper.

At my uncle's signal, we called it a day. We ate without much talk and slept without much thought.

Our nighttime arrangements were quite simple; each man rolled himself up in a travel blanket, which was his only bedding. We didn't have to worry about freezing temperatures or untimely visitors. When explorers are out in the wilds of Africa or deep in the forests of the New World, they need to watch over each other during bedtime hours.

Here, however, we had perfect solitude and total safety. There were no evildoers to fear, neither ferocious beasts nor savage humans.

The next morning we woke up fit as a fiddle. We took to the trail again. Just as we'd done the day before, we went down a path the lava had followed. We hadn't any way of identifying the types of rock it went over. Instead of plunging into the bowels of the globe, this tunnel showed signs of becoming perfectly horizontal. It dawned on me that it was even heading back toward the surface of the earth. Near ten o'clock in the morning, this tendency became so obvious—and consequently so tiring—that I had to adopt a slower pace.

"Well, Axel?" the professor said impatiently.

"Well, I can't keep this up," I replied.

"What! After a three-hour stroll over such gentle terrain?"

"I don't know about gentle, but it's definitely tiring."

"Excuse me? When everything's downhill?"

"Uphill, with all due respect."

"Uphill!" my uncle put in, shrugging his shoulders.

"Certainly. Half an hour ago the slope changed, and if we keep following it this way, I'm positive we'll be right back in the nation of Iceland."

The professor shook his head like a man who isn't about to be persuaded. I tried to continue the conversation. He didn't answer me and gave the signal to start off. I could plainly see that his silence was just an effort to rein in his bad temper.

Even so, I resolutely picked up my load and hurried after Hans, who was in front of my uncle. I was determined not to fall behind. My main concern was to stay in sight of my companions. I shuddered at the thought of going astray in the depths of this labyrinth.

What's more, when this upward route got more arduous, I comforted myself with the belief that it was bringing me closer to the surface of the earth. There was hope. Every step said so, and I was overjoyed at the idea of seeing my little Grauben again.

At noon the walls of this hallway underwent a change in appearance. I noticed that our electric light wasn't reflecting as brightly off its sides. The lava retaining wall had been replaced by the existing rock. This section of stone was made up of layers that slanted and often stood on end. We were deep in a time of transition, deep in the Silurian Period.[22]

"It's obviously sedimentary rock!" I exclaimed. "This shale, limestone, and sandstone were formed by marine deposits during the second age on earth! We're turning our backs on the section of granite! We're like somebody from Hamburg taking the Hanover road to get to Lübeck."[23]

I should have kept my findings to myself. But my geologist's temperament got the better of my good sense, and Uncle Lidenbrock heard my exclamations.

"What is it now?" he said.

"Look," I replied, showing him the different sequences of sandstone and limestone, plus the first clues pointing to a slate deposit.

"Well?"

"We're right in the period when the first plants and first animals appeared."

"Oh you think so, do you?"

"But look at it, inspect it, study it!"

I made the professor sweep his lamp over the walls of the hallway. I expected some sort of exclamation from him. But he didn't say a word and continued on his way.

Had he understood me or not? He didn't want to admit he was wrong in picking the eastern tunnel—was he trying to save face as both uncle and scientist? Or was he bent on scouting out this passageway to the very end? It was obvious that we'd left the lava path behind, that this trail couldn't lead to the core of Snaefells.

Even so, I wondered if I wasn't attaching too much importance to this change in terrain. Was I in the wrong myself? Were we

---

[22] So named because the rocks of this period are quite extensive in areas of England that used to be populated by a Celtic tribe called the Silures.

[23] *Translator's note.* Hanover and Lübeck lie in opposite directions from Hamburg.

truly crossing those layers of rock that overlie the section of granite?

If I'm right, I thought, I'm bound to find the remains of some primitive plants, then we'll have to bow to the evidence. Let's take a look.

I hadn't gone a hundred steps before irrefutable proof was offered to my eyes. This was a foregone conclusion, because the seas in Silurian times featured more than 1,500 vegetable and animal species. My feet had gotten used to the hard surface of the lava, but suddenly they were trampling on a sort of powder composed of plant and seashell remains. The fossilized imprints of fucus plants and club mosses were distinctly visible on the walls. Professor Lidenbrock couldn't mistake them; but he shut his eyes, I suspect, and continued right on without breaking his stride.

This was taking bullheadedness beyond any reasonable limit. I'd had it. I picked up a perfectly preserved shell, which had once belonged to a creature generally resembling today's sow bug; then, rejoining my uncle, I told him:

"Look!"

"Fine," he replied serenely. "It's the shell of a trilobite, an extinct order of crustaceans. Nothing more."

"But don't you conclude—"

"—what you yourself conclude? I do. Absolutely. We've left the lava path and the layer of granite behind. It could be that I'm mistaken; but I won't know if I'm wrong till I've reached the end of this hallway."

"What you're doing makes sense and I would support you, uncle, if we weren't facing a danger that's growing more and more threatening."

"What's that?"

"A shortage of water."

"Well then, Axel, we'll ration it."

20

WE DID INDEED have to ration it. Our water supply couldn't last more than three days. I realized as much at suppertime that evening. And there was an even greater source of uncertainty: we had little hope of meeting up with an active spring in the rocks from that time of transition.

All next day the endless arches of this hallway unfolded in front of our steps. We barely said a word as we walked. Close-mouthed Hans had won us over.

The path wasn't rising, at least in any noticeable way. At times it even seemed to be heading downward. But this tendency wasn't very marked in any case and offered the professor scant comfort, because the character of the strata didn't change and increasingly confirmed that we were in a time of transition.

Our electric light made the shale, limestone, and old red sandstone in the walls sparkle marvelously. You would have sworn you were on a dig out in the middle of Devonshire, which this type of terrain is named after. Magnificent specimens of marble covered the walls, some an agate gray whimsically accented with white veins, others a crimson color or a yellow mottled with patches of red; farther off were samples of dark-colored griotte marble in which some brighter shades of limestone stood out.

Most of this marble featured the fossilized imprints of primitive animals. Creation had made obvious progress since the day before. Instead of rudimentary trilobites, I spotted the remains of higher life forms—among others ganoid fish and marine lizards from the order Sauropterygia, which keen-eyed paleontologists have been able to identify as early representatives of the reptile class. The Devonian seas teemed with a large number of such animal specimens, depositing them by the thousands in these newer rock formations.

It became obvious that we were climbing up the ladder of animal life, a ladder where man sits on the top rung. But Professor Lidenbrock didn't seem to be paying the slightest attention.

He was waiting for one of two things: either a vertical shaft that opened at his feet and let him resume his descent, or an obstacle that kept him from continuing along this route. But evening arrived without his hopes being fulfilled.

On Friday, following a night in which I started to feel the pangs of thirst, our little band plunged once more into the hallway's twists and turns.

After a ten-hour hike I noted that the reflections of our lamps were significantly fainter on the walls of the hallway. The marble, shale, limestone, and sandstone in its sides had changed into a retaining wall that was dark and dingy. At a point where the tunnel got quite narrow, I leaned on the rock face to my left.

When I took my hand away, it was completely black. I looked closer. We were smack in the middle of a coalfield.

"A coal mine!" I exclaimed.

"A mine without any miners," my uncle replied.

"Huh? Who says?"

"I say," the professor remarked in a curt tone. "And I'm positive it wasn't the hand of man that cut this hallway through these coal beds. But whether or not it's the work of nature is of little consequence. It's dinnertime. Let's dine."

Hans fixed us some food. I scarcely ate a thing, then drank the few drops of water that made up my ration. Our guide had half a flask left, which was all that remained to slake the thirst of three men.

After their meal my two companions lay down on their blankets and found solace in slumber from their weariness. As for me, I couldn't sleep and counted off the hours till morning.

At six o'clock on Saturday, we set out again. Twenty minutes later we arrived at a huge cavity; by this point I'd realized that human hands couldn't have excavated this coalfield; they would have braced the vaulting, and in all honesty it seemed to stay up only by some miracle of balance.

This particular cavern measured 100 feet wide by 150 high. The earth had been forcefully pushed aside by an underground disturbance. Yielding to some powerful upthrust, the bedrock had broken apart, leaving this huge void that earthlings were probing for the first time.

The whole history of the coal age was written on these dark walls, and a geologist could easily have traced its different phases. Beds of sandstone or dense clay separated the seams of coal, which seemed to have been squashed together by the layers above them.

During the era on earth before the second age, an immense amount of vegetation covered the globe, thanks to the twofold contributions of the tropical heat and the constant humidity. A steamy atmosphere wrapped the entire globe, hiding it as yet from the sun's rays.

Ergo the logical conclusion that the high temperatures didn't come from that recently formed heat source. Maybe that shining orb wasn't even ready to play its brilliant role. There weren't any "climates" as yet, and a sweltering heat spread evenly over the whole surface of the globe from the equator to the poles. Where did this heat come from? The globe's interior.

Despite Professor Lidenbrock's suppositions, an intense fire smoldered in the bowels of our sphere; its effects could be felt as far as the upper layers of the earth's crust; shielded from the sun's wholesome outpourings, the plants didn't generate any blossoms or scents, but their roots drew much energy from the blazing terrain of those ancient days.

There were few trees, just herbaceous plants: immense grasses, bracken, and club mosses, plus prehistoric stand-ins for the tree fern and horsetail—not many families, but their species ran into the thousands.

Now then, coal owes its origin specifically to this abundant plant life. Our globe's crust was still elastic and reacted to movements in the mass of liquid it covered. Ergo the many crevices and cave-ins. Dragged under the waters, considerable amounts of vegetation accumulated little by little.

Then came the naturally occurring chemical processes; in the depths of the seas, those masses of plants initially turned into peat; then, thanks to the interaction of gases and the heat caused by fermentation, they underwent a thorough petrifying.

That's how these immense beds of fossil fuel were formed; but in less than three centuries, they're sure to run out due to overconsumption, if the industrial nations aren't careful.

These thoughts popped into my head while I was pondering the wealth of coal piled up in this part of the earth's bedrock. Surely none of it would ever come to light. Working a mine this remote would entail too many hardships. But why bother in the first place, since the surface of the globe still has loads of coal—so to speak—in a large number of regions? Accordingly these pristine beds won't look any different at the tolling of the earth's last hour.

But on we went, and I was alone among my companions in whiling away our lengthy trek by getting caught up in issues of geology. The temperature hadn't changed noticeably from what it was when we'd crossed through the lava and shale. Except that my nostrils were bothered by a very marked odor of methane. In this hallway I immediately recognized the presence of a significant amount of that hazardous elastic fluid that miners call firedamp, whose explosions have caused so many frightful catastrophes.

Fortunately Ruhmkorff's clever devices lit our way. If we'd had the bad luck and carelessness to explore this hallway with torches in hand, a dreadful explosion would have concluded these travels by wiping out the travelers.

Our excursion through this coalfield lasted till evening. My uncle could barely contain his impatience with the route's horizontal character. Twenty steps away it was invariably as dark as the pit, which kept us from estimating the hallway's length, and by six o'clock I was starting to think it went on forever, when all at once a wall loomed unexpectedly in front of us. We couldn't go any farther, not right or left, up or down. We'd come to a dead end.

"Fine, all the better!" my uncle exclaimed. "At least I know where things stand. We aren't on Saknussemm's route and all we have to do is retrace our steps. Let's get a good night's sleep, and in less than three days we'll be back where the two hallways make a fork in the road."

"Yes," I said, "if we have the strength!"

"And why wouldn't we?"

"Because tomorrow we'll be completely out of water."

"And out of courage as well?" the professor said, looking sternly at me.

I didn't dare answer him back.

21

THE NEXT MORNING we started off bright and early. We had to hurry. It would take us over three days to walk back to the intersection.

I'm not going to dwell on the woes of our return trip. My uncle endured them with the sour temper of a man who wasn't enjoying his finest hour, Hans with the forbearance of his placid personality, and I myself in all honesty by moaning and groaning; this stroke of bad luck was more than I could face.

As I predicted, we ran completely out of water by the end of our first day on the trail. After that the only liquid we had with us was gin, but this hellish liquor burned my throat and I couldn't stand even the sight of it. I found the temperature suffocating. Exhaustion paralyzed me. More than once I almost fell in a dead faint. Then we took a break; my uncle and the Icelander did their best to buck me up. But I could already see that the former was reacting negatively to his tremendous exhaustion and the agonies caused by dehydration.

Finally on Tuesday, July 7, dragging ourselves on our hands and knees, we arrived half dead at the junction point of the two hallways. I stretched out on the lava floor and lay there like an inanimate object. It was ten o'clock in the morning.

Leaning against the rock face, Hans and my uncle tried to nibble a few bites of biscuit. A long wail escaped from my swollen lips. I fell into a deep swoon.

A little while later my uncle came over to me and lifted me in his arms:

"My poor boy!" he muttered in a genuinely compassionate voice.

I was touched by these words, not used to such affection from the fierce professor. I clutched his trembling hands in mine. He let me do so while looking at me. His eyes were moist.

Then I saw him take the flask hanging at

his side. Much to my astonishment he held it up to my lips.

"Have a drink," he put in.

Had I heard him right? Was my uncle going insane? I looked at him with a dazed expression. I couldn't believe my ears.

"Have a drink," he repeated.

And tipping his flask, he emptied it out between my lips.

O infinite bliss! A swallow of water had just moistened my burning mouth—just one swallow, but it was enough to bring me back to life, a life that had been slipping away.

I clasped my hands in thanks to my uncle.

"Yes," he put in, "one swallow of water! The last one, you hear me, the last one! I kept it faithfully in the depths of my flask. Twenty times, a hundred times, I've had to withstand a fearful craving to drink it. But no, Axel, I saved it for you."

"Oh, uncle!" I mumbled, while large tears moistened my eyes.

"Yes, my poor boy, I knew that when you reached this intersection, you would collapse half dead, so I kept those last drops of water to revive you."

"Thank you!" I exclaimed. "Thank you!"

Though I'd quenched my thirst only a little, I'd recovered some of my strength. Till then my throat muscles had been constricted, but now they relaxed, and the burning in my lips eased up. I was able to speak.

"Look here," I said, "at this point we have only one option: we've run out of water; we've got to go back the way we came."

As I said these words, my uncle glanced away; he hung his head; he wouldn't look me in the eye.

"We've got to go back," I snapped, "and retrace our steps to Snaefells. May God give us the strength to climb to the top of the crater again!"

"Go back?" my uncle put in, as if responding to himself rather than to me.

"Yes, go back—and without wasting another second."

At this juncture there was a longish moment of silence.

"Hence, Axel," the professor went on in a peculiar tone, "those few drops of water didn't restore your courage and energy?"

"My courage?"

"I find you just as demoralized as before, still giving voice to words of despair!"

What sort of human being was I dealing with, and what plans were still brewing in his daredevil mind?

"What! You aren't willing to—?"

"—relinquish this expedition, just when everything indicates it can succeed? Never!"

"Then we must lay down our lives?"

"No, no, Axel! Leave. I don't want to be the death of you. Take Hans with you. Let me go on alone!"

"You want me to desert you?"

"Let me be, I tell you. I've started this journey; I'll carry it to its conclusion or I'm not coming back. Go home, Axel, go home!"

My uncle was in a tremendous state of excitement as he spoke. His voice, which had been gentle for a second, turned hard and threatening. He was fighting the impossible with grim fortitude! I didn't want to leave him down in these depths, but my instincts for self-preservation, on the other hand, were urging me to clear out.

Our guide watched this drama with his usual lack of concern. But he could grasp what was going on between his two companions. Our gestures were enough to indicate the different paths down which each of us was trying to tug the other; yet, though his life was on the line, Hans seemed to take little interest in the matter—he was ready to get moving at the signal to start off, or ready to stay put at his employer's tiniest whim.

If I could only have made him understand me just then! My words, my anguish, my tone of voice would have overcome his icy temperament. There were dangers our guide didn't even seem to suspect, and I would have made them clear and tangible. Maybe the two of us could have persuaded the bull-headed professor. In a pinch we could have forced him to head back to the upper reaches of Snaefells!

I went over to Hans. I put my hand on his. He didn't stir. I showed him the path up to the crater. He stayed motionless. My gasping features revealed all that I was suffering. The Icelander gently shook his head, pointing serenely to my uncle:

"*Mester,*" he put in.

"Master!" I exclaimed. "No, you madman! He isn't the master of your destiny! We've got to get out of here! We've got to drag him with us! Don't you hear me? Don't you understand me?"

I'd grabbed Hans by the arm. I tried to force him to his feet. I struggled with him. My uncle stepped in.

"Calm down, Axel," he said. "You'll get nowhere with this unemotional employee of mine. So listen to what I'm proposing to you."

I folded my arms and looked my uncle straight in the eye.

"This lack of water," he said, "is the only thing that stands in the way of my carrying out my plans. Lava, shale, and coal make up the eastern hallway, and we didn't find a single molecule of liquid. It's possible we'll have better luck taking the western tunnel."

I shook my head with an attitude of utter disbelief.

"Listen to me till I'm through," the professor went on, raising his voice. "While you lay here motionless, I scouted out the contours of that hallway. It plunges straight into the bowels of the globe and in a few hours it'll lead us to the section of granite. There we're bound to find plenty of springs. The character of the rock insists on it, and both my instincts and my reasoning support this belief. Now then, here's what I propose to you. Columbus once asked his crewmen to give him three more days to look for new lands, and though his crewmen were frightened and in poor health, they nevertheless granted him what he asked and he discovered the New World. I'm the Columbus of these underground regions and I'm asking you for just *one* more day. If I haven't found the water we need by the end of that time, I swear to you we'll return to the surface of the earth."

Despite my anger I was moved by these words and by the exertion it cost my uncle to deliver such a speech.

"All right!" I snapped. "We'll do it your way, and may God reward these superhuman efforts of yours. You have only a few hours to tempt fate. Off you go!"

22

OUR DESCENT RESUMED, this time down the new hallway. Hans took the lead as usual. We hadn't gone a hundred steps when, sweeping his lamp over the walls, the professor exclaimed:

"It's the original rock! We're on the right track! Keep going!"

When the earth was gradually cooling during the first days of the world, its shrinking volume caused its crust to shift, split, sink, and crack. Our current corridor was a crevice of this type, and molten granite used to pour through it. There were a thousand twists and turns, forming a hopelessly tangled labyrinth in the primeval stone.

As we descended, the sequence of layers making up the original terrain got clearer and clearer. The science of geology regards this original terrain as the basis of the earth's rocky crust and has determined that it consists of three different layers, shale, gneiss, and mica schist, all resting on that unshakable bedrock known as granite.

Now then, no mineralogists had ever before met up with such wondrous conditions for studying nature on the spot. Our own two hands, our own two eyes, were going to touch and study aspects of the earth's inner texture that no borings by crude, mindless machinery could bring to the surface.

The shale system was tinted with lovely shades of green, and winding through it were iridescent veins of copper and manganese with a few traces of platinum and gold. I thought about this fortune that lay stashed in the bowels of the globe, this wealth that greedy humanity would never enjoy! The upheavals of the first days had buried this treasure so deep, no mattock or pick could wrest it from its grave.

After the shale came the gneiss, whose formations were laid out in sheets notable for the orderliness and parallel lines of each layer, then the mica schist, organized into big plates made pleasing to the eye by the glitter of white mica.

Reflecting off the tiny facets in the mass of rock, the light from our Ruhmkorff devices sent fiery jets crisscrossing from every direction, and I fancied I was traveling inside a hollow diamond whose rays had shattered into a thousand dazzling sparks.

Near six o'clock this festival of light noticeably died down and all but faded out; the walls took on a dark yet crystalline hue; mica was mingling more intimately with feldspar and quartz to form the rock beyond compare, the stone that's hardest of all, the substance that supports the four systems in our globe's crust without being crushed. We were walled up in an immense prison of granite.

It was eight o'clock in the evening. Still no water. I was suffering horribly. My uncle forged ahead. He wasn't willing to stop. He cocked an ear and listened for the babbling of some spring. There wasn't a sound.

But my legs kept refusing to carry me. I endured my afflictions so my uncle wouldn't have to call a halt. Had he done so, it would have been a crushing blow to his hopes, because the day was drawing to a close, the last one allotted to him.

Finally my strength left me. I gave a yell and collapsed.

"Help! I'm dying!"

My uncle retraced his steps. He regarded me with his arms folded; then these muffled words fell from his lips:

"It's all over!"

A fearfully angry gesture was the last thing I saw, then I closed my eyes.

When I opened them again, I found my two companions motionless and rolled up in their blankets. Were they sleeping? For my part I couldn't doze off for a second. I was in too much pain, especially from the thought that there would be no remedy for what ailed me. My uncle's last words rang in my ears: "It's all over!" Because I was in such a weakened state, going back up to the surface of the globe was unthinkable.

We were beneath more than 3½ miles of the earth's crust! The whole weight of this mass seemed to be pressing down on my shoulders. I felt I was being crushed and I wore myself out with strenuous efforts to turn over on my granite mattress.

A few hours went by. A deep silence reigned around us, the silence of the grave.

Nothing could get through these walls; the thinnest one was five miles thick.

Yet in the midst of my swoon, I thought I heard a noise. It was dark in the tunnel. I looked more intently and I seemed to see the Icelander vanishing into the distance, lamp in hand.

Why was he going off? Was Hans leaving us? My uncle was sleeping. I tried to shout. My voice wouldn't come out from between my parched lips. It was getting extremely dark, and the last sounds were now dying away.

"Hans is leaving us!" I yelled. "Hans! Hans!"

I was yelling these words in my mind. They went no farther. However, after my first second of panic, I felt ashamed for suspecting a man whose behavior till then had been above suspicion. His going off couldn't have been an escape attempt. Instead of heading back up the hallway, he was heading down it. If he'd harbored any ill intentions, they would have taken him higher, not lower. This line of reasoning calmed me down a little, and I came around to a different way of thinking. Only some serious purpose could have snatched Hans, that placid man, from his rest. Was he investigating something? In the still of the night had he heard some low sound that hadn't intruded on my awareness?

23

FOR AN HOUR my delirious brain imagined all the reasons that could have made our tranquil hunter act this way. The silliest notions got tangled up in my head. I felt I was about to lose my mind!

But some footsteps finally rang out in the depths of the pit. Hans was coming back up. A wavering light started to glide over the walls, then it emerged from the mouth of the corridor. Hans appeared.

He went over to my uncle, put a hand on his shoulder, and roused him gently. My uncle sat up.

"What is it?" he put in.

"*Vatten!*" the hunter replied.

I'm forced to conclude that the influence of intense suffering can turn anybody into a polyglot. I didn't know a single word of Danish, yet I instinctively understood the word our guide had spoken.

"Water! Water!" I shouted, clapping my hands and waving them around like a madman.

"Water!" my uncle repeated. "*Hvar?*" he asked in Icelandic.

"*Nedat,*" Hans replied.

Where? Farther down! I understood completely. I clutched the hunter's hands and kept squeezing them while he calmly looked at me.

Getting ready to leave didn't take long, and soon we were proceeding down a corridor with a slope of one foot for every yard.

An hour later we'd gone a bit more than a mile and descended 2,000 feet.

Just then I distinctly heard an unfamiliar sound running through the innards of the granite wall, a sort of dull rumble like distant thunder. During that first half hour on the trail, not meeting up with the promised spring, I felt my afflictions taking over again; but then my uncle told me what was causing this noise.

"Hans isn't mistaken," he said. "What you're hearing is the rumble of a torrent."

"A torrent?" I exclaimed.

"There isn't the slightest doubt. An underground river is flowing around us!"

We picked up the pace, charged with hope. I didn't feel tired anymore. That sound of babbling water had already refreshed me. It was getting noticeably louder. After staying overhead for a good while, the torrent now ran through the rock face on our left, rumbling and tumbling as it went. I often stroked the rock with my hand, hoping to find traces of slickness or dampness. To no avail.

Again half an hour went by. Again we covered a bit more than a mile.

Then it became obvious that when the hunter had left us, he hadn't been able to search beyond this point. Guided by those instincts characteristic of mountaineers and human divining rods, he'd "sensed" this torrent inside the rock; but he hadn't actually

seen the precious liquid; he hadn't slaked his thirst with it.

In addition it soon became clear that if we kept on walking, we would go farther away from the stream, whose babbling was starting to grow fainter.

We turned back. Hans stopped at the exact location where the torrent seemed the closest.

I sat down next to the wall; two feet away from me, water was flowing past with tremendous force. But a barrier of granite still separated it from us.

Without thinking it through, without wondering if there was some way of getting at that water, I started giving in to despair.

Hans looked at me, and I thought I saw a smile flicker over his lips.

He got up and took the lamp. I followed him. He headed toward the wall. I watched what he did. He glued his ear to the dry stone, moving slowly while listening with great care. I could see that he was searching for the exact spot where the torrent made the most noise. He found this spot on the side wall to the left, three feet above the ground.

How excited I felt! I didn't dare guess what the hunter was trying to do! But I couldn't help realizing, applauding, and clapping him on the back when I saw him wield his pick to attack the rock itself.

"We're saved!" I yelled.

"Yes," my uncle echoed in high excitement, "Hans is right! Ah, that gallant hunter! We would never have thought of this ourselves!"

It was too true! As simple as it was, such an approach wouldn't have entered our heads. Nothing could be riskier than taking swings of the mattock at the framework of our globe. What if a cave-in took place and crushed us? What if the torrent gushed out of the rock and then overwhelmed us? These definitely weren't make-believe dangers; but by that point no fear of cave-ins or floods could hold us back—our thirst was so intense, we would have dug right through the ocean floor to quench it.

Hans started in on the task at hand, which neither my uncle nor I could have carried out. Our hands would have run wild with impatience, chips of rock would have flown all over from our hasty strokes. By contrast our guide was calm and temperate, gradually wearing down the rock with a sequence of short, rhythmic strokes, digging an opening six inches wide. I could hear the torrent getting louder, and in my mind I could almost feel that wholesome water gushing against my lips.

Soon Hans had driven his pick two feet into the granite wall. He'd been working for over an hour. I was writhing in impatience. My uncle wanted to use more extreme measures. I had trouble restraining him and he'd already grabbed his pick, when suddenly there was a hissing sound. A jet of water shot out of the wall and smacked against the rock face opposite.

Nearly toppled by the impact, Hans couldn't help giving a cry of pain. I realized why when I dipped my hands into this jet of liquid, then uttered a loud exclamation in my turn. The spring was scalding hot.

"This water's at the boiling point!" I yelled.

"Well, it'll cool down," my uncle replied.

Steam was filling up the corridor; meanwhile a brook took form, went off, and vanished into the underground windings; soon we downed our first swallows.

Ah, what joy! What rapture beyond compare! Where did this water come from? What kind was it? No matter. It was water, and though it was still warm, it refilled our hearts with a life that was on the verge of slipping away. I drank without stopping, without even tasting.

It was after sixty seconds of delight that I finally exclaimed:

"Why, this water has iron in it!"

"Splendid for the stomach," my uncle remarked, "plus it has a high mineral content. This is like going to the health resorts in Spa or Toplița."

"Oh, how good it is!"

"I would think so—this is water coming from five miles underground! It has an ink-like taste that isn't at all unpleasant. Hans has provided us with a first-class fountainhead. I propose we name this health-giving stream after him."

"Excellent!" I exclaimed.

And we immediately dubbed it the Hansbach.[24]

Hans didn't let it go to his head. After temperately refreshing himself, he propped himself in a corner with his customary calm.

"Now," I said, "this water mustn't go to waste."

"Why worry?" my uncle responded. "I doubt that this spring will ever run dry."

"That's not the point. Let's fill up our flasks and the goatskin water bag, then we'll try to plug this hole."

They took my advice. Using chips of granite and strips of burlap, Hans tried to stanch the wound he'd made in the rock face. This wasn't an easy thing to accomplish. All we did was scald our hands; the water pressure was so considerable, our efforts proved fruitless.

"Judging from the force of this jet," I said, "it's obvious that the upper reaches of this watercourse are located at a great height."

"No question," my uncle remarked. "If this column of water is 32,000 feet high, its pressure is equal to a thousand atmospheres. But a thought occurs to me."

"What?"

"Why are we so dead set on plugging this hole?"

"It's because . . . uh . . ."

I was at a loss to come up with a reason.

"When our flasks are empty, is there any guarantee we can fill them again?"

"Of course not."

"All right, let's allow this water to flow! Naturally it will run downward and it will both guide and refresh us on the way."

"Good thinking!" I exclaimed. "With this brook as our traveling companion, there's no further reason why our plans won't succeed."

"Oho, you're coming along, my boy," the professor said with a smile.

"Better yet, I'm way ahead of you."

"One moment! First let's get a few hours' rest."

I'd genuinely forgotten it was nighttime. Our chronometer proceeded to set me straight. Amply refreshed and recharged, each of us soon fell sound asleep.

---

[24] *Translator's note.* German: "the Hans Stream."

24

BY THE NEXT MORNING we'd already forgotten our past sufferings. Right off I was surprised not to feel thirsty anymore and I wondered why. The babbling brook that flowed at my feet proceeded to answer me.

We had breakfast and drank that splendid, iron-rich water. I was in high spirits and determined to walk a long way. How could a confident man like my uncle not succeed, given such an efficient guide as Hans and such a "motivated" nephew as me? These were the bright ideas that darted through my brain! If anybody had proposed that I climb back to the summit of Snaefells, I would have scornfully declined.

But luckily all we had to do was descend.

"Let's go!" I shouted, my enthusiastic tones waking the ancient echoes inside the earth.

On Thursday, at eight o'clock in the morning, we took to the trail again. Twisting and turning, the winding ways of that granite corridor were full of unexpected jogs and featured as many complications as a labyrinth; but by and large its chief direction was steadily to the southeast. To keep track of the route we were following, my uncle continually checked his compass with the greatest care.

Barely slanting, the hallway stayed nearly horizontal and had a maximum slope of one inch for every yard. The babbling brook flowed unhurriedly at our feet. To me it was like some familiar spirit guiding us through the earth, and my hand felt the gentle warmth of this water nymph whose song accompanied our steps. Whenever I'm in a good mood, I'm apt to get off into folklore.

As for my uncle, being "the defender of the upright," he railed at our route's horizontal character. This path seemed to drag on indefinitely, and instead of shooting straight down at a right angle to the earth's surface, it was, as he put it, taking the long way down the hypotenuse. But we had no choice, and provided that we kept getting closer to the center, no matter how gradually, we couldn't complain.

From time to time, though, the slopes got steeper; then our water nymph would let out a shriek and take a tumble, and we went down into the depths along with her.

By and large, over that day and the next, we made a good deal of sideways progress and comparatively little downward progress.

On Friday evening, July 10, we estimated we had to be nearly seventy-five miles southeast of Reykjavik and some six miles down.

Then a rather daunting shaft opened at our feet. Once my uncle had determined how precipitous its slopes were, he couldn't help clapping his hands.

"This will take us a long way," he exclaimed, "and easily too, because those ledges in the rock provide an honest-to-goodness staircase!"

Hans strung up the ropes to prevent any accidents. Our descent started. I wouldn't go so far as to say it was hazardous, because I was already at home with this variety of athletic activity.

This shaft was a narrow crack cut into the mass of stone and it was the type called a "fault." Apparently it had been caused by the shrinkage of the earth's framework back when our globe was cooling off. If it had formerly been a passageway for eruptive materials spewed out by Snaefells, I couldn't account for why that volcanic waste hadn't left any traces. We were going down a sort of spiral staircase, which you would have sworn had been made by human hands.

Every fifteen minutes we had to halt in order to take a much-needed breather and limber up our knee joints. At these times we sat down on some ledge or other, dangled our legs, talked, ate, and slaked our thirst with water from the brook.

Inside this fault, needless to say, the Hansbach had turned into a waterfall at the expense of its volume; but it was more than adequate for quenching our thirst; besides, it was sure to resume its placid course once the inclines were less drastic. Just then it reminded me of my good uncle with his impatience and temper, but on a gentle slope it was as calm as our Icelandic hunter.

Over July 11 and 12, we wound our way down this fault, going another five miles into

the earth's crust, which put us about twelve miles below sea level. But toward noontime on the 13th, the fault took on a far gentler slant, sloping in a southeasterly direction at about a 45° angle.

Then the trail got both easy and utterly monotonous. It could hardly have been otherwise. There weren't many changes of scenery to add variety to our trip.

Finally, on Wednesday the 15th, we were some seventeen miles underground and about 125 miles away from Snaefells. Though we were a little tired, our state of health was still encouraging and our traveling medicine chest remained unopened.

Every hour my uncle jotted down the readings given by his compass, chronometer, pressure gauge, and thermometer, the same ones he has published in his scientific report of our journey. Therefore he could easily work out our position. When he informed me that we'd gone a horizontal distance of 125 miles, I couldn't help letting out an exclamation.

"What's wrong?" he asked.

"Nothing, I just had a thought."

"What, my boy?"

"Just this: if your calculations are correct, we're no longer under Iceland."

"You think so?"

"It's easy for us to make sure."

I did some measuring on the map with a pair of compasses.

"I'm not mistaken," I said. "We've gone past Cape Portland, and those 125 miles to the southeast put us in the open sea."

"*Under* the open sea," my uncle countered, rubbing his hands.

"Which means," I exclaimed, "that the ocean's spreading overhead!"

"Phooey, Axel, nothing could be more natural! Aren't there coal mines in Newcastle that go out a long way under the waves?"

This state of affairs may have been perfectly acceptable for the professor, but the thought of my strolling around under a huge mass of water didn't fail to concern me. And yet it generally made little difference whether the plains and mountains of Iceland were hanging over our heads or the waves of the Atlantic; all that counted was that the frame-

work of granite held firm. What's more, I soon got used to this idea—because, though the corridor was sometimes straight, sometimes winding, and had gradients as unpredictable as its twists and turns, it always went southeast and farther down, quickly taking us to great depths.

Four days later, on Saturday evening, July 18, we reached a biggish sort of cave; my uncle paid Hans his three weekly riksdalers, and it was decreed that the next day would be a day of rest.

25

SO I WOKE UP Sunday morning without the usual bother of starting off immediately. And this remained a pleasant feeling even in the deepest of chasms. As a matter of fact, we were getting used to this cave-dwelling lifestyle. I barely thought about the sun, moon, and stars, or trees, houses, and towns, or any of those aboveground frills that mortal beings see as necessities. In our capacity as potential fossils, we turned up our noses at such worthless wonders.

The cave was shaped like a huge hall. Our loyal brook flowed smoothly over the granite floor. At this distance from the spring, its water had cooled to air temperature and was no problem to drink.

After breakfast the professor wanted to devote a few hours to putting his field notes in order.

"First," he said, "I'll work out the exact bearings of this location; back home I want to be able to draft a map of our journey, a sort of vertical cross section of the globe, which will provide a side view of our travels."

"That'll be intriguing, uncle; but will your readings be accurate enough?"

"Yes. I've carefully jotted down the angles and inclines. I'm sure I haven't made any errors. First let's find out where we are. Fetch the compass and see what direction it's showing."

I looked at the instrument and after a careful inspection I replied:

"East by southeast."

"Fine," the professor put in, jotting the

reading down and doing a little quick calculating. "I conclude, then, that we've gone 211 miles from our starting point."

"So we're traveling under the Atlantic?"

"Correct."

"And maybe there's a hurricane unleashed right now, and overhead ships are rocking in the waves and storm winds?"

"It could be."

"And whales coming to slap our prison walls with their tails?"

"Calm down, Axel, they won't manage to knock anything loose. But let's get back to our calculating. We've gone some 210 miles southeast from the base of Snaefells, and working from my earlier notes, I estimate we've reached a depth of forty miles."

"Forty miles!" I exclaimed.

"Undoubtedly."

"But that's the absolute limit science ascribes to the thickness of the earth's crust."

"I don't say nay."

"And at this point, according to the law of rising temperatures, it should be hotter than 2,700° Fahrenheit!"

"It *should*, my boy."

"And none of this granite could stay in a solid state but would be completely liquefied."

"You can see that it isn't so—as usual, the facts happen to contradict the fancies."

"I'm forced to agree, but it amazes me all the same."

"What does our thermometer read?"

"It says 81.7° Fahrenheit."

"The experts are therefore off by 2,618.3°. Therefore those proportional rises in temperature are a fallacy. Therefore Sir Humphry Davy wasn't mistaken. Therefore I was right to listen to him. What's your response to that?"

"Nothing."

Actually I had plenty of things to say. I didn't believe Davy's suppositions for a second and I still swore by a central heat source, though I definitely wasn't experiencing its effects. In actuality, since the chimney of this extinct volcano was covered with a coat of fireproof lava, I preferred to think that its walls wouldn't let the heat spread beyond them.

But without pausing to look for fresh arguments, I confined myself to sizing up our circumstances as they actually were.

"Uncle," I went on, "I grant the accuracy of your calculations, but allow me to draw a valid conclusion from them."

"Go on, my boy, have at it."

"Below the latitude of Iceland, at this spot where we are, isn't the earth's radius about 3,926 miles?"

"It's 3,926⅔."

"Let's round it up to 4,000. Out of a journey of 4,000 miles, we've gone 40?"

"That's right."

"And this at a cost of some 210 miles diagonally?"

"Exactly."

"In about twenty days?"

"Twenty days."

"Now then, 40 miles are 1/100 of the earth's radius. So if we keep this up, we'll take 2,000 days, or nearly 5½ years, for our descent alone!"

The professor didn't reply.

"Not to mention that we can get 40 miles down only by going 200 miles sideways, which means we'll head southeast some 20,000 miles, and we'll pop out at some point on the earth's exterior long before we reach its center!"

"To blazes with your calculations!" my uncle countered with an angry gesture. "To blazes with your theories! What are they based on? Who says this corridor doesn't go straight to our destination? Besides, there's a precedent for my expedition. I'm doing what somebody else has done, and where he succeeded, I'll succeed in my turn."

"I hope so; but all the same, if you'll allow me to—"

"I'll allow you to hold your tongue, Axel, anytime you're inclined to spout this kind of nonsense."

I clearly saw the dreaded professor threatening to take over from the uncle and I kept quiet as ordered.

"Now," he went on, "check our pressure gauge. What does it show?"

"Considerable pressure."

"Fine. You can see that by gently descending and gradually acclimating ourselves to the atmosphere's density, we aren't suffering from it in the least."

"Not in the least, except for my ears popping a little."

"That's nothing, and you can make your discomfort go away by putting the outside air in quick contact with the air held in your lungs."

"Exactly," I replied, thoroughly determined to avoid any more clashes with my uncle. "In fact it's a genuinely pleasant sensation being immersed in this denser atmosphere. Have you noticed how clearly sounds carry around us?"

"Absolutely. A deaf man would end up with wonderful hearing."

"But undoubtedly this density will increase?"

"Yes, according to a law that needs rather a bit more testing. It's a fact that the force of gravity decreases the deeper we go. You're aware that its effect is most keenly felt at the surface, while objects at the center of the globe no longer have any weight."

"I'm aware of that; but tell me, won't this air end up having the density of water?"

"Certainly, under a pressure of 710 atmospheres."

"What about farther down?"

"Farther down its density will increase even more."

"In that case how will we keep descending?"

"Well then, we'll stick pebbles in our pockets."

"Ye gods, uncle, you have an answer for everything."

I didn't dare go any farther into the realm of speculation, because I was bound to bump into some other impossibility that would make the professor leap to his feet.

Yet it was obvious that if the air was under a pressure that could reach thousands of atmospheres, it would end up converting into a solid state; and at that point, assuming our bodies lived through it, we would have to call a halt, despite all the arguments in the world.

But I didn't exploit this line of reasoning. Once again my uncle would have fired back with his eternal Saknussemm—a precedent of no value, because, even granting that the Ice-

landic scholar actually went on such a journey, there was a perfectly simple thing that could be said in reply:

In the 16th century neither the barometer nor the pressure gauge had been invented; so how could Saknussemm have figured out when he'd reached the center of the globe?

But I kept this objection to myself and waited for developments.

We spent the rest of the day calculating and conversing. I invariably sided with Professor Lidenbrock and envied Hans's utter lack of concern—he rarely went looking for causes or effects and blindly followed wherever fate led him.

26

I MUST ADMIT, things had gone well so far, and it would have been ill-mannered of me to complain. If our "problem ratio" didn't increase, we couldn't fail to achieve our goal. And then what glory would be ours! I'd finally enrolled in the Lidenbrock school of thought. It was official. Did this come from living in these strange surroundings? Maybe.

For a couple days some steeper slopes—a few of them fearfully close to downright vertical—drew us deep into the interior bedrock. There were workdays when we got from 3½ to 5 miles closer to the center. These involved dangerous descents in which Hans's skill and wondrous composure were very useful to us. That unemotional Icelander put himself at risk with inconceivable nonchalance, and thanks to him, we handled more than one bad patch we couldn't have gotten though on our own.

But by thunder, he grew more close-mouthed every day! I think he even won us over to his ways. External things have a real effect on the brain. A person locked up between four walls ultimately loses his ability to put thoughts into words. A good many prisoners in solitary confinement turn into half-wits, if not madmen, from failing to exercise their mental abilities.

During the two weeks that followed our last conversation, no incidents worth mentioning took place. Just one ultraserious development comes to mind, and with good reason. It would be hard for me to forget the tiniest details of it.

By August 7 our consecutive descents had taken us to a depth of nearly seventy-five miles, in other words, there were seventy-five miles of rocks, seas, landmasses, and towns overhead. By then we must have been about 500 miles from Iceland.

That day the tunnel was going along a level plane that barely sloped.

I was walking in the lead. My uncle carried one of the two Ruhmkorff devices and I had the other. I was studying the layers of granite.

All at once, turning around, I saw that I was alone.

Great, I thought, I've been walking too fast, or else Hans and my uncle have stopped along the way. Oh well, I'd better rejoin them. Luckily the path's barely rising.

I retraced my steps. I walked for a quarter of an hour. I looked around. Nobody. I called out. No answer. My voice died away in the midst of the cavernous echoes it suddenly aroused.

I was starting to get worried. I shivered all over.

"Take it easy," I said out loud. "I'll find my companions again, I'm bound to. There aren't two paths! Now then, since I'm out in front, let's try going to the rear."

I went back up the trail for half an hour. I listened for somebody calling to me, and in that ultradense atmosphere a voice could travel far. An abnormal silence reigned in that immense hallway.

I came to a halt. I couldn't believe how alone I felt. I was hoping I'd simply gone astray, not gotten lost. If it was the former, we would find each other again.

"Look here," I kept saying, "there's only one path and they're taking it, so I'm sure to rejoin them. I just need to go farther on up. Unless they forgot I was ahead of them, and when they didn't see me, they figured they should search to the rear. All right, even if that's the case I can hurry and find them again. That's obvious!"

I repeated these last words like a man far

from convinced. What's more, it had taken me an awfully long time to gather these perfectly simple ideas and put them together in rational form.

Then a doubt came over me. Was I really in the lead? Yes, Hans had been behind me and ahead of my uncle. He'd even paused for a few seconds to refasten his baggage on his shoulders. This detail came back to me. This was the very moment when I must have continued on my way.

Even so, I thought, I have a safeguard against getting lost, a thread that can guide me through this labyrinth and can't be snapped—my loyal brook. All I have to do is go back upstream and I'll automatically track down my companions.

This line of reasoning revived me and I decided to set out again without wasting another second.

And how I blessed my uncle's foresight when he'd kept the hunter from plugging up that gash in the granite wall! Thus, along with slaking our thirst on the way, this wholesome spring was about to guide me through the winding ways of the earth's crust.

Before heading back up, I thought a wash would do me good.

So I bent down to dunk my face in the waters of the Hansbach.

The reader can imagine my astonishment!

I was standing on dry, rugged granite. The brook was no longer flowing at my feet.

27

I CAN'T EXPRESS MY DESPAIR. No words in any human language could convey my feelings. I was buried alive, with the prospect of dying in the torments of hunger and thirst.

I swept my feverish hands mechanically over the ground. How arid this rock seemed to me!

But how had I gotten away from where the stream was running? Because, in a nutshell, it was gone. Then I realized why the tunnel had been so strangely silent that last time I'd listened, hoping some call from my companions would reach my ears. Thus, at the moment I'd taken my first steps along this rash route, I'd failed to notice that the stream wasn't at my side. At that moment, obviously, I'd come to a fork in the hallway and had headed down one slope while the Hansbach had obeyed the whims of another and had gone off with my companions toward depths unknown!

How could I get back to them? There wasn't any trail. I hadn't left a single footprint on this granite. I racked my brains looking for a solution to this insoluble problem. One word summed up my situation: lost!

Yes, lost at a depth that seemed inconceivable to me! Those seventy-five miles of the earth's crust weighed down on my shoulders with frightful heaviness. I felt I was being crushed.

I tried to turn my thoughts to terrestrial things. I could barely manage it. Hamburg, the house on Königstrasse, my poor Grauben, and that whole world under which I'd lost my way all passed swiftly through my frightened memory. I saw the incidents of our journey again in a single vivid vision—crossing the ocean, Iceland, Mr. Fridriksson, Snaefells! In my circumstances, I told myself, it would be a sign of insanity to hang onto even a shadow of hope—it was better to give in to despair!

Honestly, what human power could bring me back to the surface of the globe, breaking apart those enormous arches shored up over my head? Who could put me on the right track again and help me rejoin my companions?

"Oh, uncle!" I called out in a despairing voice.

This was the only word of complaint that came to my lips, because I knew the poor man had to be suffering in his turn as he searched for me.

Consequently, when I saw that I was beyond all human aid, unable to make any attempt to save myself, I turned to Heaven for assistance. Memories of my childhood came back to me, of my mother whom I'd known only in the nursery. I took refuge in prayer and fervently begged for God's help, though, being so behindhand in my appeals, I hadn't much claim on His attention.

This recourse to Providence calmed me down a little, and I could focus on my circumstances with all my strength of mind.

I had a three-day supply of provisions and my flask was full. However I couldn't stay on my own any longer than that. But should I go upward or downward?

Upward obviously! Always upward!

I was sure to reach the spot where I'd gotten away from the spring, that fatal fork in the road. Once I had the stream at my feet, I could always get from there to the top of Snaefells again.

Why hadn't I thought of this sooner? Here, clearly, was a chance to save myself. So my most pressing task was to make it back to where the Hansbach was running.

I got to my feet, shoved off with my alpenstock, and retreated up the hallway. The slope was fairly steep. I walked full of hope and free of doubt, like a man who hasn't any choice about which path to take.

For half an hour no obstacles impeded my steps. I tried to identify my route from the tunnel's shape, from certain rocky ledges, from the layout of the crevices. But no distinctive features jarred my memory, and I soon discovered that this hallway couldn't bring me back to the fork. It was a blind alley. I banged into an impregnable wall and fell on the rocky ground.

I can't describe the horror and despair that gripped me at that moment. I lay there, overwhelmed. My last remaining hope had just dashed to pieces against that granite wall.

I was lost in this labyrinth, whose windings crisscrossed in every direction, and I gave up my impossible escape attempt. Ahead of me was a most appalling way to die, and my death was inevitable! And strange to say, it occurred to me that if my fossilized carcass were someday found again seventy-five miles down in the bowels of the earth, it would give rise to some major scientific arguing!

I tried to say something out loud, but only wheezing sounds would come from between my parched lips. I gasped for breath.

In the midst of these afflictions, a new terror came and took hold of me. When I'd fallen, my lamp had gone on the fritz. I didn't have any way of fixing it. The light inside it was dimming and going out on me!

I watched its glowing current fade from the glass spiral inside the device. A parade of moving shadows unfolded over the darkening walls. I didn't dare blink my eyes, afraid to miss the tiniest particle of this fleeting light. It looked ready to vanish any second now, then I would be plunged in "pitch-blackness."

Finally the last glimmers trembled inside the lamp. I watched them, I inhaled them with my eyes, I focused the full power of my vision on them, as if they were the last light rays I would ever be given to experience, then I was left in a deep, vast darkness.

A dreadful yell broke loose from me! Aboveground, even in the middle of the gloomiest nights, the light never gives up all its prerogatives. It can be hazy, it can be tenuous, but no matter how faint it becomes, the retina of a person's eye will end up detecting it. Here I had nothing. This total blackout had struck me blind in the strictest sense of the word.

Then I lost my head. Holding my arms out in front of me, I made an excruciating attempt to grope my way. I took to my heels, rushing helter-skelter into that hopelessly tangled labyrinth, going still deeper underground, racing through the earth's crust like some creature of the crevices, calling, yelling, howling, promptly banging into the rocky ledges, bleeding as I fell down and got up, trying to drink the blood that drenched my face, and constantly expecting some wall to provide an obstacle for my skull to smash against!

Where did this mad dash take me? I have no idea to this day. Several hours later, my strength absolutely spent, I dropped alongside the wall like an inanimate object and lost all consciousness.

28

WHEN I CAME BACK to life, my face was damp, but damp with tears. How long I'd been in that comatose state I can't say. I no longer had any way of telling the time. Never had there been such solitude as mine, never such utter isolation!

After my collapse I'd lost a lot of blood. I felt it drenching me. Oh, how sorry I was that I hadn't passed away, that my death was "still to come." I didn't want to think anymore. I emptied my mind, surrendered to my grief, and rolled over next to the opposite wall.

I was already blacking out again, and this time heading for ultimate oblivion, when a loud noise assaulted my eardrums. It was like a drawn-out thunderclap, and I heard its resonant sound waves gradually fading away into the far-off depths of the chasm.

What had caused that noise? No doubt some natural phenomenon occurring deep in the earth's bedrock! A gas explosion, or the collapse of some section of our globe's mighty foundation!

I kept listening. I wanted to see if the noise would be repeated. Fifteen minutes went by. Silence reigned in the hallway. I couldn't hear even my own heartbeats anymore.

All at once, as my ear happened to brush against the wall, I thought I detected some muffled words, elusive and distant. I gave a start.

I'm hallucinating, I thought.

But I wasn't. Listening more intently, I actually heard the muttering of voices. But in my weakened condition I couldn't grasp what they were saying. Yet people were talking. I was sure of it.

For a second I was afraid the words were my own, carried back to me by some echo. Maybe I'd called out without realizing it. I clamped my lips together and put my ear against the wall again.

"Yes, definitely! Somebody's talking!"

When I shifted just a few feet farther along the wall, I could hear clearly. I managed to catch some words, but they were indistinct, peculiar, unintelligible. They reached me as if they'd been spoken in a low voice, literally murmured. The word *förlorad* was repeated several times with a doleful inflection.

What did it mean? Who was saying it?

My uncle or Hans obviously. But if I heard them, that meant they could hear *me*.

"Help!" I shouted with all my strength. "Help!"

I listened in the darkness, on the alert for any answer, call, or grunt. I didn't hear a thing. A few minutes went by. A host of ideas were hatching in my head. I wondered if my feeble voice would be able to reach my companions.

"It's got to be them," I said over and over. "What other human beings could be buried seventy-five miles underground?"

I knuckled down to listening again. I swept my ear over the wall, I found the mathematical point where the voices seemed to reach their maximum loudness. The word *förlorad* fell on my ears again, then the thunderclap that had yanked me out of my swoon.

"No, no," I said. "Those voices couldn't be audible through such a mass of rock. This wall's made of granite and wouldn't let the loudest explosion get past. Those sounds are coming down the hallway itself! It must be creating some absolutely unique acoustic effect!"

I listened again, and this time—yes, this time!—I distinctly heard my name shooting through the void.

It was my uncle who had spoken it! He was chatting with our guide, and the word *förlorad* was a Danish word![25]

Then I understood. To be audible, I had to speak straight along this wall, which would function to conduct my voice the same way a wire conducts electricity.

But I had no time to lose. If my companions backed a few steps away, the acoustic phenomenon would be destroyed. So I went up to the wall and spoke these words as clearly as I could:

"Uncle Lidenbrock!"

I waited with the keenest anxiety. Sound doesn't travel tremendously fast. Dense layers of air don't actually increase its speed, they just magnify its loudness. A few sec-

onds—whole centuries—went by, and at last these words reached my ears:

"Axel, Axel! Is that you?"

· · · · · · ·

"Yes, yes!" I replied.

· · · · · · ·

"Where are you, my boy?"

· · · · · · ·

"Lost in utter darkness!"

· · · · · · ·

"But what happened to your lamp?"

· · · · · · ·

"It went out."

· · · · · · ·

"And what about the stream?"

· · · · · · ·

"It's gone."

· · · · · · ·

"Axel, my poor Axel! Summon your courage again!"

· · · · · · ·

"Wait a minute, I'm exhausted! I haven't the strength to answer back. Just talk to me!"

· · · · · · ·

"Courage!" my uncle went on. "Don't talk, listen to me. We've searched for you up and down this hallway. You were nowhere to be found. Oh, how I wept for you, my boy! Finally we assumed you were still walking alongside the Hansbach and we came back down, firing rifle shots on the way. Now, thanks to a simple acoustic effect, we can reconnect by voice even though our hands can't touch! But don't despair, Axel! The fact that we can hear each other is already a step up!"

· · · · · · ·

Meanwhile I'd been thinking things over. Though still hazy, a sense of hope was wak-

[25] *Translator's note*. It means "lost" and is actually Swedish.

ing again in my heart. Right off there was one thing it behooved me to know. I put my lips close to the wall and said:

"Uncle?"

. . . .

"My boy?" he answered me after a few seconds.

. . . .

"First we need to know the distance separating us."

. . . .

"That's easy."

. . . .

"Do you have your chronometer?"

. . . .

"Yes."

. . . .

"All right, hold it in your hand. Call my name, remembering the exact second when you speak. As soon as it travels to me, I'll say it back, and you'll likewise note the exact moment when you get my response."

. . . .

"Fine, and once we know the time that went by between my call and your response, we'll divide it in half—which will tell us how long my voice took to reach you."

. . . .

"That's the idea, uncle."

. . . .

"Are you ready?"

. . . .

"Yes."

. . . .

"All right, pay attention. I'm going to call your name."

. . . .

I put my ear next to the wall, and as soon as the word "Axel" traveled to me, I instantly said "Axel" in return, then waited.

. . . .

"Forty seconds," my uncle said. "Forty seconds went by between the two words; so the sound took twenty seconds to go one way. Now then, at 1,020 feet per second, that makes 20,400 feet or 3.86 miles."

. . . .

"Three point eight six miles!" I muttered.

. . . .

"Oh, you can walk that far, Axel!"

. . . .

"But should I go up or down?"

. . . .

"Down, and here's why. We've arrived at a huge open area, and a large number of hallways feed into it. The one you're following can't fail to lead you here, since every incline and crevice in the globe seems to radiate from this immense cavern we're in. So on your feet and get going. Keep moving, drag yourself along if you need to, slide down the steep slopes, and at the end of the trail you'll find us waiting for you with open arms. Off you go, my boy, off you go!"

. . . .

These words brought me back to life.

"Good-bye, uncle," I called. "I'm on my way. Once I've left this spot, we'll no longer be able to make contact with our voices. So good-bye!"

. . . .

"See you soon, Axel! See you soon!"

. . . .

Those were the last words I heard.

Carried on within the earth's bedrock and over a distance of more than three miles, that astounding conversation ended on this note of hope. I offered a prayer of gratitude to God for guiding me through this inky vastness to maybe the only place where my companions' voices could have reached me.

This highly startling acoustic effect can be easily explained by the laws of physics; it was caused by the corridor's shape and the rock's conducting power. There are many examples of sounds that carry from one point to another yet aren't audible in between. I can recall quite a few localities where this phenomenon has been noted, including the hallway inside the dome of St. Paul's Cathedral in London, and especially throughout those intriguing caverns in the limestone quarries near Syracuse in Sicily, the most wondrous specimen of which is known as the Ear of Dionysius.

These memories popped back into my head, and since my uncle's voice had genuinely reached me, it was clear that there couldn't have been any obstacle in between us. If I went the way the sound had come, I would logically and inevitably meet up with him, provided my strength didn't give out on me.

So I got to my feet. I dragged myself more than I walked. The slope was fairly steep. I let myself slide down it.

The speed of my descent soon picked up to a frightful degree, threatening to turn into an actual fall. I didn't have any power to stop myself.

All at once there was no ground under my feet. I felt myself rolling and rebounding from the jagged surfaces of a vertical hallway, an honest-to-goodness well. My head banged against a sharp rock and I passed out.

29

LATER I CAME BACK to life and found myself in semidarkness, lying on heavy blankets. My uncle was watching over me, alert for any vital spark in my face. When I started to moan, he grabbed my hand; when my eyes started to open, he gave a cry of delight.

"He's alive, he's alive!" he exclaimed.

"Yes," I replied in a weak voice.

"We've saved you, my boy!" my uncle said, giving me a bear hug.

I was deeply touched by his inflection as he said these words, and even more by the solicitude that went along with them. But it took this kind of ordeal to inspire such an outpouring of emotion from the professor.

Just then Hans arrived. He saw my hand in my uncle's; I'll go so far as to say that his eyes expressed hearty satisfaction.

"*God dag,*" he said.

"Good day to you, Hans," I mumbled. "And now, uncle, tell me where we are at present."

"Tomorrow, Axel, tomorrow; right now you're still too weak; I've wrapped compresses around your head and they mustn't be disturbed; so go to sleep, my boy, and tomorrow you'll know everything."

"But," I went on, "at least say what time it is, and what day."

"It's eleven o'clock in the evening, today is Sunday, August 9, and I'm not allowing any further questions till it's the 10th of the month."

In all honesty I *was* quite weak, and my eyes shut instinctively. I needed a good night's rest; so I let myself doze off with the thought that I'd been on my own for three long days.

When I woke up the next morning, I looked around me. Consisting of all our travel blankets, my sickbed had been set up inside a delightful cave adorned with magnificent stalagmites, its floor covered with fine-grained sand. Twilight reigned hereabouts. No lamp or torch had been lit, yet some bewildering rays of light were reaching me from outside, coming in through the cave's narrow entrance. In addition I could hear low sounds, muffled and indistinct, like waves moaning as they break over a beach, and sometimes the whispering of a breeze.

I wondered whether I was fully awake, whether I was still dreaming, or whether I'd fractured my brain in my fall and was picking up totally imaginary sounds. Yet in this case my eyes and ears couldn't both be wrong.

It's a ray of sunlight, I thought, and it's

spilling through a chink in the rock! That's really the lapping of waves! That's a breeze blowing! Am I deluded, or are we back on the surface of the earth? So has my uncle given up his expedition, or will he bring it to a successful conclusion?

I was asking myself these baffling questions when the professor came in.

"Good day, Axel," he put in gleefully. "I'll be willing to bet you feel just fine!"

"Actually I do," I said, sitting up on the blankets.

"You were bound to, because you've been sleeping serenely. Hans and I took turns watching over you, and we could tell you were clearly on the mend."

"It's true, I feel raring to go—and to prove it, I'll do justice to any breakfast you see fit to serve me!"

"We'll feed you, my lad! You're over your fever. Hans has rubbed your cuts with some ointment or other that Icelanders alone have the secret to, and you're miraculously healed. He's quite a man, our hunter!"

While talking, my uncle fixed me some food, and I wolfed it down despite his advice to the contrary. At the same time I bombarded him with questions, which he was quick to answer.

I learned that my fortuitous fall had taken me right to the far end of a hallway that was nearly vertical; I'd arrived in the middle of a rockslide, whose smallest fragments would have been big enough to pulverize me, so it could be concluded that a section of bedrock must have slid along with me. This fearful vehicle had transported me straight into my uncle's arms, where I lay half dead and covered with blood.

"In all honesty," he told me, "it's astounding you weren't killed a thousand times over. But for God's sake, let's not get separated again, because there's a good chance we'll never get back together!"

Not get separated again! So the journey wasn't over? My eyes opened wide with surprise, which instantly elicited this question:

"What's wrong, Axel?"

"I've got something to ask you. You say I'm safe and sound at the moment?"

"Without a doubt."

"And my limbs are completely intact?"

"Surely."

"And what about my head?"

"Your head has a few bruises, but it's in its proper place on your shoulders."

"Well then, I'm afraid I've gone off my rocker."

"Off your rocker?"

"Yes. Are we back on the surface of the globe?"

"Certainly not."

"Then I must be out of my mind, because I can see sunlight and I can hear winds blowing and waves crashing!"

"Aha, so that's it."

"Can you tell me what's going on?"

"I can't tell you what I don't understand myself; but you'll find out with your own two eyes that the science of geology hasn't had its final say."

"Let's go outside," I snapped, abruptly getting up.

"No, no, Axel! The open air could be bad for you."

"Open air?"

"Right, and the wind's pretty fierce. I don't want you out there under these conditions."

"But I swear to you I'm feeling fine."

"Have a little patience, my boy. A relapse could leave us in an awkward spot, and we have no time to lose, because it might take a good while to get to the other side."

"The other side?"

"Yes, so rest up today and we'll sail tomorrow."

"Sail!"

This last word yanked me to my feet.

What! We were going on a boat? Did we have a river, lake, or sea at our disposal? Was there a craft at anchor in some harbor down here?

My curiosity had been aroused to a fever pitch. My uncle vainly tried to hold me back. When he saw that my impatience would do me more harm than his complying with my wishes, he gave in.

I instantly got dressed. As an extra precaution I wrapped myself in one of the blankets and walked outside the cave.

30

AT FIRST I DIDN'T see a thing. My eyes were out of practice at dealing with light and closed abruptly. When I could open them again, I wasn't just surprised, I was astounded.

"A sea!" I exclaimed.

"Yes," my uncle replied, "the Lidenbrock Sea, and I trust no later navigator will begrudge me the honor of being its official discoverer, or the right to name it after myself."

A vast sheet of water, the beginnings of a lake or an ocean, stretched as far as the eye could see. Waves undulated against the coastline—a spacious cove offering an expanse of fine-grained sand, gold in color, sprinkled with those little seashells that housed the first life forms in creation. The breakers came ashore with that resonant murmuring characteristic of huge enclosed spaces. Blown by a mild breeze, light flecks of foam flew through the air and a few drops of spray fell on my face. 600 feet from the tidemark, petering out on this gently sloping shore, the spurs of an enormous, sprawling mass of rock rose to an inconceivable height. Some of these sharp ridges cut across the beach, forming capes and promontories eaten into by the teeth of the surf. Farther off you could see their forms clearly outlined against the misty background of the horizon.

It was a genuine ocean whose shores had the erratic contours of coastlines aboveground, but it looked desolate and fearfully rough.

If I could see a long way across this body of water, that's because a sort of "artificial light" was illuminating the tiniest details. It didn't have the brilliant rays and resplendent aura of sunlight, nor the pale, subdued glow of moonlight, which is simply a chilly reflection. Not at all. The illuminating power of this light source, its vibrant coverage, its crisp white clarity, the fact that it wasn't much warmer than the air, and the reality that it shone more brightly than lunar light all clearly implied an electrical origin. It was like an aurora borealis, an ongoing cosmic phenomenon, and it filled up a cavern that was spacious enough to hold an ocean.

The ceiling overhead—or sky, if you prefer—seemed to consist of big clouds, swirls of traveling, shifting steam, which, after condensing, must have turned into torrential downpours at times. Given the powerful atmospheric pressure, I wouldn't have thought that water evaporation could take place, yet, due to some law of physics that eluded me, wide storm clouds were spreading across the sky. But just then we had "fair weather." Sheets of electricity created an amazing play of light on the very highest clouds. Deep shadows were etched along their curling undersides, and rays of unusual brightness often stole down to us from between two separate cloudbanks. But by and large this wasn't like sunshine, since it gave light without heat. Its effect was mournful, supremely melancholy. Instead of a firmament twinkling with stars, I sensed the granite ceiling above those clouds, a ceiling that could crush me with every ounce of its weight—and as immense as that space was, it wouldn't have been big enough for the humblest moon to move around in.

Then I remembered the ideas of that English sea captain who had likened the earth to a huge hollow sphere: inside it the air pressure lit up the sky while two heavenly bodies, Pluto and Proserpine, went along their secret orbits. Could he have been right?

No getting around it, we were trapped inside an enormous cavity. You couldn't gauge its width, since the shore continued to widen out as far as the eye could see, nor its length either, because your line of sight soon ended at a slightly blurred horizon line. As for its height, it must have been a good several miles. Nor could a person's eyes see where that ceiling came to rest on the spurs of granite; but heavy clouds were hanging in the air at an elevation, we estimated, that had to be some 12,000 feet up—higher than any clouds aboveground and surely caused by the considerable density of the atmosphere.

The word "cavern" clearly isn't up to the task of representing this immense place. But no words in any human language are good enough for folks who have ventured into the depths of the earth.

What's more, I couldn't tell what geological event had brought such a cavity into existence. Had it come about while our globe was cooling? I was well acquainted with certain famous caverns from travelers' reports, but none that boasted dimensions like these.

True, Guácharo Cave in Venezuela kept its depth a secret from Humboldt when that visiting scientist scouted it out down to 2,500 feet, but in all likelihood it didn't go much deeper. Mammoth Cave, that immense formation in Kentucky, boasted pretty gigantic proportions, since its ceiling rose 500 feet above a lake of immeasurable depth, and travelers have gone over twenty-five miles inside without coming to the end of it. But what were those caverns next to the one I was now marveling at, with its sky full of clouds, its electric splendor, and a huge sea inside its walls? My imagination felt feeble in the face of such vastness.

I contemplated all these wonders in silence. I didn't have the vocabulary to express my feelings. I felt like I was on some distant planet, Uranus or Neptune, where I was witnessing phenomena that were unknown to my "earthbound" self. These new experiences called for new words, and my imagination couldn't come up with them. I watched, I thought, I marveled, my astonishment mixed with a certain amount of apprehension.

The unexpectedness of this sight brought healthy colors back to my face; I was undergoing a course of "shock therapy" and I was on the mend thanks to this newfangled cure; what's more, the dense, bracing air made me feel better just by supplying more oxygen to my lungs.

You can easily understand that after being incarcerated for forty-seven days in a cramped hallway, it gave me infinite pleasure to inhale a moist, salty sea breeze.

Accordingly I wasn't sorry to be leaving my dark cave. My uncle was already used to these wonders and they no longer amazed him.

"Do you feel strong enough for a short walk?" he asked me.

"Yes, definitely," I replied. "Nothing would please me more."

"All right, Axel, take my arm and we'll go along this winding shoreline."

I jumped at the opportunity, and we started skirting this new seacoast. On our left steep rocks rose one on top of the other, forming a titanic heap of boulders whose effect was prodigious. Countless waterfalls poured over their sides, heading down in noisy, transparent sheets. Wafting from one rock to another, a few light wisps of steam revealed the locations of hot springs, and brooks flowed gently toward the communal basin, looking for a chance on these slopes to do their merriest babbling.

Among these brooks I identified our faithful traveling companion, the Hansbach, now serenely vanishing into the sea as if it had never done anything else since the world began.

"We're going to miss it," I said with a sigh.

"Nonsense," the professor replied. "One stream or another, what difference does it make!"

A rather ungrateful response, I thought.

But just then an unexpected sight caught my attention. 500 steps away, in the crook of a lofty promontory, a tall, dense, tangled forest came into view. It consisted of medium-sized trees that had geometrically perfect contours and were shaped like authentic umbrellas; the air currents didn't seem to have any effect on their foliage, and during a high wind they stood as still as a clump of petrified cedars.

I hurried closer. I couldn't put a name to these unusual specimens. Didn't they belong to any of the 200,000 species of vegetation described to date? Should they be given a special plant group in the family of lakeside flora? No need. By the time we'd arrived beneath their shady boughs, my wonderment was as great as my surprise.

In actuality I was looking at a standard produce item, but these samples were for a giant-sized customer. My uncle instantly sang out their name.

"It's just a forest of mushrooms," he said.

And he wasn't mistaken. As the reader can imagine, these valued vegetables had sprouted to quite a size in such a warm,

damp setting. Thanks to the botanist Pierre Bulliard, I knew that the *Lycoperdon giganteum*[26] grew to eight or nine feet around; but in this case we were dealing with white mushrooms that stood thirty to forty feet high and had caps just as wide. There were thousands of them. Their shade was so dense that no light could penetrate it, and utter darkness reigned under these domes, which grew side by side like the round roofs of an African town.

However I wanted to go deeper inside. A deathly chill descended from that fleshy ceiling. We wandered through the dank gloom for half an hour, and I ended up back on the seashore with a real feeling of relief.

But the vegetation in this underground region wasn't limited to these mushrooms. Farther on, standing in clusters, were a large number of other trees with pallid foliage. They were easy to identify—these were humble terrestrial shrubs that had grown to phenomenal dimensions: club mosses a hundred feet high, giant forebears of the tree fern, specimens of treelike bracken that grew as big as firs in the upper latitudes, scale trees with forked, cylindrical trunks, which ended in long leaves and were garnished with a rough pelt like some plump, plantlike monster.

"Stunning! Magnificent! Superb!" my uncle exclaimed. "Here are all the flora of the second age on earth, a time of transition. Here are humble plants from today's gardens that grew into trees during the first centuries of the world! Look and marvel, Axel! No botanist has ever sat down to such a feast!"

"You're right, uncle. Providence seems to have intended this as an immense greenhouse—a nursery for those prehistoric plants our scientists have reconstructed with such skill and forethought."

"You're correct, my lad, it's a greenhouse; but you would be more correct to say that it's maybe a menagerie as well."

"A menagerie?"

"Yes, no doubt about it. Look at this dirt we've been trampling underfoot, these bones scattered over the ground."

"Bones!" I exclaimed. "Yes, the bones of prehistoric animals!"

I rushed over to the age-old remains, now changed into an indestructible mineral substance.[27] Without hesitation I put names to these gigantic bones, which looked like dried-up tree trunks.

"This is the lower jaw of a mastodon," I said. "These are the molars from another ancient elephant, the dinotherium; this is a femur that could have belonged to the biggest of those beasts, a giant ground sloth called the megatherium. Yes, it's a menagerie all right, because these bones definitely weren't transferred to this spot by some cataclysm. They belonged to beasts that lived on the shores of this underground sea, that sat in the shade of these treelike plants. Hold on, I can even see complete skeletons! And yet . . ."

"And yet?" my uncle said.

"I don't understand what these quadrupeds are doing in this granite cavern."

"Why not?"

"Because animal life didn't exist on the earth till the second age, when sedimentary rock formed from alluvial deposits and replaced the white-hot rock of earlier times."

"Well, Axel, there's a perfectly simple answer to your objection, namely that the rock here *is* sedimentary rock."

"Excuse me? So far under the surface of the earth?"

"Surely, and this fact has a geological explanation. At some point in time, the earth consisted of simply an elastic crust, which, thanks to the laws of gravity, was subject to upward and downward movements in succession. Very likely these led to cave-ins on the surface, and portions of sedimentary rock were dragged down into the chasms that suddenly opened up."

"It must have happened that way. But if prehistoric animals lived in these underground regions, who's to say one of those monsters still isn't roaming around these gloomy forests or behind these steep rocks?"

At this thought I nervously examined the different corners of the horizon; but not a

---

[26] *Translator's note.* Giant puffball.

[27] Phosphate of lime.

single living thing appeared on these deserted shores.

I felt a little tired. So I went to sit on the tip of a promontory, while waves came and broke noisily against the foot of it. From there my eyes could take in this whole bay, which had formed from an indentation in the coastline. A little harbor was at hand among the pyramid-shaped boulders at the far end. Its calm waters lay protected from the winds. A brig and two or three schooners could easily have anchored there. I half expected to see some ship leaving under full sail and putting to sea with a south wind behind it.

But this daydream quickly faded. We truly were the only living creatures in this underground world. During various lulls of the wind, a silence deeper than the silence in any wilderness fell over these barren rocks and weighed heavily on the surface of the ocean. Then I tried to penetrate the far-off mists and rip open that curtain drawn across the secret reaches of the horizon. What questions sprang to my lips! How far did this sea go? Where did it end up? Could we ever scout out the other side?

For his part, my uncle hadn't the slightest doubt that we could. As for me, it was something I both desired and dreaded.

After we spent an hour contemplating this wondrous sight, we made our way back up the beach and into the cave again, where I fell sound asleep under the sway of the strangest thoughts.

31

THE NEXT DAY I woke up fully recovered. I thought a bath would do me a lot of good, so I went and swam for a few minutes in the waters of this "mediterranean" sea. With the earth both above and below, it definitely deserved the name.

I came back for breakfast with a hearty appetite. Hans got busy cooking our modest menu; he had water and fire at his disposal, so he could furnish a little change of pace from our standard fare. He served us a couple cups of coffee with dessert, and never was

this delectable drink more pleasing to my palate.

"It's time for the tide to come in," my uncle said, "and now's our chance to study this phenomenon."

"Excuse me? The tide?" I exclaimed.

"Surely."

"The influence of the sun and moon can be felt down here?"

"Why not? Aren't all solid objects subject to the same gravitational pull? This mass of water isn't exempt from the laws of the universe. Accordingly, despite the air pressure exerted on its surface, you'll see it rise just like the Atlantic itself."

Right then we were striding along the sandy shore, and little by little the breakers were closing in on the beach.

"The level really is starting to go up!" I exclaimed.

"Yes, Axel, and from the way the waves keep cresting, you can expect the sea to get some ten feet higher."

"It's wonderful!"

"On the contrary, it's normal."

"No matter what you say, uncle, it's absolutely amazing to me and I can hardly believe my eyes. Who would ever have imagined there's an actual ocean inside the earth's crust, an ocean that ebbs and flows, that has winds and storms!"

"Why not? Is there any law of physics that forbids it?"

"None that I can see, once we're forced to give up the concept of a central heat source."

"So Humphry Davy's suppositions have been borne out till now?"

"Obviously—and from this point on, nobody can dispute the presence of lands and seas inside the globe."

"Certainly not, nor that they're inhabited."

"True! And why couldn't these waters easily give us a few fish of unknown species?"

"Even so, we haven't spotted a single one as yet."

"All right, we can fix up some fishing lines, then let's see if hooks work as well down here as in a terrestrial ocean."

"We'll give it a try, Axel, because we

need to probe all the secrets of these new territories."

"But where are we? Because, uncle, I haven't asked you this question till now, and your instruments should already have given you the answer."

"We've gone 870 miles sideways from Iceland."

"As far as that?"

"My margin of error is under a thousand yards, I'm positive of it."

"And our compass is still pointing southeast?"

"Yes, with a westerly declination of 19° 42', exactly the same as aboveground. As for its dip, there's something odd going on that I've been watching with the keenest attention."

"And what's that?"

"The needle isn't dipping toward the pole the way it does in the northern hemisphere—it's rising instead."

"So we're forced to conclude that the source of this magnetic attraction lies somewhere between the surface of the globe and this spot we've gotten to?"

"Exactly, and it's quite likely that if we get closer to the arctic regions, to that 70th parallel where Sir James Clark Ross discovered the magnetic pole, we'll see the needle stand straight up. Therefore this mysterious center of attraction doesn't lie at any great depth."

"No, and it's a fact science doesn't even suspect."

"Science, my lad, is built on errors, but errors that are worth committing because they gradually lead to the truth."

"And what depth have we reached?"

"Our depth is eighty-seven miles."

"So the Scottish highlands are above us," I said, studying the map, "where the snow-covered peaks of the Grampian Hills rise to a prodigious height."

"Yes," the professor replied with a smile. "They're a bit of a burden to bear, but that ceiling is solid; the great architect of the universe built it with sound materials, and no human beings could ever have given it such a span! What are the arches of bridges or the domes of cathedrals compared to a nave

that's fifteen miles across? Under this roof there's enough elbow room for a whole ocean and all its storms!"

"Then I'm not worried the sky will fall on my head. Now, uncle, what are your plans? You aren't figuring to go back to the surface of the globe, are you?"

"Go back? By thunder, we'll do just the opposite and continue our journey; everything has gone excellently so far."

"But I don't see how you're going to get below this stretch of water."

"Well, I have no intention of diving in headfirst. But if oceans are literally just lakes because they're surrounded by land, it follows all the more that this inner sea is fenced in by the section of granite."

"Without a doubt."

"Well then, I'm sure to find other passageways on the opposite shore."

"So how wide would you say this ocean is?"

"Seventy-five to a hundred miles."

"Uh huh," I put in, figuring this estimate couldn't be any too accurate.

"Therefore we have no time to lose and we'll put to sea tomorrow."

I automatically looked around for the ship that was to carry us.

"Oh, so we're going on a cruise?" I said. "Fine. And what liner are we leaving on?"

"It won't be a liner, my boy, just a good sturdy raft."

"A raft!" I exclaimed. "A raft is as impossible to build as a ship, and I don't see—"

"You never see, Axel, but if you listened, you might just hear something!"

"Hear something?"

"Yes, assorted whacks of the hammer, which would inform you that Hans is already on the job."

"He's building a raft?"

"That's right."

"Excuse me? Has he already taken his ax and chopped some trees down?"

"Oh, the trees were on the ground waiting for him. Come along and you'll see him at work."

After a fifteen-minute walk we reached the far side of the promontory that formed the little natural harbor, and there I saw Hans toiling away. A couple more steps took me to his side. Much to my surprise a half-finished raft lay on the sand; it was made with logs of some strange wood, and material for a large number of floorboards, angle brackets, and all sorts of braces had been literally flung across the ground. We had enough there to build a whole navy.

"Uncle," I exclaimed, "what kind of wood is this?"

"Pine, fir, birch, and every other species of northern coniferous tree, and the action of salt water has turned this timber to stone."

"It can't be!"

"This is known as *surtarbrandur*, or petrified wood."

"But then it must be as hard as a rock, just like brown coal—how could it float?"

"At times it manages to; some specimens of this wood have transformed into genuine anthracite; but others, such as these, have started to fossilize only recently." My uncle tossed a piece of this precious flotsam into the sea. "Now watch," he added.

After sinking out of sight, the fragment of wood came back to the surface, bobbing around as the waves undulated.

"Are you convinced?" my uncle said.

"Convinced even though it's incredible!"

Thanks to our guide's skill, the raft was finished the next evening; it was ten feet long by five wide; lashed together with strong rope, those logs of *surtarbrandur* provided a solid surface, and when it was launched, this makeshift barge cruised serenely on the waters of the Lidenbrock Sea.

32

ON AUGUST 13 we woke up bright and early. We were scheduled to break in a new way of getting places that would be quicker and easier.

Our mast was two tree limbs fitted together, a third limb furnished the yard, and one of our blankets served as the sail—that's how the raft was rigged. There was no shortage of rope. Everything was secure.

At six o'clock the professor gave the signal to board ship. In place on deck were our provisions, baggage, instruments, weapons, and a substantial supply of fresh water we'd collected up in the rocks.

Hans had installed a rudder so he could steer his aquatic contraption. He took the tiller. I untied the mooring line attaching us to the shore. We trimmed the sail and instantly shoved off.

Just as we were leaving the little harbor, my uncle, who was big on geographic nomenclature, wanted to give it a name—mine, for instance.

"Ye gods," I said, "I have a different suggestion to make."

"What's that?"

"Name it after Grauben. Port Grauben will look quite nice on your map."

"Port Grauben it is."

And that's how we commemorated my darling Virlander on this adventurous expedition.

The breeze was blowing from the northwest. We ran ahead of the wind at a tremendous clip. The ultradense layers of atmosphere had considerable thrust and acted on our sail like a powerful fan.

At the end of an hour, my uncle was able to estimate our speed pretty accurately.

"If we keep on like this," he said, "we'll do at least seventy-five miles every twenty-four hours, and it won't be long before we raise the opposite shore."

I didn't reply and went to take a seat in the bow of the raft. The northerly coast was already gravitating below the horizon. The two arms of the shoreline were spread wide as if to make our leave-taking easier. In front of my eyes lay an immense sea. The grayish shadows of big swift clouds swept over its surface and seemed to weigh heavily on these sullen waves. Here and there water drops reflected the silvery rays from that electrical illumination overhead, and specks of light glittered in the boat's backwash. Soon the shore was completely out of sight, every landmark had vanished, and if it hadn't been for the trail of foam left by our raft, I would have sworn we were standing perfectly still.

Toward noontime immense seaweeds came into view, undulating over the surface of the waves. I'd heard about the proliferating power of these plants, which creep across sea bottoms more than 12,000 feet down, procreate under a pressure of 400 atmospheres, and often form shoals considerable enough to hinder the movements of ships; but never, I think, have there been marine weeds more gigantic than those in the Lidenbrock Sea.

Our raft traveled past fucus plants 3,000 or 4,000 feet in length, immense snakes uncoiling as far as the eye could see; I had fun watching these infinitely long ribbons, continually thinking I'd gotten to the end of them, and for whole hours they tried my patience and provoked my amazement.

What natural forces could have generated plants like these, and what had the earth looked like during its earliest formative years, when the heat and humidity encouraged only the vegetable kingdom to spread over its surface?

Evening arrived, and as I'd noted the night before, the sky remained just as brightly lit. It was an ongoing phenomenon and you could bank on its staying around.

After supper I stretched out at the foot of the mast, drifted off into idle fancies, and soon fell asleep.

Motionless by the tiller, Hans let the raft have its head; besides, it had a tailwind and didn't need to even be steered.

After our departure from Port Grauben, Professor Lidenbrock entrusted me with keeping "the ship's log," which involved jotting down our tiniest findings, entering unusual phenomena, recording wind direction, sailing speed, and miles made good—in a nutshell, describing all the incidents of our strange navigating.

Therefore, in order to give the most accurate account of our crossing, I'll limit myself now to copying out my field notes, in which I took dictation from events, so to speak.

Friday, August 14. Steady breeze from the northwest. Our raft is holding on a swift, straight course. The coastline is still seventy-five miles to leeward. Nothing on the horizon. No change in the bright daylight. Fair weather—in other words, the clouds are quite high, not very heavy, and bathing in a pale sky suggestive of molten silver. Thermometer: 89.6° Fahrenheit.

At noon Hans gets a hook ready on the end of a fishing line. He baits it with a little piece of meat and tosses it into the sea. For two hours he doesn't catch a thing. Which means these waters are uninhabited? Not so. There's a tug on the line. Hans pulls it in and lands an energetically struggling fish.

"A fish!" my uncle exclaims.

"It's a sturgeon!" I exclaim in my turn. "An undersized sturgeon!"

The professor looks the creature over carefully and doesn't share my views. The fish has a flat, rounded head, and the front part of its body is covered with bony plates; its mouth doesn't have any teeth; its pectoral fins are pretty hefty and well suited to its tailless body. This creature belongs to the same order in which naturalists have classified the sturgeon, but it differs from that fish in some pretty basic ways.

My uncle isn't mistaken, because, after a fairly brief examination, he says:

"It belongs to a family of armored fish that's been extinct for a long time, and its fossil traces are found only in rocks from the Devonian Period."

"What!" I say. "We can bring ancient sea creatures back alive?"

"Yes," the professor replies, continuing his analysis. "And you'll note that these fossil fish aren't like any of today's species. So catching a live specimen would be a genuine windfall for a naturalist."

"But what family does it belong to?"

"It's in the order of Ganoid fish, family Cephalaspida, genus . . ."

"Well?"

"Genus *Pterichthys*, I'll swear. But this one has a characteristic that's found, I'm told, in the fish of underground waters."

"What characteristic?"

"It's blind!"

"Blind?"

"Not only blind—it hasn't any visual organs at all."

I look. It's as true as true can be. But maybe this is a special case. Consequently we put more bait on our fishing line and toss it back into the sea. No doubt about it, this ocean is positively teeming with fish, because in two hours we catch a large number of genus *Pterichthys*, as well as some ancient lungfish that belong to the family Dipnoia and are likewise extinct, though my uncle can't determine their genus. All of them are lacking visual organs. This unlooked-for haul is a timely addition to our provisions.

Hence it seems to be a given that this sea contains only species we know as fossils, species of both fish and reptiles that are all the more advanced the farther back they were created.

Maybe we'll encounter some of those saurians science has managed to re-create from bits of bone or cartilage?

I take our spyglass and examine the sea. It's deserted. No doubt we're still too close to land.

I look at the skies. Why couldn't some of those birds reconstructed by the immortal Cuvier be flapping their wings through those heavy layers of air? The fish would furnish enough food for them. I examine the atmosphere, but the skies aren't any more populated than the shores.

Even so, my imagination carries me off into the wondrous theories of paleontology. I'm wide awake, but I dream away. I fancy I see enormous prehistoric turtles from the family Chersites, and they're drifting like islands on the surface of the waters. Along the gloomy beaches walk the great mammals from the beginning of time, an elklike leptotherium found in the caverns of Brazil and a llamalike mericotherium hailing from the icy regions of Siberia. Farther away a giant tapir, the elephantine lophiodon, lurks behind the boulders, ready to fight for its prey with an anoplotherium, an odd beast that takes after the rhinoceros, horse, hippopotamus, and camel—as if our Creator was in an all-fired hurry at the start of things and lumped several beasts into one. Twirling its trunk, a gigantic mastodon breaks up the rocks along the shore with its tusks; meanwhile, propped on its enormous paws, a megatherium rummages in the earth while echoes of its bellowing bounce off the resonant granite. Higher up, a protopithecus, the first ape to appear on the surface of the globe, is scaling the steep crags. Higher still, a flying reptile with winged hands, the pterodactyl, glides through the oppressive air like a large bat. In the topmost strata, finally, are immense birds, mightier than a cassowary and bigger than an ostrich—they unfurl their huge wings and proceed to bump their heads against the barrier of that granite ceiling.

This whole fossil world is born again in my imagination. I revisit the days of creation in the Bible, well before the birth of man and when the unfinished earth wouldn't have been good enough for him yet. Then my dream carries me back before the appearance of moving creatures. The mammals vanish, then the birds, then the reptiles of the second age, and finally the fish, crustaceans, mollusks, and articulata. During this time of transition, the zoophytes revert to nothingness in their turn. I'm the sum total of all animate objects on earth, and my heart is the only one left pounding in this world where animals have been eradicated. There are no more seasons; there are no more climates; the globe itself keeps getting hotter, negating the heat from Old Sol. Vegetation grows like crazy. I pass like a phantom through the treelike bracken, stepping gingerly on the lustrous marl and multicolored sandstone beneath me; I lean against the trunks of immense evergreens; I see the 100-foot-tall forerunners of scouring rushes, horsetails, and club mosses, and I lie in their shade.

Centuries go by like days! I head back up the whole sequence of the earth's transformations. Plant life vanishes; the granite bedrock loses its integrity; affected by the increasing heat, matter in a solid state starts to change into a liquid state; seas overrun the surface of the globe; they boil, they evaporate; fumes engulf the earth, which little by little becomes simply a gaseous mass, rising to a white heat, looking as big as the sun and just as brilliant!

I'm at the center of this nebula, which is 1,400,000 times more considerable than this globe it will someday form, and I'm swept off into interplanetary space! My body disintegrates, vaporizes in its turn, and merges like an indefinable atom with those immense fumes tracing their fiery orbit into infinity!

What a dream! Where's it taking me? My feverish fingers are putting its strange details on paper! I've forgotten everything else, professor, guide, and raft! These hallucinations have laid hold of my brain . . .

"What's wrong?" my uncle says.

My wide-open eyes focus on him but don't see him.

"Careful, Axel, or you'll fall overboard!"

At the same instant I feel Hans's fingers clutch me firmly. If it hadn't been for him, I would have tumbled into the ocean under the sway of my dream.

"Have you gone crazy?" the professor snaps.

"What happened?" I say, coming to at last.

"Are you ill?"

"No, I was hallucinating for a moment, but it's over. So everything's going all right?"

"Yes! Good breeze, smooth sea! We're making rapid headway, and if my calculations are correct, we'll reach land in no time."

At these words I get up and check the horizon line; but along it the waves are still merging with the clouds.

33

SATURDAY, AUGUST 15. The sea preserves its monotonous sameness. No land is in sight. The horizon seems extremely far away.

My wits are still dull from the intensity of my dream.

My uncle hasn't been dreaming, not him, but he's in a bad mood. He sweeps his spyglass over every inch of the skyline, then folds his arms with an exasperated expression.

I note that Professor Lidenbrock is tending to backslide into his old impatient self, and I enter the fact in my log. To draw a glimmer of humanity out of him, I had to be in danger or in pain; but now that I've recovered, his basic nature has taken over again. But even so, why fly off the handle? Aren't we carrying out our journey under optimum conditions? Isn't the raft making marvelous headway?

"You seem worried, uncle," I say, watching him frequently lift his spyglass to his eye.

"Worried? Not at all."

"Impatient, then?"

"Who wouldn't be, and for less reason!"

"But we're moving at a good speed—"

"You're missing the point! It's not that our speed is too slow—it's just that this sea is too wide!"

Then I remember that before we started out, the professor had put the width of this underground ocean at seventy-five miles. Now then, we've already gone three times that distance and the southern shores still aren't in sight.

"We're not descending!" the professor continues. "All we're doing is wasting time, and to put it bluntly, I haven't come as far as I have just to take a boat ride over a pond!"

He calls this crossing a boat ride and this sea a pond!

"However," I say, "since we've followed the route Saknussemm indicated—"

"That's the problem. *Have* we followed his route? Did Saknussemm meet up with this expanse of water? Did he cross it? That stream we let guide us—did it lead us completely astray?"

"In any event we can't regret we've come this far. The view's magnificent, and—

"This isn't about sightseeing. I set myself a goal and I mean to achieve it! So don't talk to me about admiring the scenery!"

I consider the matter closed and leave the professor to bite his lips in impatience. At six o'clock in the evening, Hans asks for his wages, and his three riksdalers are doled out to him.

Sunday, August 16. Nothing new. Weather the same. The wind is showing a slight tendency to pick up. When I awake, my first concern is to verify the brightness of the light. I'm continually afraid the electrical illumination will start to grow darker and then die out. There's nothing in it. The raft's shadow is clearly outlined on the surface of the waves.

This sea is truly infinite! It must be as wide as the Mediterranean or even the Atlantic. Why not?

My uncle takes several soundings. He ties

one of our heaviest picks to the end of a rope, then pays it out 1,200 feet. No bottom. We have a lot of trouble hauling in our sounding line.

When the pick is up on board again, Hans shows me some clearly defined indentations on its surface. You would have sworn this piece of iron had been tightly squeezed between two hard objects.

I look at the hunter.

"*Tänder!*" he says.

I don't understand. I turn to my uncle, who's all wrapped up in his thoughts. I don't care to disturb him. I swing back to the Icelander. The latter makes his meaning clear to me by opening and shutting his mouth several times.

"Teeth!" I say in astonishment, inspecting the iron head more closely.

Yes! Clearly these are bite marks engraved in the metal! The teeth and jaws that left them must be prodigiously strong! Is some long-lost species of monster thrashing around in the lower strata of these waters, a creature more voracious than a shark, more awesome than a whale? I can't take my eyes off this half-chewed length of metal. Is last evening's dream about to turn into reality?

These thoughts keep me on edge all day long, and my imagination doesn't get much calmer even when I nap for a few hours.

Monday, August 17. I'm trying to recall the traits characteristic of those prehistoric animals in the second age, animals that came after the mollusks, crustaceans, and fish but before mammals had appeared on the globe. At that point the earth belonged to the reptiles. Those monsters lorded it over the Jurassic seas.[28] Nature gave them the most complete organisms. What gigantic builds! What prodigious strength! Today's saurians, our biggest and scariest alligators or crocodiles, are no more than puny miniatures of their forefathers in the distant past!

I shiver at my mental images of those monsters. No human eyes have ever seen them alive. They appeared on the earth thousands of centuries before man, but their fossils have been found in that clayish limestone the English refer to as Liassic;[29] these petrified remains have allowed scientists to reconstruct them anatomically and to learn about their colossal frames.

At the Hamburg Museum I've seen a skeleton of one of these saurians that's thirty feet long. So am I destined—I, a modern-day earthling—to stand face to face with representatives of this prehistoric family? No, it isn't possible! Yet the marks of powerful teeth are etched in that iron head, and from their indentations I realize those teeth are conical like a crocodile's.

My eyes focus on the sea in dread. I'm fearful one of those creatures will leap into sight from some underwater cavern.

I imagine Professor Lidenbrock shares my thoughts if not my fears, because, after examining the pick, his eyes travel over the ocean.

"Holy smoke," I say to myself. "That was a bad idea of his to take soundings! He disturbed some animal in its lair, and if we aren't attacked on the way . . ."

I glance over our weapons and make sure they're in good working order. My uncle watches me do this and signals his approval.

The waves are already turning choppy over a wide surface area, indicating some disturbance in the strata far below. We're in imminent danger. We need to stand guard.

Tuesday, August 18. Evening arrives, or rather the moment when drowsiness weighs down our eyelids, because there isn't any nighttime on this ocean, and the implacable light wearies our eyes with its persistence, as if we were navigating under the midnight sun in the arctic seas. Hans is at the tiller. During his spell on watch, I fall asleep.

Two hours later a frightful jolt wakes me up. The raft has been lifted above the waves with indescribable force, then tossed down again 120 feet away.

"What happened?" my uncle shouts. "Did we run aground?"

Hans points his finger at a blackish mass

---

[28] Seas of the second age that formed the rock making up the Jura Mountains.

[29] *Translator's note.* Subdivision of the Jurassic Period.

alternately rising and falling barely a quarter of a mile off. I look and exclaim:

"It's a colossal porpoise!"

"Yes," my uncle remarks, "and here comes an unusually big sea lizard!"

"And farther away a monstrous crocodile! Look at those wide jaws, those rows of teeth inside . . . hey, it's gone!"

"A whale, a whale!" the professor exclaims at this point. "I can see its enormous fins! Look at all that air and water it's expelling from its blowholes!"

Indeed two waterspouts are rising to a considerable height above the sea. We stand in amazement, stunned and appalled by the presence of this band of marine monsters. Their dimensions are unearthly and the smallest of them could pulverize our raft with one snap of its jaws. Hans steers to windward, trying to get out of this bad neighborhood; but he sees other enemies on the other side of us, and they're just as alarming: a turtle forty feet wide, plus a thirty-foot snake shooting its enormous head above the waves.

Running away is impossible. These reptiles close in; they go around our raft with a speed that couldn't be matched by trains racing at full throttle; they sweep around us in concentric circles. I pick up my rifle. But what effect could a bullet have on the scales covering these animals' bodies?

We're speechless with fright. Now they're in close! The crocodile is on one side, the snake on the other. The rest of the briny band have vanished. I'm all set to fire at them. Hans stops me with a gesture. The two monsters pass within 300 feet of the raft and rush at each other, too infuriated to notice us.

The battle breaks out 600 feet away from the raft. We clearly see the two monsters coming to grips.

But now it seems like the other animals have come to join in the fight, the porpoise, whale, lizard, and turtle. I glimpse them every second or so. I point them out to the Icelander. The latter shakes his head no.

"*Tva*," he says.

"What! Two? He's claiming there are only two animals . . ."

"He's right," my uncle snaps, his spyglass never leaving his eye.

"By thunder!"

"Yes! The first of these monsters has a snout like a porpoise, a head like a lizard, and teeth like a crocodile—that's what fooled us. It's the most awesome of these prehistoric reptiles—an ichthyosaurus!"

"What about the other?"

"The other's like a snake lurking in the carapace of a turtle, the ruthless foe of the first—a plesiosaurus!"

Hans is correct. Only two monsters are agitating the surface of the sea, and in front of my eyes I have two reptiles from the oceans of long ago. I see the ichthyosaurus's bloodshot eye, as big as a man's skull. Nature has given it optical equipment of tremendous power, visual organs able to withstand the water pressure in the deep strata where it lives. Because it has a cetacean's size and speed, it can aptly be described as a whale of a lizard. This one is at least a hundred feet long, and I can tell its length when its vertical tail fins stick out of the waves. Its jaws are enormous, and according to naturalists, they boast no less than 182 teeth.

The plesiosaurus, a snake strung through a cylindrical torso, has a stubby tail and oar-shaped flippers. Its whole body is covered with a carapace, and its neck rises thirty feet above the waves, as flexible as a swan's.

These animals attack each other with indescribable fury. They stir up mountainous waves that sweep as far as our raft. Twenty times we're on the point of capsizing. Hissing sounds of prodigious intensity fill the air. The two brutes are intertwined. I can't tell which is which. All I know is, we'd better beware of the victor's wrath.

One hour goes by, then two. The fight rages as relentlessly as ever. By turns the brawlers come close to our raft, then move off. We keep still, ready to fire away.

Suddenly the ichthyosaurus and plesiosaurus vanish, churning up a genuine maelstrom in the heart of the waves. Several minutes go by. Will the battle draw to a close in the depths of the sea?

All at once an enormous head shoots back up, the plesiosaurus's head. The monster is fatally wounded. I don't see its immense carapace anymore. Only its long neck rises, falls, lifts again, droops once more, lashes the waves like a gigantic whip, writhes like a worm cut in half. Water spatters to a considerable distance. It blinds us. But soon the reptile's death throes come to an end, its movements get weaker, its contortions grow calmer, and that long piece of snake lies like an inanimate object on the quiet waves.

As for the ichthyosaurus, has it retired to its underwater cavern—or will it reappear on the surface of the sea?

34

WEDNESDAY, AUGUST 19. Luckily a strong wind is blowing, which helps us quickly get away from the battle site. Hans never leaves the tiller. Distracted from his all-consuming thoughts by the incidents of that encounter, my uncle lapses back into his impatient contemplation of the sea.

Our journey resumes its monotonous sameness; but I'm not in favor of livening things up, if the price we pay is more of yesterday's dangers.

Thursday, August 20. Wind north-northeast and rather erratic. High temperatures. We're moving at a speed of nearly nine miles per hour.

Toward noontime a noise is audible from far away. I record the fact here but can't supply an explanation. It's a continuous rumbling sound.

"There's some rock or islet off in the distance," the professor says, "which the sea is breaking against."

Hans hauls himself up to the masthead but doesn't sight any reefs. The ocean is smooth all the way to the horizon line.

Three hours go by. The rumbling sound seems to be coming from a distant waterfall.

I point this out to my uncle, who shakes his head. But I'm sure I'm not mistaken. So are we speeding toward some cataract that will hurl us into the depths? It's possible this method of heading downward will please the professor since it approaches the vertical, but speaking for myself . . .

In any event there must be some sort of noisy phenomenon a number of miles to windward, because now the rumbling sound is getting terrifically loud. Is it coming from the sky or the ocean?

I lift my eyes to the mists hanging in the air and try to sound their depths. The sky is serene. Rising all the way to the ceiling, the clouds seem motionless and adrift in the light's intense aura. So we need to look elsewhere for the cause of this phenomenon.

Then I examine the unbroken horizon, which is completely clear of fog. Its appearance hasn't changed. But if this noise comes from a falls, an actual cataract, if this whole ocean is rushing down into some lower basin, if this rumbling sound is caused by a mass of cascading water, then the current should be picking up—which means its increasing speed can help me gauge the peril that's threatening us. I check the current. There isn't any. I toss an empty bottle overboard and it stays to leeward.

Near four o'clock Hans gets up, grabs the mast, and climbs to the top of it. From there he scans the circular horizon traced by the ocean in front of our raft; then his eyes halt at one particular spot. His face doesn't express any surprise, but his look turns into a stare.

"He's spotted something," my uncle says.

"I believe so."

Hans descends again, then stretches his arm southward, saying:

"*Der nere!*"

"Down there?" my uncle echoes.

And clutching his spyglass, he looks through it carefully for a minute, which feels like a century to me.

"Yes, yes!" he exclaims.

"What do you see?"

"An immense spray of water rising above the waves."

"Yet another marine animal?"

"Maybe."

"Then let's point our prow to the west— we know where we stand on the dangers of bumping into prehistoric monsters!"

"Let's hold our course," my uncle answers.

I turn to Hans. Never wavering, Hans keeps the tiller exactly as is.

Yet quite a distance separates us from that

animal, a distance that must be at least thirty miles, so if we can see the waterspout expelled by its blowholes, that means its size is unearthly. If we run away, we'll be abiding by the laws of common sense. But we haven't come this far just to be sensible.

So on we go. The closer we get, the higher that spray of water looks. What monster could take in and shoot out so much liquid without breaking off for a second?

By eight o'clock in the evening, we're less than five miles away from it. Its huge, blackish, mound-shaped body stretches over the sea like an islet. Is this an illusion, our fears at work? It looks more than a mile long to me! It's a cetacean unknown to Cuvier, Blumenbach, or any other naturalist—so what is it? It doesn't move and appears to be sleeping; the waves don't seem able to rock it, though their crests undulate along its sides. Hurtling 500 feet into the air, the waterspout rains back down with an earsplitting noise. A hundred whales per day wouldn't be enough to feed that mighty bulk, and like madmen we're sailing right up to it.

Terror grips me. I'm not willing to go any farther! If need be, I'll cut the rope that hoists the sail! I rebel against the professor, who doesn't answer me back.

All at once Hans stands and points a finger at the danger zone:

"*Holme!*" he says.

"An island!" my uncle exclaims.

"An island?" I say in my turn, shrugging my shoulders.

"It's as plain as day," the professor replies, breaking into hearty laughter.

"But what about that waterspout?"

"*Geyser,*" Hans puts in.

"Of course it's a geyser!" my uncle fires back. "A geyser just like those in Iceland."[30]

At first I can't accept that I'm so hopelessly wrong. To mistake an island for a sea monster! But the evidence is conclusive and I have to own up to my error. It's nothing more than a natural phenomenon.

As we draw nearer, the dimensions of this liquid bouquet become still more impressive.

---

[30] A very famous erupting spring is located at the foot of Mt. Hekla.

The islet looks deceptively like an immense cetacean whose head towers sixty feet above the waves. Its geyser—a word whose Icelandic form is *geysir*, which means "fury"—rises majestically from one end. Dull explosions burst out every so often, and then that enormous jet of water gives way to a violent fit of temper, shakes off its wreath of mist, and leaps as high as the first cloud layers. It's a solitary phenomenon. No curls of steam or hot springs surround it, and all the volcanic energy is concentrated in its innards. Rays of electric light come and mingle with that dazzling spray, shading every droplet with all the colors of the prism.

"Let's pull alongside," the professor says.

But we need to carefully dodge that waterspout, which could sink our raft in a second. Maneuvering skillfully, Hans brings us to the tip of the islet.

I jump onto the rock. My uncle follows me nimbly, while the hunter stays at his post, a man nothing can amaze.

We walk over granite that's mixed with tuff composed of silica; the ground trembles underfoot like the sides of a boiler filled with writhing, supercharged steam; it's sweltering. We come in sight of a little basin in the middle, the spot where the geyser shoots up. I dip a discharge thermometer into the water bubbling around, and it registers a temperature of 325° Fahrenheit.

Hence this water comes from a fiery core. That significantly contradicts Professor Lidenbrock's suppositions. Which I can't resist pointing out.

"All right," he counters, "and exactly how does this disprove my beliefs?"

"Never mind," I say in a dry tone, seeing that I'm up against pure pigheadedness.

Nevertheless I'm forced to admit that so far we've been unusually lucky, that our journey, for some reason that eludes me, is proceeding under exceptional temperature conditions; but it seems obvious—inevitable even—that sooner or later we'll come to those regions where the central heat reaches its upper limits and goes beyond the degrees on any thermometer.

We'll see. That's the professor's watchword; and after baptizing this volcanic islet with his nephew's name, he gives the signal to board ship.

I stay behind for a few minutes, still contemplating the geyser. I note that its jet is erratic and fitful, that at times its intensity decreases and then returns with new energy, which I attribute to the varying pressures of the steam building up in its storage tank.

Finally we leave, bypassing the ultra steep rocks to the south. Hans has taken advantage of this layover to straighten up the raft.

But before heading out, I take a few readings, calculate our miles made good, and jot them down in my log. Since leaving Port Grauben, we've gone 670 miles over this sea, plus we're 1,540 miles from Iceland and right below England.

35

FRIDAY, AUGUST 21. The next day that magnificent geyser is out of sight. The wind has picked up, and we're soon far away from Axel Island. The rumbling sound dies out little by little.

The weather, if we can call it that, is about to change before much longer. The misty atmosphere is reeking with electricity generated by the evaporation of salt water; the clouds are sinking noticeably and consistently taking on an olive-colored hue; the electric rays are barely able to pierce this solid curtain, lowered over this stage on which a tempestuous drama will be played.

I feel unusually keyed up, as every earthly creature does when a cataclysm draws near. In the south, presenting a grim appearance, cumulus clouds are gathering;[31] they have that "glowering" look I've often noted at the onset of storms. The air is heavy, the sea is still.

Those far-off clouds look like big cotton balls piled in picturesque disarray; little by little they swell up, becoming larger in size but fewer in number; they've gained so much weight, they can't rise above the horizon; but due to air streams from on high, they gradually melt together, grow darker, and soon

---

[31] Clouds with billowy shapes.

make up a single cloudbank of alarming appearance; now and then a little ball of mist, still catching the light, bounces onto that grayish carpet and quickly vanishes into its deep pile.

Obviously the air is steeped in current; it's running all through me; my hair is bristling on my head as if a dynamo were nearby. If my companions were to touch me right now, I suspect they would get a severe shock.

By ten o'clock in the morning, the signs of a squall are more pronounced; the wind seems to be pausing to take a good deep breath; the storm clouds look like an immense goatskin water bag, filled to the brim with hurricanes.

I don't want to give any credence to that threatening sky, yet I can't help saying:

"There's foul weather on the way."

The professor doesn't reply. He's in a vile mood at the sight of this ocean going on indefinitely in front of his eyes. He shrugs his shoulders at my words.

"We're in for a storm," I say, motioning toward the horizon. "Those clouds are swooping on the sea like they want to pummel it!"

All is silence. The wind falls still. Nature seems to have breathed her last and expired. I can already see a faint glimmer of St. Elmo's fire on top of the mast, from which our slack sail is falling in heavy folds. The raft stands still in the middle of a turbid sea that's no longer undulating. But if we aren't moving anymore, why bother staying under full canvas? The first time the storm cuts loose, it could be the death of us!

"Haul in the sail and strike the mast!" I say. "It'll be safer!"

"No, by Lucifer!" my uncle shouts. "A hundred times no! Let the wind take hold of us! Let the storm carry us off! Just show me the rocks of some coastline, and I don't care if they smash this raft into a thousand pieces!"

These words aren't out of his mouth when the appearance of the southern horizon suddenly changes. The gathering mists condense into rainwater; forcefully summoned to fill the void left by the condensation, the air turns into a hurricane. It comes from the farthest reaches of the cavern. The darkness increases. I can barely take a few sketchy notes.

The raft rises, leaps. My uncle is thrown flat on his face. I drag myself toward him. Tightly grasping the end of a rope, he seems to be taking pleasure in this sight of the elements being unleashed.

Hans doesn't move a muscle. The hurricane whips his long hair back and forth over his motionless features—which gives him a weird appearance, because the end of each strand is garnished with a little glowing tuft. In this frightening guise he's like a prehistoric man, a contemporary of the ichthyosaurus and megatherium.

But the mast is still standing. The sail swells like a bubble ready to pop. The raft is traveling faster than I can estimate, though not yet as swiftly as those water drops displaced from underneath it, which our speed turns into straight, clear lines of spray.

"The sail, the sail!" I say, signaling for it to be lowered.

"No!" my uncle replies.

"*Nej,*" Hans puts in, calmly shaking his head.

Meanwhile the rain forms a roaring cataract in front of that horizon we're madly racing toward. But before it reaches us, the veil of clouds rips apart, the sea comes to a boil, and wide-ranging chemical processes in the upper strata bring electricity into play. Thunderclaps mix with brilliant lightning bolts; countless flashes crisscross through the explosions; the fogbanks get white-hot; hailstones start to glow after hitting our metal tools and weapons; the surging breakers look like so many burning bosoms, inner fires smoldering in their troughs, flaming plumage on each of their crests.

My eyes are dazzled by the light's intensity, my eardrums are shattered by the thunderous uproar! I have to hang onto the mast, which bends like a reed under the hurricane's force!!!

. . . .

[Here my travel notes become very sketchy. I've recovered only a few fleeting comments, scribbled by reflex action so to speak. But their brevity and their very lack of clarity are stamped with the excitement that dominated me, and they give the feel of our situation better than my memory could.]

. . . .

Sunday, August 23. Where are we? We're being carried along with inconceivable speed.

It has been an awful night. The storm isn't calming down. We're living in a world of noise, one continual explosion. Our ears are bleeding. Nobody can exchange a single word.

The flashes of lightning don't leave off. I see rebounding zigzags that shoot swiftly down, then go back up and strike the granite ceiling. What if it were to collapse? Other flashes take the form of forked lightning or balls of fire that explode like bombshells. The overall noise level doesn't seem to be increasing; it has exceeded the limit of loudness that human ears can process, and if every powder magazine on earth were now to blow up in unison, *we wouldn't hear any difference.*

There's an ongoing discharge of light along the surface of the clouds; their molecules continually give off electrical matter; the sources of atmospheric gases are obviously shifting; countless waterspouts shoot into the sky, then drop back in a mass of foam.

Where are we heading . . . ? My uncle is stretched out full length at one end of the raft.

It's getting hotter. I look at our thermometer; it reads . . . [The figure has been obliterated.]

Monday, August 24. It's never ending! Once this ultradense atmosphere has changed, does that mean its new condition will be permanent?

We're broken men from our exhaustion. Hans is his usual self. The raft races invariably toward the southeast. We've done over 500 miles since leaving Axel Island.

At noon the hurricane increases in force. Every item making up our cargo needs to be tightly secured. We tie ourselves down as well. The waves sweep completely over us.

For the last three days, it has been impossible to speak a single word. We open our mouths, we move our lips; no noticeable sounds come out. Even talking straight into a person's ear doesn't make us audible.

My uncle comes closer to me. He enunciates a few words. I think he's telling me, "We're done for." I can't be sure.

I decide to write him out these words: "Let's haul in the sail."

He nods to me in agreement.

Before he has time to lift his chin again, a fiery disk appears on one side of the raft. Our mast and sail fly off in a single piece, and I see them carried to a prodigious height, looking like a pterodactyl, that fantastic bird from our planet's first centuries.

We're frozen with fear. The ball is half white, half azure, and as big as a ten-inch bombshell; it moves about slowly, spinning with unexpected speed as the hurricane whips it around. It wanders here and there, climbs one of the raft's braces, leaps onto the bag of provisions, flits back down, bounces, brushes the powder keg. Horrors! We'll blow up! Not yet. The dazzling disk veers away; it goes over to Hans, who watches it intently . . . to my uncle, who falls on his knees to dodge it . . . to me, pale and trembling in the brilliance of its light and heat; it whirls near my foot, which I try to pull away. I'm unable to.

The smell of nitrous gas fills the air; it gets into our throat and lungs. It's suffocating.

Why can't I pull my foot away? It feels riveted to the raft! Aha, I see! When that electric globe descended on us, it magnetized every piece of iron on board; the instruments, tools, and weapons are in motion, banging together with a sharp clatter; the nails in my boot are stuck fast to a strip of iron embedded in the wood. I can't pull my foot away!

I finally tear it loose with a frenzied exertion, just as the ball's gyrations are about to grab it and carry me off, when . . .

Oh, what a dazzling light! The globe has exploded! We're covered with streams of flame!

Then everything goes dark. I just have time to see my uncle stretched out on the raft and Hans still at the tiller, where he's "spitting fire" thanks to the electricity inside him.

Where are we heading, where are we heading?

. . . .

Tuesday, August 25. I emerge from an extended blackout. The storm still rages; it unleashes lightning bolts like broods of snakes running loose in the sky.

Is there ocean still overhead? Yes, and we're being carried along with incalculable speed. We've gone under Great Britain, under the English Channel, under France, maybe under all Europe!

. . . .

A new noise reaches our ears! It's obviously the sea crashing against a mass of rocks . . . ! But in that case . . .

. . . .

36

THIS ENDS WHAT I've nicknamed "the ship's log," luckily saved from the wreckage. I now resume my narrative as before.

As for what happened when our raft collided with these coastal reefs, I can't say. I felt myself tumbling into the waves, and if I came out of them alive, if my body wasn't ripped to pieces on the sharp rocks, it was because Hans's powerful arms pulled me from the depths.

That courageous Icelander transferred me out of reach of the waves, to a patch of hot sand where my uncle and I lay side by side.

Then, intent on saving a few items from the wreckage, Hans headed back to those rocks the billows were pounding so angrily. I couldn't speak; I was a broken man from my excitement and exhaustion; it took me a good hour to recover.

Meanwhile the flood rains kept falling, but with the increased intensity that announces the end of a storm. A couple of overhanging rocks afforded us shelter from the torrents out of the sky. Hans fixed us some food, which I couldn't touch; and each of us, worn out from staying up for three whole nights, fell into a troubled slumber.

The next day the weather was magnificent. Sky and sea were at peace as if by mutual agreement. Every trace of the storm was gone. When I woke up, the professor greeted me with these cheerful words. He was dreadfully jolly.

"Well, my boy," he exclaimed, "did you sleep well?"

You would have thought we were in our house on Königstrasse, that I was serenely coming down to breakfast, that my marriage to poor Grauben was going to be celebrated that very day!

Alas! If the storm had tossed our raft slightly to the east, we *would* have gone under Germany, under my dear city of Hamburg, under the street that held everything I loved in this world. Barely 100 miles would have separated us just then! But they were 100 vertical miles through a barrier of granite, an actual travel distance of more than 2,500 miles!

All these troubling thoughts instantly crossed my mind before I could answer my uncle's question.

"Drat the boy!" he resumed. "Why won't you say if you slept well?"

"I slept very well," I replied. "I'm still stiff, but it's nothing to worry about."

"Absolutely nothing, a little overexertion, that's all."

"But you seem quite cheerful this morning, uncle."

"I'm delighted, my lad, just delighted! We've made it!"

"To the goal of our expedition?"

"No, to the end of this sea that went on forever. Now we'll continue by land and genuinely descend into the bowels of our globe."

"Allow me to ask you a question, uncle."

"You're allowed, Axel."

"What about our return trip?"

"Return trip! Heavens, you're thinking about coming back before we even get there?"

"No, I just want to find out how we'll handle it."

"In the world's simplest manner. Once we've reached the center of our planet, either we'll find a new route up to its surface, or we'll use the conventional approach of going back the way we came. I trust it won't have closed behind us."

"Then we'll have to get the raft in shape again."

"Unquestionably."

"But what about provisions—do we have enough left to accomplish all these great things?"

"Yes, of course. Hans is a skillful fellow, and I'm positive he has saved most of our cargo. But let's go make sure."

We went outside that rock shelter, which was open to every breeze. I felt hopeful and fearful at the same time; the raft had crashed so dreadfully, I didn't think it was possible that anything on board could have escaped destruction. I was mistaken. When I arrived at the beach, I spotted Hans in the midst of a heap of objects, all laid out in orderly fashion. Deeply appreciative, my uncle shook his hand. With a superhuman dedication that was close to incomparable, this man had toiled away while we slept, risking his life to save our most precious possessions.

Not that we hadn't suffered some pretty noticeable losses; our weapons, for instance; but in the final analysis, we could manage without them. Our supply of gunpowder was still intact, after nearly blowing up during the storm.

"Oh well," the professor snapped. "Since we don't have any guns, we just won't do any hunting."

"Fine, but what about the instruments?"

"Here's the pressure gauge, the most valuable of the whole lot, the one I would have given all the rest to keep! With it, I can calculate our depth and know when we've reached the center. Without it, we would risk going too far and popping out at the Antipodes!"

He was in a wildly good mood.

"But what about the compass?" I asked.

"It's in perfect condition on this rock over here, likewise the chronometer and thermometers. Yes, our hunter is a man of worth!"

There was no getting around it, not a single one of our instruments was missing. As for our tools and equipment, I saw them spread out across the sand—ladders, ropes, picks, mattocks, etc.

However the issue of food remained to be clarified.

"What about our provisions?" I said.

"Let's take a look at them," my uncle replied.

The containers of provisions were lined up along the beach in perfectly preserved condition; by and large the sea hadn't disturbed them, and there was quite enough in the way of biscuits, salted meat, gin, and dried fish to feed us reliably for another four months.

"Four months!" the professor exclaimed. "We'll have time to go there and back, then I'll take what's left over and throw a big banquet for all my colleagues at the Johanneum!"

I should have been used to my uncle's personality by this time, and yet the man still surprised me.

"Now," he said, "we'll replenish our water supply with the rain that storm poured into all these granite hollows; this way we won't have any worries about suffering from thirst. As for our raft, I'll urge Hans to do his best to repair it, though it won't be a great deal more help to us, I expect."

"Why is that?" I exclaimed.

"Just an idea of mine, my boy. I don't think we'll go out the same way we came in."

I looked at the professor with definite distrust. I wondered if he wasn't losing his mind. And yet "truer words were never spoken."

"Let's go eat breakfast," he went on.

After he'd issued his instructions to the hunter, I followed him to a lofty headland. There some dried meat, biscuits, and tea added up to an excellent meal, one of the best, I must admit, that I've eaten in my life. An empty belly, the open air, and the calm after the chaos all contributed to giving me a hearty appetite.

While my uncle and I ate breakfast, I brought up the question of figuring out where we were just then.

"I suspect it'll be hard to calculate," I said.

"Yes," he replied. "To calculate it exactly is downright impossible, since I couldn't record the raft's speed or heading during three days of the storm; but nevertheless we can estimate our current bearings."

"Right, and we took our last sights on that island with the geyser—"

"Axel Island, my boy. It's the first island discovered in the middle of the earth's bedrock, so don't turn down the honor of baptizing it with your name."

"So be it. When we got to Axel Island, we'd done about 670 miles at sea and we were over 1,500 miles from Iceland."

"Fine! Then let's proceed from that point and allow four days for the storm, during which our speed had to be at least 200 miles every twenty-four hours."

"I think so. Which would make an additional 800 miles."

"Yes, and the Lidenbrock Sea would be nearly 1,500 miles from one shore to the other. Do you realize, Axel, that it could be big enough to rival the Mediterranean?"

"Yes, especially if we've only traveled it widthwise."

"Which is entirely possible."

"And by an odd coincidence," I added, "if our calculations are correct, we've got the Mediterranean overhead right now."

"Really!"

"Really, because we're over 2,200 miles from Reykjavik.

"Which is a healthy piece of traveling, my boy; but as for being under the Mediterranean rather than Turkey or the Atlantic, we can only be sure of that if we haven't changed direction."

"We haven't, the wind seems to have held steady; consequently I think this shore must be located to the southeast of Port Grauben."

"Good, we can easily make certain by checking our compass. Let's go do a compass check."

The professor headed toward the rock where Hans had set out the instruments. He was brisk and cheerful, he rubbed his hands, he struck poses. He was like a kid again! I followed him, rather interested in seeing if my assessment was correct.

Reaching the rock, my uncle took the compass, held it level, and studied the needle, which oscillated and came to rest at the spot determined by the earth's magnetic influence.

My uncle looked at it, then rubbed his eyes and looked again. Finally he turned in my direction, dumbfounded.

"What's wrong?" I asked.

He motioned me over to examine the instrument. A surprised exclamation burst from my lips. As marked by the tip of the needle, north lay in the opposite direction to what we'd assumed! It was now toward the beach instead of the open sea!

I shook the compass and inspected it; it was in perfect condition. No matter how you positioned it, the needle kept stubbornly pointing in this same unexpected direction.

Hence there was no room for doubt: the wind had shifted during that storm, none of us had noticed, and it had carried our raft back to the very shores my uncle thought he'd left behind.

37

I DON'T THINK there's any possible way I can convey the sequence of feelings aroused in Professor Lidenbrock—his astonishment, his disbelief, and finally his wrath. Never have I seen a man so nonplussed at first, so infuriated afterward. The hardships of our crossing, the dangers we ran—everything had to be done all over again! We'd gone backward instead of forward!

But my uncle quickly got a grip on himself.

"Aha, so these are the sorts of tricks fate is playing on me!" he exclaimed. "The elements are conspiring against me! Air, fire, and water are joining forces to stand in my way! All right, they'll find out what my will can do. I'll never give up, I won't retreat a fraction of an inch, and we'll see who wins out, man or nature!"

Standing on that rock, raging, threatening, as fierce as Ajax, Otto Lidenbrock looked ready to take on the gods. But I deemed it appropriate to step in and throw the brakes on this lunatic outburst.

"Listen to me," I told him in a decisive tone. "There's a limit to what anybody's ambitions can achieve in this world; it's no use fighting the impossible; we're poorly equipped for an ocean voyage; we'll never go 1,200 miles on that sorry batch of logs, with a blanket for a sail, a stick pretending to be a mast, and unleashed winds in our face. We can't steer, we'll be the plaything of storms, and if we attempt that impossible crossing a second time, we'll be acting like madmen!"

I managed to lay out this whole irrefutable line of reasoning for over ten uninterrupted minutes, but this was entirely due to the professor's paying no attention; he didn't hear a word of my argument.

"Back to the raft!" he snapped.

That was his reply. No matter how I behaved, pleaded, or carried on, I was up against a will more unyielding than granite.

Just then Hans finished repairing the raft. You would have sworn this peculiar individual had read my uncle's mind. He'd reinforced the vessel with a few pieces of *surtarbrandur*. A sail had already been unfurled, and the wind was playing in its billowy folds.

The professor said a few words to our guide, and the latter immediately loaded the baggage on board and was all set to leave. The skies were tolerably clear, and a nice steady wind blew out of the northwest.

What could I do? Stand up to these two all by myself? Not possible. If only Hans was on my side. But he wasn't! The Icelander seemed to have taken a vow of self-denial and no longer had a will of his own. He was his master's vassal, and I couldn't expect a thing from an indentured servant like him. I had no choice but to forge ahead.

I went to take my usual place on the raft, when my uncle reached out and stopped me.

"We aren't shoving off till tomorrow," he said.

I threw up my hands like a man resigned to the worst.

"I mustn't overlook a thing," he went on, "and since fate has cast me up on this part of the coast, I won't leave before scouting it out."

This comment will make sense when you realize we'd come back to a different spot on the northern shore than the site we'd originally set out from. Port Grauben had to be located more to the west. It was perfectly reasonable, then, to carefully inspect the neighborhood of our new landing place.

"Let's take a look around," I said.

And leaving Hans to his labors, off we went. The area that lay between the lapping waves and the foot of the spurs was quite wide. You could walk half an hour before coming to the wall of rock. Our feet trampled countless shells of every shape and size, which had housed the animal life of far-off times. I also saw enormous carapaces that often exceeded fifteen feet in diameter. They'd belonged to glyptodons from the Pliocene Epoch, those gigantic armadillos next to which today's turtles are no more than pint-sized miniatures. In addition a large amount of rocky rubble littered the ground, a kind of gravel polished by the billows and laid out in consecutive rows. From this I drew the inference that the sea must have occupied this area in the past. The waves had left clear traces of their passing on the scattered stones now beyond their reach.

Which, up to a point, could explain the presence of this ocean a hundred miles under the surface of the globe. But to my mind this mass of liquid must have leaked little by little into the bowels of the earth, the water obviously coming from the oceans above and making its way down some crevice. However I'll concede that this crevice must be currently plugged up, because this whole cavern—or, more accurately, this immense tank—would have filled completely in a fairly short time. Maybe, after it had to do battle with underground fires, part of that water converted into steam. Ergo the clouds hanging overhead and the release of electricity that creates storms inside the earth's bedrock.

This interpretation of the phenomena we'd witnessed struck me as satisfactory, because no matter how stupendous nature's marvels may be, they can always be explained by the laws of physics.

Consequently we were walking over a type of sedimentary rock that had been formed by the seas, like all the rock hailing from this time and distributed so widely across the surface of the globe. The professor carefully examined every gap in the terrain. Wherever there was an opening, it became important for him to plumb its depths.

We'd been skirting the coast of the Lidenbrock Sea for over a mile, when the appearance of the soil suddenly changed. It looked like it had been overturned, contorted by violent upheavals of the strata underneath. Sinkholes or outcrops in many locations testified to some powerful disruption of the earth's bedrock.

We were moving forward, not without some difficulty, over this fractured granite, which was mixed with flint, quartz, and alluvial deposits, when we caught sight of a field—no, a whole prairie—of bones. You would have thought it was an immense cemetery in which endless refuse from the generations of twenty centuries had gotten all jumbled together. Towering mounds of rubble rose into the distance, each higher than the one before. They undulated all the way to the horizon and vanished into a thinning mist. There, piled up over maybe three square miles, lay the whole history of the animal kingdom, a saga barely recorded in the too-recent rock of the world above.

In the meantime we were carried away with impatient curiosity. With a dry sound our feet trampled these relics of ancient animals, these fossils, these rare and intriguing remains so fought over by the museums of our major cities. A thousand Cuviers would have been too few to rebuild the skeletons of the organic life lying in this magnificent boneyard.

I was stunned. My uncle raised his big arms toward the heavy ceiling that served as our sky. His jaw dropped to his knees, his eyes flashed behind the lenses of his glasses, his head kept moving up, down, left, right—in short, his whole bearing conveyed boundless amazement. He was standing in front of a priceless assortment of such prehistoric monsters as the leptotherium, mericotherium, lophiodon, anoplotherium, megatherium, mastodon, protopithecus, and pterodactyl—all gathered together for his own private pleasure. Picture to yourself a rabid book collector suddenly admitted into the legendary Library of Alexandria that Caliph Omar had burned down—and it had been miraculously reborn from its ashes! That was my uncle, Professor Lidenbrock, all over.

But another wonder lay ahead: dashing through this organic refuse, he snatched up a fleshless skull and exclaimed in a trembling voice:

"Axel, Axel! It's the head of a human being!"

"The head of a human being? Oh, uncle!" I responded, every bit as astonished.

"Yes, nephew! O Professor Milne-Edwards! O Professor de Quatrefages! If only you were here now, at the side of Otto Lidenbrock!"

38

TO APPRECIATE WHY my uncle invoked these renowned French experts, you need to learn about an event of the highest importance to paleontology, an event that took place a little while before our departure.

On March 28, 1863, near Abbeville in the Department of the Somme in France, road crews under the supervision of Jacques Boucher de Perthes had been digging in the quarries of Moulin-Quignon, when they found a human jaw fourteen feet beneath the surface of the ground. It was the first fossil of this type to see the light of day. Near it they turned up some stone axes and pieces of sharpened flint, stained and coated with a uniform patina by the passage of time.

This discovery made a big noise, not only in France but in England and Germany. Several experts from the French Institute, among them Messrs. Milne-Edwards and de Quatrefages, took the matter to heart, proved the remains in question were indisputably au-

thentic, and became the keenest witnesses for the defense in this "jawbone trial," as the English expressed it.

Geologists in the United Kingdom who viewed the matter as an established fact—Messrs. Falconer, Busk, Carpenter, etc.—were joined by experts in Germany, and at the front of their ranks, the most spirited and zealous of them all, was Uncle Lidenbrock.

So the authenticity of this humanoid fossil from the Quaternary Period seemed indisputably proven and accepted.

This school of thought, it's true, had a relentless opponent in Professor Élie de Beaumont. An expert of towering authority, he insisted that the rock of Moulin-Quignon didn't belong to any of the "water-based" varieties but to a more recent layer of terrain—and, together with Cuvier, he refused to accept that any human species had coexisted with the animals of the Quaternary Period. In company with the vast majority of geologists, Uncle Lidenbrock stood his ground, argued, and fought back, so Professor Élie de Beaumont remained pretty much alone in his views.

We knew all these aspects of the matter, but we didn't realize there had been new developments in the business since we'd left. Though belonging to individuals with different characteristics and of varying nationalities, other and identical jaws had been found in the gray, shifting earth of certain caves in France, Switzerland, and Belgium, along with weapons, utensils, tools, and the bones of children, adolescents, adults, and seniors. So every day brought more proof of man's presence in the Quaternary Period.

And this wasn't all. New remains had been unearthed from terrain of the Pliocene Epoch in the Tertiary Period, and these had led some even more daring experts to assign a greater age to the human race. These remains, it's true, weren't the bones of human beings, just samples of their handiwork: tibias and femurs of fossil animals that had been etched and carved in craftsmanlike fashion, so to speak—a clear sign of human activity.

Thus, in one fell swoop, man climbed a good many centuries farther down the ladder of time; he predated the mastodon; he turned out to be a contemporary of the southern mammoth; he lived 100,000 years ago, since that's when our most esteemed geologists say those Pliocene rocks were formed!

This, then, was the state of the science of paleontology, and what we knew of it was enough to explain our attitude toward this boneyard by the Lidenbrock Sea. So you can appreciate my uncle's astonishment and delight, especially when he took twenty more steps and ran—literally head-on—into a specimen of Quaternary man.

It was a totally recognizable human body. Did the soil have special properties—as in the cemetery of Saint-Michel in Bordeaux—that let it preserve a specimen this way down through the centuries? I couldn't say. But with its taut, wizened skin, limbs that were still robust (or at least looked it), complete set of teeth, full head of hair, and fearfully big fingernails and toenails, this corpse still showed us the figure it had cut in life.

I stood speechless in front of this apparition from another age. My long-winded uncle, that chronic chatterbox, didn't say anything either. We lifted the body. We stood it up. It looked at us from its cavernous eye sockets. We jiggled its resonant torso.

After a few seconds of silence, my uncle knuckled under to Professor Otto Lidenbrock, let his personality run away with him, and forgot the circumstances of our journey, our immediate vicinity, and the immense cavern housing us. In his own mind, it was clear, he was back at the Johanneum and giving a talk in front of his pupils, because he adopted an academic tone and orated to an imaginary audience:

"Gentlemen," he said, "I have the honor to present you a man from the Quaternary Period. Distinguished scientists have claimed he didn't exist, others just as distinguished have insisted he did. If any of paleontology's doubting Thomases were here, they could put their fingers on his body—and then they would have to own up to their error. I'm well aware that science needs to be ultracautious with discoveries of this type. I'm familiar with how P. T. Barnum and other charlatans of that ilk have cashed in on humanoid fossils. I know the stories about Ajax's kneecap, about the so-called body of Orestes that the Spartans discovered, about the body of the giant Asterius, which the Greek explorer Pausanias says had a length of ten cubits, or some fifteen feet. I've read accounts of the skeleton found in Trapani, Sicily during the 14th century, which people tried to identify as the cyclops Polyphemus, as well as the story of that giant uncovered in the neighborhood of Palermo during the 16th century. You're as familiar as I am, gentlemen, with those huge bones found outside Lucerne in 1577, which, according to an analysis by the famous Swiss physician Dr. Félix Platter, belonged to a giant nineteen feet tall! I've devoured the treatises by Cassanion and all the recollections, pamphlets, arguments, and counterarguments published about the bones of King Teutobochus, who led a Celtic tribe called the Cimbri in an invasion of Gaul, and whose skeleton was unearthed in 1613 from a sandpit in the old French province of Dauphiné. In the 18th century I would have done battle with the Dutch naturalist Peter Camper over the existence of those fossil men that Johann Scheuchzer said came before Adam. I've had in my hands a booklet entitled *Gigan . . . gan . . .*"

Here my uncle's congenital defect reappeared, his inability to pronounce difficult words in public.

" . . . a booklet," he resumed, "entitled *Gigan . . .* "

He couldn't get any farther.

"*Giganto . . .*"

Not possible. The ill-fated word just wouldn't come out. How they would have laughed at the Johanneum!

"*Gigantosteology*," the professor finished up between two cusswords.

Then, continuing more confidently and moving right along:

"Yes, gentlemen, I'm aware of all these things! I'm likewise aware that Cuvier and Blumenbach have identified those remains as merely the bones of mammoths and other beasts of the Quaternary Period. But in this case the slightest doubt would be an insult to science. We have the complete carcass! You can see it, touch it. It isn't a skeleton, it's a human body in one piece, preserved just for the benefit of anthropologists!"

I wasn't of a mind to contradict this assertion.

"If I could wash it in a solution of sulfuric acid," my uncle said further, "I would get rid of all the particles of dirt and these gleaming shells that are embedded in it. But I'm lacking that invaluable solvent. Yet such as it is, this body can speak for itself."

Here the professor grabbed the fossil carcass and handled it as deftly as a sideshow exhibitor.

"As you can see," he continued, "it's less than six feet in length, and we're a long way from our so-called giants. As for the race of this individual, it's indisputably Caucasian. It's our own white race! The skull of this fossil is perfectly oval shaped, without expanding cheekbones or protruding jaw. It doesn't show any signs of the prognathism that changes the facial angle.[32] Measure this angle. It's nearly 90°. But I'll go farther still in the way of inferences and I'll be so bold as to say that this specimen of humanity belongs to the Japhetic family, which has since spread from the East Indies all the way to western Europe. Spare me your smiles, gentlemen!"

Nobody had smiled, but the professor automatically expected to see smirking faces during his scholarly disquisitions!

"Yes," he went on with new zest, "this is a fossil man, the contemporary of the mastodons whose remains fill this amphitheater. But to tell you the way he got here, how the strata in which he lay buried slid into this enormous planetary cavity—these matters are beyond me. During the Quaternary Period, no doubt, considerable disturbances were still taking place in the earth's crust; the globe's continual cooling produced fractures, cracks,

and faults, and in all likelihood part of the upper terrain tumbled into them. I don't know that for a fact, but here in a nutshell is the man himself, surrounded by his handiwork, these axes and pieces of sharpened flint that are the essence of the Stone Age—and unless he came here as a tourist and scientific pioneer like me, I can't cast the slightest doubt on the authenticity of his ancient origin."

The professor fell silent, and I burst into a round of "unanimous applause." But my uncle was right, and wiser heads than his nephew would have had some trouble taking him on.

Another giveaway. This fossilized body wasn't the only one in this immense boneyard. At every step we took through this refuse, we kept coming across other human bodies—to confound the skeptics, all my uncle had to do was pick out the most marvelous specimens.

In truth it was an amazing sight, these generations of men and animals all jumbled together in this cemetery. But a serious question came up, which we weren't bold enough to answer. During some earthquake, had these life forms tumbled down to the shores of the Lidenbrock Sea after they'd already passed away? Or, instead, had they lived in this underground world, dwelling under its artificial sky, going from cradle to grave like other residents of the earth? So far the only living creatures we'd seen had been sea monsters and fish! Was some man of the chasms still wandering along these empty beaches?

39

FOR ANOTHER HALF an hour, our feet trampled these beds of bones. We forged ahead, driven by burning curiosity. What other marvels did this cavern hold, what scientific treasures? My eyes were on the lookout for any surprise, my imagination for any wonder.

The seashore had long since vanished behind the hills of that boneyard. Not too worried about getting lost, the reckless professor took me a good distance. We moved forward

---

[32] The facial angle is formed by two planes, one more or less vertical that's at a tangent to the forehead and incisors, the other horizontal that goes from the opening of the ear ducts to the bottom of the nasal ridge. In the language of anthropology, the condition where a protruding jaw changes the facial angle is known as "prognathism."

quietly, bathing in the waves of that electric light. Just then, due to some phenomenon I can't explain, its coverage was so comprehensive, it gave uniform illumination to all the different sides of an object. This particular light source didn't occupy a fixed point in space and it didn't create any shadow effects. You would have sworn it was high noon, the time was midsummer, you were in the heart of the equatorial regions, and the sun's rays were absolutely vertical. Every trace of mist had vanished. The masses of rock, the far-off mountains, the blurred shapes of a few forests in the distance all looked unnatural under that fluid, evenly distributed light. We were like that fantastic character in the tale by E. T. A. Hoffmann, the man who had lost his shadow.

A mile farther along, the outskirts of an immense forest appeared, but it wasn't one of those woods of mushrooms that grew around Port Grauben.

This was vegetation of the Tertiary Period in all its magnificence. Tall, proud palm trees belonged to a now-vanished species in the genus *Palmacites;* firs, yews, cypress trees, and cedars represented the conifer family and were linked to each other by a hopelessly tangled network of tropical creepers. A carpet of moss and liverwort cushioned the ground. A few brooks babbled in the shade, hardly worthy of the name since no shadows were being cast. Tree ferns grew along the banks, looking like those in the greenhouses of the world above. Except that these trees, bushes, and plants didn't have any color, since the sun's vital warmth was denied them. Everything blended into the same faded, brownish hue. The leaves didn't have any greenness, and at this point even the flowers (so plentiful during this Tertiary Period that had witnessed their birth) didn't have any color or scent, looking like they were made out of paper that had been bleached from exposure to the air.

Uncle Lidenbrock ventured into this gigantic thicket. I followed him, not without some trepidation. Since nature had stocked the place with edible vegetation, why wouldn't some awe-inspiring mammals be here as well? Fallen trees had been eroded by the passage of time, leaving wide glades in which I saw leguminous plants, maples, coffee trees, and a thousand edible shrubs so dear to the ruminants of every epoch. Then, merging and intermingling, trees were on view from wildly different regions on the surface of the globe—an oak tree growing next to a palm tree, a eucalyptus from Australia leaning across a fir from Norway, the branches of a birch from up north merging with the branches of a kauri pine from New Zealand. The world's sharpest specialist in botanical classification would have gone out of his mind.

Suddenly I stopped. I reached out and held my uncle back.

The diffuse light let us view the tiniest objects in the depths of that thicket. I thought I saw some immense forms stirring under the trees . . . no, I actually *did* see them, and with my own two eyes! In point of fact they were gigantic animals, a whole herd of mastodons like the ones whose remains were discovered in the marshes of Ohio back in 1801, only these weren't fossilized but alive! I watched their huge elephant trunks milling around under the trees like an army of snakes. I could hear the racket they made when their long ivory tusks jabbed the ancient tree trunks. Branches snapped and leaves ripped as considerable masses of both plunged down the huge gullets of those monsters.

That dream in which I watched the rebirth of this whole world from ancient times through the Tertiary and Quaternary periods—it had finally come true! And there we were, on our own, in the bowels of the globe, at the mercy of its fierce denizens!

My uncle took one look.

"Come on!" he said suddenly, clutching my arm. "Let's get closer!"

"No, no!" I exclaimed. "We're unarmed! What could we do inside that herd of giant quadrupeds? Let's get out of here, uncle! No human being could brave the fury of those monsters with impunity."

"No human being?" my uncle responded in a low voice. "You're wrong, Axel! Look! Over there! I think I see a living creature! A creature like ourselves! A man!"

I looked, shrugging my shoulders, determined to be a skeptic to the last. But as leery as I was, I had to bow to the evidence.

In essence, barely a quarter of a mile off, leaning against the enormous trunk of a kauri pine, a human creature—another of Neptune's sons, the Proteus of these underground regions—was watching over the countless mastodons in that herd!

Immanis pecoris custos, immanior ipse![33]

Yes! *Immanior ipse!* This wasn't a fossilized creature like that carcass we'd turned up in the boneyard, it was a giant, somebody who could take charge of those monsters. He stood over twelve feet tall. His head was as big as a buffalo's and hidden in the brambles of his unkempt hair. It looked like an honest-to-goodness mane, like a mammoth's in an earlier age. His hand brandished an enormous tree limb, a shepherd's crook worthy of this prehistoric herdsman.

We stood stock-still in astonishment. But he could have spotted us. It was time to go.

"Come on, come on," I snapped, tugging my uncle, who for once was open to persuasion.

Fifteen minutes later, we were out of sight of that alarming foe.

And now that I can quietly ponder the matter, now that my wits have calmed down again, now that months have gone by since this strange, uncanny encounter, what should I think, what should I believe? Nothing! It's an impossibility! Our senses were deceived, our eyes didn't see what they saw! No human beings live in this underground world! No generations of cavemen reside in these lower depths, not concerned and out of contact with the residents of the earth's surface! That's insane, utterly insane!

I'm more inclined to accept the existence of some animal of quasi-human shape, some ape living at an earlier time in geological history, some protopithecus, or some mesopithecus like the one discovered by Professor Lartet in the bone beds of Sansan, France. But the size of the creature we saw exceeded

every measurement known to modern paleontology. Which makes no difference! It was an ape, no matter how unlikely that may seem, just an ape! But could there be a man, a living man—and along with him a whole generation of men—buried in the bowels of the earth? Never!

Meanwhile we left that brightly lit forest behind, speechless with amazement, dazed and overwhelmed to a debilitating degree. In spite of ourselves we rushed away. We truly ran for our lives, as if compulsively fleeing in some nightmare. We instinctively headed back toward the Lidenbrock Sea, and Lord knows where my scattered wits would have taken me if another concern hadn't brought me around to more practical considerations.

Though I was sure our feet were striding through totally virgin territory, I often noticed clusters of rocks whose shapes reminded me of those near Port Grauben. This was further corroboration of what our compass had indicated, that we'd accidentally returned to the northern shore of the Lidenbrock Sea. At times it seemed unmistakable. Hundreds of streams and waterfalls were tumbling over the rocky ledges. I thought I spotted where the *surtarbrandur* lay, our loyal Hansbach, and the cave in which I'd come to. Then, just a few steps farther along, the layout of the spurs, the look of a stream, or the surprising outlines of a mass of rock would plunge me back into doubt.

I shared my misgivings with my uncle. He felt as uncertain as I did. He couldn't be sure of anything in this repetitious panorama.

"Obviously we didn't come ashore at our starting point," I told him. "The storm carried us a bit below it, so if we follow the coastline, we'll find our way back to Port Grauben."

"In that case," my uncle replied, "it's pointless to continue our exploring and we'd best return to the raft. But could you be wrong, Axel?"

"It's hard to say, uncle, because all these rocks look alike. Yet I seem to recognize that promontory—I think Hans built our vessel at the foot of it." Then, after examining a cove I thought I also recognized, I added, "If that

---

[33] *Translator's note.* Latin: "Tending a huge herd, even huger himself!"

isn't our little harbor, it must be close at hand."

"That's not it, Axel. At least we would find our own footprints, and I don't see a thing . . ."

"But *I* can see something!" I exclaimed, shooting over to an object that glittered in the sand.

"What are you talking about?"

"This," I replied.

And I showed my uncle what I'd just picked up—a knife covered with rust.

"Say," he said. "Did you bring this weapon along with you?"

"Me? Absolutely not. But how about you?"

"No, not that I'm aware," the professor replied. "I've never had this item in my possession."

"How very odd!"

"Not really, Axel, it's quite simple. Icelanders often carry this kind of weapon, so it belongs to Hans, and he must have lost—"

I shook my head. Hans had never had this knife in his possession.

"So is this the weapon of some prehistoric warrior?" I exclaimed. "A man who's still alive, a contemporary of that gigantic shepherd? But it can't be! This isn't a tool from the Stone Age! Not even the Bronze Age! This blade is steel . . ."

My uncle stopped me dead before I headed up this new garden path, telling me in an icy tone:

"Calm down, Axel, and come to your senses. This knife is a weapon from the 16th century, an actual dagger, like the ones noblemen carried in their belts to deliver the finishing stroke. It was made in Spain. It doesn't belong to you, me, our hunter, or even some human being who might be living in the bowels of our globe!"

"You're daring to suggest—"

"Look here, it didn't get chipped like this from cutting people's throats; its blade is covered with a layer of rust that's older than a day, a year, or even a century!"

As usual when the professor got excited, he let his imagination run away with him.

"Axel," he continued, "we've picked up the trail of a great discovery! This blade has been on its own in this sand for a century, maybe two or three centuries—and it got chipped from scraping the rocks of this underground sea!"

"But it didn't *come* here on its own," I snapped. "It didn't get bent all by itself. Somebody was here ahead of us!"

"Yes, a man!"

"What man?"

"The man who carved his name with this knife! The man whose hand tried to mark the way to the earth's center one more time! Let's start searching!"

And there we were, prodigiously motivated, skirting that lofty wall, examining any tiny crevice that had the potential to turn into a hallway.

In this fashion we arrived at a locality where the beach was narrower. The sea came almost close enough to lap the foot of the spur, leaving a pathway that was six feet wide at best. Between two protruding rocks you could see the entrance to a dark tunnel.

There, on a slab of granite, appeared two secretive, half-eroded letters, the two initials of a bold, fantastic explorer:

$$\cdot \ \text{↓} \cdot \text{Ϧ} \cdot$$

"A. S.!" my uncle exclaimed. "Arne Saknussemm! Arne Saknussemm as always!"

40

SINCE THIS JOURNEY BEGAN I'd had many amazing experiences: I was starting to think I was immune to surprise, too jaded to be astonished by anything. Yet I stood awestruck, almost in a daze, at the sight of these two letters carved 300 years ago. Not only had the learned alchemist left his signature on the rock for all to read, but the stiletto in my hands was the stylus that had scribbled it. Without showing flagrant bad faith, I couldn't doubt the existence of the traveler or the reality of his travels any longer.

While these thoughts were whirling around in my brain, Professor Lidenbrock flew into a sort of exalted fit on the topic of Arne Saknussemm.

"O you wonderful genius!" he exclaimed. "You haven't forgotten a single thing that could clear the way through the earth's crust for other men, and your fellow mortals can find the footprints you've left, even after three centuries and in the darkness of these underground depths! You've saved the contemplation of these wonders for other eyes besides yours! At stage after stage you've carved your name, guiding any explorer daring enough to follow you straight to his destination, and he'll find that name again, written by your own hand, at the very center of our planet. Very well, I too will go and sign my name on that final page of granite! But as for this cape you sighted next to this sea you discovered, from now on let it always be known as Cape Saknussemm!"

That's what I heard—or something to the same effect—and I was won over by the fervor radiating from these words. An inner fire stirred again in my heart! I forgot everything else, both the dangers of our journey and the hazards of our return. If somebody else had done it, I was willing to do it too, and none of it seemed outside the bounds of human possibility!

"Forward march!" I exclaimed.

I was already scooting over to that gloomy hallway when the professor stopped me; he, the man who flew off the handle, was counseling patience and a cool head.

"First let's get back to Hans," he said, "and bring the raft around to this location."

I followed orders, not with any great pleasure, and scrambled quickly through the rocks along the shore.

"You know, uncle," I said as we walked, "it's strange how circumstances have worked out in our favor up to now!"

"Oh? You think so, Axel?"

"No doubt about it, and even that storm got us going the right way again. Heaven bless that hurricane! It brought us back to this coast while fair weather would have taken us far away! Imagine for a second if our raft had run its prow aground—if you can call it a prow—on the southern shores of the Lidenbrock Sea! What would have happened to us?

We never would have seen Saknussemm's name and now we would be stranded on a seacoast with nowhere to go."

"Yes, Axel, it was a fortuitous thing that we set sail for the south and instead went due north, right to Cape Saknussemm. This fact, I must say, is more than surprising, and its explanation eludes me completely."

"Well, that's beside the point. We don't have to explain it, just use it to our advantage!"

"Of course, my boy, however—"

"However we're about to make our way north again, heading under the subarctic regions of Europe—Sweden, Siberia, and Lord knows where—instead of going below Africa's deserts or the ocean's waves; so I don't want to hear another thing!"

"Fine, Axel, you're right, and all's for the best since we're leaving this sideways sea that doesn't lead anywhere. Now we'll start descending, keep on descending, and never stop descending! Are you aware that to reach the center of the globe, we have barely 3,800 miles left to cover?"

"Phooey!" I exclaimed. "That honestly isn't worth mentioning. Off we go!"

This lunatic conversation was still in progress when we rejoined the hunter. Everything was ready for our immediate departure. Not one package remained to be put on board. We took our places on the raft, then Hans hoisted sail and headed along the coast toward Cape Saknussemm.

The breeze wasn't helpful for a type of craft that couldn't sail close into the wind. In many spots, accordingly, we had to push ourselves along with our alpenstocks. Lying flush with the water, the rocks often forced us to make pretty extensive detours. Finally, after navigating for three hours—in other words, near six o'clock in the evening—we reached a promising locality for landing.

I leaped ashore, followed by my uncle and the Icelander. This cruise hadn't dampened my zeal. On the contrary, I even proposed "burning our boats" to cut off any possibility of retreat. But my uncle was against it. I thought he was showing unusual restraint.

"At least," I said, "let's get going without wasting another second."

"Yes, my boy; but beforehand let's examine this new hallway and see if we need to break out the ladders."

My uncle activated his Ruhmkorff device; we left the raft to itself, tied up along the shore; however the mouth of the hallway wasn't twenty steps off, and with me in the lead, our little band headed over to it without delay.

The opening was nearly circular and about five feet wide; this gloomy tunnel had been cut into the existing rock, then carefully reamed by the eruptive materials that used to pass through it; since its floor was flush with the ground, you could go inside it without difficulty.

We walked along a surface that was nearly horizontal, then, after just six steps, our trek was interrupted by an enormous mass of stone blocking our way.

"Curse this rock!" I exclaimed angrily, finding that I'd been brought to a sudden stop by an insurmountable obstacle.

We took good looks to the right, left, up, and down, but there wasn't any passageway, any fork in the road. I felt bitterly disappointed and I wasn't willing to accept the reality of this obstacle. I bent over. I looked underneath the mass of stone. Not a cranny. Above it. The same granite barricade. Hans swept the light from his lamp over every inch of the wall; but the latter didn't reveal any break in continuity. We had to abandon all hope of getting past it.

I sat on the ground; my uncle paced swiftly up and down the corridor.

"But how did Saknussemm manage it?" I exclaimed.

"Yes," my uncle put in. "Did he let this stone barrier stop him?"

"No, no!" I went on excitedly. "This hunk of rock closed up the passageway suddenly, due to some tremor or other, or one of those magnetic phenomena that shake the earth's crust. Many years went by between the time Saknussemm returned through here and the time this mass of stone fell into place. Isn't it obvious that this hallway used to be a lava path, that in those days the eruptive materials flowed freely along it? Look, there are recent crevices streaking the granite in the ceiling;

it's made up of imported fragments, enormous stones, as if some giant had carried them here while working on the support structure; but one day the pressure increased, and like the keystone of an arch giving way, a rockslide took place and this mass of stone plugged up the whole passageway. It's an accidental obstacle that Saknussemm didn't encounter, and if we don't knock it for a loop, we don't deserve to reach the center of the world!"

That's how I was talking! The professor's entire soul had transmigrated into me. I was imbued with the spirit of discovery. I forgot the past, I sneered at the future. Nothing existed for me anymore on the surface of this sphere into whose heart I'd plunged, not its towns, not its countrysides, not Hamburg, not Königstrasse, not even my poor Grauben, who must have thought I'd gotten lost for good in the bowels of the earth!

"Fine," my uncle went on. "A swing of the mattock, a swing of the pick, and we'll make our way—we'll knock this wall down!"

"It's too hard for a pick," I snapped.

"A mattock, then!"

"It's too thick for a mattock."

"But what—"

"Oh, all right: our gunpowder! It's an explosive! We'll set off an explosion and blow this obstacle sky-high!"

"Our gunpowder?"

"Yes, all we have to do is break up a bit of rock!"

"Hans, get to work!" my uncle called.

The Icelander returned to the raft, soon came back with a pick, and used it to hollow out a shothole for the explosive. This was no easy task. It came down to making a cavity sizeable enough to hold fifty pounds of guncotton, whose expansive power is four times greater than conventional gunpowder.

I was in a prodigious state of mental excitement. While Hans toiled away, I was busily helping my uncle fix up a long fuse made of moistened powder and enclosed in a linen tube.

"We'll get past it!" I said.

"We'll get past it," my uncle repeated.

By midnight we were all set to put our explosive ideas into practice; the guncotton charge lay buried in its shothole, and the fuse wound along the hallway, ending up outside.

One spark was all it took now to activate this fearsome mechanism.

"Till tomorrow," the professor said.

I had to resign myself to waiting for another six long hours.

41

THE NEXT DAY, Thursday, August 27, was a notorious date in our underground journey. It never pops back into my head without my heartbeat speeding up in terror. From that point on our reason, judgment, and powers of invention no longer had any say in the matter, and we were to become the playthings of geological phenomena.

We were on our feet by six o'clock in the morning. It was time for the gunpowder to clear a path through the granite crust.

I applied for the honor of igniting the explosive. This done, I was to rejoin my companions on the raft, which we hadn't unloaded; then we would put to sea so as to stay clear of any dangers that arose from the powder's blowing up, aftereffects that might not be confined just to the interior of that mass of rock.

According to our calculations, the fuse was to burn for ten minutes before the flame reached the powder chamber. So I had enough time to make it back to the raft.

I got ready to perform my role, not without a certain uneasiness.

After a quick meal, my uncle and the hunter went on board while I stayed on shore. I carried a lantern with a lighted wick, which I was to use in setting fire to the fuse.

"Go, my boy," my uncle told me, "then come rejoin us immediately."

"Don't worry," I answered. "I won't do any sightseeing."

Seconds later I was at the threshold of the hallway. I opened my lantern and grabbed the end of the fuse.

The professor held his chronometer in his hand.

"Are you ready?" he called to me.

"I'm ready."

"All right, my boy, light it!"

I instantly dipped the fuse into the burning wick; it fizzed into flame on contact, and I raced for the shore.

"Hop on board," my uncle put in, "and we'll shove off!"

Hans gave an energetic push and we were back at sea. The raft went 120 feet out.

It was a suspenseful moment. The professor kept his eye on the second hand of his chronometer.

"Five more minutes . . . " he said. "Four more . . . three more . . . "

My pulse was ticking off the half seconds.

". . . two more . . . one more . . . down you go, you granite crags!"

What happened just then? I don't think I heard any sound of an explosion. But right in front of my eyes, the shape of the rocks abruptly altered; they fell open like a curtain. I saw a bottomless pit gape in the middle of the shore. The sea whirled around and turned into a single enormous wave, while our raft rode on the back of it and rose straight up in the air.

All three of us fell on our faces. In less than a second, daylight had changed into the most utter darkness. Then it felt like there wasn't any solid support under me—I don't mean under my feet but under the raft itself. I thought it was sinking straight to the bottom. Nothing of the sort. I tried to say something to my uncle, but he couldn't hear me above the roar of the waters.

Despite the darkness, noise, shock, and excitement, I realized what had just happened.

There had been a chasm beyond that rock we just blew up. The blast triggered a sort of earthquake in a terrain riddled with crevices, the gorge gaped open, and the sea rushed into it like a torrent, taking the three of us along.

I felt I was done for.

An hour went by in this way . . . two hours . . . who knows? We linked elbows and joined hands to keep from being tossed off the raft. Whenever it collided with the wall, there was a tremendously sharp jolt. Yet these collisions were infrequent, from which

I concluded that the hallway was getting considerably wider. No doubt this was the way Saknussemm had gone; but instead of descending by ourselves, we'd had the poor judgment to take a whole sea along with us.

As you can appreciate, these ideas popped into my head in the most hazy, murky form. I had difficulty piecing them together during this dizzying ride (nosedive would be more like it). To judge by the air buffeting my face, we must have been going faster than any high-speed train. So it would have been impossible to light a torch under these conditions, and our last electrical device had gotten smashed when the powder blew up.

Consequently I was quite startled to see a light suddenly gleaming next to me. It shone on Hans's calm face. Our skillful hunter had managed to get a flame going in the lantern, and though it kept threatening to flicker out, it shed a little illumination on that frightful darkness.

The hallway was wide. I'd been right in figuring it was. Our deficient light didn't let us see both sides at the same time. The waters were carrying us down a slope more precipitous than the most insurmountable rapids in America. Its surface was like a volley of liquid arrows fired with tremendous force. I don't know any better simile for conveying how it looked. Caught in various eddies, the raft sometimes spun around. When it drew near the walls of the hallway, I flashed the light of our lantern over them and I could gauge our speed by watching how the rocky ledges changed into continual streaks, as if we were enmeshed in a spiderweb whose threads were in motion. I estimated we were going at least seventy-five miles per hour.

My uncle and I looked at each other, wild-eyed, pressed against the stump of the mast—which had broken off at the time of the catastrophe. No human power could halt that moving air, and we turned our backs to it so that its speed didn't suffocate us.

Meanwhile the hours went by. Our circumstances didn't change, but there was a hitch that complicated them.

Trying to put our cargo in a little better order, I discovered that most of our belongings had gone overboard when the sea assaulted us so fiercely after the powder blew up. I wanted to find out exactly where we stood with our resources, so I took the lantern and started investigating. Among our instruments only the compass and chronometer remained. The ladders and ropes had been reduced to a length of line coiled around the stump of the mast. Not a mattock, not a pick, not a hammer, and one irreparable loss—we had only a day's supply of food left!

I ransacked every cranny in the raft, down to the tiniest slits where the planks were fastened to the logs! Not a thing! Our only remaining provisions were a piece of dried meat and a few biscuits.

I looked around with a dazed expression. I wasn't willing to face the facts. And yet what did it really amount to, this danger that had me so concerned? Even if our food were to last us for months, for years, how could we get out of these depths where this torrent had irresistibly taken us? Why worry about hunger pangs when we had so many other ways to die already? Would we honestly have enough time to starve to death?

Nevertheless, by some bewildering freak of fancy, I forgot our present perils and focused on future threats, which rose up now in all their horror. After all, couldn't we maybe escape from this furious torrent and get back to the surface of the globe? How? I hadn't the faintest idea. Where? It made no difference. A chance in a thousand is still a chance, while dying from hunger wouldn't leave us with any hope whatever, not the tiniest shred.

It occurred to me to tell my uncle everything, to show him how strapped we were at this juncture, to work out exactly how much time we had left to live. But I had the courage to keep still. I wanted to leave his composure intact.

At this point the light in our lantern gradually grew lower, then went out entirely. The wick had burned all the way down. It was as dark as the pit. We had no conceivable way of dispelling this dense blackness. We still had a torch left, but we couldn't have kept it lit. So, just like a child, I closed my eyes to shut all the darkness out.

After a fairly long stretch of time, our ride got even faster. I could tell from the air whipping my face. The waters were going down a slope that had grown extremely steep. I seriously doubted that we were sliding anymore. We were dropping. It felt like we were falling almost straight down. Reaching out and clamping onto my arms, Hans and my uncle got a tight grip on me.

All at once, after a barely noticeable interval, I felt a sort of jolt; the raft hadn't bumped into something hard—it had suddenly quit falling. A cloudburst, an immense column of liquid, crashed on top of it. I felt suffocated. I was drowning . . .

But this abrupt downpour didn't last long. A few seconds later I was back out in the open air and I inhaled a lungful. Hans and my uncle kept a stranglehold on my arms, and the raft still had all three of us on board.

42

BY THEN I GUESSED it had to be ten o'clock in the evening. Following that last onslaught, my sense of hearing was the first of my senses to function. Almost immediately I heard (because this was a genuine aural event) the hallway fall silent after all the roaring that had filled my ears for so long. Finally these muffled words from my uncle got through to me:

"We're rising!"

"What do you mean?" I exclaimed.

"We're rising! Yes, we're rising!"

I reached out; I touched the wall; I ended up with a bleeding hand. We were rising again with tremendous speed.

"Light the torch!" the professor shouted.

Hans managed to get it going, not without difficulty; despite our ascending motion, the flame stood straight up and was bright enough to shed some light on the whole picture.

"Just as I thought," my uncle said. "We're in a narrow shaft that's barely twenty-five feet wide. After reaching the bottom of the pit, the water's heading back to sea level, and we're going up with it."

"Where to?"

"I have no idea, but we need to be ready for any development. I estimate we're rising at a speed of 12 feet per second—hence 720 feet per minute, or over eight miles per hour. At this rate we'll get somewhere."

"Yes, if nothing stops us and if this shaft has a way out. But what if it's plugged up, what if the air pressure gradually increases under this column of water, what if we're crushed?"

"Axel," the professor replied with great calmness, "our situation is close to hopeless, but there's a chance or two we can make it and that's what I'm evaluating. If we can perish any second, we can be saved any second. So we need to be in a position to take advantage of the tiniest opportunity."

"But what can we do?"

"Eat and build our strength back up."

At these words I looked at him, wild-eyed. I hated to come out with it, but finally I had to tell him:

"Eat?" I echoed.

"Yes, without delay."

The professor added a few words in Danish. Hans shook his head.

"What!" my uncle exclaimed. "We've lost our provisions?"

"Yes, and here's the food we've got left—one piece of dried meat for all three of us!"

My uncle looked at me, not wanting to take in what I'd said.

"Well," I said, "do you still think we can make it?"

My question went unanswered.

An hour slipped by. I started to feel agonizingly hungry. My companions were suffering too, and not one of us dared touch that last wretched bit of food.

Meanwhile we were still rising with tremendous speed. At times we were left short of breath by the air rushing past, which happens to balloonists who ascend too quickly. But if the latter feel proportionally colder as they rise through the layers of atmosphere, we were experiencing exactly the opposite effect. The temperature had increased in a disturbing fashion, and I was sure by then that it was as high as 104° Fahrenheit.

What did such a change mean? Up to this point events had borne out Davy's and Lidenbrock's suppositions; up to this point these unconventional conditions of heat-resistant rock, electricity, and magnetic impulses had altered the overall laws of nature, leaving us only moderately warm—because, to my thinking, the concept of a central fire remained the only true one, the only defensible one. Were we going back into an environment where these phenomena were fully and properly operational, where heat reduced the rock to a completely molten state? That's what I was afraid of, and I told the professor:

"If we don't drown, if we aren't crushed, and if we don't die of starvation, we still have a good chance of being burned alive."

He was content to shrug his shoulders and lapse back into his thoughts.

An hour went by uneventfully; except for a mild increase in temperature, there wasn't any change in our circumstances. Finally my uncle broke the silence.

"Look here," he said, "we need to make a decision."

"Is that so," I remarked.

"Yes. We've got to build our strength back up. If we ration the rest of our food and try to live a few hours longer, we'll stay weak right to the end."

"Yes, right to the end, and it won't be long now."

"Well, suppose we get a chance to save ourselves, suppose the time comes when we need to take action—where will we find the energy to act if we've let ourselves grow weak from hunger?"

"Come on, uncle! Once we've gobbled up this piece of meat, what else is there?"

"Nothing, Axel, nothing. But will it nourish you any better to devour it with your eyes? Yours is the logic of a man without willpower, a creature without spirit!"

"Don't you ever give up hope?" I snapped in exasperation.

"No!" was the professor's forceful remark.

"What! You still think we have a chance to save ourselves?"

"Yes I do! Definitely! So long as his heart beats and his flesh quivers, it's unacceptable for a creature with free will to give up hope!"

What a thing to say! Only an uncommonly tough man could air such thoughts at a time like this.

"In a nutshell," I said, "what are your plans?"

"To eat the rest of our food down to the last crumb and build up our failing strength again. If this proves to be our last meal, so be it! But at least we won't be worn out, we'll be men again."

"All right, let's dig in!" I exclaimed.

My uncle took the piece of meat and the few biscuits that hadn't gone overboard; he divided them into three equal portions, then distributed them. This gave each of us about a pound of food. The professor ate greedily in a sort of high-strung frenzy; me, without enjoyment and almost with revulsion, despite my hunger; Hans, serenely and temperately, noiselessly chewing small mouthfuls, relishing them with the calm of a man who couldn't be bothered with worrying about the future. After carefully rummaging around, he found a half-full flask of gin; he offered it to us, and this bracing liquor was able to revive me a little.

"*Forträfflig!*" Hans said, drinking in his turn.

"Excellent!" my uncle shot back.

I had a little hope again. But our last meal was now over. It was five o'clock in the morning.

A man is built in such a way that he notices his physical condition only when something's wrong; once he has eaten his fill, he has trouble even recalling his horrible hunger; to recognize it, he has to experience it. Accordingly, even though we'd gone without food for quite a while, all of our past sufferings were wiped out by a couple mouthfuls of biscuit and meat.

After this meal, however, each of us sank into his own thoughts. What was on Hans's mind, this far-western man governed by the fatalistic resignation of the East? As for me, only memories filled my brain and they took me back to that surface realm I wished I'd never left. The house on Königstrasse, my poor Grauben, and old Martha all passed like phantoms in front of my eyes, and in the mournful rumblings that ran through this section of rock, I thought I detected sounds from the cities above.

As for my uncle, he "took care of business," intently examining the nature of the terrain with torch in hand; he tried to scout out the area by studying the layers of rock sitting on top of each other. This assessment —or, more accurately, this estimate—was bound to be pretty tentative; but an expert is still an expert, and when Professor Lidenbrock managed to stay composed, he certainly functioned in this capacity to an exceptional degree.

I heard him mumbling words from the science of geology; I understood them and couldn't help taking an interest in this crowning piece of research.

"Eruptive granite," he said. "We're still in primitive times; but we're rising, we're rising! Who knows . . ."

Who knows? Hope sprang eternal in him. He ran his hand over that vertical surface and a few seconds later he resumed as follows:

"Here's the layer of gneiss! Here's the mica schist! Good! Soon the rock will enter a time of transition, and then . . ."

What was the professor going on about? Could he measure the thickness of the earth's crust hanging overhead? Had he any way of making such an assessment? Hardly. Our pressure gauge was gone and no amount of rough guessing could make up for it.

Meanwhile it was getting hotter by leaps and bounds, and I felt like I was bathing in air that was on fire. I can compare it only to the heat given off by furnaces in a foundry at metal-pouring time. Hans, my uncle, and I were gradually forced to take off our jackets and vests; the tiniest piece of clothing became a source of discomfort, even pain.

"Are we rising toward some high-temperature heat source?" I exclaimed at one point as it kept getting warmer.

"No, it's not possible," my uncle replied. "Not possible!"

"However," I said, touching one side of the shaft, "this wall's on fire!"

Just as I said these words, my hand brushed the water and I had to snatch it back.

"And the water's on fire!" I exclaimed.

This time the professor's only reply was an angry gesture.

Then an uncontrollable foreboding took hold of my brain and wouldn't let go. I sensed a catastrophe drawing near, something so inconceivable that it was beyond the most daring imagination. An idea that originally was vague and uncertain had grown into a certainty in my mind. I brushed it aside, but it stubbornly came back. I didn't dare put it into words. Even so, I'd instinctively noticed a few things that strengthened my conviction. By our torch's uncertain light, I picked up chaotic movements in the granite beds; clearly a phenomenon was about to take place where electricity played a role; then there was this outrageous heat, this boiling water . . . ! I felt a need to look at the compass.

It was going berserk!

43

YES, BERSERK! With a sudden lurch the needle was leaping from one pole to the other, traveling past every notch on the dial, and whirling around in the throes of a severe dizzy spell.

According to prevailing notions, as I was well aware, the earth's mineral crust is never in a state of absolute rest; the changes brought about by substances decomposing inside it, the disturbances caused by major fluctuations of liquid, and the play of magnetic impulses all tend to unsettle it constantly, even though the life forms scattered over its surface don't have any inkling of these disturbances. So this phenomenon wouldn't otherwise have alarmed me, or at least it wouldn't have put such a dreadful idea in my head.

But other facts, certain details that were *sui generis*,[34] couldn't be overlooked any longer. Explosions were proliferating with

---

[34] *Translator's note.* Latin: "in a class of their own."

fearful intensity. I can compare them only to the racket made by a large number of buggies driven at high speed down a cobblestone street. It was one endless roll of thunder.

And whenever some electrical phenomenon made it lurch around, that berserk compass also lent credence to my views. The mineral crust was threatening to crack, the sections of granite would come back together, the crevice would fill in, this whole space would be packed solid, and us wee mites were about to be crushed in its fearsome clutches.

"Uncle, uncle!" I exclaimed. "We're done for!"

"What are you afraid of now?" he answered me with surprising calmness. "What is it this time?"

"Here's what it is! Look at these shaking walls, this mass of rock coming apart, this sweltering heat, this bubbling water, this steam that's growing denser, this needle that's out of its mind—all these clues point to an earthquake!"

My uncle shook his head gently.

"Is that so," he said.

"Yes!"

"I think you're mistaken, my boy."

"What! Don't you recognize the signs?"

"Of an earthquake? Not at all. I'm expecting something better."

"What do you mean?"

"An eruption, Axel."

"An eruption?" I said. "We're in the chimney of an active volcano?"

"I believe so," the professor said with a smile, "and it's the best thing that could happen to us."

The best thing! Had my uncle gone insane? What was the meaning of these words? Why was he so calm, why was he smiling?

"Excuse me?" I snarled. "We've gotten trapped in an eruption! Fate has dumped us right in the way of molten lava, burning stones, bubbling water, and all sorts of eruptive materials! We're going to be chucked, disgorged, ejected, spewed, and spat into the air along with hunks of rock, showers of ash or slag, and whirlwinds of flame—and it's the best thing that could happen to us?"

"That's right," the professor replied, looking at me over his eyeglasses. "Because it's the only chance we have of getting back to the surface of the earth!"

I'll skip the thousand different ideas that crossed my mind. My uncle was right, absolutely right, and never had he struck me as more daring and more confident than at this moment when he was waiting for an eruption and calmly figuring out his chances!

Meanwhile we kept rising; this ascending movement continued through the night; the uproar increased around us; I was close to suffocating, I felt that my last hour was about to toll—and yet so peculiar is the human mind, I indulged in some truly infantile guesswork. But I was the slave of my thoughts, I had no control over them!

Obviously we were being ejected by eruptive pressures; under the raft were bubbling waters, then under the waters nothing but lava, a batter with rocks mixed in that would be scattered every which way at the top of the crater. So we were in the chimney of a volcano. No doubts on that score.

But instead of an extinct volcano like Snaefells, this time we were dealing with a volcano that was fully active. So I wondered what mountain this could be, and into what part of the world we would be disgorged.

Into the northerly regions, without a doubt. Before it went berserk, our compass had never wavered in this respect. From Cape Saknussemm it took us due north for many hundreds of miles. Now then, were we back under Iceland? Were we destined to be ejected from the crater of Mt. Hekla or from one of the seven other fire-breathing mountains on that island? West along this parallel, within a radius of some 1,200 miles, I was aware of only the poorly known volcanoes on the northwest coast of America. To the east there was just the one at latitude 80°, Esk Crater on Jan Mayen Island—not far from Spitsbergen! Of course such craters weren't in short supply and some are spacious enough to spew up an entire army! But which of them would serve as our way out? That's what I was trying to predict.

Toward morning the ascending movement picked up speed. As we neared the surface of the globe, it was getting hotter instead of cooler, which meant the effect was entirely local, the result of volcanic activity. Our current way of getting places removed every doubt from my mind. Generated by steam building up in the heart of the earth, an enormous pressure—a pressure equal to several hundred atmospheres—was propelling us irresistibly. But it left us vulnerable to countless dangers!

Lurid glimmers were soon filling this vertical hallway, now getting wider; to the right and left, I saw deep corridors that looked like immense tunnels with dense fumes wafting from them; tongues of crackling flame licked at the walls.

"Uncle! Look, look!" I exclaimed.

"Fine, we've got some sulfurous flames! Nothing could be more normal during an eruption."

"But what if they surround us?"

"They won't surround us."

"But what if we suffocate?"

"We won't suffocate. The hallway's growing wider, and if necessary we'll get off the raft and take shelter in some crevasse."

"What about the water? The water's rising!"

"There *is* no more water, Axel, just a sort of lava batter that's taking us up with it to the mouth of the crater."

The column of liquid had indeed vanished, to be replaced by eruptive materials that were of some density and yet still bubbling. The heat was getting unbearable, and if we'd held out a thermometer in this air, it would have registered over 160° Fahrenheit. I was dripping with sweat. If we hadn't been ascending so swiftly, we surely would have suffocated.

But the professor didn't follow through on his proposition to get off the raft, which was all to the good. These few poorly fastened logs gave us a solid surface, a form of support we otherwise would have lacked.

Around eight o'clock in the morning, for the first time, there was a new hitch. All at once the ascending movement ceased. The raft stood absolutely still.

"What's going on?" I asked, as jarred by this sudden stop as if we'd had a collision.

"Time for a break," my uncle replied.

"Is the eruption slacking off?"

"I certainly hope not."

I stood up. I tried to see around me. Maybe the raft had gotten caught on some protruding rock, creating a temporary roadblock for the eruptive materials. If so, we needed to get loose on the double.

Nothing of the sort. The column of ash, slag, and rocky rubble had ceased rising on its own.

"Has the eruption come to a halt?" I exclaimed.

"Oh, so that's what worries you, my boy," my uncle put in, gritting his teeth. "Trust me, this peaceful interlude is only temporary; it has lasted for five minutes already, and before long we'll resume our ascent to the mouth of the crater."

While he was saying this, the professor kept checking his chronometer; his latest prophecies were to come true as well. Soon our raft got caught up again in a quick, erratic movement that lasted about two minutes, then it stopped once more.

"Good," my uncle put in, noting the time. "We'll get going again in another ten minutes."

"Ten minutes?"

"Right. We're dealing with a volcano whose eruptions are sporadic. We can catch our breath when it does."

It was as true as true can be. At the designated minute we shot upward again with tremendous speed. We had to clamp onto the raft's logs so we weren't tossed overboard. Then the pressure let up.

Since then I've pondered this odd phenomenon without finding a satisfactory explanation. Anyhow it struck me as obvious that weren't situated in the volcano's main chimney but in a secondary conduit where we were experiencing a recoil effect.

As for how often this process was repeated, I can't say. All I know is that every time the movement resumed, we shot upward with increasing force, as if we were flying off on some projectile. During rest breaks we suffocated; during flight times the burning air left me short of breath. For a second I thought how delightful it would feel to suddenly be in the High Arctic regions with a cold snap of around -20° Fahrenheit. In my overwrought imagination I was strolling across the snowy plains of the far north, eager for a chance to roll around on those frozen carpets at the pole! But I'd been jarred by so many repeated jolts, my mind seemed to be going little by little. If Hans hadn't grabbed me, I would have smashed my skull more than once against those granite walls.

Consequently I don't have any exact memory of what took place during the hours that followed. I have a confused impression of continual explosions, of the mountain shaking, of our raft getting caught up in a circular motion. It undulated on the waves of lava, ash falling all around us. Fires roared on every side. You would have sworn some immense fan was stirring up a hurricane of underground flames. I saw Hans's face one last time in the glimmers from the blaze, and the only feeling left in me was the ghastly terror that fills a condemned man when he's tied to the muzzle of a cannon, then it fires and scatters his limbs across the sky.

44

WHEN I OPENED my eyes again, I felt our guide's sinewy fingers clutching my belt. His other hand was holding onto my uncle. Though I didn't have any grievous injuries, I was a broken man whose muscles ached all over. I saw that I was lying on a mountain slope, two steps away from a chasm that the tiniest movement would have pitched me into. When I'd started rolling down the side of that crater, Hans had saved my life.

"Where are we?" my uncle asked, sounding thoroughly peeved at being back in the outside world.

The hunter shrugged his shoulders, conveying that he had no idea.

"Is this Iceland?" I said.

"*Nej*," Hans replied.

"Excuse me? Did you say no?" the professor exclaimed.

"Hans has to be wrong," I said, getting up.

After the countless surprises of this journey, a shock still lay in store for us. I'd assumed we would see a volcanic cone that was covered with perpetual snow, surrounded by the barren wastelands of the far north, lit up by the pale rays of a polar sky, and located above the highest latitudes; but contrary to all these expectations, the Icelander, my uncle, and I were lying midway down a mountainside baked by a hot sun whose fiery rays were eating us alive.

I refused to believe what I saw; but since my body was being subjected to some serious charbroiling, the facts weren't in dispute. We'd emerged from the crater half naked and had done without that shining orb for two whole months—and now it was lavishing its heat and light on us, drenching us in waves of dazzling radiance.

Once my eyes readjusted to this brilliance that they'd forgotten about, I used them to see where I'd gone wrong in my thinking. I prayed we were at least near Spitsbergen, and I wasn't in a mood to give up this idea easily.

The professor was the first of us to open his mouth and he said:

"This really doesn't look much like Iceland."

"How about Jan Mayen Island?" I responded.

"Also wrong, my boy. This definitely isn't a northern volcano—they have granite hillsides and snowcaps on top!"

"But—"

"Use your eyes, Axel!"

Over our heads, no more than 500 feet up, gaped the volcano's crater; every fifteen minutes, along with quite a loud explosion, a tall pillar of flame burst out of it, pumice stones, ash, and lava included in the mix. I could feel spasmodic movements from the mountain, which seemed to take breaths in good whale fashion, then periodically exhale wind and fire from its enormous blowhole. Below us sheets of eruptive materials stretched 700 or 800 feet down a pretty steep slope, indicating that the volcano had a total elevation of some 1,800 feet. Its base vanished beneath an honest-to-goodness plantation of green trees, among which I made out some olive trees, fig trees, and vines loaded with ruby red grapes.

Not exactly reminiscent of the arctic regions, you must admit.

As soon as a person's eyes had traveled past this lush locality, they instantly started roving across the waters of a wonderful sea or lake, which converted this magic land into an island several miles wide. To the east a little harbor was on display, in front of it a few houses, inside it vessels of a strange class swaying with the undulations of the azure waves. Beyond it chains of islets emerged from this liquid expanse, so plentiful that they looked like a huge colony of ants. To the west a distant coastline curved toward the horizon; on one part of it sat the pleasingly shaped outline of a blue mountain range; on a more remote part stood a prodigiously tall volcanic cone, a wreath of smoke quivering around its summit. Up north lay an immense expanse of water, sparkling in the sunlight, broken up here and there by mastheads or the bulging shapes of sails swelling in the wind.

The unexpectedness of this sight made its beauties a hundred times more remarkable.

"Where are we?" I kept saying under my breath.

Hans closed his eyes, not concerned; my uncle looked around, not understanding.

"Whatever mountain this is," he finally said, "it's getting a little hot hereabouts; the discharges haven't let up, and we surely didn't go to the trouble of exiting during an eruption just to be hit on the head by pieces of falling rock. Let's climb down and find out where we stand. Besides, I'm dying of hunger and thirst."

Clearly the professor wasn't blessed with a contemplative nature. If it was up to me, I would have forgotten my exhaustion and bodily needs and stayed in that location a good while longer—but I had to go with my companions.

The volcano's sides were made up of steeply pitched slopes; we skidded through real quagmires of ash, dodging the lava flows that stretched out like fiery snakes. I talked nonstop as we descended, because my mind was so full of ideas that I just had to put them into words.

"We're in Asia," I exclaimed, "on the shores of India, among the islands of Malaysia, or in the heart of Oceania! We've gone halfway around the globe from Europe and we've ended up at exactly the opposite location."

"But what about our compass?" my uncle responded.

"Yes, what about it!" I said in a baffled voice. "Abiding by our compass, we've consistently traveled north."

"So it isn't telling the truth?"

"The truth? Uh . . ."

"Unless this happens to be the North Pole!"

"The pole? No, but . . ."

It was a bewildering turn of events. I wasn't sure what to think.

Meanwhile we'd drawn nearer to that greenery our eyes found so pleasing. I was feeling pangs of both hunger and thirst. Luckily, after a two-hour walk, we came in view of a lovely countryside totally covered with olive trees, pomegranate trees, and grapevines, all looking as if they were free to the public. As strapped as we were, however, we weren't about to read the fine print. What a joy it was to press those tasty fruits against our lips, to sink our teeth into bunches of grapes from those ruby red vines! In the grass not far off, under some delectable shade trees, I discovered a freshwater spring, and we dipped our hands and faces into it with rapturous delight.

While we were wallowing in all these soothing forms of relaxation, a youth appeared between two clumps of olive trees.

"Aha!" I exclaimed. "Here's a native of this happy land!"

He was a shabby little specimen, quite wretchedly dressed and rather sickly—and our appearance seemed to frighten him a good deal; half naked and unshaven as we were, we cut very poor figures indeed, and unless this country was the headquarters for a gang of thieves, there was a good chance we would scare the daylights out of the residents.

Just as the urchin was taking to his heels, Hans ran after him and brought him back while he helplessly kicked and hollered.

My uncle began by comforting the boy as well as he could, saying to him in his best German:

"My little friend, what's the name of this mountain?"

The youth didn't reply.

"Fine," my uncle said. "We're definitely not in Germany."

He repeated the question in English.

The youth still didn't reply. It was very puzzling to me.

"Is he a deaf-mute, then?" snapped the professor, who was quite proud of his status as a polyglot and threw out the same question in French.

The youth remained silent.

"All right, let's try Italian," my uncle continued, and he said in that language:

"*Dove siamo?*"

"Yes, where are we?" I echoed impatiently.

Again no reply from the youth.

"Oh drat! Will you say something!" my uncle shouted, starting to get angry and shaking the youth by the ears. "*Come si noma questa isola?*"[35]

"*Stromboli,*" the little shepherd replied, then broke free from Hans's grasp and ran through the olive trees toward the meadow.

We didn't give him a thought. Stromboli! What an effect this unexpected name had on my mind! We were in the heart of the Mediterranean, out among those Aeolian Islands of mythological fame, off Sicily on that ancient isle also known as Strongyle where the god of the winds, Aeolus, stood ready to unleash his squalls and downpours. And those blue mountains curving to the east were the Calabrian Mountains. And that volcano rearing above the southern horizon was Mt. Etna, ferocious Mt. Etna itself.

"Stromboli! Stromboli!" I said over and over.

My uncle chimed in with both words and gestures. We were practically singing a duet!

Oh, what a journey, what a wondrous journey! Going in by one volcano, we'd come out by another—another located over 3,000 miles away from Snaefells, from that barren country of Iceland dumped at the edge of the earth! Explorer's luck had transferred us right to the heart of the most pleasing region in the world. We'd exchanged the land of perpetual snow for one of endless greenery; we'd left those gray fogs that overhang the polar zones and we'd come to the azure skies of Sicily!

After a sumptuous meal of fruit and sparkling water, we took to the trail again, heading for the harbor of Stromboli. It didn't strike us as a good idea to say how we'd arrived on this island: Italians are superstitious souls and they wouldn't fail to view us as demons spewed up from the depths of hell; regretfully, therefore, we had to give out that we were humble castaways. It was less glorious but safer.

On the way I heard my uncle mumbling:

"But the compass! The compass pointed north! How can that occurrence be explained?"

"Ye gods," I said, looking down my nose. "Just don't bother explaining, that's the easiest way!"

"By thunder! A professor at the Johanneum who can't find the reason for a universal phenomenon? How humiliating that would be!"

Talking away like this, half naked, leather moneybags down around his hips, my uncle straightened his glasses on his nose and turned back into the dreaded professor of mineralogy

An hour after we'd left the grove of olive trees, we arrived at the harbor of San Vincenzo, where Hans demanded payment for his thirteenth week of service; it was doled out to him along with our hearty handshakes.

If he didn't share our own very natural feelings at that instant, at least he indulged in a gesture that was, for him, amazingly expressive.

As he lightly pressed our two hands with his fingertips, he cracked a smile.

---

[35] *Translator's note.* Italian: "What's the name of this island?"

45

WHICH BRINGS US to the conclusion of a narrative that will provoke disbelief even among people who normally are amazed at nothing. But I'm armed in advance against human skepticism.

The Stromboli fishermen welcomed us with the compassion castaways deserve. They gave us clothing and food. On August 31, following a 48-hour wait, we traveled to Messina aboard a little speronara;[36] after resting up there for a few days, we were completely over our exhaustion.

On Friday, September 4, we left aboard the *Volturne*, a mailboat in the French imperial shipping line, and three days later we set foot in Marseilles without a worry in our heads other than that damned compass. This bewildering topic continued to seriously irk me. On the evening of September 9, we arrived in Hamburg.

Martha's astonishment and Grauben's delight are matters I won't even attempt to describe.

"Now that you're a hero, Axel," my darling fiancée told me, "you won't ever have to leave me again!"

I looked at her. She was smiling with tears in her eyes.

As the reader can imagine, Professor Lidenbrock's return created a sensation in Hamburg. Thanks to Martha's lack of discretion, the news of his departure for the center of the earth had spread all over the world. Folks refused to believe it, and when they saw him again, they still refused.

Even so, Hans's presence and various disclosures arriving from Iceland gradually changed public opinion.

By then my uncle had become a great man, and as for me, I was the nephew of a great man, which is already a step up. Hamburg threw a banquet in our honor. A public meeting took place at the Johanneum and there the professor gave an account of his expedition, omitting only the details that con-

cerned our compass. This same day he deposited Saknussemm's document in the town archives, expressing his deep regret that due to circumstances more powerful than his willpower, he couldn't follow in the Icelandic explorer's footsteps all the way to the center of the earth. He was humble in his moment of glory and his reputation grew.

Inevitably, all these honors made him some jealous enemies. He had more than his fair share: since his ideas were based on hard facts and yet bucked scientific trends on the issue of a central fire, he waged some notable arguments, both in print and in person, with experts from every country.

For my part I can't accept his concept of falling temperatures: despite what I've witnessed, I believe—and will always believe—in a central heat source; but I concede that under certain conditions that are still poorly defined, the workings of natural phenomena can alter this law.

While academia was all aquiver with these issues, my uncle experienced some genuine grief. Despite his entreaties, Hans left Hamburg; the man to whom we owed everything wouldn't let us pay off our debt. He'd gotten homesick for Iceland.

"Farval," he said one day. And with this simple word of parting, he set out for Reykjavik and arrived there undamaged.

We'd grown exceptionally attached to our gallant eiderdown hunter; though he's gone, he'll never be forgotten by those whose lives he saved, and I certainly will see him one last time before I die.

To conclude, I must add that this *Journey to the Center of the Earth* created an enormous sensation around the world. It was translated and printed in every language; top-ranking newspapers excerpted the highlights, which were dissected, debated, denounced, and defended with equal conviction in the camps of both believers and skeptics. For a rarity, my uncle enjoyed the glory he'd won in his own lifetime—and Mr. P. T. Barnum even proposed to "exhibit" him at top dollar across the states of the Union!

But in the midst of all this glory, a fly kept flitting into the ointment—a gadfly, you could say. One topic was still a source of

---

[36] *Translator's note:* Single-masted Italian sailboat.

bewilderment, the issue of our compass, and a baffling phenomenon can be mental torture for a scientist. Well, a life of perfect happiness was in store for my uncle, thank Heaven.

One day, while tidying up an assortment of minerals in his study, I noticed the notorious compass and gave it another look.

It had lain in its corner there for six months, little suspecting what a nuisance it had been.

Suddenly I froze, dumbfounded! I let out a yell. The professor ran up.

"What is it?" he asked.

"This compass . . . !"

"Well?"

"The needle's pointing south instead of north!"

"What do you mean?"

"Look—the poles are reversed!"

"Reversed?"

My uncle looked, compared, and gave a magnificent leap that shook the house.

What a light went on in both of our minds at the same instant!

"Hence," he exclaimed after he got his voice back, "when we arrived at Cape Saknussemm, the needle on this blasted compass pointed south instead of north?"

"Obviously."

"Then that explains our error. But what phenomenon could have caused this reversal of the poles?"

"Nothing could be simpler."

"Out with it, my boy."

"During that hurricane in the Lidenbrock Sea, the ball of fire that magnetized the iron on our raft simply disoriented the compass!"

"Aha!" the professor exclaimed with a burst of laughter. "It had an electrifying experience, you might say!"

From that day forward my uncle was the happiest scholar alive, and I was the happiest man, because my pretty Virlander resigned her post as ward and accepted an appointment at the house on Königstrasse in the two-fold capacity of niece and wife. Her uncle, needless to add, was the renowned Professor Otto Lidenbrock, corresponding member of every scientific, geographical, and mineralogical society in the five corners of the world.

From the Earth to the Moon

A Direct Flight in 97 Hours and 13 Minutes

First published in 1865

From the Earth to the Moon is a masterpiece of gallows humor. At bottom it's an antiwar satire, only it doesn't lampoon politicians or soldiers but the American weapons industry, manufacturers of guns, shells, and explosives. So Verne gives us a group protagonist, a band of Civil War arms dealers named the Gun Club, God-fearing fellows who would like to play God themselves: they see the bombshell as "the most brilliant manifestation of human power . . . by creating it, man becomes more like our Creator." They're the prototype of our military-industrial complex and they have an exalted mission: "the sole concerns of this learned society were the destruction of mankind for philanthropic purposes and the improvement of wartime weapons to help spread the benefits of civilization."

Verne's comedy gets even blacker as he goes into specifics about his gun clubbers. For instance, one weapon they hope to improve is a cannonball for taking out cavalry, but they have trouble arranging a field trial: "even if the horses had been agreeable to the experiment, there was an unfortunate shortage of amenable men." Otherwise they're delighted to participate in the ongoing conflict: "they felt legitimate pride whenever a battle report put the victim count at ten times the number of projectiles dispensed." And they themselves are eloquent testimony to their wartime achievements: "wooden legs, hinged arms, hooks in place of hands . . . the Gun Club's membership boasted barely one arm for every four people and just two legs for every six."

Which means they're cripples, and in more than one sense. When the Civil War ends and peace finally comes, they see it as "disastrous," something "woeful and lamentable." What are they to do with themselves? Their most militant member argues for commencing new hostilities against assorted foreign powers (England, France, and Mexico in that order), but it's no use. Since they haven't any human targets to shoot at, our out-of-work manufacturers settle for firing a shell at the moon.

Of course schemes for making contact with the moon have been around since caveman days, but Verne's two lunar novels were the first to apply industrial-strength science and engineering to the prospect. Down through the years, therefore, these books have garnered detailed attention, some of it carping: issues of air resistance and gees acceleration make Verne's method impossible for manned flights. But much of this attention has been admiring: astronaut Frank Borman praised Verne's uncanny anticipation of the 1968 moon mission, the fictional vehicle's resemblance to the Apollo 8 capsule, their startling similarities in dimensions, flight duration, takeoff, and splashdown. In the same vein space scientist Wernher von Braun concluded that Verne's fiction is about "as accurate as knowledge of the time permitted." Closer to our day Gerald Bull, John Hunter, and other North American engineers continue to investigate Verne's MacGuffin of a giant cannon that can shoot objects into space: they insist it's an achievable and cost-effective concept.

So the Gun Club marches on. Likewise the black comedy. Yet as the book proceeds, Verne doesn't target America alone: Chapter 12 makes clear that he was peeved at other nations as well, including England and his own homeland under Napoleon III. At times, then, he aims his shafts at most of industrialized humanity—as when he summarizes his novel's bottom-line approach to making contact with our satellite: "It came down to firing a projectile at her . . . a rather harsh way of initiating relations, though quite popular in civilized countries." *Translator*.

1

THE GUN CLUB

DURING THE CIVIL WAR in the United States, a highly influential new club sprang up in the town of Baltimore in the heart of Maryland. You know how energetically the military spirit spread through this population of shipowners, shopkeepers, and mechanics. Ordinary tradesmen vaulted over their counters and became makeshift captains, colonels, and generals without ever visiting the admissions office at West Point;[1] it wasn't long before they matched their Old World colleagues at "the art of war," and like the latter, they won their victories through lavish outlays of munitions, money, and manpower.

But where the Americans conspicuously outdid the Europeans was in the science of ballistics. It wasn't that their weapons were more perfectly designed, but that they boasted exceptional dimensions and consequently reached ranges unheard of till then. When it comes to grazing, plunging, or head-on fire, to diagonal, flank, or rear-guard shooting, the English, French, and Prussians know all there is to know; but their cannons, howitzers, and mortars are just pocket pistols next to the fearsome mechanisms of the American artillery.

This shouldn't amaze anybody. As the world's foremost mechanics, Yankees are to engineering what Italians are to music and Germans to metaphysics—it's in their blood. So nothing could be more natural than for them to apply their daring cleverness to the science of ballistics. Ergo these gigantic cannons—a good deal less beneficial than their sewing machines but just as amazing and even more acclaimed. Parrott, Dahlgren, and Rodman worked wonders in their field, as you know. Such European gun makers as Armstrong, Palliser, and Treuille de Beaulieu could only bow to their competitors across the sea.

So in that dreadful conflict between Northerners and Southerners, artillerymen looked down on everybody else; Union newspapers heartily applauded their latest inventions, and from the lowliest shopkeeper to the greenest nincompoop, folks racked their brains day and night calculating demented flight paths.

Now then, when an American gets an idea, he looks for a second American to share it. If there are three of them, they elect a president and two secretaries. If four, they add on a filing clerk, and the office is up and running. If five, they call a general meeting, and the club is in full swing. That's how it went in Baltimore. The first man to invent a new cannon formed an alliance with the first man to cast it and the first man to bore it. This was the nucleus of the Gun Club.[2] One month after it had been formed, it boasted 1,833 full members and 30,575 corresponding members.

The association insisted on one condition as a *sine qua non*[3] for anybody who wanted to join: the individual needed to have designed—or, at the very least, improved—a cannon; failing a cannon, a firearm of some sort. But to tell the truth, inventors of fifteen-round revolvers, swivel rifles, or sword guns didn't get much respect. Artillerymen took precedence over them in all circumstances.

"The esteem they enjoy," one of the Gun Club's shrewdest speakers said one day, "is in strict proportion to the size of their cannons and in direct ratio to the square of the distances reached by their projectiles!"

This amounted to turning Newton's law of universal gravitation into a code of etiquette.

Once the Gun Club had been established, you can easily imagine the results achieved in their field by the inventive genius of the Americans. Their engines of war took on colossal proportions, while their projectiles shot beyond any acceptable limits and sliced innocent bystanders in half. All their inventions left the timid instruments of Europe's artilleries far behind. Judge for yourself from the following figures.

---

[1] Military academy in the United States.

[2] Actually a "Cannon Club."

[3] *Translator's note.* Latin: an "absolute essential."

Formerly, in the "good old days," a 36-pound shell fired from 300 feet away could go through the flanks of 36 horses plus 68 men. This was the art in its infancy. Projectiles have come a long way since then. Rodman's cannon shoots a half-ton shell seven miles and would easily topple 150 horses and 300 men. There was actual talk at the Gun Club of conducting serious tests. But even if the horses had been agreeable to this experiment, there was an unfortunate shortage of amenable men.

Be that as it may, these cannons had a thoroughly murderous effect, and at each barrage foes fell like wheat under a scythe. Next to such projectiles, who gave a fig for the notorious shell that put 25 men out of action near Coutras in 1587, or the one that killed 40 foot soldiers near Zorndorf in 1758, or that Austrian cannon outside Kesselsdorf in 1745, which laid 70 enemies low every time it fired? Who cared about those startling volleys in Jena or Austerlitz that determined the outcomes of the battles? The Civil War in America had something very different to show. During the Battle of Gettysburg, a rifled cannon fired a conical projectile that hit 173 Confederates; and at the crossing of the Potomac, a Rodman shell sent 215 Southerners to an obviously better world. We also need to mention that fearsome mortar invented by J. T. Maston, a distinguished member and secretary for life of the Gun Club: it achieved still more murderous results and at its test firing killed 337 people—simply by blowing up!

What can we add to these figures, so eloquent in themselves? Nothing. Accordingly you can accept without argument the following calculation worked out by the statistician Pitcairn: by dividing the number of Gun Club members into the number of victims downed by their shells, you'll find that each of the former has personally killed an average of 2,375-and-a-fraction men.

Looking at such a figure, it's obvious that the sole concerns of this learned society were the destruction of mankind for philanthropic purposes and the improvement of wartime weapons to help spread the benefits of civilization.

It was a gathering of Exterminating Angels who were the jolliest good fellows deep down.

We should add that these Yankees faced every ordeal gallantly, did more than simply work out formulas, and paid their dues in person. They included in their number officers of all ranks from lieutenants to generals, and military men of all ages from those just getting started in the profession of arms to those who had grown gray behind their gun carriages. A good many had gone to their rest on the battlefield and their names appear on the Gun Club's honor roll; as for those who made it back, most of them wore the badges of their indisputable bravery. Crutches, wooden legs, hinged arms, hooks in place of hands, india-rubber jaws, silver braincases, platinum noses—this assemblage had them all, and the aforesaid Mr. Pitcairn likewise calculates that the Gun Club's membership boasted barely one arm for every four people and just two legs for every six.

But these valiant artillerymen weren't finicky about such things and they felt legitimate pride whenever a battle report put the victim count at ten times the number of projectiles dispensed.

One day, however, one woeful and lamentable day, the war's survivors made peace, the barrages gradually came to a halt, mortars fell silent, howitzers were muzzled for the long term, cannons lowered their heads and reentered their arsenals, piles of cannonballs adorned the public parks, bloodstained memories faded away, magnificent cotton crops sprang up in the richly fertilized fields, mourners packed away their funeral garb along with their grief, and the Gun Club sank into a state of total lethargy.

Some drudges, relentless overachievers, went right back to their ballistics calculations; they kept envisioning gigantic bombshells and matchless missiles. But what good were theories that couldn't be put into practice? Accordingly the meeting halls emptied out, their attendants dozed off in the anterooms, newspapers mildewed on the tables, dismal sounds of snoring came from the dark corners, and the once-boisterous members of the Gun Club, now reduced to silence by a disastrous peace, drifted off into daydreams of firearms they would never fire!

"It's depressing!" said gallant Tom Hunter one evening, his wooden legs charring in front of the smoking-room hearth. "There's nothing to do! Nothing to look forward to! What a boring existence! Where are the days when we woke up every morning to the joyful boom of cannons?"

"Those days are no more," replied the swaggering Bilsby, trying to stretch the arms he now lacked. "What fun it used to be! You designed a howitzer, and the instant it was cast, you dashed off to try it out on the other side; then you returned to camp after some encouraging words from Sherman or a handshake from McClellan. But today our generals are back behind their counters, and instead of shooting projectiles, they're shipping harmless bales of cotton. St. Barbara help us! There's no future left for artillery in America!"

"You're right, Bilsby!" Colonel Blomsberry exclaimed. "What a cruel letdown! One day you give up your quiet routine, you work to master the use of arms, you leave Baltimore for the battlefield, you perform like a hero, then two or three years later you fritter away the fruits of all that experience, end up not doing a stinking thing, and stand around with your hands in your pockets."

Despite these words, the valiant colonel would have had a hard time indicating his idleness in this way, though he wasn't short of pockets.

"And not another war in sight!" said the notorious J. T. Maston, scratching his gutta-percha skull with his iron hook. "Not a cloud on the horizon, and right when the science of artillery has so much work to do! Just this morning I myself finished the design for a new mortar, complete with ground plan, cross section, and side view—and it's destined to change the laws of warfare!"

"Really?" Tom Hunter remarked, automatically thinking of that last effort by the honorable J. T. Maston.

"Really," the latter replied. "But what good did it do to finish all that research, to solve all those problems? Wasn't it just wasted effort? The citizens of the New World seem bent on living in peace, and our warmongering *Tribune* has sunk to predicting that the next catastrophes will only come from a shameful increase in population."[4]

"But Maston," Colonel Blomsberry went on, "they're always fighting in Europe to defend the principle of national independence."

"So?"

"So maybe there'll be something to get into over there, and if they accept our services . . ."

"What are you saying?" Bilsby snapped. "We should offer our ballistics know-how to foreigners?"

"It would beat doing nothing at all," the colonel shot back.

"Certainly it would," J. T. Maston said, "but that's an expedient we mustn't ever resort to."

"And why not?" the colonel asked.

"Because in the Old World their notions of bettering themselves are the opposite of all our customs in America. Those fellows think you can't become a four-star general unless you start out as a second lieutenant, which is as good as saying you can't holler 'Fire!' unless you've cast the cannon yourself! Now then, that's simply—"

"—ridiculous!" finished Tom Hunter, nicking the arms of his easy chair with jabs of his bowie knife.[5] "And since it's the way things are, all that's left for us is to grow tobacco or process whale oil!"

"What!" J. T. Maston orated in a ringing voice. "We won't use our declining years to make new and improved firearms? We won't get another opportunity to test out the range of our projectiles? Our blazing cannons will never again light up the skies? No international difficulty will ever give us a chance to declare war against some overseas power? The French won't sink a single one of our steamers, or the English defy international law and hang three or four of our citizens?"

---

[4] The *New York Tribune* was the most aggressive abolitionist newspaper in the Union.

[5] Dagger with a wide blade.

"No such luck," Colonel Blomsberry replied. "No, Maston, not one of those incidents will happen, and if it did, we wouldn't even take advantage of it! America is becoming more and more oblivious every day—we're turning into old women!"

"We've gotten humble!" Bilsby remarked.

"And they're humiliating us!" Tom Hunter shot back.

"It's only too true, every bit of it!" J. T. Maston contended with fresh fervor. "There are a thousand reasons in the air to have a fight and nobody's fighting! We're sparing the arms and legs of people who aren't putting them to any good use! And look here, we needn't go very far to find grounds for war—didn't North America once belong to the English?"

"Sure," Tom Hunter replied, angrily stoking the fire with the tip of his crutch.

"All right," J. T. Maston went on, "why shouldn't it be England's turn to belong to Americans?"

"It would only be fair," Colonel Blomsberry shot back.

"Go propose it to the President of the United States," J. T. Maston snapped, "and see the reception he gives you!"

"It won't be a warm one," Bilsby muttered between the four teeth he'd brought back from the battlefield.

"Ye gods," J. T. Maston exclaimed, "at the next election he's not getting *my* vote!"

"Nor ours either!" replied these warmongering amputees with one voice.

"In conclusion, meanwhile," J. T. Maston went on, "if I'm not given an opportunity to try out my new mortar on an actual battlefield, I'll resign my membership in the Gun Club, then go out to some savanna in Arkansas and die!"

The daring J. T. Maston got this reply from his conversation partners: "We'll be right behind you!"

Now then, that was where things stood, attitudes were getting worse and worse, and there was a growing danger of the club's being disbanded, when an unexpected development occurred just in time to avert such a grievous catastrophe.

The day right after the foregoing conver-sation, every member of the organization received a notice that read as follows:

Baltimore
October 3

The President of the Gun Club has the honor to inform his colleagues that at this month's meeting on the 5th, he'll make an announcement on a subject that will keenly interest them. Consequently he hereby begs them to set aside any other business and accept his invitation to attend.

Very cordially,
IMPEY BARBICANE,
P.G.C.

2

PRESIDENT BARBICANE'S ANNOUNCEMENT

AT EIGHT O'CLOCK in the evening on October 5, jam-packed crowds piled into the Gun Club's lounges at 21 Union Square. All the members of the organization living in Baltimore had accepted their president's invitation. As for corresponding members, express trains were unloading them by the hundreds into the city streets, and as big as the "meeting room" was, it couldn't seat this host of learned visitors; accordingly they spilled into the neighboring halls, down the corridors, and across the courtyards outside; there they bumped into the general public piling through the doors, everybody trying to get to the front of the line, all eager to hear President Barbicane's important announcement, pushing, shoving, and jostling with that freedom of action characteristic of crowds reared on notions of "self-government."[6]

That evening a stranger passing through Baltimore couldn't have gotten into the main hall even by paying through the nose; it was exclusively reserved for local or corresponding members; there were no seats left

---

[6] Government by the people.

for anybody else, and town dignitaries, including officers on the board of selectmen,[7] had to mingle with crowds of their own constituents in order to catch the news from inside on the fly.

Meanwhile that immense "meeting room" offered the eyes an unusual sight. Its huge premises were wonderfully suited to their purpose. Secured to the ceiling by slender fastenings of die-cut wrought iron, its lofty columns consisted of cannons upended on bases supplied by heavy mortars. Arranged over the walls were picturesque panoplies of arms—networks of blunderbusses, muskets, matchlocks, carbines, every type of firearm old or new. The gaslight came full blast from a thousand revolvers grouped to form chandeliers, while bouquets of pistols topped off this marvelous light show, along with candelabra made from rifles tied in bunches. There were models of cannons, bronze reproductions, bullet-riddled gun sights, armor plate shattered by Gun Club shells, assortments of ramrods and swabs, strings of bombshells, necklaces of projectiles, garlands of missiles—in short, a whole artilleryman's tool kit dazzled the eyes, and you almost thought the true purpose of this amazing display was decorative rather than deadly.

In the place of honor and housed inside a splendid showcase, you could see a shard from the base of a mortar barrel, all smashed and twisted from the pressure of the gunpowder—precious rubble from J. T. Maston's cannon.

At the end of the hall, the president sat in a broad open area, four secretaries nearby. His seat of office was held aloft by a sculpted gun carriage and its overall shape emulated the mighty outlines of a 32-inch mortar; it was aimed at a 90° angle and suspended on metal pegs, which meant the president could sway back and forth as if he were in a "rocker," a very pleasant sensation during hot weather.[8] His desk was a huge piece of sheet

iron resting on six short-bodied naval cannons; on top of it you saw an exquisitely designed, delicately engraved inkstand—made from a Biscayan musket ball—and an exploding hand bell, which, if need be, could emit a bang like a revolver. During heated arguments even this new breed of bell was barely enough to drown the voices of that legion of agitated artillerymen.

In front of the desk, benches were set out in zigzags—like ramparts guarding an entrenched position—and formed a sequence of bastions and connecting walls where every Gun Club member sat; and this particular evening, you might say, all of them were "manning their battle stations." They were familiar enough with their president to know that he wouldn't have troubled his colleagues without the most serious reasons.

Impey Barbicane was a man of forty, cool, calm, severe, exceptionally earnest and single-minded; as accurate as a chronometer, his nerve equal to anything, his will unshakeable; adventurous but not starry-eyed, always bringing practical ideas to his most reckless undertakings; your New Englander beyond compare, a colonial Northerner, the descendant of those Roundheads who gave such grief to the Stuarts in Britain, and the implacable enemy of Southern gentlemen, those old Cavaliers in his new homeland. In short, he was a thoroughgoing Yankee.

Barbicane had made a huge fortune in the lumber business; appointed director of artillery during the war, he turned out to be a gold mine of ideas; a daring inventor, he contributed mightily to the advances made in that wing and gave a unique impetus to experimental matters.

He was an individual of medium stature and one of those rare exceptions in the Gun Club who had all his limbs intact. His facial features stood out sharply, as if they'd been marked off with a T square and an awl; and if it's true that you need to see a man in profile in order to guess his disposition, this view of Barbicane gave the clearest signs of energy, daring, and composure.

Just then he was keeping still in his easy chair, silent, engrossed, meditating in the shade of his stovepipe hat—one of those

---

[7] City administrators elected by the citizenry.

[8] In the United States rocking chairs are in wide use.

black silk cylinders that always seem tightly screwed onto American skulls.

Nearby his colleagues were chatting noisily without disturbing him; they questioned each other, they threw out guesses about what was up, they studied their president and tried—vainly—to figure out that x factor from his unflappable facial expression.

When the booming clock in the main hall chimed the hour of eight, Barbicane shot to his feet as if set in motion by a spring; there was total silence, and in a mildly oratorical tone, the speaker opened his remarks as follows:

"Gallant colleagues, for too long now a fruitless peace has managed to plunge Gun Club members into a sorry state of lethargy. After a period of several years that were highly eventful, we've had to give up our work and go no farther on the highway of progress. I have no qualms about speaking my mind—any war that would call us to arms again would be most welcome . . . "

"Yes, any war!" exclaimed the hotheaded J. T. Maston.

"Hush!" people countered throughout the hall.

"But war," Barbicane said, "isn't possible under today's conditions, and even though my honorable interrupter may get his hopes up, many years will go by before our cannons thunder again on the battlefield. So we must resign ourselves to satisfying our appetite for work in a different line of endeavor."

The audience sensed their president was getting closer to the good part. They listened twice as intently.

"For the past few months, my gallant colleagues," Barbicane went on, "I've wondered if we could stay in our field of expertise yet undertake some great experiment worthy of the 19th century, and if the advances made in ballistics might not allow us to see things through to a successful conclusion. So I've been hunting, working, calculating, and my research ended up convincing me there's one undertaking we should be able to pull off that would seem unachievable in any other country. This plan of mine has been under development for a good while and it'll be the subject of my announcement; it's wor-

thy of you, worthy of the Gun Club's best days, and it can't fail to make a noise in the world!"

"A big noise?" called an excited artilleryman.

"A big noise," Barbicane replied, "in every sense of the word."

"Stop interrupting!" several voices repeated.

"Therefore, my gallant colleagues," Barbicane went on, "I beg you to give me your full attention."

A tingle ran through the audience. With a quick movement Barbicane clamped his hat more tightly on his head, then continued his speech in a calm voice:

"There's nobody among you, my gallant colleagues, who hasn't scrutinized the moon or at least heard discussions about her. Don't be amazed if I converse with you now about that silver orb. Maybe it's ordained for us to be the Columbuses of that undiscovered world. Understand me, back me with all your energy, and I'll lead you to conquer her— then we'll add her name to the roster of those thirty-six states that make up this great Union of ours!"

"Hooray for the moon!" the Gun Club shouted in unison.

"The moon has been studied extensively," Barbicane went on. "Her mass, density, weight, volume, composition, movements, distance, and the role she plays in the solar system all have all been worked out to perfection; charts of the moon's physical features have been drafted no less accurately—if not more so—than earth maps; cameras have given us uniquely beautiful images of our satellite.[9] In a nutshell, we know everything about the moon that the sciences of mathematics, astronomy, geology, and optics can teach us; but till now nobody has ever set up any direct contact with her."

A sharp stirring of interest and surprise greeted these remarks.

"Let me remind you in a few words," he went on, "how certain eager souls went off on imaginary journeys and claimed to have

---

[9] Witness the superb photographic plates of the moon obtained by Mr. Warren De la Rue.

probed our satellite's mysteries. In the 17th century a certain David Fabricius bragged that he'd seen the moon's residents with his own two eyes. In 1649 a Frenchman named Jean Baudoin published his *Journey to the Lunar World by Domingo Gonzalez, Spanish Adventurer*. During that same period Cyrano de Bergerac served up his famous tale of a moon expedition, and it enjoyed a great success in France. Later on Fontenelle, another Frenchman (those people are fixated on the moon), wrote his *Plurality of Worlds*, a masterpiece in its day; but science marches on and tramples even masterpieces! Around 1835 a leaflet—translated from an article in the *New York American*—described how the renowned astronomer Sir John Herschel was sent to the Cape of Good Hope to study the skies; there, thanks to an improved telescope with inner illumination, he brought the moon within a viewing distance of eighty yards! Then he could clearly make out some caves with hippopotamuses living inside, green mountains trimmed with gold lace, sheep with horns made of ivory, albino deer, and natives with membranous wings like bats. This pamphlet was the work of an American named Locke and it had quite a success.[10] But people soon realized it was a scientific hoax, and the French were the first ones to laugh!"

"They laughed at an American?" J. T. Maston exclaimed. "Why, that's grounds for war!"

"Don't worry, my good friend. Before the French did their laughing, our countryman had them completely fooled. Meanwhile, to bring this brief chronicle to a close, I'll add that a certain Hans Pfaall from Rotterdam took off in a balloon filled with nitrogen gas—which is thirty-seven times lighter than hydrogen—and reached the moon after a trip lasting nineteen days. Like all the earlier attempts, this journey was just an imaginary one, but it was the work of a popular American author, a strange dreamy genius. I mean Poe!"

"Hooray for Edgar Allan Poe!" the audience shouted, galvanized by their president's words.

"Which wraps up those endeavors," Barbicane continued, "that I would label as strictly literary and no help at all in setting up serious relations with that silver orb. However I should add that a few practical souls *have* tried to make serious contact with her. To this end, some years back a German student of geometry proposed sending a panel of experts to the steppes of Siberia. There on those wide plains they were to use light-reflecting substances to form immense geometric figures—including, among others, the square of the hypotenuse, popularly known as the 'Donkey's Bridge' in France. 'Every sentient being,' the student of geometry said, 'is bound to understand the scientific purpose of that figure. If moonpeople really exist, they'll reply with a similar figure, and once we've made contact, we'll easily create an alphabet that will let us converse with the moon's residents.' Thus spoke the German student of geometry, but his plans were never put into execution, and to this day there's no direct link between the earth and the moon. It's ordained for the practical genius of Americans to set up relations with the starry realm. The way we'll manage this is so simple, easy, and sure that it can't miss—and it'll be the subject of my proposition."

A hullabaloo greeted this statement, a storm of exclamations. There wasn't a single listener who hadn't been overcome, carried off, and held captive by the speaker's words!

"Hush! Be quiet!" people exclaimed throughout the hall.

When the excitement had died down, Barbicane picked up the thread of his speech in a more solemn voice:

"You know the advances made in ballistics these past few years," he said, "and what heights of perfection firearms would have reached if the war had continued. You're aware that as a general rule, the resisting capability of a cannon and the explosive force of gunpowder are both limitless. All right, proceeding from this starting point, and assuming we'll have a large enough weapon with the needed resisting capacity, I won-

[10] In France this pamphlet was published by the Republican journalist Gabriel Laviron, who was killed during the siege of Rome in 1840.

dered if it wouldn't be possible to fire a shell to the moon."

At these words a "Wow!" of astonishment escaped from a thousand heaving chests; then came a moment of silence like the deep calm before a round of thunderclaps. And in fact there *was* a burst of thunder—but it was thunderous applause, then shouts and roars that rocked the meeting hall. Their president tried to speak; he couldn't. Ten minutes went by before he managed to make himself heard.

"Let me finish," he went on coolly. "I've looked at every aspect of the problem, I've tackled it without flinching—and by my indisputable calculations, I conclude that if we aim a projectile at the moon and give it an initial velocity of 12,000 yards per second, it will inevitably arrive there. So I have the honor to propose, my gallant colleagues, that we give this little experiment a try!"

3

HOW BARBICANE'S ANNOUNCEMENT WAS RECEIVED

IT'S IMPOSSIBLE to convey the audience's reception of these last remarks by their honorable president. What yelling! What howling! What a sequence of roars, cheers, hip-hips, and all that onomatopoetic language so plentiful in America! It was a riot, an indescribable hullabaloo! Mouths shouted, hands clapped, feet stamped on the hall floors. If every weapon in this artillery museum had gone off at the same instant, it wouldn't have set louder sound waves in motion. This needn't surprise you. There *are* gunners nearly as noisy as their cannons.

Barbicane kept calm in the midst of these impassioned outbursts; maybe he wanted to make a few further remarks to his colleagues, because his gestures were calling for silence and his exploding hand bell was running out of bangs. Nobody even heard it. Before long he was snatched from his seat of office, carried in triumph by his loyal colleagues, and passed from hand to hand into the arms of a crowd that was just as excited.

Nothing can amaze an American. Over and over people say that the word "impossi-ble" doesn't exist in French; they've obviously got their dictionaries mixed up. In America everything's easy, everything's simple, and mechanical difficulties are dead on arrival. Between Barbicane's plan and its realization, no genuine Yankee would have acknowledged even the shadow of a difficulty. The thing was no sooner said than done.

Their president's march of triumph went on all evening. It was a genuine torchlight parade. Irishmen, Germans, Frenchmen, Scots, the whole melting pot of Maryland's populace, were shouting in their mother tongues, mixing together cheers, hoorays, and bravos in a frenzy beyond words.

Sure enough, as if realizing that she was the topic of conversation, the moon came out in all her serene magnificence, her intense radiance overpowering the firelight on the ground. Every Yankee raised his eyes to her gleaming disk; some waved at her, others spoke to her in the most endearing terms; many gave her appraising glances, a number shook their fists; between eight o'clock and midnight, an optician on Jones Falls St. made a fortune selling spyglasses. That silver orb was ogled like a royal beauty. These Americans treated her as chummily as if she were one of their own. It was as if fair Phoebe belonged to these daring conquerors and was already Union territory. And yet it came down to firing a projectile at her, which, even with humble satellites, was a rather harsh way of initiating relations, though quite popular in civilized countries.

Even at the stroke of midnight the furor didn't abate; it continued in equal measure through every segment of the population; judges, scientists, tradesmen, shopkeepers, porters, sophisticates, and even "greenhorns" were thrilled to the bottoms of their hearts;[11] this business was a national undertaking; accordingly, uptown and downtown, along wharves washed by the Patapsco River, even aboard ships held captive at dockside, milling crowds were tipsy with joy, gin, and whiskey; everybody was talking, expounding, bickering, brawling, agreeing, applaud-

---

[11] "Greenhorn" is the all-American term for simpleton.

ing, from the gentleman lounging casually on a barroom couch behind his tankard of sherry cobbler[12] to the boatman in a filthy dive on Fells Point getting soused on his "gut buster."[13]

However, near two o'clock in the morning, the excitement died away. President Barbicane managed to get back home, battered, crushed, aching all over. Hercules couldn't have withstood such a furor. Little by little the crowds cleared out of the squares and streets. The four railroads converging on Baltimore—from the Ohio and Susquehanna rivers, Philadelphia, and Washington, D.C.—packed these combustible folks off to the four corners of the United States, and the town sank back into comparative tranquillity.

Even so, it would be a mistake to think that during this unforgettable evening, only Baltimore was in the grip of these frenzied feelings. From Texas to Massachusetts, from Michigan to Florida, every major town in the Union—New York, Boston, Albany, Washington, D.C., Richmond, the Crescent City,[14] Charleston, and Mobile—took part in these hysterics. Indeed the Gun Club's 30,000 corresponding members all knew about their president's note and were waiting for the notorious announcement on October 5 with identical impatience. On that evening, accordingly, as soon as the words escaped from the speaker's lips, they were racing along telegraph lines across the states of the Union at a speed of 248,447 miles per second.[15] So we can say with absolute certainty that the United States of America (ten times bigger than France) gave a single simultaneous cheer, and 25,000,000 hearts, swollen with pride, were pounding in the very same rhythm.

The next day 1,500 daily, weekly, twice-monthly, and monthly newspapers took over the matter; they examined its different aspects from the perspectives of physics, astronomy, economics, or ethics, as well as from the viewpoints of its political importance or role in the march of civilization. They wondered if the moon was a finished world, if she was no longer subject to further transformation. Did she resemble the earth at a time before our atmosphere had come into existence? What sights would her invisible face offer to our planet? Though it was still only a matter of firing a shell at that silver orb, everybody saw this as the starting point of a whole series of experiments; everybody hoped that one day America would probe the ultimate secrets of that mysterious disk, and some even seemed afraid that her conquest might noticeably upset the balance of power in Europe.

While discussing Barbicane's plan, not a single paper questioned that it would come to pass; its benefits were repeatedly pointed out in the digests, pamphlets, bulletins, and "newsletters" published by scientific, literary, or religious societies; meanwhile the Boston Society of Natural History, the association for American science and art in Albany, the American Geographical and Statistical Society in New York, the American Philosophical Society in Philadelphia, and the Smithsonian Institution in Washington, D.C. sent the Gun Club a thousand congratulatory letters along with immediate offers of money and assistance.

Accordingly you could say that no proposition had ever put together such an army of backers; misgivings, second thoughts, and anxieties weren't even in the picture. In Europe—France especially—jokes, cartoons, and ditties would have greeted this idea of firing a projectile at the moon, but here their creators would have landed in big trouble; given the wholesale fury sure to ensue, they couldn't have protected themselves with all the blackjacks on earth.[16] In the New World some things are no laughing matter. From

---

[12] Mixture of rum, orange juice, sugar, cinnamon, and nutmeg. Yellow in color, this drink is served in tankards and sipped through a glass straw.

[13] Frightful drink of the lower classes. In English it's officially called a "Thorough Knock Me Down."

[14] Nickname for New Orleans.

[15] 100,000 geographic leagues. Which is the speed of electricity.

---

[16] A blackjack is a pocket-sized weapon made of flexible whalebone and capped with a metal head.

that day forward Impey Barbicane became a leading citizen of the United States, a sort of scientific Washington, and a single indication out of many will show just how far a nation can go in its sudden fealty to one man.

A few days after that notorious session at the Gun Club, the director of an English acting company announced a run of performances at the Baltimore Theater of Shakespeare's comedy *Much Ado About Nothing*. But the townspeople saw this title as an offensive allusion to President Barbicane's plans, overran the playhouse, smashed up the seats, and induced the hapless director to change his playbill. Being a witty fellow, the latter bowed to popular demand, replaced that ill-fated comedy with *As You Like It*, and for the next several weeks box-office receipts were phenomenal.

4

ANSWERS FROM THE CAMBRIDGE OBSERVATORY

MEANWHILE, in the midst of all this acclaim pouring over him, Barbicane didn't waste a second. His first concern was to schedule a conference in the Gun Club's offices. There, after talking things over, his colleagues agreed to consult with astronomers on aspects of the undertaking related to astronomy; armed with answers from the experts, the club would then discuss the mechanical means, neglecting nothing that could insure the success of this great experiment.

The club then listed its specific questions in a meticulously drafted letter addressed to the observatory in Cambridge, Massachusetts. This town, the location of the oldest university in the United States, is justly famous for its team of astronomers. There under one roof you'll find experts of outstanding ability; there the powerful giant spyglass is at work that allowed Bond to see individual stars in the Andromeda Galaxy, Clark to discover Sirius's satellite. So the Gun Club's confidence in this famous institution was justified in every respect.

Accordingly, two days later, its impatiently awaited answers were in President Barbicane's hands. Its memo ran as follows:

Cambridge
October 7

TO: the President of the Gun Club in Baltimore

FROM: the Director of the Cambridge Observatory

After receiving your flattering note dated the 6th of this month and addressed to the Cambridge Observatory on behalf of the Gun Club's membership in Baltimore, our staff immediately convened and deemed it expedient to reply in the following manner.

These are the questions that have been presented to us:

1. Is it possible to fire a projectile to the moon?

2. What's the exact distance separating the earth from its satellite?

3. If the projectile is given sufficient initial velocity, how long will its flight take, and consequently just when should it be launched in order to meet up with the moon at a specified point?

4. Exactly when will the moon be in the most promising position for the projectile to hit her?

5. At what point in the sky should we aim the cannon that's entrusted with launching the projectile?

6. What place will the moon occupy in the sky right when the projectile leaves?

Your 1st question asks: "Is it possible to fire a projectile to the moon?"

Yes, it's possible to fire a projectile to the moon, if you manage to impel this projectile at an initial velocity of 12,000 yards per second. Our calculations show this speed to be sufficient. As you get farther from the earth, its gravitational pull decreases in inverse ratio to the square of its distance, in other words, at triple the distance that pull is only one-ninth as strong. Consequently the shell's weight will quickly decrease and will

143

end up right at zero when the moon's force of attraction balances the earth's, in other words, at 47/52 of the flight distance. At this juncture the projectile will be weightless, and if it clears this point, it will fall to the moon solely as a result of her gravitational pull. So the experiment's theoretical potential is unequivocally established; as for its actual accomplishment, that depends entirely on the power of the weapon employed.

Your 2nd question asks: "What's the exact distance separating the earth from its satellite?"

The moon doesn't sweep in a circle around the earth but rather in an ellipse, and our planet is at one of the foci; ergo the moon sometimes lies closer to the earth and sometimes farther away, or, in astronomer's parlance, sometimes she's at her perigee, sometimes at her apogee. Now then, the difference between her greatest distance and her shortest is too considerable in this case to be ignored. In fact, at her apogee the moon is 247,552 miles (99,640 geographic leagues) away, and at her perigee, only 218,657 miles (88,010 geographic leagues) away, making a difference of 28,895 miles (11,630 geographic leagues), or more than one-ninth of the trip. So it's the moon's distance at her perigee that should serve as the basis for calculations.

Your 3rd question asks: "If the projectile is given sufficient initial velocity, how long will its flight take, and consequently just when should it be launched in order to meet up with the moon at a specified point?"

If the shell consistently maintained the initial velocity of 12,000 yards per second that it will have been given at firing, it would only need about nine hours to make it to its destination; but since that initial velocity will be continually decreasing, all our calculations reveal that the projectile will take 300,000 seconds, hence 83 hours and 20 minutes, to reach the point of equal attraction between the earth and moon; and from this point it will fall to the moon in 50,000 seconds, or 13 hours, 53 minutes, and 20 seconds. So it's advisable to launch it 97

hours, 13 minutes, and 20 seconds before the moon's arrival at the target point.

Your 4th question asks: "Exactly when will the moon be in the most promising position for the projectile to hit her?"

After what has just been said above, you'll first need to select a time when the moon will reach her perigee at the same instant she reaches the zenith,[17] which will further shorten the trip by a distance equal to the earth's radius, hence 3,919 miles; this will result in an ultimate flight total of 214,976 miles (86,410 geographic leagues). However, though the moon arrives at her perigee every month, she doesn't always reach the zenith at this time. These two lunar conditions occur together only at infrequent intervals. So you'll need to wait for a moment when her arrivals at perigee and zenith coincide. Now then, by a stroke of luck, on December 4 next year both of these lunar conditions will be available: at midnight the moon will be at her perigee, in other words, her shortest distance from the earth, and she'll reach the zenith at the same time.

Your 5th question asks: "At what point in the sky should we aim the cannon that's entrusted with launching the projectile?"

In accordance with the foregoing remarks, the cannon should be aimed at the zenith of the launch site; in this way it will fire at a right angle to the plane of the horizon, and the projectile will escape more quickly from the earth's gravitational pull. But for the moon to ascend to the zenith of a given site, the site's latitude mustn't be higher than our satellite's declination—to put it plainly, the site has to be situated between latitude 0° and 28° north or south.[18] In any other locality the cannon would inevitably have to fire at an inclined angle, which

---

[17] The zenith is the point in the sky located directly over the viewer's head.

[18] In essence, at its highest altitude the moon rises to the zenith only in regions of the globe situated between the equator and the 28th parallel; beyond 28° the moon peaks farther and farther from the zenith the nearer you come to the poles.

would be detrimental to the experiment's success.

Your 6th question asks: "What place will the moon occupy in the sky right when the projectile leaves?"

The moon moves forward 13° 10' 35" every day, so right when the projectile is launched into space, she'll need to be four times that far from your zenith point, hence 52° 42' 20" away, a figure corresponding to the distance she'll cover over the duration of the projectile's trip. But it's equally essential to take into account the change in course that the shell will undergo due to the earth's spinning motion, since the shell will only reach the moon after having made a course correction equal to sixteen times the earth's radius, which, in terms of the moon's orbit, amounts to about 11°; so you need to add this 11° to the above-mentioned total representing the moon's lag distance, which makes 64° in round numbers. Hence, at the time of firing, a straight line drawn to the moon will be at a 64° angle to the site's vertical.

These are our answers to the questions presented to the Cambridge Observatory by the Gun Club's membership.

To summarize:

1. The cannon needs to be set up in a region located between latitude 0° and 28° north or south.

2. It needs to be aimed at the site's zenith.

3. The projectile needs to be impelled at an initial velocity of 12,000 yards per second.

4. It needs to be launched on December 1 next year at 10:46:40 in the evening.

5. It will meet up with the moon four days after its departure, right at midnight on December 4, just when she reaches the zenith.

So the Gun Club's membership should start the necessary work for this experiment at once and they should be ready to proceed at the time specified, because if they miss this date of December 4, they won't find the moon again under the same conditions of perigee and zenith for another eighteen years and eleven days.

The Cambridge Observatory staff place themselves completely at the club's disposal on issues of theoretical astronomy, and they join all America in hereby offering their congratulations.

On behalf of the staff,
J. M. BELFAST,
Director of the Cambridge Observatory.

5

THE TALE OF THE MOON

BACK DURING THE ERA when the universe was in chaos, a skywatcher gifted with an infinite range of vision—and stationed in that undiscovered center around which all creation revolves—would have seen that myriads of atoms were drifting in space. But as the centuries went by, a change gradually took place; a law of attraction went into effect, and those formerly footloose atoms obeyed it: the atoms got together in chemical combinations according to their affinities, turned into molecules, and formed those nebulous clusters that are scattered across deep space.

These clusters were impelled at once into a spinning motion around their center point. Made up of disorganized molecules, this center started revolving around itself as it progressively contracted; in accordance with the unchanging laws of mechanics, however, the more volume it lost as it contracted, the more its spinning motion gathered speed—and these two effects kept on, resulting in a major star at the center of the nebulous cluster.

Then, paying closer attention, our skywatcher would have noticed the other molecules in the cluster behaving just like the central star, contracting in the same way through a spinning motion that progressively gathered speed, then revolving around the chief star in the form of countless smaller stars. A nebula had taken shape, one of nearly 5,000 that astronomers have tallied to date.

Among these 5,000 nebulae is one that human beings have named the Milky Way and that includes 18,000,000 stars, each now the center of a solar system.[19]

Then, if our skywatcher had specifically examined one of the more modest, less brilliant of these 18,000,000 heavenly bodies, that fourth-class star we proudly call the sun,[20] he would witness all the consecutive phenomena responsible for the universe's formation.

In fact, while our sun was still in its gaseous state and made up of moving molecules, he would have seen it turning on its axis in order to finish its consolidating work. True to the laws of mechanics, this motion gathered speed following the loss of volume, and the time would come when centripetal force—which tends to drive molecules toward the center—would knuckle under to centrifugal force.

Then another phenomenon would have taken place as our skywatcher looked on: the molecules level with the solar equator would suddenly fly off like a stone from the snapping cords of a sling, forming several concentric rings around the sun like those around Saturn. In turn these rings of cosmic matter, which had started spinning around the central mass, would have broken up and deteriorated into lesser commodities—in other words, planets.

If our skywatcher had then paid exclusive attention to these planets, he would have noticed them behaving exactly like the sun and giving birth to one or more cosmic rings, creating those lower-class heavenly bodies known as satellites.

Hence, by proceeding from atom to molecule, molecule to nebulous cluster, nebulous cluster to nebula, nebula to major star, major star to sun, sun to planet, and planet to satellite, we've got the whole sequence of transformations undergone by cosmic entities since the first days of the universe.

The sun seems lost in the vastness of the starry realm, and yet current scientific thinking attaches it to the Milky Way galaxy. The center of a solar system, it may seem tiny out in those regions of ether, but it's actually enormous, because it's 1,400,000 times bigger than the earth. Around the sun revolve eight planets, which came from its very bowels during the early days of creation. Going from the nearest to the farthest, these heavenly bodies are Mercury, Venus, the earth, Mars, Jupiter, Saturn, Uranus, and Neptune. What's more, between Mars and Jupiter there are other, less considerable objects that are in regular motion—maybe the wandering rubble from some star shattered into several thousand pieces—and telescopes have identified ninety-seven of these to date.[21]

Thanks to the universal law of gravitation, the sun restrains its subordinates in their elliptical orbits, and some have satellites of their own. Uranus has eight of them, Saturn eight, Jupiter four, Neptune maybe three, the earth one; this last is called the moon and ranks with the least significant satellites in the solar system, yet it's her domain that America's daredevil spirit meant to conquer.

Due to her comparative nearness and the swiftly recurring sight of her different phases, that silver orb instantly competes with the sun for the attention of earthlings; but the sun is taxing to look at and its magnificent light forces viewers to glance away.

By contrast fair Phoebe is more personable, revealing herself considerably, the soul of gracious modesty; she's easy on the eyes and seldom aggressive, though she sometimes indulges in eclipsing her brother, radiant Apollo, who never eclipses her back. Realizing how much appreciation they owe this loyal friend of the earth, followers of Mohammed have based their calendar months on the duration of her orbit.[22]

The earliest tribes set up a religious cult

---

[19] Milky Way comes from the Greek word γάλα [gala], combination form γάλακτος [galaktos], meaning milk.

[20] According to the English physicist William Wollaston, the diameter of Sirius has to be twelve times bigger than the sun's, hence some 10,700,000 miles.

[21] Some of these asteroids are so small, you could go all the way around them in a single day by marching double time.

[22] About 29½ days.

specifically devoted to this chaste goddess. Egyptians called her Isis; Phoenicians named her Astarte; Greeks worshipped her as Phoebe, daughter of Latona and Jupiter, and they claimed her eclipses occurred when Diana visited handsome Endymion on the sly. If we're to believe the legends of mythology, the Nemean lion traveled the lunar countryside before showing up on the earth, and the Greek poet Agesianax, whom Plutarch mentions, penned verses honoring the gentle eyes, lovely nose, and sweet mouth formed by the shining parts of the moon goddess's adored surface.

From a mythological viewpoint the ancients fully grasped the moon's personality and temperament—in a word, her mental attributes—but even the wisest among them remained thoroughly ignorant of her physical features.

However several astronomers in the distant past discovered certain characteristics that modern science bears out. Though the Greeks in Arcadia claimed they lived on the earth before the moon had come into existence, though the Roman ruler Tatius viewed her as a fragment that had come loose from the sun's disk, though Aristotle's follower Clearchos thought of her as a glossy mirror that reflected images of the ocean, though others ended up seeing her simply as an accumulation of steam exhaled by the earth, or as a sphere that was half fire, half ice, and spinning on its own axis, there were a few scholars whose shrewd moonwatching—even without optical instruments—gave them an inkling of most of the laws that govern that silver orb.

Thus in 460 B.C. Thales the Milesian expressed the view that the moon was lit up by the sun. Aristarchus of Samos hit on the true explanation of her phases. Cleomedes held that her shine was just reflected light. Berosus of Chaldea discovered that her spinning motion and revolving motion had the same duration, and in this way he explained the fact that the moon always shows the same side. Finally, two centuries before the Christian era, Hipparchus identified a few irregularities in our satellite's visible movements. These various findings were subsequent-

ly borne out, and later astronomers benefited. Ptolemy in the 2nd century, then the Arab Abu'l-Wafa in the 10th, finalized Hipparchus's comments on the irregularities affecting the moon as she travels her undulating orbit under the sun's influence. Then Copernicus in the 15th century and Tycho Brahe in the 16th developed a complete picture of the solar system and the role played by the moon in this assembly of heavenly bodies.[23]

By this time her movements were nearly worked out; but few things were known about her physical makeup. Then Galileo explained that the luminous phenomena occurring during certain lunar phases were caused by the presence of mountains, to which he attributed an average elevation of 27,000 feet.

Later Johannes Hevelius, an astronomer from Danzig, shrank the highest elevations to 15,600 feet; but his cohort Father Riccioli inflated them to 42,000 feet.

At the close of the 18th century, Herschel worked with a high-powered telescope and sharply reduced the preceding measurements. He attributed 11,400 feet to the loftiest mountains and brought the average elevation down to a mere 2,400 feet. But Herschel was mistaken too, and it took the findings of Schröter, Louville, Halley, Nasmyth, Bianchini, Pastorff, Lohrmann, Gruithuisen, and especially the painstaking research of Messrs. Beer and Mädler, to conclusively settle the matter. Thanks to these experts, the elevations of the lunar mountains are now fully known. Messrs. Beer and Mädler determined 1,095 different elevations, of which six are higher than 15,600 feet and twenty-two higher than 14,400 feet.[24] Their loftiest peak towers 22,806 feet above the surface of the lunar disk.

During this same period moonwatchers scouted her out thoroughly; this heavenly body seemed riddled with craters, and her

---

[23] See *The Founders of Modern Astronomy*, a wonderful book by Mr. Joseph Bertrand of the French Institute.

[24] Mt. Blanc's elevation is 15,790 feet above sea level.

basically volcanic character was borne out everywhere you looked. Due to the absence of refracted light from planets occulted by her,[25] people concluded she must have practically no atmosphere. This absence of air meant an absence of water. So it was crystal clear that if moonpeople could live under such conditions, they had to have a unique organism and must differ significantly from earthlings.

Finally, thanks to innovative methods, new and improved instruments ransacked the moon relentlessly, not leaving a single part of her visible side unexplored, though her diameter measures around 2,150 miles,[26] her surface area is 1/13 that of the planet earth's,[27] and her volume 1/49 that of our globe's; but none of her secrets could elude the eyes of astronomers, and these skilled experts carried their prodigious investigations to even greater lengths.

In this way they noted that certain parts of her disk seemed to be streaked with white lines during a full moon, then with black lines during her phases. After studying them in greater detail, they managed to nail down the exact nature of these lines. They were long narrow furrows dug with parallel edges and generally ending at the brink of a crater; they ran from ten to a hundred miles long and were up to 4,800 feet wide. Astronomers called them rills, but naming them was as far as they got. As for the question of verifying whether or not these rills were old dried-up riverbeds, they couldn't settle this in any conclusive way. Accordingly, one day or another the Americans hoped they could determine the geological truth of the matter. They likewise had a stake in scouting out that sequence of parallel ramparts discovered on the surface of the moon by Gruithuisen, a learned Munich professor who considered them to be a system of fortifications erected by lunar engineers. These two unresolved matters—and

no doubt many others—could only be decisively cleared up after making direct contact with the moon.

As for the brightness of her light, there we know all there is to know; as you're aware, her beams are 1/300,000 the strength of sunlight and their heat has no noticeable influence on thermometers; as for the phenomenon known by name as earthshine, this is easily explained: it results from sunlight reflecting off the earth onto the lunar disk, an effect that seems to fill out the moon's full shape when the latter appears in the form of a crescent during her first and last phases.

This was the state of acquired knowledge concerning the earth's satellite, which the Gun Club proposed to round out from the viewpoint of every discipline: cosmography, geology, politics, and ethics.

6

WHERE IGNORANCE IS IMPOSSIBLE AND OLD BELIEFS ARE NOW IMPROPER IN THE UNITED STATES

AS AN IMMEDIATE RESULT of Barbicane's proposition, all the facts concerning the astronomy of that silver orb became the talk of the town. Everybody started to study her industriously. It was as if the moon were appearing on the horizon for the first time and nobody had ever glimpsed her in the heavens before. She was the latest rage; she became the lady of the hour without any show of vanity and she took her place among the "stars" without getting a swelled head. The newspapers resurrected the old fables that featured this "sun of the wolves"; they reminded you of the mystic powers our ignorant ancestors claimed she had; they went on and on about her; they were almost to the point of putting quotable words in her mouth; all America had gone moon-mad.

For their part, the scientific journals concentrated mostly on matters that affected the Gun Club's undertaking; they published the Cambridge Observatory's letter, commented on it, and gave it their wholehearted approval.

In short, it was now improper for even the

---

[25] *Translator's note.* The planets are hidden or eclipsed due to the moon's passing in front.

[26] About 869 geographic leagues, in other words, slightly more than a quarter of the earth's radius.

[27] Over 14,500,000 square miles.

least literate Yankee to stay ignorant of one single fact relating to his satellite, or for the most narrow-minded old wife to keep swallowing superstitious nonsense about her. The scientific truth came at them from all sides; they couldn't help seeing and hearing it; to remain a donkey was impossible . . . in astronomy.

Till then many people had no idea how science could have figured out the distance separating the moon from the earth. Science availed itself of the opportunity to teach them that this distance could be gotten by measuring the moon's parallax. If they seemed dumbfounded by this word parallax, they were told it was the angle formed by two straight lines drawn from both ends of the earth's radius to the moon. Should they question the accuracy of this method, they were given immediate proof that not only was the average distance a good 234,347 miles (94,330 geographic leagues), but furthermore that the astronomers' margin of error was under 75 miles (30 geographic leagues).

For those who weren't familiar with how the moon moves, the newspapers gave daily explanations of her two distinct motions, one spinning on her axis, the other revolving around the earth, both accomplished in the same period of time, hence 27⅓ days.[28]

Her spinning motion is what creates daytime and nighttime on the surface of the moon; except that a lunar month has just one day and one night, each lasting 354½ hours. But fortunately for her, the side facing the earth is illuminated by our planet with a light that's fourteen times brighter than moonlight. As for her other side, it's always invisible to us, so naturally it has 354 hours of total nighttime, relieved only by that "pallid glow dropping from the stars."[29] This phenomenon is due solely to that characteristic of her spinning and revolving motions taking exactly the same amount of time, which

Herschel and Giovanni Cassini say is a phenomenon common to Jupiter's satellites, and very likely to all other satellites.

A few well-meaning but slightly recalcitrant souls didn't understand at first that as the moon revolves, she always shows the same face to the earth because she does a full turn around herself during the same stretch of time. These people were told: "Go into your dining room and walk around the table while always looking at its center; when you've completely circled it, you'll have done a full turn around yourself, since you'll have looked consecutively from every side of the room. All right, your room is outer space, the table is the earth, and you're the moon!" And they went away delighted with this comparison.

Hence the moon continually shows the same face to the earth; but for the sake of accuracy, we should add that because of her socalled "swaying motion," a sort of swinging from north to south and west to east, she reveals a bit more than half of her disk, namely about 57%.

Once the know-nothings were as familiar with the moon's spinning motion as the director of the Cambridge Observatory himself, they worried their heads over her revolving motion around the earth, and twenty scientific journals were quick to feed them the facts. The public then learned how the firmament and its infinite number of stars could be regarded as a huge clock face, which the moon travels over to mark the correct time for all earthlings; how, while moving along, that silver orb displays her different phases; how the moon is full when she's in opposition to the sun, in other words, when the three heavenly bodies lie in a straight line and the earth is in the middle; how the moon is new when she's in conjunction with the sun, in other words, when she comes between it and the earth; finally how the moon is in her first or last quarter when the sun and earth form a right angle with her and she's the apex.

From this a few astute Yankees deduced that eclipses could only take place at times of conjunction or opposition, and their reasoning was sound. In conjunction the moon can eclipse the sun, while in opposition the earth

---

[28] Which is the duration of her sidereal revolution, in other words, the time it takes the moon to come back to the same position in relation to a particular star.

[29] *Translator's note.* A pet line by the 17th century playwright Pierre Corneille.

can eclipse her in return, and if these eclipses don't occur twice in each lunar month, it's because the moon moves on a plane tilted toward the ecliptic, that is, the plane of the earth's orbit.

As for the altitude that silver orb can reach above the horizon, the Cambridge Observatory's letter had exhausted the topic. Everybody knew this altitude differed according to the latitude of the site from where you're watching her. But the only zones on the globe where the moon ascends to the zenith—in other words, reaches a position directly over the spectators' heads—are necessarily situated between the 28th parallels and the equator. Ergo that major recommendation to attempt the experiment at some point or other in this part of the globe, so the projectile could be launched vertically and thus break loose more quickly from the force of gravity. This was a necessary prerequisite for the undertaking's success and it always bulked large in the public's thinking.

As for the path taken by the moon while she revolves around the earth, the Cambridge Observatory had satisfactorily explained—even to know-nothings of every nation—that this path isn't a circle but a returning curve, a definite ellipse where the earth is at one of the foci. These elliptical orbits are common to all the planets as well as to all their satellites, and rational mechanics absolutely proves it couldn't be any other way. People clearly understood that the moon is farthest from the earth at her apogee, nearest at her perigee.

So somehow or other that's what every American had learned, and that's where nobody could decently plead ignorance. But though these factual principles quickly became common knowledge, many fallacies and certain imaginary fears weren't as easy to root out.

Thus a few good people maintained, for instance, that the moon used to be a comet that had been going along its lengthy orbit around the sun, had chanced to pass near the earth, and had gotten caught in our gravitational field. These armchair astronomers claimed this explained the moon's scorched appearance, an irreparable misfortune they blamed on Old Sol. However, if you pointed out to them that comets have an atmosphere and the moon little or none, they were left without a comeback.

Others, members of the scaredy-cat species, expressed some fears about the moon's location; they'd heard that since those readings taken in the days of the caliphs, her revolving motion had speeded up to some extent; from this they deduced, logically enough, that her speedier motion had to be accompanied by a reduction in the distance between the two heavenly bodies, and that if this twofold effect kept on indefinitely, the moon would someday end up falling to the earth. But they were eventually reassured and stopped fearing for future generations, after they learned about the calculations of a famous French mathematician, Laplace, who found that this speeding up is confined within quite narrow limits and that a proportionate reduction in speed would shortly follow it. Hence the solar system couldn't be thrown out of balance in centuries to come.

On the bottom rung of these know-nothings perched the clan of the superstitious; they aren't content with staying ignorant, they believe fictitious things about the moon and they've held these beliefs a long time. Some regarded her disk as a glossy mirror in which people can see one another from different parts of the earth and can send their thoughts back and forth. Others claimed that out of every 1,000 times we've had a new moon, 950 have led to notable upheavals, such as cataclysms, revolutions, earthquakes, floods, etc.; therefore they were convinced that silver orb had some mysterious power over people's destinies; they regarded her as an actual "system of checks and balances" on our lives; they thought that each moonperson was connected by a sympathetic tie to each earthling; along with Dr. Richard Mead, they held that the whole process of existence was under lunar control, tenaciously claiming that boys tended to be born during a new moon, girls during her last quarter, etc., etc. But they had to give up these low-grade fallacies and finally come around to the simple truth, and though the moon lost her clout, though she went down in the eyes of those who groveled before any mystic power, though a few turned their backs on her, the vast majority were still on her side. As for the Yankees, their sole ambition was to stake a claim on that new landmass in the skies, to plant on her loftiest peak the star-spangled banner of the United States of America.

7

THE ANTHEM OF THE SHELL

IN ITS MEMORABLE LETTER of October 7, the Cambridge Observatory dealt with the matter from the viewpoint of astronomy; from then on it came down to settling its mechanical aspects. At this juncture the practical difficulties might have seemed insurmountable in any other country except America. Here they were child's play.

Wasting no time, President Barbicane appointed an operations committee from the Gun Club's core membership. Over three sessions this committee was to clarify the three major issues of the cannon, projectile, and gunpowder; it consisted of four members who were very knowledgeable on these topics: Barbicane (whose vote would prevail in case of ties), General Morgan, Major Elphiston, and finally the inescapable J. T. Maston, who was entrusted with the duties of secretary/recorder.

On October 8 the committee met in President Barbicane's home at 3 Republican St. Since it was important that such a crucial discussion not be disturbed by growling stomachs, the four Gun Club members took their seats at a table covered with sandwiches and substantial teapots. J. T. Maston immediately screwed his pen into his iron hook, and the meeting came to order.

Barbicane opened the proceedings:

"My dear colleagues," he said, "we're here to solve one of the most important problems in ballistics, this science beyond compare that deals with the motion of projectiles, in other words, objects launched into space by some sort of propulsive force, then left to themselves."

"Ah, ballistics, ballistics!" J. T. Maston exclaimed, sounding deeply moved.

"Maybe it would seem more logical," Barbicane went on, "to devote this first session to discussing the weapon . . . "

"Agreed," General Morgan replied.

"But after mature consideration," Barbicane continued, "it strikes me that the question of the projectile should have priority over that of the cannon, since the dimensions of the latter inevitably depend on those of the former."

"I ask for the floor!" J. T. Maston exclaimed.

It was given him with the speed his splendid record deserved.

"My gallant friends," he said in exalted tones, "our president is right to place the question of the projectile ahead of all others! This shell we're going to shoot to the moon is our messenger, our ambassador, and I ask your permission to consider it strictly from a philosophical viewpoint."

This new way of looking at a projectile noticeably piqued the committee members' interest; so they paid the keenest attention to J. T. Maston's words.

"My dear colleagues," the latter went on, "I'll be brief; I'll skip over the physical shell, the shell that kills, in order to look at the statistical shell, the philosophical shell. For me the shell is the most brilliant manifestation of human power; it sums up everything such power entails; by creating it, man becomes more like our Creator!"

"Very true!" Major Elphiston said.

"In essence," the speaker exclaimed, "God made the stars and planets, but man made the shell, this standard for earthly speed, this miniature version of those heavenly bodies wandering through space, which, honestly, are nothing more than projectiles! God generates the speed of electricity, the speed of light, the speed of sound, the speed of the wind, the speeds of the stars, comets, and planets! But we generate the speed of the shell, a hundred times greater than the speed of the fastest horses and trains!"

J. T. Maston was getting carried away; his voice took on a lyrical quality as he sang this sacred anthem of the shell.

"You want figures?" he went on. "Here are some eloquent ones! Simply take your humble 24-pounder;[30] it travels 1/800,000 as fast as electricity, 1/640,000 as fast as light, 1/76 as fast as the earth's orbiting motion around the sun, but when it leaves the cannon, it *does* exceed the speed of sound,[31] since it's doing 1,200 feet per second, 12,000 feet in ten seconds, 14 miles (or 6 aerial leagues) per minute, 840 miles (or 360 aerial leagues) per hour, 20,100 miles (or 8,614 aerial leagues) per day, in other words, the speed of any part of the equator during our globe's spinning motion, and 7,336,500 miles (or 3,155,760 aerial leagues) per year. So it would take eleven days to make it to the moon, twelve years to manage the sun, and 360 years to reach Neptune at the edge of the solar system. That's what this humble shell will do—the work of our own hands! So what would happen if it went twenty times faster, if we fired it at a speed of seven miles per second? O splendid shell, magnificent projectile! I like to think you would be welcomed on high with all the honor an earthly ambassador deserves!"

Cheers greeted this bombastic windup, and J. T. Maston, deeply touched, took his seat in the midst of his colleagues' congratulations.

"And now that we've waxed poetic," Barbicane said, "let's get down to the business at hand."

"We're all set," the committee members replied, consuming half a dozen sandwiches apiece.

"You're aware of the problem we need to solve," continued the Gun Club's president. "It concerns giving a projectile the speed of 12,000 yards per second. I have grounds for thinking we'll pull it off. But for the moment let's examine the speeds achieved to date; General Morgan will be able to enlighten us on this point."

"And even more readily," the general replied, "because during the war I was a member of the commission for experimental research. I'll have you know, then, that Dahlgren's 100-pounder cannons, which had a range of 15,000 feet, gave their projectiles an initial velocity of 500 yards per second."

"Fine. And what about Rodman's columbiad?" their president asked.[32]

"When Rodman's columbiad was tested at Fort Hamilton near New York, it fired a half-ton shell a distance of six miles at a speed of 800 yards per second, more than Armstrong and Palliser were ever able to achieve in England."

"Who needs the English!" J. T. Maston put in, his alarming hook aimed at the eastern horizon.

"Hence," Barbicane went on, "800 yards per second would be the maximum speed reached to date?"

"Right," Morgan replied.

"I'll mention, however," J. T. Maston remarked, "that if my mortar hadn't blown up . . . "

"Yes, but it did blow up," Barbicane replied, gently waving this away. "So let's take this speed of 800 yards as our starting point. We need to increase it twenty times over. Saving discussion of just how we'll generate this speed for another session, I'll accordingly call your attention, my dear colleagues, to the dimensions our shell should properly have. As you can well imagine, it's no longer a matter of projectiles weighing as little as half a ton."

"Why not?" the major asked.

"Because this shell," J. T. Maston replied instantly, "has to be big enough to catch the attention of the moon's residents, if there actually are any."

"Right," Barbicane replied, "and there's another, even more important reason."

"What do you mean, Barbicane?" the major asked.

"I mean it isn't enough to fire a projectile and then forget about it; we need to follow it during its trip till the moment it reaches its destination."

"Huh?" the general and major put in, a bit startled by this proposition.

---

[30] In other words, a shell weighing twenty-four pounds.

[31] So if you hear the gun going off, the shell has already missed you.

[32] Americans gave the name "columbiad" to these enormous engines of destruction.

"Surely," Barbicane went on, radiating self-confidence, "or our experiment won't have any verifiable result."

"But in that case," the major remarked, "won't you be giving this projectile enormous dimensions?"

"Not at all. Kindly hear me out. You're aware that optical instruments have achieved a high degree of perfection; certain telescopes have already managed to magnify things 6,000 times, bringing the moon within a viewing distance of about forty miles (sixteen geographic leagues). Now then, at that distance any object sixty feet square would be perfectly visible. If telescopes haven't been given still more enlarging power, it's because that power has an adverse effect on their clarity, and the moon, which is simply a reflecting mirror, doesn't give off a light bright enough to handle magnifying things beyond this limit."

"Well then, what'll you do?" the general asked. "Will you make your projectile sixty feet in diameter?"

"Of course not!"

"So you'll have a crack at making the moon brighter?"

"Correct."

"That's ridiculous!" J. T. Maston exclaimed.

"Yes, ridiculously simple," Barbicane replied. "In essence, if I manage to reduce the density of the atmosphere moonlight travels through, won't I make that light brighter?"

"Obviously."

"Well, to get this result, I merely have to set up a telescope on some lofty mountaintop. That's how we'll handle it."

"You win, you win," the major replied. "You do have a way of simplifying things! And what magnification are you hoping to get, then?"

"A magnification of 48,000 times, which will bring the moon within a viewing distance of just five miles, and to be visible, objects won't need to be more than nine feet in diameter."

"Perfect!" J. T. Maston exclaimed. "So our projectile will be nine feet in diameter?"

"Exactly."

"But allow me to say," Major Elphiston went on, "that it'll still weigh so much that—"

"Please, major," Barbicane replied. "Before discussing its weight, I'll have you know that our forefathers worked wonders in this regard. Far be it from me to claim that ballistics hasn't made advances, but it's worth recalling that during the Middle Ages, they achieved some startling things, more startling, I daresay, than we have."

"Like what?" Morgan remarked.

"Show us some proof!" J. T. Maston exclaimed instantly.

"Nothing could be easier," Barbicane replied. "I've got some examples to back up my proposition. For instance when Mohammed II laid siege to Constantinople in 1453, he fired shells made of stone that weighed 1,900 pounds and must have been pretty sizeable."

"Wow!" the major put in. "1,900 pounds is a hefty figure!"

"Back in the days of the Knights of Malta, there was a cannon at Fort St. Elmo that launched projectiles weighing 2,500 pounds."

"Not possible!"

"Finally, according to a French historian, under King Louis XI a mortar launched a bombshell weighing just 500 pounds; but this bombshell was hurled from the Bastille, a place where fools imprisoned wise men, and it landed in the asylum of Charenton, a place where wise men imprison fools."

"Good line," J. T. Maston said.

"Since then, what have we seen by and large? Armstrong's cannons shoot 500-pound shells, Rodman's columbiads fire projectiles weighing half a ton! So it seems that what projectiles have gained in range, they've lost in weight. Now then, if we apply ourselves in that direction, our scientific advances should let us come up with shells ten times heavier than those fired by Mohammed II and the Knights of Malta."

"That's obvious," the major replied, "but what metal are you figuring to use for our projectile?"

"Cast iron, nothing more" General Morgan said.

"Ugh! Cast iron!" J. T. Maston exclaimed with utter scorn. "That's so humdrum for a shell destined to reach the moon."

"Let's not overdo it, my honorable friend," Morgan replied. "Cast iron will be fine."

"All right," Major Elphiston went on, "but since its weight is in proportion to its volume, a cast-iron shell nine feet in diameter would still be frightfully heavy."

"Yes, if it's solid; no, if it's hollow," Barbicane said.

"Hollow? So it would be like a capsule?"

"Where we could put messages," J. T. Maston remarked, "and samples of what earthlings have manufactured."

"Right, a capsule," Barbicane replied. "It absolutely has to be; a solid 108-inch shell would weigh more than 200,000 pounds, a weight that's obviously excessive; but since the projectile needs to keep some degree of stability, I propose we give it a weight of 20,000 pounds."

"Then how thick would its walls be?" the major asked.

"If we stick to standard proportions," Morgan continued, "a 108-inch diameter would call for two-foot walls at the very least."

"Which would be too much," Barbicane replied. "Don't forget, we aren't dealing here with a shell that's meant to pierce armor plate; so all we have to do is make its walls strong enough to withstand the pressure of the gases from the gunpowder. So this is our problem: how thick should this cast-iron capsule be in order to weigh only 20,000 pounds? Our gallant Mr. Maston is a skilled mathematician and he'll give us the answer on the spot."

"Nothing to it," remarked the committee's distinguished secretary,

And with that he scrawled a few algebraic formulas on a sheet of paper; in front of their eyes his pen conjured up π's and x's raised to the second power. After pulling a cube root practically out of thin air, he said:

"The walls will be under two inches thick."

"Will that be enough?" the major asked, looking dubious.

"No," President Barbicane replied, "obviously not."

"Well then, what can we do?" Elphiston went on, looking baffled.

"Use a different metal than iron."

"Brass?" Morgan said.

"No, that's still too heavy, and I've got something better to propose."

"What?" the major said.

"Aluminum," Barbicane replied.

"Aluminum!" exclaimed the president's three colleagues.

"Surely, my friends. You're aware that in 1854 Henri Sainte-Claire Deville, a famous French chemist, managed to work aluminum into a compact mass. Now then, this valuable metal is as white as silver, as permanent as gold, as tough as iron, as fusible as copper, and as light as glass; it's highly malleable, it's extremely abundant in nature since aluminum is a basic ingredient in most rocks, it's one-third the weight of iron, and it seems to have been created for the express purpose of furnishing material for our projectile."

"Three cheers for aluminum!" exclaimed the committee's secretary, always very noisy in his moments of enthusiasm.

"But my dear president," the major said, "isn't aluminum pretty costly to come by?"

"It used to be," Barbicane replied. "Back when it was first discovered, it ran $260 to $280 per pound, then it dropped to $27, and finally it now goes for $9."

"But," remarked the major, who didn't give in easily, "$9 per pound is still an enormous expense."

"Certainly, my dear major, but it isn't beyond our reach."

"Then how much will the projectile weigh?" Morgan asked.

"Here's what my calculations come up with," Barbicane replied. "Made of cast iron, a shell 108 inches in diameter and 12 inches thick would weigh 67,440 pounds; cast from aluminum, its weight would be reduced to 19,250 pounds."

"Perfect!" Maston exclaimed. "Just what the doctor ordered!"

"It *is* perfect!" the major remarked. "But don't forget that at $9 per pound, this projectile will cost—"

"Exactly $173,250. I know that. But don't worry, my friends, I guarantee there'll be no shortage of money for our undertaking."

"It'll pour into our coffers," J. T. Maston remarked.

"Well," asked the Gun Club's president, "what do you think of aluminum?"

"Motion carried!" replied the three committee members.

"As for the shell's shape," Barbicane went on, "that makes little difference, because once it goes through the atmosphere, the projectile will be in a vacuum; consequently I propose a round shell that can rotate any which way and do whatever it likes."

That ended the committee's opening session; the projectile issue was settled conclusively, and J. T. Maston was thoroughly delighted with the idea of sending moonpeople an aluminum shell, "which would give them a mental picture of what earthlings are like!"

8

THE SAGA OF THE CANNON

THE DECISIONS MADE in that session had a great impact on the world at large. A few skittish folks were a bit appalled at the thought of a 20,000-pound shell shooting through space. People wondered what cannon could *ever* convey enough initial velocity to such a mass. The proceedings of the committee's second session were to provide a triumphant answer to such questions.

The next evening the four Gun Club members were at table in front of new mountains of sandwiches and on the shores of an authentic ocean of tea. Their discussion got back under way immediately, this time without any preamble.

"My dear colleagues," Barbicane said, "we'll now deal with the weapon we're going to build, its length, shape, composition, and weight. It's pretty likely that we'll end up giving it gigantic dimensions; but however great the difficulties may be, our technological genius will easily prevail. So kindly hear me out and don't shrink from firing your objections point-blank. I'm not afraid of them."

A grunt of approval greeted this statement.

"Let's not forget," Barbicane went on, "just where our discussion led us yesterday; the problem now takes on this form: how to impart an initial velocity of 12,000 yards per second to a 20,000-pound capsule that's 108 inches in diameter."

"Yes, that's our problem all right," Major Elphiston replied.

"Then I'll continue," Barbicane went on. "When a projectile is launched into space, what happens? It's courted by three independent forces: the environmental resistance, the earth's gravity, and the propulsive force impelling it. Let's examine these three forces. The environmental resistance—in other words, the air resistance—will be of little importance. In fact the earth's atmosphere extends for only forty miles (or about sixteen geographic leagues). Now then, it'll take just five seconds to cross this—since the projectile's speed is 12,000 yards per second—and that time is short enough for the environmental resistance to be viewed as insignificant. So let's move on to the earth's gravity, in other words, to our capsule's weight. We know this weight will decrease in inverse ratio to the square of its distance; in essence here's what physicists tell us: when you let go of an object and it falls to the surface of the earth, it drops fifteen feet the first second, and if this same object were transferred to a distance of 247,552 miles up, that is, to the distance of the moon herself, it would drop at the slower rate of about 1/24 of an inch the first second. Which is practically standing still. So we're faced with progressively overcoming this gravitational pull. How will we manage this? By the propulsive force we create."

"That's our challenge," the major replied.

"It is indeed," continued the Gun Club's president, "but we'll pull it off, because the propulsive force we need will result from the length of the weapon and the amount of gunpowder used, the latter being limited only by the resisting capability of the former. So today let's deal with the dimensions our cannon will have. As you're well aware, we can set it up so that its resisting capacity is virtually unlimited, because it isn't meant to be moved around."

"That's perfectly clear," the general replied.

"Till now," Barbicane said, "the longest cannons, our enormous columbiads, haven't exceeded twenty-five feet in length; so the dimensions we'll need to adopt are going to amaze a good many people."

"That's for sure!" J. T. Maston exclaimed. "Speaking for myself, I want a cannon that's at least half a mile long!"

"Half a mile!" exclaimed the general and the major.

"Yes, half a mile! And it'll still be 50% too short."

"Come on, Maston," Morgan replied, "you're overdoing it!"

"Not one bit!" contended their hotheaded secretary. "Honestly, I don't know how you can say I overdo things!"

"Because you go too far!"

"Sir," J. T. Maston replied, getting on his high horse, "kindly note that an artilleryman is just like a shell—he can never go too far!"

The discussion was starting to get personal, but their president stepped in.

"Calm down, my friends, and let's use our heads; it obviously needs to be a long-barreled cannon, since the piece's length will increase the pressure of the gases expanding beneath the projectile; but it's pointless to go beyond certain limits."

"Exactly," the major said.

"What's the rule of thumb in this matter? Ordinarily a cannon's length is twenty to twenty-five times the diameter of its shells, and it weighs 235 to 240 times what they do."

"That's not enough!" J. T. Maston snapped with his usual impulsiveness.

"There I agree, my good friend, and if we actually duplicated these proportions with a projectile that was nine feet wide and weighed 20,000 pounds, the weapon would have a length of only 225 feet and a weight of 4,800,000 pounds."

"That's nonsense!" J. T. Maston shot back. "It might as well be a handgun!"

"I think so too," Barbicane replied, "which is why I propose to quadruple that

length and build a cannon 900 feet long."

The general and the major raised a few objections; but nevertheless, thanks to the energetic support of the Gun Club's secretary, this proposition was decisively adopted.

"Now," Elphiston said, "how thick will its walls be?"

"Six feet thick," Barbicane replied.

"Surely you don't plan to mount a whopper like that on a gun carriage?" the major asked.

"It would be a sight to see, though!" J. T. Maston said.

"But not feasible," Barbicane replied. "No, my idea is to cast this weapon by pouring it into the ground itself, bracing it with wrought-iron hoops, and ultimately surrounding it with a thick casing of limestone brickwork, all so that it will fully benefit from the resisting capacity of the earth around it. Once the piece is cast, its bore will be carefully reamed and calibrated in order to prevent any windage[33] around the shell; this way no gas will escape, and the gunpowder's full expanding power will be used to provide thrust."

"Hooray!" J. T. Maston put in. "We've got our cannon!"

"Not yet," Barbicane replied, hushing his impatient friend with his hand.

"Why not?"

"Because we haven't discussed what form it will take. Will it be a cannon, a howitzer, or a mortar?"

"A cannon," Morgan contended.

"A howitzer," the major shot back.

"A mortar!" J. T. Maston exclaimed.

Another high-energy argument was all set to break out, each man going to bat for his favorite weapon, when their president stopped it cold.

"My friends," he said, "I'm going to bring you into full agreement; our columbiad will take after all three of these guns equally. It will be a cannon, since its powder chamber will be the same diameter as its bore. It will be a howitzer, since it will shoot a shell that's hollow. Finally it will be a mortar, since it

---

[33] The space sometimes found between a projectile and the gun bore.

will be aimed at a 90° angle; and because it's solidly embedded in the ground with no possibility of recoil, it will transmit to the projectile the full force of the cumulative thrust inside it."

"Motion carried, motion carried!" the committee members replied.

"One minor consideration," Elphiston said. "Will the barrel of this can-mort-itzer be rifled?"

"No, no," Barbicane replied. "We need an enormous initial velocity, and as you're well aware, a shell shoots less swiftly from a rifled cannon than from a cannon with a smooth bore."

"True enough."

"This time we've finally got it!" J. T. Maston said again.

"No, not quite," remarked the Gun Club's president.

"And why not?"

"Because we still don't know what metal it'll be made from."

"Let's decide right now."

"I was about to suggest it."

The four committee members gobbled a dozen sandwiches apiece followed by bowlfuls of tea, then resumed their discussion.

"My gallant colleagues," Barbicane said, "our cannon has to be tremendously tough, tremendously hard, impervious to heat, unable to liquefy, and incapable of oxidizing under the corrosive action of acids."

"There's no doubt on that score," the major replied, "and since we'll have to use a considerable amount of metal, we won't have much choice in the matter."

"All right then," Morgan said, "I propose we manufacture our columbiad from the best alloy yet known, in other words, a hundred parts copper, twelve parts tin, and six parts brass."

"My friends," their president replied, "I'll admit this combination has yielded first-rate results; but in this instance it would be too costly and also very hard to work with. So I think we need to select a material that's both first-rate and low-cost, such as cast iron. Isn't that your feeling, major?"

"Completely," Elphiston replied.

"In fact," Barbicane went on, "cast iron

sells for a tenth as much as bronze; it's simple to pour, it flows easily into molds made of sand, it's quickly shaped—so it saves both time and money. Furthermore it's a first-rate material, and at the Battle of Atlanta during the war, I recall that cast-iron pieces fired a thousand rounds each at the rate of one every twenty minutes, and they didn't suffer a bit."

"Cast iron is very brittle, however," Morgan replied.

"Yes, but also very rugged; so I'll answer for it that we won't blow up."

"You could blow up and still be decent fellows," J. T. Maston remarked pointedly.

"Of course," Barbicane replied. "So I'm going to beg our good secretary to calculate how much a cast-iron cannon would weigh if it's 900 feet long, 9 feet across inside, and has walls 6 feet thick."

"Coming right up," J. T. Maston replied.

And just as he'd done the day before, he strung his formulas together with wondrous ease, then said a minute later:

"This cannon will weigh 75,001.26 tons."

"And at two cents per pound, its cost will be . . . ?"

"It will cost $3,000,050.40."

J. T. Maston, the major, and the general gave Barbicane worried looks.

"Well, gentlemen," said the Gun Club's president, "I'll repeat what I told you yesterday—relax, those millions won't be lacking!"

With this assurance from their president, the committee scheduled their third session for the next evening, then adjourned.

9

THE GUNPOWDER QUESTION

THE QUESTION of gunpowder was still to be dealt with. The public waited anxiously for this final decision. Given the projectile's size and the cannon's length, what amount of gunpowder would be needed to furnish the propulsion? Abnormal quantities of this dreadful ingredient, whose effects human beings have nevertheless harnessed, would be called on to play their role.

It's widely believed and bandied about

that gunpowder was invented in the 14th century by a German monk named Friar Schwarz, whose great discovery cost him his life. But today it's pretty well proven that this story needs to be classed with the folk tales of the Middle Ages. Gunpowder wasn't invented by anybody; it's a direct descendant of Greek fire, a sort of 7th century flame-thrower likewise composed of sulfur and saltpeter. Except, since that time, these mixtures have transformed from simple burning mixtures into exploding ones.

But if academics are thoroughly familiar with the fictitious history of gunpowder, few people are aware of its mechanical power. Now then, that's just the knowledge needed for grasping the importance of this question before the committee.

Thus a quart of gunpowder weighs close to two pounds; when it ignites, it produces around a hundred gallons of gaseous matter; once these gases are released and heated by a temperature of 4,400° Fahrenheit, they occupy a space of about a thousand gallons. So the gunpowder's volume is 1/4,000 that of the gases produced by its combustion. The reader can imagine, then, the fearful pressure of these gases when they're squeezed into a space 4,000 times too cramped.

The committee members were perfectly cognizant of these things when they opened their third session the following day. Barbicane gave the floor to Major Elphiston, who had been director of gunpowder production during the war.

"My dear comrades," said this noted chemist, "I'll start with some indisputable figures we can use as a jumping-off point. The day before yesterday our honorable J. T. Maston described the 24-pound shell for us in the most poetic terms—well, a gun discharges this shell with only 16 pounds of powder."

"You're positive of this figure?" Barbicane asked.

"Absolutely positive," the major replied. "Armstrong's cannon uses only 75 pounds of gunpowder for an 800-pound projectile, and Rodman's columbiad expends only 160 pounds of gunpowder in order to fire a half-ton shell six miles. These facts are beyond

dispute, since I turned them up myself in the proceedings of the artillery committee."

"Good work," the general replied.

"All right," the major went on, "if there's a conclusion to be drawn from these figures, it's that the amount of gunpowder doesn't increase with the weight of the shell: in essence, if a 24-pound shell needs 16 pounds of gunpowder—put another way, if our regular cannons use an amount of gunpowder equal to two-thirds of the projectile's weight—this proportion isn't consistent. Run the numbers and you'll see that a half-ton shell doesn't take 666 pounds of gunpowder to fire, but a reduced amount of only 160 pounds."

"What are you getting at?" their president asked.

"If you take your premise to its logical extreme, my dear major," J. T. Maston said, "you'll reach a point where your shell will be so heavy, you won't need any gunpowder at all."

"Even in serious matters my friend Maston has to have his little joke," the major remarked. "But he can rest assured, I'll soon propose enough gunpowder to make any artilleryman proud. Only I still maintain that for the biggest cannons during the war, the gunpowder's weight was reduced, after experimenting, to a tenth of the shell's weight."

"You're as right as can be," Morgan said. "But before we determine the amount of gunpowder needed to provide the propulsion, I think we'd better agree on what type we want."

"We'll use coarse-grained gunpowder," the major replied. "Its combustion is quicker than the kind that's finely ground."

"No doubt," Morgan remarked, "but it's highly explosive and ends up affecting the bore of the piece."

"True, and that would be a drawback for a cannon built to see years of action, but it isn't for our columbiad. We don't run any danger of blowing up, and the gunpowder needs to ignite instantly so as to have its full mechanical effect."

"We could drill several holes for fuses," J. T. Maston said, "then it could be set off in different places at the same time."

"Of course," Elphiston replied, "but that

makes the operation more difficult. Consequently I keep coming back to my coarse-grained gunpowder, which does away with these difficulties."

"So be it," the general replied.

"To load his columbiad," the major went on, "Rodman used a gunpowder with grains the size of chestnuts—it was made of willow-tree charcoal that had simply been roasted in cast-iron boilers. This gunpowder was hard and shiny, didn't rub off on your hands, contained large quantities of hydrogen and oxygen, caught on fire instantly, was highly explosive, and yet didn't noticeably harm the guns."

"Well then," J. T. Maston replied, "it looks like we're all set to go and we've made our choice."

"At least you didn't ask for gold dust," the major remarked with a grin, which earned him a threatening wave of the hook from his touchy friend.

Till then Barbicane had stayed out of the discussion. He listened and let them do the talking. Obviously he had his own ideas. Accordingly he was content just to say:

"Now, my friends, what amount of gunpowder are you proposing?"

The three Gun Club members traded looks for an instant.

"Two hundred thousand pounds," Morgan finally said.

"Five hundred thousand," the major contended.

"Eight hundred thousand pounds!" J. T. Maston snapped.

This time Elphiston didn't dare accuse his colleague of overdoing things. In essence it came down to firing a 20,000-pound projectile to the moon and giving it an initial force of 12,000 yards per second. So a moment of silence followed this threefold proposition from our trio of colleagues.

It was finally broken by President Barbicane.

"My gallant comrades," he said in a serene voice, "my starting point is that the cannon will be built to our specifications and will have a resisting capacity that's unlimited. So I'll surprise the honorable J. T. Maston by telling him his calculations are timid,

and I propose to double his 800,000 pounds of gunpowder."

"You want 1,600,000 pounds?" J. T. Maston put in, bounding out of his chair.

"Not an ounce less."

"But then we'll have to go back to my idea of a cannon half a mile long."

"Obviously," the major said.

"One million six hundred thousand pounds of gunpowder," the committee's secretary went on, "takes up about 22,000 cubic feet of space; now then, since your cannon has a capacity of only 54,000 cubic feet, that would fill it halfway—and the bore wouldn't be long enough anymore for the gases to expand and give sufficient thrust to the projectile."

There was no comeback to this. J. T. Maston spoke the truth. They looked at Barbicane.

"However," their president went on, "I'll stand by that amount of gunpowder. Think about it—1,600,000 pounds of gunpowder will generate some 1.5 billion gallons of gaseous matter. 1.5 billion! Is that clear to you?"

"But how will we handle it, then?" the general asked.

"It's quite simple; we need to reduce this enormous amount of gunpowder without losing any of its mechanical power."

"Fine, but by what method?"

"I'm about to tell you," Barbicane merely replied.

His conversation partners devoured him with their eyes.

"In fact nothing is easier," he went on, "than to shrink this mass of gunpowder to a fourth of its volume. You're familiar with the interesting substance that makes up the rudimentary tissue of plants and is called cellulose?"

"Aha!" the major put in. "I see where you're heading, my dear Barbicane."

"This substance," their president said, "occurs in an absolutely unadulterated state in various sources, and especially in cotton where it's nothing more than the stubble on the cotton plant's seeds. Now then, if cotton is combined with cold nitric acid, it's transformed into a substance that's exceptionally

160

insoluble, exceptionally combustible, and exceptionally explosive. A few years back in 1832, a French chemist named Henri Braconnot discovered this commodity, which he called xyloidine. In 1838 another Frenchman, T.-J. Pelouze, studied its various attributes, and finally in 1846 a chemistry professor in Basel, Christian Schönbein, proposed its use as gunpowder. This powder, this nitric cotton—"

"—is also known as pyroxile," Elphiston responded.

"Or guncotton," Morgan remarked.

"So haven't any Americans signed their names to this discovery?" J. T. Maston exclaimed, motivated by a keen sense of national pride.

"Unfortunately not a single one," the major replied.

"But to keep Mr. Maston happy," continued the Gun Club's president, "I'll mention to him that one of our citizens can be credited with contributions to the research on cellulose—because collodion, which is one of the chief ingredients in photography, is quite simply pyroxile dissolved in ether with a dash of alcohol, and it was discovered by a Boston medical student named Maynard."

"All right! Three cheers for Maynard and guncotton!" shouted the Gun Club's raucous secretary.

"Let's get back to pyroxile," Barbicane went on. "You're familiar with the attributes it has that'll make it so valuable to us; it's extremely easy to prepare: soak some cotton in smoking nitric acid[34] for fifteen minutes, rinse thoroughly with water, dry, and that's that."

"In fact nothing could be simpler," Morgan said.

"What's more, pyroxile isn't affected by moisture, a valuable characteristic from our standpoint since it will take several days to load the cannon; its ignition temperature is 340° Fahrenheit instead of 465°, and its combustion is so sudden, you can light it on top of regular gunpowder

without the latter having time to catch fire."

"Perfect!" the major replied.

"Only it's more costly."

"Makes no difference!" J. T. Maston put in.

"Finally it gives projectiles four times the speed that gunpowder will. I would even add that if you mix it with 80% of its weight in potassium nitrate, its expanding power is increased to a much higher degree."

"Will we need to do that?" the major asked.

"I doubt it," Barbicane replied. "Hence, instead of 1,600,000 pounds of powder, we'll have only 400,000 pounds of guncotton, and since we can safely squeeze 500 pounds of guncotton into twenty-seven cubic feet, this substance will take up only 180 feet of the columbiad's length. Under the pressure of 1.5 billion gallons of gaseous matter, the shell will thus have over 700 feet of bore to go through before it starts its flight toward that silver orb!"

By this point J. T. Maston couldn't hide his feelings; he shot into his friend's arms with the force of a projectile—and would have staved him in if Barbicane hadn't been blessed with a bulletproof build.

This incident ended the committee's third session. Barbicane and his daring colleagues, to whom nothing seemed impossible, had just settled the ultra complex questions of the projectile, cannon, and gunpowder. Their plans were laid and had only to be put into execution.

"A mere detail, a technicality," J. T. Maston said.

* * *

NOTE: During this discussion President Barbicane alleges that one of his countrymen invented collodion. With all due respect to our gallant J. T. Maston, this is an error and it comes from the similarity of two names.

In 1847 while studying medicine in Boston, J. P. Maynard did get the idea of using collodion in the treatment of skin disorders, but collodion had been identified in 1846. The man who deserves the credit for this major discovery was a Frenchman, a thinker of great distinction, a combination scholar, painter, poet, philosopher, classicist, and chemist—Monsieur Louis Ménard. *J.V.*

---

[34] So named because when it comes in contact with moisture in the air, it gives off a dense, whitish smoke.

10

1 FOE OUT OF 25,000,000 FRIENDS

THE AMERICAN PUBLIC took an intense interest in the tiniest details of the Gun Club's undertaking. It kept daily tabs on the committee's discussions. The simplest preparations for this great experiment, the arithmetical questions it raised, the mechanical difficulties to be settled—in a nutshell, the whole "set-up operation"—aroused their feelings to a fever pitch.

More than a year would go by between the start and finish of these activities; but this stretch of time wasn't to be lacking in excitement; a location had to be selected for drilling the hole, for constructing the mold, for casting the columbiad, and for the highly dangerous task of loading it—this was more than enough to pique public curiosity. Once the projectile was launched, it would be out of sight in a few tenths of a second; what happened to it then, how it behaved in space, and how it went about reaching the moon, these were things only a handful of privileged people would see with their own eyes. Hence the preparations for the experiment, the exact details of its execution, were what really held the interest in this business.

But the undertaking's purely scientific appeal was heightened by a sudden development.

As you know, Barbicane's plan had won its creator many legions of admirers and friends. Yet as estimable and unusual as this majority was, it didn't amount to unanimous support. Alone in all the states of the Union, a single man objected to the Gun Club's endeavor; he attacked it vehemently at every opportunity; and human nature being what is, Barbicane paid more attention to this single source of opposition than to everybody else's applause.

However he was well aware of the motive behind this hostility, the origin of this unique enmity, why it was so personal and of such long standing, and finally the competitiveness and pride that had given rise to it.

The Gun Club's president had never met his dogged foe. Which was lucky, because a meeting between the two men would definitely have had a regrettable outcome. Barbicane's competitor was an intellectual like himself, a proud, daring, persuasive, and forceful personality, an unadulterated Yankee. His name was Captain Nicholl. He lived in Philadelphia.

There isn't a soul alive who doesn't know about the odd conflict that took place during the Civil War between projectiles and the armor that covered ironclad ships, the former bent on piercing the latter, the latter thoroughly determined to withstand any such piercing. This led to a drastic transformation of national navies in both the New World and the Old. It was an unprecedented fight to the finish between shells and armor plate, the one getting bigger and the other thicker in ongoing proportions. Ships went into battle equipped with fearsome firepower and protected by invulnerable carapaces. Vessels like the *Merrimack*, the *Monitor*, the ram *Tennessee*, and the *Weehawken*[35] were armored against enemy projectiles, then fired enormous projectiles themselves. They did unto others as they would *not* have others do unto them—that unethical precept underlying the whole art of war.

Now then, if Barbicane was a great caster of projectiles, Nicholl was a great forger of armor plate. The one cast night and day in Baltimore, the other forged day and night in Philadelphia. Each hewed to a diametrically opposed school of thought.

As soon as Barbicane invented a new shell, Nicholl invented new armor plate. The Gun Club's president spent his life punching holes, the captain spent his thwarting that aim. This grew into an hourly competitiveness that was at the point of getting personal. In Barbicane's dreams Nicholl appeared in the guise of an impregnable piece of armor against which he dashed to pieces, and in Nicholl's fantasies Barbicane turned into a projectile that ran him clean through.

However, though they followed diverging paths, these two experts would have ended up meeting despite all those axioms in geometry; but it would have taken place on the du-

---

[35] Ships in the American navy.

eling ground. Luckily for these two citizens who were so useful to their country, a distance of fifty to sixty miles separated them from each other, and their friends threw such obstacles in the way, they'd never met.

Now it wasn't quite clear which of these two inventors had won out over the other; the results achieved made it hard to arrive at a just verdict. But in the final analysis, it seemed that the armor had to end up caving in to the shells.

Nevertheless some knowledgeable men weren't so sure. In the most recent tests, Barbicane's cylindro-conical projectiles ended up sticking in Nicholl's armor plate like pins in a pincushion; on this occasion the forger from Philadelphia figured that he'd triumphed, that no amount of contempt was too great for his competitor; but later on the latter simply substituted 600-pound hollow cannonballs for conical shells, and the captain had to back down. In fact, though impelled at a moderate speed,[36] these projectiles cracked, breached, and pulverized the finest metal plate.

Now then, things were at this point, the shell seemingly triumphant, when the war ended—on the very day Nicholl had completed a new piece of armor made of hammered steel! It was a masterpiece of its kind; it could defy any projectile in the world. The captain had it transferred to the firing range in Washington, D.C. and challenged the Gun Club's president to put a crack in it. Since peace had been declared, Barbicane wasn't willing to attempt the experiment.

Furious, Nicholl then offered to expose his armor plate to the impact of any outlandish shell imaginable, solid, hollow, round, or conical. Not willing to endanger his recent success, the club's president refused.

Inflamed by this unspeakable stubbornness, Nicholl tried to tempt Barbicane by giving him every advantage. He proposed to set up his armor plate only 200 yards away from the cannon. Barbicane kept on refusing. 100 yards? Not even 75.

"Fifty, then!" the captain shrieked from

the pages of the newspapers. "All right, I'll put my armor plate 25 yards away and stand behind it!"

Barbicane responded that he wouldn't fire even if Captain Nicholl stood in front of it.

At this comeback Nicholl went over the edge; he got personal; he insinuated that nothing but cowardice lay behind this, that a man who refuses to fire a cannonball is pretty clearly afraid to, that those artillerymen who fight these days from six miles off are, in short, discreetly substituting mathematical formulas for personal courage, and moreover that it's far braver to wait serenely for a shell behind some armor plate than to fire one strictly by the book.

Barbicane didn't reply to these innuendos; maybe he wasn't even aware of them, since by then he was totally caught up in the calculations for his great undertaking.

When he made his notorious announcement to the Gun Club, it spurred Captain Nicholl's anger to a point of frenzy. The captain's feelings were a mixture of all-out jealousy and total helplessness! How could he invent something better than that 900-foot columbiad? What armor plate could ever withstand a 20,000-pound projectile? At first Nicholl was floored, shattered, and overwhelmed by this "shot across his bow," then he dusted himself off and decided to squelch the proposition with crushing arguments.

So he attacked the Gun Club's efforts with great vehemence; he published many letters that the newspapers didn't shrink from reprinting. He tried to tear down Barbicane's work on scientific grounds. Once hostilities had commenced, he shored up his case with any justifications he could find, and to tell the truth, they were very often underhanded and bogus.

First Barbicane's figures came under vehement attack; by juggling $a+b$'s, Nicholl tried to prove that his foe's formulas were wrong, then accused him of not knowing the basic precepts of ballistics. Among other mistakes, according to Nicholl's own calculations, it was absolutely impossible to give any object whatever a speed of 12,000 yards per second; ready with his algebra, the captain held that even at such a speed, no projec-

---

[36] The weight of the gunpowder used was only a twelfth of the cannonball's weight.

tile this weight could ever clear the outer limits of the earth's atmosphere! It wouldn't get even twenty miles up! And that's not all. Even supposing this speed was attained (and assuming it was sufficient), the capsule wouldn't withstand the pressure of the gases generated by igniting 1,600,000 pounds of gunpowder, and if it *did* withstand this pressure, it simply wouldn't tolerate the high temperature—it would melt as it left the columbiad and fall back in a boiling shower onto the heads of unwary spectators.

Barbicane didn't bat an eye at these attacks and went on with his work.

Then Nicholl turned to other aspects of the matter; without getting into its total lack of practical value, he viewed the experiment as extremely dangerous—for the citizens whose presence gave their blessing to such a shameful exhibition, ditto for the towns in the vicinity of this vile cannon; he also pointed out that if the projectile didn't reach its destination—which was an absolutely impossible objective—it obviously would fall back to the earth, and the descent of such a mass, multiplied by the square of its speed, would put some part of the globe in conspicuous jeopardy. Given such a situation, therefore, and without trampling on the rights of a free citizenry, this was one of those instances where government intervention becomes necessary, since indulging the whims of an individual shouldn't affect the safety of all.

As you can see, Captain Nicholl had gone overboard with his exaggerating. He was alone in his views. Accordingly nobody heeded his ill-omened prophesies. People didn't care if he hollered away till he was hoarse, if that's what suited him. He was the self-appointed defender of a cause that was lost from the outset; everybody heard him but nobody listened, and he didn't steal a single admirer from the Gun Club's president. What's more, the latter didn't even take the trouble to rebut his competitor's arguments.

As a last-ditch effort, not even able to lay down his life for his cause, Nicholl decided to lay down his hard-earned cash. So he publicly proposed in the *Richmond Enquirer* a series of bets on an increasing scale, which ran as follows.

He made bets:

1. That the needed funds won't be found for the Gun Club's undertaking . . .   for $1,000.

2. That there's no feasible process for casting a 900-foot cannon and the attempt will fail . . .   for $2,000.

3. That it won't be possible to load the columbiad, and that the pyroxile will self-ignite under the projectile's weight . . .   for $3,000.

4. That the columbiad will blow up the very first time it's fired . . .   for $4,000.

5. That the shell won't get even six miles up and will fall to the earth a few seconds after being launched . . .   for $5,000.

As you can see, it was a sizeable sum the captain was risking in his indomitable stubbornness. It came to no less than $15,000.[37]

Despite the size of this bet, on May 19 he received a sealed envelope containing a note that was magnificent in its brevity; it read as follows:

> *Baltimore*
> *October 18*
>
> *Done.*
>
> BARBICANE.

11

FLORIDA AND TEXAS

ONE QUESTION, however, still remained to be decided: the club had to pick a promising locality for the experiment. In line with the Cambridge Observatory's recommendations, the gun had to be pointed at a right angle to the plane of the horizon, in other words, toward the zenith; now then, the moon ascends

---

[37] *Translator's note.* In today's dollars comparable to about $300,000.

to the zenith only at sites located between latitude 0° and 28°, meaning her declination is only 28°.[38] So it was a question of determining the exact spot on the globe where the immense columbiad would be cast.

When the Gun Club met in a general session on October 20, Barbicane brought along Z. Belltropp's magnificent map of the United States. But J. T. Maston gave him no time to unfold it, asked for the floor with his usual pushiness, and spoke as follows:

"Honorable colleagues, the issue we're going to deal with today is truly of national importance, and it'll give us the opportunity to make a great patriotic gesture."

The Gun Club's membership looked at each other, not clear on where the speaker was going with this.

"None of you," he went on, "would dream of gambling with our country's glory, and if there's one right the Union can claim, it's to harbor our Gun Club's fearsome cannon inside its own borders. Now then, under current circumstances—"

"My gallant Maston . . . " their president said.

"Let me expand on this thought," the speaker continued. "Under current circumstances we're forced to pick a site close enough to the equator that the experiment can proceed under decent conditions—"

"If you would kindly . . . " Barbicane said.

"I insist on a free discussion of ideas!" countered the hotheaded J. T. Maston. "And I maintain that the land from which our glorious projectile will be launched should belong to the Union."

"No doubt about it!" a few members replied.

"All right, since our boundaries don't extend far enough, since the sea to the south throws up a barricade we can't overcome, since we need to look for this 28th parallel outside the United States in an adjacent country, that gives us legitimate grounds for war, and I move we commence hostilities against Mexico!"

"No way! Hell no!" voices exclaimed all around him.

"No?" J. T. Maston countered. "That's a word I'm shocked to hear inside these walls!"

"Just hold on now—"

"Never!" the speaker snapped fiercely. "Sooner or later that war will break out, and I move we wage it this very day."

"Maston," Barbicane said, firing a bang from his hand bell, "you no longer have the floor!"

Maston tried to answer back, but some of his colleagues managed to shut him up.

"I agree," Barbicane said, "that this experiment can and should be attempted only on Union soil, but if my impatient friend had let me speak, if he'd taken a look at a map, he would have realized that's it's utterly pointless to declare war on our neighbors, because certain U.S. boundaries *do* extend beyond the 28th parallel. See—we've got the whole southern part of Texas and Florida at our disposal."

The incident came to nothing, though J. T. Maston wasn't persuaded without some regret on his part. The club decided, therefore, that the columbiad would be poured right into the ground of either Texas or Florida. But this decision was destined to create an unprecedented competition between the towns in these two states.

After reaching the American coastline, the 28th parallel crosses Florida's peninsula and divides it into two roughly equal parts. Next, plunging into the Gulf of Mexico, it adds a lower limit to the arc formed by the coastlines of Alabama, Mississippi, and Louisiana. Then, coming to Texas, it cuts off a corner of that state, stretches across Mexico, clears Sonora, straddles Baja California, and vanishes into the waves of the Pacific. So only the portions of Texas and Florida located below this parallel met the latitude conditions recommended by the Cambridge Observatory.

The southern part of Florida has no major cities to its credit. It's garnished merely with forts built to guard against prowling Indians. Only one town, Tampa, could argue on behalf of its location and make a good case for itself.

---

[38] A heavenly body's declination is its latitude in the celestial sphere; its right ascension is the longitude.

In Texas, by contrast, towns are bigger and more plentiful; Corpus Christi in Nueces County and all the cities located on the Rio Bravo del Norte[39]—Laredo, Comalites, and San Ygnacio in Webb County, Roma and Rio Grande City in Starr County, Edinburg in Hidalgo County, Santa Rita, El Panda, and Brownsville in Cameron County—formed an imposing alliance against Florida's claims.

Accordingly the decision was no sooner announced than representatives from Texas and Florida arrived in Baltimore by the shortest routes; from then on President Barbicane and the Gun Club's leading members were besieged day and night by fearsome demands. If seven cities in Greece contended for the honor of being Homer's birthplace, here two whole states were threatening to come to blows over a cannon.

Consequently you saw their "blood brotherhoods" strolling the city streets weapon in hand. Every time they met up, there was the risk of a confrontation that might have had disastrous consequences. Luckily President Barbicane's shrewdness and discretion dispelled this danger. But such personal shows of force would have by-products in the newspapers of the various states. Thus New York's *Herald* and *Tribune* backed Texas, while the *Times* and the *American Review* sided with Florida's representatives. The Gun Club's membership didn't know who to believe anymore.

Texas proudly presented its twenty-six counties, trotting them out with a figurative drumroll; but Florida replied that its twelve counties counted for more than Texas's twenty-six, since they were in a region only one-sixth the size.

Texas really preened itself on its 330,000 residents, but Florida, being smaller, boasted that it was more densely populated with 56,000. Further, it accused Texas of specializing in malarial fever, which cost it several thousand citizens year after year. And Florida wasn't mistaken.

In its turn Texas answered that when it came to fever, Florida had no grounds for feeling left out, that it was unwise, to say the least, for this state to call other regions unsanitary when Floridians were honored to have *vómito negro*[40] on a chronic basis. And Texas was in the right.

"Besides," the Texans added in the pages of the *New York Herald*, "some respect should be shown to a state that grows the finest cotton in all America, a state that produces the best live oak for shipbuilding, a state that has superb coal deposits and iron mines whose yield is 50% pure ore."

To which the *American Review* replied that Florida's soil, though it wasn't as rich, offered the best conditions for molding and casting the columbiad, since the terrain was made up of sand and clayish earth.

"But," the Texans continued, "before you do any casting in a particular region, you need to get to that region; now then, Florida is hard to reach, while the Texas coastline offers Galveston Bay, which is thirty-five miles around and could berth every fleet in the world!"

"Swell," repeated the newspapers committed to Florida. "You're a big help with your Galveston Bay—it's located above the 29th parallel! Don't we have the Bay of Espiritu Santo,[41] which opens right at latitude 28° and lets ships go straight to Tampa?"

"Some bay!" Texas replied. "It's half choked with sand!"

"Go choke yourselves!" Florida yelled. "Next you'll be saying we're a land of savages!"

"Ye gods, you still have Seminoles running around the countryside!"

"Right, and you've got Apaches and Comanches—you call that civilized?"

They waged war in this fashion for a few days, then Florida tried to lure its opponent onto lower ground, and one morning the *Times* insinuated that since the undertaking was "intrinsically American," it could only be attempted on "intrinsically American" land.

---

[39] *Translator's note.* Mexico's name for the Rio Grande.

[40] *Translator's note.* Spanish: "black vomit," better known as yellow fever.

[41] *Translator's note.* Now called Tampa Bay.

At these words Texas shot to its feet: "American!" it howled. "Aren't we just as American as you? Weren't both Texas and Florida admitted to the Union in 1845?"

"Certainly," the *Times* answered, "but America has owned us since 1820."

"Don't we know it," the *Tribune* remarked. "For two hundred years before that, you belonged to either Spain or England, then you were sold to the United States for $5,000,000!"

"Makes no difference!" the Floridians would answer back. "Why should we be ashamed? In 1803 didn't the nation pay Napoleon Bonaparte $16,000,000 for Louisiana?"

"It's a disgrace!" shrieked the representatives from Texas. "A wretched piece of land like Florida daring to compare itself to Texas! Instead of being sold, Texas announced its own independence, drove out the Mexicans on March 2, 1836, and declared itself a unified republic after Sam Houston defeated Santa Anna's troops on the banks of the San Jacinto! A country, in short, which joined the United States of America of its own free will!"

"Because it was afraid of Mexico!" Florida replied.

Afraid! This really was too harsh a word, and from the day it was uttered, the situation became intolerable. You were waiting for the two factions to spill blood in Baltimore's streets. You couldn't let their representatives out of your sight.

President Barbicane didn't know which way to turn. Threatening letters, notes, and documents poured into his home. Whose side should he take? From the viewpoints of acquiring the land, ease of contact, and speed of shipping, the truth was that both states made equally good cases. As for the politicos, it was none of their business.

Now then, this indecision and befuddlement had already gone on for a good while when Barbicane decided on a way out; he called his colleagues together, and the solution he proposed to them was thoroughly sensible, as you'll see.

"After taking a close look," he said, "at what's happening now between Florida and Texas, it's obvious the same problems will be repeated between the individual towns in the state we choose. There's no getting around it, this competitiveness will pass from genus down to species, from state down to city. Now then, Texas has eleven towns that meet the desired conditions, they'll fight over the honor of hosting the undertaking, and they'll make new enemies for us—whereas Florida has only one town. So my vote goes to Florida and Tampa!"

When this decision was made public, the representatives from Texas were bowled over. They flew into an indescribable rage, singled out various Gun Club members, and challenged them to duels. There was only one course of action the Baltimore judiciary could take and they took it. They chartered a special train, loaded the Texans on board whether they liked it or not, and ran the whole bunch out of town at a speed of thirty miles per hour.

But despite the swiftness of their departure, the Texans had time to toss a last snide threat at their opponents.

Since Florida was a mere peninsula confined between two seas, they alluded to its slim width and claimed that it couldn't handle the jolt at launching, that it would snap in two the first time the cannon was fired.

"Fine, let it!" the Floridians replied, with a brevity worthy of old Sparta.

12

URBI ET ORBI

ONCE THE PROBLEMS relating to astronomy, mechanics, and topography were settled, the issue of money came up. Putting these plans into execution called for raising an enormous sum. No individual, no nation even, could have doled out the millions necessary.

Therefore, though it was an American undertaking, President Barbicane chose to make it a matter of worldwide concern and to ask for every country's financial cooperation. The entire planet had both the right and the responsibility to mind its satellite's business. With this objective the club launched a funding drive that reached from Baltimore to everywhere, *urbi et orbi.*[42]

This funding drive was to succeed beyond anybody's expectations. Yet it involved donating money, not lending it. The transaction was totally unselfish in the strictest sense of the word and didn't offer any chance for a profit.

But the impact of Barbicane's announcement ranged beyond the boundaries of the United States; it had crossed the Atlantic and Pacific, simultaneously infiltrating Asia, Europe, Africa, and Oceania. The Union observatories immediately got in touch with observatories in foreign countries; some of them—like the ones in Paris, St. Petersburg, Cape Town, Berlin, Altona, Stockholm, Warsaw, Hamburg, Budapest, Bologna, Malta, Lisbon, Benares, Madras, and Peking—sent the Gun Club their congratulations; the others stayed cautiously expectant.

As for the Greenwich Observatory, endorsed by the twenty-two other institutions devoted to astronomy in Great Britain, it made no bones about its position; it boldly denied any possibility of success and fell in with Captain Nicholl's thinking. Accordingly, while various scholarly societies were promising to send delegations to Tampa, the Greenwich office met in private session, had just one item on the agenda, and gave Barbicane's proposition the brush off. But this was good old English jealousy. Nothing else.

All in all the reaction of the scientific world was excellent, and from there it spread to the public, who, by and large, were enthusiastic about the business. A fact of great importance since the public would be called on to pledge a considerable amount of capital.

On October 8 President Barbicane issued an impassioned statement in which he called on "men of good will" throughout the world. This document, translated into every language, was a huge success.

Funding drives were launched in the Union's chief towns, central headquarters being the Bank of Baltimore at 9 Baltimore St.; then drives got under way in the various nations of the New World and the Old:

---

[42] *Translator's note.* Latin: "to city and world."

in Vienna—banking house of S. M. von Rothschild

in St. Petersburg—banking house of Stieglitz & Co.

in Paris—Crédit Mobilier

in Stockholm—banking house of Tottie & Arfvedson

in London—banking house of N. M. Rothschild & Sons

in Turin—banking house of Ardouin & Co.

in Berlin—banking house of Mendelssohn & Co.

in Geneva—banking house of Lombard, Odier & Co.

in Constantinople—The Ottoman Bank

in Brussels—banking house of S. Lambert

in Madrid—banking house of Daniel Weisweiller

in Amsterdam—Netherlands Credit

in Rome—banking house of Torlonia & Co.

in Lisbon—banking house of Lecesne

in Copenhagen—The Private Bank

in Buenos Aires—The Mauá Bank

in Rio de Janeiro—same banking house

in Montevideo—same banking house

in Valparaiso—banking house of Thomas La Chambre & Co.

in Mexico City—banking house of Martin, Daran & Co.

in Lima—banking house of Thomas La Chambre & Co.

Three days after President Barbicane's statement, $4,000,000 had been deposited in the various towns of the Union. With this kind of front money, the Gun Club was already in a position to get started.

But a few days later, telegrams informed America that the funding drives in foreign parts were proceeding with real alacrity. Certain countries stood out in their generosity; others kept a tighter grip on their purse strings. A matter of national character.

Even so, figures are more eloquent than

words, and here's the official status report of the sums recorded on the credit side of the Gun Club's ledger after the funding drive was over.

As its share, Russia deposited the enormous sum of 368,733 rubles (about $272,000). For this to be a surprise, you would need to be ignorant of the Russians' taste for science and the advances they've written up in the discipline of astronomy, thanks to their many observatories, the chief one of which cost 2,000,000 rubles.

France started out by laughing at the Americans' ambitions. The moon served as the excuse for a thousand puns and twenty song-and-dance routines in which bad taste and ignorance ran neck and neck. But just as the French used to pay dearly after singing their national anthem to foreign enemies, now they paid dearly after having a good laugh—they pledged the sum of 1,253,930 francs (about $231,000). At that price they were entitled to a little fun.

Austria proved generous enough in the midst of its financial troubles. For its part it raised 216,000 florins (about $96,000) for the public fund, which gave this sum a hearty welcome.

Sweden and Norway's contribution was 52,000 riksdalers (about $54,000). In relation to the region involved, this figure was considerable; but surely it would have been higher had there been a drive in Oslo at the same time as the one in Stockholm. For some reason or other, Norwegians don't like sending their money to Sweden.

Prussia sent in 250,000 talers (about $173,000), testifying to its high regard for the undertaking. Its various observatories eagerly contributed a sizeable sum and gave President Barbicane their most enthusiastic encouragement.

Turkey acted with generosity, but it had a vested interest in the business; in essence the moon regulates this country's annual calendar and its fast of Ramadan. It managed to give no less than 1,372,640 piasters (about $63,000), though it gave them with a fervor that indicated a fair amount of pressure from the Ottoman government.

Belgium stood out among the second-tier nations with its gift of 513,000 francs (about $95,000), which amounted to around twelve centimes (about two cents) per citizen.

Holland and its colonies took an interest in the operation amounting to 110,000 florins (about $43,000), insisting only on the bonus of a 5% discount for paying cash.

Demonstrating its love of scientific exploration, Denmark gave a good 9,000 ducats (about $22,000), though the Danes are hard pressed for land these days.[43]

The German Confederation promised 34,285 florins (about $13,000); you couldn't have asked for more; they wouldn't have given it anyway.

Though very badly off, Italy turned the pockets of its families inside out and found 200,000 liras (about $38,000). Had it owned the Venetian States, it could have done better; but it didn't so it couldn't.[44]

The Papal States felt they should send at least 7,040 Roman scudi (about $7,000), and Portugal expressed its dedication to science with thereabouts of 30,000 crusados (about $21,000).

As for Mexico, it cried poverty with just eighty-six sure piasters (about $319); but self-made empires are always a little hard up.

Switzerland's modest contribution to the American project was 257 francs (about $47). It must be admitted, in all honesty, that the Swiss didn't see the operation's practical side; they doubted that the move of firing a shell at the moon would help in setting up a business relationship with that silver orb, and they deemed it unwise to put their capital into such a chancy undertaking. All things considered, maybe Switzerland was right.

As for Spain, there was no possibility that it could dig up more than 110 reals (about $11). It gave the excuse that it had to finish its railroads. Actually science isn't very highly regarded in this country. It's still a little backward. Furthermore certain Span-

---

[43] *Translator's note.* Prussia and Austria had annexed big chunks of Danish territory in recent invasions.

[44] *Translator's note.* At the time Venice belonged to Austria.

iards—and not the least educated—didn't have an accurate notion of the projectile's size compared to the moon's; they were afraid it might disrupt the moon's orbit, meddle with its role as our satellite, and make it fall to the surface of the planet earth. So the wisest course was to stay out of it. Which, aside from a few reals, is what they did.

That leaves England. You're aware of the sneering hostility with which it greeted Barbicane's proposition. Great Britain contains 26,000,000 people, but the English have one and the same soul. They let it be known that the Gun Club's undertaking ran contrary to their "policy of nonintervention" and they didn't pledge a single farthing.

At this news the Gun Club was content to shrug its shoulders and get on with its tremendous task. When South America—in other words, Peru, Chile, Brazil, Colombia, and the provinces along the Rio de la Plata—had deposited its share (the sum of $300,000) in the club's coffers, the association was in command of a considerable amount of capital, and here's the breakdown:

United States pledges	$4,000,000
Foreign pledges	$1,446,675
Total	$5,446,675

So the public by itself had deposited $5,446,675 in the Gun Club's cash box.[45]

The size of this sum shouldn't startle anybody. According to the estimates, almost the entire amount had to be earmarked for the work of casting, drilling, bricklaying, transporting laborers, housing them in a virtually uninhabited area, constructing furnaces and buildings, plus equipment for the factories, the gunpowder, the projectile, and incidental operating expenses. Certain Civil War cannons cost $1,000 a shot; President Barbicane's, unique in the annals of artillery, could easily run 5,000 times that much.

On October 20 the club finalized a contract with the Cold Spring factory near New York City, which had supplied Parrott during

the war with his finest cast-iron cannons.

As stipulated between the contracting parties, the Cold Spring factory promised to ship the material needed for the columbiad's casting to Tampa in the southerly part of Florida. The factory was to complete this operation no later than October 15 of the following year, the cannon to be handed over in good working order, or they would pay a penalty of $100 per day till the time the moon would reappear under the same circumstances, in other words, after another eighteen years and eleven days. It was incumbent on the Cold Spring Co. to hire workmen, handle payroll, and make other necessary arrangements.

I. Barbicane, the Gun Club's president, and J. Murchison, the Cold Spring factory's director, signed two copies of this good-faith contract after the wording had been approved on both sides.

13
STONY HILL

ONCE THE GUN CLUB'S membership had decided against Texas, everybody in America—where the whole country knows how to read—made it a point of honor to study Florida's geography. Never had the bookshops sold so many copies of Bartram's *Travels*, Romans's *A Concise Natural History of East and West Florida*, Williams's *Territory of Florida*, and *Cleland on the Cultivating of Sugarcane in East Florida*. New editions had to be printed. They were the latest craze.

Barbicane didn't have time for books; he wanted to see and confirm the site for the columbiad with his own two eyes. Accordingly he didn't waste another second, putting the needed funds for building a telescope at the Cambridge Observatory's disposal, and signing a contract with the firm of Breadwill & Co. in Albany for manufacturing an aluminum projectile; then he left Baltimore along with J. T. Maston, Major Elphiston, and the director of the Cold Spring factory.

The next day our four traveling companions arrived in New Orleans. There they immediately boarded the *Tampico*, a gunboat in the national navy that the government had

---

[45] *Translator's note.* This is roughly comparable to $110,000,000 in today's dollars.

put at their disposal; it got up steam and the shores of Louisiana were soon out of sight.

It wasn't a long trip; two days after leaving, the *Tampico* had covered 480 miles [46] and raised the Florida coast. Drawing nearer, Barbicane saw they were facing a low, flat landscape that looked pretty barren. After hugging a coastline with a series of coves full of oysters and lobsters, the *Tampico* stood into the Bay of Espiritu Santo.

This bay is divided into two extensive offshore moorings, one for Tampa, the other for Hillsborough, and the steamer soon cleared the channel leading to them. A little while later the squat guns of Fort Brooke stood out above the waves, and the town of Tampa appeared, sprawling lackadaisically at the far end of a small natural harbor formed by the mouth of the Hillsborough River.

It was here that the *Tampico* dropped anchor on October 22 at seven o'clock in the evening; the four passengers went ashore immediately.

When Barbicane stepped onto Florida soil, he felt his heart pounding fiercely; he seemed to be probing the earth with his foot, just as the architect of a new house might check its stability. J. T. Maston scraped the ground with the tip of his hook.

"Gentlemen," Barbicane said, "we have no time to lose and starting tomorrow, we'll scout out the country on horseback."

Just as Barbicane set foot on land, Tampa's 3,000 residents came down to meet him, an honor the Gun Club's president richly deserved since he'd paid them the compliment of choosing them. They welcomed him with a fearsome round of applause; but Barbicane shrank from all this acclaim, retired to a room at the Franklin Hotel, and wasn't willing to receive any visitors. The calling of celebrity definitely didn't suit him.

The next day, October 23, some small Spanish-bred horses, exceptionally hardy and spirited, were prancing under his windows. But instead of four there were fifty, each with a rider. Barbicane went downstairs along with his three companions and was amazed at

first to find himself in the middle of such a caravan. What's more, he noted that every rider had a rifle slung over his shoulder and pistols in his holsters. The reason for this show of armed force was immediately supplied by a young Floridian, who told him:

"Sir, we've got Seminoles out there."

"Seminoles?"

"Savages running around the countryside, and it seemed wise to give you an escort."

"Nonsense!" J. T. Maston put in, climbing onto his steed.

"Still," the Floridian went on, "it'll be safer this way."

"Gentlemen," Barbicane replied, "thank you for looking after us, and now let's get moving!"

The little band started out immediately and vanished in a cloud of dust. It was five o'clock in the morning; the sun was already shining, and thermometers read 84° Fahrenheit; but cool sea breezes took the edge off this extreme temperature.

Leaving Tampa, Barbicane went southward and along the coastline down to the Alafia River. [47] This little stream flows into Hillsborough Bay twelve miles below Tampa. Barbicane and his escort stuck close to its right bank, heading east. The waves of the bay soon vanished behind an outcrop, and only the Florida countryside remained in view.

Florida is divided into two sections: the part to the north is more heavily populated and less deserted, featuring the capital city of Tallahassee as well as Pensacola, one of the chief marine arsenals in the United States; the other part is crammed between the Atlantic and the Gulf of Mexico, whose waters give it a bear hug, and it's simply a slender peninsula eroded by the Gulf Stream's current, a headland lost in the middle of a small island group and continually doubled by the many ships in Old Bahama Channel. It's the gulf's early-warning lookout for big storms. This state's surface area is 38,033,267 acres, and the club had to choose one of these acres that was both suitable for the undertaking and located on this side of the 28th parallel; accord-

---

[46] Around 200 geographic leagues.

[47] More a creek or small brook.

ingly, as Barbicane rode along, he kept a watchful eye on the lay of the land and its specific texture.

Discovered on Palm Sunday in 1513 by Juan Ponce de León, Florida was originally named "Flowering Easter." Its shores were barren and scorched, hardly deserving of such a delightful moniker. But a few miles from the riverbank, the character of the terrain changes little by little and the region lives up to its name; the ground was disrupted by a network of creeks, rivers, watercourses, ponds, and little lakes; you would have sworn you were in Holland or Guiana; but the countryside rose appreciably and soon revealed its tilled plains where all sorts of crops from both the north and south were thriving, its immense fields where the tropical sun and the water trapped in the clayish soil took care of all the farming, then finally its prairies of pineapples, yams, tobacco, rice, cotton, and sugarcane that stretched as far as the eye could see, displaying their treasures with lighthearted extravagance.

Noticing that the terrain was steadily rising, Barbicane seemed quite pleased, and when J. T. Maston questioned him on this subject:

"My good friend," he answered him, "it's in our very best interests that we cast our columbiad in the uplands."

"To get closer to the moon?" exclaimed the Gun Club's secretary.

"Not really," Barbicane replied, smiling. "What difference would a handful of extra yards make? None at all, but on higher terrain we'll have an easier job of it; we won't need to contend with any groundwater, so we'll be spared having to lay a lot of expensive drainpipe, and that's important to remember when it comes to digging a well 900 feet deep."

"You're right," said Murchison the engineer. "As far as possible, we need to stay away from watercourses when we drill; but it won't matter if we run into any springs since our equipment will divert them or pump them out. We aren't talking about an artesian well here;[48] this won't be a dark, narrow shaft

where your bits, bushings, and bores—in short, all your drilling tools—work out of sight. Not at all. We'll operate in the open air, in broad daylight, mattock or pick in hand, and with the help of explosives we'll get the job done fast."

"However," Barbicane went on, "if the elevation or character of the land can spare us from contending with underground water, the work will go more quickly and accurately; so let's try to cut our trench on terrain located several hundred yards above sea level."

"You're right, Mr. Barbicane, and if I'm not mistaken, we'll soon find us a suitable site."

"Oh, I can't wait for the first stroke of the mattock!" said the Gun Club's president.

"And I can't wait for the last!" J. T. Maston exclaimed.

"We'll get there, gentlemen," the engineer replied, "and believe you me, the Cold Spring Co. won't have to pay you any penalties for being late."

"I pray to St. Barbara you're right!" J. T. Maston remarked. "It's $100 per day till the moon appears again under the same circumstances, in other words, after another eighteen years and eleven days; did you realize that'll amount to $658,100?"

"No, sir, we didn't realize that," the engineer replied, "and we'll never need to."

By around ten o'clock in the morning, the little band had covered twelve miles or so; then the lush countryside gave way to forest regions. There a wide variety of trees were growing in tropical profusion. These virtually impregnable forests consisted of pomegranate trees, orange trees, lemon trees, fig trees, olive trees, apricot trees, banana trees, and vines with big stalks, their blossoms and fruits competing with each other in color and fragrance. In the sweet-smelling shade of their magnificent trunks, a host of bright-colored birds chirped and fluttered; among them you could especially make out some herons whose plumage had such a gemlike sparkle, jewel coffers would be the only nests worthy of them.

J. T. Maston and the major couldn't stand in the presence of this natural abundance without marveling at its superb beauty. But

---

[48] It took nine years to dig the well at Grenelle; it's 1,795 feet deep.

President Barbicane wasn't attuned to these wonders and wanted to keep pressing on; this ultra lush region displeased him by its very lushness; he'd never been a human divining rod, yet he sensed water underfoot and looked in vain for signs of an area that was indisputably dry.

But on they went; they had to ford several rivers, which had its risks because these watercourses were swarming with gators fifteen to eighteen feet long. J. T. Maston threatened them with bold swipes of his alarming hook, but he only managed to scare away the wildlife on the riverbanks, the pelicans, teal, and tropic birds; and while he did so, big red flamingos looked at him with blank expressions.

Finally the occupants of these damp regions vanished in their turn; trees that weren't so tall were scattered through woodlands that weren't so dense; a few lonely clumps stood out in the midst of unending plains where herds of startled deer went by.

"Finally!" Barbicane exclaimed, standing up in his stirrups. "Here's a region of pine trees!"

"And savages," the major replied.

Sure enough, a few Seminoles had appeared on the horizon; they were all aquiver, racing back and forth on their swift horses, brandishing long spears, or firing their rifles with a dull boom; but they confined themselves to these shows of hostility and didn't disturb Barbicane and his companions.

By then the latter were out in the middle of a rocky plain, a huge multi-acre expanse of open ground drenched in scorching sunlight. It was formed by a wide bulge in the terrain and seemed to offer the Gun Club's membership all the conditions required for constructing their columbiad.

"Stop!" Barbicane said, coming to a halt. "What do the locals call this spot?"

"Its name is Stony Hill," one of the Floridians replied.

Without saying a word, Barbicane dismounted, grabbed his instruments, and started to take his bearings with the utmost care; pulling up around him, the little band looked on while keeping absolutely still.

Just then the sun reached the meridian. A few seconds later Barbicane quickly worked out the results of his sights and said:

"This location is situated 1,800 feet above sea level in latitude 27° 7′ and longitude 5° 7′ west;[49] it strikes me that the barren, rocky character of this site offers every condition favorable to our experiment; so it's on this plain that we'll build our warehouses, workshops, furnaces, and crew shacks, and it's from here, right here," he repeated, stamping his foot on the summit of Stony Hill, "that our projectile will take off into the vast reaches of the solar system!"

14
MATTOCK AND TROWEL

THAT SAME EVENING Barbicane and his companions returned to Tampa, and Murchison the engineer sailed back to New Orleans on the *Tampico*. He needed to hire an army of workmen and to fetch the better part of the materials. The Gun Club members stayed in Tampa to organize the preliminary work with help from people in the area.

Eight days after leaving, the *Tampico* came back into the Bay of Espiritu Santo with a flotilla of steamboats. Murchison had rounded up 1,500 workmen. In the bad old days of slavery, he would have been wasting his time and energy. But since America was the land of freedom and now had only free men in its midst, the latter flocked to any place where there were generous wages and a demand for manpower. Now then, the Gun Club wasn't short of money; it offered its employees top salaries and considerable performance bonuses. After the job was done, the men hired to work in Florida could count on tidy sums being deposited in their names at the Bank of Baltimore. So Murchison simply had more candidates than he could use and he could be picky about the skill and shrewdness of his workmen. We have reason to believe he recruited a labor force of the finest mechanics, stokers, smelters, limekiln

---

[49] West of the meridian of Washington, D.C. It differs from the meridian of Paris by 79° 22′. So in French measurements this longitude is 83° 25′.

workers, miners, brick makers, and hired hands of every type, blacks or whites, their color didn't matter. Many of them brought their families along. It was an honest-to-goodness migration.

At ten o'clock in the morning on October 31, the troops landed at Tampa pier; you can imagine the fuss and bother reigning in this little town whose population had doubled in just one day. As a matter of fact, Tampa stood to profit enormously from the Gun Club's venture, not because of the many workmen (who would head immediately for Stony Hill), but thanks to the flood of curiosity seekers who were gradually converging on Florida's peninsula from everywhere on earth.

Early on, crews were busy unloading the equipment, machinery, and provisions brought by the flotilla, as well as a good many sheet-metal houses that had been disassembled and their pieces numbered. Meanwhile Barbicane was laying the groundwork for a fifteen-mile railroad intended to connect Stony Hill with Tampa.

You know how American railways are built; featuring eccentric curves, full of brash inclines, showing no respect for guardrails and niceties of workmanship, scaling peaks, plunging into valleys, their rails race along like a blind man and have no use for straight lines; not much effort is spent on them, or many dollars either; the only problem is they jump the tracks and blow up with carefree abandon. This railroad from Tampa to Stony Hill was a mere technicality and didn't need a great deal of time or money to put in place.

What's more, Barbicane was the soul of this host of workers at his command; he spurred them on, blew his own breath of life into them, his enthusiasm, his conviction; he popped up all over as if could be everywhere at the same time, and J. T. Maston, his buzzing fly, always tagged along. Barbicane's practical mind hatched a thousand innovations. No obstacles existed for him, not a single difficulty, never a tight spot; he wasn't just an artilleryman, he was a miner, bricklayer, or mechanic who had answers to every question and solutions for every problem. He

carried on a brisk correspondence with the Gun Club or the Cold Spring factory, and the *Tampico* kept its furnaces going and steam up day and night, waiting for orders at its offshore mooring by Hillsborough.

On November 1 Barbicane left Tampa with a detachment of workmen, and by the next day they'd built a town of prefabricated homes around Stony Hill; a stockade encircled it, and soon there was so much hustle and bustle, you would have sworn it was a major Union city. Life here followed a strict routine, and work got under way with perfect discipline.

They did some careful boring, which allowed them to identify the character of the terrain, and they were in a position to break ground as early as November 4. That day Barbicane gathered his shop foremen and told them:

"You all know, my friends, why I've gathered you in this patch of Florida wilderness. Our job is to cast a cannon that measures 9 feet across inside, has walls 6 feet thick, and boasts a stone retaining wall 19½ feet thick; so we need to dig a well with a total width of 60 feet and a depth of 900 feet. This considerable task has to be accomplished within eight months; now then, you've got 2,543,400 cubic feet of earth to pull out in 255 days, hence, in round numbers, 10,000 cubic feet per day. Which wouldn't present any problems to a thousand workmen operating with reasonable elbow room, but it'll be harder in a comparatively restricted area. Nevertheless that's the job to be done, it *will* be done, and I'm counting on both your courage and your skill."

At eight o'clock in the morning, the Florida soil received its first stroke of the mattock, and from then on that valiant tool wasn't idle for a second in the miners' hands. There were four shifts per workday, which the crews split up.

Besides, as colossal as the operation was, it didn't exceed the bounds of human ability. Far from it. Many tasks have presented greater actual difficulties, have called for battling the elements head-on, yet have been seen through to completion! And staying just with comparable achievements, we need mention only Joseph's Well, which Sultan Saladin sank outside Cairo in an era before the machinery had arrived that could have increased his manpower a hundredfold—and yet it descends 300 feet to the level of the Nile itself! And don't forget that other well Margrave John of Baden dug at Koblenz, which was 600 feet deep! All right then, what did it come down to here? Three times the Cairo depth with ten times its width, which made for easier drilling! Accordingly there wasn't a single supervisor or workman who doubted that the operation would succeed.

With President Barbicane's agreement, Murchison the engineer made a major decision that got the work going even faster. A clause in the contract held that the columbiad would be laced around with wrought-iron hoops applied while hot. A needlessly extravagant precaution since the weapon clearly could dispense with these ring-shaped restrictions. So the clause was waived.

Ergo much time was saved, because this meant they could employ the new excavating process now used for constructing wells where you lay your bricks as you drill. Thanks to this very simple procedure, it's no longer necessary to prop up the earth by using struts; the brick retaining walls hold it back with unshakable strength and sink by themselves from their own weight.

This operation was due to start only when the mattocks had reached the hard layer underground.

On November 4 fifty workmen dug a circular hole sixty feet wide in the exact center of the surrounding wall, in other words, that stockade encircling the upper reaches of Stony Hill.

Right off the mattocks ran into a sort of black loam, a six-inch layer they easily disposed of. After this loam came two feet of fine-grained sand, which the men removed with care because it was to be used in manufacturing the inner mold.

After this sand a heavyish white clay appeared, a seam four feet thick that looked like the marl found in England.

Then the iron picks gave off sparks against the hard bedrock, a type of very dry, solid stone that's made of petrified shells and

that the tools had to deal with from here on out. At this point the hole boasted a depth of 6½ feet, and the bricklaying chores started.

On the floor of this pit, the men built a sort of oaken "wheel," a firmly bolted disk of proven stability; in its center a hole had been cut whose diameter was the same as the columbiad's outside diameter. On this wheel they laid the first sections of brickwork, cementing the stones with hydraulic concrete of unyielding strength. After laying bricks from the rim to the center hole, the workmen stood inside a well twenty-one feet wide.

When this task was completed, the miners took up their picks and mattocks again, then started in on the rock right under the wheel, taking care to support it as they went with "trestles" of tremendous stability;[50] every time the hole got two feet deeper, they removed these trestles one after the other; the wheel gravitated downward little by little, along with the circular casing of brickwork on top of which the bricklayers toiled continually, meanwhile leaving "air holes" that were to let gases escape during the casting process.

This type of work called for tremendous skill and constant alertness on the laborer's part; while digging under the wheel, more than one man was dangerously or even fatally injured by flying chips of stone; but their energy didn't flag for a single minute day or night: by day they were under sunlight, which a few months later immersed these scorched plains in a 99° heat; by night they were under pale sheets of electric light, while the noise of picks against rock, the boom of explosives, the grinding of machinery, and the scattered swirls of smoke in the air all drew a frightening cordon around Stony Hill that the herds of bison or the detachments of Seminoles no longer dared cross.

But the work went steadily forward; steam cranes briskly cleared away the rubble. Unexpected obstacles were seldom in the picture, just difficulties that had been foreseen and skillfully eliminated.

The first month went by, and the well had reached the scheduled depth for this period

---

[50] A trestle is a type of framework.

of time, namely 112 feet. In December this depth doubled, in January it tripled. During the month of February, the workmen had to contend with a spray of water gushing out of the earth's crust. They needed to use powerful pumps and compressed-air devices to drain it, then they were able to plaster concrete over the opening to the underground spring, as you would patch a leak aboard a ship. They finally disposed of those ill-omened streams of water. Only, due to the unsettled terrain, the wheel partly gave way, and there was a partial cave-in. The reader can imagine the awful weight of that diskful of brickwork 450 feet high! This accident cost several workmen their lives.

It took three weeks to prop up the stone retaining wall, redo its underpinnings, and return the wheel to its former stable condition. The structure had been in temporary jeopardy, but thanks to skillful engineering and the use of powerful machinery, it stood up straight again and drilling resumed.

After that no new hitches impeded the operation's progress, and by June 10, twenty days before the deadline set by Barbicane, a stone facing lined the entire well, which now reached 900 feet underground. At the bottom the brickwork rested on a massive block thirty feet thick, while its top part was exactly flush with the surface.

President Barbicane and the Gun Club members gave Murchison the engineer their heartiest congratulations; he'd finished his cyclopean task under amazingly speedy circumstances.

During these eight months Barbicane hadn't left Stony Hill for a second; while keeping close watch on the drilling operations, he worried continually about his workers' health and well being, and luckily he was spared those epidemics common to big groups of people and so disastrous in areas of the globe open to all kinds of contamination from the tropics.

True, several laborers paid with their lives for the risktaking built into this hazardous work; but these grievous misfortunes are impossible to avoid, and they're details Americans seldom bother with. They care about humanity in general more than individuals in

particular. But Barbicane held contrary beliefs and put them into practice at every opportunity. Accordingly, thanks to his concern, his shrewdness, his prodigious common sense, and his helpful intervention when difficulties came up, his accident average didn't exceed the norm in those overseas countries noted for taking extravagant precautions—including France, where they figure on about one mishap per every $40,000 worth of work.

15

THE CASTING CARNIVAL

DURING THE EIGHT MONTHS devoted to drilling operations, preparatory work for the casting had been going on at the same time with tremendous speed; a stranger arriving on Stony Hill would have been quite surprised at the sight presented to his eyes.

Six hundred yards from the well and arranged in a circle around this midpoint, there stood 1,200 reverberatory furnaces, each six feet wide and separated from its neighbors by a distance of three feet. These 1,200 furnaces were laid out in a curving line that was two miles long. They were all manufactured to the same specifications and featured tall rectangular chimneys, so they created a most distinctive effect. J. T. Maston deemed it a splendid architectural arrangement. It reminded him of the monuments in Washington, D.C. For him nothing more beautiful could exist, not even in Greece, "though," he said, he'd "never been there."

You'll recall that during its third session, the committee had decided to use cast iron for the columbiad, specifically gray iron. In essence it's the most resilient, malleable, cooperative, and readily bored metal there is, so it's suitable for any molding operation and when processed with mineral coal, it's a high-quality material for major showpieces like cannons, steam-engine boilers, hydraulic presses, etc.

But if the iron undergoes smelting only once, it rarely has enough consistency and it needs a second smelting, which purifies and refines it by getting rid of leftover mineral residue.

Accordingly, before being shipped to Tampa, the iron ore had been processed by blast furnaces in Cold Spring, had interacted with coal and silicon heated to a high temperature, and had been carburized and transformed into cast iron.[51] After these preliminary procedures the metal headed off to Stony Hill. But this involved delivering 136,000,000 pounds of iron, an amount too expensive to ship by rail; the transportation costs would be twice the cost of the materials themselves. It seemed preferable to charter ships out of New York City and load the metal on board in the form of iron bars; this called for no less than sixty-eight 1,100-ton vessels, an actual fleet, which on May 3 exited the narrows to Upper New York Bay, took the ocean route south, hugged the American coastline, entered Old Bahama Channel, doubled the tip of Florida, and on the 10th of the same month headed up into the Bay of Espiritu Santo, anchoring undamaged at the port of Tampa.

There the ships' cargoes were unloaded into the freight cars of the Stony Hill railroad, and by mid-January this enormous mass of metal had reached its destination.

You can readily grasp that 1,200 furnaces weren't too many to melt these 68,000 tons of cast iron at the same time. Each of these furnaces could hold close to 114,000 pounds of metal; they'd been built to the specifications of those used in casting Rodman's cannon; they took on the shape of a very squat trapezoid. The heating mechanism and the chimney were at opposite ends of the furnace, insuring that the latter was evenly heated over its entire length. Built of fire-resistant brick, these furnaces consisted solely of a grate for burning mineral coal and a "hearth" where the iron bars were to be deposited; this hearth slanted at a 25° angle, allowing the metal to flow into the receiving tanks; from there it headed down 1,200 troughs converging on the well in the center.

The day after completing the bricklaying and drilling work, Barbicane got going on constructing the inner mold; this involved erecting a cylinder in the center of the well and up its axis point, a cylinder 900 feet high, nine wide, and exactly filling the space reserved for the columbiad's bore. This cylinder was made from a mixture of sand and clayish earth with hay and straw thrown in. The molten metal was to fill in the gap left between the cylindrical mold and the brickwork, thus forming walls six feet thick.

To stabilize it, this cylinder had to be braced with iron fastenings and secured from point to point by crossbeams embedded in the stone retaining wall; after the casting process these crossbeams would be buried inside the mass of metal, no problem for anybody.

This operation was finished on July 8, and the following day was earmarked for pouring the metal.

"It'll be a splendid ceremonial occasion, a sort of casting carnival," J. T. Maston told his friend Barbicane.

"Without the slightest doubt," Barbicane replied, "but this carnival will be closed to the public."

"What! You aren't going to open the doors of the enclosure to all comers?"

"I've got to be very careful, Maston; casting this columbiad is a delicate operation, not to say a hazardous one, and I would prefer we handled it in private. When it's time to fire the projectile, we'll have a carnival if you like—but till then, no."

The Gun Club's president was right; the operation could present unexpected dangers, which might be difficult to address with a large number of spectators on site. Maintaining freedom of action was essential. So nobody was allowed into the enclosure except a delegation of Gun Club members who had made the trip to Tampa. Among them you saw the swaggering Bilsby, Tom Hunter, Colonel Blomsberry, Major Elphiston, General Morgan, and *tutti quanti*[52] for whom casting this columbiad had turned into a personal affair. J. T. Maston was their designated tour guide; he didn't spare them the tiniest details; he led them everywhere, through warehouses, workshops, the innards

---

[51] By removing this coal and silicon during refining operations in a puddling furnace, you transform cast iron into malleable iron.

[52] *Translator's note*. Italian: "all and sundry."

of machinery, and he forced them to inspect all 1,200 furnaces one after the other. By the 1,200th inspection they were a teensy bit fed up.

The casting process was to take place exactly at noon; the night before, each furnace had been loaded with 114,000 pounds' worth of metal bars, which were arranged into crosswise piles so the hot air could freely circulate in between them. All morning the 1,200 chimneys spewed their torrents of flame into the air, and the ground quivered with dull vibrations. They had as many pounds of coal to burn as pounds of metal to cast. So there were 68,000 tons of this fossil fuel, which flung a dense curtain of black smoke in front of the sun's disk.

The heat soon became unbearable inside this circle of furnaces, whose throbbings sounded like rolls of thunder; powerful fans joined in with their continual blowing, and every one of these white-hot stoves was steeped in oxygen.

To succeed, the operation needed to be carried out at great speed. The signal to start would be the boom of a cannon, then each furnace was to release its liquid iron and empty itself out.

These arrangements in place, overseers and workmen waited for the appointed time, their impatience mixed with a pinch of excitement. Nobody else was left inside the enclosure, and all the foundry supervisors were stationed next to their tapholes.

Taking up residence on a nearby overlook, Barbicane and his colleagues were in attendance at the operation. They had a cannon in front of them, ready to fire it at the engineer's signal.

A few minutes before noon, the first droplets of metal started to pour out; the receiving tanks filled up little by little, and when the iron was completely liquid, the workmen let it stand for a few seconds, making it easier to remove foreign substances.

Twelve o'clock sounded. There was a sudden boom from the cannon, which launched a lurid lightning flash into the heavens. 1,200 tapholes opened at the same instant and 1,200 fiery snakes unwound their white-hot coils, crawling toward the well in the center. Once there, they rushed 900 feet downward with a frightful hubbub. It was an exciting and magnificent sight. The ground shook while these waves of iron, shooting swirls of smoke skyward, simultaneously turned the mold's moisture to steam and drove it up the air holes of the stone retaining wall in the form of impregnable mists. Rising to the zenith, this artificial cloudbank unwound its thick spirals 3,000 feet into the air. Any savage roaming beyond the edge of the horizon would have thought some new crater was forming in the heart of Florida, and yet there were no eruptions, tornadoes, thunderstorms, battles of the elements, or any of those dreadful phenomena nature is capable of generating. None! Mankind alone had created these reddish mists, these gigantic flames worthy of any volcano, these noisy vibrations like the jolting of an earthquake, this roaring that rivaled any hurricane or storm—and human hands had heaved this whole Niagara of molten metal into these man-made depths!

16

THE COLUMBIAD

HAD THE CASTING OPERATION succeeded? They could only speculate. But everything pointed to success, since the mold had consumed the whole mass of metal the furnaces had turned to liquid. Be that as it may, for a good while there wouldn't be any possibility of personally making sure.

In fact, when Major Rodman cast his 160,000-pound cannon, the cooling process took a full two weeks. Then how long would this monstrous columbiad, wreathed in swirls of steam and protected by its intense heat, stay hidden from the eyes of its admirers? It was hard to calculate.

The impatience of our Gun Club members was sorely tested during this period of time. But there wasn't a thing they could do. J. T. Maston's dedication to duty almost got him roasted. Two weeks after the casting process, an immense plume of smoke was still rising into the open air, and the ground burned your feet inside a radius of 200

steps around the summit of Stony Hill.

The days went by, adding up to one week after another. There was no way to cool off that immense cylinder. It was impossible to get near the thing. Everybody was forced to wait, and the Gun Club members were champing at the bit.

"It's now August 10," J. T. Maston said one morning. "Barely four months to go till December 1! We need to remove the inner mold, calibrate the bore of the piece, load the columbiad—there's all this work to do! We won't be ready! Nobody can even get near the cannon! Suppose it never cools off! What a cruel trick that would be!"

They tried to calm their impatient secretary, to no avail. Barbicane didn't say a thing, but his silence hid his underlying annoyance. To be brought to a dead stop by an obstacle that time alone could dispose of (time, an alarming foe under the circumstances), and to lie at the mercy of an enemy—that was hard for these old campaigners.

But thanks to their daily inspections, they could verify a definite change in the condition of the ground. Around August 15 it was giving off steam that had noticeably less heat and density. A few days later the terrain exhaled only a thin mist, the last breath of that monster closed up in its stone casket. Little by little the earth tremors died away and the circle of heat contracted; the most impatient bystanders moved in; one day they got twelve feet closer; the next day twenty-four; and on August 22 Barbicane, his colleagues, and the engineer were able to stand on that crest of cast iron gracing the summit of Stony Hill, which, so far, was quite a salutary place to be—no danger of cold feet, that's for sure.

"Finally!" exclaimed the Gun Club's president with an immense sigh of pleasure.

Work resumed the same day. They immediately set about extracting the inner mold so as to free up the bore of the piece. Picks, mattocks, and drilling tools worked around the clock; the clayish soil and sand had gotten extremely hard from the action of the heat; but with the help of machinery, they disposed of this earthy mixture, still hot from its contact with the cast-iron walls; the extracted rubble was quickly taken away in steam-driven carts, and there was such efficiency, the workers showed such energy, Barbicane intervened with such urgency, and his arguments in the form of cash bonuses had such great impact, by September 3 every trace of the mold was gone.

They started right in on the job of reaming the bore; the machinery was soon in place, applying powerful high-speed drills whose sharpness started to shave the rough edges off the cast iron. A few weeks later the inner surface of that immense tube was perfectly cylindrical, and the bore of the piece had acquired a perfect polish.

Finally on September 22, less than a year after Barbicane had made his announcement, the enormous weapon was ready for action, meticulously calibrated and flawlessly vertical thanks to the use of precision instruments. All that remained was to wait for the moon, and they were sure she wouldn't miss her appointment.

J. T. Maston's delight was boundless and he narrowly escaped a terrifying fall while peering down into that 900-foot tube. If he hadn't been caught by Blomsberry's right arm, which luckily still remained to the good colonel, the Secretary of the Gun Club would have gone to his doom in the columbiad's depths like a modern-day Erostratus.[53]

So the cannon was finished; beyond all doubt it had been completed to perfection; this being the case, on October 6 Captain Nicholl duly paid what he owed to President Barbicane, and the latter entered the sum of $2,000 on his books in the receivables column. We have reason to believe the captain's fury had reached such a fever pitch, he was physically ill. However he still had three bets left for $3,000, $4,000, and $5,000, and if he won any two of these, his financial position would still be respectable if not exactly outstanding. But money didn't enter at all into Nicholl's calculations, and his competitor's success—his casting a cannon that armor plate couldn't withstand if it were sixty feet thick—had dealt the captain a dreadful blow.

After September 23 the Stony Hill enclo-

---

[53] *Translator's note.* Ancient Ephesian who went to extreme lengths to achieve lasting fame.

sure was wide open to the public, and the reader can easily imagine the flood of visitors.

In essence countless curiosity seekers converged on Florida, hurrying from every part of the United States. The town of Tampa had grown prodigiously during this year given over to the Gun Club's labors, and by then the local population numbered 150,000 souls. After it had merged Fort Brooke into a network of streets, the city now stretched along that strip of land separating those two offshore moorings in the Bay of Espiritu Santo; under the hot American sun, additional neighborhoods, new squares, and a whole forest of houses had taken root on these recently empty beaches. Construction companies set up shop to build churches, schools, private homes, and in less than a year the town had gotten ten times bigger.

As you know, Yankees are born businesspeople; anywhere fate takes them, from the ice cap to the torrid zone, their moneymaking tendencies are bound to come into play. That's why simple curiosity seekers, folks coming to Florida for the sole purpose of watching the Gun Club at work, were getting involved in commercial ventures just as soon as they'd taken up residence in Tampa. The ships chartered to transport laborers and materials were filling the harbor with unparalleled activity. Laden with provisions, supplies, and merchandise, other craft of every size and tonnage would soon be gliding into the bay and its two offshore moorings; shipowners and brokers set up huge counters and bureaus in town, and every day the *Shipping Gazette* recorded the latest arrivals at the port of Tampa.

While roads were proliferating around the town, the latter, given its prodigious population and trade growth, finally got rail connections to the Union's southerly states. Trains ran from Mobile to Pensacola, the South's great marine arsenal; then they headed from this major stop to Tallahassee. There a short 21-mile section of track already existed, which put Tallahassee in contact with St. Marks on the seacoast. That was the end of the line for this roadbed stretching as far as Tampa, and on its way it

revived and awakened the dead or dormant parts of central Florida. Accordingly, thanks to these technological marvels coming from an idea hatched one fine day in the brain of a single man, Tampa had a perfect right to put on airs as a big town. It was nicknamed "Moon City," and Florida's capital suffered a total eclipse that was visible the world over.

Everybody will now understand why there was such intense competition between Florida and Texas, and why the Texans were furious when they saw their claims thrown out by the Gun Club's decision. They had the shrewdness and foresight to realize how much an area stood to gain from the experiment Barbicane was attempting, all the good that would accrue from such a cannon blast. So Texas missed out on a huge commercial hub, railroads, and considerable population growth. All of this redounded to the benefit of that wretched Florida peninsula, dumped like a boat slip between the waves of the gulf and the billows of the Atlantic Ocean. Accordingly Barbicane's unpopularity in Texas was on a par with General Santa Anna's.

However, though it had gotten caught up in the area's commercial frenzies and industrial furors, Tampa's new populace was careful not to forget the intriguing activities of the Gun Club. On the contrary. Down to the smallest stroke of the mattock, the undertaking's tiniest details held the town spellbound. To and fro between Tampa and Stony Hill, there was a continual procession, better yet, a pilgrimage.

You could already foresee that on the day of the experiment, the crowds of spectators would number in the millions, because they were already gathering on this cramped peninsula from everywhere on earth. Europe was migrating to America.

But so far, it should be recorded, these hordes of newcomers hadn't found very much to satisfy their curiosity. Many of them had counted on viewing the casting process and were rewarded with nothing but smoke. Their eager eyes had little to look at; but Barbicane wasn't willing to let anybody near the operation. Ergo much cursing, discontent, and criticism; they denounced the Gun

Club's president; they accused him of being a totalitarian dictator; his conduct was declared "un-American." There was practically a mob around the Stony Hill stockade. Barbicane, as you know, stood firm in his decision.

But when the columbiad was totally finished, the closed-door policy couldn't continue; besides, it would be ill-mannered to keep the gates shut—even worse, it would be unwise to offend public opinion. So Barbicane opened his enclosure to all comers; but given his practical mind, he decided to make money off the public's curiosity.

Just to look at this immense columbiad was quite an experience—but to descend into its depths, this struck Americans as the *ne plus ultra*[54] of earthly delight. Accordingly there wasn't a single curiosity seeker who didn't want the selfish pleasure of inspecting the insides of this metal chasm. Lifts dangling from a steam-driven winch allowed sightseers to satisfy their curiosity. It was the latest fad. Women, children, and oldsters all made it a point of honor to get to the bottom of the colossal cannon's mysteries. The fare for this descent was five dollars per person; despite this high price, the flood of visitors allowed the Gun Club to rake in nearly $500,000 over that two-month period before the experiment took place

Needless to say, the columbiad's first visitors were members of the Gun Club, a privilege appropriately reserved for that renowned association. This solemn moment occurred on September 25. An elevator of honor lowered President Barbicane, J. T. Maston, Major Elphiston, General Morgan, Colonel Blomsberry, Murchison the engineer, and other distinguished members of the famous club. Ten in all. It was still quite hot at the bottom of that long metal tube. You felt half suffocated! But what joy, what rapture! Standing on the section of stone that supported the columbiad, a table with ten place settings was illuminated *a giorno*[55] by a stream of electric light. As if descending from Heaven, many exquisite dishes took

their consecutive places in front of the dinner guests, and France's finest wines flowed copiously during this superb meal served 900 feet underground.

The feast was quite lively, even quite noisy; many toasts were exchanged; they drank to the planet earth, they drank to its satellite, they drank to the Gun Club, they drank to the Union, to the moon, to Phoebe, to Diana, to Selene, to the silver orb, to "the firmament's messenger of peace!" All their hip-hips and hoorays, borne aloft by the sound waves in that immense acoustic tube, reached the top of it like a thunderclap, and the crowds standing around Stony Hill joined in, yelling just as heartily as the ten dinner guests down at the bottom of their gigantic columbiad.

J. T. Maston couldn't control himself; whether he yelled more than he clapped, or drank more than he ate, would be hard to establish. In any event he wouldn't have traded his circumstances for an empire, "not even if the cannon was loaded, primed, and fired," and they were to shoot pieces of him "through interplanetary space right this instant!"

17

A TELEGRAM

TO ALL INTENTS AND PURPOSES, the Gun Club was done with the tremendous task it had undertaken, yet it still had two months to go till that day when the projectile would be launched at the moon. Two months that must have seemed as long as years to the impatient world! Till this point the daily newspapers had reported the operation's tiniest details, and enthusiastic readers had devoured them with eager eyes; but from then on there was a danger that this "interest payment" doled out to the public might significantly depreciate, and everybody was afraid they wouldn't get their daily dose of excitement.

Not to worry; the most unexpected, unusual, unbelievable, and unimaginable incident occurred, filling people's flagging spirits with new fanaticism and throwing the whole world into a state of acute agitation.

---

[54] *Translator's note*. Latin: "acme."

[55] *Translator's note*. Italian: "as bright as day."

At 3:47 in the afternoon on the day of September 30, a telegram traveled the undersea cable from Valentia, Ireland to Newfoundland and the coast of America, then arrived at President Barbicane's address.

President Barbicane tore open the envelope, read its contents, and despite his self-control, the blood drained from his lips and his vision blurred as he scanned the twenty words of this telegram.

Here's the text of that wire, which now resides in the Gun Club's files:

Paris, France
September 30, 4 A.M.

Barbicane
Tampa, Florida
United States

Replace spherical shell with cylindro-conical projectile. Will travel inside. Arriving steamer Atlanta.

MICHEL ARDAN.

18

THE *ATLANTA*'S PASSENGER

IF THIS ELECTRIFYING NEWS hadn't sped along the telegraph lines but had simply arrived by mail in a sealed envelope, or if the French, Irish, Newfoundlander, and American clerks hadn't automatically been privy to the contents of their wires, Barbicane wouldn't have hesitated for one second. He very sensibly would have kept quiet about it so as not to undermine his work. This telegram could be part of a hoax, especially since it came from a Frenchman. How plausible was it that any human being would be daring enough to even think of such a journey? And if this human being did exist, wasn't he a madman who should be put in a padded cell rather than a projectile?

But this wire was public knowledge, because the transmitting machinery is indiscreet by its very nature and Michel Ardan's proposition had already raced across the various states of the Union. Therefore Barbicane no longer had any reason to keep quiet. So he gathered those of his colleagues who were present in Tampa, and without revealing his thoughts, without discussing what greater or lesser credence should be given this telegram, he coolly read them its brief text.

"Not possible!—It's inconceivable!—Nothing but a joke!—Somebody's poking fun at us!—Idiotic!—Silly!" Over a few minutes they trotted out the whole litany of expressions that serve to convey doubt, suspicion, distrust, and ridicule—along with the standard gestures for such occasions. Each man smirked, grinned, shrugged his shoulders, or laughed out loud depending on the mood he was in. Only J. T. Maston put in a positive word.

"Now *there's* an idea!" he exclaimed.

"Yes," the major answered him, "but it's only acceptable to have ideas like this if you don't make the slightest attempt to carry 'em out."

"And why not?" the Gun Club's secretary remarked noisily, all set to argue. But nobody wanted to press the issue.

Meanwhile the name Michel Ardan was already circulating around the town of Tampa. Outsiders and locals looked at each other, traded questions, and cracked jokes, not over this European—a fantasy, a phantom individual—but over J. T. Maston who entertained the belief that this fairytale character actually existed. When Barbicane proposed firing a projectile to the moon, everybody viewed the undertaking as realistic, feasible, a strict matter of ballistics! But the idea of any rational person offering to travel inside the projectile, to attempt such an inconceivable journey—it was a ludicrous proposition, a joke, a prank, and to use a word for which everyday French has exactly the right translation, a "humbug."[56]

The jeering kept on till evening without letup, and the whole Union went on a laughing jag, you might say—which is far from normal in a country where outlandish undertakings find willing promoters, defenders, and supporters.

But as with any new idea, some were bound to find Michel Ardan's proposition intellectually disturbing. It upset the way they

---

[56] In France the term is *mystification* [hoax].

normally felt—"We never dreamed of such a thing!" Due to its very novelty, people quickly became fixated on this incident. They mulled it over. So many things had been scoffed at one day, only to turn into realities the next! Why shouldn't such a journey be made sooner or later? But even so, any man willing to risk his life in this way had to be insane, and since his plan definitely couldn't be taken seriously, it was best to shut him up rather than trouble a whole country with his idiotic nonsense.

But did this individual actually exist in the first place? Excellent question. The name "Michel Ardan" wasn't unfamiliar in America. It belonged to a European whose daring deeds had been on many lips. Then there was the telegram that shot through the depths of the Atlantic, the name of that ship on which the Frenchman said he was traveling, the date announced for its impending arrival—all these circumstances gave the proposition a definite air of verisimilitude. It was essential to thrash this out. Soon scattered individuals were collecting in groups; the groups, driven by curiosity, were contracting into clusters like atoms drawn by molecular attraction; and the ultimate result was a jam-packed crowd heading over to President Barbicane's residence.

The latter hadn't spoken his mind since the wire's arrival; he'd let J. T. Maston air his views without a word of praise or blame; Barbicane intended to lie low and wait for developments; but he hadn't reckoned on the public's impatience and wasn't pleased to see the whole population of Tampa congregating under his windows. They were muttering and calling out, which soon forced him to make an appearance. As you can see, he had all the responsibilities, and consequently all the annoyances, that go with being a celebrity.

So he put in an appearance; silence fell and a citizen took the floor, asking the following question straight out: "This person identified in the wire by the name of Michel Ardan—is he on his way to America? Yes or no."

"Gentlemen," Barbicane replied, "I don't know any more than you do."

"We need to find out!" shouted some impatient voices.

"Time will tell," the Gun Club's president answered coolly.

"Time has no right keeping a whole country in suspense," the speaker went on. "Have you changed the projectile's design the way the telegram asks?"

"Not yet, gentlemen; but you're correct, we need to find out what's behind this; the telegraph caused all this excitement and it has an obligation to give us the full story."

"Let's go to the telegraph office!" the crowd shouted.

Barbicane went downstairs, took charge of this immense gathering, and led it over to the headquarters of the cable service.

A few minutes later they'd fired off a telegram to the shipbrokers' agency in Liverpool. They requested answers to the following questions:

"What sort of ship is the *Atlanta*? When did it leave Europe? Was there a Frenchman on board named Michel Ardan?"

Two hours later Barbicane received such exact information, there was no room left for the slightest doubt:

"The steamer *Atlanta* hails from Liverpool, put to sea on October 2, is bound for Tampa, and has on board a Frenchman whose name the passenger list gives as Michel Ardan."

At this corroboration of the first wire, President Barbicane's eyes lit up with a sudden flame, he clenched his hands into tight fists, and you could hear him mutter:

"So it's true . . . it's a possibility . . . this Frenchman exists . . . and he'll be here in two weeks! But he's insane! He's got brain fever! I'll never agree to . . . "

And yet that same evening he wrote to the firm of Breadwill & Co., asking that they hold off on casting the projectile till further notice.

Now, it would be impossible to describe the excitement that gripped every American, how they exceeded their reception of Barbicane's announcement ten times over, what the Union newspapers said, the way they embraced this news, and how they played up the arrival of this hero from the Old World; impossible to depict the state of feverish agitation in which everybody lived, counting off the hours, minutes, and seconds; impossible to give even a feeble idea of this exhausting fixation that had turned everybody's brain into a one-track mind; impossible to show how folks had traded their occupations for a single *pre*occupation, their work grinding to a halt, all business in abeyance, ships ready to sail still moored in port so as not to miss the *Atlanta*'s arrival, trains pulling in full and leaving empty, the Bay of Espiritu Santo continually plowed by steamers, mailboats, luxury yachts, and small craft of all dimensions; impossible to total up the thousands of curiosity seekers who had quadrupled Tampa's population in just two weeks, camping out in tents like an army in the field—to convey all this is a task beyond human strength, something you would be foolhardy to undertake.

At nine o'clock in the morning on October 20, the semaphores along Old Bahama Channel reported dense smoke on the horizon. Two hours later they'd traded identification signals with a big steamer. The name *Atlanta* was instantly relayed to Tampa. By four o'clock the English ship had stood into the offshore mooring of Espiritu Santo. By five it had gone full steam ahead through the narrows to Hillsborough Bay. By six it had berthed at the port of Tampa.

Before its anchor could catch on the sandy bottom, 500 boats had surrounded the *Atlanta* and the steamer was under assault. Barbicane was the first to get over the rails, and in a voice whose excitement he vainly tried to control:

"Michel Ardan!" he called.

"Right here!" an individual replied up on the afterdeck.

With folded arms, questioning eyes, and tight lips, Barbicane looked intently at the *Atlanta*'s passenger

He was a man of forty-two, tall but already a little stooped, like those sculpted priestesses that carry balconies on their shoulders. His mighty head, a truly leonine noggin, gave his fiery shock of hair a periodic toss, turning it into an authentic mane. His face was squat, wide at the temples, and embellished with a mustache that bristled like a tabby's whiskers, little bunches of yellowish fur that grew midcheek, and round, darting eyes that squinted myopically, topping off his exceptionally catlike facial features. But his nose stood out boldly, his mouth suggested unusual kindness, his high forehead indicated shrewdness and was as furrowed as a field that never lies fallow. Finally his well-built torso was solidly stationed on long legs, his muscular arms were like strong, securely attached levers, and his stride was forceful, turning this European into a big strapping fellow, "a one-of-a-kind piece," to borrow an expression from the craft of metalworking.

From this individual's skull and facial features, a disciple of such character-judging anatomists as Lavater or Gratiolet would easily have deciphered undeniable signs of a fighting spirit—in other words, courage in the face of danger and an urge to crush opposition; also signs of generosity and those hinting at the gift of wonder, that itch filling certain personalities with a passion for superhuman deeds; but in exchange, the bump of acquisitiveness, that need to buy and own, was missing completely.

To finish off the physical characteristics of this passenger on the *Atlanta*, it's appropriate to note the baggy fit of his clothes, their loose armholes, his jacket and trousers made of so much fabric that Michel Ardan proclaimed himself "death on cloth," his floppy necktie, his shirt collar open wide around his sturdy neck, his cuffs that were always unbuttoned, and the pair of overactive hands that stuck out of them. You sensed that the iciest winters or the scariest dangers would never send chills down this man's spine—not even the figurative kind.

Meanwhile he paced back and forth through the crowd on the steamer's deck, never standing still, "dragging his anchors" as seamen say, waving at people, chummy with everybody, nibbling his fingernails in restless eagerness. He was one of those eccentrics our Creator invents in a moment of whimsy, then immediately breaks the mold.

In essence Michel Ardan's mental attributes afforded full scope to the student of character analysis. This startling man lived in a perpetual state of extreme exaggeration and still hadn't outgrown his boyish love of superlatives: the objects pictured in the retina of his eye boasted extravagant dimensions; ergo many of his ideas were on gigantic lines; he overestimated everything except difficulties and human nature.

Beyond this he had an exuberant personality and was a born showman, a witty fellow, not somebody who keeps up a constant barrage of quips but a skirmisher who hits and runs. In disputes he rarely bothered with being logical, scorned deductive reasoning (which he couldn't have dreamed up in a million years), but landed a punch in his own way. Genuinely adept at raising a fuss, he loved to fight tooth and nail for lost causes, and he aimed straight for the heart with *ad hominem* arguments that never missed.[57]

Among other foibles he called himself a Shakespearean "wise fool," and he expressed contempt for academics: "All they do," he said, "is keep score while the rest of us play the game." In sum, he was a gypsy from the land of hopes and dreams, a risk taker but not a rascal, a swashbuckler, a Phaëthon driving his sun-chariot at top speed, an Icarus with a spare set of wings. What's more, he paid his dues in full and in person, he dived headfirst into crazy undertakings, he burned his ships with more alacrity than Agathocles,[58] and since he was ready to bust his backside day or night, he invariably ended up landing on his feet, like those little birchwood figurines on strings that children play with.

His motto was just two words: *No problem!* And a love for impossible deeds was his "ruling passion," as Alexander Pope aptly expressed it.

But in addition this resourceful fellow definitely had the vices that went with his virtues! Nothing ventured, nothing gained, as people say. Ardan ventured much but never came out ahead. He was an abuser of money, a leaky jug worthy of the daughters of Danaus.[59] He was utterly unselfish to boot, somebody who followed the promptings of his heart more than those of his head; a good Samaritan, a knight in shining armor, he wouldn't have signed a death warrant for his most bloodthirsty enemy, and he would have sold himself into slavery to ransom a single Negro.

In France, in Europe, everybody had heard of this flashy, noisy character. Didn't he go about his day while hundreds of gossips spread his fame till they were hoarse? Didn't he live in a glass house, the whole universe privy to his most intimate secrets? But didn't he also have a splendid collection of enemies, including people whom, in varying degrees, he'd jostled, bruised, or ruthlessly knocked down while elbowing his way through the crowd?

However people generally liked him, indulging him like a pampered child. "Take him or leave him," the old saying goes, and they took him. Everybody was interested in his bold endeavors and kept an anxious eye on him. They knew how daring and reckless he was! When a friend of his tried to rein him in with a prediction of impending disaster, he replied with a cheery smile, "If a forest catches on fire, it's own trees are to blame," never suspecting he'd quoted the subtlest of Arab proverbs.

There you have him, this passenger on the *Atlanta*—all aquiver, all aboil with deep-seated fervor, all excited, not over what he'd come to do in America—he hadn't even given it a thought—but because of his overactive temperament. If ever two individuals stood in striking contrast, it was the Frenchman Michel Ardan and the Yankee Barbicane, yet each of them was resourceful, bold, and daring in his own way.

The Gun Club's president had been lost in thought while facing this competitor who had just thrust him into the background, but the crowd's cheers and applause soon broke in on him. Their yelling became so frenzied, their enthusiasm took on such a physical

---

[57] *Translator's note.* Latin: arguments that attack an opponent's character rather than his case.

[58] *Translator's note.* Eccentric ruler of ancient Syracuse around 300 B.C.

[59] *Translator's note.* In Greek myth their punishment after death was to carry water in jugs full of holes.

form, that Michel Ardan (after a thousand handshakes that nearly cost him his ten fingers) was forced to hide out in his cabin.

Barbicane followed him without saying a word.

"Are you Barbicane?" Michel Ardan asked him when they were alone, in the same tone he would have used with a friend he'd known for twenty years.

"I am," replied the Gun Club's president.

"Then hello there, Barbicane! How are you? Just fine? All the better!"

"Does this mean," Barbicane said without any further lead-in to his topic, "that you're determined to go?"

"Absolutely determined."

"Nothing will stop you?"

"Nothing. Have you changed your projectile the way my wire specified?"

"I've been waiting for you to arrive. But," Barbicane stressed further, "have you given this careful thought?"

"Careful thought? Do I have any time to lose? I get the opportunity to go on an outing to the moon, I take advantage of it, and that's that. There's no call for much thought, it seems to me."

Barbicane's eyes devoured this man who talked about his travel plans so blithely, who was so utterly carefree, who didn't have a worry in the world.

"But at least," he said to him, "you've got a program of action, a method of proceeding?"

"Excellent point, my dear Barbicane. But let me share something with you: I would rather tell my tale to everybody once and for all, then be out of the picture. This way I avoid saying the same thing over and over. So, unless you've got a better suggestion, summon your friends, your colleagues, the whole town, all Florida, all America if you like—and tomorrow I'll be ready to elaborate on my methods while answering whatever objections people may raise. Don't worry, I'll be waiting for them with a rock-solid case. Does this sound all right to you?"

"It does," Barbicane replied.

With that the Gun Club's president left the cabin and shared Michel Ardan's proposition with the crowd. They greeted his words by howling in glee and jumping for joy. This strategy took care of all the problems. Tomorrow people could inspect this heroic European at their leisure. But some of the more stubborn onlookers weren't willing to leave the *Atlanta*'s deck; they spent the night on board. Among them was J. T. Maston: he'd screwed his hook into the after rail, and it would have taken a winch to tear him away.

"He's a hero!" he kept on exclaiming. "And we're just doddering old women next to that European!"

As for the Gun Club's president, after encouraging visitors to run along, he reentered the passenger's cabin and didn't leave it till the ship's bell sounded the midnight watch.

But by then the two rivals in popularity were old chums, and Michel Ardan shook hands heartily with President Barbicane.

19

A RALLY

THE NEXT DAY the sun's golden orb dawned too slowly for the liking of the impatient public. For a heavenly body scheduled to illuminate such a festive event, it didn't seem to be rising to the occasion. Afraid that Michel Ardan might face too many prying questions, Barbicane would have preferred restricting the audience to a handful of specialists, his own colleagues for instance. It would have been easier to stop Niagara Falls from flowing. Consequently he had to give up this plan and let his new friend take his chances in a public forum. Despite its colossal dimensions, the trading floor of Tampa's new stock exchange wasn't deemed big enough for the proceedings, because the planned meeting was taking on the proportions of an honest-to-goodness rally.

The site chosen was a wide plain located outside town; in a few hours they'd managed to shield it from the sun's rays; since ships in the harbor had plenty of sails, tackle, spare masts, and yards, these furnished the necessary materials for pitching a colossal tent. Soon an immense firmament of canvas stretched over the charred prairie and protected it from the blazing daylight. 300,000 people squeezed underneath and braved the suffocating heat for several hours, waiting for the Frenchman to arrive. Out of this crowd of onlookers, a third could see and hear; another third had trouble seeing and couldn't hear; as for the final third, it saw nothing and heard less. This last group, however, was just as hearty in its applause.

At three o'clock Michel Ardan appeared along with the Gun Club's chief members. He was flanked on the right by President Barbicane and on the left by J. T. Maston, beaming like the noonday sun and almost as shiny. Ardan climbed onto a stage and from the top of it looked out over an ocean of black hats. He didn't seem the least bit uncomfortable; he didn't put on airs; he acted like he was in his own home, jolly, relaxed, friendly. He responded to the cheers greeting him with a courteous bow; then, waving his hand for silence and speaking in English with perfect fluency, he opened his remarks as follows:

"Gentlemen," he said, "though it's very hot out, I'm going to take up your time with a few explanations of these plans of mine that you seem to find so interesting. I'm neither a speaker nor a scientist and I certainly wasn't expecting to give a public talk; but my friend Barbicane told me it would please you, and I'm at your service. So lend me your 600,000 ears and please excuse any deficiencies in my presentation."

This easygoing preamble sat well with the attendees, who registered their pleasure with an immense murmur of appreciation.

"Gentlemen," he said, "feel free to express your approval or disapproval whenever you wish. With this understanding I'll get started. First off, don't forget you're dealing with a know-nothing, but one who's so lacking in knowledge that he simply knows no difficulties. Consequently he felt it was an easy, natural, and uncomplicated business to climb aboard a projectile and head off to the moon. This is a journey that needs to be made sooner or later, and as for the form of transportation involved, it's a natural result of the laws of progress. Man started by traveling on all fours, then one fine day on two feet, then in a cart, then in a buggy, then in a carriage, then in a stagecoach, then in a passenger train; all right, the projectile is the conveyance of the future, and to tell the truth, the planets themselves are just projectiles, simply cannonballs fired by the hand of our Creator. But let's get back to our vehicle. A few among us, gentlemen, may entertain the belief that the speed it'll be given is outrageous; it's nothing of the sort; every heavenly body can outrace it, and the earth itself, in its orbiting motion around the sun, carries us along three times faster. Here are a few examples. Only I ask your permission to present them in geographic leagues, because I haven't had much practice with American measurements and I'm afraid I'll get mixed up in my calculations."[60]

This seemed a simple enough request and it ran into no difficulties. The speaker went on with his talk:

"Here, gentlemen, are the speeds of the different planets. Though I'm a know-nothing, I must confess I've got an unusually accurate grasp of these little details from the science of astronomy; but in less than two minutes, you'll be as brainy as I am. Understand, then, that Neptune travels 5,000 geographic leagues per hour, Uranus 7,000, Saturn 8,858, Jupiter 11,675, Mars 22,011, the earth 27,500, Venus 32,190, Mercury 52,520, and certain comets 1,400,000 geographic leagues per hour at their perihelion. As for us in our space vehicles, we'll be real loafers, folks never in a hurry, because our top speed won't exceed 9,900 geographic leagues per hour and it'll always decrease from there. I ask you, is this anything to get excited about, and isn't it obvious all these figures will be exceeded someday by still faster speeds, whose mechanical force will most likely be light or electricity?"

Nobody seemed to question this assertion of Michel Ardan's.

"My dear audience," he went on, "if we're to believe certain narrow-minded people—that's the appropriate adjective for them—the

---

[60] *Translator's note:* For a rough conversion into miles, multiply the given leagues in this chapter by 2½.

human race is stuck in a sort of circle of Popilius[61] with no way out, condemned to stagnate on this globe without ever being able to shoot into interplanetary space! That isn't the case at all! You're about to go to the moon, you'll go to the planets, you'll go to the stars just as easily, quickly, and safely as you now go from Liverpool to New York, and we'll soon cross the celestial ocean as well as the lunar oceans! Distance is just a relative term and it'll end up shrinking down to nothing."

Though firmly siding with this heroic Frenchman, the gathering was a bit taken aback by such a daring idea. Michel Ardan seemed to understand this.

"You look unconvinced, my gallant visitors," he went on with a friendly smile. "All right, let's try a little logic. Do you know how long an express train would take to reach the moon? 300 days. No more. A flight of 86,410 geographic leagues, or some 215,000 miles—but so what? That's less than nine times the earth's circumference, and even weekend sailors and travelers have gone farther in their lifetimes. Yet consider this— my trip will take only ninety-seven hours! Ah, but you're telling yourself the moon's a long way from the earth and I'd better think twice before attempting this adventure. But what would you say, then, if it were an issue of going to Neptune, which revolves around the sun from 1,147,000,000 geographic leagues away—nearly three billion miles! Even if it didn't cost much more than ten cents per mile, that's a trip few people could go on. Though he's worth a fifth of a billion dollars, Baron Rothschild himself couldn't afford a ticket, and unless he scraped up an extra thirty million, he would be left by the roadside!"

This form of argument seemed to please the gathering tremendously; meanwhile, all caught up in his topic, Michel Ardan plunged into it with splendid zest and abandon; he felt they were hanging on his every word and

continued with wonderful confidence:

"Well then, my friends, Neptune's distance from the sun is nothing at all compared to that of the stars; in fact, to estimate just how far away such heavenly bodies are, we need to get into those dizzying figures where the shortest number has nine digits and a billion serves as your smallest quantity. Forgive me for having thoroughly boned up on this matter, but it's of thrilling interest. Listen and judge for yourself! Alpha Centauri is 8 trillion geographic leagues away, Vega 50 trillion, Sirius 50 trillion, Arcturus 52 trillion, Polaris 117 trillion, Capella 170 trillion, and the other stars are billions of leagues away multiplied by thousands, millions, and more billions! And yet people will babble about the distance separating the planets from the sun! And they'll insist this distance is of real consequence! A fallacy! A deception! A mental aberration! Do you know what my thoughts are on this planetary system that starts with Old Sol and ends with Neptune? Would you like to hear my thinking? It's quite simple! To my mind our solar system is a solid, integral object; the planets that compose it are rubbing, brushing, and clinging to each other, and the space existing between them is simply the space that separates the molecules in such ultradense metals as silver, gold, or platinum! So I have the qualifications and the conviction to make this statement, and I'll shout it again from the rooftops: 'Distance is a meaningless term, there's no such thing as distance!'"

"Well put! Bravo! Hooray!" the gathering yelled in unison, galvanized as much by the speaker's gestures and inflections as by the boldness of his ideas.

"No!" J. T. Maston shouted more forcefully than anybody else. "There's no such thing as distance!"

And carried away by the vehemence of his movements, by his body's barely controlled momentum, he almost tumbled off the stage onto the ground. But he managed to regain his balance and to avoid a nasty fall that would have shown him that distance wasn't a meaningless term. Then the speaker picked up the compelling thread of his talk.

"My friends," Michel Ardan said, "I think

---

[61] *Translator's note:* Ancient Roman diplomat who drew a circle in the sand around a stalling negotiator, then wouldn't let the fellow step out of it till he'd reached a decision. He soon did.

this issue is now settled. If I haven't utterly convinced everybody, it's because my explanations were timid, my arguments have been feeble, and my inadequate studies of theory are to blame. Be that as it may, I'll tell you again that the distance between the earth and its satellite is truly insignificant and doesn't deserve any serious consideration. Consequently I don't think it's far-fetched to say that we'll soon be running whole passenger trains of projectiles, and people will journey in comfort from the earth to the moon. There won't be any jolting or jostling or jumping the tracks, and you'll reach your destination quickly, without physical strain, and by a direct route, a "bee line," to use the lingo of your trappers. Before twenty years are up, half the earth will have visited the moon!"

"Hooray! Hooray for Michel Ardan!" the attendees shouted, even those who were less than convinced.

"Hooray for Barbicane!" the speaker replied modestly.

This gesture of recognition for the undertaking's promoter was greeted by unanimous applause.

"Now, my friends," Michel Ardan went on, "if you have a few questions to ask me, you'll clearly put a poor fellow like myself on the spot, but I'll try to answer you all the same."

Till this point the Gun Club's president had good reason to be highly pleased with how the discussion was shaping up. It had stayed in the realm of theoretical speculation, and Michel Ardan, carried away by his keen imagination, had given quite a stellar performance. So it was essential to keep him from veering into practical issues, where he surely wasn't as adept. Barbicane hurried to get a word in edgewise and he asked his new friend if he thought life existed on the moon or the planets.

"That's a tremendous riddle you're posing me, my fine president," the speaker replied with a grin. "But if I'm not mistaken, highly intelligent men like Plutarch, Emanuel Swedenborg, Bernardin de Saint-Pierre, and many others have answered yes. Coming at it from the standpoint of the natural sciences,

I would be inclined to agree with them; I would conclude that nothing in this universe goes to waste, and replying to your question by raising another question, Barbicane my friend, I would state that if those are livable worlds, life either exists on them, has existed, or will exist."

"Well said!" exclaimed the front rows of the audience, whose views laid down the law for the back rows.

"Nobody could give a more logical and appropriate answer," the Gun Club's president responded. "So the question comes back around to this: are those other worlds livable? Speaking for myself, I think they are."

"As for me, I'm sure of it," Michel Ardan replied.

"However," one of the attendees remarked, "there are arguments against those other worlds being livable. Obviously their basis for life would have to be different in most ways. Therefore, to take just the planets, some must be roasting and others freezing, depending on their greater or lesser distance from the sun."

"I'm sorry," Michel Ardan replied, "that I'm not personally acquainted with my honorable challenger, yet I'll try to answer him. His objection has its points, but I think we can successfully overcome it, likewise all the rest that argue against other worlds being livable. If I were a physicist, I would say that if there's less heat set in motion on the planets nearest the sun, and by contrast more on the distant planets, this simple phenomenon is enough to balance things out and keep the temperature on those worlds bearable for creatures with an organism like ours. If I were a naturalist, I would say to him that according to many renowned experts, nature has furnished us with examples on earth of creatures that thrive under highly varied living conditions; that fish breathe in an environment fatal to other creatures; that amphibians lead a double life very hard to explain; that some denizens of the seas survive in ultra deep strata and tolerate a pressure of fifty or sixty atmospheres without being squashed; that a number of aquatic insects are immune to extreme temperatures and are found simultaneously in bubbling hot springs and the icy

tundras by the polar ocean; in short, we need to acknowledge that nature has different ways of proceeding that are often inscrutable, that are nonetheless real, and that seemingly can conquer all. If I were a chemist, I would say to him that meteorites, objects obviously not created on the planet earth, have revealed undeniable traces of carbon under analysis; that this substance only comes into being in the presence of organic life, and that according to Georg Reichenbach's experiments, it automatically must have been "livened up." Finally, if I were a theologian, I would say to him that in St. Paul's opinion, God's plan of redemption seems to apply not just to the earth but to all heavenly bodies. But I'm not a theologian, chemist, naturalist, or physicist. Accordingly, being an absolute know-nothing as regards the great laws that govern the universe, I'll confine myself to replying: 'I don't know whether life exists on other worlds, and since I don't know, I'll go see!'"

Did Michel Ardan's opponent venture some different arguments against his ideas? It's impossible to say, because the crowd's frenzied yelling would have kept any additional views from being aired. When silence had been restored to the outer reaches of the audience, the triumphant speaker was content to tack on these further thoughts:

"You may well feel, my gallant Yankees, that I've merely skated over this major question; I'm certainly not here to give you a public presentation and to articulate a position on this huge subject. There's a whole series of extra arguments in favor of life existing on other worlds. I'm skipping over them. Let me stress just one thing. To people who insist the planets are unlivable, we need to reply: you could be right, if it's proven the earth is the best of all possible worlds, but it isn't, no matter what Voltaire wrote. We've got only one satellite, while Jupiter, Uranus, Saturn, and Neptune have several at their service, a privilege that's not to be sneered at. But our particular source of discomfort with the earth is the slant of its axis during its orbit. Ergo our days and nights are unequal in length; ergo we have our inconvenient changes of season. On this poor globe of ours, it's always too hot or too cold; we freeze in the winter, roast in the summer; this is the planet of sniffles, head colds, and pneumonia, but compare our situation with, say, the surface of Jupiter, whose axis slants only a little—there the residents can enjoy uniform temperatures;[62] there they have year-round zones for spring, summer, autumn, and winter; each Jovian can pick whatever climate he likes and for the rest of his life be protected from any changes in temperature. You'll readily agree that Jupiter is superior in this way to our own planet, without even getting into the length of its year, which is twelve times longer than ours! What's more, it's obvious to me that with such guardianship and such marvelous living conditions, the residents of this lucky world are superior beings—its scholars are more scholarly, artists more artistic, evildoers less evil, and do-gooders the best ever. Alas, what's keeping our planet from achieving such perfection? Nothing much! It just needs to rotate on an axis that slants less during its orbit."

"Fine!" yelled a headstrong voice. "Let's put our heads together, invent the right machinery, and straighten out the earth's axis!"

Thunderous applause erupted at this bold proposition, whose source was and could only have been J. T. Maston. Very likely the Gun Club's fiery secretary had ventured it because his engineering instincts had run away with him. But we must add—since it's the truth—that many others shouted their support, and if they'd had the fulcrum specified by Archimedes, the Americans would surely have built a lever capable of raising our globe and straightening its axis. But a fulcrum was the one thing these reckless mechanics lacked.

Nevertheless this "exceptionally practical" idea was a huge hit; the main discussion hung fire for a good fifteen minutes, and for a long time afterward—a very long time—people across the United States of America talked about this proposition so forcefully advanced by the Gun Club's secretary for life.

---

[62] The slant of Jupiter's axis during its orbit is only 3° 5′.

20

ATTACK AND COUNTERATTACK

THIS INCIDENT seemed destined to end the discussion. It was the "parting shot," and you couldn't have asked for more. But when the excitement had died down, you heard a loud, stern voice say these words:

"Now that the speaker has given us so many flights of fancy, will he kindly get back to his subject, spend less time on guesswork, and discuss the practical aspects of his expedition?"

Everybody looked at the individual who had just spoken. He was a thin, wiry man with strong features and an American-style beard flourishing under his chin. Thanks to the various surges of excitement running through the gathering, he'd gradually made it to the front row of the audience. There, arms folded and eyes boldly gleaming, he kept the rally's hero under unruffled scrutiny. After voicing his question, he fell silent and didn't seem affected by the thousands of people looking his way or by the murmurs of disapproval his words had aroused. No answer forthcoming, he asked his question once more with the same clear, crisp inflection, then he added:

"We're here to deal with the moon, not the earth."

"You're right, sir," Michel Ardan replied, "the discussion has gotten off track. Let's get back to the moon."

"Sir," the stranger went on, "you claim life exists on our satellite. Fine. But if there really are moonpeople, one thing's for sure: they're a species who live without breathing, because—I'm warning you in your own best interests—there isn't the tiniest particle of air on the surface of the moon."

At this assertion Ardan smoothed his tawny mane; he realized a fight was about to break out with this man, and it would focus on the crux of the matter. He looked intently at the fellow in his turn, then said:

"Oh, so there's no air on the moon? And who makes that claim, if you please?"

"Scientists."

"Really?"

"Really."

"Sir," Michel went on, "all joking aside, I have deep respect for scientists who are scientific, but deep contempt for those who aren't."

"Do you know any who belong to your second category?"

"Intimately. In France there's one who insists it's 'mathematically impossible' for birds to fly, and another whose suppositions show that fish aren't designed to live underwater."

"They're irrelevant to this, sir, and in support of my proposition, I could mention some names you'll find irreproachable."

"In that case, sir, you'll thoroughly overwhelm a poor know-nothing who asks only to be taught the truth."

"Then why do you bring up scientific issues if you haven't done your homework?" the stranger asked with some rudeness.

"Why?" Ardan replied. "Because a man is always brave if he doesn't suspect danger. I'm uneducated, true, but this very deficiency gives me an advantage."

"Your deficiency borders on insanity," the stranger snapped in a bad-tempered voice.

"All the better," the Frenchman fired back, "if my insanity gets me to the moon!"

Devouring him with their eyes, Barbicane and his colleagues sized up this intruder who had just taken such a bold stand against the undertaking. Nobody knew who he was, and the Gun Club's president looked at his new friend with some trepidation, uneasy about the consequences of such an open-ended debate. The gathering was all ears and sincerely worried, because this conflict had ended up calling attention to the expedition's dangers, or even its actual impossibilities.

"Sir," Michel Ardan's opponent went on, "there are many irrefutable reasons that prove the moon hasn't any atmosphere surrounding her. I'll even say *a priori*[63] that if such an atmosphere ever existed, it must have been siphoned off by the earth's gravity. But I would rather dispute you using incontestable evidence."

"Dispute away, sir," Michel Ardan replied

---

[63] *Translator's note.* Latin: "before the fact."

with faultless courtesy, "dispute me all you like!"

"You're aware," the stranger said, "that when light rays go through a medium such as air, they veer off at an angle, or put another way, they undergo refraction. All right, when stars are occulted by the moon, their rays skim the edges of her disk yet never show the slightest tendency to veer off, nor do they reveal the tiniest signs of refraction. Ergo the obvious conclusion that the moon hasn't any atmosphere covering her."

Everybody looked at the Frenchman, because if he conceded this point, the results could be dire.

"As a matter of fact," Michel Ardan replied, "that's your best argument, if not your only one, and maybe some specialists would have trouble answering back; speaking for myself, I'll just say that this argument has absolutely no validity, because it assumes the moon's angular diameter has been flawlessly determined, which isn't the case. But let that be and tell me, my dear sir: do you accept the existence of volcanoes on the surface of the moon?"

"Extinct volcanoes, yes; active ones, no."

"Isn't it within the bounds of logic, then, to believe those volcanoes were active at one time?"

"Certainly, but they themselves could furnish the oxygen needed for their combustion, so the fact that they've erupted in no way proves the presence of a lunar atmosphere."

"Then let that be as well," Michel Ardan replied. "We'll set aside this type of argument and move on to eyewitness testimony. But I warn you, I'm going to name names."

"Go ahead."

"Here goes. While the astronomers Louville and Halley were watching the eclipse of May 3, 1715, they noted a peculiar type of flashing. These bursts of light were repeated quickly and often, and the two men attributed them to thunderstorms unleashed in the moon's atmosphere."

"In 1715," the stranger contended, "what the astronomers Louville and Halley mistook for lunar phenomena were just earthly phenomena—meteors and the like occurring in our own atmosphere. That's how scientists

have responded to the description of those events, and my response is the same."

"Let that be also," Ardan replied, shrugging off this counterattack. "In 1787 didn't Herschel detect a good many specks of light on the surface of the moon?"

"Surely, but Herschel didn't suggest a cause for those specks of light and he himself never concluded that the sight called for a lunar atmosphere."

"Good answer," Michel Ardan said, complimenting his opponent. "I see you're well up on the moon's physical features."

"Well up, sir, and I'll add that Messrs. Beer and Mädler, our ablest moonwatchers, our foremost students of that silver orb, agree she has absolutely no air on her surface."

There was a shift among the attendees, who seemed influenced by the arguments put forward by this unusual individual.

"Letting all those things be," Michel Ardan replied with supreme calm, "we now come to a major event. While watching the eclipse of July 18, 1860, an adroit French astronomer, Mr. Aimé Laussedat, verified that the horns of the solar crescent were curved and shortened. Now then, this phenomenon could only have been caused by the sun's rays veering off while crossing through the moon's atmosphere, and that's the only possible explanation."

"But has this event been confirmed?" the stranger asked sharply.

"Completely confirmed!"

There was a shift in the gathering back toward our hero, whose opponent stayed silent. Ardan took the floor again and without crowing over the advantage he'd just gained, he merely said: "So you can plainly see, my dear sir, that one mustn't make hard-and-fast statements denying there's an atmosphere on the surface of the moon; very likely this atmosphere hasn't much density and is pretty depleted, but modern science largely accepts that it exists."

"Not up in the mountains, with all due respect," the stranger remarked, unwilling to give in.

"No, but on the floors of valleys and going no higher than a couple hundred feet."

"In any event you'd better take every precaution, because that air will be dreadfully thin."

"Oh, my good sir, there'll always be enough for a single man; besides, once I get there, I'll do my best to be thrifty and breathe only on important occasions!"

A fearsome roar of laughter rang in the ears of his mysterious conversation partner, whose eyes darted around the gathering, proudly defying it.

"Then," Michel Ardan continued in an easygoing manner, "since we agree on the presence of some sort of atmosphere, we're also forced to accept the presence of some sort of water supply. That's a conclusion I'm personally very glad to reach. Further, my well-meaning challenger, let me make an additional comment to you. We're acquainted with only one side of the moon's disk, and if there's a little air on the face looking at us, it's possible there's plenty on the opposite face."

"And why is that?"

"Because, due to the earth's gravitational pull, the moon has taken on the shape of an egg, which we view from the small end. Ergo it follows, thanks to Peter Hansen's calculations, that her center of gravity is located in her other half. Ergo the conclusion that whole masses of air and water must have been pulled over to our satellite's other face during the first days of her creation."

"Pure imagination!" the stranger exclaimed.

"No, pure analysis based on the laws of mechanics, and it strikes me as hard to refute. So I appeal to this gathering and I call for a vote on the matter: do you believe that life, as it exists on the earth, is possible on the surface of the moon?"

Three hundred thousand listeners instantly applauded the proposition. Michel Ardan's opponent tried to speak further but couldn't make himself heard. Shouts and threats drummed on him like hail.

"That's enough of this!" some said.

"Get rid of that intruder!" others repeated.

"Kick him out!" exclaimed the angry crowd.

But he stood firm, clung to the stage, didn't stir, and let the storm pass over, which

would have grown to fearsome proportions if Michel Ardan hadn't hushed it with a gesture. He was too good-hearted a fellow to leave his challenger in such a pickle.

"Would you like to add a few words?" he asked the man in his politest tone.

"Yes, a hundred, a thousand!" the stranger replied hotly. "Or no, I would rather say just one! To keep on with this undertaking, you would have to be—"

"—foolhardy? How can you call me that! Haven't I asked my friend Barbicane for a cylindro-conical shell, so that on the way I don't spin around like a squirrel in a cage?"

"But you poor man, the frightful recoil will pulverize you the instant you take off!"

"My dear challenger, you've just put your finger on the only real difficulty; but I have too high an opinion of America's technological genius to believe they won't manage to solve this problem."

"But what about the heat generated by the projectile's speed while going through those layers of air?"

"Oh, its walls are thick, and I'll get through the atmosphere in no time."

"But what about provisions? Water?"

"I've calculated I could bring a year's supply, and my trip will take just four days."

"But what about the air you'll breathe on the way?"

"I'll produce it by a chemical process."

"But what about your fall to the moon, if you ever get there?"

"It'll be one-sixth as fast as a fall to the earth, since gravity is one-sixth as strong on the surface of the moon."

"It'll still be enough to shatter you like glass!"

"And what's to keep me from slowing my fall by using shrewdly positioned rockets, which I'll fire at the just the right moment?"

"But ultimately, assuming that you've solved every problem, that you've smoothed over every bump in the road, that you've had luck completely on your side, and that you've unquestionably reached the moon safe and sound, how will you come back?"

"I won't come back!"

At this reply, almost sublime in its simplicity, the gathering was speechless. But its silence was more eloquent than its most enthusiastic acclaim. The stranger made the most of this and raised one last protest:

"You'll be killed without fail," he exclaimed, "and your death will be the death of a madman, no help even to science!"

"Keep it up, kindly stranger, you really have a way of making the most comforting predictions."

"Oh, this is too much!" snarled Michel Ardan's opponent. "I don't know why I'm continuing such a flippant debate! Do as you please with this insane undertaking! You aren't the one who should be held accountable!"

"Oh, you don't need to spare my feelings."

"No, it's somebody else who's responsible for your actions!"

"And who's that, if you please?" Michel Ardan asked in an insistent voice.

"The know-nothing who organized this ridiculous and impossible endeavor!"

This was a direct assault. Ever since the stranger first intervened, Barbicane had been desperately trying to control himself, "fuming inwardly" as some boiler furnaces do; but hearing himself so outrageously characterized, he jumped to his feet and was about to approach this opponent who defied him to his face, when the two of them were abruptly separated.

All at once a hundred muscular arms had lifted up the stage as if it were a warrior's shield, then they carried the Gun Club's president in triumph, an honor he had to share with Michel Ardan. It was a heavy load, but the shield bearers continually relieved each other, bickering, quarreling, and battling among themselves over whose shoulders would lend support to this grand gesture.

Meanwhile the stranger hadn't taken advantage of the uproar and left the site. In the midst of this jam-packed crowd, how could he? Surely there was no way. In any event he stood his ground in the front row, arms folded, eyes devouring President Barbicane. The latter didn't lose sight of his foe, and the two men's eyes were locked like crossed, quivering swords.

During that triumphal march the immense crowd kept the cheers at a fever pitch. Obviously Michel Ardan was delighted to go along with it all. His face was beaming. At times the stage seemed to roll and pitch like a ship tossed by the waves. But the rally's two heroes had good sea legs; they kept their footing and the vessel arrived undamaged at the port of Tampa. Luckily Michel Ardan managed to elude the last-minute clutches of his energetic admirers; he fled to the Franklin Hotel, speedily retired to his room, promptly slid under the bedcovers, and meanwhile an army of 100,000 men stood watch beneath his windows.

Simultaneously a short, solemn, and decisive drama was playing out between the mystery man and the Gun Club's president.

Free at last, Barbicane had gone right over to his opponent.

"Come along!" he said in a curt voice.

The other man followed him to the dockside, and soon the two were alone at the entrance to a pier opening off Jones Falls St.

There the two enemies, who had never met before, looked at each other.

"What's your name?" Barbicane asked.

"Captain Nicholl."

"I suspected as much. Our paths just never happened to cross till now . . ."

"That's why I came."

"You've insulted me."

"Publicly."

"And you'll give me satisfaction for that insult."

"This instant."

"No. I want everything that transpires to remain our secret. There's a forest called Skersnaw Woods located three miles outside Tampa. You know it?"

"I know it."

"Would you kindly go inside it at five o'clock tomorrow morning?"

"Yes, if you'll go in the far side at the same hour."

"And you won't forget your rifle?" Barbicane said.

"No more than you'll forget yours," Nicholl replied.

After coolly speaking these words, the captain and the Gun Club's president went their separate ways. Barbicane returned to his residence; but instead of grabbing a few hours of sleep, he spent the night thinking about how to circumvent the projectile's recoil and to solve that difficult problem Michel Ardan had raised during the rally's debate.

21

HOW A FRENCHMAN DEALS WITH A DUEL

WHILE THE TERMS of this shootout were under discussion between the captain and the Gun Club's president—a dreadful, barbaric shootout in which both opponents turn into manhunters—Michel Ardan was resting from the exertions of his triumph. But the verb "rest" clearly isn't an appropriate choice of word, because American beds are hard enough to rival a premium slab of marble or granite.

So Ardan didn't sleep very well, tossing and turning between the dishtowels that served as his sheets, and he was dreaming of outfitting his projectile with an ultra comfortable pallet, when a thunderous sound yanked him out of his fantasies. His door shook from somebody knocking wildly. An iron implement seemed to be striking it. Fearsome outcries added to this early-morning ruckus.

"Open up!" a voice bawled. "For heaven's sake, will you open up!"

Ardan had no reason to honor such an earsplitting request. But he got out of bed and opened the door, just as it was ready to cave in under his caller's persistent efforts. The Gun Club's secretary barged into the room. A bombshell couldn't have made a less decorous entrance.

"Yesterday afternoon," J. T. Maston blurted out *ex abrupto*,[64] "our president was publicly insulted during the rally! He challenged his opponent to a duel, and it's none other than Captain Nicholl! They're fighting this morning in Skersnaw Woods! I heard all about it from Barbicane's own lips! If he

gets killed, it'll be the ruination of our plans! We've got to prevent this duel! Now then, only one man alive has enough influence on Barbicane to stop him, and that man's Michel Ardan!"

While J. T. Maston was getting these words out, Michel Ardan refrained from interrupting him and scrambled into his capacious trousers; going at top speed, the two friends reached the outskirts of Tampa in less than two minutes.

It was during this breakneck race that Maston brought Ardan up to date on the situation. He informed the Frenchman of the actual reasons for the enmity between Barbicane and Nicholl, how this enmity was of long standing, and why, thanks to mutual friends, the captain and the Gun Club's president had never met face to face previously; he added that it all came down to a competition between shells and armor plate, and finally that the scene at the rally had simply been a long-sought opportunity for Nicholl to settle an old score.

Nothing could be more dreadful than the duels characteristic of this part of America—the two opponents stalk each other through the thickets, lie in wait behind patches of underbrush, and exchange shots among the brambles as if they were hunting wild game. And during it all, both duelists must deeply envy those wonderful innate abilities of the prairie Indians—their mental alertness, their cleverness and cunning, their tracking instincts, their nose for an enemy! One mistake, one hesitation, one false move could lead to disaster. During these contests Yankees often bring their dogs along, act as both hunter and hunted, and return fire for hours at a time.

"What fiends you people are!" Michel Ardan exclaimed, after his companion had set the stage for him with so much energy.

"That's us all right," J. T. Maston replied sheepishly. "But let's hurry!"

The plain was still wet with dew, and though he and Michel Ardan crossed it at a good clip, taking every possible shortcut over the creeks and rice fields, they couldn't get to Skersnaw Woods before 5:30. Barbicane must have gone inside it half an hour earlier.

---

[64] *Translator's note.* Latin: "without any preliminaries."

An old forester was at work there, busy making firewood out of some trees he'd chopped down with his ax. Maston ran toward him, yelling:

"Did you see a man with a rifle go into the woods—Barbicane our president, my best friend . . . ?"

The Gun Club's distinguished secretary had innocently assumed their president was known to the whole planet. But the forester didn't seem to understand him.

"Did you see a hunter?" Ardan said.

"A hunter? Right," the forester replied.

"Some time ago?"

"Close to an hour."

"We're too late!" Maston exclaimed.

"Have you heard any gunshots?" Michel Ardan asked the forester.

"No."

"Not even one?"

"Not even one. Your hunter doesn't seem to have his mind on hunting."

"What should we do?" Maston said.

"Go into the woods," Ardan replied, "and risk stopping a bullet not intended for us."

"Oh," Maston exclaimed in a voice that honestly meant it, "I would rather have ten bullets in my brain than a single one in Barbicane's!"

"Then on we go," Ardan resumed, clutching his companion's hand.

A few seconds later the two friends had vanished into the thicket. The underbrush was extremely dense, with giant cypresses, sycamores, tulip trees, olive trees, tamarinds, live oaks, and magnolias. These different trees intertwined their branches into a hopelessly tangled jumble that didn't allow for seeing very far. Michel Ardan and Maston walked side by side, tiptoeing amid the tall weeds, clearing paths through the tough creepers, looking suspiciously into bushes or up at branches lost in the dark, dense foliage, waiting at every step for the alarming sound of rifles going off. As for the footprints that Barbicane must have left in his trek through the woods, they were impossible to make out, and our two friends went blindly down trails that were barely blazed—over which an Indian, however, could have tracked every single step of his enemy's movements.

After an hour of searching in vain, the two companions halted. They were now twice as worried.

"It must be over and done with," Maston said despondently. "A man like Barbicane wouldn't trick his enemy, or lay a trap for him, or even use any strategies! He's too direct, too courageous. He just went straight ahead, right into danger—and no doubt he was so far away, the wind kept the forester from hearing any firearms going off."

"But what about us? What about ourselves?" Michel Ardan replied. "After we went into these woods, we should have heard . . . "

"But what if we got here too late?" Maston exclaimed in a despairing voice.

Michel Ardan was at a loss for a reply; he and Maston resumed their interrupted walk. From time to time they shouted at the tops of their lungs; they called out for Barbicane, then for Nicholl; but neither of the two opponents answered their appeals. Aroused by the sound, birds flew merrily past, vanishing among the branches, and a few frightened deer instantly fled through the thicket.

For another hour their search continued. By then they'd explored most of the woods. There wasn't a sign of the duelists. They were starting to doubt what the forester had said, and Ardan was ready to give up completely on this futile scouting expedition, when all at once Maston halted.

"Shh!" he put in. "There's a person down there!"

"A person?" Michel Ardan replied.

"Yes, a man! He seems to be perfectly still. His rifle isn't in his hands. So what's he up to?"

"But can you see who it is?" Michel Ardan asked, his nearsighted eyes not much help under circumstances like these.

"Yes, yes! He's turning around," Maston replied.

"And it's . . . ?"

"It's Captain Nicholl!"

"Nicholl?" Michel Ardan exclaimed, feeling a sharp pang.

And Nicholl wasn't carrying his weapon! So he no longer had anything to fear from his opponent?

"Let's go over to him," Michel Ardan said, "and find out where things stand."

But he and his companion hadn't taken fifty steps when they halted to watch the captain more closely. They'd expected to find a man thirsting for blood and obsessed with revenge! They were astonished when they saw what he was doing.

A closely woven net stretched between two gigantic tulip trees, and in the middle of it a little bird, whose wings had gotten ensnared in its meshes, was struggling and uttering plaintive chirps. The bird catcher who had spun this hopelessly tangled web wasn't a human being—it was a poisonous spider characteristic of this region, as big as a pigeon egg and equipped with enormous legs. Just as it was rushing at its prey, the hideous creature was forced to back away and take refuge in the upper branches of one of the tulip trees, because it was now under threat from an alarming enemy of its own.

In essence Captain Nicholl had left his gun on the ground, forgotten his perilous circumstances, and with all possible care was trying to free the victim trapped in the toils of that monstrous spider. When he'd done so, he let the little bird fly off, and it vanished, merrily fluttering its wings.

Nicholl was affectionately watching it flee through the branches, when he heard these words spoken in a voice that sounded genuinely touched:

"You're a gallant fellow, yes you are!"

He turned around. Michel Ardan stood in front of him, saying over and over:

"And a kindhearted fellow, too!"

"Michel Ardan!" the captain blurted out. "Why are you here, sir?"

"To shake your hand, Nicholl, and to keep you from killing or being killed by Barbicane."

"Barbicane!" the captain exclaimed. "I've been looking for him the past two hours and haven't found him! Where did he sneak off to?"

"Nicholl," Michel Ardan said, "that's not good manners! You should always speak civilly of your opponent; don't worry, if Barbicane's alive, we'll find him, and all the more readily since he must be looking for you as well—unless, like yourself, he has a fondness for saving oppressed wildfowl. But once we've found him, you can take Michel Ardan's word for it, there'll be no more talk of your dueling."

"There's been such a feud between President Barbicane and me," Nicholl replied solemnly, "that only the death of one of us—"

"Oh come on!" Michel Ardan continued. "Gallant gentlemen like yourselves can both detest and respect each other. You're not going to fight."

"I *will* fight, sir!"

"No way."

"Captain," J. T. Maston said straight from the heart, "I'm our president's trusted friend, his *alter ego*, his second self; if you absolutely insist on killing somebody, shoot me—it'll amount to exactly the same thing!"

"Sir," Nicholl said, gripping his rifle with hands that shook, "these jokes of yours—"

"Our friend Maston isn't joking," Michel Ardan replied, "and I appreciate his idea of laying down his life for a man he loves! But neither he nor Barbicane will bite the dust from your bullets, Captain Nicholl, because I have a proposition for you two competitors that's so enticing, you'll both jump at it."

"What proposition?" Nicholl asked, visibly skeptical.

"Patience," Ardan replied. "I can't tell you about it till Barbicane's present."

"Then let's look for him," the captain snapped.

The three men immediately took to the trail; after uncocking his rifle, the captain slung it over his shoulder and moved forward haltingly, not saying a word.

For another half an hour, they searched in vain. Maston was consumed with gruesome forebodings. He looked grimly at Nicholl, wondering whether the captain hadn't already taken his revenge, whether the unfortunate Barbicane, already shot down, wasn't lying lifeless on the floor of some blood-spattered thicket. Michel Ardan seemed to have the same thought, and both men had been giving Nicholl the eye, when Maston suddenly came to a halt.

A man's motionless head and shoulders

were visible twenty steps away, a man propped against the foot of a gigantic catalpa tree, half hidden in the weeds.

"That's him!" Maston put in.

Barbicane didn't stir. Ardan looked deep into the captain's eyes, but the latter didn't flinch. Ardan took a few steps, calling:

"Barbicane! Barbicane!"

No answer. Ardan rushed toward the man; but just as he was about to grab his friend by the arms, he stopped short and let out a cry of surprise.

Pencil in hand, Barbicane was scribbling formulas and geometric figures in a notebook, his uncocked firearm lying on the ground.

Caught up in his work, likewise forgetting his duel and his quest for revenge, the scholarly fellow was deaf and blind to the world.

But when Ardan reached out and stopped his hand from writing, he sat up and stared at the Frenchman in amazement.

"Ah," he exclaimed at last, "you're here! I've found it, my friend, I've found it!"

"What did you find?"

"A way to do it!"

"A way to do what?"

"A way to nullify the impact of the recoil when the projectile takes off!"

"Really?" Michel said, giving the captain a sidelong glance.

"Yes, it's water! Plain water will act as a set of springs . . . ah, Maston," Barbicane exclaimed, "you're here too!"

"None other," Michel Ardan responded, "and while we're at it, let me introduce the esteemed Captain Nicholl!"

"Nicholl!" Barbicane exclaimed, instantly jumping to his feet. "I beg your pardon, captain," he said. "I'd forgotten . . . I'm ready . . . "

Michel Ardan stepped in before the two enemies had time to provoke each other.

"By George," he said, "we're lucky you two gallant fellows didn't meet up earlier! We would now be mourning one or the other of you. But thanks to a little divine intervention, there's nothing more to worry about. Anytime a fellow forgets his hatred in order to dive into engineering problems or to fool

around with spiders, it's because that hatred isn't a danger to anybody."

And Michel Ardan told the captain's tale to President Barbicane.

"Now I ask you," he said in conclusion, "were you two decent people created just to blow each other's brains out with potshots from a rifle?"

There was something so surprising in this rather silly situation, Barbicane and Nicholl weren't too sure how to behave toward each other. Michel Ardan had a clear inkling of this and was determined to bring about an immediate reconciliation.

"My gallant friends," he said, trotting out his finest smile, "there's never been anything between you other than a misunderstanding. Nothing more. All right, since you're folks who don't seem to mind risking your hides, I've got a proposition for you—and if you accept it wholeheartedly, you'll prove that everything's cleared up between you."

"Go on," Nicholl said.

"Our friend Barbicane believes his projectile will go right straight to the moon."

"Yes, absolutely," remarked the Gun Club's president.

"And our friend Nicholl is convinced it'll fall back to the earth."

"I'm positive of it," the captain snapped.

"Fine," Michel Ardan went on. "I don't claim I can bring you into agreement; but I'll make you this simple offer: travel along with me, and see for yourselves whether we make it all the way."

"Huh?" J. T. Maston put in, stunned.

The two competitors exchanged glances at this unexpected proposition. They watched each other carefully. The Gun Club's president was waiting for the captain to reply. Nicholl was on the lookout for Barbicane's answer.

"Well," Michel put in as seductively as he could, "since we don't have to worry about the recoil any longer . . . "

"Done!" Barbicane exclaimed.

But as quickly as he got this word out, Nicholl was just as quick with the same word.

"Hooray! Bravo! Good work! Three cheers!" Michel Ardan exclaimed, shaking hands with the two opponents. "And now that we've dealt with your duel, my friends, let me take care of you like a good Frenchman. I'll treat you to breakfast!"

22
THE NEW CITIZEN OF THE UNITED STATES

THAT DAY ALL AMERICA learned at the same instant of the duel between Captain Nicholl and President Barbicane, likewise its unusual outcome. The role played in this encounter by the great-hearted European, his unexpected proposition that resolved the difficulty, its simultaneous acceptance by the two competitors, and France's collaborating with the United States to conquer those lunar landmasses all combined to increase Michel Ardan's popularity still further.

As you know, Yankees can become passionately dedicated to an individual. In a country where solemn magistrates harness themselves to a ballerina's buggy and pull her along in triumph, you can imagine the passions unleashed by our daring Frenchman! If they didn't unhitch his horses, most likely it's because he didn't own any, but they lavished every other form of approval on him. Each citizen was his mental and emotional ally. *E pluribus unum*, as the motto of the United States says.

From that day forward Michel Ardan no longer had a moment's peace. Delegations arrived from every corner of the Union and badgered him without rest or respite. Like it or not, he had to receive them. The hands he shook, the folks he was chummy with, were beyond counting; he soon ran out of steam; his voice grew hoarse from making endless speeches, nothing but garbled noises escaped from his lips, and he almost came down with gastroenteritis after drinking toasts to every county in the Union. Anybody else would have been "drunk with success" from the first day, but he managed to limit himself to a charming and witty state of partial intoxication.

Out of all the assorted delegations that waylaid him, a contingent called the "Luna-

tics" was careful to acknowledge its debt to the moon's future conqueror. One day a few of these poor fellows, who are fairly plentiful in America, called on him and asked to go back with him to their native land. Some of their number even claimed to "speak moonpeople" and wanted to teach it to Michel Ardan. The latter good-naturedly went along with their wide-eyed fixations and took down messages for their friends on the moon.

"What an odd form of insanity!" he told Barbicane after seeing them out. "And it's an insanity that often strikes the keenest minds. One of our most renowned scientists, François Arago, told me there have been many well-educated people with quite conservative beliefs who got tremendously excited and incredibly eccentric anytime the moon captivated them. You don't think the moon influences sickness, do you?"

"Hardly," replied the Gun Club's president.

"I don't either, and yet history records some facts that are amazing to say the least. Thus, during an epidemic in 1693, the largest number of people died on January 21 at the time of an eclipse. The famous Sir Francis Bacon blacked out during eclipses of the moon and only came to after that heavenly body had completely reemerged. King Charles VI suffered six spells of mental illness over the year 1399, during either the new moon or the full moon. Physicians have classified epilepsy among illnesses that follow the phases of the moon. Neurological disorders often seem to be subject to her influence. Richard Mead tells of a child who went into convulsions when the moon was in opposition. Franz Gall has noted that decrepit people get more energetic twice a month, when the moon is new and when she's full. Finally there are a thousand more studies of this sort on dizzy spells, deadly fevers, and sleepwalking, going to show that this silver orb has some mysterious influence on our planet's health problems."

"But how? Why?" Barbicane asked.

"Why?" Ardan replied. "Ye gods, I'll give you the same answer Arago resurrected nineteen centuries after Plutarch first came up with it: 'Maybe it's because it just couldn't be true!'"

In the midst of his triumph, Michel Ardan had to cope with all the annoyances that are part of a celebrity's life. Big-time impresarios wanted to put him on display. P. T. Barnum offered him a million to go on the road from town to town across the United States, like an exotic animal exhibit. Michel Ardan called him an elephant keeper and told him to hit the road himself

Yet if he refused to appease public curiosity in this way, at least his photographs circulated everywhere, occupying the place of honor in albums worldwide; prints were available in all dimensions, life-size down to microscopic miniatures as small as a postage stamp. You could have your hero in every imaginable pose—mug shot, head and shoulders, whole body, full face, profile, three-quarters, or rear. Over 1,500,000 copies of these were on sale, plus Michel had a fine opportunity to market parts of himself as relics, but he failed to take advantage of it. If all he did was peddle the hairs on his head for a dollar apiece, he had enough of them still left to make a fortune!

To tell the truth, his popularity didn't upset him. On the contrary. He put himself at the public's disposal and answered correspondence from everywhere on earth. His witty remarks were quoted and widely publicized, especially those he didn't actually make. He was given credit for them on the usual grounds that one lends only to the rich.

In addition to men, women were all for him as well. There were an infinite number of "ideal marriages" on offer if he ever took a notion to "get hitched." Old maids in particular, those who had been waiting in the wings for forty years, swooned over his snapshots night and day.

No doubt about it, he could have had helpmates by the hundreds, even if he'd required them to go with him into outer space. When they aren't scared of everything that moves, women are dauntless. But he had no intention of establishing a bloodline in the lunar regions and transplanting a race of crossbred Franco-Americans to those parts. So he declined all offers.

"Me go up there and play Adam to some daughter of Eve?" he said. "No thanks, I'm bound to run into some snake or other . . ."

The instant he could finally turn his back on the long-winded joys of victory, he went with his friends to pay a visit to the columbiad. He owed it that much. Besides, he'd gotten quite savvy on ballistics after he started spending his days with Barbicane, J. T. Maston, and *tutti quanti*. He took the keenest pleasure in reminding these gallant artillerymen that they were just methodical, mild-mannered murderers. He never ran out of jokes on this topic. The day he inspected the columbiad, he truly marveled at it and was lowered all the way into the bore of this gigantic mortar, which soon was to launch him toward the earth's satellite.

"At least," he said, "this cannon won't harm anybody, which is already a pretty amazing feat for a cannon. But as for your engines of destruction that burn, crush, and kill, I don't want to hear about 'em—and above all don't ever come tell me a gun has a 'sensitive' mechanism, because I know better!"

We need to take note here of a proposition originating with J. T. Maston. When the Gun Club's secretary heard Barbicane and Nicholl accept Michel Ardan's proposition, he was determined to join them and make it "a party of four." One day he asked to go along too. Distressed at having to refuse him, Barbicane explained to his friend that the projectile couldn't carry that many passengers. In despair J. T. Maston sought out Michel Ardan, who encouraged him to accept the situation, then went to town with some *ad hominem* arguments.

"Look here, Maston old boy," he said, "you mustn't take my words the wrong way, but honestly now, just between ourselves—you're too incomplete to make an appearance on the moon!"

"Incomplete!" exclaimed the valiant amputee.

"Yes, my gallant friend! Suppose we ran into some residents up there. Do you want to give them such a dismal impression of what's going on down here, to teach them what war is, to show them how we spend most of our days devouring each other, chewing each other up, breaking each other's arms and legs, and all on a planet that could nurture 100 billion residents yet barely has 1.2 billion? Come now, my fine friend, you would cause them to kick us out!"

"But if you don't get there in one piece," J. T. Maston contended, "you'll be as incomplete as I am!"

"No doubt," Michel Ardan replied, "but we'll get there in one piece."

In fact a preliminary experiment attempted on October 18 had yielded optimum results and provided legitimate grounds for the highest hopes. Wanting to assess the impact of the recoil just as the projectile takes off, Barbicane got hold of a 32-inch mortar from the Pensacola arsenal. They set it up on the beach facing the offshore mooring of Hillsborough; this way the bombshell dropped back into the sea, which would deaden its fall. The sole objective was to test the jolt at departure, not the impact on arrival. With the greatest care they fixed up a hollow projectile for this interesting experiment. The inside walls were lined with heavy padding over a network of top-grade steel springs. It was an honest-to-goodness nest that had been meticulously upholstered.

"What a shame there isn't more room inside!" J. T. Maston said, sorry that his size wouldn't let him attempt the adventure.

Into this delightful bombshell, which they closed up by the simple method of screwing its lid into place, they first inserted a good-sized cat, then the Gun Club's secretary for life also thrust in his pet squirrel, the apple of J. T. Maston's eye. But they wanted to see how this little animal—which isn't exactly troubled by fear of heights—would bear up on this experimental journey.

They loaded the mortar with 160 pounds of gunpowder, then placed the bombshell in the piece. They fired it.

At once the projectile shot swiftly into the air, swept around in its majestic parabola, reached an altitude of about a thousand feet, executed a graceful curve, then plummeted into the heart of the waves.

Without wasting another second, a longboat headed toward the spot where it had fallen; skilled divers plunged underwater and attached cables to appendages on the bombshell, which was quickly hauled on board. Five minutes hadn't gone by between the moment the animals were locked up and the moment humans were unscrewing the lid of their prison.

Ardan, Barbicane, Maston, and Nicholl were aboard the longboat and in attendance at the operation, feeling an interest easy to understand. The bombshell was no sooner opened than the cat sprang out, a little scruffy but full of energy, in no way looking like he'd come back from an expedition in the sky. Not so the squirrel. They looked inside. No trace of it. They had to face the facts. The cat had eaten his traveling companion.

Heartbroken at the loss of his poor squirrel, J. T. Maston proposed to inscribe its name on the honor roll of martyrs to science.

Be that as it may, after this experiment all their doubts and fears vanished; besides, Barbicane's plans were bound to improve the projectile still further, to eliminate the impact of the recoil almost completely. So there was nothing else to do but take off.

Two days later Michel Ardan received a message from the President of the Union, an honor he appeared to distinctly appreciate.

As they'd done with his great-hearted countryman, the Marquis de Lafayette, the government conferred on him the title of citizen of the United States of America.

23

THE PROJECTILE COACH

ONCE THE FAMOUS COLUMBIAD was finished, public interest immediately shifted to the projectile, that new-fangled vehicle destined to carry our three bold adventurers through space. Nobody had forgotten that in his telegram on September 30, Michel Ardan asked for a change in the plans drawn up by the committee members.

With good reason President Barbicane figured back then that the projectile's shape mattered little, because, once it had spent a few seconds crossing through the atmosphere, its trip was to take place in an absolute vacuum. The committee had adopted a round shape, so the shell could rotate any which way and do whatever it liked. But from the instant they'd transformed the projectile into a vehicle, it was another story. Michel Ardan had no desire to travel like a squirrel in a cage; he wanted to take off with his head held high and his feet underneath him, as poised and confident as if he were in the basket of a hot air balloon—going more quickly, no doubt, but without indulging in an undignified sequence of side leaps like a ballet dancer.

So new plans were sent to the firm of Breadwill & Co. in Albany, along with instructions to put them into execution without delay. In its changed form the projectile was cast on November 2, then immediately shipped to Stony Hill over the east-coast railroads. On the 10th it arrived safely in the vicinity of its destination. Michel Ardan, Barbicane, and Nicholl were waiting with the keenest impatience for this "projectile coach," aboard which they were to set out on a flight to discover a new world.

It was a magnificent piece of metal, you had to admit, and a metalworking achievement that paid the highest compliment to American technological genius. It was the first time a factory had amassed such a considerable amount of aluminum, which in itself could be justly regarded as a prodigious feat. The precious projectile gleamed in the sunlight. Seeing its imposing shape, its conical cap on top, you could easily have mistaken it for one of those squat turrets shaped like pepper shakers that medieval architects hung on the corners of their fortified castles. The only things missing were gun slits and a weather vane.

"I keep waiting," Michel Ardan exclaimed, "for soldiers to come out of it complete with harquebuses[65] and steel breastplates. We'll be like feudal warlords inside that, and with a few pieces of artillery we could stand up to whole armies of moonpeople, assuming our satellite has any!"

"So our vehicle pleases you?" Barbicane asked his friend.

---

[65] *Translator's note.* 15th century matchlock rifles.

"Yes, yes, certainly," Michel Ardan replied, examining it with an artist's eye. "I'm just sorry its shape isn't more tapered, its cone more graceful; it'll need to be topped off by an ornamental crest with interlacing metal trim and featuring a gargoyle, for instance, or a chimera, or one of those mythical fire-loving salamanders darting out of the flames with spreading wings and gaping maw . . . "

"What for?" Barbicane said, his practical mind not very attuned to artistic refinements.

"What for, Barbicane my friend? Alas, if you have to ask me such a question, I'm afraid you'll never understand the answer."

"Tell me anyhow, my gallant companion."

"Well, to my thinking, folks ought to add a few artistic touches to everything they do, that's the preferred way. Are you acquainted with an East Indian play entitled *The Child's Wagon?*"

"Not even by name," Barbicane replied.

"That doesn't surprise me," Michel Ardan went on. "Understand, then, that in this play there's a burglar who's about to cut through the wall of a house, then wonders whether to saw his hole in the shape of a flower, a bird, a lyre, or an ancient Greek vase. All right, Barbicane my friend, tell me—if you'd been a member of the jury at that time, would you have brought in a guilty verdict against this burglar?"

"Without any hesitation," replied the Gun Club's president, "and thrown the book at him for breaking and entering."

"And I myself would have acquitted him, Barbicane my friend! That's why you'll never be able to understand me."

"I wouldn't even try, my dashing showman."

"But since the outside of our projectile coach leaves something to be desired," Michel Ardan went on, "at least you'll let me furnish the inside as I see fit, and with all the luxury appropriate to ambassadors from the earth!"

"In that respect, my gallant Michel," Barbicane replied, "you do as you think best— we'll give you a free hand."

But the functional still took precedence

over the decorative, and with unfailing shrewdness the Gun Club's president set about implementing the methods he'd devised to lessen the impact of the recoil.

Barbicane had told himself, not without good reason, that no springs would be strong enough to deaden the jolt, and during his notorious stroll in Skersnaw Woods, he'd ended up cleverly solving this major difficulty. He intended to call on water to perform this notable service for him. Here's how.

The projectile was to be filled with a cushion of water three feet deep, which was intended to buoy up a wooden disk that was completely watertight, fitted snugly against the projectile's inside walls, yet could slide downward. The travelers would be stationed on an honest-to-goodness raft. As for the mass of liquid underneath, it was divided into layers by horizontal partitions that were to collapse consecutively under the impact at take off. From lowest to highest, each layer of water would then escape through drainpipes near the top of the projectile, acting in this way like springs, and the movable disk (itself equipped with exceptionally strong buffers) couldn't hit the shell's base underneath till the different partitions had consecutively caved in. No doubt the travelers would still experience a sharp recoil after that mass of liquid had totally escaped, but the initial impact should have been deadened almost completely by this tremendously powerful set of springs.

True, three feet of water over a surface area of fifty-four square feet had to weigh close to 11,500 pounds; but the expansion of the gas accumulating in the columbiad would be enough, in Barbicane's view, to overcome this weight increase; besides, the impact should expel all that water in less than a second, and the projectile would promptly recover its normal weight.

This is what the Gun Club's president had come up with, the way he planned to settle this important issue of the recoil. What's more, engineers at the Breadwill firm took the job shrewdly in hand and executed it marvelously; once this countermeasure had taken place and the water was expelled from the shell, the three men could easily clear away the collapsed partitions, then dismantle the movable disk that the travelers had ridden on at departure time.

As for the projectile's upper walls, they were lined with heavy leather padding that covered top-grade steel coils as supple as watch springs. The drainpipes were hidden behind this padding, not giving the tiniest hint of their presence.

Hence every imaginable precaution had been taken to deaden the initial impact, and if the travelers got squashed, it would have to be, as Michel Ardan said, "because we're made of inferior materials."

On the outside the projectile measured nine feet wide by twelve high. In order to not exceed the agreed-upon weight, they'd slightly reduced the walls' thickness and reinforced the bottom section, which had to handle the full force of the gas generated by the pyroxile's combustion. Besides, this is the standard design for bombshells and cylindro-conical missiles—their bases are always thicker.

You climbed inside this metal tower through a narrow opening contrived in the wall of the cone and resembling the "manhole" of a steam boiler. It was hermetically sealed with the help of an aluminum hatch plate, which was firmly fastened from inside simply by screwing it into place. So once they'd arrived on that silver orb, the travelers could leave their movable prison whenever they wished.

But it isn't enough just to travel, you need to see where you're heading. Nothing could be simpler. In essence there were four portholes sunk in the padding and made of extremely heavy biconvex glass, two cut in the projectile's circular walls, a third in its bottom, a fourth in its conical cap. During the trip, therefore, our travelers would actually be able to study that earth they were leaving, that moon they were nearing, and those star-spangled vistas out in space. Moreover the portholes were protected from the impact at departure by plates that were tightly inset and that easily opened outward after you undid the screws inside. This way the air contained in the projectile couldn't escape, and it became possible to do a little skywatching.

All these wonderfully devised mechanisms functioned with the greatest of ease, and the engineers proved just as shrewd in fitting out the projectile coach.

Firmly secured containers were designed to hold the water and provisions our three travelers needed; the latter could even get warmth and illumination with the help of gas, which was stored in a special container under a pressure of several atmospheres. All they had to do was turn on a spigot, and for six days this gas would light and heat their cozy vehicle. As you can see, they had everything they needed for survival and even for comfort. What's more, thanks to Michel Ardan's aesthetic instincts, the decorative and the functional joined hands in the form of assorted knick-knacks; if he'd had the space for it, he would have turned the projectile into a real artist's studio. Even so, you would be wrong to assume that three people were destined to find it cramped inside this metal tower. It had fifty-four square feet of floor space and a height of nearly ten feet, which gave its guests a definite freedom of movement. They wouldn't have been more at ease inside the coziest carriage in the United States.

Issues of lighting and provisions being settled, all that remained was the issue of air. Obviously the air that the projectile contained wouldn't be enough to keep the travelers breathing for four days; in fact, over an hour or so, a single human being uses up all the oxygen found in 25 gallons of air. Every twenty-four hours Barbicane, his two companions, and two dogs he planned to take along each would use up 600 gallons of oxygen, or in terms of weight, nearly seven pounds. It was essential to renew the air in the projectile. How? By a perfectly simple process—the one invented by Messrs. Reiset and Regnault, which Michel Ardan alluded to during the debate at the rally.

In the main, as you know, air consists of twenty-one parts oxygen and seventy-nine parts nitrogen. Now then, what happens in the course of breathing? An extremely simple phenomenon. A human being consumes the oxygen from the air, which is exceptionally suited to sustaining life, then expels the nitrogen intact. The exhaled air has lost about 5% of its oxygen and now contains an almost equal volume of carbon dioxide, the end result of the combustion of the blood's elements by the inhaled oxygen. So in a closed environment, after a certain period of time, all the oxygen in the air will end up being replaced by carbon dioxide, a basically noxious gas.

The issue boiled down to this: since the nitrogen stays intact, 1) you need to replace the consumed oxygen; 2) you need to eliminate the exhaled carbon dioxide. With the help of potassium chlorate and potassium hydroxide, nothing could be easier.

Potassium chlorate is a salt that appears in the form of white flakes; when you heat it to a temperature above 750° Fahrenheit, it's transformed into potassium chloride, and the oxygen it contains is completely released. Now then, eighteen pounds of potassium chlorate gives seven pounds of oxygen, in other words, the amount our travelers would each need over twenty-four hours. This takes care of replenishing the oxygen.

As for potassium hydroxide, it's a substance that consumes carbon dioxide in the air with great eagerness, and if you merely shake it, it lays hold of that noxious gas and forms potassium bicarbonate. This takes care of consuming the carbon dioxide.

By combining these two processes, you're sure to give the foul air all its vital attributes again. This is what the two chemists Messrs. Reiset and Regnault proved in their successful experiments. But it should be mentioned that up to that time, these experiments had only been carried out *in anima vili*.[66] Regardless of their scientific accuracy, nobody knew for certain how human beings would bear up.

Which was the comment made at a special session dealing with this important issue. Michel Ardan didn't want any leftover doubts about the possibility of their surviving on this artificial air, so he offered to do a trial run before their departure. But the honor of putting it to the test was vigorously claimed by J. T. Maston.

---

[66] *Translator's note.* Latin: "with laboratory animals."

"Since I'm not going on the projectile," said that gallant artilleryman, "the least you can do is let me spend a week inside it."

It would have been ill-mannered to turn him down. They gave in to his wishes. Adequate amounts of potassium chlorate and potassium hydroxide were put at his disposal, along with a good week's provisions; then at six o'clock in the morning on November 12, he shook hands with his friends, expressly instructed them to not open his prison before six o'clock in the evening on the 20th, slid inside the projectile, and hermetically sealed its hatch plate.

What went on during that week or so? It was impossible to determine. The thickness of the projectile's walls meant that no sounds could travel from the inside to the outside.

At exactly six o'clock on November 20, the hatch plate was removed; J. T. Maston's friends were more than a little worried. But they were promptly reassured when they heard a gleeful voice let out a fearsome hooray.

Soon the Gun Club's secretary appeared at the top of the cone and struck a triumphant pose. He'd gotten fatter!

24

THE TELESCOPE IN THE ROCKY MOUNTAINS

ON OCTOBER 20 the year before, after the funding drive had ended, the Gun Club's president had provided the Cambridge Observatory with the sums needed to build a huge optical instrument. Spyglass or telescope, this device had to be powerful enough to reveal an object on the surface of the moon more than nine feet across.

There's a major difference between a spyglass and a telescope; we would do well to recall it here. A spyglass consists of a tube with a convex lens at its upper end (known as the objective) and a second lens at its lower end (named the eyepiece) that the skywatcher looks into. Light rays pouring from an object go through the first lens, then, thanks to refraction, end up forming an upside-down image at the focal point.[67] You view this image with the eyepiece, which enlarges it just as a magnifying glass would. So the tube of a spyglass is closed off at both ends by an objective lens and an eyepiece.

A telescope's tube, on the other hand, is open at its upper end. Light rays from the object viewed can freely enter it, then end up striking a concave metal mirror—in other words, they converge. From there these reflected rays meet up with a smaller mirror that sends them to the eyepiece, which is positioned so as to magnify the image produced.

In spyglasses, accordingly, refraction plays the chief role, in telescopes, reflection. Ergo the name refractor given the first and the name reflector assigned the second. The whole challenge of manufacturing these optical devices lies in crafting the objectives, whether they're lenses or metal mirrors.

However, at the time the Gun Club was attempting its great experiment, these instruments had been improved to a notable extent and were providing magnificent results. Gone were the days when Galileo watched the stars through some paltry spyglass that magnified seven times at best. Since the 16th century optical devices had gotten considerably bigger and longer, letting astronomers assess the depths of the starry void to a degree previously unheard of. Among the refracting instruments in operation at the time, people singled out the giant spyglass at the Pulkovo Observatory in Russia, whose objective lens measures fifteen inches across,[68] the giant spyglass built by the French optician Jean-Noël Lerebours, which features an objective equal to the foregoing, and finally the giant spyglass at the Cambridge Observatory, which is equipped with an objective nineteen inches across.

Among the telescopes, two were known for their remarkable power and gigantic dimensions. The first, built by Herschel, was 36 feet long and had a mirror 4½ feet wide; it was able to magnify 6,000 times. The second

---

[67] The point where light rays recombine after being refracted.

[68] It cost 80,000 rubles (about $59,000).

belonged to the Earl of Rosse and had been set up in Ireland at Birr Castle in Parsonstown Park. Its tube was 48 feet long and its mirror 6 feet wide;[69] it magnified 6,400 times, and they had to put up an immense brick building to house the devices needed to operate the instrument, which weighed 28,000 pounds.

But despite these colossal dimensions, you'll note that it couldn't magnify more than 6,000 times in round numbers; now then, a magnification of 6,000 times only brings the moon within a viewing distance of thirty-nine miles (sixteen geographic leagues), which won't let you see objects under sixty feet wide unless those objects are of substantial length.

Now then, the case at hand involved a projectile nine feet wide and fifteen long; so the moon needed to be brought within a viewing distance of at least five miles (two geographic leagues), which called for magnifying it 48,000 times.

This was the problem presented to the Cambridge Observatory. There weren't any financial difficulties stopping them; all that remained were physical difficulties.

And first off they had to choose between a telescope and a spyglass. A spyglass has certain advantages over a telescope. With the same size objective it can magnify to a more considerable degree, because fewer light rays are absorbed and lost by passing through its lenses than by reflecting off the metal mirror in a telescope. But there are limitations to how thick a lens can be, because if it's too thick, it no longer lets light rays pass through. What's more, producing such huge lenses is extremely difficult and takes a con-

---

[69] We often hear of giant spyglasses that are a good deal longer still; among others, one with a 300-foot focal length was set up under Domenico Cassini's supervision at the Paris Observatory; but it should be understood that such giant spyglasses didn't have tubes. The objective lens hung in the air from poles, and the skywatcher held the eyepiece in his hand, positioning himself at the objective's focal point as accurately as he could. You can appreciate how awkward these instruments were to use, and how difficult it was to align the two lenses with this kind of arrangement.

siderable period of time, a period reckoned in years.

Though images are better lit in a spyglass, this isn't a notable advantage when it comes to moonwatching, since our satellite offers merely reflected light—so the observatory opted to use a telescope, which can be manufactured more quickly and can provide greater magnifying power. Moreover, since light rays lose a large part of their brightness when they go through the atmosphere, the Gun Club decided to set up their instrument on one of the Union's loftiest mountains, which would reduce the density of the layers of air.

With a telescope, as you've seen, it's the eyepiece—in other words, the magnifying glass in front of the skywatcher's eye—that does the enlarging; and the objective that can magnify to the highest degree is the one with the greatest diameter and focal length. To magnify 48,000 times, you need an objective significantly bigger than those used by Herschel and the Earl of Rosse. There lay the difficulty, because casting these mirrors is a very delicate operation.

Luckily, a few years earlier Léon Foucault, a scientist at the French Institute, had invented a procedure that made it very quick and easy to polish an objective: he replaced the metal mirror with silver-plated mirrors. All he had to do was pour a piece of glass to the desired size, then give it a metallic finish with silver nitrate. It was this procedure—whose results are excellent—that the observatory followed in crafting the objective.

What's more, they designed it following the system Herschel developed for his own telescopes. In the huge device that this astronomer set up in Slough, England, objects were reflected off the tilted mirror at the bottom of its tube, then their images took form at the other end where its eyepiece was located. Consequently, instead of standing at the tube's lower end, the skywatcher hoisted himself to its upper end, and from there he looked through its magnifying glass down into the enormous cylinder. This arrangement had the advantage of doing away with the smaller mirror that was intended to send images to the eyepiece. Objects underwent only one reflection instead of two. So fewer light rays died out. So the image was less faded. So you ended up with a clearer view, an invaluable advantage in the moonwatching to be done.[70]

Once these decisions were made, the work got under way. According to the calculations of staff members at the Cambridge Observatory, the new reflector's tube needed to be 280 feet long and its mirror 16 feet across. As colossal as such an instrument was, it couldn't compare to that 10,000-foot telescope the astronomer Robert Hooke proposed building a few years back. Nevertheless, setting up this type of device presented major difficulties.

As for its location, that matter was promptly settled. It involved picking a lofty mountaintop, and lofty mountains aren't plentiful in the states.

In essence the mountain systems of this great country boil down to two chains with moderate elevations, and between them flows the magnificent Mississippi, which Americans might have dubbed "the king of rivers" if they'd had the slightest use for royalty.

To the east are the Appalachians, whose loftiest peak—which is in New Hampshire—doesn't exceed a thoroughly modest 5,600 feet.

To the west, on the other hand, you meet up with the Rocky Mountains, an immense chain that starts at the Strait of Magellan, follows the westerly coast of South America under the guise of the Andes or the Cordillera ranges, clears the Isthmus of Panama, and runs all the way up North America to the shores of the polar sea.

These mountains aren't very high, and the Alps or the Himalayas would look down on them with the greatest scorn from their towering pinnacles. In fact the loftiest peak in this range rises only 10,701 feet, while Mt. Blanc measures 14,439 feet, and Kanchenjunga is 26,776 feet above sea level.[71]

But since the Gun Club insisted that the

telescope, as well as the columbiad, should be set up inside the states of the Union, they had to rest content with the Rocky Mountains, and all the necessary materials headed off to the summit of Long's Peak in the Missouri Territory.

Neither the written word nor the spoken can describe the full range of difficulties the American engineers would overcome, the prodigious feats of daring and skill they would accomplish. It truly was a towering achievement. They had to lift enormous stones, heavy metalwork, angle irons of considerable weight, huge sections of cylinder, and an objective mirror that in itself weighed close to 30,000 pounds; then they had to carry these items above the snow line to an elevation of over 10,000 feet—after they'd crossed empty prairies, impregnable forests, terrifying rapids, and after they'd traveled far from all population centers out into wilderness areas where every detail of survival becomes an almost insoluble problem. And yet, despite these countless obstacles, the American spirit was triumphant. In the closing days of the month of September, less than a year after work started, the gigantic reflector reared its 280-foot tube into the air. It hung from an enormous iron framework; thanks to a cleverly designed mechanism, it could easily target any point in the heavens, plus it could track heavenly bodies from one horizon to the other as they moved through space.

It had cost over $400,000. The first time they aimed it at the moon, the skywatchers experienced simultaneous feelings of curiosity and anxiety. What would they find in the field of this telescope, which magnified any object viewed 48,000 times? People, herds of lunar animals, towns, lakes, oceans? No, nothing science didn't already know about, and on every part of the moon's disk her volcanic nature could be determined with absolute accuracy.

But before it was of service to the Gun Club, this telescope in the Rocky Mountains performed a great service for astronomy. Thanks to its far-reaching power, it plumbed the outer limits of deep space, let viewers meticulously measure the visible diameters of

---

[70] These telescopes are called "front-view" reflectors.

[71] It's the highest peak in the Himalayas.

many heavenly bodies, and Mr. Clark on the Cambridge staff saw individual stars inside the Crab Nebula in Taurus,[72] which the Earl of Rosse's reflector had never been able to differentiate.

25

FINISHING TOUCHES

IT WAS NOVEMBER 22. The departure of departures was due to take place in another ten days. Just one more operation had to be seen through to completion, an operation that was delicate and dangerous, which called for infinite precautions, and against whose success Captain Nicholl had placed his third bet. In essence it was the challenge of loading the columbiad, of inserting 400,000 pounds of guncotton into it. Nicholl had thought, and not without good reason, that handling such a fearsome amount of pyroxile would maybe lead to serious catastrophes, that in any event this exceptionally explosive mass would self-ignite under the projectile's weight.

The serious dangers ahead were further increased by the carelessness and lightheartedness of the Americans, who, during the Civil War, didn't balk at loading bombshells with cigars between their lips. But Barbicane had his heart set on success and wasn't about to sink in sight of shore; so he selected his best men, put them to work right under his eyes, didn't look away for a second, and by taking pains and precautions got all the odds on his side.

And first of all he carefully held off bringing his whole load into the Stony Hill stockade. He had it arrive little by little in fully enclosed wagons. Those 400,000 pounds of pyroxile had been split up into 500-pound allotments, a total of 800 large canisters all meticulously produced by the foremost explosives manufacturers in Pensacola. There were ten to a wagon, which arrived one by one on the railroad from Tampa; in this way there were never more than 5,000 pounds of pyroxile coming into the enclosure at any given time. As soon as each wagon arrived, barefoot workers unloaded it and transferred each canister over to the columbiad's muzzle, into which it was lowered with the help of hand-run cranes. Every steam-powered mechanism had been moved far away and the tiniest fires snuffed out for two miles around. The crews already had their hands full protecting this mass of guncotton from the hot sunlight, even in November. Accordingly they chose to toil by night in the lamplight of their Ruhmkorff devices, which produce a bright glow in a vacuum and created an artificial daytime even at the bottom of the columbiad. There the canisters had been positioned at regular intervals, then connected to each other by wires that would simultaneously carry an electric spark to the heart of each of them.

In essence a battery was to take care of igniting this mass of guncotton. Covered with insulating material, all these wires were combined into one, threaded through a narrow flue in the heavy cast-iron side, a flue that had been cut level with where the projectile was to sit, then sent up to the surface through an air hole left for this purpose in the stone retaining wall. After the wire reached the top of Stony Hill, it was strung over poles for a distance of two miles, run through a switch, and connected to a powerful Bunsen battery. So if your finger merely pressed the button on the device, you would instantly restore the current and ignite the 400,000 pounds of guncotton. Needless to say, the battery wasn't to be activated till the last moment.

By November 28 the 800 canisters were in place at the bottom of the columbiad. This part of the operation was a success. But what tensions, what worries, what conflicts President Barbicane put up with! He stationed guards at the entrance to Stony Hill, but to no avail; every day curiosity seekers scaled the stockade walls, and a few of them took carelessness to the point of insanity, actually smoking among the bales of guncotton. Barbicane flew into daily rages. J. T. Maston did his best to help out, chasing trespassers away with great energy, then picking up the still-lit cigar butts the Yankees tossed here and there.

---

[72] A nebula that appears in the shape of a crawfish.

A cruel chore, since over 300,000 people were crowding around the stockade. Michel Ardan volunteered to escort the wagons over to the columbiad's muzzle; but he set a dismal example for these heedless onlookers as he ran them off—he himself got caught with an enormous cigar between his lips; the Gun Club's president realized he couldn't rely on this brazen smoker and was reduced to keeping an exceptionally close eye on him

Ultimately, since there must be a God who watches over artillerymen, nothing blew up and the workers saw the loading through to completion. So Captain Nicholl's third bet was in real danger. All that remained was to insert the projectile into the columbiad and place it on its heavy layer of guncotton.

But before proceeding with this operation, items essential to the trip were stowed aboard the projectile coach in orderly fashion. There were quite a few of them, and if it had been left to Michel Ardan, they would have taken up all the space reserved for the travelers. You wouldn't believe the things that easygoing Frenchman wanted to bring to the moon. A positive junkyard of useless stuff! But Barbicane stepped in, and they had to confine themselves to bare necessities.

In the instrument chest they stowed several thermometers, barometers, and spyglasses.

The travelers were interested in scrutinizing the moon during their flight, so to make it easier to scout out this new world, they took along Beer and Mädler's *Mappa Selenographica*,[73] an excellent chart published in four sections from separate printing plates and rightly regarded as an authentic masterpiece of painstaking investigation. With scrupulous accuracy it duplicated the tiniest details on the side of the moon that faces the earth; mountains, valleys, basins, craters, peaks, and rills were on view with their exact dimensions, their correct bearings, and their proper nomenclature, from Mt. Dörfel and Mt. Leibnitz, whose lofty summits rise on the easternmost side of the lunar disk, to *Mare Frigoris*, the Sea of Cold, which stretches

[73] *Translator's note.* Latin: "map of the moon's physical features."

into the circumpolar regions up north.

Consequently this was an invaluable document for our travelers, because they could learn the lay of the land before ever setting foot on it.

They also took three rifles and three bird guns that fired exploding bullets; plus they had plenty of gunpowder and lead shot.

"We don't know what we'll be dealing with," Michel Ardan said. "If there are men or animals up there, they may not appreciate our dropping in on them! We need to take precautions."

In addition to these instruments for the defense of their persons, they took along picks, mattocks, handsaws, and other indispensable tools, not to mention clothing suitable for every temperature, from the cold of the polar regions to the heat of the torrid zone.

Michel Ardan had intended to bring a number of animals on his expedition, though not two of every species, because he saw no need to acclimate snakes, tigers, alligators, and other malignant critters to the moon.

"No," he told Barbicane, "but a few beasts of burden, whether oxen or cattle, horses or donkeys, would do well out in the country and might come in extremely handy."

"Agreed, my dear Ardan," replied the Gun Club's president, "but our projectile coach isn't Noah's ark. It doesn't have the same proportions or purpose. So let's stay within the bounds of possibility."

Finally, after lengthy debates, the travelers settled for a first-class hunting dog belonging to Nicholl and a frisky, powerfully built Newfoundland. Several highly useful packets of seeds took their places among the indispensable items. If it had been left to Michel Ardan, he also would have brought along a few bags of soil in which to plant them. In any event he did take a dozen shrubs, which he carefully packed in a box of straw and put in a corner of the projectile.

The major issue of provisions still remained, since they had to prepare for the possibility of landing in a sector of the moon that was completely barren. Barbicane outdid himself, managing to take along enough food for a year. But lest this surprise anybody, we should add that these provisions consisted of canned meats and vegetables, reduced to their minimum volume with the help of a hydraulic press yet still containing large amounts of essential nutrients; there wasn't much variety, but you couldn't be picky on an expedition like this. Likewise there was a stock of brandy, upwards of fifty gallons' worth, and enough water for just two months; actually, according to the latest investigations by astronomers, a certain amount of water unquestionably existed on the surface of the moon. As for provisions, it would have been silly to think that earthlings couldn't find something to eat up there. Michel Ardan had never harbored any doubts on the matter. If he had, he wouldn't have decided to go.

"Besides," he told his friends one day, "we won't be utterly neglected by our comrades on the earth, they'll take care to not forget us."

"Definitely," J. T. Maston replied.

"What's your point?" Nicholl asked.

"Nothing could be simpler," Ardan answered. "Won't the columbiad still be in place? All right, anytime the moon's position offers promise of reaching the zenith, if not her perigee—in other words, about once a year—couldn't you send us a capsule loaded with provisions, which we would look for on some prearranged day?"

"Hooray, hooray! Excellent plan!" J. T. Maston shouted, like somebody who has just seen the light. "My gallant friends, we definitely won't forget you!"

"I'm counting on it! This way, you see, we'll get regular news from the earth, and speaking for ourselves, we'll be real bunglers if we can't find a way to contact our good friends down here on the ground!"

Michel Ardan's words inspired so much confidence, he looked so determined, and his nerve was so exceptional, the whole Gun Club would have followed anywhere he led. In truth, what he said seemed so simple, basic, easy, and foolproof, only the most earthbound mercenary would have shrunk from going along with the three travelers on their lunar expedition.

Once they'd stowed the various items in the projectile, they piped water in between the partitions to act as a set of springs, then filled a container with compressed gas for lighting. As for the potassium chlorate and potassium hydroxide, Barbicane was worried about unexpected delays on the way and took along enough to replenish the oxygen and consume the carbon dioxide for two months. Designed with exceptional inventiveness and functioning automatically, a mechanical device was responsible for restoring the air's vital attributes and for cleansing it in a thorough manner. So the projectile was all set and only needed to be lowered into the columbiad. Which, even so, was an operation full of dangers and difficulties.

The enormous capsule was taken to the top of Stony Hill. There powerful cranes clutched it and held it in the air above that metal well.

It was a suspenseful moment. If the chains happened to snap from that enormous weight, the fall of such a mass would certainly set off the guncotton.

Luckily nothing went wrong, and in a few hours the projectile coach, gently lowered into the cannon's bore, was resting on its layer of pyroxile, a sort of explosive feather bed. Its weight had no effect other than to tamp down the columbiad's powder charge more firmly.

"I've lost," the captain said, handing over to President Barbicane the sum of $3,000.

Barbicane didn't like taking money from somebody who was now his traveling companion; but he had to give in to Nicholl's stubbornness—the fellow wanted to honor all his commitments before leaving the earth.

"In that case," Michel Ardan said, "I've got just one thing more to ask of you, my gallant captain."

"What?" Nicholl asked.

"Please lose your other two bets. Then we'll be sure to make it all the way!"

26
FIRE!

DECEMBER 1 had arrived, the day of destiny, because if the projectile's departure didn't take place that same evening at 10:46:40, more than eighteen years would go by before the moon would reappear under the same simultaneous conditions of zenith and perigee.

The weather was magnificent; despite the coming of winter, the sun was shining brightly, its radiant rays bathing this earth that three of its residents were ready to leave behind for a new world.

During the night preceding this impatiently desired day, many folks didn't sleep very well. The burden of waiting weighed so heavily on people's spirits! Every heart was pounding anxiously except Michel Ardan's. That unemotional individual paced back and forth with his normal hyperactivity but gave no sign of anything unusual on his mind. He'd slept peacefully, like Marshal Turenne sleeping over his gun carriage on the eve of battle.[74]

Since morning endless crowds had been spreading over the prairies, which stretched around Stony Hill as far as the eye could see. Every fifteen minutes the railroad from Tampa brought new curiosity seekers; this migration soon took on fantastic proportions, and according to reports in the *Tampa Observer*, five million spectators set foot on Florida soil during that unforgettable day.

For a month now the better part of this crowd had been camping around the enclosure, laying the groundwork for a community that has since been named Ardantown. Huts, shanties, shacks, and tents garnished the plains, and these temporary residences housed a populace big enough to inspire envy in Europe's leading cities.

Representatives of every nation on earth had arrived and they were speaking every world dialect at the same time. There was such linguistic confusion, you would have compared it to the Tower of Babel in biblical times. On this occasion the various classes of American society were mixing with each other in total equality. Bankers, farmers, sailors, agents, brokers, cotton planters, traders, ferrymen, and magistrates were rubbing elbows with easygoing naturalness. Louisiana

Creoles fraternized with Indiana homesteaders; bluebloods from Kentucky or Tennessee and snooty, fashionable Virginians traded banter with cattle traders from Cincinnati and half-civilized trappers from the Great Lakes. Topped by white, wide-brimmed beaver hats or standard panamas, wearing blue trousers from the cotton mills of Opelousas, garbed in their smart holland jackets, shod in bright-colored boots, they sported lavish cambric ruffles, and their shirts, cuffs, ties, ten fingers, and even their ears glittered with a full array of rings, pins, diamonds, chains, buckles, and trinkets whose high cost was matched only by their bad taste. Costumed just as luxuriously, women, children, and servants walked beside, behind, and ahead of their husbands, fathers, and employers, who looked like tribal chieftains in the midst of their endless families.

At mealtimes you had to gape as these hosts of humans pounced on dishes characteristic of the southern states, gobbling them up with appetites that threatened the Florida food supply—fare that would have turned European stomachs, such as fricasseed frog, stuffed monkey, "fish chowder," raccoon steak, and possum cooked rare or well done.

But, in addition, what a lineup of different liqueurs and alcoholic beverages came to the aid of these indigestible feasts! What exciting yells, what enticing shouts, rang out in the barrooms and taverns, all adorned with glasses, tankards, flasks, decanters, outlandishly shaped bottles, mortars for crushing sugar, and packs of straws!

"Julep with mint leaves right here!" one vendor called out in ringing tones.

"Here's your red wine sangaree!" countered a second in a barking voice.

"Your gin sling's ready!" repeated this one.

"Cocktail and a brandy smash coming up!" yelled that one

"Who wants to try a genuine, newfangled mint julep?" hollered another of these cunning salespeople, his hands quicker than a magician's, pouring from glass to glass the nutmeg, sugar, lemon, green mint, crushed ice, water, cognac, and fresh pine-

---

[74] *Translator's note.* Turenne was a French war hero famed for being calm under pressure.

apple that made up this cooling drink.

Aimed at throats affected by the fiery action of southern spices, these inducements normally rang out over and over, filling the air with a deafening racket. But on this day of December 1, such appeals were rare. The vendors could have hollered themselves hoarse trying to drum up business, but their efforts would have been in vain. Nobody gave a thought to food or drink, and by four o'clock in the afternoon, many spectators moving through the crowd still hadn't eaten a normal lunch! And an even more significant sign: that intense American passion for gambling had lost out in the excitement. You saw bowling pins lying on their sides, dice for crap games dozing in their cups, roulette wheels sitting stock-still, cribbage boards suffering from neglect, and decks of cards for blackjack, whist, red and black, monte, and faro all serenely ensconced in their unopened wrappers—then you realized the day's developments had upstaged every other concern and left no room even for diversions.

Till evening a dull, noiseless tension ran through the anxious crowd, like the suspense before a major catastrophe. An indescribable uneasiness reigned in people's minds, an agonizing numbness, an elusive feeling that clawed at their hearts. Everybody wanted to "get it over with."

However, near seven o'clock, this dull silence abruptly dispersed. The moon rose above the horizon. Several million cheers greeted her appearance. She was on time for her appointment. The uproar climbed into the heavens; applause broke out on all sides as fair Phoebe gleamed peacefully in the clearest of skies and caressed the intoxicated crowd with her most loving rays.

Just then our three dauntless travelers showed up. At their appearance the shouts swelled in intensity. Instantly, unanimously, the national air of the United States pealed forth from every heaving chest, and "Yankee Doodle," taken up by 5,000,000 performers in unison, rose like a roaring thunderstorm to the farthest reaches of the atmosphere.

Then, after this irresistible burst of energy, the anthem sank into silence, the last harmonies gradually died away, the noises faded out, and a hushed murmur drifted over the deeply affected crowd. Meanwhile the Frenchman and the two Americans had made it inside the secured enclosure around which this immense crowd was clustering. Members of the Gun Club were with them, plus delegations sent by Europe's observatories. Cool and calm, Barbicane serenely gave his final orders. Tight lipped, hands clasped behind his back, Nicholl walked with a firm, measured step. As carefree as ever, Michel Ardan was dressed like the perfect tourist—leather gaiters on his feet, game bag hanging from one shoulder, cigar between his lips, lounging along in his capacious clothes of chestnut-colored velvet; as he went, he doled out hearty handshakes with princely generosity. His verve and good cheer were inexhaustible, he laughed, joked, played juvenile pranks on dear old J. T. Maston, and in short was "typically French" to the last second—worse yet, "hopelessly Parisian."

Ten o'clock sounded. Time for them to get situated in the projectile; it would take a while to lower them properly, to close the hatch plate, to screw it into place, then to clear away the cranes and scaffolding that were leaning over the columbiad's muzzle.

Barbicane and Murchison had synchronized their chronometers to within a tenth of a second; the engineer was responsible for igniting the gunpowder with the help of an electric spark; confined in the projectile, the travelers could accordingly keep an eye on their timepiece's second hand, which would calmly mark the exact instant of their departure.

The moment had come to say good-bye. It was a touching scene; despite his feverish good cheer, even Michel Ardan felt moved. The dry-eyed J. T. Maston found a single ancient tear beneath his eyelids; no doubt he'd saved it for the occasion. He let it fall on the brow of his dear, gallant president.

"What if I came along?" he said. "There's still time!"

"Not possible, Maston old fellow," Barbicane replied.

A few seconds later the three traveling companions had taken up residence in the projectile; they'd screwed the hatch plate into place from inside, and the columbiad's muzzle, now completely clear, was wide open to the heavens.

Nicholl, Barbicane, and Michel Ardan were locked up for good in their metal coach.

Who could possibly depict the crowd's excitement, which by then was reaching a point of frenzy!

The moon moved forward over a firmament of transparent clarity, snuffing out the twinkling lights of the stars as she went; then she traveled past the constellation Gemini and hovered nearly midway between horizon and zenith. So it had to be plain to everybody that they were aiming ahead of the target, as a hunter aims ahead of the jackrabbit he's trying to bag.

A fearful silence hung over the whole scene! Not a breath of wind on the earth! Not a breath of air in any lungs! Hearts were afraid to beat! Everybody stared in apprehension at the columbiad's gaping maw.

Murchison kept his eye on the second hand of his chronometer. Till the moment of departure sounded, there were barely forty seconds to go, and each of them lasted a century.

At the twentieth everybody shivered, and it occurred to this crowd that the daring travelers closed up inside the projectile were also counting off these dreadful seconds. These clipped words burst out:

"Thirty-five — thirty-six — thirty-seven — thirty-eight—thirty-nine—forty—*fire!*"

At once Murchison's finger pressed the switch on the device, restoring the current and shooting an electric spark into the columbiad's depths.

A frightful explosion instantly took place, unprecedented, superhuman, comparable to nothing else, neither the peal of a booming thunderclap nor the roar of an erupting volcano! An immense spray of flame shot out of the bowels of the earth as if out of a crater. The ground heaved, and for an instant a few people could catch just a glimpse of the projectile as it tore triumphantly through the air surrounded by blazing waves of steam.

27
OVERCAST SKY

WHEN THAT GLOWING spray reached a prodigious height in the heavens, a bouquet of flame lit up all Florida, and for one immeasurable moment, night turned into day over a considerable stretch of country. This immense plume of fire could be seen a hundred miles offshore in both the gulf and the Atlantic, and more than one sea captain entered the appearance of this gigantic meteor in his ship's log.

The columbiad's explosion was followed by a genuine earthquake. Florida felt the jolt down to its bowels. Expanding from the heat, the gunpowder's gases thrust aside the atmospheric layers with incomparable force, and this manufactured hurricane, a hundred times faster than any storm-bred hurricane, passed through the air like a tornado.

Not a single bystander was still on his feet; men, women, and children all were laid low like ears of grain under a cloudburst; there was unspeakable pandemonium, a large number of people were seriously injured, and J. T. Maston—who, contrary to all common sense, had been standing far out in front— was flung 120 feet backward, traveling over the heads of his fellow citizens like a cannonball. 300,000 people were left temporarily deaf and in a daze.

After toppling huts, flattening shanties, uprooting trees for twenty miles around, and pushing railroad trains back into Tampa, this air current swooped on that town like an avalanche and wiped out a hundred buildings, including St. Mary's Church and the new home of the stock exchange, which cracked open from end to end. Banging against each other, a few vessels in the harbor sank straight down, and some ten ships anchored offshore ran up onto the beach after snapping their chains as if they were cotton thread.

But this circle of devastation reached farther still, beyond the borders of the United States. Helped by winds out of the west, the impact of the recoil could be felt in the Atlantic over 300 miles off the American coastline.

It was a storm even Robert Fitzroy couldn't have predicted,[75] a man-made storm, an unexpected storm that pounced on ships with record-setting force; caught in these frightful whirlwinds with no time to take in their sails, several vessels foundered under full canvas, among others the *Childe Harold* out of Liverpool, an unfortunate catastrophe that became the subject of some extremely harsh accusations on England's part.

Finally, though only a few natives vouched for the event, we'll mention in the interests of completeness that half an hour after the projectile's departure, residents of Sierra Leone and Gorea Island in Senegal claimed they heard a dull rumbling, the death rattle of sound waves that had crossed the Atlantic Ocean and died away on the African coastline.

But we need to get back to Florida. As soon as the pandemonium had abated, the injured, the deaf, and in short the whole crowd woke up with a frenzied outburst: shouts of "Hooray for Ardan! Hooray for Barbicane! Hooray for Nicholl!" rose into the sky. Their noses in the air, equipped with telescopes, spyglasses, and pocket binoculars, several million human beings were inspecting the heavens, forgetting their hard knocks and high spirits in their concern for the projectile. But they looked in vain. Nobody could see it anymore, and they had no choice but to wait for telegrams from Long's Peak. The Cambridge Observatory's director[76] was at his workstation in the Rocky Mountains; an astronomer of skill and tenacity, he was the man entrusted with keeping an eye on the sky.

But soon the public's impatience was sorely tested by an unexpected phenomenon, which, though it easily could have been predicted, couldn't have been prevented.

The weather, so clear till then, abruptly changed; the sky got darker, filling up with clouds. How could it have been otherwise, after the atmospheric layers had been so drastically rearranged and such an enormous amount of steam had been dispersed by the combustion of 400,000 pounds of pyroxile! The entire natural order had been disrupted. Which isn't surprising, since, during naval battles, you often see atmospheric conditions change sharply due to gunfire.

The next day the sun rose above a horizon piled with dense clouds, which flung a heavy, impregnable curtain between earth and sky, and which, unfortunately, stretched as far as the Rocky Mountain regions. It was sheer bad luck. A chorus of complaining wafted from every corner of the globe. But nature was unmoved: since human beings had disrupted the atmosphere with their explosion, obviously they were obliged to suffer the consequences.

During that first day every one of them tried to see through the dense cloud cover, but every one of them found it a waste of energy, and furthermore every one of them was wrong to focus on the sky overhead, because by that point, due to the earth's daily rotation, the projectile had to be traveling straight above the Antipodes.

Be that as it may, once night had fallen over the earth, a deep and impregnable night, the moon rose again on the horizon—but it was impossible to see her; you would have sworn she was deliberately hiding from the eyes of those daredevils who had opened fire on her. So no skywatching was possible, and the wires from Long's Peak confirmed this aggravating setback.

But the travelers had left on December 1 at 10:46:40 in the evening, and if the experiment had succeeded, they were due to reach their destination at midnight on the 4th. Till that time, therefore, everybody quit griping and waited patiently, since, after all, it would have been hard under the circumstances to spot something as small as the capsule.

On December 4, from eight o'clock in the evening till midnight, it might have been possible to track the projectile, which by then would be showing up like a black dot against the moon's shining disk. But the sky stayed cruelly overcast, increasing public exasperation to a point of frenzy. People actually

---

[75] *Translator's note.* Admiral Fitzroy had recently published his *Weather Book.*

[76] Mr. Belfast.

shouted insults at the moon just because she stayed out of sight. It was a sad state of affairs down on the ground.

Desperate, J. T. Maston left for Long's Peak. He wanted to see for himself. There was no doubt in his mind that his friends had reached the end of their journey. Besides, there hadn't been any word of the projectile's falling back onto some island or landmass on the earth, and J. T. Maston didn't accept for a second the possibility of its dropping into one of those oceans that cover three-quarters of the globe.

On the 5th, same weather. The great telescopes in the Old World—those of Herschel, Rosse, and Foucault—were perpetually aimed at that silver orb, because the weather in Europe was downright magnificent; but the comparative weakness of those instruments kept them from seeing anything helpful.

On the 6th, same weather. Impatience consumed three-quarters of the globe. People started coming up with the silliest schemes for dispersing that cloud cover in the air.

On the 7th the sky seemed to change a bit. People were hopeful, but they didn't hope for long, and that evening dense clouds shielded the starry firmament from all eyes.

Then things got serious. In essence, at 9:11 in the morning on the 11th, the moon was to enter her last quarter. After that point she would be on the wane, and even if the sky cleared up, there would be significantly fewer opportunities for examining her; by that point, in fact, the moon would reveal only an ever-shrinking portion of her disk and would end up turning into a new moon— in other words, she would set and rise with the sun, whose rays would leave her totally invisible. So before they could start watching her, they had to wait till January 3 at 12:44 in the afternoon, when she would be full again.

The newspapers published these thoughts along with a thousand editorial comments, not concealing from the public that it needed to gird itself with an angelic amount of patience.

On the 8th, nothing. On the 9th the sun reappeared for a second, as if thumbing its nose at the American public. It was roundly booed, undoubtedly took offense at this reception, and reacted by keeping its rays to itself.

On the 10th, no change. J. T. Maston was close to going insane, and everybody feared for the dear fellow's mental health, which, till then, had been well protected by his gutta-percha cranium.

But on the 11th one of those frightful storms common to the subtropical regions was unleashed in the sky. Strong east winds swept up the clouds that had been accumulating for so long, and that evening the moon's disk, half gnawed away, moved majestically through the translucent constellations out in space.

28
A NEW HEAVENLY BODY

THAT SAME NIGHT the thrilling news folks couldn't wait to hear exploded like a lightning bolt over the states of the Union—and shooting overseas from there, it raced along every telegraph line on the globe. Thanks to that gigantic reflector on Long's Peak, the projectile had been sighted.

Here's the note drafted by the Cambridge Observatory's director. It contains his scientific assessment of this great experiment by the Gun Club.

Longs Peak
December 12

TO: *Staff members at the Cambridge Observatory.*

The projectile fired by the Stony Hill columbiad was sighted by Messrs. J. M. Belfast and J. T. Maston on December 12 at 8:47 in the evening, the moon having entered her last quarter.

This projectile didn't reach its destination. It passed to the side of it, though near enough to get caught in the moon's gravitational pull.

At that juncture its vertical motion changed into a dizzyingly fast circular mo-

tion, and it's sweeping in an elliptical orbit around the moon and is literally now her satellite.

As yet it hasn't been possible to determine the characteristics of this new heavenly body. We don't know the speed of its orbiting motion or the speed of its spinning motion. The distance separating it from the surface of the moon can be put at about 2,833 miles (some 1,100 geographic leagues).

Now, there are two theoretical possibilities that could bring about a change in the state of things:

* Either the moon's gravity will ultimately win out and the travelers will reach their scheduled destination.

* Or the projectile will stay in its holding pattern and will revolve around the lunar disk till the end of time.

One day our moonwatching will tell us which it is, but so far the only result of the Gun Club's experiment has been its contribution of a new heavenly body to our solar system.

J. M. BELFAST.

This unexpected outcome raised so many questions! The overall circumstances held such a wealth of mysteries for science to investigate someday! Thanks to the courage and dedication of three men, their seemingly impractical undertaking of firing a shell at the moon had just paid off in a huge way, and the consequences were incalculable. Locked up inside their new satellite, the travelers were at least part of the lunar world, even if they hadn't reached their destination; they were revolving around that silver orb, and for the first time human eyes could probe all its mysteries. So the names Nicholl, Barbicane, and Michel Ardan were destined for eternal fame in the annals of astronomy, because these bold explorers had been eager to widen the

circle of human knowledge, had daringly shot off into space, and had staked their lives in the most unusual endeavor in modern times.

Be that as it may, once the note from Long's Peak had been made public, the whole world felt surprised and frightened. Was it possible to go to the assistance of those bold earthlings? Definitely not, because they were beyond human aid and outside the bounds God had imposed on terrestrial beings. They had an air supply good for two months. They had food for a year. But afterward . . . ? Even the hardest hearts pounded faster at this dreadful question.

Only one man refused to see the situation as hopeless. Only one individual kept faith, a friend of theirs who was as dedicated, daring, and determined as they were—the gallant J. T. Maston.

What's more, he didn't let them out of his sight. From that day forward his abode was the workstation on Long's Peak, his horizon the mirror of that immense reflector. As soon as the moon rose above the horizon, he framed her in the field of the telescope and didn't take his eye off her for a second, diligently following her as she traveled through the starry void; with infinite patience he watched the projectile move across her silver disk, and the good fellow truly stayed in constant contact with his three friends, never losing hope he would see them again someday.

"As soon as circumstances allow, we'll be in touch with them!" he told anybody willing to listen. "We'll get the latest news from them, and they'll get the latest from us! Anyhow I know them, they're clever fellows. Between the three of them, they took into space every resource of art, science, and technology. With help like that you can do anything you please—and they'll pull this business off, you'll see!"

Circling the Moon

Part Two of
From the Earth to the Moon

First published in 1869

Here Verne tackles one of the trickiest technical challenges for a storyteller: *Circling the Moon* takes place in a severely restricted setting. His whole travel narrative unfolds inside a projectile ten feet high and with fifty-four square feet of floor area—not much bigger than an elevator with a high ceiling. Looking out the portholes of their space capsule, his characters are almost as confined as if they were aboard an amusement park ride. To spin a lively, varied tale under these claustrophobic conditions will take stupendous skill—what can Verne do? A good deal, as it turns out: he milks every action and suspense possibility from his material . . . mines it for gags and fascinating tidbits . . . makes the most of the moon's scientific mysteries . . . gives full play to his theatrical and comic instincts . . . and keeps us on tenterhooks about the outcome.

His concerns are different from those in the earlier moon novel: no more antiwar satire, no more gallows humor, though he still has plenty of hijinks up his sleeve. His three astronauts—two stiff-necked Yankee engineers and a motor-mouthed French adventurer—return from the first book, and their lopsided interactions are a prime source of comedy. The Americans view things with scientific fussiness, the Frenchman lets his imagination run away with him. So when the former get too technical, the latter steps in with a zany analogy for the general public—explaining, for instance, the relative sizes of the sun and planets with a lineup of pumpkins, apples, peas, and other produce.

Verne hatches plot complications both inside and outside his space capsule. Outside, his projectile is twice threatened by near collisions with meteors, the second one resulting in a gorgeous light show. Inside, meanwhile, his astronauts discover that their takeoff speed was miscalculated, cope with an outer-space burial, suffer a respiratory catastrophe, and grapple with temporary weightlessness. This last they treat blasphemously: floating above the floor, the Frenchman compares the experience to the Virgin Mary's assumption into Heaven; to which one of the Yankees replies: "This assumption isn't likely to hold up."

And all the while Verne peppers his yarn with question marks. Is there air on the moon? How about water? Active volcanoes? Does she have any colors or are they optical illusions? Are there any plants, animals, or sentient creatures? Did she *ever* have any life? Verne hems, haws, cops out, and keeps his options open. Finally he stages an amusing academic inquiry in Chapter 18 and emerges with some cunningly phrased conclusions. The upshot is that we can read this story today and still find it plausible, whereas the luscious floral descriptions, top-heavy moonpeople, and B-movie chase scenes in Wells's *First Men in the Moon* (1901) come off as fantasy.

Underneath it all Verne keeps us wondering how the journey will turn out. Will they reach the moon? Get back to earth safely? Or orbit our satellite forever? Verne seems to set this last possibility aside in his Preliminary Chapter, calling it "a total contradiction of the laws of rational mechanics." Yet he keeps revisiting the issue, suggesting that his projectile will "sweep in an elliptical orbit around the moon," that his astronauts will be left "revolving forever around that silver orb." We remain on pins and needles.

The book stumbles only when its factual tidbits and educational passages aren't dramatized or enlivened but simply doled out: the rundown of moonwatchers tacked onto Chapter 10, for example, or the stats on moon mountains versus earth mountains at the close of Chapter 16. Otherwise this oracular little novel has many marvels and few missteps. That metaphor above of an amusement park attraction is completely appropriate: for the vast majority of us, Verne's tale is the closest we'll ever come to an authentic aerial tour of the moon. And he takes us on quite a ride. *Translator*.

PRELIMINARY CHAPTER

*Which summarizes
the first part of this business
as an introduction to the second*

DURING THE COURSE of the year 186–, a scientific endeavor unprecedented in the annals of science had the whole world unusually excited. Members of the Gun Club, an association of artillerymen formed in Baltimore after the Civil War, had come up with the idea of making contact with the moon—that's right, the moon—by firing a shell at her. After consulting astronomers at the Cambridge Observatory on this subject, Barbicane—the undertaking's promoter and the club's president—took every step necessary for the success of this extraordinary undertaking, which had been deemed feasible by most qualified individuals. After he'd launched a funding drive that raised almost $6,000,000, he started in on his gigantic task.

According to a memo drafted by members of the observatory, the cannon that was to fire the projectile had to be stationed in an area located between latitude 0° and 28° north or south, so as to target the moon at the zenith. The shell's initial velocity had to be 12,000 yards per second. Fired on December 1 at 10:46:40 in the evening, it was to meet up with the moon four days after its departure, exactly at midnight on December 5 and just as the moon had reached her perigee—in other words, her closest point to the earth, a distance of just 216,025 miles away.

Over several sessions the Gun Club's chief members—President Barbicane, Major Elphiston, the club's secretary J. T. Maston, and other experts—discussed the shape and makeup of the shell, the positioning and nature of the cannon, and the quality and quantity of gunpowder to be used. They decided: 1) that the projectile would be an aluminum capsule with a diameter of 108 inches, with walls a foot thick, and with a weight of 19,250 pounds; 2) that the cannon would be a cast-iron, 900-foot columbiad that had been poured right into the ground itself; 3) that the charge would use 400,000 pounds of guncotton, which would generate some 1.5 billion gallons of gaseous matter under the projectile, easily propelling it up to that silver orb.

These issues settled, President Barbicane, aided by Murchison the engineer, picked a Florida location in latitude 27° 7′ north and longitude 5° 7′ west. At this site, thanks to marvelous workmanship, they cast the columbiad with complete success.

That's where things stood, when an incident occurred that made this huge undertaking a hundred times more interesting.

A Frenchman—a Parisian eccentric, a witty and daring showman—asked to be closed up inside the shell in order to reach the moon and conduct a scouting expedition on our planet's satellite. This stalwart adventurer was named Michel Ardan. He arrived in America, got an enthusiastic welcome, held rallies, was carried in triumph, reconciled President Barbicane with his mortal foe Captain Nicholl, and as a token of their reconciliation, urged both men to travel along with him inside the projectile.

They accepted his proposition. The shell underwent a change of shape. It took on a cylindro-conical form. A sort of airborne coach, it boasted powerful springs and collapsible partitions to deaden the recoil at departure. It carried a year's supply of food, water for a few months, gaslight for a few days. An automatic device produced and circulated air for the three travelers to breathe. Simultaneously the Gun Club had a gigantic telescope built on one of the loftiest peaks in the Rocky Mountains, allowing members to follow the projectile's flight through space. Everything was ready.

On November 30, at the appointed hour and in the midst of an extraordinary gathering of spectators, the departure took place, and for the first time three human beings left the earth and shot into interplanetary space with a near certainty of reaching their destination. These daring travelers, Michel Ardan, President Barbicane, and Captain Nicholl, were to accomplish their flight in *97 hours, 13 minutes, and 20 seconds*. Consequently they couldn't arrive on the surface of the lunar disk till midnight on December 5, right when the moon would be full, rather than on the 4th as some misinformed newspapers had announced.

But there was one unexpected circumstance: the explosion produced by the columbiad immediately had a disruptive effect on the earth's atmosphere, filling the skies with an enormous number of clouds. This phenomenon caused wholesale exasperation, because it hid the moon from the eyes of skywatchers for several nights.

Dear old J. T. Maston, the staunchest friend of the three travelers, left for the Rocky Mountains along with the honorable J. M. Belfast, the Cambridge Observatory's director, and he reached the outpost on Long's Peak where the telescope had been set up, an instrument that brought the moon within a viewing distance of five miles. The honorable secretary of the Gun Club personally wanted to keep an eye on the space vehicle of his daring friends.

The heavy cloud cover prevented any skywatching on December 5, 6, 7, 8, 9, and 10. The skywatchers themselves figured they would have to cool their heels till January 3 of the new year, because the moon would enter her last quarter on the 11th and would display only a shrinking portion of her disk, not enough light for tracking the projectile's course.

But to everybody's delight a fierce storm finally cleared the skies on the night of December 11–12, and a half moon stood out clearly against the black background of the heavens.

That same night Belfast and J. T. Maston sent a telegram from the outpost on Long's Peak to staff members at the Cambridge Observatory.

Now then, just what did their telegram announce?

It announced this: that on December 11 at 8:47 in the evening, Messrs. J. M. Belfast and J. T. Maston had sighted the projectile fired by the Stony Hill columbiad; that the shell had gone off course for some unknown reason and hadn't reached its destination but had passed so close to the moon, it had gotten caught in her gravitational pull; that its vertical motion had changed into a circular one; and that it had gone into an elliptical orbit around the moon and was now her satellite.

The telegram added that it wasn't yet possible to establish the characteristics of this new heavenly body—and in fact it was essential to take three sights, each of the heavenly body at a different position, in order to learn these characteristics. Then the wire noted that the distance separating the projectile from the lunar surface "could be put" at about 2,833 miles, hence some 1,100 geographic leagues.

Finally the telegram concluded with this twofold theory: either the moon's gravity would end up winning out and the travelers would reach their destination; or the projectile would stay in an unchanging orbit and would revolve around the moon's disk till the end of time.

Given these different alternatives, what would happen to the travelers? True, their food would last them a good while. But even assuming their reckless undertaking was a success, how would they come back? Would it ever be *possible* to come back? Would the earth hear from them again? Debated in print by the most scholarly pens of the day, these questions held the public spellbound.

It's appropriate to make a comment here that eager skywatchers would do well to ponder. When an expert announces a highly speculative discovery to the public, he can't exercise too much discretion. Nobody *has* to discover a planet, comet, or satellite, and anybody who makes a mistake in this activity is fair game for public ridicule. So it's best to bide your time, and that's what our impatient J. T. Maston should have done before firing off this telegram to the world, a telegram he believed was the last word on the undertaking.

In reality this telegram contained two kinds of errors, as was later confirmed: 1) eyewitness errors regarding the projectile's distance from the surface of the moon, because it couldn't possibly have been sighted on that particular date of December 11—so what J. T. Maston saw, or thought he saw, couldn't have been the shell fired by the columbiad; 2) theoretical errors with regard to the fate in store for the aforesaid projectile, because calling it the moon's satellite was a total contradiction of the laws of rational mechanics.

Just one theory offered by the skywatchers on Long's Peak had the potential to come true: the prediction that the travelers—if still alive—could combine their efforts with the moon's gravitational pull to reach the surface of the lunar disk.

Now then, these shrewd, bold men had survived the dreadful recoil at their departure, and what follows is the story of their journey in the projectile coach down to its strangest, most dramatic details. This account will shatter a good many illusions and surmises; but it will also give a fair idea of the complications in store for such an undertaking, and it will showcase Barbicane's scientific instincts, Nicholl's energetic resourcefulness, and the playful daring of Michel Ardan.

Beyond this, it will also demonstrate that their dear old friend J. T. Maston was wasting his time when, bending over his gigantic telescope, he watched the moon making her way through the starry void.

1

FROM 10:20 TO 10:47 IN THE EVENING

AT THE STROKE OF ten o'clock, Michel Ardan, Barbicane, and Nicholl said good-bye to the many friends they were leaving on the earth. The two dogs—who had the job of getting the canine race acclimated to those lunar landmasses—were already confined inside the projectile. The three travelers went up to the mouth of that enormous cast-iron tube, and a crane lowered them to the shell's conical cap.

There an opening had been contrived for the purpose of giving them access to the aluminum coach. The crane hauled its tackle back outside, and the last pieces of scaffolding were immediately cleared away from the columbiad's muzzle.

After entering the projectile with his companions, Nicholl started to close the opening,

lowering a heavy hatch plate that was firmly fastened from inside simply by tightening its screws. Other securely fitting plates covered the biconvex glass of the portholes. Hermetically sealed in their metal prison, the travelers were plunged in total darkness.

"And now, my dear companions," Michel Ardan said, "let's make ourselves at home. Me, I'm the indoor type and housekeeping is my strong suit. It's time we made the most of our new quarters and got comfortable. But first let's try to get a little clearer view of things. Hell's bells, if we're supposed to be moles, God wouldn't have invented gaslight!"

With that the carefree fellow lit a match by striking it on the sole of his boot; then he went over to the gas jet, which was attached to a container storing enough high-pressure acetylene to light and heat the shell for 144 hours, hence six days and six nights.

The gas lit up. Illuminated in this way, the projectile looked like a cozy room furnished with padded walls, circular couches, and a dome-shaped ceiling.

The articles it contained—weapons, instruments, utensils—were fastened securely and held in place against the curves of the padding, where they would brave the impact of departure with impunity. The club had taken every precaution humanly possible to make this reckless endeavor a success.

Michel Ardan examined everything and stated he was highly pleased with the arrangements.

"It's a prison," he said, "but a traveling prison, and so long as I can stick my nose out the window, I wouldn't mind signing a hundred-year lease. You're smiling, Barbicane? So you're having second thoughts? Are you telling yourself this prison could turn into our coffin? So be it, but I wouldn't trade it for Mohammed's, which floats in midair but stays put!"

While Michel Ardan rattled on in this way, Barbicane and Nicholl were making their final preparations.

By the time our three travelers were closed up in their shell for good, Nicholl's timepiece said it was 10:20 in the evening. This chronometer and the one belonging to Murchison the engineer had been synchronized to within a tenth of a second. Barbicane checked it.

"My friends," he said, "it's 10:20. At 10:47 Murchison will shoot an electric spark down the wire that connects to the columbiad's powder charge. At that exact moment we'll part company with our globe. Therefore we still have twenty-seven minutes left on earth."

"Twenty-six minutes and thirteen seconds," replied the meticulous Nicholl.

"Fine!" Michel Ardan exclaimed in a good-humored tone. "In twenty-six minutes you can do many things! You can discuss the most serious ethical and political issues, and even settle them! Twenty-six minutes put to good use are worth more than twenty-six years with nothing to show for them. A few seconds of Pascal or Newton are more valuable than the lifetimes of a whole pack of your average dimwits—"

"And what do you conclude from this, you eternal chatterbox?" President Barbicane asked.

"I conclude we've got twenty-six minutes left," Ardan answered.

"Only twenty-four," Nicholl said.

"Twenty-four if you say so, my gallant captain," Ardan replied, "twenty-four minutes in which we can delve into—"

"Michel," Barbicane said, "during our trip we'll have all the time we need to delve into the knottiest questions. Right now let's concentrate on our departure."

"Aren't we ready?"

"Certainly. But there are a few precautions we still need to take, to lessen the initial impact as much as possible."

"That cushion of water between the collapsible partitions—hasn't it enough elasticity to protect us?"

"I hope so, Michel," Barbicane replied softly, "but I'm not quite sure."

"Oh, what a trickster!" Michel Ardan exclaimed. "He hopes! He's not sure! And he waits till right when we're locked in to make this dismal confession! Excuse me, but I want out!"

"And how will you manage that?" Barbicane countered.

"There are difficulties, it's true," Michel Ardan said. "We're aboard the train, and the conductor will blow his whistle before twenty-four minutes are up . . ."

"Twenty," Nicholl put in.

For a few seconds the three travelers looked at each other. Then they examined the articles locked in along with them.

"Everything's in place," Barbicane said. "Now it's time to decide on our most effective position for handling the impact at departure. Our postures can't be a casual matter, and as much as possible, we need to keep the blood from suddenly rushing to our heads."

"Right," Nicholl put in.

"In that case," Michel Ardan replied, ready to suit the action to the word, "let's put our heads down and feet in the air, like clowns at the big top!"

"No," Barbicane said, "let's lie on our sides. We'll withstand the impact better that way. Don't forget, even though we're riding inside it rather than standing in front of it, when the shell's fired, it's still going to be a bit of a shock."

"So long as it's only 'a bit,' I have no complaints," Michel Ardan remarked.

"You approve of my idea, Nicholl?" Barbicane asked.

"Completely," the captain replied. "13½ minutes to go."

"That Nicholl isn't human!" Michel exclaimed. "He's a chronometer with a second hand, escape wheel, lever, roller, and eight jewels . . ."

But his companions weren't listening anymore and were making their final arrangements with inconceivable composure. They acted like two meticulous travelers on a train, folks who had taken their seats in a passenger car and were trying to get as comfortably situated as possible. Honestly, you have to wonder what substances these Americans are made of, when the most appalling danger can draw near and not make their hearts pound one beat faster!

Three sturdy, securely assembled pallets had been put in the projectile. Nicholl and

Barbicane positioned them in the middle of the disk that formed the movable floor. There the three travelers were to lie down a few moments before departure time.

Meanwhile Ardan, incapable of sitting still, paced around his cramped prison like a wild animal in a cage, exchanging chit-chat with his friends, talking to the dogs Diana and Satellite, whom he'd given meaningful names some time before, as you can see.

"Hey, Diana! Hey, Satellite!" he called out, taunting them. "So you're going to show your lunar relatives what good manners earth dogs have? That'll be a triumph for the canine race! By God, if we ever do get home again, I want to bring back a cross-bred 'moon mongrel,' and it'll cause a sensation!"

"Assuming there *are* dogs on the moon," Barbicane said.

"There are," Michel Ardan asserted, "along with horses, cows, donkeys, and chickens. I'll put money on the chickens!"

"A hundred dollars says we won't find a single one," Nicholl said.

"Done, my dear captain," Ardan replied, shaking Nicholl's hand. "But while we're on the subject, you've already lost three bets with our president, since he raised the funds needed for the undertaking, since the casting operation succeeded, and lastly since they loaded the columbiad without any accidents; hence you're out $6,000."

"Yes," Nicholl replied. "It's 10:37 and six seconds."

"Very good, captain. Well, in less than fifteen minutes you'll have to hand over an additional $9,000 to our president—$4,000 because the columbiad won't blow up and $5,000 because the shell will rise higher than six miles into the air."

"I've got the money," Nicholl replied, slapping his coat pocket. "I'll be only too happy to pay up."

"Nice going, Nicholl, I can see you're an orderly man, something I could never be; but let me point out that all in all, you've made a series of bets here that won't be very profitable for you."

"How so?" Nicholl asked.

"Because if you win the first one, that means the columbiad will have blown up and the shell along with it, so Barbicane will no longer be around to dole out your money."

"My stake is deposited at the Bank of Baltimore, and if Nicholl can't collect, it will go to his heirs," Barbicane merely replied.

"Oh, what sensible men! What practical minds!" Michel Ardan exclaimed. "I marvel at you all the more because you're so beyond my understanding!"

"Ten forty-two," Nicholl said.

"Five minutes to go," Barbicane responded.

"Yes, five tiny minutes!" Michel Ardan remarked. "And we're closed up inside a shell at the bottom of a 900-foot cannon! And piled under this shell are 400,000 pounds of guncotton, which is equivalent to 1,600,000 pounds of regular gunpowder! And our friend Murchison, holding his chronometer, eye focused on its second hand, finger resting on the electrical device, is counting off the seconds and preparing to launch us into interplanetary space . . . !"

"Enough, Michel, enough!" Barbicane said in a stern voice. "Let's get ready. Only a few seconds separate us from this crowning moment. Let's shake hands, my friends."

"Yes!" Michel Ardan exclaimed, more affected than he wanted to let on.

The three bold companions came together and clasped hands one last time.

"May God be with us!" said the reverent Barbicane.

Michel Ardan and Nicholl stretched out on the pallets positioned in the middle of the disk.

"Ten forty-seven," the captain muttered.

"Twenty seconds to go!" Barbicane quickly turned off the gas and lay down near his companions.

The heavy silence was broken only by the chronometer's ticking as it marked the seconds.

Suddenly there was a frightful jolt; under the thrust of 1.5 billion gallons of gaseous matter generated by the pyroxile's combustion, the projectile took off into space.

2

THE FIRST HALF HOUR

WHAT HAD HAPPENED? What was the result of that awful lurch? Had the projectile's manufacturers brought about a favorable outcome with their clever safeguards? Had the impact been deadened by the springs, the four buffers, the cushion of water, the collapsible partitions? Had they tamed the fearful thrust of that initial velocity of 12,000 yards per second, which was fast enough to cross Paris or New York City in the blink of an eye? Clearly these were the questions worrying the thousand witnesses of this gripping drama. They forgot about the trip's purpose and thought only of the travelers! And if one man among them—J. T. Maston, for instance—could have taken a look inside the projectile, what would he have seen?

Nothing just then. It was completely dark inside the shell. But its cylindro-conical walls had held up splendidly. Not a gash, dent, or bulge. The wonderful projectile wasn't even affected by the gunpowder's violent combustion, nor, as some seemed to fear, had it changed into liquid and rained aluminum.

All in all there was little disorder inside. A few items had been roughly hurled to the ceiling; but the most important didn't seem to have suffered from that jolt. Their fastenings were intact.

The movable disk had sunk to the bottom of the shell after the partitions had collapsed and the water escaped; on it lay three motionless bodies. Were Barbicane, Nicholl, and Michel Ardan still breathing? Was the projectile nothing more than a metal coffin carrying three corpses into space?

A few minutes after the shell's departure, one of these bodies stirred; it moved its arms, raised its head, and managed to get on its knees. It was Michel Ardan. He checked himself for broken bones, uttered a resonant "ahem," then said:

"Michel Ardan is present and accounted for. Let's see about the others!"

The courageous Frenchman tried to get up but couldn't keep his balance. His head was spinning, the blood was rushing violently to his brain, he couldn't see, he was like a man who'd had one too many.

"Whew!" he said. "I feel like I've polished off two bottles of Corton. Only it maybe didn't go down as smoothly!"

He mopped his brow several times, massaged his temples, then called out in a forceful voice:

"Nicholl! Barbicane!"

He waited anxiously. No answer. Not even a groan to show that his companion's hearts were still beating. He repeated his appeal. The same silence.

"Holy smoke!" he said. "They act like they've fallen on their heads from a fifth-floor window. Phooey," he added with that unflappable confidence nothing could shake. "If a Frenchman can get on his knees, two Americans won't have any trouble getting on their feet! But first of all let's shed some light on the situation."

Ardan felt life coursing through his veins again. His blood settled down and resumed its normal circulation. With additional exertions he got his balance back. He managed to stand, took a match out of his pocket, struck its phosphorous tip, and watched it flare up. Then he went over and lit the gas jet. The container hadn't suffered in the slightest. No gas had escaped. If it had, the smell would have given it away, the place would be full of hydrogen, and Michel Ardan wouldn't be waltzing around match in hand with impunity. Mixed together, the air and gas would have formed an explosive combination, and maybe the blast would have finished what the jolt hadn't.

After lighting the gas, Ardan stooped over his companions' bodies. They'd toppled on top of each other, inanimate objects, Nicholl above, Barbicane below.

Ardan sat the captain up, leaned him against a couch, and gave him an energetic massage. Shrewdly executed, this back rub revived Nicholl, who opened his eyes, instantly came to his senses, and clutched Ardan's hand. Then, looking around:

"What about Barbicane?" he asked.

"One at a time," Michel Ardan replied serenely. "I started with you, Nicholl, because you were on top. Now let's move on to Barbicane."

With that Ardan and Nicholl picked up the Gun Club's president and dropped him off on the couch. He seemed to have suffered more than his companions. There had been some bleeding, but Nicholl was relieved to confirm that it was only from a mildly hemorrhaging cut on Barbicane's shoulder. A mere scratch, which the captain dressed carefully.

Nevertheless Barbicane didn't come to for a good while—which alarmed his two friends, who didn't skimp on the massaging.

"He's breathing, though," Nicholl said, putting his ear close to the ailing man's chest.

"Yes," Ardan replied, "he's breathing like a man who's fairly used to that everyday operation. Let's rub him harder, Nicholl, harder."

And the two makeshift healers worked so long and so well, Barbicane recovered the full use of his faculties. He opened his eyes, sat up, clutched the hands of his two friends, and delivered this opening remark:

"Nicholl," he asked, "are we in motion?"

Nicholl and Ardan traded looks. As yet they hadn't given a thought to the projectile. Their primary concern hadn't been the vehicle but its passengers.

"Are we actually in motion?" Michel Ardan repeated.

"Or still sitting quietly on the ground in Florida?" Nicholl asked.

"Or on the floor of the Gulf of Mexico?" Michel Ardan added.

"By thunder!" exclaimed President Barbicane.

And this twofold theory suggested by his companions had the immediate result of snapping him back to reality.

Be that as it may, they still couldn't say what the shell's circumstances were. Its seeming stillness and the lack of any outside contact didn't allow them to settle this issue. Maybe the projectile was tooling along its flight path through space; maybe, after a brief ascent, it had fallen back to the earth—or even into the Gulf of Mexico, a real possibil-

ity given the narrowness of Florida's peninsula.

The situation was serious, the problem intriguing. It needed to be settled before much longer. Stirred into action, overcoming his bodily weakness with strength of mind, Barbicane got up. He cocked an ear. It was totally silent outside. But the padding on the walls was heavy enough to block any sounds from the earth. But one circumstance struck Barbicane. The temperature inside the projectile was unusually hot. The Gun Club's president took a thermometer out of its case and checked it. The instrument read 113° Fahrenheit.

"Yes!" he exclaimed. "Yes, we *are* in motion! This suffocating heat is seeping through the projectile's walls. It comes from our friction against the layers of air. It will soon cool down, because we're already cruising in space; then, after nearly suffocating, we'll be subjected to intense cold."

"What!" Michel Ardan asked. "Barbicane, are you saying we're already outside the bounds of the earth's atmosphere?"

"No doubt about it, Michel. Hear me out. It's 10:55. We left about eight minutes ago. Now then, if the friction hadn't reduced our initial velocity, we would have taken only six seconds to pass through the forty miles of atmosphere around our globe."

"Exactly," Nicholl replied, "but how much *has* the friction reduced our velocity, do you figure?"

"By a third, Nicholl," Barbicane replied. "It's a considerable reduction, but according to my calculations, that's the truth of the matter. So if our initial velocity was 12,000 yards per second, by the time we'd left the earth's atmosphere, we would have slowed down to 8,018 yards per second; be that as it may, we've already crossed this expanse, and—"

"—and in that case," Michel Ardan said, "our friend Nicholl has lost his other two bets: $4,000 since the columbiad didn't blow up, $5,000 since the projectile has risen higher than six miles into the air. Come on, Nicholl, fork over."

"Let's verify it first," the captain replied, "then I'll produce the money. It's quite possible Barbicane's analysis is correct and I've

lost my $9,000. But another theory occurs to me, and it could invalidate the wager."

"What?" Barbicane asked instantly.

"The theory that for some reason or other, the gunpowder never got ignited, and we haven't left."

"By God, captain," Michel Ardan exclaimed, "that theory isn't even worthy of *my* brain! You can't be serious! Didn't that jolt knock us half silly? Didn't I revive you? Isn't our president's shoulder still bleeding from something it banged into?"

"Agreed, Michel," Nicholl echoed, "but I've got one question."

"Ask it, my good captain."

"There had to have been a fearsome explosion—did you hear it?"

"No," Ardan replied, quite surprised. "As a matter of fact, I didn't hear any explosion."

"How about you, Barbicane?"

"I didn't either."

"Well then?" Nicholl put in.

"It's true," muttered the Gun Club's president. "Why didn't we hear an explosion?"

The three friends looked at each other with rather flustered expressions. They were faced with a bewildering phenomenon. Yet the projectile had left, consequently there should have been an explosion.

"First let's lower the panels," Barbicane said, "and find out where we are."

This extremely simple operation instantly got under way. Using a monkey wrench, they loosened the nuts securing the bolts of the plate outside the right-hand porthole. They pushed the bolts out, and india-rubber plugs stopped up the holes that admitted those bolts. Instantly the outside plate fell back on its hinges like a hatch lid, revealing biconvex glass inset in the porthole. There was an identical porthole in the heavy wall on the opposite side of the projectile, another in its dome above, and finally a fourth in the middle of its base. So they could look out in four different directions—at the firmament through the side windows, and closer to hand, at the moon or the earth through the shell's openings overhead or underneath.

Barbicane and his two companions instantly rushed to the uncovered window. Not a single ray of light livened things up. Utter darkness surrounded the projectile. Which didn't keep President Barbicane from exclaiming:

"No, my friends, we haven't fallen back to the earth! And no, we aren't submerged under the Gulf of Mexico! And yes, we're ascending into space! Look at those stars twinkling in the night, and that impregnable darkness coming between us and the earth!"

"Hooray, hooray!" Nicholl and Michel Ardan shouted in unison.

In essence this intense blackness proved the projectile had left the earth, because if the travelers were still sitting on its surface, then the ground would have been visible in the bright moonlight. This darkness also showed that the projectile had gone through the atmospheric layers, because the diffuse light scattered in the air would have reflected off the metal walls, an effect also lacking. This light would have shone on the porthole window, but the window was dark. There was no more room for doubt. The travelers had left the earth.

"I've lost," Nicholl said.

"And I offer my congratulations!" Ardan replied.

"Here's your $9,000," the captain said, pulling a roll of dollar bills out of his pocket.

"Would you like a receipt?" Barbicane asked, taking it all.

"If you don't mind," Nicholl answered. "It's just good business."

As seriously and stoically as if he'd been at his desk, President Barbicane took out his notebook, tore off a blank page, wrote an official receipt in pencil, dated, signed, and initialed it, then handed it over to the captain, who placed it carefully in his wallet.

Michel Ardan tipped his hat and bowed to his two companions without saying a word. These financial formalities under such unusual circumstances left him literally speechless. He'd never seen anything so *American*.

This transaction completed, Barbicane and Nicholl took their places again by the window and looked at the constellations. The stars stood out like brilliant sparks against the black background of the sky. But from that side they couldn't see the earth's satellite, which was moving from east to west while gradually rising to the zenith. Accordingly her absence caused Ardan to remark:

"What about the moon?" he said. "By any chance will she miss our appointment?"

"Rest assured," Barbicane replied, "our future world is in position, we just can't see her from this side. Let's open the opposite porthole."

Just as Barbicane was about to leave the window and start uncovering the porthole on the other side, a glowing object came into view and caught his attention. It was an enormous disk whose dimensions were too colossal to calculate. It was facing the earth and shining brightly. You would have sworn it was some smaller moon reflecting light from the bigger one. It was coming on with prodigious speed and seemed to be orbiting the earth along a route that would intercept the projectile's flight path. As it followed its orbit, this moving object was spinning on its axis. So it was behaving like any heavenly body running loose in space.

"Hey!" Michel Ardan called out. "What's that? Another projectile?"

Barbicane didn't reply. The appearance of this enormous object surprised and alarmed him. A collision was possible and it would have had deplorable results: either the projectile would be driven off course, or the impact would break its momentum and knock it back down to the earth, or it would end up being irresistibly dragged along in the asteroid's gravitational field.

President Barbicane was quick to grasp the consequences of these three theoretical possibilities, which, one way or another, meant that his endeavor was doomed to failure. His speechless companions looked out into space. The object grew prodigiously as it came nearer, and by some sort of optical illusion, the projectile seemed to be rushing to meet it.

"Ye gods and little fishes!" Michel Ardan exclaimed. "It's going to be a real train wreck!"

Instinctively the travelers shrank back. They were in tremendous fear, but not for much longer than a few seconds. Several hundred yards away from the projectile, the asteroid shot by and vanished—which was due less to its speed and more to the fact that it faced the moon and was suddenly lost in the absolute darkness of space.

"Good riddance!" Michel Ardan called, heaving a sigh of relief. "Imagine that! Infinity isn't big enough for this poor little shell to take a carefree stroll in! Drat, what was that overbearing sphere that almost ran us down?"

"I know what it is," Barbicane replied.

"Of course. You know everything."

"It's simply a meteor," Barbicane said, "but an enormous one that the earth's gravity keeps up here in the capacity of a satellite."

"It can't be!" Michel Ardan exclaimed. "So the earth has two moons like Neptune?"

"That's right, my friend, two moons, though it's generally believed to have only one. But this second moon is so small and fast moving, people on earth can't see it. By accounting for certain disturbances, a French astronomer named Frédéric Petit was able to detect the presence of this second satellite and to determine its characteristics. His findings indicate that this meteor will orbit the earth in just three hours and twenty minutes, which implies a prodigious rate of speed."

"Do all astronomers," Nicholl asked, "accept the existence of this satellite?"

"No," Barbicane replied, "but if they'd met up with it as we just did, they wouldn't have any further doubts. In fact, though this meteor could have caused major problems if it had hit the projectile, I think it will allow us to pinpoint our position in space."

"How?" Ardan said.

"Because its distance is a matter of record, so when we met up with it, we were exactly 5,058 miles from the surface of our planet."

"Over 2,000 geographic leagues!" Michel Ardan exclaimed. "Which would be a tall order for express trains back on that pitiful globe we call the earth."

"I imagine so," Nicholl replied, checking his chronometer. "It's eleven o'clock, just thirteen minutes since we left the continent of North America."

"Only thirteen minutes?" Barbicane said.

"Yes," Nicholl replied, "and if we've kept

up our initial velocity of 12,000 yards, we'll have been doing nearly 25,000 miles per hour."

"That's all well and good, my friends," said the Gun Club's president, "but we're still left with that unanswered question. Why didn't we hear the columbiad's explosion?"

No reply was forthcoming, so the conversation ground to a halt; his thoughts elsewhere, Barbicane set about lowering the lid from that second porthole on the opposite side. He was successful in this activity and radiant moonlight poured into the projectile through the uncovered glass. Nicholl, a thrifty fellow, turned off the gaslight, now unnecessary and furthermore too bright to allow any scrutiny of interplanetary space.

At that point the lunar disk was shining with incomparable clarity. No longer diluted by the earth's hazy atmosphere, moonlight filtered through the glass, and the air inside the projectile was steeped in silvery glimmers. The black curtain of the firmament actually heightened the moon's brightness—though, since there isn't any diffuse light in this ethereal void, she didn't outshine the stars nearby. Viewed under these conditions, the heavens had a whole new look no human eye could have anticipated.

The reader can imagine how intently these daredevils contemplated that silver orb, their journey's ultimate destination. Moving along her orbit, the earth's satellite was inching closer to the zenith, the mathematical point she was to reach some ninety-six hours later. Her mountains, her plains, and all her surface features didn't stand out any more clearly than if the men had been eyeing them from somewhere on the earth; but her light radiated through space with incomparable intensity. Her disk was shining like a platinum mirror. Already our travelers had forgotten about the earth, which was now receding beneath their feet.

It was Captain Nicholl who first reminded them about their vanishing planet.

"Yes," Michel Ardan replied, "let's show it a little gratitude! Since we're leaving our homeland, we owe it one last look. I want to see the earth again before it's completely out of sight."

To fulfill his companions' wishes, Barbicane set about uncovering the window in the projectile's base, which would give them a direct view of the earth. Not without some difficulty, he dismantled the movable disk, which the powerful thrust at takeoff had driven to the bottom of the shell. Set carefully against the walls, its separate parts could still come in handy on occasion. A circular opening then appeared, about twenty inches across and cut into the shell's underside. It was covered by six-inch glass reinforced with brass fastenings. Attached underneath was an aluminum plate secured by bolts. Once the nuts were unscrewed and the bolts removed, the plate fell open, and visual contact was restored between inside and outside.

Michel Ardan knelt on the glass. It was so dark, it seemed opaque.

"Well," he exclaimed, "what happened to the earth?"

"The earth," Barbicane said, "is over there."

"What!" Ardan put in. "That skinny sliver, that silvery crescent?"

"Undoubtedly, Michel. In four days, right when we reach her, the moon will be full and the earth will be new. Our planet will be visible only in the form of a slender crescent, which will soon vanish and be submerged for a few days in impregnable blackness,"

"That's the earth?" Michel Ardan repeated, his eyes popping at that skinny remnant of his home planet.

President Barbicane's explanation was correct. In relation to the projectile, the earth had entered its last phase. It was in its octant and looked like a lightly sketched crescent against the black background of the sky. Tinted a bluish color by the heavy layer of atmosphere, the light it gave off wasn't as bright as that from a crescent moon. This particular crescent boasted considerable dimensions. It reminded you of an enormous longbow stretching across the firmament. A few parts—especially in its concave portion—were brightly lit and proclaimed the presence of lofty mountains; but they sometimes vanished behind dense patches unlike anything seen on the surface of the moon's disk. These came from belts of clouds forming concentric rings around the earth.

However, due to a natural phenomenon—identical to what occurs on the moon during her octants—you could make out our planet's full contours. The shape of its entire disk was fairly easy to see, thanks to an effect comparable to earthshine on the moon but less pronounced. And the reason for this lesser intensity is simple to understand. When earthshine occurs on the moon, it's caused by the sun's rays reflecting off the earth onto its satellite. Here the opposite applies: the sun's rays reflect off the moon onto the earth. Now then, light coming from the earth is about thirteen times stronger than that from the moon, due to the different sizes of these two entities. Ergo the result that in this phenomenon of reflected light, the dark part of the earth's disk is less clearly outlined than that of the moon's disk, since the phenomenon's intensity is directly proportional to the illuminating power of these two heavenly bodies. We should add that the earth's crescent seemed to form a longer curve than that of its disk. Simple irradiation at work.[1]

While the travelers were trying to peer through the intense darkness of space, a dazzling bouquet of shooting stars blossomed in front of their eyes. Ignited by contact with the atmosphere, hundreds of meteors streaked the blackness with their light trails, scrawling fiery stripes across the dark part of the earth's disk. During this time the earth was at its perihelion, and the month of December is so conducive to the appearance of shooting stars, astronomers have counted up to 24,000 per hour. But Michel Ardan, sneering at all scientific logic, preferred to think the earth was saying good-bye to three of its children with a glittering display of fireworks.

In short, this was all they saw of that sphere vanishing into the darkness, that minor member of the solar system, which rises and sets on the horizons of the bigger planets like a humble morning or evening star! A barely visible speck in space, it was nothing more than a fading crescent, this globe where they'd left everything they loved!

For a good while the three friends kept watch, silent but single-minded, while the projectile moved farther away at a speed that was steadily decreasing. Then an irresistible drowsiness came over them. Were they exhausted in body and mind? Surely, after the high excitement of those last hours spent on the earth, a reaction was bound to set in.

"Well," Michel said, "since we're sleepy, let's sleep."

And stretching out on their pallets, all three of them were soon deep in slumber.

But they hadn't been dozing for more than fifteen minutes, when Barbicane suddenly sat up and roused his companions with a fearsome shout:

"I've got it!" he yelled.

"Got what?" Michel Ardan asked, bounding from his pallet.

"The reason why we didn't hear the columbiad's explosion."

"And it's because . . . ?" Nicholl put in.

"It's because our projectile traveled faster than the speed of sound!"

3

IN WHICH THEY TAKE UP RESIDENCE

AFTER THIS UNUSUAL but unquestionably accurate explanation, the three friends fell sound asleep again. Where could they have found a calmer spot, a more peaceful setting in which to bed down? On the earth both urban homes and rustic cottages feel every tremor running through the planet's crust. Out at sea a ship tossing on the waves goes by fits and starts. In the sky a hot air balloon shifts continually between wind currents of different densities. Only this projectile, cruising in a perfect void, surrounded by perfect silence, could offer its guests the ideal retreat.

Accordingly our three venturesome travelers maybe would have slept on indefinitely, if an unexpected sound hadn't woken them up near seven o'clock in the morning on December 2, eight hours after their departure.

---

[1] *Translator's note.* In this case "irradiation" refers to the optical illusion where a bright object seems bigger when viewed against a dark background.

It was the unmistakable sound of barking.

"The dogs! It's the dogs!" Michel Ardan exclaimed, getting up immediately.

"They're hungry," Nicholl said.

"By God," Michel replied, "we forgot about them!"

"Where are they?" Barbicane asked.

They looked around and found one of the animals cowering under the couch. Unnerved and immobilized by that initial jolt, it had stayed in its hideout till the point where it had gotten hungry enough to announce the fact.

It was sweet Diana, still pretty dispirited, who emerged from her cubbyhole after some persuasion. Michel Ardan had to coax her with his most honeyed words.

"Here, Diana!" he said. "Here, girl! You're about to go down in the history of hounds! You're a pooch that pagans would have made a house pet of the god Anubis, Christians a mascot for St. Roch! You deserve to be cast in bronze by the lord of the underworld, like that magic mutt Jupiter gave lovely Europa in exchange for a kiss! You'll be more famous than the sleuthhound of Montargis or the heroic rescuers of the St. Bernard passes! You're shooting into interplanetary space and maybe you'll be the Eve of moondogs! Out here you're going to live up to that saying of Professor Toussenel's: 'In the beginning God created man, then saw how imperfect he was and created dog.' Here, Diana, here!"

Flattered or not, Diana came out little by little, whimpering plaintively.

"Good," Barbicane put in. "I can see Eve all right, but where's Adam?"

"Adam?" Michel responded. "Adam can't be far off! He's around somewhere, let's give him a call! Satellite! Come here, Satellite!"

But Satellite didn't appear. Diana kept on whimpering. They verified, however, that she hadn't been hurt in any way, and a tasty serving of dog chow put a stop to her complaints.

As for Satellite, he seemed to have vanished completely. They had to search a good while before finding him in one of the projectile's upper compartments, where, in some

bewildering manner, the recoil had forcefully hurled him. The poor animal was badly injured and in pitiful condition.

"Holy blazes!" Michel said. "So much for acclimating a race of canines!"

They carefully lowered the unfortunate dog. He'd cracked his skull against the ceiling and didn't seem likely to recover from such a blow. All the same they stretched him out comfortably on a cushion, where he gave a moan.

"We'll take care of you," Michel said. "We're responsible for your existence. I would rather lose a whole arm than one paw of my poor Satellite!"

And with that he offered a few sips of water to the injured animal, who lapped them up eagerly.

After tending to him, the travelers studied the earth and moon intently. The earth was now represented only by a disk of reflected light ending in a crescent that was narrower than on the previous evening; but its size was still enormous compared to that of the moon, which was nearer and nearer to becoming a perfect circle.

"Actually," Michel Ardan said, "it's a shame we didn't take off just as the earth was full, in other words, when our globe was in opposition to the sun."

"Why is that?" Nicholl asked.

"Because we could have viewed our continents and oceans from a new perspective, the former shining in the direct sunlight, the latter looking darker, just as they're shown on some world maps. I wish I could have seen those poles of rotation that mankind still hasn't clapped eyes on!"

"No doubt," Barbicane replied, "but if the earth had been full, the moon would have been new, in other words, invisible in the midst of the sun's rays. Now then, it's better for us to see our scheduled destination rather than our starting point."

"You're right, Barbicane," Captain Nicholl replied. "And besides, once we've reached the moon, we'll have some leisure time during those long lunar nights and we can examine that globe crowded with folks like us."

"Folks like us!" Michel Ardan exclaimed.

"Why, they're no more like us now than moonpeople are! We live in a new world populated only by ourselves—this projectile! I'm like Barbicane and Barbicane's like Nicholl. Over and beyond ourselves, humanity is no more, and we're the only citizens of this miniature cosmos till the time we turn into regular moonpeople."

"In about eighty-eight hours," the captain remarked.

"What do you mean?" Michel Ardan asked.

"That it's 8:30 in the morning," Nicholl answered.

"All right," Michel shot back, "then I can't see even the shadow of a reason for not eating breakfast this second."

In essence the citizenry of this new heavenly body had to eat to live, and their bellies had to abide by the all-powerful laws of hunger. Being the only Frenchman on the premises, Michel Ardan elected himself chief cook, a high office for which he ran uncontested. The gas jet furnished the few degrees of heat needed for his culinary artistry, and the supply chest provided the ingredients for this first-time feast.

Breakfast started with three cups of excellent beef broth, brewed by dissolving in hot water some of those invaluable Liebig cubes that are made with the best cuts from the cattle of the Pampas. After the soup came some slices of steak, shaped into patties by a hydraulic press, as tender and juicy as if they hailed from the kitchen of the Café Anglais. Michel, a man with an imagination, even claimed they were "pink inside."

Canned vegetables ("fresher tasting than nature's," added the tolerant Michel) followed the meat course, and after that came cups of tea with bread and butter in the American style. This drink, which they found superb, was an herbal tea made with the choicest leaves, and the Tsar of Russia had donated a couple cases for the travelers' consumption.

Finally, to top off this meal, Ardan dug up a splendid bottle of Nuits-Saint-Georges, which "just happened" to be in the supply chest. The three friends drank to the partnership of the earth and its satellite.

And as if it hadn't done enough by fermenting this full-bodied wine on the slopes of Burgundy, the sun decided to join the party. Just then the projectile had emerged from the conical shadow cast by our planet, and thanks to the angle that the moon's orbit makes with the earth's, the solar rays struck the base of the shell head-on.

"The sun!" Michel Ardan exclaimed.

"Certainly," Barbicane replied. "I've been expecting it."

"But," Michel said, "what about this conical shadow the earth casts in space—does it reach beyond the moon?"

"A good distance beyond, if you don't count the atmosphere's refraction," Barbicane said. "But when the moon is covered by this shadow, it's because the centers of three heavenly bodies, the sun, earth, and moon, are lying in a straight line. Then the nodes coincide with the phases of the full moon and we get an eclipse. If we'd departed just as there was a lunar eclipse, our whole flight would have taken place in the dark, which would have been a nuisance."

"Why?"

"Because, though we're cruising in space, our projectile is bathing in the sun's rays, getting both light and heat. This saves on gas, an invaluable savings in every respect."

In fact, under these rays whose temperature and intensity no atmosphere can tame, the projectile got warmer and brighter as if winter had suddenly changed into summer. The moon above and the sun below were flooding it with light.

"It's pleasant in here," Nicholl said.

"I think so too!" Michel Ardan exclaimed. "If we spread a little vegetable soil over our aluminum planet, we could grow green peas in twenty-four hours. I've got only one fear, namely that the shell's walls might melt."

"No need to worry, my good friend," Barbicane replied. "Our projectile handled a much higher temperature as it flew through the atmospheric layers. To the eyes of those spectators in Florida, I wouldn't be surprised if it looked like a fiery meteor."

"Then J. T. Maston must have figured we'd roasted to death."

"What does surprise me," Barbicane responded, "is that we didn't. It was a danger we hadn't anticipated."

"I worried about it," Nicholl merely replied.

"And you didn't say a thing, O noblest of captains!" Michel Ardan exclaimed, shaking his companion's hand.

Meanwhile Barbicane proceeded to take up residence inside the projectile as if he were destined to live there in perpetuity. You'll recall that this airborne coach had a base with a surface area of fifty-four square feet. Twelve feet high at the apex of its ceiling, cleverly laid out inside, instruments and traveling gear kept out of the way in their specific places, it gave its three guests reasonable freedom of movement. The heavy window inset in part of the base could bear a considerable amount of weight with impunity. Accordingly Barbicane and his companions walked on its surface as if it were solid flooring—but the sun's rays, striking it head-on, illuminated the projectile's interior from underneath and created some unusual lighting effects.

They started by double-checking the condition of their water tank and supply chest. These containers hadn't suffered at all, thanks to the measures taken to deaden the impact at takeoff. They held ample provisions, enough to feed three travelers for a whole year. Barbicane wasn't taking any chances in case the projectile landed in a sector of the moon that was completely barren. As for the water and their fifty-gallon stock of brandy, they had enough for just two months. But according to the latest research by astronomers, the moon maintained a low, dense, heavy atmosphere—at least in her deep valleys—and there would be no shortage of brooks or springs. For the remainder of their flight, then, and for the first year of their residence in that lunar landscape, these venturesome explorers wouldn't suffer from hunger or thirst.

One issue remained: the air inside the projectile. Again there was no problem. The Reiset and Regnault device for producing oxygen had a two-month supply of potassium chlorate. Inevitably it consumed a fair amount of gas, because it needed to keep the producing compound hotter than 750° Fahrenheit. But here, too, they were on firm footing. Besides, the device required minimal attention. It functioned automatically. At that high temperature the potassium chlorate turned into potassium chloride, releasing all the oxygen it contained. Now then, how much oxygen would eighteen pounds of potassium chlorate provide? The exact seven pounds that made up the daily oxygen requirement of each of the projectile's guests.

But it wasn't enough to replenish the spent oxygen: they also had to consume the carbon dioxide produced by exhaling. Now then, some twelve hours had gone by and the shell's air was full of this absolutely noxious gas, which ultimately results from the combustion of the blood's elements by the inhaled oxygen. Nicholl realized the air was in this state when he saw Diana panting laboriously. In essence, due to the same phenomenon that occurs inside the renowned "Dog's Cave" near Mt. Vesuvius, the carbon dioxide—being heavier than air—had collected close to the floor of the projectile. Poor Diana carried her head much lower than did her masters, so she was bound to suffer sooner from the presence of this gas . . . but Captain Nicholl was quick to remedy this state of affairs. On the projectile's floor he placed several containers of potassium hydroxide, which he shook for a while, and this substance consumed all the carbon dioxide with great eagerness, thus cleansing the air inside.

Next they started in on an inventory of the instruments. Their thermometers and barometers had made it safely, except for a minimum thermometer whose glass had shattered. They took an excellent aneroid barometer out of its padded case and hung it on one of the walls. Naturally it could sense and measure only the air pressure inside the projectile. However it also showed how much moisture the shell contained. Just then its needle was wavering between 29.9 and 30.1 inches. This promised "fair weather."

Barbicane had also packed several compasses that were in one piece. You can appreciate that under the current circumstances their needles were going berserk, in other words, they weren't pointing in one continuous direction. At the shell's distance from the earth, in fact, the magnetic pole couldn't have exercised any noticeable control over the devices. But if they were transferred to the lunar disk, maybe these compasses could record some unusual phenomena. In any event it would be interesting to see if the earth's satellite was subject to magnetic influences just like the planet itself.

A hypsometer for measuring the elevations of lunar mountains, a sextant for taking the sun's altitude, a surveyor's theodolite for mapping terrain and plotting angles at a distance, spyglasses that were bound to come in handy as the projectile neared the moon—the travelers carefully inspected all these instruments and found them in good condition, despite the force of that initial jolt.

As for the utensils, picks, mattocks, and assorted tools that Nicholl had expressly selected, plus the shrubs and various sacks of grain that Michel Ardan banked on transplanting to those lunar lands, they occupied their proper places in the projectile's upper reaches. A sort of loft gaped up there, piled with things the extravagant Frenchman had crammed into it. What they were nobody knew, and the lighthearted fellow wasn't telling. Every so often he climbed the iron steps clamped to the wall, then crept into this hideaway that he alone was allowed to visit, his own private Capernaum. He tidied, he organized, he rummaged through various mysterious boxes, livening things up with an old French song crooned in a voice hopelessly out of tune.

Barbicane was interested to note that his rockets and other explosives hadn't suffered any damage. With their powerful charges these important items were meant to break the projectile's fall, once it had gone past the point of neutral attraction and the moon's gravity started pulling it down to the ground. Besides, the shell was due to fall only a sixth as fast as it would on the earth's surface, thanks to the difference in mass between these two heavenly bodies.

So their inspection ended on an overall note of satisfaction. Then everybody went back and peered into space through the side windows and the glass below.

Same sight as before. The whole dome of the heavens swarmed with stars and constellations of such wonderful clarity, an astronomer would have come unhinged. On one side was the sun, like the open maw of a blazing furnace, a brilliant disk without its earthly halo, standing out from the black background of the sky! On the other side, the moon threw back this radiance by reflecting it, seemingly motionless in the middle of the starry universe. Then, fairly prominent and still edged with a silvery border, a dark patch seemed to puncture the firmament: it was the earth. Here and there floated cloudy masses like huge flakes of interstellar snow, and from zenith to nadir stretched an immense ring made up of infinitesimal powdery stars—that Milky Way galaxy in which the sun ranks as a star of merely the fourth magnitude!

Our skywatchers couldn't take their eyes off this unique sight, which no description can hint at. What thoughts it brought to mind! What strange feelings it aroused in their souls! Barbicane wanted to keep a record of his journey while under the sway of these impressions, and hour after hour he took notes on all the events that distinguished this first stage of his undertaking. He wrote serenely in his large square script and matter-of-fact style.

In the meantime Nicholl the calculating machine was reviewing his flight formulas, manipulating figures with matchless skill. Michel Ardan chatted in turn with Barbicane who didn't answer him, with Nicholl who didn't hear him, with Diana who didn't grasp any of his theories, then finally with himself, asking and answering, coming and going, busy with a thousand details, sometimes bent over the glass below, sometimes perched high in the projectile, singing constantly all the while. In this miniature cosmos he stood for Gallic talkativeness and impulsiveness, and believe me, these attributes were adequately represented.

That day—or more accurately, that lapse of the twelve hours making up daytime on the earth—ended with a bounteous, nicely cooked supper. As yet no incident of any kind had occurred to shake the travelers' confidence. Full of hope, already sure of success, they accordingly fell into a peaceful sleep, as the projectile made its way through the heavens at a speed that was steadily decreasing.

4

A LITTLE ALGEBRA

THE NIGHT WENT BY uneventfully. This word "night," though, is misleading.

The projectile's position in relation to the sun hadn't changed. To an astronomer's eyes it was daytime in the lower half of the shell, nighttime in the upper. So when these two words are used in this narrative, they represent the period of time that elapses between sunrise and sunset on the earth.

The travelers slept all the more peacefully, because, though the projectile was going extremely fast, it seemed perfectly still. No movements revealed that it was proceeding through space. Not even the swiftest speed can be detected by an organism if it takes place in a vacuum, or when the air mass around the traveling object flows along with it. What earthling notices how fast his planet is carrying him, even though its speed is nearly 56,000 miles per hour? Under such conditions neither motion nor stillness can be "sensed." Here, accordingly, all objects are neutral. If an object is standing still, it will remain in that state so long as no outside force moves it. If it's in motion, it won't stop till some obstacle gets in its way. This neutrality with respect to motion or stillness is called inertia.

Therefore, since Barbicane and his companions were closed up inside their projectile, it could easily have seemed to them they were standing perfectly still. Even so, the effect would have been the same if they were on the outside. If the moon hadn't been growing bigger overhead, they would have sworn they were absolutely stationary.

That morning, December 3, a cheerful but unexpected sound woke the travelers up. The crowing of a rooster rang through the coach's interior.

Michel Ardan was on his feet first, clambered to the top of the projectile, and closed a partly open crate:

"Pipe down, will you!" he said in a low voice. "This creature's going to spoil all my arrangements!"

But Nicholl and Barbicane were awake.

"A rooster?" Nicholl was saying.

"Heavens no, my friends!" Michel replied hastily. "I was the one who tried to wake you up with this barnyard vocalizing!"

And with that he let out a choice cock-a-doodle-doo, which would have done credit to a prize specimen of the genus *Gallus*.

The two Americans couldn't help laughing.

"That's quite a talent," Nicholl said, giving his companion a sidelong glance.

"Yes," Michel replied, "it's an old joke in my country. Typical French fun. That's how we play cock of the walk in high society!"

Then, quickly changing the subject:

"Barbicane," he said, "do you know who I thought about all last night?"

"No," replied the Gun Club's president.

"Our Cambridge friends. You've already commented that I'm a champion know-nothing in mathematical matters. So I can't even guess how the experts at the observatory calculated what the projectile's initial velocity had to be for it to reach the moon after leaving the columbiad."

"You mean," Barbicane countered, "for it to reach that neutral point where the moon's gravity equals the earth's, since from that point on—which is about nine-tenths of the way there—the projectile would fall to the moon simply because of its weight."

"So be it," Michel replied. "But once again, how did they manage to calculate the initial velocity?"

"Nothing could be easier," Barbicane answered.

"And could you have worked that calculation?" Michel Ardan asked.

"Absolutely. Nicholl and I would have done so if that memo from the observatory hadn't saved us the trouble."

"Well, Barbicane old boy," Michel replied, "they could slice me from top to bottom before I could solve a problem like that."

"Because you don't know your algebra," Barbicane remarked serenely.

"Oh, there you go again, you gluttons for

x's! You think you've said it all when you've said *algebra*."

"Michel," Barbicane countered, "do you think you could be a blacksmith without a hammer or a farmer without a plow?"

"Hardly."

"Well, algebra is a tool like your plow or hammer, and a good tool for people who know how to use it."

"You're serious?"

"Perfectly serious."

"And you can work with this tool in front of me?"

"If you're interested."

"And show me how they calculated our coach's initial velocity?"

"Yes, my good friend. By taking into account all the elements of the problem—the distance from the center of the earth to the center of the moon, the earth's radius, the earth's mass, the moon's mass—I can establish just what the projectile's initial velocity has to be, thanks to a simple formula."

"Let's see this formula."

"You're about to. Only I won't give you the curve our shell actually makes to account for the earth and moon orbiting the sun. No, I'll regard these two heavenly bodies as stationary, which will be good enough for us."

"And why is that?"

"Because otherwise we would be grappling with that problem called 'the problem of the three bodies,' which integral calculus still hasn't advanced far enough to solve."

"My, my," Michel Ardan put in with a bantering air. "Mathematics hasn't had its final say?"

"Of course not," Barbicane replied.

"Great. Maybe the moonpeople have taken their integral calculus farther than you. And by the way, what *is* this integral calculus?"

"It's a computation that's the reverse of differential calculus," Barbicane answered solemnly.

"Thanks a lot."

"Put another way, it's a computation in which you look for finite quantities whose differential you know."

"That's clearer at least," Michel replied with a smug expression.

"Now it's time to put pencil to paper," Barbicane went on. "And in less than half an hour, I'll have the formula we want."

With that Barbicane got down to work, leaving Nicholl to peer out into space and his companion to take care of breakfast.

Half an hour hadn't gone by before Barbicane looked up and showed Michel Ardan a page covered with algebraic signs, in the midst of which this overall formula stood out:

$$\frac{1}{2}(v^2 - v_0^2) = gr\left\{\frac{r}{x} - 1 + \frac{m'}{m}\left(\frac{r}{d-x} - \frac{r}{d-r}\right)\right\}$$

"And this means . . . ?" Michel asked.

"This means," Nicholl replied, "that half of *v* to the second power minus *v* zero squared equals *gr*, times *r* over *x* minus 1 plus *m* prime over *m*, times *r* over *d* minus *x* minus *r* over *d* minus *r*—"

"—plus *x* over *y* climbing on *z* and sitting astride *p*," Michel Ardan exclaimed, bursting into laughter. "And you can understand all this, captain?"

"Nothing could be clearer."

"Positively!" Michel said. "It's as plain as day and I couldn't ask for more."

"You incurable comedian!" Barbicane countered. "You wanted algebra and now you're in it up to the neck."

"I would rather be hanged by the neck."

"As a matter of fact," replied Nicholl, who was examining the formula with a connoisseur's eye, "this strikes me as nicely worked out, Barbicane. It's the integral of the momentum equation, and I'm sure it will give us the desired result."

"But I want to understand it!" Michel exclaimed. "I'll put in ten years of a life like Nicholl's if it'll help!"

"Then listen," Barbicane went on. "Half of *v* to the second power minus *v* zero squared—this is the formula that gives us fractional variations in momentum."

"Fine, and Nicholl knows what it means?"

"Surely, Michel," the captain replied. "All these signs may seem like cabalistic symbols to you, but they form the clearest, simplest, and most logical language to folks who know how to read it."

"And you're claiming, Nicholl," Michel

asked, "that through these hieroglyphics, which are about as intelligible as the squawks of an Egyptian ibis, you can find what initial velocity the projectile has to be given?"

"Indisputably," Nicholl replied. "And by using this same formula, I can always tell you its speed at any given point in its trip."

"Word of honor?"

"Word of honor."

"So you're as crafty as our president?"

"No, Michel. The hard part is what Barbicane did, which is to set up an equation that accounts for all the conditions of the problem. The rest is nothing more than a little arithmetic and calls only for knowledge of the four processes."

"That sounds promising already!" replied Michel Ardan, who couldn't do simple addition to save his life and who defined the process as follows: "a riddle in Chinese that allows for an endless variety of answers."

In the meantime Barbicane insisted that if Nicholl had put his mind to it, he would certainly have hit on this formula.

"I'm not so sure," Nicholl said, "because the more I study it, the more I marvel at how you've set it up."

"Now listen," Barbicane told his know-nothing comrade, "and you'll see that each of these letters has a meaning."

"I'm all ears," Michel said, looking resigned.

"*d*," Barbicane put in, "is the distance from the center of the earth to the center of the moon, because we must use their centers to calculate their gravitational pull."

"That I can follow."

"*r* is the radius of the earth."

"*r*, radius. Granted."

"*m* is the earth's mass, *m* prime the moon's. In essence we need to take the masses of these two magnetic objects into account, since their gravitational pull is in direct proportion to their masses."

"Got it."

"*g* represents gravity—the speed per second of an object falling to the earth's surface. Is that clear?"

"As mineral water," Michel replied.

"Now, I use *x* to represent the variable distance separating the projectile from the center of the earth, and *v* stands for the projectile's velocity at that distance."

"All right."

"Finally the expression *v* zero figuring in this equation is the shell's velocity on leaving the atmosphere."

"In essence," Nicholl said, "it's from there that we need to calculate this velocity, since we already know that our velocity at departure is exactly 1½ times greater than our velocity on leaving the atmosphere."

"I've quit understanding!" Michel put in.

"Yet it's quite simple," Barbicane said.

"Not as simple as I am," Michel remarked.

"It means that once our projectile has gone past the bounds of the earth's atmosphere, we've already lost a third of our initial velocity."

"As much as that?"

"Yes, my friend, merely because of our friction against the atmospheric layers. Please understand that the faster we go, the more resistance we get from the air."

"That I can accept and understand," Michel replied, "though your *v* to the second power and your *v* zero squared are jangling around in my head like nails in a sack."

"Algebra's initial effect," Barbicane went on. "And now to finish you off, we're going to establish the numerical values of these different expressions, in other words, put them into figures."

"Go on, finish me off!" Michel replied.

"Some of these expressions are already known," Barbicane said, "the others need to be worked out."

"I'll look after the latter," Nicholl said.

"Let's take *r*," Barbicane went on. "*r* is the earth's radius, which at our starting point, Florida's latitude, equals 20,899,000 feet. *d*, in other words, the distance from the center of the earth to the center of the moon, is equal to fifty-six times the earth's radius, hence . . ."

Nicholl quickly worked it out.

"Hence," he said, "1,170,340,000 feet just as the moon has reached her perigee, in other words, her closest point to the earth."

"Good," Barbicane put in. "Now *m* prime over *m*—in other words, the ratio of the earth's mass to the moon's—equals 1/81."

"How wonderful," Michel said.

"*g*, the gravity, is 32.18 feet in Florida. From which it follows that *gr* is—"

"—equal to 671,948,000 square feet," Nicholl responded.

"And now what?" Michel Ardan asked.

"Now that the expressions have been put into figures," Barbicane replied, "I'm going to look for the velocity *v* zero, in other words, the velocity our projectile needs on exiting the atmosphere to reach the point where the gravitational pull is equivalent to an absence of velocity. Since velocity at that juncture is nonexistent, I'll make it equal to zero, then I'll let *x*—the distance at which this neutral point is found—be represented by 9/10 of *d*, in other words, the distance separating the two centers."

"I have a vague notion that's got to be right," Michel said.

"Which gives me, then: *x* equals 9/10 of *d*, and *v* equals zero, and my formula will become . . ."

Barbicane wrote quickly on his piece of paper:

$$v_0^2 = 2gr \left\{ 1 - \frac{10r}{9d} - \frac{1}{81} \left(\frac{10r}{d} - \frac{r}{d-r} \right) \right\}$$

Nicholl scanned it eagerly.

"That's it, that's it!" he exclaimed.

"Is it clear?" Barbicane asked.

"It's inscribed in letters of fire!" Nicholl replied.

"What helpful fellows," Michel mumbled.

"Do you finally understand it?" Barbicane asked.

"Understand it?" Michel Ardan snapped. "It's giving me a splitting headache!"

"Thus," Barbicane went on, "*v* zero squared equals *2gr*, times 1 minus *10r* over *9d* minus 1/81, times *10r* over *d* minus *r* over *d* minus *r*."

"And now," Nicholl said, "to get the shell's velocity as it leaves the atmosphere, we only have to do a little calculating."

The captain, a seasoned all-around problem solver, started writing with fearful speed. Divisions and multiplications stretched into the distance under his fingers. Figures fell like hail onto the blank spots on his sheet of paper. Barbicane kept an eye on him, while Michel Ardan pressed both hands against his temples, which were now starting to throb severely.

"Well?" Barbicane asked after a few minutes of silence.

"Well, according to the finished calculation," Nicholl replied, "*v* zero, in other words, the velocity the projectile needs on leaving the atmosphere to reach the neutral point, should be . . ."

"Yes . . . ?" Barbicane put in.

". . . should be 12,085 yards per second."

"*What!*" Barbicane put in, jumping up. "You're telling me—"

"It should be 12,085 yards."

"Curse the rascals!" exclaimed the Gun Club's president, making a gesture of despair.

"What's wrong?" Michel Ardan asked, quite startled.

"Wrong? If right now the friction has already reduced our speed by a third, then our initial velocity should have been . . ."

"It should have been 18,128 yards per second," Nicholl replied.

"But the Cambridge Observatory stated that 12,000 yards was enough at departure, so our shell took off with only that much speed!"

"Well?" Nicholl asked.

"Well, it won't be enough."

"Good heavens."

"We aren't going to reach the neutral point."

"Blast!"

"We won't even get halfway."

"Son of a gun!" Michel Ardan exclaimed, leaping up as if the projectile were already colliding with their planet.

"And we'll fall back to the earth!"

5

THE COLDNESS OF SPACE

THIS REVELATION was like a lightning bolt. Who could have anticipated such a calculating error? Barbicane refused to believe it. Nicholl reviewed his figures. They were correct. As for the formula that had generated them, its accuracy was above suspicion, and after verifying it, they'd confirmed that an initial velocity of 18,000 yards per second was needed to reach the neutral point.

The three friends looked at each other in silence. Breakfast wasn't in the picture anymore. Barbicane peered out a porthole, gritting his teeth, knitting his brow, convulsively clenching his fists. Nicholl examined his calculations, arms folded. Michel Ardan muttered:

"So much for your so-called experts! Those good-for-nothings! I would give twenty gold pieces for this shell to fall right on the Cambridge Observatory and pulverize every pencil pusher inside!"

All at once the captain had a thought, which he conveyed immediately to Barbicane.

"Hold on!" he said. "It's seven o'clock in the morning. So we've been gone thirty-two hours. Our flight is more than half over, yet as far as I can tell, we aren't falling."

Barbicane didn't answer. But after a quick glance at the captain, he picked up a pair of compasses he used for measuring the angular distance of the earth. Then he got a highly accurate reading through the lower window, since the projectile seemed to be stock-still. Afterward he straightened, mopped the beads of sweat forming on his brow, and juggled some figures on his piece of paper. Nicholl saw that the Gun Club's president was trying to compute from the length of the earth's diameter just how far the shell had traveled. The captain watched him anxiously.

"No!" Barbicane exclaimed a few seconds later. "No, we're *not* falling! We're already over 125,000 miles from the earth! We've gone past the point where the projectile should have halted if its initial velocity had been just 12,000 yards per second. We're still ascending!"

"Obviously," Nicholl replied. "So we're forced to conclude that the thrust from those 400,000 pounds of guncotton produced an initial velocity greater than the promised 12,000 yards. That explains why it took us just thirteen minutes to meet up with our second satellite, whose orbit is more than 5,000 miles above the earth."

"And this explanation is all the more likely," Barbicane added, "because by expelling the water stored between the collapsible partitions, the projectile suddenly lost considerable weight."

"Right," Nicholl put in.

"Ah, my gallant Nicholl," Barbicane exclaimed, "we're saved!"

"Well then," Michel Ardan replied serenely, "since we're saved, it's time for breakfast."

In fact Nicholl wasn't mistaken. By a stroke of luck, their initial velocity had been greater than the speed specified by the Cambridge Observatory, but the Cambridge Observatory had made a mistake all the same.

Recovering from this false alarm, our travelers sat down to a hearty breakfast. If they ate a good deal, they talked even more. Their confidence was even greater now than before "the algebra incident."

"Why shouldn't we succeed?" Michel Ardan kept saying. "Why shouldn't we arrive safely? We've taken off. There are no obstacles in front of us. There are no stumbling blocks in our way. We've got an easy road to travel, easier than a ship struggling against the sea, easier than a balloon fighting with the wind! Now then, if a ship can sail where it wants and a balloon can soar where it pleases, why can't our projectile hit the target it's aiming at?"

"It will hit the target," Barbicane said.

"If only to do credit to the American people," Michel Ardan added, "the only people who could see such an undertaking through to completion, the only ones who could bring forth a man like President Barbicane. And come to think of it, what's going to happen to us now that our worries are over? We'll end up being bored stiff."

Barbicane and Nicholl waved this away.

"But I've foreseen this state of affairs, my friends," Michel Ardan went on. "Just say the word. You've got chess, checkers, card games, and dominoes at your disposal. All we're lacking is a billiard table."

"What!" Barbicane asked. "You brought such frivolous things along?"

"Certainly," Michel replied, "and not just to entertain ourselves, but also with the praiseworthy intention of bequeathing them to the moonpeople's clubhouses."

"My friend," Barbicane said, "if there *are* people on the moon, they appeared thousands of years before people on the earth, because they live on a heavenly body that's unquestionably older than ours. So if these moonpeople have existed for hundreds of thousands of years, and if their brains are put together like human brains, they've already invented everything we've invented, and even what we'll invent in centuries to come. They have nothing to learn from us, and we have everything to learn from them."

"What!" Michel responded. "You think they've got artists like Phidias, Michelangelo, or Raphael?"

"They do."

"Writers like Homer, Virgil, Milton, Lamartine, and Victor Hugo?"

"I'm sure of it."

"Philosophers like Plato, Aristotle, Descartes, and Kant?"

"I haven't any doubt of it."

"Scientists like Archimedes, Euclid, Pascal, and Newton?"

"I would swear to it."

"Comedians like Étienne Arnal and photographers like . . . like that Nadar fellow?"[2]

"I'm sure of it."

"Then, Barbicane my friend, if these moonpeople are as good as we are, or even better, why haven't they tried to contact the earth? Why haven't they fired a lunar projectile at our planet?"

"Who says they haven't?" Barbicane replied in all seriousness.

"That's right," Nicholl added. "It would be easier for them than for us, and for two reasons: first, because the gravity on the surface of the moon is a sixth of the earth's gravity, which would allow a projectile to take off more easily; second, because they would need to send this projectile a mere 20,000 miles instead of 200,000, which would require only a tenth as much thrust at departure."

"Then I repeat," Michel continued, "why haven't they done it?"

"And I repeat," Barbicane countered, "who says they haven't?"

"When?"

"Thousands of years before man appeared on the earth."

"What about the shell? Where's the shell? I insist on seeing the shell."

"My friend," Barbicane replied, "the sea covers five-sixths of our globe. That gives us five good reasons for assuming that if a lunar projectile was fired, it's now sitting on the floor of the Atlantic or the Pacific. Unless it got buried in some crevasse during that era when the earth's crust still hadn't hardened sufficiently."

"Barbicane old boy," Michel replied, "you have an answer for everything and I bow to your wisdom. All the same here's one theory that suits me better than the rest: since moonpeople are older and therefore wiser than we are, they simply decided not to invent gunpowder!"

Just then Diana butted into the conversation, barking noisily. She was clamoring for her breakfast.

"Ah!" Michel Ardan put in. "While we were arguing away, we forgot about Diana and Satellite."

They immediately dished out a decent helping of dog chow, which Diana devoured ravenously.

"Look here, Barbicane," Michel said, "we ought to have turned this projectile into a second Noah's ark and taken two of every domestic animal to the moon."

"No doubt," Barbicane answered, "but there wouldn't be enough room."

"True," Michel said, "it might be a bit of a squeeze."

"The fact is," Nicholl replied, "such ruminants as oxen, cows, bulls, and horses would be mighty useful on those lunar landmasses. It's a shame this coach couldn't be made into a stable or a cowshed."

"But at least," Michel Ardan said, "we might have brought a donkey along, just one little donkey, one of those courageous, patient creatures old Silenus liked to ride. I'm partial to those poor donkeys! They're abso-

---

[2] *Translator's note.* Félix Nadar (1820–1910) was Verne's model for Michel Ardan, whose last name is an anagram of "Nadar."

lutely the unluckiest animals in creation. They get beaten not only while they're alive, but even after they're dead."

"How do you figure that?" Barbicane asked.

"It's the truth," Michel put in. "Their hides are used for drums!"

Barbicane and Nicholl couldn't help laughing at this silly statement. But an exclamation from their lighthearted companion cut them off. The latter was stooping over the nook where Satellite lay; he straightened up, saying:

"Fine. Satellite isn't ailing anymore."

"Good," Nicholl put in.

"No, he's dead," Michel went on. "That's going to be awkward," he added in a doleful tone. "I'm afraid, my unlucky Diana, you aren't going to establish a bloodline in the lunar regions!"

In essence poor Satellite hadn't recovered from his injury. He was stone dead. Very flustered, Michel Ardan looked at his friends.

"This presents a problem," Barbicane said. "We can't keep this dog's carcass with us for another two days."

"No, surely not," Nicholl replied, "but our portholes are on hinges. We can lower them. We'll open one of them and toss his body out into space."

The Gun Club's president thought for a few seconds and said:

"Yes, that's how we'll proceed, but we'll need to take the most meticulous precautions."

"Why?" Michel asked.

"For two reasons you'll soon understand," Barbicane replied. "The first concerns the air inside the projectile—we need to lose as little of it as possible."

"But we renew our air."

"Only partially. We renew just the oxygen, my gallant Michel—and pertinent to this, let's take good care the device doesn't furnish an excessive amount of oxygen, because too much could cause us very serious physiological problems. But though we renew the oxygen, we don't renew the nitrogen, this carrier that the lungs don't consume and that needs to stay intact. Now then, this ni-

trogen will swiftly escape through the open porthole."

"Oh I see—while we're tossing out poor Satellite," Michel said.

"Right, so we'll need to act quickly."

"And how about your second reason?" Michel asked.

"The second reason is that we mustn't let the intense cold outside get into the projectile, otherwise we'll freeze to death."

"But what about the sun . . . ?"

"The sun warms our projectile, which absorbs its rays, but it doesn't warm the vacuum in which we're cruising right now. There's no air, so heat can't spread any more than light can, and wherever the sun's rays don't shine directly, it's not only dark, it's cold as well. This temperature, then, is simply what's produced by stellar radiation, in other words, it's what the planet earth would experience if the sun faded out one day."

"Which isn't a cause for concern," Nicholl replied.

"Who knows?" Michel Ardan said. "Even so, assuming that the sun doesn't fade out, couldn't the earth move farther away from it?"

"Oh good," Barbicane put in. "Michel's daydreaming again!"

"Wait!" Michel went on. "Isn't it a fact that the earth passed through the tail of a comet in 1861? Now then, if we ever ran into a comet with a gravitational pull greater than the sun's, our orbit could shift toward this rambling space rock, the earth could become its satellite, and our planet could be dragged so far away that the sun's rays wouldn't have any further effect on its surface."

"That actually could happen," Barbicane replied, "but the consequences of such a change needn't be quite as alarming as you assume."

"And why not?"

"Because heat and cold would remain in balance on our planet. Scientists calculate that if the earth had been carried off by that comet in 1861, we would have felt, even when we were farthest from the sun, a heat barely sixteen times greater than what we get from moonlight—which even the strongest magnifying lens can't increase to any appreciable extent."

"So?" Michel put in.

"Wait a second," Barbicane replied. "Scientists also calculate that at the earth's perihelion, when we're closest to the sun, we'll face a heat 28,000 times greater than what we feel during the summer. But this heat, which is enough to fuse solid matter and turn the seas into steam, will form heavy belts of clouds that reduce the intense temperature. Ergo the coldness of the aphelion compensates for the warmth of the perihelion, and we're likely to reach a happy medium."

"But how cold," Nicholl asked, "do scientists estimate that it gets in outer space?"

"In the past," Barbicane replied, "they thought temperatures fell tremendously. In calculating low thermometer readings, they got to the point of juggling figures millions of degrees below zero. It was Joseph Fourier, one of Michel's countrymen and a famous expert at the French Academy of Sciences, who turned these numbers back into reasonable estimates. According to him, the temperature in space isn't any lower than -76° Fahrenheit."

"Piddling," Michel put in.

"It's pretty close to the temperature," Barbicane replied, "that was recorded in the arctic regions at Melville Island and Fort Reliance, hence about -69° Fahrenheit."

"It remains to be seen," Nicholl said, "if Fourier's assessments were well founded. If I'm not mistaken, another French scientist, Claude Pouillet, puts the temperature in space at -256° Fahrenheit. However we'll be able to find out for ourselves."

"Not right now," Barbicane replied, "because the sun's rays are shining directly on our thermometer, so I'm afraid they would give an overly high temperature. But each side of the moon is dark for two weeks at a time, and once we've landed, we'll have the leisure to conduct this experiment, because the earth's satellite is moving in a vacuum."

"But what do you mean by a vacuum?" Michel asked. "Is it an absolute void?"

"It's absolutely without air."

"And the air isn't replaced by anything?"

"Yes. By ether," Barbicane replied.

"Aha! And just what is this ether?"

"Ether, my friend, is a cluster of infinitesimal atoms, which, according to books on molecular physics, are as far from each other, relative to their dimensions, as celestial bodies are in space. But this distance is less than one 75,000,000th of an inch. It's the vibrating motion of these atoms that generates both light and heat, undulating 430 trillion times per second, though they're only two or three 125,000ths of an inch in size."

"Billions of billions!" Michel Ardan exclaimed. "So they've measured and counted all those fluctuations, have they? These, Barbicane my friend, are typical scientific figures—they grate on the ears and people can't relate to them."

"But you have to work with figures—"

"No you don't. You're better off comparing them to something. A trillion doesn't mean a thing. Comparisons say it all. For instance: if you keep telling me that Uranus is 76 times bigger than the earth, Saturn 900 times bigger, Jupiter 1,300 times bigger, the sun 1,300,000 times bigger, I won't be much farther along. Accordingly I prefer—and by far—those old-fashioned comparisons in the almanacs that just talk down to you: the sun is a pumpkin two feet wide, Jupiter is an orange, Saturn is a lady apple, Neptune is a black cherry, Uranus is a Barbados cherry, the earth is a pea, Venus is a smaller pea, Mars is a bulbous pinhead, Mercury is a mustard seed, Juno, Ceres, Vesta, and Pallas are simply grains of sand. This way, at least, you know where you stand!"

After Michel Ardan's sally against scientists and the trillions they reel off without batting an eye, it was time to bury Satellite. This was a simple matter of tossing him out into space, just as sailors toss a corpse into the sea.

But as President Barbicane had advised, they needed to work fast so as to lose as little air as possible, since that elastic fluid would quickly pour out into the void. They carefully unscrewed the bolts in the right porthole, whose opening measured about a foot across; in the meantime Michel, full of remorse, got ready to launch the dog into space. Raised by a powerful lever that helped it overcome the interior air pressure on the projectile's walls, the window swung swiftly on its hinges and out went Satellite. Only a few molecules of air had escaped, and the operation was so successful, Barbicane had no qualms later on about likewise dumping any needless rubbish that cluttered the coach.

6

QUESTIONS AND ANSWERS

ON DECEMBER 4, when the travelers woke up after fifty-four hours of traveling, the chronometers said five o'clock in the morning earth time. As for the scheduled length of their stay aboard the projectile, they'd gone five hours and forty minutes past its halfway point; but as for their flight plan, they'd already covered nearly seven-tenths of its distance. This oddity was due to their gradual decrease in speed.

When they studied the earth through the lower window, it looked like nothing more than a dark patch washed out by the sun's rays. No more crescent, no more reflected light. At midnight the next day, exactly when they would have a full moon, they also would have a new earth. Overhead, that silver orb drew nearer and nearer to the path being taken by the projectile, getting ready to meet up with it at the appointed hour. The dark dome all around them was spangled with shimmering sparks that seemed to be slowly moving. But they were at such considerable distances, their comparative sizes didn't seem to have changed. The sun and stars looked the same as they do from the earth. As for the moon, she was considerably bigger; but our travelers' spyglasses simply didn't have the power to examine her surface, so it was too soon to conduct a productive survey of her topography and geology.

Accordingly they passed the time in endless conversations. They especially chatted about the moon. Each man trotted out his own special brand of knowledge. Barbicane and Nicholl were always in earnest, Michel Ardan always fanciful. The projectile, its position, its heading, possible developments, and what precautions to take while falling to

the moon all were unlimited subjects for speculation.

Sure enough, during breakfast one of Michel's questions about the projectile provoked a rather unusual answer from Barbicane, an answer worth quoting.

Michel wanted to know what the consequences would have been, supposing the shell had suddenly come to a halt while it was still going at its fearsome initial velocity.

"But," Barbicane replied, "I don't see how the projectile could have come to a halt."

"Suppose it had," Michel responded.

"That isn't a feasible supposition," remarked the practical Barbicane. "Unless there was a loss of thrust. But even then its speed would have decreased little by little and it wouldn't have come to a sudden stop."

"Let's assume it had bumped into an object in space."

"What object?"

"That enormous meteor we met up with."

"Then," Nicholl said, "the projectile would have been smashed into a thousand pieces and the three of us along with it."

"Worse than that," Barbicane replied. "We would have burned up."

"Burned up!" Michel exclaimed. "By God, I'm sorry it didn't take place, so we could have 'seen for ourselves.'"

"And it would have been something to see," Barbicane replied. "Nowadays it's a known fact that heat is simply motion converted. When you warm water—in other words, when you add heat to it—that means you set its molecules in motion."

"Say," Michel put in, "that's a clever way of looking at it!"

"And it's accurate, my good friend, because it explains every phenomenon associated with high temperatures. Heat is only molecular motion, a simple fluctuation of the particles in an object. When you throw on a train's brakes, the train comes to a stop. But what happens to the motion impelling it? It's transformed into heat and the brakes get hot. Why do they grease the axles of the wheels? To keep them from getting hot, since the loss of motion will transform into heat. Do you understand?"

"I do understand," Michel replied, "I understand perfectly. To give an example, when I've been running for so long that I'm dripping wet, that I'm sweating in big drops, why do I need to stop? Quite simply because my motion has transformed into heat!"

Barbicane couldn't help smiling at Michel's comeback. Then, continuing with his supposition:

"Hence," he said, "in the event of a collision, our projectile would have been in the same shoes as a bullet that falls smoking to the ground after hitting a piece of armor plate. Its motion has turned into heat. Consequently I maintain that if our shell had bumped into that meteor, its sudden loss of speed would have created enough heat to turn it instantly into steam."

"Then," Nicholl asked, "what would happen if the earth were to suddenly stop orbiting?"

"Its temperature would shoot so high," Barbicane replied, "it would immediately be reduced to vapor."

"Fine," Michel put in. "That's a way for the world to end that thoroughly simplifies things."

"And what if the earth plummeted into the sun?" Nicholl said.

"It's calculated," Barbicane replied, "that its fall would generate the same heat as 1,600 lumps of coal the same size as the planet earth."

"A handy increase in temperature for the sun," Michel Ardan remarked. "And the residents of Uranus or Neptune surely won't have any grounds for complaint, because they must be freezing to death on their planets."

"Hence, my friends," Barbicane went on, "any motion that's suddenly halted will generate heat. And this formulation leads us to believe that the sun's heat is fed by a hailstorm of meteors falling continually on its surface. They've even calculated . . . "

"Look out," Michel muttered, "here come the figures."

"They've even calculated," Barbicane went on unflappably, "that each meteor's collision with the sun should generate the same heat as 4,000 loads of coal the same size."

"And how hot is the sun?" Michel asked.

"As hot as if you'd burned a seam of coal around it that's over sixteen miles deep."

"And this heat—"

"—could bring 695 billion cubic miles of water to a boil in one hour."

"And it doesn't roast you?" Michel exclaimed.

"No," Barbicane replied, "because the earth's atmosphere absorbs four-tenths of the sun's heat. Besides, the amount of heat the earth intercepts is only two billionths of the sun's total output."

"I can see that all's for the best," Michel remarked, "and our atmosphere is a handy concoction, because it not only lets us breathe, it also keeps us from cooking."

"Yes," Nicholl said. "Unfortunately it won't be the same on the moon."

"Phooey," Michel put in, always optimistic. "If creatures live on her, they're breathing. If they've died off, they're bound to have left enough oxygen for three people, if only at the bottom of gullies where it'll accumulate because of its weight. So we won't do any mountain climbing, that's all!"

And getting up, Michel went to study the moon's disk, which was shining with unbearable brilliance.

"Good grief," he said, "it must be warm up there!"

"Not to mention," Nicholl replied, "that each day lasts 360 hours!"

"Plus, by way of compensation," Barbicane said, "the nights are just as long, and since the moon's heat is restored only through solar radiation, her temperature has to be the same as it is in outer space."

"Not exactly paradise," Michel said. "Never mind! I wish I was there already! Hoho, my dear comrades, it'll be pretty strange to have the earth as our moon, to see it rise above the horizon, to make out the shapes of the continents, and to tell yourself, 'There's America, there's Europe,' then to watch it go and get lost in the sunlight! Speaking of that, Barbicane, do moonpeople ever have a chance to see eclipses?"

"Yes, eclipses of the sun," Barbicane replied, "when the centers of the three heavenly bodies are in a line and the earth is in the middle. But they're only annular eclipses in which the earth hides just a portion of the sun's disk, leaving a large outer ring still visible."

"And why aren't there any total eclipses?" Nicholl asked. "Doesn't that conical shadow cast by the earth stretch beyond the moon?"

"Yes, if we don't count the refraction caused by the earth's atmosphere. No, if we do count that refraction. Therefore, if we let *delta* prime be the horizontal parallax, and *p* prime the apparent semidiameter—"

"Whew!" Michel put in. "We're back to half of *v* zero squared! Speak English, you fiend for algebra!"

"All right," Barbicane replied. "In layman's terms the average distance from the moon to the earth is sixty times the earth's radius, but after refraction the length of the conical shadow shrinks to less than forty-two times that radius. During an eclipse, then, the moon ends up protruding beyond the original conical shadow, and the rays she receives come not only from the edges of the sun but from its center."

"Then," Michel said in a mocking tone, "why are there eclipses at all, if there shouldn't be any?"

"Solely because the sun's rays are weakened by the refraction, so most of them fade out after they enter the atmosphere!"

"That's a convincing reason," Michel replied. "Anyhow we'll find out when we get there. Meanwhile tell me this, Barbicane—do you think the moon was once a comet?"

"Now there's an idea!"

"Oh," Michel remarked with smug cheeriness, "I get a few now and then."

"But this particular idea doesn't originate with Michel," Nicholl responded.

"Great. So I'm plagiarizing it?"

"Without any doubt," Nicholl replied. "According to the ancients, the Greeks in Arcadia claimed their ancestors lived on the earth before the moon became its satellite. Based on this fact certain scientists have viewed the moon as a comet, a comet whose orbit brought her so near the earth one day, she was caught in its gravitational pull."

"And is there any truth to this theory?" Michel asked.

"None whatever," Barbicane replied, "and

as proof, the moon doesn't reveal any trace of the gaseous covering that always surrounds a comet."

"But," Nicholl went on, "before the moon became the earth's satellite, couldn't she have passed so near the sun during her perihelion that all this gaseous matter evaporated?"

"It could have happened, Nicholl my friend, but it isn't likely."

"Why not?"

"Because . . . ye gods, I don't know."

"Ah, how many hundreds of volumes," Michel exclaimed, "we could publish about everything we don't know!"

"Oh drat! What time is it?" Barbicane asked.

"Three o'clock," Nicholl replied.

"How time flies," Michel said, "when scholars like us put our heads together! No doubt about it, I feel loaded down with learning! I feel like I've become a well of knowledge!"

With that Michel hoisted himself up to the ceiling of the projectile, "to get a better look at the moon," he claimed. Meanwhile his companions were peering into space through the lower window. Nothing new to report.

When Michel Ardan came back down, he went over to a side porthole and suddenly let out a cry of surprise.

"What's the matter?" asked Barbicane.

The Gun Club's president went over to the window and saw a sort of flattened-out bag floating in space a few yards away from the projectile. This object seemed as motionless as the shell, so it had to be heading upward in the same way.

"What *is* that thingamajig?" Michel Ardan kept saying. "Is it some sort of space particle our projectile has attracted to us, something that'll go with us to the moon?"

"What amazes me," Nicholl replied, "is that the specific gravity of this object is clearly much less than the shell's, yet it's staying exactly level with us."

"Nicholl," Barbicane replied after a moment's thought, "I don't know what that object is, but I definitely know why it's staying level with the shell."

"Why?"

"Because we're floating in a vacuum, my dear captain, and in a vacuum objects fall or move—which is the same thing—at the identical speed regardless of their gravity or shape. It's the air resistance that generates differences in weight. When you create a vacuum in a tube pneumatically, the objects you throw into it, whether they're specks of dust or lead pellets, all fall at the same speed. Out here in space you've got the same cause and the same effect."

"Quite right," Nicholl said, "and everything we toss out of the projectile will go with us all the way to the moon."

"Oh, what blockheads we've been!" Michel exclaimed.

"Why do you call us that?" Barbicane asked.

"Because we could have filled up the projectile with useful objects—books, instruments, tools, etc. We could have dumped them all out, and they all would have lined up behind us. But here's a thought. Why can't we ourselves roam around outside like that meteor? Why can't we shoot into space through one of these portholes? What fun it would be to hang out in the ether like that—and we're luckier than birds are, since they always have to flap their wings to stay up!"

"Agreed," Barbicane said, "but how would we breathe?"

"If there's no air out there, a thousand curses on the stuff!"

"But your density is less than the projectile's, Michel, so if there *were* air out there, you would soon be left far behind."

"Then it's a vicious circle."

"As vicious as can be."

"And we must stay locked up in our coach?"

"We must."

"Ah! Of *course!*" Michel blurted out in a fearsome voice.

"What's wrong?" Nicholl asked.

"Now I see, now I can guess what that so-called space particle is! It isn't an asteroid that's going along with us. It isn't a piece of some planet."

"Then what is it?" Barbicane asked.

"It's our unfortunate dog! It's Diana's mate!"

Shapeless, unrecognizable, reduced to nothingness, the object was indeed Satellite's carcass, flattened out like a deflated set of bagpipes, yet rising higher and higher!

7

AN INTOXICATING MOMENT

HENCE THESE STRANGE conditions gave rise to a phenomenon that was unusual but logical, peculiar but understandable. Any objects tossed out of the projectile had to follow its flight path and could come to a halt only when it did. Here was a topic of conversation good for a whole evening. Besides, the three travelers were growing more excited the nearer they got to their journey's end. They were on the alert for anything new and unexpected, and nothing would have surprised them in their current frame of mind. Their feverish fancies were going faster than the projectile itself, which had slowed down significantly without their noticing. But the moon was getting bigger in front of their eyes, and they already imagined that if they simply stretched out their hands, they could practically grab it.

The next day, December 5, all three were on their feet by five o'clock in the morning. If their calculations were correct, this was to be the last day of their journey. In eighteen hours, at midnight that very evening and right when the moon was full, they would arrive on its shining disk. This coming midnight would see them complete their journey, the most amazing of all time. Bright and early that morning, therefore, they looked out the portholes, which were tinted silver by the moon's rays, and they greeted her with a hearty and hopeful cheer.

The earth's satellite was proceeding majestically across the starry firmament. A few more degrees and she would reach the exact point in space where she was due to meet up with the projectile. By Barbicane's own reckoning they would make contact in her northern hemisphere, where mountains are scarce and wide plains stretch into the distance. A promising state of affairs, if, as they believed, the moon stored her atmosphere exclusively in the lowlands.

"Besides," Michel Ardan pointed out, "it's better to land on a plain than a mountain. If a moonperson got dropped off on the summit of Mt. Blanc in Europe or on top of the Himalayas in Asia, he wouldn't really have arrived yet!"

"What's more," Captain Nicholl added, "on level terrain the projectile would stay stationary once it descended. By contrast, if we alighted on a slope, our shell would roll down it like an avalanche, and since we aren't squirrels in a cage, we wouldn't arrive safe and sound. So all's for the best."

In fact the success of their daring endeavor no longer seemed doubtful. But Barbicane was bothered by one thought; however, not wanting to worry his two companions, he kept silent on the matter.

In essence their moving toward the moon's northern hemisphere proved that the projectile's flight path had changed slightly. As worked out by the mathematicians, the blast at takeoff was supposed to carry the shell to the very center of the lunar disk. If it didn't arrive there, that meant it had gone off course. What was the cause? Due to the shortage of landmarks, Barbicane couldn't gauge or even guess the magnitude of this change in course. Nevertheless he hoped it would result only in taking them toward the topside of the moon, a region more suitable for landing.

Therefore, without sharing his worries with his friends, Barbicane was content to keep a close watch on the moon, trying to see if the projectile had truly changed direction. Because if the shell missed its target, overshot the moon, and flew off into interplanetary space, they would be in a dreadful position.

Just then, instead of looking flat like a disk, that silver orb was already hinting at her convexity. If the sun's rays had struck her at an angle, the shadows cast would have highlighted her lofty mountains and made them stand out sharply. A person's eyes could have dipped into the yawning depths of her craters or followed those erratic crevices that streak across her wide plains. But the intense brightness still flattened everything. You could barely see those wide blotches that make our satellite look like a human face.

"A face it may be," Michel Ardan said, "but with apologies to the charming goddess of the moon,[3] a pockmarked face!"

But the travelers were so close to their destination, they couldn't take their eyes off this new world. They strolled in their imaginations through its unknown lands. They scaled its lofty peaks. They descended into its wide basins. Here and there they thought they saw huge seas barely coalescing in its thin atmosphere, and watercourses pouring out their contributions from the mountains. Peering into the depths, they hoped to detect some sounds from this heavenly body, eternally silent in the solitude of space.

That last day left them with thrilling memories. They took note of the tiniest details. A vague uneasiness came over them as the time drew nearer. This uneasiness would have been even greater if they'd sensed how their speed was slackening. They wouldn't have thought it at all sufficient to take them to their destination. This was because the projectile no longer "carried any weight" by that point. It kept getting lighter, and at that boundary line where the moon's gravity and the earth's neutralize each other, the shell would become completely weightless, creating some highly startling effects.

But despite his various involvements, Michel Ardan didn't forget to fix their morning meal with his usual punctuality. They ate heartily. Nothing could have been more excellent than that beef broth brewed over the gas jet, nothing finer than those canned meats. A couple glasses of good French wine topped off this meal. And pertinent to this, Michel Ardan pointed out that under such blazing sunlight, even more robust wines were sure to be fermenting in the moon's vineyards, assuming they existed in the first place. In any event the farsighted Frenchman had taken pains to pack some precious cuttings from Médoc and Cote d'Or for which he had especially high hopes.

The Reiset and Regnault device continued to operate with tremendous efficiency. The

---

[3] *Translator's note.* Diana, sister of Apollo.

air was always perfectly fresh. Not a molecule of carbon dioxide eluded the potassium hydroxide, and as for the oxygen, Captain Nicholl called it "definitely high quality." The traces of water vapor inside the projectile mixed with the air, tempering its dryness, and it's a fact that few apartments and auditoriums in London, Paris, or New York could have offered such sanitary conditions.

But for it to operate reliably, the device had to be kept in perfect working order. Accordingly Michel inspected the escape valves every morning, tested the spigots, and adjusted the gas temperature on the pyrometer. Everything had gone well till then, and like dear old J. T. Maston, the travelers were starting to put on weight—and if they stayed locked in a few months longer, they would end up unrecognizable. In short, they acted like chickens in a coop: they got fatter.

Glancing out the portholes, Barbicane saw the ghostly carcass of the dog and various other objects that had been tossed out of the projectile, all stubbornly tagging along. Diana gave a mournful howl at seeing Satellite's remains. This flotsam and jetsam looked as motionless as if it were lying on solid ground.

"Do you realize, my friends," Michel Ardan said, "that if one of us had died from the recoil at our departure, we would have had a hard time burying him, or rather 'etherizing' him, since out here we've got ether instead of dirt. As you can see, the incriminating corpse would have followed us into space like a guilty conscience."

"That would have been distressing," Nicholl said.

"But," Michel went on, "the thing I miss is being able to go for a stroll outdoors. What rapture to float through this radiant ether, to bathe in it, to roll around in the sun's pure rays! If only Barbicane had thought to provide us with diving gear and an air pump, I could venture outside, pretend to be a gargoyle, and pose on top of the projectile like a chimera or a hippogriff."

"Well, Michel old fellow," Barbicane replied, "you wouldn't play hippogriff for long, because, despite your diving suit, the air would expand inside you, then you would inflate and explode like a shell from a mortar, or rather like a hot air balloon that has gone too high in the skies. Therefore you aren't missing anything, and remember this: so long as we're cruising in space, we need to prohibit any starry-eyed strolling outside the projectile."

Michel Ardan let himself be partially persuaded. He conceded the thing was difficult though not "impossible," a word that wasn't in his vocabulary.

The conversation shifted from this topic to another, not faltering for a second. Right then the three friends felt that ideas were sprouting in their brains the way leaves sprout during the first warm spell in spring. They were starting to get all tangled up.

In the midst of the questions and answers crisscrossing each other that morning, Nicholl pointed out a problem that didn't have an immediate solution.

"Of course," he said, "it's all fine and dandy to go to the moon, but how do we get back?"

His two conversation partners looked at each other in surprise. You would have thought this possibility had never occurred to them before.

"What do you mean, Nicholl?" Barbicane asked in all seriousness.

"It strikes me as premature," Michel added, "to think about leaving a place before we even get there."

"I'm not saying we shouldn't keep on," Nicholl remarked, "but I'll repeat my question and ask: how do we get back?"

"I haven't a clue," Barbicane replied.

"As for me," Michel said, "if I'd known how to come back, I never would have gone."

"That's not much help," Nicholl snapped.

"I'm on Michel's side," Barbicane said, "and I'll add that the problem has no current relevance. Later on, when we judge it's time to go back, we'll put our heads together. Though we don't have the columbiad, we'll still have the projectile."

"There's a step in the right direction. A bullet without a gun!"

"The gun we can build," Barbicane replied. "The gunpowder we can make. There should be no shortage of metal, saltpeter, or coal in the bowels of the moon. Besides, in order to go back all we have to do is overcome the moon's force of attraction, and we only need to go 20,000 miles before we'll fall to the earth simply because of the laws of gravity."

"That's enough," Michel said heatedly. "Let's table this question of getting back! We've spent too much time on it already. As for contacting our old colleagues on the ground, that won't be hard."

"And how would you do it?"

"With meteors launched out of lunar volcanoes."

"Good thinking, Michel," Barbicane replied in a decisive tone. "Pierre Laplace calculated that a force five times greater than that of today's cannons would be enough to shoot a meteor from the moon to the earth. Now then, every volcano has more propulsive force than that."

"Hooray!" Michel shouted. "What handy mailmen these meteors will make, plus they won't cost a cent! And what fun we'll have with the postal authorities! But come to think of it . . . "

"Think of what?"

"I've just had a marvelous idea! Why didn't we hook a wire to our shell? We could have traded telegrams with the earth!"

"Damnation!" Nicholl shot back. "A wire 215,000 miles long—do you think it would weigh nothing at all?"

"Nothing at all! We could have tripled the columbiad's powder charge! Even quadrupled or quintupled it!" Michel exclaimed, each of his verbs getting higher in pitch.

"There's just one small objection to make to your plan," Barbicane replied. "As our globe rotates, the wire will wind itself around it like a chain on a winch—and that'll bring us back down to earth for sure."

"God bless the Union and its thirty-nine stars!" Michel said. "I'm having nothing but unrealistic ideas today—ideas worthy of J. T. Maston! But I guess if we don't make it back to the earth, J. T. Maston could come and fetch us."

"Yes, he'll come!" Barbicane remarked. "He's a dear and courageous comrade! Be-

sides, what could be simpler? Isn't the columbiad still buried in Florida soil? Is there any shortage of cotton and nitric acid for manufacturing pyroxile? Won't the moon reappear at the zenith above Florida? Eighteen years from now won't she be in exactly the same place she's in today?"

"Yes," Michel echoed. "Yes, Maston will come—along with our friends Elphiston, Blomsberry, and all the members of the Gun Club, and they'll get a hearty welcome! Then later on we'll run trains of projectiles between the earth and the moon! Hooray for J. T. Maston!"

It's likely that if the honorable J. T. Maston didn't hear the cheers uttered on his behalf, at least his ears were burning. What was he doing at that juncture? No doubt he was stationed in the Rocky Mountains at the outpost on Long's Peak, still trying to find that invisible shell drifting in space. If he was thinking of his dear companions, it must be conceded that they weren't far behind—all three were in the grip of a strange exhilaration and were sending him their best wishes.

But what was the reason for this lively behavior, now visibly increasing in the projectile's guests? Their sobriety couldn't be doubted. Should this odd intellectual sensitivity be blamed on their unusual circumstances, on the nearness of that moon just a few hours away, on some mysterious lunar influence now affecting their nervous systems? Their faces were as red as if they'd been exposed to heat from an oven; their breathing had quickened, and their lungs were pumping like a blacksmith's bellows; an abnormal light gleamed in their eyes; their voices were exploding with fearsome emphasis; their words were popping out like champagne corks expelled by carbon dioxide; their sweeping gestures were becoming dangerous. And strangely enough, none of them noticed this mental hypertension.

"Now," Nicholl said in a curt tone, "now that I'm not so sure we'll get back from the moon, I want to know what we'll do there."

"What we'll do there?" Barbicane replied, stamping his foot like a swordsman at a fencing club. "I have no idea!"

"You have no idea?" Michel exclaimed,

bellowing the words so that they reverberated noisily around the projectile.

"No, I haven't the foggiest notion!" Barbicane shot back, matching the volume level of his conversation partner.

"Well, I know what we'll do," Michel replied.

"So tell us," Nicholl snapped, no longer able to keep a snarl out of his voice.

"I'll tell you if I feel like it," Michel exclaimed, grabbing his companion fiercely by the arm.

"You'd *better* feel like it," Barbicane said, eyes fiery, fists raised. "You're the one who dragged us on this fearsome journey, and we want to know why!"

"That's right!" the captain put in. "Since I'm not sure where I'm going, I want to know *why* I'm going!"

"Why?" Michel exclaimed, jumping a yard off the floor. "Why? To lay claim to the moon in the name of the United States! To add a fortieth state to the Union! To colonize these lunar regions, farm them, populate them, send them all our prodigious achievements in art, science, and technology! To bring civilization to the moonpeople, unless they're more civilized than we are, and to set them up in a republic, if they haven't got one already!"

"And what if there aren't any moonpeople?" Nicholl shot back, turning very argumentative under the sway of this bewildering intoxication.

"Who says there aren't any moonpeople?" Michel snapped in a threatening tone.

"I do!" Nicholl roared.

"Captain," Michel said, "if you continue this insolent behavior, I'll ram it down your throat along with your teeth!"

The two opponents were about to rush at each other, and this disjointed debate was all set to deteriorate into a fistfight, when Barbicane made a fearsome leap in between them.

"Stop, you miserable fools!" he said, causing his two companions to turn their backs on each other. "If there aren't any moonpeople, we'll manage without them."

"Right," snapped Michel, who had no strong feelings either way. "We'll manage

without them. Who needs moonpeople anyway? Down with all moonpeople!"

"The lunar empire is ours," Nicholl said.

"The three of us will set up a republic!"

"I'll be the congress," Michel exclaimed.

"I'm the senate," Nicholl shot back.

"And Barbicane's president," Michel roared.

"Not a president elected by the nation!" Barbicane replied.

"All right, a president elected by congress," Michel snapped. "And since I'm the congress, you're elected unanimously!"

"Three cheers for President Barbicane!" Nicholl shouted.

"Hip hip hooray!" Michel Ardan howled.

Afterward president and senate, both in dreadful voice, sang a rabble-rousing "Yankee Doodle," while the virile strains of the "Marseillaise" rang out from congress.

Then they started a chaotic round dance, making demented gestures, stomping insanely, turning somersaults like rubber-boned clowns. Howling in her turn, Diana joined the dance and leaped to the ceiling of the projectile. Then came a bewildering ruckus of flapping wings and a peculiar clamor like a rooster crowing. Five or six hens were fluttering around, knocking against the walls like crazed bats . . .

Their lungs out of order from some perplexing cause, more than just intoxicated, scorched by the air that was burning their respiratory organs, the three traveling companions fell motionless to the projectile's floor.

8

195,285 MILES AWAY

WHAT WAS GOING ON? What had caused this strange intoxication that could have had such disastrous consequences? A simple blunder on Michel's part, which Nicholl was luckily able to remedy in time.

After a genuine swoon that lasted a few minutes, the captain came back to life first and gathered his wits about him.

Though he'd had breakfast two hours earlier, he felt his stomach growling dreadfully, as if he hadn't eaten for several days. From belly to brain his whole system was in an extreme state of hyperactivity.

So he stood up and ordered Michel to fix a light snack. Michel, wiped out, didn't reply. Nicholl then tried to brew a couple cups of tea, intending it to ease his consumption of a dozen or so sandwiches. First he set about lighting the gas and briskly struck a match.

He was startled to see its sulfur shine with such amazing brilliance, he could barely stand to look at it. When he lit the gas jet, a flame shot out of it like a beam of electric light.

An explanation dawned in Nicholl's mind. That bright light, the physiological problems he was experiencing, the hyperactivity of all his mental and emotional processes—now he understood.

"The oxygen!" he exclaimed.

And bending over the air device, he saw that this colorless, tasteless, odorless gas was pouring full blast from the spigot—a substance essential to life but in an unadulterated state causing the severest organic disorders. Michel had inadvertently left the spigot on the device wide open!

Nicholl hurriedly turned off the oxygen, which was saturating the atmosphere and would have led to the deaths of the travelers, not from asphyxiation but from combustion.

An hour later the air was thinner and their lungs back to normal. Little by little the three friends got over their intoxication; but they had to sleep off their oxygen like a drunk with his wine.

When Michel learned about the role he'd played in this incident, he didn't seem put out in the least. This unscheduled spree broke the monotony of their journey. Under its influence many foolish words had been spoken, but they were no sooner said than forgotten.

"Then again," added the lighthearted Frenchman, "I'm not sorry I sampled a little of that heady gas. You know, my friends, it would be interesting to set up an emporium with oxygen rooms, where folks with weak constitutions could lead a more active life for a few hours! Imagine a gathering where the air was steeped in this noble elastic fluid, or a theater where the management would always add a stiff dose—what passions would fill the souls of the actors and the audience, what fire and enthusiasm! And if instead of a mere crowd we could saturate a whole community, how vigorously it would behave, what extra vitality it would gain! Maybe we could turn a worn-out nation into a big strong one, and I know more than one old European country that needs to go on an oxygen regimen for health reasons!"

Michel babbled so energetically, you would have sworn the spigot was still wide open. But a single sentence from Barbicane threw the brakes on his enthusiasm.

"That's all well and good, Michel my friend," he told Ardan, "but how do you explain the presence of these hens that joined in our music making? "

"Hens?"

"Yes."

It was true, half a dozen hens and a handsome rooster were strutting around, clucking and flapping their wings.

"Oh, the spoilsports!" Michel exclaimed. "That oxygen incited them to rebellion!"

"But what did you bring these hens for?" Barbicane asked.

"To acclimate them to the moon, of course!"

"Then why hide them?"

"It was a prank, my dear president, simply a prank that backfired pitifully. I meant to turn them loose on the moon without saying anything. Goodness, how amazed you would have been to see these earth birds pecking away at your moon meadows!"

"You scamp, you eternal scamp!" Barbicane replied. "You don't need any oxygen going to your head! The way we acted under the influence of that gas is the way you always act! You're always out of your mind!"

"Ah, but what if that's a way to wisdom?" Michel Ardan remarked.

After this philosophical thought the three friends put the projectile back in order. Hens and rooster were reinstated in their chicken coop. But while proceeding with this operation, Barbicane and his two companions became distinctly aware of a new phenomenon.

Since the moment they'd left the earth, their own weight, the shell's, and that of the objects inside all had been progressively decreasing. Though they couldn't verify this weight loss in the projectile's case, the time would come when they would feel its effect on their own persons and on the tools and instruments they'd been using.

Needless to say, a scale couldn't have registered this loss, because the weights used to measure the object's heaviness would have lost the same amount as the object itself. But a spring balance, for instance, keeps its tension regardless of the gravitational pull and could have assessed this loss accurately.

We know that an object's force of attraction, also called its specific gravity, is in direct proportion to the object's mass and in inverse ratio to the square of its distance. From this it follows: if all other celestial bodies had been suddenly wiped out and our planet were alone in space, the projectile, in accordance with Newton's law, would weigh less and less the farther it got from our globe—yet it would never be completely weightless, because the earth's gravitational pull would always be felt no matter how far away.

But in the present instance, there had to come a time when the projectile was no longer subject to the laws of gravity, disregarding other celestial bodies, which could be viewed as having zero influence.

In essence the projectile was following a path between the earth and the moon. As it traveled away from our planet, the earth's gravitational pull decreased in inverse ratio to the square of its distance, but the moon's influence increased by the same proportion. So there had to come a point where these two forces of attraction would neutralize each other and the shell would no longer have any weight. If the moon and the earth had been equal in mass, this point would be found halfway between the two heavenly bodies. But after accounting for their difference in mass, it's easy to calculate that this point would be located at 47/52 of the way there— hence, to run the numbers, 195,285 miles away from the earth.

At this point an object without any built-in source of speed or motion would stay stationary forever, pulled equally by both heavenly bodies and drawn neither to one nor the other.

Now then, if the projectile's thrust had been accurately calculated, it was due to reach this point when its speed was gone and it had lost every ounce of its weight, like all the objects it carried inside.

Then what would happen? There were three theoretical possibilities.

Either the projectile would still keep some of its speed, go past the point of equal attraction, and fall to the moon—because the earth's gravitational pull would be less than its satellite's.

Or, running out of speed and failing to reach the point of equal attraction, the shell would fall back to the earth—because the moon's gravitational pull would be less than its planet's.

Or finally, impelled by enough speed to reach the neutral point but not enough to go past it, the projectile would stay eternally suspended in midair between zenith and nadir, like the fabled coffin of Mohammed.

That was the situation, and Barbicane clearly explained the consequences to his traveling companions. They were extremely concerned. Now then, when would they know that the projectile had reached this neutral point, which was located 195,285 miles away from the earth?

Exactly when they and the objects inside the projectile were no longer governed by the laws of gravity.

Till then, though the travelers all could tell this force was having less and less effect, they were still aware of its presence. But that day, near eleven o'clock in the morning, Nicholl let a glass slip out of his hand, and instead of falling, the glass stayed suspended in the air.

"Aha!" Michel Ardan exclaimed. "Now there's an entertaining lesson in physics."

And right away, when they let go of various objects, weapons, and bottles, the articles stayed miraculously aloft. Released in space by Michel, even Diana herself duplicated— but without any sleight of hand—that marvelous suspension trick worked by such magicians as Alfred de Caston and Jean Robert-Houdin. What's more, the dog didn't seem to even realize she was floating in the air.

Despite their scientific sophistication, our three venturesome companions were startled and astonished themselves, feeling swept off into a realm of wonders, their bodies weightless. If they held out an arm, it hadn't any inclination to drop. Their heads bobbed around on their shoulders. Their feet no longer stayed on the projectile's floor. They were like drunkards who had lost their sense of balance. Fantastic tales have featured people who had no reflections, others who had no shadows. But here, by neutralizing the force of gravity, real life had created human beings for whom nothing had any weight, who weighed nothing themselves!

Suddenly Michel gathered himself, leaped off the floor, and stayed suspended in the air like the floating monk in Murillo's painting *Angels' Kitchen*.

His two friends joined him instantly, and right in the middle of the projectile, all three enacted a miraculous ascension into Heaven.

"Is this credible? Is this feasible? Is this possible?" Michel exclaimed. "No, and yet it's happening! Oh, if only Raphael had seen us like this, what an 'assumption' he could have put on canvas!"

"This assumption isn't likely to hold up," Barbicane replied. "If the projectile goes past the neutral point, the moon's gravity will pull us toward her."

"Then our feet will stand on the ceiling of the projectile," Michel answered.

"No," Barbicane said, "because the projectile's center of gravity is quite low, so it will swing around little by little."

"Then it'll turn all our arrangements upside down, literally!"

"Relax, Michel," Nicholl replied. "Nothing's going to overturn, don't worry. Not a single object will move, because the projectile will change position without our even noticing."

"That's right," Barbicane went on. "And once it has cleared the point of equal attraction, its base, being comparatively heavier,

will draw it vertically down to the moon. But for this phenomenon to occur, we need to have gone past the neutral line."

"Past the neutral line!" Michel exclaimed. "Then let's do what seamen do when they cross the equator. Let's drink to the occasion!"

An easy sideways movement took Michel to the padded wall. There he found a bottle and glasses, set them "out in the open" for his companions, and they gleefully greeted the boundary line with a round of toasts followed by three cheers.

These gravitational effects lasted barely an hour. The travelers felt themselves gradually settling back onto the floor, and Barbicane thought he saw the projectile's conical end veer a little from its usual position of pointing toward the moon. With a counter-movement the base was coming around. So the moon's gravity was winning out over the earth's. They were starting their fall toward the lunar disk, though it was still barely noticeable; they must have been going only fifteen feet per hour. But little by little this gravitational influence would grow stronger, their descent would become more pronounced, the projectile's base would be pulled downward and its cone would point toward the earth, then the shell would fall with increasing speed to the surface of the lunar landscape. Therefore they would reach their destination. Now nothing could impede the undertaking's success, and both Nicholl and Michel Ardan shared Barbicane's delight.

Then they chatted about all those phenomena they'd marveled at one after another. In particular they couldn't say enough about that neutral point where the laws of gravity weren't enforced. Michel Ardan, always the enthusiast, tried to draw some conclusions that were simply sheer imagination.

"Ah, my good friends," he exclaimed, "what progress we could make back home if we could get rid of gravity, that chain shackling us to the earth! We would be like prisoners set free! Our arms and legs would never get tired again. No doubt it's true we would need to be 150 times stronger to fly over the earth's surface, to stay in the air just by using our muscles—but if there weren't any gravity, we could go off into space on a mere whim, simply by an act of will."

"That's right," Nicholl said, grinning. "If we managed to eliminate gravity the way we eliminate pain with an anesthetic, modern society would certainly be in for a change!"

"Yes," Michel exclaimed, all caught up in his argument. "Let's abolish gravity, then we'll have no more burdens to carry! Which means no more cranes, jacks, winches, hand cranks, or other outmoded gadgets!"

"Well put," Barbicane remarked. "But if nothing had any weight, nothing would hold still anymore—not even the hat on your head, my good Michel, nor your house, whose bricks stay in place simply because of their weight! Nor even a boat, which keeps steady on the water merely as a result of gravity. Nor the ocean itself, whose waves would no longer be regulated by the earth's gravitational pull. Nor finally even the atmosphere, whose molecules would no longer cling together and would scatter into space!"

"How inconvenient," Michel remarked. "There's nothing like these practical folks for bringing you back to reality with a thud."

"But take heart, Michel," Barbicane went on. "Though there's no heavenly body where the laws of gravity have been repealed, at least you're going to visit one with much less gravity than the earth."

"The moon?"

"Right. On the surface of the moon, objects weigh a sixth of what they do on the earth, a phenomenon you'll quite easily verify."

"Then we'll notice it ourselves?" Michel asked.

"Obviously, since 450 pounds will weigh only 75 on the surface of the moon."

"And our muscles won't have less strength?"

"Not at all. Instead of jumping three feet off the ground, you'll jump eighteen."

"Why, I'll be a regular Hercules on the moon!" Michel exclaimed.

"To say the least," Nicholl replied. "Because if a moonperson's size is in proportion to his sphere's mass, he'll be barely a foot tall."

"Like the people of Lilliput!" Michel remarked. "So I'll get to play the role of Gulliver! We'll bring those fairy tales about giants to life! That's the advantage of leaving our planet and roaming the solar system!"

"Hold on, Michel," Barbicane responded. "If you want to play Gulliver, visit just the smaller planets such as Mercury, Venus, or Mars, whose masses are a bit less than the earth's. But don't venture onto the big planets of Jupiter, Saturn, Uranus, or Neptune, because there you'll swap roles and you'll be the one from Lilliput."

"What about the sun?"

"Though the sun has a quarter of the earth's density, it has 1,324,000 times the volume, and its gravity is twenty-seven times stronger than on the surface of our globe. Keeping everything in proportion, the natives there should boast an average height of two hundred feet."

"Damnation!" Michel exclaimed. "I would be nothing more than a pygmy, a house pet!"

"Gulliver in Brobdingnag," Nicholl said.

"Exactly," Barbicane replied.

"So it would be helpful to take along a couple cannons for protection."

"Oh good," Barbicane remarked. "Your shells would be completely ineffectual on the sun—they would travel only a few yards before they fell to the ground."

"That's a strong statement."

"That's a true statement," Barbicane replied. "The gravity on that huge heavenly body is so considerable, an object weighing 150 pounds on the earth would weigh over 4,200 pounds on the surface of the sun. Your hat would weigh over 20 pounds, your cigar half a pound. In short, if you slipped and fell on that solar soil, you would be so heavy— over 5,500 pounds—that you couldn't pick yourself up again."

"Holy smoke!" Michel put in. "So I would need to pack a small portable crane! All right, my friends, let's be happy with the moon for right now. At least, we'll cut an impressive figure there. Later on we'll see if there's any point in going to the sun, where nobody can have a drink without a winch to hoist his glass to his lips!"

9

THE CONSEQUENCES OF GOING OFF COURSE

BARBICANE HAD REGAINED his confidence, if not in the journey's outcome, at least in the projectile's thrust. Its speed had the potential to take it past the neutral line. Therefore it wouldn't fall back to the earth. Therefore it wouldn't stay stationary at the point of equal attraction. This left only one theoretical possibility with a chance of becoming reality: the shell would arrive at its destination through the workings of the moon's gravity.

Actually this meant a fall of 20,740 miles—onto a heavenly body, it's true, whose gravity must be reckoned at just a sixth of the earth's. A fearsome fall nevertheless, and one for which they needed to take every conceivable precaution.

These precautions were of two kinds: some were to deaden the impact right when the projectile landed on the lunar soil, others were to slow their fall and thus reduce its force.

With regard to deadening the impact, it was a shame Barbicane couldn't use the same methods that had so effectively lessened the jolt at departure, in other words, collapsible partitions and the use of water as springs. The partitions were still available but not the springs, because the travelers couldn't use their water supply for this purpose—a supply that would prove invaluable, if, during their first days on the moon, they found this liquid element lacking in her soil.

What's more, this supply would have been quite inadequate as a set of springs. The cushion of water stored in the projectile at departure—underneath the watertight disk— was a good three feet deep, with a surface area of fifty-four square feet. Its volume was nearly eight cubic yards, its weight 6.3 tons. Now then, their containers of drinking water didn't hold a fifth of this amount. So they had to do without this potent method of deadening the jolt on arrival.

Luckily, since Barbicane hadn't been content with using just water, the movable disk featured highly resilient buffers, designed to lessen the jolt at the shell's base when the horizontal partitions slammed into it. These buffers were still available; the travelers simply needed to readjust them and put the movable disk back in position. All these parts were easy to handle, weighed nothing to speak of, and could be quickly reassembled.

This took place. Readjusting the various pieces wasn't a problem. It was literally a nuts-and-bolts affair. And tools weren't in short supply. Soon the reconditioned disk lay on its steel buffers like a table on its legs. One problem resulted from the presence of this disk. It blocked the lower window. So even when they were rushing straight at the moon, it would be impossible for the travelers to keep an eye on her through this opening. Consequently they had to make do without it. However they could still see the vast lunar landscape out the side openings, just as you can look at the earth from an airship's gondola.

Positioning this disk was a good hour's work. It was afternoon by the time everything was ready. Barbicane took new readings on the projectile's tilt; but much to his annoyance, it hadn't swung around enough to start falling; it seemed to be traveling along a curve that ran parallel to the moon's disk. That silver orb was gleaming radiantly in space, while the golden orb opposite was a blazing fire.

The situation didn't inspire confidence.

"Will we get there?" Nicholl said.

"We'll proceed on that assumption," Barbicane replied.

"You scaremongers," Michel Ardan remarked. "We'll get there, and faster than we may like."

This response sent Barbicane back to his preparatory work, and he got busy readying the devices designed to slow their fall.

You may recall the drama at that rally held in Tampa, Florida, during which Captain Nicholl played the role of Barbicane's foe and Michel Ardan's opponent. When Captain Nicholl argued that the projectile would shatter like glass, Michel had replied he would slow its fall by using shrewdly positioned rockets.

In essence, with the projectile's base

262

as their launchpad, powerful explosives could blow up outside, create a recoil, and check the shell's speed to some extent. True, these rockets would have to burn in a vacuum, but they wouldn't be short of oxygen since they supplied it themselves, like those lunar volcanoes that can burn despite the moon's lack of atmosphere.

So Barbicane had come equipped with these explosives, which were packed in small tubes of threaded steel that could be screwed into the projectile's base. On the inside of the shell, these tubes were flush with the floor. Outside, they jutted six inches. There were twenty of them. An opening contrived in the disk allowed you to light the fuse on each. The result took place entirely outdoors. They'd tamped the detonation charges into the tubes beforehand. So all they had to do was pull out the metal plugs lodging in the base and replace them with these tubes, which fitted snugly into their holes.

Near three o'clock they'd finished this new chore, and after taking all these precautions, they had nothing left to do except wait.

Meanwhile the projectile was visibly closing in on the moon. To some extent it was obviously subject to her gravity, but its own impetus was also tugging it at an angle. The line of travel resulting from these two influences could take the shell off on a tangent. But the projectile definitely wasn't going to fall to the surface of the moon in the normal way, because its lower end, being heavier, already should have swung around toward her.

Barbicane's confidence shrank as he watched his shell withstand the moon's gravitational pull. The unknown was opening up in front of him, the unknown of interstellar space. He, the expert, thought he'd foreseen the three theoretical possibilities—falling back to the earth, falling to the moon, or staying stationary at the neutral line! And now a fourth possibility, fraught with all the terrors of the infinite, had unexpectedly surged into view. To face up to it without flinching, you needed to be a determined professional like Barbicane, a confirmed stoic like Nicholl, or a daring adventurer like Michel Ardan.

This now became the topic of conversation. Other men would have explored the question from a practical viewpoint. They would have wondered where their projectile coach was carrying them. Not these three. They looked for the cause that had produced this effect.

"So we've jumped the tracks," Michel said. "But why?"

"Despite all the precautions that were taken," Nicholl replied, "I very much fear the columbiad wasn't correctly angled. No matter how small the error was, it must have been enough to make us overshoot the moon's gravitational field."

"Then their aim was off?" Michel asked.

"I don't think so," Barbicane replied. "The cannon was absolutely vertical, it was unquestionably directed at the zenith overhead. Now then, once the moon reaches that zenith, we should hit her dead center. There's an additional argument, but it eludes me."

"Aren't we arriving too late?" Nicholl asked.

"Too late?" Barbicane put in.

"Yes," Nicholl went on. "The memo from the Cambridge Observatory maintains that we're to accomplish this flight in 97 hours, 13 minutes, and 20 seconds. Which means that if we arrive any sooner, the moon won't have made it to the point in question, and any later, she'll already be gone."

"Agreed," Barbicane replied. "But we left on December 1 at 10:46:40 in the evening, and we're supposed to arrive at midnight on the 5th, right when the moon is full. Now then, today is December 5. It's 3:30 in the afternoon, and another 8½ hours should be enough to take us to our destination. Why isn't it happening?"

"Could we be going too fast?" Nicholl responded. "Because we now know that our initial velocity was greater than it should have been."

"No, a hundred times no!" Barbicane responded. "Even if the projectile's going too fast, this wouldn't keep us from reaching the moon if our direction's right. No, our course has changed! Something has driven us off course."

"How? Why?" Nicholl asked.

"I can't say," Barbicane replied.

"Well then, Barbicane," Michel said, "would you like to know my views on this question of what drove us off course?"

"Go on."

"I wouldn't give fifty cents for the answer. We're off course and that's that. It makes no difference where we're heading! We'll soon find out. Hell's bells, we're being dragged through space, so we'll definitely end up falling into some gravitational field or other."

Michel Ardan's lack of concern didn't appease Barbicane. It wasn't that he was worried about the future, but about why his projectile had gone off course—he wanted to figure this out at any cost.

Meanwhile the shell continued to move sideways toward the moon, escorted by the retinue of objects tossed out of it. From prominent landmarks on the moon, now less than 5,000 miles away, Barbicane could even verify that they'd started moving at a uniform speed. Fresh proof they weren't falling. The projectile's thrust was still winning out over the moon's gravitational pull, but its flight path was definitely bringing it closer to the lunar disk, and there was a chance that when it got closer still, the force of gravity would take over and ultimately cause it to fall.

Having nothing better to do, our three friends stayed on watch. But they still couldn't make out the details of the moon's topography. All her surface features were flattened by the direct sunlight.

Consequently they peered out the side windows till eight o'clock in the evening. By then that silver orb had grown so big as they looked, it concealed a good half of the firmament. From opposite sides both sun and moon flooded the projectile with light.

By this point Barbicane thought he could put the distance separating them from their destination at just 1,750 miles. He judged that the projectile's speed was over 200 yards per second, hence about 410 miles per hour. Under the influence of centripetal force, the shell's base was showing a tendency to swing toward the moon; but centrifugal force was still winning out, so their linear flight path

seemed likely to change into some sort of curve, its nature still undetermined. . . .

Barbicane kept looking for a solution to his insoluble problem.

The hours went by to no effect. The projectile was obviously closing in on the moon, but it was equally obvious that they wouldn't reach her. As for how near they would come, this depended on the two forces, one attracting and one repelling, that were courting this moving object.

"All I want," Michel kept saying, "is to get close enough to probe the moon's secrets!"

"A thousand curses on whatever caused our projectile to go off course!" Nicholl exclaimed.

"In that case," Barbicane replied, as if an idea had suddenly occurred to him, "curse that meteor we passed on the way!"

"Huh?" Michel Ardan put in.

"What do you mean?" Nicholl snapped.

"I mean," Barbicane said in a decisive tone, "that our going off course is entirely due to our meeting up with that rambling space rock."

"But it didn't even graze us," Michel replied.

"That makes no difference. Compared to our projectile, its mass was enormous, so its gravitational pull was enough to affect our course."

"Only minimally!" Nicholl exclaimed.

"Yes, Nicholl, but as minimal as it was," Barbicane replied, "over a distance of 210,000 miles, that's all it took to make us miss the moon!"

10

THE MOONWATCHERS

CLEARLY BARBICANE HAD hit on the only plausible reason for their going off course. As small as it was, it had been enough to change the projectile's flight path. This was sheer bad luck. Due to a completely accidental occurrence, their daring endeavor had gone haywire, and unless there were some exceptional developments, they would no longer be able to reach the moon's disk.

Would they pass near enough to resolve certain matters of physics or geology that hadn't been settled as yet? This was the only question currently worrying these bold travelers. As for whatever fate the future had in store for them, they didn't give it a thought. But what would happen to them in the midst of this infinite emptiness, these men whose air would soon run out? A few more days and they would die of asphyxiation in this shell, which was now wandering at random. But for these stalwarts a few days were as good as centuries, and they devoted every second of their time to examining that moon they no longer had any hope of reaching.

By that point you could put the distance separating the projectile from the earth's satellite at about 500 miles. When it came to viewing the moon's surface features, our travelers were farther away under these circumstances than earthlings equipped with high-powered telescopes.

In fact, as you know, the Earl of Rosse assembled an instrument in Parsonstown, Ireland that magnifies 6,500 times, bringing the moon within forty miles; better still, the high-powered mechanism set up on Long's Peak can magnify that silver orb 48,000 times, making for a viewing distance of less than five miles, and objects over thirty feet across are distinct enough to be studied.

Hence, at their current distance the details of the moon's topography couldn't be closely scrutinized without a spyglass. A person's eyes grasped the general outlines of those huge hollows incorrectly called "seas" but couldn't identify their actual nature. The mountains lost their upthrust in that magnificent glare caused by the sun's reflected rays. An onlooker instinctively turned away, as dazzled as if peering into a pool of molten silver.

Even so, the oval shape of that heavenly body was already apparent. She looked like a gigantic egg, her small end facing the earth. In reality, when the moon was first being formed, she had the appearance of a perfect sphere and was either liquid or ductile; but she soon got caught in the earth's gravitational pull and was stretched out of shape by its force of attraction. Turning into a satellite,

she lost the symmetrical contours of her birth; her center of gravity was distinctly *off* center, and due to this state of things, some experts drew the conclusion that the moon's air and water had managed to take refuge on her opposite side, which can't be seen from the earth.

This modification of our satellite's original contours was noticeable for only a few seconds. The moon very quickly drew closer thanks to the projectile's speed, which was considerably slower than its initial velocity though eight or nine times faster than any express train. The shell's going off at an angle—due to the very nature of the angle itself—left Michel Ardan hopeful of bumping into the lunar disk at some point or other. He refused to believe they weren't going to reach her. Yes, he refused to believe it and said so time and again! But Barbicane, a better judge of the facts, never failed to answer him with pitiless logic:

"No, no, Michel! We can reach the moon only by falling to her surface and we aren't doing so. Centripetal force keeps us within range of the moon's gravity, while centrifugal force pulls us irresistibly away."

This was said in a tone that removed Michel Ardan's last hopes.

The projectile was closing in on our satellite's northern hemisphere, which moon maps place at the bottom, because these maps are generally drafted to match the images supplied by spyglasses, and as you know, spyglasses show things upside down. This was the case with Beer and Mädler's *Mappa Selenographica*, which Barbicane consulted. On this map the northerly hemisphere displayed wide plains broken up by isolated mountains.

At midnight the moon was full. Right then the travelers should have been setting foot on her, if that ill-omened meteor hadn't driven them off course. So the earth's satellite was arriving under the conditions meticulously calculated by the Cambridge Observatory. With mathematical precision she'd reached her perigee at the zenith of the 28th parallel. An eyewitness standing at the bottom of that enormous columbiad—whose aim was at an exact right angle to the horizon—would have

265

seen the moon framed in the cannon's mouth. A straight line from the axis point of the piece would have gone right through the center of that silver orb.

No need to mention that during the night of December 5–6, our travelers didn't rest for a second. How could they shut their eyes while so near to this new world? No way. They put every ounce of their energy into a single objective: keep looking! These three represented the entire earth, they stood for all mankind past and present, through their eyes the whole human race was gaping at those lunar regions and probing our satellite's secrets! Their hearts throbbed with excitement and they went silently from one window to the other.

Their findings, which Barbicane recorded, were meticulously accurate. They had spyglasses for making them, maps for double-checking them.

The first moonwatcher was Galileo. His inadequate spyglass magnified only thirty times. Nevertheless, seeing those patches scattered over the lunar disk "like the eyes on a peacock's tail," he was the first to identify them as mountains and he estimated the elevations of a few peaks, giving them an exaggerated height equal to 1/20 of the disk's visible width, hence about 27,000 feet. Galileo didn't draw up any map of his findings.

A few years later Johannes Hevelius, an astronomer from Danzig, used procedures that were correct only twice a month during the moon's first and last quarters, reducing Galileo's peaks to just 1/26 of that disk width. An exaggeration in the other direction. Even so, he's the scholar we have to thank for our first moon map. On it the clear round patches represent circular mountains, and the dark patches indicate wide seas, which in reality are only plains. He named these mountains and expanses of water after surface features on the earth. On his map you'll see a Mt. Sinai in the middle of a second Arabia, a Mt. Etna in the center of another Sicily, new versions of the Alps, Apennines, and Carpathians, then the Mediterranean, Sea of Azov, Black Sea, and Caspian Sea. But these monikers are misnomers, because neither the mountains nor the seas

have shapes resembling their namesakes on the earth. Take that wide white spot on his map, which joins still-bigger landmasses to its south and ends in a cape—it's hard to recognize this as an upside-down image of India's peninsula, the Bay of Bengal, and Cochin China. Accordingly these names were dropped. Another mapmaker, somebody with a better knowledge of what makes people tick, proposed a new naming system that had instant appeal to human vanity.

This skywatcher was Father Riccioli, one of Hevelius's contemporaries. The map he drew up was crude and crammed with errors. But he named the lunar mountains after great men of antiquity and the scientists of his own era, a custom mostly followed to this day.

A third moon map appeared in the 17th century, the work of Domenico Cassini; though better drawn than Riccioli's, its proportions aren't accurate. Several miniature versions of it were published, and the royal press at the Louvre kept its brass printing plates for many years, then finally sold them by the pound for scrap metal.

Philippe de La Hire, a famous draftsman and mathematician, drew up a moon map thirteen feet high, but it was never engraved.

Following him, about midway through the 18th century, a German astronomer named Tobias Mayer undertook to publish a magnificent map of the moon's physical features, using measurements he'd meticulously verified; but his death in 1762 kept him from finishing this worthy task.

Next came Johann Schröter from Lilienthal, who sketched many moon maps, then one Lorhmann from Dresden, whom we have to thank for a layout divided into twenty-five sections, four of which have been engraved.

It was in 1830 that Messrs. Beer and Mädler rendered their famous *Mappa Selenographica* by tracing over an orthographic projection.[4] This map faithfully reproduces the lunar disk as it appears to our eyes, but the shapes of its mountains and plains are accurate only in the central part; elsewhere in the northern, southern, eastern, or western

---

[4] *Translator's note.* View of an object projected onto a drawing surface.

parts, these shapes are foreshortened and aren't comparable to those in the center. Thirty-seven inches high and divided into four parts, this topographic map is a masterpiece of lunar cartography.

Among later experts, we'll mention the relief maps of the moon's surface features by the German astronomer Julius Schmidt, the topographic work of Father Secchi, those magnificent photographic prints by the English enthusiast Warren De la Rue, and finally a map based on an orthographic projection by Messrs. Lecouturier and Chapuis—issued in 1860, it was an unusually fine example of clear draftsmanship and cogent design.

So much for this laundry list of different maps depicting the lunar world. Barbicane had two in his possession, Beer's and Mädler's plus the one by Messrs. Chapuis and Lecouturier. They were to make his moonwatching work a good deal easier.

As for the optical instruments at their disposal, there were some excellent nautical spyglasses manufactured specifically for this journey. They magnified objects a hundred times. Consequently they could bring the moon within a viewing distance of less than 2,500 miles from the earth. But just then, around three o'clock in the morning, their distance didn't exceed 75 miles, and in a setting that never suffered from bad weather, their instruments were to bring the ground on the moon within 5,000 feet.

11

FACT AND FANCY

"HAVE YOU EVER seen the moon?" a teacher sarcastically asked one of his pupils.

"No, sir," the pupil remarked even more sarcastically. "But I have to admit I've heard about the place."

In a sense the pupil's humorous answer could be given by the vast majority of mortal beings. How many people have heard about the moon but have never seen her . . . at least not through the eyepiece of a spyglass or telescope! How many have never even examined a map of the earth's satellite!

When we look at a map of the moon's physical features, one oddity strikes us right off.

In contrast to the arrangement adopted on the earth and Mars, the moon's continents lie primarily in the southern hemisphere of her globe. These continents don't boast the clean, clear outlines of South America, Africa, and India's peninsula. Their angular, erratic, deeply chiseled coasts are full of bays and capes. They're instantly reminiscent of the mass confusion in the Sunda Islands of Malaysia, where the land is extremely broken up. If any ships ever navigated over the surface of the moon, it must have been an exceptionally difficult and dangerous activity, and those lunar seamen and hydrographers were to be pitied—the latter as they surveyed the tortuous shorelines, the former as they made for those hazardous landing places.

You'll also note that on the lunar globe, her south pole is a much fuller landmass than her north pole. This last is nothing but a skimpy patch of ground separated from the other continents by wide seas.[5] To the south landmasses cover nearly the whole hemisphere. So it's possible moonpeople have already planted a flag on one of their poles, while the likes of such terrestrial explorers as Franklin, Ross, Kane, Dumont d'Urville, and Lambert still haven't managed to reach that unknown spot on the planet earth.

As for islands, they're plentiful on the surface of the moon. Nearly all of them are oval or as circular as if drawn with a pair of compasses, and they seem to form a huge group similar to those delightful isles scattered between Greece and Asia Minor, a region mythology once livened up with its most appealing legends. The names of such islands as Naxos, Tenedos, Milo, and Karpathos automatically spring to mind, and you instantly look around for the vessel captained by Ulysses or the "clipper" of the Argonauts. At least that's the effect this region had on Michel Ardan—they were the Greek Isles that he saw on the map. To the eyes of his

---

[5] It's understood, of course, that this word "seas" refers to those huge areas that most likely were underwater in the past but today are only wide plains.

less fanciful companions, the appearance of these coastlines was more reminiscent of the sliced-up lands of New Brunswick and Nova Scotia, and where our Frenchman found the traces of fabled heroes, these Americans were pointing out the most favorable sites for opening trading posts in the interests of lunar commerce and industry.

To finish this description of the land-locked part of the moon, here are a few words on the layout of her mountains. Her chains of pinnacles, solitary peaks, basins, and crevices are easy to spot. The moon's most rugged terrain is confined to this section. Here it's amazingly craggy. You've got an immense Switzerland, an ongoing Norway where volcanic action has affected everything. This deeply carved surface came from consecutive contractions of the moon's crust back when this heavenly body was in the process of being formed. Therefore this lunar disk is a promising locale for studying your major geological phenomena. As certain astronomers have noted, her surface, though older than the earth's, has actually aged less. There are no seas to spoil her primitive features and increasingly smooth everything over, nor any air with a corroding effect that could change the outlines of her mountains. Here the fruits of volcanic activity can be seen in all their original glory, unchanged by water erosion. The earth was like this before swamps and streams coated it with layers of sediment.

After roaming these wide landmasses, a person's eyes are caught by even wider seas. Their organization, location, and appearance are all reminiscent of the earth's oceans; like the earth's, moreover, these seas take up the greater part of the globe. And yet they aren't bodies of water but plains, whose nature the travelers soon hoped to determine.

Astronomers, it must be conceded, have adorned these so-called seas with names that are peculiar to say the least, though science honors them to this day. Michel Ardan was right to compare a moon map to that board game "The Map of the Heart," which was played by romantic folks like Madeleine de Scudéry or Cyrano de Bergerac.

"Only," he added, "it's no longer the maudlin map of the 17th century, it's the map of life, quite neatly divided into two parts, one feminine and the other masculine. The right half of the moon's sphere is for women, the left for men!"

Whenever he went on like this, Michel left his matter-of-fact companions shrugging their shoulders. Barbicane and Nicholl looked at a moon map from a viewpoint quite unlike their fanciful friend's. However their fanciful friend may have been right about a few things. You be the judge.

In the left half of the lunar globe sat the "Sea of Clouds," where human reason so often founders. Not far away appeared the "Sea of Rain," fed by all the cares of life. Nearby lay the "Ocean of Storms," where folks wage continual war with their passions, too often losing the battle. Then, exhausted by deceit, treachery, infidelity, and the whole retinue of worldly woes, what do people find at the end of their careers? That vast "Sea of Moods," barely sweetened by a few drops from the "Bay of Dew." Clouds, rain, storms, moods—does a human life include anything else, and don't these four words say it all?

The right half, "for ladies only," contains smaller seas, whose meaningful names take in all the incidents of a feminine existence. There's the "Sea of Serenity," a mirror into which young women peer, and the "Lake of Dreams," which reflects a smiling future! There's the "Sea of Nectar" with its waves of affection and breezes of love! There's the "Sea of Fertility," the "Sea of Crises," then the "Sea of Low Spirits," whose dimensions are maybe too modest, and finally that vast "Sea of Tranquillity," which swallows up every false passion, futile dream, and unquenched desire, and whose waves empty peacefully into the "Lake of Death!"

What an odd sequence of names! What a quaint way of characterizing the moon's two halves, pairing them like husband and wife, fashioning this realm of existence out in space! As for our fanciful Michel, wasn't he right to interpret the old astronomers' whimsies in this manner?

But while his imagination was "roving the seas," his earnest companions were looking at things more geographically. They were learning this new world by heart. They were measuring her angles and diameters.

For Barbicane and Nicholl, the Sea of Clouds was an immense hollow in the ground that was dotted with a few circular mountains while largely covering the west side of the southern hemisphere; it took up about 1,150,000 square miles and its center was located in latitude 15° south and longitude 20° east. The Ocean of Storms, *Oceanus Procellarum*, the widest plain on the moon's disk, embraced a surface area of some 2,050,000 square miles, its center being in latitude 10° north and longitude 45° east. From the heart of it rose those wonderfully luminous mountains named after Kepler and Aristarchus.

More to the north and separated from the Sea of Clouds by lofty mountain chains, the Sea of Rain, *Mare Imbrium*, had its center point in latitude 35° north and longitude 20° east; it was almost circular in shape and covered an area of over 1,200,000 square miles. Not far off was the Sea of Moods, *Mare Humorum*, a little bowl only measuring about 275,000 square miles and located in latitude 25° south and longitude 40° east. Finally three bays stood out as well on the shores of this half of the moon's sphere: the Bay of Heat, the Bay of Dew, and the Bay of Rainbows, little plains fenced in by lofty mountain chains.

The "feminine" half—with a mind of its own, naturally—featured seas that were smaller and more plentiful. These were: to the north the Sea of Cold, *Mare Frigoris*, in latitude 55° north and longitude 0°, boasting a surface area of about 475,000 square miles, and bordering on the Lake of Death and the Lake of Dreams; the Sea of Serenity, *Mare Serenitatis*, found in latitude 25° north and longitude 20° west and encompassing a surface area of some 537,000 square miles; the Sea of Crises, *Mare Crisium*, in latitude 17° north and longitude 55° west, well defined, quite round, and embracing a surface area of nearly 250,000 square miles—an honest-to-goodness Caspian Sea hidden inside a belt of mountains. Then at the equator the Sea of Tranquillity, *Mare Tranquillitatis*, could be

seen in latitude 5° north and longitude 25° west, taking up some 759,000 square miles; to the south this sea connected with the Sea of Nectar, *Mare Nectaris*, an expanse of about 180,000 square miles in latitude 15° south and longitude 35° west, and to the east it connected with the Sea of Fertility, *Mare Fecunditatis*, the widest in this half of the moon's sphere, taking up around 1,370,000 square miles in latitude 3° south and longitude 50° west. Finally, to the far north and far south, two other seas were visible—the Sea of Humboldt, *Mare Humboldtianum*, whose surface area was over 40,000 square miles, and the Southern Sea, *Mare Australe*, with a surface area of more than 160,000 square miles.

In the middle of the lunar disk, straddling the equator and the zero meridian, lay the Bay of the Center, *Sinus Medii*, a kind of hyphen linking the two halves.

That's how Nicholl's and Barbicane's eyes sorted out the whole visible surface of the earth's satellite. When they added up the different measurements, they found that the area of this half was some 29,610,000 square miles, of which about 20,720,000 square miles were volcanoes, mountain chains, basins, and islands—in short, everything that seemed to make up the solid part of the moon—while about 8,810,000 square miles were seas, lakes, and swamps—everything that seemed to make up the liquid part. None of this, however, was of the slightest interest to our good Michel.

This half sphere, as you can see, is less than a thirteenth the size of the earth's. Even so, lunar scholars have already counted over 50,000 craters! Consequently this surface is blistered, cracked, and as full of holes as a skimming spoon; in other words, it's worthy of that far from poetic designation the English have given it—"green cheese."

Michel Ardan leaped up when Barbicane spoke this discourteous name.

"So this is the respect," he exclaimed, "that 19th century Anglo-Saxons show to lovely Diana, fair Phoebe, sweet Iris, charming Astarte, the Queen of the Night, Jupiter's daughter by Latona, and the little sister of glorious Apollo!"

12

MOUNTAIN MATTERS

THE PROJECTILE'S HEADING, as we've already indicated, was taking it toward the moon's northern hemisphere. Our travelers were far from that center point they were scheduled to hit before their flight plan suffered an irreparable change in course.

It was 12:30 in the morning. At this juncture Barbicane put their distance at 870 miles, a little longer than the moon's radius and sure to decrease as they drew nearer to her north pole. By then the projectile wasn't level with the equator but abreast of the 10th parallel—and from this latitude up to the pole, as they carefully reckoned on their map, Barbicane and his two companions could study the moon under optimum conditions.

With the help of their spyglasses, in fact, this distance of 870 miles shrank to 8.7 miles, hence 3½ geographic leagues. That telescope in the Rocky Mountains could bring the moon closer still, but the earth's atmosphere significantly weakened its optical power. Stationed in his projectile and looking through his pocket binoculars, Barbicane could accordingly view certain surface features that weren't visible to moonwatchers on the earth.

"My friends," said the Gun Club's president in a solemn voice, "I don't know where we're heading, I don't know if we'll ever see the planet earth again. Nevertheless let's proceed as if our research will someday benefit our fellow mortals. Let's forget all our worries and free up our minds. We're astronomers. This shell is a workroom at the Cambridge Observatory transferred into outer space. Let's start our investigations."

After that they conducted their research with tremendous diligence, faithfully recording changes in the moon's appearance at the different distances where the projectile hovered in relation to her.

Right when the shell was level with the 10th parallel north, it seemed to be heading faithfully up longitude 20° east.

Here we'll make an important comment about the chart they were using in their investigations. In moon maps based on images supplied by spyglasses, the south is above and the north below, because these instruments show things upside down; given this inversion, it would seem natural for the east to be on the left and the west on the right. But this isn't the case. If the map were turned downside up and it displayed the moon as we see her, the east would still be on the left and the west still on the right, the opposite of earth maps. Here's the reason for this anomaly. Skywatchers located in the northern hemisphere—in Europe, say—see the moon to the south in relation to themselves. When they study her, their backs are to the north, the reverse of where they'll be when these folks look at an earth map. Since their backs are to the north, the east is on their left and the west on their right. To skywatchers located in the southern hemisphere—in Patagonia, for instance—the moon's west would be properly on their left and her east on their right, since the south is behind them.

That's the reason for this seeming reversal of the two compass points, and it's essential to take this into account while keeping an eye on President Barbicane's investigations.

With the help of Beer and Mädler's *Mappa Selenographica*, the travelers could instantly identify any portion of the lunar disk framed in the fields of their spyglasses.

"What are we seeing right now?" Michel asked.

"The northerly part of the Sea of Clouds," Barbicane replied. "We're too far away to determine its character. Are those plains composed of dry sand, as the earliest astronomers claimed? Are they only immense forests, in line with Mr. Warren De la Rue's thinking, which gives the moon a very dense but low-lying atmosphere? That's something we'll find out later. We won't draw any conclusions till we're qualified to."

This Sea of Clouds is rather sketchily defined on the maps. Supposedly this wide plain is littered with chunks of lava spewed out of those volcanoes close to its right-hand side, Ptolemy, Purbach, and Arzachel. But the projectile was moving ahead, drawing noticeably nearer, and soon some peaks appeared, closing off the northerly end of this sea. To the front stood a luminous mountain in all its beauty, its summit hidden from sight behind an outburst of solar rays.

"That's . . . ?" Michel asked.

"Copernicus," Barbicane replied.

"Let's give Copernicus a look."

Located in latitude 9° north and longitude 20° east, this pinnacle rises to a height of 11,280 feet above the level of our satellite's surface. It's quite visible from the earth, and astronomers can study it thoroughly, especially during the phase that occurs between the last quarter and the new moon, because at that point shadows fall lengthwise from east to west, letting you calculate its elevation.

After Tycho, which is located in the southern hemisphere, Copernicus boasts the most prominent network of bright rays on the moon. Like a gigantic lighthouse, it towers in isolation over the part of the Sea of Clouds that's next to the Ocean of Storms, and it sheds its magnificent radiance on both oceans at the same time. Those long luminous trails were a matchless sight, so dazzling during the full moon, crossing over the boundary of mountain chains to the north and going as far as the Sea of Rain before fading out. It was one o'clock in the morning earth time, and like a hot air balloon carried off into space, the projectile looked down on this splendid mountain.

Barbicane could accurately identify its chief characteristics. Copernicus belongs to the category of circular mountains, the first order in the division of large basins. Like Kepler and Aristarchus, which overlook the Ocean of Storms, it has sometimes gleamed through the gray light like a blazing spark, causing it to be mistaken for a volcanic eruption. But it's only an extinct volcano like all the others on that side of the moon. It measured about fifty-five miles across, rampart to rampart. Their spyglasses revealed traces of stratification produced by consecutive outpourings, and the whole neighborhood seemed to be littered with volcanic waste, a fair amount still visible inside the crater itself.

"There are several kinds of basins on the surface of the moon," Barbicane said, "and it's easy to see that Copernicus belongs to the variety notable for its bright rays. If we were closer, we could spot those cones that garnish its insides and that used to be volcanic vents. An unusual characteristic, which is consistent on the moon, is that the inner surfaces of these basins go significantly below ground level, unlike the structure seen in craters on the earth. As a result, the overall curve at the bottom of each basin is a miniature version of the moon's spherical shape."

"And what's the reason for this distinctive characteristic?" Nicholl asked.

"Nobody knows," Barbicane replied.

"What marvelously bright rays!" Michel kept saying. "A lovelier sight would be hard to imagine!"

"Then what would you say," Barbicane responded, "if traveler's luck takes us to the southern hemisphere?"

"Hopefully I'll say it's lovelier still!" Michel Ardan remarked.

Just then the projectile looked straight down on this basin. The ramparts of Copernicus formed a nearly perfect circle and its ultra steep walls stood out clearly. You could even detect a second ring of rock inside. All around it stretched a grayish, wild-looking plain whose surface features were highlighted in yellow. On the basin's floor, like jewels in a case, two or three volcanic cones sparkled for a second as if they were enormous dazzling gemstones. To the north the walls receded, forming a valley that very likely gave access to the crater's interior.

While passing over the surrounding plains, Barbicane could take note of a good many less-important mountains, among others a small circular one named Gay-Lussac that measured some fourteen miles across. To the south the plain looked extremely flat, not a single bulge, not a single projection above ground. To the north as far as the Ocean of Storms, however, it resembled a liquid surface agitated by a hurricane, and its peaks and swellings looked like a sequence of waves suddenly taking form. Across this whole expanse, luminous trails ran in from every direction, converging on the summit of Copernicus. Some were over eighteen miles wide, their lengths incalculable.

Our travelers discussed the origin of these strange rays, no more able to determine their nature than moonwatchers on the earth.

"But why," Nicholl said, "couldn't these rays simply be spurs of mountains that reflect sunlight more intensely?"

"Not possible," Barbicane replied. "If that were the case, these ridges would cast shadows under certain lunar conditions. Now then, they don't do any such thing."

In essence these rays are visible only when the sun is directly opposite the moon, and they vanish as soon as the sunlight shines at an angle.

"But what have they come up with to explain those light trails?" Michel asked. "Because I refuse to believe scientists are ever at a loss for an explanation!"

"It's true," Barbicane replied, "that Herschel made his views known, but he didn't dare offer them as conclusive."

"Never mind. What were his views?"

"He thought those rays must have been streams of hardened lava that glittered under normal sunlight. Maybe so, but it's far from a certainty. If we pass nearer to Tycho, however, we'll be in a better position to identify what's causing those bright rays."

"My friends," Michel said, "do you know what that plain looks like from this far up?"

"No," Nicholl replied.

"Well, since all those bits of lava are as skinny as spindles, it looks like an immense game of pick up sticks tossed around helter-skelter. All that's missing is a hook for pulling them out one by one."

"Can't you ever be serious!" Barbicane said.

"Seriously then," Michel remarked in a serene voice, "let's say bones instead of sticks. This way the plain could simply be a vast cemetery covered with the mortal remains of a thousand deceased generations. Do you like this highfalutin comparison better?"

"One's as bad as the other," Barbicane remarked.

"Holy smoke, you're hard to please!" Michel replied.

"My good friend," continued the practical Barbicane, "it makes no difference what it looks like, when we don't know what it *is*."

"Excellent answer!" Michel exclaimed. "That'll teach me to argue with an expert."

Meanwhile the projectile was moving ahead, going around the lunar disk at a speed that was nearly uniform. As you can readily imagine, our travelers didn't dream of resting, not for a second. Every minute brought a change in the scenery speeding by under their eyes. Near 1:30 in the morning, they glimpsed the upper reaches of another mountain. Checking his map, Barbicane identified it as Eratosthenes.

It was a circular mountain over 14,700 feet high, one of those basins so plentiful on the earth's satellite. Pertinent to this, Barbicane told his friends about Kepler's odd views on the formation of these basins. According to that famous mathematician, these crater-shaped cavities had been dug by human hands.

"For what purpose?" Nicholl asked.

"For a perfectly understandable purpose," Barbicane replied. "The moonpeople would have undertaken these immense labors and dug these enormous holes in order to take refuge in them—to stay protected from the sun's rays, which beat down on them for two weeks at a time."

"Those moonpeople were no fools!" Michel said.

"An odd notion," Nicholl replied. "But it's likely that Kepler didn't know the real dimensions of these basins, because digging them would have been a job for giants, hardly feasible for moonpeople!"

"Why not?" Michel said. "On the surface of the moon, isn't gravity only a sixth of what it is on the earth?"

"But what if moonpeople are only a sixth as big?" Nicholl remarked.

"And what if there *aren't* any moonpeople?" Barbicane added. Which shut down the discussion.

Soon Eratosthenes vanished below the horizon without the projectile's getting close enough for them to carefully scrutinize it. This peak separated the Apennines from the Carpathians.

Among the moon's pinnacles you can make out several mountain chains distributed chiefly over her northern hemisphere. However some also reside in certain parts of her southern hemisphere.

Here's a table of these different chains listed from south to north, along with their latitudes and the elevations of their loftiest peaks:

Mountains:	Latitudes:	Elevations:
Dörfel	84° south	24,944 ft.
Leibnitz	65° "	24,934 "
Rook	20° to 30° "	5,249 "
Altai	17° to 28° "	13,278 "
Cordillera	10° to 20° "	12,789 "
Pyrenees	8° to 18° "	11,913 "
Ural	5° to 13° "	2,749 "
D'Alembert	4° to 10° "	19,183 "
Haemus	8° to 21° north	6,631 "
Carpathian	15° to 19° "	6,362 "
Apennine	14° to 27° "	18,048 "
Taurus	21° to 28° "	9,009 "
Ripheus	25° to 33° "	13,684 "
Hercynian	17° to 33° "	3,839 "
Caucasus	32° to 41° "	18,264 "
Alps	42° to 49° "	11,867 "

The most prominent of these different chains are the Apennines, 375 miles in length—which is less, however, than the major mountain systems on the earth. The Apennines skirt the east coast of the Sea of Rain and continue to the north as the Carpathians, whose geological profile measures about 250 miles.

The travelers could glimpse only the upper part of these Apennines, which are laid out between longitude 10° west and longitude 16° east; but the Carpathian chain stretched under their eyes from longitude 18° to 30° east, and they could appreciate its characteristics.

One theory struck them as thoroughly justified. Noticing that here and there this Carpathian chain took on a circular shape and was overlooked by peaks, they concluded this range used to feature prominent basins. These circular mountains must have partially broken up during the huge eruption that created the Sea of Rain. In appearance these Carpathians were what the Purbach, Arzachel, and Ptolemy basins might have been, assuming some cataclysm had knocked down their left-hand ramparts and transformed them into a continuous chain. They boasted an average elevation of 10,500 feet, an elevation comparable to certain parts of the Pyrenees on the earth, such as the valley of Pineda. Their southerly slopes dropped abruptly down to the immense Sea of Rain.

Near two o'clock in the morning, Barbicane found they were level with the 20th lunar parallel and not far from a small mountain 5,115 feet high, which goes by the name Pythias. The projectile's distance from the moon didn't exceed 750 miles, which their spyglasses reduced to 7½.

The *Mare Imbrium*, or Sea of Rain, spread out under our travelers' eyes like an immense valley whose features were still barely visible. Near it on the left stood Mt. Lambert, whose elevation has been put at 5,948 feet, and farther on by the edge of the Ocean of Storms, luminous Mt. Euler shines in latitude 23° north and longitude 29° east. This mountain rose just 5,955 feet above the lunar surface and was the subject of some interesting research by the astronomer Johann Schröter. Trying to identify how these lunar mountains had originated, this scientist wondered if each crater always ended up having the right amount of space to hold the ramparts forming it. Now then, this perfect fit turned out to be generally the case, so Schröter concluded that a single outpouring of volcanic waste was all it took to form these ramparts, because additional outpourings would have upset the balance. Only Mt. Euler belied this general rule—it must have required several consecutive outpourings when it was formed, since its cavity had twice the space needed to hold its surrounding wall.

These various theories were all very well for some earthbound skywatcher whose instrument functioned only in a limited way. But Barbicane wasn't willing to settle for them, and seeing that his projectile was drawing steadily nearer to the moon's disk, he hoped that if he couldn't reach her, at least he could discover the secrets of her formation.

13

LUNAR SCENERY

BY 2:30 IN THE MORNING, the shell hovered abreast of the 13th lunar parallel, at an actual distance of some 620 miles but a viewing distance their optical instruments had reduced to about 6¼. There still seemed to be no possibility they could reach any part of the lunar disk. They were orbiting at a comparatively moderate speed, which President Barbicane found bewildering. At this distance from the moon, it would take considerable velocity to withstand her gravitational pull. So the reason for this phenomenon remained elusive. Anyhow there wasn't time to look for the cause. The moon's surface features were parading under our travelers' eyes, and they didn't want to miss a single detail.

As seen through their spyglasses, then, the lunar disk was 6¼ miles away. If a balloonist were carried that far above the earth, how much could he make out on its surface? We can't say, since the highest flights haven't gone more than 5 miles up.

Meanwhile here's an accurate description of what Barbicane and his companions saw from that altitude.

Broad swatches of pigment appeared over the moon's disk, covering a fair range of colors. Lunar scholars aren't in agreement on the nature of these pigments. There are a variety of them and they're pretty sharply contrasted. Julius Schmidt claims that if the earth's oceans dried up and a lunar skywatcher compared those oceans to our globe's inland plains, they wouldn't offer as great a range of distinct shades as the moon shows to skywatchers on the earth. According to him, the color common to those wide plains called "seas" is a dark gray mixed with green and brown. A few big craters also feature this pigmentation.

Barbicane was acquainted with the views of this lunar specialist from Germany, views shared by Messrs. Beer and Mädler. His own eyes verified that they were right and not certain astronomers who acknowledged only gray pigments on the surface of the moon. In some areas the color green was exception-

ally distinct, being conspicuous, according to Julius Schmidt, in the Sea of Serenity and Sea of Moods. Barbicane likewise noticed some wide craters that hadn't any cones inside and were giving off a bluish color, like the gleam from a shiny new piece of boiler plate steel. These pigments were truly intrinsic to the moon's disk and weren't caused, as some astronomers say, by a spyglass's flawed objective lens or by the intervention of the earth's atmosphere. Barbicane had no doubts on this score. He was viewing them out in space and couldn't have made any optical errors. He accepted these different pigments as a proven scientific fact. Did that mean these shades of green came from tropical vegetation thriving in a dense, low-lying atmosphere? He still couldn't make up his mind.

Farther off he noted a reddish hue that was distinct enough. A comparable shade had already been spotted on the floor of a remote basin named Lichtenberg Crater, which is located near the Hercynian Mountains on the edge of the moon; even so, he couldn't discover its nature.

He wasn't any luckier with another lunar oddity whose cause he couldn't accurately define. Here's that oddity.

Michel Ardan was on watch next to the Gun Club's president, when he noticed some long white lines shining intensely in the direct sunlight. It was a sequence of luminous furrows very different from the bright rays Copernicus had recently displayed. They lay parallel to each other.

With his usual breeziness Michel didn't fail to exclaim:

"Say! Tilled fields!"

"Tilled fields?" Nicholl responded, shrugging his shoulders.

"Plowed at least," Michel Ardan contended. "But what farmhands these moon-people have got to be, and what gigantic oxen they must hitch to their plows to cut such furrows!"

"They aren't furrows," Barbicane said, "they're rills."

"Go on with your rills," Michel replied genially. "Just what do you mean by rills, in a scientific sense?"

Barbicane promptly told his companion

what he knew about lunar rills. He knew that such furrows had been spotted on every lowland part of the moon's disk; that isolated examples of these furrows very often measured from 10 to 125 miles in length; that they ran from 3,000 to 5,000 feet wide, and that their edges were absolutely parallel; but he didn't know anything more about their formation or their nature.

Using his spyglass, Barbicane examined these rills with the greatest care. He noticed that their edges consisted of ultra steep slopes. They were long parallel ramparts, and with a little imagination you could accept them as lengthy lines of fortifications erected by lunar engineers.

Some of these different rills were as flawlessly straight as if they'd been drawn with a tape measure. Others had gentle curves, though their edges always stayed parallel. The latter intersected each other; the former cut across craters. Here, they plowed through routine cavities such as the Posidonius or Petavius basins; there, they streaked over whole seas such as the Sea of Serenity.

These local irregularities inevitably fired the imaginations of astronomers on the earth. Their initial moonwatching hadn't turned up these rills. Neither Hevelius, Cassini, La Hire, nor Herschel seems to have been aware of them. It was Schröter who first brought them to scientific notice in 1789. After him others such as Pastorff, Gruithuisen, Beer, and Mädler studied these furrows. As many as seventy have been counted to date. But though we know their number, we still haven't determined their nature. They definitely aren't fortifications, any more than they're old dried-up riverbeds, because for one thing, water is so scarce on our satellite's surface that it couldn't have carved itself any spillways, and for another, these furrows often go across craters located at high elevations.

It must be acknowledged, however, that Michel Ardan came up with an explanation— and without realizing it, this time he fell in with Julius Schmidt's thinking.

"Why couldn't those bewildering sights," he said, "simply be a phenomenon caused by vegetation?"

"What do you mean?" Barbicane asked instantly.

"Easy, my dear president," Michel replied. "Couldn't those dark lines making up that barricade be trees planted in neat rows?"

"So you're in favor," Barbicane said, "of calling them vegetation?"

"I'm in favor," Michel Ardan remarked, "of explaining what all you experts can't! At least my theory would have the advantage of suggesting why these rills vanish, or seem to vanish, at regular intervals."

"And what's your reason for this?"

"The reason is that the trees become invisible when they lose their leaves, and visible when they get them back."

"Your explanation is clever, my dear companion," Barbicane replied, "but it's unacceptable."

"Why?"

"Because there literally are no seasons on the surface of the moon, so that vegetation of yours couldn't cause any phenomenon whatever."

In fact the minimal angle of the moon's axis keeps the sun virtually at a constant elevation in every latitude. Over the equatorial regions that shining orb is almost always found at the zenith, and in the polar regions it barely goes past the horizon line. So depending on the particular region, winter, spring, summer, or autumn will reign all year long, as they do on the planet Jupiter, which likewise orbits on an axis that's minimally tilted.

How did these rills originate? Hard question to answer. They definitely arrived after the craters and basins were formed, because several have invaded these cavities by busting through their circular ramparts. So this occurrence could have been contemporary with recent geological history and may have been due simply to the encroachment of natural forces.

Meanwhile the projectile had pulled level with the 40th lunar parallel, hovering at a distance that couldn't have been more than 500 miles. Framed in their spyglasses, objects seemed to be located only 5 miles away. At this juncture Helicon rose to a height of 1,657 feet right underneath where they stood, and on its left curved those medium-sized hills that surround a small portion of the Sea of Rain known as the Bay of Rainbows.

If astronomers are to thoroughly examine the surface of the moon, the earth's atmosphere would need to be 170 times more transparent than it actually is. But in this vacuum where the projectile was cruising, no moisture intervened between the eye of the beholder and the object beheld. What's more, Barbicane enjoyed a viewing distance that the highest-powered telescopes had never afforded, neither the one built by the Earl of Rosse nor the one in the Rocky Mountains. So he had absolutely optimum conditions for settling that crucial question of whether or not life could exist on the moon. But the answer still eluded him. He could make out only an empty expanse of immense plains plus some barren mountains to the north. No artifacts revealed the hand of man. No ruins gave evidence of human beings passing that way. No herds of animals indicated that at least the lower life forms had developed. Nowhere any movement, nowhere a trace of vegetation. Out of the three kingdoms sharing the planet earth, only one was represented in this lunar world: the mineral kingdom.

"Oh drat!" Michel Ardan said, looking a little flustered. "Isn't anybody home?"

"Not so far," Nicholl replied. "No human beings, no animals, no trees. After all, we still haven't any way of knowing if there's air hidden deep in those cavities, inside those basins, or even on the other side of the moon."

"Besides," Barbicane added, "even for the keenest eyes, a human being isn't visible more than 4½ miles off. So if any moonpeople exist, they can see our projectile, but we can't see them."

Near four o'clock in the morning, level with the 50th parallel, their distance had shrunk to some 370 miles. On the left, prominent in the broad daylight, a row of erratically shaped mountains unfolded. To the right, by contrast, a dark hole punctured the ground like a huge murky pit, impossible to plumb, drilled far into the lunar soil.

That hole was Plato, the Black Lake, a deep basin earthlings can properly study between the last quarter and the new moon, when shadows fall from west to east.

This black pigment is seldom found on our satellite's surface. It has been identified elsewhere only in the depths of Endymion Crater, east of the Sea of Cold in the northern hemisphere, and on the floor of Grimaldi Basin, at the equator near the eastern edge of the moon.

Plato is a circular mountain located in latitude 51° north and longitude 9° east. Its basin is fifty-seven miles long and thirty-eight wide. Barbicane was sorry they weren't passing directly over this huge opening. There were depths to plumb, maybe some mysterious phenomenon to discover. But the projectile's course couldn't be changed. They had to resign themselves completely to this fact. Even hot air balloons can't be steered, much less a shell when you're closed up inside its walls.

By around five o'clock in the morning, they'd finally gone past the northerly limits of the Sea of Rain. La Condamine Crater and Fontenelle Crater were still to come, one on the left, the other on the right. Starting with the 60th parallel, that part of the moon's disk was turning completely mountainous. Their spyglasses brought it within 2½ miles, less than what separates the summit of Mt. Blanc from sea level. This whole region was garnished with peaks and basins. Near latitude 70° Philolaus Crater towered to a height of 12,140 feet, revealing an oval basin forty miles long and ten wide.

Viewed from that distance, though, the moon's disk had an extremely peculiar appearance. Her scenery was visible under far different, far poorer conditions than on the earth.

Since the moon hasn't any atmosphere, this absence of a gaseous covering has consequences that already have been shown. There isn't any twilight on her surface, so night follows day and day follows night with the abruptness of a lamp turned off or on in the midst of utter darkness. There's no transition from hot to cold, so the temperature drops in a second from the boiling point to the coldness of outer space.

This absence of air has another consequence: wherever the sun's rays don't reach, it's as dark as the pit. What we refer to on the earth as diffuse light, the luminous matter hanging in the air that creates dusk and dawn, that produces shadows, half-lights, and all the magic of chiaroscuro—this doesn't exist on the moon. Ergo these stark contrasts of hers that feature just two colors, black and white. If moonpeople were to shade their eyes from the sun's rays, the sky would seem completely black to them, and the stars would look as bright as they do on the darkest nights.

You can gather what an impact this strange vista had on Barbicane and his two friends. Their eyes were befuddled. They couldn't tell foregrounds from backgrounds. No landscape painter on earth could render a piece of lunar scenery that lacks the softening effects of chiaroscuro. The result would be nothing more than ink blotches on a blank sheet of paper.

This vista didn't change, not even when the projectile drew level with the 80th parallel and was separated from the moon by little more than sixty miles. Nor even at six o'clock in the morning when it came within thirty miles of Gioja Crater, a distance their spyglasses reduced to some 1,600 feet. They practically could reach out and touch the moon! It seemed impossible that the shell wouldn't bump into her before long, if only at her north pole whose brilliant crest stood out sharply against the black background of the sky. Michel Ardan wanted to open a porthole and dive down to our satellite's surface. A 30-mile fall? No problem. But it wouldn't have been worth the effort, because Michel would have been dragged along in their wake; if the projectile couldn't reach any part of the moon, he couldn't either.

Just then, at six o'clock, the lunar pole appeared. Sharply lit up, only half of the moon's disk was offered to the travelers' eyes, while the other half was lost in shadow. All at once the projectile crossed the line of demarcation between bright light and utter darkness, then abruptly plunged into the blackest of nights.

14

THE NIGHT LASTING 354½ HOURS

AT THE MOMENT this phenomenon suddenly occurred, the projectile had been skimming the lunar north pole, barely thirty miles up. So it took only a few seconds for them to plunge into the utter blackness of space. This transition happened so swiftly, without any stages in between, any fading of brightness, any softening of light waves, it was as if that silver orb had been blown out by a stupendous puff of air.

"The moon vanished!" Michel Ardan exclaimed, absolutely astounded. "It dissolved into nothingness!"

True enough, there wasn't a glimmer or a shadow. Not another thing was visible of that disk whose light had recently been so dazzling. It was as dark as the pit, and stellar radiation made the darkness even deeper. This was "that pitch-blackness" in which the lunar night is steeped, a period lasting 354½ hours on every part of her hidden disk, a night whose length comes from the equal speeds of her spinning and orbiting motions, one on her axis, the other around the earth. Since the projectile hovered deep inside the moon's conical shadow, the sun's rays didn't have any more effect on it than they had on that whole invisible side of the earth's satellite.

Inside the shell it was, then, as dark as the pit. They couldn't see each other anymore. Ergo they needed to dispel this darkness. As badly as Barbicane wanted to conserve his limited supply of gas, he had to call on it for some artificial light, a costly replacement for that sunshine currently denied them.

"The sun can go to blazes!" Michel Ardan snapped. "Making us spend our gas allowance instead of giving us daylight for free!"

"Don't blame the sun," Nicholl continued. "It isn't Old Sol's fault, it's the moon's—she came between us and the sun like a shield."

"It's the sun!" Michel insisted.

"It's the moon!" Nicholl shot back.

This was a pointless dispute, which Barbicane squelched by saying:

"My friends, it isn't the sun's fault *or* the

moon's. It's our projectile's fault—instead of faithfully staying on its flight path, it clumsily veered away. Or to be fair about it, it's the fault of that ill-omened meteor, which drove us so dismally off our original course."

"Fine!" Michel Ardan replied. "Since that settles the matter, let's eat breakfast. After being on the lookout all night, it's time we had a little sustenance."

This proposition met with no resistance. In a few minutes Michel had fixed their meal. But they ate for the sake of eating, they drank without proposing any toasts or rounds of cheers. Carried off into these gloomy regions, lacking their usual escort of light rays, our bold travelers felt a vague uneasiness coming over them. Those "savage shadows" so dear to Victor Hugo's pen were clawing at them from all sides.

Meanwhile they chatted about this endless night of 354½ hours—hence nearly two weeks—that the laws of physics had inflicted on moon dwellers. Barbicane gave his friends some information on the causes and consequences of this unusual phenomenon.

"Unusual is the word for it," he said. "During her long nights, each half of the moon goes without sunlight for two weeks, and the side we're over right now can't enjoy even the sight of the earth brilliantly lit up. In short, only one side of the lunar disk has a big heavenly body in the sky—I'm referring to our planet. Now then, suppose this were the case on the earth; suppose, for example, the moon never beamed on Europe and she was visible only in the Antipodes, can you imagine how amazed Europeans would be when they arrived in Australia?"

"Folks would make the trip just to see the moon!" Michel replied.

"Well," Barbicane continued, "this same amazement lies in store for moonpeople who live on the lunar face that looks away from the earth, a face that's never visible to our countrymen down on the ground."

"But which we ourselves would have seen," Nicholl added, "if we'd arrived here during a new moon, in other words, two weeks later."

"To even things up," Barbicane went on, "I'll add that residents of the visible face are exceptionally blessed by nature at the expense of their brethren on this invisible face. As you can see, the latter have absolute darkness for 354 hours without a single glimmer cutting through the nighttime. By contrast, after the sun has shone for two weeks and sunk below the horizon, the former see a brilliant orb rise on the opposite horizon. It's the earth, thirteen times bigger than that small-scale moon we're familiar with; the earth, looking as wide as two lunar degrees, bathing the moon in a light thirteen times brighter than any light filtered through its own layers of atmosphere; the earth, which only vanishes just as the sun reappears in its turn!"

"Very eloquent," Michel Ardan said, "though maybe a bit technical."

"It follows from this," Barbicane continued without missing a beat, "that the visible face of the lunar disk must be quite pleasant to live on, since this side is always lit up, either by the sun when the moon is full, or by the earth when the moon is new."

"But," Nicholl said, "this advantage must be totally offset by the unbearable heat the light brings with it."

"That particular drawback is the same for both faces, because light reflected by the earth obviously has no heat. Even so, this invisible face will still experience more heat than the visible face. I say this for your benefit, Nicholl, because Michel isn't likely to understand."

"Thanks," Michel put in.

"In essence," Barbicane went on, "when this invisible face gets light and heat from the sun simultaneously, it's because the moon is new, in other words, she's in conjunction, she's located between the sun and the earth. So in relation to where she's located when she's in opposition—when she's full—she's situated closer to the sun by twice her distance from the earth. Now then, we can put this distance at 1/200 of the distance separating the sun from the earth, or in round numbers, 500,000 miles. Therefore this invisible face is 500,000 miles closer to the sun when she gets its rays."

"Quite right," Nicholl replied.

"On the other hand . . . ," Barbicane continued.

"Just a second," Michel said, interrupting his earnest companion.

"What is it?"

"I insist on continuing the explanation."

"Why is that?"

"To prove that I *do* understand."

"Go ahead," Barbicane put in, smiling.

"On the other hand," Michel said, mimicking President Barbicane's tone and gestures, "on the other hand, when the sun shines on the moon's visible face, it's because the moon is full, in other words, she's located opposite to the sun in relation to the earth. So the round number for the distance separating her from that shining orb is 500,000 miles greater, and the heat she gets has to be a little less."

"Well put!" Barbicane exclaimed. "You know, Michel, for a showman you've got some sense!"

"Yes," Michel replied nonchalantly, "we all do around the Boulevard des Italiens." [6]

Barbicane solemnly shook hands with his easygoing companion, then continued to spell out some of the benefits in store for residents of the moon's visible face.

Among others he mentioned the sight of solar eclipses, which take place only on that side of the moon's disk, since she needs to be in opposition for them to occur. Caused by the earth's intervening between the moon and the sun, these eclipses can last two hours; during this time, thanks to the rays refracted by the earth's atmosphere, our planet looks like nothing more than a black dot on the sun.

"Thus," Nicholl said, "there's half of the moon, this invisible half, that nature has really shortchanged, really neglected!"

"Yes," Barbicane replied, "but not completely. In fact, by a kind of swaying motion, by a kind of swinging on her midpoint, the moon shows somewhat more than half of her disk to our planet. She's like a pendulum whose center of gravity tends toward the earth and fluctuates rhythmically. What's the source of this fluctuation? The fact that her spinning motion on her axis stays at a uniform speed, whereas her orbiting motion—along an oval path around the earth—isn't uniform. At her perigee, the moon's closest point to the earth, her orbiting speed wins out and she shows a portion of her western edge. At her apogee, by contrast, her spinning speed wins out and a piece of her eastern edge appears. These slivers, which cover about eight lunar degrees, sometimes appear to the west, sometimes to the east. Consequently 56.9% of the moon is on view."

"It makes no difference," Michel replied. "If we ever change into moonpeople, we'll live on the visible face. Me, I like the limelight."

"Unless," Nicholl countered, "the atmosphere happens to have condensed on the other side, as some astronomers claim."

"We'll take that into consideration," Michel merely replied.

Meanwhile, breakfast over, the moonwatchers went back to their posts. They tried to see through the murky portholes by quenching all light in the projectile. But in the darkness outside, nothing so much as glimmered.

One bewildering fact bothered Barbicane. Since they'd passed so close to the moon—within about thirty miles of her—why hadn't the projectile fallen to her surface? If their speed had been tremendous, it was understandable that such a fall wouldn't occur. But since their speed was comparatively moderate, this resistance to the moon's gravity remained baffling. Was the projectile subject to some foreign influence? Was some sort of alien entity keeping it out in the ether? Obviously it wasn't destined to reach any part of the moon. Where was it heading? Was it getting closer to the lunar disk or farther away? Would it be carried off into that black night and across infinity? How could they learn the truth, how could they figure it out in the midst of this darkness? All these questions worried Barbicane, but he couldn't answer them.

Though invisible, the earth's satellite was definitely there, maybe no farther away than a few geographic leagues, a few miles; but neither he nor his companions could see her anymore. If her surface gave off any noises,

<hr />

[6] *Translator's note.* Parisian theater district.

they weren't audible. There was no air, no sound-conducting medium, to transmit any rumblings from the moon, which Arabic legends characterize as "a living, breathing human being who's already half granite."

It was enough, you must admit, to aggravate the most patient skywatchers. Nothing less than this whole unknown side of the moon was hidden from their eyes! The face that the sun's rays brilliantly light up—as they had two weeks earlier and would two weeks later—was currently lost in utter darkness. Where would the projectile be in another two weeks? Where would these different forces of gravity chance to take it? Who could say?

Thanks to the findings of lunar scholars, it's generally conceded that our satellite's invisible half has absolutely the same makeup as her visible half. In fact about a seventh of this side is revealed by that swaying motion Barbicane spoke of. Now then, on those slivers that have been glimpsed, there were simply plains, mountains, basins, and craters—similar to the ones already recorded on the maps. So we can expect the same sort of world, the same dry, dead habitat. And yet what if the moon's atmosphere had taken refuge on this face? What if a combination of air and water had brought life to this reborn landscape? What if vegetation continued to thrive here? What if animals populated these lands and seas? What if such good living conditions meant that man still existed hereabouts? So many intriguing questions were left to be clarified! So many answers could be derived from studying this half of the moon! How enthralling to take a look at this world no human eyes have ever glimpsed!

The reader can imagine, then, how annoyed the travelers felt in the midst of this pitch-black night. All scrutiny of the lunar disk was prohibited. Only the constellations made a bid for their attention, and it must be acknowledged that not even such astronomers as Faye, Chacornac, or Father Secchi ever found such promising conditions for studying them.

In fact nothing could match the magnificence of that starlit world bathing in the translucent ether. Set in the dome of the skies, those diamonds sparkled with superb fire. A person's eyes took in the firmament from the Southern Cross to the North Star, those two constellations that in another 12,000 years, thanks to the precession of the equinoxes, will relinquish their roles as pole stars, one to Canopus in the southern hemisphere, the other to Vega in the northern hemisphere. A person's imagination could get lost in this sublime infinity where the projectile was revolving, a new heavenly body created by the hand of man. Due to natural causes, the constellations gleamed with a gentle glow; since there wasn't any atmosphere, they didn't twinkle, which is caused by intervening layers of air that differ in density and humidity. Those stars were gentle eyes, gazing into that deep night through the absolute stillness of space.

Our travelers were speechless for a good while, in this state examining that star-spangled firmament where the huge shield of the moon made an enormous dark hole. But a painful sensation finally tore them away from their contemplating. It was bitterly cold, and thick coats of ice were soon covering the insides of the glass portholes. In essence there was no longer any direct sunlight to warm the projectile, which, little by little, was losing the heat stored between its walls. This heat was radiating into the void and swiftly evaporating, and the result was a significantly lower temperature. Coming in contact with the glass windows, the moisture in the shell had consequently changed into ice, which made it impossible to see outside.

Nicholl checked the thermometer and saw it had dropped to 1.4° above zero. Therefore, despite all the reasons for practicing thrift, Barbicane had to call on their gas not only for light but for heat. The shell's low temperature was no longer bearable. Its guests would have frozen to death.

"We can't complain that this trip has been monotonous," Michel Ardan pointed out. "We've had plenty of variety, at least in temperature! Sometimes we're blinded by the light and suffocated by the heat, like Indians on the Pampas! Sometimes we're surrounded by absolute darkness in the middle of an arctic chill, like Eskimos at the pole! No, we

really haven't any right to complain, and nature has put on quite a show in our honor."

"But," Nicholl asked, "what's the temperature outside?"

"Exactly that of interplanetary space," Barbicane replied.

"Then," Michel Ardan went on, "wouldn't this be the time to conduct that experiment we couldn't attempt when the sun's rays were flooding over us?"

"It's now or never," Barbicane replied, "because we're in a viable position to verify the temperature in space—and to see whether it's Fourier's or Pouillet's calculations that are correct."

"It's cold in any event," Michel replied. "Look how the moisture inside is condensing on the glass portholes. If the temperature drops even a little more, the steam of our breath will turn into snowflakes and fall all around us!"

"Let's get a thermometer ready," Barbicane said.

As you can easily imagine, a standard thermometer wouldn't have been any help under the conditions the instrument would soon be exposed to. The mercury would have frozen in its bulb, since it can't stay liquid below -38° Fahrenheit. But Barbicane had come equipped with a discharge thermometer based on Walferdin's design, which gives the minimum readings of extremely low temperatures.

Before starting the experiment, they compared this instrument to a standard thermometer, then Barbicane got set to use it.

"How will we manage this?" Nicholl asked.

"Nothing could be simpler," Michel Ardan replied, never at a loss. "We quickly open the porthole; we toss out the instrument; it follows the projectile with exemplary obedience; fifteen minutes later we yank it back in—"

"With your hand?" Barbicane asked.

"With my hand," Michel answered.

"Well, my friend, that's a risk you'd better not run," Barbicane replied. "Because the hand you'll yank in will be nothing more than a stump, frozen and deformed by this frightful cold."

"Really!"

"You'll feel a dreadful burning sensation, as if from a white-hot iron; because whether heat abruptly leaves or enters our flesh, the effect is absolutely the same. Besides, I'm not certain the objects we tossed outside the projectile are still escorting us."

"Why not?" Nicholl said.

"Because if we're passing through any sort of atmosphere, even if it has very little density, those objects will lag behind. Now then, this darkness keeps us from verifying whether they're still floating around us. So to avoid any risk of losing our thermometer, we'll attach it, then we can pull it back inside more easily."

They took Barbicane's advice. Through a quickly opened porthole, Nicholl tossed out the instrument, which was on the end of a short string so it could be quickly yanked back in. The porthole was open only a second, but that second was enough to let the intense cold get into the projectile.

"Damnation!" Michel Ardan yelled. "It's cold enough to freeze a polar bear!"

Barbicane waited till half an hour had gone by, ample time for the instrument to drop to the temperature level out in space. At this point, then, they quickly yanked the thermometer back inside.

Barbicane calculated the amount of alcohol discharged into the tiny vial that was soldered to the instrument's lower end, then he said:

"It reads -220° Fahrenheit!"

Claude Pouillet was right and not Joseph Fourier. This was the alarming temperature of interstellar space! And maybe this was the figure for those lunar landmasses, when, after basking in two weeks of sunlight, that silver orb lost all her heat by its radiating into the void.

15

HYPERBOLA OR PARABOLA

MAYBE IT SURPRISES YOU that while Barbicane and his companions were shooting through the infinite ether, they were so unconcerned about the future in store for them inside their metal prison. Instead of wondering where they were heading, they spent their time conducting experiments, as if they were serenely ensconced in their workrooms.

We could reply that these stouthearted men were above such concerns, that they didn't bother with trivia, that they had other things to do besides worrying about their future lot in life.

The truth is, they weren't in control of their projectile, they couldn't check its speed or change its direction. A seaman can adjust his vessel's heading at will; a balloonist can make his airship go up and down. Our travelers, by contrast, were powerless over their vehicle. Every possible maneuver was prohibited. Ergo this inclination to let things be, or as sailors say, "ride it out."

Where were they hovering just then, at eight o'clock in the morning on that earth day reckoned as December 6? Very definitely in the vicinity of the moon, and so close even that she looked like a huge black shield covering the firmament. As for the distance separating them, it was impossible to estimate. Kept aloft by some bewildering force, the projectile had skimmed our satellite's north pole, barely thirty miles up. But during their two hours inside this conical shadow, had their distance increased or decreased? There weren't any landmarks to help them gauge the projectile's direction and speed. Maybe it was hurrying away from the lunar disk and would soon leave this unbroken shadow. On the other hand, maybe it was drawing appreciably closer to the moon and was about to bump into some lofty peak on her invisible side—which would bring this journey to a close, no doubt at our travelers' expense.

This topic came up for discussion; Michel Ardan, always chock-full of explanations, offered his view that since the shell was caught in the moon's gravity, it would end up falling to her surface as a meteor falls to the earth.

"First of all, my dear comrade," Barbicane answered him, "not all meteors fall to the earth, just a small number. So even if we're transformed into a meteor, it doesn't follow that we're sure to reach the surface of the moon."

"But," Michel responded, "what if we get close enough . . . "

"A fallacy," Barbicane replied. "Haven't you seen thousands of shooting stars streak through the sky at various times?"

"Right."

"Well, those stars—or rather those particles—only shine after they've heated up from flying through layers of air. Now then, if they enter the earth's atmosphere, they come within forty miles of the ground yet rarely fall on it. The same goes for our projectile. It could get very close to the moon yet not fall on her."

"In that case," Michel insisted, "I would be pretty curious to know how our vagabond vehicle will behave out in space."

"I see only two theoretical possibilities," Barbicane replied after thinking for a few seconds.

"Which are?"

"The projectile has a choice of two mathematical curves, and it will go along one or the other depending on the speed impelling it, which I can't estimate just now."

"Yes," Nicholl said, "it will go along a parabola or a hyperbola."

"Right," Barbicane replied. "At a certain speed it will take the parabola, and at a more considerable speed the hyperbola."

"I love these big words," Michel Ardan snapped. "Right off they're so self-explanatory. And what, if you please, is this parabola of yours?"

"My friend," the captain replied, "a parabola is a curve of the second order that results from slicing a cone with a plane parallel to one of its sides."

"Aha!" Michel put in smugly.

"It's almost the same," Nicholl went on, "as the flight path taken by a bombshell fired from a mortar."

"Wonderful. And how about your hyperbola?" Michel asked.

"A hyperbola, Michel, is a curve of the second order produced by the intersection of a conical surface and of a plane parallel to its axis, which forms two separate and distinct branches that extend indefinitely in opposite directions."

"It can't be!" Michel Ardan cooed in the

most solemn tone, as if he'd learned of some awe-inspiring development. "But bear this in mind, Captain Nicholl. What I love about your definition of hyperbola—I almost said hyperbaloney—is that it's even less clear than the word you're claiming to define!"

Nicholl and Barbicane ignored Michel Ardan's jokes. They'd launched into a scientific discussion. Which curve would the projectile take: that's what had them fired up. One favored a hyperbola, the other a parabola. The reasons they gave each other were garnished with x's. They couched their arguments in language that made Michel jumpy. It was a heated discussion, and neither opponent would back down from his curve of choice.

This scientific conflict wore on, and Michel finally got impatient, saying:

"Oh drat! Will you fiends for trigonometry stop throwing parabolas and hyperbolas at each other? There's just a single interesting thing in this whole business, and I want to hear about it. We'll go along one or the other of your curves. Fine. But where will they lead us?"

"Nowhere," Nicholl replied.

"Excuse me? Nowhere?"

"Obviously," Barbicane said. "They're open curves that continue indefinitely."

"Oh, you scientists, you're so dear to my heart!" Michel exclaimed. "Come on! Out in space what difference does it make if it's a parabola or hyperbola, since they'll both carry us off into infinity!"

Barbicane and Nicholl couldn't help smiling. They'd just been indulging in "art for art's sake." Never had a more needless question been raised at a less timely moment. Here was the grim truth: whether their projectile was carried off hyperbolically or parabolically, they were never again to meet up with the earth or its moon.

Now then, what would happen to these bold travelers in the not-too-distant future? If they didn't die from hunger or thirst, it's because by the time their gas ran out in a few days, they would be dead from lack of air, if the cold didn't kill them first.

Yet as crucial as it was to conserve this gas, the extremely low temperature of their surroundings required them to consume a certain amount. In a pinch they could do without its light, but not its heat. Luckily the warmth generated by the Reiset and Regnault device raised the projectile's interior temperature a little, and they managed to keep it at a bearable level without burning too much gas.

But it had gotten very difficult to look out the portholes. The moisture inside the shell was condensing on the windows and immediately freezing. They had to scrape ice off the panes time and again. However this allowed them to verify some phenomena of the greatest interest.

Actually, if the moon's invisible half were supplied with an atmosphere, shouldn't you see the light trails of meteors streaking over it? If the projectile itself had gone through those shifting layers of air, wouldn't you detect some noises transmitted by echoes from the moon—the rumbling of a storm, for instance, or the hubbub of an avalanche, or the explosions of an erupting volcano? And if some fire-breathing mountain threw in a few lightning bolts, wouldn't you notice their intense flashing? Carefully validated, such data could significantly clarify that murky issue of the moon's composition. Accordingly Barbicane and Nicholl were stationed at their porthole like true-blue astronomers, studying her with scrupulous patience.

But so far her disk remained dark and silent. She wasn't answering the assorted questions posed by these eager brains.

Which provoked this remark by Michel, an apt one on the face of it:

"If we ever make this trip again, we'll be better off picking a time when the moon's new."

"Actually," Nicholl replied, "that *would* be a more promising circumstance. Since the sun's rays will wash out the moon, I admit she won't be visible during the flight, but as compensation we'll see the earth when it's full. What's more, if we're forced to circle the moon—which is happening right now—at least we'll have the benefit of seeing her invisible half magnificently lit up!"

"Well put, Nicholl," Michel Ardan remarked. "Barbicane, what think you?"

"I think this," replied the Gun Club's solemn president. "If we ever make this trip again, we'll start out at the same time and under the same conditions. Suppose we'd reached our destination, wouldn't it have been better to find these landmasses in broad daylight rather than plunged in the blackest of nights? Wouldn't we have taken up residence under better circumstances to begin with? Yes, obviously. As for this invisible side, we could have inspected it during our scouting expeditions over the lunar globe. So that period of the full moon was the right choice. But it called for reaching our destination, and to do so, not going off course."

"I can't argue with that," Michel Ardan said. "Nevertheless we've missed a fine opportunity for studying the other side of the moon. Who knows if the residents of other planets aren't farther along than our earth scientists when it comes to their satellites."

To Michel Ardan's comment we could easily reply as follows: yes, other satellites are easier to study simply because they're closer to their planets. The residents of Saturn, Jupiter, and Uranus—assuming there are any—would have less trouble setting up contact with their moons. Jupiter's four satellites revolve at distances of 270,650 miles, 430,500 miles, 686,750 miles, and 1,200,325 miles. But these distances are computed from the planet's center, and after subtracting the length of the radius (which is between 42,500 and 45,000 miles), you'll find that the first satellite isn't as far from Jupiter's surface as the moon is from the earth's. Out of Saturn's eight moons, four are likewise closer: Dione is 211,500 miles away, Tethys 157,415, Enceladus 120,478, and finally Mimas with an average distance of just 86,250. Out of Uranus's eight satellites, Ariel, the first, is only 128,800 miles away from its planet.

On the surface of these three heavenly bodies, therefore, an experiment similar to President Barbicane's presented fewer difficulties. So if their residents have made such an attempt, maybe they've identified the composition of that half of their satellite's disk that's perpetually hidden from their eyes.[7] But if they've never left their planet, they're no farther along than astronomers on the earth.

In the darkness, meanwhile, the shell was going along that incalculable flight path no landmark helped them work out. Had its heading shifted, whether from the tug of the moon's gravity or the influence of some alien entity? Barbicane couldn't tell. But a change had taken place in the vehicle's relative position, and Barbicane verified the fact around four o'clock in the morning.

The change amounted to this: the projectile's base had swung toward the surface of the moon, its axis point staying at a right angle to her. Her force of attraction—in other words, her specific gravity—had brought about this shift. The heaviest part of the shell was facing her invisible disk, exactly as if it was falling toward her.

Was it falling, then? Were the travelers finally going to reach their deeply desired destination? Not so. And the sight of a landmark (which in itself was rather bewildering) soon showed Barbicane that his projectile wasn't closing in on the moon, that it had headed off along a nearly concentric curve.

This landmark was a bright gleam Nicholl suddenly spotted on the edge of that horizon formed by the black disk. This speck of light couldn't be confused with a star. It was a reddish glow that increased little by little, irrefutable proof the projectile was moving toward it and not falling to the surface of the moon in the normal way.

"A volcano! It's an active volcano!" Nicholl exclaimed. "An outpouring of our satellite's inner fires! So this world still isn't completely dead."

"Yes, it's an eruption!" Barbicane replied,

---

[7] As a matter of fact, Herschel has verified that a satellite's spinning motion on its axis is always equal to its revolving motion around the planet. Consequently it always shows the same face. Only the planet Uranus offers a pretty distinct difference: its moons move almost at right angles to the paths of their orbits, plus they move in reverse, in other words, these satellites head in the opposite direction of other heavenly bodies in the solar system.

carefully studying the phenomenon through his night glasses. "Honestly, what else could it be except a volcano?"

"But in that case," Michel Ardan said, "there has to be air for it to keep burning. So an atmosphere *is* covering that part of the moon."

"Maybe," Barbicane replied, "but not necessarily. By decomposing certain ingredients, a volcano can supply its own air and thus shoot up flames in a vacuum. That blaze strikes me as definitely having the intensity and brilliance caused by objects burning in unadulterated oxygen. So we mustn't be too hasty about proclaiming the existence of a lunar atmosphere."

This fire-breathing mountain had to have been located around latitude 45° south on the invisible part of the lunar disk. But much to Barbicane's displeasure, the curve taken by the projectile led it far away from the scene of the eruption. Therefore he couldn't determine its nature more specifically. Half an hour after they'd spotted it, this brilliant speck of light vanished below the dark horizon. But their sighting of this phenomenon was a notable event in lunar research. It proved that heat still hadn't completely vanished from the bowels of this sphere, and where there's heat, who can say that the vegetable kingdom—even the animal kingdom—isn't still withstanding the forces of destruction? Conclusively identified by experts on the earth, the presence of this erupting volcano would surely lead to many affirmative theories on that important issue of whether life could exist on the moon.

Barbicane let his thoughts run away with him. He was lost in silent reverie, all aquiver with the fateful mysteries of the lunar world. He was trying to piece together the evidence gathered to this point, when a new incident brought him sharply back to reality.

This incident was more than a cosmic phenomenon, it was an impending danger whose consequences could be disastrous.

Out in the ether, in that deep darkness, an enormous mass had suddenly appeared. It looked like a moon, but a white-hot moon whose brilliance was even more unbearable by contrast with the stark blackness of space.

Circular in shape, this mass gave off so much light that it filled up the projectile. Bathed in harsh white rays, the faces of Barbicane, Nicholl, and Michel Ardan took on a pale, ghastly, bluish gray appearance, which physicists can create with that artificial light produced by mixing salt in alcohol.

"Damnation, we look hideous!" Michel Ardan exclaimed. "What *is* that ill-omened moon?"

"A meteor," Barbicane replied.

"A meteor burning in a vacuum?"

"Yes."

That ball of fire was indeed a meteor. Barbicane wasn't mistaken. Seen from the earth, shooting stars out in the cosmos generally give off a bit less light than the moon, but here in this dark ether, they dazzle the eyes. These rambling space rocks carry their own source of incandescence. They don't need oxygen around them in order to burn. And while it's true that some meteors cross through the atmospheric layers five to eight miles above the earth, others, by contrast, go along flight paths at a distance where the atmosphere can't reach. Examples of the latter include the meteor on October 27, 1844, which appeared at an altitude of 320 miles up, and another on August 18, 1841, which vanished at a distance of 455 miles up. Some of these shooting stars are around 1¾ to 2½ miles wide and reach speeds greater than 45 miles per second, moving in a direction opposite to the earth's.[8]

More than 250 miles away from them, this spinning ball was suddenly visible in the darkness, so Barbicane estimated that it had to measure over 6,500 feet across. It came on at a speed of about 1¼ miles per second, hence 75 miles per minute. It was cutting across the projectile's path and was bound to reach them in a few minutes. As it closed in, it grew at a tremendous rate.

Imagine, if you can, the predicament our travelers were in! It's impossible to describe. Despite their courage, their composure, their jauntiness in the face of danger, they stood silent and motionless, muscles clenched, in

---

[8] The earth moves along its ecliptic at an average speed of only 18½ miles per second.

the grip of wild terror. Their projectile—whose course they couldn't change—was racing straight at that flaming mass, which was brighter than the gaping maw of a reverberatory furnace. They seemed to be rushing into a fiery chasm.

Barbicane clutched the hands of his two companions, and all three looked through half-closed eyelids at that white-hot asteroid. If their thought processes hadn't been eradicated, if their brains still functioned in this frightful situation, they must have figured they were done for!

Two minutes after the meteor's abrupt appearance—two centuries of agony—the projectile seemed on the verge of colliding with it, when that ball of fire burst like a bombshell, but without making the slightest noise out in that vacuum where sounds can't occur, since they're simply layers of vibrating air.

Nicholl gave a shout. He and his companions rushed to the glass portholes. What a sight! What pen could ever describe it, what palette had colors rich enough to duplicate such magnificence?

It was like a crater gaping wide, like a huge fire scattering sparks. Thousands of glowing fragments lit up the void, streaking it with their embers. Every size, every color, was in the mix. There were rays tinted yellow, ivory, red, green, gray, a royal crown of multicolored fireworks. As for that enormous, alarming ball of fire, nothing was left of it except pieces flying in all directions, now changed to asteroids in their turn, some like flaming swords, others surrounded by whitish clouds, a number leaving brilliant trails of cosmic dust in their wake.

These luminous lumps were crisscrossing, colliding, scattering into smaller fragments, a few even striking the projectile. One piece hit the left window so forcefully, it actually cracked the glass. They seemed to be cruising through a hailstorm of shrapnel, and the tiniest shard could wipe them out in a second.

The ether was steeped in light that was expanding with incomparable intensity, these asteroids spreading it in all directions. At one point it was so bright, Michel dragged Barbicane and Nicholl over to his window, exclaiming:

"The invisible moon—it's finally visible!"

During an outpouring of light that lasted a couple seconds, all three glimpsed the moon's secret side, which human eyes were seeing for the first time.

What could they make out from that incalculable distance? A few slender bands over her disk, actual clouds forming in an environment with very little air, an environment where whole mountains emerged as well as less important surface features, where basins and yawning craters were laid out in erratic patterns, just like on the moon's visible side. Then there were immense open spaces, no longer barren plains but actual seas, oceans distributed far and wide, reflecting in their liquid mirrors all the dazzling magic of the bonfires in space. Finally, on the surface of those landmasses, there were huge dark forms, like immense forests swiftly seen beneath flashes of lightning . . .

Was it a mirage, a hallucination, an optical illusion? Could they give scientific credence to a discovery so hastily made? Did they dare decide that question of life on the moon after such a faint view of her invisible disk?

Meanwhile those flashes out in space gradually grew weaker; their periodic brilliance died away; the asteroids fled down different flight paths and faded into the distance. The ether finally resumed its usual murkiness; momentarily outshone, the stars twinkled in the firmament, and the moon's disk, barely glimpsed, vanished once more into the impregnable night.

16

THE SOUTHERN HEMISPHERE

THE SHELL HAD JUST escaped a dreadful danger, a danger totally unforeseen. Who would have imagined these brushes with meteors? Such wandering space rocks could pose major hazards for the projectile. They were scattered over this ocean of ether like so many reefs, and our travelers—less fortunate than navigators at sea—had no way of avoiding them. But did these space explorers com-

plain? Not since nature had given them that superb sight of a meteor explosion on a fearsome scale, not since they'd seen those cosmic fireworks even the Ruggieri Brothers couldn't have duplicated, not since those incomparable skyrockets had shed a couple seconds of light on the moon's invisible glory. That swift flash had shown them landmasses, seas, and forests. Did this mean an atmosphere had brought its bracing particles to the moon's unseen face? These were issues that still couldn't be settled, riddles eternally nagging at mankind's curiosity!

By then it was 3:30 in the afternoon. The shell headed along the curving line of its course around the moon. Due to that meteor, were they again on a new flight path? They feared so. However the projectile had to be sweeping in a steady curve determined by the laws of rational mechanics. Barbicane was inclined to think that this curve would be a parabola rather than a hyperbola. Assuming it *was* a parabola, however, pretty soon the shell would have to emerge from the conical shadow, which, here in space, fell away from the sun. In actuality this cone is quite narrow, since the moon's angular diameter is so small compared to the diameter of that golden orb. Now then, the projectile was still hovering in absolute darkness. Whatever their speed had been—and it couldn't have been negligible—the shell wasn't coming out into the sunlight. This was obvious enough, yet shouldn't things maybe have been otherwise, given that their flight path was supposed to be a strict parabola? It was a new problem pestering Barbicane's brain, caught up in a cycle of mysteries he honestly couldn't unravel.

Our travelers didn't dream of resting, not for a second. Each was on the alert for some unforeseen event that could shed new light on the layout of the heavens. Near five o'clock Michel Ardan distributed, under the guise of dinner, some cold cuts and slices of bread, which were swiftly consumed without any of them leaving their portholes, whose windowpanes continually iced over from vapor condensing.

Around 5:45 in the evening, Nicholl aimed his spyglass at the southerly edge of the moon—the direction in which the projectile was heading—and he sighted a few brilliant specks of light puncturing the dark shield of the sky. You would have sworn it was some jagged mountain range with a profile like a squiggle. It was shining pretty brightly. Which is how the moon's horizon line looks during one of her octants.

The cause was unmistakable. This time they weren't dealing with a simple meteor, because that glittering ridge didn't boast any color or motion. Nor was it an erupting volcano. Accordingly Barbicane gave his verdict without hesitation.

"It's the sun!" he exclaimed.

"What! The sun?" Nicholl and Michel Ardan responded.

"Yes, my friends, it's that shining orb in person, lighting up the tips of those mountains located on the moon's southerly edge. Obviously we're closing in on her south pole."

"After having gone over her north pole," Michel replied. "So we've done a full circle around our satellite!"

"Yes, my gallant Michel."

"Then we haven't any more hyperbolas, parabolas, or open curves to worry about!"

"No, just a closed curve."

"Meaning what?"

"An ellipse. Instead of getting lost in interplanetary space, most likely the projectile will sweep in an elliptical orbit around the moon."

"Oh really?"

"And it'll become *her* satellite."

"The moon's moon!" Michel Ardan exclaimed.

"Only I'll remind you, my good friend," Barbicane remarked, "that despite this turn of events, we're still done for."

"True, but at least we'll go out in warmth and comfort," replied the carefree Frenchman with his cheeriest smile.

President Barbicane was right. In sweeping along its elliptical orbit, the projectile would undoubtedly revolve around the moon for all eternity like a junior satellite. A new heavenly body had been added to the solar system, a miniature cosmos housing three occupants—who would soon die from lack of air. So Barbicane couldn't have been overjoyed at this permanent state of affairs, which had been inflicted on the shell by the twofold influence of centripetal force and centrifugal force. He and his companions were going to see daylight again on the face of that lunar disk. Maybe they could even stay alive till they took one last look at the entire earth, splendidly lit by the sun's rays. Maybe they could bid a final farewell to that globe they were never to see again! Then their projectile would be nothing more than a snuffed-out mass, as inert as some lifeless asteroid circulating in the ether. Their only consolation was that they were finally leaving this bottomless darkness, going back into daylight, reentering zones bathed by the sun's rays.

Meanwhile those mountains Barbicane had identified were standing out more and more from the mass of blackness. They were Mt. Dörfel and Mt. Leibnitz, which garnish the moon's circumpolar regions to the south.

All the mountains on the visible half have been measured with flawless accuracy. Maybe you'll find this perfection surprising, yet a hypsometer is an infallible instrument for determining heights. You could even say that the elevations of the moon's mountains have been worked out just as accurately as those of the earth's.

The method usually favored is to measure shadows that the mountains cast, while accounting for the sun's altitude at the time of your readings. Assuming the correct diameter of the lunar disk has been accurately established, such measurements are easily gotten by using a spyglass that has a reticular eyepiece with two parallel crosshairs. This method likewise allows for calculating the depth of craters and cavities on the moon. Galileo put it to good use, and since then Messrs. Beer and Mädler have utilized it with the greatest success.

Another approach, known as the "tangent rays method," can also be employed in measuring the moon's surface features. You employ it just as the mountains turn into specks of light that stand out from the boundary line of night and day, shining above the dark part of the lunar disk. These specks of light are caused by solar rays higher than those marking the edge of the phase. So if we measure the interval of darkness left between the speck of light and the lighted portion of the phase that's nearest, we'll get the locale's exact elevation. Understand, however, that this procedure can be employed only with mountains near the boundary line of night and day.

A third method consists of using a micrometer to measure the profiles of lunar mountains outlined against the background; but it doesn't work with elevations near the moon's rim.

In any event you'll note that this measuring of shadows, intervals, or profiles can be executed only when the sun's rays, in relation to the onlooker, strike our satellite at an angle. When they strike her directly—in a word, when she's full—every shadow is summarily dismissed from her disk and no more readings are possible.

After Galileo had identified the existence of mountains on the moon, he was the first to calculate their elevations by measuring the shadows they cast. He attributed to them, as we've already said, an average height of 27,000 feet. Hevelius reduced these figures significantly, but on the other hand Father Riccioli doubled them. Their measurements were exaggerations in both directions. Equipped with new and improved instruments, Herschel came much closer to the hypsometric truth of the matter. But we ultimately need to look for it in the reports by modern skywatchers.

Messrs. Beer and Mädler, the foremost lunar scholars on the entire planet, have measured 1,095 of the moon's mountains. From their calculations it emerges that six of these mountains are higher than 19,000 feet, and twenty-two higher than 15,700 feet. The moon's loftiest summit measures 24,944 feet; consequently it's smaller than those on the earth, some of which exceed it by 3,000 to 3,500 feet. But one comment is called for. If you put these pinnacles alongside the respective masses of the two heavenly bodies, the moon's mountains are comparatively higher than the earth's. The former make up 1/470 of the moon's diameter, the latter only 1/1,440 of the earth's. To match the comparative proportions of a lunar mountain, an earthly mountain would have to measure 85,800 feet straight up. Now then, the highest we've got is less than 30,000 feet.

Hence, to continue with the comparisons, the Himalayan chain includes three peaks higher than any lunar peak: Mt. Everest at 28,993 feet high, Kanchenjunga at 28,176 feet, and Dhaulagiri at 26,860 feet. Mt. Dörfel and Mt. Leibnitz on the moon have an elevation comparable to Mt. Jewahir's in this same chain, hence around 24,940 feet. The chief lunar peaks in her Caucasus and Apennine ranges—Newton, Casatus, Curtius, Short, Tycho, Clavius, Blancanus, Endymion—are higher than Mt. Blanc, which measures 15,781 feet. Equal to Mt. Blanc are: Moretus, Theophilus, Catharnia; equal to Monte Rosa, hence 15,210 feet: Piccolomini, Werner, Harpalus; equal to the Matterhorn at 14,836 feet: Macrobius, Eratosthenes, Albategnius, Delambre; equal to the peak in Tenerife, which stands 12,172 feet high: Baco, Cysatus, Philolaus, and the summits of the lunar Alps; equal to Mt. Perdido in the Pyrenees, hence 10,994 feet: Römer and Boguslawsky; equal to Mt. Etna at 10,620 feet: Hercules, Atlas, Furnerius.

These comparative examples can help us appreciate the elevations of mountains on the moon. Now then, the projectile's flight path was taking it straight toward the upland regions of her southern hemisphere, where the finest samples of these lunar pinnacles rise into the air.

17

TYCHO

AT SIX O'CLOCK in the evening, the projectile passed over the moon's south pole, less than thirty miles up. They'd come within the same distance of her north pole. So that elliptical curve was flawlessly designed.

Just then our travelers reemerged into a wholesome outpouring of sunshine. Once again they saw those stars that slowly move from east to west. They greeted Old Sol with three cheers. Both light and heat came their way, soon seeping through the metal walls.

The windows recovered their usual transparency. Those coatings of ice magically melted away. Resuming their thrifty habits, the travelers immediately turned off the gas. Only the air device needed to keep up its standard rate of consumption.

"Ahhh!" Nicholl put in. "These heat rays feel so good! After such a long night, how impatient moonpeople must get, waiting for that golden orb to reappear!"

"Yes!" Michel Ardan replied, figuratively inhaling this radiant ether. "Light and heat, they're life itself!"

Just then the projectile's base was showing a slight tendency to veer away from the surface of the moon, so as to stay on its longish elliptical orbit. If the earth had been full at this juncture, Barbicane and his companions could have seen it again. But the sun's rays washed it out and their planet remained completely invisible. Another sight inevitably caught their eyes—the picture offered by this southern section of the moon, which their spyglasses brought within a third of a mile. They didn't budge from their portholes and noted all the details of this peculiar landmass.

Mt. Dörful and Mt. Leibnitz make up two separate systems that unfold almost to the lunar south pole. The first system reaches from the pole to the 84th parallel on the moon's east side; the second, laid out along the eastern border, goes from latitude 65° to the pole.

Dazzling white sheets covered the irregular contours of these ridges, as Father Secchi has reported. Barbicane was on a firmer footing than that famous Italian astronomer and could identify what they were.

"They're blankets of snow!" he exclaimed.

"Snow?" Nicholl echoed.

"Yes, Nicholl, snow whose surface has frozen solid. Look at the light rays reflecting on it. Hardened lava would never give off such bright reflections. So there has to be water on the moon, there has to be air. Not much if you like, but the facts are now indisputable."

No, they couldn't be disputed! And if Barbicane ever laid eyes on the earth again, his notes would testify to this significant event in lunar studies.

Mt. Dörful and Mt. Leibnitz stood in the middle of moderately wide plains bordered by a muddled sequence of basins and circular ramparts. These two mountain chains are the only ones coming together in this land of basins. Offering comparatively little variety, a few sharp peaks jut here and there, the loftiest among them measuring 24,944 feet high.

But the projectile looked right down on this whole panorama, whose surface features vanished in the brilliant glare from the moon's disk. Under our travelers' eyes the lunar scenery reappeared in its primitive state, raw toned, with no intermediate colors, no gradual shading, stark blacks and whites, all due to the shortage of diffuse light. However the vista of this desolate world couldn't help captivating them by its very strangeness. They were cruising over this chaotic region as if carried along by hurricane winds, watching summits go past beneath their feet, their eyes digging into cavities, darting into clefts, scaling ramparts, plumbing those mysterious holes, surveying all those crevices. But not a trace of vegetation, not a sign of any cities; only sheets of rock, lava flows, outpourings as shiny as immense mirrors and reflecting the sun's rays with unbearable brilliance. Not a thing belonging to a living world, everything part of a dead world where avalanches, rolling silently down from the mountaintops, were disgorged deep into the gorges. The movements remained, the sounds were still missing.

After repeated scrutiny Barbicane verified that along the edges of the lunar disk, the surface features had been subject to different forces from those governing such features in the central region, yet they all displayed the identical structure. Same circular clusters, same projections above ground. Even so, you might suspect that these arrangements weren't necessarily comparable. In fact, back when the moon's crust was malleable, her center was subject to the twofold gravitational pull of the moon and the earth, which tugged in opposite directions along a straight line running from one to the other. At the edges of her disk, by contrast, the moon's

gravity operates virtually at a right angle to the earth's. Supposedly, surface features created under these separate circumstances should have taken on different forms. Now then, this isn't what happened. So the moon herself was the sole source of her formation and composition. She owed nothing to any outside influences, living up to that noteworthy proposition by the French scientist Arago: "No external force has contributed to the creation of the moon's features."

Be that as it may, in her current state she was the picture of a dead world, and it wasn't possible to tell if organic life had ever livened up the place.

Nevertheless Michel Ardan thought he identified a cluster of ruins, which he called to Barbicane's attention. It was near the 80th parallel in longitude 30°. Laid out in a fairly regular arrangement, this pile of stones looked like a huge fortress towering over one of those long clefts that used to serve as riverbeds in prehistoric times. Not far off, circular Short Crater rose to an elevation of 18,524 feet, as high as the Caucasus range in Asia. With his usual gusto Michel Ardan trotted out "the evidence" for his fortress. Behind it, he detected the demolished ramparts of a town; here, the curving shape of a still-intact portico; there, two or three columns lying below their support structure; farther on, a sequence of arches that must have held up the conduits of an aqueduct; elsewhere, the fallen pillars of a gigantic bridge running the width of the cleft. He made all this out, but with such imaginative eyes and through such a fanciful spyglass that we're forced to take his findings with a grain of salt. And yet who could claim, who would dare insist, that the dear boy hadn't actually spotted a few things his two companions weren't willing to see?

Their time was too valuable to waste in needless debate. Fanciful or not, the lunar city had already vanished into the distance. The projectile was showing a tendency to pull away from the moon's disk, and the details of her terrain were starting to fade into a confused jumble. Only the contours of her major features, craters, and plains continued to stand out clearly.

Off to the left just then, one of the finest

293

basins in the lunar uplands came into view, one of this continent's points of interest. It was Newton Crater, which, after revisiting the *Mappa Selenographica*, Barbicane had no trouble identifying.

Newton is located right in latitude 77° south and longitude 16° east. It forms a circular crater whose ramparts rose to a height of 23,832 feet and seemed to be insurmountable.

Barbicane pointed out to his companions that this mountain's height above the surrounding plain was far less than its crater's depth. This enormous hole was impossible to plumb and formed a black chasm whose bottom the sun's rays could never reach. As Humboldt has noted, utter darkness reigns there, and neither sunlight nor earthlight can break in. A mythmaker would have made it—and with good reason—the entrance to his underworld.

"Newton Crater," Barbicane said, "is the foremost example of these circular mountains, no specimens of which are found on the earth. They prove that in the process of cooling, the moon's formation took place under violent circumstances, because while her internal fires were making these surface features jut to considerable heights, their bottoms were receding and sinking far below ground level."

"I don't say nay," Michel Ardan replied.

A few minutes after passing over Newton, the projectile looked straight down on circular Moretus Crater. They skirted the summits of Blancanus from a fair distance away, then reached the basin of Clavius near 7:30 in the evening.

One of the most notable on the lunar disk, this basin is located in latitude 58° south and longitude 15° east. Its estimated elevation is 23,264 feet. From a distance of nearly 250 miles, which their spyglasses reduced to 2½, the travelers could marvel at this huge crater in its entirety.

"Volcanoes on the earth," Barbicane said, "are just molehills compared to the ones on the moon. If you measure those old craters formed by the first eruptions of Vesuvius and Etna, you'll find they're barely four miles wide. In France the Cantal crater is around six miles wide; in Ceylon the island's basin is about forty-four miles wide and it's considered the largest on the globe. These diameters are nothing next to Clavius's, which we're looking down on right now!"

"So how wide is it?" Nicholl asked.

"One hundred forty-one miles," Barbicane said. "This basin, in fact, is the most substantial on the moon, though quite a few others measure 120, 90, and 60 miles wide."

"Ah, my friends," Michel exclaimed, "imagine what this peaceful satellite must have been like when thunder filled these craters, when they simultaneously spewed out torrents of lava, hailstorms of stones, clouds of smoke, and sheets of flame! What a prodigious sight it was back then, and now what a comedown! This moon is nothing more than the pitiful tube of a firecracker, one of those squibs, skyrockets, snakes, or pinwheels that explode splendidly, then leave only pathetic shreds of cardboard behind. Who knows the cause, the reason, the justification for cataclysms like that?"

Barbicane wasn't listening to Michel Ardan. He was contemplating Clavius's ramparts, which consisted of squat mountains several geographic leagues wide. A hundred little extinct craters punctured the floor of this immense cavity and the ground had as many holes as a skimming spoon, while over it all towered a 16,000-foot peak.

All around, the plains had a desolate look. Nothing could be more barren than these surface features, more dreary than these remnants of mountains and—if we can put it this way—these tidbits of pinnacles littering the ground! At this locality the moon seemed to have exploded.

The projectile kept moving forward and this chaos didn't change. There were continual sequences of basins, craters, and crumbling mountains. No more plains, no more seas. An endless Norway and Switzerland. Finally, smack in the middle of this ruptured region, there was its high point—dazzling Tycho, the most magnificent mountain on the moon's disk, in which posterity will forever enshrine the name of that famous Danish astronomer.

While watching the full moon in a cloudless sky, nobody can help noticing this brilliant speck in her southern hemisphere. To characterize it, Michel Ardan used every metaphor his imagination could conjure up. For him Tycho was a blazing core of light, the center of a halo, a crater spewing sunbeams. It was the hub of a glittering wheel, a starfish squeezing the lunar disk with silver tentacles, an immense flame-filled eye, a circle of radiance to fit around the head of Pluto! It was a fireball hurled by the hand of our Creator, only to squash against the face of the moon!

Tycho's glow is so focused, earthlings can see it without a spyglass even though it's 250,000 miles away. Imagine, then, how bright it must look to the eyes of moonwatchers stationed only 375 miles away! Across this unadulterated ether its brilliance was unbearable, and before they could stand its brightness, Barbicane and his friends needed to darken the eyepieces of their spyglasses with smoke from the gas jet. Then they fell silent, rarely letting out even exclamations of wonderment, and they looked, they contemplated. All their feelings, all their reactions, were centered in their eyes—just as our whole beings, when deeply moved, are centered in our hearts.

Tycho belongs in the category of mountains with networks of bright rays, like Aristarchus and Copernicus. But it's the most comprehensive and characteristic of all, furnishing unimpeachable evidence of the appalling volcanic activity that led to the moon's formation.

Tycho is located in latitude 43° south and longitude 12° east. In its center is a crater fifty-four miles wide. Slightly oval-shaped, its surrounding wall is a ring of ramparts that towers 16,000 feet above the outer plains to the east and west. It's a collection of Mt. Blancs, circling the same midpoint and topped by a radiant headdress.

The character of this incomparable mountain, the panorama of surface features converging on it, the bulges inside its crater, are things even a photograph could never capture. In essence it's during a full moon that Tycho is revealed in all its splendor. Now

then, at that juncture there aren't any shadows or foreshortenings of perspective, and prints from negatives look overexposed. An inconvenient state of things, because it would be interesting to have accurate photographs of this alien realm. It's nothing but a cluster of holes, craters, and basins, a dizzying web of ridges; then, vanishing into the distance, a whole string of volcanoes flung across the blistered landscape. As you can see, then, those bubbles that burst during the central outpouring have kept their original shape. After cooling and hardening, they've typified how the moon used to look while under the influence of eruptive forces.

The travelers weren't so far away from Tycho's circular summit that they couldn't pick out its chief details. On the very embankment forming Tycho's ramparts, the slopes of both the inner and outer mountainsides were arranged in tiers like gigantic terraces. They seemed 300 or 400 feet higher to the west than to the east. No military campsite on earth could compare to this natural fortification. A town built on the floor of this circular cavity would have been completely out of reach.

Out of reach and marvelously situated on this broken terrain with its picturesque projections! In essence nature hadn't left the floor of this crater flat and empty. It enjoyed its own personal mountain range, highland regions that virtually turned it into a separate world. Our travelers could clearly make out some cones, hills in the center, notable fluctuations of the terrain, natural settings ready for any architectural masterpieces the moonpeople could design. There, a spot marked out for a temple; here, the site of a forum; in this locality, the support structure of a palace; in that one, the plateau of a citadel. Towering above everything, a 1,500-foot mountain rose in the middle. In this huge circular area, there was enough space for all of ancient Rome ten times over!

"Ah," Michel Ardan exclaimed, carried away at the sight. "What an impressive town you could construct inside that ring of mountains! A serene metropolis, a quiet refuge, located far from all human misery! In such a city everybody who's full of distrust, everybody who hates humanity, everybody with a loathing for social intercourse, could live in peace and solitude!"

"Everybody?" Barbicane merely replied. "There wouldn't be enough room!"

18
IMPORTANT ISSUES

MEANWHILE THE PROJECTILE had gone past Tycho's surrounding wall. With the most scrupulous care, Barbicane and his two friends examined those glowing streaks the famous mountain scatters so intriguingly to every horizon.

What *was* this radiant halo? What geological phenomenon had designed this blazing headdress? These issues had Barbicane legitimately concerned.

Under his eyes, in fact, shiny furrows ran off in all directions, each sporting raised edges and sunken middles, some of them twelve miles wide, others thirty. In certain localities these glittering trails stretched as far as 750 miles from Tycho and seemed to take in—especially toward the east, northeast, and north—a good half of the southern hemisphere. One of them spurted as far as Neander Crater, located on the 40th meridian. Another made a turn and went off to plow the Sea of Nectar, crashing against the Pyrenees range after a thousand-mile run. To the west still others covered the Sea of Clouds and Sea of Moods with a network of light.

Over the plains as well as over surface features of every height, these glittering rays stood out—how had they originated? All of them shared the same center, Tycho's crater. This was their starting point. Herschel attributed their shining appearance to old lava flows frozen by the cold, a view that's far from official. Other astronomers have regarded these bewildering streaks as similar to glacial deposits, rows of erratic rubble that would have been dumped at the time of Tycho's formation.

"And why not?" Nicholl asked Barbicane, who was reporting these different views, then rejecting them.

"Because the symmetry of these shiny lines is so bewildering, given the force that's needed to shoot volcanic material to such a distance."

"Of course I myself," Michel Ardan replied, "can easily explain how these rays originated."

"You don't say," Barbicane put in.

"I do say," Michel went on. "All we have to do is view them as a huge star-shaped fracture, like you get when a ball or a stone hits a pane of glass."

"Fine," Barbicane remarked with a smile. "And whose hand would be strong enough to throw a stone that could cause such a fracture?"

"The hand isn't essential," Michel replied, unflustered. "And as for the stone, let's assume it's a comet."

"Oh, those poor overworked comets!" Barbicane exclaimed. "My gallant Michel, your explanation isn't bad, but your comet's superfluous. The impact that caused this rupture could have come from *inside* the heavenly body. While the moon's crust was cooling and shrinking, some powerful contraction would have been sufficient to etch this gigantic star shape."

"A contraction I can go along with," Michel Ardan replied. "Something like a lunar bellyache."

"Besides," Barbicane added, "this is the view of an English expert, James Nasmyth, and it seems to me that it adequately explains the bright rays of these mountains."

"That Nasmyth was no dummy," Michel replied.

For a good while the travelers marveled at Tycho's splendors, never tiring of the sight. Steeped in outpourings of light, in rays from both the sun and moon, their projectile must have looked like a ball of fire. So they'd suddenly gone from considerable cold to intense heat. Nature was preparing them in this way to become moonpeople.

To become moonpeople! The thought took them back to the issue of whether life could exist on the moon. After what they'd seen, could our travelers settle this? Could they decide the matter one way or the other? Michel Ardan urged his two friends to clarify their views, asking them straight out if they thought animals and human beings were present in the lunar world.

"I think we can answer you," Barbicane said. "But to my mind that isn't how the question should be couched. I would like to rephrase it."

"Phrase it any way you want," Michel replied.

"Here goes," Barbicane went on. "The problem is twofold and calls for a twofold solution. Can life exist on the moon? Has life ever actually done so?"

"Good," Nicholl replied. "First off, let's look into whether life can exist on the moon."

"To tell the truth, I haven't a clue," Michel remarked.

"And I myself say no," Barbicane went on. "In the moon's current condition, her atmospheric cover is definitely quite reduced, her seas mostly dried up, her water supply inadequate, her vegetation minimal, her temperature abruptly shifting from cold to hot, her nights and days lasting 354 hours. So she doesn't strike me as a place where life can thrive; she doesn't seem to offer any promise for propagating the animal kingdom or for adequately supplying the necessities of existence as we understand them."

"Agreed," Nicholl replied. "But couldn't creatures live on the moon whose organisms are different from ours?"

"That's a harder question to answer," Barbicane contended. "I'll give it a try, however, but I would ask Captain Nicholl if *motion* strikes him as an essential byproduct of life, no matter what organisms are involved?"

"Without the slightest doubt," Nicholl replied.

"Well then, my fine companion, I'll answer you that we've studied the lunar landmasses from as close as 1,600 feet, and nothing seemed to be moving on the surface of the moon. The presence of any humanity whatever would have been revealed by some earmarks, by various artifacts, by actual ruins. Now then, what did we see? In every locality always the geological achievements of nature, never any human achievements. So if representatives of the animal kingdom live on the moon, they must be hiding out of sight in those bottomless cavities. Which I can't ac-cept, because over these plains they would have left traces of their movements that a layer of atmosphere is bound to protect, no matter how thin it may be. Now then, no such traces are anywhere to be seen. So only one theoretical possibility remains—a species of living beings to whom motion, the essence of life, is alien!"

"That's as good as saying," Michel remarked, "living creatures who are lifeless."

"Exactly," Barbicane replied. "Which from our standpoint is nonsense."

"Then may we clarify our views?" Michel said.

"We may," Nicholl replied.

"All right then," Michel Ardan went on. "Regarding the issue of whether life can currently exist on the moon, this scientific commission has convened in the Gun Club's projectile, conducted an analysis based on freshly discovered facts, and reached a unanimous decision: no, it can't."

This decision was entered in President Barbicane's notebook, where the proceedings of this meeting on December 6 are still to be found.

"Now," Nicholl said, "let's attack the second question, the inevitable counterpart of the first. Therefore I ask the honorable commission: if life can't exist on the moon today, has it ever done so in the past?"

"Citizen Barbicane has the floor," Michel Ardan said.

"My friends," Barbicane replied, "I didn't plan this journey to form my views on whether life could have previously existed on the earth's satellite. I'll add that our personal investigations could only confirm the views I'd already held. I believe—nay, I insist—that the moon was inhabited by human civilizations like our own, that she brought forth animals anatomically similar to animals on the earth, but I would add that both her human and her animal species have had their day and are extinct for good."

"Then," Michel asked, "does this mean the moon's older than the earth?"

"No," Barbicane answered with conviction, "but a world that has aged faster, that has developed and deteriorated with greater speed. The matter-shaping forces inside the moon have been far more violent, comparatively speaking, than those inside the planet earth. The cracked, craggy, bloated condition of our satellite today is overwhelming proof of this. Originally the earth and moon were only gaseous masses. Due to various influences, these gases changed into a liquid state, then into a solid mass later on. But gases or liquids very definitely remained on the moon after she cooled down, solidified, and became able to support life."

"That's how I see it," Nicholl said.

"Then," Barbicane went on, "an atmosphere surrounded her. Confined inside this gaseous covering, the seas couldn't evaporate. Thanks to the influence of her air, water, light, solar heat, and central heat, vegetation took root on any landmass ready to welcome it, and life definitely appeared around this time, because nature is never wasteful, and a world so wonderfully suited to supporting life needs some life to support."

"However," Nicholl replied, "many phenomena hailing from our satellite's movement patterns must have hampered the development of the plant and animal kingdoms. For example, how about these days and nights lasting 354 hours?"

"In the polar regions on the earth," Michel said, "they go for six months!"

"An argument that carries little weight, since the poles aren't inhabited."

"Let's take note of one thing, my friends," Barbicane continued. "In the moon's current condition, these long nights and days create temperature differences no organism can handle, but this wasn't the case at an earlier time in her history. An atmosphere covered the lunar disk with a shifting mantle. Steam condensed into banks of clouds. This natural shield tempered the sunlight's heat and restrained its rays at nighttime. Plus the light in the air could grow just as diffuse as the heat. Ergo, now that this atmosphere has almost totally vanished, the balance between these influences no longer exists. What's more, I'm going to add something amazing . . ."

"Amaze us," Michel Ardan said.

"Well, I'm inclined to think that back when there was life on the moon, her nights and days didn't last 354 hours!"

"And why is that?" Nicholl asked instantly.

"Because in those days the moon's spinning motion on her axis very likely wasn't equal to her revolving motion—that state of equality where each part of her disk feels the sunlight's effects for a couple weeks at a time."

"Right," Nicholl replied, "but why wouldn't these two motions have been equal the way they are today?"

"Because this state of equality has been determined solely by the earth's gravitational pull. Now then, who knows if this gravity was strong enough to change the moon's movements back when the earth still hadn't solidified?"

"True," Nicholl remarked, "and who knows if the moon has always been the earth's satellite?"

"And who knows," Michel Ardan exclaimed, "if the moon wasn't around long before the earth was?"

Their imaginations were carrying them off into an infinite realm of possibilities. Barbicane tried to rein them in.

"We're getting into extravagant speculating," he said, "and problems that are genuinely insoluble. Let's not go there. Let's simply acknowledge that the earth's original gravity was inadequate, therefore the moon's spinning and revolving motions weren't equal, and her nights and days back then could follow each other just as they do on the earth. What's more, life was possible even without those conditions."

"Hence," Michel Ardan asked, "human beings have vanished from the moon?"

"Right," Barbicane replied, "after enduring, no doubt, for thousands of centuries. Then as the air got thinner, the lunar disk gradually became unlivable, as the planet earth will someday become when it cools off."

"When it cools off?"

"Undoubtedly," Barbicane replied. "As the moon's inner fires went out and their molten materials contracted, her crust cooled. Little by little these phenomena led to consequences: organic life vanished, vegetation vanished. Soon the air got thinner, very likely siphoned off by the earth's gravity; oxygen vanished, water vanished simply by evaporating. At this point in time the moon had become lifeless and unlivable. It was a dead world, just as it appears to us today."

"And you're saying the same fate is in store for the earth?"

"Very likely."

"But when?"

"When the cooling of its crust will have made it unlivable."

"And has anybody calculated when our hapless globe will get around to cooling?"

"Surely."

"And you're familiar with these calculations?"

"Completely."

"Then speak out, you scaremongering scientist," Michel Ardan exclaimed, "because you've got me boiling with impatience!"

"All right, my gallant Michel," Barbicane replied serenely, "we know how much the earth's temperature decreases in the course of a century. Now then, according to some calculations, in another 400,000 years this average temperature will have gone down to zero!"

"Four hundred thousand years!" Michel exclaimed. "Oh, I can breathe again! You had me honestly terrified! To hear you, I figured we had barely 50,000 years left!"

Barbicane and Nicholl couldn't help laughing at their companion's trepidations. Then, wanting to finish things up, Nicholl restated the second question, which had just been under consideration.

"Has life ever existed on the moon?" he asked.

The answer was a unanimous yes.

Though their discussion was full of theories that were a bit chancy, it summed up the general drift of scientific thinking on this topic; in the meantime the projectile was swiftly nearing the moon's equator, while steadily moving farther away from her surface. It went over Wilhelm Crater and the 40th parallel, 500 miles up. Then, leaving Pitatus to the right at 30°, it skirted the southern end of the Sea of Clouds, whose northern regions they'd already approached. Various basins looked blurred in the brilliant

white of the full moon: Bullialdus, Purbach (shaped almost like a square with a crater in the middle), then Arzachel whose inner mountain shines with indescribable brilliance.

While the projectile kept getting farther away, these surface characteristics finally faded as the travelers watched, the mountains melted into the distance, and out of that whole wonderful, peculiar, alien panorama of the moon, soon there was nothing left but the undying memory.

19

FIGHTING THE IMPOSSIBLE

FOR A FAIRLY LONG TIME, Barbicane and his companions were silent and thoughtful, looking at that world they'd seen only from afar like Moses with the land of Canaan, that world they were leaving never to return. The projectile's position in relation to the moon had shifted and its base had swung toward the earth.

This change, which Barbicane verified, didn't fail to surprise them. Since the shell was supposed to be revolving around the moon along an elliptical orbit, why wasn't its heaviest part facing her, as our satellite herself does with respect to the earth? This detail was unclear.

Watching the projectile's course, they could see it veering away from the moon and going along a curve similar to the one it made when approaching her. Consequently it was sweeping around in an ultra long ellipse that most likely would reach to the point of equal attraction, where the gravitational fields of both the earth and its satellite are nullified.

This was the conclusion Barbicane appropriately drew from the facts they'd gathered, a conviction that his two friends shared.

Immediately the questions rained down.

"And when we're back at the neutral point, what will happen to us?" Michel Ardan asked.

"That we don't know," Barbicane answered.

"But we can sketch some theories, I presume?"

"Two," Barbicane replied. "Either the projectile won't have enough speed and therefore it'll stay stationary forever on this line of equal attraction—"

"Whatever the other theory is, I prefer it," Michel remarked.

"Or," Barbicane went on, "it *will* have enough speed and it'll resume its elliptical path, revolving forever around that silver orb."

"Not a very comforting turnabout," Michel said. "Reduced to the position of humble lackeys to a moon we're used to regarding as our handmaid! And that's the future waiting for us?"

Neither Barbicane nor Nicholl responded.

"You're not saying anything," Michel went on impatiently.

"There's nothing to be said," Nicholl replied.

"Which means there's nothing to be done?"

"Nothing," Barbicane replied. "Are you claiming you can fight the impossible?"

"Why not? We're a Frenchman and two Americans—we should sneer at the very word!"

"But what would you do?"

"Get control over this motion that's sweeping us along."

"Control?"

"Yes," Michel continued more heatedly, "check it or change it, then ultimately use it to carry out our plans."

"How?"

"That's your department! If artillerymen can't control where their shells go, they aren't artillerymen. If the projectile's in charge of the gunner, we might as well load the gunner in the cannon instead. Ye gods, you're a fine pair of experts! You haven't a clue what will happen next, after coercing me—"

"Coercing you!" Barbicane and Nicholl exclaimed. "What are you talking about?"

"No criticism intended!" Michel said. "I'm not complaining! This outing has been a delight! The projectile suits me fine! But let's do everything humanly possible to fall to the ground somewhere, even if it's not on the moon."

"There's nothing we would like better, my gallant Michel," Barbicane replied, "but there's no way to do it."

"Can't we change the projectile's motion?"

"No."

"Or slow it down?"

"No."

"Or even lighten it, like they lighten a ship with too much cargo?"

"What would you toss out?" Nicholl responded. "We don't have any ballast on board. And besides, it seems to me that if the projectile were lighter, we would move faster."

"Slower," Michel said.

"Faster," Nicholl contended.

"Neither slower nor faster," Barbicane replied, trying to get his two friends on the same page. "Because we're hovering in space, where we don't need to take our specific gravity into account."

"All right," Michel Ardan snapped in a decisive tone, "there's only one thing left to do."

"What?" Nicholl asked.

"Eat breakfast," our daring Frenchman answered unflappably, always coming up with this solution when circumstances were at their most trying.

In fact, though this activity wasn't destined to influence the projectile's course, it was a sure-fire, trouble-free undertaking from a gastric standpoint. No doubt about it, that Michel had the right priorities.

So they ate breakfast at two o'clock in the morning, but never mind the time. Michel dished out his standard menu, topped off by a hearty bottle extracted from his private cellar. If their brains weren't spinning with ideas, we give up on Chambertin 1863.

Their meal finished, they went back on watch.

Around the projectile, the objects tossed outside stayed at a distance that never varied. As it circled the moon during its orbiting motion, the shell obviously hadn't gone through any atmosphere, because the specific gravities of these different objects would have changed their relative speeds.

There was nothing to see on the side facing their planet. New the previous midnight, the earth was just a day old, and two more days needed to go by before its crescent could move out of the sunlight and serve as a clock for moonpeople, since, during its spinning motion, every part of it goes past the same lunar meridian over a 24-hour period.

There was a different sight on the side facing the moon. That silver orb was shining in all her splendor amid countless constellations whose purity couldn't be disturbed by her rays. Over the moon's disk her plains were already recovering that dark shade visible from the earth. The remainder of her halo still glittered, and in the midst of this overall glittering, Tycho continued to stand out like a sun.

Barbicane didn't have any way of gauging the projectile's speed, but common sense told him it had to be steadily decreasing in line with the laws of rational mechanics.

In essence, conceding that the shell would sweep in an orbit around the moon, this orbit would need to be elliptical. Science proves it has to be this way. No moving thing that travels around an attracting object disobeys this law. Every orbit sweeping around in space is elliptical, whether it's a satellite circling its planet, a planet circling its sun, or a sun circling some unknown heavenly body that serves as its central pivot. Why should the Gun Club's projectile be exempt from the natural order of things?

Now then, with an elliptical orbit the attracting object is always at one of the foci of the ellipse. At one moment, then, the satellite is closer to the heavenly body it's revolving around, at another it's farther away. When the earth is nearest the sun, it's at its perihelion, then its aphelion when it's farthest removed. In the moon's case, she's closest to the earth at her perigee and farthest at her apogee. To coin a couple of comparable expressions that will improve every astronomer's vocabulary, if the projectile remains in the role of a lunar satellite, you ought to

say that it's at its "periselene" when at its nearest point, its "aposelene" when at its farthest point.

In the latter case the projectile should reach its minimum speed, in the former its maximum. Now then, the shell was obviously moving toward its aposelenical point, and Barbicane had grounds for thinking they would lose speed up to that moment, gradually regaining it as they drew nearer to the moon. If the point itself coincided with the point of equal attraction, their speed would actually go all the way down to zero.

Barbicane was pondering the consequences of these different scenarios and wondering what conclusions to draw, when he was sharply interrupted by a shout from Michel Ardan.

"By God!" Michel exclaimed. "We're absolute numbskulls, I have to admit!"

"I don't say nay," Barbicane replied. "But what brings this on?"

"We've got a very simple way to curb this speed that's taking us farther from the moon—and we aren't using it!"

"What way is that?"

"We could utilize the recoil power contained in our rockets."

"That's it!" Nicholl said.

"So far we haven't utilized this power, it's true," Barbicane said, "but we'll do so."

"When?" Michel asked.

"When the time is right. My friends, notice the position our projectile's in, a position still at an angle to the lunar disk—while changing our direction, the rockets could make us veer away from the moon instead of drawing nearer. Now then, you *do* want to reach the moon, don't you?"

"That's the idea," Michel replied.

"Then wait. Due to some bewildering influence, the projectile is tending to keep its base toward the earth. At the line of equal attraction, its conical cap will very likely point straight at the moon. By then, hopefully, our speed will be zero. That will be the moment to take action, and with the thrust from our rockets, maybe we can make the shell fall right to the surface of the lunar disk."

"Bravo!" Michel put in.

"We didn't do this—we couldn't do

this—when we crossed the neutral point before, because the speed impelling our projectile was still so considerable."

"Makes sense," Nicholl said.

"Let's wait patiently," Barbicane went on. "Let's get the odds on our side, and after so much despair, I'm now inclined to think we'll reach our destination!"

This conclusion prompted a round of hip-hips and hoorays from Michel Ardan. But not one of these daring lunatics remembered that they'd answered no on a crucial issue: no, life doesn't exist on the moon; no, it isn't likely life *can* exist on the moon. Yet they were willing to try anything to reach her!

There was one matter left to settle: exactly when would the projectile reach that point of equal attraction where the travelers would risk all?

In order to calculate this to within a few seconds, Barbicane had to merely revisit his travel notes and check the various entries he'd made at the lunar parallels. Thus the time it took to cover the distance between the neutral point and the moon's south pole should be equal to the distance separating her north pole from that neutral point. He'd carefully jotted down the hours representing their travel time, and the calculation turned out to be easy.

Barbicane found that their projectile would reach the neutral point at one o'clock in the morning on the night of December 7–8. Now then, at that moment it was three o'clock in the morning on the night of December 6–7. So if nothing impeded its progress, the projectile would reach the desired position in twenty-two hours.

The rockets had originally been put in place to slow the shell's fall to the moon, and now these daredevils were going to use them to create exactly the opposite effect. Be that as it may, the devices were all set and our travelers simply had to wait for the right moment to ignite them.

"Since there's nothing left to be done," Nicholl said, "I have a proposition to make."

"What's that?" Barbicane asked.

"I propose we take a nap."

"By thunder!" Michel Ardan exclaimed.

"We haven't shut our eyes in forty hours,"

Nicholl said. "A couple hours' sleep will build our strength back up."

"Never," Michel snapped back.

"Fine, suit yourself," Nicholl went on. "Me, I'm for a nap."

Nicholl stretched out on a couch and before long was whistling like a 48-pound shell.

"That Nicholl's a sensible man," Barbicane said after a short while. "I'm doing likewise."

A few seconds later his snores were adding a ground bass beneath the captain's baritone.

"No doubt about it," Michel Ardan said, seeing he was on his own, "these practical fellows know an idea whose time has come."

Stretching his long legs and folding his big arms behind his head, Michel dozed off in his turn.

But their slumber wasn't to be long or restful. Too many worries were swirling around in the brains of these three men, and a few hours later around seven o'clock in the morning, all three were on their feet at the same instant.

The projectile was still heading away from the moon, its conical end leaning toward her more and more. It was a phenomenon that remained bewildering, though luckily it served Barbicane's purposes.

Seventeen hours to go, then it would be time to take action.

How long that day seemed. Daredevils they might be, but our travelers were on pins and needles over the coming of this moment that was to decide everything—either they would fall to the moon or they would be permanently trapped in an unchanging orbit. So they counted off the hours, which went by too slowly for their liking; Barbicane and Nicholl were stubbornly immersed in their calculations, Michel paced back and forth between the cramped walls, contemplating the unresponsive moon with an eager eye.

Sometimes fleeting memories of the earth crossed their minds. They saw their friends from the Gun Club again—especially J. T. Maston, their dearest friend of all. Just then the distinguished secretary should have been manning his post in the Rocky Mountains. If he spotted the projectile in the mirror of his gigantic telescope, what would he make of it? He'd seen it vanish beyond the lunar south pole, only to see it reappear over her north pole! So it was our satellite's satellite! Had J. T. Maston fired off this unexpected news to the world at large? Was this the outcome, then, of that great undertaking?

Meanwhile the day had gone by uneventfully. It was midnight earth time. December 8 was just starting. In another hour they would reach the point of equal attraction. What was the projectile's current speed? They couldn't estimate it. But no error could have blemished Barbicane's calculations. By one o'clock in the morning their speed should and would be zero.

What's more, another phenomenon would mark the projectile's arrival on the neutral line. At this locality the gravitational fields of both moon and earth would be negated. Our travelers wouldn't be dealing with "weighty things" anymore. This distinctive circumstance, which Barbicane and his companions were fascinated to experience on their outbound journey, would be duplicated on their return trip under identical conditions. Which was exactly when they needed to take action.

Already the projectile's conical cap was noticeably swinging toward the lunar disk. The shell would be in a position to take full advantage of the recoil from the thrust of the explosive devices. So the odds favored the travelers. If the projectile's speed at the neutral point was right at zero, any distinct movement toward the moon, no matter how slight, would be enough to make them fall.

"Twelve fifty-five," Nicholl said.

"We're all set," Michel Ardan replied, holding a taper in readiness near the gas jet's flame.

"Wait!" Barbicane said, chronometer in hand.

By then gravity was creating no further effects. The travelers felt it completely vanishing from their persons. They were quite close to the neutral line, if not right on it . . . !

"One o'clock," Barbicane said.

Michel Ardan lowered the flaming taper to a fuse in direct contact with the rockets.

No explosion was audible outside where there wasn't any air. But through the portholes Barbicane saw a protracted flash of light, which soon faded away.

The projectile gave a definite lurch that was distinctly noticeable inside.

The three friends looked and listened without saying a word, almost without breathing. In the utter silence you could have heard their heartbeats.

"Are we falling?" Michel Ardan finally asked.

"No," Nicholl replied, "because the projectile's base hasn't swung back toward the moon!"

Just then Barbicane left the window of his porthole and faced his two companions. He was fearfully pale, frowning, tight lipped.

"We *are* falling!" he said.

"Aha!" Michel Ardan exclaimed. "Toward the moon?"

"Toward the earth!" Barbicane replied.

"Blast!" Michel Ardan exclaimed. Then he added philosophically, "Fine. When we got inside this shell, we suspected it wouldn't be easy to come back out!"

That frightful descent was indeed under way. The projectile had kept enough speed to take it past the neutral point. The exploding rockets couldn't hold it in check. Its outbound speed had carried the projectile beyond the point of equal attraction, and its inbound speed was carrying it back again. The laws of physics decreed that *it must return to every point on its elliptical orbit that it had already gone past.*

It was a dreadful fall from 195,000 miles up, and no springs could soften it. According to the laws of ballistics, the projectile was due to hit the earth at the same speed that had impelled it from the columbiad's muzzle, a terminal velocity of "nearly 18,000 yards per second."

To provide a basis for comparison, it's calculated that an object tossed from the tip of a steeple at Notre Dame Cathedral—which is only 200 feet high—will reach the pavement at a speed of 300 miles per hour. Here the projectile was due to hit the earth at a speed of *144,000 miles per hour.*

"We're done for!" Nicholl said coolly.

"All right, if we die," Barbicane replied in a kind of religious ecstasy, "the outcome of our journey will increase in magnificence! We'll learn the ultimate secret from God's own lips! In the next life our souls will have no need for machines or engines to gain knowledge! We'll become one with eternal wisdom!"

"In fact," Michel Ardan remarked, "the next world and everything it entails might be a pretty fair substitute for that lowly satellite known as the moon!"

As a gesture of sublime acceptance, Barbicane folded his arms over his chest.

"May Heaven's will be done!" he said.

20

THE *SUSQUEHANNA*'S SOUNDINGS

"WELL, LIEUTENANT, where are we with this sounding?"

"I think the operation's about over, sir," Lieutenant Bronsfield replied. "But who would have expected it to be this deep so close to land, just 250 miles off the American coast!"

"You're right, Bronsfield, it's a huge depression," Captain Blomsberry said. "In this locality there's an underwater valley cut by the Humboldt Current, which runs down the American coastline as far as the Strait of Magellan."

"Bottoms this deep," the lieutenant went on, "aren't much good for laying telegraph cables. A level plateau works better, like the one bearing up the Atlantic Cable between Valentia Island and Newfoundland."

"There I agree, Bronsfield. And by your leave, lieutenant, how do things stand at this time?"

"Right now, sir," Bronsfield replied, "we've payed out 21,500 feet of sounding line, and the sinker tugging it still hasn't hit bottom, because it would have come back up on its own."

"That Brooke device is a clever piece of equipment," Captain Blomsberry said. "It lets us take highly accurate soundings."

Overseeing the operation, a helmsman in the bow shouted just then: "We've hit bottom!"

The captain and the lieutenant made their way to the quarterdeck.

"What's the depth?" the captain asked.

"It's 21,762 feet," the lieutenant replied, writing this figure in his notebook.

"Good, Bronsfield," the captain said. "I'll record this total on my chart. Now haul in the sounding line. It's several hours' work. In the meantime the engineer can light the furnaces, and we'll be ready to go as soon as you're through. It's ten o'clock, and by your leave, lieutenant, I'm turning in."

"Go right ahead, sir!" Lieutenant Bronsfield replied obligingly.

Always at his officers' service and a gallant man if there ever was one, the *Susquehanna*'s captain retired to his cabin, downed a brandy toddy that earned his chief steward no end of praise, turned in after complimenting his manservant on his bed-making skills, and fell peacefully asleep.

By then it was ten o'clock in the evening. That day of December 11 would be changing into a magnificent night.

A 500-horsepower sloop of war in the United States Navy, the *Susquehanna* had been busy taking soundings in the Pacific about 250 miles off the American coast, level with that lengthy peninsula laid out along the coast of Mexico.

The wind had died down little by little. No turbulence was stirring up the layers of air. Motionless, inanimate, the warship's pennant dangled from the mast of the topgallant sail.

Captain Jonathan Blomsberry was a first cousin of that same Colonel Blomsberry who was a stalwart of the Gun Club—the colonel had married the captain's aunt, the daughter of a respectable Kentucky merchant named Horschbidden; Captain Blomsberry couldn't have asked for better weather for seeing his tricky sounding operations through to completion. His sloop of war hadn't felt even a drop of the huge storm that had cleared those piles of clouds away from the Rocky Mountains, making it possible to track the progress of the notorious projectile. Everything had gone to his liking, and with typical Presbyterian fervor he didn't neglect to thank Heaven for his blessings.

This series of soundings carried out by the *Susquehanna* aimed to locate the most promising parts of the seafloor for laying an underwater cable that would link the Hawaiian Islands with the coast of America.

This was a tremendous scheme, thanks to the initiative of a mighty corporation. Its chief executive officer, shrewd Cyrus Field, even claimed this vast electrical network would cover all the islands in Oceania, an immense undertaking worthy of America's technological genius.

The sloop of war *Susquehanna* had been entrusted with the initial sounding operations. During that night of December 11–12, the ship lay right in latitude 27° 7′ north and longitude 41° 37′ west of the meridian of Washington, D.C.[9]

The moon, then in her last quarter, was starting to peek above the horizon.

After Captain Blomsberry's departure, the lieutenant and a few officers gathered on the afterdeck. When the earth's satellite appeared, their thoughts turned to that heavenly body the eyes of a whole hemisphere were contemplating by then. The finest naval spyglasses couldn't have detected the projectile roaming around its half of the moon and yet they were all aimed at that glittering disk, which millions of eyes were ogling simultaneously.

"They've been gone ten days," Lieutenant Bronsfield said. "What happened to them?"

"They've arrived, lieutenant!" a young midshipman exclaimed. "And they're doing what every traveler does after arriving in a new country—they've gone for a stroll!"

"Of course, my young friend, if you say so," Lieutenant Bronsfield replied with a smile.

"But," another officer went on, "there's no question about them arriving. The projectile was due to reach the moon at midnight on the 5th, just as she was full. It's now December 11, which makes six days. Now then, in twenty-four hours of daylight times six,

you've got a comfortable amount of time for taking up residence. I can see them now, our gallant countrymen—they're camped at the bottom of some valley on a lunar riverbank, next to them the projectile's half buried in volcanic rubble after its crash landing, Captain Nicholl's starting his survey work, President Barbicane's putting his travel notes into final form, and Michel Ardan's perfuming the lunar wastes with the smell of his Havanas . . . "

"Yes, it's bound to be like that—just like that!" the young midshipman cut in, excited by his superior's rose-colored description.

"I wish I could believe it," Lieutenant Bronsfield replied, less carried away. "Unfortunately we're still lacking any direct news from the lunar world."

"Pardon me, lieutenant," the midshipman said, "but can't President Barbicane write us?"

A burst of laughter greeted this response.

"Not letters!" the young man went on hastily. "The post office isn't involved yet."

"So they're going to run telegraph lines?" asked one of the officers sarcastically.

"Not that either," the midshipman replied, unflustered. "But it's very easy to set up visual contact with the earth."

"How?"

"By using the telescope on Long's Peak. As you know, it brings the moon within a viewing distance of just five miles from the Rocky Mountains, which makes it possible to see objects on her surface that are nine feet across. All right, if our resourceful friends build an alphabet of gigantic letters, if they spell out words 600 feet long and sentences 2½ miles long, that's how they could send us the latest news."

The young midshipman, who was blessed with quite an imagination, got a hearty round of applause. Even Lieutenant Bronsfield agreed the idea was doable. He added they could also set up direct contact by sending light rays focused into beams with the aid of parabolic mirrors; in fact these rays would be as visible on the surface of Venus or Mars as the planet Neptune is from the earth. He finished by saying that the specks of light already spotted on nearby planets might well

---

[9] Right at longitude 119° 55′ west of the meridian of Paris.

be signals aimed at the earth. But he pointed out that though we could get news from the lunar world with such a method, the earthly world couldn't send any news back, unless people on the moon were equipped with decent instruments for long-distance viewing.

"Obviously," one of the officers replied. "But what happened to the travelers, what have they done, what have they seen? That's got to be the most intriguing thing about this. What's more, if this experiment was successful—which I don't question—they'll try again. The columbiad is still embedded in Florida soil. So it's only a matter of shells and gunpowder, and every time the moon ascends to the zenith, we can send her a shipment of visitors."

"It's obvious," Lieutenant Bronsfield replied, "that one of these days J. T. Maston will be rejoining his friends."

"If he's open to it," the midshipman exclaimed, "I'm all set to go along!"

"Oh, there'll be no shortage of takers," Bronsfield remarked. "If we let them, half the people on earth would migrate to the moon in no time!"

The *Susquehanna*'s officers kept up this conversation till around one o'clock in the morning. We can't say what scatterbrained schemes and cockeyed theories these daring thinkers put forward. After Barbicane's endeavor nothing seemed impossible to an American. They were already planning a landing on the moon's beaches, no longer by a committee of scientists but by a whole colony, plus a whole army complete with enough infantry, artillery, and cavalry to conquer the lunar world.

By one o'clock in the morning, they still weren't through hauling in the sounding line. 10,000 feet were out as yet, which meant several hours' more work. In compliance with their commander's orders, the furnaces had been lit and were already up to pressure. The *Susquehanna* could have gotten under way immediately.

Just then—it was 1:17 in the morning—Lieutenant Bronsfield was all set to go off watch and retire to his cabin, when his attention was caught by a totally unexpected noise, a far-away hissing.

At first he and his comrades thought a steam leak was the cause of this hissing; but when they raised their heads, they could tell this noise was coming from the upper layers of the atmosphere.

Before they had any time to question each other, this hissing became fearfully intense; dazzling the eyes, an enormous meteor suddenly shot into view, on fire from the speed of its descent and from its friction against the layers of air.

This blazing mass grew as they watched, with a thunderous sound struck the sloop of war right on the bowsprit, snapped it off just shy of the stempost, and plunged into the waves with a deafening crash!

A few feet nearer and the *Susquehanna* would have gone down with all hands.

Just then Captain Blomsberry appeared, half dressed, hurrying to the forecastle where all his officers had rushed.

"By your leave, gentlemen—what happened?" he asked.

And the midshipman, taking it on himself to speak for everybody, blurted out:

"Skipper, it's *them*—they're back!"

21
REENTER J. T. MASTON

THERE WAS TREMENDOUS excitement aboard the *Susquehanna*. Officers and sailors forgot the dreadful danger they'd just run—the possibility of being pulverized and sent to the bottom. They thought only about the catastrophe concluding that moon journey. Hence the most daring undertaking of all time had cost the lives of the bold adventurers who had attempted it.

"It's *them*—they're back!" the young midshipman had said, and everybody knew what he meant. Nobody questioned that this meteor was the Gun Club's projectile. Regarding the travelers locked up inside, there were differing views as to their fate.

"They're dead!" this one said.

"They're alive," said that one. "The water's deep in this area and it softened their fall."

"But they were short of air," another went

on, "so they must have died of asphyxiation!"

"They burned to death!" somebody else contended. "When the projectile crossed through the atmosphere, it was nothing but a mass of flame."

"What difference does it make!" the crew replied to a man. "Whether they're alive or dead, we've got to pull them out!"

Meanwhile Captain Blomsberry had gathered his officers and—by their leave—was conferring with them. This involved their agreeing on an immediate course of action. The most urgent concern was to fish up the projectile—an operation that was difficult though not impossible. But their sloop of war didn't have the requisite equipment, which needed to be both powerful and precise. So they decided to make for the nearest port and send word to the Gun Club that its shell had fallen out of the sky.

This verdict was unanimous. The choice of a port came under discussion. The nearby coast didn't offer any anchorage at latitude 27°. Higher up, on the far side of Monterey Peninsula, sat the major town it's named after. But this community lay on the borders of an honest-to-goodness desert, no network of telegraph lines linked it with cities inland, and only electricity could spread this crucial news swiftly enough.

San Francisco Bay opened a few degrees farther north. This metropolitan area in the California gold country was in easy contact with the heart of the Union. By running at full steam, the *Susquehanna* could reach the port of San Francisco in less than two days. So they had to leave without delay.

The furnaces had been stoked. They could get going immediately. 10,000 feet of sounding line were still left in the depths. Unwilling to waste valuable time hauling it in, Captain Blomsberry decided to cut it.

"We'll secure the end to a buoy," he said, "and this buoy will mark exactly where the projectile fell."

"What's more," Lieutenant Bronsfield responded, "we know our exact position: latitude 27° 7′ north and longitude 41° 37′ west."

"Fine, Mr. Bronsfield," the captain replied, "and by your leave let's get that line cut."

The crew deposited a sizeable buoy, reinforced by a couple of spare yards, on the surface of the ocean. The end of the sounding line was tightly lashed to the top of the buoy, which, being subject solely to the comings and goings of the billows, wasn't destined to drift significantly.

Just then the engineer notified the captain they were up to pressure and could depart. The captain thanked him for this excellent news. Then he set their course for north-northeast. Tacking about, the sloop of war headed at full steam for San Francisco Bay. It was three o'clock in the morning.

There were 550 miles to cover, a minor matter for a good racer like the *Susquehanna*. It gobbled up this distance in thirty-six hours, and at 1:27 in the afternoon on December 14, it stood into San Francisco Bay.

The sight of an American naval craft arriving at top speed, bowsprit shorn and foremast braced, excited substantial public curiosity. A jam-packed crowd had soon gathered along the wharves, waiting for the crew to come on land.

After dropping anchor, Captain Blomsberry and Lieutenant Bronsfield got down into a dinghy equipped with eight oars, which swiftly carried them ashore.

They leaped onto the wharf.

"Where's the telegraph?" they asked, without answering a single one of the thousand questions coming their way.

In the midst of an immense gathering of curiosity seekers, the harbormaster himself led them to the telegraph office.

Blomsberry and Bronsfield went into the office while the crowd clustered around the door.

In a few minutes they'd fired off a telegram in quadruplicate: the first to the Secretary of the Navy in Washington, D.C.; the second to the Vice President of the Gun Club in Baltimore; the third to the honorable J. T. Maston on Long's Peak in the Rocky Mountains; the fourth to the deputy director of the Cambridge Observatory in Massachusetts.

It ran as follows:

On December 12 at 1:17 in the morning, the projectile from the columbiad fell into the Pacific in latitude 27° 7' north and longitude 41° 37' west. Send instructions.

BLOMSBERRY,
Commander Susquehanna.

Five minutes later the whole town of San Francisco had heard the news. Before six o'clock that evening, the various states of the Union knew about this crowning catastrophe. After midnight all Europe learned by cablegram how the great American experiment had concluded.

We'll make no attempt to describe the effect this unexpected outcome had on the whole world.

After receiving the telegram, the Secretary of the Navy wired the *Susquehanna*, ordering it to wait in San Francisco Bay without shutting down its furnaces. It needed to be ready day or night to put to sea.

The Cambridge Observatory met in a special session and with that stateliness typical of scholarly gatherings, placidly discussed the scientific aspects of the matter.

At the Gun Club there was an explosion. All the artillerymen were convened. Sure enough, the honorable Mr. Wilcome—their vice president—was reading that premature telegram in which Belfast and J. T. Maston announced they'd just spotted the projectile in their gigantic reflector on Long's Peak. This message further conveyed that the shell had gotten caught in the moon's gravitational pull and was playing the role of a junior satellite in the solar system.

You already know the truth of the matter.

But when Blomsberry's wire arrived and flatly contradicted J. T. Maston's telegram, two factions took form in the Gun Club's bosom. On one side were those who accepted that the projectile had fallen to the earth and that the travelers had therefore come back. On the other were the ones who swore by the findings from Long's Peak and concluded that the *Susquehanna*'s commander was mistaken. To this latter group the so-called projectile was just a meteor, nothing more, a shooting star that had fallen out of the sky

and smashed the sloop of war in the bow. There weren't many facts that could refute this argument, because the moving object had to have been traveling so swiftly, it would've been very hard to make out. Certainly the *Susquehanna*'s commander and his officers could have committed an error in good faith. Nevertheless one argument worked in their favor: namely, if the projectile *had* fallen to the earth, it could meet up with our planet only in latitude 27° north and—taking into account the lapse of time and the earth's spinning motion—between longitude 41° and 42° west.

Be that as it may, the Gun Club unanimously decided that cousin Blomsberry, Bilsby, and Major Elphiston should get to San Francisco without delay and settle on a way of pulling up the projectile from the ocean depths.

These dedicated men wasted no time in starting out, and the railroad—which soon would run all across the center of America—took them to St. Louis, where speedy stagecoaches were waiting for them.

Practically at the same instant that the Secretary of the Navy, the Gun Club's vice president, and the observatory's deputy director got their telegrams from San Francisco, the honorable J. T. Maston was experiencing the most intense excitement he'd known in his entire existence, an excitement he hadn't felt even when his notorious cannon blew up, an excitement that once again nearly cost him his life.

As you'll recall, the Gun Club's secretary had left a few seconds after the projectile had (and almost as quickly) for the workstation at Long's Peak in the Rocky Mountains. J. M. Belfast, the Cambridge Observatory's scholarly director, went with him. Arriving at the outpost, the two friends took up residence in short order and didn't leave the topside of their enormous telescope for a moment.

In essence, as you know, this gigantic instrument was set up to be a "front-view" reflector, as the English term it. With this arrangement objects were subjected to just a single reflection, thereby providing a sharper image. Consequently, when J. T. Maston and Belfast watched the skies, they didn't stand

309

at the lower end of the instrument but the upper. They reached this by a spiral staircase, a masterpiece of light construction, and beneath them, culminating in an iridescent mirror, gaped a metal well that was 280 feet deep.

Now then, positioned above the telescope was a cramped platform where the two experts spent their lives, cursing the sunlight for hiding the moon from their eyes, the clouds for stubbornly concealing her at night.

Then, after a few days of suspense, how gleeful they felt on the night of December 5 when they spotted the space vehicle carrying their friends! But their glee gave way to deep disappointment when, relying on their sketchy findings, they fired off their first telegram to the world, which mistakenly claimed the projectile had turned into the moon's satellite and was revolving in an unchanging orbit.

After that the shell was no longer in view, a vanishing act easily explained since by then it had gone behind the moon's invisible side. But when the time came for it to reappear in front of the visible one, the reader can imagine J. T. Maston's seething impatience and the similar impatience of his companion! Every sixty seconds that night they thought they'd spotted the projectile again—but they hadn't! Ergo there were endless debates and vicious quarrels between the two. Belfast insisted the projectile was out of sight, J. T. Maston maintained it was "right under his nose."

"That's the shell!" J. T. Maston kept saying.

"No!" Belfast replied. "That's an avalanche breaking loose from a lunar mountain!"

"Then we'll see it tomorrow."

"No, we'll never see it again! It flew off into space."

"We will!"

"We won't!"

And during these times when exclamations were raining down like hail, the well-known temper of the Gun Club's secretary posed a perpetual danger for the honorable Mr. Belfast.

Their joint existence would soon have become impossible, but an unexpected development cut short their constant feuding.

During the night of December 14–15, the two estranged friends were busy studying the moon's disk. As usual J. T. Maston had been insulting the scholarly Belfast, who was fuming at his side. The Gun Club's secretary was maintaining for the thousandth time that he'd just spotted the projectile, even adding that Michel Ardan's face was visible through one of the portholes. He was backing up his arguments with a series of gestures rendered quite bothersome by his alarming hook.

Just then Belfast's manservant appeared on the platform—it was ten o'clock in the evening—and handed him a wire. It was the telegram from the *Susquehanna*'s commander.

Belfast tore open the envelope, read its contents, and let out a shout.

"Huh?" J. T. Maston put in.

"The shell!"

"What about it?"

"It just fell to the earth!"

He was answered by a second shout, which this time changed into a howl.

He turned to J. T. Maston. The poor fellow had been recklessly leaning out over the metal tube and he'd vanished into that immense telescope. A 280-foot drop! Belfast rushed frantically to the reflector opening.

He breathed again. J. T. Maston had caught himself with his metal hook and was hanging from one of the struts that regulated the telescope's range. He was emitting fearsome shrieks.

Belfast called for help. His assistants came running. They set up pulleys and hauled out the Gun Club's reckless secretary, not without some difficulty.

He reemerged unhurt at the top of the opening.

"Say," he put in, "what if I'd broken the mirror?"

"You would have to pay for it," Belfast replied sternly.

"So that damned shell fell out of the sky?" J. T. Maston asked.

"Into the Pacific!"

"Let's get going."

Fifteen minutes later the two experts were

heading down the slopes of the Rocky Mountains; and two days later, at the same instant as their Gun Club friends, they arrived in San Francisco—after working five horses to death on the way.

Elphiston, cousin Blomsberry, and Bilsby rushed up to them on their arrival.

"What's the plan?" they snapped.

"Fish up the shell," J. T. Maston replied, "and as fast as possible!"

22

THE RESCUE

THE ACTUAL LOCALITY where the projectile had plunged under the waves was certain knowledge. The instruments for clutching and carrying it back to the surface of the ocean were still lacking. They had to be invented, then manufactured. This was a minor matter, no problem for American engineers. Once the grappling hooks were in place and steam power applied, they were sure to raise the projectile regardless of its weight, which in any case was lessened by the density of the liquid engulfing it.

But it wasn't enough to fish up the shell. In the travelers' best interests, it was essential to act promptly. Nobody questioned that they were still alive.

"Yes!" J. T. Maston repeated continually, his confidence winning everybody over. "They're skillful men, our friends, and they wouldn't handle this fall like simpletons. They're alive, definitely alive, but we've got to move fast if we're to find them in that state. Food and water don't worry me. They have enough for a good while. But air, air— that's what they'll soon run out of! So let's hurry, let's hurry!"

And hurry they did. They modified the *Susquehanna* for its new assignment. Its powerful engines were ready to work the hauling chains. That aluminum projectile weighed only 19,250 pounds—much less than the Atlantic Cable, which had been raised under similar circumstances. So the only difficult thing about fishing up this cylindro-conical shell was that its walls were so smooth, they might be hard to grip.

Racing to San Francisco with this in mind, Murchison the engineer devised some enormous grappling hooks that worked automatically—they were designed so that they would never relax their hold once they'd managed to clutch the projectile in their powerful pincers. He also got some diving suits ready, which offered strong waterproof protection for undersea explorers scouting out the ocean floor. He likewise put some cleverly designed compressed-air chambers aboard the *Susquehanna*. Inset with portholes, these were actual rooms that could plummet far into the depths by letting water into various compartments. These diving chambers were already available in San Francisco, where they'd been used in building an underwater jetty. And this was a real stroke of luck because there wouldn't have been time to manufacture any.

But despite the excellence of these devices, despite the cleverness of the experts assigned to work with them, the success of this operation was anything but assured. The odds were iffy, since it was a matter of recovering that projectile from 20,000 feet down! Then, even supposing the shell were brought back to the surface, how would the travelers have borne up under that dreadful impact, if those 20,000 feet of water hadn't softened it sufficiently?

In short, they had to work faster. J. T. Maston drove his hired hands day and night. He was all set to put on a diving suit or test a compressed-air chamber himself, in order to scout out the predicament his courageous friends were in.

But despite all the diligence displayed in readying these various pieces of equipment, despite the considerable sums placed at the Gun Club's disposal by the Union government, five long days—five centuries—went by before preparations were complete. In the meantime public interest had surged to a fever pitch. Telegrams continually shot back and forth over wires and electric cables around the world. Rescuing Barbicane, Nicholl, and Michel Ardan was an international affair. Every participant in the Gun Club's funding drive had a personal stake in the travelers' welfare.

Finally the hauling chains, the compressed-air chambers, and the automatic grappling hooks had been loaded aboard the *Susquehanna*. J. T. Maston, Murchison the engineer, and the Gun Club delegation were already occupying their cabins. They had only to set sail.

On December 21 at eight o'clock in the evening, the sloop of war got under way with a smooth sea, a breeze out of the northeast, and a fairly sharp chill in the air. The whole population of San Francisco crowded the wharves, excited but silent, saving their cheers for the ship's return.

Steam up to maximum pressure, the *Susquehanna*'s propeller swiftly carried them out of the bay.

It's pointless to describe the shipboard conversations between officers, sailors, and passengers. Every man had only one thought. Every heart throbbed with the same emotion. While the vessel was racing to their rescue, what were Barbicane and his companions up to? What had happened to them? Were they in a position to attempt some daring move to win their freedom? Nobody could say. The truth is, anything they tried would have failed! Submerged nearly five miles down, that metal prison could defy its prisoners' best efforts.

On December 23 at eight o'clock in the morning, after a quick run, the *Susquehanna* arrived at the supposed site of the calamity. They needed to wait till noon to get their exact bearings. They still hadn't discovered the buoy with the sounding line lashed to it.

At noon, assisted by the officers who double-checked his readings, Captain Blomsberry took his sights in the presence of the Gun Club delegation. It was an anxious moment for them. According to their position fix, the *Susquehanna* lay a few minutes west of the actual locality where the projectile had vanished under the waves.

So the sloop of war changed course in order to reach this exact spot.

At 12:47 in the afternoon they turned up the buoy. It was in perfect condition and must have drifted very little.

"Finally!" J. T. Maston exclaimed.

"Shall we get started?" Captain Blomsberry asked.

"Without wasting another second," J. T. Maston replied.

They took every precaution to keep the sloop of war absolutely still.

First of all, before trying to grab hold of the projectile, Murchison the engineer wanted to scout out its location on the ocean floor. The underwater chamber assigned to this search was supplied with air. Working this equipment had its dangers, because at 20,000 feet below the surface of the waves, it's under considerable pressure and vulnerable to rupturing, with dreadful consequences.

Not worrying about these dangers, J. T. Maston, cousin Blomsberry, and Murchison the engineer took their places in the compressed-air room. Stationed on the bridge, the skipper directed the operation, ready to stop lowering or to haul in the chains at the tiniest signal. The propeller had been thrown in gear, and with the engines' full power put on the winch, they could quickly bring the diving chamber back on board.

The descent began at 1:25 in the afternoon; once its ballast tanks were full of water, the chamber sank below the surface of the ocean and vanished from view.

The officers and sailors on board now divided their anxieties between the projectile's inmates and those in the underwater chamber. As for the latter, they hadn't a thought for themselves, stayed glued to the panes of their portholes, and carefully scanned the mass of liquid they were going through.

It was a swift descent. J. T. Maston and his companions had reached the floor of the Pacific by 2:17. But all they saw was a barren wasteland no longer livened up by marine flora or fauna. In the light from their lamps, which were equipped with powerful reflectors, they could inspect the murky underwater strata over a pretty extensive radius, but the projectile was nowhere to be seen.

These bold divers were consumed with indescribable impatience. Their chamber was in electrical contact with the sloop of war, so they sent it a prearranged signal, and the *Susquehanna* moved their underwater room here and there over a one-mile area, dangling it a few yards above the seafloor .

That's how they explored this whole underwater plain, fooled every second by heartbreaking optical illusions. Here a rock, there a bulge on the bottom, looked to them like the dearly desired projectile; then they quickly realized their mistake and were in despair.

"But where are they? Where are they?" J. T. Maston demanded.

And the poor fellow called for Nicholl, Barbicane, and Michel Ardan at the top of his lungs, as if his unlucky friends could have heard him or answered him back through that impregnable medium!

They continued to search under these conditions till the foul air in the chamber forced the divers to ascend again.

The winch started hauling them in around six o'clock in the evening and didn't finish till past midnight.

"We'll try again tomorrow," J. T. Maston said, setting foot on the warship's deck.

"Right," Captain Blomsberry replied.

"And at another location."

"Right."

J. T. Maston still felt confident of success, but his companions—no longer as tipsy with excitement as they'd been early on—had already grasped the full difficulty of this undertaking. What seemed easy in San Francisco looked almost unattainable here in midocean. The odds that they would succeed were shrinking tremendously, and they could only hope some stroke of luck would lead them to the projectile.

Despite their exhaustion from the day before, they resumed operations the next morning, December 24. The sloop of war shifted a few minutes to the west, and after the diving chamber was refilled with air, it carried the same explorers back into the ocean depths.

They spent the whole day in fruitless searching. The seabed was empty. Their workday on the 25th didn't produce any results either. Nor did the 26th.

It was agonizing. Think of those unfortunate men closed up in that shell for the past twenty-six days! Maybe at this point they were feeling the first symptoms of asphyxia-

tion—if they'd survived their dangerous fall in the first place. Their air was running out, and along with it, no doubt, their courage and strength of mind.

"Air possibly," J. T. Maston invariably replied. "But strength of mind never!"

On the 28th, after two more days of searching, they abandoned all hope. That projectile was a flyspeck in the vastness of the sea! They had to give up their quest.

But J. T. Maston wouldn't hear of heading back. He wasn't willing to leave the area without at least finding the grave of his friends. Yet Captain Blomsberry couldn't stay out any longer, and over the good secretary's objections, he had no choice but to get his vessel under way.

On December 29 at nine o'clock in the morning, the *Susquehanna* aimed its prow to the northeast and plied a course back toward San Francisco Bay.

It was ten o'clock in the morning. The sloop of war was going off under half steam, as if grieving the site of the catastrophe, when there came a sudden shout from the sailor on watch in the crosstrees of the topgallant sail:

"Buoy abreast of us to leeward!"

The officers peered in the direction indicated. Using their spyglasses, they found that the object sighted did indeed look like one of those buoys used for marking entrances to bays or rivers. But oddly enough, a flag was fluttering in the wind on top of its cone, which emerged five or six feet above water. This buoy gleamed in the sunlight as if its walls were made of silver plate.

Captain Blomsberry, J. T. Maston, and the Gun Club delegation climbed onto the bridge and examined this object, which was wandering over the waves at random.

They all looked with feverish anxiety but without saying a word. Nobody dared voice the thought that had occurred to every one of them.

Closing in, the sloop of war lay less than a quarter of a mile from the object.

The whole crew shook with excitement.

That flag was the American flag!

Just then an authentic bellow of pain rang out. It came from our gallant J. T. Maston,

who had just fallen in a heap. Forgetting in the first place that an iron hook had replaced his right arm, and in the second that only a gutta-percha cap covered his braincase, he'd just given his forehead a fearsome smack.

They rushed over to him. They lifted him up. They revived him. And what were his first words?

"Oh, we're donkeys three times over, morons four times over, and nincompoops five!"

"What's wrong?" exclaimed everybody around him.

"Wrong?"

"Come on, out with it!"

"You numbskulls," howled the dreaded secretary, "the shell weighs only 19,250 pounds!"

"So?"

"Yet it displaces twenty-eight tons, the same as 56,000 pounds, and consequently *it will float!*"

Oh, how the good fellow underlined this verb "float!" And it was the truth! Every one of these experts—yes, every one of them—had forgotten this fundamental law: namely, the projectile had a low specific gravity, so after its fall had dragged it far into the ocean depths, it naturally had to come back to the surface! And now it was floating serenely, at the mercy of the waves . . .

After J. T. Maston and his friends had hurried into them, the longboats were put to sea. Excitement was running high. All hearts were pounding as the dinghies moved toward the projectile. What did it hold? The living or the dead? The living surely—unless death had claimed Barbicane and his two friends after they'd displayed that flag!

Utter silence reigned on the longboats. Every heart had a seizure. Eyes couldn't see straight. One of the projectile's portholes was open. A few shards were still in the frame, showing that the glass had been knocked out. This porthole was currently located at a height of five feet above the waves.

The longboat carrying J. T. Maston pulled alongside. J. T. Maston lunged at the shattered window . . .

Just then a bright, cheerful voice rang out; it was Michel Ardan's voice, exclaiming in triumphant tones:

"Double blank, Barbicane, double blank!"

Barbicane, Michel Ardan, and Nicholl were playing a game of dominoes.

23

TO CONCLUDE

YOU'LL RECALL THE enormous sympathy that had gone along with our three travelers on their departure. If they aroused such feelings in the New World and the Old at the start of their undertaking, imagine the furor that would greet them on their return! Those millions of spectators overrunning Florida's peninsula—wouldn't they rush to meet these exalted adventurers? Those legions of foreigners racing from every corner of the globe toward the shores of America—would they leave Union territory without getting a look at Barbicane, Nicholl, and Michel Ardan? Of course not, and the public's fiery enthusiasm was to prove an appropriate response to the greatness of this undertaking. Any human being leaving our planet, then returning from such a strange journey into outer space, was sure to be welcomed as if he were the prophet Elijah come down to earth again. To see them first, then to hear them—that was the world's dearest wish.

This wish was to become reality very quickly for almost every citizen of the Union.

Going back to Baltimore without delay, Barbicane, Michel Ardan, Nicholl, and the Gun Club delegation were greeted by an indescribable furor. President Barbicane was ready to hand over his travel notes to the press. Since this manuscript was destined to be extremely significant, the *New York Herald* bought it for a price that still hasn't been disclosed. In fact, during its publication of "Journey to the Moon," this newspaper increased its circulation to 5,000,000 copies. Three days after the travelers had returned to the earth, the tiniest details of their expedition were general knowledge. Nothing remained other than to lay eyes on the heroes of this superhuman undertaking.

While Barbicane and his friends were circling the moon, their investigations allowed them to double-check the body of accepted theories regarding the earth's satellite. These scholars had carried out their examination under absolutely unique conditions and *de visu*.[10] As for the creation of that heavenly body, her origins, her ability to support life, people now knew which formulations to reject and which to retain. Her past, present, and future had likewise yielded up their ultimate secrets. How could you argue with these diligent witnesses who from barely twenty-five miles away had surveyed that strange peak of Tycho, the oddest mountain system on the moon? How could anybody talk back to these experts whose eyes had probed the depths of Plato's basin? What human being could contradict these daredevils whose risky endeavor actually took them over the moon's invisible face, which no mortal eyes had glimpsed till that moment? Our travelers were now qualified to have the last word in that science of lunar studies—which had reconstructed the world of the moon as Cuvier had his fossil skeletons—and they were able to say: "The moon was once a world that could support life and it did so before the earth could! The moon is now a world that's lifeless and unlivable!"

To celebrate the return of its most famous member and his two companions, the Gun Club decided to throw a banquet for them, but a banquet worthy of both the victors and the American public—and the circumstances would allow every citizen of the Union to personally participate.

All the main railroad lines in the nation were joined together by temporary tracks. At every train station, now decked out with matching flags and dolled up with matching decorations, stood tables that were identically laid. At consecutive, carefully determined times (designated by electric clocks synchronized to the second), the townspeople were invited to take their seats at the banquet tables.

For four days from January 5 to the 9th, the regular trains didn't run, as they don't every Sunday on Union railroads, and all the tracks stayed free.

During these four days just one high-speed locomotive, pulling a single passenger car of honor, had permission to ride the rails in the United States.

Aboard this locomotive were an engineer and a fireman, plus, as a token of esteem, the honorable J. T. Maston, the Gun Club's secretary.

The passenger car was exclusively for President Barbicane, Captain Nicholl, and Michel Ardan.

After the hip-hips, hoorays, and every onomatopoetic form of praise in the American language, the engine driver blew the whistle and the train left Baltimore Station. It traveled at a speed of 200 miles per hour. But what was this speed compared to the velocity of our three heroes shooting out of the columbiad?

Thus they went from one town to the other, finding the citizenry at table along the way, greeted by identical applause, showered with identical bravos. In this manner they crossed the eastern part of the Union through Pennsylvania, Connecticut, Massachusetts, Vermont, Maine, and New Hampshire; they headed north and west through New York, Ohio, Michigan, and Wisconsin; they went back down south through Illinois, Missouri, Arkansas, Texas, and Louisiana; they dashed southeast through Alabama and Florida; they went up through Georgia, then North and South Carolina; they visited the interior by way of Tennessee, Kentucky, Virginia, and Indiana; then after pulling out of the station in Washington, D.C., they reentered Baltimore, and over those four days they must have thought the whole United States of America were at the same table during the same immense banquet, greeting them simultaneously with identical hoorays!

It was a glorification of these heroes worthy of them, these three men whom legend would have raised to the rank of demigods.

And now will this endeavor of theirs, unprecedented in the history of travel, lead to any practical result? Will we ever set up direct contact with the moon? Will we open a service for navigating through space, with stopovers across the solar system? Will we go from planet to planet—Jupiter to Mer-

---

[10] *Translator's note.* Latin: "with their own eyes."

cury—and later from one star to another—the polestar to Sirius? Will this way of getting places allow us to visit those suns the firmament is swarming with?

These are questions we can't answer. But knowing the daring inventiveness of the Anglo-Saxon race, nobody will be surprised that the Americans tried to make profitable use of President Barbicane's endeavor.

Accordingly, some time after the travelers returned, the public reacted with clear approval to a prospectus from a limited partnership company, with $100,000,000 in capital, split into 100,000 shares of stock at $1,000 per share, and bearing the name National Interstellar Transportation Co. Barbicane was president; Captain Nicholl, vice president; J. T. Maston, recording secretary; Michel Ardan, traffic director.

And since it's the American way to plan for every business contingency, even bankruptcy, the honorable Harry Trollope and Mr. Francis Drayton were appointed in advance as presiding judge and trustee!

20,000 Leagues Under the Seas

A World Tour Underwater

First published in 1870

The underwater set pieces in this haunting novel rank with the most imaginative achievements in literature. As usual Verne did his homework—here in the areas of marine science and nautical engineering—but the unforgettable scenes in the book are his own brainchildren. Yes, underwater boats and diving outfits were in use long before he went to press, but that use was dismally restricted—nobody inside the contraptions dared travel out of sight of shore. But in *20,000 Leagues Under the Seas*, Verne's futuristic submarine, the *Nautilus*, goes on an ocean voyage covering 49,000+ miles, and its diving-suited passengers hike across the seafloor at depths of 500 to 1,000 feet.

Real life would take many decades to catch up. The 19th century's top submersible performance was an 1898 run along the Atlantic seaboard from Norfolk to Sandy Hook—barely 120 nautical leagues, let alone 20,000. Only in the 1950s would nuclear subs and atmospheric diving suits match the undersea doings in Verne's story. Consequently the novel's highlights are spectacular feats of imagination: when the *Nautilus* goes aground on a reef, streaks through an underwater tunnel, descends into a miles-deep trench, or gets sealed up in antarctic ice, Verne had nobody's true-life example to lean on—he took a few bits of décor from the textbooks, but he himself conceived or extrapolated the action at stage center.

In the process he gives us a pageant of the deep, and his sequences for hard-hat divers are especially vivid: they're set in undersea forests, coral graveyards, oyster beds—even the sunken ruins of Atlantis, here making their first appearance in popular fiction. Verne sprinkles his backgrounds with fish, seashells, and zoophytes lifted from the treatises of Buffon, Lacépède, and the ranking French scientists of his day, but he puts together his foreground events and effects on his own.

So *20,000 Leagues Under the Seas* presents a uniquely rich, crowded panorama. Alone among the five yarns in this volume, the novel was first serialized in the *Magasin d'éducation et de récréation:* the science here is extensive, in line with the educational side of the periodical's mission. Accordingly the tale is told by a leading marine biologist, his field notes heighten the story's verisimilitude, and there are frequent checklists of aquatic life forms. They're "on the dry side," the narrator admits, hinting that it's okay to skate over them. Some readers find them fascinating all the same: big-name fans of the novel have included such undersea specialists as Jacques Cousteau, William Beebe, and Robert Ballard.

In one additional way *20,000 Leagues* differs from the other novels in this volume: its plot isn't goal-driven. There's no equivalent here to aiming at the moon, heading for the earth's core, or going on a global junket with an 80-day deadline—instead we experience an unprecedented state of being, a new *alternative existence*. The *Nautilus* belongs to a shadowy, mystical, preternaturally imposing man who calls himself Captain Nemo: his destiny, we're told, is to "live out his entire life in the heart of this immense sea, and even his grave lay ready in its impregnable depths." Nemo heads up a multinational crew who share his values, speak their own private dialect, even have a sign language for treks on the ocean floor. Who are these refugees? What are they after? Why do they lead this alternative lifestyle beneath the sea? These mysteries are the book's undertow, and Chapter 45, just before the end, gives the outlines of an answer. This, too, will prove an innovative and imaginative achievement. *Translator.*

Note. In this novel of undersea exploration, Verne reports travel distances using a 19th century "nautical league," which is equivalent to roughly 2½ statute miles.

.

PART ONE

1

A Runaway Reef

THE YEAR 1866 was marked by a peculiar development, a baffling, bewildering phenomenon that surely nobody has forgotten. Without getting into those rumors that troubled civilians in the seaports and muddled public thinking even far inland, it must be said that professional seamen were especially alarmed. Traders, shipowners, sea captains, skippers and master mariners from Europe and America, naval officers everywhere, and at their heels the various national governments on those two continents all were extremely disturbed by the business.

In essence, over a period of time several ships had met up with "an enormous thing" at sea, a long spindle-shaped object that sometimes gave off a phosphorescent glow and was infinitely larger and faster than a whale.

As entered in various logbooks, the relevant data on this apparition agreed pretty closely as to the makeup of the object or creature in question, the record-setting speed of its movements, its startling ability to get from one location to another, and the unique energy it seemed to enjoy. If it was a cetacean, it exceeded in bulk any whale classified by science to that day. No naturalist, not Cuvier or Lacépède or Messrs. Duméril and de Quatrefages, would have accepted the existence of such a monster unless he'd seen it himself—seen it, let's emphasize, with his own trained scientific eyes.

After striking an average of the estimates made on various occasions—ignoring the timid appraisals that gave the object a length of only 200 feet and excluding the exaggerated claims that it was a mile wide and three long—you could state that this phenomenal creature exceeded by far any dimensions previously acknowledged by ichythologists, assuming it existed in the first place.

Now then, it *did* exist, this was an undeniable fact, and since the human mind is auto-matically partial to wondrous things, you can appreciate the worldwide excitement caused by this uncanny apparition. As for relegating it to the realm of fish stories, that charge had to be dropped.

To get down to cases, on July 20, 1866, the steamer *Governor Higginson* from the Calcutta & Burnach Steam Navigation Co. met up with this moving mass 500 miles off the east coast of Australia. At first Captain Baker thought he was facing an unknown reef; he was even getting ready to fix its exact position, when two waterspouts shot out of this bewildering object and sprang hissing into the air some 150 feet. So unless this reef was subject to the sporadic eruptions of a geyser, the *Governor Higginson* had fair and honest dealings with some aquatic mammal, unknown till that moment, whose blowholes spurted waterspouts mixed with air and steam.

Similar events were likewise witnessed in Pacific seas, on July 23 of the same year, by the *Christopher Columbus* from the West India & Pacific Steam Navigation Co. Consequently this extraordinary cetacean could transfer itself from one locality to another with surprising speed, since, within the space of just three days, the *Governor Higginson* and the *Christopher Columbus* had spotted it at two positions on the charts separated by a distance of more than 700 nautical leagues.

Two weeks later and 2,000 leagues farther, the *Helvetia* from the French transatlantic line and the *Shannon* from the Royal Mail fleet, running on opposite tacks in that part of the Atlantic lying between the United States and Europe, respectively signaled each other that they'd sighted the monster in latitude 42° 15′ north and longitude 60° 35′ west of the meridian of Greenwich. In their simultaneous estimates they were able to put the mammal's minimum length at more than 350 English feet, since both the *Shannon* and the *Helvetia* were of smaller dimensions, though each measured 330 feet from stem to stern. Now then, the largest whales, those rorqual whales that frequent the waterways of the Aleutian Islands, have never exceeded a length of 185 feet—if they even reach that.

One by one reports arrived that would

deeply affect public opinion: new estimates made by the transatlantic liner *Pereire*, the Inman line's *Etna* running afoul of the monster, a sworn statement drawn up by officers on the French frigate *Normandy*, ultracareful reckonings obtained by Commodore Fitz-James's staff aboard the *Lord Clyde*. In more lighthearted countries people joked about this phenomenon, but such serious, practical countries as England, America, and Germany were keenly concerned.

In every big city the monster was the latest rage; they sang about it in the coffee houses, they ridiculed it in the newspapers, they dramatized it in the theaters. The tabloids found it a fine opportunity for chasing wild geese. Since news editors are always short of copy, you saw the reappearance of every gigantic imaginary creature within memory, from "Moby Dick," the dreadful white whale of the High Arctic regions, to the stupendous kraken whose tentacles could entwine a 550-ton craft and drag it down into the ocean depths. They even reprinted statements from ancient times: the views of Aristotle and Pliny accepting the existence of such monsters, then the Norwegian narratives of Bishop Pontoppidan, the descriptions of Paul Egede, and finally the reports of Captain Harrington—whose good faith is above suspicion—in which he claims he saw, while aboard the *Castilian* in 1857, one of those enormous serpents that till then had frequented only the seas of France's old extremist newspaper, the *Constitutionalist*.

An endless debate then broke out between believers and skeptics in the scholarly societies and scientific journals. The "monster matter" had everybody fired up. During this unforgettable crusade journalists who specialized in science battled with those who specialized in humor, spilling waves of ink and some of them even two or three drops of blood, since they went from sea serpents to the most offensive personal remarks.

For six months the war seesawed. With untiring zest the popular press took potshots at feature articles from the Geographic Institute of Brazil, the Royal Academy of Science in Berlin, the British Association, the Smithsonian Institution in Washington, D.C., at

discussions in the *Indian Archipelago*, in *Cosmos* published by Father Moigno, in Petermann's *Mitteilungen*,[1] and at the science sections of the major French and foreign newspapers. When the monster's opponents quoted a saying by the zoologist Linnaeus that "nature doesn't make leaps," humorous writers in the popular periodicals parodied it, maintaining in essence that "nature doesn't make lunatics," then ordering their contemporaries to never give the lie to nature by believing in krakens, sea serpents, "Moby Dicks," and other all-out efforts from drunken seamen. Finally, in a much-feared satirical journal, an article by its most popular columnist squelched the monster for good, attacking it like the old dragon slayer Hippolytus and polishing it off it in the midst of worldwide laughter. Humor had defeated science.

During the first months of the year 1867, the whole matter seemed to be dead and buried—and it didn't seem due for resurrection—when new facts came to the public's attention. It was no longer an issue of a scientific problem to be solved, but of a real and serious danger to be avoided. The matter took a completely new turn. Once again the monster became an islet, rock, or reef, but a runaway reef, shifty and hard to pin down.

On March 5, 1867, the *Moravian* from the Montreal Ocean Co., lying during the night in latitude 27° 30′ and longitude 72° 15′, ran its starboard quarter afoul of a rock not marked on any charts of those waterways. Under the combined efforts of its 400-horsepower steam and the wind, it was going at a speed of fifteen miles per hour. If its hull hadn't been of exceptional quality, the *Moravian* would surely have cracked open from the impact and gone down along with the 237 passengers it was bringing back from Canada.

This accident happened around five o'clock in the morning, just as day was beginning to break. The officers on watch rushed to the craft's stern. They examined the ocean with the most scrupulous care. All they saw was a strong eddy about a third of a mile away, as if those sheets of water had been forcefully churned. They took the site's exact

---

[1] *Translator's note*. German: "Newsletter."

bearings, and the *Moravian* continued on course apparently undamaged. Had it run afoul of an underwater rock or the wreckage of some huge derelict ship? They couldn't say; but when they examined its underside in the service yard, they found that part of its keel had been smashed.

Though this event was tremendously serious in itself, it still might have been forgotten like so many others, if, three weeks later, it hadn't been duplicated under identical circumstances. Only this time, thanks to the nationality of the ship victimized by this new ramming, and thanks to the reputation of the company to which this ship belonged, the development caused a huge uproar.

There isn't a soul alive who hasn't heard of the famous English shipowner Cunard. In 1840 this shrewd businessman launched a postal service between Liverpool and Halifax using three wooden ships with 400-horsepower paddle wheels and a burden of 1,281 tons. Eight years later the company increased its assets by adding four 650-horsepower ships at 2,006 tons, and in two more years two other vessels of still greater power and tonnage. In 1853 the Cunard Co., whose mail-carrying charter had just been renewed, consecutively added to its assets the *Arabia*, the *Persia*, the *China*, the *Scotia*, the *Java*, and the *Russia*, all ships of top speed and after the *Great Eastern* the largest to ever plow the seas. Hence, in 1867 this company owned twelve ships, eight with paddle wheels and four with propellers.

I'm providing these heavily condensed details to help everybody understand the importance of this maritime transportation company, known the world over for its shrewd management. No transoceanic navigational undertaking has been conducted with greater skill, no business dealings have been crowned with greater success. In twenty-six years Cunard ships have made 2,000 Atlantic crossings, never canceling a voyage, never experiencing a delay, never losing a man, a vessel, or even a letter. Accordingly, despite strong competition from France, passengers still pick the Cunard line over all others, as a survey of official documents from recent years will confirm. Given that, nobody will

be surprised at the uproar caused by this accident involving one of its finest steamers.

On April 13, 1867, with a smooth sea and a moderate breeze, the *Scotia* lay in longitude 15° 12′ and latitude 45° 37′. It was going at a speed of 15½ miles per hour under the thrust of its thousand-horsepower engines. Its paddle wheels were churning the sea with perfect steadiness. Its draft of water was 22 feet and its displacement 233,924 cubic feet.

At 4:17 in the afternoon during a high tea for passengers gathered in the main lounge, a collision occurred, barely noticeable on the whole, affecting the *Scotia*'s hull in the quarter a little astern of its port paddle wheel.

The *Scotia* hadn't run afoul of something, it had *been* fouled, and by a cutting or puncturing instrument rather than a blunt one. This encounter seemed so minor that nobody on board would have been troubled by it—if it hadn't been for the shouts of crewmen in the hold, who climbed on deck yelling:

"We're sinking! We're sinking!"

At first the passengers were quite frightened, but Captain Anderson hastened to reassure them. In reality there couldn't be any pressing danger. Divided into seven compartments by watertight bulkheads, the *Scotia* could brave any leak with impunity.

Captain Anderson immediately made his way into the hold. He found that the sea had invaded the fifth compartment, and the speed of this invasion proved the leak was considerable. Luckily this compartment didn't contain the boilers, because their furnaces would have gone out instantly.

Captain Anderson called an immediate halt, and one of his sailors dived down to appraise the damage. A few seconds later he'd verified that there was a hole 6½ feet wide in the steamer's underside. A leak that big couldn't be patched, so with its paddle wheels half swamped, the *Scotia* had no choice but to continue its voyage. By then it lay 300 miles from Cape Clear, and after three days of delay that filled Liverpool with acute anxiety, it entered the company docks.

The engineers then proceeded to inspect the *Scotia*, which had been put in dry dock. They couldn't believe their eyes. Eight feet below its waterline gaped an orderly gash in the shape of an isosceles triangle. This breach in the sheet iron was perfectly formed and couldn't have been cleaner if it had been die cut. So it must have been produced by a puncturing tool of uncommon toughness—plus, after being launched with prodigious power and then piercing 1½ inches of sheet iron, this tool had to have withdrawn itself by a backward movement truly bewildering.

This was the last straw and it ended up arousing public passions all over again. From then on, in fact, any marine casualty without an established cause was charged to the monster's account. This outrageous animal had to shoulder responsibility for all missing vessels, whose number is unfortunately considerable—some 3,000 shipwrecks are recorded annually at the maritime information bureau, and the number of steam or sailing ships presumed lost with all hands, in the absence of any news, totals at least 200!

Now then, fairly or unfairly, it was the "monster" who stood accused of their disappearance; and since the creature was making it more and more dangerous to travel between the various continents, the public spoke its mind and demanded straight out that this fearsome cetacean be removed from the seas at any cost.

2

THE PROS AND CONS

AT THE TIME these developments were occurring, I'd come back from a scientific excursion to the Nebraska badlands in the United States. The French government had attached me to this expedition in my capacity as assistant professor at the Paris Museum of Natural History. After spending six months in Nebraska, I arrived in New York near the end of March, loaded down with valuable collections. I was scheduled to leave for France at the beginning of May. So in the meantime I was busy classifying my mineralogical, botanical, and zoological treasures, when that incident took place with the *Scotia*.

I was fully up to date on this matter, which was the talk of the town, and how could I not have been? I'd read and reread every American and European newspaper without being any farther along. This mystery puzzled me. Finding it impossible to form any views, I drifted from one extreme to the other. Something was out there, that much was certain, and any doubting Thomas was invited to put his finger on the *Scotia*'s wound.

When I arrived in New York, the issue was at the boiling point. The theory of a drifting islet or an elusive reef—put forward by people not quite in their right minds—was completely eliminated. And in truth, unless this reef had an engine in its belly, how could it get around with such prodigious speed?

Also discredited was the presence of a floating hull or some other huge piece of wreckage, and again because of this speed of movement.

So only two possible solutions to the problem were left, creating two very distinct groups of supporters: on one side, those favoring a monster of colossal strength; on the other, those favoring an "underwater boat" of tremendous motor power.

Now then, though the latter theory was perfectly reasonable, it couldn't stand up to inquiries conducted in both the New World and the Old. It was hardly likely that a private individual had such a mechanism at his disposal. Where and when had he built it, and how could he have built it in secret?

Only some government could have owned such an engine of destruction, and in these catastrophic times when men tax their ingenuity to build increasingly powerful aggressive weapons, it was possible that some nation, unbeknownst to the rest of the world, was testing out such a fearsome machine. The Chassepot rifle led to the torpedo, and the torpedo has led to this underwater battering ram, which in turn will lead to the world's putting its foot down. At least I hope so.

But this theory of a war machine collapsed in the face of firm denials by the various governments. Since the public interest was involved and transoceanic travel was suffering, the sincerity of those governments couldn't be doubted. Besides, how could the construction of this underwater boat have eluded public notice? Keeping a secret of this kind would be hard enough for an individual, and downright impossible for a nation whose every move is under constant surveillance by competing powers.

So after inquiries conducted in England, France, Russia, Prussia, Spain, Italy, America, and even Turkey, the theory of an underwater *Monitor* was decisively rejected.

And so the monster surfaced again, despite the never-ending jokes heaped on it by the popular press, and people's imaginations soon got caught up in the most ridiculous ichthyological fantasies.

After I arrived in New York, several individuals paid me the honor of consulting me on the phenomenon in question. In France I'd published a two-volume work in quarto entitled *The Mysteries of the Great Ocean Depths*. Well received in scholarly circles, this book had established me as a specialist in this pretty obscure field of natural history. My views were in demand. So long as I could dispute the reality of the business, I confined myself to sweeping denials. But I was soon backed into a corner and urged to explain my position straight out. And right on cue the *New York Herald* summoned "the honorable Pierre Aronnax, professor at the Paris Museum," to clarify his views no matter what.

I complied. Since I could no longer hold my tongue, I let it wag. I discussed every aspect of the matter, both political and scientific, and I'll now quote a passage from the well-padded article I published in the issue of April 30:

Hence, I said, after examining these different theories one by one, and after refuting every other supposition, we're forced to accept the existence of an extremely powerful marine animal.

The ocean's deepest recesses are completely unknown to us. No soundings have ever been able to reach them. What's going on in those distant depths? What creatures dwell, or could dwell, in those regions twelve to fifteen miles under the surface of the water? What kind of organism do those animals have? We can barely even guess.

However the solution to this problem presented to me can take the form of a choice between two alternatives.

Either we know all the varieties of creatures that live on our planet, or we don't.

If we don't *know them all, if nature still keeps ichthyological secrets from us, nothing is more reasonable than to accept the existence of fish or cetaceans of new species or even new genera, animals with a basically "cast-iron" organism that can live in strata beyond the reach of our soundings and that some development or other—an itch or a whim, if you prefer—can bring to the upper levels of the ocean at periodic intervals.*

If, on the other hand, we do *know every living species, we need to look for the animal in question among those marine creatures already cataloged, and in that event I would be inclined to accept the existence of a* giant *narwhal.*

The common narwhal, or sea unicorn, often reaches a length of sixty feet. If you increase its dimensions fivefold or even tenfold, then give this cetacean strength in proportion to its size while enlarging its offensive weapons, you'll get just the animal we're looking for. It would have the proportions determined by the Shannon's *officers, the requisite instrument for puncturing the* Scotia, *and enough power to pierce a steamer's hull.*

In essence the narwhal is armed with a sort of ivory sword, or lance, as some naturalists put it. It's a king-sized tooth as hard as steel. Some of these teeth have been found buried in the bodies of baleen whales, which the narwhal attacks with invariable success. Others have been yanked, not without some difficulty, from the undersides of vessels that narwhals have pierced clean through, the way a gimlet pierces a wine barrel. The museum at the Faculty of Medicine in Paris has one of these tusks 7 feet 4½ inches long and 19 inches around at the base!

All right then! Imagine this weapon to be ten times stronger and the animal ten times more powerful, launch it at a speed of twenty miles per hour, multiply its mass times its velocity, and you'll get just the impact we need to create the specified catastrophe.

So till I have fuller information, I'll plump for a sea unicorn of colossal dimensions, no longer armed with simply a lance but an actual spur, like ironclad frigates or those warships called "rams," whose mass and motor power it would also have.

This bewildering phenomenon can thus be accounted for—unless it's something else altogether, which, despite everything that has been sighted, studied, explored, and experienced, is still possible!

These last words were cowardly of me; but as far as I could, I wanted to protect my academic dignity and not lay myself open to laughter from the Americans, who, when they do laugh, laugh their heads off. I'd left myself a loophole. Yet deep down I'd accepted the existence of "the monster."

My article was hotly debated and caused a major uproar. It won over a number of supporters. What's more, the solution it proposed allowed for free play of the imagination. The human mind loves the impressive prospect of uncanny creatures. Now then, the sea is exactly their best environment, the only appropriate setting for the breeding and rearing of such giants—next to which land animals such as elephants or rhinoceroses are pip-squeaks by comparison. Those masses of liquid provide transportation for the biggest known species of mammals and maybe harbor mollusks of incomparable size or crustaceans too frightful to contemplate, such as 300-foot lobsters or crabs weighing 200 tons! Why not? Back in prehistoric times, land animals (quadrupeds, apes, reptiles, birds) were built on a gigantic scale. Our Creator cast them using a colossal mold that time has gradually made smaller. In its untold depths why couldn't the sea preserve those huge life forms from another age, this sea that never changes while the landmasses are undergoing almost continual alteration? Couldn't the heart of the ocean hide the last-remaining varieties of those titanic species, for which years are centuries and centuries millennia?

But I mustn't let these fantasies run away with me! Enough of these phantoms that time has changed for me into harsh realities. I repeat, public opinion had firmed up as to the nature of this phenomenon, and people accepted without argument the existence of a prodigious creature that had nothing in common with the sea serpents of fable.

Yet if some saw it strictly as a scientific problem to be solved, more practical people, especially in America and England, were determined to rid the ocean of this alarming monster in order to insure the safety of transoceanic travel. The industrial and commercial newspapers dealt with the issue chiefly from this viewpoint. The *Shipping & Mercantile Gazette*, *Lloyd's List*, France's *Ocean Liner* and *Maritime & Colonial Review*, all the periodicals devoted to insurance companies—who threatened to raise their premium rates—were unanimous on the point.

The public had spoken, and the states of the Union were the first to jump in. Preparations got under way in New York for an expedition to track down this narwhal. A high-speed frigate, the *Abraham Lincoln*, was fitted out for putting to sea as soon as possible. The navy unlocked its arsenals for Commander Farragut, who moved energetically ahead with arming his frigate.

But it never fails—just when a decision had been made to hunt the monster, the monster didn't put in any further appearances. For two months nobody heard a word about it. Not a single ship met up with it. Apparently the unicorn had gotten wise to these plots being hatched against it. People kept yammering about the creature, even over the Atlantic Cable! So the comics claimed that slippery rascal had waylaid a passing telegram and made the most of it.

Therefore the frigate was equipped for a far-off voyage and armed with fearsome fishing gear, but nobody knew where to steer it. And the public's impatience grew till on June 2, word came that the *Tampico*, a steamer on the San Francisco line running from California to Shanghai, had sighted the animal again, three weeks earlier in the northerly seas of the Pacific.

This news caused tremendous excitement. Commander Farragut didn't get even a 24-hour breather. His provisions were on board. His coal bunkers were overflowing. Not a single crewman had failed to report for duty. To cast off, all he had to do was light and stoke his furnaces. So if he'd delayed even half a day, it would have been unforgivable! But Commander Farragut wanted nothing more than to be on his way.

I received a letter three hours before the *Abraham Lincoln* left its Brooklyn pier;[2] the letter read as follows:

Pierre Aronnax
Professor at the Paris Museum
Fifth Avenue Hotel
New York

Sir:

If you would like to join the expedition on the Abraham Lincoln, *the government of the Union will gladly accept you as France's representative in this undertaking. Commander Farragut is holding a cabin for you.*

Very cordially yours,
J. B. HOBSON,
Secretary of the Navy.

3

AS MASTER WISHES

THREE SECONDS before the arrival of J. B. Hobson's letter, I'd no more dreamed of tracking down the unicorn than of trying for the Northwest Passage. Three seconds after reading this letter from the honorable Secretary of the Navy, I understood at last that my true vocation, my sole purpose in life, was to hunt this disturbing monster and rid the world of it.

Even so, I'd just come back from an arduous trip, exhausted and badly needing a rest. My only wish was to see my country again, my friends, my little flat by the nature gardens, my beloved collections! But nothing could hold me back. I forgot all of the above, and without another thought for my exhaustion, friends, or collections, I accepted the American government's offer.

"Besides," I mused, "all roads lead home

---

[2] Type of wharf earmarked for a particular vessel.

to Europe, and our unicorn may be gracious enough to take me toward the coast of France! That fine animal might even let itself be captured in European seas—as a personal favor to me—and I'll bring back to the Museum of Natural History at least twenty inches of its ivory lance!"

But in the meantime I would have to hunt for this narwhal in the northern Pacific Ocean, which meant going back to France by way of the Antipodes.

"Conseil!" I called in an impatient voice.

Conseil was my manservant. A dedicated lad who went with me on all my trips; a gallant Flemish boy whom I genuinely liked and who returned the compliment; a born stoic, meticulous as a matter of principle, habitually hardworking, rarely startled by life's surprises, very skillful with his hands, efficient in all his duties, and despite his having a name that means "counsel," never giving advice—not even the unsolicited kind.

From rubbing shoulders with scientists in our miniature world by the nature gardens, Conseil had managed to learn a few things. The boy was a seasoned specialist in biological classification and he could run with acrobatic agility up and down the whole ladder of branches, groups, classes, subclasses, orders, families, genera, subgenera, species, and varieties. But there his science came to a halt. Classifying was everything to him, so he knew nothing else. Well versed in the theory of classification, he was poorly versed in its practical application, and I doubt that he could tell a sperm whale from a right whale! And yet what a fine, gallant lad!

For the past ten years, Conseil had gone with me wherever science beckoned. Not once had he commented on the length or the difficulty of a trip. Never had he objected to buckling up his suitcase for any country whatever, China or the Congo, no matter how far off it was. He went here, there, and everywhere in perfect contentment. What's more, he enjoyed excellent health that defied all illness, had strong muscles, but didn't have a nerve in his body, not even a hint of one—the mental type, I mean.

The lad was thirty years old, and his age

compared to his employer's was as fifteen is to twenty. Please forgive me for this under-handed way of admitting I'd turned forty.

But Conseil had one flaw. He was a fanatic on formality and he addressed me only in the third person—to the point where it got tiresome.

"Conseil!" I repeated, while feverishly starting my preparations for departure.

To be sure, I had confidence in this dedicated lad. Ordinarily I never asked if it suited him to go with me on my trips; but this time an expedition was involved that could drag on indefinitely, a risky undertaking whose purpose was to hunt down an animal that could sink a frigate as easily as a walnut shell! This was food for thought, even for the world's least emotional man. How would Conseil react?

"Conseil!" I called a third time.

Conseil appeared.

"Did master summon me?" he said, coming in.

"Yes, my boy. Get my things ready, yours as well. We're leaving in two hours."

"As master wishes," Conseil replied serenely.

"We haven't a moment to lose. Pack as much into my trunk as you can, my traveling kit, my suits, shirts, and socks, don't bother counting, just squeeze them all in—and hurry!"

"What about master's collections?" Conseil pointed out.

"We'll deal with them later."

"What! The skeletons of archaeotherium, hyracotherium, oreodon, choeropotamus, and master's other fossil bones?"

"The hotel will take care of them."

"What about master's live babirusa?"

"They'll feed it during our absence. Anyhow we'll leave instructions to ship the whole menagerie to France."

"Then we aren't going back to Paris?" Conseil asked.

"Yes we are ... certainly ... ," I replied evasively, "but after we make a detour."

"Whatever detour master wishes."

"Oh, it's nothing much! A route slightly less direct, that's all. We're leaving on the *Abraham Lincoln*."

"As master thinks best," Conseil replied placidly.

"You see, my friend, it concerns the monster . . . the notorious narwhal. We're going to rid the seas of it! The author of a two-volume work in quarto on *The Mysteries of the Great Ocean Depths* has no excuse for not setting sail with Commander Farragut. It's a glorious mission but also a dangerous one! We don't know where it'll take us! Those beasts can be very unpredictable! But we're going just the same! We have a commander who's game for anything . . . !"

"What master does, I'll do," Conseil replied.

"But give it some thought, because I don't want to hide anything from you. This is one of those voyages from which people don't always come back!"

"As master wishes."

Fifteen minutes later our trunks were ready. Conseil did them in a flash, and I was sure the lad hadn't left out a thing, because he classified shirts and suits as expertly as birds and mammals.

The hotel elevator dropped us off in the main vestibule on the mezzanine. I went down the few steps leading to the ground floor. I settled my bill at that huge counter always under siege by a considerable crowd. I left instructions for shipping my containers of stuffed animals and dried plants to Paris, France. I opened a line of credit sufficient to cover the babirusa, and with Conseil right behind me, I jumped into a carriage.

For a fare of four dollars, the vehicle went down Broadway to Union Square, took Fourth Ave. to its junction with Bowery St., turned into Catherine St., and halted at Pier 34. There the Catherine ferry transferred men, horses, and carriage to Brooklyn, that major New York annex located on the left bank of the East River, and in a few minutes we arrived at the wharf alongside which the *Abraham Lincoln* was spewing torrents of black smoke out of its two funnels.

They immediately transferred our baggage to the frigate's deck. I rushed on board. I asked for Commander Farragut. One of the sailors led me to the afterdeck, where I stood in the presence of a smart-looking officer who held out his hand to me.

"Professor Pierre Aronnax?" he said to me.

"The same," I replied. "Commander Farragut?"

"None other. Welcome aboard, professor. Your cabin's ready for you."

I bowed, and letting the commander attend to getting under way, I was taken to the cabin being held for me.

The *Abraham Lincoln* had been perfectly chosen and fitted out for its new mission. It was a high-speed frigate furnished with supercharging equipment that could build its steam tension to seven atmospheres. Under this pressure the *Abraham Lincoln* reached an average speed of 18.3 miles per hour, a considerable speed but still not enough to contend with our gigantic cetacean.

The frigate's living arrangements complemented its nautical virtues. I was very happy with my cabin, which was located in the stern and opened into the officers' mess.

"We'll be quite cozy here," I told Conseil.

"With all due respect to master," Conseil replied, "as cozy as a hermit crab in the shell of a whelk."

I left Conseil with the task of properly stowing our luggage and I climbed on deck to watch the preparations for getting under way.

Just then Commander Farragut was issuing orders to loose the last moorings that held the *Abraham Lincoln* to its Brooklyn pier. Hence, if I'd been delayed by fifteen minutes or even less, the frigate would have gone without me, and I would have been absent from this extraordinary, uncanny, and inconceivable expedition, a truthful account of which may well meet with some skepticism.

But Commander Farragut didn't want to waste a single day or even a single hour in making for those seas where the animal had just been sighted. He sent for his engineer.

"Are we up to pressure?" he asked the man.

"Aye, sir," the engineer replied.

"Then go ahead!" Commander Farragut called.

This order was relayed to the engine room with the help of a compressed-air device, and the mechanics activated the start-up wheel. Steam rushed whistling into the gaping valves. Long horizontal pistons groaned and pushed the tie rods of the drive shaft. The propeller blades churned the waves with increasing speed and the *Abraham Lincoln* moved out majestically, escorted by over a hundred ferries and tenders all crammed with spectators.[3]

The wharves in Brooklyn and every part of New York bordering the East River were covered with curiosity seekers. Exiting from 500,000 chests, three cheers burst forth in succession. Thousands of handkerchiefs were waving above those jam-packed masses, hailing the *Abraham Lincoln* till it reached the waters of the Hudson River, at the tip of the long peninsula that forms New York City.

Then the frigate went along the New Jersey coast—the wonderful right bank of this river, all loaded down with country homes—and passed between the forts to salutes from their biggest cannons. The *Abraham Lincoln* replied by three times lowering and hoisting the American flag, whose thirty-nine stars twinkled from the gaff of the mizzen sail; then it slowed down to take the channel marked with buoys, entered the curving inner bay formed by the spit of Sandy Hook, and hugged this sand-covered strip of land where thousands of spectators acclaimed us one more time.

The escort of boats and tenders kept following the frigate and left us only when we came abreast of the lightship, whose two signal lights mark the entrance of the narrows to Upper New York Bay.

Three o'clock sounded. The harbor pilot went down into his dinghy and rejoined the little schooner waiting for him to leeward. The stokers prodded the furnaces; the propeller churned the waves with greater speed; our frigate skirted the flat, yellow coast of Long Island; and by eight o'clock in the evening, after the lights on Fire Island had vanished into the northwest, we were running at full steam over the dark waters of the Atlantic.

---

[3] Tenders are little steamboats that assist the big liners.

4

NED LAND

COMMANDER FARRAGUT was a fine seaman, worthy of the frigate he commanded. His ship and he were one. He was its soul. On the cetacean matter no doubts ever sprang up in his mind, and he didn't allow the animal's existence to be disputed aboard his vessel. He believed in it as certain pious women believe in the leviathan from the Book of Job—out of faith, not reason. The monster existed, and he'd vowed to rid the seas of it. The man was a sort of Knight of Rhodes, a modern-day Dieudonné of Gozo on his way to face the dragon devastating his island. Either Commander Farragut would slay the narwhal, or the narwhal would slay Commander Farragut. No middle of the road for these two.

The ship's officers shared the views of their leader. While they scanned the vast expanse of the ocean, you couldn't help hearing them chatter, bicker, debate, and calculate the various chances of meeting up with the creature. Voluntary watches from the crosstrees of the topgallant sail were self-imposed by more than one who would have cursed this chore under any other circumstances. As often as the sun swept over its daily arc, the masts were populated with seamen whose feet itched and couldn't hold still on the planking of the deck below. And the *Abraham Lincoln*'s stempost hadn't even cut the suspicious waters of the Pacific.

As for the crew, all they wanted was to find the unicorn, harpoon it, haul it on board, and slice it up. They surveyed the sea with scrupulous care. What's more, Commander Farragut had mentioned that a certain sum of $2,000 was waiting for whoever sighted the animal first, whether cabin boy or sailor, mate or officer. I'll let the reader decide if people's eyes got proper exercise aboard the *Abraham Lincoln*.

As for me, I wasn't far behind the others and I delegated to nobody my share in this daily watching. Our frigate would have had fivescore good reasons for rechristening itself the *Argus*, after that mythological beast with a hundred eyes! The lone rebel among us was Conseil, who seemed completely uninterested in the issue exciting us and was out of step with the overall enthusiasm on board.

As I said, Commander Farragut had carefully equipped his ship with the proper gear for catching a gigantic cetacean. No whaling vessel could have been better armed. We had every known mechanism from the hand-hurled harpoon to the blunderbuss that fired barbed arrows and the duck gun with exploding bullets. Mounted on the forecastle was a new and improved breech-loading cannon with a very heavy barrel and narrow bore, a weapon that would figure in the Universal Exhibition of 1867. Made in America, this valuable instrument could fire a nine-pound conical projectile an average distance of ten miles without the least bother.

So the *Abraham Lincoln* wasn't lacking in engines of destruction. But there was still more. There was Ned Land, the King of Harpooners.

Gifted with rare manual ability, Ned Land was a Canadian who had no equal in his perilous trade. Skill, poise, daring, and shrewdness were virtues he possessed to a high degree, and it took an unusually crafty right whale or an exceptionally sly sperm whale to dodge the thrusts of his harpoon.

Ned Land was about forty years old. A man of great stature—over six English feet—he was powerfully built, earnest in manner, not very sociable, sometimes headstrong, and thoroughly bad-tempered when crossed. His looks caught your attention, and above all his sharp eyes, which gave an odd intensity to his facial expression.

To my way of thinking, Commander Farragut had made a wise move in hiring on this man. With his eye and throwing arm, he was worth the whole crew all by himself. I can't do better than compare him to a high-powered telescope that could double as a cannon always ready to fire away.

A Canadian is practically a Frenchman, and as unsociable as Ned Land was, I must admit he took a definite liking to me. No doubt it was my nationality that attracted him. It was a chance for him to speak, and for me to hear, that old 16th century dialect used by Rabelais and still spoken in some Canadian provinces. The harpooner's family originated in Quebec and they were already a line of bold fishermen back in the days when this town belonged to France.

Little by little Ned grew fond of chatting, and I loved hearing the tales of his adventures in the polar seas. He described his fishing trips and battles with great natural lyricism. His tales took on the form of an epic poem, and I felt I was hearing some Canadian Homer spinning his *Iliad* of the High Arctic regions.

I'm writing of this bold companion as I know him today. Because we've become old friends, bonding in that permanent comradeship born and cemented only during the most fearful crises! Ah, my gallant Ned! All I ask is to live a hundred years more, the longer to remember you!

And now what were Ned Land's views on this matter of a marine monster? I must admit that he flatly didn't believe in the unicorn, and he was the only man who didn't share the overall conviction on board. He avoided even dealing with the topic, for which I felt compelled to take him to task one day.

One magnificent evening on June 25—in other words, three weeks after our departure—the frigate lay off Cabo Blanco, thirty miles to leeward of the coast of Patagonia. We'd crossed the Tropic of Capricorn, and the Strait of Magellan opened less than 700 miles to the south. Before the week was out, the *Abraham Lincoln* would be plowing the waves of the Pacific.

Seated on the afterdeck, Ned Land and I chatted about this and that, looking at the mysterious sea whose depths are still beyond the reach of human eyes. Quite naturally I led our conversation around to the giant unicorn and I weighed our expedition's various chances for success or failure. Then, seeing that Ned just let me talk without saying much himself, I went at him more directly.

"Ned," I asked him, "how can you still doubt the existence of this cetacean we're after? Do you have any specific reasons for being so skeptical?"

The harpooner looked at me for a few seconds before replying, slapped his broad forehead in one of his standard gestures, shut his eyes as if to collect his thoughts, and finally said:

"Just maybe, Professor Aronnax."

"But Ned, you're a professional whaler, a man who's acquainted with all the big marine mammals—your mind should easily accept this theory of an enormous cetacean, and you should be the last one to doubt it under circumstances such as these."

"That's just where you're wrong, professor," Ned replied. "It's all very well for the man in the street to think there are oversized comets in outer space or prehistoric monsters living inside the earth, but no astronomer or geologist believes in such phantoms. The same goes for whalers. I've hunted plenty of cetaceans, I've harpooned a large number, I've killed quite a few; but no matter how powerful and well armed they were, neither their tails or their tusks could puncture the sheet-iron plates of a steamer."

"Even so, Ned, people talk of vessels that narwhal tusks have run clean through."

"Wooden ships maybe," the Canadian replied. "But I've never seen the like. So till I have proof to the contrary, I'll deny that baleen whales, sperm whales, or unicorns can do any such thing."

"Listen to me, Ned—"

"No, no, professor. I'll go along with anything you want except that. Some gigantic devilfish maybe . . . ?"

"Even less likely, Ned. A devilfish is simply a mollusk, and this name in itself hints at its semiliquid flesh because it's Latin meaning *soft one*. Devilfish don't belong to the vertebrate branch, and even if one were 500 feet long, it still couldn't do the slightest harm to ships like the *Scotia* or the *Abraham Lincoln*. Consequently the feats of krakens or other monsters of that ilk must be relegated to the realm of fish stories."

"So, Mr. Naturalist," Ned Land continued in a mocking tone, "you'll just keep on believing in the existence of some enormous cetacean . . . ?"

"Yes, Ned, I repeat it with a conviction based on reasoning from the facts. I believe in the existence of a mammal with a mighty organism, belonging to the vertebrate branch like baleen whales, sperm whales, or dolphins, and armed with a tusk made of horn that has tremendous penetrating power."

"Humph!" the harpooner put in, shaking his head with the attitude of a man who isn't open to being persuaded.

"Note well, my fine Canadian," I went on, "if there *is* such an animal, if it lives deep in the ocean, if it frequents the liquid strata located a couple miles under the surface of the water, it needs to have an organism so strong that it defies all comparison."

"And why such a mighty organism?" Ned asked.

"Because it takes incalculable strength just to live in those deep strata and withstand their pressure."

"Really?" Ned said, tipping me a wink.

"Really, and I can easily prove it to you with a few figures."

"Bosh!" Ned countered. "You can make figures do anything you want!"

"In business, Ned, but not in mathematics. Hear me out. Let's accept that the pressure of one atmosphere is represented by the pressure of a column of water 32 feet high. In reality this column of water wouldn't be quite so high because here we're dealing with salt water, which is denser than fresh water. Well then, when you dive under the waves, Ned, for every 32 feet of water above you, your body is tolerating the pressure of one more atmosphere, in other words, 14.2 pounds per each square inch on your body's surface. So it follows that at 320 feet down, this pressure is equal to ten atmospheres, to a hundred atmospheres at 3,200 feet, and to a thousand atmospheres at 32,000 feet, hence at around six miles down. Which is tantamount to saying that if you could reach this depth in the ocean, each square inch on your body's surface would be experiencing 14,200 pounds of pressure. Now then, my gallant Ned, do you know how many square inches there are on the surface of your body?"

"I haven't the foggiest notion, Professor Aronnax."

"About 2,600."

"As many as that?"

"Yes, and since the atmosphere's pressure actually weighs slightly more than 14.2 pounds per square inch, right now your 2,600 square inches are tolerating 38,730 pounds."

"Without my noticing it?"

"Without your noticing it. And if you aren't crushed by all that pressure, it's because the air penetrates inside your body with equal pressure. Ergo there's a perfect balance between inside and outside pressures, which neutralize each other and allow you to handle them without discomfort. But in the water it's another story."

"Yes, I see," Ned replied, getting more interested. "Because the water surrounds me but doesn't penetrate me."

"Exactly, Ned. Hence, at 32 feet beneath the surface of the sea, you'll experience a pressure of 38,730 pounds; at 320 feet, or ten times greater pressure, it's 387,300 pounds; at 3,200 feet, or a hundred times greater pressure, it's 3,873,000 pounds; finally at 32,000 feet, or a thousand times greater pressure, it's 38,730,000 pounds; in other words, you would be squeezed as flat as if you'd been yanked from between the plates of a hydraulic press!"

"Holy smoke!" Ned put in.

"All right, my fine harpooner, if vertebrates several hundred yards long and proportionate in bulk live at those depths, their surface areas make up hundreds of thousands of square inches, and the pressure they experience must be measured in *billions* of pounds. Figure out for yourself, then, what a resistant bone structure and what a mighty organism they would need in order to withstand such pressures!"

"They would need to be manufactured," Ned Land replied, "from sheet-iron plates eight inches thick, like ironclad frigates."

"That's right, Ned, and then imagine the damage that kind of mass could inflict if it were speeding as fast as an express train and it struck a ship's hull."

"Yes . . . really . . . maybe," the Canadian replied, staggered by these figures but still not ready to give in.

"Well, have I persuaded you?"

"You've persuaded me of one thing, Mr. Naturalist. That deep in the sea, such animals would need to be just as strong as you say—*if* they exist."

"But if they don't exist, you stubborn harpooner, how do you explain the accident that happened to the *Scotia?*"

"It's maybe . . . ," Ned said, hesitating.

"Go on!"

"Because . . . it just couldn't be true!" the Canadian replied, not realizing he'd just aped a famous catchphrase of the scientist Arago.

But his answer didn't prove a thing, other than how bullheaded the harpooner could be. That day I didn't go at him again. The *Scotia*'s accident couldn't be denied. Its hole was real enough that it had to be plugged up, and I don't think a hole's existence can be more emphatically proven. Now then, that hole didn't just make itself, and since it hadn't resulted from underwater rocks or underwater machines, it must have been caused by the puncturing tool of some animal.

Now then, for all the reasons given to this point, I believed that animal was a member of the branch Vertebrata, class Mammalia, group Pisciforma, and finally order Cetacea. As for the family in which it would be placed (baleen whale, sperm whale, or dolphin), the genus in which it belonged, and the species in which it would find its proper home, these issues had to be left for later. To answer them called for dissecting this unknown monster; to dissect it called for catching it; to catch it called for harpooning it—which was Ned Land's business; to harpoon it called for sighting it—which was the crew's business; and to sight it called for meeting up with it— which was a chancy business.

5

AT RANDOM

FOR A WHILE the *Abraham Lincoln*'s voyage was uneventful. But one circumstance arose that displayed Ned Land's marvelous skills and showed just how much confidence we could have in him.

Off the Falkland Islands on June 30, the frigate came in contact with a fleet of American whalers, and we learned that they hadn't any knowledge of the narwhal. But one of them, the captain of the *Monroe*, knew Ned Land had shipped aboard the *Abraham Lincoln* and asked his help in hunting a baleen whale that was in sight. Eager to see Ned Land at work, Commander Farragut allowed him to make his way aboard the *Monroe*. And the Canadian had such good luck that with a right-and-left shot, he harpooned not one whale but two, striking the first straight to the heart and catching the other after a chase lasting just a few minutes!

No doubt about it, if the monster ever had to deal with Ned Land's harpoon, I wouldn't put my money on the monster.

Our frigate sailed down the east coast of South America with prodigious speed. By July 3 we were at the entrance to the Strait of Magellan off Cabo de las Virgenes. But Commander Farragut didn't want to attempt this winding passageway and maneuvered to double Cape Horn.

The whole crew agreed with him. In all honesty were we likely to run into the narwhal inside such a cramped strait? Many of the sailors swore that the monster couldn't negotiate this passageway simply because "he's too big for it!"

Near three o'clock in the afternoon on July 6, fifteen miles south of shore, the *Abraham Lincoln* doubled the solitary islet at the tip of the South American continent, that stray rock Dutch seamen had named Cape Horn after their hometown of Hoorn. We set our course for the northwest, and by the next day the frigate's propeller was finally churning the waters of the Pacific.

"Open your eyes! Open your eyes!" the *Abraham Lincoln*'s sailors kept saying.

And they opened amazingly wide. Eyes and spyglasses (a bit dazzled, it's true, by the outlook of $2,000) didn't remain at rest for a second. Day and night we scanned the surface of the ocean, and those with nyctalopic eyes, whose ability to see in the dark increased their chances by 50%, had an excellent shot at winning the prize.

For me personally the money didn't have any allure, yet I was hardly the least watchful on board. Grabbing only a few minutes for meals and a few hours for sleep, come rain or come shine, I stayed put on deck. Sometimes bending over the forecastle railings, sometimes leaning against the sternrail, I eagerly scoured that cotton-colored wake whitening the ocean as far as the eye could see. And how many times I shared the excitement of the staff and crew when some unpredictable whale would lift its blackish back above the waves. In a second the frigate's deck would become densely populated. The cowls over the companionways would spew out a torrent of sailors and officers. With panting chests and anxious eyes, we would watch the cetacean's movements. I looked; I looked so hard, I nearly went blind from a run-down retina—while Conseil, as stoic as ever, kept repeating to me in a calm tone:

"If master's eyes would kindly stop bulging, master will see farther!"

But what a waste of energy! The *Abraham Lincoln* would change course and race after the animal we'd sighted, only to find an ordinary right whale or a common sperm whale that soon vanished in the midst of extensive cursing.

But the good weather held up. Our voyage was proceeding under optimum conditions. By then it was the bad season in these southernmost regions, because July in this zone corresponds to our January in Europe; but the sea stayed smooth and offered an unobstructed view over a wide perimeter.

Ned Land continued to display the most stubborn skepticism; outside his spells on watch, he even kept up a pretense of never looking at the surface of the waves—at least while no whales were in sight. And yet the marvelous power of his vision would have performed a real service. But that obstinate Canadian spent eight hours out of every twelve reading or sleeping in his cabin. A hundred times I scolded him for his lack of interest.

"Phooey!" he replied. "Nothing's out there, Professor Aronnax, and even if there *is* some animal, what chance would we have of spotting it? Can't you see we're just wandering around at random? Folks say they've sighted this slippery beast again in the Pacific high seas—I'm truly willing to believe it; but two months have already gone by since then, and judging from your narwhal's personality,

it hates getting moldy from hanging out too long in the same waterways! It's blessed with a terrific gift for getting around. Now then, professor, you know better than I that nature doesn't do senseless things, and she wouldn't give some naturally slow animal the talent to move quickly if it didn't need to. So if the beast does exist, it's already long gone!"

I had no reply to this. Obviously we were groping in the dark. But what else could we do? All the same our chances were automatically pretty limited. Yet everybody still felt confident of success, and not a single sailor on board would have bet against the narwhal appearing, and soon.

On July 20 we cut the Tropic of Capricorn at longitude 105°, and by the 27th of the same month, we'd crossed the equator on the 110th meridian. These bearings determined, the frigate took a more decisive westward heading and tackled the seas of the central Pacific. With good reason Commander Farragut felt it would be better to stay in deep waters and keep his distance from continents or islands, whose neighborhoods the animal always seemed to avoid—"No doubt," our bosun said, "because there isn't enough water for him!" So the frigate kept well out when going past the Tuamotu, Marquesas, and Hawaiian islands, then cut the Tropic of Cancer at longitude 132° and headed for the seas of China.

We were finally in the area of the monster's latest antics! And in all honesty life became impossible on board. Hearts were pounding so frightfully, they risked developing aneurysms. The whole crew suffered from a nervous excitement that it's beyond me to describe. Nobody ate, nobody slept. Twenty times a day some error in perception or the optical illusions of some sailor perched in the crosstrees would cause unbearable anguish, and with this emotion repeated twenty times over, we stayed in a state of irritability so intense that a reaction was bound to follow.

And in fact this reaction wasn't long in coming. For three months during which every day seemed like a century, the *Abraham Lincoln* plowed all the northerly seas of the Pacific, racing after whales we'd sighted,

suddenly veering off course, swerving sharply from one tack to another, stopping abruptly, putting on steam and reversing engines in quick succession—at the risk of stripping its gears—and not leaving a single sector unexplored from the beaches of Japan to the coasts of America. And we found nothing! Nothing except vast, deserted waters! Nothing remotely like a gigantic narwhal, or an underwater islet, or a derelict ship, or a runaway reef, or anything even the least bit uncanny!

So a reaction set in. At first discouragement took hold of people's minds, opening the door to skepticism. A new feeling appeared on board, three parts shame and seven parts fury. The crew called themselves "out-and-out fools" for being hoodwinked by a phantom, then they got even angrier. Those mountains of arguments built up over a year collapsed all at once, and after that people only wanted to catch up on their eating and sleeping, to make up for all the time they'd so stupidly sacrificed.

With typical human fickleness they jumped from one extreme to the other. The undertaking's heartiest supporters inevitably turned into its noisiest opponents. This reaction surged upward from the bowels of the ship, from the stokers' quarters to the staff mess room, and if it hadn't been for Commander Farragut's characteristic stubbornness, the frigate would definitely have headed right back to that cape in the south.

But this pointless search couldn't drag on much longer. The *Abraham Lincoln* had done everything it could to succeed and hadn't any reason to blame itself. Never had the crew of an American naval vessel shown more patience and zeal; they weren't responsible for this failure; there was nothing left to do but go home.

The crew presented the commander with a petition to that effect. The commander stood his ground. His sailors couldn't hide their discontent and their work suffered as a result. I don't mean to imply that there was a mutiny on board, but after a reasonable period of intransigence, Commander Farragut, like Christopher Columbus before him, asked for a grace period of just three days more. If the monster hadn't appeared by this deadline three days off, our helmsman would give the wheel three turns, and the *Abraham Lincoln* would chart a course for European seas.

This promise was given on November 2. It had the immediate result of reviving the crew's failing spirits. They scanned the ocean with renewed care. Every man wanted one last look in which to sum up his experience. Spyglasses went to work with feverish energy. We'd issued a crowning challenge to the giant narwhal, and the latter had no acceptable excuse for ignoring this Summons to Appear!

Two days went by. The *Abraham Lincoln* stayed at half steam. On the off chance that the animal might be found in these waterways, we used a thousand methods to spark its interest or rouse it from its apathy. We trailed huge sides of bacon in our wake, much to the satisfaction, I must say, of assorted sharks. While the *Abraham Lincoln* heaved to, its longboats radiated around it in all directions and didn't leave a corner of the sea unexplored. But the evening of November 4 arrived with this underwater mystery still unsolved.

At noon the next day, November 5, the promised deadline would come and go. As good as his word, Commander Farragut would fix his position, set his course for the southeast, and leave the northerly regions of the Pacific decisively behind.

By then the frigate lay in latitude 31° 15' north and longitude 136° 42' east. The Japan coast was less than 200 miles to our leeward. Night was falling. Eight o'clock had just sounded. Huge clouds covered the moon's disk, then in her first quarter. The sea undulated placidly beneath the frigate's stempost.

Just then I was in the bow and leaning over the starboard rail. Conseil was stationed next to me and looking straight ahead. The crew were perched in the shrouds and examining the horizon, which was gradually shrinking and darkening. Officers scoured the gathering gloom with their night glasses. Sometimes the murky ocean sparkled under moonbeams that darted between the fringes of two clouds. Then all traces of light vanished into the darkness.

I looked at Conseil and saw that the gallant lad showed signs of falling under the popular influence. At least I thought so. Maybe his nerves were twitching with curiosity for the first time in history.

"Come on, Conseil!" I told him. "Here's your last chance to pocket that $2,000!"

"If master will allow me to say so," Conseil replied, "I never expected to win that prize, and the Union government could have promised $100,000 and been none the poorer."

"You're right, Conseil. It turned out to be a foolish business after all, and we jumped into it too hastily. What a waste of time, what a pointless outlay of energy! Six months ago we already would have been back in France . . ."

"In master's little apartment," Conseil remarked. "In master's museum! And by now I would have classified master's fossils. And master's babirusa would be ensconced in its cage at the nature gardens and it would have attracted every curiosity seeker in town!"

"No question, Conseil, and I imagine they'll have some fun with us as well."

"To be sure," Conseil replied serenely, "I do think they'll have fun at master's expense. And must it be said . . . ?"

"It must be said, Conseil."

"Well then, it will serve master right."

"How true!"

"When one has the honor of being an expert as master is, one mustn't lay himself open to—"

Conseil wasn't able to finish his compliment. In the midst of the overall silence, a voice rang out. It was Ned Land's voice and it shouted:

"Ahoy! There's the thing we're after, abreast of us to leeward!"

6

AT FULL STEAM

AT THIS SHOUT the whole crew rushed toward the harpooner—commander, officers, mates, sailors, cabin boys, down to engineers leaving their machinery and stokers neglecting their furnaces. The order to stop went forth, and the frigate simply coasted.

By then it was completely dark, and as good as the Canadian's eyes were, I still wondered how he could see—and what he'd seen. My heart was pounding fit to burst.

But Ned Land hadn't been mistaken, and we all spotted the object he was pointing to.

Astern to starboard, less than a quarter of a mile from the *Abraham Lincoln*, the sea seemed to be lit up from underneath. This was no simple phosphorescent phenomenon, that much was unmistakable. Submerged several yards under the surface of the water, the monster gave off that same intense, bewildering glow that several captains had mentioned in their reports. This magnificent radiance had to come from some force with a great illuminating capacity. The area of its luminiscence swept over the sea in an immense slender oval whose middle was a concentrated, blazing core of light, an unbearable glow that gradually faded as it spread out from the center.

"It's only a cluster of phosphorescent particles!" one of the officers exclaimed.

"No, sir," I countered with conviction. "No marine creatures, not even salps or piddocks, have ever given off such a strong light. That glow is basically electrical in nature. Besides . . . look, look! It's shifting! It's moving back and forth! It's darting at us!"

A shout went up from the whole frigate.

"Quiet!" Commander Farragut said. "Helm hard to windward! Reverse engines!"

Sailors rushed to the helm, engineers to their machinery. Under reverse steam immediately, the *Abraham Lincoln* beat to port, sweeping in a semicircle.

"Right your helm! Engines forward!" Commander Farragut called.

These orders were executed, and the frigate quickly retreated from that blazing core of light.

My mistake. It *tried* to retreat, but the uncanny creature came toward us at a speed twice our own.

We gasped. More astonished than afraid, we stood hushed and motionless. The animal easily caught up with us. It circled the frigate—then doing sixteen miles per hour—and wrapped us in sheets of electricity that looked like luminous dust. Then it retreated two or three miles, leaving a phosphorescent trail like the swirls of steam that shoot behind the locomotive of an express train. Suddenly, all the way from the dark horizon where it had gone to gather momentum, the monster dashed abruptly toward the *Abraham Lincoln* at a frightening speed, stopped sharply twenty feet from our side plates, and quenched its light—not by diving under the waves, since its glow didn't recede gradually, but all at once, as if the source of that brilliant outpouring had suddenly been shut off. Then it reappeared on the other side of the ship, either by circling us or by gliding under our hull. Any second a collision could have occurred that would have been fatal to us.

Meanwhile I was amazed at the frigate's maneuvers. It wasn't fighting, it was fleeing. The hunter had become the hunted, and I said as much to Commander Farragut. His face, ordinarily so unemotional, was stamped with indescribable amazement.

"Professor Aronnax," he answered me, "I don't know what sort of fearsome creature I'm up against and I don't want my frigate running foolish risks in all this darkness. Besides, how can you go on offense or defense when you're facing the unknown? Let's wait for daylight, then we'll swap roles."

"You have no further doubts, commander, as to the nature of this animal?"

"No, sir, it's apparently a gigantic narwhal, and an electric one to boot."

"Maybe," I added, "it's no more approachable than an electric eel or an electric ray!"

"Right," the commander replied. "And if it has their electrocuting power, it's definitely the most dreadful animal ever conceived by our Creator. That's why I'll keep on my guard, sir."

The whole crew stayed on their feet all night long. Nobody even thought of sleeping. Unable to match the monster's speed, the *Abraham Lincoln* slowed down and stayed at half steam. For its part the narwhal emulated the frigate, simply rode with the waves, and

seemed determined not to leave the field of battle.

But toward midnight it vanished, or to use a more appropriate expression, it "went out," like some huge glowworm. Had it left us? It was our duty to fear so rather than hope so. But at 12:53 in the morning, we heard a loud hissing sound, like the noise made by a waterspout expelled with tremendous force.

By then Commander Farragut, Ned Land, and I were on the afterdeck, peering eagerly into the deep gloom.

"Ned Land," the commander asked, "have you often heard whales bellowing?"

"Often, sir, but never a whale that netted me $2,000 just for sighting it!"

"That's right, the prize goes to you. But tell me, isn't that the sound cetaceans make when they spurt water out of their blowholes?"

"The same sound, sir, but this one's way louder. So it's as plain as day. There's definitely a whale lurking in these waters. With your permission, sir," the harpooner added, "tomorrow at sunrise I'll have words with the critter."

"Assuming it's in a mood to listen to you, Mr. Land," I replied in a dubious tone.

"If I get within four harpoon lengths of it," the Canadian shot back, "it had *better* listen!"

"But to get near it," the commander went on, "wouldn't I need to put a whaleboat at your disposal?"

"Certainly, sir."

"That would be gambling with the lives of my men."

"Mine too!" the harpooner merely replied.

Near two o'clock in the morning, that blazing core of light reappeared, just as intense, five miles to windward of the *Abraham Lincoln*. Despite the distance, despite the noise of wind and sea, we could clearly hear the fearsome thrashings of the animal's tail and even its panting breath. When that enormous narwhal came up to breathe at the surface of the ocean, the air it sucked into its lungs sounded like steam going into the huge cylinders of a 2,000-horsepower engine.

"Hmm!" I said to myself. "A cetacean as

powerful as a whole cavalry regiment—now that's a whale of a whale!"

We stayed on the alert till daylight, getting ready for action. Whaling gear sat lined up along the railings. Our chief officer loaded the blunderbusses, which can shoot harpoons as far as a mile, and long duck guns with exploding bullets that can mortally wound even the strongest animals. Ned Land was content to sharpen his harpoon, a dreadful weapon in his hands.

At six o'clock dawn began to break, and with the first rays of sunrise, the narwhal's electric glow vanished. By seven o'clock it was light enough, but a very heavy morning fog restricted the horizon, and our finest spyglasses couldn't see through it. The outcome: disappointment and anger.

I hoisted myself up to the crosstrees of the mizzen sail. A few officers were already perched on the mastheads.

By eight o'clock the fog was rolling ponderously across the waves and its huge curls were gradually lifting. The horizon grew wider and clearer all at once.

Suddenly, just as on the previous evening, Ned Land's voice rang out.

"There's the thing we're after, astern to port!" the harpooner shouted.

Every eye looked toward the area indicated.

There, a mile and a half from the frigate, a long blackish body emerged a yard above the waves. Quivering forcefully, its tail created a considerable eddy. No caudal equipment had ever thrashed the sea with such strength. An immense wake of glowing whiteness marked the animal's track, which swept in a long curve.

The frigate drew nearer to the cetacean. I examined it with a completely open mind. The reports from the *Shannon* and the *Helvetia* had slightly exaggerated its dimensions, and I put its length at only 250 feet. Its girth was harder to judge, but on the whole the animal seemed wonderfully proportioned in all three dimensions.

While I was studying this phenomenal creature, two jets of steam and water sprang from its blowholes and rose to an altitude of about 130 feet, which settled its system of breathing for me. So I concluded once and for all that it belonged to the branch Vertebrata, class Mammalia, subclass Monodelphia, group Pisciforma, order Cetacea, family . . . but here I couldn't make up my mind. The order Cetacea consists of three families, baleen whales, sperm whales, and dolphins, and it's in this last group that narwhals are placed. Each of these families is divided into several genera, each genus into species, each species into varieties. So I was still missing variety, species, genus, and family, but I was sure I would complete my classifying with the aid of Heaven and Commander Farragut.

The crew were waiting impatiently for orders from their leader. The latter, after carefully studying the animal, called for his engineer. The engineer raced over.

"Sir," the commander said, "are you up to pressure?"

"Aye, sir," the engineer replied.

"Fine. Stoke your furnaces and clap on full steam!"

Three cheers greeted this order. The hour of battle had sounded. A few seconds later the frigate's two funnels spewed out torrents of black smoke, and the deck shook from the vibrations of its boilers.

Driven forward by its powerful propeller, the *Abraham Lincoln* headed straight for the animal. Unconcerned, the latter let us get within a hundred yards; then, not bothering to dive, it picked up a little speed, retreated, and was content to simply keep its distance.

This chase dragged on for about three-quarters of an hour without the frigate's gaining twelve feet on the cetacean. At this rate it was obvious we would never catch up with it.

Infuriated, Commander Farragut kept twisting the thick tuft of hair that flourished under his chin.

"Ned Land!" he called.

The Canadian reported for duty.

"Well, Mr. Land," the commander asked, "do you still advise me to break out the longboats?"

"No, sir," Ned Land replied, "because we aren't going to catch that beast against its will."

"Then what should we do?"

"Stoke up more steam if you can, sir. As for me, with your permission I'll get situated in the bobstays under the bowsprit, and if we come within a harpoon length, I'll harpoon the brute."

"Go to it, Ned," Commander Farragut replied. "Engineer," he called, "keep the pressure mounting!"

Ned Land made his way to his post. The stokers prodded the furnaces more energetically; the propeller did forty-three revolutions per minute, and steam burst from the valves. Heaving the log, we saw that the *Abraham Lincoln* was going at the rate of 18.5 miles per hour.

But that damned animal also did a speed of 18.5.

For the next hour our frigate kept up this pace without gaining two yards! This was mortifying for one of the fastest racers in the American navy. The crew were seething with surly anger. Sailor after sailor threw insults at the monster, which couldn't be bothered with answering back. Commander Farragut wasn't content to simply twist his goatee; he chewed on it.

He summoned the engineer once again.

"You're up to maximum pressure?" the commander asked him.

"Aye, sir," the engineer replied.

"And your valves are charged to . . . ?"

"Six and a half atmospheres."

"Charge them to ten atmospheres."

A typical American order if I ever heard one. We might as well have been in a Mississippi paddleboat race, trying to "outstrip the competition!"

"Conseil," I said to my gallant servant, now at my side, "you realize we're likely to blow ourselves sky-high?"

"As master wishes!" Conseil replied.

All right, I admit it—I did wish to run that risk!

They charged the valves. The furnaces gobbled up more coal. Fans sent streams of air over the braziers. The *Abraham Lincoln* picked up speed. Its masts trembled down to their blocks, and the swirls of smoke could barely squeeze through the narrow funnels.

We heaved the log a second time.

"Well, helmsman?" Commander Farragut asked.

"It's doing 19.3 miles per hour, sir."

"Keep stoking the furnaces."

The engineer did so. Our pressure gauge read ten atmospheres. But no doubt the cetacean itself had "stoked up," because without the least trouble it also did 19.3.

What a chase! No, I can't describe the excitement that made me tremble from head to toe. Ned Land stayed at his post, harpoon in hand. Several times the animal let us close in.

"We're overhauling it!" the Canadian would shout.

Then, just as he was about to strike, the cetacean would dash away so swiftly, I estimated it was going at least thirty miles per hour. And even at our maximum speed, it took the liberty of thumbing its nose at the frigate by running a full circle around us. A howl of fury burst from every chest!

By noon we weren't any farther along than at eight o'clock in the morning.

Commander Farragut decided to take a more direct approach.

"So," he said, "that animal's faster than the *Abraham Lincoln*. All right, let's see if it can outrun our conical shells. Mate, man the foreward gun!"

They immediately loaded and leveled our forecastle cannon. The cannoneer fired a shot, but his shell passed a few feet above the cetacean, which lay half a mile off.

"Over to somebody with better aim!" the commander shouted. "And $500 to the man who can pierce that infernal beast!"

Steady of eye, cool of expression, an old gray-bearded gunner—I can see him to this day—went up to the cannon, put the piece in position, and took aim for a good while. There was a loud explosion, mixed with cheers from the crew.

The shell reached its target; it hit the animal, but not in the usual manner—it bounced off that rounded surface and vanished into the sea two miles out.

"Oh drat!" said the old gunner in his anger. "That rascal must be covered with six-inch armor plate!"

"Curse the beast!" Commander Farragut shouted.

Once again the hunt was on, and Commander Farragut leaned over to me, saying:

"I'll chase that animal till my frigate explodes!"

"Right," I replied, "and nobody will blame you!"

We still could hope the animal would tire out and not be as immune to exhaustion as our steam engines. No such luck. Hour after hour went by without its showing the tiniest sign of weariness.

But to the *Abraham Lincoln*'s credit, I must say that it struggled on with unflagging persistence. I estimate that we covered over 300 miles during that ill-fated day of November 6. But night fell and wrapped the rolling ocean in its shadows.

By then I figured that our expedition had come to an end, that we would never see the fantastic creature again. I was mistaken.

At 10:50 in the evening, that electric light reappeared three miles to windward of the frigate, as clear and intense as the night before.

The narwhal seemed perfectly still. Maybe it was asleep, weary from its workday, just riding with the waves? This was our chance, and Commander Farragut was determined to make the most of it.

He issued his orders. Staying at half steam, the *Abraham Lincoln* moved forward cautiously so as to not awaken its opponent. In midocean it isn't unusual to come across whales so sound asleep that they can be attacked successfully, and Ned Land had harpooned more than one in its slumber. The Canadian went back to his post in the bobstays under the bowsprit.

The frigate closed in without making a sound, stopped less than a quarter of a mile from the animal, and coasted. Nobody breathed on board. Absolute silence reigned over the deck. We weren't a hundred feet from that blazing core of light, whose glow intensified, dazzling the eyes.

Just then, leaning over the forecastle railing, I saw Ned Land below me, one hand gripping the martingale, the other brandishing his dreadful harpoon. Barely twenty feet separated him from the motionless animal.

All at once his arm shot forward and the harpoon was in the air. I heard the weapon collide resonantly, as if it had hit some hard substance.

The electric light suddenly went out, and two enormous waterspouts crashed onto the frigate's deck, racing like a torrent from stem to stern, toppling crewmen, breaking spare masts and yards from their lashings.

An appalling collision occurred, and before I could catch hold of anything, I was thrown over the rail and into the sea.

7

A WHALE OF UNKNOWN SPECIES

THOUGH I WAS startled by that unexpected descent, at least I have a very clear memory of my sensations during it.

At first I was dragged about twenty feet down. I'm a good swimmer—without claiming to equal such other authors as Byron and Edgar Allan Poe, who were masters of the sport—and that nosedive didn't cause me to lose my head. Two vigorous kicks of the heel brought me back to the surface of the sea.

My first concern was to look for the frigate. Did the crew see me go overboard? Was the *Abraham Lincoln* tacking about? Would Commander Farragut put a longboat to sea? Had I any hope of being rescued?

It was extremely dark. I glimpsed a black shape vanishing eastward, where its running lights were fading out in the distance. It was the frigate. I felt I was done for.

"Help! Help!" I shouted, swimming desperately toward the *Abraham Lincoln*.

My clothes were weighing me down. The water glued them to my body, they were paralyzing my movements. I was sinking! I was suffocating . . . !

"Help!"

This was the last shout I gave. My mouth filled up with water. I was floundering, I was being dragged into the depths. . . .

Suddenly a pair of energetic hands grabbed my clothes. I felt myself being pulled forcefully back to the surface of the sea, and yes, I heard these words spoken in my ear:

"If master would be so kind as to lean on

my shoulder, master will swim with much greater ease."

I reached out and clutched my loyal Conseil by the arm.

"You!" I said. "It's you!"

"The same," Conseil replied, "and at master's command."

"Did that collision throw you overboard along with me?"

"Not at all. But being in master's employ, I followed master."

The fine lad thought this was only natural!

"What about the frigate?" I asked.

"The frigate?" Conseil replied, rolling over on his back. "I think master had better not depend on it to any great extent!"

"What do you mean?"

"I mean that just as I jumped overboard, I heard the men at the helm shout, 'Our propeller and rudder have been smashed!'"

"Smashed?"

"Yes, smashed by the monster's tusk! I believe it's the only injury the *Abraham Lincoln* has sustained. But what's inconvenient for us is that the ship can no longer steer."

"Then we're done for!"

"Maybe," Conseil replied serenely. "However we still have a few hours in front of us, and in a few hours one can do a good many things!"

Conseil's unflappable composure cheered me up. I swam more energetically, but I was hampered by clothes as restricting as a cloak made of lead, so I was managing with only the greatest difficulty. Conseil noticed this.

"If master will allow me, I'll do a little cutting," he said.

And he slipped an open clasp knife under my clothes, slitting them from top to bottom with one swift stroke. Next he deftly undressed me while I swam for the two of us.

Then I did Conseil the same favor, and we continued to "navigate" side by side.

But our circumstances weren't any less dreadful. Maybe they hadn't seen us go overboard; and even if they had, the frigate—being undone by its rudder—couldn't return to leeward after us. So its longboats were the only thing we could rely on.

Conseil had coolly reasoned out this theory and had laid his plans accordingly. An amazing character, this boy—in midocean the stoic lad seemed right at home!

We concluded that our only chance of being rescued was to be picked up by the *Abraham Lincoln*'s longboats, so we had to take steps to wait for them as long as we could. Consequently I decided to divide our energies so we wouldn't both get tired at the same time, and this was the arrangement: while one of us lay on his back, staying motionless with arms folded and legs outstretched, the other would swim and propel his partner forward. This towing role was to last no longer than ten minutes, and by relieving each other in this way, we could stay afloat for some hours, maybe even till daybreak.

Our chances were slim, but hope springs eternal in the human breast! Besides, there were two of us. And I must admit—as unlikely as it sounds—that even if I'd wanted to destroy all my illusions, even if I'd been willing to "give in to despair," I couldn't have!

The cetacean had rammed our frigate around eleven o'clock at night. So I was figuring on eight hours of swimming till sunrise. It was hard work but still doable, thanks to our relieving each other. The sea was pretty smooth and barely tired us. Now and then I tried to peer through the dense gloom, which was broken only by the phosphorescent flickers coming from our movements. I looked at the shining ripples breaking over my hands, glistening sheets spotted with patches of bluish gray. You would have sworn we'd plunged into a pool of quicksilver.

Around one o'clock in the morning, I got tremendously tired. My limbs stiffened in the grip of intense cramps. Conseil had to keep me going, and attending to our self-preservation became his sole responsibility. I soon heard the poor lad gasping; he was taking short, hurried breaths. I knew he couldn't hold out much longer.

"Go on! Go on!" I told him.

"Leave master behind?" he replied. "Never! I'll drown before he does!"

Just then, past the fringes of a huge cloud that the wind was driving eastward, the moon appeared. The surface of the sea sparkled under her rays. That wholesome light rekindled our strength. I held my head high again. My eyes flew to every corner of the horizon. I spotted the frigate. It was five miles away from us, no more than a dark, barely visible mass. But as for longboats, there wasn't a single one in sight!

I tried to call out. It was no use at such a distance! My swollen lips wouldn't let any sounds through. Conseil could still enunciate a few words, and I heard him shout again and again:

"Help! Help!"

Holding still for a second, we listened. And it may have been a ringing in my ears from their filling with congested blood, but it seemed to me that Conseil's shout had gotten an answer back.

"Did you hear that?" I mumbled.

"Yes, yes!"

And Conseil sent another desperate plea into space.

This time there couldn't be any mistake! A human voice had answered us! Was it the voice of some poor devil left behind in mid-ocean, another victim of the collision suffered by our ship? Or was it one of the frigate's longboats, hailing us out of the gloom?

Conseil made one crowning effort; bracing his hands on my shoulders while I offered resistance with my last ounce of strength, he raised himself half out of the water, then fell back exhausted.

"What did you see?"

"I saw," he muttered, "I saw . . . but we mustn't talk . . . save our strength . . . !"

What had he seen? Then, Lord knows why, thoughts of the monster came into my head for the first time . . . ! But even so, that voice . . . ? Gone are the days when Jonahs could take refuge in the bellies of whales!

Nevertheless Conseil kept towing me. Sometimes he lifted his chin, looked straight ahead, and shouted a request for directions, which was answered by a voice getting closer and closer. I could barely hear it. I'd reached the end of my strength; my fingers gave out; my hands were no help to me; my mouth opened convulsively, filling with brine; its coldness ran through me; I raised my head one last time, then I collapsed. . . .

Right that instant something hard banged into me. I held onto it. Then I felt myself being pulled upward, back to the surface of the water; my chest caved in and I fainted. . . .

I must have come to quickly, because somebody was massaging me so energetically that it left furrows in my flesh. I half opened my eyes. . . .

"Conseil!" I muttered.

"Did master ring for me?" Conseil replied.

Just then, in the last light of the moon as she gravitated toward the horizon, I spotted a face that wasn't Conseil's, a face I recognized immediately.

"Ned!" I exclaimed.

"None other, sir, and still trying to claim my prize!" the Canadian replied.

"You were thrown overboard after the frigate's collision?"

"Yes, professor, but I was luckier than you and right away I managed to set foot on this floating islet."

"Islet?"

"Or in other words, on our gigantic narwhal."

"What do you mean, Ned?"

"I mean that I soon realized why my harpoon got blunted and couldn't puncture its hide."

"Why, Ned, why?"

"Because, professor, this beast is made of boiler plate steel!"

And now I need to get a good grip on myself, carefully reconstruct my experiences, and personally double-check every statement I make.

The Canadian's last words caused a sudden upheaval in my brain. I swiftly hoisted myself to the top of this half-submerged creature or object that was serving as our refuge. I tested it with my foot. Obviously it was some hard, impregnable substance, not the soft matter that makes up the bodies of our big marine mammals.

But this hard substance could have been a bony carapace, like those that covered certain prehistoric animals, and I might have left it at that and classified this monster among such amphibious reptiles as turtles or alligators.

Well, hardly. The blackish back supporting me was smooth and polished, without any overlapping scales. On impact it made a metallic sound, and as incredible as this may seem, it appeared, I swear, to be made of riveted plates.

No doubts were possible! This animal, this monster, this natural phenomenon that had puzzled the whole scientific world and boggled the minds of seamen in both hemispheres, was now revealed to be an even more astounding phenomenon—a phenomenon made by human hands.

Even if I'd discovered that some fabulous mythological creature actually existed, it wouldn't have given me such a mental jolt. It's easy enough to accept that prodigious things can come from our Creator. But to find, all at once, under your very eyes, that the impossible has been mysteriously accomplished by man himself, this was a staggering thought!

But there was no question now. We were lying on the back of some sort of underwater boat, which, as far as I could judge, boasted the shape of an immense steel fish. Ned Land had clear views on the matter. Conseil and I could only fall into line behind him.

"But then," I said, "wouldn't this contraption have some propulsion units and a crew to operate them?"

"You would think," the harpooner replied. "And yet for the three hours I've lived on this floating island, it hasn't shown a sign of life."

"This boat hasn't moved?"

"No, Professor Aronnax. It just rides with the waves and doesn't do a blessed thing."

"But we definitely know it can travel at great speed. Now then, it needs an engine to generate that speed and a mechanic to run the engine, therefore I conclude: we're saved."

"Humph!" Ned Land put in, his tone indicating reservations.

Just then, as if to take my side in the argument, the water started bubbling to the rear of this strange submersible—whose drive mechanism was obviously a propeller—and the boat began to move. We had barely time to hang onto its topside, which emerged about 2½ feet above water. Luckily its speed wasn't excessive.

"So long as it navigates horizontally," Ned Land muttered, "I have no complaints. But if it gets the urge to dive, I wouldn't give two dollars for my hide!"

The Canadian could have named a far lower price. So it was essential to make contact with whatever beings were confined inside the plating of this machine. I searched its surface for an opening or a hatch, a "manhole" to use the official term; but the lines of rivets had been firmly driven into the sheet-iron joins and were straight and uniform.

What's more, the moon vanished at this point and left us in absolute darkness. We had to wait for daylight to find some way of getting inside this underwater boat.

Hence our lives were totally in the hands of the mysterious helmsmen steering this submersible, and if it made a dive, we were done for! But aside from that I didn't doubt the possibility of our making contact with them. In fact, if they didn't produce their own air, they inevitably had to pay periodic visits to the surface of the ocean to replenish their oxygen supply. Consequently there had to be an opening that put the boat's interior in contact with the outside air.

As for our being rescued by Commander Farragut, there we had to abandon all hope. We were being carried westward, and I estimate that our comparatively moderate speed reached twelve miles per hour. The propeller churned the waves with mathematical steadiness, sometimes emerging above the surface and spraying phosphorescent water to great heights.

Near four o'clock in the morning, the submersible picked up speed. We could barely cope with this dizzying rush, and the waves pummeled us with everything they had. Luckily Ned's hands found a big mooring ring fastened to the topside of that sheet-iron back, and we all could hang on tight.

Finally that long night was over. My faulty memory won't let me recall all my impressions of it. A single detail sticks in my mind. Several times, during various lulls of wind and sea, I thought I heard faint sounds, fleeting harmonies produced by distant musical chords. What was the secret behind this underwater navigating that the whole world had vainly tried to explain? What beings lived inside this strange boat? What mechanical force allowed it to move about with such prodigious speed?

Daylight appeared. Morning mists surrounded us but soon broke apart. I was about to begin a careful examination of the hull, whose topside formed a sort of horizontal platform, when I felt it sinking little by little.

"Oh damnation!" Ned Land shouted, stamping his foot on the resonant sheet iron. "Open up, you unsociable navigators!"

But it was hard to make yourself heard above the deafening beats of the propeller. Luckily the submerging movement stopped.

Suddenly, from inside the boat, we heard the sound of iron fastenings being forcefully pushed aside. One of the steel plates flew up, a man appeared, gave a peculiar yell, and instantly vanished.

A few seconds later eight strapping fellows appeared silently, their faces like masks, and dragged us inside their fearsome machine.

8

MOBILIS IN MOBILI

THIS BRUTALLY EXECUTED capture was carried out with lightning speed. My companions and I had no time to collect our thoughts. I don't know how they felt about being shoved inside that aquatic prison; but as for me, I had goose bumps and was shivering uncontrollably. Who were we dealing with? Surely some new breed of pirates ravaging the sea in their own way.

The narrow hatch had scarcely closed over me when I was surrounded by absolute darkness. Steeped in the outside light, my eyes couldn't make out a thing. I felt my bare feet clinging to the steps of an iron ladder. Tightly gripped, Ned Land and Conseil were right behind me. At the foot of the ladder, a door opened and instantly closed after us with a loud clang.

We were alone. Where? I couldn't say, could scarcely even imagine. Everything was in darkness, such utter darkness that after several minutes, my eyes still couldn't catch

a single one of those hazy gleams that drift through even the blackest nights.

Meanwhile, furious at this treatment, Ned Land gave free rein to his exasperation.

"Damnation!" he exclaimed. "These people are about as sociable as the savages of New Caledonia! All that's lacking is for them to be cannibals! I wouldn't be surprised if they were, but believe you me, they won't eat me without my kicking up a protest!"

"Calm down, Ned my friend," Conseil replied serenely. "It's too soon to fly off the handle. We aren't in a kettle yet."

"In a kettle no," the Canadian shot back, "but in an oven for sure! It's dark enough for one. Luckily my bowie knife is still with me, and I don't need to see much to put it to good use.[4] The first one of these bandits who lays a hand on me—"

"Don't be so irritable, Ned," I told the harpooner, "and don't ruin things for us with senseless violence. Who knows, they might be listening to us. Instead let's try to find out where we are."

I started moving, groping my way. After five steps I came to an iron wall made of riveted boiler plate. Then, turning around, I bumped into a wooden table with several stools set out next to it. The floor of this prison lay hidden under thick hempen matting that deadened the sound of footsteps. The bare walls didn't reveal any trace of a door or window. Going around the opposite way, Conseil met up with me and we went back to the center of this cabin, which had to be twenty feet long by ten wide. As for its height, not even Ned Land with his great stature could determine it.

Half an hour had already gone by without any change in our circumstances, when our eyes were suddenly spirited from total darkness into blinding light. Our prison lit up all at once; in other words, it filled with luminescent matter so brilliant, I couldn't stand it at first. From its whiteness and intensity, I recognized the electric glow that had spread around this underwater boat like some magnificent phosphorescent phenomenon. After

---

[4] A bowie knife is a wide-bladed dagger that Americans never leave home without.

instinctively closing my eyes, I opened them again and saw that this luminous force came from a frosted half globe curving out of the cabin's ceiling.

"Finally! It's light enough to see something!" Ned Land exclaimed, knife in hand, staying on the defensive.

"Yes," I replied, then ventured the opposite view. "But as for our situation, we're still in the dark."

"Master needs to be patient," said the unemotional Conseil.

This sudden illumination of our cabin allowed me to examine its tiniest details. It contained only a table and five stools. Its invisible door must have been hermetically sealed. Not a single sound reached our ears. Everything seemed dead inside this boat. Was it in motion, or stationary on the surface of the ocean, or sinking into the depths? I hadn't a clue.

But that shining globe hadn't been turned on without good reason. Consequently I hoped some crewmen would soon make an appearance. If you want to forget about somebody, you don't light up his dungeon.

I wasn't mistaken. There were unlocking sounds, a door opened, and two men appeared.

One was short and stocky, powerfully muscled, broad of shoulder, robust of limbs, head squat, hair black and luxuriant, mustache bushy, eyes bright and piercing, and his whole personality stamped with the southern-blooded zest that in France typifies the people of Provence. The philosopher Diderot has very aptly claimed that a person's bearing is a clue to his character, and this stocky little man was certainly living proof of that claim. You sensed that his everyday conversation must have been packed with vivid figures of speech such as personification, symbolism, and misplaced modifiers. But I was never in a position to verify this, because around me he used only an odd and completely unintelligible dialect.

The second stranger deserves a more detailed description. A disciple of such character-judging anatomists as Gratiolet or Engel could have read this man's features like an open book. Without hesitation I identified his dominant qualities: self-confidence, since his head soared like a nobleman's above the arc formed by the lines of his shoulders, and his black eyes had an icy assurance; calmness, since his skin was pale rather than ruddy, indicating tranquillity of blood; energy, shown by the swiftly knitting muscles of his brow; finally courage, since his deep breathing revealed tremendous stores of vitality.

In line with the findings of physiognomists, those analysts of facial character, I might add that this was a man of great pride, that his calm, firm look seemed to reflect thinking on a lofty plane, and along with this, that the harmony of expression in his facial and bodily movements gave a feeling of unimpeachable sincerity.

I felt "instinctively reassured" in his presence, a good omen for our interview.

Whether this individual was thirty-five or fifty years of age, I couldn't tell. He was tall, his forehead broad, his nose straight, his mouth clearly etched, his teeth magnificent, his hands slender, tapered, and to use a word from palmistry, exceptionally "psychic," in other words, worthy of serving a lofty and passionate spirit. This man was certainly the most wonderful physical specimen I'd ever met up with. One unusual detail: his eyes were spaced rather far from each other and could instantly take in nearly a quarter of the horizon. This ability—as I later verified—was enhanced by a range of vision even greater than Ned Land's. When this stranger focused on an object, his eyebrows gathered into a frown, his heavy eyelids closed around his pupils to contract his huge field of vision, and he *looked!* What a look—as if he could magnify objects shrinking into the distance; as if he could probe your very soul; as if he could pierce those sheets of water so murky to our eyes and scan the deepest seas . . . !

Wearing caps made of sea-otter fur and shod in sealskin fishing boots, the two strangers were dressed in clothes made from some unique fabric that flattered the figure and allowed great freedom of movement.

The taller of the two—apparently the leader on board—examined us with the greatest care but without saying a word. Then, turning to his companion, he conversed with him in a language I didn't recognize. It was a sonorous, harmonious, flexible dialect whose vowels seemed to undergo a highly varied accentuation.

The other replied with a shake of the head and added two or three completely unintelligible words. Then he seemed to question me directly with a long look.

I answered in my best French that I wasn't familiar with his language; but he didn't seem to understand me, and the situation got a little awkward.

"Even so, master should tell our story," Conseil said to me. "Maybe these gentlemen will grasp a few words of it!"

I tried again, telling the tale of our adventures, clearly enunciating every syllable, and not leaving out a single detail. I gave our names and titles; then, in order, I formally presented Professor Aronnax, his manservant Conseil, and Mr. Ned Land, harpooner.

The man with calm, gentle eyes listened to me serenely, even courteously, and paid remarkable attention. But nothing in his facial expression indicated he understood my story. When I finished, he didn't say a single word.

One resource still left was to speak English. Maybe they would be familiar with this nearly universal language. But I knew it, as I did the German language, well enough only to read it fluently, not well enough to speak it properly. Here, however, our overriding need was to make ourselves understood.

"Come on, it's your turn," I told the harpooner. "Over to you, Mr. Land. Pull out of your bag of tricks the best English ever spoken by an Anglo-Saxon, and let's see if you have better luck than I had."

Ned didn't need any persuading and started our story all over again, most of which I understood. Its substance was the same, but its style differed. Carried away by his volatile temperament, the Canadian put great passion into it. He complained vehemently about being imprisoned without any regard for his civil rights, asked what law justified their detaining him, invoked writs of *habeas corpus*, threatened to press charges against anybody holding him in illegal custody, ranted, shouted, flailed about, and finally conveyed with an expressive gesture that we were starving to death.

This was perfectly true, but we'd nearly forgotten the fact.

Much to his astonishment, the harpooner didn't seem to have gotten through to them any better than I had. Our visitors didn't bat an eye. Apparently they were engineers who didn't know the languages of either the French physicist Arago or the English physicist Faraday.

Thoroughly baffled after vainly exhausting our linguistic resources, I didn't know what tactic to try next, when Conseil said to me:

"If master will allow me, I'll tell the whole business in German."

"What! You know German?" I exclaimed.

"Like most Flemish people, with all due respect to master."

"On the contrary, my respect is due you. Go to it, my boy."

And in a serene voice Conseil described for the third time the various complications of our story. But despite our narrator's fine accent and stylish turns of phrase, the German language also missed the mark.

Finally, as a last resort, I hauled out everything I could remember from my early schooldays and attempted to narrate our adventures in Latin. Cicero would have covered his ears and sent me to the scullery, but somehow I managed to pull through. With the same negative result.

This last effort ultimately backfiring, the two strangers exchanged a few words in their unintelligible language and took their leave, not favoring us even with one of those encouraging gestures that are known the world over. The door closed again.

"This is outrageous!" Ned Land shouted, exploding for the twentieth time. "I ask you! We speak French, English, German, and Latin to those rogues, and neither of them has the decency to even answer back!"

"Calm down, Ned," I told the seething harpooner. "Getting angry won't accomplish a thing."

"But professor," our irascible companion continued, "can't you see, we could actually die of hunger in this iron cage!"

"Nonsense!" Conseil put in philosophically. "We can hold out a good while yet."

"My friends," I said, "we mustn't lose heart. We've gotten out of tighter spots. So please do me the favor of waiting a little before you form your views on the commander and crew of this boat."

"My views are fully formed," Ned Land shot back. "They're rogues!"

"Oh good. And from what country?"

"Roguedom!"

"My gallant Ned, as yet that country isn't clearly marked on maps of the world, but I'll admit that the nationality of those two strangers is hard to make out. They aren't English, French, or German, that's all we can say. However I'm tempted to believe that both the commander and his chief officer were born in the low latitudes. There's southern blood in them. But as for whether they're Spaniards, Turks, Arabs, or East Indians, their physical characteristics don't give me enough to go on. And as for their speech, it's completely unintelligible."

"That's the problem with not knowing every language," Conseil responded, "or the drawback in not having one universal language!"

"Which would all go out the window!" Ned Land replied. "Don't you see, these people have a language all to themselves, a language they've come up with just to cause despair in decent folks who ask for a bite of dinner! Why, in every country on earth, when you open your mouth, snap your jaws, smack your lips and teeth, isn't that the world's clearest message? From Quebec to the Tuamotu Islands, from Paris to the Antipodes, doesn't it mean: I'm hungry, give me some grub!"

"Oh," Conseil put in, "there are people so naturally dense . . ."

As he was saying these words, the door opened. A steward came in.[5] He brought us some clothes—jackets and sailor's pants made from a fabric whose nature I couldn't identify. I hurriedly changed into them, and my companions followed suit.

Meanwhile our silent steward, maybe a

---

[5] Waiter aboard a steamer.

deaf-mute, set the table and laid three place settings.

"There's something serious afoot," Conseil said, "and it bodes well."

"Phooey!" replied our hostile harpooner. "What the blazes do you suppose they eat around here? Turtle livers, loin of shark, dogfish steak?"

"We'll soon find out!" Conseil said.

Under silver dish covers, platters were neatly positioned on the tablecloth, and we sat down to eat. Obviously we were dealing with civilized people, and if it hadn't been for the electric light flooding over us, I would have sworn we were in the dining room of the Adelphi Hotel in Liverpool or the Grand Hotel in Paris. But I feel compelled to mention that bread and wine were totally absent. The water was fresh and clear, but it was still water—which wasn't what Ned Land had in mind. Among the foods we were served, I could identify various delicately prepared fish; however I couldn't make up my mind about certain otherwise excellent dishes and I couldn't even say whether their contents belonged to the vegetable or the animal kingdom. As for the tableware, it was elegant and in perfect taste. Each utensil, whether spoon, fork, knife, or plate, bore on its reverse a letter with a Latin motto curving around it, and here's exactly how it looked:

Moving within a moving element! It was a highly appropriate motto for this underwater machine, so long as the preposition *in* is translated as *within* and not *upon*. No doubt the letter *N* was the initial of that mystifying individual in command under the seas!

Ned and Conseil had no time for such musings. They wolfed down their food, and without further ado I did the same. By now I felt reassured about our fate, and it seemed obvious that our hosts didn't intend to let us die of starvation.

But all earthly things come to an end, all things must pass, even the hunger of people who haven't eaten in fifteen hours. Our appetites appeased, we felt an urgent need for sleep. A perfectly natural reaction after that endless night of fighting for our lives.

"Ye gods, I'll sleep like the dead," Conseil said.

"I'm passing out already!" Ned Land replied.

My two companions stretched out on the cabin's carpeting and were soon deep in slumber.

As for me, I gave in less easily to this intense need for sleep. Too many thoughts had crowded into my brain, too many insoluble questions had come up, too many images were keeping my eyelids open! Where were we? What strange power was carrying us along? I felt—or at least thought I felt—the submersible sinking into the sea's deepest strata. I kept having intense nightmares. In these mysterious marine sanctuaries I glimpsed a host of unknown animals, and this underwater boat seemed to be their blood relation, living, breathing, just as fearsome . . . ! Then my mind grew calmer, my imagination melted into a dim drowsiness, and I soon fell into an uneasy slumber.

9

NED LAND'S TEMPER

I HAVE NO IDEA how long we slumbered, but it must have been a good while because we were completely over our exhaustion. I was the first one to wake up. My companions weren't yet stirring and still lay in their corners like inanimate objects.

I'd barely gotten up from my tolerably hard mattress when I felt my mind clearing, my brain going on the alert. So I started a careful reexamination of our cell.

Nothing had changed in its interior arrangements. The prison was still a prison and its prisoners still prisoners. But the steward had made the most of our slumber and cleared the table. So nothing indicated any forthcoming improvement in our situation, and I seriously wondered if we were doomed to spend the rest of our lives in this cage.

This prospect seemed increasingly painful to me, because, even though my brain was free of its fixations from the night before, I was feeling an odd short-windedness in my chest. It was getting hard for me to breathe. The heavy air was no longer sufficient for the full play of my lungs. Though our cell was sizeable, we'd obviously used up most of the oxygen it contained. In essence, over an hour's time a single human being consumes all the oxygen found in 25 gallons of air, at which point that air is full of a nearly equal amount of carbon dioxide and is no longer fit for breathing.

So it was now essential to replenish the air in our prison, and no doubt the air in this whole underwater boat as well.

Here a question popped into my head. How did the commander of this seagoing residence go about it? Did he obtain air using chemical methods, releasing the oxygen contained in potassium chlorate by heating it, meanwhile absorbing the carbon dioxide with potassium hydroxide? If so, he would have to keep up some sort of relationship with the shore, to come by the materials required for this operation. Did he limit himself to storing his air in high-pressure tanks, dispensing it as his crew needed it? Maybe. Or, proceeding in a more convenient, more economical, and therefore more likely manner, was he content with simply returning to breathe at the surface of the water like a cetacean, replenishing his oxygen supply every twenty-four hours? In any event, whatever his method was, it seemed sensible to me that he use this method without delay.

In fact I'd already resorted to speeding up my inhalations, to extract from the cell what little oxygen it contained, when suddenly I felt refreshed by a current of clean air scented with a salty aroma. It was a bracing sea breeze with a high iodine content! I opened my mouth wide and my lungs gorged themselves on the fresh particles. At the same time I felt a swaying, a rolling of moderate magnitude but definitely noticeable. This boat, this sheet-iron monster, had obviously just risen to the surface of the ocean to breathe in good whale fashion. So the ship's system of ventilation was conclusively established.

When I'd consumed a chestful of this clean air, I looked for the conduit—the "air carrier," if you prefer—that allowed this wholesome influx to reach us, and I soon found it. Above the door opened an air vent that let in a fresh current of oxygen, replenishing the thin air in our cell.

I'd gotten to this point in my inspection when Ned and Conseil woke up almost at the same instant, under the influence of that invigorating air purification. They rubbed their eyes, stretched their arms, and were on their feet in a second.

"Did master sleep well?" Conseil asked me with his never-failing good manners.

"Extremely well, my gallant lad," I replied. "And how about you, Mr. Ned Land?"

"Like a log, professor. But I must be imagining things, because it seems like I'm breathing a sea breeze!"

On this topic a seaman couldn't be wrong, and I told the Canadian what had gone on while he was sleeping.

"Good!" he said. "That explains perfectly all those bellowing sounds we heard when our so-called narwhal lay in sight of the *Abraham Lincoln*."

"Perfectly, Mr. Land. It was catching its breath."

"Only I have no idea what time it is, Professor Aronnax—isn't it at least dinnertime?"

"Dinnertime, my fine harpooner? Say at least breakfast time, because we've definitely woken up to a new day."

"Which indicates," Conseil replied, "that we've slept around the clock."

"That's my assessment," I responded.

"You won't get any arguments from me," Ned Land remarked. "But whether it's dinner or breakfast, that steward will be plenty welcome whether he brings the one or the other."

"The one *and* the other," Conseil said.

"Well put," the Canadian responded. "They owe us two meals, and speaking for myself, I'll do justice to 'em both."

"All right, Ned, let's wait and see," I replied. "It's obvious these strangers don't intend to let us die of hunger, otherwise last evening's dinner wouldn't make any sense."

"Unless they're fattening us up!" Ned shot back.

"I object," I replied. "We haven't fallen into the hands of cannibals."

"Just because they don't make a habit of it," the Canadian replied in all seriousness, "doesn't mean they don't indulge from time to time. Who knows? Maybe these people have gone without fresh meat for a good while, and in that case three healthy, well-built specimens like the professor, his man-servant, and me—"

"Get rid of those ideas, Mr. Land," I answered the harpooner. "And above all don't let them lead you into flaring up against our hosts, which will only make things worse."

"Anyhow," the harpooner said, "I'm as hungry as all blazes, and dinner or breakfast, there isn't a meal in sight!"

"Mr. Land," I remarked, "we have to adjust to the schedule on board, and I imagine our bellies are running ahead of the chief cook's dinner bell."

"Well then, we'll adapt our bellies to the chef's timetable," Conseil replied serenely.

"There you go again, Conseil my friend!" the impatient Canadian fired back. "You never have any attacks of nerves or displays of bile. You're everlastingly calm! You would say your after-meal grace even if you didn't get any food for your before-meal blessing—and you would starve to death rather than complain!"

"What good would it do?" Conseil asked.

"Complaining doesn't need to do any good, it just *feels* good! And if these pirates—I say pirates out of consideration for the professor since he won't let us call them cannibals—if these pirates think they can smother me in this cage without hearing what cusswords spice up my outbursts, they've got another think coming! Look here, Professor Aronnax, level with me. How long do you figure they'll keep us in this big iron box?"

"To tell the truth, friend Land, I don't know much more about it than you do."

"But in a nutshell, what do you suppose is going on here?"

"My supposition is that sheer chance has made us privy to an important secret. Now then, if the crew of this underwater boat have a vested interest in keeping that secret, and if their vested interest has a higher priority than the lives of three men, I think our very existences are in jeopardy. If that isn't the case, then this monster that has swallowed us up will take us back to our own world at the first available opportunity."

"Unless they recruit us for the crew," Conseil said, "and keep us here—"

"Till the moment," Ned Land contended, "when some frigate that's faster or more agile than the *Abraham Lincoln* captures this den of buccaneers, then hangs the whole pack of us from the tip of a mainmast yardarm!"

"Well thought out, Mr. Land," I replied. "But so far we haven't been tendered any enlistment offers, therefore it's pointless to argue about what tactics we should try in such a case. I repeat, let's wait and be guided by events, and let's do nothing right now—since right now there's nothing we *can* do."

"On the contrary, professor," the harpooner replied, unwilling to give in. "There *is* something we can do."

"Oh? And what, Mr. Land?"

"Break out of here!"

"Breaking out of a prison on shore is hard enough, but with an underwater prison, it strikes me as flatly impossible."

"Come on, Ned my friend," Conseil asked, "what's your answer to master's objection? I can't believe that an American could ever be at the end of his rope!"

Visibly baffled, the harpooner didn't say anything. Under the conditions in which fate had left us, escaping was totally out of the question. But a Canadian is half French, and Mr. Ned Land made this clear in his reply.

"So, Professor Aronnax," he continued after thinking for a few seconds, "you haven't figured out what folks do when they can't escape from their prison?"

"No, my friend."

"Easy. They fix things so they stay there."

"Of course!" Conseil put in. "Since we're deep in the ocean, being inside this boat is vastly preferable to being above it or below it!"

"But we'll fix things by kicking out all the jailers, guards, and warders," Ned Land added.

"What's this, Ned?" I asked. "You're se-

riously thinking of taking over this craft?"

"Very seriously," the Canadian replied.

"It's impossible."

"And why is that, sir? Some promising opportunity might come up, and I don't see what could keep us from making the most of it. If there are only about twenty men aboard this machine, I doubt that they can stave off two Frenchmen and a Canadian!"

It seemed wiser to accept the harpooner's proposition than to debate it. Accordingly I was content to reply:

"We'll let such circumstances come, Mr. Land, then we'll see. But till that time I beg you to control your impatience. We need to act shrewdly, and your flare-ups won't bring us any promising opportunities. So give me your word that you'll accept our situation without losing your temper over it."

"I give you my word, professor," Ned Land replied in an unenthusiastic tone. "No nasty comments will leave my mouth, no rude gestures will give my feelings away, not even when they don't feed us on time."

"I have your promise, Ned," I answered the Canadian.

Then our conversation broke off and each of us sank into his own private thoughts. For my part, despite the harpooner's confident talk, I admit that I didn't entertain any illusions. I hadn't any faith in those promising opportunities Ned Land kept going on about. To operate as efficiently as it did, this underwater boat had to have a sizeable crew, so if it came to a physical contest, we would be facing an overwhelming opponent. Besides, before we could take action we had to be free, and that certainly wasn't the case. I couldn't see any way out of this sheet-iron, hermetically sealed cell. And if the strange commander of this boat *did* have a secret to keep—which seemed pretty likely—he would never give us freedom of movement aboard his vessel. Now, would he resort to violence in order to get rid of us, or would he drop us off one day on some patch of solid ground? There lay the unknown. All these theories seemed extremely plausible to me, and to hope for freedom through use of force, you had to be a harpooner.

Moreover I realized that Ned Land's brooding was getting him madder by the minute. I could hear those aforementioned cusswords gradually welling up from the depths of his gullet, and I saw his movements turn threatening again. He got up, pacing in circles like a wild animal in a cage, striking the walls with his foot and fist. Meanwhile the hours went by, our hunger nagged unmercifully, and this time the steward didn't appear. Which amounted to forgetting our castaway status for much too long, if they really had good intentions toward us.

Tormented by the growling of his well-built belly, Ned Land was getting more and more riled, and despite his promise to me, I was in real dread of an explosion when he stood in the presence of one of the men on board.

For two more hours Ned Land's temper got worse and worse. The Canadian shouted and pleaded, but to no avail. The sheet-iron walls were deaf. I didn't hear a single sound inside that dead-seeming boat. The vessel hadn't stirred, because I obviously would have felt its hull vibrating from the beat of the propeller. No doubt it had sunk into the watery deep and didn't belong to the outside world anymore. All this dismal silence was terrifying.

As for our neglect, our isolation in the depths of this cell, I was afraid to guess at how long it might last. The hopes I'd entertained after our interview with the ship's commander were gradually fading away. The gentleness in the man's eyes, the generosity expressed in his facial features, the nobility of his bearing all vanished from my memory. I viewed that mystifying individual in a new light, as somebody who must have been cruel and merciless. I saw him as outside humanity, beyond all feelings of compassion, the implacable foe of his fellow man, against whom he must have sworn an oath of undying hatred!

But even so, was the man going to let us die of starvation, locked up in this cramped prison, vulnerable to those horrible temptations to which people are driven by overpowering hunger? This gruesome thought took on a dreadful intensity in my mind, and fired by my imagination, I felt an unreasoning terror race through me. Conseil stayed calm. Ned Land bellowed.

Just then there were sounds outside. Footsteps rang on the metal tiling. The locks turned, the door opened, the steward appeared.

Before I could make a single movement to prevent him, the Canadian rushed at the poor man, threw him down, grabbed him by the throat. The steward was choking in that powerful grip.

Conseil was already trying to pry the harpooner's hands from his half-throttled victim, and I was about to lend my assistance, when I was suddenly frozen in place by these words spoken in French:

"Calm down, Mr. Land! And you, professor, kindly listen to me!"

10

THE MAN OF THE WATERS

IT WAS THE ship's commander who had just spoken.

At these words Ned Land got up hastily. Nearly strangled, the steward staggered out at a signal from his superior; but the commander had such authority aboard his vessel, that crewman didn't give a single sign of the resentment he must have felt toward the Canadian. I stood there dumbfounded, and in spite of himself Conseil seemed almost interested, as we silently waited for the outcome of this drama.

Arms folded, leaning against a corner of the table, the commander studied us with great care. Was he reluctant to say more? Did he regret those words he'd just spoken in French? It seemed like it.

After a few seconds of silence, which none of us would have dreamed of breaking:

"Gentlemen," he said in a calm, penetrating voice, "I speak French, English, German, and Latin with equal fluency. So I could have answered you at our earlier interview, but first I wanted to make your acquaintance and then think things over. Your four narratives agreed in every essential and established your personal identities for me. I now know that sheer chance has put in my presence Professor Pierre Aronnax, specialist in natural history at the Paris Museum and entrusted with a scientific mission abroad, his manservant Conseil, and Ned Land, a harpooner of Canadian origin aboard the *Abraham Lincoln*, a frigate in the national navy of the United States of America."

I nodded in agreement. The commander hadn't asked me a question, so no answer was called for. This man expressed himself with perfect ease and without any accent. His phrasing was clear, his words well chosen, his delivery remarkably fluent. And yet he didn't have "the feel" of a countryman.

He went on with the conversation as follows:

"No doubt you've felt, sir, that I took too long to pay you this second visit. After learning your identities, I wanted to weigh carefully what policy to adopt toward you. I had difficulty deciding. Some highly inconvenient circumstances have put you in the presence of a man who has cut himself off from humanity. You've disrupted my whole existence."

"We didn't mean to," I said.

"You didn't mean to?" the stranger replied, raising his voice a little. "Didn't the *Abraham Lincoln* mean to hunt me across the seven seas? Didn't you mean to travel aboard that frigate? Didn't your shells mean to strike my hull? Didn't Mr. Ned Land mean to hit me with his harpoon?"

I detected a repressed anger in these words. But there was a perfectly natural answer to these accusations, and I gave it.

"Sir," I said, "you undoubtedly have no idea of the discussions about you that have been going on in Europe and America. You aren't aware of the public passions aroused on both of those continents by various collisions with your underwater machine. I won't go into the countless theories with which we've tried to explain this bewildering phenomenon, whose secret is yours alone. But please understand that the *Abraham Lincoln* chased you over the Pacific high seas in the belief it was hunting some powerful marine monster, which had to be removed from the ocean at any cost."

A half smile loosened the commander's lips; then, in a calmer tone:

"Professor Aronnax," he replied, "do you dare claim that your frigate wouldn't have chased and cannonaded an underwater boat just as it would a monster?"

This question baffled me, since I knew Commander Farragut wouldn't have hesitated for a second. He would have seen it as his sworn duty to destroy a contraption of this sort just as promptly as a gigantic narwhal.

"So you understand, sir," the stranger went on, "that I have a right to treat you as my enemies."

I kept quiet, with good reason. What was the point of debating this proposition when superior force can crush the best arguments?

"It took me a good while to decide," the commander went on. "I was under no obligation to offer you my hospitality. If I were to part company with you, I wouldn't have any reason to see you again. I could put you back on the platform of this ship that has served as your refuge. I could sink under the sea, and I could forget you ever existed. Wouldn't that be my right?"

"Maybe it would be the right of a savage," I replied, "but not of a civilized man."

"Professor," the commander countered instantly, "I'm not what you term a civilized man! I've severed all ties with society for reasons that I alone am qualified to appreciate. Therefore I don't follow its rules and I ask that you never refer to them in front of me!"

This was plain speaking. A flash of anger and scorn lit up the stranger's eyes, and I glimpsed a fearsome past in this man's life. Not only had he put himself outside human laws, he'd rendered himself independent, unreachable, free in the strictest sense of the word! Because who would dare chase him into the depths of the sea, when he could thwart all attacks on the surface? What ship could survive a collision with his underwater *Monitor?* What armor plate, no matter how heavy, could withstand a thrust from his spur? No man among men could require him to account for his actions. God, if he believed in Him, his conscience if he had one—these were the only judges to whom he was answerable.

These thoughts swiftly crossed my mind, while this strange individual fell silent, like somebody completely self-absorbed. I regarded him with a mixture of fear and fascination, in the same way, no doubt, that Oedipus regarded the Sphinx.

After a tolerably long silence, the commander went on with our conversation.

"So I had difficulty deciding," he said. "But I felt that my best interests could be reconciled with that natural compassion to which all human beings have a right. Since fate has brought you here, you'll stay on my vessel. You'll be free on board, and in exchange for this comparative freedom, I'll lay just one condition on you. Your word that you'll agree to it will be sufficient."

"Go on, sir," I replied. "I assume it's a condition any decent person can accept?"

"Yes, sir. It's this. There's a possibility that certain unforeseen events may require me to confine you to your cabins for a few hours, or even a few days as the case may be. Since I never want to use force, I expect from you in such a situation, even more than in any other, your unquestioning obedience. By acting in this way, I protect you from any involvement, I clear you of all responsibility, since I myself make it impossible for you to see what you aren't meant to see. Do you accept this condition?"

So things happened here that were quite odd to say the least, things not fit to be seen by people who hadn't put themselves outside society's laws! Among all the surprises the future had in store for me, this wouldn't be the mildest.

"We accept," I replied. "But with your permission, sir, I'll ask you a question—just one."

"Go ahead, sir."

"You said we would be free aboard your vessel?"

"Completely."

"Then I would like to know what you mean by this freedom."

"Why, the freedom to come, go, see, and even study everything happening here—except under certain rare circumstances. In short, the same freedom we ourselves enjoy, my companions and I."

We clearly weren't talking about the same thing.

"Excuse me, sir," I went on, "but that's merely the freedom any prisoner has, the freedom to walk around his cell. That's not enough for us."

"Nevertheless it will have to do."

"What! We must give up seeing our homeland, friends, and relatives ever again?"

"Yes, sir. But giving up that intolerable earthly yoke that some people call freedom may not be as painful as you think."

"By thunder!" Ned Land shouted. "I'll never promise I won't try getting out of here!"

"I didn't ask for such a promise, Mr. Land," the commander replied icily.

"Sir," I responded, flaring up in spite of myself, "you're taking unfair advantage of us! This is sheer cruelty!"

"No, sir, it's an act of mercy! You're my prisoners of war! I've cared for you when a single word of mine could have plunged you back into the ocean depths! You attacked me! You've just unearthed a secret no living man must probe, the secret of my whole existence! And you think I'll send you back to a world that mustn't know anything more of me? Never! By keeping you here, it isn't *you* I care for, it's myself!"

As these words indicated, the commander had adopted a policy that brooked no opposition.

"Then, sir," I went on, "you give us, quite simply, a choice between life and death?"

"Quite simply."

"My friends," I said, "when the question's put like that, our answer can be taken for granted. But we haven't made any promises to the commander of this vessel."

"None, sir," the stranger replied.

Then, in a gentler voice, he went on:

"Now let me finish what I have to tell you. I've heard of you, Professor Aronnax. You, if not your companions, may not be so inclined to complain about the stroke of fate that has brought us together. Among the books that make up my favorite reading, you'll find the work you've published on the great ocean depths. I often refer to it. You've taken your research as far as terrestrial science can go. But you don't know everything because you haven't seen everything. Let me assure you, professor, you won't regret the time you spend aboard my vessel. You're going to voyage through a land of wonders. Stunned amazement will most likely be your habitual state of mind. It will be a long while before you tire of the sights continually in front of your eyes. Once again I'll be going on a world tour underwater—maybe my last, who knows?—and I'll review everything I've studied in the depths of these seas I've crossed so often, and you can be my fellow student. Starting today you'll enter a new element, you'll see what no human being has ever seen before—since my men and I don't count anymore—and thanks to me, you're about to learn our planet's ultimate secrets."

I can't deny it, the commander's words had a tremendous effect on me. He'd hit me on my weak spot, and for a second I forgot that not even such sublime sights as these could repay me for the loss of my freedom. Anyhow I relied on the future to settle that major issue. So I was content to reply:

"Sir, even though you've cut yourself off from humanity, I'm willing to believe you haven't given up all humanitarian feelings. We're castaways you've charitably taken on board—we'll never forget that. And speaking for myself, I won't deny that my scientific interests can even override my desire for freedom, so I'm positive our association will have plenty of compensations for me."

I thought the commander would offer me his hand to seal our bargain. He did nothing of the sort. That disappointed me.

"One last question," I said, just as this bewildering individual seemed ready to take his leave.

"Ask it, professor."

"What name am I to call you?"

"Sir," the commander replied, "to you, I'm simply Captain Nemo;[6] to me, you and your companions are simply passengers on the *Nautilus*."

Captain Nemo called out. A steward appeared. The captain issued his orders in that strange language I couldn't even recognize. Then, turning to the Canadian and Conseil:

"A meal is waiting for you in your cabin," he told them. "Kindly follow this man."

"That's an offer I can't refuse!" the harpooner replied.

After being locked up for over thirty hours, he and Conseil were finally out of this cell.

"And now, Professor Aronnax, our own breakfast is ready. Allow me to lead the way."

"Yours to command, captain."

I followed Captain Nemo, and after I stepped through the doorway, I went down a sort of electrically lit passageway that resembled a corridor on a ship. Some thirty feet farther along, a second door opened in front of me.

I went into a dining room that was austerely decorated and furnished. Inlaid with ebony trim, tall oaken sideboards stood at both ends of this room, and on their shelves sparkled undulating rows of crockery, porcelain, and glassware of incalculable value. A silver-plated dinner service gleamed under the rays pouring from light fixtures in the ceiling, whose glare was softened and tempered by delicately painted designs.

In the center of the room stood a table, richly spread. Captain Nemo pointed out the place I was to occupy.

"Sit down and eat," he told me, "you must be famished."

Our breakfast consisted of several dishes whose contents were all supplied by the sea, and some foods whose nature and derivation were unknown to me. They were good, I admit, but with an odd flavor I would soon get used to. These various food items seemed to be rich in phosphorous, and I thought that they too must have been of marine origin.

Captain Nemo looked at me. I hadn't said a thing to him, but he read my thoughts and on his own answered the questions I was itching to ask him.

"Most of these dishes are new to you," he

---

[6] *Translator's note.* Latin: nemo means "no one."

told me. "But you can consume them without fear. They're wholesome and nourishing. I gave up terrestrial foods long ago and I'm none the worse for it. My crew are strong and full of energy, and they eat what I eat."

"So," I said, "all these foods are the handiwork of the sea?"

"Yes, professor, the sea supplies me with everything I need. Sometimes I cast my nets in our wake and I pull them up ready to burst. Sometimes I go hunting right in the midst of this element that has seemed so far out of man's reach, and I corner the game that dwells in my underwater forests. Like the flocks of old Proteus, Neptune's shepherd, my herds graze without fear over the ocean's immense prairies. There I have vast properties that I harvest myself, properties that are continually sown by the hand of the Creator of All Things."

I looked at Captain Nemo in definite amazement and I answered him:

"Sir, I fully understand how your nets can furnish excellent fish for your table; I understand less how you can hunt aquatic game in your underwater forests; but how a piece of red meat, no matter how small, can figure in your menu—that I don't understand at all."

"Nor I, sir," Captain Nemo answered me. "I never touch the flesh of land animals."

"Nevertheless *this* . . . ," I went on, pointing to a dish where some slices of loin were still left.

"What you believe to be red meat, professor, is simply loin of sea turtle. Likewise here are some dolphin livers you might mistake for stewed pork. My chef is a skillful food processor who specializes in pickling and preserving these different items from the ocean. Feel free to sample all of these foods. Here are some preserves of sea cucumber that a Malay would call unmatched in the whole world, here's cream from milk furnished by the udders of cetaceans, and sugar from the huge fucus plants in the North Sea; and finally let me offer you some marmalade of sea anemone, equal to that made from the tastiest fruits."

So I sampled away, more as a curiosity seeker than an epicure, while Captain Nemo delighted me with his incredible anecdotes.

"But this sea, Professor Aronnax," he told me, "this prodigious, inexhaustible wet nurse of a sea not only feeds me, she dresses me as well. The clothes you have on were woven from the masses of filaments anchoring certain seashells; in the style of the ancients, they were colored with dye from purpura shells and shaded with violet tints that I extract from a marine slug known as the Mediterranean sea hare. The lotions you'll find on the washstand in your cabin were produced from the oozings of marine plants. Your mattress was made from the ocean's softest eelgrass. Your quill pen will be whalebone, your ink a fluid secreted by cuttlefish or squid. Everything comes to me from the sea, just as someday everything will go back to it!"

"You're in love with the sea, captain."

"Deeply in love! The sea is the be all and end all! It covers seven-tenths of the planet earth. Its breath is clean and wholesome. It's an immense wilderness where a man is never alone because he feels life stirring all around him. The sea is simply the vehicle for a prodigious, uncanny mode of existence; it's simply movement and love; it's living infinity, as one of your poets put it. And in essence, professor, it showcases all three of nature's kingdoms, mineral, vegetable, and animal. The last of these is well represented by the four zoophyte groups, three classes of articulata, five classes of mollusks, and three vertebrate classes, mammals, reptiles, and those countless legions of fish, an infinite order of creatures totaling more than 13,000 species, only a tenth of which belong to fresh water. The sea is a huge natural preserve. In a sense our planet started with the sea, and who can say we won't end with it! Here I find supreme tranquillity. The sea doesn't belong to tyrants. On its surface they can still stake their evil claims, battle each other, devour each other, haul every earthly horror. But thirty feet below sea level, their power ceases, their influence fades, their domination vanishes! Ah, sir, live! Live in the heart of the seas! Here alone do I find independence! Here I recognize no superiors! Here I'm free!"

Captain Nemo suddenly fell silent in the midst of this enthusiastic outpouring. Had he let down his guard and gotten carried away? Had he said too much? For a few seconds he paced around, all aquiver. Then his agitation subsided, his facial expression recovered its usual icy composure, and turning to me:

"Now, professor," he said, "if you would like to inspect the *Nautilus*, I'm yours to command."

11

THE *NAUTILUS*

CAPTAIN NEMO got up. I followed him. Contrived at the rear of the dining room, a double door opened and I went into a room with the same dimensions as the one I'd just left.

It was a library. Tall bookcases, made of black rosewood inlaid with brass, held on their wide shelves a large number of uniformly bound books. These furnishings followed the contours of the room, and at their base were huge couches upholstered in chestnut leather and curved for maximum comfort. Light, movable reading stands could be pushed away or pulled closer at will, and books could be placed on them for easy study. In the center stood a huge table covered with pamphlets, among which some out-of-date newspapers were visible. Electric light flooded this whole pleasing picture, falling from four frosted half globes set in the scrollwork of the ceiling. I looked in genuine wonderment at this room so cleverly laid out and I couldn't believe my eyes.

"Captain Nemo," I told my host, who had just stretched out on a couch, "this library would do credit to several palaces on land, and I'm truly amazed to think it can go with you into the deepest seas."

"Where could you find greater solitude or silence, professor?" Captain Nemo replied. "Did your study at the museum offer you such a perfect retreat?"

"No, sir, and I must say that it's a very humble one next to yours. You have 6,000 or 7,000 volumes here . . ."

"Twelve thousand, Professor Aronnax. They're the only ties I have left with the shore. But I was done with dry land the day my *Nautilus* submerged for the first time un-der the waters. That day I bought my last volumes, my last pamphlets, my last newspapers, and ever since I've chosen to believe that human beings no longer think or write. In any event, professor, these books are at your disposal, feel free to use them."

I thanked Captain Nemo and went up to the shelves of this library. Written in every language, books on science, ethics, and literature were there in profusion, but I didn't see a single work on economics—they seemed to be strictly banned on board. One odd detail: all these books were shelved indiscriminately without any regard for the language in which they were written, and this jumble showed that the *Nautilus*'s captain could fluently read any volume he happened to pick up.

Among these books I noted masterpieces by the greats of ancient and modern times, in other words, all of mankind's finest achievements in history, poetry, fiction, and science, from Homer to Victor Hugo, from Xenophon to Michelet, from Rabelais to Madame George Sand. But science especially predominated in this library: books on mechanics, ballistics, hydrography, meteorology, geography, geology, etc., took up as much space as works on natural history, and I realized they were the captain's main interests. There I saw the complete works of Humboldt, all of Arago, and works by Foucault, Henri Sainte-Claire Deville, Chasles, Milne-Edwards, de Quatrefages, John Tyndall, Faraday, Berthelot, Father Secchi, Petermann, Commander Maury, Louis Agassiz, etc., as well as the transactions of France's Academy of Sciences, bulletins from the various geographical societies, etc., and in a prime location, those two volumes on the great ocean depths that maybe had earned me this comparatively warm welcome from Captain Nemo. Among the works of Joseph Bertrand, his book entitled *The Founders of Modern Astronomy* even gave me a definite date; and because I knew it had appeared in the course of 1865, I concluded that the *Nautilus* hadn't been fitted out before then. Hence Captain Nemo had begun his underwater existence three years ago at the most. Moreover I hoped some even more recent books would let me pinpoint the date exactly;

but I had plenty of time to look for them and I didn't want to put off any longer our stroll through the *Nautilus*'s wonders.

"Sir," I told the captain, "thank you for placing this library at my disposal. There are scientific treasures here, and I'll make the most of them."

"This room isn't just a library," Captain Nemo said, "it's also a smoking room."

"A smoking room?" I exclaimed. "Then people may smoke on board?"

"Surely."

"In that case, sir, I'm forced to believe you've kept up relations with Havana."

"None whatever," the captain replied. "Try this cigar, Professor Aronnax, and even though it doesn't come from Havana, you'll enjoy it if you're a connoisseur."

I accepted the cigar he offered me, whose shape recalled those from Cuba; but it looked like it was made of gold leaf. I lit it at a small brazier sitting on a stylish bronze stand and I took my first draws with the relish of a smoker who hasn't had a puff in two days.

"It's excellent," I said, "but it isn't from the tobacco plant."

"No," the captain replied, "this tobacco doesn't come from either Cuba or the East. It's a sort of nicotine-rich seaweed that the ocean supplies me, sparingly I'm afraid. Do you still miss your Havanas, sir?"

"Captain, I'll sneer at them from this day forward."

"Then smoke these cigars whenever you like and without quibbling about their origin. They don't have any government seal of approval, but I imagine they're none the worse for it."

"On the contrary."

Just then Captain Nemo opened a door facing the one through which I'd entered the library, and I went into an immense, splendidly lit lounge.

It was a huge rectangle with canted corners, thirty-three feet long, twenty wide, sixteen high. Decorated with delicate arabesques, an illuminated ceiling shed a soft, clear daylight over all the wonders gathered in this museum. For a museum it truly was, in which clever hands had spared no expense to accumulate every natural and artistic treasure, displaying them with the helter-skelter picturesqueness that marks a painter's studio.

Some thirty pictures by the masters, uniformly framed and separated by gleaming panoplies of arms, adorned walls on which were stretched tapestries of austere design. There I saw canvases of the highest value, the likes of which I'd marveled at in private European collections and art exhibitions. The various schools of the old masters were represented by a Raphael Madonna, a Virgin by Leonardo da Vinci, a nymph by Correggio, a woman by Titian, an adoration of the Magi by Veronese, an assumption of the Virgin by Murillo, a Holbein portrait, a monk by Velazquez, a martyr by Ribera, a village fair by Rubens, two Flemish landscapes by Teniers, three small genre paintings by Gerard Dow, Metsu, and Paul Potter, two canvases by Géricault and Prud'hon, plus seascapes by Backhuysen and Vernet. Among the works of modern art were pictures signed by Delacroix, Ingres, Decamps, Troyon, Meissonier, Daubigny, etc., and some wonderful statues in marble or bronze—miniature copies of antiquity's finest originals—stood on pedestals in the corners of this magnificent museum. As the *Nautilus*'s commander had predicted, my mind was already falling into that promised state of stunned amazement.

"Professor," this strange man said, "you must excuse the informal way I've welcomed you, as well as the disorder reigning in this lounge."

"Sir," I replied, "without prying into your identity, might I venture to call you an artist?"

"A collector, sir, nothing more. In the past I loved acquiring these beautiful works created by the hand of man. I hunted them greedily, ferreted them out tirelessly, and I was able to gather some objects of great value. They're my last mementos of those shores that are now dead for me. In my eyes your modern artists are already as old as the ancients. They've existed for 2,000 or 3,000 years and I mix them up in my mind. The masters are ageless."

"What about these composers?" I said, pointing to sheet music by Weber, Rossini, Mozart, Beethoven, Haydn, Meyerbeer, Hérold, Wagner, Auber, Gounod, Victor Massé, and a number of others scattered over an ultra large piano-organ that took up one of the wall panels in this lounge.

"These composers," Captain Nemo answered me, "are the contemporaries of Orpheus, because all chronological differences fade in the annals of the dead—and I too am dead, professor, just as dead as those friends of yours sleeping six feet under!"

Captain Nemo fell silent and seemed lost in a deep reverie. I regarded him with intense emotion, quietly analyzing his strange facial expression. Leaning his elbow on the corner of a valuable mosaic table, he no longer saw me, he'd forgotten my very presence.

I didn't disturb his meditations but continued my inspection of the curiosities adorning this lounge.

After works of art, natural rarities were the main attraction. They consisted chiefly of plants, shells, and other exhibits from the ocean that must have been Captain Nemo's own personal finds. In the middle of the lounge, an electrically lit jet of water fell back into a basin made from a single giant clam. The delicately festooned rim of this shell, supplied by the biggest mollusk in the class Acephala, measured about twenty feet around; so it was even bigger than those fine giant clams given King François I by the Republic of Venice, clams whose shells the Church of Saint-Sulpice in Paris made into two gigantic holy water fonts.

Around this basin, inside stylish glass cases reinforced with brass fastenings, were classified and labeled the most valuable marine exhibits ever put under the eyes of a naturalist. As you can imagine, I was in a state of academic ecstasy.

The zoophyte branch offered some highly unusual specimens from its two groups, the polyps and the echinoderms. In the first group: organ-pipe coral, gorgonian fan coral, soft sponges from Syria, coral of the genus *Isis* from the Molucca Islands, sea-pen coral, wonderful coral of the genus *Virgularia* from the waters of Norway, various coral of the genus *Ombellularia*, some octocoral, then a full series of those madrepores that my mentor Professor Milne-Edwards has so shrewdly classified into divisions, among which I noted the captivating genus *Flabellina*, the genus *Oculina* from Réunion Island, and a "Neptune's chariot" from the Caribbean Sea—every magnificent variety of coral and in short all the species of these unusual polyparies that congregate to form entire islands, which will turn into continents someday. Among the echinoderms, notable for being covered with spines, some starfish, sand stars, feather stars, sea lilies, basket stars, sea urchins, sea cucumbers, etc., represented a complete collection of the individuals in this group.

An excitable conchologist would surely have fainted dead away in front of the many other glass cases in which were classified specimens from the mollusk branch. There I saw a collection of incalculable value that I haven't time to describe completely. Among these exhibits I'll mention just for the record: an elegant royal hammer shell from the Indian Ocean, its uniform white spots standing out sharply against a background of red and brown; an imperial thorny oyster, brightly colored, garnished with spines, a specimen rare to European museums and whose value I put at $4,000; a common hammer shell from the seas near Australia, very hard to come by; exotic cockles from Senegal, fragile white bivalve shells that a single breath could pop like a soap bubble; several varieties of watering-can shell from Java, a sort of limestone tube fringed with leafy folds and much fought over by collectors; a whole series of top shells—greenish-yellow ones fished up from American seas, others colored reddish brown and patronizing the waters off Australia, the former coming from the Gulf of Mexico and notable for their overlapping shells, the latter some sun-carrier shells found in the southernmost seas, finally and rarest of all, the magnificent spur shell from New Zealand; then marvelous tellin shells from the species *Tellina sulphurea*, some valuable species of smooth clams and venus shells, trellislike sundial snails from Tranquebar on India's east coast, a mottled turban snail gleaming with mother-of-pearl, green parrot shells from the seas of China, the all-but-unknown cone snail from the genus

Cœnodulli, every variety of cowry used as money in India and Africa, a "glory of the seas," the most valuable shell in the East Indies; finally periwinkles, snails from the genus *Delphinula*, screw shells, purple snails, egg cowries, volute shells, olive shells, miter shells, helmet shells, purpura shells, whelks, harp shells, rock snails, triton shells, telescope shells, spindle shells, conch shells, spider conchs, limpets, snails from the genus *Hyala*, sea butterflies—every kind of delicate, fragile seashell that science has baptized with the most delightful names.

Aside and in special compartments, strings of supremely beautiful pearls lay spread out, the electric light flecking them with little fiery sparks: pink pearls extracted from saltwater fan shells in the Red Sea; green pearls from the blackfoot abalone; yellow, blue, and ebony pearls, the unusual handiwork of various mollusks from every ocean and of certain mussels from rivers up north; in short, several specimens of incalculable value that had been oozed by the rarest of shellfish. Some of these pearls were bigger than a pigeon egg; they more than equaled the one that the explorer Tavernier sold the Shah of Persia for $600,000 and they surpassed that other pearl owned by the Imam of Muscat, which I'd thought unmatched in the whole world.

Hence it was literally impossible to calculate the value of this collection. Captain Nemo had to have spent millions in acquiring these different specimens, and I was wondering what financial resources he tapped to satisfy his collector's fancies, when these words interrupted me:

"You're examining my shells, professor? Certainly they're of interest to a naturalist; but for me they have an added charm because I've collected every one of them with my own two hands, and not a sea on the globe has eluded my investigations."

"I understand, captain, I understand your delight at strolling in the midst of all this wealth. You're a man who gathers his treasure in person. No museum in Europe has such a collection of exhibits from the ocean. But if I use up all my wonderment on them, I won't have anything left for the vessel itself!

I don't want to pry into those secrets of yours, but I confess my curiosity is aroused to a fever pitch by this *Nautilus*, the motor power it contains, the equipment allowing it to operate, the ultrapowerful force that brings it to life. I see some instruments hanging on the walls of this lounge and their purposes are unknown to me. Might I learn—"

"Professor Aronnax," Captain Nemo answered me, "I've said you'll be free aboard my vessel, so no part of the *Nautilus* is out of bounds for you. You may give it a detailed inspection, and I'll be delighted to act as your guide."

"I can't thank you enough, sir, but I don't want to abuse your good nature. I'll ask you only about the uses for these instruments of physical measure—"

"Professor, these same instruments are also in my stateroom, where I'll have the pleasure of explaining their functions to you. But beforehand, come inspect the cabin I've set aside for you. You need to learn how you'll be lodged aboard the *Nautilus*."

I followed Captain Nemo, who went through one of the doors cut into the lounge's canted corners, then led me back down the ship's corridors. He took me to the bow, and there, instead of just a cabin, I found a stylish stateroom with a bed, a washstand, and various other furnishings.

I could only thank my host.

"Your stateroom adjoins mine," he told me, opening a door, "and mine leads into that lounge we've just left."

I went into the captain's stateroom. It had an austere, almost monastic appearance. An iron bedstead, a worktable, some washstand appurtenances. Subdued lighting. No luxuries. Just the bare necessities.

Captain Nemo showed me to a bench.

"Kindly be seated," he told me.

I sat, and he started speaking as follows:

12

ENTIRELY BY ELECTRICITY

"SIR," CAPTAIN NEMO SAID, showing me the instruments hanging on the walls of his stateroom, "these are the devices needed to navigate the *Nautilus*. Here, as in the lounge, I always have them in front of my eyes, and they show my position and exact heading in the midst of the ocean. You're familiar with some of them, such as the thermometer, which gives the temperature inside the *Nautilus;* the barometer, which measures the heaviness of the outside air and forecasts changes in the weather; the humidistat, which shows the degree of dryness in the air; the storm glass, whose mixture decomposes to announce the arrival of hurricanes; the compass, which directs my course; the sextant, which takes the sun's altitude and tells me my latitude; chronometers, which let me calculate my longitude; and finally spyglasses for both day and night, allowing me to scrutinize every corner of the horizon once the *Nautilus* has risen to the surface of the waves."

"These are your normal navigational instruments," I replied, "and I'm familiar with their uses. But no doubt these others answer the *Nautilus*'s special needs. That dial I see there, with the needle moving over it—isn't it a pressure gauge?"

"It is indeed a pressure gauge. We put it in contact with the water, and it shows the outside pressure on our hull, which in turn gives me the depth at which my submersible is traveling."

"And are these some new breed of sounding line?"

"They're thermometric sounding lines that report water temperatures in the different strata."

"And these other instruments, whose functions I can't even guess?"

"Here, professor, I need to do a bit of explaining," Captain Nemo said. "So kindly hear me out."

He fell silent for a few seconds, then he said:

"There's a force that's powerful, obedient, quick, and effortless, that can be bent to any use, and that reigns supreme on board. My ship is run entirely by this force. It lights me, it heats me, it's the soul of my mechanical equipment. This force is electricity."

"Electricity!" I exclaimed in some surprise.

"Yes, sir."

"But, captain, you have a tremendous speed of movement that doesn't square with the strength of electricity. Till now its dynamic potential has been very limited, capable of generating only a small amount of power!"

"Professor," Captain Nemo replied, "my electricity isn't the run-of-the-mill variety, and with your permission I'll leave it at that."

"I won't insist, sir, and I'll rest content with simply being flabbergasted at your results. I would like to ask one question, however, which you needn't answer if it's out of line. The electrical cells you use to generate this marvelous force must run down very quickly. Their zinc, for example—how do you replace it, since you're no longer in contact with the shore?"

"That question I'll answer," Captain Nemo replied. "First off, I'll mention that at the bottom of the sea there are veins of zinc, iron, silver, and gold that I would quite certainly be capable of mining. But I haven't tapped any of these terrestrial metals and I've chosen to make demands only on the sea itself for the sources of my electricity."

"The sea itself?"

"Yes, professor, and there was no shortage of such sources. In fact, by establishing a circuit between two wires immersed to different depths, I could have obtained electricity from the divergent temperatures they experience; but I preferred to use a more practical procedure."

"And what's that?"

"You're familiar with the composition of salt water. In thirty-five ounces you'll find 96.5% water and about 2.66% sodium chloride; then small amounts of magnesium chloride, potassium chloride, magnesium bromide, sulfate of magnesia, calcium sulfate, and calcium carbonate. So you can see that sodium chloride is found there in significant proportions. Now then, it's this sodium that I extract from salt water and use in making my electrical cells."

"Sodium?"

"Yes, sir. Mixed with mercury it forms an amalgam that can take the place of zinc in Bunsen cells. The mercury is never used up.

Only the sodium is consumed, and the sea itself gives me that. Beyond this, I'll mention that sodium batteries have been found to generate the greater energy, and their electromotor strength is twice that of zinc batteries."

"Captain, I fully understand the value of sodium under the conditions in which you're placed. The sea contains it. Fine. But it still has to be produced, in short, extracted. And how do you accomplish this? Obviously your batteries could do the extracting; but if I'm not mistaken, the consumption of sodium needed by your electrical equipment would be greater than the quantity you would extract. So in the process of producing your sodium, you would use up more than you would make!"

"Accordingly, professor, I don't extract it with batteries; quite simply, I utilize the heat from mineral coal."

"Mineral coal?" I said, my voice going up on the words.

"We'll say sea coal, if you prefer," Captain Nemo replied.

"And you can mine these seams of underwater coal?"

"You'll watch me work them, Professor Aronnax. All I ask is a little patience, and you'll have plenty of time to cultivate that virtue. Just remember this: I owe everything to the ocean; it generates electricity, and electricity gives the Nautilus heat, light, movement, and in a word, life itself."

"But not the air you breathe?"

"Oh, I could produce the air needed on board, but there wouldn't be any point in it, since I can rise to the surface of the sea whenever I like. But even though electricity doesn't supply me with breathable air, at least it operates the powerful pumps that store air under pressure in special tanks—which, in a pinch, will allow me to stay down in the lower strata for as long as I want."

"Captain," I replied, "I'll rest content with marveling. You've obviously found what all mankind will surely find someday, the true dynamic power of electricity."

"I'm not so sure they'll find it," Captain Nemo replied icily. "Be that as it may, you're already familiar with the first use I've discovered for this valuable force. It lights us, and with a uniformity and continuity not offered even by sunlight. Now look at this clock: it's electric, it runs with an accuracy challenging the finest chronometers. I've had it divided into twenty-four hours like Italian clocks, since neither day nor night, sun nor moon, exist for me, but only this artificial light I import into the depths of the seas! See, right now it's ten o'clock in the morning."

"On the dot."

"Another use for electricity: that dial hanging in front of our eyes shows how fast the Nautilus is going. An electric wire puts it in contact with the patent log; this needle tells me the actual speed of my submersible. And . . . hold on . . . just now we're proceeding at the moderate pace of fifteen miles per hour."

"It's marvelous," I replied, "and you're so right to use this force, captain—it's destined to take the place of wind, water, and steam."

"But there's more, Professor Aronnax," Captain Nemo said, getting up. "And if you'll kindly follow me, we'll inspect the Nautilus's stern."

In essence I was already familiar with the whole forward part of this underwater boat, and here are its exact subdivisions going from amidships to its spur: the dining room, 16½ feet long and separated from the library by a watertight bulkhead, in other words, it couldn't be penetrated by the sea; the library, 16½ feet long; the main lounge, 33 feet long and separated from the captain's stateroom by a second watertight bulkhead; the aforesaid stateroom, 16½ feet long; mine, 8 feet long; and finally air tanks 24½ feet long and reaching to the stempost. Total: a length of 115 feet. The doors cut in the watertight bulkheads closed hermetically with the help of india-rubber seals, which insured complete safety on board in case the Nautilus sprang a leak.

I followed Captain Nemo down corridors located close at hand and I arrived amidships. There I found a sort of shaft heading upward between two watertight bulkheads. An iron ladder clamped to the wall led to the shaft's upper end. I asked the captain what this ladder was for.

"It leads to the skiff," he replied.

"What! You have a skiff?" I remarked in some amazement.

"Surely. A first-class longboat, light and unsinkable, which we use for excursions and fishing trips."

"But when you want to set out, don't you need to go back to the surface of the sea?"

"By no means. The skiff is attached to the topside of the *Nautilus*'s hull and it occupies a cavity designed specifically to hold it. It's completely decked over, absolutely watertight, and held solidly in place by bolts. This ladder leads to a manhole cut in the *Nautilus*'s hull and corresponding to a similar hole cut in the skiff's side. Through this double opening I insert myself into the longboat. My crew close up the hole belonging to the *Nautilus*; I close up the one belonging to the skiff by merely tightening its screws; I undo the bolts holding the skiff to the submersible, and the longboat rises with prodigious speed to the surface of the sea. Then I open the cover panel, which has stayed carefully closed till that point; I up mast and hoist sail—or I take out my oars—and I go for a spin."

"But how do you come back to the ship?"

"I don't, Professor Aronnax; the *Nautilus* comes to me."

"At your command?"

"At my command. An electric wire connects me to the ship. I fire off a telegram and that's that."

"Right," I said, dazed by all these wonders. "Nothing to it!"

After going past the well of the companionway that led to the platform, I saw a cabin 6½ feet long in which Conseil and Ned Land, enraptured with their meal, were busy devouring it to the last crumb. Then a door opened into the galley, 10 feet long and located between the vessel's huge storage lockers.

There, even more powerful and obedient than gas, electricity took care of all the cooking. Wires under the stoves transmitted to platinum griddles a heat that was distributed and maintained with perfect consistency. It also heated a distilling mechanism, which, through an evaporation process, supplied excellent drinking water. Next to the galley was a bathroom, conveniently laid out, with faucets supplying hot or cold water at will.

After the galley came the crew's quarters, 16½ feet long. But the door was closed and I couldn't see its furnishings, which might have told me the number of men it took to operate the *Nautilus*.

At the far end stood a fourth watertight bulkhead separating the crew's quarters from the engine room. A door opened and I went into the compartment where Captain Nemo, indisputably a world-class engineer, had set up his propulsion units.

Brightly lit, the engine room measured a good 65 feet in length. It was appropriately divided into two parts: the first held the cells for generating electricity; the second, the mechanism that transmitted motion to the propeller.

Right off I detected an odor permeating this compartment that was *sui generis*.[7] Captain Nemo noticed the negative impression it made on me.

"That's a gaseous discharge caused by our use of sodium," he told me, "but it's only a mild inconvenience. In any case we cleanse the ship every morning by ventilating it in the open air."

Meanwhile I examined the *Nautilus*'s engine with an interest you can easily imagine.

"You'll note," Captain Nemo told me, "that I use Bunsen rather than Ruhmkorff cells. The latter would be ineffective. Bunsen cells are fewer in number but large and powerful, which makes them superior in my experience. The electricity generated here proceeds to the stern, where electromagnets of huge size activate a special system of levers and gears that transmit motion to the propeller shaft. The latter has a diameter of 20 feet, a pitch of 24½ feet, and can do up to 120 revolutions per minute."

"And you get?"

"A speed of fifty miles per hour."

Here lay a mystery, but I didn't insist on investigating it. How could electricity work with such power? Where did this nearly unlimited energy come from? Was it from some new kind of high-voltage induction

---

[7] *Translator's note.* Latin: "in a class of its own."

coil? Could its transmission be immeasurably increased by some unknown system of levers?[8] This was the part that was beyond me.

"Captain Nemo," I said, "I can vouch for the results and I won't try to figure them out. I've seen the *Nautilus* in operation near the *Abraham Lincoln* and I know where I stand on its speed. But it isn't enough just to move, we need to see where we're going! We have to be able to steer right or left, up or down. How do you reach the lower depths, where you meet an increasing resistance that's measured in hundreds of atmospheres? How do you come back to the surface of the ocean? Finally, how do you stay at whatever level suits you? Am I out of line in asking you all these things?"

"Not in the least, professor," the captain answered me after a slight hesitation, "since you'll never leave this underwater boat. Come into the lounge. It's actually our workroom, and there you'll get the full story on the *Nautilus!*"

13

A Few Figures

A SECOND LATER we were seated on a couch in the lounge, cigars between our lips. The captain laid under my eyes a working drawing that gave a ground plan, cross section, and side view of the *Nautilus*. Then he began to describe the ship as follows:

"Here, Professor Aronnax, are the different dimensions of this boat now carrying you. It's a very lengthy cylinder with conical ends. As you can see, it's shaped like a cigar, a shape already used in London for several projects of the same type. From one end to the other, this cylinder measures exactly 230 feet, and its maximum breadth of beam is 26 feet. Consequently it isn't quite built on the ten-to-one ratio of your high-speed steamers, but its lines are sufficiently long and their tapering gradual enough that the displaced wa-

ter easily slips past and poses no obstacle to the ship's movements.

"These two dimensions allow you to obtain, by a simple calculation, the *Nautilus*'s surface area and volume. Its surface area totals 10,887 square feet, its volume 53,226 cubic feet—which is tantamount to saying that when it's completely submerged, it displaces 53,226 cubic feet of water, or weighs 1,661.4 tons.

"In drawing up plans for a ship meant to navigate underwater, I wanted it, when floating on the waves, to lie nine-tenths below the surface and to emerge only one-tenth. Under these conditions, consequently, it needed to displace only nine-tenths of its volume, or 47,903 cubic feet; in other words, it had to weigh only 1,495.26 tons. So I was obliged to not exceed this weight while building it to the aforesaid dimensions.

"The *Nautilus* is made up of two hulls, one inside the other; between them, joining them together, are iron T-bars that give this ship the utmost rigidity. In fact, thanks to this cellular arrangement, it's as resistant as a mass of stone, as if it were a solid object. Its plating can't cave in; it's self-adhering and doesn't depend on the tightness of its rivets; and due to the perfect union of its materials, the solidarity of its construction allows it to challenge the roughest seas.

"The two hulls are manufactured from boiler plate steel, whose relative density is 7.8 times that of water. The first hull is no less than two inches thick and weighs 435.37 tons. My second hull, the outer skin, features a keel twenty inches high by ten inches wide and weighing 68 tons in itself; this hull, the engine, the ballast, the various accessories and furnishings, plus the bulkheads and inner braces, have a combined weight of 1,059.89 tons, which, when added to 435.37 tons, gives us the requisite total of 1,495.26 tons. Clear?"

"Clear," I replied.

"So," the captain went on, "when the *Nautilus* lies on the waves under these conditions, a tenth of it does emerge above water. Now then, if I provide some ballast tanks equal in capacity to that tenth, hence able to hold 166.14 tons, and if I fill them up with

---

[8] And sure enough, there are now rumors of such a discovery, in which a new set of levers generates considerable power. Did its inventor bump into Captain Nemo?

water, the boat then displaces 1,661.4 tons, or it weighs that much, and it would be completely submerged. That's what takes place, professor. These ballast tanks are close at hand in the lower reaches of the *Nautilus*. I open some stopcocks, the tanks fill up, the boat sinks, and it's exactly flush with the surface of the water."

"Fine, captain, but now we come to the real difficulty. You're able to lie flush with the surface of the ocean, that much I understand. But while diving into the depths beneath that surface, isn't your submersible going to encounter a pressure (and therefore experience an upward thrust) that's measured at one atmosphere per every 32 feet of water, or at about 14.2 pounds per square inch?"

"Exactly, sir."

"Then unless you fill up the whole *Nautilus*, I don't see how you can drive it down through those masses of liquid."

"Professor," Captain Nemo replied, "static objects mustn't be confused with dynamic ones or we'll be vulnerable to serious errors. Comparatively little effort is spent in reaching the ocean's lower depths, because all objects have a tendency to become 'sinkers.' Here's how I reasoned it out."

"I'm all attention, captain."

"When I wanted to determine what increase in weight the *Nautilus* needed to have in order to submerge, all I had to do was take note of the progressive reduction in volume that salt water experiences in deeper and deeper strata."

"That's obvious," I replied.

"Now then, if water isn't absolutely incompressible, at least it compresses very little. In fact, according to the latest calculations, this reduction is only .0000436 per atmosphere, or per every 32 feet of depth. To go 3,200 feet down, I have to take into account the reduction in volume that occurs under a pressure equivalent to a 3,200-foot column of water, in other words, under a pressure of a hundred atmospheres. In this instance the reduction would be .00436. Consequently I would need to increase my weight from 1,661.4 tons to 1668.64. So the additional weight would only be 7.24 tons."

"That's all?"

"That's all, Professor Aronnax, and the calculation is easy to check. Now then, I have supplementary ballast tanks capable of shipping 110 tons of water. So I can descend to considerable depths. When I want to rise again and lie flush with the surface, all I have to do is expel that water; and if I want the *Nautilus* to emerge above the waves to a tenth of its total capacity, I empty all the ballast tanks completely."

This line of reasoning, backed up by figures, left me without a single objection.

"I accept your calculations, captain," I replied, "and I would be ill-mannered to question them since your daily experience bears them out. But I have a hunch we're still left with one real difficulty."

"What, sir?"

"When you're at a depth of 3,200 feet, the *Nautilus*'s plating bears a pressure of a hundred atmospheres. If at this point you want to empty the supplementary ballast tanks to lighten your boat and rise to the surface, your pumps have to overcome that pressure of a hundred atmospheres, which amounts to 1,420 pounds per square inch. This demands a strength—"

"—that only electricity can give me," Captain Nemo said instantly. "I repeat, sir, the dynamic power of my engines is nearly infinite. The *Nautilus*'s pumps have prodigious strength, as you must have noticed when their waterspouts rushed like a torrent over the *Abraham Lincoln*. But with a view to conserving my machinery, I use my supplementary ballast tanks only to reach an average depth of 5,000 to 6,500 feet. Accordingly, when I feel like visiting the ocean depths five or six miles under the surface, I use procedures that are more time-consuming but no less infallible."

"What are they, captain?" I asked.

"Here I'm naturally led into telling you how the *Nautilus* is maneuvered."

"I can't wait to find out."

"In order to steer this boat to port or starboard, in short, to make turns on a horizontal plane, I use an ordinary wide-bladed rudder that's fastened to the rear of the sternpost and worked by a wheel and tackle. But I can also move the *Nautilus* upward and downward on a *vertical* plane by the simple method of slanting its two fins, which are attached to its sides at its center of flotation; these fins are adjustable, able to assume any position, and operated from inside with the help of powerful levers. If the fins stay parallel to the boat, the latter moves horizontally. If they slant, the *Nautilus* follows the angle of that slant and under its propeller's thrust either sinks or rises on a diagonal that's as steep as I wish. And likewise if I want to return more quickly to the surface, I throw the propeller in gear, and the water pressure makes the *Nautilus* rise vertically, as a gas balloon filled with hydrogen lifts swiftly into the skies."

"Bravo, captain!" I exclaimed. "But in the midst of the waters, how can your helmsman follow the course you've given him?"

"My helmsman is stationed behind the windows of a pilothouse, which protrudes from the topside of the *Nautilus*'s hull and is fitted with biconvex glass."

"Can glass withstand such pressures?"

"Absolutely. Though fragile when struck, crystal still offers considerable resistance. In 1864, during experiments on fishing by electric light in the middle of the North Sea, glass panes less than a third of an inch thick were seen to withstand a pressure of sixteen atmospheres, all the while letting through strong, heat-generating rays whose warmth was unevenly distributed. Now then, I use glass windows measuring more than eight inches at their centers—in other words, they're thirty times thicker."

"Fair enough, captain, but in order to see, we need a little light to dispel the darkness, and in the midst of the murky waters, I wonder how your helmsman—"

"Astern of the pilothouse is a powerful electric searchlight whose rays light up the sea for a distance of half a mile."

"Oh bravo! Bravo three times over, captain! That explains the phosphorescent glow from this so-called narwhal that was so puzzling to us scientists! Pertinent to this, I would like to ask you if the *Nautilus*'s running afoul of the *Scotia*, which caused such a great uproar, was accidental?"

"Completely accidental, sir. I was navigating 6½ feet under the surface of the water when the collision occurred. But I could see that it had no dire consequences."

"None, sir. But as for your run-in with the *Abraham Lincoln* . . . ?"

"Professor, that bothered me, because it's one of the best ships in the gallant American navy, but I was under attack and I had to defend myself! Even so, I was content to simply put the frigate in a condition where it couldn't do me any harm—it won't have trouble getting repairs at the nearest port."

"Ah, commander," I exclaimed with conviction, "your *Nautilus* is truly a marvelous boat!"

"Yes, professor," Captain Nemo replied with genuine feeling, "and I love it like my own flesh and blood! If danger threatens one of your ships on the surface of the sea, your only thoughts are of the cold, remorseless depths, as the Dutchman Jansen so aptly put it; but under the waves on the *Nautilus*, a man can throw his cares away! There are no structural weaknesses to fear, because our double hull has the rigidity of iron; no rigging strained by rolling and pitching on the waves; no sails for winds to carry off; no boilers for steam to blow up; no fires to fear, because the submersible is made of sheet iron, not wood; no coal to run out of, since its propulsive power is electricity; no collisions to fear, because it navigates the watery deep all by itself; no storms to brave, because just a few yards under the waves, it finds absolute tranquillity! There, sir, there's a ship beyond compare! And if it's true that the engineer has more confidence in a craft than the builder, and the builder more than the captain himself, you can appreciate the utter abandon with which I put my trust in this *Nautilus*, since I'm its captain, builder, and engineer all in one!"

Captain Nemo spoke with spellbinding eloquence. The fire in his eyes and the passion in his gestures transformed him. Yes, he loved his ship the way a father loves his child!

But one question naturally popped up, and though it may have been out of line, I couldn't help asking it.

"So you're an engineer, Captain Nemo?"

"Yes, professor," he answered me. "I studied in London, Paris, and New York back in the days when I lived on dry land."

"But how did you manage to build this wonderful *Nautilus* in secret?"

"Each piece of it, Professor Aronnax, came from a different part of the globe and reached me at a cover address. Its keel was forged by Creusot in France, its propeller shaft by Penn & Co. in London, the sheet-iron plates for its hull by Laird's in Liverpool, its propeller by Scott's in Glasgow. Its tanks were manufactured by Cail & Co. in Paris, its engine by Krupp in Prussia, its spur by the Motala workshops in Sweden, its precision instruments by Hart Bros. in New York, etc.; and each of these suppliers received my specifications under a different name."

"But," I continued, "once these parts were manufactured, didn't they have to be assembled and adjusted?"

"Professor, I set up my workshops on a deserted islet in midocean. There my workmen—in other words, my gallant companions whom I've molded and trained—helped me complete our *Nautilus*. Then, when the operation was over, we burned every trace of our stay on that islet, which, if I could have, I would have blown up."

"So I can assume that this vessel was quite an expensive proposition?"

"An iron ship, Professor Aronnax, runs $204 per ton. Now then, the *Nautilus* has a burden of 1,660 tons. So it cost $338,000, or $400,000 including its furnishings, and $800,000 to $1,000,000 with all the collections and works of art it holds."[9]

"One final question, Captain Nemo."

"Ask, professor."

"You're a wealthy man?"

"Wealthy beyond measure, sir—and without the slightest trouble I could pay off the two-billion-dollar French national debt!"

I looked intently at the peculiar individual who had just spoken these words. Was he playing on my credulity? Time would tell.

---

[9] *Translator's note.* The total would be roughly comparable to $20,000,000 in today's dollars.

14
THE BLACK TIDE

THE PART OF THE planet earth that the seas cover is estimated to be 147,975,892 square miles, hence more than 94 billion acres. This mass of liquid totals 2,250,000,000 cubic miles and could form a globe with a diameter of 150 miles, whose weight would be over three quintillion tons. To grasp such a number, we need to remember that a quintillion is to a billion as a billion is to one, in other words, there are as many billions in a quintillion as ones in a billion! Now then, this mass of liquid nearly equals the total amount of water that has flowed through all the earth's rivers for the past 40,000 years!

In prehistoric times an era of fire led to an era of water. At first there was ocean everywhere. Then, during the Silurian Period, mountaintops gradually appeared above the waves, islands emerged, vanished under temporary floods, rose again, fused together to form continents, and finally the earth's geography settled into what we have today. Solid matter had confiscated from liquid matter some 37,000,657 square miles, hence about 24 billion acres.

The shapes of the continents allow the seas to be divided into five major parts: the frozen Arctic and Antarctic oceans, the Indian Ocean, the Atlantic Ocean, and the Pacific Ocean.

The Pacific Ocean stretches north to south between the two polar circles and east to west between America and Asia over an expanse of 145 degrees of longitude. It's the most tranquil of the seas; its currents are wide and slow moving, its tides moderate, its rainfall abundant. And this was the first ocean I was destined to cross under these extremely unusual conditions.

"If you don't mind, professor," Captain Nemo told me, "we'll determine our exact position and fix the starting point of our voyage. It's fifteen minutes before noon. I'm going to rise to the surface of the water."

The captain pressed an electric bell three times. The pumps started to expel water from the ballast tanks; a needle on the pressure gauge marked the decreasing pressures that showed the *Nautilus*'s upward progress; then the needle stopped.

"Here we are," the captain said.

I proceeded to the central companionway, which led to the platform. I climbed its metal steps, went through the open hatches, and arrived topside on the *Nautilus*.

The platform emerged only 2½ feet above the waves. The *Nautilus*'s bow and stern were spindle-shaped, causing the ship to be aptly compared to a long cigar. I noted the slight overlap of its sheet-iron plates, which resembled the scales covering the bodies of our big land reptiles. So I had a perfectly natural explanation for why, despite the finest spyglasses, this boat had always been mistaken for a marine animal.

Near the middle of the platform, the skiff was half set in the ship's hull, making a slight bulge. Fore and aft stood two cupolas of moderate height, their sides slanting and inset with windows of heavy biconvex glass: one was for the helmsman steering the *Nautilus*, the other for the powerful electric beacon lighting his way.

The sea was magnificent, the skies clear. That long aquatic vehicle barely felt the ocean's broad undulations. A mild breeze out of the east rippled the surface of the water. Free of any trace of fog, the horizon was ideal for taking sights.

There wasn't a thing to be seen. Not a reef, not an islet. No more *Abraham Lincoln*. Just a vast emptiness.

Raising his sextant, Captain Nemo took the altitude of the sun, which would give him his latitude. He waited a few minutes till that golden orb touched the rim of the horizon. While he was taking his sights, he didn't move a muscle, and the instrument wouldn't have been steadier if his hands had been made of marble.

"Noon," he said. "Professor, whenever you're ready. . . ."

I took one last look at the sea, a little yellowish near the landing places of Japan, and I went below again to the main lounge.

There the captain fixed his position and used a chronometer to calculate his longitude, which he double-checked against his previous readings of hour angles. Then he told me:

"Professor Aronnax, we're in longitude 137° 15′ west—"

"West of which meridian?" I asked instantly, hoping the captain's reply would maybe reveal his nationality to me.

"Sir," he answered me, "I have chronometers variously set to the meridians of Paris, Greenwich, and Washington, D.C. But in your honor I'll use the one for Paris."

His answer didn't tell me a thing. I nodded, and the commander went on:

"We're in longitude 137° 15′ west of the meridian of Paris, and latitude 30° 7′ north, in other words, about 300 miles from the shores of Japan. At noon on this day of November 8, we hereby begin our voyage of underwater exploration."

"May God be with us!" I replied.

"And now, professor," the captain added, "I'll leave you to your intellectual pursuits. I've set our course east-northeast at a depth of 165 feet. Here are some large-scale charts on which you can follow that course. The lounge is at your disposal, and with your permission I'll take my leave."

Captain Nemo bowed. I was on my own, lost in my thoughts. They all centered on the *Nautilus*'s commander. Would I ever learn the nationality of this strange man who boasted that he didn't have any? His sworn hatred for humanity, a hatred that maybe was bent on some dreadful program of revenge—what had caused it? Was he one of those unappreciated scholars, one of those geniuses "wounded by the world," as Conseil put it, a modern-day Galileo, or maybe one of those men of science, like America's Commander Maury, whose careers were ruined by political revolutions? It was too early to say. As for me, whom fate had just brought aboard his ship and whose life he'd held in the balance, the captain had given me a cool but courteous welcome. Only he never took the hand I offered him. He never offered me his own.

For a whole hour I was deep in these musings, trying to probe this mystery that had me so intrigued. Then my eyes focused on a huge world map displayed on the table, and I put my finger on the exact spot where our just-determined longitude and latitude intersected.

Like the landmasses the sea has its rivers. These are special currents that can be identified by their temperature and color, and the most remarkable one is known as the Gulf Stream. Science has determined the global paths of five chief currents: one in the north Atlantic, a second in the south Atlantic, a third in the north Pacific, a fourth in the south Pacific, and a fifth in the southern Indian Ocean. It's even likely that a sixth current used to exist in the northern Indian Ocean, when the Caspian and Aral seas joined up with certain large Asian lakes to make one uniform expanse of water.

Now then, at the spot shown on the world map, one of these seagoing rivers was rolling by, the *Kuroshio* of the Japanese, the Black Tide; warmed by vertical rays from the tropical sun, it leaves the Bay of Bengal, crosses the Strait of Malacca, goes up the shores of Asia, and curves into the north Pacific as far as the Aleutian Islands, carrying along trunks of camphor trees and other local items, the deep indigo of its warm waters contrasting sharply with the ocean's waves. This was the current the *Nautilus* was about to cross. I followed it on the map with my eyes, I saw it vanish into the vastness of the Pacific, and I felt myself carried along with it, when Ned Land and Conseil appeared in the lounge doorway.

My two gallant companions stood petrified at the sight of the wonders spread out in front of their eyes.

"Where are we?" the Canadian exclaimed. "In the Quebec Museum?"

"Begging master's pardon," Conseil countered, "but this seems more like the Sommerard artifacts exhibition!"

"My friends," I replied, motioning them to come in, "you're in neither Canada nor France but securely aboard the *Nautilus*, 165 feet below sea level."

"If master says so, then so be it," Conseil remarked. "But in all honesty this lounge is enough to amaze even somebody Flemish like me."

"Go ahead and be amazed, my friend, and take a good look around, because there's plenty of work here for a champion classifier like you."

Conseil didn't need any encouragement. Bending over the glass cases, the gallant lad was already mumbling choice words from the naturalist's vocabulary: class Gastropoda, family Buccinoidea, genus cowry, species *Cypræa madagascariensis*, etc.

In the meantime Ned Land, less infatuated with conchology, questioned me about my interview with Captain Nemo. Had I found out who he was, where he came from, where he was heading, how deep he was taking us? In short, a thousand questions I would need a year to answer.

I told him everything I'd learned—or rather hadn't learned—and I asked him what he'd seen or heard on his part.

"Didn't see or hear a thing," the Canadian replied. "I haven't even spotted the crew of this boat. Could they be electrical too by any chance?"

"Electrical?"

"I swear I'm half tempted to believe it! But back to you, Professor Aronnax," Ned Land said, still hanging onto his old ideas. "Can't you tell me how many men are on board? Ten, twenty, fifty, a hundred?"

"I can't answer that, Mr. Land. And trust me on this, for the time being get rid of those notions of taking over the *Nautilus* or escaping from it. This boat is a masterpiece of modern technology, and I would hate to have missed it. Many people would jump at this chance that has been handed to us, just to walk in the midst of these wonders. So keep calm, and let's see what's going on around here."

"See!" the harpooner exclaimed. "There's nothing to see, nothing we'll *ever* see from this sheet-iron prison! We're simply running around blindfolded—"

Ned Land was just saying these last words when we were suddenly plunged in darkness—total darkness. The ceiling lights went out so quickly, my eyes literally ached, just as if we'd experienced the opposite sensation of going from the deepest gloom into the brightest sunlight.

We stood stock-still, not knowing what

surprise was waiting for us, pleasant or unpleasant. Then there was a sliding sound. You could tell that some panels were shifting over the *Nautilus*'s sides.

"It's the beginning of the end!" Ned Land said.

". . . order Hydromedusae," Conseil mumbled.

Suddenly, through two oval openings, daylight appeared on both sides of the lounge. Masses of liquid came into view, brightly lit by the rays pouring from the ship's beacon. Two panes of glass separated us from the sea. At first I shuddered at the thought that those fragile partitions might shatter; but strong brass fastenings secured them, giving them nearly infinite resistance.

The sea was clearly visible for a one-mile radius around the *Nautilus*. What a sight! What pen could ever describe it? Who could possibly depict the effects of the light passing through those translucent sheets of water, or the subtlety of its progressive shadings into the ocean's upper and lower strata?

The transparency of salt water is well known. It's thought to be even clearer than spring water. The mineral and organic substances it holds in suspension actually increase its translucency. In certain parts of the Caribbean, you can see the sandy bottom with surprising distinctness as deep as 475 feet down, and the penetrating power of the sun's rays seems to give out only at a depth of about 1,000 feet. But in this fluid setting where the *Nautilus* was traveling, our electric glow was being generated in the very heart of the waves. It was no longer illuminated water, it was liquid light.

If we accept the theories of the microbiologist Ehrenberg—who believes the ocean depths are lit up by phosphorescent organisms—nature has certainly saved one of her most prodigious sights for residents of the sea, as I could judge for myself from the thousand ways the light was playing about. On both sides I had windows opening over those unexplored depths. The darkness in the lounge made the light outside seem even brighter, and we looked through that clear glass as if it were the window of an immense aquarium.

The *Nautilus* didn't seem to be moving. This was due to the lack of landmarks. But streaks of water, parted by the ship's spur, sometimes shot past our eyes with extraordinary speed.

In sheer wonderment we leaned on our elbows in front of those display windows, and our stunned silence remained unbroken till Conseil said:

"You wanted to see something, Ned my friend—well, now you can feast your eyes!"

"Fascinating!" the Canadian put in, forgetting his temper tantrums and getaway schemes while giving in to this irresistible allure. "It's worth coming as far as we have, just to see a sight like this!"

"Ah!" I exclaimed. "I understand our captain's way of life. He has found himself a separate world that saves its most amazing wonders just for him!"

"But where are the fish?" the Canadian pointed out. "I don't see any fish!"

"Why would you care, Ned my friend?" Conseil replied. "Since you have so little knowledge of them."

"Me? I'm a fisherman!" Ned Land exclaimed.

And on this topic a dispute arose between the two friends, since both were knowledgeable about fish but from completely different viewpoints.

Everybody knows that fish make up the fourth and last class in the vertebrate branch. They've been very aptly defined as "cold-blooded vertebrates with a double circulatory system, breathing through gills, and built to live in water." They consist of two distinct categories: the category of *bony fish*, in other words, those whose spines have vertebrae made of bone; and *cartilaginous fish*, in other words, those whose spines have vertebrae made of cartilage.

Maybe the Canadian was acquainted with this distinction, but Conseil knew far more about it; and since he and Ned were now fast friends, he just had to show off. Accordingly he told the harpooner:

"Ned my friend, you're a slayer of fish, a highly skilled fisherman. You've caught a large number of those interesting creatures.

But I'll bet you don't know how they're classified."

"Sure I do," the harpooner replied in all seriousness. "They're classified into fish we eat and fish we don't eat!"

"Spoken like a true glutton," Conseil replied. "But tell me, do you know the difference between bony fish and cartilaginous fish?"

"Just maybe, Conseil."

"And how about the subdivisions of these two large classes?"

"I haven't the foggiest notion," the Canadian replied.

"All right, listen and learn, Ned my friend! Bony fish are subdivided into six orders. *Primo*, the acanthopterygians, whose upper jaw is fully formed and free moving, and whose gills are shaped like a comb. This order consists of fifteen families, in other words, three-quarters of all known fish. Example: the common perch."

"Pretty fair eating," Ned Land replied.

"*Secundo*," Conseil went on, "the abdominals, whose pelvic fins hang under the abdomen to the rear of the pectorals but aren't attached to the shoulder bone—an order that's divided into five families and makes up the great majority of freshwater fish. Examples: carp, pike."

"Ugh!" the Canadian put in with distinct scorn. "You can keep the freshwater fish!"

"*Tertio*," Conseil said, "the subbrachians, whose pelvic fins are attached under the pectorals and hang directly from the shoulder bone. This order has four families. Examples: flatfish such as plaice, dab, turbot, brill, sole, etc."

"Excellent, really excellent!" the harpooner exclaimed, interested in fish only from an edible standpoint.

"*Quarto*," Conseil went on, unabashed, "the apods, which have long bodies that lack pelvic fins and are covered with a heavy, often sticky skin—an order consisting of only one family. Examples: common eels and electric eels."

"So-so, just so-so!" Ned Land replied.

"*Quinto*," Conseil said, "the lophobranchians, which have fully formed, free-moving jaws but whose gills are made up of little tufts arranged in pairs along their gill arches. This order has only one family. Examples: seahorses and sea moths."

"Bad, very bad!" the harpooner remarked.

"*Sexto* and last," Conseil said, "the plectognaths, whose maxillary bone is firmly attached to the side of the intermaxillary that forms the jaw and whose palate arch is locked to the skull by sutures that render the jaw immovable—an order lacking true pelvic fins and that consists of two families. Examples: puffers and sunfish."

"They're an insult to a frying pan!" the Canadian exclaimed.

"Are you grasping all this, Ned my friend?" asked the erudite Conseil.

"Not a lick of it, Conseil my friend," the harpooner replied. "But keep on going, you're just too interesting for words."

"As for cartilaginous fish," Conseil went on unflappably, "they consist of only three orders."

"All the better," Ned put in.

"*Primo*, the cyclostomes, whose jaws are fused into a flexible ring and whose gill openings are simply a large number of holes—an order consisting of only one family. Example: the lamprey."

"An acquired taste," Ned Land replied.

"*Secundo*, the selacians, with gills like those of the cyclostomes but whose lower jaw is free moving. This order, which is the most important in the class, consists of two families. Examples: the ray and the shark."

"What!" Ned Land exclaimed. "Rays and man-eaters in the same order? Well, Conseil my friend, on behalf of the rays, I wouldn't advise you to put them in the same fish tank!"

"*Tertio*," Conseil replied, "The sturionians, whose gill opening is the usual single slit adorned with a gill cover—an order consisting of four genera. Example: the sturgeon."

"Ah, Conseil my friend, you saved the best for last, in my opinion anyhow! And that's all of 'em?"

"Yes, my gallant Ned," Conseil replied. "And note well, even when you've grasped all this, you're still ignorant, because these families are subdivided into genera, subgenera, species, varieties—"

"All right, Conseil my friend," the harpooner said, leaning toward the glass panel, "here come a couple of your varieties now!"

"Yes, fish at last!" Conseil exclaimed. "It's as if we're in front of an aquarium!"

"No," I replied, "because an aquarium is just a cage, and these fish are as free as birds in the air."

"Well, Conseil my friend, identify them! Start naming them!" Ned Land said.

"Me?" Conseil replied. "I can't. That's my employer's bailiwick."

It was true, though the fine lad was a classifying maniac, he was no naturalist, and I doubt that he could tell a bonito from a tuna. In short, he was the exact opposite of the Canadian, who didn't know a thing about classification but could instantly put a name to any fish.

"A triggerfish," I said.

"It's a Chinese triggerfish," Ned Land replied.

"Genus *Balistes*, family Sclerodermi, order Plectognathi," Conseil muttered.

No doubt about it, Ned and Conseil in combination added up to one exceptional naturalist.

The Canadian wasn't mistaken. Playing around the *Nautilus* was a school of triggerfish with flat bodies, grainy skins, stings on their dorsal fins, and four quivery rows of quills garnishing both sides of their tails. Nothing could have been more wondrous than the skin covering them: gray above, white underneath, with spots of gold that sparkled in the dark eddies of the waves. Around them rays were undulating like sheets flapping in the wind, and among these I spotted, much to my delight, a Chinese ray, yellowish on its topside, a delicate pink on its belly, and with three stings behind its eyes; a rare species whose very existence was doubted in Lacépède's time, since that pioneering classifier of fish had seen one only in a portfolio of Japanese drawings.

For two hours a whole aquatic army escorted the *Nautilus*. In the midst of their leaping and playing, while they competed with each other in beauty, radiance, and speed, I made out some green wrasse, goatfish marked with pairs of black lines, rock gobies with curved caudal fins and violet spots on their white backs, wonderful Japanese mackerel from the genus *Scomber* that had blue bodies and silver heads, the glittering blue-and-gold fusilier whose name by itself gives its full description, lousy fish with fins variously blue and yellow, red-breasted wrasse enhanced by black stripes on their tail fin, barred thicklips stylishly corseted in their six waistbands, trumpetfish that were sometimes a yard long and whose flute-shaped beaks made them look like seagoing woodcocks, Japanese salamanders, six-foot moray eels from the genus *Echidna* that had keen little eyes and huge mouths bristling with teeth, etc.

Our wonderment stayed at an all-time fever pitch. Our exclamations were endless. Ned identified the fish, Conseil classified them, and as for me, I was in ecstasy over the verve of their movements and the beauty of their forms. Never before had I been able to glimpse these creatures alive and at large in their natural element.

Given such a complete collection from the seas of Japan and China, I won't mention every variety that passed in front of our dazzled eyes. More plentiful than birds in the air, those fish raced right up to us, no doubt attracted by the bright glow of our electric beacon.

Suddenly daylight appeared in the lounge. The sheet-iron panels slid shut. The magic vision vanished. But for a good while I kept dreaming away, till the moment my eyes focused on the instruments hanging on the wall. The compass still showed our heading as east-northeast, the pressure gauge indicated a pressure of five atmospheres (corresponding to a depth of 165 feet), and the electric log gave our speed as fifteen miles per hour.

I waited for Captain Nemo. But he didn't appear. The clock pointed to the hour of five.

Ned Land and Conseil went back to their cabin. I retired in turn to my stateroom. There I found dinner ready for me. It consisted of

turtle soup made from the most delicate hawksbill, a red mullet with white, slightly flaky meat, whose liver when separately prepared makes delicious eating, plus loin of imperial angelfish whose flavor struck me as even better than salmon.

I spent the evening in reading, writing, and thinking. Then I got drowsy, I stretched out on my eelgrass mattress, and I fell sound asleep, while the *Nautilus* glided through the swift current of the Black Tide.

15

An Invitation in Writing

THE NEXT DAY, November 9, I woke up only after a long twelve-hour slumber. Conseil, a creature of habit, came to ask "how master's night went" and to offer his services. He'd left his Canadian friend sleeping like a man who had never done anything else.

I let the gallant lad babble away without putting much energy into answering him. I was concerned about Captain Nemo's absence during our session the previous afternoon and I hoped to see him again today.

I'd soon put on my clothes, which were woven from strands of seashell tissue. More than once their composition drew comments from Conseil. I informed him that they were made from the smooth, silken filaments with which the fan mussel, a type of seashell very plentiful along Mediterranean beaches, attaches itself to rocks. In olden times folks made fine fabrics, stockings, and gloves from these filaments, because they were both very soft and very warm. So the *Nautilus*'s crew could dress themselves on the cheap, without needing a thing from cotton growers, sheep, or silkworms on shore.

As soon as I'd gotten dressed, I made my way to the main lounge. It was empty.

I plunged into studying the conchological treasures amassed in the glass cases. I also investigated the huge plant albums filled with the rarest marine herbs, which still kept their wonderful colors even though they were pressed and dried. Finally I noted a complete series of seaweeds among these valuable water plants: some *Cladostephus verticillatus*, peacock's tails, vine-leafed caulerpa, red algae from the species *Callithamnion granulatum*, delicate ceramiums tinted scarlet, dulse arranged into fan shapes, mermaid's cups that looked like the caps of squat mushrooms and for years had been classified among the zoophytes.

The entire workday went by without my being honored by a visit from Captain Nemo. The panels in the lounge didn't open. Maybe they didn't want us to get tired of all those lovely things.

The *Nautilus* kept to an east-northeasterly heading, a speed of twelve miles per hour, and a depth between 165 and 200 feet.

The next day, November 10, the same neglect, the same solitude. I didn't see a soul from the crew. Ned and Conseil spent most of the day with me. They were amazed at the captain's bewildering absence. Was that strange man ill? Did he want to change his plans concerning us?

But after all, as Conseil noted, we enjoyed complete freedom, we were delicately and abundantly fed. Our host was keeping his side of the bargain. We had no grounds for complaint, and furthermore our lot was so unique and promised us such generous rewards, we didn't have any reason to be critical.

That day I started my journal of these adventures, which has allowed me to describe them with the most scrupulous accuracy. And here's an odd detail: I wrote it on paper manufactured from marine eelgrass.

Early in the morning on November 11, fresh air poured through the *Nautilus*'s interior, informing me that we'd come back to the surface of the ocean to replenish our oxygen supply. I headed for the central companionway and climbed onto the platform.

It was six o'clock. I found the sky overcast, the sea gray but calm. Barely a billow. I was hoping to run into Captain Nemo there—would he come on deck? I saw only the helmsman closed up in his glass-windowed pilothouse. Seated on the ledge furnished by the skiff's hull, I inhaled the sea's salty aroma with great pleasure.

Little by little the fog dispersed under the

action of the sun's rays. That shining orb cleared the eastern horizon. Under its glance the sea caught on fire like a trail of gunpowder. Scattered on high, the clouds were tinted with bright, wonderfully shaded colors, and a large number of "cat's tongues" warned of winds all day long.[10]

But what were mere winds to this *Nautilus* that no storms could faze!

I was marveling at this delightful sunrise, so cheery and refreshing, when I heard somebody climbing onto the platform.

I was all set to greet Captain Nemo, but it was his chief officer who appeared—whom I'd already met during our first visit with the captain. He moved forward across the platform, not seeming to notice my presence. A powerful spyglass up to his eye, he scrutinized every corner of the horizon with the utmost care. His examination finished, he went over to the hatch and uttered a sentence whose exact wording follows below. I remember it because he repeated it every morning under the same circumstances. It went like this:

"*Nautron respoc lorni virch.*"

As for what it meant, I couldn't say.

These words spoken, the chief officer went below again. I figured the *Nautilus* was about to resume its underwater navigating. So I headed down the hatch and back through the corridors to my stateroom.

Five days went by in this way without any change in our circumstances. Every morning I climbed onto the platform. The same individual uttered the same sentence. Captain Nemo didn't appear.

I'd adopted the policy that we'd seen the last of him, when on November 16 while going back into my stateroom with Ned and Conseil, I found a note addressed to me on the table.

I opened it impatiently. It was written in a script that was clear and neat but a bit "Old English" in style, its characters reminding me of German calligraphy.

This note read as follows:

November 16, 1867

Professor Aronnax
Aboard the Nautilus

Captain Nemo invites Professor Aronnax on a hunting trip that will take place tomorrow morning in his Crespo Island forests. He hopes nothing will keep the professor from attending and he looks forward with pleasure to the professor's companions joining him.

CAPTAIN NEMO,
Commander of the Nautilus.

"A hunting trip!" Ned exclaimed.

"And in his forests on Crespo Island!" Conseil added.

"But does this mean the old boy goes ashore?" Ned Land went on.

"That seems to be the gist of it," I said, re-reading the letter.

"Well, we've got to accept!" the Canadian remarked. "Once we're on solid ground, we can figure out our next move. Besides, it wouldn't pain me to eat a couple slices of fresh venison!"

I didn't try to reconcile the contradiction between Captain Nemo's open aversion to continents or islands and his invitation to go hunting in a forest; instead I was content to reply:

"First of all, let's look into this Crespo Island."

I checked the world map, and in latitude 32° 40′ north and longitude 167° 50′ west, I found an islet that Captain Crespo had scouted out in 1801 and that old Spanish charts called *Roca de la Plata*, in other words, "Silver Rock." So we were about 1,800 miles from our starting point, and by a slight change of heading, the *Nautilus* was taking us back toward the southeast.

I showed my companions this small stray rock in the middle of the north Pacific.

"If Captain Nemo does go ashore sometimes," I told them, "at least he only picks desert islands!"

Ned Land shook his head without replying, then he and Conseil left me. After supper was served me by the mute and unresponsive

---

[10] "Cat's tongues" are light little white clouds with ragged edges.

steward, I fell asleep, but not without a few anxieties.

When I woke up the next day, November 17, I found the *Nautilus* completely motionless. I dressed quickly and went into the main lounge.

Captain Nemo was waiting for me. He got up, bowed, and asked if it suited me to come along.

Since he'd made no allusion to his absence the past week, I also refrained from mentioning it and I simply answered that my companions and I were ready to go with him.

"Only, sir," I added, "I'll take the liberty of asking you a question."

"Fire away, Professor Aronnax, and I'll answer if I can."

"Well then, captain, how is it that you've severed all ties with dry land, yet you own forests on Crespo Island?"

"Professor," the captain answered me, "these forests of mine don't bask in the warmth and brightness of the sun. No lions, tigers, panthers, or other quadrupeds frequent them. They're known to me alone. They grow for me alone. These forests aren't on land—they're underwater forests."

"Underwater forests!" I exclaimed.

"Yes, professor."

"And you're offering to take me to them?"

"Exactly."

"On foot?"

"Without getting your feet wet."

"While hunting?"

"While hunting."

"Rifles in hand?"

"Rifles in hand."

I looked at the *Nautilus*'s commander with an attitude anything but flattering to the man.

"He has brain fever, no doubt about it," I said to myself. "He had an attack a week ago and he isn't over it even yet. What a shame! I liked him better unconventional than unhinged!"

These thoughts could be clearly read on my face; but Captain Nemo seemed content with inviting me to go with him, which I did like somebody resigned to the worst.

We arrived at the dining room, where we found breakfast ready.

"Professor Aronnax," the captain told me, "let's have breakfast together without any formality. We can chat while we eat. Because, though I promised you a stroll in my forests, I didn't agree to find you a restaurant there. So eat your breakfast like a man who'll most likely eat dinner only when it's extremely late."

I did justice to the meal. It consisted of assorted fish and some slices of sea cucumber, that praiseworthy zoophyte, all garnished with such highly appetizing seaweeds as *Porphyra laciniata* and *Laurencia primafetida*. Our drink was clear water, to which, following the captain's example, I added a few drops of a fermented liquor extracted by the Kamchatka method from a seaweed known by name as *Rhodymenia palmata*.

At first Captain Nemo ate without saying a word. Then he told me:

"Professor, when I proposed that you go hunting in my Crespo forests, you thought I was contradicting myself. When I informed you that the forests in question were underwater, you thought I'd gone insane. Professor, you must never make snap judgments about your fellow man."

"But, captain, believe me—"

"Kindly listen to me, and you'll see if you have any grounds for accusing me of insanity or self-contradiction."

"I'm all attention."

"Professor, you know as well as I that a man can survive underwater so long as he carries with him his own supply of air to breathe. For underwater work projects, the workman wears a waterproof suit with his head enclosed in a metal helmet, while he gets air from above with the help of force pumps and flow controls."

"That's the standard equipment for a diving suit," I said.

"Exactly, but under such conditions the man has no freedom. He's attached to a pump that sends him air through an india-rubber hose—it's a literal chain that shackles him to the shore, and if we were tied down to the *Nautilus* in this way, we couldn't get very far."

"Then how do you break free?" I asked.

"By using the Rouquayrol-Denayrouze device, invented by two of your countrymen but perfected by me for my own special uses, thereby allowing you to risk these new physiological conditions without experiencing any organic disorders. It consists of a tank built from heavy sheet iron in which I store air under a pressure of fifty atmospheres. This tank is fastened onto your back with straps, like a soldier's knapsack. Its upper part forms a container where the air is controlled by a bellows mechanism and can be released only at its proper tension. In the Rouquayrol device that has been in general use, two india-rubber hoses leave this container and feed to a sort of tent that covers the operator's nose and mouth; one hose is for the entrance of air to be inhaled, the other for the exit of air to be exhaled, and the tongue shuts off the former or the latter depending on the breather's needs. But in my case, since I face considerable pressures on the seafloor, I needed to enclose my head in a brass globe like those found on standard diving suits, and the two hoses for inhalation and exhalation now feed to that globe."

"That's perfect, Captain Nemo, but the air you carry must be quickly consumed, and once it's less than 15% oxygen, it becomes unfit for breathing."

"Surely, but as I told you, Professor Aronnax, the *Nautilus*'s pumps allow me to store air under considerable pressure; given this fact, the tank on my diving equipment can supply breathable air for nine or ten hours."

"I have no more objections to raise," I replied. "I'll only ask you this, captain: how can you light your way on the ocean floor?"

"With the Ruhmkorff device, Professor Aronnax. If the other is carried on your back, this one is fastened to your belt. It features a Bunsen battery that I activate not with potassium dichromate but with sodium. An induction coil gathers the electricity generated and directs it to a specially designed lantern. In this lantern there's a glass spiral that has just a slight residue of carbon dioxide gas. When the device is turned on, this gas becomes luminous and gives off a continual whitish light. Thus equipped, I can both breathe and see."

"Captain Nemo, you meet all my objections with such overwhelming answers, I don't dare have any doubts. But even though I'm forced to accept both your Rouquayrol and Ruhmkorff devices, I'm still dubious about the rifle you're going to give me."

"But it isn't a rifle that uses gunpowder," the captain replied.

"So it's an air gun?"

"Surely. How could I make gunpowder on my ship when I don't have any saltpeter, sulfur, or charcoal?"

"Even so," I said, "to fire underwater in a medium that's 855 times denser than air, you would have to overcome considerable resistance."

"That doesn't necessarily follow. Using Fulton's designs, the Englishmen Philippe-Coles and Burley, the Frenchman Furcy, and the Italian Landi have perfected guns that are equipped with a special system of airtight fastenings and can fire in underwater conditions. But I repeat, since I don't have any gunpowder, I've replaced it with air at high pressure, which is generously supplied me by the *Nautilus*'s pumps."

"But this air must run out very quickly."

"Well, in a pinch can't I get more from my Rouquayrol tank? All I have to do is draw it from an *ad hoc*[11] spigot. Besides, Professor Aronnax, you'll see for yourself that during these underwater hunting trips, we use little air and few bullets."

"But in this semidarkness, in the midst of this liquid that's so dense in comparison to the open air, it seems to me that gunshots couldn't carry very far and would seldom be fatal!"

"On the contrary, sir, with this rifle every shot is fatal; as soon as an animal is hit, no matter how lightly, it drops as if struck by lightning."

"Why?"

"Because this rifle doesn't shoot ordinary bullets but little glass capsules invented by the Austrian chemist Leniebroek, and I have a considerable supply of them. These glass

---

[11] *Translator's note.* Latin: "purpose-built."

capsules are covered with a strip of steel and weighted with a lead base; they're genuine little Leyden jars charged with high-voltage electricity. They go off at the slightest impact, and the animal drops dead, no matter how strong it is. These capsules, I might add, are no bigger than no. 4 shot, and the chamber of any ordinary rifle could hold ten of them."

"I'll quit debating," I replied, getting up from the table. "All that's left is for me to shoulder my rifle. Where you go, I'll go."

Captain Nemo led me to the *Nautilus*'s stern, and going past Ned and Conseil's cabin, I called to my two companions, who instantly fell in behind us.

Then we arrived at a cell located close to the engine room, and in this cell we were to get dressed for our stroll.

16
Strolling the Plains

THE CELL PROPER was the *Nautilus*'s arsenal and wardrobe. A dozen diving suits were hanging on its walls, waiting for anybody who wanted to take a stroll.

As soon as he saw them, Ned Land revealed a clear aversion to the idea of putting one on.

"But my gallant Ned," I told him, "the forests of Crespo Island are simply underwater forests!"

"Swell!" put in the disappointed harpooner, watching his dreams of fresh meat fade away. "And what about you, Professor Aronnax, are you going to stick yourself inside one of those outfits?"

"That's how it's done, Mr. Ned."

"Have it your way, sir," the harpooner replied, shrugging his shoulders. "But speaking for myself, I'll never get into those things unless they force me!"

"Nobody will force you, Mr. Land," Captain Nemo said.

"And is Conseil up for it?" Ned asked.

"Where master goes, I go," Conseil replied.

At the captain's summons, two crewmen came to help us put on these heavy waterproof clothes, made from seamless india rubber and expressly designed to bear up under considerable pressure. They were like suits of armor that were both strong and supple. These clothes consisted of a jacket and pants. The pants ended in bulky footwear adorned with heavy lead soles. The jacket's fabric was reinforced with brass plating that shielded the chest, protected it from the water pressure, and let your lungs function freely; the sleeves ended in supple gloves that didn't impede hand movements.

These perfected diving suits, it was easy to see, were a far cry from such misbegotten costumes as the cork breastplates, protective vests, undersea tunics, barrel helmets, etc., invented and acclaimed in the 18th century.

Conseil and I were soon dressed in these diving suits, as were Captain Nemo and one of his companions—a Herculean type who must have been prodigiously strong. All that remained was to lower the metal globes over our heads. But before proceeding with this operation, I asked the captain for permission to examine the rifles set aside for us.

One of the *Nautilus*'s men presented me with a rifle of simple design whose butt was boiler plate steel, hollow inside, and of pretty large dimensions. This served as a tank for the compressed air, which a trigger-operated valve released into the metal tube. Inset in the butt's widest part, a cartridge clip held some twenty electric bullets, which, with the help of a spring, automatically took their places in the rifle barrel. As soon as one shot had been fired, another was ready to go.

"Captain Nemo," I said, "this is an ideal, easy-to-use weapon. All I ask is to put it to the test. But how will we reach the seafloor?"

"Right now, professor, the *Nautilus* is aground in thirty feet of water, and we've only to be on our way."

"But how will we get outside?"

"You'll see."

Captain Nemo inserted his skull into its spherical headwear. Conseil and I did the same, but not before we heard the Canadian wish us a sarcastic "happy hunting." On top the suits ended in collars of threaded brass, and we screwed our metal helmets onto them.

Three holes covered with heavy glass allowed us to see in any direction by simply turning our heads inside the globes. Placed on our backs, the Rouquayrol devices went into operation as soon as they were in position, and for my part I could breathe with ease.

Rifle in hand, the Ruhmkorff lamp hanging from my belt, I was ready to go forth. But in all honesty, while trapped in these heavy clothes and nailed to the deck by my lead soles, it was impossible for me to take a single step.

But this circumstance had been foreseen, because I felt myself being shoved into a little room adjoining the wardrobe. Towed in the same way, my companions went with me. I heard a door with watertight seals close after us, and we were immersed in absolute darkness.

After a few minutes a sharp hissing sound reached my ears. I felt a sort of coldness rising from my feet to my chest. Obviously a stopcock inside the boat was letting in water from outside, which flooded the room and soon filled it up. Contrived in the *Nautilus*'s hull, a second door opened. We were bathed in twilight. An instant later our feet were walking on the bottom of the sea.

And now, how can I possibly convey the impressions left on me by this stroll under the waters? Words are powerless to describe such wonders! When the effects of this liquid element are too unique even for the painter's brush to portray, how can the writer's pen ever hope to depict them?

Captain Nemo took the lead, and his companion followed us a few steps to the rear. Conseil and I walked side by side, as if daydreaming that through our metal carapaces a little polite conversation might still be possible. Already I no longer felt the bulkiness of my clothes, footwear, and air tank, nor the weight of that heavy globe in which my head was rattling around like an almond in its shell. Once they were underwater, all these objects lost a part of their weight equal to the weight of the liquid they displaced, and thanks to this law of physics discovered by Archimedes, I did just fine. I wasn't an inert mass anymore and I had, comparatively speaking, great freedom of movement.

Lighting up the seafloor even thirty feet under the surface of the ocean, the sun amazed me with its power. The solar rays easily crossed that aqueous mass and dispersed its dark colors. I could clearly make out objects 300 feet away. Farther on, the bottom was tinted with fine shades of ultramarine; then, off in the distance, it turned blue and faded in the midst of a hazy darkness. To tell the truth, this water surrounding me was simply a kind of air, denser than the atmosphere on land but nearly as transparent. Overhead I could see the calm surface of the ocean.

We were walking on sand that was fine-grained and smooth, not rippled like beach sand, which retains the imprint of the waves. That dazzling carpet was a genuine mirror and it threw back the sun's rays with startling intensity. Ergo this immense vista of reflections, a glinting radiance that penetrated every liquid molecule. Will anybody believe me if I insist that at this thirty-foot depth, I could see as if it were broad daylight?

For a quarter of an hour, I hiked over this blazing sand, which was sprinkled with the evanescent powder of finely ground seashells. Looming like a long reef, the *Nautilus*'s hull gradually vanished, but when night fell in the midst of the waters, the ship's beacon would surely help us find our way back on board, since its rays carried with perfect distinctness. This effect is hard to understand for anybody who has never seen a light beam so sharply defined on shore. There the air is so steeped in dust, it makes such rays look like a luminous fog; but over the water as well as under it, shafts of electric light are transmitted with incomparable clarity.

Meanwhile we kept on going, and the wide sandy plains seemed endless. My hands parted liquid curtains that closed again behind me, and my footprints faded swiftly under the water pressure.

Soon, scarcely blurred by their distance from us, the forms of a few objects took shape under my eyes. I made out a magnificent foreground of rocks carpeted by the loveliest zoophyte specimens, and right off I was struck by an effect unique to this medium.

By then it was ten o'clock in the morning. The sun's rays were hitting the surface of the waves at a fairly sharp angle, decomposing by refraction as if passing through a prism; and when this light came in contact with flowers, rocks, seedlings, shells, and polyps, the edges of these objects were shaded with all seven hues of the solar spectrum. This riot of rainbow tints was a marvel, a feast for the eyes: a genuine kaleidoscope of red, green, yellow, orange, violet, indigo, and blue—in short, a full palette of colors for a madcap painter! If only I'd been able to tell Conseil about the vivid sensations rising in my brain, matching him in exclamations of wonderment! If only I'd known how to communicate in that sign language used by Captain Nemo and his companion! Accordingly, having nothing better to do, I talked to myself, orating inside that brass container over my head, foolishly wasting my air on empty words.

Conseil, like me, had stopped in front of this splendid sight. In the presence of these zoophyte and mollusk specimens, the fine lad obviously was classifying his heart out. Polyps and echinoderms packed the seafloor. There were various corals: assorted isis, cornularia living in isolation, tufts of virginal genus *Oculina* formerly known by the name "white coral," prickly fungus coral shaped like mushrooms, plus sea anemones hanging on by their muscular disks, all making up an authentic flowerbed that was adorned with blue-button jellyfish wearing collars of azure tentacles, with starfish spangling the sand, including warty basket stars from the genus *Astrophyton* that were like fine lace embroidered by the hands of water nymphs, their festoons swaying in the gentle undulations caused by our walking. It filled me with real regret to crush underfoot the gleaming mollusk specimens that littered the seafloor by the thousands: scallops from the species *Pecten concentricus*, hammer shells, coquina (seashells that can actually hop around), top shells, red helmet shells, roostertail conchs, sea hares, and so many other items from this inexhaustible ocean. But we had to keep going and we forged ahead, while above us

scudded schools of Portuguese men-of-war that let their ultramarine tentacles drift in their wakes, medusas whose milky white or dainty pink parasols were festooned with azure tassels and shaded us from the sun's rays, plus purple-striped jellyfish, which, in the dark, would have sprinkled our path with phosphorescent glimmers!

I glimpsed all these wonders in the space of a quarter of a mile, barely pausing, following Captain Nemo whose gestures kept beckoning me onward. Soon the character of the seafloor changed. After the plains of sand came a bed of that viscous slime Americans call "ooze," which is composed exclusively of seashells rich in limestone or silica. Then we crossed a prairie of algae, open-sea plants that the ocean hadn't yet uprooted, so they were growing lustily. This soft, richly textured lawn would have matched the most luxuriant carpets woven by human hands. But while this greenery was spreading under our steps, it didn't neglect us overhead. The surface of the water was crisscrossed by a floating arbor of marine plants belonging to that superabundant algae family that includes more than 2,000 known species. I saw long ribbons of fucus drifting above me, some globular, others tubular, *Laurencia*, *Cladostephus* with the slenderest foliage, *Rhodymenia palmata* resembling the fan shapes of cactus. I noticed that the green plants kept close to the surface of the sea, while the reds were at a medium depth, leaving the blacks and browns to design gardens and flowerbeds on the ocean floor.

These algae are truly one of the most prodigious things in creation, one of the wonders of world flora. This family produces both the biggest and smallest plants on earth. On one hand, a million near-invisible seedlings have been counted in the space of a fifth of a square inch, on the other, fucus plants have been gathered that were a third of a mile long!

We'd been gone from the *Nautilus* for about an hour and a half. It was close to noon. I deduced this from the verticality of the sun's rays, which weren't refracted anymore. The magic of those solar colors gradually vanished, with emerald and sapphire shades fading from our surroundings altogether. We walked with steady steps that rang on the seafloor with amazing intensity. The tiniest sounds were transmitted with a speed the ear isn't used to on land. Actually water is a better conductor of sound than air, and noises carry four times as fast under the waves.

Just then the seafloor started to slope sharply downward. The light took on a uniform hue. We reached a depth of 300 feet, by which point we were undergoing a pressure of ten atmospheres. But my diving suit was built in such a way that I never suffered from this pressure. I felt only a sort of tightness in the joints of my fingers, and even this discomfort soon vanished. As for the exhaustion that should have resulted from a two-hour stroll in such unfamiliar trappings, it didn't happen. Helped by the water, I could move with startling ease.

Arriving at this 300-foot depth, I still detected the sun's rays, but just barely. Their intense brightness had given way to a reddish twilight, a midpoint between day and night. But we could see well enough to keep on going, and it still wasn't necessary to activate the Ruhmkorff device.

Just then Captain Nemo stopped. He waited till I caught up with him, then he pointed to some dark masses outlined in the shadows a short distance away.

It's the forest of Crespo Island, I thought. And I wasn't mistaken.

17

AN UNDERWATER FOREST

WE'D FINALLY ARRIVED on the outskirts of this forest, surely one of the finest in Captain Nemo's immense domain. He regarded it as his own and had laid the same claim to it that, in the first days of the world, the first men had laid to their forests on land. Besides, who else could dispute his ownership of this underwater property? What other, bolder pioneer would come, ax in hand, to clear away its dark thickets?

This forest consisted of big treelike plants, and when we went under their huge arches, my eyes were instantly struck by the odd arrangement of their branches—an arrangement I'd never witnessed before.

None of the weeds that carpeted the seafloor, none of the branches garnishing the shrubbery, crawled, leaned, or stretched on a horizontal plane. They all rose right up toward the surface of the ocean. Every filament or ribbon, no matter how thin, stood ramrod straight. Fucus plants and creepers were growing in stiff vertical lines, controlled by the density of the element that generated them. After I parted them with my hands, those otherwise motionless plants would shoot straight back to their original positions. It was the land of the upright.

I soon got used to this peculiar arrangement, likewise to the comparative darkness surrounding us. Sharp chunks of rock were scattered across the seafloor in this forest and they were hard to avoid. Here the range of underwater flora seemed pretty comprehensive to me, as well as more plentiful than it might have been in arctic or tropical zones where there's less variety. But for a few minutes I kept accidentally confusing the two kingdoms, mistaking zoophytes for water plants, animals for vegetables. And who hasn't made the same blunder? Flora and fauna are so closely associated in this underwater world!

I noticed that all these commodities from the vegetable kingdom were attached to the seafloor by only the most makeshift methods. They hadn't any roots and didn't care which solid objects secured them, sand, shells, pods, or pebbles; they didn't ask their hosts for a livelihood, just a point of purchase. These plants are self-propagating and owe their existence to the water that supports and feeds them. In place of leaves most of them sprouted whimsically shaped blades that were confined to a narrow gamut of colors consisting only of pink, crimson, green, olive, tan, and brown. There I saw again, but not yet pressed and dried like the *Nautilus*'s specimens, some peacock's tails spread open like fans to stir up a cooling breeze, scarlet ceramiums, sea tangle stretching out their edible young shoots, twisting strings of bull kelp that bloomed to a height of fifty feet, bouquets of mermaid's cups whose stems grew wider at the top, and a number of other open-sea plants, all without flowers. "It's an odd anomaly in this peculiar element!" as one humorous naturalist puts it. "The animal kingdom blossoms, and the vegetable kingdom doesn't!"

These various types of shrubbery were as big as trees in the temperate zones, and in their moist shade were clustered actual bushes of moving flowers, hedges of zoophytes featuring growths of cauliflower coral that were streaked with twisting furrows, yellowish cup coral with transparent tentacles, plus stony coral from the order *Zoantharia* with grassy tufts; and to top off the illusion, fish flies flew from branch to branch like a swarm of hummingbirds, while yellow cardinalfish with bristling jaws and sharp scales, flying gurnards, and pinecone fish rose underfoot like a covey of snipe.

Around one o'clock Captain Nemo gave the signal to halt. Speaking for myself, I was glad to oblige, and we stretched out under a bower of winged kelp, whose long slender shoots stood up like arrows.

This short break was a delight. The only thing missing was the charm of conversation. But it was impossible to speak, impossible to reply. I simply nudged my big brass headpiece against Conseil's. I saw a happy gleam in the gallant lad's eyes, and to convey his pleasure, he jiggled around inside his carapace in the world's silliest way.

After four hours of strolling, I was quite amazed not to feel any intense hunger. I have no idea why my belly stayed in such a good mood. But in exchange I experienced that irresistible desire for sleep that overcomes every diver. Accordingly my eyes soon closed behind their heavy glass windows and I fell into an uncontrollable doze, which, till then, I'd been able to fight off only through the movements of our walking. Captain Nemo and his muscular companion were already stretched out in the crystal-clear water, setting us a fine naptime example.

I can't estimate how long I was deep in slumber; but when I awoke, the sun seemed to be gravitating toward the horizon. Captain Nemo was already up, and I'd started to stretch my limbs, when an unexpected sight yanked me suddenly to my feet.

A few steps away a monstrous sea spider, three feet high, was watching me with beady eyes, ready to spring at me. Though my diving suit was heavy enough to protect me from the creature's bites, I couldn't help flinching in horror. Just then Conseil woke up along with the *Nautilus*'s sailor. Captain Nemo alerted his companion to this hideous crustacean, which a swing of the rifle butt instantly mowed down, and I watched the monster's horrible legs writhing in dreadful convulsions.

This confrontation reminded me that other, more alarming creatures had to be lurking in these dark reaches, and my diving suit might not be adequate protection against their attacks. Thoughts such as these hadn't previously crossed my mind, and I was now determined to keep on my guard. Meanwhile I'd figured this rest period would be the turning point in our stroll, but I was wrong; instead of heading back to the *Nautilus*, Captain Nemo continued his daring excursion.

The seafloor kept sinking, and its significantly steeper slope took us to greater depths. It must have been nearly three o'clock when we reached a narrow valley scooped out between high vertical walls and located 500 feet down. Thus, thanks to the perfection of our equipment, we'd gone 300 feet below the limit that nature had previously set on man's underwater excursions.

I say 500 feet, even though I didn't have any instruments for determining this distance. But I knew that even in the clearest seas the sun's rays couldn't reach any deeper. Now then, at exactly this point it got completely dark. Not a single object was visible more than ten steps ahead. So I'd started groping my way when I suddenly saw the glow of a bright white light. Captain Nemo had just activated his electrical device. His companion did likewise. Conseil and I followed suit. By turning a switch I established contact between the induction coil and the glass spiral, and the light from our four lanterns illuminated the sea for a radius of eighty feet.

Captain Nemo kept plummeting into the dark depths of the forest, whose shrubbery grew sparser and sparser. I noticed that vegetable life was vanishing faster than animal life. The open-sea plants had already given up on the increasingly arid seafloor, where a prodigious number of animals were still swarming—zoophytes, articulata, mollusks, and fish.

As we walked along I figured the lights from our Ruhmkorff devices were bound to attract some of the denizens of these dark strata. But if they did come near us, at least they kept at a distance regrettable from the hunter's standpoint. Several times I saw Captain Nemo stop and take aim with his rifle; then, after sighting down its barrel for a few seconds, he would straighten up and resume his walk.

By around four o'clock this marvelous excursion had finally run its course. Imposing in its sheer mass, a wall of magnificent rocks stood in front of us, a pile of gigantic boulders, an enormous granite cliffside pitted with dark caves but not offering a single gradient we could climb up. This was the underpinning of Crespo Island. This was land.

The captain stopped suddenly. A signal from him brought us to a halt, and however much I wanted to go up that wall, I had to stop. Captain Nemo's domain ended here. He had no desire to go outside it. Farther on was a part of the globe where he would no longer set foot.

Our return trip began. Captain Nemo resumed the lead in our little band, always heading forward without hesitation. I noted that we didn't follow the same path in going back to the *Nautilus*. This new route, very steep and therefore very arduous, quickly took us up toward the surface of the sea. But this return to the upper strata wasn't so sudden that decompression took place too quickly, which could have led to serious organic disorders and given us those internal injuries so fatal to divers. With great promptness the light reappeared and grew stronger; and the refraction of the sun, already low on the horizon, again ringed the edges of various objects with the whole color spectrum.

At a depth of thirty feet, we walked through a swarm of small fish from every species, more plentiful than birds in the air,

more agile too; but no aquatic game worthy of a gunshot had come in sight as yet.

Just then I saw the captain's weapon spring to his shoulder and track a moving object through the bushes. A shot went off, I heard a faint hissing sound, and an animal dropped a few steps away, literally struck by lightning.

It was a magnificent sea otter from the genus *Enhydra*, the only exclusively marine quadruped. Almost five feet long, this otter had to be worth a good high price. Its coat was chestnut brown above, silver underneath, and would have made one of those marvelous fur pieces so sought after in the Russian and Chinese marketplaces; the fineness and luster of its pelt guaranteed that it would go for at least $400. I was full of wonderment at this unusual mammal, with its circular head adorned with short ears, its round eyes, its white whiskers like those on a cat, its webbed and clawed feet, its bushy tail. Hunted and trapped by fishermen, this valuable carnivore has gotten extremely scarce and it takes refuge chiefly in the northernmost parts of the Pacific, where in all likelihood its species will soon be facing extinction.

Captain Nemo's companion picked the animal up, loaded it on his shoulder, and we took to the trail again.

For an hour plains of sand unrolled under our steps. Often the seafloor rose to within six feet of the surface of the water. Then I saw our images clearly reflected on the underside of the waves, but upside down, and an identical band appeared above us that duplicated all our movements and gestures—a perfect likeness, in short, of the quartet over which it walked, but with heads down and feet in the air.

Another noteworthy effect. Heavy clouds went by above us, forming and fading swiftly; but after thinking it over, I realized those so-called clouds were simply caused by the changing densities of the long ground swells, and I even spotted the foaming "white caps" their breaking crests were spreading over the surface of the water. What's more, I actually saw the shadows of large birds going by overhead and swiftly skimming the surface of the ocean.

On this occasion I witnessed one of the finest gunshots to ever thrill a hunter to the marrow. A large bird with a wide wingspan, quite clearly visible, drew near and hovered over us. When it was just a few yards above the waves, Captain Nemo's companion took aim and fired. The creature dropped, electrocuted, and its descent brought it within reach of our skillful hunter, who then grabbed hold of it. It was an albatross of the finest species, a wonderful specimen of these open-sea fowl.

This incident didn't interrupt our walk. For two hours we sometimes went over plains of sand, sometimes over prairies of seaweed that were quite arduous to cross. In all honesty I was dead tired by the time I spotted, half a mile away, a faint glow cutting through the darkness of the waters. It was the *Nautilus*'s beacon. In twenty minutes we would be back on board, and there I would literally be able to breathe easier, because my tank's current air supply seemed very low in oxygen. But I hadn't reckoned on a run-in that slightly delayed our arrival.

I was lagging about twenty steps behind when I saw Captain Nemo suddenly come back toward me. With his powerful hands he pushed me to the ground, while his companion did the same to Conseil. At first I didn't know what to make of this sudden attack, but I was reassured to see the captain lying down and staying motionless next to me.

I was stretched out on the seafloor right under some bushes of algae, when I raised my head and spotted two enormous masses hurtling by, throwing off phosphorescent glimmers.

My blood turned to ice in my veins! I saw that two fearsome sharks were threatening us. They were blue sharks, dreadful man-eaters with enormous tails, dull glassy eyes, and phosphorescent matter oozing from holes around their snouts. Monstrous fireflies that could grind up an entire man in their iron jaws! I don't know if Conseil was busy with their classification, but as for me, I looked at their silver bellies and their fearsome, teeth-studded mouths from a viewpoint not exactly scientific—more as a food item than as a naturalist.

Luckily these voracious creatures have poor eyesight. They went by without noticing us, brushing us with their brownish fins; miraculously, we escaped a danger greater than meeting up with a tiger deep in the jungle.

Guided by its electric trail, we reached the *Nautilus* half an hour later. The outside door had been left open, and Captain Nemo closed it after we went back into the first cell. Then he pressed a button. I heard pumps operating inside the ship, I felt the water lowering around me, and in a few seconds the cell was completely empty. The inside door opened and we went into the wardrobe.

There our diving suits were removed, not without some difficulty, and I retired to my stateroom, thoroughly worn out, weak from lack of food and rest, and full of wonder at this startling excursion in the ocean depths.

18

4,000 Leagues Under the Pacific

BY THE NEXT MORNING, November 18, I'd fully recovered from my exhaustion of the day before and I climbed onto the platform just as the *Nautilus*'s chief officer was uttering his daily sentence. Then it occurred to me that these words referred to the state of the sea, or more specifically that they meant "there's nothing in sight."

And the ocean was truly empty. Not a sail on the horizon. The upper reaches of Crespo Island had vanished during the night. Swallowing up every color of the prism except its blue rays, the sea reflected the latter in all directions and sported a wondrous indigo tint. Time and again the undulating waves looked like watered silk with wide stripes.

I was marveling at this magnificent ocean view when Captain Nemo appeared. He didn't seem to notice my presence and started taking a series of celestial sights. When he'd finished his operations, he went and leaned his elbows on the beacon housing, his eyes straying over the surface of the ocean.

Meanwhile some twenty of the *Nauti-*

lus's sailors—all husky, energetic fellows—climbed onto the platform. They'd come to pull up the nets left in our wake during the night. These seamen obviously were of different nationalities, though they all had European characteristics. If I'm not mistaken, I recognized some Irishmen, some Frenchmen, a few Slavs, and a native of either Greece or Crete. Even so, these men were frugal of speech and among themselves used only that peculiar dialect whose origin I couldn't even guess. Accordingly I had to give up any notions of questioning them.

They hauled the nets on board. These were a type of trawl similar to the ones used off the Normandy coast, huge pouches held half open by a floating pole and a chain pulled through their lower meshes. Trailing in this way from these iron glove makers, the resulting receptacles scoured the ocean floor and collected every marine item in their path. That day they gathered up some unusual specimens from these fish-filled waterways: goosefish whose comical movements qualify them for the designation "clowns," black anglers equipped with antennas, red-lined triggerfish encircled by little crimson stripes, balloonfish whose venom is extremely insidious, a couple of olive-colored lampreys, pipefish covered with silver scales, cutlass fish with the electrocuting power of an electric eel or electric ray, scaly featherbacks with crosswise brown stripes, greenish codfish, several varieties of goby, etc.; finally a few fish of larger proportions, including a three-foot bar jack with a prominent head, several handsome bonito from the genus *Scomber* decked out in the colors blue and silver, and three magnificent tuna whose high speeds couldn't save them from our trawl.

I estimate that this cast of the net brought in more than a thousand pounds of fish. It was a fine catch but hardly surprising. In essence those nets stayed in our wake for several hours, incarcerating a whole aquatic world in prisons made of thread. So we were never short of high-quality provisions, which the *Nautilus*'s speed and the allure of its electric light could continually replenish.

These various items from the sea were immediately lowered down the hatch in the direction of the storage lockers, some to be eaten fresh, others to be preserved.

When its fishing was done and its air supply replenished, I figured the *Nautilus* would resume its underwater excursion and I was all set to head back to my stateroom, when Captain Nemo turned to me and said without any further preamble:

"Look at this ocean, professor! Doesn't it literally have a life of its own? Doesn't it feel both anger and affection? Last evening it went to sleep just as we did, and now it's waking up after a peaceful night!"

No hellos or good mornings for this character! You would have sworn this strange individual was simply continuing a conversation we'd already started!

"See!" he went on. "It's awakening under the sun's caresses! It's ready to relive its daily existence! What a fascinating field of study lies in watching the play of its organism. It has a pulse and arteries, it has spasms, and I side with the scholarly Commander Maury, who found that it has a circulation as real as the blood circulation in animals."

I'm sure Captain Nemo didn't expect any responses from me, and it seemed pointless to keep popping in with "Of course," "Certainly," or "Right you are." In actuality he was talking to himself and taking long pauses between sentences. He was thinking out loud.

"Yes," he said, "the ocean has an authentic circulation, and to trigger it, the Creator of All Things had only to increase its heat, salt, and microscopic animal life. In essence heat creates the different densities that cause currents and countercurrents. Evaporation, which is nonexistent in the High Arctic regions and very active in equatorial zones, produces a continual exchange of tropical waters with polar waters. What's more, I've detected those rising and falling currents that make the ocean actually seem to be breathing. I've seen a molecule of salt water heat up at the surface, sink back into the depths, reach maximum density at 28° Fahrenheit, then cool off, grow lighter, and rise again. At the poles you'll note the consequences of this phenomenon, and thanks to this law of far-seeing nature, you'll understand why water can freeze only at the surface!"

As the captain finished his sentence, I said to myself, "The pole! Is this daredevil claiming he'll take us even to that location?"

Meanwhile the captain fell silent and looked at that liquid element he'd studied so thoroughly and unceasingly. Then, going on:

"Salts," he said, "fill the sea in considerable quantities, professor, and if you removed every dissolved grain, you could create a mass totaling some 28,000,000 cubic miles, which, if it were spread out over the globe, would form a layer nearly thirty-five feet thick. And don't assume that the presence of these salts is simply due to some whim of nature. Hardly. Salts make seawater less vulnerable to evaporation and keep the wind from carrying off excessive amounts of steam, which, on condensing, would flood the temperate zones. Salts play a leading role, the role of stabilizing force in the overall management of our planet!"

Captain Nemo stopped, straightened up, took a few steps down the platform, then came back to me:

"As for those billions of tiny animals," he went on, "those infusoria that live by the millions in one droplet of water, twenty billion of which weigh barely an ounce, their role is equally important. They consume the salt in the sea, they assimilate the solid elements in the water, and since they produce coral and madrepores, they're the actual creators of limestone continents! And then, once they've deprived our water drop of its mineral nutrients, the droplet gets lighter, rises to the surface, there consumes more salt left behind through evaporation, gets heavier, sinks again, and brings those tiny animals new elements to consume. Ergo these two currents, rising and falling, continually moving, continually alive! More intense than on land, more plentiful, more infinite, this energy flourishes in every part of this ocean, a fatal element for man, it's said, but a vital element for myriads of creatures—and for me!"

When Captain Nemo spoke in this way, he was transformed and he aroused extraordinary feelings in me.

"Out there is true existence!" he added. "And I can envision the founding of nautical towns, clusters of underwater homes, which, like the *Nautilus*, would come back to the surface of the sea to breathe each morning, free towns if ever there were, independent cities! Then again, who knows if some tyrant . . ."

Captain Nemo finished his sentence with a vehement gesture. Then, instantly speaking to me as if to drive away an ugly thought:

"Professor Aronnax," he asked me, "do you know how deep the ocean is?"

"I only know, captain, what the major soundings have told us."

"Could you quote them, so I can double-check them if need be?"

"Here are a few that stick in my memory," I replied. "If I'm not mistaken, an average depth of 27,000 feet was found in the north Atlantic, and 8,200 feet in the Mediterranean. The most remarkable soundings were taken in the south Atlantic near the 35th parallel and they gave 39,000 feet, 46,230 feet, and 49,701 feet. All in all it's estimated that if the whole sea bottom were made level, its average depth would be about 4½ miles."

"Well, professor," Captain Nemo replied, "I'm in hopes of showing you something better than that. As for the average depth of this part of the Pacific, I'll have you know that it's only 13,000 feet."

With that Captain Nemo headed to the hatch and vanished down the ladder. I followed him and went back to the main lounge. The propeller instantly started turning, and the log showed our speed as twenty miles per hour.

Over the ensuing days and weeks, Captain Nemo was very frugal with his visits. I saw him only at rare intervals. His chief officer regularly fixed the positions I found reported on the chart, and in such a way that I could exactly plot the *Nautilus*'s course.

Conseil and Land spent many long hours with me. Conseil had told his friend about the wonders of our undersea stroll, and the Canadian was sorry he hadn't gone along. But I hoped we would have a chance to visit the forests of Oceania.

Almost every day the panels in the lounge stayed open for a few hours, and our eyes never tired of probing the mysteries of the underwater world.

The *Nautilus*'s overall heading was southeast and it kept at a depth between 300 and 500 feet. But one day, from Lord knows what whim, it did a diagonal dive with the help of its slanting fins, reaching strata located 6,500 feet underwater. The thermometer gave a temperature of 40° Fahrenheit, which at this depth seemed to be a temperature common to all latitudes.

On November 26 at three o'clock in the morning, the *Nautilus* crossed the Tropic of Cancer at longitude 172°. On the 27th it passed in sight of the Hawaiian Islands, where the famous Captain Cook met his death on February 14, 1779. By then we'd fared 4,860 leagues from our starting point. When I arrived on the platform that morning, I saw the island of Hawaii two miles to leeward, the biggest of the seven islands that form this group. I could clearly make out the tilled soil on its fringes, the various mountain chains running parallel with its coastline, and its volcanoes with Mauna Kea towering over them, 16,000 feet above sea level. Among other specimens from these waterways, our nets brought up some fan coral from the species *Flabellaria pavonia*, polyps flattened into graceful shapes and characteristic of this part of the ocean.

The *Nautilus* kept to its southeasterly heading. On December 1 it cut the equator at longitude 142°, and on the 4th of the same month, after a swift and uneventful crossing, we raised the Marquesas Islands. Three miles off in latitude 8° 57′ south and longitude 139° 32′ west, I spotted Martin Point on Nuku Hiva, chief member of this island group that belongs to France. I saw only its wooded mountains outlined on the horizon, because Captain Nemo hated hugging shore. Here our nets brought up some fine fish specimens—dolphinfish with azure fins, gold tails, and meat that's unmatched in the whole world, wrasse that have almost no scales but are exquisitely tasty, coachwhip cardinalfish

with bony jaws, yellowish frigate mackeral as good as bonito, all fish worth classifying in the ship's pantry.

After leaving these delightful islands to the protection of the French flag, the *Nautilus* covered about 2,000 miles from December 4 to the 11th. Its navigating was marked by an encounter with an immense school of squid, unusual mollusks that are close relatives of the cuttlefish. French fishermen nickname them "cuckoldfish," and they belong to the class Cephalopoda, family Dibranchiata, consisting of themselves along with cuttlefish and argonauts. The naturalists of antiquity made a special study of them, and these creatures furnished many earthy figures of speech for soapbox orators in the Greek marketplace, as well as excellent dishes for the tables of wealthy citizens, if we're to believe Athenaeus, a Greek physician predating Galen.

It was during the night of December 9–10 that the *Nautilus* met up with this army of largely nocturnal mollusks. They numbered in the millions. They were migrating from the temperate zones toward zones still warmer, following the itineraries of herring and sardines. We looked at them through our heavy glass windows—they swam backward with tremendous speed, moving with the help of their propulsion tubes, chasing fish and mollusks, eating the little ones, eaten by the big ones, and tossing around in indescribable confusion the ten feet nature has rooted in their heads like a hairpiece of pneumatic snakes. Despite its speed the *Nautilus* navigated for several hours in the midst of this school of creatures, and its nets brought up an incalculable number, among which I identified all nine species that Professor d'Orbigny has classified as living in the Pacific Ocean.

During this crossing the sea continually lavished the most marvelous sights on us. Its variety was infinite. It changed its setting and decor for the mere pleasure of our eyes, and we were called upon not simply to contemplate the works of our Creator in the midst of the liquid element, but also to probe the ocean's most alarming mysteries.

During the day of December 11, I was busy reading in the main lounge. Ned Land

and Conseil were studying the luminous waters through the gaping panels. The *Nautilus* wasn't moving. Its ballast tanks full, it was sitting at a depth of 3,300 feet in a comparatively unpopulated region of the ocean where only bigger fish put in occasional appearances.

Just then I had my nose in a delightful book by Jean Macé, *The Servants of the Stomach*, and was savoring its clever contents, when Conseil interrupted my reading.

"Would master kindly come here a second?" he said to me in an odd voice.

"What is it, Conseil?"

"It's something master should see."

I got up, went, leaned on my elbows in front of the window, and saw it.

In the broad electric daylight, a huge, motionless black shape was hanging in the midst of the waters. I studied it carefully, trying to figure out the nature of this gigantic cetacean. Then a thought suddenly crossed my mind.

"A ship!" I exclaimed.

"Yes," the Canadian replied, "a disabled craft that's sinking straight down!"

Ned Land wasn't mistaken. We were in the presence of a ship whose severed shrouds still dangled from their clasps. Its hull seemed in good condition, so it must have gone under just a few hours before. Chopped off a couple feet above the deck, three wooden stumps indicated a flooding ship that had been forced to sacrifice its masts. But it had heeled sideways, filled completely, and was listing to port even yet. It was a sad sight, this carcass lost under the waves, but sadder still was the view on its deck, where, lashed with ropes to keep from washing overboard, a few corpses still lay! I counted four of them—four men, one still standing at the helm—then a woman, halfway out of the skylight on the afterdeck and holding a child in her arms. This woman was young. Under the brilliant lighting of the *Nautilus*'s rays, I could make out her features, which the water hadn't yet decomposed. With her last ounce of strength, she'd lifted her child above her head, and the poor little creature still had its arms entwined around its mother's neck! The postures of the four seamen seemed ghastly

to me, contorted from convulsive movements as if making one last effort to break loose from the ropes tying them to their ship. And then the helmsman—alone, calmer, his face smooth and solemn, his grizzled hair plastered to his forehead, his hands gripping the wheel, he seemed even yet to be steering his wrecked three-master through the ocean depths!

What a picture! We stood speechless, hearts pounding, in front of that shipwreck caught in the act, photographed in its final moments as it were! And already I could see enormous sharks moving in with fiery eyes, drawn by the lure of human flesh!

Turning in the meantime, the *Nautilus* circled the sinking ship, and for a second I could read its stern board:

The Florida
Sunderland, England

19
VANIKORO

THIS DREADFUL SIGHT ushered in a whole series of maritime catastrophes that the *Nautilus* would encounter on its run. After it entered more heavily traveled seas, we often saw wrecked hulls rotting in midwater, and at greater depths, cannons, shells, anchors, chains, and a thousand other iron objects being eaten up by rust.

Meanwhile, continually carried along by this *Nautilus* where we lived in near isolation, we raised the Tuamotu Islands on December 11, that old "dangerous group" associated with the French global navigator Commander Bougainville; it reaches from Ducie Island to Lazareff Island over a distance of 1,200 miles from the east-southeast to the west-northwest, between latitude 13° 30′ and 23° 50′ south, and between longitude 125° 30′ and 151° 30′ west. This island group covers a surface area of 2,300 square miles and it's made up of some sixty subgroups, among which we noted the Gambier group, a French protectorate. These are coral islands. Their slow but continual upheaval will someday connect them to each other, thanks to the efforts of the polyps. Later on this new island will be fused to its neighboring island groups, and a fifth continent will stretch from New Zealand and New Caledonia all the way to the Marquesas Islands.

The day I explained this theory to Captain Nemo, he answered me coldly:

"The earth doesn't need new continents, it needs new men!"

Sailors' luck led the *Nautilus* straight to Reao Island, one of the most unusual in this group, which was discovered in 1822 by Captain Bell aboard the *Minerva*. So I could study the madreporic process that has produced the islands in this ocean.

Madrepores, which you must guard against confusing with precious coral, clothe their tissue in a limestone crust, and their variations in structure have led my famous mentor Professor Milne-Edwards to class them in five divisions. The microscopic animals that secrete this polypary live by the billions in the depths of their cells. Their limestone deposits become rocks, reefs, islets, and islands. In some places they form atolls, a circular ring surrounding a lagoon or small inner lake that gaps put in contact with the sea. Elsewhere they take the shape of barrier reefs, like those along the coasts of New Caledonia and several of the Tuamotu Islands. In still other localities, such as Réunion Island and the island of Mauritius, they build fringing reefs, high straight walls next to which the ocean descends to considerable depths.

While cruising about a quarter of a mile from the underpinnings of Reao Island, I marveled at the gigantic piece of work accomplished by these microscopic laborers. These walls were the express achievements of madrepores going by the names fire coral, finger coral, star coral, and cauliflower coral. These polyps grow exclusively in the agitated strata at the surface of the sea, and so it's in the upper reaches that they start these support structures, which gradually sink along with the secreted rubble binding them. At least that's the theory of Mr. Charles Darwin, who explains the formation of atolls in this manner—a theory superior, in my view, to the one that says these madreporic edifices sit on volcanoes or mountain peaks submerged a few feet below sea level.

I could study these strange walls quite closely, since our sounding lines showed that they dropped straight down for more than a thousand feet, and our electric beams made their bright limestone positively sparkle.

In answer to a question Conseil asked me about the growth rate of these colossal barricades, I thoroughly amazed him by saying that scientists put it at an eighth of an inch per biennium.

"Therefore," he said to me, "in order to build these walls, it took . . . ?"

"A hundred and ninety-two thousand years, my gallant Conseil, which significantly stretches out those days of creation in the Bible. Besides, the formation of coal—in other words, the petrifying of forests swallowed up by floods—and the cooling of basaltic rocks both call for a much longer period of time. I might add that those days in the Bible must stand for whole eras and not just the time between two sunrises, because according to the Bible itself, the sun doesn't date from the first day of creation."

When the *Nautilus* came back to the surface of the ocean, I could take in Reao Island over its whole flat, wooded expanse. Obviously its madreporic rocks had been fertilized by tornadoes and thunderstorms. One day, carried off by a hurricane from neighboring shores, some seed fell onto the limestone beds, mixing with those decomposed particles of fish and marine plants that form vegetable humus. Propelled by the waves, a coconut arrived on this new coast. Its germ took root. Its tree grew tall, catching steam off the water. A brook was born. Gradually vegetation spread. Tiny animals—worms, insects—rode ashore on tree trunks the winds had uprooted from other islands. Turtles came to lay their eggs. Birds nested in the young trees. In this way animal life developed, and drawn by the greenery and fertile soil, man appeared. And that's how these islands were formed, the immense achievement of microscopic animals.

Toward evening Reao Island melted into the distance, and the *Nautilus* changed course in a noticeable fashion. After reaching the

Tropic of Capricorn at longitude 135°, it headed west-northwest, going back up the whole intertropical zone. Though the summer sun lavished its rays on us, we never suffered from the heat, because 100 to 130 feet underwater, the temperature stayed in a range between 50° and 55° Fahrenheit.

By December 15 we'd left the alluring Society Islands in the east, likewise gracious Tahiti, queen of the Pacific. That morning I spotted this island's lofty mountain peaks a few miles to leeward. Its waters furnished excellent fish for the ship's tables—mackerel, bonito, albacore, and some varieties of that sea serpent known as the moray eel.

The *Nautilus* had covered 8,100 miles. We logged 9,720 miles as we went among the Tonga Islands, where crews from the *Argo*, *Port-au-Prince*, and *Duke of Portland* had perished, and the island group of Samoa, scene of the slaying of Captain de Langle, friend of that long-lost navigator, the Count de La Pérouse. Then we raised the Fiji Islands, where savages slaughtered sailors from the *Union*, as well as Captain Bureau, commander of the *Sweet Josephine* out of Nantes, France.

Stretching over a distance of 250 miles north to south and 225 miles east to west, this island group lies between latitude 2° and 6° south, and between longitude 174° and 179° west. It consists of a number of islands, islets, and reefs, among which we noted the islands of Viti Levu, Vanua Levu, and Kadavu.

It was the Dutch navigator Tasman who discovered this group in 1643, the same year the Italian physicist Torricelli invented the barometer and King Louis XIV ascended the French throne. I'll let the reader decide which of these deeds was more helpful to humanity. Later came Captain Cook in 1774, Rear Admiral d'Entrecasteaux in 1793, and finally in 1827 Captain Dumont d'Urville, who untangled the whole chaotic geography of this island group. The *Nautilus* drew near Wailea Bay, an unlucky place for England's Captain Dillon, who was the first to shed light on the longstanding mystery surrounding the disappearance of ships under the Count de La Pérouse.

Dredged several times, this bay furnished a huge supply of excellent oysters. As the Roman playwright Seneca recommended, we opened them right at the table and ate way too many. These mollusks belonged to the species known by name as *Ostrea lamellosa*, whose members are quite common off Corsica. This Wailea oyster bed must have been substantial, and if these clusters of shellfish hadn't had so many natural enemies, they surely would have ended up jam-packing the bay, since close to 2,000,000 eggs have been counted in a single individual.

And if Mr. Ned Land didn't repent of his gluttony this time around, it's because oysters are the only dish that never causes indigestion. In fact it takes at least sixteen dozen of these mollusks from the class Acephala to supply the 315 grams that satisfy one man's minimum daily requirement for nitrogen.

On December 25 the *Nautilus* navigated in the midst of the island group of the New Hebrides, which the Portuguese seafarer Queirós discovered in 1606, which Commander Bougainville explored in 1768, and which got its current name from Captain Cook in 1773. This group consists chiefly of nine big islands and forms a 300-mile strip from the north-northwest to the southsoutheast, lying between latitude 2° and 15° south, and between longitude 164° and 168°. At the moment of our noon sights, we passed fairly close to the island of Aurou, which looked like a mass of green woods with a very high mountain peak towering over them.

That day it was yuletide, and it struck me that Ned Land badly missed celebrating "Christmas," that true family holiday where Protestants are such zealots.

I hadn't seen Captain Nemo for over a week when, on the morning of the 27th, he entered the main lounge, as usual acting as if he'd been gone for just five minutes. I was busy working out the *Nautilus*'s course on the world map. The captain came up, put his finger over a spot on the chart, and said just one word:

"Vanikoro."

This name was magic! It was the name of those islets where vessels under the Count de La Pérouse had miscarried. I straightened instantly.

"The *Nautilus* is bringing us to Vanikoro?" I asked.

"Yes, professor," the captain replied.

"And I can visit those famous islands where the *Compass* and the *Astrolabe* came to grief?"

"If you like, professor."

"When will we reach Vanikoro?"

"We already have, professor."

Followed by Captain Nemo, I climbed onto the platform, and from there my eyes eagerly scanned the horizon.

In the northeast emerged two different-sized volcanic islands that were encircled by a coral reef forty miles around. We were facing the island of Vanikoro proper, which Captain Dumont d'Urville had named "Island of the Search"; we lay right in front of the little harbor of Vana, located in latitude 16° 4' south and longitude 164° 32' east. Its shores seemed to be covered with greenery from its beaches to its inland peaks, with Mt. Kapogo towering over them, 2,856 feet high.

After taking a narrow passageway through the outer belt of rocks, the *Nautilus* lay inside the breakers where the sea's depth ranged from 180 to 240 feet. Under the green shade of some mangroves, I spotted a few savages who looked tremendously startled at our coming. As this long blackish object moved forward flush with the water, didn't they see it as some fearsome cetacean that they'd better treat with respect?

Just then Captain Nemo asked me what I knew about the shipwreck of the Count de La Pérouse.

"What everybody knows, captain," I answered him.

"And could you kindly tell me what everybody knows?" he asked me with a touch of sarcasm in his tone.

"Very easily."

I described to him what the last efforts of Captain Dumont d'Urville had brought to light, efforts detailed here in this heavily condensed summary of the whole business.

In 1785 King Louis XVI of France sent the Count de La Pérouse and his subordinate Captain de Langle on a voyage to circum-navigate the globe. They boarded two sloops of war, the *Compass* and the *Astrolabe*, which were never seen again.

In 1791, justly concerned about the fate of those two sloops of war, the French government fitted out two large cargo boats, the *Search* and the *Hope*, which left Brest on September 28 under the command of Rear Admiral Bruni d'Entrecasteaux. Two months later testimony from a certain Commander Bowen, aboard the *Albemarle*, alleged that rubble from shipwrecked vessels had been seen on the coast of New Georgia. But d'Entrecasteaux hadn't heard this news—which wasn't too reliable in any case—and headed toward the Admiralty Islands, which had been named in a report by one Captain Hunter as the site of the Count de La Pérouse's shipwreck.

He searched in vain. The *Hope* and the *Search* traveled right past Vanikoro without stopping there; and in short, this voyage was plagued by misfortune, ultimately costing the lives of Rear Admiral d'Entrecasteaux, two of his subordinate officers, and several seamen from his crew.

It was an old hand at the Pacific, the English adventurer Captain Peter Dillon, who was the first to pick up an actual trail left by castaways from the wrecked vessels. On May 15, 1824, his ship, the *St. Patrick*, went past Tikopia Island, one of the New Hebrides. There a local boatman pulled alongside in a dugout canoe and sold Dillon a silver sword hilt, which bore the imprint of characters engraved with a burin, a type of cutting tool. What's more, this boatman claimed that during a stay in Vanikoro six years earlier, he'd seen two Europeans belonging to ships that had run aground on the island's reefs many years before.

Dillon guessed that the ships in question were those under the Count de La Pérouse, ships whose disappearance had stirred up the whole world. He tried to reach Vanikoro, where the boatman had told him a good deal of rubble from the shipwreck could still be found; but winds and currents kept him from doing so.

Dillon went back to Calcutta. There he was able to interest the Asiatic Society and the East India Company in his discovery. They put a ship named after the *Search* at his disposal, and he left on January 23, 1827, along with a French deputy.

This second *Search* made several Pacific stops, then dropped anchor in front of Vanikoro on July 7, 1827, in the same harbor of Vana where the *Nautilus* was currently floating.

There Dillon collected many relics of the shipwreck, including iron utensils, anchors, eyelets from pulleys, swivel guns, an eighteen-pound shell, the remains of some astronomical instruments, a piece of sternrail, and a bronze bell bearing the inscription "Made by Bazin," the foundry mark at Brest Arsenal around 1785. There could be no further doubt.

Dillon finished his investigations, staying at the site of the casualty till the month of October. Then he left Vanikoro, headed toward New Zealand, anchored off Calcutta on April 7, 1828, and went back to France, where he received a very cordial welcome from King Charles X.

But by that point the renowned French explorer Captain Dumont d'Urville, unaware of Dillon's activities, had already set sail to search elsewhere for the site of the shipwreck. In essence a whaling vessel had reported that some medals and a Cross of St. Louis had been seen in the possession of savages in the Louisiade Islands and New Caledonia.

So Captain Dumont d'Urville had put to sea in command of a ship named after the *Astrolabe*, and within two months of Dillon's departure from Vanikoro, Dumont d'Urville dropped anchor in front of Hobart. There he heard about Dillon's findings and he also learned that a certain James Hobbs, chief officer on the *Union* out of Calcutta, had put to shore on an island located in latitude 8° 18′ south and longitude 156° 30′ east, and had noted the natives of those waterways making use of iron bars and red fabrics.

Pretty perplexed, Dumont d'Urville didn't know if he should give any credence to these reports, which had been carried in some of the less dependable newspapers; nevertheless he decided to start on Dillon's trail.

On February 10, 1828, this second *Astrolabe* pulled up in front of Tikopia Island, took on a guide and interpreter in the person of a deserter who had settled there, plied a course toward Vanikoro, raised it on February 12, sailed along its reefs till the 14th, and only on the 20th dropped anchor inside its barrier in the harbor of Vana.

On the 23rd several officers circled the island and brought back some rubble of little consequence. The natives adopted a system of denial and evasion, refusing to guide the Frenchmen to the site of the casualty. This rather shady behavior aroused the suspicion that the natives had mistreated the castaways, and in fact the natives seemed afraid that Dumont d'Urville had come to avenge the Count de La Pérouse and his unfortunate companions.

But on the 26th, persuaded by presents and seeing that they didn't need to fear any retaliatory measures, the natives led the chief officer, Mr. Jacquinot, to the site of the shipwreck.

At that location, in twenty to twenty-five feet of water between the Paeu and Vana reefs, there lay some anchors, cannons, and ingots of iron and lead all caked with limestone concretions. A launch and whaleboat from the second *Astrolabe* were steered to this locality, and after going to exhausting lengths, their crews managed to dredge up an anchor weighing 1,800 pounds, a cast-iron eight-pounder cannon, a lead ingot, and two brass swivel guns.

Questioning the natives, Captain Dumont d'Urville also learned that after La Pérouse's two ships had miscarried on the island's reefs, the count had built a smaller craft, only to go off and miscarry a second time. Where? Nobody knew.

Then the commander of the second *Astrolabe* had a monument erected under a tuft of red mangrove, in memory of the famous navigator and his companions. It was a simple four-sided pyramid set on a coral base, with no metalwork that could be a temptation to some greedy native.

Afterward Dumont d'Urville tried to set sail; but his crews were run down from the fevers raging on those unsanitary shores, and since he was quite ill himself, he couldn't weigh anchor till March 17.

Meanwhile, afraid that Dumont d'Urville wasn't up to date on Dillon's activities, the French government sent a sloop of war to Vanikoro, the *Daughter of Bayonne*, which was stationed on the American west coast under Commander Le Goarant de Tromelin. Dropping anchor in front of Vanikoro a few months after the second *Astrolabe* had left, the *Daughter of Bayonne* didn't find any additional evidence but verified that the savages hadn't disturbed the memorial honoring the Count de La Pérouse.

This is the gist of the account I gave Captain Nemo.

"So," he said to me, "the castaways built a third ship on Vanikoro Island, and to this day nobody knows where it went and perished?"

"Nobody knows."

Captain Nemo didn't reply but motioned me to follow him to the main lounge. The *Nautilus* sank a few yards under the waves, and the panels opened.

I rushed to the window and saw crusts of coral, including fungus coral, lichen coral, leather coral, and cup coral; under this coral covering, beneath myriads of delightful fish such as wrasse, tilapia, sweepers, snappers, and squirrelfish, I detected some rubble the old dredges hadn't managed to tear loose— iron stirrups, anchors, cannons, shells, tackle from a capstan, a stempost, all objects hailing from the wrecked ships and now carpeted in moving flowers.

And as I looked at this desolate wreckage, Captain Nemo told me in a solemn voice:

"Commander La Pérouse set sail on December 7, 1785, with his ships, the *Compass* and the *Astrolabe*. He dropped anchor first in Botany Bay, visited the Tonga Islands and New Caledonia, headed toward the Santa Cruz Islands, and put into Nomuka, one of the islands in the Ha'apai group. Then his ships arrived at the unknown reefs of Vanikoro. Traveling in the lead, the *Compass* slammed into rocks off the southerly coast. The *Astrolabe* went to its rescue and also ran aground. The first ship went to pieces almost

immediately. The other, stranded to leeward, held up for a few days. The natives gave the castaways a fair enough welcome. The latter took up residence on the island and built a smaller craft with rubble from the two full-size ones. A few seamen stayed willingly in Vanikoro. The others, weak and ailing, set sail with the Count de La Pérouse. They headed for the Solomon Islands and they perished with all hands on the westerly coast of the chief island in that group, between Cape Deception and Cape Satisfaction."

"And how do you know these things?" I exclaimed.

"Here's what I found at the very site of that final shipwreck!"

Captain Nemo showed me a tin box, stamped with the coat of arms of France and all corroded by salt water. He opened it, and I saw a bundle of papers, yellowed but still readable.

They were the actual military orders given Commander La Pérouse by France's Minister of the Navy, with notes along the margin in the handwriting of King Louis XVI!

"Ah, what a splendid way for a seaman to die!" Captain Nemo said. "A coral grave is a tranquil grave, and may Heaven grant that my companions and I lie in no other!"

20

TORRES STRAIT

DURING THE NIGHT of December 27–28, the *Nautilus* left the waterways of Vanikoro with extraordinary speed. Its heading was southwesterly and in three days it had covered the 750 leagues that separate La Pérouse's islands from the southeastern tip of Papua.

On January 1, 1868, bright and early, Conseil joined me on the platform.

"Will master allow me," the gallant lad said, "to wish him a happy new year?"

"Heavens, Conseil, it's just like old times at my office by the nature gardens in Paris! I accept your good wishes and I thank you for them. Only I would like to know what you mean by a 'happy year' under our current circumstances. Is it a year that'll bring our imprisonment to an end, or a year that'll see this strange voyage continue?"

"Ye gods," Conseil replied, "I'm not sure what to tell master. We're certainly seeing some unusual things and for two months we haven't had a moment of boredom. The latest wonder is always the most amazing, and if this progression keeps up, I can't imagine what its climax will be. In my opinion we'll never again have such an opportunity."

"Never, Conseil."

"What's more, Mr. Nemo really lives up to his Latin name, since he couldn't be less in the way if he didn't exist."

"True enough, Conseil."

"Therefore, with all due respect to master, I think a 'happy year' would be a year that lets us see everything . . ."

"Everything, Conseil? No year could be that long. But what does Ned Land think of it all?"

"Ned Land's thoughts are exactly the opposite of mine," Conseil replied. "He has a practical mind and a domineering stomach. He isn't content with looking at fish and eating nothing else day after day. This shortage of wine, bread, and meat isn't suitable for an upstanding Anglo-Saxon, a man used to beefsteak and unfazed by regular doses of brandy or gin!"

"Speaking for myself, Conseil, that doesn't bother me in the least, and I've adjusted very nicely to the diet on board."

"I have too," Conseil replied. "Accordingly I think as much about staying as Mr. Land does about escaping. So if this new year isn't a happy one for me, it will be for him, and vice versa. No matter what happens, one of us will be pleased. In conclusion, then, I wish master to have whatever his heart desires."

"Thank you, Conseil. Only I need to ask you to put off the matter of new year's gifts and for right now make do with just a hearty handshake. That's all I have on me."

"Master has never been more generous," Conseil replied.

And with that the gallant lad went away.

By January 2 we'd fared 11,340 miles, hence 5,250 leagues, from our starting point in the seas of Japan. In front of the *Nautilus*'s

spur stretched the dangerous waterways of the Coral Sea off the northeast coast of Australia. Our boat cruised along a few miles away from that alarming shoal where Captain Cook's ships nearly miscarried on June 10, 1770. The craft that Cook was aboard crashed into some coral rock, and if his vessel didn't go down, it was because a piece of coral broke off from the impact and stayed stuck in the hull, plugging up the puncture.

I dearly wanted to visit this long 900-mile reef, which the continually choppy sea dashed against with the fearsome intensity of thunderclaps. But just then the *Nautilus*'s slanting fins took us to great depths, and I couldn't see anything of those high coral walls. I had to be content with the various specimens of fish hauled up by our nets. Among others I noted some long-finned albacore, a species in the genus *Scomber*, as big as tuna, bluish on the flanks, and streaked with crosswise stripes that vanish when the creature dies. Schools of these fish followed us and supplied our table with exceptionally delicate meat. We also caught a large number of yellow-green sea bream, two inches long and tasting like dorado, plus some kitefish, authentic underwater swallows that on dark nights streak both air and water with their phosphorescent glimmers. Among mollusks and zoophytes, I found in our trawl's meshes various species of octocoral, sea urchins, hammer shells, spur shells, sundial snails, telescope shells, and snails from the genus *Hyala*. The local flora was represented by fine floating algae, including sea tangle and giant kelp steeped in the mucilage their pores perspire, from which I collected a wonderful *Nemastoma geliniaroidea* to classify with the natural curiosities in the museum.

On January 4, two days after crossing the Coral Sea, we raised the coast of Papua. At this juncture Captain Nemo told me he intended to reach the Indian Ocean by way of Torres Strait. That was the extent of his remarks. Ned saw with pleasure that this course would bring us closer again to European seas.

Torres Strait is regarded as dangerous not only for the reefs garnishing it but for the savages dwelling along its coasts. It separates

Australia from the large island of Papua, also known as New Guinea.

Papua is 1,000 miles long by 325 miles wide, with a surface area of 250,000 square miles. It's located between latitude 0° 19′ and 10° 2′ south, and between longitude 128° 23′ and 146° 15′. At noon while the chief officer was taking the sun's altitude, I spotted the tops of the Arfak Mountains, rising in terraces and ending in sharp pinnacles.

Discovered in 1511 by the Portuguese Francisco Serrano, this country was consecutively visited by Don Jorge de Meneses in 1526, by Juan de Grijalva in 1527, by the Spanish general Alvaro de Saavedra in 1528, by Iñigo Ortiz in 1545, by the Dutchman Schouten in 1616, by Nicolas Struyck in 1753, by Tasman, Dampier, Fumel, Carteret, Edwards, Bougainville, Cook, Forrest, and John McCluer, by Rear Admiral d'Entrecasteaux in 1792, by Louis-Isidore Duperrey in 1823, and by Captain Dumont d'Urville in 1827. "It's the stronghold of the blacks who live all over Malaysia," Mr. de Rienzi has said; and little did I suspect that sailors' luck was about to bring me into contact with those alarming Andaman aborigines.

So the *Nautilus* pulled up in front of the entrance to the world's most dangerous strait, a passageway that even the boldest navigators shrank from going into, the strait that Luis Vaez de Torres faced on returning from the South Seas in Melanesia, the strait where sloops of war under Captain Dumont d'Urville ran aground in 1840 and nearly miscarried with all hands. And even the *Nautilus*, rising superior to every danger in the sea, was about to make the acquaintance of those coral reefs.

Torres Strait is around eighty-five miles wide, but it's clogged with an incalculable number of islands, islets, breakers, and rocks that make it nearly impossible to navigate. Consequently Captain Nemo took every desirable precaution in crossing it. Floating flush with the water, the *Nautilus* moved ahead at a moderate pace. Like a cetacean's tail, its propeller slowly churned the waves.

Taking advantage of this circumstance, my two companions and I stationed ourselves on the ever-deserted platform. In front of us stood the pilothouse, and unless I'm badly mistaken, Captain Nemo must have been inside, steering his *Nautilus* himself.

Under my eyes I had the excellent charts of Torres Strait surveyed and drawn up by the hydrographic engineer Vincendon Dumoulin and Sublieutenant (now Admiral) Coupvent-Desbois, who were on Dumont d'Urville's staff during his last voyage to circumnavigate the globe. These, along with Captain King's efforts, are the best charts for untangling the snarl of this narrow passageway, and I consulted them with scrupulous care.

Around the *Nautilus* the sea was boiling furiously. Bearing from southeast to northwest at a speed of 2½ miles per hour, a stream of waves broke over heads of coral emerging here and there.

"That's one rough sea!" Ned Land told me.

"Downright abominable," I replied, "and hardly suited to a craft like the *Nautilus*."

"That damned captain must really be sure of his course," the Canadian went on, "because if these clumps of coral so much as brush us, they'll rip our hull into a thousand pieces!"

It was truly a dangerous situation, but as if by magic the *Nautilus* seemed to glide right down the middle of those rampaging reefs. It didn't follow the exact course of the *Zealous* and the second *Astrolabe*, which had proven so disastrous for Captain Dumont d'Urville. It went more to the north, hugged the Murray Islands, and headed back to the southwest near Cumberland Passage. I thought it was all set to charge wholeheartedly into this opening, but it went up to the northwest through a large number of little-known islands and islets, then steered toward Tound Island and the Bad Channel.

I was already wondering if Captain Nemo, reckless to the point of sheer insanity, wanted his ship to tackle the narrows where Dumont d'Urville's two sloops of war had gone aground, when he changed direction a second time and cut straight to the west, heading toward Gueboroa Island.

By then it was three o'clock in the after-

noon. The current was slacking off and it was almost full tide. The *Nautilus* drew near that island, which I can see to this day with its remarkable fringe of screw pines. We hugged it from less than two miles out.

A sudden jolt toppled me off my feet. The *Nautilus* had just struck a reef and it lay motionless, listing slightly to port.

When I got up, I saw Captain Nemo and his chief officer on the platform. They were examining the ship's circumstances, exchanging a few words in their unintelligible dialect.

Here's what those circumstances entailed. Two miles to starboard lay Gueboroa Island, its coastline curving north to west like an immense arm. To the south and east, heads of coral were already on display, left uncovered by the ebbing waters. We'd run aground at full tide and in one of those seas whose tides are moderate, an inconvenient state of things when it came to floating the *Nautilus* off. However its hull was so solidly joined, the ship hadn't suffered in any way. But even though it couldn't sink or crack open, the vessel was in serious danger of being permanently attached to these reefs, in which case it would be all over for Captain Nemo's submersible.

I was thinking this through when the captain came up, cool and calm, forever in control of himself, looking neither alarmed nor annoyed.

"An accident?" I said to him.

"No, an incident," he answered me.

"But an incident," I remarked, "that may require you to become a resident again of those shores you've been avoiding!"

Captain Nemo gave me an odd look and waved this away. Which told me pretty clearly that nothing would ever force him to set foot on a landmass again. Then he said:

"No, Professor Aronnax, the *Nautilus* isn't on the road to perdition. It will still carry you through the ocean's wonders. Our voyage has just begun, and I wouldn't want to deprive myself so soon of the honor of your company."

"Even so, Captain Nemo," I went on, ignoring his sardonic turn of phrase, "the *Nautilus* has run aground at a time when the sea

is full. Now then, the tides aren't strong in the Pacific, and if you can't unballast the *Nautilus*, which doesn't seem possible to me, I don't see how it will float off."

"You're right, professor, the Pacific tides aren't strong," Captain Nemo replied. "But in Torres Strait there's still a five-foot difference in level between high and low seas. Today is January 4, and in five days the moon will be full. Now then, I'll be quite amazed if our kindhearted satellite doesn't sufficiently raise these masses of water and do me a favor for which I'll be forever grateful."

With that Captain Nemo went back down inside the *Nautilus*, followed by his chief officer. As for our craft, it stayed put, as motionless as if those coral polyps had already walled it in with their indestructible cement.

"Well, sir?" Ned Land said to me, coming up after the captain had left.

"Well, Ned my friend, we'll serenely wait for the tide on the 9th, because it seems the moon will have the kindness of heart to float us free."

"It's as simple as that?"

"It's as simple as that."

"So our captain isn't going to drop his anchors, put his engines on the chains, and do anything to haul us off?"

"Since the tide will be sufficient," Conseil merely replied.

The Canadian looked at Conseil, then he shrugged his shoulders. The seaman in him was talking now.

"Sir," he answered, "you can trust me when I say this hunk of iron will never navigate again, on the seas or under them. It's only fit to be sold by the pound. So I think it's time we gave Captain Nemo the slip."

"Ned my friend," I replied, "unlike you, I haven't given up on our valiant *Nautilus*, and in four days we'll know where we stand on these Pacific tides. Besides, an escape attempt might be timely if we were in sight of the coasts of England or Provence, but in the waterways of Papua it's another story. And we can always try such a thing as a last resort if the *Nautilus* doesn't right itself, which I would regard as a real calamity."

"But couldn't we at least get the lay of the

land?" Ned went on. "Here's an island. On this island there are trees. Under those trees land animals loaded with cutlets and roast beef, which I would be happy to sink my teeth into."

"In this instance our friend Ned is right," Conseil said, "and I'm on his side. Couldn't master persuade his friend Captain Nemo to send the three of us ashore, just so our feet don't lose the knack of walking on the solid parts of our planet?"

"I can ask him," I replied, "but he'll refuse."

"Let master take the risk," Conseil said, "and we'll know where we stand on the captain's good nature."

Much to my surprise Captain Nemo gave me the permission I asked for and he did so with a good deal of grace and alacrity, not even making me promise to come back on board. But escaping across the New Guinea territories would have been highly dangerous, and I wouldn't have advised Ned Land to attempt it. Better to be prisoners aboard the *Nautilus* than to fall into the hands of Papuan natives.

The skiff would be at our disposal the following morning. I hardly needed to ask if Captain Nemo planned on coming along. I likewise figured that no crewmen would be assigned to us, that Ned Land would be in sole charge of piloting the longboat. Besides, the shore lay no more than two miles off, and it would be child's play for the Canadian to guide that nimble skiff through those rows of reefs so disastrous for full-size ships.

The next day, January 5, after its deck paneling had been opened, we yanked the skiff out of its niche and put it to sea from the top of the platform. Two of us were sufficient for that operation. The oars were inside the longboat and all we had to do was take our seats.

By eight o'clock, armed with rifles and axes, we'd pulled clear of the *Nautilus*. The sea was fairly calm. A mild breeze blew from shore. In place by the oars, Conseil and I rowed energetically, and Ned steered us into the narrow lanes between the breakers. The skiff handled easily and moved swiftly along.

Ned Land couldn't hide his glee. He was like a prisoner escaping from prison and never imagining he would have to go back.

"Meat!" he said over and over. "Now we'll eat red meat! Actual game! A real mess call, by thunder! I'm not saying fish aren't a good thing, but we mustn't overdo 'em, and a slice of fresh venison grilled over live coals will be a nice change from our standard fare."

"You glutton," Conseil replied, "you're making my mouth water!"

"It remains to be seen if those forests actually have any game," I said, "and if the kinds of game might not be big enough to turn the tables on the hunter."

"Fine, Professor Aronnax!" replied the Canadian, whose teeth seemed as honed as the edge of an ax. "But if there's no other quadruped on that island, I'll eat tiger—tiger sirloin."

"Our friend Ned is starting to concern me," Conseil responded.

"Whatever it is," Ned Land went on, "any animal having four feet without feathers, or two feet *with* feathers, will be greeted by my very own one-gun salute."

"Oh good," I replied, "the reckless Mr. Land is at it again!"

"Don't worry, Professor Aronnax, just keep on rowing!" the Canadian replied. "I only need twenty-five minutes to serve you one of my own special creations."

By 8:30 the *Nautilus*'s skiff had just run gently aground on a sandy beach, after successfully getting through the ring of coral that encircles Gueboroa Island.

21

A FEW DAYS ASHORE

STEPPING ASHORE was exhilarating for me. Ned Land tested the soil with his foot as if he were laying claim to it. Yet it had been only two months since we'd become, as Captain Nemo put it, "passengers on the *Nautilus*," in other words, the literal prisoners of its commander.

In a few minutes we were a gunshot away from the coast. The soil was almost completely madreporic, but some dry streambeds were sprinkled with granite rubble, proving that this island was of primeval origin. The whole horizon was hidden behind a curtain of wonderful forests. Enormous trees, sometimes as high as 200 feet, were linked to each other by garlands of tropical creepers, genuine natural hammocks rocking in a mild breeze. There were mimosas, banyan trees, ironwoods, teakwoods, hibiscus, screw pines, and palm trees all mingling in wild profusion; meanwhile orchids, leguminous plants, and ferns grew at the foot of their gigantic trunks and in the shade of their green canopies.

But the Canadian passed over all these fine specimens of Papuan flora, preferring the functional to the decorative. He spotted a coconut palm, beat down and broke open some of its fruit, then we drank their milk and ate their meat with a pleasure that was like a protest against our standard fare on the *Nautilus*.

"Excellent!" Ned Land said.

"Exquisite!" Conseil replied.

"And I don't imagine," the Canadian said, "that your Nemo would object to us stashing a cargo of coconuts on board?"

"I wouldn't think so," I replied, "but he won't want to sample them."

"Too bad for him," Conseil said.

"And all the better for us!" Ned Land shot back. "There'll be more left over!"

"A word of caution, Mr. Land," I told the harpooner, who was all set to ravage another coconut palm. "Coconuts are admirable things, but before we stuff the skiff with them, it would be sensible to find out if this island offers other items just as useful. Some fresh vegetables would be well received in the *Nautilus*'s pantry."

"Master is right," Conseil replied, "and I propose we set aside three places in our longboat, one for fruit, another for vegetables, and a third for venison, of which I still haven't glimpsed the tiniest specimen."

"Hang in there, Conseil," the Canadian replied.

"So let's continue our excursion," I went on, "but let's keep our eyes peeled. This island seems uninhabited, but there still could be individuals around who aren't so finicky about what type of game they eat!"

"Heehee!" Ned Land put in with a highly meaningful movement of his jaws.

"Ned! Oh horrors!" Conseil exclaimed.

"Ye gods," the Canadian shot back, "I'm starting to appreciate the charms of cannibalism!"

"Ned, Ned! Don't say that!" Conseil responded. "You a cannibal? Why, I'll no longer be safe with you, I who share your cabin! Does this mean I'll wake up half devoured one fine day?"

"I'm awfully fond of you, Conseil my friend, but not enough to eat you when there's better food around."

"Then I daren't delay," Conseil replied. "The hunt is on! We absolutely must bag some game to pacify this man-eater, or one of these mornings master won't have enough pieces of his manservant left to serve him."

While exchanging this chitchat, we went under the dark canopies of the forest and for two hours we explored it in all directions.

We couldn't have been luckier in our search for edible plants, and some of the most useful produce in the tropical zones furnished us with a valuable foodstuff missing on board.

I mean the breadfruit tree, which is quite plentiful on Gueboroa Island, and there I noted chiefly the seedless variety that Malays call *rima*.

You can tell this tree from other trees by its straight, forty-foot trunk. Its crown is gracefully rounded and made up of big multilobed leaves, which allows a naturalist to easily identify it as the artocarpus that has been so successfully transplanted to the Mascarene Islands east of Madagascar. Huge globular fruit stood out from its mass of foliage, four inches wide and covered with a skin that's wrinkled into hexagonal patterns. It's a handy plant that nature bestows on regions lacking in wheat—without needing to be tended, it bears fruit eight months out of the year.

Ned Land was on familiar terms with this fruit. He'd already eaten it on his many voyages and knew how to cook the edible part of it. Accordingly the mere sight of this plant aroused his appetite, and he couldn't control himself.

"Sir," he told me, "I'll die if I don't sample a few pieces of breadfruit toast!"

"Sample away, Ned my friend, sample all you like. We're here to conduct experiments, let's conduct them."

"It won't take a minute," the Canadian replied.

Using a lens, he lit a fire of deadwood that was soon crackling merrily. Meanwhile Conseil and I selected the finest artocarpus fruit. Some still weren't ripe enough and their heavy skins covered white, slightly fibrous pulps. But a good many others were yellowish and jellylike, just begging to be picked.

This fruit didn't have any pits. Conseil brought a dozen of them to Ned Land, who cut them into thick slices and put them on the live coals, the whole time repeating:

"You'll see, sir, how tasty this bread is!"

"Especially since we've gone without baked goods for so long," Conseil said.

"It's more than just bread," the Canadian added. "It's a dainty pastry. Haven't you ever eaten any, sir?"

"No, Ned."

"All right, get ready for a real treat! If you don't come back for more, I'm not the King of Harpooners!"

After a few minutes the parts of the fruit exposed to the fire were completely baked. The inside had turned into white toast, a sort of soft bread center whose flavor reminded me of artichoke.

This bread was excellent, I must admit, and I ate it with great pleasure.

"Unfortunately," I said, "this toast will get stale, so it seems pointless to make a supply for on board."

"By thunder, sir!" Ned Land exclaimed. "There you go, talking like a naturalist! But meantime I'll be working like a baker—Conseil, harvest some more of this fruit to take with us when we go back."

"And how are you going to fix it?" I asked the Canadian.

"I'll make a fermented batter from its pulp that'll keep indefinitely without spoiling. When I want some, I'll just cook it in the galley on board—it'll have a slightly tart flavor, but you'll find it's excellent."

"So, Mr. Ned, I can see this bread is all we need . . ."

"Not quite, professor," the Canadian replied. "We need some fruit to go with it, or at least some vegetables."

"Then let's start looking for fruit and vegetables."

When our breadfruit harvesting was done, we took to the trail to complete this "dry-land dinner."

We didn't search in vain and toward noontime we had an ample supply of bananas. This delicious produce from the Torrid Zones ripens all year round, and Malays, who give bananas the name *pisang*, eat them without bothering to cook them. Along with these bananas we collected some enormous jackfruit with a very tangy flavor, some tasty mangoes, and some pineapples of unbelievable size. All this foraging took up a good deal of our time, which, even so, we had no reason to regret.

Conseil kept an eye on Ned. The harpooner walked in the lead, and during his stroll through the forest, he picked some excellent fruit with a sure touch, which should have rounded out his provisions.

"So," Conseil asked, "you have everything you need, Ned my friend?"

"Humph!" the Canadian put in.

"What! You're still not happy?"

"All this vegetation doesn't make a meal," Ned replied. "Just side dishes, dessert. But where's the soup course? Where's the roast?"

"Right," I said. "Ned promised us cutlets, which strikes me as pretty doubtful."

"Sir," the Canadian replied, "our hunting not only isn't over, it hasn't even started! Patience! We're bound to end up running into some creature with either feathers or fur, if not here, then somewhere else."

"And if not today, then tomorrow, because we mustn't wander too far off," Conseil added. "So I propose we return to the skiff."

"What! Already!" Ned exclaimed.

"We ought to be back before nightfall," I said.

"But what hour is it, then?" the Canadian asked.

"At least two o'clock," Conseil answered.

"How time flies on solid ground!" exclaimed Mr. Ned Land with a sigh of regret.

"Off we go!" Conseil replied.

We went back through the forest and we finished our harvest by making a clean sweep of some palm cabbages that had to be picked from the crowns of their trees, some small beans that I recognized as the kind Malays call *abrou*, and some high-quality yams.

We were overloaded when we arrived at the skiff. However Ned Land still found these provisions inadequate. But lady luck smiled on him. Just as we were boarding, he spotted several trees twenty-five to thirty feet high and belonging to the palm species. As valuable as the artocarpus, these trees are justly ranked with the most useful produce in Malaysia.

They were sago palms, vegetation that grows without being tended; like mulberry trees, they reproduce through shoots and seeds.

Ned Land knew how to handle these trees. Taking his ax and wielding it with great energy, he soon felled two or three sago palms, whose maturity was revealed by the white powder sprinkled over their palm fronds.

I watched him more as a naturalist than as a man in hunger. He started by peeling from each trunk an inch-thick strip of bark, which covered a network of long, hopelessly tangled fibers that were puttied with a sort of gummy flour. This flour was the starchlike sago, a food item that's a chief feature of meals eaten by the peoples of Melanesia.

For the time being Ned Land was content to chop these trunks into pieces, as if he were making firewood; later he would extract the flour, sift it through cloth to separate it from its fibrous ligaments, let it dry out in the sun, and leave it to harden inside molds.

Loaded down with all our treasures, we finally left the beach at five o'clock in the afternoon, and half an hour later we pulled alongside the *Nautilus*. Nobody appeared on our arrival. That enormous sheet-iron cylinder seemed deserted. Once our provisions were loaded on board, I went below to my stateroom. There I found my supper ready. I ate it, then fell asleep.

The next day, January 6, nothing new on board. Not a single sound inside, not a single sign of life. The skiff was still alongside in the same place we'd left it. We decided to go back to Gueboroa Island. Ned Land hoped he would have better luck in his hunting than on the day before and he wanted to visit a different part of the forest.

By sunrise we were off. Carried along by an inbound current, the longboat reached the island in seconds.

We got out, and thinking it would be better to follow the Canadian's nose, we let Ned Land take the lead, and his long legs threatened to leave us to the rear.

Ned Land went westward up the coast, forded a few streambeds, then reached some open plains bordered by wonderful forests. A few kingfishers lurked along the watercourses, but they didn't let us get near. Their cautious behavior told me these winged creatures knew where they stood on bipeds of our species, and I concluded that if this island wasn't actually inhabited, human beings at least paid it frequent visits.

After crossing a fairly lush prairie, we arrived on the outskirts of a small wood, livened up by the singing and soaring of a large number of birds.

"Just birds and nothing else," Conseil said.

"But you can eat some of 'em," the harpooner replied.

"Wrong, Ned my friend," Conseil countered, "because all I see are ordinary parrots."

"Conseil my friend," Ned replied with complete seriousness, "parrots are like pheasant to folks with nothing else on their plates."

"And I might add," I said, "that when these birds are properly cooked, they're at least worth a stab of the fork."

Under the dense foliage of this wood, in fact, a host of parrots fluttered from branch to branch, needing only a decent upbringing to break into human speech. For the moment they were cackling in chorus with parakeets of every color and with solemn cockatoos that seemed to be pondering some philosophical problem, while bright red lories flew past like pieces of bunting borne on the breeze, in the midst of great-billed parrots raucously on the wing, Papuan lorikeets painted the subtlest shades of azure, and a delightful variety of other winged creatures, none especially edible.

But one bird was missing from this collection, a bird that's characteristic of these shores and never goes past the boundaries of the Aru and Papuan islands. However I had a chance to marvel at it soon enough.

After going through a moderately heavy thicket, we found some plains clogged with bushes. There I saw some magnificent birds soaring aloft, the arrangement of their long feathers requiring them to head into the wind. Their undulating flight, their graceful curves in the air, and their glistening colors caught and delighted the eye. I had no trouble identifying them.

"Birds of paradise!" I exclaimed.

"Order Passeriformes, division Clystomores," Conseil replied.

"Partridge family?" Ned Land asked.

"I doubt it, Mr. Land. Nevertheless I'm counting on your hunting skills to catch me one of these delightful representatives of tropical nature!"

"I'll give it a try, professor, though I'm handier with a harpoon than a rifle."

Malays, who do a booming business in these birds with the Chinese, have various methods for catching them, none of which we could emulate. Sometimes they set snares on top of the tall trees where the bird of paradise likes to perch. At other times they capture it with a sticky glue that paralyzes its movements. They even go so far as to poison the springs where these fowl tend to drink. But in our case all we could do was fire at them on the wing, which left us little chance of nabbing one. And in truth we used up a good part of our ammunition in vain.

Near eleven o'clock in the morning, we made it to the foothills of the mountains forming the center of the island, and we still hadn't bagged a thing. Our hunger spurred us on. The hunters had counted on consuming the proceeds of their hunting and they'd miscalculated. Luckily, and much to his surprise, Conseil pulled off a right-and-left shot and guaranteed us lunch. He brought down a white pigeon and a ringdove, which were deftly plucked, hung from a spit, and roasted over a blazing fire of deadwood. While these interesting creatures were cooking, Ned fixed some bread from the artocarpus. Then we devoured the pigeon and ringdove down to the bones and found them superb. These birds like to gorge themselves on nutmeg, which flavors their meat and makes it delicious eating.

"They taste like chicken stuffed with truffles," Conseil said.

"All right, Ned," I asked the Canadian, "what's next on the program?"

"Game with four paws, Professor Aronnax," Ned Land replied. "All these pigeons are just appetizers, snacks. So I won't be happy till I've bagged a creature with cutlets!"

"Nor I, Ned, till I've caught a bird of paradise."

"Then let's keep on hunting," Conseil replied, "but while heading back toward the sea. We've arrived at the foothills of these mountains, and I think we'll do better if we return to the forest regions."

This was good advice and we took it. After walking for an hour, we reached a whole forest of sago palms. A few harmless snakes fled underfoot. Birds of paradise flew off as we got near, and I was in real despair of catching one when Conseil, who was walking in the lead, stooped suddenly, gave a triumphant shout, and came back to me carrying a magnificent bird of paradise.

"Oh bravo, Conseil!" I exclaimed.

"Master is too kind," Conseil replied.

"Not at all, my boy. That was a brilliant feat, catching one of these live birds with your bare hands!"

"If master will examine it closely, he'll see I deserve no great praise."

"Why not, Conseil?"

"Because this bird is as drunk as a lord."

"Drunk?"

"Yes, master, drunk from the nutmegs it was devouring under that nutmeg tree where I caught it. See, Ned my friend, see the monstrous results of intemperance!"

"Damnation!" the Canadian shot back. "Considering the amount of gin I've had these past two months, you've got nothing to complain about!"

Meanwhile I examined this unusual bird. Conseil wasn't mistaken. Tipsy from that potent juice, our bird of paradise had been reduced to helplessness. It couldn't fly. It could barely walk. But this didn't worry me, and I just let it sleep off its nutmeg.

This bird belonged to the finest of the eight species credited to Papua and its neighboring islands. It was a "great emerald," one of the scarcest birds of paradise. It measured a foot long. Its head was comparatively small, and its eyes, placed near the opening of its beak, were also small. But it offered a wonderful medley of colors: yellow beak, brown feet and claws, hazel wings with purple tips, light yellow head and scruff of the neck, emerald throat, the belly and breast chestnut to brown. Made of horn covered with down, two long strands rose over its tail, which was lengthened by light, slender feathers of wonderful fineness, and these topped off the costume of this marvelous bird that the islanders have poetically named "the sun bird."

I dearly wanted to take this magnificent bird of paradise back to Paris and donate it to the nature gardens, which doesn't have a single live specimen.

"I guess they must be scarce, right?" the Canadian asked, in the tone of a hunter who's inclined to give the game a pretty low rating.

"Very scarce, my gallant comrade, and above all very hard to capture alive. And even when they're dead, there's still a major market for these birds. So the natives have figured out how to make imitations, like people make imitation pearls or diamonds."

"What!" Conseil exclaimed. "They make counterfeit birds of paradise?"

"That's right, Conseil."

"And does master know how the islanders go about it?"

"He does. During the easterly monsoon season, birds of paradise lose those magnificent feathers around their tails that naturalists call 'below-the-wing' feathers. These feathers are gathered up by the fowl forgers and skillfully fitted onto some poor, previously mutilated parakeet. Then they paint over the joins, varnish the bird, and ship the fruits of their unique labors to museums and collectors in Europe."

"Good enough!" Ned Land put in. "If it isn't the right bird, it's still the right feathers, and so long as the merchandise isn't meant to be eaten, I don't see any problem."

But if my desires were fulfilled by catching this bird of paradise, the wants of our Canadian hunter were still unsatisfied. Luckily, around two o'clock Ned Land brought down a magnificent wild pig of the type the natives call *bari-outang*. This animal came in the nick of time for us to bag some real quadruped meat, and it was warmly welcomed. Ned Land proved himself quite gloriously with his gunshot. Hit by an electric bullet, the pig dropped dead on the spot.

The Canadian thoroughly skinned and cleaned it, after removing half a dozen cutlets destined to provide the grilled meat course of our evening meal. Then the hunt was on again and would be marked by the further exploits of Ned and Conseil.

In essence, by beating the bushes the two friends flushed a herd of kangaroos that fled by bounding away on their elastic paws. But these animals didn't flee so quickly that our electric capsules couldn't stop them in their tracks.

"Oh, professor!" shouted Ned Land, whose hunting fever had gone to his brain. "What marvelous game, especially in a stew! What supplies for the *Nautilus!* Two, three, five down! And just think how we'll eat all this meat ourselves, while those numbskulls on board won't get a shred!"

In his uncontrollable glee I think the Canadian might have slaughtered the whole horde, if he hadn't been so busy talking! But he was content with a dozen of these interesting marsupials, which make up the first order of aplacental mammals, as Conseil just had to tell us.

They were smallish animals, a species of wallaby whose members usually dwell in the hollows of trees and are tremendously fast; though they're of middling size, at least they furnish a meat that's highly prized.

We were quite pleased with the results of our hunting. Ned gleefully proposed that we return the next day to this magic island, whose edible quadrupeds he planned to eradicate. But he hadn't reckoned on developments still to come.

By six o'clock in the evening, we were back on the beach. The skiff was aground in its usual place. Looking like a long reef, the *Nautilus* emerged above the waves two miles offshore.

Without any further ado Ned Land got down to the major business of dinner. He came wonderfully to terms with its entire cooking. Grilling over the coals, those cutlets from the *bari-outang* were soon giving off a succulent aroma that perfumed the air . . .

And here I am, following in the Canadian's footsteps—look at me, gushing over freshly grilled pork! Please pardon me as I've already pardoned Mr. Land, and on the same grounds!

In short, dinner was excellent. Two ringdoves rounded out this extraordinary menu. Toasted sago, bread from the artocarpus, mangoes, half a dozen pineapples, and the fermented liquor from certain coconuts all heightened our glee. I suspect that my two fine companions weren't quite as clearheaded as one might wish.

"What if we don't go back to the *Nautilus* tonight?" Conseil said.

"What if we don't ever go back?" Ned Land added.

Just then a stone whizzed toward us, landed at our feet, and cut short the harpooner's proposition.

22

CAPTAIN NEMO'S LIGHTNING BOLTS

WITHOUT GETTING UP, we looked in the direction of the forest, my hand stopping midway to my mouth, Ned Land's completing its assignment.

"Stones don't fall from the sky," Conseil said, "or else they deserve to be called meteorites."

A second well-polished stone knocked a tasty ringdove leg out of Conseil's hand, giving still greater relevance to his comment.

All three of us got up, rifles to our shoulders, ready to answer any attack.

"Apes maybe?" Ned Land exclaimed.

"Nearly," Conseil replied. "Savages."

"Head for the skiff!" I said, moving toward the sea.

It was definitely necessary to beat a retreat, because some twenty natives armed with bows and slings had appeared barely a hundred steps away, on the outskirts of a thicket covering the horizon to our right.

The skiff was beached sixty feet from us.

The savages came nearer, not running but favoring us with a tremendous show of hostility. It was raining stones and arrows.

Ned Land wasn't willing to leave his provisions behind, and despite the impending danger he gripped his pig on one side, his kangaroos on the other, and scampered off with respectable speed.

In two minutes we were on the beach. Loading provisions and weapons into the skiff, pushing it to sea, and readying its two oars were the work of an instant. We hadn't gone a quarter of a mile when a hundred savages, shouting and waving at us, came into the water up to their waists. I looked to see if their appearance would draw some of the *Nautilus*'s men onto the platform. It didn't. Lying well out, the enormous machine still seemed completely deserted.

Twenty minutes later we boarded ship. The hatches were open. After tying up the skiff, we got back inside the *Nautilus*.

I went below to the lounge, from which some chords were wafting. Captain Nemo was there, bending over the organ and deep in a musical trance.

"Captain!" I said to him.

He didn't hear me.

"Captain!" I went on, reaching out and touching him.

He trembled, and turning around:

"Ah, it's you, professor!" he said to me. "Well, did you have a happy hunt? Was your herb gathering a success?"

"Yes, captain," I replied, "but unfortunately we've flushed out a horde of bipeds whose presence has me worried."

"What sort of bipeds?"

"Savages."

"Savages!" Captain Nemo replied in a sardonic tone. "You set foot on one of the shores of this globe, professor, and you're surprised to find savages? Where *aren't* there savages? And besides, are they any worse than men elsewhere, these people you call savages?"

"But captain—"

"Speaking for myself, sir, I've found them everywhere."

"Well then," I replied, "if you don't want to welcome them aboard the *Nautilus*, you'd better take some precautions!"

"Easy, professor, no cause for alarm."

"But there are a large number of these natives."

"What's your count?"

"At least a hundred."

"Professor Aronnax," replied Captain Nemo, whose fingers had taken their places again on the organ keys, "even if every islander in Papua were to gather on that beach, the *Nautilus* would have nothing to fear from their attacks!"

Then the captain's fingers ran over the instrument's keyboard, and I noticed that he touched only its black keys, which gave his melodies a basically Scottish quality. Soon he'd forgotten my presence and was lost in a reverie that I no longer tried to dispel.

I climbed onto the platform. Night had already fallen, because in this low latitude the sun sets quickly, without any twilight. I saw Gueboroa Island only dimly. But many fires had been kindled on the beach, indicating that the natives had no thoughts of leaving it.

For several hours I was on my own, sometimes thinking about the islanders—but no longer fearing them, because the captain's unflappable confidence had won me over—and sometimes forgetting about them to marvel at the splendors of that tropical night. My memories took wing toward France in the wake of those zodiacal stars due to twinkle over it in a few hours. The moon was shining in the midst of the constellations at the zenith. Then I remembered that the day after tomorrow, our loyal, kindhearted satellite would come back to this same place to raise the tide and snatch the *Nautilus* from its bed

of coral. Toward midnight, seeing that everything was quiet over the darkened waves as well as under the waterside trees, I retired to my cabin and fell peacefully asleep.

The night went by without mishap. No doubt the Papuans had been scared off by the mere sight of this monster aground in the bay, because our hatches stayed open, offering easy access to the *Nautilus*'s interior.

At six o'clock in the morning, January 8, I climbed onto the platform. The morning shadows were lifting. The island soon came into view through the dissolving mists, first its beaches, then its mountain peaks.

The islanders were still there, in greater numbers than on the day before, maybe 500 or 600 of them. Taking advantage of the low tide, some of them had moved forward over the heads of coral to less than a quarter of a mile from the *Nautilus*. I could easily make them out. They clearly were true Papuans, men of fine stock, their builds athletic, foreheads high and broad, noses large but not flat, teeth white. Their woolly, red-tinted hair contrasted sharply with their bodies, which were as black and glistening as a Nubian's. Strings of beads made from bone dangled under their sliced, lengthened earlobes. Generally these savages were naked. I noted some women among them, clothed from hip to knee in grass skirts held up by belts made from vegetation. Some of the chieftains adorned their necks with crescents and with necklaces made from beads of red and white glass. Armed with bows, arrows, and shields, nearly all of them carried from their shoulders a sort of net, which held those polished stones their slings hurl with such skill.

One of those chieftains came pretty close to the *Nautilus*, examining it with care. He must have been a *mado* of high rank, because he was decked out in a mat of banana leaves that had notched edges and was highlighted with bright colors.

This islander was standing at such close range, I easily could have picked him off; but I thought it would be better to wait for an actual show of hostility. Between Europeans and savages, it's acceptable for Europeans to shoot back but not to attack first.

During this whole time of low tide, the is-

landers lurked near the *Nautilus*, but they behaved themselves. I frequently heard them repeat the word *assai*, and from their gestures I understood they were inviting me to go ashore, an invitation I firmly declined.

So the skiff didn't leave shipside that day, much to the displeasure of Mr. Land who couldn't top off his provisions. Our handy Canadian used the time to process the meat and flour products he'd brought from Gueboroa Island. As for the savages, they went back ashore near eleven o'clock in the morning, once the heads of coral began to vanish under the waves of the rising tide. But I saw their numbers swell considerably on the beach. Very likely they'd come from neighboring islands or from the mainland of Papua proper. However I didn't see a single local canoe.

Having nothing better to do, I decided to dredge these lovely clear waters, which exhibited a profusion of seashells, zoophytes, and open-sea plants. Besides, it was the last day the *Nautilus* would be spending in these waterways, if it still floated off to the open sea tomorrow as Captain Nemo had promised.

So I summoned Conseil, who brought me a small light dragnet like the ones used in oyster fishing.

"What about these savages?" Conseil asked me. "With all due respect to master, they don't strike me as very wicked!"

"They're cannibals even so, my boy."

"A cannibal can be a decent man," Conseil replied, "just as a glutton can be an upstanding citizen. The one doesn't exclude the other."

"Fine, Conseil. I'm sure there are upstanding cannibals who do a very decent job of devouring their prisoners. However I'm not keen on being devoured, even by paragons of decency, so I'll stay on my guard—since it seems that the *Nautilus*'s commander isn't taking any precautions. And now to work!"

For two hours we fished industriously but didn't turn up any rarities. Our dragnet filled with midas abalone, harp shells, melania snails, and especially the finest hammer shells I'd seen to that day. We also gathered a few sea cucumbers, some pearl oysters, and a dozen small turtles we set aside for the ship's pantry.

But just when I least expected it, I laid my hands on a marvel, or I should say, on a natural deformity that's very rarely encountered. Conseil had just made a cast of the dragnet, and his gear had come back up loaded with a variety of fairly ordinary seashells, when all at once he saw me thrust my arms hurriedly into the net, pull out a shelled animal, and give a conchological yell, in other words, the noisiest yell a human throat can produce.

"Goodness, what happened to master?" Conseil asked, quite startled. "Did master get bitten?"

"No, my boy, but I would be willing to lose a finger for a find like this!"

"What find?"

"This shell," I said, holding up the subject of my triumph.

"But that's nothing more than a porphyry olive shell, genus *Oliva*, order Pectinibranchia, class Gastropoda, branch Mollusca—"

"Yes, yes, Conseil! But instead of coiling from right to left, this olive shell rolls from left to right!"

"It can't be!" Conseil exclaimed.

"Yes, my boy, it's a left-handed shell!"

"A left-handed shell!" Conseil repeated, his heart skipping a beat.

"Look at its spiral!"

"Oh, master can trust me on this," Conseil said, taking the valuable shell in his trembling hands, "but never have I felt such excitement!"

And there was good reason to be excited! In fact, as naturalists have pointed out, "right-handedness" is a well-known law of nature. In their orbiting and spinning motions, stars and their satellites go from right to left. Man uses his right hand more often than his left, and so his various gadgets and contraptions (staircases, locks, watch springs, etc.) are designed to be used in a right-to-left manner. Now then, nature has generally obeyed this law in coiling her shells. They're right-handed with rare exceptions, and if a shell's spiral should chance to be left-handed, collectors will pay its weight in gold for it.

So Conseil and I were intently examining our treasure, and I'd solemnly promised myself to adorn the Paris Museum with it, when an ill-omened stone, hurled by one of the islanders, whizzed over and shattered the valuable object in Conseil's hands.

I gave a yell of despair! Conseil pounced on his rifle and aimed at a savage swinging a sling about thirty feet away from him. I tried to stop him, but his shot went off and shattered a bracelet of amulets hanging from the islander's arm.

"Conseil!" I shouted. "Conseil!"

"Goodness, what's wrong? Didn't master see that this man-eater initiated the attack?"

"A shell isn't worth a human life!" I told him.

"Oh, the rascal!" Conseil exclaimed. "I would rather he'd cracked my shoulder!"

Conseil was in dead earnest, but I didn't subscribe to his views. However our circumstances had changed in just a few seconds and we hadn't noticed. Some twenty dugout canoes were surrounding the *Nautilus*. Hollowed from tree trunks, these canoes were long, narrow, and well designed for speed, keeping their balance with the help of two bamboo poles that floated on the surface of the water. They were manned by skillful, half-naked paddlers, and I viewed their coming with definite alarm.

It was obvious that these Papuans had already been in contact with Europeans and knew their ships. But this long iron cylinder lying in the bay and having no masts or funnels—what were they to make of it? Nothing good, because at first they kept at a respectful distance. But seeing that it didn't move, they gradually gained confidence and tried to get more familiar with it. Now then, this familiarity was exactly what we needed to prevent. Since our guns made no sound when they went off, they would have only a middling effect on these islanders, who are said to respect nothing but weapons that make a racket. Without thunderclaps, lightning bolts would be far less frightening, though the danger lies in the flash, not the noise.

Just then the dugout canoes drew nearer to the *Nautilus*, and a cloud of arrows burst over it.

"Great Lucifer, it's hailing!" Conseil said. "And maybe it's poisoned hail!"

"We need to alert Captain Nemo," I said, going back inside the hatch.

I went below to the lounge. I didn't find anybody there. I ventured a knock on the door opening into the captain's stateroom.

I heard the words "Come in!" I complied and found Captain Nemo busy with calculations in which there was no shortage of x's and other algebraic signs.

"Am I disturbing you?" I said out of politeness.

"You are, Professor Aronnax," the captain answered me. "But I imagine you have pressing reasons for looking me up?"

"Extremely. We're surrounded by natives in dugout canoes, and in a few minutes we're sure to be attacked by several hundred savages."

"Ah!" Captain Nemo put in serenely. "They've come out in their canoes?"

"Yes, sir."

"Well, sir, closing the hatches should do the trick."

"Exactly, and that's what I came to tell you—"

"Nothing could be easier," Captain Nemo said.

And he pressed an electric button, transmitting an order to the crew's quarters.

"There, sir, everything's under control!" he told me after a few seconds. "The skiff is in its place, and the hatches are closed. I don't imagine you're worried these gentlemen will stave in walls that your frigate's shells couldn't breach?"

"No, captain, but there's one danger that still remains."

"What, sir?"

"Tomorrow at around this time, we'll need to open the hatches again to replenish the *Nautilus*'s air."

"Positively, sir, since our craft breathes in the manner favored by cetaceans."

"But if the Papuans are on the platform at that moment, I don't see how you can prevent them from coming inside."

"Then, sir, you assume they'll board us?"

"I'm certain of it."

"Well, sir, let them come. I see no reason

to prevent them. Deep down they're just poor devils, these Papuans, and I don't want my visit to Gueboroa Island to cost the life of a single one of these unfortunate creatures!"

On that note I was about to take my leave, but Captain Nemo detained me and invited me to have a seat by him. He asked me solicitously about our excursions ashore and our hunting, but didn't seem to understand the Canadian's passionate craving for red meat. Then our conversation touched on various topics, and Captain Nemo seemed friendlier than usual, though no more forthcoming.

Among other things we got to talking about the *Nautilus*'s current circumstances, aground in the same strait where Captain Dumont d'Urville had nearly miscarried. Then, pertinent to this:

"He was one of your great seamen," the captain said to me, "one of your shrewdest navigators, that d'Urville. He was France's answer to Captain Cook. Brilliant but unlucky! Braving the ice barriers of the South Pole, the coral of Oceania, the cannibals of the Pacific, only to perish wretchedly in a train wreck! If that dynamic man was able to look back on his life during its last seconds, imagine what his final thoughts must have been!"

As he spoke Captain Nemo seemed quite moved, an emotion I felt was to his credit.

Then, chart in hand, we went back to the French navigator's achievements: his voyages to circumnavigate the globe, his two tries at the South Pole that led to his discovery of the Adélie Coast and the Louis-Philippe Peninsula, and finally his hydrographic surveys of the chief islands in Oceania.

"What your d'Urville did on the surface of the sea," Captain Nemo told me, "I've done inside the ocean, but more easily and completely than he. Tossed about by one hurricane after another, the *Zealous* and the second *Astrolabe* couldn't hold a candle to the *Nautilus*—a quiet workroom genuinely at rest in the midst of the waters!"

"Even so, captain," I said, "there's a major similarity between Dumont d'Urville's sloops of war and the *Nautilus*."

"What, sir?"

"The *Nautilus* has run aground just as they did!"

"Sir, the *Nautilus* isn't aground," Captain Nemo replied icily. "The *Nautilus* was built to rest on the ocean floor, and I don't need to perform the arduous labors and maneuvers d'Urville had to undertake in order to float off his sloops of war. The *Zealous* and the second *Astrolabe* nearly perished, but my *Nautilus* is in no danger. Tomorrow, at the appointed hour on the appointed day, the tide will quietly lift it off and it will resume its navigating through the seas."

"Captain," I said, "I don't doubt—"

"Tomorrow," Captain Nemo added as he got up, "tomorrow at 2:40 in the afternoon, the *Nautilus* will float off and exit Torres Strait undamaged."

Saying these words in a very sharp tone, Captain Nemo gave me a curt bow. This was my dismissal and I went back to my stateroom.

There I found Conseil, who wanted to know the outcome of my interview with the captain.

"My boy," I replied, "when I expressed the belief that these Papuan natives were a threat to his *Nautilus*, the captain gave me a highly sarcastic answer. So I've got just one thing to say to you: have faith in him and enjoy a good night's rest."

"Master has no need for my services?"

"No, my friend. What's Ned Land up to?"

"Begging master's indulgence," Conseil replied, "but our friend Ned is concocting a kangaroo pie that will be the eighth wonder!"

I was on my own; I went to bed but didn't sleep very well. I kept hearing sounds from the savages, who were stamping on the platform and letting out earsplitting yells. The night went by in this way without the crew ever shaking off their usual inertia. They were no more bothered by the presence of those man-eaters than soldiers in an armored fortress are troubled by ants running over the armor plate.

I got up at six o'clock in the morning. The hatches weren't open, so the air inside hadn't been replenished. But the air tanks were kept full for any eventuality and went right to work pumping a few cubic yards of oxygen into the *Nautilus*'s thin atmosphere.

I stayed busy in my stateroom till noon without seeing Captain Nemo for even a second. Nobody on board seemed to be making any preparations for departure.

I waited a while longer, then I made my way to the main lounge. Its timepiece said 2:30. In ten minutes the tide would reach its maximum elevation, and if Captain Nemo hadn't made a rash promise, the *Nautilus* would immediately break free. If not, many months might go by before it could leave its bed of coral.

But soon a few preliminary vibrations could be felt over the boat's hull. I heard its plating grind against the limestone roughness of that coral base.

At 2:35 Captain Nemo appeared in the lounge.

"We're ready to leave," he said.

"Ah!" I put in.

"I've issued orders to open the hatches."

"What about the Papuans?"

"What about them?" Captain Nemo replied with a slight shrug of his shoulders.

"Won't they come inside the *Nautilus?*"

"How will they manage that?"

"By jumping down the hatches you're going to open."

"Professor Aronnax," Captain Nemo replied serenely, "the *Nautilus*'s hatches aren't to be entered in that manner even when they're open."

I looked at the captain.

"You don't understand?" he said to me.

"Not in the least."

"Well, come along and you'll see!"

I headed to the central companionway. There, very puzzled, Ned Land and Conseil watched a couple crewmen opening the hatches, while frightful howls and shouts of anger were erupting outside.

The hatch lids fell back onto the outer plating. Twenty horrible faces appeared. But when the first islander laid hands on the companionway railing, he was flung backward by some invisible force, Lord knows what! He ran off, shrieking in terror and wildly prancing around.

Ten of his companions followed him. All ten met the same fate.

Conseil was in ecstasy. Ned Land, carried away by his violent tendencies, leaped up the companionway. But as soon as his hands grabbed the railing, he was thrown backward in his turn.

"Damnation!" he exclaimed. "I've been hit by a lightning bolt!"

These words explained everything. It wasn't just a railing that led up to the platform, it was a metal cable fully charged with the ship's electricity. Anybody who touched it got a fearsome shock—a shock that would have been fatal if Captain Nemo had thrown the full current from his equipment into this conducting cable! Between him and his attackers, he'd set up a network of electricity that literally nobody could pass through with impunity.

In the meantime, wild with terror, the unhinged Papuans beat a retreat. As for us, in between laughing we massaged and comforted poor Ned Land, who was cussing like a man possessed.

But just then, lifted off by the tide's last undulations, the *Nautilus* rose from its bed of coral exactly at that fortieth minute pinpointed by the captain. Its propeller churned the waves with leisurely majesty. Gathering speed little by little, the ship navigated on the surface of the ocean, and safe and sound, it left the dangerous narrows of Torres Strait.

23

ÆGRI SOMNIA[12]

THE NEXT DAY, January 10, the *Nautilus* resumed its travels in midwater but at a remarkable speed I estimated to be at least thirty-five miles per hour. The propeller was going so fast, I couldn't count or even follow its revolutions.

I thought about how this marvelous electrical force not only gave motion, heat, and light to the *Nautilus* but even protected it against outside attacks, transforming it into a

---

[12] *Translator's note.* Latin: "under sedation."

sacred ark that no profane hands could touch without being blasted; my wonderment was boundless and it went from the submersible itself to the engineer who had created it.

We were traveling due west and on January 11 we doubled Cape Wessel, located in longitude 135° and latitude 10° north, the western tip of the Gulf of Carpentaria. Reefs were still common but more scattered and were fixed on the chart with the greatest accuracy. The *Nautilus* easily dodged the Money breakers to port and the Victoria reefs to starboard, positioned at longitude 130° on the 10th parallel, which we went along faithfully.

Arriving in the Timor Sea on January 13, Captain Nemo raised the island of that name at longitude 122°. This island, whose surface area measures 10,150 square miles, is governed by rajas. These aristocrats boast that they're descended from crocodiles, in other words, blessed with the loftiest origins a human being can claim. Accordingly their scaly ancestors infest the island's rivers and are the subjects of unusual veneration. They're sheltered, nurtured, flattered, pampered, and offered a steady diet of nubile maidens; and woe to the foreigner who lifts a finger against these sacred saurians.

But the *Nautilus* didn't want anything to do with these nasty animals. Timor Island was visible for only a second at noon while the chief officer took our position. I likewise barely caught a glimpse of little Roti Island, part of this same group, whose women have a well-established reputation for beauty in the marketplaces of Malaysia.

From then on the *Nautilus* adjusted its latitude bearings toward the southwest. It pointed its prow toward the Indian Ocean. Where would Captain Nemo's fancies take us? Would he head back up to the shores of Asia? Would he draw nearer to the beaches of Europe? Neither decision was very likely for a man who steered clear of populated areas! So would he go south? Would he double the Cape of Good Hope, then Cape Horn, and push on to the antarctic pole? Would he finally go back to Pacific seas, where his *Nautilus* could navigate freely and easily? Time would tell.

After cruising past the Cartier, Hibernia, Seringapatam, and Scott reefs, the solid element's last efforts against the liquid, we were beyond all sight of shore by January 14. The *Nautilus* slowed down in an odd manner, and very eccentric in its ways, it sometimes swam in the midst of the waters, sometimes drifted on their surface.

During this segment of our voyage, Captain Nemo conducted interesting experiments on the different temperatures in various strata of the sea. Under ordinary circumstances these readings are obtained using some pretty complicated instruments whose findings are dubious to say the least, whether they come from thermometric sounding lines, whose glass often shatters under the water pressure, or from those devices based on the changing resistance of metals to electric currents. Either way the results can't be adequately double-checked. By contrast Captain Nemo could find the sea's temperature by going himself into its depths, and when he put his thermometer in contact with the various layers of liquid, he found the desired degree immediately and with certainty.

So by loading up its ballast tanks or by sinking on an angle with the help of its slanting fins, the *Nautilus* reached the consecutive depths of 10,000, 13,000, 16,000, 23,000, 30,000, and 33,000 feet, and the conclusive result of these experiments was that the sea had a constant temperature of 40° Fahrenheit at depths of over 3,000 feet in all latitudes.

I watched these experiments with the deepest interest. Captain Nemo brought a real passion to them. I often wondered why he conducted these studies. Were they for the benefit of his fellow man? It wasn't likely, because sooner or later his work would perish with him in some unknown sea! Unless he intended the results of his experiments for me. But that meant this strange voyage of mine would come to an end, and no such end was in sight.

Be that as it may, Captain Nemo also introduced me to the different data he'd obtained on the relative densities of the water in our planet's chief seas. From this news I derived some personal enlightenment that had nothing to do with science.

It happened the morning of January 15. The captain and I were strolling on the platform, and he asked me if I knew how the density of salt water differs from sea to sea. I said no, adding that there was a shortage of controlled scientific studies on this subject.

"I've conducted such studies," he told me, "and I can vouch for their accuracy."

"Fine," I replied, "but the *Nautilus* lives in a separate world, and the secrets of its scientists don't make their way ashore."

"You're right, professor," he told me after a few seconds of silence. "This *is* a separate world. It's as alien to the earth as the planets accompanying our globe around the sun, and we'll never know the accomplishments of scientists on Saturn or Jupiter. But since fate has linked our two lives, I can share the results of my studies with you."

"I'm all attention, captain."

"As you know, professor, salt water is denser than fresh water, but this density isn't uniform. In essence, if I represent the density of fresh water by 1.000, then I find 1.028 for the waters of the Atlantic, 1.026 for the waters of the Pacific, 1.030 for the waters of the Mediterranean—"

Aha, I thought, so he ventures into the Mediterranean?

"—1.018 for the waters of the Ionian Sea, and 1.029 for the waters of the Adriatic."

No doubt about it, the *Nautilus* didn't avoid the heavily traveled seas of Europe, and I concluded from this that the ship would take us back—maybe quite soon—to more civilized shores. I expected Ned Land to greet this news with undisguised satisfaction.

For several days we spent our work hours doing all sorts of experiments—on the degree of salinity in waters of different depths, or on their electrical properties, coloration, and transparency—and in every instance Captain Nemo displayed a resourcefulness matched only by his courtesy toward me. Then I didn't see anything more of him for several days and once again lived on board in isolation.

On January 16 the *Nautilus* seemed to have fallen asleep a few yards under the surface of the water. Its electrical equipment had been turned off, and the motionless propeller let it ride with the waves. I figured the crew were busy with interior repairs required by the engine's strenuous mechanical action.

Then my companions and I witnessed an unusual sight. The panels in the lounge were open, and since the *Nautilus*'s beacon was off, a hazy darkness reigned in the midst of the waters. Covered with heavy clouds, the stormy sky gave only the faintest light to the ocean's upper strata.

I was studying the state of the sea under these conditions, and even the biggest fish were no more than ill-defined shadows, when the *Nautilus* was suddenly transferred into broad daylight. At first I thought the beacon had gone back on and was casting its electric light into this mass of liquid. I was wrong and saw my mistake after a quick inspection.

The *Nautilus* had drifted into the midst of some phosphorescent strata, which, in this darkness, came off as downright dazzling. This effect was caused by myriads of luminous microscopic animals whose brightness intensified as they glided over the submersible's metal hull. In the midst of those luminous sheets of water, I then glimpsed flashes of light, like the flickerings inside a blazing furnace that are caused by streams of molten lead or from masses of metal brought to a white heat—but these flashes were so intense that some parts of the light turned into shadows by contrast, in this fiery setting that supposedly should have eliminated all shadows. No, this was no longer the steady radiance of our normal lighting. This light throbbed with unusual energy and activity. You sensed it was alive!

In essence it was a cluster of countless open-sea infusoria, of seedlike noctiluca, actual balls of transparent jelly equipped with a threadlike tentacle—up to 25,000 of them have been counted in two cubic inches of water. And their light was further intensified by those glimmers characteristic of medusas, starfish, moon jellyfish, common piddocks, and other phosphorescent zoophytes, which were soaked with grease from organic matter decomposed by the sea, and maybe with mucus secreted by fish.

For several hours the *Nautilus* drifted in that glittering tide, and our wonderment grew when we saw huge marine creatures playing in it like the fire-loving salamanders of myth. In the midst of this fire that didn't burn, I could see smart, swift porpoises, the tireless pranksters of the seas, and ten-foot sailfish, those shrewd heralds of hurricanes, whose fearsome broadswords sometimes banged against the lounge window. Then smaller fish appeared: assorted triggerfish, talang queenfish, bulbnose unicornfish, and a hundred others that left streaks on the luminous air as they swam.

Some magic lay behind this dazzling sight! Maybe some atmospheric condition had intensified this phenomenon? Maybe a storm was unleashed on the surface of the waves? But only a few yards down, the *Nautilus* didn't feel its fury and the ship rocked peacefully in the midst of the calm waters.

And so it went, some new wonder continually delighting us. Conseil studied and classified his zoophytes, articulata, mollusks, and fish. The days went by quickly, and I no longer kept track of them. Ned, as usual, kept looking for changes of pace from our standard fare. Like regular snails we were at home in our shell, and I can vouch that it's easy to turn into a full-fledged snail.

So this way of living started to seem simple and natural to us, and we no longer envisioned a different lifestyle on the surface of the planet earth, when something happened to remind us of our strange circumstances.

On January 18 the *Nautilus* lay in longitude 105° and latitude 15° south. The weather was threatening, the sea rough and billowy. The wind was blowing a strong gust from the east. Our barometer, which had been falling for a few days, forecast an oncoming battle of the elements.

I'd climbed onto the platform just as the chief officer was taking his readings of hour angles. Out of habit I waited for him to utter his daily sentence. But that day he replaced it with a different sentence, just as unintelligible. Almost immediately I saw Captain Nemo appear, raise his spyglass, and inspect the horizon.

For a minute or two the captain stood motionless, rooted to the spot contained within the field of his objective lens. Then he lowered his spyglass and exchanged about ten words with his chief officer. The latter seemed in the grip of an excitement he was vainly trying to control. More in command of himself, Captain Nemo stayed cool. In addition he seemed to be raising certain objections that his chief officer kept answering with sweeping assurances. At least that's what I gathered from their differences in tone and gesture.

As for me, I looked carefully in the same direction but without spotting a thing. Sky and water merged into a perfectly clean horizon line.

Meanwhile Captain Nemo strolled from one end of the platform to the other, not looking at me, maybe not even seeing me. His step was firm but less rhythmic than usual. Sometimes he would stop, fold his arms over his chest, and study the sea. What could he be looking for in that immense expanse? By then the *Nautilus* lay hundreds of miles from the nearest coast!

The chief officer kept raising his spyglass and stubbornly examining the horizon, pacing back and forth, stamping his foot, in his nervous agitation a sharp contrast to his superior.

But this mystery was soon to be cleared up, because Captain Nemo issued orders to increase speed, and the engine boosted its drive power, setting the propeller in swifter rotation.

Just then the chief officer drew the captain's attention once again. The latter interrupted his strolling and aimed his spyglass at the place indicated. He studied it a good while. As for me, I was deeply puzzled, went below to the lounge, and fetched an excellent long-range telescope that I often used. Leaning my elbows on the beacon housing, which jutted from the stern of the platform, I got set to scour that whole stretch of sky and sea.

But I'd no sooner peered into the eyepiece than the instrument was rudely snatched out of my hands.

I turned around. Captain Nemo was standing in front of me, but I almost didn't recognize him. His facial features were transformed. Gleaming with dark fire, his eyes had shrunk beneath his frowning brow. His teeth were half bared. His rigid body, clenched fists, and hunched shoulders revealed that his whole being was in the grip of intense hatred. He didn't move. My spyglass had slipped out of his hand and was rolling at his feet.

Had I accidentally caused these signs of anger? Did this baffling individual think I'd detected some secret forbidden to guests on the *Nautilus?*

Not so! I wasn't the target of his hatred, because he wasn't looking at me; his eyes were stubbornly focused on that inscrutable corner of the horizon.

Finally Captain Nemo recovered his self-control. His facial appearance, so deeply changed, now resumed its usual calm. He spoke a few words to his chief officer in their strange language, then he turned to me:

"Professor Aronnax," he told me in a tone of some urgency, "I ask that you now honor one of the binding agreements between us."

"Which one, captain?"

"You and your companions must be placed in confinement till I see fit to set you free."

"You're in command," I answered, looking at him intently. "But may I ask you a question?"

"You may not, sir."

After that I stopped objecting and started obeying, since resistance was useless.

I went below to the cabin occupied by Ned Land and Conseil, and I informed them of the captain's decision. The reader can imagine how the Canadian took this news. In any case there was no time for explanations. Four crewmen were waiting at the door and they led us to the cell where we'd spent our first night aboard the *Nautilus.*

Ned Land tried to register a complaint, but the only answer he got was a door shut in his face.

"Will master tell me what this means?" Conseil asked me.

I told my companions what had happened. They were as amazed as I was and just as much in the dark.

Then my thoughts descended into the realm of speculation, and Captain Nemo's strange facial seizure stayed in the forefront of my mind. I couldn't connect two ideas in

logical order and I'd wandered off into the silliest theories, when Ned Land snapped me out of my mental struggles with these words:

"Hey, look here! It's lunchtime!"

The table had indeed been laid. Apparently Captain Nemo had issued this order at the same time he'd commanded the *Nautilus* to pick up speed.

"Will master allow me to make a recommendation?" Conseil asked me.

"Yes, my boy," I replied.

"Well, master needs to eat lunch. It's the sensible thing to do, because we have no idea what the future holds."

"You're right, Conseil."

"Unfortunately," Ned Land said, "they've only given us the standard menu."

"Ned my friend," Conseil remarked, "what would you say if they'd given us no lunch at all?"

This dose of sanity cut the harpooner's complaints clean off.

We took our seats at the table. Our meal proceeded pretty much in silence. I ate very little. Conseil, everlastingly sensible, "force-fed" himself, and despite the menu Ned Land didn't waste a bite. Lunch over, each of us propped himself in a corner.

Just then the luminous globe lighting our cell went out, leaving us in absolute darkness. Ned Land soon dozed off, and to my amazement Conseil also fell sound asleep. I was wondering what could have caused this urgent need for slumber, when I felt a heavy drowsiness seeping into my brain. I tried to keep my eyes open, but they closed in spite of me. I was in the grip of anguished hallucinations. Obviously some sort of sleeping potion had been mixed into the food we'd just eaten! So imprisonment wasn't enough to hide Captain Nemo's plans from us—sleep was needed as well!

Then I heard the hatches close. The sea's undulations had been creating a gentle rocking motion, now they ceased. Had the *Nautilus* left the surface of the ocean? Was it reentering the motionless depths of the sea?

I tried to fight off this sleepiness. It was impossible. My breathing grew fainter. I felt a deathly chill freezing my dull, nearly paralyzed limbs. Like little lead skullcaps, my eyelids closed. I couldn't open them. A morbid sleep, full of hallucinations, gripped my whole being. Then the visions vanished and left me in utter oblivion.

24

THE CORAL REALM

THE NEXT DAY I woke up with my head unusually clear. Much to my surprise I was in my stateroom. No doubt my companions had been reinstated in their cabin without noticing it any more than I had. Like me, they would have no idea what had taken place during the night, and I could only hope that some future happenstance would unravel this mystery.

Then I considered leaving my stateroom. Was I free or still a prisoner? Completely free. I opened my door, headed down the corridors, and climbed the central companionway. The hatches, which had been closed the day before, were now open. I arrived on the platform.

Ned Land and Conseil were there waiting for me. I questioned them. They didn't know a thing. They'd fallen into a deep sleep that had left them with no memories and they were quite surprised to wake up in their cabin.

As for the *Nautilus*, it seemed as tranquil and mysterious as ever. It was cruising on the surface of the waves at a moderate speed. Nothing seemed to have changed on board.

Ned Land examined the sea with his keen eyes. It was deserted. The Canadian didn't sight anything new on the horizon, neither sail nor shore. A breeze was blowing noisily from the west, and disheveled by the wind, long billows made the submersible roll very noticeably.

After replenishing its air, the *Nautilus* stayed at an average depth of fifty feet, which allowed it to get back quickly to the surface of the waves. And contrary to custom, it executed such a maneuver several times during that day of January 19. Then the chief officer would climb onto the platform, and his usual sentence would echo around inside the ship.

As for Captain Nemo, he didn't appear.

Of the other men on board, I saw only my unemotional steward, who waited on me with his usual mute efficiency.

At about two o'clock I was busy organizing my notes in the lounge when the captain opened the door and appeared. I nodded to him. He gave me an almost invisible nod in return, without saying a single word to me. I went back to work, hoping he would give me an explanation of the previous afternoon's events. He did nothing of the sort. I glanced at him. His face looked tired; his reddened eyes hadn't been refreshed by sleep; his features expressed deep sadness, genuine grief. He paced back and forth, sat and stood, picked up a book at random, put it down right away, checked his instruments without taking his usual notes, and apparently couldn't stand still for a second.

Finally he came over and said to me:

"Are you a physician, Professor Aronnax?"

This question was so unexpected, I looked at him for some while without replying.

"Are you a physician?" he said again. "Several of your scientific colleagues took their degrees in medicine, such as Gratiolet, Moquin-Tandon, and others."

"That's right," I said. "I'm a doctor, I used to be on call at the hospitals. I was in practice for several years before joining the museum."

"Very good, sir."

My reply apparently pleased Captain Nemo. But not knowing what he was driving at, I waited for further questions, ready to answer as circumstances dictated.

"Professor Aronnax," the captain said to me, "would you be willing to examine one of my men?"

"Somebody is sick?"

"Yes."

"I'm ready to go with you."

"Come along."

I admit my heart was pounding. Lord knows why, but I saw a definite connection between this sick crewman and yesterday's happenings, and the mystery of those events concerned me at least as much as the man's sickness.

Captain Nemo led me to the *Nautilus*'s

stern and invited me into a cabin located next to the sailors' quarters.

On a bed lay a man some forty years old with strongly marked features, the very image of an Anglo-Saxon.

I bent over him. He wasn't just sick, he was injured. His head was swathed in blood-soaked linen and was resting on a folded pillow. I undid the linen bandages, while the injured man looked up with great staring eyes and let me proceed without making a single complaint.

It was a horrible injury. His skull had been cracked open by some blunt instrument, his brain was left exposed, and the cerebral matter had incurred deep abrasions. Blood clots had formed in this liquefying mass, turning the color of wine dregs. Simultanous contusion and concussion of the brain had taken place. The sick man's breathing was labored, and a few spasmodic muscle movements quivered in his face. The cerebral inflammation was complete and had brought about a paralysis of movement and sensation.

I took the injured man's pulse. It was sporadic. Already the body's extremities were growing cold, and I saw that death was coming on without any possibility of my holding it in check. After dressing the poor man's injury, I redid the linen bandages around his head and I turned to Captain Nemo.

"How did he get this injury?" I asked him.

"What difference does it make," the captain replied evasively. "The *Nautilus* was in a collision that cracked one of the engine levers, and it struck this man. My chief officer was standing beside him. This man leaped forward to intercept the blow. A brother lays down his life for his brother, a friend for his friend, what could be simpler? That's the law for everybody aboard the *Nautilus*. But what's your diagnosis of his condition?"

I hesitated to speak my mind.

"You can talk freely," the captain told me. "This man doesn't understand French."

I took one last look at the injured man, then I replied:

"This man will be dead in two hours."

"Nothing can save him?"

"Nothing."

Captain Nemo clenched his fists, and tears glistened in his eyes, which I hadn't thought were capable of weeping.

For a few seconds I still watched the dying man, whose life was waning little by little. He grew even paler under the electric light bathing his deathbed. I looked at his intelligent head, furrowed with premature wrinkles that misfortune, maybe suffering, had etched long before. I was hoping to learn about his secret existence from any last words that might escape from his lips!

"You may go, Professor Aronnax," Captain Nemo told me.

I left the captain in the dying man's cabin and I retired to my stateroom, very moved by this scene. All day long I was aquiver with grim forebodings. That night I didn't sleep well, and in between my fitful dreams, I thought I heard a distant moaning like a funeral dirge. Was it a prayer for the dead, murmured in that language I couldn't understand?

The next morning I climbed on deck. Captain Nemo was there already. He came over as soon as he saw me.

"Professor," he said to me, "would it be convenient for you to go on an underwater excursion today?"

"With my companions?" I asked.

"If they're amenable."

"We're yours to command, captain."

"Then kindly put on your diving suits."

As for the dead or dying man, he hadn't come into the picture. I rejoined Ned Land and Conseil. I informed them of Captain Nemo's proposition. Conseil was eager to accept, and this time the Canadian was perfectly willing to come along.

It was eight o'clock in the morning. By 8:30 we were suited up for this new stroll and equipped with our two devices for lighting and breathing. The double door opened, and accompanied by Captain Nemo with a dozen crewmen following, we set foot on the firm seafloor where the *Nautilus* was resting at a depth of thirty feet.

A gentle slope gravitated to an uneven bottom about ninety feet down. This bottom was totally different from the one I'd visited during my first excursion beneath the waves of the Pacific Ocean. Here I didn't see any fine-grained sand, underwater prairies, or open-sea forests. I immediately recognized the wondrous region in which Captain Nemo did the honors that day. It was the coral realm.

In the zoophyte branch, class Octo-corallia, you'll find the order Gorgonacea, which has three coral groups, the gorgonians, isidians, and corallians. It's in this last group that precious coral belongs, an unusual substance that has alternately been classified in the mineral, vegetable, and animal kingdoms. Medicine in ancient times, jewelry in the modern era, it wasn't conclusively assigned to the animal kingdom till Peysonnel of Marseilles did so in 1694.

A coral is an assemblage of microscopic creatures organized over a polypary with a brittle, stony composition. These polyps have a unique generating mechanism that produces them through the budding process and they lead an individual existence while also participating in a communal life. Therefore they embody a sort of natural socialism. I was acquainted with the latest research work on this peculiar zoophyte—which turns to stone while taking on a tree form, as some naturalists have very aptly commented—and nothing could have been more interesting to me than to visit one of these petrified forests that nature has planted on the bottom of the sea.

We turned on our Ruhmkorff devices and went along a coral shoal in the process of forming, which, given time, will someday close off this whole part of the Indian Ocean. Our path was bordered by hopelessly tangled bushes, which were formed from snarls of shrubs all covered with little star-shaped, white-leafed flowers. Only, contrary to plants on shore, these tree forms become attached to rocks on the seafloor by heading from top to bottom.

Our lights created a thousand delightful effects while playing over these brightly colored boughs. I fancied I could see those cylindrical, membranous tubes quivering beneath the water's undulations. I was tempted to pick their fresh petals that were adorned with delicate tentacles, some newly in bloom, others barely open, while slender fish with fast-moving fins brushed past them like flocks of birds. But if my hands drew near the moving flowers of those spirited, sensitive creatures, an alarm instantly sounded throughout the colony. The white petals retracted into their red sheaths, the flowers vanished in front of my eyes, and the whole bush changed into a chunk of stony nipples.

Sheer chance had brought me into contact with the most valuable variety of this zoophyte. It equaled the coral fished up from the Mediterranean off the Barbary Coast or off the shores of France and Italy. With its bright colors it lived up to those poetic names of *blood flower* and *blood foam* that the industry gives its finest exhibits. Precious coral goes for as much as $45 a pound, and in the watery deep at this locality, a host of coral fishermen could make a fortune. This invaluable substance often merges with other polyparies to form compact, hopelessly tangled assemblages known as *macciota*, and I noted some wonderful pink samples of this coral.

But as the bushes shrank, the tree forms magnified. Actual petrified thickets and long alcoves from some freakish school of architecture kept opening up in front of us. Captain Nemo went down a dark hallway whose gentle slope took us to a depth of over 300 feet. The light from our glass spirals created magical effects at times, lingering on the wrinkled roughness of some natural arch or some overhang suspended like a chandelier, which our lamps would fleck with fiery sparks. Among these bushes of precious coral, I saw other polyps just as unusual—red coral, iris coral with jointed outgrowths, and then a few tufts of genus *Corallina*, some green and others red, actually a type of seaweed encrusted with limestone salts, which, after years of arguing, naturalists have finally assigned to the vegetable kingdom. Yet as one intellectual has commented, "This could be the actual point where life rises humbly out of sleeping stone, but without completely breaking away from its primitive starting point."

After two hours of walking, we finally reached a depth of about a thousand feet, in other words, the lowermost limit at which coral can begin to form. But here it was no longer an isolated bush or a modest thicket of low timber. It was an immense forest, huge mineral vegetation, enormous petrified trees linked by stylish garlands of hydras from the genus *Plumularia*, those tropical creepers of the sea all decked out in shadings and glimmers. We walked freely under their lofty boughs lost up in the shadows of the waves, while at our feet organ-pipe coral, cauliflower coral, star coral, fungus coral, and cup coral formed a carpet of flowers sprinkled with dazzling gemstones.

What an indescribable sight! Oh, if only we could share our feelings! Why did we have to be trapped behind these masks of metal and glass? Why were we forbidden to talk with each other? At least allow us to lead the lives of the fish populating this liquid element, or better still the lives of amphibians, which can spend long hours at sea or on shore, traveling around their double domain as their fancy takes them!

Meanwhile Captain Nemo had called a halt. My companions and I stopped walking, and I turned to watch the crewmen form a semicircle around their leader. Looking more carefully, I saw that four of them were carrying on their shoulders an object that was oblong in shape.

At this locality we stood in the center of a huge clearing surrounded by the tall tree forms of that underwater forest. Our lamps cast a sort of brilliant twilight over the area, making outrageously long shadows on the seafloor. Past the boundaries of the clearing, the darkness deepened again, brightened only by tiny sparkles winking on sharp crests of coral.

Ned Land and Conseil stood beside me. As we watched, it dawned on me that I would be in attendance at a strange drama. Studying the seafloor, I saw that it swelled here and there into low bulges that were encrusted with limestone deposits and laid out in an orderly arrangement that indicated the hand of man.

In the middle of the clearing, a cross of coral stood on a pedestal of roughly piled rocks, spreading long arms you would have sworn were made of petrified blood.

At a signal from Captain Nemo, one of his men stepped forward, detached a mattock from his belt, and started to dig a hole a few feet from that cross.

Now I understood! The clearing was a cemetery, this hole a grave, that oblong object the body of the man who must have died during the night! Captain Nemo and his men had come to bury their companion in this communal resting place on the unreachable ocean floor!

No! My brain was reeling! Never before had such staggering thoughts raced through my mind! I didn't want to see what my eyes were taking in!

Meanwhile the grave digging went slowly. Fish fled here and there as their retreat was disturbed. I heard the pick ringing out on the limestone soil, its iron tip sometimes giving off sparks when it hit a stray piece of flint on the seafloor. The hole grew longer, wider, and soon was deep enough to hold the body.

Then the pallbearers drew near. Wrapped in white cloth made from filaments of the fan mussel, the body was lowered into its watery grave. Arms folded over his chest, Captain Nemo knelt in a posture of prayer, along with all the friends of him who had loved them. . . . My two companions and I bowed our heads reverently.

They covered up the grave with the rubble dug from the seafloor, and it formed a low mound.

When this was done, Captain Nemo and his men stood again; then they went over to the grave, knelt once more, and held out their hands in final farewell. . . .

Then the funeral party went back up the path to the *Nautilus*, heading under the arches of the forest, through the thickets, along the coral bushes, always going higher.

Finally the ship's rays appeared. Their luminous trail guided us to the *Nautilus*. By one o'clock we'd returned.

After changing clothes, I climbed onto the platform and sat next to the beacon, in the grip of my dreadfully obsessive thoughts.

Captain Nemo rejoined me. I got up and said to him:

"So as I predicted, that man died during the night?"

"Yes, Professor Aronnax," Captain Nemo replied.

"And now he's resting next to his companions in that coral cemetery?"

"Yes, forgotten by the world but not by us! We dig the graves, then the polyps are in charge of sealing them up for all eternity!"

With a sudden movement the captain hid his face in his clenched fists, vainly trying to keep back a sob. Then he added:

"It's our peaceful cemetery, hundreds of feet under the surface of the waves!"

"At least, captain, your dead sleep serenely there, out of the reach of sharks!"

"Yes, sir," Captain Nemo replied solemnly, "of sharks and men!"

PART TWO

25

THE INDIAN OCEAN

NOW WE BEGIN the second part of this voyage under the seas. The first ended with that affecting drama at the coral cemetery, which made such a deep impression on my mind. Hence Captain Nemo would live out his entire life in the heart of this immense sea, and even his grave lay ready in its impregnable depths. There the last sleep of the *Nautilus*'s occupants, those friends bound to each other in death as well as in life, would be safe from monsters of the deep. "And men!" the captain had added.

Always the same fierce, implacable defiance of human society!

As for me, I was no longer content with the theories that satisfied Conseil. That fine lad still saw the *Nautilus*'s commander as simply one of those unappreciated innovators who repay the world's indifference with contempt. For him the captain was still a misunderstood genius who had tired of men's deceptions, fled beyond their reach, and taken refuge in an environment where he was free to follow his heart. But to my way of

thinking, this theory explained only one side of Captain Nemo.

In essence the mystery of the previous afternoon when we were locked up and dosed with a sleeping potion, the captain's violent precaution of snatching away from my eyes a spyglass poised to scour the horizon, and the fatal injury given that man during some unexplained collision experienced by the *Nautilus* all led me down a plain trail. No, Captain Nemo wasn't content with simply fleeing from humanity! His fearsome submersible was an instrument not only in his quest for freedom, but maybe also in some sort of dreadful vendetta, Lord knows what.

Right now nothing is clear to me, I still can catch only glimmers in the dark, and I need to restrict my pen to taking dictation from events, so to speak.

But we don't have any formal ties to Captain Nemo. He believes that escaping from the *Nautilus* is impossible. We aren't even bound by our word of honor. No promises shackle us. We're simply captives, prisoners masquerading under the name "guests" for the sake of common politeness. However Ned Land hasn't given up all hope of recovering his freedom. He's sure to take advantage of the first chance that comes his way. No doubt I'll do the same. And yet I'll feel some regret at going off with the *Nautilus*'s secrets, so generously shared with us by Captain Nemo! Which raises the question, should we ultimately detest or admire this man? Is he the persecutor or the persecuted? And to be truthful, before leaving him for good I want to finish this underwater tour of the world, whose first stages have been so magnificent. I want to witness a full cycle of the undersea wonders on our planet. I want to see what no man has seen before, even if this insatiable curiosity costs me my life! What are my discoveries to date? Practically nothing, since so far we've gone only 6,000 leagues across the Pacific!

Nevertheless I'm well aware that the *Nautilus* is heading toward populated areas, and if some chance to escape becomes available to us, it would be inhuman to sacrifice my companions to my obsession with exploring the unknown. I'll have to go with them, maybe even lead them. But will this opportunity ever come up? Robbed of his freedoms, the man in me yearns for such an opportunity; but the scientist, hungry for knowledge, dreads it.

At noon that day, January 21, 1868, the chief officer went up to take the sun's altitude. I climbed onto the platform, lit a cigar, and watched him at work. It seemed obvious to me that this man didn't understand French, because I made several comments out loud that should have triggered some automatic reaction if he'd understood them; but he remained silent and unresponsive.

While he was taking his sights with his sextant, one of the *Nautilus*'s sailors—that muscular man who had gone with us to Crespo Island on our first underwater excursion—came up to clean the glass panes of the beacon. I examined the fittings of this mechanism, whose power was increased a hundredfold by biconvex lenses that functioned like those in a lighthouse and kept its rays productively focused. This electric lamp had been designed so as to maximize its illuminating power. In essence its light was generated in a vacuum, guaranteeing both its steadiness and intensity. The vacuum also reduced wear on the graphite points between which the luminous arc stretches. This was an important savings for Captain Nemo, who would have had trouble refurbishing them. But under these conditions wear and tear were almost nonexistent.

When the *Nautilus* was ready to resume its underwater travels, I went below again to the lounge. The hatches closed once more, and we set our course due west.

Then we plowed the waves of the Indian Ocean, a huge stretch of water with an area of about 1.3 billion acres, whose surface is so transparent that you'll get dizzy if you lean over it and look down. The *Nautilus* drifted around, generally at depths between 300 and 600 feet. It behaved this way for a few days. To anybody without my immense love for the sea, these hours would surely have seemed long and monotonous; but my daily strolls on the platform where I was refreshed by the bracing ocean air, the sights in the rich waters beyond the lounge windows, the books available in the library, and the maintenance of my journal took up all my time and didn't leave me a single moment of boredom or idleness.

All in all we enjoyed a highly satisfactory state of health. The diet on board agreed with us perfectly, and speaking for myself, I could easily have managed without those changes of pace that Ned Land, in a spirit of rebellion, kept taxing his ingenuity to supply us. What's more, in this regulated temperature we didn't even have to worry about catching colds. Besides, the ship had a good stock of the madrepore *Dendrophyllia*, known in Provence by the name sea fennel, and lozenges prepared from the dissolved flesh of its polyps make a first-class cough medicine.

Over a few days we saw a large number of web-footed aquatic birds known as gulls or sea mews. Some were skillfully slain, and when cooked a certain way, they're a perfectly acceptable platter of water game. Among the great wind riders—soaring far from any land and resting on the waves when they're tired of flying—I spotted some magnificent albatross, birds belonging to the Longipennate (long-winged) family, whose raucous calls sound like a donkey braying. In the Totipalmate (fully webbed) family were speedy frigate birds, deftly catching fish at the surface, and many tropic birds from the genus *Phaethon*, among others the red-tailed tropic bird, the size of a pigeon, its white plumage tinted a shade of pink that contrasted with the black color of its wings.

The *Nautilus*'s nets hauled in several types of sea turtle from the hawksbill genus with arching backs whose scales are highly prized. Diving easily, these reptiles can stay a good while underwater by closing the fleshy valves located at the outside openings of their nasal passages. When they were captured, some hawksbills were still asleep inside their carapaces, a refuge from other marine animals. Generally the meat of these turtles was only so-so, but their eggs made for an excellent feast.

As for fish, they always filled us with wonderment when the open panels let us spy out the secrets of their aquatic lives. I noted several species I hadn't been able to study previously.

I'll mention chiefly some trunkfish characteristic of the Red Sea, the Indian Ocean, and those seas lapping the shores of equinoctial America. Like turtles, armadillos, sea urchins, and crustaceans, these fish are protected by armor plate that's neither chalky nor stony but actual bone. Sometimes this armor is shaped like a solid triangle, sometimes like a solid quadrangle. Among the triangular type I noticed individuals two inches long with brown tails, yellow fins, and wholesome, exquisitely tasty meat; I even recommend acclimating them to fresh water, a change, by the way, that a number of saltwater fish can make with ease. I'll also mention some quadrangular trunkfish with four big protuberances on top of the back; trunkfish that have white spots on the underside and that do as well in captivity as birds; boxfish equipped with stings formed from extensions of their bony crusts and whose odd grunting has earned them the nickname "sea pigs"; then some trunkfish known as dromedaries with tough, leathery meat and big conical humps.

From the field notes kept by Mr. Conseil, I'll also single out certain fish from the genus *Tetradon* characteristic of these seas, especially some Guinean puffers with red backs and white chests distinguished by three lengthwise rows of filaments, plus jugfish seven inches long and adorned with the brightest colors. Then, as specimens of other genera, blowfish looking like a dark brown egg, streaked with white stripes, and lacking tails; globefish, authentic porcupines of the sea, armed with stings and able to inflate themselves till they look like pincushions bristling with needles; seahorses common to every ocean; longtail sea moths with lengthy snouts and very extended pectoral fins shaped like wings, which allow them, if not to fly, at least to shoot into the air; slender sea moths whose tails are covered with many scaly rings; spiny eels with long jaws, superb creatures ten inches long and gleaming with the most cheerful colors; bluish gray dragonets with wrinkled heads; myriads of leaping blennies with black stripes and long pectoral

fins, gliding over the surface of the water with prodigious speed; delicious sailfish that can hoist their fins in a favorable current like so many unfurled sails; splendid nurseryfish on which nature has lavished yellow, azure, silver, and gold; gourami with wings made of filaments; bullheads that are eternally spattered with mud and that make distinct moaning sounds; gurnards whose livers are thought to be poisonous; Spanish ladyfish that can flutter their eyelids; finally snipefish with long tubular snouts, real oceangoing flycatchers packing a rifle unknown to both Remington and Chassepot: it bags insects by shooting them with a simple drop of water.

From the eighty-ninth genus in Lacépède's classification system, belonging to his second subclass of bony fish (characterized by gill covers and a bronchial membrane), I noted some scorpionfish whose heads are embellished with stings and that sport only one dorsal fin; these creatures are covered with small scales or have none at all depending on which subgenus they belong to. The second subgenus gave us some specimens of sea goblin that were twelve to sixteen inches long, boasted yellow stripes, and had heads with a phantasmagoric appearance. As for the first subgenus, it furnished several specimens of that peculiar fish aptly nicknamed the "toadfish," whose big head is sometimes pitted with deep cavities, sometimes swollen with protuberances; it's garnished with stings and studded with nodules; it sports hideously misshapen horns; its body and tail are embellished with calluses; its stings inflict dangerous injuries; it's repulsive and horrible.

From January 21 to the 23rd, the *Nautilus* traveled at the rate of 250 leagues every twenty-four hours, hence 540 miles at twenty-two miles per hour. During our trip we could identify these different varieties of fish because they were drawn by our electric light and tried to follow alongside; outstripped by our speed, most of them soon fell behind; but a few managed to keep up with the *Nautilus* for some while.

On the morning of the 24th, in latitude 12° 5′ south and longitude 94° 33′, we raised Keeling Island, a madreporic outcrop that's covered with magnificent coconut trees and was once visited by Mr. Darwin and Captain Fitzroy. The *Nautilus* cruised a little ways off the coast of this desert island. Our dragnets hauled in many specimens of polyps and echinoderms plus some unusual shells from the mollusk branch. Some valuable new exhibits enhanced Captain Nemo's treasures—a species of snail from the genus *Delphinula* onto which I fastened some pointed star coral, a sort of parasitic polypary that often latches onto seashells.

Soon Keeling Island vanished below the horizon, and we set our course for the northwest, toward the tip of India's peninsula.

"Civilization!" Ned Land told me that day. "Much better than those Papuan islands where we came across more savages than venison! India, professor, is a land with roads and railways, English, French, and Hindu towns. We wouldn't go five miles without bumping into a countryman. Come on now, isn't it time we said good-bye to Captain Nemo?"

"No, no, Ned," I replied in a very firm tone. "Let's ride it out as you seamen say. The *Nautilus* is nearing populated areas. It's heading back toward Europe, let it take us there. Once we're in our own waters, we'll figure out what our best move is. Besides, I can't see Captain Nemo letting us hunt along the coasts of Malabar or Coromandel the way we did in the forests of New Guinea."

"Well, sir, do we always need his permission?"

I didn't answer the Canadian. I didn't feel like arguing. Deep down I was determined to fully exploit the good fortune that had put me aboard the *Nautilus*.

After leaving Keeling Island, our pace generally got slower. It also got more unpredictable, often taking us to great depths. Several times we used our slanting fins, which levers inside could set at an angle to our waterline. In this way we went as deep as one or two miles down but without ever verifying the Indian Ocean's lowest depths, which soundings of 43,000 feet haven't been able to reach. As for the temperature in the lower strata, our thermometer always and invariably read 39° Fahrenheit. I noted only that the water in the upper layers was always colder over shallows than in the open sea.

On January 25 the ocean was completely deserted, so the *Nautilus* spent the day on the surface, churning the waves with its powerful propeller and making them spurt to great heights. Under these conditions who wouldn't have mistaken it for a gigantic cetacean? I spent three-quarters of that day on the platform. I watched the sea. There was nothing on the horizon, till around four o'clock in the afternoon when a long steamer appeared to the west, running on our opposite tack. Its masts were visible for a second, but it couldn't have seen the *Nautilus*, which was lying too low in the water. I figured that steamship belonged to the Peninsular & Oriental line, which runs between the island of Ceylon and Sidney, also calling at King George Sound and Melbourne.

At five o'clock in the afternoon, just before the brief twilight that connects day with night in tropical zones, Conseil and I marveled at an unusual sight.

It was a delightful creature whose discovery, according to the ancients, is a sign of good luck. Aristotle, Athenaeus, Pliny, and Oppian studied its habits and lavished on it all the scholarly poetry of Greece and Italy. They called it "nautilus" and "pompilius." But modern science hasn't approved these monikers, and this mollusk now goes by the name argonaut.

Anybody checking with Conseil would soon learn from the gallant lad that the branch Mollusca is divided into five classes; that the first class features the Cephalopoda (whose members are sometimes bare, sometimes covered with a shell), which consists of two families, the Dibranchiata and the Tetrabranchiata, which you can tell apart by the number of gills they have; that the family Dibranchiata features three genera, the argonaut, the squid, and the cuttlefish, and that the family Tetrabranchiata has only one genus, the nautilus. After this laundry list, if some recalcitrant listener confuses the argonaut, which is *acetabuliferous* (in other words, a bearer of suction tubes), with the nautilus, which is *tentaculiferous* (a bearer of tentacles), it will be simply unforgivable.

Now then, a whole school of these argonauts was voyaging on the surface of the sea. Numbering several hundred, they belonged to a species that's covered with protuberances and is specific to the Indian Ocean.

These graceful mollusks swam backward with the help of their propulsion tubes, sucking water into these tubes and then expelling it. Six of their eight tentacles were long, thin, and floating on the waves, while the other two were rounded into palms and spread out to the wind like light sails. I had a perfect view of their undulating, spiral-shaped shell, which Cuvier aptly compared to a smart cockleboat. And it really *is* like a boat. It transports the creature that secretes it, but the creature isn't attached to it.

"The argonaut is free to leave its shell," I told Conseil, "but it never actually does."

"Not unlike Captain Nemo," Conseil replied sagely. "Which is why he should have christened his ship the *Argonaut*."

For about an hour the *Nautilus* cruised in the midst of this school of mollusks. Then, Lord knows why, they were gripped by a sudden fear. As if at a signal, every sail was suddenly lowered; arms curled up, bodies contracted, shells flipped over by shifting their center of gravity, and the whole flotilla vanished under the waves. It was instantaneous, and no warships doing maneuvers were ever more in unison.

Just then night suddenly fell, and the waves barely surged in the breeze, spreading peacefully around the *Nautilus*'s side plates.

The next day, January 26, we cut the equator on the 82nd meridian and we reentered the northern hemisphere.

During that day a fearsome school of sharks provided us with an escort. The dreadful creatures teem in this ocean and make it mighty dangerous. There were Port Jackson sharks with a brown back, a whitish belly, and eleven rows of teeth, epaulet sharks with necks marked by a big black spot encircled in white and resembling an eye, and carpet sharks whose rounded snouts were dotted with dark specks. Often these powerful creatures rushed at the lounge window with a violence not exactly comforting. By this point Ned Land couldn't control himself. He wanted to rise to the surface of the waves and harpoon the monsters, especially some smoothhound sharks whose mouths were paved with teeth arranged like a mosaic, and some big sixteen-foot tiger sharks that insisted on personally provoking him. But the *Nautilus* soon picked up speed and easily left the fastest of these man-eaters astern.

On January 27, at the entrance to the huge Bay of Bengal, we repeatedly met up with a grim sight: human corpses floating on the surface of the waves! Carried out to sea by the Ganges, these were East Indian villagers who had passed away yet hadn't been fully devoured by vultures, the only morticians in these parts. But there were plenty of sharks to assist them with their undertaking chores.

Near seven o'clock in the evening, the *Nautilus* lay half submerged, navigating in the midst of creamy white waves. As far as the eye could see, the ocean seemed to have turned into milk. Was it an effect of the moon's rays? Hardly, because the new moon was barely two days old and was still out of sight below the horizon. Though lit by starlight, the whole sky seemed pitch-black in comparison to the whiteness of the waters.

Conseil couldn't believe his eyes and he asked me about the causes of this odd phenomenon. Luckily I was in a position to answer him.

"It's called a milk sea," I told him, "a huge expanse of white waves frequently seen off the shores of Amboina and in these waterways."

"But could master tell me what causes this effect?" Conseil asked. "I assume this water hasn't really changed into milk."

"No, my boy, and this whiteness that surprises you is simply due to the presence of myriads of tiny creatures called infusoria, a sort of microscopic glowworm that's colorless and jellylike in appearance, as thick as a strand of hair, and less than a hundredth of an inch long. Some of these tiny creatures stick to each other over a distance of several leagues."

"Several leagues!" Conseil exclaimed.

"Yes, my boy, and don't bother trying to calculate how many infusoria are out there. You won't be able to, because, if I'm not mistaken, navigators have cruised through milk seas for over forty miles."

I'm not sure that Conseil heeded my recommendation because he seemed to be deep in thought, no doubt trying to figure out how many creatures a hundredth of an inch long could fit in forty square miles. As for me, I kept on studying this phenomenon. For several hours the *Nautilus*'s spur sliced those whitish waves, and I watched it glide noiselessly over that soapy water, as if cruising through the eddies of foam that a bay's currents and countercurrents sometimes leave between each other.

Toward midnight the sea suddenly resumed its normal color, but behind us all the way to the horizon, the skies kept mirroring the whiteness of the waves and for a good while seemed filled with the dim glow of an aurora borealis.

26

A New Proposition from Captain Nemo

AT NOON ON January 28, when the *Nautilus* came back to the surface of the sea, it lay at latitude 9° 4′ north, and land was in sight eight miles to the west. Right off I noticed a cluster of mountains that had a very irregular outline and were about 2,000 feet high. After our position fix I went back down to the lounge, and once our bearings were reported on the chart, I realized we were facing the island of Ceylon, that pearl dangling from the earlobe of India's peninsula.

I went looking in the library for a book about this island, one of the most fertile on earth. Sure enough, I found a volume entitled *Ceylon and the Cingalese* by H. C. Sirr, Esq. Going back into the lounge, I first noted the bearings of Ceylon, on which the ancients lavished so many different names. It's located between latitude 5° 55′ and 9° 49′ north, and between longitude 79° 42′ and 82° 4′ east of the meridian of Greenwich; its length is 275 miles; its maximum width, 150 miles; its circumference, 900 miles; its surface area, 24,448 square miles—in other words, it's a little smaller than Ireland.

Just then Captain Nemo and his chief officer appeared.

The captain glanced at the chart. Then, turning to me:

"The island of Ceylon," he said, "is famous for its pearl fisheries. Would you be open to visiting one of those fisheries, Professor Aronnax?"

"Certainly, captain."

"Fine. It's easily arranged. But when we see the fisheries, we won't see any fishermen. The annual harvest hasn't started yet. Not to worry. I'll issue orders to make for the Gulf of Mannar, and we'll arrive there late tonight."

The captain said a few words to his chief officer, who left immediately. Soon the *Nautilus* reentered its liquid element, and the pressure gauge showed that it was staying at a depth of thirty feet.

With the chart under my eyes, I looked for the Gulf of Mannar. I found it by the 9th parallel off the northwestern shores of Ceylon. It was formed by the long curve of little Mannar Island. To reach it we had to go all the way up Ceylon's west coast.

"Professor," Captain Nemo told me, "there are pearl fisheries in the Bay of Bengal, the Indian Ocean, the Japan and China seas, plus those seas south of the United States, the Gulf of Panama and the Gulf of California; but it's off Ceylon that this fishing reaps the richest rewards. No doubt we'll be arriving a bit early. Fishermen gather in the Gulf of Mannar only during the month of March, and for thirty days some 300 boats concentrate on the lucrative harvest of this ocean treasure. Each boat is manned by ten oarsmen and ten fishermen. The latter divide into two groups, dive in rotation, and go down to a depth of forty feet with the help of a heavy stone gripped between their feet and attached by a rope to their boat."

"You mean they still use such primitive methods?" I said.

"Still," Captain Nemo answered me, "though these fisheries belong to the most industrialized people on earth, the English, to whom the Treaty of Amiens granted them in 1802."

"Yet it strikes me that diving suits like

yours could perform a real service in such work."

"Yes, since those poor fishermen can't stay very long underwater. In writing about his trip to Ceylon, the Englishman Percival speaks highly of a Kaffir who stayed under five minutes before coming back to the surface, but I find this feat hard to believe. I know that some divers can last as long as fifty-seven seconds and very skillful ones as long as eighty-seven; but such men are rare, and when the poor fellows climb back on board, the water dripping out of their noses and ears is stained with blood. I believe the average time underwater that these fishermen can tolerate is thirty seconds, during which they hurriedly stuff their little nets with all the pearl oysters they can tear loose. But these fishermen generally don't live into ripe old age; their vision weakens, ulcers break out on their eyes, sores form on their bodies, and some of them even have strokes on the ocean floor."

"Yes," I said, "it's a sad occupation, especially since it's all done simply to pander to human vanity. But tell me, captain, how many oysters can a boat fish up in a single workday?"

"About 40,000 to 50,000. It's even said that in 1814, when the English government went fishing on its own behalf, its divers worked just twenty days and brought up 76,000,000 oysters."

"Are the fishermen at least decently paid?" I asked.

"Hardly, professor. In Panama they make just a dollar a week. More often they earn only a penny for each oyster that has a pearl, and they bring up so many that have none!"

"Only a penny to those poor people who make their employers rich? That's atrocious!"

"On that note, professor," Captain Nemo told me, "you and your companions will visit the Mannar oyster bed, and if some eager fisherman happens to arrive early, well, we can watch him in operation."

"That's fine with me, captain."

"By the way, Professor Aronnax, you aren't afraid of sharks, are you?"

"Sharks?" I exclaimed.

This was a needless question if I ever heard one.

"Well?" Captain Nemo went on.

"I admit, captain, I'm not yet on very familiar terms with that breed of fish."

"We're used to them, the rest of us," Captain Nemo remarked. "And you will be too in time. Anyhow we'll be armed and on our way we might hunt a man-eater or two. It's an interesting sport. Hence, professor, I'll see you tomorrow bright and early."

Tossing this off in a carefree tone, Captain Nemo left the lounge.

If you're invited to hunt bears in the Swiss Alps, you might say to yourself, "Oh good! I get to go bear hunting tomorrow!" If you're invited to hunt lions on the Atlas plains or tigers in the jungles of India, you might say, "Ha! Now's my chance to hunt lions and tigers!" But if you're invited to hunt sharks in their natural element, you might want to think it over before accepting.

As for me, I started mopping my brow, where a few beads of cold sweat were busy forming.

"Let's think this through," I said to myself, "and let's take our time. It's all very well to hunt otters in underwater forests, as we did in the forests of Crespo Island. But to run around the ocean floor when you're almost certain to meet up with man-eaters, that's another story! I'm quite aware that in some countries, especially the Andaman Islands, Negroes don't hesitate to attack sharks, knife in one hand and noose in the other; but I'm also aware that many people who face those fearsome creatures don't come back alive. Anyhow I'm not a Negro, and even if I were, in this instance I don't think a little hesitation on my part would be out of place."

And there I was, daydreaming about sharks, envisioning huge jaws armed with multiple rows of teeth and capable of biting a man in half. I already felt a distinct pain around my pelvic girdle. And how I resented the offhand way in which the captain had extended his deplorable invitation! One would have thought he was talking about going into the woods on some harmless foxhunt!

"Well," I mused, "Conseil definitely won't be up for it—and that'll give me an excuse for not going with the captain."

As for Ned Land, I admit I felt less confident of his wisdom. Danger, no matter how great, held a perennial attraction for his aggressive nature.

I went back to reading Sirr's book, but I paged through it mechanically. Between the lines I kept seeing fearsome, wide-open jaws.

Just then Conseil and the Canadian arrived, looking calm and even gleeful. Little did they know what they were in for.

"Ye gods, sir!" Ned Land told me. "Your Captain Nemo—may he go to blazes—has just made us quite a pleasant proposition!"

"Oh!" I said, "You know about . . ."

"With all due respect to master," Conseil replied, "the *Nautilus*'s commander has invited us, along with master, to visit Ceylon's magnificent pearl fisheries tomorrow. He did so in the most cordial terms and behaved like a true gentleman."

"He didn't tell you anything else?"

"Nothing, sir," the Canadian replied. "He said you'd already discussed this little stroll."

"True," I said. "But didn't he give you any details on—"

"Not a one, Mr. Naturalist. You *will* be going with us, right?"

"Me? Why certainly, of course! Uh, I see that this appeals to you, Mr. Land."

"It does! The whole thing sounds really interesting."

"And maybe dangerous!" I added in a tone full of implications.

"Dangerous?" Ned Land replied. "A simple trip to an oyster bed?"

Clearly Captain Nemo hadn't seen fit to bring up that little matter of sharks with my companions. For my part I looked at them anxiously, as if they were already short a couple of limbs. Should I alert them? Yes, surely, but I didn't know how to go about it.

"Would master," Conseil said to me, "give us a little background on pearl fishing?"

"On the fishing itself?" I asked. "Or on the occupational hazards that—"

"On the fishing," the Canadian replied. "Before we tackle the terrain, it helps to know the lay of the land."

"All right, have a seat, my friends, and I'll tell you everything I've just learned from the Englishman H. C. Sirr."

Ned and Conseil sat down on a couch, and the Canadian started off by saying to me:

"Sir, just what *is* a pearl exactly?"

"My gallant Ned," I replied, "for poets a pearl is a tear wept by the sea; for the people of the East, it's a drop of solidified dew; for the ladies it's a jewel that they wear on their fingers, necks, or ears and that has an oval shape, a glassy sheen, and is formed from mother-of-pearl; for chemists it's a mixture of calcium phosphate and calcium carbonate with a dash of gelatin protein; and finally for naturalists it's a simple festering secretion from the organ that produces mother-of-pearl in certain bivalves."

"Branch Mollusca," Conseil said, "class Acephala, order Testacea."

"Correct, O scholarly Conseil. Now then, the Testacea that can produce pearls include blackfoot abalone, turbo snails, giant clams, and saltwater scallops—in short, all the ones that secrete mother-of-pearl, in other words, that blue, azure, violet, or white substance lining the insides of their valves."

"Are mussels included too?" the Canadian asked.

"Absolutely! The mussels of certain streams in Scotland, Wales, Ireland, Saxony, Bohemia, and France."

"Good!" the Canadian replied. "From now on I'll pay attention to 'em."

"But," I continued, "when it comes to secreting pearls, the mollusk beyond compare is the pearl oyster *Meleagrina margaritifera*, that invaluable shellfish. Pearls result simply from mother-of-pearl solidifying into a globular shape. Either they stick to the oyster's shell or they get buried inside the creature's folds. On the valves a pearl sticks fast; on the flesh it lies loose. But its nucleus is always some small hard object, say a sterile egg or a grain of sand, around which the mother-of-pearl is deposited in thin, concentric layers over a period of several consecutive years."

"Can one find several pearls in the same oyster?" Conseil asked.

"Yes, my boy. There are certain shellfish

that turn into real jewel coffers. They even talk of one oyster, about which I remain dubious, that supposedly had at least 150 sharks in it."

"A hundred and fifty sharks!" Ned Land exclaimed.

"Did I say sharks?" I cut in hastily. "That's nonsense. I meant 150 pearls."

"Of course," Conseil said. "But will master now tell us how one goes about extracting these pearls?"

"One proceeds in several ways, and often, when pearls stick to the valves, fishermen even pull them loose with pliers. But usually they spread the shellfish out on mats made from the esparto grass covering the beaches. In this way the creatures die in the open air and after ten days they've decomposed to the proper point. Then they're dumped into huge tanks of salt water, opened up, and washed. At this juncture the sorters take over and do double duty. First they remove the layers of mother-of-pearl, which are known in the industry by the names *legitimate silver*, *bastard white*, or *bastard black* and are shipped out in cases weighing some 300 to 350 pounds. Then they remove the oyster's fleshy tissue, boil it, and strain it in order to extract even the tiniest pearls."

"Are pearls priced differently depending on their size?" Conseil asked.

"Not only depending on their size," I replied, "but also according to their shape, their *water*—in other words, their color—and their *orient*—in other words, that dappled, glistening luster that makes them so delightful to the eye. The loveliest pearls are called virgin pearls, or paragons; they form in isolation inside the mollusk's tissue. They're white, often opaque, sometimes of opalescent transparency, but usually globular or pear-shaped. The globular ones are made into bracelets, the pear-shaped ones into earrings, and since they're the most valuable, they're priced individually. Those other pearls that stick to the oyster's shell aren't as symmetrical and are priced by weight. Finally, classed in the lowest order, the tiniest pearls go by the name seed pearls; they're priced by the measuring cup and are mostly used in the creation of embroidery for church vestments."

"But that must be a long, hard job, sorting out pearls by size," the Canadian said.

"No, my friend. That task is performed with eleven strainers, or sieves, that are pierced with varying numbers of holes. Those pearls staying in the strainers with 20 to 80 holes are in the first order. Those not slipping through the sieves pierced with 100 to 800 holes are in the second order. Finally those pearls for which you use strainers pierced with 900 to 1,000 holes make up the seed pearls."

"How clever," Conseil said, "to turn separating and classifying pearls into a mechanical operation. And could master tell us the profits brought in by harvesting these beds of pearl oysters?"

"According to Sirr's book," I answered, "these Ceylon fisheries are farmed for a total profit of 600,000 man-eaters a year."

"Dollars a year!" Conseil amended.

"Right, dollars!" I continued. "$600,000! But I doubt that these fisheries bring in the returns they once did. Likewise the American fisheries used to make an annual profit of $800,000 during the reign of King Charles V, but now they bring in only two-thirds of that amount. All in all it's estimated that $1,800,000 is the current yearly return for the whole pearl-harvesting industry."

"But," Conseil asked, "haven't some famous pearls been quoted at extremely high prices?"

"Yes, my boy. They say Julius Caesar gave Servilia a pearl worth $24,000 in our currency."

"I've even heard tell," the Canadian said, "of a lady in ancient times who drank pearls in vinegar."

"Cleopatra," Conseil shot back.

"It must have tasted awful," Ned Land added.

"Abominable, Ned my friend," Conseil replied. "But when a little glass of vinegar is worth $300,000, its taste is a small price to pay."

"I'm sorry I didn't marry the gal," the Canadian said, throwing up his hands and looking discouraged.

"Ned Land married to Cleopatra?" Conseil exclaimed.

"But I was supposed to walk down the aisle, Conseil," the Canadian replied in all seriousness, "and it wasn't my fault the whole business fell through. I even bought a pearl necklace for my fiancée, Kate Tender, but she married somebody else instead. Well, that necklace cost me only $1.50, but you can absolutely trust me on this, professor—its pearls were so big, they wouldn't have gone through that strainer with twenty holes."

"My gallant Ned, those were imitation pearls," I replied, laughing. "Ordinary glass beads whose insides are coated with a product called Essence of the East."

"Golly," the Canadian replied, "that Essence of the East must go for quite a price."

"Next to nothing! It comes from the scales of a European carp, it's merely a silvery substance that collects in the water and is preserved in ammonia. It's practically worthless."

"Maybe that's why Kate Tender married somebody else," Mr. Land replied philosophically.

"But getting back to pearls of real value," I said, "I don't think any sovereign ever owned a finer one than the pearl belonging to Captain Nemo."

"This one?" Conseil said, pointing to a magnificent jewel ensconced in its glass case.

"Exactly, and I wouldn't be far off if I put its value at 400,000 . . . uh . . ."

"Dollars!" Conseil said instantly.

"Right," I said, "$400,000! And no doubt all it cost our captain was the effort of picking it up."

"Ha!" Ned Land exclaimed. "During our stroll tomorrow, who says we won't run into one just like it?"

"Nonsense!" Conseil put in.

"And why not?"

"What good would a pearl worth millions do us here on the *Nautilus?*"

"Here, not much," Ned Land said. "But elsewhere . . ."

"Oh, elsewhere!" Conseil put in, shaking his head.

"Actually," I said, "Mr. Land is right. And if we ever brought back to Europe or America a pearl worth millions, it would make the story of our adventures more believable—and a bit more rewarding."

"That's how I see it," the Canadian said.

"But," said Conseil, who always got back to the educational side of things, "is this pearl fishing ever dangerous?"

"No," I replied quickly, "especially if you take definite precautions."

"What risks would there be in a job like that?" Ned Land said. "Swallowing a couple gulps of salt water?"

"If you say so, Ned." Then, trying to mimic Captain Nemo's carefree tone, I asked, "By the way, gallant Ned, you aren't afraid of sharks, are you?"

"Me?" the Canadian replied. "I'm a professional harpooner. It's my job to poke fun at 'em!"

"It isn't a matter," I said, "of fishing for them with a swivel hook, hoisting them onto the deck of a ship, chopping their tails off with a swipe of the ax, slicing their bellies open, tearing their hearts out, and tossing them into the sea."

"So it's a matter of . . . ?"

"Yes, exactly."

"In the water?"

"In the water."

"Ye gods, just give me a good harpoon! You see, sir, sharks are poorly designed. In order to snap you up, they have to flip their bellies over, and in the meantime . . ."

Ned Land had a way of saying the word "snap" that sent chills down your spine.

"Well, how about you, Conseil? What are your feelings about these man-eaters?"

"Me?" Conseil said. "I'm afraid I must be frank with master."

Good for you, I thought.

"If master faces those sharks," Conseil said, "I see no reason why his loyal manservant shouldn't face them with him!"

27

A Pearl Worth $2,000,000

NIGHT FELL. I went to bed. I didn't sleep very well. Man-eaters played a major role in my dreams. And I found it more or less appropriate that the French word for shark, *requin*, has its linguistic roots in the word *requiem*.

The next day at four o'clock in the morning, I was awakened by the steward whom Captain Nemo had assigned expressly to me. I quickly got up, dressed, and went into the lounge.

Captain Nemo was waiting for me.

"Are you ready, Professor Aronnax?" he said to me.

"I'm ready."

"Kindly follow me."

"What about my companions, captain?"

"They've been alerted and they're waiting for us."

"Aren't we going to put on our diving suits?" I asked.

"Not yet. I haven't let the *Nautilus* pull too near the coast, and we're fairly well out from the Mannar oyster bed. But I have the skiff ready, and it will take us right to our jumping-off place and spare us a fairly long trek. It's carrying our diving equipment, and we'll suit up just before we start our underwater exploring."

Captain Nemo took me to the central companionway, whose steps led to the platform. Ned and Conseil were there, excited about the "pleasure trip" getting under way. Oars poised, five of the *Nautilus*'s sailors were waiting for us aboard the skiff, which was tied up alongside.

The night was still dark. Layers of clouds blanketed the sky and left only a few stars in view. My eyes flew to the side where land lay, but all I saw was a fuzzy line covering three-quarters of the horizon from southwest to northwest. Going up Ceylon's west coast during the night, the *Nautilus* lay west of the bay, or rather that gulf formed by the mainland and Mannar Island. Under these dark waters stretched the bed of shellfish, an inexhaustible field of pearls over twenty miles long.

Captain Nemo, Conseil, Ned Land, and I sat in the stern of the skiff. The longboat's coxswain took the tiller; his four companions leaned into their oars; we loosed our moorings and pulled clear.

The skiff headed southward. The rowers were in no hurry. I watched their oars vigorously catch the water, but they always paused ten seconds between strokes, following the practice used in most navies. While the longboat coasted, water drops flicked from the oars and hit the dark troughs of the billows, pitter-pattering like trickles of molten lead. A mild swell, coming in from well out, made the skiff roll gently, and the crests of a few waves lapped at its bow.

We sat in silence. What was Captain Nemo thinking about? Maybe that this nearby shore was too close for comfort, contrary to the Canadian's views in which it still seemed too far away. As for Conseil, he was there out of simple curiosity.

Near 5:30 the first tints on the horizon gave clearer emphasis to the upper edge of the coastline. It was fairly flat to the east but swelled a little toward the south. Five miles still separated it from us, and its beach merged with the misty waters. Between there and our skiff, the sea was deserted. Not a boat, not a diver. Absolute solitude reigned over this gathering place of pearl fishermen. As Captain Nemo had commented, we were arriving in these waterways a month too soon.

At six o'clock daylight suddenly appeared, with that speed characteristic of the tropical regions, which experience no actual dawn or dusk. The sun's rays pierced the curtain of clouds piled up on the easterly horizon and Old Sol rose swiftly.

I could clearly see the shore, which featured a few sparse trees here and there.

The skiff moved on toward Mannar Island, which curved to the south. Captain Nemo got up from his thwart and scanned the sea.

He gave the signal to drop anchor, but its chain barely ran because the bottom lay little more than a yard down; this locality was one of the shallowest spots near the bed of shellfish. The skiff immediately wheeled around in the outbound pull of the ebb tide.

"Here we are, Professor Aronnax," Captain Nemo said. "You see this confined bay? A month from now in this same spot, all the fishing boats of the harvesters will gather, and these are the waters their divers will ransack so daringly. This bay is conveniently laid out for their type of fishing. It's sheltered from strong winds, and the sea is never very rough, highly favorable conditions for diving work. Now let's put on our underwater suits and we'll begin our stroll."

I didn't reply, and while looking at those suspicious waves, I started to put on my heavy aquatic clothes, helped by the longboat's sailors. Captain Nemo and my two companions suited up as well. None of the *Nautilus*'s men were to go with us on this new excursion.

Soon we were enclosed up to the neck in india-rubber clothing, and the air devices were strapped on our backs. As for the Ruhmkorff device, it didn't seem to be in the picture. Before I stuck my head into its brass covering, I commented on this to the captain.

"Our lanterns won't be necessary," the captain answered me. "We aren't going very deep, and the sun's rays will be sufficient to light our path. Besides, it isn't a good idea to carry an electric lamp under these waves. Its glow might accidentally attract certain dangerous denizens of these waterways."

As Captain Nemo spoke these words, I turned to Conseil and Ned Land. But my two friends had already stuffed their skulls into their metal headgear and they couldn't hear me or answer me back.

I had one question left to ask Captain Nemo.

"How about our weapons?" I inquired. "Our rifles?"

"Rifles! What for? Don't your mountaineers attack bears knife in hand, and isn't steel surer than lead? Here's a sturdy blade. Slip it under your belt and let's be off."

I looked at my companions. They were armed in the same way, and furthermore Ned Land was brandishing an enormous harpoon he'd stowed in the skiff before leaving the *Nautilus*.

After that, following the captain's example, I went ahead and donned my heavy brass helmet; our air tanks immediately started to operate.

A second later the longboat's sailors helped us overboard one at a time, and we stood on level sand in about five feet of water. Captain Nemo gave us a hand signal. We followed him down a gentle slope and vanished under the waves.

There my obsessive fears left me. I grew surprisingly calm again. The ease with which I could move increased my confidence, and the many strange sights captivated my imagination.

The sun was already sending sufficient light beneath the waves. The tiniest objects remained visible. After ten minutes of walking, we were about sixteen feet under, and the terrain was now nearly level.

Like a covey of snipe in a marsh, schools of unusual fish rose under our feet, members of the swamp eel genus that have no fin besides their tail. I identified a Javanese moray, a thirty-inch snake with a bluish gray belly, which, without the gold stripes down its sides, you could easily confuse with the conger eel. From the butterfish genus, whose bodies are flat and oval-shaped, I noticed several adorned with dazzling colors and sporting a sickle-shaped dorsal fin, edible fish that when dried and marinated make a splendid dish known by the name *karawade;* then some alligatorfish from the genus *Aspidophoroides* whose bodies are covered with a suit of scaly armor that's divided into eight lengthwise sections.

Meanwhile the sun got progressively higher, lighting up this mass of water more and more. The seafloor changed gradually. Its fine-grained sand turned into an actual causeway of smooth crags covered with a carpet of mollusks and zoophytes. Among other specimens in these two branches, I noted some windowpane shells with thin, different-sized valves, a type of oyster characteristic of the Red Sea and the Indian Ocean, orange lucina clams with circular valves, auger shells, some of those Persian purpura shells that furnish the *Nautilus* with such wonderful dye, six-inch spiky rock snails that reared up under the waves like hands ready to grab you, turban snails with shells made of horn and garnished with spines all over, lamp shells, edible duck clams that feed the Hindu marketplace, purple-striped jellyfish that were mildly luminous, and finally some wonderful *Oculina flabelliforma,* magnificent sea fans that fashion one of the lushest tree forms in this ocean.

In the midst of this moving vegetation, legions of clumsy articulata darted under the arbors of water plants, especially some spanner crabs whose carapaces form a slightly rounded triangle, robber crabs specific to these waterways, and horrible elbow crabs whose appearance was repulsive to the eye. One equally hideous creature I saw several times was the enormous crab that Mr. Darwin came across, a crab which nature has given the instinct and strength needed to feed on coconuts; it scrambles up trees on the beach and knocks their coconuts down—they hit the ground and crack, then the creature opens them with its powerful pincers. Here, beneath these clear waves, this crab raced around with matchless agility, while green turtles from the species that frequents the Malabar coast moved slowly among the loose boulders.

Around seven o'clock we finally surveyed the bed of shellfish, where pearl oysters reproduce by the millions. These valuable mollusks cling to rocks, where they're firmly attached by a mass of brown filaments that keeps them from moving around. In this respect nature has made oysters inferior even to mussels, which can still go off for a change of scene.

The shellfish *Meleagrina*, a womb for pearls whose valves are nearly the same size, has a round shell with thick walls and a very rough outside. Some of these shells had layered surfaces and were furrowed with greenish bands that radiated down from the top. These were the young oysters. The others had black, rugged exteriors, measured up to six inches across, and were ten or more years old.

Captain Nemo pointed to this prodigious heap of shellfish, and I saw that these mines were literally inexhaustible, since nature's creative powers outstrip man's destructive tendencies. True to those tendencies, Ned Land promptly stuffed the finest of these mollusks into a net he carried at his side.

But we couldn't stop. We had to follow the captain, who seemed to be heading down paths only he knew. The seafloor rose sharply, and when I raised my arms, they sometimes reached above the surface of the sea. Then that eccentric oyster bed sank again. Often we went around high pointed rocks rising like pyramids. In their dark crevices huge crustaceans were poised on their long legs like engines of war and watched us with unblinking eyes, while under our feet crawled bloodworms, annelid worms, and bristleworms from the genus *Myrianida* and the genus *Aricia*, whose antennas and tentaclelike feelers were unbelievably long.

Just then a huge cave opened up in front of us, scooped out of a picturesque heap of rocks whose smooth heights were completely covered with underwater vegetation. At first it seemed pitch-black in this cave. The sun's rays inside seemed to fade gradually. Their faint transparency became nothing more than a blurred, far-away light.

Captain Nemo went in. We followed him. My eyes soon got used to this comparative gloom. I could make out the eccentrically contoured springings of a vault that was supported by natural pillars standing on a firm foundation of granite, like the heavy columns of Tuscan architecture. Why had our inscrutable guide taken us into the depths of this underwater crypt? I would soon find out.

After going down a fairly steep slope, our feet stepped onto the floor of a sort of circular pit. There Captain Nemo stopped and pointed to an object I hadn't yet noticed.

It was an oyster of extraordinary dimensions, a stupendous giant clam, a holy water font that could have held a lake, a basin more than six feet across, hence even bigger than the one adorning the *Nautilus*'s lounge.

I went up to this phenomenal mollusk. Its mass of filaments attached it to a slab of granite and there it grew by itself in the midst of the cave's calm waters. I estimated that this giant clam weighed over 650 pounds. Consequently such an oyster held more than 30 pounds of meat, and you would need the belly of King Gargantua to eat a couple dozen.

Captain Nemo was clearly aware of this bivalve's existence. It wasn't the first time he'd paid the creature a visit, and I figured his only reason for leading us to this locality was to show us a natural curiosity. I was wrong. Captain Nemo had a vested interest in checking on the current status of this giant clam.

The mollusk's two valves were half open. The captain went up and stuck his knife between the shells to discourage any ideas about closing; then with his other hand he raised the fringed, membranous tunic that made up the creature's mantle.

There, between its leafy folds, I saw a loose pearl as big as a coconut. Its globular shape, perfect clarity, and wonderful orient made it a jewel of incalculable value. Carried away by curiosity, I reached out a hand to take it, weigh it, fondle it! But the captain stopped me, signaled no, removed his knife in one quick motion, and let the two valves snap shut.

I realized what Captain Nemo's objective was. By leaving the pearl buried beneath the giant clam's mantle, he allowed it to grow gradually. With each year that went by, the mollusk's secretions added new concentric layers. The captain alone knew about the cave where this wonderful fruit of nature was "ripening"; he alone was rearing it, so to speak, in order to transfer it one day to his beloved museum. Maybe, following the examples of oyster farmers in China and India, he'd even predetermined the creation of this pearl by sticking some piece of glass or metal under the mollusk's folds, where it was gradually covered with mother-of-pearl. In any event, comparing this pearl to others I'd heard of and to those gleaming in the captain's collection, I estimated it was worth at least $2,000,000. It was a marvelous natural curiosity rather than a luxurious jewel, because I don't know of any woman with an ear that could handle it.

Our visit to this well-to-do giant clam was over. Captain Nemo left the cave, and we went back up to the bed of shellfish, in the midst of those clear waters not yet troubled by divers at work.

We walked by ourselves, honest-to-goodness loiterers stopping or straying as our fancies dictated. Speaking for myself, I no longer worried about those dangers my imagination had so ridiculously exaggerated. The shallows drew noticeably closer to the surface of the sea, and soon I was walking in little more than three feet of water, my head well above the level of the ocean. Conseil rejoined me, and gluing his huge brass helmet to mine, he gave me a friendly hello with his eyes. But this elevated plateau was only several yards long, and soon we reentered Our Element. I believe I'm now qualified to give it that label.

Ten minutes later Captain Nemo came to a sudden stop. I thought he'd called a halt so we could turn and start back. Not so. He motioned for us to crouch beside him at the foot of a wide crevice. He gestured toward a spot within the mass of liquid, and I looked hard in that direction.

Sixteen feet away a shadow appeared and dropped to the seafloor. The alarming idea of sharks crossed my mind. But I was wrong, and once again we didn't have to deal with monsters of the deep.

It was a man, a living man, an East Indian Negro, a poor devil of a fisherman who undoubtedly had come to gather what he could before harvest time. I saw the bottom of his dinghy, moored a few feet above his head. He would dive and go back up in quick succession. A stone cut in the shape of a sugar loaf (which he gripped between his feet while a rope connected it to his boat) helped him sink more quickly to the ocean floor. That was the extent of his equipment. Arriving on the sea bottom at a depth of about sixteen feet, he dropped to his knees and stuffed his sack with shellfish gathered at random. Then he went back up, emptied his sack, reeled in his stone, and started all over again, the whole process lasting just thirty seconds.

This diver didn't see us. The crags cast a shadow that hid us from his view. And besides, how could this poor East Indian ever have guessed that human beings, creatures like himself, were near him under the waters, eavesdropping on his movements, not missing a single detail of his fishing!

So he went up and down several times. He only gathered about ten shellfish per dive, because he had to tear them from the beds where each clung with its tough mass

of filaments. And how many oysters were lacking those pearls for which he risked his life!

I watched him intently. His movements were methodical, and for half an hour no danger seemed to threaten him. So I'd gotten used to the sight of this interesting fishing, when all at once, just as the East Indian was kneeling on the seafloor, I saw him make a gesture of alarm, stand, and gather himself to spring back to the surface of the waves.

I understood his fear. A gigantic shadow appeared above the poor diver. It was a shark of huge size, moving in diagonally, eyes fiery, jaws wide open!

I was speechless with horror and couldn't move a muscle.

With one mighty stroke of its fins, the voracious creature shot toward the East Indian, who jumped aside and dodged the shark's teeth but not its thrashing tail, which struck him across the chest and laid him out on the seafloor.

This episode took barely a few seconds. The shark returned, flipped over on its back, and was getting ready to bite the East Indian in half, when Captain Nemo, who was stationed next to me, suddenly stood up. Then, knife in hand, he went straight for the monster, all set to fight it at close quarters.

Just as it was going to snap up the poor fisherman, the man-eater saw its new opponent, flipped onto its belly again, and headed swiftly toward him.

I can see Captain Nemo's bearing to this day. Bracing himself, he waited for the fearsome man-eater with wonderful composure, and when the latter rushed at him, the captain jumped aside with prodigious agility, dodged the blow, and buried his knife in its belly. But that wasn't the end of the story. A dreadful battle broke out.

The shark bellowed, so to speak. Blood poured into the waves from its wounds. The sea was dyed red, and through that opaque liquid I couldn't see a thing.

Not till there was a rift in the clouds, and I spotted the daring captain clinging to one of the creature's fins, fighting his foe at close quarters, riddling the monster's belly with thrusts from his knife yet unable to deliver the finishing stroke, in other words, stab it to the heart. The man-eater struggled so furiously, it churned up a swirling mass of water that threatened to topple me over.

I wanted to run to the captain's rescue. But I was transfixed with horror and couldn't move.

I watched, wild-eyed. I saw the fight enter a new phase. The captain fell to the seafloor, toppled by the enormous mass weighing him down. Then the shark's jaws opened astoundingly wide, like a pair of industrial shears, and it would have been all over for the captain, if Ned Land hadn't rushed forward as quick as thought and driven the dreadful point of his harpoon into the shark's underside.

Masses of blood filled the surging waves while the man-eater thrashed around with indescribable fury. Ned Land hadn't missed his target. This was the monster's death rattle. Pierced to the heart, it was writhing in frightful spasms whose aftershocks toppled Conseil off his feet.

Meanwhile Ned Land pulled the captain clear. Unharmed, the latter got up, went right to the East Indian, quickly cut the rope tying the man to his stone, took the fellow in his arms, gave a sharp kick of the heel, and rose to the surface of the sea.

The three of us followed him, and in a few seconds, miraculously safe, we'd reached the fisherman's longboat.

Captain Nemo's first priority was to revive that unfortunate man. I wasn't too sure he would succeed. But I hoped so since the poor devil hadn't been underwater very long. However that stroke from the shark's tail could have been his deathblow.

Luckily, thanks to energetic massaging by Conseil and the captain, the nearly drowned man came to little by little as I watched. He opened his eyes. How startled he must have been, how terrified even, at seeing four huge brass heads leaning over him!

And above all, what was he to think when Captain Nemo took a bag of pearls from a pocket in his diving suit and gave it to him? The poor East Indian from Ceylon accepted these magnificent alms from the Man of the Waters with trembling hands. His frightened eyes further revealed that he didn't know to what superhuman beings he owed both his life and his fortune.

At the captain's signal we went back to the bed of shellfish; returning in our tracks, we walked for half an hour till we came to the anchor connecting the seafloor with the *Nautilus*'s skiff.

Back on board, the sailors helped us remove our heavy brass carapaces.

Captain Nemo spoke first to the Canadian.

"Thank you, Mr. Land," he told him.

"Tit for tat, captain," Ned Land replied. "I owed it to you."

The ghost of a smile glided over the captain's lips, and that was all.

"Back to the *Nautilus*," he said.

The longboat flew over the waves. A few minutes later we came across the shark's carcass, floating.

From the black markings on the tips of its fins, I identified it as one of those dreadful reef sharks found in the Indian Ocean, a variety in the species of sharks proper. It was over twenty-five feet long; its enormous mouth took up a third of its body. We could tell it was an adult from the six rows of teeth that formed an isosceles triangle in its upper jaw.

Conseil looked at it with a purely scientific interest, and I'm sure he placed it, not without good reason, in the class of cartilaginous fish, order Chondropterygii with fixed gills, family Selachii, genus *Squalus*.

While I was studying this inert mass, a dozen of those voracious reef sharks suddenly appeared around our longboat; but they paid no attention to us, pounced on the carcass, and quarreled over every scrap of it.

By 8:30 we were back aboard the *Nautilus*.

There I got to thinking about the incidents marking our excursion over the Mannar oyster bed. Two impressions were unavoidable. One concerned Captain Nemo's matchless bravery, the other his dedication to a human being, a representative of that race from which he'd fled under the seas. Despite what he'd said, this strange man still hadn't managed to fully do away with his heart.

When I shared these impressions with him, he answered me in a tone touched with emotion:

"That East Indian, professor, lives in the land of the oppressed, and till my last breath I'll remain a native of that same land!"

28
THE RED SEA

DURING THE DAY of January 29, the island of Ceylon vanished below the horizon, and at a speed of twenty miles per hour, the *Nautilus* glided into that labyrinth of channels separating the Maldive and Laccadive islands. It even hugged Kiltan Island, madreporic in origin, discovered by Vasco da Gama in 1499, and one of nineteen chief islands in the island group of the Laccadives, which are located between latitude 10° and 14° 30′ north, and between longitude 50° 72′ and 69° east.

By then we'd fared 16,220 miles, or 7,500 leagues, from our starting point in the seas of Japan.

The next day, January 30, when the *Nautilus* rose to the surface of the ocean, there was no more land in sight. Setting its course to the north-northwest, the ship headed toward the Gulf of Oman, scooped out between India's peninsula and Arabia and providing access to the Persian Gulf.

Obviously this was a blind alley with no possible way through. So where was Captain Nemo taking us? I couldn't say. Which didn't please the Canadian, who asked me that day where we were heading.

"We're heading, Mr. Ned, wherever the captain's fancy takes us."

"His fancy won't get us very far," the Canadian replied. "The Persian Gulf hasn't any way through, and if we go into it, we'll be back out again in no time."

"All right, so we will, Mr. Land, and if the *Nautilus* wants to visit the Red Sea after the Persian Gulf, the Strait of Bab el Mandeb will still be there to let us in."

"I don't need to tell you, sir," Ned Land replied, "that the Red Sea is as landlocked as the gulf, since the Isthmus of Suez still isn't cut through all the way; and even if it was, a boat as secretive as ours wouldn't dare go into a canal intersected with locks. So the Red Sea won't be our route back to Europe either."

"But I didn't say we were going back to Europe."

"What do you figure, then?"

"I figure that after visiting these unusual waterways of Arabia and Egypt, the *Nautilus* will head back down to the Indian Ocean, maybe through Mozambique Channel, maybe off the Mascarene Islands, and then make for the Cape of Good Hope."

"And once we've reached the Cape of Good Hope?" the Canadian asked with typical stubbornness.

"Well then, we'll enter that Atlantic Ocean we haven't yet gotten to know. What's wrong, Ned my friend? Are you tired of this voyage under the seas? Are you bored with this constantly changing parade of underwater wonders? Speaking for myself, I'll be tremendously sorry to see the end of a voyage like this, which so few men will ever be able to make."

"But don't you realize, Professor Aronnax," the Canadian replied, "that soon we'll have been imprisoned for three whole months aboard this *Nautilus?*"

"No, Ned, I didn't realize it, I would rather not realize it, and I don't keep track of every hour in the day."

"But when will it be over?"

"In its own good time. Meanwhile there's nothing we can do about it, and these discussions are pointless. My gallant Ned, if you come and tell me, 'We have a chance to escape,' then I'll discuss it with you. But this isn't the case, and to tell the truth, I don't think Captain Nemo ever ventures into European seas."

As you can see from this brief exchange, in my obsession with the *Nautilus* I'd turned into the spitting image of its commander.

As for Ned Land, he ended our dialogue with a solo number: "That's all fine and dandy. But in my humble opinion, a life in jail is a life without joy."

For four days till February 3, the *Nautilus* inspected the Gulf of Oman at various speeds and depths. It seemed to be traveling at random, as if hesitating over which course to follow, but it never went beyond the Tropic of Cancer.

After leaving this gulf, we raised Muscat for an instant, the most important town in the country of Oman. I marveled at its strange appearance, its white houses and forts standing out against the black rocks surrounding it. I spotted the curving domes of its mosques, the stylish spires of its minarets, and its fresh, leafy terraces. But it was only a fleeting vision, and the *Nautilus* soon plunged under the dark waves of those waterways.

Then our ship cruised along six miles off the Arabic coasts of Mahra and Hadhramaut, the undulating lines of their mountains relieved by a few ancient ruins. On February 5 we finally stood into the Gulf of Aden, a genuine funnel inserted in the neck of Bab el Mandeb and bottling India's waters in the Red Sea.

On February 6 the *Nautilus* cruised in sight of Aden, perched on a promontory that was connected to the mainland by a narrow isthmus, a sort of impregnable Gibraltar whose fortifications the English rebuilt after capturing it in 1839. I glimpsed the octagonal minarets of this town, which used to be the wealthiest, busiest emporium on this coast, as the Arab historian Idrisi tells it.

I was positive that once Captain Nemo made it to this point, he would back out again; but I was mistaken, and much to my surprise he did nothing of the sort.

The next day, February 7, we entered the Strait of Bab el Mandeb, whose name means "Gate of Tears" in the Arabic language. It's twenty miles wide but only thirty-two long, so with the *Nautilus* launched at full speed, going through it was the work of barely an hour. But I didn't see a thing, not even Perim Island where the British government built fortifications to bolster Aden's position. Many English and French steamers were plowing this narrow passageway, liners going from Suez to Bombay, Calcutta, Melbourne, Réunion Island, and Mauritius—far too much traffic for the *Nautilus* to make an appearance on the surface. So it wisely stayed in midwater.

439

By noon we were finally plowing the waves of the Red Sea.

The Red Sea, that huge lake so famous from biblical times, is rarely replenished by rains, fed by no major rivers, continually drained by a high rate of evaporation, and afflicted with a water level that drops five feet every year! If it were totally landlocked like a lake, this odd gulf maybe would have dried up completely; on this score it's inferior to its neighbors, the Caspian Sea and the Dead Sea, whose levels lower only to the point where their evaporation exactly equals the amount of water they take in.

This Red Sea is 1,600 miles long with an average width of 150. In the days of the Ptolemies and the Roman emperors, it was the world's foremost commercial thoroughfare, and when its isthmus has been cut all the way through, it will completely regain that bygone importance, which the Suez railways have already brought back in part.

I wouldn't even attempt to understand the whim that influenced Captain Nemo to take us into this gulf. But I wholeheartedly approved of the *Nautilus*'s entering it. The ship adopted a moderate pace, sometimes staying on the surface, sometimes diving to dodge some vessel, and so I could study both the inside and topside of this highly unusual sea.

On February 8, right at the first hours of daylight, Mocha came in sight, a town now in ruins—whose walls will crumble at the mere sound of a cannon—and which shelters a few leafy date trees here and there. This once-important city used to have six public marketplaces, twenty-six mosques, and fourteen forts protecting its walls, which fashioned a two-mile girdle around it.

Then the *Nautilus* drew near the shores of Africa, where the sea is considerably deeper. Through the open panels and in a midwater as clear as crystal, we were able to study wonderful shrubs of shining coral and huge slabs of rock wrapped in splendid green furs of algae and fucus. What an indescribable sight, and what a variety of settings and scenery where the reefs and volcanic islands level off by the Libyan coast! But soon the *Nautilus* was hugging the eastern shore where these tree forms appeared in all their glory.

This was off the coast of Tihama, and there these zoophyte displays not only flourished below sea level, they also fashioned picturesque networks that unreeled as high as sixty feet *above* it; the latter were more whimsical but less colorful than the former, which kept their bloom thanks to the vital moisture of the waters.

How many delightful hours I spent in this way at the lounge window! How many new specimens of underwater flora and fauna I marveled at under the light of our electric beacon! Mushroom-shaped fungus coral, some slate-colored sea anemones including the species *Thalassianthus aster* among others, organ-pipe coral arranged like flutes and just begging for a puff from the god Pan, some shells characteristic of this sea that dwell in madreporic cavities and whose bases are shaped like squat spirals, and finally a thousand samples of a polypary I hadn't noticed till then—the common sponge.

First division in the polyp group, the class Spongiaria has been established by scientists just for this interesting item whose usefulness is beyond dispute. The sponge definitely isn't a plant, as some naturalists still believe, but an animal of the lowest order, a polypary inferior even to coral. Its animal nature isn't in doubt, and we can't accept even the views of the ancients, who regarded it as halfway between plant and animal. But I must admit that naturalists aren't in agreement on the structural makeup of sponges. For some it's a polypary, and for others such as Professor Milne-Edwards, it's a single solitary individual.

The class Spongiaria has about 300 species that are found in a large number of seas and even in certain streams, where they've been given the name freshwater sponges. But their waters of choice are the Red Sea and the Mediterranean near the Greek Isles or the coast of Syria. The specimens that reproduce and grow up in these parts are the soft, delicate bath sponges whose prices run as high as thirty dollars apiece—yellow sponges from Syria, hard sponges from Barbary, etc. But since I didn't have any hope of examining these zoophytes in the seaports of the Levant, from which we were separated by the uncrossable Isthmus of Suez, I had to be content with studying them in the waters of the Red Sea.

So I called Conseil to my side, while at an average depth of twenty-five to thirty feet, the *Nautilus* slowly skimmed all those lovely rocks along the easterly coast.

There sponges grew in all sorts of shapes, stalklike, leafy, globular, fingerlike. With reasonable accuracy they lived up to their nicknames of basket sponges, chalice sponges, cattail sponges, elk horn sponges, lion's paws, peacock's tails, and Neptune's gloves—monikers bestowed on them by fishermen, who are more poetically inclined than scientists. Smeared with a semiliquid, jellylike substance, the fibrous tissue of these sponges leaked continual trickles of water that had carried nutrients to each cell, then had been expelled by a contracting motion. This jellylike substance vanishes when the polyp dies, giving off ammonia as it decomposes. Finally all that's left are the fibers, either jellylike or made of horn, that constitute your household sponge, which turns a russet color and is used for various tasks depending on how elastic, porous, and durable it is.

These polyparies were clinging to rocks, the shells of mollusks, and even the stalks of water plants. They adorned the tiniest crevices, some spreading out, others standing or hanging like coral outgrowths. I told Conseil that sponges are fished up in two ways, by dragnet or by hand. The latter method calls for the services of a diver, but it's preferable because it's easier on the polypary's tissue, leaving it with a much higher market value.

Other zoophytes milling around these sponges consisted chiefly of a very elegant species of medusa; mollusks were represented by varieties of squid that are specific to the Red Sea, according to Professor d'Orbigny, and reptiles by green turtles that belonged to the species *Chelonia virgata* and that furnished our table with a dainty but wholesome dish.

As for fish, they were plentiful and often noteworthy. Here are the ones that the *Nautilus*'s nets most often hauled on board: rays, including blue-spotted rays that were oval in shape and brick red in color, their bodies dotted with irregular blue specks and recognizable from their jagged double stings, marbled stingrays with silver backs, blue stingrays with freckled tails, butterfly rays that looked like huge seven-foot cloaks flapping at middepth, totally toothless manta rays that were a type of cartilaginous fish closer to the shark, eighteen-inch trunkfish known as dromedaries that had humps ending in backward-curving stings, snakelike moray eels with silver tails and bluish backs plus brown pectorals edged in gray, harvestfish from the genus *Stromateus* decked out in thin gold stripes and the three colors of the French flag, sixteen-inch blennies from the species *Blennius garamit*, magnificent bar jacks handsomely embellished by seven black crosswise stripes with blue and yellow fins plus gold and silver scales, snooks, Red Sea goatfish with yellow heads, parrotfish, wrasse, triggerfish, gobies, etc., plus a thousand other fish common to the oceans we'd already visited.

On February 9 the *Nautilus* cruised through the widest part of the Red Sea, which is 190 miles across and lies between Suakin on the west coast and Qunfidha on the east coast.

At noon that day after our position fix, Captain Nemo climbed onto the platform, where I just happened to be. I vowed to not let him go below again without at least getting him to hint at his future plans. He came over as soon as he saw me, graciously offered me a cigar, and said to me:

"Well, professor, are you enjoying this Red Sea? Have you seen enough of its hidden wonders, its fish, zoophytes, gardens of sponges, and forests of coral? Did you get a glimpse of the towns built on its banks?"

"Yes, Captain Nemo," I replied, "and the *Nautilus* is wonderfully suited to this whole survey. Ah, it's a clever boat!"

"Yes, sir, clever, daring, and invulnerable! It has no fear of the Red Sea's dreadful storms or its currents and reefs."

"As a matter of fact," I said, "this sea is spoken of as one of the worst, and in the days of the ancients, if I'm not mistaken, it had an abominable reputation."

"Thoroughly abominable, Professor Aronnax. The Greek and Latin historians can't find a single thing to say in its favor, and the Greek geographer Strabo adds that it's especially rough during the rainy season and the period of summer prevailing winds. The Arab Idrisi, referring to it by the name Gulf of Colzoum, states that ships perished in large numbers on its sandbanks and that nobody risked navigating it by night. This, he claims, is a sea subject to frightful hurricanes, sprinkled with forbidding islands, and 'with nothing good to offer,' either on its surface or in its depths. And in all honesty the same views can also be found in Arrian, Agatharchides, and Artemidorus."

"It's easy to see," I remarked, "that those historians hadn't navigated aboard the *Nautilus*."

"True," the captain replied with a smile, "and in this respect the moderns aren't much farther along than the ancients. It took many centuries to discover the mechanical power of steam. Who knows if we'll see a second *Nautilus* in the next hundred years! Progress is slow, Professor Aronnax."

"That's a fact," I replied. "Your ship is a century ahead of its time, maybe several centuries. It would be a real shame if such a secret were to die with its inventor!"

Captain Nemo didn't reply. After a few minutes of silence:

"You were alluding," he said, "to the views of ancient historians on the dangers of navigating this Red Sea?"

"Right," I replied. "But weren't their fears exaggerated?"

"Yes and no, Professor Aronnax," answered Captain Nemo, who seemed to know "his Red Sea" by heart. "For a modern ship, well rigged, solidly built, and in control of its course thanks to obedient steam, some conditions are no longer hazardous that offered all sorts of perils to the vessels of the ancients. Just picture those early navigators venturing out in sailboats made of planks tied together with ropes of palm leaves, caulked with powdered resin, and smeared with dogfish grease. They didn't even have any instruments for taking their bearings, so they went by guesswork in the midst of currents they barely knew. Under such conditions shipwrecks must have been commonplace. But these days steamers running between Suez and the South Seas have nothing to fear from this bad-tempered gorge, despite the contrary winds of its monsoons. Their captains and passengers no longer prepare for departure with sacrifices to appease the gods, and after coming home, they don't traipse in wreaths and gold ribbons to say thanks at the local temple."

"Agreed," I said. "And steam seems to have done away with the gratitude in seamen's hearts. But since you appear to have made a special study of this sea, captain, could you tell me how it came by its name?"

"Many explanations exist on the subject, Professor Aronnax. Would you like to hear the views of a chronicler in the 14th century?"

"Gladly."

"This tale spinner claims the sea was given its name after the crossing of the Israelites, when the pharaoh perished in those waves that closed up again at Moses' command:

> *As a sign of this marvel, it's said*
> *that the sea turned a fiery red.*
> *And afterward it got its name*
> *from the color it became.*"

"An artistic explanation, Captain Nemo," I replied, "but I'm not quite content with it. So I'll ask you for your own personal views."

"Here they come. To my way of thinking, Professor Aronnax, this name 'Red Sea' should be regarded as a translation of the Hebrew word *Edrom*, and the ancients called it that simply because of the distinctive color of its waters."

"But so far all I've seen are clear waves, without any distinctive hue."

"No doubt, but as we move on to the far end of this gorge, you'll note its odd appearance. I can recall seeing the bay of El Tur totally red, like a lake of blood."

"And you attribute this color to the presence of microscopic algae?"

"Yes. It's a purplish, sticky substance produced by those puny seedlings known as trichodesmia, a million of which are needed to fill up 1/25 of a square inch. Maybe you'll run into some when we get to El Tur."

"So, Captain Nemo, this isn't the first time you've gone through the Red Sea aboard the *Nautilus?*"

"No, sir."

"Then, since you've already brought up the crossing of the Israelites and the catastrophe that befell the Egyptians, I would like to know if you've ever found any traces under the waters of that great historical event?"

"No, professor, and for an excellent reason."

"What?"

"That same locality where Moses crossed with all his people is now so full of sand, camels can barely get their legs wet. As you can appreciate, my *Nautilus* wouldn't have enough water for itself."

"And that locality is . . . ?" I asked.

"That locality lies a little above Suez in a sound that used to form a deep estuary when the Red Sea reached as far as the Bitter Lakes. Now, whether or not their crossing was literally miraculous, the Israelites did cross there on their way back to the Promised Land, and the pharaoh's army did perish at exactly that locality. So I think that excavating those sands would bring to light a good many weapons and tools of Egyptian origin."

"Clearly," I replied. "And for the sake of archaeology, let's hope that sooner or later such excavations really take place, once new towns are settled on the isthmus after the Suez Canal is cut through—a canal, by the way, of little use to a ship such as the *Nautilus!*"

"Surely, but highly useful to the world at large," Captain Nemo said. "The ancients fully understood the commercial value of connecting the Red Sea with the Mediterranean, but it never occurred to them to dig a canal between the two and instead they picked the Nile as their go-between. If we can trust tradition, it was most likely Egypt's King Sesostris who began digging the canal needed to join the Nile with the Red Sea. What's certain is that in 615 B.C., King

Necho II was hard at work on a canal that was fed by Nile water and ran through the Egyptian plains facing Arabia. This canal could be traveled in four days and it was so wide, two triple-tiered galleys could pass through it abreast. Its construction was continued by Darius the Great, son of Hystaspes, and very likely finished by King Ptolemy II. Strabo saw ships navigating through it; but the weakness of its slope between its starting point, near Bubastis, and the Red Sea left it navigable only a few months out of the year. This canal was open for business till the century of Rome's Antonine emperors; at that point it was closed down and covered with sand, subsequently reopened by Caliph Omar I of Arabia, then filled in for good around 761 or 762 A.D. by Caliph Al-Mansur—with the motive of cutting off supplies to Mohammed ibn Abdullah, who had rebelled against him. During his Egyptian campaign your General Napoleon Bonaparte found traces of the old works in the Suez desert, and when the tide caught him by surprise, he nearly perished just a few hours before rejoining his regiment in Hadjaroth, the very place where Moses had pitched camp 3,300 years before him."

"Well, captain, what the ancients didn't dare undertake, Mr. de Lesseps is now finishing up—when he connects these two seas, he'll shorten the route from Cadiz to India by 5,600 miles and he'll soon change Africa into an overgrown island."

"Yes, Professor Aronnax, and you have every right to be proud of your countryman. Such a man brings a nation more honor than even the greatest military commanders! Like so many others he started with problems and setbacks, but he triumphed because he has the volunteer spirit. And it's a sad thought that this endeavor, which should have been the work of an international body and which would have guaranteed that any administration went down in history, will succeed only because of the efforts of one man. So all hail to Mr. de Lesseps!"

"Yes, all hail to that great French citizen," I replied, quite surprised by the intensity with which Captain Nemo had just spoken.

"Unfortunately," he went on, "I can't take

you through that Suez Canal, but you'll be able to see the long jetties of Port Said when we're in the Mediterranean the day after tomorrow."

"In the Mediterranean!" I exclaimed.

"Yes, professor. Does that amaze you?"

"What amazes me is the idea that we'll be there the day after tomorrow."

"Oh really?"

"Yes, captain, though since I've been aboard your vessel, I should have formed the habit of not being amazed by anything!"

"But what is it that you find so startling?"

"The thought of how appallingly fast the *Nautilus* will need to go, if it's to double the Cape of Good Hope, circle Africa, and lie in the open Mediterranean by the day after tomorrow!"

"And who says it will circle Africa, professor? What's this talk about doubling the Cape of Good Hope?"

"But unless the *Nautilus* navigates on dry land and crosses over the isthmus—"

"Or under it, Professor Aronnax."

"Under it?"

"Surely," Captain Nemo replied serenely. "Long ago under this tongue of land, nature made the same thing that man is now making on its surface."

"What! There's a passageway?"

"Yes, an underground passageway I've named the Arabian Tunnel. It starts below Suez and ends in the Bay of Pelusium."

"But isn't that isthmus composed only of quicksand?"

"To a certain depth. But at just 165 feet down, you'll find a firm foundation of rock."

"And it's by luck that you discovered this passageway?" I asked, more and more surprised.

"Luck plus logic, professor, and logic even more than luck."

"Captain, I hear you, but I can't believe my ears."

"Oh, sir! *Aures habent et non audient!*[13] The old saying still holds true. Not only does this passageway exist, I've taken advantage

of it several times. Without it I wouldn't have ventured today into such a blind alley as the Red Sea."

"Am I out of line in asking how you discovered this tunnel?"

"Sir," the captain answered me, "there can be no secrets between men who will never leave each other."

I ignored this innuendo and waited for Captain Nemo's explanation.

"Professor," he told me, "the simple logic used by naturalists led me to discover this passageway, and only I know of its existence. I'd noted that in the Red Sea and the Mediterranean there are a number of absolutely identical species of fish, such as eels, harvestfish, wrasse, sand perch, smelt, and flying fish. Given this fact, I wondered if there wasn't some connection between the two seas. If there was, its underground current had to go from the Red Sea to the Mediterranean simply because of their difference in level. So I caught a large number of fish in the vicinity of Suez. I slipped brass rings over their tails and tossed them back into the sea. A few months later off the coast of Syria, I recaptured a few specimens of my fish, adorned with their telltale rings. This proved to me that some connection existed between the two seas. I searched for it with my *Nautilus*, I discovered it, I ventured into it; and soon, professor, you too will have gone through my Arabic tunnel!"

29

ARABIAN TUNNEL

THE SAME DAY, I reported to Conseil and Ned Land that part of the foregoing conversation that would immediately interest them. When I told them we would be lying in Mediterranean waters within two days, Conseil clapped his hands, but the Canadian shrugged his shoulders.

"An underwater tunnel!" he exclaimed. "A connection between two seas! Who ever heard of such malarkey!"

"Ned my friend," Conseil replied, "had you ever heard of the *Nautilus?* No, yet here it is! So don't shrug your shoulders

---

[13] *Translator's note.* Latin: "They have ears, but they hear not."

so blithely, and don't discount something with the feeble excuse that you've never heard of it."

"We'll see!" Ned Land fired back, shaking his head. "After all, I would like nothing better than to believe in your captain's passageway, and I hope to Heaven it really *does* take us to the Mediterranean."

The same evening, at latitude 21° 30′ north, the *Nautilus* cruised on the surface of the sea, drawing nearer to the Arab coast. I spotted Jidda, a major financial center for Egypt, Syria, Turkey, and India. I could make out its blocks of buildings pretty clearly, the ships tied up along its wharves, and those whose draft of water required them to drop anchor at the port's offshore mooring. The sun was fairly low on the horizon and beat down heavily on the houses in this town, bringing out their whiteness. Outside the city limits a few huts made of wood or reeds indicated the quarter where the bedouins lived.

Soon Jidda faded into the evening gloom, and the *Nautilus* went back beneath the mildly phosphorescent waters.

The next day, February 10, several ships appeared, running on our opposite tack. The *Nautilus* resumed its underwater navigating; but at the moment of our noon sights, the sea was deserted and the ship rose to its waterline again.

Along with Ned and Conseil, I went to sit on the platform. The coast to the east looked like a shapeless blur in the damp fog.

Leaning against the sides of the skiff, we were chatting about this and that, when Ned Land pointed to a spot at sea and said to me:

"Notice anything out there, professor?"

"No, Ned," I replied, "but I don't have your eyes, you know."

"Take a good look," Ned went on. "There, ahead to starboard, almost level with the beacon! Don't you see something moving around?"

"Right," I said after looking intently, "I can make out a long blackish object on the surface of the water."

"A second *Nautilus?*" Conseil said.

"No," the Canadian replied, "unless I'm badly mistaken, that's some marine animal."

"Are there whales in the Red Sea?" Conseil asked.

"Yes, my boy," I replied, "they're sometimes found here."

"That's no whale," continued Ned Land, whose eyes never strayed from the object they'd sighted. "We're old chums, whales and I, and I know their little ways."

"Let's wait and see," Conseil said. "The *Nautilus* is heading that direction, and before long we'll know what we're in for."

In fact that blackish object was soon just a mile away from us. It looked like a huge reef stranded in midocean. What was it? I still couldn't make up my mind.

"Oh no, it's moving off! It's diving!" Ned Land exclaimed. "Damnation! What kind of animal is it? It hasn't got a forked tail like baleen whales or sperm whales, and its fins look like amputated limbs."

"But if that's so—" I put in.

"Good Lord," the Canadian went on, "it's flipping over on its back and raising its breasts in the air!"

"It's a siren!" Conseil exclaimed. "With all due respect to master, it's an actual mermaid!"

This word "siren" got me on track, and I realized the animal belonged to the order Sirenia, marine creatures that folktales have turned into mermaids, half woman, half fish.

"No," I told Conseil, "it isn't a mermaid, it's a strange creature that's now very scarce in the Red Sea. That's a dugong."

"Order Sirenia, group Pisciforma, subclass Monodelphia, class Mammalia, branch Vertebrata," Conseil replied.

And when Conseil has spoken, there's nothing left to be said.

Meanwhile Ned Land kept on looking. His eyes were burning with desire at the sight of that animal. His hands were all set to hurl a harpoon. You would have sworn he was waiting for the right moment to jump overboard and attack the creature in its own element.

"Oh, sir," he told me in a voice trembling with excitement, "I've never hunted anything like *that!*"

His whole harpooner's soul was bound up in this last word.

Just then Captain Nemo appeared on the platform. He spotted the dugong. He understood the Canadian's frame of mind and spoke to him immediately:

"If you had a harpoon, Mr. Land, wouldn't your hands be itching to put it to work?"

"Positively, sir."

"So just for one day, it wouldn't displease you to go back to your fisherman's trade and add this cetacean to the list of your successes?"

"It wouldn't displease me a bit."

"All right, you can give it a try."

"Thank you, sir," Ned Land replied, his eyes ablaze.

"Only," the captain went on, "I urge you to take careful aim at this animal, in your own best interests."

"Are dugongs dangerous to attack?" I asked, despite the Canadian's shrug of the shoulders.

"Sometimes they are," the captain replied. "The beasts can turn on their attackers and capsize their longboats. But there's no danger of that with Mr. Land on the case. His eye is sharp, his arm is sure. If I recommend he aim carefully at this creature, it's because the dugong is justly regarded as a fine game animal, and I know Mr. Land never passes up a chance for a choice morsel."

"Aha!" the Canadian put in. "This critter offers the added luxury of being good to eat?"

"Yes, Mr. Land. Its flesh is actual red meat, highly prized and set aside throughout Malaysia for the tables of aristocrats. As a consequence this excellent animal has been hunted relentlessly, and just like its manatee relatives, it's growing scarcer and scarcer."

"If that's the case, captain," Conseil said in all seriousness, "on the off chance that this creature might be the last of its line, wouldn't it be advisable to spare its life, in the interests of science?"

"Maybe," the Canadian contended, "it would be better to hunt it down, in the interests of mealtime."

"Then proceed, Mr. Land," Captain Nemo replied.

Just then, as silent and unresponsive as ever, seven crewmen climbed onto the platform. One carried a harpoon and line like those used in whale fishing. After opening the skiff's cover panel, they yanked the longboat out of its niche and put it to sea. Six rowers sat down on the thwarts, and the coxswain took the tiller. Ned, Conseil, and I got situated in the stern.

"Aren't you coming, captain?" I asked.

"No, sir, but I wish you happy hunting."

The skiff pulled clear, and driven along by its six oars, it headed quickly toward the dugong, which by then was floating two miles from the *Nautilus*.

About a quarter of a mile from the cetacean, our longboat slowed down and the sculls dipped noiselessly into the tranquil waters. Harpoon in hand, Ned Land went and stood in the skiff's bow. Harpoons used for hunting whales are normally attached to a very long rope that pays out quickly when the wounded animal drags it after him. But this rope wasn't much longer than sixty feet, and its other end had simply been fastened to a small barrel, which would stay afloat and indicate the dugong's whereabouts underwater.

I got up and took a good look at the Canadian's opponent. This dugong, which also goes by the name halicore, closely resembled a manatee. Its oval body ended in an exceptionally long caudal fin and its side fins in actual fingers. It differs from a manatee in that its upper jaw boasts two long, pointed teeth that diverge to form tusks on either side.

This dugong Ned Land was about to attack was of colossal dimensions, easily exceeding twenty feet in length. It didn't stir and seemed to be sleeping on the surface of the waves, a circumstance that should make it easier to capture.

The skiff came up cautiously to within twenty feet of the animal. The oars hung in the air above their rowlocks. I stood up halfway. Arching his body slightly backward, Ned Land brandished his harpoon with expert hands.

Suddenly there was a hissing sound and the dugong vanished. Though the harpoon had been forcefully hurled, apparently it hit only water.

"Damnation!" yelled the furious Canadian. "I missed it!"

"No," I said, "the animal's wounded, there's its blood; but your weapon didn't stay in its body."

"My harpoon! Get my harpoon!" Ned Land exclaimed.

The sailors went back to their sculling, and the coxswain steered the longboat over to the floating barrel. The harpoon fished up, our skiff took off again after the animal.

From time to time the latter came back up to breathe at the surface of the sea. Its wound hadn't weakened it because it moved with tremendous speed. Propelled by powerful arms, the longboat flew on its trail. Several times we got within four or five yards of it, and the Canadian was all set to strike; but then the dugong would take his leave with a sudden dive, and it was impossible to catch up with the brute.

As you would expect, our impatient Ned Land lost his temper. He hurled at the hapless animal the noisiest cusswords in the English language. As for me, I was simply annoyed at seeing this dugong outsmart us time and again.

We chased it for a full hour without stopping, and I'd started to think it would be very hard to capture, when the animal got the ill-fated idea of taking revenge on us, a notion it would soon have good reason to regret. It wheeled on the skiff to attack us in its turn.

This move didn't escape the Canadian.

"Look alive!" he said.

The coxswain said a few words in his peculiar language, undoubtedly alerting his men to stay on their guard.

Arriving within twenty feet of the skiff, the dugong stopped and sharply sniffed the air with its huge nostrils, which weren't located on the tip but the topside of its muzzle. Then it gathered itself and sprang at us.

The skiff couldn't dodge the blow. Half overturned, it shipped a ton or two of water that we had to bail out. But thanks to our coxswain's skill, we were fouled at an angle rather than broadside, so we didn't capsize. Hanging onto the stempost, Ned Land thrust his harpoon again and again into the gigantic animal, which buried its teeth in our gunwale and lifted the longboat out of the water the way a lion would lift a deer. We were thrown on top of each other, and I'm not too sure how the venture would have ended, if the Canadian hadn't kept on relentlessly and finally stabbed the beast to the heart.

I heard a grinding of teeth on sheet iron, and the dugong vanished, taking our harpoon along with it. But the barrel soon came back to the surface, and a few seconds later the animal's body appeared, rolling belly up. The skiff rejoined it, took it in tow, and headed toward the *Nautilus*.

It required pulleys of great strength to hoist that dugong onto the platform. The beast weighed 5½ tons. They carved it up in sight of the Canadian, who stayed to oversee every detail of the operation. At dinner the same day, my steward served me a couple slices of this meat, skillfully prepared by the ship's cook. I found it excellent, better even than veal, if not beef.

The next morning, February 11, some additional pieces of delicate game enriched the *Nautilus*'s pantry. A covey of terns alighted on the *Nautilus*. They were a variety of *Sterna nilotica* characteristic of Egypt's shores: black beak, head gray and speckled, eyes encircled by white dots, back, wings, and tail grayish, belly and throat white, feet red. We also caught a couple dozen Nile duck, superior-tasting wildfowl whose neck and crown of the head are white with black spots.

By then the *Nautilus* had slowed down. It was just moseying along, you might say. I noticed that the Red Sea's water was growing less salty the closer we got to Suez.

Around five o'clock in the afternoon, we sighted Cape Ras Mohammed to the north. This cape forms the tip of Arabia Petraea, which lies between the Gulf of Suez and the Gulf of Aqaba.

The *Nautilus* entered the Strait of Jubal, which leads to the Gulf of Suez. I clearly made out a high mountain towering over Ras Mohammed between the two gulfs. It was Mt. Horeb, in the Bible called Mt. Sinai, the mountaintop where Moses met God face to face, that peak we always picture in our minds as being wreathed in lightning.

At six o'clock, sometimes floating and sometimes submerged, the *Nautilus* passed well out from El Tur, which sat at the far end of a bay whose waters seemed to be dyed red, as Captain Nemo had already commented. Then night fell in the midst of a heavy silence sometimes broken by the calls of pelicans and nocturnal birds, by the sound of surf dashing against rocks, or by the faraway moan of a steamer churning the waves of the gulf with noisy blades.

From eight to nine o'clock, the *Nautilus* stayed a few yards under the waters. According to my calculations we had to be very close to Suez. Through the panels in the lounge, I could see the rocky bottom in the brilliant lighting of our electric rays. It looked like the strait was getting narrower and narrower.

At 9:15, when our boat went back to the surface, I climbed onto the platform. I couldn't wait to go through Captain Nemo's tunnel, felt very restless, and had come up to breathe the fresh night air.

In the gloom I soon spotted a pale signal light glimmering a mile away, half discolored by the mist.

"A floating lighthouse," said somebody beside me.

I turned and found the captain.

"That's the floating signal light of Suez," he went on. "We'll be at the entrance to the tunnel before much longer."

"It can't be very easy to enter."

"No, sir. Accordingly it's my practice to stay in the pilothouse and direct operations myself. And now if you'll kindly go below, Professor Aronnax, the *Nautilus* is ready to sink under the waves and it will come back to the surface only after we've traveled through the Arabian Tunnel."

I followed Captain Nemo. The hatch closed, the ballast tanks filled with water, and the submersible sank some thirty feet down.

Just as I was getting ready to retire to my stateroom, the captain stopped me.

"Professor," he said to me, "would you like to go with me to the wheelhouse?"

"I was afraid to ask," I replied.

"Then come along. This way you'll get the full story on this combination underwater and underground navigating."

Captain Nemo led me to the central companionway. In midstair he opened a door, went along the upper corridors, and arrived at the wheelhouse, which, as you know, juts from one end of the platform.

It was a cabin six feet square and closely resembling those manned by the helmsmen of paddleboats on the Mississippi or Hudson rivers. An upright wheel stood in the center, connected to rudder chains that ran to the *Nautilus*'s stern. Four deadlights were inset in the cabin's walls, windows of biconvex glass that allowed the man at the helm to see in all directions.

The cabin was dark; but my eyes soon got used to this darkness and I saw the pilot, a muscular man whose hands were resting on the pegs of the wheel. Outside, the sea was brightly lit by the beacon shining behind the cabin at the other end of the platform.

"Now," Captain Nemo said, "let's look for our passageway."

Electric wires connected the pilothouse with the engine room, and from this cabin the captain could simultaneously signal heading and speed to his *Nautilus*. He pressed a metal button and at once the propeller slowed down significantly.

I looked in silence at the high sheer wall we were skirting just then, the firm base of the sandy mountains on the coast. For an hour we went along it in this manner, staying only a few yards away. Captain Nemo kept an eye on the two concentric circles of the compass hanging in the cabin. At a simple gesture from him, the helmsman would instantly change the *Nautilus*'s heading.

Standing by the port deadlight, I spotted magnificent support structures made of coral, plus zoophytes, algae, and crustaceans with enormous quivering claws that reached out from crevices in the rock.

At 10:15 Captain Nemo took the helm himself. A wide hallway, dark and deep, opened up in front of us. The *Nautilus* plunged boldly into it. There was a strange rumbling all around us. It was water from the Red Sea rushing down the tunnel's slope to the Mediterranean. Our engines tried to offer resistance by churning the waves with propeller in reverse, but the *Nautilus* went with the torrent, as swift as an arrow.

Along the narrow walls of this passageway, I saw only glittering streaks, hard lines, fiery furrows, all scribbled by our fast-moving electric light. My heart was pounding, and I pressed my hand against it.

At 10:35 Captain Nemo left the steering wheel and turned to me:

"The Mediterranean," he told me.

In less than twenty minutes, swept along by the torrent, the *Nautilus* had just gone under the Isthmus of Suez.

30
The Greek Isles

AT SUNRISE the next morning, February 12, the *Nautilus* rose to the surface of the waves. I rushed onto the platform. The blurred silhouette of Pelusium stood out three miles to the south. The torrent had carried us from one sea down to the other. But though that tunnel was easy to descend, going back up must have been impossible.

Around seven o'clock Ned and Conseil joined me. Those two inseparable companions had slept serenely, completely unaware of the feat that the *Nautilus* had performed.

"Well, Mr. Naturalist," the Canadian asked in a mildly mocking tone, "and how about that Mediterranean?"

"We're floating on its surface, Ned my friend."

"What!" Conseil put in. "Last night . . . ?"

"Yes, last night, in a matter of minutes, we went under that uncrossable isthmus."

"I don't believe a word of it," the Canadian responded.

"Then you're in the wrong, Mr. Land," I went on. "That flat coastline curving southward is the coast of Egypt."

"Tell it to the marines," countered the stubborn Canadian.

"But if master says so," Conseil told him, "then so be it."

"What's more, Ned," I said, "Captain Nemo himself did the honors in his tunnel, and I was right beside him in the pilothouse while he steered the *Nautilus* through that narrow passageway."

"You hear, Ned?" Conseil said.

"And you, Ned, who have such sharp eyes," I added, "you can spot the jetties of Port Said stretching out to sea."

The Canadian took a good look.

"It's the truth," he said. "You're right, professor, and your captain's a superman. We're in the Mediterranean. Fine. So now let's have a chat about our little doings, if you please, and let's be careful that nobody overhears us."

I could see what was coming. In any event I thought it would be better to let the Canadian have his chat, so the three of us went and sat next to the beacon, where we were less exposed to the damp spray from the billows.

"Now, Ned, we're all ears," I said. "What have you got to say?"

"What I've got to say is very simple," the Canadian replied. "We're in Europe, and before Captain Nemo's whims drag us deep into the polar seas or back to Oceania, I say we should leave this *Nautilus*."

I must admit that these discussions with the Canadian always baffled me. I didn't want to restrict my companions' freedom in any way, yet I had no desire to leave Captain Nemo. Thanks to him and his submersible, I was finishing my undersea research by the day and I was rewriting my book on the great ocean depths in the midst of the very element I was describing. Would I ever again have such an opportunity to study the ocean's wonders? Never! So I simply couldn't entertain this idea of leaving the *Nautilus* before completing our course of inquiry.

"Ned my friend," I said, "tell me the truth. Are you bored with this ship? Are you sorry that fate has left you in Captain Nemo's hands?"

The Canadian paused for a few seconds before replying. Then, folding his arms:

"To tell the truth," he said, "I'm not sorry about this voyage under the seas. I'll be glad to have done it, but in order to have done it, it's got to finish. That's my feeling."

"It will finish, Ned."

"Where and when?"

"Where, I don't know. When, I can't say. Or rather I suppose it will be over when these seas don't have anything left to show us. Everything that begins in this world has to come to an end."

"I agree with master," Conseil replied, "and it's highly likely that after we cross every sea on the globe, Captain Nemo will bid the three of us a fond farewell."

"Bid us a fond farewell?" the Canadian exclaimed. "You mean beat us to a fare-thee-well!"

"Let's not exaggerate, Mr. Land," I went on. "We have nothing to fear from the captain—but even so, I don't share Conseil's views. We're privy to the *Nautilus*'s secrets, and I don't expect that its commander, just to set us free, will meekly stand by while we spread those secrets all over the world."

"Then what *do* you expect?" the Canadian asked.

"That we're just as likely to find favorable conditions for escaping in six months as now."

"Great Scott!" Ned Land put in. "And where, if you please, will we be in six months, Mr. Naturalist?"

"Maybe here, maybe in China. You know how quickly the *Nautilus* moves. It crosses oceans the way swallows cross the air or express trains continents. It has no fear of heavily traveled seas. Who can say it won't hug the coasts of France, England, or America, where we could make our escape just as effectively as here."

"Professor Aronnax," the Canadian replied, "your arguments are rotten to the core. You talk way off in the future—'We'll be here, we'll be there!' Me, I'm talking about right now—here we are, and we've got to make the most of it!"

I was hard pressed by Ned Land's common sense and felt I was losing ground. I no longer knew what arguments to put forward on my behalf.

"Sir," Ned went on, "let's suppose that Captain Nemo, by all that's fantastic, offered your freedom to you right now. Would you accept?"

"I don't know," I replied.

"And suppose he adds that this offer he's making you right now won't ever be repeated, then would you accept?"

I didn't reply.

"And what thinks our friend Conseil?" Ned Land asked.

"Your friend Conseil," the fine lad replied serenely, "has nothing to say on this issue. He's a completely disinterested party. Like his master, like his comrade Ned, he's a bachelor. No wife, parents, or children are waiting for him back home. He's in master's employ, he thinks like master, he talks like master, and much to his regret, he can't be counted on to form a majority. Only two people are in this dispute: master on one side, Ned Land on the other. That said, your friend Conseil is all set to listen and keep score."

I couldn't help smiling as Conseil wiped himself out of existence. Deep down the Canadian must have been overjoyed at not having to contend with him.

"Then, sir," Ned Land said, "since Conseil is no more, we'll finish this discussion just between the two of us. I spoke my piece, you heard me out. What's your answer?"

It was obvious the matter had to be settled, and I hated the idea of stalling.

"Ned my friend," I said, "here's my answer. You're in the right, and my arguments don't hold up next to yours. It will never do to count on Captain Nemo's benevolence. The most ordinary good sense would keep him from setting us free. On the other hand, it also makes sense that we take advantage of the first opportunity we get to leave the *Nautilus*."

"Good, Professor Aronnax, now you're talking."

"But I have one comment," I said, "just one. The opportunity must be the real thing. Our first try has to succeed—if it backfires, we won't get a second chance, because Captain Nemo will never forgive us."

"That's also right on the money," the Canadian replied. "But your comment applies to any escape attempt, whether it's in two years or two days. So this question still has the same answer: if a promising opportunity comes up, we need to jump on it."

"Agreed. And now, Ned, will you tell me what you mean by a promising opportunity?"

"One that brings the *Nautilus* close to the coast of Europe on some cloudy night."

"And you'll try to get away by swimming?"

"Yes, if we're near enough to shore and the ship's floating on the surface. No, if we're well out and the ship's navigating underwater."

"And in that case?"

"In that case I'll try to lay hold of the skiff. I know how to handle it. We'll stick ourselves inside, undo the bolts, and rise to the surface, without the helmsman in the bow seeing a thing."

"Fine, Ned. Keep your eyes peeled for such an opportunity; but don't forget, one slipup will be the end of us."

"I won't forget, sir."

"And now, Ned, would you like to know my overall thinking on your plan?"

"Gladly, Professor Aronnax."

"Well then, I think—and I don't mean 'I hope'—that your promising opportunity won't ever come up."

"Why not?"

"Because Captain Nemo surely recognizes that we haven't given up all hope of recovering our freedom, and he'll keep on his guard, especially while navigating in sight of the European coast."

"I agree with master," Conseil said.

"We'll see," Ned Land replied, shaking his head with a determined expression.

"And now, Ned Land," I added, "let's leave it at that. Not another word on any of this. The day you're ready, alert us and we're with you. I leave it all up to you."

That's how we ended this conversation, which was to have such serious consequences later on. Right then, I must admit, events seemed to confirm my predictions, much to the Canadian's despair. Did Captain Nemo view us with distrust in those heavily traveled seas, or was he simply trying to keep out of sight of those ships of all nations that plow the Mediterranean? I have no idea, but usually he stayed in midwater and well out from any coast. The *Nautilus* would surface only

far enough for its pilothouse to emerge, or it would head for the lower depths, though between the Greek Isles and Asia Minor, we didn't find bottom even at 6,500 feet down.

Accordingly I became aware of the isle of Karpathos, one of the Sporades Islands, only when Captain Nemo put his finger over a spot on the world map and quoted me this verse by Virgil:

Est in Carpathio Neptuni gurgite vates Caeruleus Proteus...[14]

It really was that bygone abode of Proteus, the old shepherd of Neptune's flocks— an island located between Rhodes and Crete that Greeks now call Karpathos, Italians Scarpanto. Through the lounge window I could see only its granite bedrock.

The next day, February 14, I decided to spend a few hours studying the fish of this island group; but for whatever reason, the panels stayed hermetically sealed. After determining the *Nautilus*'s heading, I noted that it was proceeding toward the ancient island of Crete, also known as Candia. At the time I'd boarded the *Abraham Lincoln*, this whole island was in rebellion against its tyrannical overlords, the Ottoman Empire of Turkey. But since then I didn't have the faintest idea what had transpired with this revolution, and Captain Nemo, completely out of contact with the shore, wasn't the man to enlighten me.

So that evening I didn't allude to this event when I ended up alone with him in the lounge. Besides, he seemed closemouthed and preoccupied. Then, contrary to custom, he ordered both panels in the lounge to be opened and he went from one to the other, carefully studying that mass of water. What was he up to? I hadn't a clue and for my part I used the time to examine the fish passing in front of my eyes.

Among others I noted the three-bearded rockling that Aristotle mentions—it's popu-

---

[14] *Translator's note.* Latin: "Living in Neptune's domain by Karpathos, his agent is / sky-colored Proteus . . ."

larly known by the name sea loach and is characteristically found in the salty waters next to the Nile Delta. Nearby some semi-phosphorescent porgy were going past, a type of sea bream that the Egyptians listed with their sacred animals, honoring them in religious ceremonies when their arrival in the Nile's waters announced the fertile flood season. I likewise noted some foot-long wrasse, bony fish with transparent scales whose bluish gray color is mingled with red spots; they're enthusiastic eaters of marine vegetables, which gives them an exquisite flavor; accordingly these wrasse were much in demand among the epicures of ancient Rome, and their entrails were dressed with brains of peacock, tongue of flamingo, and testes of moray to make the divine platter that enraptured the Roman emperor Vitellius.

Another resident of these seas caught my attention and reawakened all my memories of antiquity. This was the remora, which travels attached to the bellies of sharks; as the ancients tell it, when these little fish stick to the underside of a ship, they can bring it to a halt, and by impeding Mark Antony's vessel during the Battle of Actium, one of them contributed to the victory of Augustus Caesar. From such slender threads hang the destinies of nations! I likewise noticed some wonderful snappers belonging to the family Lutjanidae, sacred fish for the Greeks, who believed these creatures could drive off sea monsters from the waters they frequent; their Greek name *Anthias* means "flower," and they live up to it with their glistening scales and the shifting gleams that turn their dorsal fins into watered silk; their coloring is confined to a gamut of reds from pale pink to radiant ruby. I couldn't take my eyes off these ocean wonders—when an unexpected sight suddenly gave me a jolt.

In the midst of the waters, a man appeared, a diver carrying a little leather bag at his belt. It wasn't a corpse lost in the waves. It was a living man, swimming energetically, vanishing at times to breathe at the surface, and instantly diving again.

I turned to Captain Nemo, and in an agitated voice:

"A man! A castaway!" I exclaimed. "We've got to rescue him at any cost!"

The captain didn't reply but went to lean against the window.

The man came up, glued his face to the panel, and looked at us.

To my deep astonishment Captain Nemo signaled to him. The diver answered with a gesture, immediately swam up to the surface of the sea, and didn't reappear.

"No need for concern," the captain told me. "That's Nicolas from Cape Matapan, nicknamed *Il Pesce*.[15] He's well known all around the Cyclades Islands. A bold diver! Water is his true element, and he lives in the sea more than on shore, going continually from one island to another, even as far as Crete."

"You know him, captain?"

"Why not, Professor Aronnax?"

With that Captain Nemo went to a cabinet standing by the lounge's left panel. Beside this cabinet I saw a chest bound with iron hoops, its lid bearing a brass plaque that displayed the *Nautilus*'s monogram with its motto *Mobilis in Mobili*.

Just then, ignoring my presence, the captain opened this cabinet, a sort of safe that held a large number of ingots.

They were gold ingots. And they represented an enormous sum of money. Where had this precious metal come from? How had the captain amassed this gold, and what was he planning to do with it?

I didn't say a word. I watched. Captain Nemo took out the ingots one by one, stacked them methodically inside the chest, and filled it to the top. At which point I estimated that it held more than 2,000 pounds of gold, in other words, close to $1,000,000.

After tightly closing the chest, Captain Nemo wrote an address on its lid in characters that had to have been modern Greek.

This done, the captain pressed a button whose wiring put it in contact with the crew's quarters. Four men appeared and tugged the chest out of the lounge, not without some difficulty. Then I heard them hoist it up the iron companionway with the help of pulleys.

---

[15] *Translator's note.* Italian: "The Fish."

At this point Captain Nemo turned to me:

"And you were saying, professor?" he asked me.

"I wasn't saying a thing, captain."

"Then, sir, with your permission I'll bid you good evening."

And with that Captain Nemo left the lounge.

I went back into my stateroom, very puzzled as you can imagine. I tried in vain to fall asleep. I kept searching for a relationship between the appearance of the diver and that chest filled with gold. Soon, from certain rolling and pitching movements, I sensed that the *Nautilus* had left the lower strata and was back on the surface of the water.

Then I heard the sound of footsteps on the platform. I realized some crew members were detaching the skiff and putting it to sea. For a second it bumped the *Nautilus*'s side, then all sounds ceased.

Two hours later the same sounds, the same comings and goings, were repeated. Crewmen hoisted the longboat on board and fitted it into its niche again, then the *Nautilus* plunged back under the waves.

Hence they'd delivered that gold to its address. At what spot on the continent? Who was the recipient of Captain Nemo's riches?

The next day I described the night's events to Conseil and the Canadian, events that had aroused my curiosity to a fever pitch. My companions were as surprised as I was.

"But where does he get that gold?" Ned Land asked.

There was no way we could answer this. After breakfast I proceeded to the lounge and knuckled down to work. I wrote up my notes till five o'clock in the afternoon. Just then— was it because of some personal indisposition?—I felt tremendously hot and had to take off my coat made of fan mussel fabric. Which was a perplexing state of affairs, because we weren't in the low latitudes—and besides, once the *Nautilus* was submerged it shouldn't have been experiencing any rise in temperature. I looked at our pressure gauge. It indicated a depth of sixty feet, a depth beyond the reach of the atmosphere's heat.

I kept on working, but the temperature rose to the point of being unbearable.

"Has a fire broken out on board?" I wondered.

I was just about to leave the lounge when Captain Nemo came in. He went over and checked the thermometer, then turned to me:

"It's 108° Fahrenheit," he said.

"I've detected that fact, captain," I replied, "and if it gets much hotter, we won't be able to handle it."

"Oh, professor, it won't get any hotter unless we want it to!"

"Then you can regulate this heat?"

"No, but I can back away from the fireplace that's producing it."

"So it's outside?"

"Certainly. We're cruising in a current of boiling water."

"It can't be!" I exclaimed.

"Look."

The panels had opened and I could see a totally white sea around the *Nautilus*. Smoky, sulfurous fumes were uncoiling in the midst of waves that were bubbling like water in a boiler. I leaned my hand against one of the windows, but I had to snatch it back because the glass was so hot.

"Where are we?" I asked.

"Near the island of Santorini, professor," the captain answered me, "and right in the channel that separates the volcanic islets of Nea Kameni and Palea Kameni. I wanted to show you the unusual sight of an underwater eruption."

"I thought that the formation of these new islands was finished," I said.

"Nothing is ever finished in the waterways near a volcano," Captain Nemo replied, "and thanks to its underground fires, our planet is continually under construction in these regions. According to the Latin historians Cassiodorus and Pliny, by the year 19 of the Christian era, a new island, the divine Thera, had already appeared in the same place these islets have formed more recently. Then Thera sank under the waves, only to rise and sink once more in the year 69 A.D. From that day to this, such volcanic construction work has been in abeyance. But on February 3, 1866, a new islet named George Island emerged in the midst of sulfurous smoke near Nea Kameni and was fused to it on the 6th of the same month. Seven days later, on February 13, the islet of Aphroessa appeared, leaving a thirty-foot channel between itself and Nea Kameni. I was in these seas when that phenomenon occurred and I was able to study all its phases. The islet of Aphroessa was circular in shape and measured 300 feet across by thirty feet high. It was composed of black, glassy lava mixed with bits of feldspar. Finally, on March 10, a smaller islet named Reka appeared next to Nea Kameni, and since then these three islets have fused to form one whole island."

"What about this channel we're in right now?" I asked.

"Here it is," Captain Nemo replied, showing me a chart of the Greek Isles. "You'll note that I've entered the new islets in their place."

"But will this channel fill up one day?"

"Very likely, Professor Aronnax, because since 1866 eight little lava islets have surged up in front of the port of St. Nicolas on Palea Kameni. So it's obvious that Nea and Palea will join together in days to come. In the middle of the Pacific, tiny infusoria build continents, but here they're built by volcanic phenomena. Look, sir! Look at the construction work going on under these waves."

I went back to the window. The *Nautilus* wasn't moving anymore. The heat had become unbearable. From the white it had recently been, the sea was turning red, a pigment resulting from the presence of iron salts. Though the lounge was hermetically sealed, it was giving off an intolerable stink of sulfur, and I saw scarlet flames that were so bright, they overpowered our electric rays.

I was dripping with sweat, I was suffocating, I was starting to cook. Yes, I felt myself cooking in actual fact!

"We can't stay any longer in this boiling water," I told the captain.

"No, it wouldn't be sensible," replied Nemo the Unemotional.

He issued an order. The *Nautilus* tacked about and retreated from this furnace it couldn't brave with impunity. Fifteen minutes later we were breathing fresh air on the surface of the waves.

Then it occurred to me that if Ned had picked these waterways for an escape attempt, we wouldn't have come out of this fiery sea alive.

The next day, February 16, we exited this basin, which tallies depths of nearly 10,000 feet between Rhodes and Alexandria, and passing well out from Cerigo Island after doubling Cape Matapan, the *Nautilus* left the Greek Isles behind.

31
THE MEDITERRANEAN IN FORTY-EIGHT HOURS

THE MEDITERRANEAN, blue sea beyond compare; to Greeks just "the sea," to Hebrews "the great sea," to Romans *mare nostrum*.[16] Fringed with orange trees, aloes, cactus, and maritime pine trees, perfumed with the scent of myrtle, framed by craggy mountains, imbued with clean, transparent air but continually under construction by fires inside the earth, this sea is a genuine battlefield where Neptune and Pluto still struggle for world domination. Here on these beaches and waters, says the French historian Michelet, humanity is refreshed by one of the most bracing climates in the world.

But as beautiful as it was, I could catch only a quick glimpse of this basin whose surface area is more than 770,000 square miles. Even Captain Nemo's personal insights were denied me, because that mystifying individual didn't appear one single time during our high-speed crossing. I estimate that the *Nautilus*'s track under the waves of this sea was about 600 leagues, and it covered this distance in just twenty-four hours times two. Leaving the waterways of Greece on the morning of February 16, we'd gone through the Strait of Gibraltar by sunrise on the 18th.

Pinned between those shores Captain Nemo wanted to avoid, the Mediterranean obviously gave him little pleasure. Its waves and breezes brought back too many memories, if not regrets. Here he no longer had the

---

[16] *Translator's note.* Latin: "our sea."

freedom of movement and ease of maneuver that the oceans allowed him, and his *Nautilus* felt fenced in by the nearby coasts of Africa and Europe.

Accordingly our speed was twenty-five miles—hence about ten geographic leagues —per hour. Needless to say, Ned Land had to give up his escape plans, much to his distress. Shooting along at some forty to forty-five feet per second, he could hardly make use of the skiff. Leaving the *Nautilus* under such conditions would have been like jumping off a train running at this speed, a rash move if there ever was one. What's more, the submersible replenished its air supply only by rising to the surface of the waves at night, and it steered by dead reckoning, relying just on its compass and log.

Under the Mediterranean, then, all I could catch of the scenery flying by was what a traveler might see from an express train; in other words, I could view only the distant horizons because the foregrounds went past like lightning. But Conseil and I could study those Mediterranean fish whose powerful fins let them keep up with the *Nautilus* for a couple seconds. We stayed on watch in front of the lounge windows, and our notes allow me to reconstruct the ichthyology of this sea in just a few words.

Among the various fish living in it, some I viewed, others I glimpsed, and the rest I missed completely thanks to the *Nautilus*'s speed. Kindly allow me to sort them out using this eccentric system of classification. At least it will indicate the fast pace of this whole survey.

In the midst of this mass of water, three-foot lampreys, common to nearly all climates, meandered past in the bright light of our electric beams. A type of ray, the long-nosed skate, was five feet wide, had a white belly with a spotted ash-gray back, and drifted along on the currents like a big wide-open shawl. Other rays went past so quickly, I couldn't tell if they deserved that name "eagle ray" coined by the ancient Greeks, or those descriptions of "rat ray," "toad ray," and "bat ray" that modern fishermen have inflicted on them. Soupfin sharks, twelve feet long and especially dreaded by divers, were

racing each other. Looking like big bluish shadows, thresher sharks went by, eight feet long and boasting a tremendously acute sense of smell. Dorado from the genus *Sparus*, some over four feet long, showed up in silver and azure costumes encircled with little bands that contrasted with the dark coloring of their fins; fish sacred to the goddess Venus, their eyes inset in brows of gold; a valuable species that patronizes both fresh and salt water, equally at home in rivers, lakes, and oceans, living in all climates, handling all temperatures, their line dating back to prehistoric times on this earth yet still keeping all its beauty from those far-off days. Magnificent sturgeons, around ten or eleven yards long and extremely fast, banged their powerful tails against our glass panels, revealing bluish backs with little brown spots; they resemble sharks without matching their strength and are found in all seas; in the spring they're fond of swimming up the major rivers, fighting the currents of the Volga, Danube, Po, Rhine, Loire, and Oder while feeding on herring, mackerel, salmon, and codfish; though they belong to the class of cartilaginous fish, they're a delicacy; folks eat them fresh, dried, marinated, or salted, and in olden times they were carried in triumph to the table of the Roman epicure Lucullus. But whenever the *Nautilus* drew near the surface, those residents of the Mediterranean I could study most productively belonged to the sixty-third genus of bony fish. They were tuna from the genus *Scomber*, blue-black on top, silver on the belly armor, their dorsal stripes giving off a golden radiance. They're reputed to follow ships in search of cooling shade from the fiery tropical sun and they did just that with the *Nautilus*, as they'd once done with the vessels of the Count de La Pérouse. For many hours they kept up with our submersible. I couldn't stop marveling at these creatures so perfectly cut out for racing, their heads small, their bodies sleek, spindle-shaped, and sometimes almost ten feet long, their pectoral fins boasting remarkable power, their caudal fins forked. Like certain flocks of birds, whose speed they match, these tuna swam in triangle formation, which led the ancients to say that they'd boned up on geometry and military strategy. And yet they can't escape the Provençal fishermen, who prize them as highly as the residents of Turkey and Italy once did; and these valuable creatures, as oblivious as if they were deaf and blind, leap right into the Marseilles tuna nets and perish by the thousands.

Just for the record I'll mention those Mediterranean fish that Conseil and I barely glimpsed. There were whitish knifefish from the species *Gymnotus fierasfer* that went by like fleeting wisps of steam, conger eels that were around ten or twelve feet long and dolled up in green, blue, and yellow, three-foot whiting with livers that make a choice morsel, red bandfish drifting like delicate seaweed, gurnards that poets call lyrefish and seamen pipers and whose snouts have two jagged triangular plates shaped like old Homer's lyre, swallowfish swimming as fast as the bird they're named after, Haifa groupers whose dorsal fins are trimmed with filaments, some shad (spotted with black, gray, brown, blue, yellow, and green) that actually respond to tinkling hand bells, splendid diamond-shaped turbot that were like aquatic pheasants with yellowish fins stippled in brown and with the left topside marbled mostly in brown and yellow, finally schools of wonderful striped mullet, real oceangoing birds of paradise for which ancient Romans paid as much as 10,000 sesterces apiece—and which they killed right at the table, so that those heartless people could watch it change color from fiery red while alive to pallid white when dead.

And as for other fish common to the Atlantic and Mediterranean, I couldn't study any brown rays, triggerfish, puffers, seahorses, jewelfish, trumpetfish, blennies, goatfish, wrasse, smelt, flying fish, anchovies, pandoras, sea bream, grass carp, or any of the chief representatives of the order Pleuronectiformes such as dab, flounder, plaice, sole, and fluke, all because of the dizzying speed with which the *Nautilus* tore through these rich waters.

As for marine mammals, while going past the mouth of the Adriatic Sea, I thought I identified two or three sperm whales

equipped with the single dorsal fin that indicates the genus *Physeter*, some pilot whales from the genus *Globicephalus* specific to the Mediterranean, the front part of the head striped with small distinct lines, and also a dozen seals with white bellies and black coats, known by the name monk seal and just as solemn as if they were ten-foot Dominicans.

For his part Conseil thought he spotted a turtle six feet wide and adorned with three protruding ridges that ran lengthwise. I was sorry I missed this reptile, because from Conseil's description I thought I recognized the leatherback turtle, a pretty scarce species. I myself noted only some loggerhead turtles with long carapaces.

As for zoophytes, for a few seconds I could marvel at a wonderful orange-tinted fanworm from the genus *Galeolaria* that clung to the glass of our port panel; it consisted of a long slender filament that spread out into countless branches and ended in the most delicate lace ever spun by the followers of Arachne. Unfortunately I couldn't fish up this wonderful specimen, and surely no other Mediterranean zoophytes would have been offered to my eyes, if, on the evening of the 16th, the *Nautilus* hadn't slowed down in an odd manner. This was the situation.

By then we were passing between Sicily and the coast of Tunisia. In that cramped space between Cape Bon and the Strait of Messina, the sea bottom rises almost instantaneously. It forms an actual ridge with only 56 feet of water left above it, while the depth on either side is 560 feet. Therefore the *Nautilus* had to maneuver carefully so as not to bang into this underwater barricade.

I showed Conseil the whereabouts of this long reef on our chart of the Mediterranean.

"But with all due respect to master," Conseil pointed out, "it's like an actual isthmus connecting Europe to Africa."

"Yes, my boy," I replied, "it cuts all the way across the Strait of Sicily, and Smyth's soundings prove that these two continents used to be genuinely connected between Cape Boeo and Cape Farina."

"I can well believe it," Conseil said.

"I might add," I went on, "that there's

a similar barricade between Gibraltar and Ceuta, and in prehistoric times it closed off the Mediterranean completely."

"Huh?" Conseil put in. "What if some volcanic upheaval were to raise those two barricades back above the waves one day?"

"That's pretty unlikely, Conseil."

"If master will let me finish, I mean that if this phenomenon were to occur, it might be upsetting to Mr. de Lesseps, who has gone to such pains to cut through his isthmus!"

"I agree, but I'll say again, Conseil, that such a phenomenon won't occur. The intensity of those underground forces is continually decreasing. Volcanoes were quite plentiful in the first days of the world, but they're going extinct one by one; the heat inside the earth is growing weaker, the temperature in its lower strata is cooling appreciably every century, which could spell the earth's ruin, because this heat is its life."

"But the sun—"

"The sun isn't enough, Conseil. Can it reheat a corpse?"

"Not that I've heard."

"Well, my friend, someday the earth will be just such a cold corpse. Like the moon, which lost her vital heat long ago, our planet will become lifeless and unlivable."

"In how many centuries?" Conseil asked.

"In hundreds of thousands of years, my boy."

"Then we have ample time to finish our voyage," Conseil replied, "if Ned Land doesn't botch things!"

And with that reassurance Conseil went back to examining the shallows that the *Nautilus* was skimming at moderate speed.

On the rocky, volcanic seafloor bloomed a complete line of moving flora—sponges, sea cucumbers, translucent comb jellies from the genus *Cydippe* that were adorned with reddish tendrils and gave off a mild phosphorescence, members of the genus *Beroe* popularly known as melon jellyfish and bathing in the shimmer of the whole color spectrum, roving feather stars that were a yard wide and that reddened the waters with their crimson hue, treelike gorgon plants of the greatest beauty, sea fans with long stalks, a large number of edible sea urchins from various species, plus green sea anemones with a grayish trunk and brown disk buried under the olive tresses of their tentacles.

Studying mollusks and articulata kept Conseil especially busy, and though his laundry list is on the dry side, it would be unfair to the gallant lad to leave out his personal comments.

In the branch Mollusca he mentions many scallops from the species *Pectunculus pectiniformis*, some European thorny oysters piled on top of each other, triangular coquina, tridentated hyales with yellow fins and transparent shrimplike shells, orange slugs from the genus *Pleurobranchus* looking like eggs spotted or sprinkled with greenish dots, members of the genus *Aplysia* also known as sea hares, other sea hares from the genus *Dolabella*, bubble shells from the species *Acera carnosa*, umbrella shells specific to the Mediterranean, European abalone whose shell produces a mother-of-pearl much in demand, scallops from the species *Pectunculus flammula*, jingle shells that diners in the French province of Languedoc are said to like better than oysters, those carpetshells so dear to the citizens of Marseilles, fat white venuses that are among those clams so plentiful off the coast of North America and so sought after in New York, variously colored scallops from the species *Pecten opercularis*, burrowing date mussels with a peppery flavor I relish, furrowed cockles whose shells have riblike ridges on their arching tops, conchs garnished with scarlet bumps, snails from the genus *Carinaria* with backward-curving tips that made them look like flimsy gondolas, crowned ferole shells, spiral-shaped snails from the family Atlantidae, gray nudibranchs from the genus *Tethys* that were covered with white spots and fringed mantles, nudibranchs from the suborder Eolidea that looked like small slugs, sea butterflies crawling on their backs, shells from the genus *Auricula* including the oval-shaped *Auricula myosotis*, tan wentletrap snails, periwinkles, purple shells, gray top shells, rock borers, transparent lamellarias, cap snails, pandora shells, etc.

As for the articulata, Conseil's notes very appropriately divide them into six classes, three of which belong to the marine world. These classes are the Crustacea, Cirripedia, and Annelida.

Crustaceans are subdivided into nine orders, and the first of these consists of the decapods, in other words, creatures whose head and thorax are usually fused, whose cheek-and-mouth mechanism is made up of several pairs of appendages, and whose thorax boasts four, five, or six pairs of walking legs. Conseil adopted the methods of our mentor Professor Milne-Edwards, who organizes the decapods into three divisions: Brachyura, Macrura, and Anomura. These names are a little hard on the eyes, but they're accurate and appropriate. Among the Brachyura Conseil lists some crabs from the genus *Amathia* whose fronts were furnished with two big diverging tips, some scorpion spider crabs that—Lord knows why—symbolized wisdom for the ancient Greeks, other spider crabs from the species *Lambrus massena* and *Lambrus spinimanus* that very likely had gone astray in these shallows because they usually live in the lower depths, coral crabs, hairy crabs, rhomboid crabs, box crabs from the species *Calappa granulosa* (easy on the digestion, as Conseil pointed out), toothless helmet crabs, nut crabs, stilt crabs, porter crabs, etc. Among the Macrura (which are subdivided into five families, armorclads, burrowers, crawfish, prawns, and sand crabs), Conseil mentions some common rock lobsters whose females supply a meat that's highly prized, slipper lobsters or common shrimp, riverside mud borers from the genus *Gebia*, and all sorts of edible species, but he doesn't say a thing about the crawfish subdivision that includes the true lobster, because rock lobsters are the only type found in the Mediterranean. Finally, among the Anomura, he saw common drocine crabs hiding out in whatever castoff seashells they could take over, bearded crabs with spiny fronts, hermit crabs, porcelain crabs, etc.

There Conseil's work came to a halt. He didn't have time to finish off the class Crustacea by examining its stomapods, amphipods, homopods, isopods, trilobites, branchiopods, ostracods, and entomostracans. And to wrap up his study of marine articulata, he

should have mentioned the class Cirripedia, which takes in water fleas and fish lice, plus the class Annelida, which he would have divided without fail into tube worms and sand worms. But the *Nautilus* went past the shallows of the Strait of Sicily, reached deeper waters, and resumed its usual speed. From then on there were no more mollusks, zoophytes, or articulata. Just a few big fish sweeping by like shadows.

During the night of February 16–17, we entered the second Mediterranean basin, which is sometimes as much as 10,000 feet deep. Driven downward by its propeller and slanting fins, the *Nautilus* descended to the lowest strata of this sea.

There, instead of natural wonders, this mass of water offered some fearfully moving pictures to my eyes. In essence we were crossing that part of the Mediterranean with the largest number of casualties. Between the shores of Algiers and the beaches of Provence, how many shipwrecks have occurred, how many vessels have vanished! Compared to such a vast stretch of water as the Pacific, the Mediterranean is a mere lake, but it's an unpredictable lake with fickle waves—today it's gentle and affectionate with the frail single-masters drifting between the twofold ultramarine of its sky and waters; tomorrow it's raging and tormented, lashed by the winds, demolishing the strongest ships under sudden waves that smash down with a headlong wallop.

So in our quick run through these deep strata, how many pieces of wreckage I saw lying on the seafloor, some already caked with coral, others clad only in a layer of rust: anchors, cannons, shells, iron fittings, propeller blades, engine parts, cracked cylinders, staved-in boilers, then hulls floating in midwater, here upright, there overturned.

Some of these wrecked ships had perished in collisions, others from striking granite reefs. I saw a number that had sunk straight down, their masts still upright, their rigging stiffened by the water. They looked like they were at anchor by some immense offshore mooring where they were waiting for their departure time. When the *Nautilus* went among them, covering them with sheets of electricity, they seemed ready to salute us with their colors and to send us their serial numbers! But no, nothing but silence and death filled this field of catastrophes!

I noticed that these Mediterranean depths got more and more cluttered with this grim wreckage as the *Nautilus* drew nearer to the Strait of Gibraltar. By then the shores of Africa and Europe were converging, and in that narrow space collisions were commonplace. There I saw a slew of iron undersides, the phantasmagoric ruins of steamers, some lying down, others rearing up like fearsome animals. One of these boats made a dreadful first impression: sides ripped open, funnel bent, paddle wheels stripped to the mountings, rudder separated from the sternpost and still hanging from an iron chain, its stern board eaten away by the sea's salts! How many lives were dashed in this shipwreck! How many victims were dragged under the waves! Did some sailor on board live to spin yarns about this dreadful disaster, or did the waves still keep this casualty a secret? It occurred to me, Lord knows why, that this boat buried under the sea might have been the *Atlas*, which went missing with all hands some twenty years back and was never heard from again! Oh, what a grim tale these Mediterranean depths could tell, this huge boneyard where so much wealth has been lost, where so many victims have met their deaths!

Meanwhile, briskly unconcerned, the *Nautilus* ran at full propeller through the midst of these ruins. On February 18, near three o'clock in the morning, it pulled up in front of the entrance to the Strait of Gibraltar.

There are two currents here: an upper current, long known to exist, that carries the Atlantic Ocean's waters into the Mediterranean basin; then a lower countercurrent, whose existence has been proven more recently by simple logic. In essence the Mediterranean receives a continual influx of water both from rivers emptying into it and from the Atlantic; since its rate of evaporation isn't enough to restore the balance, the total amount of additional water should raise the Mediterranean's level every year. Yet that isn't the case, so we're naturally led to assume the existence of some lower current that carries the Mediter-

ranean's surplus back through the Strait of Gibraltar and into the Atlantic basin.

And so it turned out. The *Nautilus* took full advantage of this countercurrent. It moved swiftly through this narrow passageway. For a second I could glimpse the wondrous ruins of the Temple of Hercules, buried undersea, as Pliny and Avianus have mentioned, along with that flat island they stand on; and a few minutes later we were cruising on the waves of the Atlantic.

32

Vigo Bay

THE ATLANTIC! A vast expanse of water whose surface area is 25,000,000 square miles, with a length of 9,000 miles and an average width of 2,700. A major sea nearly unknown to the ancients, except maybe the Carthaginians, those Dutchmen of antiquity who went along the west coasts of Europe and Africa on their commercial junkets. An ocean whose parallel winding shores make up an immense perimeter fed by the earth's major rivers, the St. Lawrence, Mississippi, Amazon, Plata, Orinoco, Niger, Senegal, Elbe, Loire, and Rhine, which bring it waters from the most civilized countries as well as from the least developed! A magnificent stretch of waves plowed continually by ships of all nations, shaded by every flag on earth, and ending in those two dreadful headlands so feared by navigators, Cape Horn and the Cape of Storms!

The *Nautilus* cut these waters with the edge of its spur after covering nearly 10,000 leagues in 3½ months, a track longer than a great circle of the earth. Where were we heading now, and what did the future have in store for us?

Exiting the Strait of Gibraltar, the *Nautilus* took to the high seas. It came back to the surface of the waves, so we could resume our daily strolls on the platform.

I climbed onto it immediately, Ned Land and Conseil along with me. Twelve miles away Cape St. Vincent was dimly visible, the southwestern tip of the Iberian Peninsula. The wind was blowing a pretty strong gust from the south. The sea was rough and running high. Its waves made the *Nautilus* roll and jerk violently. It was nearly impossible to stand up on the platform, which was continually battered by that enormously heavy sea. After grabbing a few breaths of air, we went below once more.

I retired to my stateroom. Conseil went back to his cabin; but the Canadian, looking rather distracted, followed me. Our quick trip through the Mediterranean hadn't let him put his plans into execution, and he barely hid his disappointment.

Once my stateroom door was closed, he sat and looked at me silently.

"Ned my friend," I told him, "I know how you feel, but it wasn't your fault. The way the *Nautilus* was navigating, it would have been sheer insanity to think of escaping!"

Ned Land didn't reply. His pursed lips and frowning brow indicated he was firmly in the grip of his fixation.

"Look here," I went on, "this is no time to lose heart. We're going up the Portuguese coast. France and England aren't far off, and there we'll easily find refuge. Of course if the *Nautilus* had left the Strait of Gibraltar and made for that cape in the south, if it were taking us toward regions far from any land, I would share your concern. But now we know that Captain Nemo doesn't avoid the seas of civilization, and in a few days I think we can safely take action."

Ned Land looked at me even more intently and finally unpursed his lips:

"We'll do it this evening," he said.

I shot to my feet. I admit I was far from ready for this announcement. I wanted to answer the Canadian, but words failed me.

"We agreed to wait for decent circumstances," Ned Land went on. "Those circumstances have arrived. This evening we'll be just a few miles off the coast of Spain. It'll be cloudy tonight. The wind's blowing toward shore. You gave me your promise, Professor Aronnax, and I'm counting on you."

I still hadn't said anything, so the Canadian got up and came over to me:

"We'll do it this evening at nine o'clock," he said. "I've alerted Conseil. By then Captain Nemo will be cooped up in his stateroom and most likely in bed. The mechanics and the crewmen won't be able to see us. Conseil and I will head to the central companionway. As for you, Professor Aronnax, you'll stay in the library a couple steps away from us and wait for my signal. The oars, mast, and sail are in the skiff. I've even managed to stow some provisions inside. I've gotten hold of a monkey wrench to unscrew the nuts bolting the skiff to the *Nautilus*'s hull. So everything's all set. I'll see you this evening."

"The ocean's rough," I said.

"I know," the Canadian replied, "but that's a risk we have to take. Freedom's worth paying for. In any case the longboat's well built, and going a few miles with a carrying wind is no big deal. By tomorrow who knows if this ship won't be a hundred leagues out to sea? If circumstances are in our favor, between ten and eleven this evening we'll be landing on some piece of solid ground or we'll be dead. So it's in God's hands, and I'll see you this evening!"

With that the Canadian turned and went, leaving me close to dumbfounded. I'd assumed that if it ever came to this, I would have time to think about it, to talk it over. My stubborn companion hadn't granted me this courtesy. But even if he had, what would I have said to him? Ned Land was right a hundred times over. These were promising circumstances, and he was making the most of them. Out of sheer selfishness could I go back on my word and be responsible for ruining the future lives of my companions? Tomorrow couldn't Captain Nemo take us far away from any land?

Just then a loudish hissing sound told me the ballast tanks were filling, and the *Nautilus* sank under the waves of the Atlantic.

I stayed in my stateroom. I wanted to avoid the captain so that he wouldn't see the agitation overwhelming me. What an agonizing day I spent, torn between my desire to recover my freedom and my regret at saying good-bye to this marvelous *Nautilus*, leaving my underwater research incomplete! How could I give up this ocean, "my own Atlantic," as I liked to call it, without studying its lower strata, without drawing out of it the kinds of secrets that had been revealed to me by the Indian Ocean and the Pacific! I was putting down my novel half read, I was waking up as my dream neared its climax! How painfully the hours went by, as I sometimes envisioned myself safe on shore with my companions, or, despite my better judgment, as I sometimes wished that some unforeseen circumstance would keep Ned Land from carrying out his plans.

Twice I went to the lounge. I wanted to check our compass. I wanted to see if the *Nautilus*'s heading was really taking us closer to shore instead of farther away. It was. The *Nautilus* still lay in Portuguese waters. Facing north, it was cruising just off the coast.

So I had to accept my fate and get ready to escape. My baggage wasn't heavy. My notes, nothing more.

As for Captain Nemo, I wondered how he would react to our escaping, what concern or maybe what distress it might cause him, and what he would do in the twofold event of our attempt either failing or being found out! I certainly had no complaints to register with him, on the contrary. His hospitality couldn't have been more heartfelt. Yet I couldn't be called ungrateful for leaving him. No solemn promises tied us to him. In order to hold us captive, he'd counted only on the force of circumstances and not on our word of honor. But since he plainly intended to keep us here the rest of our lives, any attempt we could make was fully justified.

I hadn't seen the captain since our visit to the island of Santorini. Would fate bring me into his presence before we left? I both desired and dreaded it. I listened for footsteps in the stateroom adjoining mine. No sounds reached my ear. His stateroom had to be empty.

Then I began to wonder if this strange individual was actually on board. Since that night when the skiff had left the *Nautilus* on some secret errand, my ideas about him had subtly changed. In spite of everything I thought Captain Nemo must have kept up some sort of relationship with the shore. Did he ever leave the *Nautilus?* Whole weeks had often gone by without my seeing him. What

was he doing at those times? On the occasions when I'd thought he was in seclusion due to his basic distrust of humanity, was he instead far away from the ship, involved in some secret activity whose nature still eluded me?

All these ideas and a thousand others invaded my brain at the same moment. In these strange circumstances I could go on guessing forever. My anxiety level was unbearable. This day of waiting seemed endless. The hours chimed too slowly for the liking of my impatient mood.

As usual dinner was served me in my stateroom. Deeply distracted, I ate little. I left the table at seven o'clock. There were 120 minutes to go—I was counting them off—before I had to rejoin Ned Land. I got more and more nervous. My pulse was throbbing fiercely. I couldn't hold still. I paced back and forth, trying to calm my troubled mind with movement. The possibility of perishing in our reckless undertaking was the least of my worries; what set my heart pounding was the thought of our plans being discovered before we'd left the *Nautilus*, the thought of being hauled in front of Captain Nemo and finding him angry, or worse yet, grieved by my desertion.

I wanted to see the lounge one last time. I went down the corridors and arrived at that museum where I'd spent so many pleasant and productive hours. I looked at all its wealth, all its treasures, like a man on the eve of his eternal exile, a man leaving never to return. For a good while now, my life had centered on these natural wonders and artistic masterworks, and I was about to leave them behind forever. I wanted to plunge my eyes through the lounge window and into those Atlantic waters; but the panels were hermetically sealed, and a mantle of sheet iron separated me from this ocean I still hadn't gotten to know.

Crossing through the lounge, I arrived at the door that was contrived in one of the canted corners and opened into the captain's stateroom. Much to my amazement this door was ajar. I instinctively shrank back. If Captain Nemo was in his stateroom, he would be able to see me. But I didn't hear a sound and drew nearer. His stateroom was empty. I pushed the door open. I took a couple steps inside. Still the same austere, monastic appearance.

Just then I caught sight of a few etchings hanging on the wall, something I hadn't noticed during my first visit. They were portraits of great men of history who had spent their lives in continual dedication to a great human ideal: Thaddeus Kosciuszko, the hero who embraced defeat with the words *Finis Poloniae;*[17] Markos Botzaris, a new King Leonidas for today's Greece; Daniel O'Connell, Ireland's defender; George Washington, founder of the American Union; Daniele Manin, the Italian patriot; Abraham Lincoln, shot dead by a supporter of slavery; and finally that martyr for the emancipation of the black race, John Brown, hanging from his gallows as Victor Hugo's pencil has so terrifyingly portrayed.

What were the ties between these valiant souls and the soul of Captain Nemo? From this collection of portraits could I finally unlock the secret of his existence? Was he a champion of the oppressed, a liberator of the enslaved? Had he taken part in the recent political or social upheavals of this century? Was he one of the heroes of that dreadful Civil War in America, a war both grievous and forever glorious . . . ?

Suddenly the clock struck eight. The first stroke of its hammer on the chime snapped me out of my daydreams. I trembled as if some invisible eye had seen into my innermost thoughts, and I rushed outside the stateroom.

There my eyes fell on the compass. Our heading was still northerly. The log showed a moderate speed, the pressure gauge a depth of around sixty feet. So circumstances were in favor of the Canadian's plans.

I retired to my stateroom. I dressed warmly—fishing boots, otter cap, coat made of fan-mussel fabric lined with sealskin. I was ready and waiting. Only the propeller's vibrations broke the heavy silence reigning on board. I cocked an ear and listened. Would some sudden outburst of voices tell me that Ned Land's escape plans had just been detected? A ghastly uneasiness crept through me. I tried in vain to recover my composure.

A few minutes before nine o'clock, I glued my ear to the captain's door. Not a sound. I left my stateroom and went back to the lounge, which was empty and plunged in near darkness.

I opened the door leading to the library. Same low lighting, same solitude. I went and took up my position near the door opening into the well of the central companionway. I waited for Ned Land's signal.

At this point the propeller's vibrations slowed down appreciably, then they died out altogether. Why was the *Nautilus* coasting to a stop? Whether this layover would help or hinder Ned Land's schemes I couldn't tell.

The only other thing that broke the silence was the pounding of my heart.

Suddenly I felt a mild jolt. I realized that the *Nautilus* had just come to rest on the ocean floor. My uneasiness grew. The Canadian's signal hadn't reached me. I dearly wanted to rejoin Ned Land and urge him to put off his attempt. I had a feeling we weren't navigating under normal conditions anymore.

Just then the door to the main lounge opened and Captain Nemo appeared. He saw me, and without any further preamble:

"Ah, professor," he said in a cheery tone, "I've been looking for you. Do you know your Spanish history?"

Even if he knew it by heart, a man in my disturbed, befuddled condition couldn't have quoted a syllable of his *own* country's history.

"Well?" Captain Nemo went on. "Did you hear my question? Do you know the history of Spain?"

"Very little of it," I replied.

"The most learned men," the captain said, "still have much to learn. Have a seat," he added, "and I'll tell you about an unusual episode in that body of history."

The captain stretched out on a couch, and I automatically took a seat near him—but in the shadows.

"Give me your best attention, professor," he said. "This piece of history will definitely

---

[17] *Translator's note.* Latin: "Poland is no more!"

hold your interest, since it answers a question you surely haven't been able to resolve."

"I'm all ears, captain," I said, not certain what my conversation partner was driving at and wondering if this incident related to our escape plans.

"Professor," Captain Nemo went on, "if you're amenable, we'll go back in time to 1702. You remember that in those days your King Louis XIV thought an imperial gesture would be enough to humble the Pyrenees in the dust, so he inflicted his grandson, the Duke of Anjou, on the Spaniards. Reigning more or less poorly under the name King Philip V, this aristocrat had to deal with mighty opponents abroad.

"In essence, a year earlier the royal houses of Holland, Austria, and England had signed a treaty of alliance at The Hague, intending to wrest the Spanish crown from King Philip V and to place it on the head of an archduke whom they prematurely named King Charles III.

"Spain needed to stand up to these allies. But the country had almost no army or navy. Yet it wasn't short of money, provided that its galleons loaded with gold and silver from America could reach its ports. Now then, late in 1702 Spain was expecting a wealthy convoy, which France undertook to escort with a fleet of twenty-three vessels commanded by Admiral de Château-Renault, because by that point the allied navies were patrolling the Atlantic.

"This convoy was scheduled to put into Cadiz, but after hearing that the English fleet lay across those waterways, the admiral decided to make for a French port.

"The Spanish commanders in the convoy objected to this decision. They demanded to be taken to a Spanish port—if not Cadiz, then Vigo Bay, which was located on Spain's northwest coast and not blockaded.

"Admiral de Château-Renault was indecisive enough to obey this directive, and the galleons entered Vigo Bay.

"Unfortunately this bay forms an offshore mooring so wide open that it's impossible to defend. It was essential, then, to hurry and empty the galleons before the allied fleets arrived, and there would have been ample time to unload them if a wretched issue of trade agreements hadn't suddenly come up.

"Are you clear on the chain of events?" Captain Nemo asked me.

"Perfectly clear," I said, still not sure why I was being given this history lesson.

"Then I'll continue. Here's what came to pass. The tradesmen of Cadiz had negotiated a charter whereby they were to receive all merchandise coming from the West Indies. Now then, unloading the ingots from those galleons at the port of Vigo would have been a violation of their rights. So they registered a complaint in Madrid and they obtained an order from the indecisive King Philip V: without unloading, the convoy was to stay in custody at the offshore mooring of Vigo till the enemy fleets had retreated.

"Now then, while this decision was being handed down, English vessels arrived in Vigo Bay on October 22, 1702. Despite his inferior forces Admiral de Château-Renault fought courageously. But when he saw that the convoy's wealth was about to fall into enemy hands, he burned and scuttled the galleons, which sank under the waves with their immense treasure."

Captain Nemo came to a stop. I must admit I still couldn't see why this piece of history should be of any interest to me.

"Well?" I asked him.

"Well, Professor Aronnax," Captain Nemo answered me, "we're now in Vigo Bay, and all that's left is for you to probe the mysteries of the place."

The captain got up and invited me to follow him. I'd pulled myself together by then. I did so. The lounge was dark, but the waves of the sea sparkled through the clear windows. I looked out.

Around the *Nautilus* for a half-mile radius, the waters were steeped in electric light. The sandy bottom was smooth and clean. Crewmen in diving suits were busy removing half-rotted barrels and disemboweled trunks from the dingy hulks of ships. Out of those trunks and kegs spilled ingots of gold and silver, cascades of jewels, pieces of eight. The sand was heaped with them. Then, loaded down with these valuable spoils, the men returned to the *Nautilus*, dropped off their burdens inside, and went back to resume this never-ending harvest of gold and silver.

I understood. This was the setting of that battle on October 22, 1702. It was here that those galleons carrying riches to the Spanish government had gone under. It was here that Captain Nemo came, whenever he needed, to withdraw those millions to ballast his *Nautilus*. America had surrendered its precious metals for him and him alone. He was the direct and sole heir to this treasure snatched from the Incas and the peoples conquered by Hernando Cortés!

"Did you know, professor," he asked me with a smile, "that the sea contained so much wealth?"

"I know it's estimated," I replied, "that there are over two million tons of silver held in suspension in salt water."

"Surely, but in extracting *that* silver, your expenses would be greater than your profits. Here, by contrast, all I have to do is pick up what other men have lost, and not just in Vigo Bay but from a thousand other shipwrecks whose positions are marked on my underwater chart. Do you understand now that I'm rich to the tune of billions?"

"I understand, captain. But let me point out that in harvesting this same Vigo Bay, you're simply beating a rival organization to the punch."

"What organization?"

"An organization chartered by the Spanish government to hunt for these sunken galleons. Its investors were lured by the bait of enormous gains, because this scuttled treasure is estimated to be worth $100,000,000."

"It *was* worth $100,000,000," Captain Nemo answered me, "but not any longer!"

"Right," I said. "So a timely warning to those investors would be an act of charity. Yet who knows if it would be well received? What gamblers usually regret the most isn't losing their money but giving up their lunatic dreams. In the long run, though, I feel less sorry for them than for the thousands of poverty-stricken people who would have benefited from a fair distribution of this wealth, but now it will be of no help to them!"

I'd no sooner voiced this regret than I felt it must have offended Captain Nemo.

"No help!" he replied heatedly. "So you think, sir, that this wealth goes to waste once I gather it? You believe I work to amass this treasure out of selfishness? Who says I don't put it to good use? Do you think I don't know about the suffering individuals and oppressed races living on this earth, poor people to comfort, victims to avenge? Don't you understand . . . ?"

Captain Nemo stopped after these last words, maybe regretting that he'd said too much. But I'd guessed. Whatever motives had driven him to look for independence under the seas, he remained a human being above all else! His heart still throbbed for the sufferings of humanity, and he offered his immense charity both to downtrodden races and to individuals!

And then I knew where Captain Nemo had delivered that chest of gold, when the *Nautilus* navigated those waters where Crete was rebelling against its Turkish overlords!

33

A LOST CONTINENT

THE NEXT MORNING, February 19, I looked up to see the Canadian coming into my stateroom. I'd been expecting this visit. He had a very long face.

"Well, sir?" he said to me.

"Well, Ned, the fates were against us yesterday."

"I'll say! That damned captain had to call a halt right when we were ready to escape from his boat."

"Yes, Ned, he had business with his banker."

"His banker?"

"Or rather his banking house. By which I mean this ocean, where his wealth is safer than in any government treasury."

I told the Canadian what had happened the night before, secretly hoping he would come around to the idea of not deserting the captain; but my narrative had no result other than Ned's voicing deep regret that he hadn't strolled across the Vigo battlefield on his own behalf.

"Anyhow," he said, "it isn't over yet! My first harpoon missed, that's all! We'll pull it off the next time, and as soon as this evening if it comes to that . . ."

"What's the *Nautilus*'s heading?" I asked.

"I have no idea," Ned replied.

"All right, at noon we'll find out what our position is."

The Canadian went back to Conseil's side. As soon as I got dressed, I went into the lounge. The compass wasn't encouraging. The *Nautilus*'s course was south-southwest. We were turning our backs on Europe.

I could hardly wait till our position was reported on the chart. Near 11:30 the ballast tanks emptied and the submersible rose to the surface of the ocean. I leaped onto the platform. Ned Land was there already.

No more shore in sight. Nothing but the immense sea. A few sails were on the horizon, undoubtedly some ships going as far as Cape São Roque to find favorable winds for doubling the Cape of Good Hope. The sky was cloudy. A squall was on the way.

Furious, Ned tried to see through the mists on the horizon. He still hoped that the land he longed for was behind all that fog.

At noon the sun appeared for an instant. Making the most of this rift in the clouds, the chief officer took his sights. Then the sea got stormier, we went below again, and the hatch closed once more.

When I checked the chart an hour later, I saw that the *Nautilus*'s position had been marked at longitude 16° 17′ and latitude 33° 22′, a good 150 leagues from the nearest coast. It wouldn't do to even dream of escaping, and the reader can imagine how thoroughly the Canadian lost his temper when I let him know where things stood.

As for me, I wasn't exactly heartbroken. It felt like a heavy weight had been lifted off of me, and I could resume my usual activities in a state of comparative calm.

Around eleven o'clock in the evening, I received a very unexpected visit from Captain Nemo. With great courtesy he asked me if I felt tired from our vigil the night before. I said no.

"Then, Professor Aronnax, I propose an unusual excursion."

"Propose away, captain."

"Till now you've visited the ocean depths only by day and under sunlight. Would you like to see them on a dark night?"

"Very much."

"I warn you, this will be a tiring stroll. We'll need to walk long hours and scale a mountain. The roads aren't terribly well kept up."

"What you're telling me, captain, makes it sound twice as interesting. Count me in."

"Then come along, professor, and we'll put on our diving suits."

Arriving at the wardrobe, I saw that neither my companions nor any crewmen would be going with us on this excursion. Captain Nemo hadn't even suggested my fetching Ned or Conseil.

In a few seconds we'd put on our equipment. The air tanks were fully charged and on our backs, but the electric lanterns weren't in readiness. I commented on this to the captain.

"We won't be needing them," he replied.

I thought I hadn't heard him right, but I couldn't repeat my comment because the captain's head had already vanished into its metal covering. I finished harnessing myself, I felt an alpenstock being put in my hand, and a few minutes later after the standard procedures, we set foot on the floor of the Atlantic, close to a thousand feet down.

It was almost midnight. The waters were extremely dark, but Captain Nemo pointed to a reddish spot off in the distance, a sort of wide glow shining about two miles from the *Nautilus*. As for what that fire was, what substances fed it, how and why it kept burning in this mass of liquid, I couldn't say. In any case it lit our way, though dimly, and I soon got used to this unique gloom; so under these circumstances I could see why we didn't need the Ruhmkorff device.

Captain Nemo and I walked side by side, heading straight for that conspicuous fire. The level seafloor rose slightly. We took long strides, helped by our alpenstocks; but generally it was slow going, because our feet kept sinking into a kind of slimy mud mixed with seaweed and assorted flat stones.

As we moved forward I heard a sort of pitter-patter overhead. Sometimes this sound speeded up and turned into a continual crackling. I soon figured out the cause. It was a heavy rainfall rattling on the surface of the waves. Instinctively I worried that I would get soaked. By water in the midst of water! I couldn't help chuckling at this outlandish notion. But to tell the truth, in these heavy diving suits you no longer feel the liquid element—you simply think you're in the midst of air a little denser than air on land.

After we walked for half an hour, the seafloor grew rocky. Medusas, microscopic crustaceans, and sea-pen coral lit it gently with their phosphorescent glimmers. I glimpsed piles of stones covered with a couple million zoophytes and tangles of algae. My feet often skidded on this viscous carpet of seaweed, and without my alpenstock I would have taken a tumble more than once. When I turned around I still saw the *Nautilus*'s whitish beacon, which was starting to turn pale in the distance.

Those piles of stones I just mentioned were laid out on the ocean floor with a distinct but bewildering symmetry. I saw gigantic furrows trailing off into the distant darkness, their length incalculable. In addition there were other peculiarities I couldn't make sense of. My heavy lead soles seemed to be trampling a blanket of bones that made a dry, crackling sound. What could they be, these wide plains I was crossing in this way? I wanted to question the captain, but I still hadn't learned the sign language that allowed him to chat with his companions when they went with him on his underwater excursions.

Meanwhile the reddish glow guiding us had spread out and lit up the horizon. The presence of that furnace under the waters had me extremely puzzled. Was it some sort of electrical discharge? Was I nearing some natural phenomenon still unknown to scientists on shore? Or was that fire—the thought *did* occur to me—caused by the hand of man? Had human beings fanned that flame? In these deep strata would I meet up with more of Captain Nemo's companions, friends he was going to visit who led lives as strange as his own? Would I find a whole colony of exiles in these nether regions, men weary of the world's woes, men who had searched for independence and found it on the ocean floor? All these insane, unacceptable ideas dogged me, and in this frame of mind, continually excited by the series of wonders passing in front of my eyes, I wouldn't have been surprised to find, right here on this sea bottom, one of those underwater towns Captain Nemo dreamed of!

Our path grew brighter and brighter. The red glow had turned white and was radiating from a mountain peak about 800 feet high. But what I saw was only a reflection produced by the crystal-clear waters of these strata. The furnace that gave off this bewildering light was located on the other side of the mountain.

Captain Nemo moved forward without hesitation through the maze of stones furrowing this Atlantic seafloor. He knew this dark path. No doubt he'd often traveled it and was incapable of losing his way. I followed him with unshakable confidence. He seemed like some Spirit of the Sea, and as he walked in front of me, I marveled at his tall figure, a black silhouette against the glowing background of the horizon.

It was one o'clock in the morning. We arrived at the mountain's lower gradients. But in grappling with them, we had to venture up difficult trails through a huge thicket.

That's right, a thicket of dead trees! Trees with no leaves, without sap, petrified by the action of the waters, with gigantic pines towering over them here and there. It was like a vertical coalfield, its roots hanging onto the broken soil, its boughs clearly silhouetted against the ceiling of the waters like thin, black, paper cutouts. Imagine a forest clinging to the sides of a peak in the Harz Mountains, but a submerged forest. Algae and fucus plants clogged the trails, a host of crustaceans swarming among them. I forged ahead, scaling rocks, straddling fallen tree trunks, snapping marine creepers that swayed from one tree to another, scaring away the fish that flew from branch to branch. In my excitement I didn't feel tired anymore. I followed a guide who was tireless.

What a sight! How can I put it into words!

How can I depict these woods and rocks in this liquid setting, their lower parts dark and menacing, their upper parts colored red by that light whose intensity increased when the waters reflected it! We scaled enormous sections of rock that collapsed behind us with the hollow rumble of an avalanche. To our right and left, gloomy hallways had been gouged out and they were too dark to peer into. Wide glades opened up, looking as if human hands had cleared them, and at times I wondered if some resident of these underwater regions might suddenly make an appearance right in front of my eyes.

But Captain Nemo kept climbing. I didn't want to fall behind. I followed him boldly. My alpenstock gave me much-needed assistance. The smallest stumble would have been disastrous on the narrow paths cut into the sides of those chasms, but I walked with a firm step and without any feeling of dizziness. Sometimes I jumped over a crevasse so deep, I would have shrunk back if I'd been in the midst of glaciers on land; sometimes I ventured out on a wobbly tree trunk fallen across some gorge, without looking down, my eyes marveling only at the wild scenery of this region. Leaning on their unevenly cut bases, monumental rocks seemed to defy the laws of balance. Between their stony knees, trees sprang up like jets of liquid under fearsome pressure, leaning on each other for support. Then came natural towers with wide, steeply hewed battlements, all slanting at angles that the laws of gravity would never have allowed on dry land.

And I personally could feel the difference created by the water's powerful density—despite my heavy clothing, brass headpiece, and metal soles, I climbed the most impossibly steep gradients with all the nimbleness, I swear it, of a chamois or a Pyrenees mountain goat!

As for my account of this excursion under the waters, I'm well aware that it sounds incredible! I'm the chronicler of events seemingly impossible yet indisputably real. This wasn't a dream. This was what I saw and felt!

Two hours after leaving the *Nautilus*, we'd made it to the timberline, and the mountain peak stood a hundred feet overhead, forming a dark silhouette against the brilliant glare that came from the other side. A few petrified shrubs rambled here and there in scowling zigzags. Fish rose in a body at our feet like birds startled in tall grass. This mass of rock was pitted with bottomless crevices, yawning caves, and holes too deep to plumb, and at their far ends I could hear fearsome things moving around. My blood would curdle as I watched some enormous antenna bar my path, or heard some frightful pincer snap shut in the shadow of some cavity! A thousand specks of light glittered in the midst of the gloom. They were the eyes of gigantic crustaceans hiding out in their lairs, giant lobsters rearing up like spear carriers and twitching their claws with a scrap-metal clanking, titanic crabs aiming their bodies like cannons on their carriages, and hideous devilfish intertwining their tentacles like bushes of writhing snakes.

What could this be, this outrageous world so new to me? In what order did these articulata belong, these creatures for which the rocks furnished a second carapace? Where had nature found the secret of their static existence, and how many centuries had they lived like this in the ocean's lower strata?

But I couldn't dawdle. Captain Nemo was on familiar terms with these dreadful creatures and no longer minded them. We'd arrived at a preliminary plateau where still more surprises were waiting for me. There picturesque ruins took shape, revealing the hand of man, not our Creator. They were huge piles of stones in which you could make out the blurred forms of palaces and temples, now adorned with a host of flowering zoophytes and covered, not by ivy, but by a heavy mantle of algae and fucus plants.

But what part of the globe could this be, this realm that cataclysms had swallowed up? Who had set up these rocks and stones like the dolmens of prehistoric times? Where was I, where had Captain Nemo's fancies taken me?

I wanted to question him. Unable to, I stopped him. I grabbed his arm. But he shook his head, pointed to the mountain's highest peak, and seemed to be telling me:

"Come on! Come with me! Come higher!"

I followed him with a last burst of energy and a few minutes later I'd scaled that peak, which towered some thirty feet above the whole mass of rock.

I looked down the side we'd just climbed. There the mountain rose only 700 or 800 feet above the plains; but on the other side it towered over the receding bottom of this part of the Atlantic by a height twice that. I peered into the distance and took in a vast area lit by fiery flashes of light. In actuality this mountain was a volcano. Fifty feet below its peak, under a shower of stones and slag, a wide crater spewed out torrents of lava that were dispersed in blazing cascades into the heart of this mass of liquid. Positioned as it was, this volcano was an immense torch that lit up the lower plains all the way to the horizon.

As I said, this underwater crater spewed lava, not flames. Flames need oxygen from the air and can't spread beneath the waves; but a lava flow has its own source of incandescence and can rise to a white heat, overpower the liquid element, and turn it into steam on contact. Swift currents carried off all that diffuse gas, and rivers of lava slid to the foot of the mountain, like the volcanic waste from Mt. Vesuvius flowing over the city limits of a second Torre del Greco.

In fact, right under my eyes was a town in ruins, demolished, overwhelmed, laid low, its roofs caved in, its temples pulled down, its arches dislocated, its columns lying on the ground; in those ruins you could still detect the solid proportions of a sort of Tuscan architecture; farther away, the remains of a gigantic aqueduct; here, the caked heights of an acropolis along with the fluid forms of a Parthenon; there, the remnants of a wharf, as if some bygone port had formerly harbored merchant vessels and triple-tiered war galleys on the shores of some lost ocean; still farther away, long rows of collapsing walls, empty boulevards, a whole Pompeii buried under the waters, which Captain Nemo had resurrected beneath my eyes!

Where was I? I wanted to find out at any cost, I wanted to speak, I wanted to tear off the brass globe imprisoning my head.

But Captain Nemo came over and stopped me with a gesture. Then he took a piece of chalky stone, went to a slab of black basalt, and scrawled this one word on the rock:

ATLANTIS

What a blaze of light flashed through my mind! Atlantis, the ancient country of Meropis spoken of by the historian Theopompus; Plato's Atlantis; the continent whose very existence has been disputed by such philosophers and scientists as Origen, Porphyry, Iamblichus, d'Anville, Malte-Brun, and Humboldt, who entered its disappearance in the ledger of myths and folk tales; the realm that such other thinkers as Posidonius, Pliny, Ammianus Marcellinus, Tertullian, Engel, Scherer, Tournefort, Buffon, and d'Avezac have accepted as real—that land lay right under my eyes, furnishing its own unimpeachable evidence of the catastrophe that had overtaken it! So this was the submerged region that had existed outside Europe, Asia, and Libya, beyond the Pillars of Hercules, the home of those mighty Atlantean people against whom ancient Greece had waged its earliest wars!

The author whose writings record the lofty deeds of those heroic times is Plato himself. His dialogues *Timaeus* and *Critias* were drafted with the poet and lawmaker Solon as their inspiration, so to speak.

One day Solon was conversing with some elderly wise men in the Egyptian capital of Sais, a town already 8,000 years of age, as documented by the annals inscribed on the sacred walls of its temples. One of these elders narrated the history of another town 1,000 years older still. That original city of Athens, ninety centuries old, had been invaded and partially destroyed by the Atlanteans. Those Atlanteans, he said, lived on an immense continent bigger than Africa and Asia combined, taking in an area that lay between latitude 12° and 40° north. Their dominion reached even to Egypt. They tried to enforce their rule as far as Greece, but they had to retreat before the indomitable resistance of the Hellenic people. Centuries went by. A cataclysm occurred—floods, earthquakes. It took

only a single night and day to wipe out this Atlantis, whose highest peaks (Madeira, the Azores, the Canaries, the Cape Verde Islands) still poke above the waves.

These were the historical memories Captain Nemo's scrawl sent pulsating through my mind. Hence, led by the strangest of fates, I'd set foot on one of the mountains of that continent! My hands were touching ruins many thousands of years old, contemporary with prehistoric times! I was walking in the same place where the contemporaries of early man had walked! My heavy soles were trampling the skeletons of animals from the age of fable, animals that used to crouch in the shade of these trees that were now petrified!

Oh, why was I so short of time! I would have gone down the steep slopes of this mountain, crossed this whole huge continent that surely connects Africa with America, and visited its great prehistoric cities. Maybe the warlike town of Makhimos lay under my eyes, or the pious village of Eusebes, whose gigantic residents lived for whole centuries and were strong enough to pile up these stones that still withstood the action of the waters. Maybe one day some volcanic phenomenon will bring these sunken ruins back to the surface of the waves! Many underwater volcanoes have been sighted in this part of the ocean, and several ships have felt terrific tremors while passing over these turbulent depths. A few have heard hollow sounds announcing some battle of the elements down below, others have hauled in volcanic ash that shot above the waves. As far as the equator, this whole seafloor is still under construction by eruptive forces. And who knows, in some far-off time these fire-breathing mountaintops, built up by volcanic waste and consecutive layers of lava, could reappear above the surface of the Atlantic!

As I daydreamed in this way, trying to establish every detail of that impressive landscape in my memory, Captain Nemo leaned his elbows on a mossy monument and sank into a silent trance, as motionless as if turned to stone. Was he thinking about those lost generations, asking them for the secret of human destiny? Was it here that this strange man came to refresh himself, basking in his-

torical memories, reliving that bygone existence, he who had no desire for our modern one? I would have given anything to learn his thoughts, to share them, understand them!

We stayed in that place a whole hour, contemplating its wide plains in the lava's glow, which sometimes took on a startling intensity. Underground bubblings sent quick shivers racing through the mountain's crust. Noises from down below, clearly transmitted by this liquid medium, boomed with majestic resonance.

Just then the moon appeared for an instant through the mass of water, casting a few pale rays over this submerged continent. It was only a glimmer, but its effect was indescribable. The captain straightened and took one last look at those immense plains; then he gave me a hand signal to follow him.

We went swiftly down the mountain. Once we were past the petrified forest, I could see the *Nautilus*'s beacon twinkling like a star. The captain walked right toward it, and we were back on board just as the first tints of dawn were whitening the surface of the ocean.

34

THE UNDERWATER COALFIELDS

THE NEXT DAY, February 20, I overslept. I was so worn out from the night before, I didn't get up till eleven o'clock. I instantly got dressed. I hurried to find out the *Nautilus*'s heading. The instruments showed that it was running southward at a speed of twenty miles per hour and a depth of 330 feet.

Conseil came in. I described our nocturnal excursion to him, and since the panels were open, he could still glimpse part of that submerged continent.

In fact the *Nautilus* was skimming those Atlantis plains just thirty feet above the seafloor. The ship scudded along like a hot air balloon carried by the wind over some prairie on land; but it would be nearer the truth to say that sitting in this lounge was like riding in a coach on an express train. As for the foregrounds passing in front of our eyes, they were fantastically carved rocks, forests of trees that had crossed from the vegetable kingdom into the mineral kingdom, their motionless silhouettes scowling under the waves. In addition there were masses of stone buried beneath carpets of sea squirts and sea anemones, all garnished with long vertical water plants, then strangely shaped lava rocks that testified to a furious amount of volcanic activity.

While these peculiar locales were glittering under our electric beams, I told Conseil the history of the Atlanteans, who had inspired the old French scientist Jean Bailly to write so many entertaining—though utterly fictitious—pages.[18] I told the lad about the wars of those valiant people. I discussed the issue of Atlantis as a man who would never again doubt its existence. But Conseil was so distracted that he barely heard me, and his lack of interest in this historical topic was soon explained.

In essence many fish were catching his eye, and when fish go by, Conseil descends into the realm of classification and leaves real life behind. In which case I could only tag along and resume our ichthyological research.

Even so, these Atlantic fish weren't noticeably different from the ones we'd studied earlier. There were rays of gigantic size, sixteen feet long and boasting such great muscle power that they could leap above the waves, sharks of various species including a fifteen-foot spiny dogfish with sharp triangular teeth and so transparent that it was almost invisible in the midst of the waters, brown lantern sharks, prickly dogfish that were prism-shaped and armored with protuberant hides, sturgeons resembling their relatives in the Mediterranean, plus broad-nosed pipefish eighteen inches long, yellowish brown with little gray fins but no teeth or tongue, and uncoiling like slim, supple snakes.

Among bony fish Conseil noticed some blackish marlin ten feet long with a sharp sword jutting from the upper jaw, bright-colored weevers known in Aristotle's day as sea dragons and whose dorsal stingers

make them very dangerous to grab, then dolphinfish that had brown backs with little blue stripes and gold borders, handsome dorado, moonfish called opahs that look like azure disks but which the sun's rays turn into spots of silver, finally swordfish from the genus *Xiphias*, over twenty-five feet long and swimming in schools—these stalwart creatures had yellowish, sickle-shaped fins and six-foot broadswords, were plant eaters rather than fish eaters, and obeyed the tiniest signals from their females like henpecked husbands.

But while studying these different specimens of marine fauna, I still kept a close eye on the long plains of Atlantis. At times some unpredictable irregularity in the seafloor would oblige the *Nautilus* to go slower, and then it would glide into the narrow channels between the hills with a cetacean's agility. If the labyrinth became hopelessly tangled, the submersible rose above it like an airship; then, after going past the obstacle, it resumed its speedy course a few yards above the ocean floor. It was an enjoyable and impressive way of navigating that did indeed recall the maneuvers of an airship ride, with the major difference that the *Nautilus* faithfully obeyed the hands of its helmsman.

The terrain consisted mostly of heavy slime interspersed with petrified branches, but it gradually changed around four o'clock in the afternoon; it grew rockier and seemed to be sprinkled with pudding stones and a basaltic gravel known as tuff, along with a few pinches of lava and sulfurous obsidian. I figured these long plains would soon lead to a mountain region, and sure enough, as the *Nautilus* turned this way and that, I saw a high wall blocking the southerly horizon and apparently closing off all exits. Its top obviously poked above the level of the ocean. It must have been a continent or at the very least an island, either one of the Canaries or one of the Cape Verde Islands. Our bearings hadn't been marked on the chart—maybe deliberately—and I had no idea what our position was. In any event that wall seemed to signal the end of Atlantis, of which, all in all, we'd crossed only the tiniest part.

Nighttime didn't interrupt my investiga-

---

[18] *Translator's note.* Bailly believed that Atlantis was located at the North Pole!

tions. I was on my own. Conseil had retired to his cabin. The *Nautilus* slowed down and hovered above the chaotic shapes on the seafloor, sometimes brushing them as if trying to come to rest, sometimes rising eccentrically to the surface of the waves. Then I glimpsed a few bright constellations through the crystal-clear waters, specifically five or six of those zodiacal stars trailing from the tail end of Orion.

I would have stayed much longer at my window, marveling at these beauties of sea and sky, but the panels closed. Just then the *Nautilus* had arrived at the vertical face of that high wall. I hadn't a clue what the ship would do next. I retired to my stateroom. The *Nautilus* didn't stir. I fell asleep with the firm intention of waking up in a couple of hours.

But it was eight o'clock in the morning when I went back to the lounge. I looked at the pressure gauge. It told me the *Nautilus* was floating on the surface of the ocean. What's more, I heard the sound of footsteps on the platform. Yet there weren't any rolling movements to indicate the presence of waves undulating overhead.

I climbed up to the hatch. It was open. But instead of the broad daylight I expected, absolute darkness surrounded me. Where were we? Had I been mistaken? Was it still night? No, not one star was twinkling, and nighttime is never as completely black as that!

I wasn't sure what to think, when a voice said to me:

"Is that you, professor?"

"Ah, Captain Nemo," I replied. "Where are we?"

"Underground, professor."

"Underground!" I exclaimed. "And the *Nautilus* is still floating?"

"It always floats."

"But I don't understand."

"Wait a few seconds. Our beacon is about to go on, and if you want some light on the subject, you'll have your wish."

I set foot on the platform and waited. It was so pitch-black, I couldn't even see Captain Nemo. But when I looked at the zenith directly overhead, I thought I caught sight of a faint glimmer, a sort of twilight filtering through a circular hole. Just then the beacon suddenly went on, and its intense brightness made that dim light vanish.

This stream of electricity dazzled my eyes, and after shutting them for a moment, I looked around. The *Nautilus* was stationary. It was floating beside an embankment made over to function as a wharf. As for the water now buoying the ship, it was a lake completely enclosed by a circular wall about two miles across, hence six miles around. Its level—as shown by our pressure gauge—would be the same as the outside level, because some connection had to exist between this lake and the sea itself. The walls slanted inward over their base, converging to form a vault shaped like an immense upside-down funnel that measured some 500 or 600 yards high. At the top was the circular opening through which I'd detected that faint glimmer, obviously daylight.

Before more carefully examining the inner features of this enormous cavern, and before deciding if it was the work of man or nature, I went over to Captain Nemo.

"Where are we?" I said.

"In the very heart of an extinct volcano," the captain answered me, "a volcano whose interior was invaded by the sea after some upheaval in the earth. While you were asleep, professor, the *Nautilus* entered this lagoon through a natural channel that opens some thirty feet below the surface of the ocean. This is our home port, secure, convenient, secret, and shielded against winds from any direction! Along the coasts of your continents or islands, show me a single offshore mooring that can match this safe refuge for withstanding the fury of hurricanes."

"It's true," I replied. "Here you're in perfect safety, Captain Nemo. Who could get at you in the heart of a volcano! But didn't I see an opening at the top?"

"Yes, its crater, a crater that used to be filled with lava, steam, and flames but that now lets in this fresh air we're breathing."

"But what volcanic mountain is this?" I asked.

"It's one of the many islets sprinkled over this sea. For ships merely a reef, for us an immense cavern. I discovered it by chance, and chance did me a good turn."

"But couldn't somebody enter through the mouth of that crater?"

"No more than I could exit through it. You can get about a hundred feet up the inner side of the mountain's base, but then the walls overhang at such a sharp angle, you can't climb any farther."

"I can see, captain, that nature is your obedient servant, anytime, anywhere. You're safe on this lake, and nobody else can visit its waters. But what's the point of this refuge? The *Nautilus* doesn't need a harbor."

"No, professor, but it needs electricity to run, batteries to generate its electricity, sodium to feed its batteries, coal to make its sodium, and coalfields to supply its coal. Now then, right at this spot the sea covers whole forests that sank underwater in prehistoric times; today, turned to stone, transformed into fossil fuel, they offer me inexhaustible coal mines."

"So, captain, your men practice the trade of miners here?"

"Exactly. These mines reach under the waves like the coalfields in Newcastle. Dressed in diving suits, pick and mattock in hand, my men go out and dig up this fossil fuel, which means I don't need a single mine on land. When I burn this combustible to produce sodium, the smoke escaping from the crater makes this mountain look like a volcano that's still active."

"And will we see your companions at work?"

"No, at least not this time, because I'm in a hurry to resume our underwater tour of the world. Accordingly I'll rest content with drawing on my reserve supply of sodium. We'll stay here long enough to load it on board—in other words, a single workday—then we'll resume our voyage. So, Professor Aronnax, if you would like to explore this cavern and circle its lagoon, seize the day."

I thanked the captain and went to look for my two companions, who hadn't left their cabin yet. I invited them to follow me, not telling them where we were.

They climbed onto the platform. Conseil, whom nothing could amaze, viewed it as a perfectly natural matter to fall asleep under the waves and wake up under a mountain.

But the only idea Ned Land had in his head was to see if there might be some way out of this cavern.

After breakfast near ten o'clock, we went down onto the embankment.

"So here we are, back on shore," Conseil said.

"I wouldn't exactly call this shore," the Canadian replied. "And besides, we aren't on it but under it."

Between the waters of the lake and the foot of the mountain's walls, a sandy beach unfolded, 500 feet across at its widest point. Going along this shoreline, you could easily circle the lake. But at the base of those high walls, the ground was broken up and littered with picturesque piles of volcanic rock and enormous pumice stones. Underground fires had given all these disintegrating masses a glazed finish, and they glittered in the stream of electric light from our beacon. Stirred up by our footsteps, the mica dust on this beach flew into the air like a cloud of sparks.

As we got farther from the sand flats by the waves, the ground rose appreciably and we soon arrived at some long winding gradients, authentic mountain trails that allowed us to go higher little by little; but we had to watch our step in the midst of the pudding stones that weren't cemented together, and our feet kept skidding on the glassy trachyte made of feldspar and quartz crystals.

The volcanic character of this enormous cavity was apparent everywhere. I commented on it to my companions.

"Can you picture," I asked them, "what this funnel must have been like when it was filled with boiling lava, and that white-hot liquid rose right to the mountain's crater, like cast iron up the insides of a blast furnace?"

"I can picture it perfectly," Conseil replied. "But will master tell me why this huge smelter suspended operations and why an oven was replaced by the tranquil waters of a lake?"

"In all likelihood, Conseil, because some upheaval created an opening below the surface of the sea, the opening that serves as a passageway for the *Nautilus*. Then the Atlantic Ocean rushed inside the mountain. A dreadful battle ensued between the elements of fire and water, a battle ending in Neptune's favor. But many centuries have gone by since then, and this submerged volcano has turned into a peaceful cavern."

"That's fine," Ned Land answered. "I can go along with that explanation, but in our own best interests, I'm sorry this opening the professor mentions wasn't made above sea level."

"But Ned my friend," Conseil contended, "if it weren't an underwater passageway, the *Nautilus* couldn't enter it!"

"And I might add, Mr. Land," I said, "that the ocean wouldn't have rushed under the mountain and the volcano would still be a volcano. So you have nothing to be sorry about."

Our climb continued. The gradients grew steeper and narrower. Cutting across them were occasional deep crevices that we had to get over. There were masses of overhanging rock we needed to work our way around. We slid on our knees, we crawled on our bellies. But thanks to Conseil's skill and the Canadian's strength, we overcame every obstacle.

About a hundred feet up, the character of the terrain changed without getting any easier to handle. The pudding stones and trachyte gave way to black basalt: here, lying in slabs all spattered with blisters; there, actually prism-shaped and organized into a series of columns that supported the springings of this immense vault, a wonderful specimen of natural architecture. Between these pieces of basalt meandered long, hardened lava flows that were lined with veins of bituminous coal and sometimes covered with wide blankets of sulfur. The sunshine coming through the crater had grown stronger, shedding a dim light over all the volcanic waste buried forever in the heart of this extinct mountain.

But when we'd gotten about 250 feet up, we were stopped by insurmountable obstacles. The converging inside walls had turned into overhangs and our climb into a circular stroll. At this uppermost level the vegetable kingdom started to challenge the mineral kingdom. A few shrubs and even some trees emerged from crevices in the walls. I identified some spurges that were letting their bitter sap trickle out. There were heliotropes that did a poor job of living up to their name—getting no sunlight, their colors had faded, plus their scents were gone and their blossoms woefully wilted. Here and there a few chrysanthemums grew timidly at the foot of aloes with long, sad, sickly leaves. But between those lava flows I spotted some little violets that still gave off a subtle fragrance and I must admit that I sniffed them with delight. The soul of a flower is its scent, and those splendid water plants, the flowers of the sea, have no souls!

We'd arrived at the foot of a sturdy clump of dragon trees, which were pushing the rocks aside with exertions of their muscular roots, when Ned Land exclaimed:

"Look, sir, a hive!"

"A hive?" I responded, making a gesture that scoffed at this.

"Yes, a hive," the Canadian said again, "with bees buzzing around!"

I went closer and had to bow to the evidence. Near a hole in the trunk of a dragon tree were swarming thousands of those clever insects so common to all the Canary Islands, where their output is especially prized.

Naturally the Canadian wanted to lay in a supply of honey, and it would have been ill-mannered of me to say no. He mixed some dry leaves with sulfur, set the concoction on fire with a spark from his tinderbox, and proceeded to smoke the bees out. Gradually the buzzing died down, and the disemboweled hive yielded several pounds of fragrant honey. Ned Land stuffed his haversack with it.

"When I've mixed this honey with our breadfruit batter," he told us, "I'll be ready to bake you a scrumptious cake."

"Of course!" Conseil put in. "We'll have gingerbread!"

"With all deference to the gingerbread," I said, "let's get back to this interesting stroll."

At various turns in the trail we were taking, the lake appeared in its full expanse. The ship's beacon lit up that whole peaceful surface, which experienced neither ripples nor undulations. The *Nautilus* stayed perfectly still. On its platform and the embankment, crewmen were bustling about, black shadows sharply silhouetted in that luminous air.

Just then we worked our way around the highest ridge of those rocky foothills that supported the vaulting. At this point I saw that bees weren't the animal kingdom's only representatives inside this volcano. Here and in the shadows, birds of prey soared and whirled, flying away from nests perched on tips of rock. There were white-bellied sparrow hawks and screeching kestrels. With all the speed their stiltlike legs could muster, fine fat bustards scampered over the slopes. The reader can imagine how quickly the Canadian's appetite was aroused by the sight of this tasty game and how he regretted not having a rifle in his hands. He tried to make do with stones in place of bullets, and after several fruitless attempts, he managed to wound one of those magnificent bustards. To say he risked his life twenty times in order to capture that bird is simply the unadulterated truth; but he fared so well, the creature went into his sack to join the honeycombs.

By then we were forced to go back down to the beach, because the ridge had become impossible to climb. Above us that yawning crater looked like the mouth of a huge well. The sky was pretty easy to make out from where we stood, and I watched some clouds race by, disheveled by the west wind, letting tatters of mist trail over the mountaintop. Proof positive that those clouds were only moderately high up, because this volcano didn't rise more than 1,800 feet above the level of the ocean.

Half an hour after the Canadian's latest exploits, we were back on the inner beach. There the local flora was represented by a wide carpet of samphire, a small carrotlike plant that keeps quite nicely and also goes by the names glasswort, saxifrage, and sea fennel. Conseil picked a couple bunches. As for the local fauna, it featured thousands of crustaceans of every type, including lobsters, brown crabs, prawns, plankton, daddy longlegs, squat lobsters, and a prodigious number of shellfish such as cowries, rock snails, and limpets.

In this locality we found the entrance to a magnificent cave. My companions and I took pleasure in stretching out on the fine-grained sand inside it. Fire had buffed its glazed, sparkling walls, sprinkled all over with mica dust. Ned Land tapped these walls and tried to probe their thickness. I couldn't help smiling. Then our conversation shifted to his eternal escape plans, and without going too far, I felt I could offer him this hope: Captain Nemo had gone down south only to replenish his sodium supplies. So I hoped he now would hug the coasts of Europe and America, where the Canadian could try again with a greater chance of success.

We were stretched out in this delightful cave for an hour. Our conversation was lively at the outset, then it wound down. A definite drowsiness overcame us. Since I didn't see any reason to fight it off, I fell sound asleep. I dreamed—one doesn't choose his dreams—that my life had been reduced to the static existence of a humble mollusk. It seemed to me that this cave formed my double-valved shell. . . .

Suddenly Conseil's voice startled me awake.

"Get up! Get up!" the fine lad shouted.

"What is it?" I asked, in a sitting position.

"The water's rising!"

I got back on my feet. The sea was rushing like a torrent into our hideaway, and since we definitely weren't mollusks, we had to clear out.

In a few seconds we'd reached safety above the cave.

"What was that about?" Conseil asked. "Some new natural phenomenon?"

"Not quite, my friends," I replied. "It was the tide, only the tide, which nearly caught us by surprise the same way it did Sir Walter Scott's hero! The ocean outside is rising, and by a perfectly natural law of balance, the level of this lake is also rising. We got off with just a mild dunking. Let's go back to the *Nautilus* and change clothes."

Three-quarters of an hour later, we'd finished our circular stroll and were back on board. At the same moment the crewmen finished loading the sodium supplies, so the *Nautilus* could have left immediately.

But Captain Nemo didn't issue any orders. Would he wait for nightfall and exit through his underwater passageway in secrecy? Maybe.

Be that as it may, by the next day the *Nautilus* had left its home port and was navigating well out from any shore, a few yards under the waves of the Atlantic.

35

THE SARGASSO SEA

THE *NAUTILUS* didn't change direction. For the time being, then, we had to set aside any hope of going back to European seas. Captain Nemo kept his prow pointing south. Where was he taking us? I was afraid to guess.

That day the *Nautilus* crossed an odd part of the Atlantic Ocean. Everybody knows about the existence of that great warm-water current called the Gulf Stream. After emerging from channels near Florida, it heads up to Spitsbergen. But before entering the Gulf of Mexico around latitude 44° north, this current divides into two arms; its chief arm makes for the shores of Ireland and Norway while the second flexes southward level with the Azores; then it reaches the coast of Africa, sweeps in a long oval, and goes back to the Caribbean Sea.

Now then, this second arm—which is more like a collar, to be exact—forms a ring of warm water around a section of cool, tranquil, motionless ocean called the Sargasso Sea. This is an honest-to-goodness lake in the open Atlantic, and the great current's waters take at least three years to circle it.

The Sargasso Sea proper covers the whole submerged region of Atlantis. Some writers have even held that the many weeds scattered over this sea were uprooted from the prairies of that ancient continent. It's more likely, however, that those grasses, algae, and fucus plants were carried off from the shores of Europe and America, then taken as far as this zone by the Gulf Stream. Which is one of the reasons why Christopher Columbus believed in the existence of a New World. When the ships of that bold investigator arrived in the Sargasso Sea, they had difficulty navigating in the midst of these weeds, which, much to their crews' dismay, brought them to a stop and made them waste three long weeks crossing this sector.

That was the region our *Nautilus* was visiting just then, an authentic prairie, a close-knit carpet of algae, float fucus, and gulfweed so dense and compact, a craft's stempost couldn't tear through it without difficulty. Accordingly, not wanting to entangle his propeller in this weed-choked mass, Captain Nemo kept his ship a few yards below the surface of the waves.

The name Sargasso comes from the Spanish word *sargazo*, meaning seaweed. This particular seaweed, called gulfweed or sea holly, is the chief substance making up this immense bed of vegetation. And here's why these water plants collect in this placid Atlantic basin, according to the expert on the subject, Commander Maury, author of *The Physical Geography of the Sea*.

The explanation he gives seems to entail a set of conditions that everybody knows. "Now," Maury says, "if bits of cork or chaff, or any floating substance, be put into a basin, and a circular motion be given to the water, all the light substances will be found crowding together near the center of the pool, where there is the least motion. Just such a basin is the Atlantic Ocean to the Gulf Stream, and the Sargasso Sea is the center of the whirl."

I share Maury's view and I was able to study the phenomenon in this unique setting where ships rarely go. Huddling among the brown weeds, objects floated above us that had originated from all over: tree trunks uprooted from the Rocky Mountains or the Andes and sent drifting down the Amazon or the Mississippi, many pieces of wreckage, remains of keels or undersides, bulwarks staved in and so weighed down with seashells and barnacles, they couldn't rise to the surface of the ocean. And the march of time will someday bear out Maury's other view that by collecting in this way down through the centuries, these substances will be petrified by the action of the waters and will form inexhaustible coalfields. Valuable reserves prepared by farseeing nature for that moment when man will have used up his mines on dry land.

Amid this hopelessly tangled fabric of weeds and fucus plants, I noted some delightful pink-tinted, star-shaped leather coral, some sea anemones trailing their tentacles like long tresses, some green, red, and blue medusas, and especially some of those giant jellyfish from the genus *Rhizostoma* that Cuvier described, whose bluish parasols are trimmed with violet festoons.

We spent that entire day of February 22 in the Sargasso Sea, where fish that hanker after marine plants and crustaceans find plenty of food. The next day the ocean resumed its customary appearance.

From then on, for nineteen days from February 23 to March 12, the *Nautilus* kept to the middle of the Atlantic, hustling us along at a constant speed of a hundred leagues every twenty-four hours. It was clear that Captain Nemo intended to stay on his underwater schedule, and I had no doubt that he planned, after doubling Cape Horn, to go back to the seas of the south Pacific.

So Ned Land had good reason to be anxious. There was no way we could jump ship in these wide seas that hadn't any islands. Nor could we oppose Captain Nemo's wishes. All we could do was play along; but if we couldn't achieve our ends through force or cunning, I hoped we could succeed through persuasion. When this voyage was over, wouldn't Captain Nemo agree to set us free in exchange for our promise to never reveal his existence? Our word of honor, which we would have kept without fail. However this delicate matter needed to be negotiated with the captain. But how would he receive our request for freedom? Right at the outset and in no uncertain terms, hadn't he stated that his secret existence required us to be permanently imprisoned aboard the *Nautilus*? Wasn't he sure to take my four-month silence as a tacit acceptance of the situation? Wouldn't bringing up this subject again only arouse suspicions that could hamper our escape plans, if we had promising circumstances for trying again later on? I weighed all these considerations, turned them over in my mind, and ran them by Conseil, but he was as baffled as I was. In short, though I'm not easily discouraged, I could see that my chances of ever rejoining the human race were shrinking by the day, especially at a time when Captain Nemo was recklessly heading for the south Atlantic!

During the nineteen days just mentioned, our voyage was fairly uneventful. I saw little of the captain. He was at work. In the library I often found books he'd left open, especially books on natural history. He'd gone page by page through my work on the great ocean depths and had covered the margins with his notes, which sometimes contradicted my suppositions and formulations. But the captain remained content with this way of editing my text and he rarely discussed it with me. Sometimes I heard melancholy sounds coming from the organ, which he played very expressively but only at night in the midst of the most secretive darkness, while the *Nautilus* was asleep in the wilds of the ocean.

During this part of our voyage, we navigated on the surface of the waves for whole days. The sea was nearly deserted. Laden for the East Indies, a few sailing ships were making for the Cape of Good Hope. One day we were chased by the longboats of a whaling vessel, which no doubt mistook us for some huge, highly valuable baleen whale. But Captain Nemo didn't want the gallant gentlemen wasting their time and energy, so he ended the hunt by diving under the waters. This event seemed to interest Ned Land intensely. I'm sure the Canadian was sorry those fishermen couldn't harpoon our sheet-iron cetacean and mortally wound it.

During this time the fish Conseil and I studied barely differed from the ones we'd already examined in other latitudes. Chief among them were specimens from the shark clan, that dreadful genus of cartilaginous fish that's divided into three subgenera numbering at least thirty-two species: striped catsharks sixteen feet long, the head flattened out and wider than the body, the caudal fin curved, the back with seven big black parallel lines that ran lengthwise; then perlon sharks, ash gray, pierced with seven gill openings, furnished with a single dorsal fin positioned almost exactly in the middle of the body.

Some big dogfish also went by, a voracious breed of shark if there ever was one. Fishing yarns are rightly regarded as untrustworthy, but here's what a few of them have to say. Inside the carcass of one of these creatures, fishermen found a buffalo head and a whole calf; in another, two tuna and a sailor in uniform; in yet another, a soldier with his saber; finally, in still another, a horse with its rider. Frankly none of this sounds like divine revelation. But the fact remains that not a single one of these creatures let itself get caught in the *Nautilus*'s nets, so I couldn't verify their voracity.

Pods of elegant, playful dolphins swam alongside us for whole days. They went in groups of five or six, hunting in packs like wolves out in the countryside; what's more, they're just as voracious as dogfish, if I can believe a certain Copenhagen professor who says he removed thirteen porpoises and fifteen seals from the belly of just one dolphin. True, it was a killer whale of the biggest known species, whose length sometimes exceeds twenty-four feet. The family Delphinidae includes ten genera, and the dolphins I saw belonged to the genus *Delphinorhynchus*, notable for an extremely narrow muzzle four times as long as the skull. Their bodies were ten feet long, black on top, and underneath a pinkish white sprinkled with small, very sparse spots.

From these seas I'll also mention some unusual specimens of drums, fish from the order Acanthopterygii, family Sciaenidae. Some writers—more artistic than scientific—claim that these fish are melodious singers, that their voices in unison put on concerts unmatched by human choristers. I don't say nay, but to my regret these drums didn't serenade us as we went by.

Finally, to conclude, Conseil classified a large number of flying fish. Nothing could have made a more unusual sight than the marvelous accuracy with which dolphins hunt them. Whatever distance it flew, whatever flight path it took (even up and over the *Nautilus*), the poor flying fish always found a dolphin ready and waiting with open mouth. These were either kitefish or gray gurnards, whose lips glowed in the dark, at night scribbling fiery lines in the air before diving into the murky waters like so many shooting stars.

Our navigating continued under these conditions till March 13. That day the *Nautilus* went to work in some depth-sounding experiments that were of keen interest to me.

By then we'd fared nearly 13,000 leagues from our starting point in the Pacific high seas. Our position fix put us in latitude 45° 37′ south and longitude 37° 53′ west. These were the same waterways where Captain Denham, aboard the *Herald*, payed out 46,000 feet of sounding line but didn't find bottom. Here too Lieutenant Parker, aboard the American frigate *Congress*, couldn't reach the ocean floor at 49,701 feet.

Captain Nemo decided to take his *Nautilus* down to the lowest depths in order to double-check these different soundings. I got ready to record all the results of this experiment. The panels in the lounge opened, and maneuvers began for reaching those prodigiously deep strata.

Apparently it was considered out of the question to dive by filling the ballast tanks. Maybe they wouldn't sufficiently increase the *Nautilus*'s specific gravity. To go back up, moreover, the excess water would need to be expelled, and our pumps might not have been strong enough to overcome the outside pressure.

Captain Nemo decided to search for the ocean floor by diving on an appropriately gradual diagonal with the help of his side fins, which he set at a 45° angle to the *Nautilus*'s waterline. Then he brought the propeller to its maximum speed, and its four blades churned the waves with indescribable force.

Under this powerful thrust, the *Nautilus*'s hull vibrated like a resonating chord as the ship sank steadily beneath the waters. Stationed in the lounge, the captain and I watched the needle move swiftly over our pressure gauge. Soon we'd gone below the livable zone where most fish reside. Some of these creatures can thrive only at the surface of seas or rivers, but a minority can dwell at fairly great depths. Among the latter I noticed a species of dogfish called the mud shark that's furnished with six gill slits, telescope fish with enormous eyes, mailed gurnards with gray thoracic fins and black pectoral fins plus protective breastplates made from pale red slabs of bone, then finally some grenadiers that were living at a depth of 3,900 feet, by that point tolerating a pressure of 120 atmospheres.

I asked Captain Nemo if he'd seen any fish at even greater depths.

"Fish? Hardly ever!" he answered me. "But given the current state of scientific thought, who are we to presume, what do we actually know of these depths?"

"Just this, captain. As we go into the ocean's deeper strata, we know that plant life vanishes more quickly than animal life. We know that moving creatures can still be found where water plants no longer grow. We know that pilgrim scallops and oysters live in 6,500 feet of water, and that Admiral McClintock, England's hero of the polar seas, pulled in a live sea star from a depth of 8,000 feet. We know that the crew of the Royal Navy's *Bulldog* brought up a starfish from 15,720 feet, hence from nearly three miles down. Would you still say, Captain Nemo, that we don't actually know anything?"

"No, professor," the captain replied, "I wouldn't be so bold. Yet can you explain how these creatures manage to live at such depths?"

"I can explain it from two standpoints," I replied. "First, vertical currents—caused by differences in the water's salinity and density—can create enough motion to support the rudimentary lifestyles of sea lilies and starfish."

"True," the captain put in.

"Second, animals need oxygen, and we know that more and more oxygen is dissolved in salt water the deeper you go, so the pressure in those lower strata actually helps to concentrate their oxygen content."

"Oho! We know that, do we?" Captain Nemo replied in a tone of mild surprise. "Well, professor, we have good reason to know it because it's the simple truth. I might add, in fact, that the air bladders of fish hold more nitrogen than oxygen when these creatures are caught at the surface of the water, and by contrast, more oxygen than nitrogen when they're hauled up from the lower

depths. Which bears out your formulation. But let's continue our investigations."

My eyes flew back to the pressure gauge. The instrument showed a depth of nearly 20,000 feet. We'd been submerging for an hour. The *Nautilus* slid downward on its slanting fins, still sinking. Those empty waters were wonderfully clear, their transparency impossible to convey. An hour later we were at 43,000 feet—over eight miles down—yet the ocean floor was nowhere in sight.

But at 46,000 feet down I saw blackish mountaintops rising in the midst of the waters. However these peaks could have belonged to mountains as high or even higher than the Himalayas or Mt. Blanc, and the depth of the seafloor remained incalculable.

Despite the powerful pressures it was experiencing, the *Nautilus* sank still deeper. I could feel its sheet-iron plates trembling down to their riveted joins; its metal braces were bending; its bulkheads groaned; the lounge windows seemed to curve inward under the water pressure. And that whole sturdy mechanism would surely have caved in, if, as its captain had said, it hadn't been capable of resisting like a solid mass.

While grazing those rocky slopes lost under the waters, I still spotted a few seashells, tube-dwelling worms from the genus *Serpula*, lively worms with coiled shells from the genus *Spirorbis*, and some specimens of starfish.

But soon these last forms of animal life vanished, and around nine miles down, the *Nautilus* went below the limits where any marine beings can exist at all, just as a hot air balloon rises into zones in the sky where a person can't breathe. We reached a depth of 52,000 feet—almost ten miles down—and by that point the *Nautilus*'s plating was withstanding a pressure of more than 1,600 atmospheres, in other words, nearly 23,000 pounds on each square inch of its surface!

"What an experience!" I exclaimed. "Roaming these deep regions where no man has ever gone before! Look, captain! Look at those magnificent rocks, those empty caves, those last places on earth where life is no longer possible! What unheard-of scenery, and isn't it a shame we're reduced to preserving it only as a memory!"

"Would you like," Captain Nemo asked me, "to bring back more than just a memory?"

"What do you mean?"

"I mean that nothing could be easier than taking a photograph of this underwater region!"

Before I had time to express my surprise at this new proposition, a camera materialized in the lounge at Captain Nemo's request. Lit by our electric rays, that liquid setting unfolded with perfect clarity through the wide-open panels. No shadows, no blurs, thanks to our artificial light. Not even sunshine would have been better suited to our purposes. The *Nautilus* stood still, the thrust of its propeller curbed by the slant of its fins. The camera took aim at the scenery on the ocean floor, and in a few seconds we had an exceptionally clear negative.

I attach a print of the positive. There you can view those primeval rocks that have never seen daylight, the underlying granite that forms the earth's mighty foundation, the deep caves gouged into the masses of stone— their shapes incomparably clear because their edges were outlined in black as if from the brushes of certain Flemish painters. A mountainous horizon is off in the distance, a marvelously undulating line that forms the background of this landscape. The overall effect of those smooth rocks is indescribable: black, polished, without any moss or other blemishes, hewed into strange shapes, resting solidly on a carpet of sand that sparkled beneath our streams of electric light.

Meanwhile, his photographic operations finished, Captain Nemo told me:

"Let's go back up, professor. We mustn't overdo things and leave the *Nautilus* vulnerable to these pressures for too long."

"Let's go back up!" I replied.

"Hold on tight."

Before I had time to understand why the captain made this recommendation, I was hurled to the carpet.

Its fins set vertically, its propeller thrown in gear at the captain's signal, the *Nautilus* rose with lightning speed, streaking upward like a hot air balloon into the sky. Vibrating resonantly, it sliced through the mass of water. Not a single detail was visible. In four minutes it had covered the ten miles separating it from the surface of the ocean, and after shooting into view like a flying fish, it fell back into the sea, making waves leap to prodigious heights.

36
SPERM WHALES AND RIGHT WHALES

DURING THE NIGHT of March 13–14, the *Nautilus* resumed its southward heading. Once it was off Cape Horn, I figured it would turn to the west, make for Pacific seas, and finish its world tour. It did nothing of the sort and kept moving toward the southernmost regions. So where were we heading? The pole? That was lunacy. I was beginning to think that the captain's recklessness more than justified Ned Land's worries.

For a good while the Canadian hadn't said anything more to me about his escape plans. He'd become less sociable, almost sullen. I could see how heavily this protracted imprisonment was weighing on him. I could feel the anger building in him. Whenever he met the captain, his eyes would flicker with a dark fire, and I was in constant dread that his explosive nature would lead him to some extreme measure.

That day, March 14, he and Conseil managed to catch me in my stateroom. I asked them the reason for their visit.

"I've got a simple question for you, sir," the Canadian answered me.

"Go on, Ned."

"How many men do you figure are aboard the *Nautilus?*"

"I can't say, my friend."

"It seems to me," Ned Land went on, "that it wouldn't take much of a crew to run a ship like this one."

"That's right," I replied. "Under existing conditions about ten men at the most should be enough to operate it."

"Well then," the Canadian said, "why would there be any more than that?"

"Why?" I responded.

I looked at Ned Land, whose motives were easy to guess.

"Because," I said, "if I can trust my hunches, if I truly understand the captain's way of life, his *Nautilus* isn't just a ship. It's meant to be a place of refuge for people like its commander, people who have severed all ties with the shore."

"Maybe," Conseil said. "But in a nutshell, the *Nautilus* can hold only a certain number of men, so couldn't master estimate their maximum?"

"How, Conseil?"

"By calculating it. Master is aware of the ship's capacity, hence the amount of air it holds; on the other hand, master knows how much air each man consumes in the course of breathing, and he can compare those totals to the fact that the *Nautilus* has to rise to the surface every twenty-four hours . . ."

Conseil left his sentence dangling, but I could easily see what he was driving at.

"I get you," I said. "But even though this calculation is simple to do, it can give us only a very rough figure."

"No problem," the Canadian went on stubbornly.

"Then here's how to calculate it," I replied. "In one hour each man consumes the oxygen in 25 gallons of air, hence during twenty-four hours the oxygen in 600 gallons. Therefore we must look for the *multiple* of 600 gallons that gives us the amount of air found in the *Nautilus*."

"Exactly," Conseil said.

"Now then," I went on, "the *Nautilus*'s capacity is 1,660 tons, and there are 226 gallons in a ton, so the *Nautilus* holds some 375,000 gallons of air, which, divided by 600 . . ."

I did a quick pencil calculation.

". . . gives us the quotient of 625. Which is tantamount to saying that the air in the *Nautilus* would be exactly enough for 625 men over twenty-four hours."

"Six hundred and twenty-five!" Ned echoed.

"But rest assured," I added, "between passengers, seamen, or officers, we don't total a tenth of that figure."

"Which is still too many for three men!" Conseil muttered.

"So, my poor Ned, I can only counsel patience."

"And not only patience," Conseil replied, "but acceptance."

Conseil had said the magic word.

"Even so," he went on, "Captain Nemo can't head south forever! Surely he'll have to stop, if only at the ice barrier, then he'll go back to the seas of civilization! And that will be our chance to resume Ned Land's plans."

The Canadian shook his head, mopped his brow, didn't answer, and left us.

"With master's permission, I'll make a comment to him," Conseil told me. "Our poor Ned broods about everything he can't have. His former life haunts him. He misses everything that's forbidden to us. He's burdened by all his old memories, and it's breaking his heart. We need to understand him. What does he have to keep him occupied? Nothing. He isn't a scientist like master, so he doesn't share our enthusiasm for the sea's wonders. He would run any risk just to go into a tavern in his own country!"

To be sure, the monotony of life on board must have seemed unbearable to the Canadian, who was used to freedom and activity. It was a rare event that could excite him. But that morning an incident occurred that reminded him of his happy harpooning days.

Around eleven o'clock, while on the surface of the ocean, the *Nautilus* fell in with a pod of right whales. This encounter didn't surprise me, because I knew these animals were being hunted so relentlessly, they took refuge in the ocean basins of the high latitudes.

In the seagoing world and in the realm of geographic exploration, whales have played a leading role. The Basques were the first to chase after these animals, then Asturian Spaniards, Englishmen, and Dutchmen, and in the process these hunters learned to brave the ocean's dangers and they sailed to the ends of the earth. Whales like to frequent the southernmost and northernmost seas. Old legends even claim these cetaceans led fishermen to within just seven leagues of the North Pole. Even though this feat is fictitious, it will someday come true, because it's quite likely that by hunting whales in the arctic or antarctic regions, human beings will finally reach this unknown spot on the globe.

We were seated on the platform next to a tranquil sea. The month of March, being the equivalent of October in these latitudes, was giving us some lovely autumn days. It was the Canadian—on this topic he was never mistaken—who sighted a baleen whale on the eastern horizon. If you looked carefully, you could see its blackish back alternately rise and fall above the waves five miles from the *Nautilus*.

"Oh man!" Ned Land exclaimed. "If I were aboard a whaler, that beast would be a golden opportunity! It's a big one! Look how high its blowholes are spouting all that air and steam! Damnation! Why am I chained to this hunk of sheet iron!"

"What's this, Ned?" I responded. "You still aren't over your old fishing urges?"

"How could a whale fisherman give up his old trade, sir? What harpooner could ever forget the thrill of the chase?"

"You've never fished these seas, Ned?"

"Never, sir. Just the northernmost seas, both in Bering Strait and Davis Strait."

"So the southern right whale is still unknown to you. Till now it's the bowhead whale you've hunted, and it won't venture past the warm waters of the equator."

"Oh, professor, what are you feeding me?" the Canadian responded in a tolerably skeptical tone.

"I'm feeding you the facts."

"By thunder! In '65, just 2½ years ago, I myself personally stepped onto the carcass of a whale off Greenland, and its flank was still carrying the marked harpoon of a whaling ship from the Bering Sea. Now I ask you, after this animal got wounded west of America, how could it get killed in the *east*, unless it had crossed the equator and doubled Cape Horn or the Cape of Good Hope?"

"I agree with our friend Ned," Conseil said, "and I'm waiting to hear how master will answer him."

"Master will answer, my friends, that whales are localized according to species within certain seas that they never leave. And if one of these animals went from Bering Strait to Davis Strait, it's quite simply because there's a passageway from one sea to the other, along either the coast of Canada or Siberia."

"You expect us to swallow that?" the Canadian asked, tipping me a wink.

"If master says so," Conseil replied.

"Which means," the Canadian went on, "since I've never fished these waterways, I'm not acquainted with the whales that frequent them?"

"That's what I'm telling you, Ned."

"All the more reason to make their acquaintance," Conseil remarked.

"Look! Look!" the Canadian exclaimed, his voice full of excitement. "Here it comes! It's swimming toward us! It's thumbing its nose at me! It knows I can't do a blessed thing to it!"

Ned stamped his foot. His hands quivered as if they were brandishing an imaginary harpoon.

"These cetaceans," he asked, "are they as huge as the ones in the northernmost seas?"

"Pretty nearly, Ned."

"Because I've seen huge baleen whales, sir, whales up to 100 feet long! I've even heard that those rorqual whales off the Aleutian Islands sometimes get over 150 feet."

"That strikes me as exaggerated," I replied. "Those animals are simply members of the genus *Balaenoptera* supplied with dorsal fins, and like sperm whales, they're generally smaller than the bowhead whale."

"Hey!" exclaimed the Canadian, whose eyes hadn't left the ocean. "It's coming even closer, it's swimming right up to the *Nautilus!*"

Then, going on with his conversation:

"You talk about sperm whales," he said, "as if they're small! But there are stories of gigantic sperm whales. They're shrewd cetaceans. I hear that some will cover themselves with algae and fucus plants. Folks mistake them for islets. They pitch camp on top, make themselves comfortable, light a fire—"

"Build houses," Conseil said.

"Yes, funny man," Ned Land replied. "Then one fine day the animal dives and drags all its occupants down into the depths."

"Like in the voyages of Sinbad the Sailor," I remarked, laughing. "Oh, Mr. Land, you're such a pushover for tall tales! What sperm whales you're handing us! I hope you don't honestly believe in them."

"Mr. Naturalist," the Canadian replied in all seriousness, "when it comes to whales, you can believe practically anything. (Look at that one move! Look at it dashing away!) Folks claim these animals can circle the earth in just two weeks."

"I don't say nay."

"But what you undoubtedly don't know, Professor Aronnax, is that at the beginning of time, whales traveled even quicker."

"Oh really, Ned! And why was that?"

"Because in those days their tails moved side to side like the ones on fish, in other words, their tails stood straight up and thrashed the water from left to right, right to left. But our Creator felt they went too blamed fast and He twisted their tails—so ever since they've been thrashing the waves up and down, at the expense of their speed."

"Fine, Ned," I said, then resurrected one of the Canadian's expressions. "You expect us to swallow that?"

"Not too terribly," Ned Land replied, "and no more than if I told you there are whales 300 feet long and weighing a million pounds."

"That's definitely on the high side," I said. "But you have to admit that certain cetaceans do grow to significant size, since they're said to supply over 130 tons of oil."

"I've seen it myself," the Canadian said.

"I can easily believe it, Ned, just as I can believe that certain baleen whales are equal in bulk to a hundred elephants. Imagine the impact of such a mass if it were going at full speed!"

"Is it true," Conseil asked, "that they can sink ships?"

"Ships? I doubt it," I replied. "However they say that in 1820, right in these southern seas, a whale charged into the *Essex* and drove it backward at a speed of thirteen feet per second. The *Essex* took on water astern and went down almost immediately."

Ned looked at me with a taunting expression.

"As for me," he said, "I once got walloped by a whale's tail—in my longboat, needless to say. My companions and I were tossed twenty feet in the air. But next to the professor's whale, mine was just a baby."

"Do those animals live a long time?" Conseil asked.

"A thousand years," the Canadian replied without hesitation.

"And how, Ned," I asked, "do you know that's so?"

"Because folks say so."

"And why do folks say so?"

"Because folks know so."

"No, Ned! They don't know so, they *suppose* so, and here's how they reason it out. When fishermen first hunted whales 400 years ago, those animals grew to bigger sizes than they do today. Sensibly enough, it's assumed that today's whales are smaller because they haven't had time to reach their full growth. That's why the Count de Buffon wrote that cetaceans could live, and even were *meant* to live, for a thousand years. You understand?"

Ned Land didn't understand. He wasn't even listening. That baleen whale kept coming closer. He devoured it with his eyes.

"Wow!" he exclaimed. "It isn't just one whale, it's ten, twenty, a whole pod! And I can't do a blasted thing! I'm tied hand and foot!"

"But Ned my friend," Conseil said, "why not ask Captain Nemo for permission to hunt—"

Before Conseil could finish his sentence, Ned Land had scooted down the hatch and hustled off to look for the captain. A few seconds later the two of them reappeared on the platform.

Captain Nemo studied the pod of cetaceans playing in the waters a mile from the *Nautilus*.

"They're southern right whales," he said. "There goes the fortune of a whole whaling fleet."

"Well, sir," the Canadian asked, "couldn't I get out and hunt them, just to keep my hand in as a harpooner?"

"Hunt them? What for?" Captain Nemo

replied. "Simply to destroy them? We have no use for whale oil on this ship."

"But, sir," the Canadian went on, "in the Red Sea you let us go after a dugong!"

"There it was a matter of getting fresh meat for my crew. Here it would be killing just for the sake of killing. I'm well aware that's a privilege reserved for mankind, but I won't tolerate such bloodthirsty pastimes. When your colleagues, Mr. Land, destroy decent, harmless creatures like the southern right whale or the bowhead whale, they're guilty of criminal behavior. Consequently they've already eradicated the stock in Baffin Bay and they'll ultimately wipe out a whole class of beneficial animals. So leave those poor cetaceans alone. They have quite enough natural enemies, such as sperm whales, swordfish, and sawfish, without your meddling with them."

The reader can imagine the faces that the Canadian made during this lecture on harpooning ethics. Using arguments such as these with a professional hunter was a waste of words. Ned Land looked at Captain Nemo and obviously didn't take his meaning. But the captain was right. Thanks to the relentless, ravenous, compulsive way they're being hunted, the last whale will someday vanish from the ocean.

Ned Land whistled "Yankee Doodle" between his teeth, shoved his hands in his pockets, and turned his back on us.

Meanwhile Captain Nemo studied the pod of cetaceans, then spoke to me:

"I was right to claim that baleen whales have enough natural enemies without counting man. These individuals will soon have to deal with mighty opponents. Eight miles to leeward, Professor Aronnax, can you see those dark spots moving around?"

"Yes, captain," I replied.

"Those are sperm whales, dreadful animals I've sometimes encountered in pods of 200 or 300! As for them, they're cruel, destructive beasts and they deserve to be exterminated."

The Canadian turned swiftly at these last words.

"Well, captain," I said, "on behalf of the right whales, there's still time—"

"No need to run any risks, professor. The *Nautilus* itself can disperse those sperm whales. It's armed with a steel spur quite equal to Mr. Land's harpoon, I expect."

The Canadian didn't even bother shrugging his shoulders. Attacking cetaceans with thrusts from a spur! Who ever heard of such malarkey.

"Just wait, Professor Aronnax," Captain Nemo said. "We'll show you a new type of hunting. We'll take no pity on those ferocious cetaceans. They're merely mouth and teeth."

Mouth and teeth! You couldn't hit on a better way to describe the long-skulled sperm whale, which sometimes exceeds eighty feet in length. The enormous head of this cetacean takes up about a third of its body. Better armed than a baleen whale, whose upper jaw is adorned only with whalebone, the sperm whale has twenty-five huge teeth that are eight inches long, have cylindrical, conical tips, and weigh two pounds each. In the upper part of its enormous head, inside big cavities separated by cartilage, you'll find some 600 to 900 pounds of that valuable oil known as "spermaceti." The sperm whale is an undignified animal, more tadpole than fish, as Professor Frédol has noted. It's poorly built, being "impaired," so to speak, over the whole left side of its anatomy, with good eyesight only in its right eye.

Meanwhile that monstrous pod kept coming closer. It had seen the baleen whales and was getting set to attack. You could tell in advance that the sperm whales would prevail, not only because they were better built for attacking than their harmless opponents, but also because they could stay longer underwater before going back to breathe at the surface.

There was just time to run to the rescue of the right whales. The *Nautilus* sank to midwater. Conseil, Ned, and I took seats in front of the lounge windows. Captain Nemo proceeded to the helmsman's side to operate his submersible as an engine of destruction. Soon I felt the beats of our propeller getting faster, and we picked up speed.

The battle between sperm whales and right whales had already started by the time the *Nautilus* arrived. It jockeyed to cut into the pod of long-skulled predators. At first the latter showed little concern at the sight of this new monster meddling in the conflict. But they soon had to dodge its thrusts.

What a fight! Ned Land quickly grew enthusiastic and even ended up applauding. Brandished in its captain's hands, the *Nautilus* was simply a fearsome harpoon. He hurled it at those masses of flesh and ran them clean through, leaving two squirming animal halves. Their fearsome tails would slam against our hull, but the submersible barely felt them. No more than the collisions we caused. After exterminating one sperm whale, the ship raced after another, turned on a dime so as to not miss its prey, went ahead or astern, obeyed its rudder, made a dive when the cetacean sank to deeper strata, rose with it when it returned to the surface, struck it head-on or slantwise, hacked at it or ripped it, and from any direction or at any speed impaled it with that dreadful spur.

What bloodshed! What a hubbub on the surface of the waves! What sharp hisses and snorts characteristic of those animals when they're frightened! Their tails were churning the normally peaceful strata into actual billows.

This Homeric slaughter lasted an hour, and the long-skulled predators couldn't get away. Several times ten or twelve of them banded together and tried to crush the *Nautilus* with a mass assault. We saw their fearsome eyes through the windows, their enormous mouths paved with teeth. Ned Land couldn't control himself, hurling threats and insults at them. You could feel them hanging onto the submersible like hounds on top of a wild boar in a thicket. But by forcing the pace of its propeller, the *Nautilus* carried them off, pulled them under, or dragged them back to the upper level of the waters, untroubled by their enormous weight or powerful grip.

Finally that mass of sperm whales thinned out. The waves grew calm again. I felt us rising to the surface of the ocean. The hatch opened and we rushed onto the platform.

The sea was covered with mutilated carcasses. A fearsome explosion couldn't have slashed, ripped, or shredded those masses of flesh with greater violence. We were floating in the midst of gigantic bodies, bluish on top, whitish on the belly, and disfigured all over by enormous protuberances. A few frightened sperm whales were fleeing toward the horizon. The waves were dyed red over an area of several miles, and the *Nautilus* was floating in the middle of a sea of blood.

Captain Nemo rejoined us.

"Well, Mr. Land?" he said.

"Well, sir," replied the Canadian, whose enthusiasm had died down, "it's a dreadful sight for sure. But I'm a hunter not a butcher, and this is plain butchery."

"It was a slaughter of destructive animals," the captain replied, "and the *Nautilus* is no butcher knife."

"I'll stick with my harpoon," the Canadian remarked.

"To each his own," the captain replied, looking intently at Ned Land.

I was in dread the latter would erupt in some vehement outburst that might have had deplorable consequences. But his anger was sidetracked by the sight of a baleen whale that the *Nautilus* had pulled alongside just then.

The animal hadn't managed to escape from the teeth of those sperm whales. I identified it as a southern right whale, its head squat, its body dark all over. It differs anatomically from the bowhead whale and the black right whale in that its seven cervical vertebrae are fused, and it has two more ribs than its relatives. Floating on its side, its belly riddled with bites, the poor cetacean was dead. Still hanging from the tip of its mutilated fin was a little baby whale that it hadn't been able to rescue from the slaughter. Its open mouth let water flow through its whalebone like the swishing of surf.

Captain Nemo guided the *Nautilus* next to the animal's carcass. Two of his men climbed onto the whale's flank, and to my amazement I saw them draw from its udders all the milk they held, in other words, enough to fill up two or three casks.

The captain offered me a cup of this milk, which was still warm. I couldn't help showing my aversion to such a drink. He assured me that this milk was excellent, that it tasted like cow milk.

I sampled it and agreed. So this milk was a worthwhile reserve ration for us, because in the form of salted butter or cheese, it would furnish a pleasant change of pace from our standard fare.

From that day forward I noted with some uneasiness that Ned Land's attitude toward Captain Nemo continued to grow worse and worse, and I decided to keep a close watch on the Canadian's movements and activities.

37

THE ICE BARRIER

THE *NAUTILUS* resumed its unflappable south-bound heading. It went along the 50th meridian with considerable speed. Would it reach the pole? I didn't think so, because every prior attempt to reach that spot on the globe had come to grief. What's more, the season was already quite advanced, since March 13 on antarctic shores corresponds to September 13 in the northernmost regions, which marks the start of the equinoctial period.

On March 14 at latitude 55°, I spotted floating ice, plain pale bits of rubble twenty to twenty-five feet long and forming reefs over which waves were breaking. The *Nautilus* stayed on the surface of the ocean. Having fished in the arctic seas, Ned Land was already familiar with the sight of icebergs. Conseil and I were marveling at them for the first time.

Toward the southern horizon a dazzling streak of white stretched across the sky. English whalers have given this sight the name "ice blink." No matter how heavy the clouds may be, they can't hide this natural phenomenon. It announces the presence of a pack, or shoal, of ice.

In fact bigger chunks of ice soon appeared, their brightness varying at the whim of the mists. Some of these masses had green veins, as if streaked with undulating lines of copper sulfate. Others looked like enormous amethysts, letting the daylight shine all the way through. The latter reflected the sun's rays off the thousand facets of their crystals.

The former, shaded a bright, shiny limestone hue, would have supplied enough building material to make a whole marble town.

The farther south we went, the more these floating islands grew in size and number. Polar birds nested on them by the thousands. These were petrels, cape pigeons, or puffins, and their calls were deafening. Some of them mistook the *Nautilus* for the carcass of a whale, alighted on it, and prodded its resonant sheet iron with pecks of their beaks.

During this navigating in the midst of the ice, Captain Nemo often stayed on the platform. He scanned those deserted waterways carefully. Sometimes I could see his calm eyes perk up. In these polar seas forbidden to man, did he feel right at home, the lord of these unreachable regions? Maybe. But he didn't say. He stood stock-still, coming to life only when his pilot's instincts took over. Then he steered his *Nautilus* with consummate skill, expertly dodging masses of ice that were sometimes several miles long and around 230 to 260 feet high. Often they seemed to completely block off the horizon. Level with latitude 60° all passageways had vanished. Captain Nemo searched with care and soon found a narrow opening into which he brazenly slipped, knowing full well, however, that it would close up behind him.

In this way, guided by his skillful hands, the *Nautilus* went past all those different masses of ice, which are classified by size and shape with an exactitude that enraptured Conseil: "icebergs," or mountains; "ice fields," or smooth, endless tracts; "drift ice," or floating floes; "packs," or broken tracts, called "patches" when they're circular and "streams" when they form long strips.

The temperature was fairly low. Exposed to the outside air, our thermometer read between 27° and 28° Fahrenheit. But we were warmly dressed in furs, for which seals and aquatic bears had paid the ultimate price. Uniformly heated by its electrical equipment, the *Nautilus*'s interior could withstand the most intense cold. Moreover we had only to sink a few yards under the waves to find a bearable temperature.

Two months earlier we would have enjoyed unbroken daylight in this latitude; but night already fell for three or four hours and later it would cast six months of darkness over these circumpolar regions.

By March 15 we'd gone beyond the latitude of the South Shetland and South Orkney islands. The captain told me that many pods of seals used to live on those shores; but in a frenzy of destruction, English and American whalers had slaughtered all the adults, including pregnant females, and where life and activity once existed, those fishermen left only silence and death.

Going along the 55th meridian, the *Nautilus* cut the Antarctic Circle on March 16 near eight o'clock in the morning. Ice completely surrounded us and blocked off the horizon. Nevertheless Captain Nemo went from passageway to passageway, always proceeding south.

"But where's he going?" I asked.

"Dead ahead," Conseil replied. "Ultimately, when he can't go any farther, he'll come to a stop."

"I wouldn't bet on it!" I replied.

And to tell the truth, this venturesome excursion didn't displease me one bit. I can't express how amazed I was at the beauties of these new regions. The ice struck wondrous poses. Here, it looked like a town in the Far East with countless minarets and mosques. There, a city in ruins, demolished by upheavals in the earth. These views kept changing as the sunlight hit them at different angles, or they were swallowed up completely by gray fogs during blizzards. Then explosions, cave-ins, and great iceberg somersaults would take place all around us, varying the scenery like the shifting landscape in a diorama.

If the *Nautilus* was submerged during these losses of balance, we heard the sound spread under the waters with frightful intensity, and the collapse of these masses created alarming eddies down to the ocean's lower strata. Then the *Nautilus* rolled and pitched like a ship left to the fury of the elements.

Often I couldn't see any way out and figured we were imprisoned for good; but Captain Nemo followed his nose and discovered new passageways from the tiniest signs. By keeping an eye on those thin threads of bluish water that streaked through the ice fields, he never went wrong. Accordingly I was sure he'd previously taken his *Nautilus* a good way into the antarctic seas.

Yet during the day of March 16, those tracts of ice completely barred our path. It wasn't the ice barrier as yet, just huge ice fields that the cold had cemented together. This obstacle couldn't stop Captain Nemo, and he launched his ship against the ice fields with appalling violence. The *Nautilus* charged into those brittle masses like a wedge, splitting them with dreadful cracklings. It was an old-fashioned battering ram propelled with unlimited power. Hurled aloft, shards of ice fell all around us like hail. Through the sheer power of its momentum, the submersible carved a channel for itself. Carried away by its own impetus, the ship sometimes mounted on top of those tracts of ice and crushed them with its weight, or at other times when cooped up beneath the ice fields, it split them open with simple pitching movements that made wide gashes.

During this period violent squalls attacked us. Occasionally the mists were so heavy, we couldn't see from one end of the platform to the other. The wind would suddenly shift to any point on the compass. The snow was piling up in such packed layers, it had to be chipped loose with blows from picks. Even in a temperature of only 23° Fahrenheit, the *Nautilus*'s whole outside was covered with ice. A ship's rigging would have been unusable because all its tackle would have gotten stuck in the grooves of the pulleys. Only a craft without sails—and powered by an electric motor that had no need for coal— could face these high latitudes.

Under these conditions our barometer generally stayed quite low. It fell as far as twenty-nine inches. Our compass readings no longer offered any guarantees. The berserk needles would mark contradictory directions as we got nearer to the southern magnetic pole, which doesn't correspond to the South Pole proper. Actually, according to the astronomer Hansteen, this magnetic pole is located fairly close to latitude 70° and longitude 130°, or abiding by the conclusions of Louis-Isidore Duperrey, in latitude 70° 30′ and longitude 135°. So we had to take many readings, transporting compasses to different parts of the ship and striking an average. But often we could chart our course only by guesswork, hardly a satisfactory method in the midst of these winding passageways whose landmarks change continually.

At last on March 17, after twenty futile offensives, the *Nautilus* was decisively held in check. There were no ice fields, streams, or patches anymore—just an endless, immovable barricade made up of frozen mountains fused to each other.

"The ice barrier!" the Canadian told me.

For Ned Land, as well as for every navigator before us, I knew that this was an insurmountable obstacle. Toward noon the sun appeared for an instant, and Captain Nemo took a reasonably accurate sight that put us in longitude 51° 30′ and latitude 67° 39′ south. This was a position already well along in these antarctic regions.

As for the sea or any sort of liquid surface, there was no longer a semblance of such a thing beneath our eyes. In front of the *Nautilus*'s spur lay vast broken plains, a confused tangle of frozen chunks with all the helter-skelter unpredictability typical of a river's surface a short while before its ice breaks up; but in this case the proportions were gigantic. Sharp peaks loomed here and there, thin spires that rose 200 feet into the air; farther away, a succession of steep cliffs with a grayish tinge, huge mirrors that reflected the meager rays of a sun half drowned in mist. Beyond, a stark silence reigned over this desolate expanse, a silence barely broken by the flapping wings of petrels or puffins. By this point everything was frozen, even sound.

So the *Nautilus* had to halt in its venturesome course through those tracts of ice.

"Sir," Ned Land told me that day, "if your captain goes any farther . . ."

"Yes?"

"He'll be a superman."

"Why, Ned?"

"Because nobody can get past the ice barrier. Your captain's a powerful man, but damnation, he isn't more powerful than nature. If she lays down a boundary line, that's where you stop, like it or not!"

"True, Ned Land, but I still want to know what's behind that ice barrier. There's my greatest source of irritation—a wall!"

"Master is right," Conseil said. "Walls were devised simply to frustrate scientists. There ought to be a law against walls."

"Fine!" the Canadian put in. "But we already know what's behind that ice barrier."

"What?" I asked.

"Ice, ice, and more ice."

"You may believe that, Ned," I remarked, "but I'm not so sure. That's why I want to see for myself."

"Well, professor," the Canadian replied, "you can just drop that idea. You've made it to the ice barrier, which is already plenty far, but you won't get any farther, not you, your Captain Nemo, or his *Nautilus*. Like it or not, we're going to head back north—in other words, to the land of sensible people."

I had to agree that Ned Land was right, and till ships are built to navigate over tracts of ice, they'll have to call a halt at the ice barrier.

Sure enough, despite its efforts, despite the powerful methods it used to split the ice, our *Nautilus* was reduced to immobility. Ordinarily, when somebody can't go any farther, he still has the option of returning in his tracks. But in this case it was just as impossible to turn back as to go forward, because all passageways had closed up behind us, and if our submersible stayed even slightly stationary, we would be promptly frozen in. Which is just what happened around two o'clock in the afternoon, and fresh ice kept forming over the ship's sides with amazing speed. I must admit that Captain Nemo's leadership hadn't exactly been a model of good judgment.

Just then I was on the platform. Studying our situation for a few seconds, the captain said to me:

"Well, professor, what think you?"

"I think we're trapped, captain."

"Trapped! What do you mean?"

"I mean we can't go forward, backward, or sideways. I believe that's the standard definition of 'trapped,' at least in the civilized world."

"So, Professor Aronnax, you think the *Nautilus* won't manage to float free?"

"It'll be difficult, captain, since the season is already too advanced for you to depend on the ice breaking up."

"Oh, professor!" Captain Nemo replied in a sardonic tone. "You're always the same! All you see are impediments and obstacles! I promise you, not only will the *Nautilus* float free, it will go farther still."

"Farther south?" I asked, looking at the captain.

"Yes, sir, it will go to the pole."

"The pole!" I exclaimed. And I couldn't help making a gesture that scoffed at this.

"Yes," the captain replied coolly, "the antarctic pole, that unknown spot crossed by every meridian on the globe. As you know, I can do anything I like with my *Nautilus*."

Yes, I knew that! I knew this man was daring to the point of being foolhardy. But to conquer all the obstacles around the South Pole—even less attainable than the North Pole, which still hadn't been reached by the boldest navigators—wasn't this a totally deranged undertaking, one that only the brain of a madman could dream up?

Then it dawned on me to ask Captain Nemo if he'd already discovered this pole, where no human being had ever set foot.

"No, sir," he answered me, "but we'll discover it together. Where others have come to grief, I'll succeed. Never before has my *Nautilus* cruised so far into these southernmost seas; but I repeat, it will go farther still."

"I would love to believe you, captain," I went on with a touch of sarcasm in my tone. "Oh, I do believe you! Let's forge on! Obstacles don't exist for us! Let's smash that ice barrier! Let's blow it to smithereens, then if it's still in the way, let's put wings on the *Nautilus* and fly over it!"

"Over it, professor?" Captain Nemo replied serenely. "No, not over it, but under it."

"Under it!" I exclaimed.

Just then a sudden insight into Captain Nemo's plans flashed through my mind. I understood. He would put the marvelous abilities of his *Nautilus* to work yet again in this superhuman undertaking!

"I can see we're starting to understand each other, professor," Captain Nemo told me with a half smile. "You already glimpse the possibilities—myself, I would say the realities—of this endeavor. Maneuvers that aren't feasible for an ordinary ship are easy for the *Nautilus*. If there's a landmass at the pole, we'll halt at that landmass. If, on the other hand, the pole is open sea, we'll go straight to the spot!"

"You're right," I said, carried along by the captain's logic. "Even though the surface of the sea has solidified into ice, its lower strata will still be open, for the fortuitous reason that salt water reaches its maximum density at one degree above its freezing point. And if I'm not mistaken, the submerged part of this ice barrier is in a four-to-one ratio to the part above water."

"Just about, professor. For every foot of iceberg above the sea, there are another three below. Now then, since these ice mountains don't exceed a height of 330 feet, they sink only to a depth of about a thousand feet. And what's a thousand feet to the *Nautilus?*"

"Practically nothing, sir."

"We could dive even deeper and look for that warm layer found in all ocean water, and there we could brave with impunity those surface temperatures of -20° to -40° Fahrenheit."

"True, sir, very true," I replied, my interest growing.

"Our only difficulty," Captain Nemo went on, "will be to stay submerged for several days without replenishing our air supply."

"That's all?" I remarked. "The *Nautilus* has huge air tanks; we'll fill them up, and they'll supply all the oxygen we could want."

"Good thinking, Professor Aronnax," the captain replied with a smile. "But since I would hate to be accused of foolhardiness, I'm giving you all my objections in advance."

"You have more?"

"Just one. If there's a sea at the South Pole, it's possible that sea may be completely frozen over, so we couldn't come up to the surface!"

"My dear sir, have you forgotten that the *Nautilus* is armed with a fearsome spur? Couldn't it be launched diagonally against those tracts of ice, which would break open from the impact?"

"Ah, professor, you're a gold mine of ideas today!"

"Besides, captain," I added with increasing enthusiasm, "why wouldn't we find open sea at the South Pole just as at the North Pole? The poles of cold don't correspond to the poles of rotation in either the northern or southern hemispheres, and till proof to the contrary, we can assume those two spots on the earth feature either a landmass or an ice-free ocean."

"I think as you do, Professor Aronnax," Captain Nemo replied. "I'll just point out that after raising so many objections to my plan, you're now burying me under arguments in its favor."

Captain Nemo was right. I was ready to outdo him in daring! I was the one tugging him to the pole. I was leading the way, I was out in front . . . oh stop it, you silly fool! Captain Nemo already knew the pros and cons of this business, and it amused him to see you flying off into impossible fantasies!

Nevertheless he didn't waste another second. At his signal the chief officer appeared. The two men held a quick exchange in their unintelligible language, and either the chief officer had been briefed previously or he found the plan feasible, because he didn't show any surprise.

But as unemotional as he was, he couldn't have been more impeccably emotionless than Conseil when I told the fine lad we intended to push on to the South Pole. He greeted this news with his standard "As master wishes," and I had to be content with that. As for Ned Land, on this occasion he gave a shrug for the ages.

"You and your Captain Nemo!" he told me. "Honestly, sir, I pity you both!"

"But we'll make it to the pole, Mr. Ned."

"Maybe, but you won't make it back!"

And Ned Land retreated to his cabin, "so I don't do something I might regret," he told me as he left.

Meanwhile preparations for this daring endeavor had gotten under way. The *Nautilus*'s powerful pumps forced air down into the tanks and stored it under high pressure. Around four o'clock Captain Nemo informed me that the platform hatches were about to be closed. I took one last look at that massive ice barrier we were getting ready to conquer. The weather was fair, the skies reasonably clear, the cold very brisk, namely 10° Fahrenheit; but after the wind let up, this temperature didn't seem too unbearable.

Ten or so men carrying picks climbed onto the *Nautilus*'s sides and chipped loose the ice around the ship's lower plating, which was soon set free. This operation was swiftly executed because the fresh ice was still thin. All of us went back inside. The main ballast tanks filled up with the water that hadn't yet congealed at our line of flotation. The *Nautilus* submerged without delay.

Conseil and I took seats in the lounge. We looked out the open window at the lower strata of this southernmost ocean. The thermometer rose again. The needle on the pressure gauge moved over its dial.

About a thousand feet down, just as Captain Nemo had predicted, we cruised beneath the undulating surface of the ice barrier. But the *Nautilus* sank even deeper. It reached a depth of 2,600 feet. At the surface the water gave a temperature of 10° Fahrenheit, but now it gave over 12°. We'd already gained two degrees. Thanks to its heating equipment, the *Nautilus*'s temperature stayed at a much higher degree, needless to say. Every maneuver was accomplished with extraordinary precision.

"With all due respect to master," Conseil told me, "we'll get past it."

"I fully expect to!" I replied in a tone of deep conviction.

Now in open water, the *Nautilus* headed straight for the pole without veering from the 52nd meridian. From 67° 30′ to 90°, there were 22½ degrees of latitude left to cover, in other words, slightly more than 500 leagues. The *Nautilus* stuck to an average speed of twenty-six miles per hour, the speed of an express train. If it maintained this pace, we would reach the pole in forty hours.

The novelty of our circumstances kept Conseil and me by the lounge window for a good part of the night. The electric rays from our beacon lit up the sea. But it was empty. Fish didn't linger in this imprisoned stretch of water. For them it was simply a channel from the Antarctic Ocean to open sea at the pole. We made rapid headway. You could feel it in the vibrations of our long steel hull.

Near two o'clock in the morning, I went to grab a few hours of sleep. Conseil did the same. I didn't run into Captain Nemo while going down the corridors. I figured he was staying in the pilothouse.

The next day, March 18, at five o'clock in the morning, I was back at my post in the lounge. The electric log revealed that the *Nautilus* had reduced speed. By that point we were rising to the surface, but cautiously, while slowly emptying our ballast tanks.

My heart was pounding. Would we come out into the open and find the polar air again?

Not yet. A sudden jolt told me the *Nautilus* had bumped the underbelly of the ice barrier, still very thick to judge from the dull sound it made. In fact we'd "struck bottom," to use nautical terminology, but in the opposite direction and at a depth of 1,500 feet. That gave us 2,000 feet of ice overhead, of which 500 feet were above water. So the ice barrier was higher here than we'd found it on its outskirts. A circumstance not exactly encouraging.

Several times that day the *Nautilus* repeated the same experiment and always it bumped against this surface that formed a ceiling above it. Occasionally the ship met ice at a depth of 3,000 feet, indicating a thickness of 4,000 feet, of which 1,000 feet rose above the level of the ocean. This height had tripled since the moment when the *Nautilus* had plunged under the waves.

I took meticulous notes on these different depths, in this way obtaining the underwater profile of that upended mountain chain spreading out beneath the sea.

By evening our circumstances still hadn't changed. The ice stayed between 1,300 and 1,600 feet thick. Clearly it was shrinking, but what a barricade still lay between us and the surface of the ocean!

By then it was eight o'clock. The air inside the *Nautilus* should have been replenished four hours earlier in line with the daily routine on board. But I wasn't too uncomfortable, though Captain Nemo still hadn't made demands on his supplementary oxygen tanks.

It was hard for me to sleep that night. Hope and fear gripped me in turn. I got up several times. The *Nautilus* kept groping. Around three o'clock in the morning, I saw that we were meeting the ice barrier's underbelly at a depth of only fifty yards. So 150 feet separated us from the surface of the water. Gradually the ice barrier was turning into an ice field again. The mountains were changing back into plains.

My eyes didn't leave the pressure gauge. We kept rising on a diagonal, going along that glossy surface sparkling under our electric rays. Above and below, the ice barrier was subsiding in long gradients. Mile after mile it kept getting thinner.

Finally, at six o'clock in the morning on that unforgettable day of March 19, the lounge door opened. Captain Nemo appeared.

"Open sea!" he told me.

38

THE SOUTH POLE

I RUSHED UP onto the platform. Yes, open sea! Only a few meager floes, some moving icebergs; a sea reaching into the distance; a host of birds in the air and myriads of fish under the waters, which varied from deep blue to olive green depending on the depth. Our thermometer read 37° Fahrenheit. It was as if a comparative springtime had been shut up behind that ice barrier, whose far-off masses were outlined on the northern horizon.

"Are we at the pole?" I asked the captain, my heart pounding.

"I have no idea," he answered me. "At noon we'll fix our position."

"But will the sun show through this mist?" I said, looking at the grayish sky.

"No matter how faintly it shines, it will be bright enough for me," the captain replied.

Ten miles south of the *Nautilus*, a lonely islet rose to a height of some 650 feet. We proceeded toward it, but cautiously, because this sea could have been sprinkled with reefs.

In an hour we'd reached the islet. Two hours later we'd circled it. It measured four to five miles around. A narrow channel separated it from a considerable stretch of land, maybe a whole continent whose far edges we couldn't see. The presence of this landmass seemed to bear out Commander Maury's theories. In essence this clever American has noted that between the South Pole and the 60th parallel, the sea is covered with floating ice whose dimensions are more enormous than any found in the north Atlantic. From this fact he drew the conclusion that the Antarctic Circle must contain a considerable body of land, since icebergs can't form on the high seas but just along coastlines. According to his calculations, this frozen mass around the southernmost pole forms a huge ice cap that must be nearly 2,500 miles wide.

Meanwhile, to avoid running aground, the *Nautilus* halted about a third of a mile from the beach, over which towered magnificent piles of rocks. The skiff was put to sea. Two crewmen carrying instruments, the captain, Conseil, and I were on board. It was ten o'clock in the morning. I hadn't seen Ned Land. No doubt, in the presence of the South Pole, the Canadian hated having to eat his words.

A few strokes of the oar took the skiff to the sand, where it went aground. Just as Conseil was getting ready to jump out, I held him back.

"Sir," I told Captain Nemo, "you deserve the honor of being the first to set foot on this shore."

"Yes, sir," the captain replied, "and if I don't hesitate to step onto this polar soil, it's because no human being has left a footprint here till now."

With that he leaped lightly onto the sand. His heart must have been throbbing with intense excitement. He scaled an overhanging rock that ended in a little promontory; and there, silent and motionless, with his arms folded and his eyes glowing, he seemed to be laying claim to these southernmost regions. After spending five minutes in this trance, he turned to us.

"Whenever you're ready, sir," he called to me.

I got out, Conseil right behind me, leaving the two men in the skiff.

For a good distance the soil consisted of that igneous gravel known as tuff, which has a reddish color as if made from crushed bricks. Slag, lava flows, and pumice stones covered the ground. Its volcanic origin was unmistakable. In certain locations a few light curls of steam gave off a sulfurous odor, showing that the inner fires still kept their explosive power. But when I scaled a lofty escarpment, I didn't see any volcanoes within a radius of several miles. In these antarctic regions, as you know, Sir James Clark Ross found the craters of Mt. Erebus and Mt. Terror in fully active condition on the 167th meridian at latitude 77° 32'.

The vegetation on this desolate continent struck me as extremely limited. A few lichens from the species *Usnea melanoxantha* were spread out on the black rocks. The whole meager flora of this locality consisted of certain microscopic seedlings, some rudimentary diatoms, a sort of cell positioned between two quartz shells, plus long purple and crimson fucus plants buoyed by small air bladders and washed ashore by the surf.

The beach was sprinkled with mollusks—little mussels, limpets, sleek heart-shaped cockles, and especially some sea butterflies that had oval, membranous bodies and heads formed from two rounded lobes. I also saw myriads of those inch-long sea butterflies from up north, which baleen whales can consume in huge quantities with a single swallow. The open waters at the shoreline were bustling with these delightful pteropods, true butterflies of the deep.

Among other zoophytes present in these shallows were a few coral tree forms, which Sir James Clark Ross describes as living in the antarctic seas at depths greater than 3,000 feet; then I saw some small leather coral belonging to the species *Procellaria pelagica*, also a large number of starfish characteristic of these climates, including some sand stars that spangled the earth.

But it was in the air that life was superabundant. Various species of birds flapped and fluttered by the thousands, deafening us with their calls. Packing the rocks, other fowl looked on fearlessly as we went by and crowded against our feet in a neighborly fashion. These were auks, as agile and supple in water—where they're sometimes mistaken for speeding bonito—as they're clumsy and heavy on land. They uttered outlandish calls and participated in many public assemblies that featured much noise but little action.

Among still other fowl I noted some sheathbills from the wading bird family, the size of pigeons, white in color, beak short and conical, eyes surrounded by red circles. Conseil laid in a supply of them, because when they're properly cooked, these winged creatures make an enjoyable dish. Flying overhead were sooty albatross that had thirteen-foot wingspans, birds aptly called "vultures of the ocean," also gigantic petrels including several with arching wings, enthusiastic eaters of seal that are known as *quebrantahuesos*,[19] and cape pigeons, a sort of duckling with a black and white topside, finally a whole series of smaller petrels, some whitish with wings trimmed in brown, others blue and specific to these antarctic seas, the former "so oily," I told Conseil, "that folks in the Faroe Islands simply fit the bird with a wick, then light it up."

"With that minor addition," Conseil replied, "these fowl would make perfect lamps! After this, all we need is for nature to equip them with wicks in advance!"

Half a mile farther on, the ground was all riddled with penguin nests, egg-laying burrows out of which popped large numbers of birds. Later Captain Nemo had a couple hundred of them hunted down, because their black flesh is quite edible. They brayed like donkeys. The size of a goose, these creatures had slate-colored bodies, white undersides, and lemon-colored neck bands, and they let themselves be stoned to death without making any effort to get away.

Meanwhile the fog didn't lift, and by eleven o'clock the sun still hadn't made an appearance. Its absence troubled me. Without it we couldn't take any sights. Then how could we tell if we'd reached the pole?

---

[19] *Translator's note.* Spanish: "ospreys."

When I rejoined Captain Nemo, I found him leaning silently against a hunk of rock and looking at the sky. He seemed impatient, baffled. But what could he do? This daring and powerful man couldn't control the sun the way he did the sea.

Noon arrived without that golden orb appearing for a single second. You couldn't even make out where it was hiding behind the curtain of mist. And soon that mist started to condense into snow.

"Till tomorrow," the captain said simply; and we went back to the *Nautilus* in the midst of flurries in the air.

During our absence the nets had been spread, and I was interested in seeing the fish just hauled on board. The antarctic seas serve as a refuge for quite a large number of migratory fish that flee from storms in the subpolar zones, in truth only to slide down the throats of porpoises and seals. I noted some four-inch southern bullheads, a species of whitish cartilaginous fish overrun with bluish gray stripes and armed with stings, then some antarctic rabbitfish, three feet long, body very slender, skin a smooth silver white, head rounded, topside sporting three fins, snout ending in a trunk that curved back toward the mouth. I sampled its meat but found it flavorless, though Conseil's views were quite positive.

The blizzard lasted till the next day. It was impossible to stay out on the platform. I wrote up the incidents of this polar excursion in the lounge, and from there I could hear the calls of petrels and albatross playing in the midst of the turmoil. The *Nautilus* didn't stay idle and moved some ten miles farther south, skirting the coast in the half-light left by the sun as it skimmed the horizon line.

The next day, March 20, it stopped snowing. The cold was a little more brisk. Our thermometer read 28° Fahrenheit. The fog had lifted, and that day I hoped we could take our noon sights.

Since Captain Nemo hadn't yet appeared, the skiff ferried only Conseil and me ashore. The soil's character was still the same—volcanic. There were traces of lava, slag, and basaltic rock everywhere, but I couldn't see the crater that had spewed them out. Here as elsewhere, myriads of birds livened up this part of the polar continent. But they had to share their dominion with huge pods of marine mammals that looked at us with gentle eyes. These were seals of different species, some lying on the ground, others stretched out on drifting ice floes, several leaving or reentering the sea. Since they'd never had any dealings with man, they didn't run off at our coming, and I estimated that there were enough of them around to provision a couple hundred ships.

"Ye gods," Conseil said, "it's a good thing Ned Land isn't with us!"

"Why, Conseil?"

"Because that madcap hunter would have slain every animal here."

"Every animal is going a bit far, but in reality I doubt that we could have kept our Canadian friend from harpooning *some* of these magnificent cetaceans. Which would be offensive to Captain Nemo, since he never spills the blood of innocent creatures without good reason."

"He's right."

"Absolutely, Conseil. But tell me, haven't you finished classifying these splendid specimens of marine fauna?"

"Master is well aware," Conseil replied, "that I haven't very much field experience. When master has told me these animals' names . . ."

"They're seals and walruses."

"Two genera," our scholarly Conseil hastened to say, "that belong to the family Pinnipedia, order Carnivora, group Unguiculata, subclass Monodelphia, class Mammalia, branch Vertebrata."

"Very nice, Conseil," I replied, "but these two genera of seals and walruses are both divided into species, and if I'm not mistaken, we now have a chance to actually look at them. Let's."

It was eight o'clock in the morning. We had four hours to ourselves till it was time for our noon sights. I led the way to a huge bay that made an indentation in the granite cliffside along the beach.

There, all about us, I swear that the shores and ice floes were packed with marine mam-

mals as far as the eye could see, and I automatically looked around for old Proteus, that mythological shepherd who watched over Neptune's immense flocks. These were predominantly seals. The males and females formed well-defined groups, the father guarding his family, the mother suckling her babies, the stronger youngsters emancipated a few steps away. When these mammals wanted to relocate, they contracted their bodies and took little jumps, awkwardly assisted all the while by their misshapen flippers, which form actual forearms on their manatee relatives. In the water, their element beyond compare, I must say that these seals swim wonderfully, thanks to their flexible spines, narrow pelvises, clean-shaven coats, and webbed feet. Resting on shore, they assumed the most graceful positions. Accordingly their gentle features, their glances as expressive as the loveliest woman's, their soft, limpid eyes, and their beguiling poses all led the ancients to glorify them by metamorphosing the males into sea gods and the females into mermaids.

I called Conseil's attention to the considerable growth of the cerebral lobes in these intelligent cetaceans. No mammal except man has more abundant cerebral matter. Accordingly seals are definitely teachable; they make good pets, and I agree with certain other naturalists that if these animals are properly trained, they can perform a real service as hunting dogs for fishermen.

Most of these seals were sleeping on the rocks or the sand. Among seals proper—which have no external ears, unlike sea lions whose ears protrude—I saw several varieties of leopard seal, ten feet long, with white coats, bulldog heads, and ten teeth in each jaw—four incisors in both the upper and lower, then two big canines shaped like a fleur-de-lis. In between them wriggled some sea elephants, a breed of seal with a short flexible trunk; these are the giants of the species, twenty feet around and over thirty feet long. They didn't move as we came near.

"Are these animals dangerous?" Conseil asked me.

"Only if they're attacked," I replied. "But

when these seals protect their babies, their fury is dreadful, and it isn't rare for them to smash a fisherman's longboat to bits."

"They have every right to," Conseil remarked.

"I don't say nay."

Two miles farther on we were stopped by a promontory that screened the bay from southerly winds. It dropped straight down to the sea and was flecked with foam by the surf. From beyond this ridge fearsome bellowings broke out, like the sounds made by a herd of cattle.

"Gracious," Conseil put in, "a choir of bulls?"

"No," I said, "a choir of walruses."

"Are they fighting with each other?"

"Either fighting or playing."

"With all due respect to master, this we must see."

"Then see it we must, Conseil."

And there we were, climbing over the blackish rocks, grappling with sudden landslides and stones slick with ice. More than once I took a tumble at the expense of my backside. Conseil, either more careful or more stable, rarely faltered and would help me up, saying:

"If master's legs would kindly adopt a wider stance, master will keep his balance."

Arriving at the topmost ridge of this promontory, I saw wide white plains covered with walruses. These animals were playing with one another. They were howling in fun, not fury.

Walruses resemble seals in their body shape and the layout of their limbs. But their lower jaws lack canines and incisors; as for their upper canines, they consist of two tusks nearly a yard long and a foot around at the socket. Made of solid ivory, without any striations, harder than elephant tusks, and less prone to yellowing, these teeth are in great demand. Accordingly walruses are the victims of a senseless hunting campaign that soon will destroy every last one of them, because their hunters indiscriminately slaughter pregnant females and youngsters, destroying over 4,000 individuals every year.

Walking near these unusual animals, I could examine them at my leisure since they didn't stir. Their hides were rough and heavy, a tan color tending toward a reddish brown; their coats were short and sparse. Some were over twelve feet long. More tranquil and less fearful than their northern relatives, they didn't post any sentinels on guard duty at the entrances to their campsite.

After examining this community of walruses, I decided to return in my tracks. It was eleven o'clock, and if Captain Nemo found favorable conditions for taking his sights, I wanted to be there when he did. But that day I had scant hope that Old Sol would make an appearance. That golden orb was hidden from our eyes by clouds piled up on the horizon. Apparently the jealous sun wasn't willing to reveal this unreachable region of the globe to any member of the human race.

Even so, I decided to head back to the *Nautilus*. We took a steep, narrow path that ran along the top of the cliff. By 11:30 we'd arrived at our landing place. The beached skiff had brought the captain ashore. I spotted him standing on a chunk of basalt. His instruments were beside him. His eyes were focused on the northern horizon, near which the sun would be sweeping in its wide arc.

I found a spot next to him and waited without saying a word. Noon arrived, and just as on the previous day, the sun didn't put in an appearance.

It was sheer bad luck. We still hadn't gotten our noon sights. If we couldn't take them tomorrow, we would have to completely give up on fixing our position.

In essence it was exactly March 20. Tomorrow, the 21st, was the day of the equinox; the sun would vanish below the horizon for six months not counting refraction, and after its disappearance the long polar night would begin. Following the September equinox, the sun had emerged above the northerly horizon, rising in wide spirals till December 21. On that date, the summer solstice of these southernmost regions, the sun had started to descend again and tomorrow it would cast its last rays.

I shared my thoughts and fears with Captain Nemo.

"You're right, Professor Aronnax," he told me. "If I can't take the sun's altitude tomorrow, I won't be able to try again for another six months. But exactly because sailors' luck has led me into these seas on March 21, it will be easy to get our bearings if the noonday sun does show itself to our eyes."

"How so, captain?"

"It comes from the fact that when that golden orb sweeps in such wide spirals, it's hard to measure the sun's exact altitude above the horizon, and our instruments are vulnerable to committing serious errors."

"Then what can you do?"

"Tomorrow I'll use only my chronometer," Captain Nemo answered me. "At noon on March 21, if, after accounting for refraction, the northern horizon cuts the sun's disk exactly in half, that will mean I'm at the South Pole."

"True," I said. "Nevertheless it isn't mathematically exact proof, because the equinox needn't fall right at noon."

"No doubt, sir, but the margin of error will be about 300 feet, and that's close enough for us. Till tomorrow, then."

Captain Nemo went back on board. Conseil and I stayed behind till five o'clock, wandering, studying, and combing the beach. The only unusual item I picked up was an auk's egg of remarkable size, for which a collector would have paid over $200. Its cream-tinted coloring, plus the streaks and markings that decorated it like so many hieroglyphics, made it a rare knickknack. I put it in Conseil's hands, and holding it like precious Chinese porcelain, that sensible, sure-footed lad got it back to the *Nautilus* in one piece.

There I put this rare egg inside one of the glass cases in the museum. I ate supper, feasting hungrily on an excellent piece of seal liver whose flavor reminded me of pork. Then I went to bed, but not before praying like a good Hindu for the sun's blessing.

The next day, March 21, I climbed onto the platform bright and early at five o'clock in the morning. I found Captain Nemo there.

"The weather is clearing a bit," he told me. "I have high hopes. After breakfast we'll make our way ashore and choose our lookout."

This matter settled, I went to find Ned Land. I wanted to take him along. The obstinate Canadian refused, and I could easily see that he was growing more closemouthed and bad tempered by the day. Under the circumstances I wasn't sorry he refused. In all honesty there were too many seals ashore, and it wouldn't do to expose that impulsive fisherman to such temptations.

Breakfast over, I made my way ashore. The *Nautilus* had gone a few more miles during the night. It lay a good league out from the coast, over which towered a sharp mountain peak some 1,300 to 1,600 feet high. Also in the skiff were Captain Nemo, two crewmen, and the instruments—in other words, a chronometer, a spyglass, and a barometer.

During our crossing I saw many baleen whales belonging to the three species characteristic of these southernmost seas: bowhead whales ("the right whale," as the English say), which have no dorsal fins; humpback whales from the genus *Balaenoptera* (in other words, "winged whales"), beasts with pleated bellies and huge whitish pectoral fins, which, genus name nothwithstanding, haven't yet developed into wings; and finback whales, yellowish brown, the fastest of all cetaceans. These powerful animals can be heard from far away when they shoot up towering spouts of air and steam that look like swirls of smoke. Pods of these different mammals were playing in the tranquil waters, and I could easily see that this antarctic polar basin now served as a refuge for those cetaceans too relentlessly tracked by hunters.

I likewise noted some long whitish strings of salps, a type of mollusk found in clusters, and some medusas of large size rocking in the eddies of the billows.

By nine o'clock we'd pulled up to shore. The sky was growing brighter. Clouds were escaping to the south. The fog was lifting off the cold surface of the water. Captain Nemo headed toward the peak, which he undoubtedly planned to use as a lookout. It was an arduous climb over sharp lava and pumice stones, through air often stinking with the sulfurous emissions carried by the curls of steam. For a man out of practice at walking on solid ground, the captain scaled the steep-

497

est slopes with a supple agility that I couldn't match and that would have been envied by hunters of Pyrenees mountain goats.

It took us two hours to reach the top of that peak, which was half crystal, half basalt. From there our eyes could take in a huge expanse of sea, which scrawled its boundary line firmly against the background of the northern sky. At our feet, dazzling tracts of white. Overhead, a pale azure, free of mists. North of us, the sun's disk, a ball of fire already cut into by the horizon line. From the heart of the waters, jets of liquid rising from various whales like hundreds of magnificent bouquets. In the distance, the *Nautilus*, looking like a cetacean still sleeping. Behind us to the south and east, an immense stretch of land, a chaotic heap of rocks and ice whose far edges we couldn't see.

Arriving at the top of this peak, Captain Nemo meticulously determined its elevation with the help of his barometer, since he had to take this into account in his noon sights.

By 11:45 the sun, at that point visible only by refraction, looked like a golden disk and dispersed its last rays over this deserted continent down to these seas not yet plowed by mankind's ships.

Captain Nemo carried a spyglass that had a reticular eyepiece, which corrected the sun's refraction with the help of a mirror, and he used this instrument to watch that golden orb sinking little by little along an extremely wide diagonal that reached below the horizon. I held the chronometer. My heart was pounding furiously. If the lower half of the sun's disk vanished just as the chronometer said noon, that meant we were right at the pole.

"Noon!" I called.

"The South Pole!" Captain Nemo replied in a solemn voice as he handed me the spyglass, which showed that golden orb cut into two exactly equal parts by the horizon.

I looked at the last rays wreathing this mountain peak, while shadows were gradually climbing its gradients.

Just then, resting a hand on my shoulder, Captain Nemo said to me:

"Sir, in 1600 the Dutchman Gherritz was carried by storms and currents as far as latitude 64° south, where he discovered the South Shetland Islands. On January 17, 1773, the famous Captain Cook went along the 38th meridian and arrived at latitude 67° 30′; and on January 30, 1774, along the 109th meridian, he reached latitude 71° 15′. In 1819 the Russian Bellinghausen lay on the 69th parallel and in 1821 on the 66th at longitude 111° west. In 1820 the Englishman Bransfield halted at 65°. That same year the American Morrel, whose reports are dubious, went along the 42nd meridian and found open sea at latitude 70° 14′. In 1825 the Englishman Powell couldn't get beyond 62°. That same year a humble seal fisherman, the Englishman Weddell, went as far as latitude 72° 14′ on the 35th meridian and as far as 74° 15′ on the 36th. In 1829 the Englishman Foster, commander of the *Chanticleer*, laid claim to the continent of Antarctica in latitude 63° 26′ and longitude 66° 26′. On February 1, 1831, the Englishman Biscoe discovered Enderby Land at latitude 68° 50′, Adelaide Land at latitude 67° on February 5, 1832, and Graham Land at latitude 64° 45′ on February 21. In 1838 the Frenchman Dumont d'Urville halted at the ice barrier in latitude 62° 57′, sighting the Louis-Philippe Peninsula; on January 21 two years later, at a new southerly position of 66° 30′, he named the Adélie Coast, and a week later the Clarie Coast at 64° 40′. In 1838 the American Wilkes progressed as far as the 69th parallel on the 100th meridian. In 1839 the Englishman Balleny discovered the Sabrina Coast at the edge of the polar circle. Finally, on January 12, 1842, with his ships, the *Erebus* and the *Terror*, the Englishman Sir James Clark Ross found Victoria Land in latitude 70° 56′ and longitude 171° 7′ east; on the 23rd of that same month, he reached the 74th parallel, which till then had been the record for Farthest South; on the 27th he lay at 76° 8′; on the 28th at 77° 32′; on February 2 at 78° 4′; and late in 1842 he returned to 71° but couldn't get beyond it. Well now! In 1868 on this 21st day of March, I, Captain Nemo, have personally reached the South Pole at 90° and I hereby claim this entire part of the globe, equal to one-sixth of the known continents."

"In the name of which sovereign, captain?"

"In my own name, sir!"

And with that Captain Nemo unfurled a black flag with a gold "N" quartered on its bunting. Then, turning toward that golden orb whose last rays were licking at the sea's horizon:

"Farewell, O sun!" he called. "Vanish, O shining orb! Sleep beneath this open sea, and let six months of night spread their shadows over my new domain!"

39

ACCIDENT OR INCIDENT?

THE NEXT DAY, March 22, preparations for departure were under way by six o'clock in the morning. The last glimmers of twilight had melted into night. The cold was brisk. The constellations shone with startling intensity. The wondrous Southern Cross, polar star of the antarctic regions, was twinkling at the zenith.

Our thermometer read 10° Fahrenheit, and the wind was picking up, leaving a sharp nip in the air. Ice floes were increasing over the open water. The sea was starting to congeal everywhere. Many blackish patches were spreading across its surface, announcing the imminent formation of fresh ice. Obviously this southernmost basin froze over completely during its six-month winter and was out of reach the whole time. Meanwhile what happened to the whales? Undoubtedly they went under the ice barrier to find more feasible seas. As for seals and walruses, they were used to living in the harshest climates and stayed on in these icy waterways. These animals know instinctively how to gouge holes in the ice fields and keep them continually open; they go to these holes to breathe. Once the birds have migrated northward to escape from the cold, these marine mammals become the sole lords of the polar continent.

Meanwhile our ballast tanks filled with water and the *Nautilus* sank slowly. At a depth of a thousand feet, it stopped. Its propeller churned the waves and it proceeded due north at a speed of fifteen miles per hour.

Toward the afternoon it was already cruising under the immense frozen carapace of the ice barrier.

As a precautionary measure the panels in the lounge stayed closed, because the *Nautilus*'s hull could run afoul of some submerged chunk of ice. Accordingly I spent that day putting my notes into final form. My mind was completely caught up in my memories of the pole. We'd made it to that unreachable spot without facing any danger or even physical strain, as if our seagoing passenger car had ridden there on railroad tracks. And now we'd actually started our return trip. Did it still have comparable surprises in store for me? I felt sure it did, so inexhaustible is this series of underwater wonders! As it was, in the 5½ months since fate had put us on board, we'd gone 14,000 leagues, and over this track longer than the earth's equator, so many fascinating or frightening incidents had beguiled our voyage: that hunting trip in the Crespo forests, running aground in Torres Strait, the coral cemetery, the pearl fisheries of Ceylon, the Arabic tunnel, the fires of Santorini, those millions in Vigo Bay, Atlantis, the South Pole! During the night all these memories darted from one dream to the next, not letting my brain rest for a second.

At three o'clock in the morning, a violent collision jarred me awake. I sat up in bed, listened in the darkness, and suddenly was heaved out into the middle of my stateroom. Obviously the *Nautilus* had gone aground, then heeled over significantly.

Leaning against the walls, I dragged myself down the corridors to the lounge, whose ceiling lights were on. The furniture had been overturned. Luckily the glass cases were firmly secured at the base and had stayed upright. Because we'd been displaced from the vertical, the starboard pictures were glued to the tapestries, while those to port had their lower edges hanging a foot out from the wall. So the *Nautilus* was lying on its starboard side, completely stationary to boot.

Inside I heard the sound of footsteps and a jumble of voices. But Captain Nemo didn't appear. Just as I was about to leave the lounge, Ned Land and Conseil came in.

"What happened?" I instantly said to them.

"That's what I came to ask master," Conseil replied.

"Damnation!" the Canadian exclaimed. "I know full well what happened! The *Nautilus* has gone aground, and judging from the way it's listing, I don't think it'll pull through like that first time in Torres Strait."

"But," I asked, "are we at least back on the surface of the sea?"

"We have no idea," Conseil answered.

"It's easy to find out," I remarked.

I checked our pressure gauge. Much to my surprise it showed a depth of 1,180 feet.

"What's the meaning of this?" I exclaimed.

"We'll have to ask Captain Nemo," Conseil said.

"But where can we find him?" Ned Land inquired.

"Follow me," I told my two companions.

We left the lounge. Nobody in the library. Nobody by the central companionway or the crew's quarters. I figured Captain Nemo had to be stationed in the pilothouse. It was best to wait. The three of us went back to the lounge.

I'll skip over the Canadian's complaints. He had good grounds for an outburst. I didn't answer him back and let him blow off all the steam he wanted.

We'd been left to ourselves for twenty minutes, trying to detect the slightest sound inside the *Nautilus*, when Captain Nemo came in. He didn't seem to see us. His face, usually so unemotional, revealed a definite uneasiness. He silently studied the compass and pressure gauge, then he went and put his finger on the world map in the part showing the southernmost seas.

I didn't want to interrupt him. But when he turned to me a few seconds later, I tossed back at him a comment that he'd made in Torres Strait:

"An incident, captain?"

"No, sir," he replied, "this time an accident."

"Serious?"

"Maybe."

"Any immediate danger?"

"No."

"The *Nautilus* is aground?"

"Yes."

"And this accident happened . . . ?"

"Through nature's unpredictability, not man's incompetence. We didn't make a single error in our maneuvers. Nevertheless we can't keep a loss of balance from taking its toll. We may defy human laws, but nobody can flout the laws of nature."

Captain Nemo had picked an odd time to get philosophical. All in all his answer didn't tell me a thing.

"Might I learn, sir," I asked him, "what caused this accident?"

"An enormous body of ice, an entire mountain, has toppled over," he answered me. "When an iceberg is eroded at the base by warmer waters or by repeated collisions, its center of gravity rises. Then it somersaults, it turns completely upside down. That's what happened here. One of those icebergs overturned and struck the *Nautilus* as it was cruising under the waters. This mass of ice then slid beneath our hull, raised us with irresistible power, and has lifted us into less congested strata where we're now lying on our side."

"But can't we float the *Nautilus* free by emptying its ballast tanks, to regain our balance?"

"We're doing that right now, sir. You can hear the pumps working. Look at the needle on the pressure gauge. It shows that the *Nautilus* is rising, but this mass of ice is rising along with us, and till some obstacle halts its upward movement, our position won't change."

It was true, the *Nautilus* had kept the same heel to starboard. Surely it would straighten up once this frozen mass came to a halt. But before that happened, who knew if we wouldn't strike the underbelly of the ice barrier and be hideously squeezed between those two frozen surfaces?

I pondered all the possible outcomes for this situation. Captain Nemo kept his eye on our pressure gauge. Since the iceberg had toppled over, the *Nautilus* had risen about 150 feet, but it still stayed at the same angle to the vertical.

Suddenly we felt a slight movement over the hull. Clearly the *Nautilus* was straightening a bit. Objects hanging in the lounge were visibly returning to their normal positions. The walls went back to being vertical. Nobody said a word. Our hearts pounding, we could see and feel the ship righting itself. Once again the floor became horizontal under our feet. Ten minutes went by.

"Finally, we're upright!" I exclaimed.

"Yes," Captain Nemo said, heading for the lounge door.

"But will we float off?" I asked him.

"Certainly," he replied, "since the ballast tanks aren't empty as yet, and when they are, the *Nautilus* will automatically rise toward the surface of the sea."

The captain went out; before long I saw that at his orders the *Nautilus* had ceased its upward movement. In fact it soon would have struck the underbelly of the ice barrier, but it had stopped in time and was floating in midwater.

"That was a close call!" Conseil said.

"Yes. We could have been crushed between those masses of ice, or at the very least imprisoned between them. And then, without any way of replenishing our air supply. . . . Yes, that *was* a close call!"

"If it's over with!" Ned Land muttered.

I didn't want to get into a pointless argument with the Canadian, so I didn't reply. What's more, the panels opened just then, and the outside light burst through the uncovered windows.

We were fully afloat as I've said; but some thirty feet away, dazzling walls of ice rose on both sides of the *Nautilus*. In addition there were walls above and below. Above, because the ice barrier's underbelly spread over us like an immense ceiling. Below, because that somersaulting iceberg had gradually shifted, had found points of purchase on both side walls, and had gotten jammed between them. The *Nautilus* was imprisoned in a literal tunnel of ice about sixty-five feet wide and filled with quiet water. So the ship could go either ahead or astern and easily leave this tunnel, then it could dive a few hundred yards deeper and take an open passageway under the ice barrier.

The ceiling lights were off, yet the lounge was still brightly lit. This was due to the reflecting power of those walls of ice, which threw the beams of our beacon right back at us. Words can't describe the effects created by our galvanic rays on those huge, eccentrically carved chunks of ice, all their corners, ridges, and facets giving off a different glimmer according to the nature of the veins running inside them. It was like a dazzling mine of gemstones, especially sapphires and emeralds that threw off crisscrossing jets of blue and green. Here and there the soft, subtle hues of opals darted among sparkling diamonds whose fiery brilliance was more than any eye could stand. The power of our beacon was magnified a hundred times over, like a lamp through the biconvex lenses of a world-class lighthouse.

"Lovely, absolutely lovely!" Conseil exclaimed.

"Yes!" I said. "It's a wonderful sight, isn't it, Ned?"

"Oh damnation, yes!" Ned Land shot back. "I hate to admit it, but it's magnificent! Nobody has ever seen the like. But this sight could cost us dearly. And to tell the truth, I think we're looking at things God never intended for human eyes."

Ned was right. It was too lovely. All at once a yell from Conseil made me turn around.

"What's wrong?" I asked.

"Master should close his eyes! Master shouldn't look!"

With that Conseil clapped his hands over his eyes.

"But what's the matter, my boy?"

"I've been dazzled, struck blind!"

Instinctively my eyes flew to the window, but I couldn't stand the fiery light devouring it.

I realized what had happened. The *Nautilus* had just started off at high speed. Then all those gentle glimmers on the ice walls had changed into flashing streaks. The fiery glints from those myriads of diamonds were merging with each other. Swept along by its propeller, the *Nautilus* was traveling through a sheath of lightning.

Then the panels in the lounge closed. We

held our hands over our eyes, which were steeped in those circular gleams that swirl in front of the retina when sunlight strikes it too intensely. It was a good while before our vision returned to normal.

Finally we lowered our hands.

"Ye gods, I never would have thought it possible," Conseil said.

"And I still don't!" the Canadian shot back.

"After we've been spoiled by all these natural wonders and we're back on shore," Conseil added, "imagine how we'll turn up our noses at those pitiful landmasses, those puny works of man! No, the civilized world won't be good enough for us!"

Such words from the lips of this unemotional Flemish boy showed that our enthusiasm was near the boiling point. But the Canadian just had to throw a little cold water over us.

"The civilized world?" he said, shaking his head. "Don't worry, Conseil my friend, that's a world we won't be seeing anymore!"

By this point it was five o'clock in the morning. Just then there was a collision in the *Nautilus*'s bow. I gathered that its spur had just bumped a chunk of ice. It must have been a faulty maneuver, because this underwater tunnel was cluttered with such chunks and didn't make for easy navigating. So I figured Captain Nemo would adjust his course and go around each obstacle by hugging the walls of the tunnel. In any case our forward progress wouldn't receive an absolute check. Nevertheless, contrary to my expectations, the *Nautilus* definitely started to move backward.

"We're going astern?" Conseil said.

"Yes," I replied. "The tunnel must not have a way out at this end."

"And so . . . ?"

"So," I said, "our maneuvers are quite simple. We'll return in our tracks and go out the southern opening. That's all."

In saying this I tried to sound more confident than I actually felt. Meanwhile the *Nautilus* was backing up more quickly and swept us along at great speed, running with propeller in reverse.

"This'll mean a delay," Ned said.

"What difference are a few hours one way or the other, so long as we get out."

"Yes," Ned Land echoed, "so long as we get out!"

I strolled for a few seconds from the lounge into the library. My companions stayed seated and kept quiet. It wasn't long before I plumped down on a couch and picked up a book, which my eyes skimmed mechanically.

Fifteen minutes later Conseil came up to me, saying:

"Is master reading something interesting?"

"Very interesting," I replied.

"I believe it. Master is reading his own book!"

"My own book?"

My hands were actually holding my own work on the great ocean depths. I hadn't even suspected. I closed the book and went back to my strolling. Ned and Conseil got up to leave.

"Stay here, my friends," I said, stopping them. "Let's stay together till we're out of this blind alley."

"As master wishes," Conseil replied.

A few hours went by. I often studied the instruments hanging on the lounge wall. The pressure gauge showed that the *Nautilus* was staying at a constant depth of a thousand feet, the compass that it kept heading south, the log that it was going at a speed of twenty miles per hour, an excessive speed for such a cramped area. But Captain Nemo knew that he couldn't possibly go too fast, because by that point minutes were worth centuries.

At 8:25 a second collision occurred. This time astern. I grew pale. My companions were at my side. I clutched Conseil's hand. We questioned each other with our eyes, and more directly than if our thoughts had been translated into words.

Just then the captain came into the lounge. I went over to him.

"Our path is barred to the south?" I asked him.

"Yes, sir. When that iceberg overturned, it closed up every exit."

"We're boxed in?"

"Yes."

40

SHORTAGE OF AIR

CONSEQUENTLY there were impregnable frozen walls above, below, and all around the *Nautilus*. We were the ice barrier's captives! The Canadian banged a table with his fearsome fist. Conseil kept still. I looked at the captain. His face was as unemotional as ever. His arms were folded. He was mulling things over. The *Nautilus* didn't stir.

Then the captain broke into speech:

"Gentlemen," he said in a calm voice, "there are two ways of dying under conditions such as these."

This bewildering individual acted like a mathematics teacher working out a problem for his pupils.

"The first way," he went on, "is death by crushing. The second is death by asphyxiation. I'll leave out the possibility of death by starvation, because the *Nautilus*'s provisions will certainly last longer than we will. So let's focus on our chances of being crushed or asphyxiated."

"As for asphyxiation, captain," I replied, "that isn't a concern because the air tanks are full."

"True," Captain Nemo went on, "but they'll supply air for only two days. Now then, we've been buried under the waters for thirty-six hours, and the *Nautilus*'s heavy atmosphere already needs replenishing. In another forty-eight hours our oxygen stores will be used up."

"Well then, captain, let's free ourselves within forty-eight hours!"

"We'll try to at least, by cutting through one of these walls of ice around us."

"Which one?" I asked.

"Borings will tell us that. I'm going to set the *Nautilus* down on the lower bed, then my men will put on their diving suits and attack whichever wall is the thinnest."

"Can the panels in the lounge be left open?"

"Without any ill effect. We're no longer in motion."

Captain Nemo went out. Hissing sounds soon told me that water was being let into the ballast tanks. The *Nautilus* slowly gravitated downward and came to rest on the icy bottom at a depth of 1,150 feet, the depth at which the lower bed of ice lay submerged.

"My friends," I said, "we're in a serious predicament, and I'm counting on your courage and energy."

"Sir," the Canadian replied, "this isn't the time to bore you with my complaining. I'm ready to do anything I can for the general welfare."

"Excellent, Ned," I said, holding out my hand to the Canadian.

"I might add," he went on, "that I'm as handy with a pick as a harpoon. If I can be helpful to the captain, he can use me any way he wants."

"He won't turn down your assistance. Come with me, Ned."

I led the Canadian to the room where the *Nautilus*'s men were putting on their diving suits. I informed the captain of Ned's proposition, which he accepted. The Canadian got into his underwater gear and was ready as soon as his fellow workers. On their backs they all carried Rouquayrol devices that the air tanks had supplied with substantial allowances of fresh oxygen. A considerable but necessary withdrawal from the *Nautilus*'s reserves. As for the Ruhmkorff lamps, they weren't needed out in those clear waters imbued with our electric rays.

Once Ned was suited up, I went back into the lounge, whose windows had been uncovered; stationed next to Conseil, I examined the strata that surrounded and supported the *Nautilus*.

A few seconds later we saw a dozen crewmen set foot on the bed of ice, among them Ned Land, recognizable from his tall figure. Captain Nemo was with them.

Before he started digging into the ice, the captain had to do some preliminary boring to make sure he was working in the best direction. They drove long bores into the side walls; but after 50 feet the instruments were still impeded by the thickness of those walls. It was futile to attack the ceiling since that surface was the ice barrier itself, over 1,300 feet high. Then Captain Nemo bored into the lower surface. There only about 33 feet separated us from the sea. That's how thick this tract of ice was. From that point on it was a matter of chopping out a piece whose surface area matched the *Nautilus*'s waterline. This meant removing about 230,000 cubic feet, to dig a hole big enough for the ship to pass through and sink below this frozen tract.

The workers started immediately and proceeded with tireless persistence. Instead of digging all around the *Nautilus*, which would have been exceptionally difficult, Captain Nemo had an immense trench outlined on the ice some 25 feet off our port quarter. Then his men simultaneously drilled into it at several spots along its edges. Soon their picks were energetically attacking that compact matter, and huge chunks of it started coming loose. These chunks of ice weighed less than the water, and due to an unusual effect of specific gravity, each piece took wing, you might say, to the roof of the tunnel, which thickened above by as much as it shrank below. But nobody cared so long as the lower surface kept getting thinner.

After two hours of hard work, Ned Land came back inside, worn out. He and his companions were replaced by new workmen, Conseil and I among them. The *Nautilus*'s chief officer supervised us.

The water struck me as unusually cold, but I warmed up promptly while wielding my pick. My movements were quite free, though they were executed under a pressure of thirty atmospheres.

After two hours of work, coming back in to grab a little food and rest, I found a noticeable difference between the clean elastic fluid supplied me by the Rouquayrol device and the *Nautilus*'s air, which was already full of carbon dioxide. Our oxygen hadn't been replenished in forty-eight hours, and its vital attributes were considerably reduced. Meanwhile, after twelve hours had gone by, we'd removed from the outlined surface area a slice of ice only a yard thick, hence about 21,000 cubic feet. Assuming we could achieve the same result every twelve hours, it would still take five nights and four days to see the undertaking through to completion.

"Five nights and four days!" I told my companions. "And we have only two days'

worth of oxygen in the air tanks."

"Without taking into account," Ned contended, "that once we're out of this damned prison, we'll still be cooped up under the ice barrier without any possible contact with the open air!"

Good point. Who could predict the minimum time we would need to free ourselves? Before the *Nautilus* could get back to the surface of the waves, wouldn't we all be dead of asphyxiation? Were this ship and everybody on board doomed to perish in this tomb of ice? It was a dreadful state of affairs. But we faced it head-on, each of us determined to do his part to the end.

As I predicted, we removed a new one-yard slice from that immense niche during the night. But in the morning, wearing my diving suit, I was crossing through the mass of liquid in a temperature ranging from 19° to 21° Fahrenheit, when I noted that the side walls were gradually closing in on each other. Not warmed by the movements of workmen and tools, pockets of water farthest from the trench were showing a tendency to freeze. In the face of this imminent new danger, what would happen to our chances for survival, and how could we keep this liquid around us from freezing solid, then cracking the *Nautilus*'s hull like glass?

I didn't tell my two companions about this new danger. There was no point in dampening the energy they were putting into our arduous rescue work. But when I went back on board, I mentioned this serious complication to Captain Nemo.

"I know," he told me in that calm tone the most dreadful outlook couldn't change. "It's one more danger, but I don't know any way of warding it off. Our only chance for salvation is to work faster than the water freezes. We need to get there first, that's all."

Get there first! By then I should have been used to this type of talk!

For several hours that day, I wielded my pick doggedly. The work kept me going. Besides, working meant leaving the *Nautilus*, which meant breathing the clean oxygen drawn from the air tanks and supplied by our equipment, which meant leaving the thin, foul air behind.

By evening we'd dug one more yard out of the trench. When I went back on board, I was nearly asphyxiated by the carbon dioxide filling the air. Oh, if only we had the chemical methods that would allow us to eliminate this noxious gas! There was no lack of oxygen. All this water contained a considerable amount, and after being decomposed by our powerful batteries, this vital elastic fluid could have been available to us again. I'd worked it out perfectly, but it was no use because the carbon dioxide produced by our breathing permeated the whole ship. To absorb it, we would need to fill containers with potassium hydroxide and shake them continually. But we didn't have this substance on board and nothing could replace it.

That evening Captain Nemo was forced to open the spigots on his air tanks and shoot a few spouts of fresh oxygen into the *Nautilus*'s interior. Without this precaution we wouldn't have woken up the following morning.

The next day, March 26, I went back to my mining chores, toiling to dig out the fifth yard. The ice barrier's side walls and underbelly had visibly thickened. Clearly they would come together before the *Nautilus* could break free. For a second I lost heart. My pick nearly slipped out of my hands. What was the point of digging if I was going to be smothered and crushed to death by this water turning to rock—a torture beyond the imaginings of the fiercest savages! I felt as if I were lying between the jaws of some fearsome monster, jaws closing irresistibly.

Supervising our work, working himself, Captain Nemo went past me just then. I reached out, touched him, and pointed to the walls of our prison. The starboard wall had moved forward to a point barely twelve feet from the *Nautilus*'s hull.

The captain understood and signaled me to follow him. We got back on board. My diving suit removed, I went with him to the lounge.

"Professor Aronnax," he told me, "this calls for heroic measures, or we'll be sealed up in this frozen water as if it were cement."

"Yes!" I said. "But what can we do?"

"Oh," he exclaimed, "if only my *Nautilus* were strong enough to handle that much pressure without being crushed!"

"Well?" I asked, not getting the captain's point.

"Don't you understand," he went on, "that the congealing of this water could come to our aid? Don't you see that by solidifying, it could burst these tracts of ice imprisoning us, just as its freezing can burst the hardest rocks? Don't you realize that this force could rescue us rather than destroy us?"

"Yes, captain, maybe so. But whatever defenses the *Nautilus* may have against being crushed, it still couldn't handle such frightful pressures and it would be squeezed as flat as a piece of sheet iron."

"I know it, sir. So we mustn't rely on nature to rescue us but on our own efforts. We must counteract this solidification. We must hold it in check. Not only are the side walls closing in, there aren't ten feet of water ahead or astern of the *Nautilus*. All around us this freeze is gaining fast."

"How long," I asked, "will the oxygen in the air tanks allow us to breathe on board?"

The captain looked me in the eye.

"After tomorrow," he said, "the air tanks will be empty!"

I broke into a cold sweat. But why should his answer have surprised me? On March 22 the *Nautilus* had submerged under the open waters at the pole. It was now the 26th. For five days we'd lived off the ship's stores! And all remaining breathable air had to be saved for the workmen. Even today as I write these lines, my sensations are so intense that an instinctive terror sweeps over me, and my lungs still seem short of air!

Meanwhile Captain Nemo stood lost in thought, not saying a thing. An idea had visibly crossed his mind. But he seemed to brush it aside. He told himself no. Finally these words escaped from his lips:

"Boiling water!" he muttered.

"Boiling water?" I exclaimed.

"Yes, sir. We're shut up in a relatively confined area. If the *Nautilus*'s pumps were to shoot continual streams of boiling water into this space, wouldn't that raise its temperature and delay its freezing?"

"It's worth a try!" I said resolutely.

"Then let's try it, professor."

At this point our thermometer gave 19° Fahrenheit outside. Captain Nemo led me to the galley where a huge distilling mechanism was at work, supplying drinking water through an evaporation process. We loaded the mechanism with water and threw the full electric heat of our batteries into coils passing through the liquid. In a few minutes the water reached its boiling point of 212° Fahrenheit. It went off to the pumps while new water replaced it in the meantime. The heat generated by our batteries was so intense that after simply going through the mechanism, water drawn cold from the sea arrived boiling hot at the brigade of pumps.

Three hours after the pumping started, our thermometer gave the outside temperature as 21° Fahrenheit. We'd gained two degrees. Two hours later the thermometer registered close to 25°.

After double-checking the operation's progress and taking many notes, I told the captain, "It's working."

"I think so," he answered me. "We won't be crushed. Now all we have to fear is asphyxiation."

During the night the water temperature rose to 30° Fahrenheit. The pumping couldn't get it to go a single degree higher. But since salt water freezes only at 28°, I was finally assured that there was no danger of its solidifying.

By the next day, March 27, we'd dug about twenty feet of ice out of the niche. There were only thirteen more feet to go. That still meant forty-eight hours of work. The air couldn't be replenished inside the *Nautilus*. Accordingly it kept getting worse and worse throughout the day.

An unbearable heaviness came over me. Around three o'clock in the afternoon, this oppressive sensation affected me to an agonizing degree. I yawned so much, I dislocated my jaws. My lungs were gasping as they hunted that elastic fluid needed for breathing but now getting scarcer and scarcer. I was in a daze. I lay outstretched, strength gone, close to unconscious. My gallant Conseil had the same symptoms, suffered the same sufferings, yet never left my side. He clutched my hand, he kept encouraging me, and I even heard him mutter:

"Ah, if only I didn't have to breathe, so I could leave more air for master!"

It brought tears to my eyes to hear him say these words.

Since conditions inside were unbearable for everybody, how eagerly, how happily, we put on our diving suits to take our turns working! Our picks rang out on that layer of ice. Our arms were aching, our hands were rubbed raw, but who cared about a little exhaustion or a few scratches? Vital air was reaching our lungs! We could breathe! We could breathe!

And yet not a single worker tried to overstay his scheduled time underwater. At the end of his shift, each man handed his life-giving air tank to a gasping companion. Captain Nemo set the example by being the first to follow this strict regimen. When his time was up, he turned over his equipment to somebody else and went back into the foul air on board, always calm, never faltering, never complaining.

That day we finished the usual work with even greater energy. Over the whole surface area, we had only six feet left to dig out. Only six feet separated us from the open sea. But the ship's air tanks were almost empty. The little air that remained had to be saved for the workmen. Not one atom for the *Nautilus!*

When I got back on board, I felt half suffocated. What a night! I can't even write about it. Such sufferings are indescribable. The next day my breathing was constricted. Headaches and ghastly fits of dizziness made me stagger around like a drunk. My companions had the same symptoms. A few crewmen were at their last gasp.

That day, the sixth of our imprisonment, Captain Nemo saw that picks and mattocks weren't working fast enough, so he decided that the layer of ice separating us from open water needed to be *crushed*. The man had kept his energy and composure. He overcame bodily pain with strength of mind. He thought, planned, and took action.

At his orders the craft was eased off, in other words, lifted up from that layer of ice by a change in its specific gravity. Once it was floating, the crew took it in tow and led it right above the huge trench that had been chopped out to match the ship's waterline. Then, after the ballast tanks let in more water, the boat sank and settled into its niche.

At this point the whole crew came back on board, closing the outside double door. The *Nautilus* rested on a layer of ice only a yard thick and drilled by bores in a thousand places.

Then the stopcocks on the ballast tanks opened wide, and 3,500 cubic feet of water rushed in, increasing the *Nautilus*'s weight by 220,000 pounds.

We waited, listened, forgot our sufferings, and were hopeful once more. We'd staked our salvation on this last throw of the dice.

Despite all the buzzing in my head, I soon heard vibrations under the *Nautilus*'s hull. It tilted. The ice cracked with an odd ripping sound like paper tearing, and the *Nautilus* gravitated downward.

"We're going through!" Conseil muttered in my ear.

I couldn't answer him. I clutched his hand. I squeezed it in a reflex action.

All at once, pulled down by its frightful excess load, the *Nautilus* plummeted under the waters like a cannonball—in other words, it dropped as if in a vacuum!

Then our full electric power was put on the pumps, which instantly started to expel water from the ballast tanks. In a few minutes we'd checked our fall. Soon the pressure gauge registered an ascending movement. Brought to full speed, the propeller made the sheet-iron hull tremble down to its rivets, and we streaked northward.

But how long would it take to navigate under the ice barrier to the open sea? Another day? I would be dead first!

Half lying on a couch in the library, I was suffocating. My face was purple, my lips blue, my faculties in abeyance. I couldn't see or hear anymore. I'd lost all sense of time. My muscles had no power to contract.

I can't estimate how many hours went by in this way. But I knew my death throes were beginning. I realized I was about to die . . .

Suddenly I came to. A couple breaths of air had entered my lungs. Had we risen to the surface of the waves? Had we gotten past the ice barrier?

No! Ned and Conseil, my two gallant friends, were sacrificing themselves to save me. A few atoms of air were still left in the depths of one of the Rouquayrol devices. Instead of breathing it themselves, they'd kept it for me; while they suffocated, they poured life into me drop by drop! I tried to push the device away. They held my hands, and for a few seconds I breathed luxuriously.

My eyes flew to the clock. It was eleven in the morning. It had to be March 28. The *Nautilus* was going at the frightful speed of forty miles per hour. It was writhing in the waters.

Where was Captain Nemo? Had he given up the ghost? Had his companions perished with him?

Just then our pressure gauge showed that we were no more than twenty feet below the surface. A mere tract of ice separated us from the open air. Could we break through it?

Maybe! In any case the *Nautilus* was going to try. I actually could feel it positioning itself at an angle, lowering its stern and raising its spur. It shifted its balance simply by letting in additional water. Then, driven by its powerful propeller, it attacked the ice field from below like a fearsome battering ram. It split that barricade little by little, backing up, then putting on full speed against the punctured tract of ice; and finally, carried away by its crowning momentum, it burst all the way through and sank onto the frozen surface, crushing the ice under its weight.

The hatch opened—or flew off its hinges, so to speak—and waves of clean air poured into every part of the *Nautilus*.

41

FROM CAPE HORN
TO THE AMAZON

AS FOR HOW I GOT onto the platform, I can't say. Maybe the Canadian transferred me there. But I could breathe, I could inhale the bracing salt air. Beside me my two companions were getting tipsy on the fresh oxygen particles. Poor souls who have gone without food for a good while daren't pounce thoughtlessly on the first thing they get. We, on the other hand, didn't have to practice such moderation—we could drink the atoms from the air by the lungful, and it was the breeze, the breeze itself, that poured this luxurious liquor down our throats!

"Ahhh!" Conseil put in. "What fine oxygen! Master needn't have any fears about breathing it. There's plenty for everybody."

As for Ned Land, he didn't say a word, but his wide-open jaws would have scared off a shark. And how noisily he inhaled! The Canadian puffed away like a furnace going full blast.

Our strength came back quickly, and when I looked around, I saw that we were alone on the platform. No crewmen. Not even Captain Nemo. Those strange seamen aboard the *Nautilus* were content with the oxygen circulating inside. Not a single one of them had come up to enjoy the open air.

The first words I spoke were words of appreciation and gratitude to my two companions. Ned and Conseil had kept me alive during the last hours of our long death throes. But no expression of thanks could ever repay such dedication.

"Good Lord, professor," Ned Land answered me. "Don't mention it! What did we do that's so praiseworthy? Not a thing. It was a simple matter of arithmetic. Your life is worth more than ours, so we had to save it."

"No, Ned," I replied, "it isn't worth more. Nobody could be superior to a decent, generous man like you!"

"All right, all right!" the Canadian repeated in embarrassment.

"And as for you, my gallant Conseil, you suffered quite a bit."

"Not that much, to be honest with master. I could have used a few throatfuls of air, but I scraped by. Besides, when I saw master go into a swoon, I lost all desire to breathe. You might say that it took the wind out of . . ."

Appalled by this descent into cheap word-play, Conseil gave up in midsentence.

"My friends," I replied, deeply touched,

"we're forever bound to each other, and I'm in your debt—"

"Which I'll take advantage of," the Canadian fired back.

"Huh?" Conseil put in.

"Yes," Ned Land went on, "and you can repay that debt by coming along when I leave this infernal *Nautilus*."

"By the way," Conseil said, "are we heading in a promising direction?"

"Yes," I replied, "because we're heading in the direction of the sun, and here the sun is due north."

"Sure," Ned Land went on, "but we still don't know whether we'll make for the Atlantic or the Pacific, in other words, whether we'll end up in well-traveled or deserted seas."

I couldn't answer this and I was afraid Captain Nemo wouldn't take us homeward but instead into that huge ocean lapping the shores of both Asia and America. In this way he would finish his underwater tour of the world, then go back to those seas where the *Nautilus* enjoyed the greatest freedom. But if we returned to the Pacific, far from any populated area, what would happen to Ned Land's plans?

We would soon settle this important point. The *Nautilus* traveled swiftly. Before long we'd gone past the Antarctic Circle as well as the promontory of Cape Horn. By seven o'clock in the evening on March 31, we were level with the tip of South America.

By then we'd forgotten all our past sufferings. The memory of that imprisonment under the ice had faded from our minds. We thought only of the future. Captain Nemo didn't appear in public anymore, neither in the lounge nor on the platform. The positions reported each day on the world map were put there by the chief officer and they allowed me to determine the *Nautilus*'s exact heading. Now then, that evening it became clear, much to my satisfaction, that we were going north again by the Atlantic route.

I shared my conclusions with the Canadian and Conseil.

"That's good news," the Canadian replied, "but where's the *Nautilus* off to?"

"I can't say, Ned."

"After the South Pole does our captain want to take on the North Pole, then head back to the Pacific through the notorious Northwest Passage?"

"I wouldn't double dare him," Conseil replied.

"Oh well," the Canadian said, "we'll give him the slip long before."

"In any case," Conseil added, "he's a superman, that Captain Nemo, and we'll never regret that we knew him."

"Especially once we've left him!" Ned Land shot back.

The next day, April 1, when the *Nautilus* rose to the surface of the waves a few minutes before noon, we raised land to the west. It was Tierra del Fuego, which means "Land of Fire," a name given it by early navigators when they saw many curls of smoke rising from the natives' huts. This Land of Fire forms a huge cluster of islands 75 miles long and 200 miles wide, stretching between latitude 53° and 56° south, and between longitude 67° 50′ and 77° 15′ west. Its coastline looked flat, but lofty mountains rose in the distance. I even thought I glimpsed Mt. Sarmiento, whose elevation is 6,791 feet above sea level—a pyramid-shaped hunk of shale with a very sharp peak, which, depending on whether it's clear or clouded over, "predicts fair weather or foul," as Ned Land told me.

"A blue-ribbon barometer, my friend."

"Yes, sir, a natural barometer that has never let me down when I've navigated the narrows of the Strait of Magellan."

Just then its peak was visible in front of us, standing out clearly against the background of the skies. This forecast fair weather. And so it turned out.

Going back under the waters, the *Nautilus* pulled near the coast, cruising along it for only a few miles. Through the lounge windows I could see long creepers and gigantic fucus plants, bulb-bearing seaweeds we'd occasionally spotted in the open sea at the pole; with their smooth, viscous filaments, they measured up to a thousand feet long; more than an inch wide and very durable, they're honest-to-goodness cables that are often used as mooring ropes for ships. Another weed, a variety of kelp, had four-foot leaves,

was crammed into the coral concretions, and carpeted the ocean floor. It provides room and board for myriads of crustaceans and mollusks, especially crabs and cuttlefish. In its foliage seals and otters can dine sumptuously, mixing meat from fish with vegetables from the sea, like the English with their stews.

The *Nautilus* passed over these lush, luxuriant depths with tremendous speed. Toward evening it drew close to the Falkland Islands, whose craggy mountaintops I recognized the next day. The sea was of moderate depth. So with good reason I figured that these two islands, along with the many islets surrounding them, used to be part of the Magellan coastline. Very likely the Falkland Islands were discovered by the famous navigator John Davis, who gave them the name Davis Southern Islands. Later Sir Richard Hawkins called them the Maidenland, after the Blessed Virgin. Subsequently, at the beginning of the 18th century, they were named the Malouines by fishermen from Saint-Malo in Brittany, then finally renamed the Falklands by the English, to whom they belong today.

In these waters our nets brought up splendid algae specimens, particularly some fucus plants whose roots were loaded with the world's finest mussels. Geese and duck alighted by the dozens on the platform and soon took their places in the ship's pantry. As for fish, I specifically studied some bony fish belonging to the goby genus, especially some black gobies about eight inches long and sprinkled with white and yellow spots.

I likewise marveled at the many medusas, including the loveliest of their kind, those sea nettles characteristic of the Falkland waterways. Some of these jellyfish looked like very smooth, bowl-shaped parasols that sported russet stripes and were fringed with twelve neat festoons. Others were like upside-down baskets from which wide leaves and long red twigs were gracefully trailing. They swam by fluttering their four leafy arms, letting the luxuriant tresses of their tentacles dangle in the drift. I was hoping to catch and preserve a few samples of these delicate zoophytes, but they were merely clouds, shadows, and illusions; removed from their natural element, they faded away and melted into nothingness.

When the upper reaches of the Falkland Islands finally vanished below the horizon, the *Nautilus* submerged to a depth between sixty-five and eighty feet, then went along the South American coast. Captain Nemo still hadn't put in an appearance.

We didn't leave those Patagonian waterways till April 3, cruising sometimes under the ocean, sometimes on its surface. The *Nautilus* went past the wide estuary formed by the mouth of the Rio de la Plata, and on April 4 the ship lay off Uruguay, though fifty miles out. Keeping to its northerly heading, it followed the long windings of South America. By that point we'd fared 16,000 leagues since coming on board in the seas of Japan.

Around eleven o'clock in the morning, we cut the Tropic of Capricorn on the 37th meridian, passing well out from Cape Frio. Much to Ned Land's displeasure, Captain Nemo had no liking for the neighborhood of Brazil's populated shores, because he shot by with dizzying speed. Not even the swiftest fish or birds could keep up with us, and we weren't able to study any of the natural curiosities in these seas.

We maintained this speed for several days and by the evening of April 9 we'd raised South America's easternmost tip, Cape São Roque. But the *Nautilus* veered away once more and went looking for the lowest depths of an underwater valley scooped out between this cape and Sierra Leone on the coast of Africa. Level with the West Indies, this valley splits into two arms and ends to the north in an enormous depression nearly 30,000 feet deep. From this locality to the Lesser Antilles, the ocean's geological profile features a sheer cliff over 3½ miles high, and off the Cape Verde Islands there's another wall just as substantial; together these two barricades fence in the whole submerged continent of Atlantis. A few mountains break up the floor of this immense valley, furnishing these underwater depths with scenic views. This description is based mostly on some handdrawn charts kept in the *Nautilus*'s library, charts obviously rendered by Captain Nemo himself from his own personal investigations.

For two days we inspected those deep, deserted waters with the help of our slanting fins. The *Nautilus* would make long diagonal dives that took us to every level. But on April 11 it rose suddenly and the shore reappeared at the mouth of the Amazon River, a huge estuary whose outflow is so considerable, you can find fresh water several leagues out to sea.

We cut the Equator. Guiana was twenty miles to the west, French territory where we could easily have taken refuge. But the wind was blowing a strong gust, and we couldn't face the raging waves in a mere skiff. Ned Land undoubtedly realized this because he didn't say a word to me. I didn't allude to his escape plans either, because I didn't want to push him into an endeavor that was bound to backfire.

I easily filled the time with interesting research. During those two workdays of April 11-12, the *Nautilus* didn't leave the surface of the sea, and its trawl brought up a positively miraculous catch of zoophytes, fish, and reptiles.

A few zoophytes got caught in the chain of our trawl. Most were lovely sea anemones belonging to the family Actinidia—including, among other species, the *Phyctalis protexta* native to this part of the ocean, a small cylindrical trunk embellished with vertical stripes, flecked with red spots, and crowned by a marvelous bouquet of tentacles. As for mollusks, they consisted of items I'd already studied: screw shells, porphyry olive shells with neat crisscrossing lines and russet spots that stood out sharply against a flesh-colored background, weird spider conchs that looked like petrified scorpions, transparent snails from the genus *Hyala*, argonauts, some goodtasting cuttlefish, and certain species of squid that the naturalists of antiquity put in the same class as flying fish and that are used chiefly as bait for catching cod.

Speaking of the fish in these waterways, I noted various species that I hadn't yet had an opportunity to study. Among cartilaginous fish: river lampreys, a sort of eel fifteen inches long, head greenish, fins violet, back bluish gray, belly a silvery brown sprinkled with bright spots, iris of the eye encircled in gold, unusual creatures that the Amazon's current had to have carried out to sea because they're freshwater dwellers; longnose stingrays with pointed snouts and delicately drawn-out tails armed with extensive jagged stings; small three-foot sharks popularly known as hammerheads, with gray and whitish hides, their teeth arranged in several backward-curving rows; batfish, a sort of reddish isosceles triangle about twenty inches long and whose pectoral fins are expanded by fleshy extensions that make these fish look like bats, though an appendage made of horn up by the nostrils has earned them the nickname sea unicorns; finally a couple species of triggerfish, the sargassum whose speckled flanks shine with a sparkling gold color, and the bright purple leatherjacket whose hues glisten like a pigeon's throat.

I'll finish up this laundry list—on the dry side but quite accurate—with the individuals I studied in the category of bony fish: ghost eels with blunt, snow-white snouts, their bodies painted a handsome black and armed with a very long, slim, fleshy whip; prickly herring from the genus *Odontognathus* that looked like foot-long sardines and shone with a bright silver glow; horse mackerel furnished with two anal fins; black kingfish you can catch by using torches, fish over six feet long with white, firm, fatty meat that tastes like eel when fresh, like smoked salmon when dried; Spanish hogfish with scales only at the bases of their dorsal and anal fins; cardinalfish from the species *Cheilodipterus chrysopterus* whose hides mingle the colors gold, silver, ruby, and topaz; yellow-tailed sea bream whose meat is extremely delicate and whose phosphorescent properties give them away in the midst of the waters; orange-tinted porgies with slender tongues; barred grunts with gold caudal fins; whitecheek surgeonfish; four-eyed fish from Surinam, etc.

This "etc." won't keep me from mentioning one more fish that Conseil will have good reason to long remember.

One of our nets had hauled up a sort of very flat ray weighing close to forty-five pounds, which, without its tail, would have formed an authentic disk. Ending in a double-lobed fin, its ultrasmooth hide was white underneath and reddish on top, with big round spots that were a deep blue encircled in black. While lying on the platform, it kept struggling with convulsive movements, trying to turn over and spending so much energy, its final lunge was about to flip it into the sea. But Conseil is very possessive of his fish, and before I could stop him, he rushed after it and grabbed it with both hands.

Instantly there he was, on his back, legs in the air, body half paralyzed, and yelling:

"Oh, sir, sir! Will you help me!"

For once in his life, the poor lad didn't address me in the third person.

The Canadian and I sat him up; we rubbed his contracted arms, and when he'd recovered the use of his faculties, that eternal classifier mumbled in a broken voice:

"Class of cartilaginous fish, order Chondropterygii with fixed gills, suborder Selachii, family Rajiiformes, genus electric ray."

"Yes, my friend," I answered, "it was an electric ray that left you in such dismal shape."

"Oh, master can trust me on this," Conseil shot back. "I'll get my revenge on that creature!"

"How?"

"I'll eat it."

Which he did that same evening, but only to get even; because, frankly, it tasted like leather.

Poor Conseil had manhandled an electric ray of the most dangerous species, the cumana. In a conducting medium like water, this peculiar creature can electrocute other fish from several yards away, so powerful is its electrical apparatus, whose two chief surfaces total no less than twenty-seven square feet.

During the course of the following day, April 12, the *Nautilus* drew near the coast of Dutch Guiana by the mouth of the Maroni River. There several groups of sea cows were living in family units. They were manatees, which belong to the order Sirenia along with the dugong and Steller's sea cow. Harmless and unaggressive, these fine animals were around twenty to twenty-five feet long and had to have weighed nearly 4½ tons apiece. I told Ned Land and Conseil that farseeing nature had given these mammals a major role to play. In essence manatees, just like seals, are responsible for grazing on underwater prairies, destroying the clusters of weeds that clog the mouths of tropical rivers.

"And do you know what happened," I added, "after human beings came close to wiping out these beneficial species? Rotting weeds poisoned the air, and that poisoned air nurtures the yellow fever that devastates these marvelous countries. This toxic vegetation continues to proliferate in these warm seas, so the epidemic has spread unchecked from the mouth of the Rio de la Plata up to Florida!"

And if we're to believe Professor Toussenel, this outbreak is nothing next to the plague that will strike our descendants once seals and whales are eradicated from the seas. Then, crowded with jellyfish, squid, and other devilfish, the oceans will become huge centers of infection, because their waves will no longer shelter "those huge stomachs that God has put in charge of scrubbing the surface of the sea."

Meanwhile, without gainsaying these theories, the *Nautilus*'s crew captured half a dozen manatees. In essence it was a matter of stocking the larder with excellent red meat, even better than beef or veal. Their hunting held little interest. The manatees let themselves be struck down without putting up any resistance. Several tons of meat were hauled below, where they were dried and stored.

That same day an odd fishing technique further increased the *Nautilus*'s stores, so full of game were these seas. The meshes of our trawl brought up a number of fish whose heads were topped by little oval slabs with fleshy rims. They were suckerfish from the third family in the order of the subbrachians, the Malacopterygii. The flat disks on their heads are formed from crosswise plates of flexible cartilage, between which the creatures can create a vacuum, allowing them to stick to things like a suction cup.

The remoras I'd studied in the Mediterranean were related to this species. But the creature at issue here was an *Echeneis osteochir* characteristic of this sea. After catching them, our seamen dumped them in buckets of water.

Its fishing finished, the *Nautilus* drew nearer to the coast. In this locality a number of sea turtles were sleeping on the surface of the waves. These valuable reptiles are hard to catch, because they wake up at the slightest sound and their solid carapaces are harpoon-proof. But our suckerfish would bring about their capture with extraordinary certainty and precision. In essence this creature is a living fishhook, a source of potential wealth and happiness for the greenest fisherman in the business.

The *Nautilus*'s men attached to each fish's tail a ring big enough to not hamper its movements, and to this ring they tied a long line secured on board at the other end.

Tossed into the sea, the suckerfish immediately started to play their roles, heading over and fastening onto the breastplates of the turtles. They were so tenacious, they would rip apart rather than let go. We hauled the creatures in, still sticking to the turtles that came on board with them.

In this way we caught several loggerheads measuring a yard wide and weighing nearly 450 pounds apiece. They're quite valuable because of their carapaces, which were covered with big thin plates of horn that were brown, transparent, and mottled with white and yellow markings. What's more, they were excellent from an edible standpoint, with an exquisite flavor comparable to the green turtle.

This fishing ended our stay in the waterways of the Amazon, and that evening the *Nautilus* took to the high seas once more.

42

THE DEVILFISH

FOR A FEW DAYS the *Nautilus* kept veering away from the American coast. Obviously it wasn't interested in frequenting the waves of the Gulf of Mexico or the Caribbean Sea. Yet there was no shortage of water under its keel, because the average depth of these seas is 5,900 feet; but since these waterways are sprinkled with islands and plowed by steamers, most likely they didn't agree with Captain Nemo.

On April 16 we raised Martinique and Guadeloupe from about thirty miles away. For one second I spotted their lofty mountain peaks.

The Canadian was thoroughly flustered, having counted on putting his plans into execution in the gulf, either by reaching land or by pulling alongside one of the many boats involved in coastal navigation between the various islands. An escape attempt would have been perfectly feasible, assuming Ned managed to lay hold of the skiff without the captain's knowledge. But in midocean this was unthinkable.

The Canadian, Conseil, and I had a pretty long conversation on this subject. For six months we'd been prisoners aboard the *Nautilus*. We'd fared 17,000 leagues, and as Ned Land put it, there was no end in sight. So he made me a proposition I hadn't expected. Namely, we should ask Captain Nemo this question straight out: did the captain intend to keep us aboard his vessel indefinitely?

I hated this tactic. In my opinion it wouldn't get us anywhere. We couldn't hope for a thing from the *Nautilus*'s commander but could depend only on ourselves. Besides, for a good while now the man had been gloomier, more remote, less sociable. He seemed to be avoiding me. I bumped into him only at rare intervals. In the past he was happy to explain the ocean's wonders to me; now he left me to my research and didn't come into the lounge anymore.

What had changed in him? And what was behind it? I hadn't done anything reprehensible. Maybe our presence on board had become a burden for him? Even so, I didn't hold out any hope that the man would set us free.

So I begged Ned to let me think things over before taking action. If this tactic failed, it could arouse the captain's suspicions, make our circumstances even more arduous, and endanger the Canadian's plans. I might add that I could hardly use our state of health as a justification. Aside from that agonizing ordeal under the ice barrier at the South

Pole, we'd never been in better shape, neither Ned, Conseil, nor I. The nutritious food, bracing air, orderly lifestyle, and uniform temperature kept sickness at arm's length; and for a man who didn't miss his past life ashore, for a Captain Nemo who was at home here, who did what he wished, who went down mysterious paths after secret goals known only to him, I could understand such a lifestyle. But the three of us hadn't severed all our ties with humanity. For my part I didn't want my new and unusual research to go to the grave with me. I was now qualified to write the ideal book on the sea, and sooner or later I wanted that book to see daylight.

Some thirty feet below the surface of the waves, through the panels opening into these Caribbean waters, I found so many interesting items to describe in my field notes! Among other zoophytes there were Portuguese men-of-war also known as *Physalia pelagica*, big oval bladders gleaming like mother-of-pearl, their membranes spread to the wind, their blue tentacles drifting like silk thread—to the eye delightful jellyfish, to the touch actual nettles that ooze a corrosive acid. Among the articulata were annelid worms nearly five feet long, sporting a pink proboscis, equipped with 1,700 feelers for crawling around, and winding through the waters while throwing off every hue in the solar spectrum. From the fish branch there were manta rays, enormous cartilaginous fish ten feet long and weighing 600 pounds, pectoral fin triangular, middle of the back slightly arched, eyes attached to the rim of the face at the front of the head; they drifted around like wreckage from a ship, sometimes clinging to our windows like storm shutters. There were clown triggerfish for which nature has ground only black and white pigments, tri-tri gobies that were long and fleshy with yellow fins and jutting jaws, five-foot mackerel that had short sharp teeth, were covered with small scales, and belonged to the same species as albacore. Then came swarms of red mullet corseted in gold stripes from head to tail, their glittering fins all aquiver, genuine masterpieces of jewelry that were formerly sacred to the goddess Diana, much sought after by wealthy Romans, and the subject of an old saying: "The man who catches them doesn't eat them!" Finally, adorned with emerald ribbons and dressed in velvet and silk, angelfish passed in front of our eyes like courtiers in the paintings of Veronese; sea bream from the species *Sparus calcaratus* were sneaking by with their quick thoracic fins; pilchards fifteen inches long were wrapped in their phosphorescent glimmers; gray mullet churned the sea with their big fleshy tails; lizardfish seemed to be mowing the waves with their sharp pectoral fins; and silver moonfish, living up to their name, rose on the horizon of the waters like the pale reflection of many moons.

How many other wondrous new specimens I still could have studied if the *Nautilus* hadn't slowly gravitated toward deeper strata! Its slanting fins took it about 6,500 feet down, then over 11,000 feet down. By that point the animal life consisted only of sea lilies, starfish, delightful feather stars with bell-shaped heads like tiny chalices sitting on straight stems, top shells, bleeding tooth shells, and keyhole limpets, a large species of coastal mollusk.

By April 20 we'd risen to an average level of about 5,000 feet. The nearest land was the island group of the Bahamas, scattered over the surface of the water like a trail of stepping-stones. There we saw high underwater cliffs, sheer walls made of rough boulders piled in wide layers like foundations; between those rocks gaped dark holes that were so deep, our electric rays couldn't light them to their far ends.

These boulders were draped with big weeds, huge sea tangle, gigantic fucus—an authentic trellis of water plants suited to a world of giants.

While Conseil, Ned, and I talked about those colossal plants, we naturally got around to the sea's gigantic animals. Obviously the former were meant to feed the latter. But through the windows of the nearly stationary *Nautilus*, all I could see among those long filaments were the chief articulata in the division Brachyura, long-legged spider crabs, violet crabs, and sea butterflies characteristic of the Caribbean Sea.

It was about eleven o'clock when Ned Land called my attention to a fearsome commotion out in that big seaweed.

"Well," I said, "those are real devilfish caverns, and I wouldn't be surprised to see a few such monsters hereabouts."

"What!" Conseil put in. "Squid, common squid from the class Cephalopoda?"

"No," I said, "devilfish of large dimensions. But friend Land is surely mistaken, because I don't see a thing."

"That's too bad," Conseil remarked. "I would love to come face to face with one of those devilfish that I've heard so much about, that can drag ships down into the depths. Those animals are known as krak—"

"And bull," the Canadian replied sarcastically.

"Krakens!" Conseil shot back, ignoring his companion's joke and getting out the rest of his word.

"You'll never convince me creatures like that really exist," Ned Land said.

"Why not?" Conseil responded. "We sincerely believed in master's narwhal."

"We were wrong, Conseil."

"No doubt, but there are others with no doubts who believe in it still!"

"Very likely, Conseil. But as for me, I'm not accepting the existence of any such monster till I've dissected it with my own two hands."

"Yet," Conseil asked me, "doesn't master believe in gigantic devilfish?"

"Come on, who the blazes ever believed in them?" the Canadian exclaimed.

"Many people, Ned my friend," I said.

"No fishermen. Scientists maybe!"

"Excuse me, Ned. Scientists *and* fishermen!"

"In fact," Conseil said with the world's straightest face, "I myself can personally recall seeing a large boat dragged under the waves by the arms of a cephalopod."

"You saw that?" the Canadian asked.

"Yes, Ned."

"With your own two eyes?"

"With my own two eyes."

"Where, if you please?"

"In Saint-Malo," Conseil answered unflappably.

"In the harbor?" Ned Land said sarcastically.

"No, in a church," Conseil replied.

"In a church!" the Canadian exclaimed.

"Yes, Ned my friend. It had a picture that portrayed the devilfish in question."

"Oh fine!" Ned Land put in, bursting into laughter. "Mr. Conseil got me that time!"

"Actually he's right," I said. "I've heard about that picture. But the subject it portrays is taken from a legend, and you know how to rate legends in matters of natural history! Besides, when it comes to monsters, people's imaginations always tend to run wild. Folks not only claimed these devilfish could drag ships down, but a certain Olaus Magnus tells of a cephalopod that was a mile long and looked more like an island than an animal. People also describe how the Bishop of Trondheim set up an altar one day on an immense rock. After he'd finished saying mass, the rock picked itself up and headed back into the sea. The rock was a devilfish."

"And that's everything we know?" the Canadian asked.

"No," I replied, "another bishop, Pontoppidan of Bergen, also tells of a devilfish that was so large, a whole cavalry regiment could maneuver on it."

"They sure did go on, those old-time bishops!" Ned Land said.

"Finally the naturalists of antiquity talk of monsters with mouths as big as a gulf—they were too huge to get through the Strait of Gibraltar."

"Give me a break!" the Canadian put in.

"But in all those stories, is there any truth?" Conseil asked.

"None whatever, my friends, at least in the ones that go beyond the bounds of credibility and fly off into fable or legend. Yet there had to be a cause, or at least an excuse, for the imaginings of those storytellers. It can't be denied that some species of squid and other devilfish are quite large, though still smaller than cetaceans. Aristotle put the dimensions of one squid at five cubits, or 10 feet 2 inches. Our fishermen often see specimens over 5½ feet long. The museums in Trieste and Montpellier have preserved some devilfish carcasses measuring over 6½ feet. Besides, according to the calculations of naturalists, one of these creatures just 6 feet long would have tentacles as long as 27 feet. Which is enough to make a fearsome monster."

"Does anybody fish for 'em these days?" the Canadian asked.

"If they don't fish for them, sailors at least sight them. A friend of mine, Captain Paul Bos of Le Havre, has often sworn to me that he came across a monster of colossal size in the Indian Ocean. But the most amazing event took place a few years back in 1861, and it proves these gigantic creatures are undeniably real."

"What event was that?" Ned Land asked.

"Just this. In 1861, to the northeast of Tenerife and fairly near the latitude where we are right now, the crew of the gunboat *Alecto* spotted a monstrous squid swimming in their waters. Commander Bouguer closed in and attacked the creature, hurling harpoons and firing rifles at it, but without much success because both bullets and harpoons skidded across its soft flesh as if it were semiliquid jelly. After several fruitless attempts the crew managed to slip a noose around the mollusk's body. This noose slid as far as the caudal fins and came to a halt. Then they tried to haul the monster on board, but when they tugged on the rope, the creature was so heavy that it parted company with its tail, and deprived of that adornment, it vanished beneath the waves."

"Finally, an actual event," Ned Land said.

"An indisputable event, my gallant Ned. Accordingly people have proposed naming that devilfish Bouguer's Squid."

"And how long was it?" the Canadian asked.

"Wasn't its length about twenty feet?" said Conseil, who was back at the window examining the crevices in the cliff.

"Exactly," I replied.

"Wasn't its head," Conseil went on, "crowned by eight tentacles that quivered in the water like a nest of snakes?"

"Exactly."

"Weren't its eyes prominently placed and highly enlarged?"

"Yes, Conseil."

"And wasn't its mouth a real parrot's beak but of fearsome size?"

"It was, Conseil."

"Well, with all due respect to master," Conseil replied serenely, "if this isn't Bouguer's Squid, it's at least one of his siblings."

I looked at Conseil. Ned Land rushed to the window.

"What an awful animal!" he exclaimed.

I looked in my turn and couldn't help shrinking back in revulsion. Quivering in front of my eyes was a horrible monster worthy of a place among the most farfetched teratological legends.

It was a squid of colossal dimensions, easily twenty-five feet long. It was moving backward with tremendous speed, going the same way as the *Nautilus*. Its enormous staring eyes were tinted sea green. Its eight arms—or feet, to be exact—were rooted in its head, which has earned these creatures the name cephalopod; its arms were twice as long as its body and were writhing like the snaky hair of the Furies. You could clearly see its 250 suckers, distributed over the inner sides of its tentacles and looking like bowl-shaped bottle caps. Sometimes those suckers fastened onto the lounge window by creating a vacuum against it. The monster's mouth—which was made of horn and shaped like a parrot's beak—opened and closed vertically. Its tongue was also made of horn, featured several rows of sharp teeth, and kept flickering out from between those phenomenal shears. What a freak of nature! A bird beak on a mollusk! Its spindle-shaped body was swollen in the middle portion, a mass of flesh that must have weighed some twenty or twenty-five tons. Its unstable color changed with tremendous speed when the creature was irritated, shifting consecutively from bluish gray to reddish brown.

What had irritated this mollusk? Undoubtedly the presence of the *Nautilus*, even more fearsome than itself and which it couldn't grip with its mandibles or the suckers on its arms. And yet what monstrosities these devilfish are, what vitality our Creator has given them, what energy in their movements, thanks to their having three hearts!

Sheer chance had put us in the presence of this squid, and I didn't want to miss this opportunity to take a close look at such a cephalopod specimen. I overcame the horror its appearance inspired in me, picked up a pencil, and started to sketch it.

"Maybe this is the same as the *Alecto*'s," Conseil said.

"No way," the Canadian replied, "because this one's complete while the other one lost its tail!"

"That doesn't necessarily follow," I said. "These creatures are able to regenerate their arms and tails, and in seven years the tail on Bouguer's Squid has surely had time to sprout again."

"Anyhow," Ned shot back, "if it isn't this fellow, maybe it's one of those!"

In fact other devilfish were appearing at the starboard window. I counted seven of them. They provided the *Nautilus* with an escort, and I could hear their beaks gnashing on our sheet-iron hull. We couldn't have asked for a more devoted following.

I went on with my artwork. The monsters kept pace in our waters so flawlessly that they seemed to be standing still, and I could have traced their outlines in miniature on the window. But we were moving at a moderate speed.

All at once the *Nautilus* came to a halt. There was a sudden jolt and the whole ship trembled.

"Did we run aground?" I asked.

"In any event we're already clear," the Canadian replied, "because we're floating."

The *Nautilus* was definitely afloat, but it was no longer in motion. Its propeller blades weren't churning the waves. A minute went by. Followed by his chief officer, Captain Nemo came into the lounge.

I hadn't seen him for a good while. He seemed gloomy. Without speaking to us, maybe without even seeing us, he went to the panel, looked at the devilfish, and said a few words to his chief officer.

The latter went out. Soon the panels closed. The ceiling lit up.

I went over to the captain.

"An interesting assortment of devilfish," I

told him, as carefree as a collector in front of an aquarium.

"Very interesting, Mr. Naturalist," he answered me, "and we're going to fight them at close quarters."

I looked at the captain. I thought my hearing had gone bad.

"At close quarters?" I echoed.

"Yes, sir. Our propeller is jammed. I think the horn-covered mandibles of one of those squid are entangled in the blades. That's why we aren't moving."

"And what are you going to do?"

"Rise to the surface and completely slaughter the vermin."

"A difficult undertaking."

"Very. Our electric bullets are ineffective against such soft flesh, because they don't meet enough resistance to go off. But we'll attack the creatures with axes."

"And harpoons, sir," the Canadian said, "if you don't turn down my help."

"I accept it, Mr. Land."

"We'll go with you," I said. And we followed Captain Nemo, heading to the central companionway.

There some ten men were standing by for the attack, armed with boarding axes. Conseil and I picked up two more axes. Ned Land grabbed a harpoon.

By then the *Nautilus* was back on the surface of the waves. Stationed on the top steps, one of the seamen undid the bolts of the hatch. But he'd scarcely unscrewed the nuts when the hatch flew up with tremendous force, obviously pulled open by the suckers on a devilfish's arm.

Instantly one of those long arms glided like a snake into the opening and twenty others were quivering above. With a swipe of the ax, Captain Nemo chopped off this fearsome tentacle, which slid writhing down the steps.

Just as we were crowding each other to reach the platform, two more arms whipped through the air, swooped on the seaman stationed in front of Captain Nemo, and carried the fellow away with irresistible force.

Captain Nemo gave a shout and leaped outside. We rushed after him.

What a picture! Clutched by the tentacle and glued to its suckers, the unfortunate man was swinging in the air at the mercy of that enormous appendage. Gasping and gagging, he yelled, "Help! Help!" These words, *spoken in French*, left me absolutely stunned! So I had a countryman on board, maybe several! I'll hear his harrowing plea the rest of my life!

The poor fellow was done for. Who could tear him from that mighty grip? Even so, Captain Nemo rushed at the devilfish and with a swipe of the ax hewed one more of its arms. His chief officer battled furiously with other monsters crawling up the *Nautilus*'s sides. The crew joined the fight, hacking away with their axes. The Canadian, Conseil, and I buried our weapons in the masses of flesh. A strong musky odor filled the air. It was horrible.

For a second I thought the poor man entwined by the devilfish would be torn loose from its powerful suction. Seven of its eight arms had been chopped off. Brandishing its victim like a feather, one last tentacle was writhing in the air. But just as Captain Nemo and his chief officer rushed at it, the creature shot off a spout of blackish liquid, which was secreted by a pouch located in its abdomen. It blinded us. By the time that cloud dispersed, the squid had vanished, and so had my poor countryman!

How furiously we pitched into those monsters! We couldn't control ourselves. Ten or twelve devilfish were overrunning the *Nautilus*'s platform and sides. We piled helter-skelter into the thick of that vipers' tangle, which tossed around on the platform amid waves of blood and sepia ink. Those viscous tentacles seemed to keep growing back like the many heads of Hydra. With each thrust Ned Land's harpoon would plunge into a squid's sea-green eye and explode it. But my daring companion was suddenly toppled by a monster whose tentacles he couldn't dodge.

Oh, my heart nearly burst from excitement and horror! The squid's fearsome beak was opening over Ned Land. The poor man was about to be bitten in half. I ran to his rescue. But Captain Nemo got there first. His ax vanished between the two enormous mandibles, and miraculously saved, the Canadian leaped to his feet and plunged his harpoon all the way into the devilfish's triple heart.

"Tit for tat," Captain Nemo told the Canadian. "I owed it to myself!"

Ned nodded without answering him.

The struggle had lasted a quarter of an hour. Defeated, mutilated, battered to death, the monsters finally gave in to us and vanished under the waves.

Red with blood, motionless by the beacon, Captain Nemo looked at the sea that had swallowed up one of his companions, and large tears streamed from his eyes.

43

THE GULF STREAM

NONE OF US will ever be able to forget that fearful drama on April 20. I wrote it up in a state of intense excitement. Later I reviewed my narrative. I read it to Conseil and the Canadian. They found it accurate in detail but deficient in impact. To convey such sights, it would take the pen of our most renowned poet, Victor Hugo, author of *The Toilers of the Sea*.

As I said, Captain Nemo wept while looking at the waves. His grief was immense. This was the second companion he'd lost since we'd come on board. And what a way to die! Smashed, throttled, crushed by the fearsome arms of a devilfish, then ground up between its iron mandibles, that friend would never rest with his companions in the peaceful waters of their coral cemetery!

As for me, what had harrowed my heart in the thick of the struggle was the despairing yell given by that unfortunate man. Forgetting his regulation language, that poor Frenchman had reverted to speaking his own mother tongue in order to fling out one crowning plea for help! Among the *Nautilus*'s crew, allied body and soul with Captain Nemo and likewise fleeing from human contact, I'd found a countryman! Was he France's only representative in this mysterious alliance, obviously made up of individuals of different nationalities? This was just

one more of those insoluble problems that kept welling up in my mind!

Captain Nemo went back inside his stateroom and I saw no more of him for a good while. But how sad, desperate, and indecisive he must have felt, to judge from this ship whose soul he was, which reflected his every mood! The *Nautilus* no longer kept to a fixed heading. It drifted back and forth, riding with the waves like a corpse. Its propeller had been disentangled but was barely put to use. The ship was navigating at random. It couldn't tear itself away from the setting of this last struggle, from this sea that had devoured one of its own!

Ten days went by in this way. It was only on May 1 that the *Nautilus* firmly resumed its northbound course, after raising the Bahamas at the mouth of Old Bahama Channel. Then we went with the current of the sea's biggest river, which has its own banks, fish, and temperature. I'm talking about the Gulf Stream.

It is indeed a river, one that runs independently through the middle of the Atlantic, its waters never mixing with the ocean's waters. It's a salty river, even saltier than the sea that surrounds it. Its average depth is 3,000 feet, its average width sixty miles. In certain areas its current moves at a speed of 2½ miles per hour. The unchanging volume of its waters is larger than that of all the world's rivers combined.

As Commander Maury discovered, the true source of the Gulf Stream—its starting point, if you prefer—is located in the Bay of Biscay. There, still cool and colorless, its waters begin to form. It heads south, skirts equatorial Africa, warms its waves in the sunshine of the Torrid Zone, crosses the Atlantic, reaches Cape São Roque on the coast of Brazil, and splits into two branches, one heading for the Caribbean Sea where it's further infused with marine heat particles. Then the Gulf Stream starts to play its stabilizing role, balancing hot and cold temperatures and blending tropical and northern waters. Reaching a white heat in the Gulf of Mexico, it heads north up the American coast, proceeds as far as Newfoundland, veers away under pressure from a cold current out of Davis

Strait, and resumes its course in midocean by going along a great circle of the earth on a rhumb line;[20] then it divides into two arms near latitude 43°; one, helped by the northeast trade winds, heads back to the Bay of Biscay and the Azores; the other pours lukewarm water over the shores of Ireland and Norway, then heads beyond Spitsbergen where it falls to 39° Fahrenheit and forms the open sea at the pole.

It was on this oceangoing river that the *Nautilus* was navigating just then. Leaving Old Bahama Channel, which is thirty-five miles wide by 1,150 feet deep, the Gulf Stream moves at a rate of five miles per hour. Its speed steadily decreases as it proceeds northward, and we can only pray that this steadiness continues, because if its speed and direction were to change, as some say they've detected, Europe's climates will suffer consequences that are incalculable.

Around noon I was on the platform with Conseil. I gave him the relevant details on the Gulf Stream. When my explanation was over, I invited him to dip his hands into its current.

Conseil did so and was quite amazed to find that it didn't feel either hot or cold.

"Which comes from the fact," I told him, "that when the Gulf Stream leaves the Gulf of Mexico, its water temperature is barely different from your blood temperature. This Gulf Stream is a huge heat generator that allows the shores of Europe to be decked out in perpetual greenery. And if we can believe Commander Maury, were one to harness the full warmth of this current, it would melt enough iron solder to make a river as big as the Amazon or the Missouri."

Just then the Gulf Stream's speed was five miles per hour. Its current is perfectly distinct from the surrounding sea, so its well-defined waters not only stand out from the ocean's colder waters but they flow on a different level. Darker too, as well as very rich in salts, its deep indigo color cuts a clear path through the green waves around it. What's more, the line of demarcation is so clear, off the Caro-

linas the *Nautilus*'s spur sliced the waves of the Gulf Stream while its propeller still churned those that belonged to the ocean.

This current carried with it a host of moving creatures. Many schools of argonauts, so common in the Mediterranean, were voyaging here. Among cartilaginous fish the most notable were rays whose ultra slender tails took up nearly a third of the body, which was shaped like a huge diamond twenty-five feet long; then came little three-foot sharks, head large, snout short and rounded, teeth sharp and laid out in several rows, body looking as if it were covered with scales.

Among bony fish I noticed some gray wrasse characteristic of these seas, red-tailed snappers whose eyes have glowing irises, three-foot drums whose wide mouths were garnished with small teeth and which let out thin cries, black kingfish like the ones I've already mentioned, blue dolphinfish with gold and silver highlights, rainbow-hued parrotfish as colorful as the loveliest tropical birds, striped blennies with triangular heads, bluish flounder without any scales, toadfish covered with a crosswise yellow band in the shape of a Greek *t*, swarms of little freckled gobies spattered with brown spots, perch with silver heads and yellow tails, assorted specimens of salmon, a variety of mullet with a slim body and a softly glowing radiance that Lacépède named after the great love of his life, and finally the ribbonfish, a handsome creature decorated by every honorary order, adorned with every commemorative medal, and frequenting the shores of this great nation where orders and medals are held in such low regard.

During the night, I might add, the phosphorescence of the Gulf Stream's waters matched the electric brightness of our beacon, especially in the stormy weather that frequently threatened us.

Off North Carolina on May 8, we were across from Cape Hatteras again. There the Gulf Stream is seventy-five miles wide and 690 feet deep. The *Nautilus* continued to wander at random. It seemed like nobody was standing watch on board. Under these conditions I admit we could have gotten away successfully. In fact the populated

---

[20] *Translator's note.* On flat maps a curving line that represents the most direct route between two locations.

shores offered easy refuge everywhere. The sea was plowed continually by the many steamers running between the Gulf of Mexico and New York or Boston, and it was crossed night and day by little schooners engaged in coastal navigation between various stops on the American shoreline. We could hope to be picked up. So it was a promising opportunity, despite the thirty miles separating the *Nautilus* from the Union coast.

But one inconvenient circumstance absolutely thwarted the Canadian's plans. The weather was thoroughly foul. We were nearing waterways where storms are commonplace, the homeland of those tornadoes and cyclones specifically generated by the Gulf Stream's current. To face a frequently raging sea in our frail skiff was to court certain disaster. Even Ned Land acknowledged this. So he was champing at the bit, in the grip of an intense homesickness that could be cured only by our escaping.

"Sir," he said to me that day, "this has got to stop. I want to thrash it out once and for all. Your Nemo's veering away from shore and heading up north. But believe you me, I had my fill at the South Pole and I'm not going with him to the North Pole."

"What can we do, Ned, since it isn't feasible to escape right now?"

"I keep coming back to my original idea. We've got to talk to the captain. When we were in your country's seas, you didn't say a thing. Now we're in my own seas, and I want to speak out. In a few days I figure the *Nautilus* will lie off Nova Scotia, and between there and Newfoundland is the mouth of a wide gulf, and the St. Lawrence empties into that gulf, and the St. Lawrence is my own river, the river running past Quebec, my hometown—and when I think about all this, I get so angry that my hair stands on end! I tell you, sir, I would rather jump overboard! I can't stay here any longer! I'm suffocating!"

The Canadian had obviously reached the end of his patience. His energetic nature couldn't adjust to this protracted imprisonment. Day by day his face kept getting longer. His moods were growing gloomier and gloomier. I understood what he was suffering because I too was gripped by homesickness. Nearly seven months had gone by without our having any news from shore. In addition Captain Nemo's reclusive behavior, his changed mood, and especially his complete silence since the battle with the devilfish all made me see things in a different light. I no longer had the enthusiasm of our first days on board. You needed to be Flemish like Conseil to accept these circumstances, living in a habitat designed for cetaceans and other residents of the sea. Honestly, if that gallant lad had been given gills instead of lungs, I think he would have made an exceptional fish!

"Well, sir?" Ned Land went on, seeing that I didn't reply.

"Well, Ned, you want me to ask Captain Nemo what he intends to do with us?"

"Yes, sir."

"Even though he has already made it clear?"

"That's right. I want it settled once and for all. Speak just for me, strictly on my behalf, if you like."

"But I seldom run into him. He positively avoids me."

"All the more reason you should go see him."

"I'll ask him about it, Ned."

"When?" the Canadian inquired stubbornly.

"When I meet up with him."

"Professor Aronnax, would you like me to go find him myself?"

"No, let me do it. Tomorrow—"

"Today," Ned Land said.

"So be it. I'll see him today," I answered the Canadian, who, if he'd taken action himself, would certainly have ruined everything.

I was on my own. His request granted, I decided to handle it immediately. I like things over and done with.

I went back into my stateroom. From there I heard movements inside Captain Nemo's quarters. I couldn't pass up this opportunity to meet with him. I knocked on his door. There was no reply. I knocked again, then turned the knob. The door opened.

I went in. The captain was there. He was bending over his worktable and hadn't heard me. Determined to not leave without questioning him, I drew closer. He looked up suddenly, frowned, and said in a rather gruff tone:

"Oh, it's you! What do you want?"

"To speak with you, captain."

"But I'm busy, sir, I'm at work. I give you the freedom to enjoy your privacy, can't I have the same for myself?"

This reception was hardly encouraging. But I was determined to give as good as I got.

"Sir," I said coolly, "I need to speak with you on a matter that simply can't wait."

"And what might that be?" he responded sardonically. "Have you made some discovery that I've overlooked? Has the sea yielded up some novel secret to you?"

We were miles apart. But before I could reply, he showed me a manuscript open on the table and told me in a more serious tone:

"Here, Professor Aronnax, is a manuscript written in several languages. It includes a summary of my undersea research, and God willing, it won't perish with me. Signed with my name, complete with my life story, this manuscript will go into a small unsinkable container. The last one of us left on the *Nautilus* will throw that container into the sea, and it will drift wherever the waves take it."

The man's name! His life story written by his own hand! So his secret existence might someday be unveiled? But just then I viewed this announcement only as a lead-in to my topic.

"Captain," I replied, "I applaud this idea you're putting into effect. The fruits of your research mustn't be lost. But the methods you're using strike me as primitive. Who knows where the winds will take that container, into whose hands it may fall? Can't you find something better? Can't you or one of your men—"

"Never, sir," the captain said, swiftly interrupting me.

"But my companions and I are ready, willing, and able to safeguard this manuscript, and if you give us back our freedom—"

"Your freedom!" Captain Nemo put in, straightening up.

"Yes, sir, and that's the subject I wanted to talk over with you. For seven months we've been aboard your vessel, and I ask you today, in the name of my companions as well as myself, if you intend to keep us here forever."

"Professor Aronnax," Captain Nemo said, "I'll answer you today the same way I did seven months ago: those who board the *Nautilus* are never to leave it."

"You're inflicting outright slavery on us!"

"Call it anything you like."

"But every slave has the right to recover his freedom! By any worthwhile available means!"

"Who has denied you this right?" Captain Nemo responded. "Did I ever try to tie you down with your word of honor?"

The captain looked at me, folding his arms.

"Sir," I told him, "taking up this subject a second time would be distasteful to both of us. So let's finish what we've started. I repeat, it isn't just for myself that I bring up this matter. For me, research is an escape, a powerful diversion, a seductive pleasure, a passion that can make me forget everything else. Like you, I'm a man neglected and unknown, living in the faint hope that someday I can bequeath the fruits of my labors to the future of humanity, by means of some figurative container left to the winds and waves of fate. In short, I can admire you and comfortably join you in an existence that makes sense to me in some ways; but I still catch glimpses of other aspects of your life that are surrounded by unknown factors and secrets that my companions and I, alone on board, aren't allowed to share. And even when our hearts have gone out to you, moved by your grief or stirred by your deeds of courage and genius, we've had to quash even the smallest signs of that fellow feeling that comes from seeing something fine and good, whether it's in a friend or a foe. All right then! It's this awareness that we're outsiders with regard to all these things concerning you that makes our position untenable, impossible—even for me but especially for Ned Land. Every man, by virtue of his very humanity, deserves fair treatment. Have you ever considered how a love of freedom and hatred of slavery could lead to plans of revenge in a personality like the Canadian's, what he might think, scheme, attempt . . . ?"

I fell silent. Captain Nemo got up.

"Ned Land can think, scheme, or attempt anything he likes, what difference does it make to me? I didn't go looking for him! I get no pleasure out of keeping him on board! As for you, Professor Aronnax, you're a learned man who can understand anything, including silence. I have nothing more to say to you. May this first time you've brought up this subject also be the last, because a second time I won't even listen."

I took my leave. From that day forward our position was very strained. I reported this conversation to my two companions.

"Now we know," Ned said, "that we can't expect a thing from that man. The *Nautilus* is nearing Long Island. We'll escape no matter what the weather's like."

But the skies got more and more threatening. There were clear signs of a hurricane coming. The air was turning white and milky. On the horizon thin sheaves of cirrus cloud gave way to layers of nimbocumulus. Other low-lying clouds fled swiftly. The sea grew rough, inflated by long swells. Every bird had vanished aside from a couple petrels, those lovers of storms. Our barometer fell significantly, revealing a tremendous tension in the hazy sky. The air was steeped in electricity, and the mixture in our storm glass decomposed under its influence. A battle of the elements was at hand.

The storm burst during the daytime of May 13, right when the *Nautilus* was cruising off Long Island, a few miles from the narrows to Upper New York Bay. I'm able to describe this battle of the elements because Captain Nemo didn't flee into the ocean depths; instead, from some bewildering whim, he chose to brave it out on the surface.

The wind was blowing from the southwest, a stiff breeze at first, in other words, with a speed close to thirty-five miles per hour, which reached fifty-five near three o'clock in the afternoon. This is the figure for major storms.

Undeterred by the squalls, Captain Nemo had stationed himself on the platform. He'd lashed himself around the waist to withstand the monstrous breakers foaming over the deck. I hoisted and tied myself to the same place, dividing my wonderment between the storm and that incomparable man who faced it head-on.

The furious sea was swept with big tattered clouds that were drowning in its waves. I didn't see any more of those small intervening billows that form in the troughs of the big crests. Nothing but long soot-colored undulations with crests so compact that they didn't foam. They grew taller. They spurred each other on. Rolling and pitching frightfully, the *Nautilus* sometimes lay on its side, sometimes stood on end like a mast.

Around five o'clock a torrential rain fell, but it lulled neither the wind nor the sea. The hurricane was unleashed at a speed of a hundred miles—hence about forty geographic leagues—per hour. Under conditions such as these, houses topple over, iron railings snap in two, flying roof tiles puncture wooden doors, and 24-pounder cannons relocate. And yet in the midst of this turmoil, the *Nautilus* lived up to that saying by an expert engineer: "A well-built hull can challenge any sea!" This submersible wasn't some stationary boulder that the waves could demolish; it was a steel spindle, agile and obedient, without masts or rigging, and able to brave their fury with impunity.

Meanwhile I carefully examined those unleashed breakers. They measured up to 50 feet in height over an approximate length of 500 to 600 feet, and they moved at a speed of almost thirty-five miles per hour, a third that of the wind. Their size and strength increased with the water's depth. Then I understood the role played by those waves, which trap air in their flanks and release it deep underwater where its oxygen brings life. It's estimated that their maximum pressure is as much as 6,600 pounds per square foot on any surface they smash against. In the Hebrides it was waves such as these that repositioned a boulder weighing forty-two tons. It was their brethren in the tidal wave on December 23, 1854, that toppled part of the Japanese city of Tokyo, then raced that same day at over 400 miles per hour to crash into the coastline of America.

At twilight the storm grew in intensity. Our barometer fell to twenty-eight inches, as barometers did during the 1860 cyclone on Réunion Island. At day's end I saw a big ship going past on the horizon, struggling painfully. It lay to at half steam, trying to face into the waves. It must have been a steamer on one of the lines running from New York to Liverpool or Le Havre. It soon vanished into the darkness.

At ten o'clock in the evening, the skies caught on fire. Violent flashes of lightning streaked through the air. I couldn't stand their brightness, but Captain Nemo looked straight at them, as if inhaling the very spirit of the storm. Dreadful sounds filled the air, complex noises made up of crashing breakers, howling winds, claps of thunder. The wind shifted to every corner of the horizon, and the cyclone whirled out of the east, only to circle back after sweeping through north, west, and south, moving in the opposite direction of revolving storms in the southern hemisphere.

Oh, that Gulf Stream! It truly lives up to its nickname, the Lord of Storms! It breeds these fearsome cyclones through the temperature differences in the air strata overlying its currents.

After the rain came a downpour of fire. Water drops changed into exploding tufts. You would have sworn Captain Nemo was seeking to be struck by lightning—a death worthy of him. In one hideous pitching movement, the *Nautilus* raised its steel spur into the air like a lightning rod, and I saw long sparks shoot down it.

Shattered, at the end of my strength, I crawled on my belly to the hatch. I opened it and went below to the lounge. By that point the storm had reached its maximum intensity. It was impossible to stand up inside the *Nautilus*.

Captain Nemo came back in near midnight. I could hear the ballast tanks gradually filling, and the *Nautilus* sank gently under the surface of the waves.

Through the lounge's open windows, I saw large frightened fish going past like phantoms in those fiery waters. Some were struck by lightning right in front of my eyes!

The *Nautilus* kept sinking. I thought it would find calm again at 50 feet down. Not quite. The upper strata were tossing around too violently. It had to sink to 165 feet, finding a resting place in the bowels of the sea.

But once there, how tranquil, silent, and peaceful it was all around us! Who would have known that a dreadful hurricane was being unleashed on the surface of this ocean?

44

In Latitude 47° 24' and Longitude 17° 28'

IN THE AFTERMATH of that storm, we were driven back to the east. Away went any hope of escaping to the landing places of New York or the St. Lawrence. In despair poor Ned went into seclusion like Captain Nemo. Conseil and I stayed together from then on.

As I said, the *Nautilus* veered to the east. To be exact I should have said to the northeast. Sometimes on the surface of the waves, sometimes under them, the ship wandered for a couple days through those fogs so dreaded by navigators. They're caused chiefly by melting ice, which keeps the air tremendously damp. How many ships have perished in these waterways as they tried to scout out the dim lights on the coast! How many casualties these heavy mists have caused! How many collisions have occurred with these reefs, where the breaking surf is covered by the noise of the wind! How many vessels have rammed each other, despite their running lights, despite the warnings given by their bosun's pipes and alarm bells!

So the floor of this sea looked like a battlefield where all the ships conquered by the ocean still lay, some already old and encrusted, others newer and reflecting our beacon light on their ironwork and brass undersides. Among these vessels how many went down with all hands—with their crews and their hosts of immigrants—at those trouble spots so prominent in the statistics, Cape Race, St. Paul Island, the Strait of Belle Isle, the St. Lawrence estuary! And in just a few years, how many victims have been added to this dismal tally by the Royal Mail, Inman, and Montreal lines; by vessels christened the

Solway, the *Isis*, the *Paramatta*, the *Hungarian*, the *Canadian*, the *Anglo-Saxon*, the *Humboldt*, and the *United States*, all run aground; by the *Arctic* and the *Son of Lyons*, gone down in collisions; by the *President*, the *Pacific*, and the *City of Glasgow*, missing for reasons unknown; in the midst of their gloomy rubble, the *Nautilus* navigated as if giving the the dead a formal inspection!

By May 15 we lay off the southern end of the Grand Banks of Newfoundland. These banks are the result of marine sedimentation, an extensive accumulation of organic waste brought from the equator by the Gulf Stream's current or from the North Pole by that countercurrent of cold water skirting the American coast. Here, after their breakup, erratically drifting chunks of ice also collect. Here an immense boneyard forms from fish, mollusks, and zoophytes dying over it by the billions.

The sea isn't very deep at the Grand Banks. Barely a third of a mile at best. But to the south there's a sudden depression, a pit whose bottom is 10,000 feet down. Here the Gulf Stream spreads out. Its waters come to full bloom. It loses its speed and temperature, but it turns into a sea.

Among the fish that the *Nautilus* scared off as it went by, I'll mention a three-foot lumpsucker that's blackish on top with orange on the belly and rare among its brethren in that it practices monogamy, a good-sized eelpout, a sort of emerald moray with an excellent flavor, a big-eyed wolffish whose head did bear a certain resemblance to a canine's, viviparous blennies that hatch their eggs inside their bodies as snakes do, black gobies (or ebony sleepers) eight inches in length, plus grenadiers with long tails and shining with a silvery glow, fast fish venturing far from their High Arctic seas.

Our nets also hauled in a bold, daring, energetic, and muscular fish armed with prickles on its head and stings on its fins, a genuine scorpion measuring seven to ten feet long, the relentless foe of cod, blennies, and salmon; it was the bullhead of the northerly seas, a fish with red fins and a brown body covered with nodules. The *Nautilus*'s fishermen had trouble laying hold of this creature,

which, thanks to the formation of its gill covers, can protect its respiratory system from any parching contact with the air and can live out of water for a fair amount of time.

And I'll mention—for the record—some little striped blennies that follow ships into the northernmost seas, sharp-nosed carp specific to the north Atlantic, scorpionfish, and finally the gadoid family, chiefly the cod species, which I detected in their waters of choice over those inexhaustible Grand Banks.

Because Newfoundland is simply an underwater peak, you could call these cod mountain fish. While the *Nautilus* was clearing a path through their tight ranks, Conseil couldn't help making this comment:

"Mercy, look at these codfish!" he said. "Why, I thought cod were flat like dab or sole!"

"Innocent boy!" I exclaimed. "Cod are flat only at the grocery store, where they've been cut open and spread out on display. But in the water they're like mullet, spindle-shaped and perfectly built for speed."

"I can well believe master," Conseil replied. "What mobs of them! What swarms!"

"That's nothing! There would be many more, my friend, if it weren't for their enemies, scorpionfish and human beings! Do you know how many eggs have been counted in a single female?"

"I'll go all out," Conseil replied. "Half a million."

"Eleven million, my friend."

"Eleven million! I refuse to believe that till I've counted them myself."

"Then count them, Conseil. But it would be less work to believe me. In any case Frenchmen, Englishmen, Americans, Danes, and Norwegians catch these cod by the thousands. They're eaten in prodigious quantities, and if the creatures weren't so amazingly fertile, they would soon be eradicated from the seas. So in England and America alone, 5,000 ships manned by 75,000 seamen are at work catching cod. Each ship brings back an average haul of 4,400 fish, making 22,000,000. Off the coast of Norway, the total's the same."

"Fine, I'll abide by master," Conseil replied. "I won't count them."

"Count what?"

"Those eleven million eggs. But I'll make just one comment."

"And that is?"

"If all their eggs hatched, only four codfish could feed England, America, and Norway."

As we skimmed the depths of the Grand Banks, I could clearly see those long fishing lines—each equipped with 200 hooks—that every boat dangled by the dozens. The lower end of each line dragged the bottom with the help of a small grappling hook, and at the surface it was secured to the buoy-rope of a cork float. The *Nautilus* had to maneuver shrewdly in the midst of this underwater spiderweb.

But the ship didn't stay long in those heavily traveled waterways. It went up to about latitude 42°. This brought it level with St. John's in Newfoundland and with Heart's Content, where the Atlantic Cable reaches its end point.

Instead of continuing to the north, the *Nautilus* took an easterly heading as if intending to go along that plateau on which the telegraph cable rests, where multiple soundings have given the contours of the terrain with the utmost accuracy.

It was on May 17, around 500 miles from Heart's Content and over 9,100 feet down, that I spotted the cable lying on the seafloor. Conseil, whom I hadn't alerted, mistook it at first for a gigantic sea snake and was all set to classify it in high style. But I enlightened the fine lad and let him down gently by giving him various details on the laying of this cable.

The first cable was put down during the years 1857–58; but after transmitting about 400 telegrams, it quit working. In 1863 engineers built a second cable that measured 2,100 miles long, weighed nearly 5,000 tons, and was shipped aboard the *Great Eastern*. This attempt also failed.

Now then, on May 25 while submerged to a depth of 12,585 feet, the *Nautilus* lay in exactly the locality where this second cable ruptured and ruined the undertaking. It happened 638 miles from the coast of Ireland. At around two o'clock in the afternoon, all contact with Europe broke off. The electricians on board decided to cut the cable before fishing it up, and by eleven o'clock that evening they'd recovered the damaged part. They repaired the joint and its splice, then submerged the cable once more. But a few days later it snapped again and couldn't be retrieved from the ocean depths.

Those Americans didn't lose heart. The daring Cyrus Field, who had risked his whole fortune to promote this undertaking, launched a new funding drive. It was an instant success. They developed another cable along better lines. Its sheaves of conducting wire were insulated inside a gutta-percha covering, which was protected by a padding of textile material that in turn was enclosed in a metal sheath. The *Great Eastern* put back to sea on July 13, 1866.

The operation proceeded apace. However there was one hitch. As they gradually unrolled this third cable, the electricians noticed several times that somebody had recently driven nails into it, trying to damage its core. Captain Anderson got together with his officers and engineers, discussed the matter, and posted a warning that if the culprit were detected, he would be tossed overboard without a trial. After that these villainous attempts weren't repeated.

By July 23 the *Great Eastern* lay no farther than 500 miles from Newfoundland, when Ireland wired it the news of an armistice signed between Prussia and Austria after the Battle of Sadova. Through the fog on the 27th, it sighted the port of Heart's Content. The undertaking had ended happily, and in its first telegram young America greeted old Europe with these wise words so seldom understood: "Glory to God in the highest, and peace on earth to men of good will."

I didn't expect to find that electric cable in pristine condition, as it looked on leaving its place of manufacture. The long snake was covered with seashell rubble and garnished with foraminifera; a crust of caked gravel shielded it from any mollusks tempted to bore into it. It rested serenely, sheltered from the sea's movements, under a pressure conducive to the transmission of that electric spark that goes from America to Europe in

32/100 of a second. No doubt this cable will last indefinitely, because, as some have noted, a stay in salt water will actually improve its gutta-percha casing.

Besides, on this happy choice of plateau the cable never lies at depths that might cause it to snap. The *Nautilus* followed it to its lowest reaches, located 14,537 feet down, and even there it rested without any tension or tugging. Then we went back to the locality where the 1863 accident had taken place.

There the ocean floor formed a valley nearly seventy-five miles wide, into which you could fit Mt. Blanc without its top poking above the surface of the waves. This valley ends to the east in a sheer wall 6,500 feet high. We arrived there on May 28, and the *Nautilus* lay no farther than ninety-five miles from Ireland.

Would Captain Nemo head up north and beach us on the British Isles? Hardly. Much to my surprise he went south again and back into European seas. As our course curved around the Emerald Isle, I spotted Cape Clear for a second, also the lighthouse on Fastnet Rock that guides those thousands of ships leaving Glasgow or Liverpool.

Then a major question popped into my head. Would the *Nautilus* dare tackle the English Channel? Ned Land, who promptly reappeared after we hugged shore, never stopped asking me. What could I say to him? Captain Nemo remained invisible. After giving the Canadian a glimpse of America's shores, was he about to show me the coast of France?

But the *Nautilus* kept gravitating southward. On May 30, in sight of Land's End, it passed between the lowermost tip of England and the Isles of Scilly, which it left behind to starboard.

If it planned to enter the English Channel, it obviously needed to head east. It didn't.

All day long on May 31, the *Nautilus* swept around the sea in a series of circles that puzzled me deeply. It seemed to be searching for some locality that it had trouble finding. At noon Captain Nemo himself came to take our bearings. He didn't say a word to me. He looked gloomier than ever. What was making him so melancholy? Was it our nearness to the European coast? Had this stirred up some memories of the country he'd left behind? If so, what was he feeling? Remorse or regret? For a good while my brain was busy with these thoughts and I had a hunch that fate would soon reveal the captain's secrets.

The next day, June 1, the *Nautilus* kept to the same tack. Obviously it was trying to locate some exact spot in the ocean. Just as on the day before, Captain Nemo came to take the altitude of the sun. The sea was smooth, the sky clear. Eight miles to the east, a big steamship was visible on the horizon line. No flag was flying from the gaff of its fore-and-aft sail, and I couldn't tell its nationality.

A few minutes before the sun reached the zenith, Captain Nemo aimed his sextant and took his sights with the utmost accuracy. The absolute calm of the waves made the operation easier. The *Nautilus* lay perfectly still, neither rolling nor pitching.

I was on the platform just then. After determining our position, the captain spoke only these words:

"Here it is!"

He went down the hatch. Had he seen that vessel, which was changing course and seemed to be heading toward us? I couldn't say.

I went back to the lounge. The hatch closed, and I heard water hissing in the ballast tanks. The *Nautilus* began to sink on a vertical line, because its propeller was in check and no longer furnished any forward motion.

A few minutes later it halted at a depth of 2,733 feet and came to rest on the seafloor.

Then the lounge's ceiling lights went out, the panels opened, and through the windows I could see the ocean brightly lit over a half-mile radius by the beacon's rays.

I looked to port and saw nothing but the vastness of those tranquil waters.

To starboard a prominent bulge on the sea bottom caught my attention. It seemed to be some old ruin buried beneath a crust of whitened seashells, as if under a blanket of snow. Carefully examining this mass, I could make out the swollen shape of a ship shorn of its masts, a ship that must have gone down bow first. This casualty definitely dated from some far-off time. To be caked with so much limestone from the water, this wreckage had to have spent many years on the ocean floor.

What ship was this? Why had the *Nautilus* come to visit its grave? Had it been something other than a maritime accident that had sent this craft to the bottom?

I wasn't sure what to think, but next to me I heard Captain Nemo's voice slowly say:

"Originally this ship was christened the *Son of Marseilles*. It carried seventy-four cannons and was launched in 1762. On August 13, 1778, commanded by La Poype-Vertrieux, it fought valiantly against the *Preston*. On July 4, 1779, with the squadron under Admiral d'Estaing, it aided in the capture of the island of Grenada. On September 5, 1781, under the Count de Grasse, it took part in the Battle of Chesapeake Bay. In 1794 the new Republic of France changed the ship's name. On April 16 of that same year, it joined the squadron in Brest under Rear Admiral Villaret de Joyeuse, whose mission was to escort a convoy of wheat coming from America under the command of Admiral Vanstabel. In this second year of the French Revolutionary Calendar, on the 11th and 12th days in the Month of Pasture, this squadron came up against English vessels. Sir, today is June 1, 1868, or the 13th day in the Month of Pasture. Seventy-four years ago to the day, at this very place in latitude 47° 24′ and longitude 17° 28′, this ship sank after a heroic battle; all three masts gone, water in its hold, a third of its crew out of action, it chose to go to the bottom with its 356 seamen rather than surrender; and with its flag nailed up on the afterdeck, it vanished under the waves to shouts of 'Long live the Republic!'"

"This is the *Avenger!*" I exclaimed.

"Yes, sir! The *Avenger!* A splendid name!" Captain Nemo murmured, folding his arms.

45

A Mass Execution

HIS MANNER OF SPEAKING, the unexpectedness of this episode, first the war record of that patriotic ship, then the intensity with which this strange individual spoke those last

words—the name *Avenger*, whose significance couldn't elude me—all these things, taken together, had a deep impact on my mind. My eyes never left the captain. Hands reaching toward the sea, he pondered that proud wreck with glowing eyes. Maybe I would never find out who he was, where he came from, or where his destiny would take him, but more and more I could see a distinction between the man and the scientist. It was no routine distrust of humanity that kept Captain Nemo and his companions sequestered inside the *Nautilus*'s plating, but a hatred that was so monstrous or sublime, age couldn't wither it.

Was this hatred still bent on revenge? Time would tell—and before much longer.

Meanwhile the *Nautilus* rose slowly to the surface of the sea, and I watched the *Avenger*'s murky shape gradually vanishing. Soon a gentle rolling motion told me we were floating in the open air.

Just then there was a hollow explosion. I looked at the captain. The captain didn't stir.

"Captain?" I said.

He didn't reply.

I left him and climbed onto the platform. Conseil and the Canadian were there already.

"What was that explosion?" I asked.

"A cannon going off," Ned Land replied.

I looked in the direction of that ship I'd spotted. It was heading toward the *Nautilus* and you could tell it had put on steam. Six miles separated it from us.

"What sort of craft is it, Ned?"

"From its rigging and its low masts," the Canadian replied, "I bet it's a warship. Here's hoping it pulls up and sinks this damned *Nautilus!*"

"Ned my friend," Conseil replied, "what harm could it do the *Nautilus?* Will it attack us under the waves? Will it cannonade us in the depths of the seas?"

"Tell me, Ned," I asked, "can you make out the nationality of that craft?"

Frowning, squinting, and puckering the corners of his eyes, the Canadian took a few seconds and focused the full power of his vision on that ship.

"No, sir," he replied. "I can't make out what nation it's from. It isn't flying any flag.

But I'll swear it's a warship, because there's a long pennant streaming from the peak of its mainmast."

For a quarter of an hour, we continued to watch that craft bearing down on us. But I couldn't believe that it had raised the *Nautilus* from so far away, still less that it knew what this underwater machine really was.

Soon the Canadian announced that the craft was a big battleship, a double-decker ironclad armed with a ram. Dark, dense smoke burst from its two funnels. Its furled sails merged with the lines of its yards. The gaff of its fore-and-aft sail wasn't flying any flag. It was too far off for us to make out the colors of its pennant, which was fluttering like a thin ribbon.

It was making rapid headway. If Captain Nemo let it close in, a chance to escape might be available to us.

"Sir," Ned Land told me, "if that boat gets within a mile of us, I'm jumping overboard and I suggest you do the same."

I didn't reply to the Canadian's proposition but kept watching the ship, which was coming increasingly into view. Whether it was English, French, American, or Russian, it would surely take us on board if only we could get to it.

"Master may recall," Conseil said, "that we've had some experience with swimming. He can trust me to tow him to that vessel, if it suits him to go with our friend Ned."

Before I could reply, white smoke gushed from the battleship's bow. A few seconds later there was a splash to the rear of the *Nautilus*, a disturbance caused by a heavy object falling into the water. Soon afterward an explosion reached my ears.

"What's going on? They're firing at us!" I exclaimed.

"Good lads!" the Canadian muttered.

"That means they don't see us as castaways hanging onto some wreckage!"

"With all due respect to master—gracious!" Conseil put in, shaking off the water that had sprayed over him from another shell. "With all due respect to master, they've discovered the narwhal and they're cannonading the beast."

"But surely they can tell that they're dealing with human beings," I exclaimed.

"Maybe that's why!" Ned Land replied, looking over at me.

The full truth dawned on me at last. Undoubtedly the world now knew where it stood on the nature of this so-called narwhal. Undoubtedly its collision with the *Abraham Lincoln*—when the Canadian tried to harpoon it—had made Commander Farragut realize that it wasn't a narwhal at all but actually an underwater boat, more dangerous than any uncanny cetacean!

Yes, this had to be the case, and undoubtedly the world was now hunting this dreadful engine of destruction across the seven seas!

And dreadful the *Nautilus* truly was, if, as we could assume, Captain Nemo had been using it in some program of revenge! That night in the middle of the Indian Ocean when he imprisoned us in the cell, hadn't he attacked some ship? That man now buried in the coral cemetery, wasn't he the victim of some collision caused by the *Nautilus?* Yes, I repeat, this had to be the case. Part of Captain Nemo's secret existence had been unveiled. And now, even though his identity was still a question mark, the nations allied against him at least knew they weren't hunting a phantom, but a man who had sworn an oath of implacable hatred against them!

This whole fearsome chain of events appeared in my mind's eye. Instead of meeting friends on that approaching ship, we would find only merciless enemies.

Meanwhile more and more shells were falling around us. Some would hit the liquid surface, then ricochet and vanish into the sea a considerable distance away. But none of them reached the *Nautilus*.

By then the ironclad was no more than three miles from us. Despite its violent cannonade Captain Nemo hadn't appeared on the platform. And yet if one of those conical shells had scored a routine hit on the *Nautilus*'s hull, it might have been fatal to him.

Then the Canadian told me:

"Sir, we need to do everything we can to get out of this jam! Let's signal them! Damnation! Maybe they'll realize we're decent people!"

Ned Land took out his handkerchief to wave it in the air. But he'd barely unfolded it when he was felled by an iron fist, and despite his great strength, he tumbled to the deck.

"Scum!" the captain exclaimed. "Do you want to be nailed to the *Nautilus*'s spur before it charges that ship?"

Captain Nemo was dreadful to hear and even more dreadful to see. His face was pale from some spasm of his heart, which must have stopped beating for a second. His pupils were appallingly contracted. His voice no longer spoke, it bellowed. Leaning forward, he reached out and shook the Canadian by the shoulders.

Then, letting Ned go, he turned to the battleship, whose shells were raining around him:

"O ship of an accursed nation, you know who I am!" he shouted in his powerful voice. "And I don't need your colors to recognize you! Look! I'll show you mine!"

And in the bow of the platform, Captain Nemo unfurled a black flag like the one he'd previously planted at the South Pole.

Just then a shell hit the *Nautilus*'s hull at an angle, failed to breach it, ricocheted near the captain, and vanished into the sea.

Captain Nemo shrugged his shoulders. Then, speaking to me:

"Go below!" he told me in a curt tone. "You and your companions, go below!"

"Sir," I exclaimed, "are you going to attack that ship?"

"Sir, I'm going to sink it."

"You wouldn't!"

"I will," Captain Nemo replied icily. "I advise you not to pass judgment on me, sir. Fate has shown you what you weren't meant to see. The attack has come. Our reply will be dreadful. Get back inside!"

"From what country is that ship?"

"You don't know? Fine, all the better! At least its nationality will remain a mystery to you. Go below!"

The Canadian, Conseil, and I had no choice but to obey. Some fifteen of the *Nautilus*'s seamen surrounded the captain and looked with an air of implacable hatred at the ship bearing down on them. You could sense the same vengeful spirit coming to life in each of their souls.

I went below just as another projectile grazed the *Nautilus*'s hull, and I heard the captain exclaim:

"Shoot, you demented vessel! Shower your useless shells! You won't escape the *Nautilus*'s spur! But this isn't the place where you'll perish! I don't want your wreckage mingling with that of the *Avenger!*"

I retired to my stateroom. The captain and his chief officer stayed on the platform. The propeller started turning. The *Nautilus* quickly retreated, taking us outside the range of the vessel's shells. But the chase continued, and Captain Nemo was content to keep his distance.

Near four o'clock in the afternoon, unable to control the impatience and anxiety devouring me, I went back to the central companionway. The hatch was open. I ventured onto the platform. The captain was still strolling there, his steps agitated. He looked at the ship, which stayed to his leeward five or six miles off. He was circling it like a wild animal, coaxing it eastward, letting it chase after him. Yet he didn't attack. Maybe he was still undecided?

I tried to intervene one last time. But I'd barely queried Captain Nemo when the man silenced me:

"I'm the law, I'm the tribunal!" he told me. "I'm the oppressed and there are my oppressors! Thanks to them, I've witnessed the destruction of everything I loved, cherished, and venerated—homeland, wife, children, father, and mother! There lies everything I hate! Now be still!"

I took one last look at the battleship, which was putting on steam. Then I rejoined Ned and Conseil.

"We've got to escape!" I exclaimed.

"Right," Ned put in. "Where's that ship from?"

"I have no idea. But wherever it's from, it will go to the bottom before nightfall. In any case we're better off perishing along with it than being accomplices in some vendetta whose fairness we have no way of judging."

"That's my feeling," Ned Land replied coolly. "Let's wait for nightfall."

Night fell. A deep silence reigned on board. Our compass indicated that the *Nautilus* hadn't changed direction. I heard the beat of its propeller, churning the waves in a quick rhythm. Staying on the surface of the water, the submersible rolled gently, sometimes to one side, sometimes to the other.

My companions and I were determined to escape the instant that warship came close enough for us to be heard—or seen, because the moon would be full in three days and was shining brightly. Once we were aboard that vessel, if we couldn't ward off the danger threatening it, at least we could do everything circumstances would allow. Several times I thought the *Nautilus* was on the verge of attacking. But it was content to simply let its opponent come near, then it would quickly resume its retreating ways.

Part of the night went by uneventfully. We kept watch for an opportunity to take action. We said little, being too keyed up. Ned Land was all for jumping overboard. I made him wait. As I saw it, the *Nautilus* would attack the double-decker on the surface of the waves, then escaping would be both possible and easy.

At three o'clock in the morning, feeling anxious, I climbed onto the platform. Captain Nemo hadn't left it. He was standing in the bow next to his flag, which a mild breeze unfurled over his head. His eyes never left that vessel. The extraordinary intensity of his look seemed to attract it, beguile it, and draw it after him more surely than if he had it in tow!

The moon reached the zenith. Jupiter was rising in the east. In the midst of that peaceful expanse, sky and ocean competed with each other in tranquillity, and the sea offered that silver orb the loveliest mirror to ever reflect her image.

And when I compared the deep calm of the elements to the wholesale fury that seethed inside the plating of this barely visible *Nautilus*, I shivered all over.

The vessel was two miles away. It drew nearer, always moving toward the phosphorescent glow that indicated the *Nautilus*'s presence. I saw its green and red running lights, also the white lantern hanging from the mainstay of its foremast. Faint gleams flickered over its rigging, revealing that its furnaces were pushed to the limit. Showers of sparks and cinders of blazing coal were escaping from its funnels, spangling the sky with stars.

I stood there till six o'clock in the morning, Captain Nemo never seeming to notice me. The vessel lay a mile and a half off, and with the first glimmers of daylight, it resumed its cannonade. It wouldn't be long before the *Nautilus* attacked its opponent, then my companions and I would take our final leave of this man I didn't dare judge.

I'd turned to go below and alert them, when the chief officer climbed onto the platform. Several sailors were with him. Captain Nemo didn't see them, or didn't choose to see them. They'd come to carry out the *Nautilus*'s version of "clearing the decks for action." Their procedures were quite simple. They took down the manropes forming a handrail around the platform. In addition they lowered the pilothouse and the beacon housing into the hull till the units were exactly flush with it. The surface of that long sheet-iron cigar no longer had any protrusions that could interfere with its maneuvers.

I went back to the lounge. The *Nautilus* still emerged above the surface. A few morning gleams were filtering through the liquid strata. Beneath the undulations of the billows, the windows were alive with the red of the rising sun. That dreadful day of June 2 was dawning.

At seven o'clock the log told me the *Nautilus* was slowing down. I realized that it was letting the warship close in. Moreover the explosions kept getting louder. Shells plowed the water around us, drilling through it with an odd hissing sound.

"It's time, my friends," I said. "Let's shake hands, and may God be with us!"

Ned Land was determined, Conseil was calm, I was nervous and barely in control of myself.

We went into the library. Just as I pushed open the door leading to the well of the central companionway, I heard the hatch suddenly close overhead.

The Canadian leaped up the steps, but I

stopped him. A well-known hissing sound told me that water was entering the ship's ballast tanks. In fact, within seconds the *Nautilus* had submerged a few yards under the surface of the waves.

I realized what this maneuver meant. It was too late to take action. The *Nautilus* had no intention of striking the doubledecker where it was clad in impregnable iron armor, but below its waterline, where that metal carapace no longer protected its planking.

We were prisoners once more, unwilling spectators at the gruesome performance now in preparation. But we barely had time to think. Taking refuge in my stateroom, we looked at each other and didn't say a word. My mind was in a total daze. My mental processes had ground to a halt. I was in that agonizing state of anticipation a person feels just before a frightful explosion. I waited, I listened, I lived only through my sense of hearing!

Meanwhile the *Nautilus* had noticeably picked up speed. That meant it was gathering momentum. Its whole hull was trembling.

Suddenly I let out a yell. There had been a collision, but it was comparatively mild. I felt the penetrating force of that steel spur. I heard scratchings and scrapings. Carried away by its driving power, the *Nautilus* had gone through the mass of that vessel like a sailmaker's needle through canvas!

I couldn't hold still. Frantic, going insane, I leaped out of my stateroom and rushed into the lounge.

Captain Nemo was there. Silent, gloomy, implacable, he was looking out the port panel.

An enormous mass was sinking under the waters, and the *Nautilus* followed it down, not missing any stage of its death throes. About thirty feet away I could see its gaping hull, where water was rushing in with a thunderous sound, then its two rows of cannons and railings. Dark, quivering shadows darted all over its deck.

The water was rising. Those poor men were leaping into the shrouds, hanging onto the masts, writhing under the waters. It was a human anthill that an invading sea had caught by surprise!

Paralyzed, rigid with anguish, my hair standing on end, my eyes popping out of my head, short of breath, suffocating, speechless, I looked—I too! An irresistible allure glued me to the window!

The enormous vessel gravitated slowly downward. Descending along with it, the *Nautilus* spied on its every movement. Suddenly there was an eruption. Air compressed inside the craft had blown up its decks, as if somebody had set a match to the powder stores. The thrust of the waters was so intense, the *Nautilus* swerved away.

Then the poor ship sank more swiftly. Its mastheads came into view, loaded with victims, then its crosstrees bending under clusters of men, finally the peak of its mainmast. Then the dark shape vanished, and along with it that crew of corpses dragged under by fearsome eddies . . .

I turned to Captain Nemo. That dreadful executioner, that authentic archangel of hatred, kept on looking. When it was all over, Captain Nemo headed to the door of his stateroom, opened it, and went in. I followed him with my eyes.

On the rear paneling under the portraits of his heroes, I saw the portrait of a still-youthful woman with two little children. Captain Nemo looked at them for a few seconds, stretched his hands toward them, fell to his knees, and dissolved into sobs.

46

Captain Nemo's Last Words

THE PANELS CLOSED over that frightful view, but the lights didn't go on in the lounge. Inside the *Nautilus* all was gloom and silence. It left that place of devastation with prodigious speed, a hundred feet underwater. Where was it going? North or south? Where would the man flee after carrying his vendetta to such horrible lengths?

I went back into my stateroom where Ned and Conseil were waiting silently. Captain Nemo filled me with overwhelming horror. Whatever he'd suffered at the hands of men, he had no right to punish them in this way. He'd made me, if not an accomplice, at least an eyewitness to his program of revenge! Even this was intolerable.

At eleven o'clock the electric lights came back on. I went into the lounge. It was empty. I checked the different instruments. The *Nautilus* was fleeing northward at a speed of twenty-five miles per hour, sometimes on the surface of the sea, sometimes thirty feet under it.

After our position had been marked on the chart, I saw that we were going into the mouth of the English Channel, that our heading would take us to the northernmost seas with incomparable speed.

I could barely catch sight of the swiftly passing marine life: longsnout dogfish, hammerhead sharks, catsharks that frequent these waters, big eagle rays, swarms of seahorses looking like knights on a chessboard, eels coiling like firecracker snakes, armies of crabs scurrying at an angle by crossing their pincers over their carapaces, finally pods of porpoises that ran races with the *Nautilus*. But by this point watching, studying, and classifying were out of the question.

By evening we'd gone 200 leagues up the Atlantic. Shadows gathered and gloom overran the sea till the moon came up.

I retired to my stateroom. I couldn't sleep. I kept having nightmares. That horrible scene of destruction flashed through my mind over and over.

From that day forward who knows where the *Nautilus* took us in the north Atlantic basin? Always at incalculable speed! Always amid the High Arctic mists! Did it call at the capes of Spitsbergen or the shores of Novaya Zemlya? Did it visit the uncharted waters of the White Sea, the Kara Sea, the Gulf of Ob, the Lyakhov Islands, or those unknown beaches on the Siberian coast? I couldn't say. I lost track of the passing hours. Time was in abeyance on the ship's clocks. As happens in the polar regions, night and day no longer seemed to follow their normal sequence. I felt myself being carried off into that strange domain where the overwrought imagination of Edgar Allan Poe was at home. Like the fictional Arthur Gordon Pym, at any moment I expected to see that "shrouded human figure, very far larger in its proportions

than any dweller among men," thrown across the cataract that guards the outskirts of the pole!

I estimate—but maybe I'm mistaken— that the *Nautilus* kept on its haphazard course for two to three weeks, and I'm not sure how long this would have gone on if it hadn't been for the catastrophe that ended our voyage. As for Captain Nemo, he was no longer in the picture. As for his chief officer, the same applied. Not a single crewman was visible for a second. The *Nautilus* cruised under the waters almost continually. When it briefly rose to the surface to replenish our air, the hatches opened and closed as if automated. No more positions were reported on the world map. I didn't know where we were.

I should also mention that the Canadian had reached the end of his strength and patience and no longer left his cabin. Conseil couldn't coax a single word out of him and feared that Ned would kill himself while delirious and under the sway of some ghastly homesickness. So Conseil kept a dedicated watch on his friend every second.

You can appreciate that under these conditions our situation had become untenable.

One morning—I don't know the date—I was slumbering near the first hours of daylight, a tormented, unhealthy slumber. Waking up, I found Ned Land leaning over me and I heard him tell me in a low voice:

"We're going to escape!"

I sat up.

"When?" I asked.

"Tonight. Nobody seems to be standing watch on the *Nautilus*. It's like the whole ship is in a daze. Will you be ready, sir?"

"Yes. Where are we?"

"In sight of land—I saw it through the fog this morning, twenty miles to the east."

"What land is it?"

"I have no idea, but whatever it is, we'll take refuge there."

"Fine, Ned! We'll escape tonight even if the sea swallows us up!"

"The sea's rough, the wind's strong; but a twenty-mile run doesn't scare me, and the *Nautilus*'s longboat is a nimble craft. I've managed to stow some food and flasks of water inside it without the crew spotting me."

"I'm ready when you are."

"What's more," the Canadian added, "if they catch me, I plan to defend myself, I'll fight them to the death."

"Then we'll die together, Ned my friend."

I was bound and determined. The Canadian left me. I went out on the platform, where I could barely stand up due to the jolting of the billows. The skies were threatening, but there was land behind that heavy fog and we had to escape. We couldn't delay a single day or even a single hour.

I went back to the lounge, desiring yet dreading a last encounter with Captain Nemo, wanting and yet not wanting to see him. What would I say to him? How could I hide the instinctive horror he inspired in me? No, it would be better to not come face to face with him! Better to forget him! And yet . . . !

How long that day seemed, the last I would spend aboard the *Nautilus!* I was on my own. Ned Land and Conseil avoided speaking to me, afraid they would give themselves away.

At six o'clock I had supper, though I wasn't hungry. Despite my revulsion I forced myself to eat, to keep up my strength.

At 6:30 Ned Land came into my stateroom. He told me:

"We won't see each other again before we go. At ten o'clock the moon still won't be up. We'll take advantage of the darkness. Come to the skiff. Conseil and I will be waiting for you inside."

Then the Canadian left, giving me no time to answer him.

I wanted to check the *Nautilus*'s heading. I made my way to the lounge. We were running north-northeast with frightful speed, 165 feet down.

I took one last look at the natural wonders and artistic treasures gathered in the museum, that matchless collection doomed to perish someday in the depths of the seas along with its curator. I tried to establish one crowning impression in my mind. I stayed there for an hour, basking in the aura of the ceiling lights, formally inspecting the treasures gleaming in their glass cases. Then I went back to my stateroom.

There I put on heavy seafaring clothes. I gathered my notes and tucked them carefully around my person. My heart was pounding fiercely. I couldn't slow it down. My anxiety and agitation would certainly have given me away if Captain Nemo had seen me.

What was he doing just then? I listened at the door to his stateroom. I heard the sound of footsteps. Captain Nemo was inside. He hadn't gone to bed. With each step I felt he was going to appear and ask me why I wanted to escape! I was in a continual state of alarm. My imagination magnified this feeling. It became so acute, I wondered if it wouldn't be better to go into the captain's stateroom, meet him face to face, and stand up to him with my eyes and bearing!

That was sheer lunacy. Luckily I got a grip on myself and stretched out on the bed to relax my physical tension. My nerves calmed a little; but in my agitated frame of mind, I did a hurried review of my whole existence on the *Nautilus*, all the pleasant or unpleasant incidents that had come my way since I went overboard from the *Abraham Lincoln:* the underwater hunting trip, Torres Strait, running aground, the savages of Papua, the coral cemetery, the Suez passageway, the island of Santorini, the Cretan diver, Vigo Bay, Atlantis, the ice barrier, the South Pole, imprisonment in the ice, the battle with the devilfish, the storm in the Gulf Stream, the *Avenger*, and that horrible scene of the vessel sinking with its crew . . . ! All those events passed in front of my eyes like backdrops rolling across the stage in a theater. Then, in that strange setting, Captain Nemo grew astoundingly. His features stood out, taking on superhuman proportions. He was no longer a fellow mortal, he was the Man of the Waters, the Spirit of the Seas.

By then it was 9:30. I held my head in both hands to keep it from exploding. I closed my eyes. I didn't want to think anymore. Half an hour still to go! Half an hour of a nightmare that could drive me insane!

Just then I heard faint chords from the organ, mournful harmonies from some unidentifiable hymn, genuine pleadings from a soul trying to sever its earthly ties. I listened with all five senses, barely breathing, immersed like Captain Nemo in that musical trance carrying him beyond the bounds of this world.

Then a sudden thought terrified me. Captain Nemo had left his stateroom. He was in that very lounge I needed to cross in order to escape. I would meet him there one last time. He would see me, maybe speak to me! One gesture from him could overwhelm me, a single word shackle me to his vessel!

Even so, ten o'clock was about to strike. It was time to leave my stateroom and rejoin my companions.

I didn't dare hesitate, even if Captain Nemo rose up in front of me. I opened the door cautiously, but as it swung on its hinges, it seemed to make an awful noise. This noise existed, maybe, only in my imagination!

I crept forward through the *Nautilus*'s dark corridors, pausing after each step to slow the pounding of my heart.

I arrived at the corner door of the lounge. I opened it gently. The lounge was plunged in total darkness. Chords from the organ were reverberating faintly. Captain Nemo was there. He didn't see me. Even in broad daylight I doubt that he would have noticed me, he was so completely immersed in his trance.

I inched over the carpet, avoiding the tiniest bump whose noise might give me away. It took me five minutes to reach the library door at the far end.

I was about to open it when a groan from Captain Nemo froze me in place. I realized that he was getting up. I even caught a glimpse of him, because a few rays of light from the library were filtering into the lounge. He was coming toward me, arms folded, silent, not walking but gliding like a ghost. His chest was heaving, swelling with sobs. And I heard him murmur these words, the last of his to ever reach my ears:

"O almighty God! Enough! Enough!"

Had a prayer of repentence just escaped from the man's conscience . . . ?

I rushed frantically into the library. I climbed the central companionway, went along the upper corridor, and arrived at the skiff. I crawled through the opening that had already given access to my two companions.

"Let's go, let's go!" I exclaimed.

"This instant!" the Canadian replied.

Using the monkey wrench he had with him, Ned Land first closed and bolted the opening cut into the *Nautilus*'s sheet iron. After he'd also closed the opening in the skiff, the Canadian started to unscrew the nuts still holding us to the underwater boat.

Suddenly there were noises inside the ship. Loud voices were answering each other. What was going on? Had they spotted our escape? I felt Ned Land slipping a knife into my hand.

"Yes," I muttered, "we know how to die!"

The Canadian had stopped what he was doing. But one word repeated twenty times over, one dreadful word, told me the cause of the agitation spreading aboard the *Nautilus*. We weren't the reason the crew were upset.

"Maelstrom! Maelstrom!" they were yelling.

The Maelstrom! Could a more frightening name have rung in our ears under more frightening circumstances? Were we lying in the dangerous waterways off the Norwegian coast? Was the *Nautilus* being dragged into that whirlpool just as the skiff was ready to detach from its plating?

At the turn of the tide, as you know, the waters cooped up between the Faroe and Lofoten islands rush out with irresistible force. They form a vortex from which no ship has ever been able to escape. Monstrous waves race together from every corner of the horizon. They form a whirlpool aptly called "the ocean's navel," which can suck things in from over nine miles away. It can drag down not only ships but whales, and even polar bears from the northernmost regions.

This was where the captain had accidentally—or maybe even deliberately—taken his *Nautilus*. The vessel was sweeping around in a spiral whose radius kept getting smaller and smaller. Since the skiff was still attached to the ship's plating, we were carried along at dizzying speed. I could feel it. I was starting to get sick to my stomach from the continual spinning. We were in dread, in the last stages of sheer horror, our blood frozen in our veins, our nerves numb, dripping with cold sweat as if we were in our death throes! And what a racket around our frail skiff! What roars echoing from several miles away! What crashes from the waters breaking against sharp rocks on the seafloor, where the hardest objects are shattered, where tree trunks are worn down and worked into "a shaggy fur," as Norwegians express it!

What a state of affairs! We were rocking frightfully. The *Nautilus* was fighting back like a human being. Its steel muscles were cracking. Sometimes it stood on end, and the three of us along with it!

"We've got to hang on tight," Ned said, "and screw the nuts back down! If we can stay attached to the *Nautilus*, we can still make it . . . !"

He hadn't finished speaking when there was a cracking sound. The nuts gave way, and the skiff was yanked out of its niche and hurled like a stone from a sling into the midst of the vortex.

My head banged against an iron timber, and from that violent blow I passed out.

47

CONCLUSION

WHICH BRINGS US to the conclusion of this voyage under the seas. As for what happened that night, how the skiff escaped from the Maelstrom's fearsome eddies, how Ned Land, Conseil, and I got out of that whirlpool, I can't say. But when I came to, I was lying in a fisherman's hut on one of the Lofoten Islands. Safe and sound, my two companions were at my bedside clutching my hands. We hugged each other heartily.

Going back to France right now is unthinkable. There are few means of transportation between upper Norway and the south. So I have to wait for the arrival of a steamer that runs twice a month from North Cape.

Consequently it's here, among these decent folks who have taken us in, that I'm reviewing my account of these adventures. It's accurate. Not a single fact has been omitted, not a single detail exaggerated. It's the faithful record of this inconceivable expedition into an element now beyond human reach, but where progress will someday make great inroads.

Will anybody believe me? I don't know. Ultimately it makes little difference. What I can now state is that I'm qualified to speak of these seas: in less than ten months, I've covered 20,000 leagues in this world tour underwater that has shown me so many wonders across the Pacific, the Indian Ocean, the Red Sea, the Mediterranean, the Atlantic, the southernmost and northernmost seas!

But what happened to the *Nautilus?* Did it elude the Maelstrom's clutches? Is Captain Nemo alive? Is he still under the ocean continuing his frightful vendetta, or did he stop after his latest mass execution? Will the waves someday deliver that manuscript containing his whole life story? Will I finally learn the man's name? Will the nationality of the ship he sank tell us Captain Nemo's nationality?

I hope so. I also hope that his powerful submersible conquered the sea inside its most dreadful whirlpool, that the *Nautilus* has survived where so many other ships have perished! If this is the case and Captain Nemo is still dwelling in the ocean—his adopted country—may the hatred be appeased in his fierce heart! May his contemplation of all those wonders snuff out his desire for revenge! May the executioner pass away and the scientist continue his peaceful exploring of the seas! If his destiny is strange, it's also sublime. Haven't I encompassed it myself? Didn't I lead ten months of that otherworldly existence? Accordingly there are two men out of all mankind who are now qualified to answer that question asked 6,000 years ago in the Book of Ecclesiastes: "Who can fathom the soundless depths?" Those two men are Captain Nemo and myself.

AROUND
THE
WORLD
IN
80 DAYS

First published in 1872

A witty mixture of manhunt, love story, social satire, and race against the clock, *Around the World in 80 Days* is the entertainment gem in Verne's output. The novel has a futuristic concept, or at least did for its time: circumnavigating the earth in a record-breaking eighty days or less. It's a feat that America's Nellie Bly actually pulled off just seven years later. How so? Because Verne plays fair and doesn't concoct any fictitious conveyances or contrivances: from schooners to steam locomotives, his tale uses only established forms of transportation; even the book's single far-fetched vehicle, a sail-powered sled, turns out after investigation to be nothing new—the Dutch had been riding on them for years.

Free of high-tech encumbrances, Verne's plot is arguably his best built. It moves with speed and economy, plus he has a matchless knack for spotting which parts of his material have the liveliest dramatic potential: an elephant ride through a murderous cult of East Indians . . . facing a rampaging storm in an undersized sailboat . . . the slapstick antics of a Japanese acrobatic troupe . . . and a rollicking wild west sequence that takes up a good fifth of the book and comes complete with mob violence, high-noon shootout, and train holdup. In this last instance, too, Verne writes of places he hadn't actually visited, yet he has a sharp eye for the most telling details in his sources, and his descriptions are convincing even to readers (such as myself) who are personally familiar with the territory.

He knows what to keep and what to dump. Right off, for example, he skips Europe and heads straight for exotic Egypt. Similarly he crosses the entire Pacific (a third of his journey) in a single chapter, the eastern U.S. in a single paragraph. Other story-telling shortcuts are downright slick: when he supplies an expository flashback in Chapter 7 to indicate the ground just covered, it's a few lines scribbled in an itinerary. Finally, at the climax of this marvelously managed yarn, everything goes hopelessly wrong—till Verne springs one of literature's choice surprise endings.

The story's linchpin is its leading man Phileas Fogg, the ultimate Britisher with stiff upper lip. Yet Fogg goes far beyond the stereotype: commentators have likened him to the author's father, hidebound attorney Pierre Verne, said to have lived a life of clockwork rigidity. Fogg is just as machinelike, in fact is continually described as a chronometer, an appliance, a robot, an icy emotional vacuum. Yet the bottled-up pressures get to him and at times he gives in to knee-jerk impulses: he tries to leap onto a burning pyre, engages in a narcissistic duel to the death, aims to single-handedly save his valet Passepartout from Sioux warriors, and, of course, pigheadedly makes the multimillion-dollar bet in Chapter 3 that causes all the trouble. He's a portrait of psychic imbalance—but curable.

As for the manhunt subplot, it's driven by relentless Inspector Fix of Scotland Yard—that's "fix" as in *fixation* or *idée fixe*. Finally, sketched with delicacy and restraint, there's an unexpectedly charming love story. En route Fogg rescues the voluptuous East Indian widow Aouda, who turns out to be surprisingly emancipated and an egalitarian partner for Fogg—she's not only a good looker, she's a good shot, a good cardplayer, and even, it's hinted, good in bed.

Social satire? Verne is full of sly wonderment at England's colonizing virtuosity. Halfway around the globe in Hong Kong, the rubbernecking Passepartout finds he's "pretty much still in Bombay, Calcutta, or Singapore. It's as if a trail of English towns runs around the globe." Does this mean Fogg winds up in exactly the same place when he gets back to Britain? Actually it doesn't . . . as you'll see. *Translator.*

1

*In which Phileas Fogg and
Passepartout mutually accept each other
as master and manservant*

IN THE YEAR 1872 the house at 7 Savile Row in Burlington Gardens—the house where Sheridan died in 1816—was the residence of Phileas Fogg, Esq., one of the most distinctive and noteworthy members of the Reform Club in London, though he seemed to shrink from doing anything that might attract attention.

One of England's greatest orators had been replaced, then, by this Phileas Fogg, a mystifying individual nobody knew anything about, except that he was quite well bred and one of the finest gentlemen in English high society.

He was said to resemble Byron—though he didn't have a clubfoot, at least his profile was Byronic—but a Byron with mustache and side-whiskers, an unemotional Byron who could have lived to a thousand without showing his age.

Though definitely English, Phileas Fogg may not have been a Londoner. You never saw him at the stock exchange, the Bank of England, or any of the financial establishments in the business district. London's docks and shipyards had never berthed a vessel owned by Phileas Fogg. The gentleman wasn't listed on any board of directors. His name never rang out in any college of lawyers, not the Temple, Lincoln's Inn, or Gray's Inn. He'd never pleaded a case in the Courts of Chancery, Queen's Bench, or Exchequer, nor in the Ecclesiastical Court. He wasn't a manufacturer, wholesaler, shopkeeper, or farmer. He didn't belong to the Royal Institution of Great Britain, the London Institution, the Artisan Society, the Russell Institution, the Western Literary Institution, the Law Society, or the Combined Society for the Arts and Sciences, which is under the direct patronage of Her Gracious Majesty. In short, he hadn't joined any of the many societies that teem in England's capital, from the Harmonic Union to the Entomological Society, which had been formed chiefly for the purpose of exterminating pesky insects.

Phileas Fogg was a member of the Reform Club and nothing more.

To anybody who might be amazed that such a secretive gentleman could be a member of this respectable association, we'll reply that he got in on the recommendation of Baring Brothers & Co., the famous bank where he had an unlimited line of credit. Ergo he enjoyed a definite "status," since his checking account always showed a positive balance and drafts ordinarily went through on sight.

Was this Phileas Fogg a wealthy man? Indisputably. But even the best informed couldn't say how he'd made his fortune, and Mr. Fogg was the last person they were inclined to approach for enlightenment. In any case he neither squandered his money nor hoarded it, because whenever funds were needed to support some noble, beneficial, or generous cause, he provided them quietly and even anonymously.

In a nutshell, nobody could be less sociable than this gentleman. He said as little as possible and his silence made him seem even more secretive. Even so, he lived his life in plain view, but since he always did the same things with mathematical predictability, people's imaginations were restless and on the lookout for something more.

Had he traveled extensively? Very likely, because nobody knew the map of the world better than he. No place was so remote that he didn't seem to have detailed knowledge of it. Sometimes—though in a few quick, clear words—he would correct the thousands of comments that flew around his club regarding some lost or missing explorer; he would pinpoint the most likely eventualities, and so frequently were his words borne out by future developments, he seemed almost clairvoyant. He must have been a man who had traveled everywhere, at least in his head.

All the same it was clear that Phileas Fogg hadn't been away from London in a good while. There were some who had the honor of knowing him a bit better than the rest of the world, and they swore that except for the direct route he traveled each day from his home to his club, nobody could ever claim they'd seen him anywhere else. His only pastimes were reading the newspapers and playing whist. This quiet game was well suited to his nature, and he often won at it; however his winnings never went into his billfold but made up a sizeable part of his charitable contributions. Even so, we must note that Mr. Fogg clearly didn't play to win but for the pleasure of playing. He saw the game as a contest, a battle against a difficulty, but a battle that didn't involve moving around, shifting ground, or getting tuckered out, and this agreed with his personality.

As far as anybody knew, Phileas Fogg had neither wife nor children (which can happen to the most decent fellows), neither relatives nor friends (which is actually much rarer). Phileas Fogg lived alone in his house on Savile Row and nobody visited him. His home life never came into the picture. A single manservant was enough for his needs. He ate lunch and dinner at his club on a schedule that had been worked out with a chronometer, and he did so in the same dining room, at the same table, never entertaining colleagues, never inviting strangers to join him, and he went home to bed at the stroke of midnight without ever using the comfortable quarters the Reform Club puts at the disposal of select members. He spent just ten hours out of every twenty-four at his residence, either in sleeping or in getting groomed and dressed for the day ahead. Anytime he went for a stroll, it was with a steady step over the parquet floor of the club's lobby or down its circular hallway, which was topped by a dome that had blue-tinted windows and rested on twenty Ionic columns of red porphyry. When he ate lunch or dinner, the club's kitchens, larder, pantry, fish market, and dairy furnished his table with their sumptuous stores; the club's waiters—solemn individuals dressed in black and shod in slippers with padded soles—served his food on exclusive china and marvelous saxony table linen; the club's goblets came from a lost line of glass molds and held his sherry, his port, and his claret, which had been seasoned with cinnamon, maidenhair, and cassia; finally the club's ice—imported at major expense from America's lakes—kept his drinks satisfactorily chilled.

If this lifestyle can be called eccentric, you must admit that eccentricity has something going for it!

Though his home on Savile Row wasn't ostentatious, it still rated as tremendously comfortable. In addition, since its tenant's habits never varied, its upkeep made fewer demands. Even so, Phileas Fogg required his single manservant to be exceptionally punctual and reliable. On this very day, October 2, Phileas Fogg had just given the boot to James Forster (the fellow had been found guilty of heating his master's shaving water to 84° Fahrenheit instead of 86°) and was waiting for his replacement, who was supposed to show up between 11:00 and 11:30.

Sitting dead center in his armchair, two feet together like a soldier on dress parade, palms resting on knees, body erect, head held high, Phileas Fogg watched the hand moving on his wall clock—a complicated mechanism that marked the hour, minute, second, day, date, month, and year. When 11:30 chimed, Mr. Fogg was to leave home and make his way to the Reform Club in line with his daily schedule,

Just then somebody knocked on the door to the little parlor where Phileas Fogg was waiting.

His ex-employee James Forster appeared.

"The new manservant," he said.

A fellow of about thirty came in and bowed.

"You're from France," Phileas Fogg asked him, "and your name is John?"

"Jean, with all due respect, sir," the newcomer replied, "but my nickname is 'Jean Passepartout.'[1] I've lived up to it with my knack for handling tight situations, so the label has stuck. I think I'm a decent fellow, sir, but to be honest with you, I've been a jack-of-all-trades. I've worked as a wandering minstrel, a horseman in a circus, a trapeze artist like Léotard, and a tightrope walker like

---

[1] *Translator's note.* French: "passkey." The literal meaning of *passepartout* is "gets through anything."

Blondin; after that, to make more profitable use of my talents, I became a gymnastics teacher and finally a sergeant in the Paris Fire Department. I've got some really notable blazes on my résumé. But I left France five years ago, wanted a taste of domestic bliss, and today earn my living in England as a personal valet. Now then, being out of work and hearing that Mr. Phileas Fogg was the most orderly and retiring gentleman in the United Kingdom, I've arrived on his doorstep in hopes of living a serene existence and forgetting the very name of Passepartout . . ."

"I'm comfortable calling you Passepartout," the gentleman replied. "You come recommended. I've received good reports on you. You know my requirements?"

"Yes, sir."

"Fine. What time do you have?"

"It's 11:22," Passepartout replied, tugging an enormous silver watch from the depths of his vest pocket.

"You're slow," Mr. Fogg said.

"Pardon me, sir, but that isn't possible."

"You're four minutes slow. Let it be. I've noted the discrepancy, enough said. Therefore, as of 11:29 this Wednesday morning, October 2, 1872, you're now in my employ."

With that Phileas Fogg got up, took his hat in his left hand, put it on his head with a robotlike motion, and vanished without another word.

Passepartout heard the front door give a slam—it was his new master leaving; then a second slam—it was his predecessor James Forster going off in his turn.

They'd left Passepartout alone in the house on Savile Row.

2

Where Passepartout is convinced
he has found perfection at last

"YE GODS," Passepartout said to himself, a bit flabbergasted at first. "I've seen folks at Madame Tussaud's with as much feeling in them as my new master!"

It's appropriate to mention at this point that the "folks at Madame Tussaud's" are wax figures, a major tourist attraction in London; the only thing they lack is the gift of speech.

During the few seconds in which he'd just caught a glimpse of Phileas Fogg, Passepartout had given his future master a quick but careful inspection. A man who might have been forty, his employer had fine aristocratic features, a tall figure not spoiled by a slight tummy, blond hair and side-whiskers, smooth brow and temples without a wrinkle in sight, pale rather than ruddy features, and magnificent teeth. To a supreme degree he seemed to have what physiognomists, those analysts of facial character, call "strength in repose," a virtue typical of folks who value deeds more than words. With his stoic calm, clear eye, and unblinking alertness, he was an ideal example of those ultra composed Englishmen you come across so often in the United Kingdom, people whose slightly pedantic outlooks the portrait painter Angelica Kauffmann has captured so wonderfully with her brush. Seen in the various activities of his daily life, this gentleman gave the impression of being fully counterbalanced, meticulously aligned, as faultless as a chronometer manufactured by a master watchmaker like Leroy or Earnshaw. In essence Phileas Fogg was the soul of precision, which was clearly visible in "the language of his hands and feet," because with both men and animals, the body parts themselves are instruments that can convey states of mind.

Phileas Fogg was one of those mathematically correct people who are never in a rush, always prepared, economical in their every step and movement. He never took a stride too many and always went by the shortest route. He didn't stare off into space. He didn't indulge in unnecessary actions. Nobody ever saw him excited or agitated. He was the least hurried person on earth, yet he always arrived on the dot. Even so, you can appreciate why he lived a solitary existence, an existence free of all social intercourse, as it were. He knew that friction was a part of life, and since friction is time-consuming, he never rubbed anybody the wrong way.

As for Jean, dubbed Passepartout, he was a thoroughgoing Parisian who had moved to

England five years earlier, had worked in London as a personal valet, and had searched in vain for a master to whom he could pledge his allegiance.

Passepartout wasn't like Frontin, Mascarille, or other stage servants in the popular French farces—high-handed, brazen-faced, wry-eyed rascals who shrug their shoulders and turn up their noses. Not at all. Passepartout was a gallant fellow with friendly features and rather full lips that were always game for a nibble or a kiss—a kindly, helpful person with one of those pleasant round noggins you like to see on a good friend's shoulders. He had blue eyes, lively coloring, a face chubby enough for him to see his own cheekbones, a broad chest, a strapping build, vigorous muscles, and that Herculean strength he'd developed so marvelously during his athletic youth. His brown hair was a little unruly. Though the sculptors of antiquity knew eighteen different ways of arranging Minerva's tresses, Passepartout knew only one way of dealing with his own: three swipes with a big-tooth comb and his grooming was done.

The most basic caution keeps us from saying whether a fellow with such an exuberant personality could get along with a man like Phileas Fogg. Would Passepartout be that stringently correct manservant his master required? The only way to find out was to put him to work. After a pretty unstable youth, as you know, he longed for peace and quiet. Hearing high praise for the methodical English and for the proverbial reserve of their gentlemen, he came to England to seek his fortune. But so far the fates had been against him. He hadn't been able to put down roots anywhere. He'd worked in ten homes. In all of them his employers had been wayward and temperamental, chasing after women or chasing off on joyrides, neither of which was acceptable to Passepartout these days. Young Lord Longsferry, a Member of Parliament and his latest master, spent his nights in Haymarket "oyster bars" and all too often came home slung over a policeman's shoulders. First and foremost Passepartout wanted a master he could respect, so he ventured a few polite comments; when these were poorly received, he quit. At this point he heard that Phileas Fogg, Esq., was looking for a manservant. He investigated the gentleman. An individual who led an orderly life, didn't sleep out, didn't travel, and never went away, not even for a day, would suit him down to the ground. He showed up and was hired under the circumstances you're acquainted with.

Eleven-thirty having chimed, Passepartout was alone in the house on Savile Row. He started to inspect it at once. He went over it from the cellar to the attic. It was a neat, clean, simple, straitlaced home laid out for easy upkeep, and it pleased him. It reminded him of a snail shell, but a high-class shell with both gaslight and a gas furnace, because carbureted hydrogen took care of all its heating and lighting needs. Passepartout had no difficulty finding the third-floor bedroom intended for him. It suited him perfectly. Electric bells and speaking tubes put him in contact with the rooms on the second and first floors. An electric clock stood on his mantel, synchronized with the clock in Phileas Fogg's bedroom, and the two timepieces ticked the same second at the same instant.

"This," Passepartout said to himself, "is just what the doctor ordered!"

In his bedroom he also noted a memo tacked above the clock. It was a schedule of his daily responsibilities. Running from 8:00 in the morning, the official time for Phileas Fogg to get up, till 11:30 when he left home to go eat lunch at the Reform Club, this schedule covered his manservant's duties in full detail—tea and toast at 8:23, shaving water at 9:37, hair care at 9:40, etc. Then, from 11:30 in the morning till midnight when the systematic gentleman went to bed, everything else was listed, anticipated, and spelled out. Passepartout took delight in studying this schedule and learning its different entries by heart.

As for his employer's wardrobe, it was meticulously hung and wondrously thorough. Each vest, dress coat, and pair of trousers bore a serial number, which had been copied into a ledger that recorded their comings and goings and showed the date, depending on the season, when each piece of clothing was to be worn in its turn. Same protocol for shoes.

All in all this house on Savile Row—which must have been a haven of chaos in the days of the notoriously loose-living Sheridan—was furnished in a comfortable style that suggested substantial means. No library and no books, though—Mr. Fogg wouldn't have had any use for them, since the Reform Club put two libraries at his disposal, one devoted to literature, the other to politics and the law. In his bedroom was a medium-sized safe, built to be both fireproof and theft-proof. There weren't any weapons in the house, no implements for hunting game or waging war. Only the most peaceful intentions were in evidence.

After he'd given the dwelling a detailed inspection, Passepartout rubbed his hands, his broad face beaming, and he said over and over in delight:

"It's a perfect fit! It's right down my alley! We'll get along famously, Mr. Fogg and I! He's a homebody, an orderly man! A real piece of machinery! Well, it won't pain me to have a domestic appliance for a master!"

3

Where a conversation takes place that could cost Phileas Fogg a fortune

LEAVING HIS HOUSE on Savile Row at 11:30, Phileas Fogg put his right foot in front of his left 575 times, and his left foot in front of his right 576 times, before he arrived at the Reform Club, a huge edifice that stood on Pall Mall and cost the equivalent of at least $600,000 to build.

At once Phileas Fogg made his way to the dining room, whose nine windows opened onto a lovely garden where the trees were already turning an autumnal gold. He sat down at his usual table, now laid and waiting for him. His lunch featured an appetizer of boiled fish sharply seasoned with a first-rate Reading Sauce, roast beef done rare and trimmed with mushroom pieces, a pastry with rhubarb and green gooseberry filling, and a wedge of Cheshire cheese—all of it washed down with a couple cups of excellent tea brewed from leaves picked exclusively for the Reform Club's pantry.

At 12:47 the gentleman got to his feet and headed for the main lounge, a lavish chamber adorned with opulently framed paintings. There an attendant gave him a brand-new copy of the *Times*, and Phileas Fogg handled the demanding task of unfolding and cutting it with a sure touch that revealed long experience at this tricky operation. Reading this newspaper kept Phileas Fogg busy till 3:45, and doing likewise with the *Evening Standard*—which was next on the bill—took him till dinnertime. This meal proceeded along the same lines as lunch, except for the addition of a "Royal British Sauce."

At 5:40 the gentleman reappeared in the main lounge and knuckled down to reading the *Morning Chronicle*.

Half an hour later various members of the Reform Club came in and drew near the hearth, where a coal fire was blazing. They were Mr. Phileas Fogg's regular partners at cards, men as addicted to playing whist as he was: Andrew Stuart the engineer, the bankers John Sullivan and Samuel Fallentin, Thomas Flanagan the brewer, and Walter Ralph, one of the Bank of England's directors—individuals of unusual wealth and influence, even in this club whose membership included the biggest names in industry and finance.

"Well, Ralph," Thomas Flanagan asked, "what's going on with that business of the robbery?"

"Well," Andrew Stuart replied, "the bank has seen the last of its money."

"On the contrary," Walter Ralph said, "I'm hopeful we'll lay our hands on the fellow who perpetrated the robbery. Our best qualified police inspectors have been dispatched to America and Europe, to all the major outbound and inbound ports, and it'll be hard for this gentleman to slip past them."

"But do they have the robber's physical description?" Andrew Stuart asked.

"First of all he isn't a robber," Walter Ralph replied in all seriousness.

"Excuse me? This party filches £55,000

in banknotes and he isn't a robber?"[2]

"Not by trade," Walter Ralph replied.

"So is he a businessman?" John Sullivan said.

"The *Morning Chronicle* is positive he's a gentleman."

The individual who gave this answer was none other than Phileas Fogg, whose head emerged at this point from the waves of newspapers heaped around him. At the same instant Phileas Fogg nodded in greeting to his colleagues, and they nodded back.

The event under discussion, which the various newspapers in the United Kingdom were hotly debating, had taken place three days earlier on September 29. A stack of banknotes, totaling the enormous sum of £55,000, had been stolen from the head teller's counter at the Bank of England.

To anybody who was amazed that such a robbery could have occurred so easily, the deputy governor Walter Ralph confined himself to replying that when it happened, the teller was busy recording a deposit of three shillings sixpence, and nobody can keep an eye on everything.

But it's appropriate to point something out at this juncture, something that makes the event more understandable: the Bank of England, that praiseworthy establishment, seems tremendously squeamish about questioning the public's honesty. It hasn't any guards, any retired military, any grilled windows. Gold, silver, and paper money are right out in the open, at the mercy of the first comer, as it were. The bank can't bring itself to doubt the respectability of any passerby. One of our foremost students of English behavior describes an instance of this very thing: in one of the bank's rooms where he was waiting one day, his interest was caught by a gold ingot that weighed seven or eight pounds and lay right out on the teller's counter; wanting a closer look, he picked the ingot up, inspected it, passed it to his neighbor, the latter gave it to somebody else, and in this manner the ingot went from hand to hand all the way to the far end of a dark corridor; it only came back to where it belonged half an hour later, and the teller hadn't looked up even once.

But on September 29 things didn't quite work out this way. The stack of banknotes didn't come back, and when the magnificent clock that loomed over "Deposits and Withdrawals" chimed the hour of five and close of business, the Bank of England was obliged to reflect that missing £55,000 in the profit and loss account.

Once the fact of the robbery had been properly established, droves of investigators—"masters of detection" handpicked from the best in the business—were dispatched to the major ports in Liverpool, Glasgow, Le Havre, Suez, Brindisi, New York, etc.; they were promised a reward of £2,000 ($10,000) for a successful capture, plus 5% of the total amount recovered. While waiting for the details sure to come from an official inquiry that instantly got under way, these police inspectors had the task of scrupulously monitoring all arriving and departing travelers.

Now then, exactly as the *Morning Chronicle* said, there were grounds for presuming that the fellow who perpetrated the robbery wasn't a member of England's criminal classes. During that day of September 29, staff had noted a well-dressed, well-mannered, refined-looking gentleman pacing back and forth in the cash payments room that was the setting of the robbery. The official inquiry had made it possible to generate a pretty accurate description of this gentleman, a description that was forwarded at once to every detective in the United Kingdom and on the continent. So a few positive thinkers—Walter Ralph among them—felt justified in hoping that the robber wouldn't get away with it.

As the reader can imagine, this event was the talk of the town in London and all England. Multitudes joined the debate, arguing for and against the likelihood of Scotland Yard's cracking the case. It won't amaze you, then, to hear that the same issue was being discussed at the Reform Club, and all the

---

[2] *Translator's note.* £55,000 was equivalent at the time to over $250,000 in U.S. currency; in today's dollars its purchasing power would be roughly comparable to $5,000,000.

more intensely because its membership included one of the bank's deputy governors.

The honorable Walter Ralph refused to harbor any doubts about the investigation's outcome, figuring that the reward on offer was sure to significantly sharpen the wits and zeal of the investigators. But his colleague Andrew Stuart was far from sharing this confident outlook. So these gentlemen kept on arguing after they sat down at a card table for their evening whist; Stuart and Flanagan were partners and faced each other, likewise Fallentin and Phileas Fogg. During play the participants didn't talk, but their interrupted conversation would resume in high style at the finish of a rubber.[3]

"The odds are in the robber's favor, I tell you," Andrew Stuart said. "Because he's got to be a smooth operator!"

"Come now!" Ralph replied. "There isn't a single country left where he can hide out."

"By thunder!"

"Where would you have him go?"

"That isn't my strong suit," Andrew Stuart answered. "But after all, the earth is a pretty huge place."

"It used to be," Phileas Fogg said under his breath. "Sir, will you cut?" he added, handing the cards to Thomas Flanagan.

The argument hung fire during the next rubber. But Andrew Stuart was soon back at it, saying:

"You muttered 'it used to be.' Has the earth gotten smaller by any chance?"

"Without a doubt," Walter Ralph replied. "I'm on Mr. Fogg's side. The world *is* smaller, because we can now travel around it ten times faster than a hundred years ago. And in the present instance, this is the thing that will speed up the whole investigation."

"And the thing that will also help the robber get away!"

"You lead, Mr. Stuart," Phileas Fogg said.

But the skeptical Stuart wasn't convinced, and when the round was over:

"I must admit, Mr. Ralph," he went on, "that you've come up with an amusing way of showing that the earth has gotten

smaller! Therefore, just because we can now go around it in three months—"

"In only eighty days," Phileas Fogg said.

"That's a fact, gentlemen," John Sullivan added. "In eighty days, since the Great Indian Peninsular Railway has opened a section of track between Rothal and Allahabad in northern India." And he showed them the timetable that the *Morning Chronicle* had worked out:

From London to Suez via Mt. Cenis and Brindisi, by railway and ocean liner	*7 days*
From Suez to Bombay, by ocean liner	*13 "*
From Bombay to Calcutta, by railway	*3 "*
From Calcutta to Hong Kong (China), by ocean liner	*13 "*
From Hong Kong to Yokohama (Japan), by ocean liner	*6 "*
From Yokohama to San Francisco, by ocean liner	*22 "*
From San Francisco to New York, by railroad	*7 "*
From New York to London, by ocean liner and railway	*9 "*
Total	*80 days*

"Yes, in eighty days!" Andrew Stuart exclaimed, not paying attention and trumping a sure winner. "But that doesn't include foul weather, contrary winds, shipwrecks, jumping the tracks, etc."

"All included," Phileas Fogg replied, pressing on with the game, because this time the argument was taking over from the whist.

"Even if some Hindus or Red Indians pull up the rails?" Andrew Stuart snapped. "Even if they hold up the train, loot the

---

[3] *Translator's note.* Best of three games.

baggage car, and scalp the passengers?"

"All included," Phileas Fogg replied, throwing down his hand. "The highest two trumps," he added.

It was Andrew Stuart's turn to deal and he gathered up the cards, saying:

"In theory you're right, Mr. Fogg, but in practice—"

"In practice as well, Mr. Stuart."

"I would like to see you try."

"It's up to you. Let's set out together."

"Heaven help me!" Stuart exclaimed. "But I would bet you a good £4,000 that it's impossible to carry out such a journey on these terms.

"On the contrary, it's perfectly possible," Mr. Fogg replied.

"Fine, then do it!"

"Go around the world in eighty days?"

"Yes."

"Glad to."

"When?"

"Right now."

"This is insanity!" Andrew Stuart exclaimed, beginning to feel annoyed at the persistence of his fellow cardplayer. "Look here, let's get on with the game!"

"Then start over," Phileas Fogg replied. "That was a misdeal."

Andrew Stuart feverishly picked the cards back up; then he suddenly put them on the table:

"All right, Mr. Fogg, fine," he said. "Fine! I'll bet you £4,000!"

"My dear Stuart," Fallentin said. "Calm down, don't be so serious!"

"When I make a bet, " Andrew Stuart replied, "I'm always serious."

"Done!" Mr. Fogg said. Then, turning to his colleagues:

"I have £20,000 in my account at Baring Brothers & Co., and I would be willing to stake it—"

"Twenty thousand pounds!" John Sullivan shrieked. "£20,000 that you could lose because of one unexpected delay?"

"Nothing is ever unexpected," Phileas Fogg merely replied.

"But Mr. Fogg, this period of eighty days is only the figure for the minimum time possible!"

"Well-managed minimums are always enough."

"But to keep from exceeding this one, you would have to hop with mathematical exactitude from the railways to the ocean liners, then from the ocean liners back to the railways!"

"I'll hop with mathematical exactitude."

"You've got to be joking!"

"No true Englishman ever jokes about something as serious as a bet," Phileas Fogg replied. "I'll bet £20,000 against all comers that I can go around the world in eighty days or less, hence in 1,920 hours, or 115,200 minutes. Do you accept?"

"We accept," replied Messrs. Stuart, Fallentin, Sullivan, Flanagan, and Ralph after putting their heads together.

"Fine," Mr. Fogg said. "The boat train leaves for Dover at 8:45. I'll take it."

"This very evening?" Stuart asked.

"This very evening," Phileas Fogg replied. Then, after studying a pocket calendar, he added, "Since today is Wednesday, October 2, I'm due back in London, in this same lounge at the Reform Club, by 8:45 on Saturday evening, December 21; failing that, gentlemen, the £20,000 currently in my personal account at Baring Brothers & Co. will be yours by right and possession. Here's a check for that same amount."[4]

The six co-participants drew up a written statement of the bet and signed it on the spot. Phileas Fogg was as cool as ever. Clearly he hadn't made this bet to increase his income and he'd limited the amount to £20,000—half of his fortune—because he anticipated that he might need to spend the other half in seeing this difficult, if not unachievable, scheme through to completion. As for his opponents, they themselves seemed on edge, not from the amount of money they'd put up, but because they were feeling some qualms about a wager along these lines.

Seven o'clock chimed at this point. The others offered to break off their whist playing

---

[4] *Translator's note.* £20,000 was equivalent at the time to about $100,000 in U.S. currency; in today's dollars its purchasing power would be roughly comparable to $2,000,000.

so that Mr. Fogg could go prepare for his departure.

"I'm always prepared!" that unemotional gentleman replied, then dealt the cards:

"Diamonds are trumps," he said. "You lead, Mr. Stuart."

4

*In which Phileas Fogg astounds
his manservant Passepartout*

AT 7:25 PHILEAS FOGG took leave of his distinguished colleagues and headed home from the Reform Club, having won twenty guineas at whist.[5] At 7:50 he opened his front door and went inside his house.

Having conscientiously studied his schedule, Passepartout was pretty startled to find Mr. Fogg guilty of incorrectness and showing up at this abnormal hour. According to the memo, the tenant at 7 Savile Row wasn't due back till the stroke of midnight.

Right away Phileas Fogg went up to his bedroom, then he called:

"Passepartout."

Passepartout didn't reply. This call couldn't be meant for him. It wasn't time.

"Passepartout," Mr. Fogg said again, still without raising his voice.

Passepartout put in an appearance.

"That's twice I've called you," Mr. Fogg said.

"But it isn't midnight," Passepartout replied, watch in hand.

"I know," Phileas Fogg went on, "and I'm not reprimanding you. We're leaving for Dover and Calais in ten minutes."

A sort of pained look spread over the Frenchman's round face. Obviously he was losing his hearing.

"You're going somewhere, master?" he asked.

"Yes," Phileas Fogg replied. "We're traveling around the world."

Passepartout gaped outrageously, eyelids and eyebrows raised, arms flung wide, body collapsing, giving every sign of someone who's amazed to the point of befuddlement.

"Around the world?" he mumbled.

"In eighty days," Mr. Fogg replied. "So we haven't a moment to lose."

"But what about packing our trunks?" Passepartout said, his head unconsciously swaying from right to left.

"There won't be any trunks. Just my overnight bag. Put two woolen shirts inside and three pairs of socks. The same for you. We'll buy what we need on the way. Fetch down my raincoat and travel blanket. Take some sturdy shoes. Even so, we won't do much walking. Go."

Passepartout wanted to reply. He couldn't. He left Mr. Fogg's bedroom, went up to his own, fell into a chair, and used an expression that was fairly popular back where he came from:

"Well, if this doesn't take the cake! And all I wanted was peace and quiet . . . !"

And moving like a machine, he prepared for his departure. Around the world in eighty days! Was he dealing with a madman? No. . . . Was it a joke? They were off to Dover—fine. To Calais—so be it. And yet it wouldn't be too awfully aggravating, because five years had gone by since the gallant fellow had set foot in his native land. Maybe they would even go to Paris, and ye gods, what fun it would be to see that great metropolis again. But a gentleman so thrifty with his footsteps was certain to come to a halt at that point. . . . Yes, definitely, though it was true nevertheless that he was leaving and running off, this gentleman who had been such a homebody till then!

By eight o'clock Passepartout had packed the humble bag that held his own wardrobe and his master's; then, still uneasy in his mind, he carefully shut his bedroom door and rejoined Mr. Fogg.

Mr. Fogg was ready. Tucked under his arm was *Bradshaw's Continental Railway, Steam Transit & General Guide*, which would provide him with all the particulars his journey needed. He took the bag from

---

[5] *Translator's note.* A guinea is one pound one shilling, so twenty were equivalent at the time to about $100 in U.S. currency; in today's dollars its purchasing power would be comparable to about $2,000.

Passepartout's hands, opened it, and slid into it a substantial stack of those handsome banknotes that are honored in every country.

"You haven't forgotten anything?" he asked.

"Nothing, sir."

"My raincoat and travel blanket?"

"Right here."

"Fine, carry this bag."

Mr. Fogg handed the bag back to Passepartout.

"And be careful with it," he added. "It has £20,000 inside."

The bag nearly slipped out of Passepartout's hands, as if the £20,000 had been solid gold and weighed accordingly.

Then master and manservant went down to the street, double locking the front door behind them.

A cabstand was at the end of Savile Row. Phileas Fogg and his manservant climbed into a carriage and drove swiftly to Charing Cross Station, the last stop on one of the branch lines of the Southeastern Railway.

At 8:20 their cab pulled up at the gate of the terminal. Passepartout jumped to the ground. His master followed suit, paying off the cabbie.

Standing barefoot in the mud was a poor beggar woman who held a child by the hand, wore a shabby hat with a pitiful drooping feather, and had a tattered shawl over her rags; just then she came up to Mr. Fogg and asked for alms.

Mr. Fogg reached into his pocket, took out the twenty guineas he'd recently won at whist, and handed them to the beggar woman:

"There you are, my good lady," he said. "Pleased to meet you!"

Then on he went.

Passepartout felt a little moisture in the vicinity of his pupils. His master had gone up a notch in his esteem.

He and Mr. Fogg immediately entered the main waiting room at the terminal. There Phileas Fogg instructed Passepartout to buy two first-class tickets to Paris. Then, turning around, he spotted his five colleagues from the Reform Club.

"Gentlemen, I'm on my way," he said.

"And when I come back, you'll be able to double-check my itinerary against the different visa stamps on the passport I'm carrying for that purpose."

"Oh, that isn't necessary, Mr. Fogg," Walter Ralph replied diplomatically. "We'll rely on your word as a gentleman."

"My procedure is best," Mr. Fogg said.

"You won't forget when you're due back . . . ?" Andrew Stuart pointed out.

"In eighty days," Mr. Fogg replied. "By 8:45 on Saturday evening, December 21. Good-bye till then, gentlemen."

At 8:40 Phileas Fogg and his manservant took their seats in the same compartment. At 8:45 a whistle blew and the train moved out.

It was a black night. A light rain fell. Propped in his corner, Phileas Fogg didn't say a word. Still in a daze, Passepartout hugged the bag of banknotes in a machinelike grip.

But before the train had gone past Sydenham, Passepartout let out a genuine howl of despair!

"What is it?" Mr. Fogg asked.

"It's . . . it's that . . . I was in such a hurry . . . I was so bothered . . . that I forgot . . ."

"Forgot what?"

"To turn off the gas jet in my bedroom!"

"Well, my lad," Mr. Fogg replied coolly, "it will burn at your own expense."

5

*In which a new share shows up
on the London stock market*

AS HE LEFT LONDON, Phileas Fogg surely had no inkling of the huge uproar his departure was about to cause. First the news of his bet flew around the Reform Club, generating real excitement among the members of that respectable fellowship. Next, thanks to various reporters, this excitement went from the club to the newspapers, then from the newspapers to the populace of London and the entire United Kingdom.

This "going-around-the-world business" gave rise to comments, arguments, and analyses that were as eager and impassioned as if they concerned a new set of *Alabama* Claims.[6] Some sided with Phileas Fogg, while others—and they soon formed a substantial majority—took stands against him. However it might look on paper or the drawing board, to actually go around the world in this minimum time, with the means of transportation currently available, was insane, simply impossible!

The *Times, Evening Standard, Morning Chronicle, Evening Star*, and twenty other newspapers of great renown came out against Mr. Fogg. Only the *Daily Telegraph* backed him to any extent. Phileas Fogg was largely regarded as a maniac, a madman, and his colleagues at the Reform Club were denounced for going along with this bet, whose initiator clearly suffered from softening of the brain.

Articles appeared on the matter that were both well reasoned and tremendously impassioned. As you know, the English are interested in anything having to do with geography. Accordingly there wasn't a reader in the land, of any economic class, who didn't gobble up the columns of print devoted to the Phileas Fogg affair.

Early on a few daring souls—chiefly female—were all for him, especially when the *Illustrated London News* borrowed a photograph on file in the Reform Club's records and published his portrait. "Hear, hear," some gentlemen also dared to say. "After all, why not? Stranger things have happened!" These were mainly the *Daily Telegraph*'s readers. But soon even this newspaper noticeably started to back off.

In essence a lengthy article appeared in the October 7th bulletin from the Royal Geographical Society. It dealt with the issue from every viewpoint and clearly established the insanity of the undertaking. According to this article, the traveler had everything going against him, both human obstacles and natu-

ral obstacles. To pull off this scheme, he needed to figure on a miraculous matching up of departure and arrival times, but there wasn't and couldn't be any such matchup. When push comes to shove, you can depend on trains in Europe arriving on schedule, since the distances they cover are comparatively short; but when they take three days to cross India and seven days to cross the United States, can you bank on the pieces of such a puzzle punctually fitting together? Engines conk out, jump the tracks, have collisions, face foul weather, run into snowdrifts—and wasn't Phileas Fogg up against all these things? Then, traveling by ocean liner, wouldn't he be at the mercy of winter blasts and fogs? In the international shipping world, was it so rare for even top-of-the-line vessels to face delays of two or three days? Now then, just one delay was all it would take to snap his chain of connections beyond repair. If Phileas Fogg missed the departure of a single ocean liner, even by a few hours, he would have to wait for the next liner, and by the same token his journey would be hopelessly jeopardized.

This article made a big noise. Nearly all the newspapers reprinted it, and Phileas Fogg's stock fell significantly.

During the days right after the gentleman's departure, the "risk factor" in his endeavor inspired some major bookmaking transactions. As you know, the English betting world has loftier, more discerning standards than the rest of the gambling world. Betting is in the English national character. Accordingly, not only did various members of the Reform Club place considerable bets for or against Phileas Fogg, but the general public climbed on the bandwagon. The name Phileas Fogg was entered in a sort of studbook as if he were a race horse. He was also converted into shares and immediately quoted on the London stock market. "Phileas Foggs" were bought and sold at face value or at a premium and they did tremendous business. But five days after his departure, after that article in the Geographical Society's bulletin, there was a rush to sell. Phileas Foggs declined. They were offered in quantity. First in batches of five, then ten,

---

[6] *Translator's note.* During the American Civil War, the UK violated its neutrality and built the warship *Alabama* for the confederacy. The U.S. government took England to international arbitration and claimed damages.

and ultimately no less than twenty, fifty, or a hundred!

He had just one supporter left. This was elderly, paralyzed Lord Albemarle. Stuck in his armchair, this distinguished nobleman would have given his whole fortune and ten years of his life to go around the world! He bet £5,000 ($25,000) that Phileas Fogg would succeed. And anytime somebody spelled out the scheme's foolishness and pointlessness for him, he was content to reply: "If the thing can be done, it would be good for an Englishman to do it first!"

Now then, that's where matters stood and supporters of Phileas Fogg were growing scarcer and scarcer; everybody sided against him, and with good reason; acceptable odds were at least 150 or 200 to 1, when, thanks to a totally unexpected incident a week after his departure, the bottom dropped out of things completely.

In essence, at nine o'clock in the evening on that day, Scotland Yard's commissioner of police received a telegram that ran like this:

Police Commissioner Rowan
Central Administration, Scotland Yard
London

Am tailing bank robber, one Phileas Fogg. Send arrest warrant immediately to Bombay, British India.

Detective Inspector Fix
Suez.

This wire had an immediate impact. The respectable gentleman vanished and in his place stood the man who stole the banknotes. His photograph was on file at the Reform Club along with those of all his colleagues, and the authorities examined it. Feature for feature it duplicated the physical description furnished by the official inquiry. People remembered Phileas Fogg's secretive lifestyle, his solitary habits, his sudden departure, and it seemed obvious that this individual, using the excuse of an around-the-world trip based on an insane bet, had the sole aim of outfoxing investigators from the English police force.

6

*In which Fix the investigator
is understandably impatient*

THE WIRE CONCERNING this Phileas Fogg fellow had been fired off under the following circumstances.

On Wednesday, October 9, at eleven o'clock in the morning, folks were waiting in Suez for the ocean liner *Mongolia* of the Peninsular & Oriental Steam Navigation Co., an iron-hulled, propeller-driven steamer that boasted an upper deck, weighed nearly 3,100 tons, and was on the books as having 500-horsepower engines. The *Mongolia* did a regular run from Brindisi to Bombay by way of the Suez Canal. It was one of the company's fastest racers and always exceeded the scheduled speeds, which were 10 miles per hour from Brindisi to Suez and 9.53 miles per hour from Suez to Bombay.

While waiting for the *Mongolia* to arrive, two men strolled along the pier through the crowds of locals and foreigners pouring into this town—recently a village but with a considerable future ahead, since, thanks to the tremendous efforts of France's Mr. de Lesseps, the canal was now open for business.

One of these two men ran the consulate that the United Kingdom had set up in Suez; in spite of dire prophecies by the British government and grim predictions from Stephenson the engineer, this official saw English ships go through the canal every day, which took only half as long as the old England-to-India route around the Cape of Good Hope.

The other, a skinny little man, had rather crafty, twitchy features and kept knitting his brow in a conspicuous way. Behind his long lashes gleamed a keen pair of eyes, but he could dim their luster at will. Just then he was showing distinct signs of impatience, pacing back and forth, unable to hold still.

The man's name was Fix and he was one of those "masters of detection," one of those investigators from the English police force who had been dispatched to various ports after that robbery committed at the Bank of

England. With the greatest care this man Fix was to keep an eye on every traveler going by way of Suez, and if one of them seemed suspicious, to "stay on his tail" till a warrant for his arrest had arrived.

Sure enough, two days earlier Scotland Yard's commissioner of police had sent Fix a physical description of the man who supposedly perpetrated the robbery. It gave particulars about that well-dressed, refined-looking individual whom bank staff had noticed in the cash payments room.

His successful capture would earn a substantial reward, and this obviously had strong appeal for the detective, who was waiting for the *Mongolia*'s arrival with an impatience you can easily appreciate.

"And you're sure, Mr. Consul," he asked for the tenth time, "that this boat can't be much longer?"

"No, Mr. Fix," the consul replied. "It was sighted yesterday off Port Said, and a hundred miles of canal are nothing for such a speedy vessel. I'll mention again that the *Mongolia* has always earned that £25 bonus the government offers whenever a ship runs twenty-four hours ahead of schedule."

"This ocean liner comes straight here from Brindisi?" Fix asked.

"Right from Brindisi, where it picked up the mail for India, and it left Brinidisi Saturday at five o'clock in the afternoon. So be patient, it'll arrive before much longer. But if your man's aboard the *Mongolia*, I honestly don't see how you'll be able to identify him from the description you've got."

"Mr. Consul," Fix replied, "we scent these fellows rather than identify them. You need to have a nose for it, and this nose is like a special organ that combines hearing, seeing, and smelling. I've arrested more than one of these gentlemen in my day, and if my robber's on board, I assure you he won't slip through my fingers."

"I hope not, Mr. Fix, because there's a major robbery involved here."

"A magnificent robbery!" the investigator replied excitedly. "£55,000! We don't get a bonanza like this very often! Our master burglars have turned into petty thieves! Escape artists like John Sheppard are a dying breed!

Today's crooks get hung for stealing a couple shillings!"

"Mr. Fix," the consul replied, "with an attitude like yours, I sincerely hope you succeed; but I'll mention again that I'm afraid it'll be difficult in your present circumstances. Based on the description you've got, surely you realize this robber looks exactly like a respectable man."

"Mr. Consul," the police inspector replied dogmatically, "accomplished robbers always look like respectable fellows. As you can easily appreciate, people with faces like scalawags have no choice but to stay honest or be arrested. Those with respectable features are the ones you especially need to see through. Hard work, I admit, but it isn't just a job—it's an art."

As you can see, the aforesaid Mr. Fix had his fair share of vanity.

Meanwhile the pier gradually got busier. Seamen of various nationalities, tradespeople, brokers, porters, and rustics were pouring in. Obviously it was nearly time for the ocean liner to arrive.

The sky was pretty clear, but the wind blew from the east and the air was chilly. In the pale sunlight a few minarets stood out above the town. A jetty to the south, 1¼ miles long, reached like an arm to the offshore mooring of Suez. Wheeling around on the surface of the Red Sea were several fishing and coastal vessels, a few of them built along the stylish lines of an old-time galley.

Out of professional habit Fix gave every passerby the once-over as he moved through these working-class crowds.

By then it was 10:30.

"And that ocean liner still hasn't arrived!" he exclaimed when he heard the harbor clock striking.

"It can't be far off," the consul responded.

"How long will it lay over in Suez?" Fix asked.

"Four hours. Long enough to take on coal. It needs to replenish its fuel supply, because it has to cover 1,310 miles from Suez to Aden at the lower end of the Red Sea."

"And does this boat go straight from Suez to Bombay?" Fix asked.

"Straight there, without any cargo stops."

"Well then," Fix said, "if the robber took this route and this boat, he must have a plan to jump ship in Suez, then go by some other way to the Dutch or French possessions in Asia. He must be well aware there's no safety for him in India, since it's English territory."

"Unless he's a very clever man," the consul replied. "As you know, an English criminal is always better off hiding in London than in foreign parts."

While the investigator gave this idea some thought, the consul headed back to his office, which was located a short distance away. Left on his own, filled with nervous impatience, the police inspector had a peculiar hunch that his robber was destined to be aboard the *Mongolia*—and in actuality, if the rogue had left England bound for the New World, he was sure to choose the route through India, which was less closely watched, or harder to watch, than the Atlantic route.

Fix wasn't lost in thought for long. Sharp toots from a whistle announced the ocean liner's arrival. The whole mob of porters and rustics rushed down to the pier, a wild dash that left a few traces on the limbs and attire of waiting passengers. Ten or so dinghies shoved off from the bank and headed out to wait for the *Mongolia*.

Soon you could see the *Mongolia*'s gigantic hull moving along between the banks of the canal, and as eleven o'clock was striking, the steamer dropped anchor at the offshore mooring, steam from its exhaust pipes making a huge racket.

There were a fair number of passengers on board. A few of them stayed on the upper deck to view the picturesque panorama of the town; but most of them went ashore in the dinghies that had pulled alongside the *Mongolia*.

Fix scrupulously examined every person who set foot on land.

Just then one of them came toward him, energetically repulsed the rustics who closed in with offers of assistance, and very courteously asked if the detective could point to the office of the English consulate. At the same time this passenger held out a passport, no doubt wanting to get a British visa stamp.

Fix automatically took the passport and read the description in it with one quick glance.

He all but jumped out of his skin. The paperwork trembled in his hand. The description set forth in the passport was identical to the one he'd gotten from Scotland Yard's commissioner of police.

"This passport isn't yours?" he said to the passenger.

"No," the latter replied, "it's my master's passport."

"And where's your master?"

"He's staying on board."

"But," the investigator went on, "he needs to show up in person at the office of the consulate, to establish his identity."

"What! Is that necessary?"

"Essential."

"And where's this office?"

"There, on that side of the square," the inspector replied, pointing to the consul's quarters some 200 steps away.

"Then I'll go get my master, but he won't take kindly to being bothered this way!"

On that note the passenger nodded to Fix and went back aboard the steamer.

7

Which demonstrates once again that passports are no help in police work

THE INSPECTOR went back down the pier and quickly headed over to the consul's office. At his urgent request he was instantly ushered into that functionary's presence.

"Mr. Consul," he told him without any further preamble, "I have solid grounds for believing our fellow's traveling aboard the *Mongolia*."

And Fix described what had gone on between the manservant and himself regarding the passport.

"Well, Mr. Fix," the consul replied, "It wouldn't pain me to see the rascal's face. But if he's the man you assume, maybe he won't show up at my office. Robbers don't like to leave trails behind them—and besides, the formality of showing your passport isn't required anymore."

"Mr. Consul," the investigator replied, "if he's the clever man we think he is, he'll come!"

"To get a visa stamp on his passport?"

"Right. Passports are good only for inconveniencing respectable folks and helping rascals get away. This one will be all in order, I assure you, but I sincerely hope you won't stamp it."

"And why not?" the consul replied. "If his passport's in order, I haven't any right to deny him his visa stamp."

"But Mr. Consul, I've got to keep this man here till I receive a warrant for his arrest from London."

"Aha! That, Mr. Fix, is *your* concern," the consul replied. "But as for me, I can't—"

The consul didn't finish his sentence. Right then there was a knock on his study door and the office boy ushered two strangers in, one of them the very manservant who had just conversed with the detective.

The master had indeed come along with his valet. The master held out his passport, requesting with Spartan brevity that the consul kindly add his visa stamp.

The latter took the passport and read it carefully, while Fix watched from a corner of the study, devouring the stranger with his eyes.

When the consul was finished reading:

"You're Phileas Fogg, Esq.?" he asked.

"Yes, sir," the gentleman replied.

"And this fellow's your manservant?"

"Yes. A Frenchman known as Passepartout."

"You've come from London?"

"Yes."

"And you're going where?"

"To Bombay."

"Very good, sir. You're aware that this formality of visa stamps isn't necessary, that we aren't required to show our passports anymore?"

"I'm aware of it, sir," Phileas Fogg replied, "but I want your visa stamp as proof that I've traveled by way of Suez."

"As you wish, sir."

And after signing and dating the passport, the consul stamped it with his seal. Mr. Fogg paid the certification fee, nodded coolly, and left with his manservant at his heels.

"Well?" the inspector asked.

"Well," the consul answered, "he looks like a perfectly respectable man!"

"Even if he does," Fix replied, "that isn't the issue. Don't you see, Mr. Consul, that this stoic gentleman resembles, feature for feature, the robber whose description I've received?"

"I grant you, but as you're aware, every description . . ."

"I'm going to get to the bottom of this," Fix responded. "The manservant strikes me as easier to puzzle out than his master. Furthermore he's a Frenchman, so he won't be able to keep his mouth shut. See you later, Mr. Consul."

With that the investigator left to start looking for Passepartout.

Meanwhile, after leaving the quarters of the consulate, Mr. Fogg headed toward the pier. There he gave a few instructions to his manservant; next, climbing into a dinghy, he went back aboard the *Mongolia* and reentered his cabin. Then he picked up his notebook, which contained the following remarks:

Left London, Wednesday, October 2, at 8:45 in the evening.

Arrived in Paris, Thursday, October 3, at 7:20 in the morning.

Left Paris, Thursday at 8:40 in the morning.

Arrived in Turin by way of Mt. Cenis, Friday, October 4, at 6:35 in the morning.

Left Turin, Friday, at 7:20 in the morning.

Arrived in Brindisi, Saturday, October 5, at 4:00 in the afternoon.

Sailed on the Mongolia, *Saturday, at 5:00 in the afternoon.*

Arrived in Suez, Wednesday, October 9, at 11:00 in the morning.

Total hours spent: 158½, hence 6½ days.

Mr. Fogg had recorded these dates in an itinerary organized into columns, which indicated (from October 2 to December 21) the month, date, day, scheduled arrival, and actual arrival at each major stop, Paris, Brindisi, Suez, Bombay, Calcutta, Singapore, Hong Kong, Yokohama, San Francisco, New York, Liverpool, and London; he was able to compute the time gained or lost on each leg of his journey.

Consequently this systematic itinerary kept track of everything, and Mr. Fogg always knew whether he was behind or ahead of schedule.

So when he recorded his arrival in Suez on that day of Wednesday, October 9, it matched the scheduled arrival and amounted to neither a gain nor a loss.

Then he had his lunch brought up to his cabin. As for looking over the town, he never even gave it a thought, since he belonged to that race of Englishmen who see the countries they cross only through the eyes of their servants.

8

*In which Passepartout says a bit
more than maybe he ought to*

IN A FEW SECONDS Fix had rejoined Passepartout on the pier, where he was sauntering along like a tourist, not feeling that he, at least, had to refrain from looking things over.

"Well, my friend," Fix said, buttonholing him, "did you get that visa stamp on your passport?"

"Oh, it's you, sir," the Frenchman replied. "Much obliged. We're fine, everything's in order."

"And you're touring the country?"

"Yes, but we're going so fast, I seem to be traveling in a dream. And as for this place, it's Suez?"

"It's Suez."

"In Egypt?"

"In Egypt, correct."

"And in Africa?"

"In Africa."

"In Africa!" Passepartout echoed. "I can't believe it! Just think, sir—I imagined we wouldn't go any farther than Paris and I revisited that famed metropolis from only 7:20 to 8:40 in the morning, between the Northern and Lyons railway terminals, through a cab window, and while it was raining cats and dogs! I was so disappointed! I would have loved to see the Père Lachaise Cemetery again and the Champs Élysées Circus!"

"So you're in quite a rush?" the police inspector asked.

"I'm not, but my master is. Speaking of which, I need to buy some socks and shirts! We left without any luggage, just an overnight bag."

"I'll take you to a bazaar where you'll find everything you need."

"Really, sir," Passepartout replied, "you're very kind . . . !"

And the two went off together. Passepartout talked nonstop.

"Above all," he said, "I must be very careful not to miss the boat!"

"You've got time," Fix replied. "It's barely noon."

Passepartout tugged out his big watch.

"Noon!" he said. "Come on! It's 9:52!"

"Your watch is slow," Fix replied.

"My watch? This watch that has been in my family, that has been handed down from my great-grandfather? After a whole year it isn't off even five minutes. It's an authentic chronometer!"

"I see what the problem is," Fix replied. "You're still on London time, which is, um, two hours behind Suez. You should make a point of resetting your watch at noon in each country."

"Me tamper with my watch?" Passepartout exclaimed. "Never!"

"Well then, it won't agree with the sun."

"Too bad for the sun, sir! It'll be the party at fault!"

And the gallant fellow put his watch back in his vest pocket with a haughty flourish.

A few seconds later Fix said to him:

"So you left London in a hurry?"

"I'll say! Last Wednesday at eight o'clock in the evening, completely contrary to his daily habits, Mr. Fogg came back from his club, and forty-five minutes later we left home."

"But where's your master off to?"

"He's just following his nose! He's going around the world!"

"Around the world?" Fix exclaimed.

"Yes, in eighty days! On a bet, he says, but between ourselves I don't buy it. It's against all common sense. There's something else going on."

"Ah, so he's eccentric, this Mr. Fogg?"

"That's what I gather."

"He's a wealthy man, then?"

"Apparently, and he's carrying a goodly sum along with him in brand-new banknotes! And he isn't pinching pennies on the way! Get this—he promised a magnificent bonus to the *Mongolia*'s head mechanic if we reach Bombay well ahead of schedule!"

"And have you known your master a long while?"

"Me?" Passepartout answered. "I started working for him the same day we left."

The reader can easily imagine the effect these answers had to have on the police inspector, whose brain was already in a tizzy.

The gentleman's hasty departure from London soon after the robbery, the large sum he carried with him, his hurry to reach these distant lands, and his excuse of an eccentric bet all inevitably corroborated what Fix had been thinking. He kept the Frenchman talking and became convinced that the fellow didn't know a thing about his master, that the latter lived a solitary life in London, that he was said to be wealthy though the source of his fortune wasn't known, that he was an impregnably secretive man, etc. But at the same time, Fix could see for certain that Phileas Fogg wasn't getting off in Suez, that he was actually going on to Bombay.

"Is Bombay far?" Passepartout asked.

"Pretty far," the investigator replied. "It'll take you about ten more days by sea."

"And just where is Bombay?"

"In India."

"Part of Asia?"

"Of course."

"Holy smoke! I have a confession to make . . . there's just one thing that has me worried . . . it's my gas jet!"

"Gas jet?"

"In my bedroom—I forgot to turn it off and it's burning at my expense. Now then, I've calculated I'll be out two shillings every twenty-four hours, exactly sixpence more than I make, and you can understand that the longer our journey goes on . . ."

Did Fix really understand this gaseous matter? It didn't seem likely. He'd stopped listening and was reaching a decision. He and the Frenchman had arrived at the bazaar. Fix left his companion to his shopping, advised him to not be late for the *Mongolia*'s departure, and returned with great speed to the office of the consulate.

Now that he was sure he was right, Fix had fully recovered his composure.

"Sir," he told the consul, "there's no longer any doubt in my mind. I've got my man. He's giving out that he's an eccentric who's trying to go around the world in eighty days."

"Then he's a trickster," the consul replied, "and after he totally outfoxes the police in both the New World and the Old, he's figuring on going back to London!"

"We'll see about that," Fix replied.

"But could you be mistaken?" the consul asked yet again.

"I'm not mistaken."

"Then why was this robber so bent on getting a visa stamp to prove he'd traveled by way of Suez?"

"Why?" the detective responded. "I haven't the faintest idea, Mr. Consul, but hear me out."

And in a few words, he reported the highlights of his conversation with the suspect Fogg's manservant.

"In essence," the consul said, "appearances are dead against this man. And what are you going to do?"

"Fire off a telegram to London, ask that an arrest warrant be sent immediately to Bombay, set sail on the *Mongolia*, tail my robber to India, and there on English soil politely pull alongside him, warrant in one hand, other hand on his shoulder."

Coolly uttering these words, the investigator took his leave of the consul and proceeded to the telegraph office. There he fired off to Scotland Yard's police commissioner the wire you're acquainted with.

Carrying his little travel bag, flush with funds, Fix climbed aboard the *Mongolia* fifteen minutes later, and that high-speed liner was soon going full steam ahead over the waters of the Red Sea.

9

Where the Red Sea and the Indian Ocean cooperate with Phileas Fogg's objectives

THE DISTANCE BETWEEN Suez and Aden is 1,310 miles on the button, and the company's specifications give ocean liners a travel time of 138 hours. Energetically pushing its furnaces, the *Mongolia* was making such good progress that it promised to arrive ahead of schedule.

Most of the passengers had come on board in Brindisi and were almost exclusively bound for India. Some were proceeding to Bombay, others to Calcutta—but by way of Bombay, because, now that a railroad runs across India's entire peninsula, it's no longer necessary to double the tip of Ceylon.

Included in the *Mongolia*'s passengers were various civil functionaries and military officers of every rank. Among the latter were some who belonged to the British Army proper, others who commanded the native Sepoy troops, all of them highly paid, even these days after the government had taken over the rights and responsibilities of the old East India Company: second lieutenants earn the equivalent of $1,400 per year, brigadiers $12,000, generals $20,000.[7]

So folks lived high on the hog aboard the *Mongolia;*[8] mixed in with this gathering of functionaries were a few young Englishmen who had millions in their pockets and were off to set up colonial trading posts. The "purser" was the company's confidential representative as well as the captain's equal on board, and he did things in grand style. At morning breakfast, 2:00 lunch, 5:30 dinner, and 8:00 supper, the ship's tables groaned under platters of cold cuts and desserts provided by the liner's meat locker and pantries. Female passengers—there were a few—changed their gowns and makeup twice a day. Folks played music and even danced when the sea was amenable.

But the Red Sea is very flighty and often thoroughly out of sorts, as is true of all long narrow channels. When the wind blew from either the Asian or African coasts, it caught the *Mongolia* at an angle and the long, spindle-shaped, propeller-driven vessel rolled frightfully. Then the ladies vanished, the pianos fell still, the singing and dancing broke off instantly. Yet despite the wind and waves, the ocean liner, driven by its mighty engines, made uninterrupted headway toward the Strait of Bab el Mandeb.

What was Phileas Fogg doing all this time? Wouldn't you expect him to be constantly worried and nervous, concerned about the wind's shifting and impeding the ship's progress, about wildly surging billows that threatened to damage the engines, about, in short, very possible form of breakdown that could force the *Mongolia* to put into some port and jeopardize his journey?

Not at all, or at the very least, the gentleman didn't let on that he was considering these possibilities. He was the same unemotional man, the same unflappable member of the Reform Club whom no incident or accident could surprise. He showed no more feeling than the ship's chronometers. You rarely saw him on deck. He didn't bother to take the briefest look at this Red Sea that was so rich in memories, this stage for the earliest dra-

---

[7] Civil functionaries are paid even higher salaries. Mere aides on the bottom rung of the hierarchy make the equivalent of $2,400 per year, magistrates $12,000, presiding court judges $50,000, governors $60,000, and the governor-general over $120,000. (Author's note)

[8] *Translator's note.* To find out *how* high, multiply these salaries by twenty; this will give their approximate purchasing power in today's dollars.

mas in human history. He didn't come up and scout out the interesting towns that were scattered along its shores, their picturesque shapes sometimes silhouetted against the horizon. He didn't even ponder the dangers of this Arabic body of water, which such ancient historians as Strabo, Arrian, Artemidorus, and Idrisi always spoke of with horror, and over which old-time navigators ventured only after blessing their voyages with sacrifices to appease the gods.

So what was this eccentric individual up to while he was confined aboard the *Mongolia?* First of all he ate his four meals per day, without the ship's rolling and pitching ever throwing his marvelously coordinated mechanism out of gear. Then he played whist.

That's right! He'd turned up some card partners who were as zealous as he was: a tax collector making his way to his post in Goa, a preacher named Reverend Decimus Smith who was heading back to Bombay, and a brigadier general in the British Army who was rejoining his unit in Benares. These three passengers shared Mr. Fogg's passion for whist and they played for hours on end, just as closemouthed as he was.

As for Passepartout, he was immune to seasickness. He occupied a cabin in the bow and likewise ate all his meals conscientiously. It definitely needs to be said that when their journey proceeded under conditions such as these, it didn't upset him anymore. He could accept it. Well fed, well housed, he saw the sights and meanwhile told himself that the whole pipedream would come to an end in Bombay.

On October 10, the day after leaving Suez, he climbed on deck and was pleasantly surprised to bump into that obliging individual he'd spoken to when he went ashore in Egypt.

"If I'm not mistaken, sir," he said, buttonholing the man with his cheeriest smile, "aren't you the fellow who was kind enough to act as my guide in Suez?"

"So I am," the detective replied. "And I remember you! You're the manservant of that eccentric Englishman . . ."

"That's right, Mr.—"

"Fix."

"Mr. Fix," Passepartout replied. "I'm delighted to find you on board. So where are you headed?"

"Why, the same place you are—Bombay."

"All the better! Have you made this voyage before?"

"Several times," Fix replied. "I'm a representative of the Peninsular & Oriental Co."

"Then you're familiar with India?"

"Why . . . yes . . . ," Fix replied, not wanting to overdo it.

"Is India an interesting place?"

"Quite interesting! Mosques, minarets, temples, beggar monks, pagodas, tigers, snakes, and dancing girls! But you'll have time to see the country, I hope?"

"I hope so too, Mr. Fix. As you're well aware, it isn't acceptable for a man of sound mind to spend his life hopping from ocean liners to railways and from railways back to ocean liners, all with some excuse of going around the world in eighty days! No, these acrobatics will come to a full stop in Bombay, count on it."

"And is he doing all right, your Mr. Fogg?" Fix asked in his most offhand tone.

"Perfectly all right, Mr. Fix. And the same goes for me. I eat like an underfed ogre. It's this salt air."

"And yet I never see your master on deck."

"Never. He isn't the inquisitive type."

"You know, Mr. Passepartout, this so-called journey in eighty days could well be a cover for some secret mission . . . a diplomatic mission, for instance!"

"Ye gods, Mr. Fix, I swear I don't know a thing about it, and when all's said and done, I wouldn't pay even half a crown to find out."

After this encounter Passepartout and Fix often chatted together. The police inspector kept up his friendship with the manservant of this Fogg fellow. It might come in handy on occasion. Consequently he often stood the Frenchman a couple rounds of whiskey or pale ale in the *Mongolia*'s taproom—the gallant lad cheerfully accepted them, returned the compliment so as not to be outdone, and all the while found this Mr. Fix a gentleman and a scholar.

In the meantime the ocean liner made rapid headway. On the 13th it raised Mocha, which came in sight with its girdle of ruined walls, a few leafy date trees standing out above them. Huge coffee plantations were thriving in the distant mountains. Passepartout found this famous town delightful to contemplate, and he even felt that with those circular walls and that broken-down fort shaped like a handle, it looked like an enormous coffee cup.

The following night the *Mongolia* cleared the Strait of Bab el Mandeb, an Arabic name that translates as "Gate of Tears," and the next day, the 14th, the ship called at Steamer Point, northwest of the offshore mooring of Aden. Which was where it would take on fuel.

When it's this far away from any mining district, feeding an ocean liner's furnace is a serious and important concern. The Peninsular Co. thinks nothing of incurring an annual expense of £800,000 (about $4,000,000) at this activity. In fact the company found it essential to set up fueling stations in several ports, and in these far-off seas coal went for $18 per ton.

The *Mongolia* still had 1,650 miles to go before reaching Bombay and it had a four-hour layover in Steamer Point for the purpose of filling up its coal bunkers.

But this delay couldn't do the slightest harm to Phileas Fogg's schedule. He was expecting it. Besides, instead of reaching Aden merely by the morning of October 15, the *Mongolia* had arrived there the evening of the 14th. Which was a gain of fifteen hours.

Mr. Fogg and his manservant went ashore. The gentleman wanted a visa stamp on his passport. Fix followed them without their noticing. Finished with the formality of the visa stamp, Phileas Fogg went back on board to resume his interrupted card game.

With regard to Passepartout, as usual he was out sauntering around, mixing with that populace of Somalis, Banyans, Parsis, Jews, Arabs, and Europeans who constitute the 25,000 residents of Aden. He marveled at the fortifications that make this town the Gibraltar of the Indian Ocean, as well as the magnificent water tanks that English engineers were working on again, 2,000 years after the engineers under King Solomon.

"It's all so interesting!" Passepartout told himself, coming back on board. "Traveling isn't as pointless as I thought, if you're open to seeing new things."

At six o'clock in the evening, the *Mongolia*'s propeller blades churned the waters of Aden's offshore mooring, and soon the ship was racing across the Indian Ocean. It had been allotted 168 hours for the run from Aden to Bombay. What's more, the Indian Ocean itself was cooperative. There was a steady wind out of the northwest. Sail power could come to the aid of steam power.

With this increased support, the ship rolled less. Female passengers freshened up and reappeared on deck. The singing and dancing started again.

Their voyage was proceeding under optimum conditions. Passepartout was delighted with the genial companion fortune had found for him in the person of Mr. Fix.

Toward noontime on Sunday, October 20, they raised the coast of India. Two hours later the harbor pilot climbed aboard the *Mongolia*. Hills ran across the far reaches of the horizon, pleasingly outlined against the background of the sky. Soon the rows of palm trees shielding the town stood out clearly. The ocean liner cruised through the offshore mooring set up between Colaba, Salsette, Butcher, and Elephanta islands, and at 4:30 it pulled alongside a Bombay pier.

Right then Phileas Fogg was finishing his thirty-third rubber of the day, and thanks to a daring move, he and his partner won all thirteen tricks, concluding this fine crossing with a marvelous grand slam.

The *Mongolia* wasn't due to arrive in Bombay till October 22. Now then, its actual arrival time was the 20th. So this amounted to a gain of two days since he'd left London, and Phileas Fogg methodically recorded the fact in the plus column of his itinerary.

10

*Where Passepartout gets off easy
with just the loss of his shoes*

AS EVERYBODY IS AWARE, India, that big upside-down triangle with its base to the north and its point to the south, covers a surface area of 1,400,000 square miles, which are occupied by an unevenly distributed population of 180,000,000 people. The British government exercises realistic control over certain parts of this immense country. It maintains a governor-general in Calcutta, governors in Madras, Bombay, and Bengal, plus a lieutenant governor in Agra.

But British India proper has a surface area of only 700,000 square miles, which are occupied by a population of 100,000,000 to 110,000,000 people. Let's just say that a significant part of this country is still outside the Queen's authority; and inland there are some dreadfully savage regions that remain completely independent, where rajas are the true rulers.

From 1756 (when the English founded their first settlement on the site where the town of Madras stands today) down to the year when the great Sepoy Rebellion broke out, the famous East India Company was all-powerful. Little by little it took over various provinces, acquiring them from the rajas in exchange for yearly payments that it seldom if ever made; it appointed its own governor-general and all his civil and military underlings; but today it's a thing of the past, and England's possessions in India answer directly to the crown.

Accordingly the peninsula's appearance, customs, and ethnographic distinctions are subject to change on a daily basis. Formerly you traveled the country using all the old-fashioned forms of transportation—on foot, on horseback, in a cart, in a wheelbarrow, in a covered litter, riding piggyback, by carriage, etc. Today high-speed steamboats ply the Indus and Ganges rivers, and a railway crosses the entire width of India with branch lines as it goes, so Bombay is only three days from Calcutta.

The roadbed of this railway doesn't go straight across India. This distance is only 1,000 to 1,100 miles as the crow flies, and a train running at just average speed would cover it in under three days; but the railway sweeps in a loop up to Allahabad in the northern part of the peninsula, which therefore increases the distance by at least a third.

Here, in a nutshell, are the high spots along the roadbed of the Great Indian Peninsular Railway. Leaving the island of Bombay, the line crosses Salsette, vaults over to the mainland opposite Thane, clears the Western Ghats mountain chain, runs northeast as far as Burhanpur, plows through the all-but-independent territory of Bundelkhand, goes up to Allahabad, adjusts its direction eastward, meets the Ganges by Benares, veers away a little, heads back down to the southeast past Burdwan and the French town of Chandernagore, then reaches the end of the line in Calcutta.

The *Mongolia*'s passengers went ashore in Bombay at 4:30 in the afternoon, and the train for Calcutta was scheduled to pull out at eight o'clock on the dot.

Mr. Fogg took leave of his card partners, got off the ocean liner, gave his manservant a few shopping instructions, expressly advised him to be at the railway terminal before eight o'clock, and headed to the passport office, his steady step ticking the seconds like the pendulum of an astronomical clock.

Hence he wasn't planning to see any of Bombay's wonders—not its city hall, magnificent library, forts, docks, cotton market, bazaars, mosques, synagogues, Armenian churches, or the splendid pagoda on Malabar Hill adorned with its two polygon-shaped towers. He wouldn't be contemplating the masterpieces of sculpture on Elephanta Island, or its secret catacombs hidden to the southeast of the offshore mooring, or the Kanheri Caves on Salsette Island, those marvelous remnants of Buddhist architecture.

No, none of it was for him! After leaving the passport office, Phileas Fogg serenely made his way to the railway terminal and there he sat down for dinner. Among other dishes, the headwaiter earnestly advised him to try the "wild rabbit in white wine," telling him it was superb.

Phileas Fogg ordered the rabbit and sampled it conscientiously; but despite its highly spiced sauce, he found it abominable.

He rang for the headwaiter.

"Sir," he said, looking intently at the man, "is this really rabbit?"

"Yes, milord," the ruffian replied brazenly. "Jungle rabbit."

"And this rabbit didn't meow when you killed it?"

"Meow? Oh, milord! A rabbit? I swear to you—"

"Don't swear, Mr. Headwaiter, and remember this one thing," Mr. Fogg continued coolly. "Cats used to be considered sacred animals in India. Those were good times."

"For cats, milord?"

"And maybe for travelers as well!"

Having passed along this comment, Mr. Fogg serenely went on with his dinner.

A few seconds after Mr. Fogg had gone ashore, Fix the investigator likewise left the *Mongolia* and raced over to the headquarters of Bombay's chief of police. He introduced himself in his capacity as detective, revealed the assignment he'd been given, and disclosed where he stood with regard to the supposed perpetrator of the robbery. Had they received an arrest warrant from London . . . ? They hadn't received a thing. And in actuality, since the warrant left after Mr. Fogg did, it couldn't have arrived as yet.

Fix was thoroughly flustered. He asked the police chief for authorization to arrest this Fogg fellow. The chief refused. The case was a Scotland Yard matter, and only they could legally issue a warrant. This insistence on sticking to principles, on strictly adhering to the letter of the law, is perfectly in keeping with English tradition, which won't tolerate anything arbitrary where personal freedoms are concerned.

Fix backed off, realizing he had no choice but to wait for his warrant. However he was determined to not lose sight of the inscrutable rascal as long as the latter remained in Bombay. He didn't doubt that Phileas Fogg would stay in town for a while (and as you know, this was also Passepartout's conviction), which would give the arrest warrant time to show up.

But after he'd received his master's latest instructions while getting off the *Mongolia*, Passepartout clearly saw that Bombay would be the same as Suez and Paris, that the journey wouldn't end here, that it would continue on at least as far as Calcutta and maybe farther. And he started to wonder if this bet of Mr. Fogg's wasn't in dead earnest, and if fate wasn't leading him—he, who wanted a life of peace and quiet—to actually go around the world in eighty days!

Meanwhile, after buying some shirts and socks, he strolled through the streets of Bombay. Hordes of working people were converging on them, including Europeans of all nationalities, Persians with pointy hats, Bunhyas with round turbans, Sindhis with square hats, Armenians in long robes, and Parsis with black miters. It so happened that these Parsis, or Ghebers, were celebrating a feast day; their sect is directly descended from Zoroaster's disciples, is the most industrious, civilized, intelligent, and ascetic of the Hindu races, and includes the wealthiest merchants currently living in Bombay. On this occasion they were celebrating a sort of religious carnival complete with processions and entertainments; the latter featured dancing girls dressed in pink gauze trimmed with gold and silver, who danced marvelously, yet with perfect decency, to the strumming of viols and the thumping of tom-toms.

As for whether Passepartout watched these unusual ceremonies, whether his eyes and ears saw and heard by opening as wide as they could, and whether his attitude and facial expression were those of the greenest nincompoop imaginable, these are things you can take for granted.

Unfortunately for him and his master, he ran the risk of jeopardizing their journey by indulging his curiosity to unacceptable lengths.

In essence, after he'd gotten a glimpse of this Parsi carnival, Passepartout was heading to the railway terminal, when he crossed in front of the wonderful pagoda on Malabar Hill and had the ill-fated idea of looking inside.

He was unaware of two things: first of all, going into certain Hindu pagodas is strictly forbidden to Christians; and beyond that, even true believers can't enter without leaving their shoes at the door. We should note here that it's the sound policy of the English government to respect the country's religion, to enforce respect for the most miniscule details of its practices, and to severely punish anybody who violates them.

Going in, meaning no harm, acting like any ordinary tourist, Passepartout stood inside the Malabar Hill temple and was marveling at the dazzling frippery of its Brahman decorations, when three priests suddenly toppled him onto its sacred flagstones. Their faces ablaze with fury, they jumped on him, tore off his shoes and socks, then started to pummel him while shrieking fiercely.

Agile and energetic, the Frenchman was back up in an instant. His opponents were seriously hampered by their long robes, and he toppled two of them with a smack of the fist and a kick of the foot, shot out of that pagoda as fast as his legs would move, and soon outstripped the third Hindu, who was hot on his heels and trying to set the crowd on him.

At 7:55, just a few minutes before the train's departure, Passepartout arrived at the railway terminal, without his hat, in his bare feet, his package of purchases left behind during the scuffle.

Fix was there on the boarding platform. Having followed this Fogg fellow to the terminal, he realized the rascal was about to leave Bombay. He instantly decided to go along with him to Calcutta, and farther if need be. Passepartout didn't see Fix, who was lurking in the shadows, but Fix heard Passepartout give his master a quick description of his adventures.

"I hope this won't happen again," Phileas Fogg merely replied, taking a seat in one of the passenger cars on the train.

Barefoot and thoroughly discomfited, the poor fellow followed his master without saying a word.

Fix was about to climb into a different passenger car, when an idea suddenly held him back and changed his travel plans.

"No, I'm staying," he said to himself.

"They broke the law on East Indian soil . . . I've got my man."

Just then the locomotive let out a mighty whistle and the train vanished into the night.

11

*Where Phileas Fogg buys a fabulously
expensive form of transportation*

THE TRAIN LEFT at the scheduled time. It carried a number of travelers, a few officers, some civil functionaries, and some traders in opium and indigo whose business called them to the eastern part of the peninsula.

Passepartout occupied the same compartment as his master. A third traveler sat in the corner facing them.

This was Brigadier General Sir Francis Cromarty, who was one of Mr. Fogg's card partners during the crossing from Suez to Bombay and who was rejoining his troops quartered near Benares.

Sir Francis Cromarty was a large, blond, fiftyish individual who had served with much distinction during the last Sepoy revolt and truly deserved to be called a native. He'd lived in India since his youth and made only rare appearances in his homeland. He was an educated man who gladly would have supplied information on the customs, history, and makeup of this Hindu country, if Phileas Fogg had been the sort to ask for it. But the gentleman didn't ask for a thing. He wasn't on a journey, he was going in a circle. He was, in all seriousness, a heavenly body following its orbit around the planet earth in line with the laws of rational mechanics. Just then he was mentally recalculating the time that had gone by since he'd left London, and if it had been in his nature to make a needless gesture, he would have rubbed his hands.

His traveling companion's eccentricity wasn't lost on Sir Francis Cromarty, though he'd studied the man only with cards in hand and in between rubbers. So he had good reason to wonder whether a human heart was throbbing under that chilly exterior, whether Phileas Fogg had a soul with any feeling for natural beauty or ethical ideals. He had his doubts. Of all the eccentrics the brigadier general had come across, none of them could compare to this exemplar of the exact sciences.

Phileas Fogg hadn't hidden from Sir Francis Cromarty his plan to travel around the world, nor the conditions under which he was proceeding. The brigadier general saw this bet as simply a form of eccentricity that served no useful purpose and was inevitably lacking in any measure of *transire benefaciendo*,[9] an ambition that ought to guide all reasonable human beings. The way this peculiar gentleman was behaving, he obviously would go though life "without doing a thing," either for himself or anybody else.

An hour after leaving Bombay, the train had crossed the viaducts, traveled through Salsette Island, and shot over to the mainland. At the station in Kalyan, a branch line on the right heads down to southeast India through Khandala and Pune, but they passed it by and went on to the station in Panvel. At this juncture their train tackled the many offshoots of the Western Ghats mountain chain, whose base is a combination of traprock and basalt and whose loftiest peaks are covered with dense woods.

Now and then Sir Francis Cromarty and Phileas Fogg exchanged a few words, and at this point, reviving a conversation that often languished, the brigadier general said:

"In this locality a few years ago, Mr. Fogg, you would have experienced a delay that very likely would have jeopardized your itinerary."

"How so, Sir Francis?"

"Because the train tracks stopped at the base of these mountains, and to cross over to the station in Khandala on the opposite slope, you had to ride a pony or travel in a covered litter."

"Such a delay wouldn't at all have upset the timing of my schedule," Mr. Fogg replied. "I never proceed without expecting that certain obstacles may arise."

"But Mr. Fogg," the brigadier general went on, "you're in danger of having a very nasty problem on your hands from this fellow's adventure."

Feet wrapped in his travel blanket, Passepartout was sound asleep and didn't dream people were talking about him.

"With that kind of infraction," Sir Francis Cromarty continued, "the English government is tremendously strict and with good reason. More than anything it insists on respect for the Hindu religious customs, and if your manservant had been caught . . ."

"Then he would have been caught, Sir Francis," Mr. Fogg replied. "He would have been found guilty, he would have served his sentence, and afterward he would have gone quietly back to Europe. I fail to see how such a business could delay his employer."

And on that note the conversation languished again. During the night the train cleared the Western Ghats mountain range, went past Nashik, and the next day, October 21, shot through the comparatively flat country that makes up the territory of Khandesh. Sizeable villages are scattered across this well-cultivated land, above which minarets and pagodas stand in for the church steeples of Europe. This fertile region is irrigated by many small watercourses, most of them branches or subbranches of the Godavari River

When he woke up, Passepartout looked out and couldn't believe he was going through this Hindu countryside in a train belonging to the Great Indian Peninsular Railway. It seemed inconceivable to him. And yet nothing could be closer to the truth! Driven by the hands of an English engineer and stoked with English coal, the locomotive blew its smoke over farms of cotton plants, coffee plants, nutmeg trees, clove trees, and red pepper bushes. Its steam curled in spirals around clumps of palm trees, and in between them you saw picturesque bungalows, a few deserted monasteries of the sort known as viharis, and some wondrous temples enhanced with the endless embellishments of India's architecture. Then immense expanses of terrain took shape as far as the eye could see, jungles with no shortage of snakes or tigers that shied away from the shrieking train, and

_____

[9] *Translator's note.* Latin: "doing good in one's lifetime."

ultimately the line's roadbed cut through some forests that were still haunted by elephants, which watched with thoughtful eyes as the whole disorderly procession went by.

That morning, beyond the station in Malegaon, our travelers crossed the deadly territory where so much blood has been spilled by followers of the goddess Kali. Not far away Ellora reared up with its marvelous pagodas, nor was famed Aurangabad far away, base of operations for the fierce Emperor Aurangzeb, now a mere county seat in one of the freestanding provinces in the Nizam of Hyderabad's realm. This region had been under the sway of Feringhea, king of stranglers and leader of the Thuggee cult. That close-knit, elusive band of assassins paid homage to the goddess of death by strangling victims of all ages without ever shedding their blood, and there was a time when you couldn't dig up the ground anywhere in this locality without finding a corpse. The English government has succeeded in preventing a significant percentage of these murders, but the frightful band is still in existence, still in operation.

By 12:30 the train had stopped at the station in Burhanpur, and there Passepartout paid an arm and a leg to acquire a pair of Turkish slippers, which were adorned with imitation pearls and which his feet clearly felt proud to wear.

The passengers ate a quick lunch and left again for the train station in Asirgarh, after momentarily hugging the banks of the Tapi, a small river that goes and empties into the Gulf of Khambhat near Surat.

This is as good a time as any to reveal a few of the thoughts taking up space in Passepartout's brain. Till his arrival in Bombay, he'd believed—and couldn't help believing—that things would end there. But now that they were going full steam ahead across India, a shift took place in his mental processes. His old self galloped back to the fore. He dusted off the fanciful tendencies of his youth, he took his master's plans seriously, he believed the bet was in earnest—and therefore so was this trip around the world *and* the need to not exceed its time limit. In fact he was already worried about possible delays, about accidents that could occur on the way. He felt as if he had a personal stake in this wager and shuddered at the thought that he could have jeopardized it by his unforgivable rubbernecking the day before. Accordingly, being far less stoic than Mr. Fogg, he was a much bigger worrywart. He counted and recounted the days that had gone by, cussed out the train when it stopped, accused it of dawdling, and since his master hadn't promised the engine driver a bonus, criticized Mr. Fogg *in petto*.[10] The gallant lad didn't realize that what was possible on an ocean liner was no longer so on a railroad train, which has to run on schedule.

Toward evening they tackled the gorges of the Satpura mountain range, which separates the territories of Khandesh and Bundelkhand.

The next day, October 22, when Sir Francis Cromarty asked him the hour, Passepartout checked his watch and answered three o'clock in the morning. But in reality, since this notorious watch was still set to Greenwich time and that meridian lay about seventy-seven degrees to the west, it would have to be—and indeed was—four hours slow.

So the brigadier general corrected the time Passepartout had given him, then followed up with the same comment the latter had already heard from Fix's lips. Sir Francis tried to make the Frenchman understand that he needed to reset his watch at each new meridian, that he was always traveling eastward—in other words, toward the sun—and that the days were shorter to the tune of four minutes for each degree he went over. It was no use. Whether or not the pigheaded fellow got the brigadier general's point, he refused to move his watch forward, and it kept faultless London time. But this was an innocent quirk that did nobody any harm.

At eight o'clock in the morning and fifteen miles shy of the station in Rothal, the train came to a stop in the middle of a wide

---

[10] *Translator's note.* Italian: "in his heart of hearts."

glade that was bordered by a few bungalows and crew shacks. Outside, walking down the line of passenger cars, the train conductor kept saying:

"Travelers get off here!"

Phileas Fogg looked at Sir Francis Cromarty, who seemed quite puzzled at their stopping in the heart of a forest of tamarind and khajour trees.

No less surprised, Passepartout scooted down the rails and came back almost immediately, exclaiming:

"Sir, there are no more tracks!"

"What do you mean?" Sir Francis Cromarty asked.

"I mean the train won't be continuing on!"

The brigadier general climbed down immediately from their passenger car. Phileas Fogg followed suit, taking his time. Both of them spoke to the conductor:

"Where are we?" Sir Francis Cromarty asked.

"By the hamlet of Kholby," the conductor replied.

"Is this a scheduled stop?"

"Certainly. The railway isn't finished."

"Excuse me? It isn't finished?"

"No. Fifty miles of track still need to be laid between this point and Allahabad, where the rails resume."

"But the newspapers announced that the railroad was open all the way through!"

"What do you want, general? The newspapers were mistaken."

"And yet you issue tickets from Bombay to Calcutta!" Sir Francis Cromarty went on, starting to get hot under the collar.

"Certainly," the conductor replied, "but our passengers are well aware they need to find transportation from Kholby to Allahabad."

Sir Francis Cromarty was furious. Passepartout gladly would have trounced the conductor, who actually couldn't do a thing. He didn't dare look at his master.

"Sir Francis," Mr. Fogg merely said, "if you're amenable, we'll inquire into some way of getting to Allahabad."

"But Mr. Fogg, won't this delay be absolutely detrimental to your best interests?"

"No, Sir Francis, I expected as much."

"What! You knew the rails wouldn't—"

"By no means, but I knew that sooner or later some sort of obstacle would spring up in my path. Now then, we're in no jeopardy at all. I have a gain of two days that I can sacrifice. There's a steamer that leaves Calcutta for Hong Kong at noon on the 25th. Today is the 22nd, and we'll reach Calcutta in time."

There was no comeback to a reply made with such utter confidence.

It was only too true that work on the railway had stopped at this point. Newspapers are like certain watches that have a quirky habit of running fast, and the press had gotten ahead of itself when it announced the line was finished. Most of the passengers knew that the rails gave out here, so they climbed down from the train and laid hold of every kind of vehicle the village had—four-wheeled buggies of the type called a *palki gharri*, carts pulled by a breed of humpbacked ox known as a zebu, coaches that looked like traveling pagodas, covered litters, ponies, etc. Accordingly Mr. Fogg and Sir Francis Cromarty scoured the whole village, but they came back without finding a thing.

"I'll go on foot," Phileas Fogg said.

Joining his master at this point, Passepartout reacted with a pained look as he regarded his magnificently inappropriate Turkish slippers. Luckily he'd also been out searching and he said a little hesitantly:

"Sir, I think I've found a means of transportation."

"What?"

"An elephant! An elephant that belongs to an East Indian living a hundred steps away."

"Let's see this elephant," Mr. Fogg replied.

Five minutes later Phileas Fogg, Sir Francis Cromarty, and Passepartout arrived at a hut that was next to a pen encircled by a high stockade. In the hut was the East Indian and in the pen an elephant. At their request the East Indian let Mr. Fogg and his two companions into the pen.

There they stood in the presence of a creature that was only half tamed, because its owner wasn't rearing it as a beast of burden but as a combat animal. With this goal in mind, he'd started changing the mammal's naturally docile personality so as to lead it gradually into that enraged condition known as *musth* in the Hindu language, and this called for feeding it sugar and butter over a three-month period. This treatment might not seem conducive to such a result, but elephant breeders have employed it with success all the same. Luckily for Mr. Fogg, the elephant in question had barely started on this diet and there were no symptoms of *musth* as yet.

Like all of its relatives, Kiouni—that was the beast's name—could move at a brisk clip for long stretches, and since no other forms of transportation were left, Phileas Fogg decided on this one.

But elephants are expensive in India, where they're starting to grow scarce. Only the males are suitable for circus events and they're in tremendous demand. Once these animals are tame and in captivity, they seldom reproduce, so you can lay hold of one only by hunting it. Accordingly they're the subject of tremendous attention, and when Mr. Fogg asked the East Indian if he would hire out his elephant, the East Indian flatly refused.

Fogg persisted, offering to pay the exorbitant hourly rate of £10 ($50) for the beast. Again refused. £20? Also refused. £40? Still refused. Passepartout jumped at each new bid. But the East Indian wouldn't give in to temptation.

This was first-class money nevertheless. Assuming the elephant took fifteen hours to do the trip to Allahabad, it would earn its owner £600 ($3,000).

Without getting riled in any way, Phileas Fogg then proposed to buy the beast from the East Indian, making him an initial offer of £1,000 ($5,000).

The East Indian wasn't willing to sell! Maybe the ruffian smelled a magnificent deal in the offing.

Sir Francis Cromarty took Mr. Fogg aside and urged him to think about it before going any farther. Phileas Fogg answered his companion that he wasn't in the habit of acting without thinking, that he was ultimately dealing with a bet of £20,000, that this elephant was essential to him, and that he would have this elephant if he had to pay twenty times what the beast was worth.

Mr. Fogg went back up to the East Indian, whose little eyes gleamed greedily and clearly revealed that with him it was all a matter of price. Phileas Fogg made consecutive offers of £1,200, then £1,500, then £1,800, and finally £2,000 ($10,000).[11] Passepartout, ordinarily quite ruddy, had turned white with emotion.

At £2,000 the East Indian gave in.

"That," Passepartout exclaimed, "is a record price for elephant meat, I swear by my slippers!"

The transaction completed, all that remained was to find a guide. This was easier. A young Parsi with shrewd features offered his assistance. Mr. Fogg agreed and promised to pay him generously, which could only sharpen his shrewdness.

The elephant was led out and equipped without delay. As a *mahout*, or elephant driver, the Parsi knew his job thoroughly. He covered the elephant's back with a kind of drop cloth and down each of its flanks rigged a sort of big side pouch that wasn't terribly comfortable.

Phileas Fogg paid the East Indian with banknotes extracted from the notorious overnight bag. Passepartout felt as if they were literally being yanked out of his innards. Then Mr. Fogg offered to give Sir Francis Cromarty a lift to the station in Allahabad. The brigadier general accepted. One more traveler wouldn't be any strain for the gigantic animal.

They bought provisions in Kholby. Sir Francis Cromarty got into one of the big side pouches, Phileas Fogg into the other. Passepartout straddled the drop cloth right between his master and the brigadier general. The Parsi took up his perch on the elephant's neck, and at nine o'clock the animal exited the village, plunging by the shortest path into the dense forest of fan palms.

---

[11] *Translator's note.* This is comparable to about $200,000 in today's dollars.

12

*Where Phileas Fogg and his companions
venture through the forests of India
and what comes of it*

TO SHORTEN THE DISTANCE they had to travel, their guide left the roadbed that was still under construction well to his right. Hindered by the many erratic offshoots of the Vindhya Mountains, this roadbed couldn't go by the quickest route, which it was in Phileas Fogg's best interests to take. Well acquainted with the region's highways and byways, the Parsi claimed that twenty miles could be saved by cutting through the forest, and they figured he knew best.

Sunk up to the neck in the big side pouches, Phileas Fogg and Sir Francis Cromarty got a thorough jostling as the elephant strode stiffly forward, its driver prodding it along at a brisk clip. But they endured the experience with true British stoicism—and furthermore seldom said a word, since they could barely see each other.

As for Passepartout, he was stationed on the creature's back and fully exposed to every bump and thump; he was ultracareful to heed his master's advice and not put his tongue between his teeth, because he would have chomped it clean off. Alternately shooting back and forth between the elephant's neck and rump, the gallant fellow did gymnastic tricks like a clown on a springboard. But he joked and laughed in the midst of his belly flops, occasionally taking a lump of sugar out of his bag for Kiouni's trunk to grab, the clever animal not breaking its steady stride for a second.

After a two-hour run, their guide pulled the elephant over and gave it a rest hour. Once it had slaked its thirst at a nearby pond, the animal dined on branches and shrubs. Sir Francis Cromarty raised no objections to this time-out. He was black and blue. Mr. Fogg seemed as fit as if he'd just gotten up.

"Why, he must be made of iron!" the brigadier general said, looking at him in wonderment.

"Wrought iron," Passepartout replied, busy fixing them a nominal lunch.

At noon their guide gave the signal to start off. The countryside soon looked much more like a wilderness area. The big forests gave way to thickets of tamarind trees and dwarf palms, then to wide arid plains garnished with sparse shrubs and scattered with huge chunks of igneous rock known as syenite. This whole part of upper Bundelkhand is rarely visited by travelers and is occupied by religious zealots who are at home with the most dreadful practices of the Hindu religion. The English haven't been able to establish any reliable sway over this territory, still under the influence of rajas who are hard to get at in their unreachable hideouts in the Vindhya Mountains.

Several times they spotted fierce-looking gangs of East Indians, who shook their fists as they watched the swift quadruped going past. However the Parsi avoided them as much as possible, regarding them as nasty folks to run into. They saw few animals that day, just some monkeys that ran off with a thousand scowls and contortions that amused Passepartout no end.

One thought in the midst of a good many troubled this individual. What would Mr. Fogg do with the elephant after he'd arrived at the station in Allahabad? Take it along? Impossible! The transportation costs on top of the acquisition costs would turn the animal into a fiscal catastrophe. Sell it or set it free? The worthy beast definitely deserved some consideration. If Mr. Fogg happened to make a gift of the creature to Passepartout himself, the latter would be totally at a loss. And this was a worry that wouldn't let him be.

By eight o'clock in the evening, the travelers had crossed the chief range of the Vindhya Mountains, and they stayed overnight in a tumbledown bungalow at the foot of the northerly slope.

That workday they'd covered a distance of about twenty-five miles, and they had just as many to go before reaching the train station in Allahabad.

It was a chilly night. Inside the bungalow the Parsi lit a fire of dry branches, and its warmth was much appreciated. The provisions they'd bought in Kholby supplied their supper. The travelers ate like men who were dog tired and aching all over. Their conversation began with a few broken sentences and soon ended with much noisy snoring. The guide kept watch next to Kiouni, who leaned against a huge tree trunk and slept standing up.

The night was uneventful. A few growling cheetahs and panthers sometimes broke the silence, along with some screeching, snickering monkeys. But the carnivores confined themselves to making noises rather than hostile advances toward the bungalow's guests. Sir Francis Cromarty slept like a log, a gallant soldier thoroughly done in. Passepartout's slumber was troubled, his dreams revisiting his somersaults of the day before. As for Mr. Fogg, his rest was as peaceful as if he were back in his tranquil home on Savile Row.

At six o'clock in the morning, they took to the trail again. Their guide hoped to reach the station in Allahabad that same evening. In this way Mr. Fogg would lose only part of the forty-eight hours he'd saved since his journey started.

They went down the last gradients of the Vindhya Mountains. Kiouni was speeding along again. Toward noontime their guide gave a wide berth to the village of Kalinjar, located on the Ken River, a subbranch of the Ganges. He always avoided population centers, feeling safer in the lonely wilderness areas that represent the outer reaches of this major river basin. The train station in Allahabad was less than twelve miles to the northeast. They stopped under a clump of banana trees, whose fruit they greatly appreciated—as tourists say, it's as wholesome as bread and "as yummy as custard."

At two o'clock the guide took cover in a dense forest he would travel through for a distance of several miles. He preferred the protection of a wooded area. At all events he hadn't run into anything troublesome so far, and it looked like the whole journey would prove uneventful, when their elephant pulled up short, showing signs of uneasiness.

By then it was four o'clock.

"What's going on?" Sir Francis Cromarty asked, sticking his head out of his big side pouch.

"I don't know, general," the Parsi replied, cocking an ear to a confused undercurrent of sound that was coming through the heavy branches.

The undercurrent grew clearer a few seconds later. Though it was still quite far away, you would have sworn it was a choir of human voices and brass percussion instruments.

Passepartout was all eyes and ears. Mr. Fogg waited patiently without saying a word.

The Parsi jumped to the ground, tied the elephant to a tree, and plunged into the deepest part of the thicket. He came back a few minutes later, saying:

"A procession of Brahmans is heading this way. If possible, we mustn't let them see us."

Advising the travelers to not set foot on the ground, their guide untied the elephant and led the beast into a grove. As for himself, if they had to make a run for it, he was all set to straddle his steed in a hurry. But they were completely concealed by the dense foliage, and he figured the band of worshippers would go by without spotting them.

The dissonant racket of the voices and instruments drew nearer. It was a mixture of toneless singing with the sound of drums and cymbals. Soon the front of the procession appeared beneath the trees, some fifty steps away from the place where Mr. Fogg and his companions were stationed. Through the branches they could easily make out the strange participants in this religious ceremony.

Moving forward at the head of the line were the priests, wearing miters on their heads and dressed in long embroidered robes. They were surrounded by men, women, and children who gave voice to a sort of dismal chant punctuated at regular intervals by the thumping of tom-toms and cymbals. Behind them, on a wide-wheeled wagon whose spokes and rims were sculpted to portray intertwining snakes, a hideous statue came into view, pulled along by two pairs of richly arrayed zebus. This statue had four arms; its body was colored dark red, it wore a wild-eyed expression, its hair was tangled, its tongue was hanging out, and its lips were tinted with reddish-brown dye from the henna plant and betel nut. Around its throat was a necklace of human skulls, and a belt of severed hands hung down its sides. It stood upright on the fallen carcass of a decapitated giant.

Sir Francis Cromarty recognized this statue.

"The goddess Kali," he muttered. "The goddess of love and death."

"Death I'll grant you, but love never!" Passepartout said. "What a nasty old harridan!"

The Parsi motioned him to keep still.

Around the statue a band of old beggar monks were all aquiver, darting and writhing, smeared with streaks of ocher, covered with cross-shaped cuts from which their blood trickled drop by drop—stupefied maniacs who still dash under the wheels of the Car of Juggernaut, a wagon carrying the statue of Krishna during major Hindu ceremonies.

Behind them, in all the sumptuousness of their eastern attire, a couple Brahmans were dragging along a woman who could barely stand up.

This woman was young and as white as a European. Her head, throat, shoulders, ears, arms, hands, and toes were loaded down with jewels, necklaces, bracelets, clasps, and rings. Under a light muslin wrap, a tunic with gold brocade outlined the curves of her figure.

Behind this young woman—and in sharp visual contrast—came guards armed with bare sabers stuck under their belts and with long pistols of Damascus steel; they carried a human corpse on a covered litter.

It was the body of an old man dressed in the luxurious garments of a raja, wearing, as he had in life, a turban embroidered with pearls, a robe woven of silk and gold, a diamond-studded cashmere belt, and the magnificent weapons of an East Indian aristocrat.

Then, at the end of the parade, there came musicians and a rear guard of religious zealots, whose shouts sometimes drowned out the deafening clamor from the instruments.

Sir Francis Cromarty looked unusually distressed as he watched all this pageantry, then he turned to the guide:

"A suttee!" he said.

The Parsi signaled yes and put a finger to his lips. The long procession slowly unwound beneath the trees and soon its rear rows vanished into the forest depths.

Little by little the singing died out. There were still a few outbursts of far-off shouting, then finally all the hubbub gave way to utter silence.

Phileas Fogg heard the word Sir Francis Cromarty had used, and as soon as the procession was gone:

"What's a suttee?" he asked.

"A suttee, Mr. Fogg, is a human sacrifice," the brigadier general replied, "though the sacrifice is voluntary. That woman you just saw will be burned tomorrow at the crack of dawn."

"Oh, the scum!" exclaimed Passepartout, who couldn't help crying out in righteous anger.

"What about that corpse?" Mr. Fogg asked.

"That was her aristocratic husband," their guide answered, "one of the independent rajas of Bundelkhand."

"Excuse me?" Phileas Fogg went on, his voice not revealing the slightest emotion. "These barbaric practices still endure in India, and the English haven't been able to stamp them out?"

"In most of India these sacrificial rites don't take place anymore," Sir Francis Cromarty replied, "but we haven't any influence over these wilderness areas and least of all over this territory of Bundelkhand. This whole northerly backside of the Vindhya Mountains is the scene of continual looting and bloodshed."

"The poor creature," Passepartout muttered. "To be burned alive!"

"Yes, burned," the brigadier general continued. "And if not, you can't believe the wretched state her relatives would reduce her to. They would shave her head, feed her just a few handfuls of rice, and cast her out—she would be regarded as an unclean thing and would die in some corner like a mangy dog. Accordingly it's the prospect of such a ghastly existence, far more than any love or religious zeal, that often leads these poor creatures to forfeit their lives. Sometimes, however, the sacrifice is genuinely voluntary, and the government must forcefully intervene to prevent it. Thus, a few years ago when I lived in Bombay, a young widow went and asked the governor for permission to be burned along with her husband's body. The governor refused, as you can well imagine. Then the widow left town, took refuge in the realm of an independent raja, and there went through with her sacrificial rites."

As the brigadier general told this story, their guide shook his head, then when the story was over:

"This sacrifice taking place at dawn tomorrow," he said, "isn't voluntary."

"How do you know that?"

"It's a situation everybody in Bundelkhand knows about," the guide answered.

"But the unfortunate woman didn't seem to be putting up any resistance," Sir Francis Cromarty pointed out.

"That's because they've drugged her on hashish and opium smoke."

"But where are they leading her?"

"To the Pillaji pagoda two miles away from here. She'll spend the night there, waiting till it's time for the sacrificial rites."

"And these rites will take place . . . ?"

"Tomorrow at daybreak."

After this reply their guide led the elephant out of the dense grove, then hoisted himself onto the animal's neck. He was just about to give the particular whistle that would get the beast moving, when Mr. Fogg stopped him and turned to Sir Francis Cromarty:

"What if we rescue this woman?" he said.

"Rescue this woman, Mr. Fogg!" the brigadier general exclaimed.

"I'm still twelve hours ahead of schedule. I can devote them to that."

"Say!" Sir Francis Cromarty put in. "You're a man with a heart after all!"

"On occasion," Phileas Fogg merely replied. "When I have time."

13

In which Passepartout proves once again that luck and pluck are partners

THEIR OBJECTIVE WAS bold, rife with difficulties, maybe unattainable. Mr. Fogg was about to risk his life or at the very least his freedom, and in the process the successful outcome of his plans—but he didn't hesitate. What's more, he had a determined ally in Sir Francis Cromarty.

As for Passepartout, he was all set and at their disposal. His master's idea thrilled him. He sensed a heart and soul under that icy exterior. He was starting to grow fond of Phileas Fogg.

Which left the guide. Whose side would he take in the business? Wouldn't he favor the Hindus? At the very least, if they couldn't get his assistance, they needed to make sure he would stay neutral.

Sir Francis Cromarty asked him this question straight out.

"General," their guide answered, "I'm a Parsi and that woman's a Parsi. I'm at your service."

"Well said, guide!" Mr. Fogg responded.

"But just be aware that if we're captured," the Parsi went on, "we'll run the risk not only of losing our lives but of being horribly tortured. So keep that in mind."

"I will," Mr. Fogg replied. "I think we need to wait till nighttime before we take action, yes?"

"I think so too," their guide answered.

Then the gallant Hindu gave them some particulars on the victim. She was an East Indian lady renowned for her beauty, a member of the Parsi race, and the daughter of wealthy merchants in Bombay. In that town she'd received a comprehensive English education, and from her behavior and upbringing you would have sworn she was a European. Her name was Aouda.

Left an orphan, she was forced to marry an elderly raja in Bundelkhand. She became a widow three months later. Knowing the fate waiting for her, she tried to escape it, was recaptured at once, and the raja's family (who would profit from her death) consigned her to this torment from which no escape seemed possible.

This account could only reinforce the generous decision that Mr. Fogg and his companions had made. They agreed that their guide should steer the elephant toward the Pillaji pagoda, getting as close to it as he could.

Half an hour later they halted in a thicket 500 steps away from the pagoda, which was out of sight; but the howls of the zealots were clearly audible.

Then they discussed ways of reaching the victim. Their guide was acquainted with the Pillaji pagoda, where he maintained that the young woman was being held prisoner. Could they go in one of its doorways while the whole band were deep in their drugged slumber, or would it be necessary to cut a hole in one of the walls? This could be determined only at the proper time and place. But one thing was for sure—they had to carry out their kidnapping scheme that very night, not the next day while the victim was being led to the slaughter. At that point she would be beyond all human aid.

Mr. Fogg and his companions waited for nightfall. Around six o'clock in the evening, as soon as it got dark, they decided to scout out the vicinity of the pagoda. By then the last yells of the beggar monks had died out. As was their custom, these East Indians must have been sinking into that intensely drugged state brought on by *bhang*—liquid opium mixed with a dose of hashish—and maybe it would be possible to sneak between them into the temple.

Leading Mr. Fogg, Sir Francis Cromarty, and Passepartout, the Parsi moved forward through the forest without making a sound. After ten minutes of crawling beneath the branches, they reached the bank of a small river, and in the glow of the resin burning on top of some iron torches, they saw a pile of stacked lumber. Built with precious sandalwood and already steeped in scented oil, this was the funeral pyre. On its upper part lay the raja's embalmed body, which was to be burned at the same time as his widow. The pagoda stood a hundred steps away from the pyre, its minarets

cutting through the shadows of the treetops.

"Come on!" their guide said in a low voice.

And with still greater caution, his companions behind him, he slipped quietly through the tall grass.

The silence was further broken only by the murmuring of the wind in the branches.

Soon their guide stopped at the edge of a glade. A couple of resin torches lit up the area. The ground was littered with groups of heavily drugged sleepers. You would have sworn it was a battlefield covered with corpses. Men, women, and children all were jumbled together. A few of these sots still let out a cough here and there.

Inside the mass of trees, the Pillaji temple loomed dimly in the background. But in the smoky torchlight, much to the guide's disappointment, the raja's guards kept watch at the doors, on patrol with bare sabers. You could assume that the priests inside were keeping watch as well.

The Parsi didn't go any farther. Realizing it would be impossible to storm their way into the temple, he ordered his companions to beat a retreat.

Phileas Fogg and Sir Francis Cromarty also understood that they couldn't try anything on this side of the pagoda.

They stopped and conversed, keeping their voices low.

"Let's wait," the brigadier general said. "It isn't eight o'clock yet, and it's possible the guards will also drop off to sleep."

"It is indeed possible," the Parsi replied.

So Phileas Fogg and his companions stretched out at the foot of a tree and waited.

How long those hours seemed! Occasionally their guide left them and went to the edge of the wood for a look. The raja's guards still kept watch in the torchlight, and a hazy glow filtered through the pagoda's windows.

In this fashion they waited till midnight. There was no change in their circumstances. The building exterior was still under surveillance. The guards clearly couldn't be relied on to doze off. In all likelihood they hadn't shared in the *bhang*'s drugging effects. So the rescuers needed to change tactics and get inside by cutting an opening in one of the pagoda walls. It remained to be seen whether the priests were keeping watch beside their victim with as much care as the soldiers at the temple door.

After one last conference their guide said he was set to go. Mr. Fogg, Sir Francis, and Passepartout followed him. They took a longish roundabout route, aiming to come at the pagoda from the sanctuary side.

About thirty minutes past midnight, they arrived at the foot of the back wall without running into a soul. Nobody was standing guard on that side—though, to tell the truth, it didn't have a single door or window.

It was a gloomy night. By then the moon was in her last quarter and barely clearing the horizon, which was cluttered with heavy clouds. The height of the trees made it even darker.

But it wasn't enough to reach the foot of the wall: they still needed to cut an opening in it. To carry out this operation, Phileas Fogg and his companions had nothing more than their pocketknives to work with. Luckily the temple walls consisted of a mixture of wood and brick that wouldn't be hard to get through. Once the first brick had been removed, the rest would come out easily.

They got down to business, keeping as quiet as possible. Toiling side by side, the Parsi and Passepartout pried loose the bricks, working to create an opening two feet wide.

They were making progress when they heard a yell inside the temple, which was answered almost immediately by other yells outside the building.

Passepartout and the guide stopped what they were doing. Had their efforts been detected? Had an alarm been given? The most ordinary good sense decreed that they back off, which they did at the same instant as Phileas Fogg and Sir Francis Cromarty. They crouched once more under the cover of the trees, waiting for the alert (if it was one) to run its course, ready to get back to work when it did.

But—a grievous setback—guards appeared on the sanctuary side of the pagoda, where they stood on watch to keep anybody from coming near.

It would be hard to describe the disappointment these four men felt when they had to break off their work. If they couldn't reach the victim, how could they rescue her? Sir Francis Cromarty gnawed his knuckles. Passepartout was hopping mad, and the guide had a hard time restraining him. As for Fogg the Unemotional, he waited and kept his feelings to himself.

"So all we can do is leave?" the brigadier general asked in a low voice.

"All we can do is leave," their guide answered.

"Wait," Fogg said. "My only requirement is to be in Allahabad before noon tomorrow."

"But what can you hope to accomplish?" Sir Francis Cromarty responded. "It'll be daylight in a few hours and—"

"We may get a chance at the crowning moment that we don't have right now."

The brigadier general wished he could read what was in Phileas Fogg's eyes.

What did this icy Englishman expect to do? At the moment of torment, did he intend to rush up to the young woman and openly snatch her from her executioners?

This was insanity, and how could anybody think the man was as insane as that? Nevertheless Sir Francis Cromarty agreed to stay around for the outcome of this fearful drama. Even so, the guide didn't leave his companions in their hiding place but led them toward the front part of the glade. There, sheltered by a clump of trees, they could keep an eye on the groups of sleepers.

Meanwhile, perched on the bottom branches of a tree, Passepartout was chewing on an idea that initially had flashed through his mind, then had ended up putting down roots in his brain.

At the outset he'd told himself, "It's sheer insanity!" Now, however, he kept saying, "But after all, why not? It's a chance, maybe the only one we'll get, and with junkies like these . . ."

In any event Passepartout didn't formulate his thoughts past this point but instantly slid with snakelike suppleness along the tree's lower branches, whose tips were bending toward the ground.

The hours went by, and soon a few lighter

tints announced that dawn was near. But it was still extremely dark.

The moment had come. A mass resurrection seemed to take place in that slumbering crowd. The groups stirred. Thumps of the tom-tom echoed again. The singing and shouting broke out once more. It was time for the poor woman to die.

In fact the pagoda doors were opening. A brighter light escaped from inside. Mr. Fogg and Sir Francis Cromarty could see the victim, brightly illuminated, two priests dragging her outdoors. From some crowning instinct for self-preservation, the unfortunate woman actually seemed to have shaken off her drugged stupor and was trying to break away from her executioners. Sir Francis Cromarty's heart gave a leap and he grabbed Phileas Fogg's hand in a reflex action, then felt an open clasp knife in that hand.

Just then the crowd started off. The young woman had sunk back into that torpor brought on by hashish smoke. She went among the beggar monks, who escorted her with their pious howling.

Mingling with the crowd at the rear of the line, Phileas Fogg and his companions followed her.

Two minutes later they reached the riverbank, then stopped less than fifty steps from the funeral pyre on which the raja's body rested. In the semidarkness they saw the victim lying completely inert beside her husband's corpse.

Then a torch materialized; steeped in oil, the lumber instantly caught on fire.

Just then Sir Francis Cromarty and the guide grabbed hold of Phileas Fogg, who was lunging toward the pyre in a temporary fit of insane generosity . . .

But Phileas Fogg had already thrown them off when the picture abruptly changed. A yell of fear went up from the onlookers. The whole crowd fell to the ground, terrified.

Could it be that the old raja wasn't dead? They suddenly saw him rise up like a phantom, lift the young woman in his arms, and step down from the pyre amid swirls of smoke that made him look like a ghost!

Guards, priests, and beggar monks were instantly filled with fear and lay there face to the ground, not daring to raise their eyes and witness such a prodigious event!

Muscular arms carried the motionless victim away as if she didn't weigh a thing. Mr. Fogg and Sir Francis Cromarty were still on their feet. The Parsi had bowed his head, and surely Passepartout was no less astonished . . . !

Thus the resurrected raja arrived in the vicinity of the place where Mr. Fogg and Sir Francis Cromarty were waiting, and in a curt voice he said:

"Let's get out of here!"

It was Passepartout himself who had stolen up to the pyre in the midst of the dense smoke! It was Passepartout who had taken advantage of the intense darkness still prevailing and had snatched the young woman from the jaws of death! It was Passepartout who had played his role with luck and pluck, making his getaway in the midst of that wholesale panic!

A second later all four men had vanished into the woods, and the elephant carried them off at a brisk clip. Then came shouts, hubbub, and a bullet that actually left a hole in Phileas Fogg's hat, informing them that the Hindus had seen through the trick.

In essence the old raja's body was now visible on the burning pyre. Recovering from their fear, the priests realized that his widow had just been kidnapped.

At once they rushed into the forest. The guards followed suit. There was a burst of gunfire, but the abductors fled swiftly and in a few seconds were out of range of both bullets and arrows.

14

In which Phileas Fogg goes down the whole wonderful valley of the Ganges without even thinking to look at it

THEIR BOLD KIDNAPPING SCHEME had worked. An hour later Passepartout was still chuckling over his success. Sir Francis Cromarty had wrung the stalwart fellow's hand. His master's comment had been "Good job," which, from that gentleman's lips, amounted to high praise. Passepartout replied that his master deserved all the glory in the business. As for him, he'd only "come up with a crazy idea," and he chuckled to think that for a few seconds he, Passepartout, former gymnast and ex-sergeant in the fire department, had been an old embalmed raja and the late spouse of a delightful woman!

As for the young East Indian, she hadn't been conscious during those goings-on. Wrapped in travel blankets, she was resting in one of the big side pouches.

Meanwhile, steered with tremendous assurance by the Parsi, the elephant was making rapid headway through the still-dark forest. An hour after leaving the Pillaji pagoda, the beast shot across an immense plain. At seven o'clock they called a halt. The young woman was still in a state of total collapse. The guide made her drink a few sips of brandy and water, but those crippling narcotics would keep her in their power for a while longer.

Sir Francis Cromarty was acquainted with the drugged state induced by breathing hashish smoke and he wasn't at all worried on her behalf.

But if the recovery of this young East Indian wasn't a concern in the brigadier general's mind, he felt less confident about her future prospects. Without hesitation he told Phileas Fogg that if Lady Aouda stayed in India, she inevitably would fall back into the hands of her executioners. Those maniacs lived all over the peninsula, and despite the English police, they would surely be able to recapture their victim, whether in Madras, Bombay, or Calcutta. And to back up what he said, Sir Francis Cromarty cited a similar case that had happened recently. In his opinion the young woman wouldn't be genuinely safe till she'd left India.

Phileas Fogg replied that he would take these comments into consideration and do what he could.

Near ten o'clock the guide announced their arrival at the station in Allahabad. There the interrupted railway tracks would resume, and trains covered the distance between Allahabad and Calcutta in less than twenty-four hours.

So Phileas Fogg would certainly arrive in time to catch an ocean liner that wasn't leaving for Hong Kong till noon the next day, October 25.

They put the young woman in a room at the railway terminal. Passepartout had the job of going shopping for her, of tracking down various bathroom articles, a frock, shawl, furs, etc., whatever he could find. His master approved him for an unlimited line of credit.

Passepartout left at once and raced through the local streets. Allahabad, meaning "City of God," is one of the most revered towns in India, due to its being built at the meeting place of two sacred rivers, the Ganges and Yamuna, whose waters draw pilgrims from all over the peninsula. What's more, according to well-known legends in the epic poem *The Ramayana*, the headwaters of the Ganges are in Heaven, from where, thanks to Brahma the Creator, they flow down to the earth.

In the process of making his purchases, Passepartout soon toured the town, a community formerly protected by a magnificent fortress that's now a national penitentiary. There isn't any business or industry left in this city, formerly so industrious and businesslike. Operating as if he were on Regent St. and only a couple steps from Farmer & Co., Passepartout looked in vain for a fashionable shop, but he found the items he needed only in a secondhand store owned by a finicky old Jew, from whom he bought a plaid frock, a bulky cloak, and a magnificent otterskin fur coat for which he didn't hesitate to pay £75 ($375). Then he returned in triumph to the railway terminal.

Lady Aouda showed signs of coming to. The narcotics that the Pillaji priests had forced on her were wearing off little by little, and her lovely eyes regained all their East Indian softness.

When the poetic monarch Yusuf Adil Shah lauds the attractions of the Queen of Ahmednagar, this is how he puts it:

Neatly parted down the middle, her glossy hair frames the pleasing contours of her delicate white cheeks, buffed to glistening freshness. Her ebony eyebrows have the shape and impact of the longbow belonging to Kama the god of love, and under her long silken lashes, the purest gleams of starlight swim in the dark pupils of her large limpid eyes as if in the holy lakes of the Himalayas. She has small, white, even teeth that glitter between her smiling lips like dewdrops in the half-closed heart of a pomegranate flower. Her dainty, symmetrically molded ears, her rosy-fingered hands, and her sweet little toes curling like lotus buds all sparkle with the brilliance of Ceylon's finest pearls and Golconda's choicest diamonds. A single hand can clasp her supple waist, whose slimness enhances the comely curves of her rounded loins and the luxuriance of her bosom, flaunting young womanhood's most flawless treasures, and under her tunic's silken folds, she seems to have been modeled from white silver by the divine hands of the eternal sculptor Viswakarma.

But without laying it on any thicker, let's just say that Lady Aouda, widow of a Bundelkhand raja, had womanly attractions in the fullest European sense of the term. She spoke absolutely flawless English, and their guide hadn't exaggerated when he claimed that this young Parsi woman had been transformed by her upbringing.

Meanwhile their train was about to leave the station in Allahabad. The Parsi was waiting. Mr. Fogg paid him according to the wage scale they'd agreed upon and didn't spend a farthing more. This rather surprised Passepartout, who knew how much his master owed to the guide's dedication. In essence the Parsi had willingly risked his life during that Pillaji business, and if those Hindus caught up with him later on, he would have a hard time eluding their vengeance.

Which left the additional matter of Kiouni. What were they to do with such an expensive elephant?

But Phileas Fogg had already made up his mind on the issue.

"Parsi," he told the guide, "you've been helpful and dedicated. I've paid for your help but not your dedication. Do you want this elephant? If so, it's yours."

The guide's eyes lit up.

"Your worship is giving me a fortune!" he exclaimed.

"Take it, guide," Mr. Fogg replied, "and I'll still be in your debt."

"Good show!" Passepartout exclaimed. "Take Kiouni, my friend. This is a gallant and courageous animal!"

And going over to the beast, he offered it a few lumps of sugar, saying:

"Here, Kiouni, here!"

The elephant let out a couple grunts of pleasure. Then, grabbing Passepartout around the waist with its trunk, it lifted him as high as its head. Not the least bit afraid, Passepartout petted the beast affectionately, then Kiouni put him gently back on the ground, and the good fellow offered his handshake in exchange for the good animal's trunk shake.

A few seconds later Phileas Fogg, Sir Francis Cromarty, and Passepartout took their places in a comfortable passenger car, let Lady Aouda have the best seat, and shot off full steam ahead for Benares.

No more than eighty miles separated that town from Allahabad, and the train covered them in two hours.

During this trip the young woman came to fully and completely; the *bhang*'s numbing fumes had worn off.

How amazed she must have felt to find herself on a train, in a passenger compartment, wearing European garments, and surrounded by travelers who were perfect strangers!

Right off her companions lavished their attentions on her, pepping her up with a few drops of liquor; then the brigadier general told her the whole story. He laid stress on Phileas Fogg's dedication, his instant willingness to gamble his life in order to rescue her, and the outcome of the venture thanks to Passepartout's daring brainstorm.

Mr. Fogg let him speak without adding a word. Thoroughly embarrassed, Passepartout kept saying, "It was nothing!"

Lady Aouda heartily thanked her rescuers, but with tears rather than words. Her lovely eyes conveyed her gratitude more eloquently than her lips. Then pictures from the suttee flashed through her mind again, and when she looked out at that land of India where so many dangers still waited for her, she couldn't help shuddering in terror.

Phileas Fogg realized what Lady Aouda was thinking, and to reassure her, he offered—though with icy formality—to take her to Hong Kong, where she could stay till the business had blown over.

Lady Aouda gratefully accepted the offer. Sure enough, she had a relative living in Hong Kong, a Parsi like herself and one of the chief merchants in that town, which is thoroughly English though it sits on a headland off the coast of China.

By 12:30 the train had halted at the station in Benares. Brahman legends assert that this town stands on the site of ancient Kashi, which used to stay suspended in midair between zenith and nadir like Mohammed's coffin. But in these more practical times, Benares (which students of the East dub the Athens of India) keeps its feet prosaically on the ground, and for a second Passepartout glimpsed its houses of brick and its huts of woven twigs and weeds, which gave it an utterly desolate appearance without any local color.

This was Sir Francis Cromarty's stop. The troops he was rejoining were camped a few miles north of town. So the brigadier general said farewell to Phileas Fogg, wishing him all possible success and expressing the desire that he travel that way again but in a less eccentric and more economical fashion. Mr. Fogg gave his companion's fingers a light squeeze. Lady Aouda's courtesies were more affectionate. Never would she forget what she owed Sir Francis Cromarty. As for Passepartout, the brigadier general honored him with an all-out handshake. Deeply touched, the Frenchman wondered where and when he could ever repay the fellow. Then they parted company.

After leaving Benares, the railway went along a portion of the Ganges valley. Through the passenger car windows, the varied countryside of Bihar came into view under reasonably clear skies, then its mountains covered with vegetation, its fields of barley, corn, and wheat, its streams and ponds populated by greenish alligators, its nicely kept-up villages, and its still-lush forests. A few elephants and some big humpbacked zebus had come to bathe in the waters of the sacred river, and despite the lateness of the season and a temperature that was already chilly, Hindu groups of both sexes were also piously performing their holy ablutions. Relentless foes of Buddhism, these fervent folks were staunch members of the Brahman religion, whose beliefs are embodied by three individuals: Visnu the sun god, Siva the divine personification of natural forces, and Brahma the supreme master of priests and lawmakers. But from what viewpoint were Brahma, Siva, and Visnu to regard today's "anglicized" India, as some steamboat went snorting by, troubling the sacred waters of the Ganges, scaring off the gulls that flew over its surface, the turtles that congregated on its banks, and the worshippers spread out along its shores!

The whole panorama unreeled in a flash, and a pale cloud of steam often hid its details. Our travelers could barely glimpse the fort in Chunar that's twenty miles southeast of Benares and a former stronghold for the rajas of Bihar, or Ghazipur with its major rosewater factories and Lord Cornwallis's tomb standing on the left bank of the Ganges, or the fortified town of Buxar, or the leading commercial and industrial city of Patna where India's opium traffic is headquartered, or the town of Munger that isn't just European but as English as Manchester or Birmingham, being renowned for its iron foundries, its manufacturers of cutlery and side arms, and its tall chimneys that soil Brahma's heavens with dark smoke—it gives this land of dreams a real black eye.

Then night fell, and tigers, bears, and wolves howled and fled in front of the locomotive, while the train shot along at full speed and they saw nothing more of Bengal's wonders, not Golconda, dilapidated Gour, Murshidabad the former capital city, Barddhaman, Hugli, nor Chandernagore—the French quarter in this land of India, where Passepartout would have been proud to see his country's flag fluttering overhead!

Finally, at seven o'clock in the morning, they reached Calcutta. The ocean liner bound for Hong Kong wouldn't weigh anchor till noon. So Phileas Fogg had five hours in front of him.

According to his itinerary, the gentleman was due to arrive in India's capital on October 25, twenty-three days after leaving London, and he arrived there right on the scheduled day. Thus he was neither late nor early. Unfortunately those two days he'd gained between London and Bombay had been lost (and you know why) while crossing India's peninsula—but presumably Phileas Fogg had no regrets.

15

Where the bag of banknotes gets lighter by another couple thousand pounds

THE TRAIN CAME to a halt in the railway terminal. Passepartout was the first one down from their passenger car, followed by Mr. Fogg who helped his young companion step onto the platform. Phileas Fogg meant to take Lady Aouda straight over to the Hong Kong ocean liner, to see that she got comfortably situated; he wasn't about to leave her while she was in this country that held such perils for her.

Just as Mr. Fogg was exiting the terminal, a policeman came up to him and said: "You're Mr. Phileas Fogg?"

"I am."

"And this fellow's your manservant?" the policeman added, indicating Passepartout.

"Yes."

"Would both of you kindly follow me."

Mr. Fogg gave no sign that he felt any surprise whatever. This officer represented the law, and for every Englishman the law is sacred. Passepartout behaved like a typical Frenchman and tried to argue, but the policeman nudged him with his billy club, and Phileas Fogg motioned him to obey.

"This young woman can come with us?" Mr. Fogg asked.

"She can come," the policeman answered.

The policeman led Mr. Fogg, Lady Aouda, and Passepartout over to a *palki gharri*, a sort of four-wheeled, four-seated buggy hitched to two horses. Off they went.

Nobody said a word during the drive, which took about twenty minutes.

First the buggy went through "blacktown," whose narrow streets ran between rows of hovels teeming with a municipal population dressed in filthy rags; then the vehicle crossed the European district, which was brightened up by brick homes, shaded by coconut palms, and garnished with flagpoles—and where, despite the morning hour, stylish riders and magnificent carriages were already out and about.

The *palki gharri* stopped in front of a plain-looking residence, which wasn't intended, however, to be anybody's living quarters. The policeman unloaded his captives (to give them their correct title), led them into a cell with barred windows, and told them:

"You'll appear before Judge Obadiah at 8:30."

Then he backed out and shut the door.

"Good grief! We're being held prisoner!" Passepartout exclaimed, collapsing onto a chair.

At once Lady Aouda turned and spoke to Mr. Fogg, her voice vainly trying to conceal her emotions:

"Sir, you must leave me! They've hunted you down on my account! Because you rescued me!"

Phileas Fogg was content to answer that such a thing wasn't possible. Hunted down over that business of the suttee? Out of the question! How would the plaintiffs dare show their faces? There must be some mistake. Mr. Fogg added that he wouldn't leave the young woman under any circumstances—he was going to take her to Hong Kong.

"But the boat's sailing at noon!" Passepartout pointed out.

"By noon we'll be on board," the unemotional gentleman merely replied.

This was such plain speaking, Passepartout couldn't help telling himself:

"Of course! No doubt about it! By noon we'll be on board!" But he felt far from confident.

At 8:30 the cell door opened. The policeman reappeared and ushered his captives into a nearby assembly hall. It was a hall for public hearings, and a largish audience of Europeans and locals already filled the courtroom.

Mr. Fogg, Lady Aouda, and Passepartout took their seats in a pew facing the bench, which was the territory of the magistrate and court clerk.

Judge Obadiah entered almost immediately, followed by the court clerk. The magistrate was a fat man who looked perfectly round. He unhooked a wig that had been hanging on a nail and briskly put it on his head.

"First case," he said.

Then, raising his hand to his head:

"Here now, this isn't my wig!"

"You're right, Mr. Obadiah," the clerk responded. "It's mine."

"My dear Mr. Oysterpuff, how do you expect a judge to hand down a just sentence when he's wearing a clerk's wig?"

They swapped wigs. Passepartout was boiling with impatience during these preliminaries, because the hands on the big courtroom clock seemed to be moving dreadfully fast.

"First case," Judge Obadiah repeated at this point.

"Phileas Fogg?" said Oysterpuff the clerk.

"I'm here," Mr. Fogg answered.

"Passepartout?"

"Present!" Passepartout replied.

"Good, the accused are in court," Judge Obadiah said. "For two days we've been looking for you on every train from Bombay."

"But what are we accused of?" Passepartout exclaimed impatiently.

"You'll find out," the judge replied.

"Sir," Mr. Fogg said at this juncture, "I'm an English citizen and I have a right—"

"Have you been inconsiderately treated?" Mr. Obadiah asked.

"Not at all."

"Fine. Bring in the plaintiffs."

A door opened at the judge's command and the bailiff ushered in three Hindu priests.

"It's them all right!" Passepartout muttered. "Those are the rogues who tried to burn our young lady!"

The priests stood in front of the judge, and the court clerk read aloud a charge of sacri-

lege drawn up against one Phileas Fogg and his manservant, who were accused of desecrating a place held sacred by the Brahman religion.

"You've heard the indictment?" the judge asked Phileas Fogg.

"Yes, sir," Mr. Fogg replied, checking his watch. "And I plead guilty."

"Oh? You plead guilty?"

"I plead guilty, and I'm waiting for these priests to plead guilty in their turn to what they were attempting at the Pillaji pagoda."

The three priests looked at each other. They didn't seem to understand a word the accused had said.

"It was as plain as day!" Passepartout shouted impulsively. "They were going to burn a human victim in front of the Pillaji pagoda!"

Further astonishment from the priests and utter surprise from Judge Obadiah.

"What victim?" he asked. "Burn who? Right in the city of Bombay?"

"Bombay?" Passepartout exclaimed.

"Certainly. This isn't about the Pillaji pagoda but the pagoda on Malabar Hill in Bombay."

"And as proof of guilt, here are the blasphemer's shoes," the court clerk added, slapping two pieces of footwear down on his desk.

"My shoes!" yelped Passepartout, who was stupendously surprised and couldn't help blurting out these words.

The reader can guess how much confusion filled the minds of both master and manservant. They'd forgotten about the incident at the pagoda in Bombay, and it was this very thing that had landed them in front of the Calcutta magistrate.

In essence Fix the investigator had recognized all the benefits he could reap from that ill-fated business. Putting off his departure for twelve hours, he'd given the priests on Malabar Hill a word of advice; well aware that the English government takes a very dim view of this type of illegality, he'd promised the three men they would be awarded considerable personal damages; then he sent them in hot pursuit of the desecrator by the next train. But due to the time Phileas Fogg had taken to rescue the young widow, Fix and the Hindus arrived in Calcutta ahead of the Englishman and his manservant, whom the judiciary had been alerted by telegram to arrest as they climbed down from their train. As you might guess, Fix was disappointed to learn that Phileas Fogg hadn't yet arrived in India's capital. He was forced to believe his robber had stopped off at one of the stations on the Peninsular Railway and was taking refuge in the northerly provinces. For twenty-four hours Fix kept watch on the railway terminal in a state of mortal anxiety. That very morning, then, how gleeful he felt when he saw his man climb down from a passenger car—along with, it's true, a young woman whose presence the investigator couldn't explain. At once he sent a policeman after the fellow, and that's how Mr. Fogg, Passepartout, and the widow of a Bundelkhand raja were brought before Judge Obadiah.

And if Passepartout hadn't been so caught up in his own affairs, he would have spotted the detective off in a corner of the courtroom, watching the proceedings with an interest you can easily appreciate—because in Calcutta just as in Bombay and Suez, he still didn't have his arrest warrant!

Meanwhile Judge Obadiah had noted the admission escaping from Passepartout's lips, though the Frenchman would have given all his worldly possessions to take back those hasty words.

"You don't dispute the facts?" the judge said.

"We don't dispute them," Mr. Fogg replied coolly.

"Insofar," the judge resumed, "insofar as the English legal system aims to give strict and equal protection to all religions practiced by India's peoples, and as this Passepartout person has admitted breaking the law by blasphemously setting foot on the floor slabs of the Malabar Hill pagoda in Bombay on the day of October 20, the aforesaid Passepartout stands convicted, and I sentence him to two weeks in jail and a fine of £300."

"Three hundred pounds!" Passepartout shrieked, this fine being the one thing that had genuinely gotten through to him.

"Silence in the court!" the bailiff put in, barking the words.

"And," Judge Obadiah added, "insofar as there's no material proof that the manservant and master weren't in collusion, and as the master in any case is to be held responsible for the deeds and activities of an employee in his pay, the court detains the aforesaid Phileas Fogg and sentences him to one week in jail and a fine of £150. The clerk may call the next case!"

Off in his corner Fix felt indescribable pleasure. Phileas Fogg detained for a week in Calcutta—that gave the warrant for his arrest more than enough time to arrive.

Passepartout was dumbfounded. This sentence spelled financial ruin for his master. A £20,000 bet lost, and all because he was a hopeless rubbernecker and had gone into that damned pagoda!

Phileas Fogg didn't even frown, his self-control as perfect as if the sentence had nothing to do with him. But just as the clerk called the next case, he stood up and said:

"I'll post bail."

"That's your prerogative," the judge replied.

Fix felt a chill go down his spine, but he recovered his confidence when he heard the judge say that "insofar as Phileas Fogg and his manservant have the status of foreigners," the bail set for each of them would be the enormous sum of £1,000 ($5,000).

If they didn't serve their sentences, Mr. Fogg would be out £2,000.

"I'll pay it," the gentleman said.

Then he took a pack of banknotes from the bag Passepartout was carrying and put it on the clerk's desk.

"This sum will be refunded to you after you've done your jail time," the judge said. "Meanwhile you're released on bail."

"Come along," Phileas Fogg said to his manservant.

"But at least I should get my shoes back!" Passepartout yelled, shaking his fist.

They gave him back his shoes.

"Here's a pricey pair!" he mumbled. "Over £1,000 per shoe! Not to mention that they pinch my toes!"

Thoroughly humbled, Passepartout followed Mr. Fogg, who had offered the young woman his arm. Fix was still hoping his robber wouldn't be willing to leave that sum of £2,000 behind and would do his week in jail. So he took off on Fogg's heels.

Mr. Fogg caught a cab and immediately climbed into it along with Lady Aouda and Passepartout. Fix ran after the buggy, which soon pulled up at one of the town piers.

In the offshore mooring half a mile out, the *Rangoon* lay at anchor, the blue flag at its masthead indicating it was ready to sail. Eleven o'clock sounded. Mr. Fogg was an hour early. Fix watched him climb down from the buggy and set out in a dinghy with Lady Aouda and his manservant. The detective stamped his foot on the ground.

"The filthy beggar!" he exclaimed. "He's leaving! He's saying good-bye to £2,000! Oh, he's a big-spending robber all right! I'll tail him to the ends of the earth if I have to; but at the rate he's going, he'll run through all the money he stole!"

The police inspector had good grounds for believing this. In fact, during the course of his journey since leaving London, Phileas Fogg had already squandered over £5,000 ($25,000) on travel expenses, bonuses, buying an elephant, posting bail, and paying fines, so the amount that could be recovered was shrinking by the day—and likewise the percentage that would go to the detectives who recovered it.

16

*Where Fix plays dumb
when he hears certain things*

THE *RANGOON* was one of the ocean liners that the Peninsular & Oriental Co. used on its run through the seas of China and Japan; it was an iron-hulled, propeller-driven steamer with a gross burden of 1,950 tons and it was on the books as having 400-horsepower engines. It matched the *Mongolia* in speed but not in comfort. Accordingly Lady Aouda wasn't as well situated as Phileas Fogg would have liked. Even so, they were faced with a crossing of only 3,500 miles, hence lasting eleven to twelve days, and it turned out that the young woman wasn't a demanding passenger.

During the first days of that crossing, Lady Aouda got better acquainted with Phileas Fogg. At every opportunity she expressed how deeply grateful she was to him. The stoic gentleman listened to her—or at least appeared to—with the iciest calm, no inflection or gesture revealing that he felt the tiniest emotion. He saw to it that the young woman had everything she could want. He visited her on a regular schedule, if not to chat at least to listen. He showed her every courtesy that the strictest good manners could require, but with the grace and spontaneity of a robot whose actions had been pre-programmed for the purpose. Lady Aouda wasn't too sure what to think, but Passepartout gave her a quick briefing on his master's personal eccentricities. He informed her of the wager that was taking the gentleman around the world. Lady Aouda had smiled at this; but after all, she did owe him her life, and her rescuer had nothing to lose by being seen through the eyes of her gratitude.

Lady Aouda corroborated the account their Hindu guide had given of her affecting life story. She did indeed belong to the race that ranks as the upper class among these native races. Several Parsi traders in the East Indies had made huge fortunes in the cotton business. One of them, Sir Jamsetji Jijibhai, had been given a peerage by the English government, and Lady Aouda was related to this wealthy individual, now living in Bombay. In fact it was one of Lord Jijibhai's cousins, the honorable Jijih, whom she banked on rejoining in Hong Kong. Would she receive assistance and protection at his hands? She couldn't say. To which Mr. Fogg responded that she wasn't to worry, that everything would work out mathematically. This was his watchword.

Did the young woman understand what he meant by that horrid adverb? Who knows. She kept her large eyes on Mr. Fogg's the whole time, her large eyes as limpid as "the holy lakes of the Himalayas." But Fogg the Incurable, as much a stuffed shirt as ever, apparently wasn't the sort to dive into such a lake.

The first stage of the *Rangoon*'s crossing took place under excellent conditions. The weather was easy to work with. Seamen call that immense bay "the Bengal lap," and this part of it fully cooperated with the ocean liner's efforts. The *Rangoon* soon raised the Andaman Islands, whose chief member, Great Andaman, features a picturesque mountain named Saddle Peak, which stands 2,400 feet high and can be spotted by far-off navigators.

Its extensive coastline lay fairly near. The Papuan savages on this island didn't put in an appearance. They sit on the bottom rung of the human ladder, but it isn't true that they're cannibals.

The panoramic layout of these islands was superb. Immense forests of fan palms, areca palms, bamboo, nutmeg, teakwood, gigantic mimosas, and tree ferns covered the foreground of this landscape, and to the rear the stylish silhouettes of mountains stood out. Along the coastline swarmed thousands of those precious swifts whose edible nests furnish a soup that's much in demand throughout the Celestial Empire. But the *Rangoon* soon went past all the different sights on view in the Andaman Islands, then steamed swiftly toward the Strait of Malacca, which would give it access to the seas of China.

As for Inspector Fix, it was his ill-omened lot to be dragged along on this journey to circumnavigate the globe—so what was he up to during this crossing? Before exiting Calcutta, he'd left instructions that once the warrant finally arrived, it should be forwarded to him in Hong Kong; then, without being spotted by Passepartout, he'd managed to get aboard the *Rangoon*, where he hoped to lie low till the ocean liner had reached its destination. The fact is, he would have had trouble explaining why he was on board without arousing Passepartout's suspicions, since the fellow was sure to think he'd remained in Bombay. But a perfectly logical chain of events led him to renew his acquaintance with the good Frenchman. How? You'll see.

All the police inspector's hopes and dreams now focused on a single part of the globe, Hong Kong, because the ocean liner's layover in Singapore would be too brief for him to accomplish anything in that town. Therefore he had to place the robber under arrest in Hong Kong, or the robber would steal away, so to speak, for good.

In essence Hong Kong was still English territory, but it was the last he would encounter on the route they were taking. Beyond it China, Japan, and America offered this Fogg fellow a refuge that was almost completely secure. Obviously the warrant for his arrest was close behind, and if it finally caught up with Fix in Hong Kong, the detective would arrest Fogg and leave him in the hands of the local police. No problem. But beyond Hong Kong a mere warrant for his arrest wouldn't be enough. A writ of extradition would be required. Ergo all sorts of delays, postponements, and roadblocks that the rogue would take advantage of to get away once and for all. If the process broke down in Hong Kong, it would be quite difficult, if not impossible, to resume operations with any chance of success.

"Therefore," Fix told himself over and over during the long hours he spent in his cabin, "therefore I'll arrest my man if the warrant's in Hong Kong; but if it isn't, this time I've got to delay his departure at any cost! I botched it in Bombay, I botched it in Calcutta! If I miss my chance in Hong Kong, my reputation's done for! Whatever it takes, I've got to pull this off. But what delaying tactics should I use with this damned Fogg, if it comes down to that?"

If all else failed, Fix was quite determined to make a clean breast of it to Passepartout and let him know what sort of master he was serving, since they clearly weren't in collusion. Enlightened by this revelation, Passepartout was sure to be afraid for his own skin and undoubtedly would come over to Fix's side. But this was a risky measure in the final analysis, one to be used only if nothing else worked. One word from Passepartout to his master would be enough to ruin things irreparably.

So the police inspector felt thoroughly baffled, but new vistas opened up in his mind when he found Lady Aouda aboard the *Rangoon* in Phileas Fogg's company.

Who *was* this woman? What convergence

of circumstances had made her Fogg's companion? Obviously they'd met somewhere between Bombay and Calcutta. But on what part of the peninsula? Was it by chance that Phileas Fogg and this young woman were now traveling together? Or, on the contrary, had the gentleman undertaken this journey across India with the aim of renewing his acquaintance with the lady's attractions? Because she did have attractions! Fix had gotten a good look at them during the court session in the hall for public hearings in Calcutta.

As you can appreciate, one aspect of the matter inevitably puzzled the investigator. He wondered if the business didn't have the makings of a felony kidnapping. Yes, this had to be the case! The idea took root in Fix's brain and he saw all the benefits he could reap from such a state of things. Whether the young woman was married or not, it added up to kidnapping, and in Hong Kong it would be possible to land her abductor in such hot water, no amount of money could get him out of it.

But he didn't dare wait till the *Rangoon* reached Hong Kong. This Fogg had an abominable habit of hopping from one boat to another, and he could be long gone before procedures even got under way.

So the main thing was to warn the English authorities and notify them of the *Rangoon*'s movements before it arrived and unloaded its passengers. Now then, nothing could be simpler: the ocean liner called at Singapore, and telegraph lines connected Singapore to the China coast.

Even so, just to play it safe, Fix decided to question Passepartout before taking any action. He knew it wouldn't be very hard to get the fellow talking, and he concluded it was time to come out of hiding and quit traveling incognito. Now then, he didn't have a moment to lose. It was October 30, and the very next day the *Rangoon* would put into Singapore.

Consequently Fix left his cabin that day, climbed on deck, and intended to "make the first contact" by running into Passepartout while playacting the most tremendous surprise. Passepartout was strolling in the bow,

when the inspector rushed up to him, exclaiming:

"What! You're on the *Rangoon?*"

"Mr. Fix? You're on board too?" Passepartout responded, utterly amazed to recognize his traveling companion from the *Mongolia.* "What's going on? I leave you in Bombay and I find you again on the way to Hong Kong? Does this mean you're traveling around the world as well?"

"No, no," Fix replied. "I plan to stop over in Hong Kong—for a few days at least."

"Ah," Passepartout said, then looked startled for a second. "But why haven't I seen you on board since we left Calcutta?"

"Ye gods, I've been so ill . . . a touch of seasickness . . . I stayed in bed inside my cabin. The Bay of Bengal doesn't agree with me as much as the Indian Ocean. And how's your master, Mr. Phileas Fogg?"

"In perfect health and smack on his itinerary! Not a day late! Oh, here's something you don't know, Mr. Fix—we also have a young lady with us."

"A young lady?" the investigator replied, acting as if he didn't understand a word his conversation partner was trying to say.

But Passepartout soon brought him up to date on the whole story. He described the incident at the Bombay pagoda, buying an elephant at a cost of £2,000, the business of the suttee, kidnapping Aouda, the sentence passed by the Calcutta court, being released on bail. Though Fix was familiar with the incidents in this last bit, he behaved as if it was all news to him, and Passepartout couldn't resist the pleasure of narrating his adventures to somebody who listened with such interest.

"But ultimately," Fix asked, "doesn't your master plan to take this young woman to Europe?"

"Not at all, Mr. Fix! We're simply going to leave her in the care of one of her relatives, a wealthy merchant in Hong Kong."

That's no help, Fix thought, hiding his disappointment. "How about a glass of gin, Mr. Passepartout?"

"Gladly, Mr. Fix. We've just met again aboard the *Rangoon*, so the least we can do is drink to the occasion!"

17

*Which deals with this and that during
the crossing from Singapore to Hong Kong*

FROM THAT DAY FORWARD Passepartout and the detective often bumped into each other, but the investigator was tremendously on guard around his companion and didn't try to get him talking. Only once or twice did he glimpse Mr. Fogg, who gladly stayed in the *Rangoon*'s main lounge and either kept Lady Aouda company or played whist in line with his set routine.

As for Passepartout, he gave very serious thought to the strange happenstance that Fix, once again, was going the same way as his master. And in all honesty it was more than surprising. This very friendly and certainly very courteous gentleman whom they'd first met in Suez, who had sailed on the *Mongolia*, who had gotten off in Bombay where he said he would stop over, who had turned up again on the *Rangoon* bound for Hong Kong, who, in a nutshell, was following Mr. Fogg's itinerary step by step—this individual deserved close consideration. It was a coincidence that was more than peculiar. What was this Fix person playing at? Passepartout was ready to bet his Turkish slippers—he'd packed them with loving care—that Fix would leave Hong Kong the same time they did, and most likely on the same ocean liner.

Passepartout could have worn his thinking cap for a whole century without ever guessing what assignment the investigator had been given. Never would he have imagined that Phileas Fogg was being "tailed" around the planet earth as a robbery suspect. But since it's human nature to seek explanations for everything, here's how Passepartout, in a sudden flash of inspiration, made sense of Fix's ongoing presence—and actually his scenario was quite plausible. In essence he believed that Fix was and could only have been a hireling in the pay of Mr. Fogg's colleagues at the Reform Club, who had sent him on the gentleman's heels to verify that this journey around the world was legitimately taking place and following the agreed-upon itinerary.

"It's obvious!" the good fellow told himself over and over, quite proud of his astuteness. "He's a spy those gentlemen have hired to dog our footsteps! How shameful of them! Mr. Fogg's so upright, so honorable! Spied on by a hireling—oh, you'll pay dearly for this, you gentlemen of the Reform Club!"

Though delighted with his discovery, Passepartout decided to say nothing about it to his master, afraid the latter would be rightly offended by this distrust on the part of his opponents. But he solemnly swore he would tease Fix when the chance came up, dropping sly hints without giving himself away.

Wednesday afternoon, October 30, the *Rangoon* entered the Strait of Malacca, which lends its name to the southern end of the Malay Peninsula and separates it from the shores of Sumatra. As for the latter, its main island was hidden from the passengers' view by islets featuring very steep, very picturesque mountains.

At four o'clock the next morning, the *Rangoon* put into Singapore to replenish its coal supply; it had finished its crossing half a day ahead of schedule.

Phileas Fogg recorded this gain in the plus column and on this occasion went ashore along with Lady Aouda, who had expressed a desire to roam around for a few hours.

Finding Mr. Fogg's every move suspicious, Fix followed him while keeping out of sight. As for Passepartout, he did his usual shopping, laughing at Fix's machinations *in petto.*

The island of Singapore is neither large nor imposing in appearance. It suffers from a shortage of geological contours—mountains, in other words. Even so, the place is attractive in its low-profile way. It's like a park with lovely paths cutting through it. Hitched to stylish horses imported from Australia, a smart rig carried Lady Aouda and Phileas Fogg through clumps of palm trees with sparkling foliage, then myrtles whose cloves consisted of partly open flower buds. Pepper bushes were standing in for the prickly hedges of Europe's countrysides; sago palms and big ferns with superb fronds added visual variety to this tropical landscape; the air was steeped in the pungent scent of nutmeg trees with lacquered foliage. Watchful, scowling mobs of monkeys were plentiful in the trees, and tigers were a possibility in the jungles. To anybody who's amazed to hear that these dreadful carnivores haven't been totally eliminated from this comparatively tiny island, we'll answer that they keep coming into Malacca by swimming across the strait.

After a two-hour drive around the countryside, Lady Aouda and her companion—who gave it a glance but saw nothing—reentered the town, a huge cluster of flat, bulky dwellings surrounded by delightful gardens full of pineapples, mangosteens, and all sorts of world-class fruit.

By ten o'clock they were back on the ocean liner, never suspecting they'd been followed by the police inspector, who had likewise needed to incur the cost of a carriage.

Passepartout was waiting for them on the *Rangoon*'s deck. The gallant lad had bought a couple dozen mangosteens: they're the size of your average apple, their rinds are dark brown outside and bright red inside, their white innards melt in your mouth, and true gourmets find them an unparalleled delight. Passepartout was overjoyed to offer them to Lady Aouda, who thanked him with great courtesy.

By eleven o'clock the *Rangoon* had a full load of coal under its belt and loosed its moorings; a few hours later its passengers lost sight of Malacca's lofty mountains, whose forests shelter the world's handsomest tigers.

About 1,300 miles lie between Singapore and the island of Hong Kong, a small English possession that's separate from mainland China. It was in Phileas Fogg's best interests to cover this distance in no more than six days, allowing him to catch the boat due to leave Hong Kong on November 5 for Yokohama, one of Japan's chief ports.

The *Rangoon* was fully booked. A large number of passengers had come on board in Singapore—Hindus, Ceylonese, Chinese, Malays, and Portuguese, most of them down in second class.

They'd had fair weather till then, but this changed when the moon entered her last quarter. The sea was running high. At times the wind rose to a stiff breeze, but luckily it blew out of the southeast quadrant and aided the steamer's efforts. The captain spread sail whenever it was feasible. Rigged like a brig, the *Rangoon* often navigated under its foresail and two topsails, and the combined action of wind and steam gave it still greater speed. Coping in this way with the choppy and sometimes very trying waves, they skirted the Vietnamese coastlines of Annam and Cochin China.

But the *Rangoon* was more at fault than the sea, and its passengers—most of whom got sick—should have blamed the ocean liner itself for the trying time they had.

In essence Peninsular Co. ships on this run through the seas of China have a serious design defect. The ratio of their depth to their draft with full cargo has been poorly calculated, and as a result they put up only the weakest resistance to a heavy sea. Their enclosed, watertight volume is insufficient. They get "swamped," as sailors say, and due to this structural inadequacy, it takes only a few waves over the deck to affect their speed. Consequently these ships are quite inferior—at least in design, if not in their engines and steam generators—to such examples from the French imperial shipping line as the *Empress* and the *Cambodia*. According to the calculations of engineers, the latter can take on their full weight in water before foundering, whereas Peninsular Co. boats—the *Golconda*, the *Korea*, and the *Rangoon* too—couldn't take on a sixth of their weight without going to the bottom.

So their procedure in foul weather was to exercise the greatest caution. Sometimes the vessel had to lie to at half steam. The loss of time didn't seem to bother Phileas Fogg in the slightest, but it angered Passepartout tremendously. After denouncing the captain, the head mechanic, and the shipping line, he damned the entire travel industry to you-know-where. Maybe that gas jet burning at his own expense in the house on Savile Row also bulked large in his impatient thinking.

"So it's quite urgent for you to reach Hong Kong?" the detective asked him one day.

"Terrifically urgent!" Passepartout replied.

"You think Mr. Fogg's in a hurry to catch the ocean liner to Yokohama?"

"An awful hurry."

"So these days you believe in this strange journey around the world?"

"Absolutely. How about you, Mr. Fix?"

"Me? Not a word of it."

"You're such a cutup!" Passepartout replied, tipping him a wink.

At this comment the investigator fell to brooding. Being branded this way bothered him, yet he couldn't say exactly why. Had the Frenchman guessed what he was up to? He wasn't sure what to think. But he alone knew he was there in his capacity as detective—how could Passepartout have found out his secret? And yet when Passepartout spoke to him that way, he clearly had some ulterior motive.

It happened that the gallant lad went even farther on another occasion, because it was just too much for him. He couldn't hold his tongue.

"Look here, Mr. Fix," he asked his companion in a sly tone, "once we get to Hong Kong, will we have to bid you a tearful goodbye?"

"Well," Fix answered in some confusion, "I don't know . . . maybe I . . . "

"Ah!" Passepartout said. "If only you could come with us, how overjoyed I would be! Look here, a representative of the Peninsular Co. can't quit while he's ahead! You were going just to Bombay and you'll be in China any minute now! America isn't far off, and it's only a short hop from America to Europe!"

Fix looked closely at his conversation partner, who wore the world's sweetest expression, and decided to laugh along with him. But the latter was going great guns and asked Fix if his job "paid pretty well."

"Yes, and no," Fix replied with a straight face. "You have to take the good with the bad. But you can easily understand that I don't travel at my own expense."

"Oh, I'm quite sure you don't!" Passepartout exclaimed, laughing even more heartily.

When their conversation ended, Fix went back into his cabin and mulled things over. Obviously the fellow was on to him. Somehow or other the Frenchman had spotted that he was there in his capacity as detective. But had he tipped off his master? What role was the manservant playing in all this? Were the two in collusion or not? If Fix's cover had been blown, did that mean it was all over? The investigator spent a few arduous hours on the issue, sometimes fearing everything was lost, sometimes hoping Fogg was in the dark on things, ultimately unable to make up his mind.

Even so, his brain calmed down again and he decided to be frank with Passepartout. If the desired circumstances didn't turn up for arresting Fogg in Hong Kong, and if Fogg this time made moves to leave English territory for good, he, Fix, would tell Passepartout everything. Either the manservant was in collusion with his master—and the latter knew everything, meaning that the business was in irreparable jeopardy—or the manservant had nothing to do with the robbery and it would be in his best interests to part company with the robber.

So that was the situation relative to these two men, while Phileas Fogg hovered above them with majestic unconcern. He was systematically orbiting the earth, never worrying his head over the asteroids that revolved around him.

And yet there was—as astronomers put it—a "disturbing body" nearby that ought to have caused some irregularities in the gentleman's very core. But not so! Lady Aouda's attractions had no such impact, much to Passepartout's surprise, and if there *were* any irregularities, they would have been harder to calculate than the ones on Uranus that led to the discovery of Neptune.

Yes, this was a source of daily amazement to Passepartout, who read in the young woman's eyes so much gratitude toward his master! No doubt about it, Phileas Fogg's heart was capable of heroic deeds but not amorous ones—he was a fighter, not a lover! As for any trepidation that this chancy trip might have aroused in him, there wasn't a sign of such a thing. But Passepartout himself lived in continual agony. One day he was leaning over the engine room guardrail and keeping an eye on the powerful machinery (which sometimes acted up), when the bow pitched sharply downward and the propeller flailed around above the waves. Then steam burst out of the valves, and this made the good fellow hit the roof.

"The valves aren't fully charged!" he howled. "We aren't budging! This is an English ship all over! Oh, if only it was an American boat—maybe we would blow up, but at least we would move faster!"

18

In which Phileas Fogg, Passepartout, and Fix go about their separate business

THE WEATHER WAS pretty foul during the last days of the crossing. The wind increased tremendously. It blew steadily out of the northwest quadrant, impeding the ocean liner's progress. The *Rangoon* was far from stable and rolled considerably, so the passengers had every right to take offense at those revoltingly long waves the wind stirred up in midocean.

During the daytime on November 3 and 4, they had something of a storm. Gusts of wind gave the sea a furious thrashing. The *Rangoon* had to lie to for half a day, holding steady while its propeller did just ten revolutions per minute in order to cut through the waves at an angle. All the sails had been taken in, yet the rigging was still under great strain and whistled during the blasts.

As the reader can imagine, the ocean liner went significantly slower, and the prognosis was that it would arrive in Hong Kong twenty hours behind schedule, later still if the storm didn't die down.

The sea seemed to be deliberately opposing him, yet Phileas Fogg took in the whole furious sight with his usual lack of emotion. His brow didn't cloud over for a second, and yet a twenty-hour delay could jeopardize his journey and make him miss the ocean liner leaving for Yokohama. But the man hadn't a nerve in his body and seemed neither impatient nor annoyed. It was as if this storm were actually listed on his schedule and he'd been expecting it. When Lady Aouda discussed this setback with her companion, she found him as calm as ever.

Fix himself didn't see things from the same viewpoint. Quite to the contrary. This storm delighted him. His pleasure would have been downright boundless had the *Rangoon* been forced to turn tail and flee from the turmoil. All these delays were fine with him, because they would force this Fogg fellow to stay in Hong Kong for a few days. The sky itself with its blasts and gusts was finally on his side. He was ill quite a bit, but it didn't make any difference! He paid no attention to his queasiness; though his body was wracked with seasickness, his mental pleasure was so great that it kept him diverted.

As for Passepartout, the reader can guess how much barefaced fury he felt during this trying time. Everything had gone so well till this point! Land and sea seemed dedicated to his master. Steamers and railways obeyed him. Wind and steam joined hands to speed his journey. Did this mean the hour of adversity had finally tolled? Life became impossible for Passepartout, as if that £20,000 bet had to be paid out of his own pocket. The storm aggravated him, the blasts threw him into a rage, and he would gladly have given the naughty sea a good whipping, like Xerxes with the Dardanelles. Poor fellow! Fix was careful to hide his personal pleasure from the Frenchman, which was just as well because if Passepartout had sensed Fix's inner happiness, Fix would have been in for a nasty quarter of an hour.

Passepartout stayed on the *Rangoon*'s deck the whole time the gusts persisted. He was incapable of remaining below; he clambered up into the masts; he amazed the crew, lending everybody a hand, as spry as a monkey. He pestered the captain, officers, and sailors with a hundred questions, and they couldn't help chuckling at the sight of such a flustered fellow. Passepartout desperately wanted to know how long the storm would last. So they referred him to the ship's barometer, which showed no inclination to rise again. Passepartout gave the barometer a shaking, but, though he piled both physical and verbal abuse on it, he couldn't do a thing with that shiftless instrument.

Finally the turmoil abated. The state of the sea underwent a change during the daytime on November 4. The wind veered two points to the south and turned helpful again.

As the weather calmed down, so did Passepartout. The crew were able to let out both the topsails and lower sails, and the *Rangoon* got back on course wonderfully fast.

But there was no way to make up all the time they'd lost. It just couldn't be helped, and they didn't raise land till five o'clock in the morning on the 6th. Phileas Fogg's itinerary had the ocean liner arriving on the 5th. Now then, since it wasn't till the 6th that the ship did arrive, he was twenty-four hours late and would inevitably miss the vessel leaving for Yokohama.

At six o'clock the harbor pilot climbed aboard the *Rangoon* and took his place on the bridge, ready to steer the ship through the narrows to the port of Hong Kong.

Passepartout had a terminal craving to question the man and ask him if the ocean liner to Yokohama had left Hong Kong. But he didn't have the nerve, preferring to hang onto a little hope till the last second. He shared his worries with Fix, and the sly dog tried to console him, saying that all Mr. Fogg had to do was take the next boat. Which sent Passepartout into conniptions.

But if Passepartout didn't dare question the harbor pilot, Mr. Fogg checked his Bradshaw, then serenely asked the aforesaid pilot if he knew when a boat would be leaving Hong Kong for Yokohama.

"Tomorrow on the morning tide," the pilot replied.

"Ah," Mr. Fogg put in, showing no surprise.

Passepartout was on hand and would have gladly hugged the pilot, whereas Fix would have liked to wring his neck.

"What's the steamer's name?" Mr. Fogg asked.

"The *Carnatic*," the pilot replied.

"Wasn't it scheduled to leave yesterday?"

"Yes, sir. But they had to repair one of the boilers, so they put its departure off till tomorrow."

"Thank you," Mr. Fogg replied. Then, with his machinelike tread, he went back down to the *Rangoon*'s lounge.

As for Passepartout, he grabbed the pilot's hand and squeezed it energetically, saying:

"Pilot, you're quite a man!"

Doubtless the pilot never found out how his remarks had earned this outburst of enthusiasm. Hearing the toot of a whistle, he went back up on the bridge and steered the ocean liner through the flotilla of junks, Tanka houseboats, fishing vessels, and ships of every description that clog the Hong Kong sluiceways.

The *Rangoon* docked at one o'clock, and its passengers went ashore.

In this instance, you must admit, chance had been exceptionally helpful to Phileas Fogg. If the *Carnatic* hadn't needed to repair its boilers, its departure date would have been November 5 and passengers bound for Japan would have needed to wait a week for the next ocean liner to leave. True, Mr. Fogg had been delayed twenty-four hours, but this delay wouldn't have any dire effect on the rest of his journey.

In actuality the steamer that did the Pacific crossing from Yokohama to San Francisco connected directly with the ocean liner from Hong Kong, so it couldn't depart till the latter had arrived. Obviously they would reach Yokohama twenty-four hours late, but this time would be easily made up during the twenty-two days it takes to cross the Pacific. So, thirty-five days after leaving London, Phileas Fogg was within twenty-four hours of where his schedule said he ought to be.

The *Carnatic* was due to leave at five o'clock the next morning. Mr. Fogg had sixteen hours ahead of him for taking care of business, in other words, matters pertaining to Lady Aouda. Getting off the boat, he offered the young woman his arm and led her to a covered litter. He asked the carriers to recommend lodgings, and they suggested the Club Hotel. With Passepartout following, the covered litter got under way and reached its destination twenty minutes later.

Phileas Fogg booked a suite for the young woman and saw to it that she had everything she could want. Then he told Lady Aouda he would immediately set about searching Hong Kong for the relative in whose care he was to leave her. At the same time he instructed Passepartout to stay at the hotel till his return, so the young woman wouldn't be left by herself.

The gentleman took a cab to the stock exchange. There they were sure to know about such an individual as the honorable Jijih, who ranked among the wealthiest businesspeople in the city.

The broker whom Mr. Fogg approached did indeed know about the Parsi merchant. But the latter had left town two years earlier and didn't live in China anymore. Having made his fortune, he'd taken up residence in Europe (in Holland, it was thought), which was understandable because he'd cultivated many acquaintances in those parts during his business career.

Phileas Fogg went back to the Club Hotel. At once he asked Lady Aouda's permission to meet with her, then informed her without any further preamble that the honorable Jijih no longer resided in Hong Kong and most likely was living in Holland.

Lady Aouda didn't reply to this at first. She mopped her brow and stood in thought for a few seconds. Then, in her gentle voice:

"What should I do, Mr. Fogg?" she said.

"It's very simple," the gentleman replied. "Come along to Europe."

"But I can't take advantage of your—"

"You aren't, and your presence won't interfere with my schedule in any way . . . Passepartout!"

"Sir?" Passepartout replied.

"Go to the *Carnatic* and book three cabins."

Since the young woman was so gracious to him, Passepartout was delighted to continue traveling in her company and he immediately set out from the Club Hotel.

19

*Where Passepartout grows
extremely concerned for his master
and what comes of it*

HONG KONG IS JUST an islet that the Treaty of Nanking made an English possession after the First Opium War ended in 1842. In a few years Great Britain's colonizing genius had created a major town here and set up a port, Victoria Harbor. This island is located at the mouth of the Pearl River, and only sixty miles separate it from the Portuguese city of Macao, which sprang up on the opposite bank. Inevitably Hong Kong was bound to defeat Macao in any trade war, and today the English town handles most of China's shipping. Docks, hospitals, wharves, warehouses, a Gothic cathedral, a "government building," and paved streets all make Hong Kong look like some mercantile city in the county of Kent or Surrey, a city that had burrowed through the planet earth and had come out more or less on the opposite side in this part of China.

Hands in his pockets, Passepartout made his way toward Victoria Harbor, looking at the covered litters, the wind-powered wheelbarrows still popular in the Celestial Empire, and all the hordes of Chinese, Japanese, and Europeans crowded together in the streets. As he went along, the good fellow found he was pretty much still in Bombay, Calcutta, or Singapore. It's as if a trail of English towns runs all around the globe.

Passepartout reached Victoria Harbor. There, at the mouth of the Pearl River, the waves were swarming with ships of all nations, English, French, American, and Dutch, warships and merchantmen, longboats from Japan or China, junks, sampans, Tanka houseboats, and even floating bordellos that looked like so many flower gardens drifting on the waters. Strolling around, Passepartout noticed that a number of locals, all of them quite elderly, were dressed in yellow. After going into a Chinese barbershop to get a China-style shave, he learned from the Figaro of the place (who spoke pretty good English) that all these elders were at least eighty years old, that at this age they'd earned the privilege of sporting the color yellow—which is the empire's official color. Passepartout couldn't quite put his finger on why he found this last fact thoroughly amusing.

Shave out of the way, he proceeded to the *Carnatic*'s loading dock and there he spotted Fix strolling to and fro, which didn't surprise the Frenchman in the slightest. But the police inspector's face revealed signs of deep disappointment.

"Good," Passepartout said to himself, "things aren't going well for the gentleman of the Reform Club!"

And he pulled alongside Fix with his merriest smile, paying no attention to the frustration in his companion's face.

Now then, the investigator had good reason to rail against the hellish luck dogging him. The warrant hadn't come! Obviously that warrant was close on his heels, but it couldn't catch up with him unless he stayed in town for a few days. Now then, Hong Kong was the last English territory on this Fogg fellow's route, so he would escape for good unless Fix managed to detain him here.

"Well, Mr. Fix, have you decided to come along with us to America?" Passepartout asked.

"Yes," Fix answered through clenched teeth.

"You don't say!" Passepartout exclaimed, bursting into hearty laughter. "I was positive you couldn't bring yourself to part with us! Come on, let's go get you a place on board!"

And the two of them went into the overseas travel office and secured cabins for four people. But the clerk pointed out that the *Carnatic*'s repairs were finished and the ocean liner would leave at eight o'clock that same evening, not the next morning as originally announced.

"Very good!" Passepartout responded. "That'll suit my master just fine. I'll go warn him."

At this point Fix came to a drastic decision. He decided to tell Passepartout everything. It seemed to be the only way he had of detaining Phileas Fogg in Hong Kong for a few days.

Leaving the travel office, Fix offered to take his companion to a tavern for a bit of refreshment. Passepartout had the time. He accepted Fix's invitation.

A tavern on the pier was open for business. It looked promising. The two men went inside. It was a huge, nicely decorated den, and a folding bed adorned with cushions stretched across the far end. A number of sleeping people had been stowed on this bed.

In the main part of the den, thirty or so customers sat at little wickerwork tables. Some were emptying pints of ale, porter, or other English beers, some jugs of gin, brandy, or similar alcoholic spirits. However the majority were smoking long pipes of red clay in which were packed little globules of opium mixed with rose oil. Every so often an enfeebled smoker would slide under his table, then the staff of the establishment would grab him by the head and feet, carry him, and put him next to a crony on the folding bed. Thus about twenty of the sots had been stowed side by side, in the last stages of debilitation.

Fix and Passepartout realized they'd gone into one of those smoking parlors haunted by the dazed, wasted, crackbrained wretches who consume that deadly drug called opium, and every year mercenary England sells them $52,000,000 worth of this narcotic! What sorry millions these are—they're the front money for one of human nature's deadliest vices.

China's government has tried hard to rectify this abuse with the harshest laws, but to no avail. Opium use has spread from the wealthy classes, who at first kept it strictly to themselves, down to the lower classes, and there's no end to the damage it can do. People smoke opium at all times and places in the Middle Empire. Both men and women are in the thrall of this dismal addiction, and once they're hooked on inhaling the drug, they can't abstain from it without experiencing horrible stomach cramps. Heavy users can smoke up to eight pipes per day, but they'll die within five years.

Now then, looking for a bit of refreshment, Fix and Passepartout had gone into one of the many smoking parlors of this type that proliferate right in Hong Kong. Passepartout didn't have any money with him, but he gladly accepted his companion's "invite," figuring to return the compliment at some future time and place.

They ordered two bottles of port, which the Frenchman did full justice to, while Fix exercised more restraint and kept a close eye on his companion. They chatted about this and that, especially about the splendid idea Fix had of sailing on the *Carnatic*. And pertinent to this, Passepartout recalled that the steamer would be leaving a few hours earlier and got up, once the bottles were empty, to go warn his master.

Fix held him back.

"One second," he said.

"What's up, Mr. Fix?"

"I have some serious concerns to talk over with you."

"Serious concerns!" Passepartout exclaimed, emptying the last few drops of wine at the bottom of his glass. "Well, let's talk 'em over tomorrow. I haven't got time right now."

"Wait," Fix replied. "It's about your master!"

When he heard this, Passepartout looked closely at his conversation partner.

The expression on Fix's face struck him as odd. He sat down again.

"So what have you got to tell me?" he asked.

Fix rested his hand on his companion's arm and lowered his voice:

"You've guessed who I am?" he asked the Frenchman.

"Of course!" Passepartout said with a grin.

"Then I'm going to confess everything to you—"

"Now that I know it already, old chum? Well, if that doesn't beat all! Never mind, keep talking. But before you do, let me tell you that those gentlemen have gone to a needless expense!"

"Needless!" Fix said. "That's easy for you to say! Anybody can see you don't know how huge the amount is!"

"Certainly I do," Passepartout replied. "It's £20,000!"

"It's *£55,000!*" Fix went on, clutching the Frenchman's hand.

"What!" Passepartout exclaimed. "How would Mr. Fogg dare . . . ? £55,000 . . . ? All right," he added as he got up again, "that's another reason for not wasting one more second."

"Fifty-five thousand pounds!" Fix continued, ordering a decanter of brandy and making Passepartout sit back down. "And if I pull this off, I'll earn a £2,000 reward. Would you like £500 of that for agreeing to help me?"

"Help you?" Passepartout exclaimed, his eyes popping out of his head.

"Yes, help me detain that Fogg fellow in Hong Kong for a few days!"

"Huh?" Passepartout put in. "What in the world are you saying? Excuse me? Those gentlemen aren't content just with doubting my master's good faith and having him followed, they're even trying to throw obstacles in his way? How shameful of them!"

"Drat the fellow! What do you mean?" Fix asked.

"I mean this is out-and-out cheating. They might as well lay hold of Mr. Fogg and take the money right out of his pocket!"

"Ah, that's just what we figure it will come to."

"Then it's a trap!" Passepartout shouted, gathering steam under the influence of the brandy Fix kept pouring and he kept absentmindedly drinking. "It's an honest-to-goodness trap! Some gentlemen and colleagues *they* are!"

Fix was starting to not get it.

"Colleagues!" Passepartout snarled. "Members of the Reform Club! You listen here, Mr. Fix—my master's a respectable man, and when he makes a bet, he aims to win it in good faith!"

"Why, who do you think I am, then?" Fix asked, looking Passepartout in the eye.

"That's easy! A hireling in the pay of members of the Reform Club—you've been assigned to double-check my master's itinerary, and the whole thing's utterly disgraceful! And so, even though I guessed your mission a while back, I've been very careful to not pass it along to Mr. Fogg."

"He knows nothing?" Fix asked instantly.

"Nothing," Passepartout replied, emptying his glass one more time.

The police inspector mopped his brow. He

hesitated before continuing the conversation. What should he do? Passepartout's mistake seemed genuine, but it made Fix's plans more complicated. Obviously this fellow was speaking in all sincerity and wasn't in collusion with his master—which was what the investigator had been afraid of.

"All right," he said to himself, "since they aren't in collusion, he'll help me."

For a second time the detective came to a decision. Besides, he couldn't delay any longer. He needed to keep Fogg in Hong Kong at any cost.

"Listen," Fix said in a curt voice, "listen closely to me. I'm not what you think I am—in other words, I'm not a hireling in the pay of members of the Reform Club . . ."

"Phooey!" Passepartout said, looking at him with a scornful expression.

"I'm a Scotland Yard police inspector working on a case . . ."

"You . . . a police inspector . . . ?"

"Yes, and I can prove it," Fix went on. "Here's my authorization."

And taking a piece of paper out of his wallet, the investigator showed his companion an authorization signed by the chief of police at central headquarters. Dumbfounded, Passepartout looked at Fix and couldn't get out a single word.

"The bet this Fogg fellow made," Fix went on, "was just an excuse and it fooled both you and his colleagues at the Reform Club, because he had a vested interest in making you his unconscious accomplices."

"But why . . . ?" Passepartout exclaimed.

"Hear me out. Just this fall, on September 29, a robbery to the tune of £55,000 took place at the Bank of England, and they were able to put together a physical description of the individual involved. Now then, here's that description, and it jibes feature for feature with this Fogg fellow."

"Oh come on!" Passepartout exclaimed, banging the table with his beefy fist. "My master's the most respectable man alive!"

"How would *you* know?" Fix responded. "You're barely even acquainted with him! He hired you the same day he left town, and he hurried off on a lunatic excuse, without packing any trunks, and carrying a huge amount

in banknotes! And you dare insist he's a respectable man?"

"Yes! Yes!" the poor fellow repeated automatically.

"Then do you want to be arrested as his accomplice?"

Passepartout held his head in both hands. He wasn't himself anymore. He didn't dare look at the police inspector. Phileas Fogg a robber? He, Lady Aouda's rescuer, that gallant, generous man? And yet appearances were against him! Passepartout tried to fight off the suspicions that were creeping into his mind. He refused to believe his master was guilty.

"Anyhow what do you want from me?" he said to the police investigator, restraining himself with a crowning effort.

"This," Fix replied. "I've tailed that Fogg fellow till now, but I still haven't received the warrant for his arrest that I requested from London. So you've got to help me detain him in Hong Kong—"

"Me? But I—"

"You'll share in that £2,000 reward the Bank of England has promised!"

"Never!" Passepartout replied, trying to get up but falling back down, feeling his strength of mind and body leaving him at the same moment.

"Mr. Fix," he said, stumbling over his words, "even if everything you've told me is true . . . if my master turns out to be the robber you're looking for . . . which I dispute . . . I was . . . I *am* in his employ . . . I've seen how decent and generous he is . . . I won't betray him . . . never . . . not for all the gold on earth. We don't sell folks down the river back where I come from!"

"You refuse?"

"I refuse."

"Let's just pretend it never happened," Fix replied. "How about another drink?"

"Yes . . . another drink!"

Passepartout was getting tipsier and tipsier. Realizing the fellow had to be separated from his master at any cost, Fix decided to finish him off. On the table were a couple of pipes filled with opium. Fix slid one of them into Passepartout's hand; the Frenchman took it, lifted it to his lips, lit it, inhaled a few draws, then sank down in his seat, his head sagging under the narcotic's influence.

"Finally," Fix said, seeing Passepartout now wiped out. "That Fogg fellow won't be warned in time about the *Carnatic*'s early departure, and if he does go anywhere, at least he'll go without this damned Frenchman!"

Then he paid his tab and left.

20

In which Fix makes direct contact with Phileas Fogg

DURING THE FOREGOING DRAMA, which had the makings, maybe, of seriously jeopardizing his future, Mr. Fogg was strolling with Lady Aouda through the streets of this English town. After Lady Aouda had accepted his offer to take her to Europe, he needed to think about every detail that might pertain to such a long journey. It was all very well for an Englishman like himself to go around the world carrying just an overnight bag, but a woman couldn't undertake such a trip on these terms. Ergo their need to buy the clothing and articles essential for such a journey. Mr. Fogg handled this task with characteristic calm, so when the young widow felt embarrassed by all his kindness and apologized or objected, he would always reply:

"It's in my journey's best interests and my schedule allows it."

Their purchases made, Mr. Fogg and the young woman reentered their hotel and dined on a fixed-price meal that was sumptuously served. Then, feeling a bit tired, Lady Aouda went back up to her suite after an "English-style handshake" with her unflappable rescuer.

As for that respectable gentleman, the whole evening he kept busy reading the *Times* and the *Illustrated London News.*

If he'd been the sort whom something could surprise, he would have felt this emotion when he didn't see his manservant appear at bedtime. But since he believed the ocean liner to Yokohama wasn't leaving Hong Kong till the next morning, he gave the matter no further thought. But when

Mr. Fogg rang for him the next morning, Passepartout didn't come.

There's no telling what the distinguished gentleman thought when he heard that his manservant hadn't returned to the hotel. Mr. Fogg was content to pick up his overnight bag, alert Lady Aouda, and send for a covered litter.

By then it was eight o'clock, and the *Carnatic* was scheduled to take advantage of the high tide and exit through the narrows at 9:30.

When a covered litter arrived at the hotel entrance, Mr. Fogg and Lady Aouda climbed into the cozy vehicle, and their baggage came after them in a wheelbarrow.

Half an hour later the travelers stepped down onto the loading dock, where Mr. Fogg learned that the *Carnatic* had left the night before.

Mr. Fogg had expected to find the ocean liner and his manservant at one go, now he was reduced to doing without both of them. But no sign of disappointment appeared on his face, and when Lady Aouda gave him a worried look, he was content to reply:

"Just an incident, my lady, nothing more."

An individual had been watching him closely and walked up to him at this point. It was Inspector Fix, who bowed and said to him:

"Sir, weren't you a passenger like myself on the ship that came in yesterday, the *Rangoon?*"

"Yes, sir," replied Mr. Fogg coolly. "But I haven't had the honor . . . "

"Pardon the intrusion, but I was expecting to find your manservant here."

"Sir, do you know where he is?" the young woman asked instantly.

"What!" Fix replied, faking surprise. "Isn't he with you?"

"No," Lady Aouda answered. "We haven't seen him since yesterday. Could he have gone off on the *Carnatic* without us?"

"Without you, ma'am?" the investigator responded. "Excuse me for asking, but were you planning to leave on that ocean liner?"

"Yes, sir."

"I was too, ma'am, and you can see how distressed I feel. The *Carnatic* finished its repairs and left Hong Kong twelve hours earlier without warning anybody, so now we'll have to wait a week for the next departure!"

As he said these words "a week," Fix felt his heart jump for joy. A week! Fogg detained in Hong Kong for a whole week! The warrant for his arrest would have time to arrive. The law's representative had finally gotten a lucky break.

We'll let the reader decide what a staggering jolt Fix received when he heard Mr. Fogg say in his calm voice:

"But it seems to me there are other vessels besides the *Carnatic* in the port of Hong Kong."

And Mr. Fogg offered Lady Aouda his arm, then headed dockside to look for an outbound ship.

Dumbfounded, Fix followed him. You would have sworn there was a wire connecting the two.

Yet luck seemed to have truly deserted this man it had served so well till then. For three hours Phileas Fogg scoured the harbor in all directions, determined, if need be, to charter a craft to take him to Yokohama; but all he saw were ships loading or unloading and therefore not able to set sail. Fix got his hopes up again.

But Mr. Fogg wasn't perturbed and intended to keep looking if he had to go all the way to Macao, when a seaman pulled alongside him in the outer harbor.

"Looking for a boat, your worship?" the seaman said to him, doffing his cap.

"Have you a boat ready to set out?" Mr. Fogg asked.

"Yes, your worship, pilot boat no. 43, the best in the whole flotilla."

"Is it fast?"

"Somewhere between eight and nine miles per hour. Want to see it?"

"I do."

"You'll be pleased, your worship. This is for a pleasure cruise?"

"No. For an ocean voyage."

"An ocean voyage?"

"Would you agree to take me to Yokohama?"

At these words the seaman stood with his arms dangling, his eyes wide open.

"Are you being humorous, your worship?" he said.

"No. I missed the *Carnatic*'s departure and I need to be in Yokohama no later than the 14th, in order to catch the ocean liner to San Francisco."

"I'm sorry," the pilot replied, "but that isn't possible."

"I'll offer you £100 per day, plus a bonus of £200 if I arrive in time."

"You're serious?" the pilot asked.

"Quite serious," Mr. Fogg answered.

The pilot went off by himself. He looked at the sea, his desire to earn an enormous sum obviously at war with his fear of venturing such a great distance. Fix was in mortal agony.

Meanwhile Mr. Fogg turned back to Lady Aouda.

"You won't be afraid, my lady?" he asked her.

"Not with you, Mr. Fogg," the young woman replied.

Twisting his cap in his hands, the pilot approached the gentleman once more.

"Well, pilot?" Mr. Fogg said.

"Well, your worship," the pilot replied, "on such a long trip at this time of year, I couldn't risk myself, you, or my men in a boat that weighs only twenty-two tons. Besides, we wouldn't arrive in time, because it's 1,650 miles from Hong Kong to Yokohama."

"Only 1,600," Mr. Fogg said.

"It amounts to the same thing."

Fix took a good deep breath.

"But," the pilot added, "maybe there's a different way to handle this."

Fix stopped breathing.

"What way?" Phileas Fogg asked.

"Go to Nagasaki at the southern tip of Japan, which is 1,100 miles from Hong Kong, or just to Shanghai, which is 800 miles. In the second of these runs, we won't stay far from the China coast, which will be a real benefit, especially because we'll have northbound currents."

"Pilot," Phileas Fogg replied, "to catch the American mail boat, I need to reach Yokohama, not Shanghai or Nagasaki."

"But why?" the pilot responded. "The ocean liner to San Francisco doesn't start out from Yokohama. It calls at Yokohama and Nagasaki, but its port of origin is Shanghai."

"You're positive of what you're saying?"

"Positive."

"And when does the liner leave Shanghai?"

"On the 11th at seven o'clock in the evening. So we have four days still to go. Four days adds up to ninety-six hours, and if we average eight miles per hour, if our luck holds up, if the wind stays in the southeast, and if the sea's calm, we can polish off those 800 miles between here and Shanghai."

"And you can leave—"

"In an hour. Enough time to buy provisions and hoist the sails."

"We have a deal. Are you the boat's skipper?"

"Yes—John Bunsby, skipper of the *Tankadère*."

"Would you like a down payment?"

"If you would be so kind, your worship."

"Here's £200 on account." Turning to Fix, Phileas Fogg added, "Sir, if you would like to take advantage of this opportunity . . . "

"Sir, I was going to ask you that favor myself," Fix answered, making a quick decision.

"Fine. We'll board in half an hour."

"But what about your poor servant . . ." Lady Aouda said, tremendously worried by Passepartout's absence.

"I'll do everything I can for him," Phileas Fogg replied.

And while the high-strung, keyed-up, teeth-gnashing Fix made his way to the pilot boat, the other two headed over to the Hong Kong police station. There Phileas Fogg left Passepartout's description along with enough money to get him back home. After they'd gone through the same formalities at the French consulate, and after they'd dropped by the hotel to pick up their baggage, the covered litter took the travelers back to the outer harbor.

Three o'clock sounded. Its crew on board and provisions stowed, pilot boat no. 43 was ready to set sail.

At twenty-two tons the *Tankadère* was an attractive little schooner, its bow quite trim, its handling very easy, its lines well tapered.

You would have sworn it was a racing yacht. Its copperwork gleamed, its ironwork had been galvanized, and its deck was as white as ivory, showing that skipper John Bunsby went all out to keep his vessel in tiptop condition. Its two masts had a slight rearward lean. It carried a spanker sail, foresail, forestaysail, jibs, and gaff topsails, plus it could rig a temporary mast in case of a tailwind. It was sure to make marvelous time, and in fact it had already won several prizes in the "pilot boat matchups."

The *Tankadère*'s crew consisted of skipper John Bunsby and four deckhands. They were able-bodied seamen who ventured out to look for arriving ships in all weather; they knew these seas wonderfully well. John Bunsby was a man of about forty-five, energetic, heavily sunburned, keen-eyed, strong-featured, completely self-assured, and a thorough professional; he would have inspired confidence in the most timid heart.

Phileas Fogg and Lady Aouda went on board. Fix was there already. They took the schooner's aft hatchway down into a square room with berths inset in the walls above a circular couch. A swinging lamp lit a table in the middle. It was small but shipshape.

"I'm sorry there's nothing better to offer you," Mr. Fogg told Fix, who nodded without answering.

The police inspector felt almost ashamed to take advantage of Mr. Fogg's kindness in this way.

He's definitely a very courteous rascal, he thought, but a rascal all the same!

At 3:10 they hoisted sail. The Union Jack was flapping from the schooner's gaff. The passengers sat out on deck. Mr. Fogg and Lady Aouda took one last look at the pier to see if Passepartout was in sight.

Fix was feeling a bit apprehensive, because he'd treated that unfortunate man disgracefully, and chance might have led the fellow to this very place—then an exchange would have broken out where the detective wouldn't have had the upper hand. But the Frenchman didn't appear, and no doubt that debilitating narcotic still had him in its grip.

Skipper John Bunsby finally reached the

open sea, where the *Tankadère* caught the wind in its spanker sail, foresail, and jibs, then went bounding over the waves.

21

Where the Tankadère*'s skipper is in real danger of losing his £200 bonus*

NAVIGATING 800 MILES in a 22-ton vessel was a venturesome expedition all right, above all at that time of year. The seas of China are rough as a rule and prone to dreadful squalls, chiefly during the equinoxes, plus it was the beginning of November to boot.

Since he was being paid by the day, obviously it would have been more profitable for the pilot to take his passengers all the way to Yokohama. But he would have been extremely unwise to attempt such a crossing under these conditions, and it was already a feat of derring-do, if not foolhardiness, to go as far up as Shanghai. But John Bunsby had confidence in his *Tankadère*, which rose to the waves like a seagull, and maybe he was in the right.

During the evening hours of that day, the *Tankadère* navigated through Hong Kong's eccentric narrows and acquitted itself admirably in every circumstance, whether sailing close into the wind or running ahead of it.

"Pilot," Phileas Fogg said as the schooner stood into the open sea, "I don't need to advise you to put on all possible speed."

"You can depend on it, your worship," John Bunsby replied. "In fact we're carrying every sail the wind will let us carry. The gaff topsails won't add anything and will just put the boat out of kilter by hurting its speed."

"It's your profession, pilot, not mine. I leave it to you."

Body erect, legs apart, as steady as a seaman, Phileas Fogg looked at the surging billows without flinching. Full of emotion, the young woman sat in the stern and contemplated that ocean she was braving in this frail boat; the waves were already grower darker in the twilight. White sails unfurled above her head, carrying her off into space like great wings. Lifted by the wind, the schooner seemed to be flying through the air.

Night fell. The moon was entering her first quarter and her inadequate rays would soon fade into the mists on the horizon. Clouds driven from the east were already overrunning part of the sky.

The pilot had put on his running lights—an indispensable precaution in ultra busy seas near landing places. Collisions between ships aren't infrequent in these waters, and at the speed it was zipping along, the schooner would have cracked open from the slightest impact.

Fix sat brooding in the craft's bow. He was keeping to himself, knowing Fogg wasn't talkative by nature. Besides, he hated speaking to this man whose help he'd accepted. Accordingly he was thinking about the future. He felt sure this Fogg fellow wouldn't stop over in Yokohama but would immediately take the ocean liner to San Francisco, aiming to reach those wide-open spaces in America that guaranteed him safety and impunity. Phileas Fogg's plan struck him as the height of simplicity.

Instead of sailing straight from England to the United States like an ordinary rascal, this Fogg had gone on a grand tour covering three-quarters of the globe, to be more certain of reaching that American continent where he could serenely squander the bank's money after outfoxing the police. But what was Fix to do once he was in Union territory? Forget about the fellow? No, a hundred times no! Till he'd gotten a writ of extradition, he would stay on Fogg's heels. This was his responsibility and he would see it through to the finish. In any case he'd had one piece of good luck: Passepartout wasn't with his master anymore, and since Fix had confided in the Frenchman, it was crucial that employer and employee never got back together.

As for Phileas Fogg, he spent no less time thinking about his manservant, who had vanished in such an odd fashion. After he'd given the matter full consideration, it didn't strike him as impossible that the poor lad, due to some misunderstanding, had gone off on the *Carnatic* at the last moment. Which was Lady Aouda's view as well, and she keenly missed that good servant whom she owed so much. So there was a possibility they would track him down in Yokohama, and it would be easy to find out whether the *Carnatic* had transported him there.

Near ten o'clock the breeze started to pick up. Maybe it would have been wise to take in a reef, but their pilot carefully examined the state of the sky, then left his sails as is. Besides, the *Tankadère* carried its canvas wonderfully, having a sizeable draft of water, and they were all set to haul in fast if a squall came up.

At midnight Phileas Fogg and Lady Aouda went below to their cabin. Fix was there already and lay on one of the berths. As for the pilot and his men, they stayed on deck all night.

By sunrise the next day, November 8, the schooner had done over a hundred miles. They often heaved the log, and it showed they were averaging eight to nine miles per hour. Every sail bellying out, the *Tankadère* had the breeze at its back and in these circumstances was going at top speed. If the wind and weather conditions held up, the odds were in their favor.

That whole workday the *Tankadère* didn't stray noticeably far from the coast, where currents were more helpful. The shore lay five miles at best off their port quarter and its jagged outlines were occasionally visible through rifts in the haze. The wind came off the land, so the sea wasn't as rough thereabouts—a lucky state of affairs for the schooner, because vessels of small tonnage are especially vulnerable in a swell, which can interrupt their headway and "stop 'em dead" as sailors put it.

Toward noontime the breeze died down a little and blew from the southeast. The pilot let out the gaff topsails; but two hours later he had to take them in because the wind picked up again.

Fortunately Mr. Fogg and the young woman weren't prone to seasickness and hungrily ate the biscuits and canned foods on board. They invited Fix to share their meal, and he had to accept, well aware that bellies need ballast as much as boats do—but it troubled him! To travel at Fogg's expense, to eat the food the man was paying for: this struck Fix as somehow a bit underhanded. He

did eat, however—just a snack, it's true—but it counted as eating all the same.

Nevertheless, once their meal was over, he felt he had to take this Fogg fellow aside, and he said to him:

"Sir . . ."

This "sir" scalded his lips, and he had to exercise self-restraint to keep from grabbing this "sir" by the collar!

"Sir, it was very kind of you to give me a lift on your boat. But though I haven't the means to travel in the style you do, I intend to pay my fair share—"

"Sir," Mr. Fogg replied, "don't give it a thought."

"But really, I—"

"No, sir," Fogg repeated in a tone that brooked no opposition. "This goes under general expenses!"

Feeling suffocated, Fix gave a nod, went and stretched out in the schooner's bow, and didn't say another word that day.

Meanwhile they were speeding along. John Bunsby had high hopes. Several times he told Mr. Fogg they would reach Shanghai within the desired time. Mr. Fogg merely replied that he expected as much. And so the whole crew of the little schooner went at it with a will. The £200 bonus was an enticement for these gallant fellows. Accordingly there wasn't a single line that hadn't been painstakingly tightened! There wasn't a single sail that hadn't been firmly stretched! There wasn't a single swerve that could be blamed on the helmsman! They wouldn't have run the vessel with more discipline in a Royal Yacht Club regatta.

That evening the pilot worked out from the log that they'd gone a distance of 220 miles from Hong Kong, and Phileas Fogg could look forward to having no delays to record in his schedule when he reached Yokohama. Hence the first major setback he'd experienced since leaving London most likely wouldn't be detrimental to him.

That night, during the early morning hours, the *Tankadère* headed right into Taiwan Strait, which separates the big island of Taiwan from the China coast, then cut the Tropic of Cancer. The sea was very troublesome in this strait, which was full of eddies caused by countercurrents. The schooner was under a lot of strain. The choppy billows demolished its momentum. They had quite a hard time standing upright on deck.

The wind picked up again at daybreak. In the sky it looked like a squall was brewing. In addition their barometer announced that atmospheric changes were imminent: the instrument's behavior was erratic all day, the mercury in it fluctuating unpredictably. What's more, you could see the ocean to the southeast rearing up in long swells that "smacked of a storm." The evening before, the sun had set in a red haze, surrounded by a sea that sparkled with phosphorescent glimmers.

For a good while their pilot studied the sky's nasty appearance, muttering unintelligible things between his teeth. At one point, finding himself next to his passenger:

"Can I be honest with you, your worship?" he said in a low voice.

"Completely," Phileas Fogg replied.

"Well then, we're in for a squall."

"Will it come from the north or south?" Mr. Fogg merely asked.

"From the south. Take a look. We've got a typhoon in the works!"

"I'm all in favor of typhoons from the south," Mr. Fogg replied. "They'll drive us in the right direction."

"If those are your feelings," the pilot remarked, "I'll leave it at that!"

John Bunsby's hunch was correct. During the warmer seasons, as a well-known meteorologist put it, typhoons fizzle out in bright showers of fiery electricity; but when they're unleashed during the winter equinox, there's a danger they'll be vicious.

The pilot took precautions ahead of time. He rolled and tied every sail on the schooner and lowered the yards to the deck. The topmasts came down. The bowsprit was retracted. They carefully battened the hatches. After that not one drop of water could get inside the craft's hull. To keep the schooner stern to the wind, they hoisted a single triangular sail—a storm jib made of heavy canvas—to act as a forestaysail. And they waited.

John Bunsby encouraged his passengers to go below to their cabin; but since they would be confined in a cramped area, would have almost no air, and would be jolted around by the swell, this wasn't something with great appeal. Neither Mr. Fogg, nor Lady Aouda, nor even Fix would agree to leave the deck.

Around eight o'clock gusts of air and rain swept down on the vessel. With nothing more than its little scrap of canvas, the *Tankadère* was borne like a feather on these winds, which words can't describe when they blow up into a storm. If you compared their speed to four times that of a locomotive shooting along at full throttle, it would still be less than the truth.

The whole day the boat raced northward in this fashion, carried by the monstrous billows, luckily keeping up the same speed they did. Twenty times it was nearly overtopped by one of those mountains of water rearing up astern; but a shrewd twitch of the rudder by their pilot would stave off disaster. Sometimes the passengers were drenched in spray, but they took it philosophically. No doubt Fix moaned and groaned, but our dauntless Aouda kept her eyes on her companion, could only marvel at his composure, and proved worthy of him by braving the turmoil at his side. As for Phileas Fogg himself, he acted as if this typhoon were simply an item on his schedule.

Till then the *Tankadère* had been on a continuous northerly course; but toward evening, as they might have feared, the wind shifted through three quadrants and blew from the northwest. Now catching the waves sideways, the schooner shook appallingly. The sea battered it with an intensity that was bound to terrorize anybody who didn't know how securely a vessel's parts are all put together.

At nightfall the storm grew in strength. When he saw darkness coming on—and the turmoil increasing along with it—John Bunsby felt deeply concerned. He wondered if it wasn't time to head for shore, so he conferred with his crew.

After this staff conference John Bunsby went up to Mr. Fogg and told him:

"I think, your worship, it would be best if

we made for one of the harbors along the coast."

"I think so too," Phileas Fogg replied

"Oh?" the pilot put in. "Which?"

"I know of only one," Mr. Fogg answered serenely.

"And it's . . . ?"

"Shanghai."

For a few seconds at first, the pilot wasn't sure what to make of this reply, or the stubbornness and determination underlying it. Then he exclaimed:

"Of course, your worship! You're right! On to Shanghai!"

And the *Tankadère* kept to its unflappable northbound heading.

They had a truly dreadful night! It was a miracle the little schooner didn't capsize. Twice they lost control, and everything would have been swept overboard had the lashings given way. It was a shattering experience for Lady Aouda, but she didn't utter a single complaint. More than once Mr. Fogg had to rush up and protect her from the ferocity of the billows.

Daylight reappeared. The storm was still being unleashed with tremendous fury. Even so, the wind dropped back to the southeast. Which was a positive change, and the *Tankadère* resumed its course over the raging sea, whose billows collided with the ones caused by that new wind now blowing. Ergo this pileup of counter swells, which would have pulverized a vessel less sturdily built.

When the mists broke apart, you could view the coastline from time to time, but there wasn't a ship in sight. Only the *Tankadère* had stayed at sea.

By noontime there were a few signs of a lull, and they were more clearly apparent as the sun sank toward the horizon.

Due to its very ferocity, the storm hadn't lasted long. Our passengers could grab a quick bite and a little rest after their shattering experience.

They had a comparatively peaceful night. Their pilot close reefed his sails again. The boat's speed was considerable. At sunrise the next morning, the 11th, they raised the Japan coast, and John Bunsby could report that they were barely a hundred miles from Shanghai.

A hundred miles and only one day left to do them in! If Mr. Fogg didn't want to miss the ocean liner setting out for Yokohama, he needed to arrive in Shanghai that same evening. He'd lost several hours during the storm, otherwise he would have been barely thirty miles from port by then.

The breeze slackened noticeably, but luckily the sea subsided along with it. The schooner ran under full canvas. It carried everything it had, gaff topsails, staysails, and false jib included, and the sea foamed beneath its stempost.

By noontime the *Tankadère* lay no more than forty-five miles from Shanghai. It still had six hours left in which to reach port before the ocean liner set out for Yokohama.

The suspense on board was tremendous. They intended to make it at any cost. You could sense everybody's heart pounding with impatience—Phileas Fogg's excepted, of course. The little schooner had to maintain an average speed of nine miles per hour, yet the wind kept dying down! It was an intermittent breeze that blew off the land in erratic puffs. The instant they wafted by, the sea smoothed out again.

Yet the current was so helpful, their boat so light, its sails so tall, their fabric so delicate and so adept at catching the fickle breezes, by six o'clock John Bunsby figured he wasn't more than ten miles from the Shanghai River, the town itself being located a good twelve miles above the river's mouth.

By seven o'clock they were still three miles from Shanghai. A fearsome swearword escaped from their pilot's lips. . . . Clearly the £200 bonus was about to elude him. He looked at Mr. Fogg. Mr. Fogg was his unemotional self, and yet his whole fortune was at stake just then . . .

Just then, too, an object appeared at the far edge of the water: it was long, black, shaped like a post, and crowned by a plume of smoke. It was a ship's funnel—the American ocean liner was leaving at the scheduled time.

"Curse it all!" John Bunsby howled at the helm, desperately flinging the wheel back around.

"Signal them!" Phileas Fogg merely said.

Mounted in the *Tankadère*'s bow was a little bronze cannon. It was used for sending signals in foggy weather.

They loaded the cannon to the muzzle, but just as the pilot was holding a hot coal to its vent:

"Fly your flag at half mast," Mr. Fogg said.

They brought the flag to mid pole. This served as a distress signal, and they could only hope the American ocean liner would see it, momentarily change direction, and attend to the pilot boat.

"Fire!" Mr. Fogg said.

And the little bronze cannon gave a boom that shattered the air.

22

*Where Passepartout finds
that even halfway around the world,
it's wise to have a little money in your pocket*

LEAVING HONG KONG at 6:30 in the evening on November 7, the *Carnatic* headed for the shores of Japan with all steam on. It carried a full load of goods and passengers. Two cabins in the stern remained unoccupied. They were the ones that had been booked on behalf of Mr. Phileas Fogg.

The next morning crewmen in the bow watched with some surprise as a tottering, bleary-eyed, tousle-headed passenger emerged from the second-class hatchway, staggered over to where a spare mast was lying, and sat down on it.

This passenger was none other than Passepartout. Here's what had transpired.

A few seconds after Fix had left the smoking parlor, two of its staff members had lifted Passepartout, now sound asleep, and laid him on the bed earmarked for opium users. But three hours later, hounded by an intense fixation even in his nightmares, Passepartout woke up and fought off the crippling effects of the narcotic. The thought of a responsibility he hadn't fulfilled roused him from his numbness. Driven by a sort of relentless, irresistible instinct, he left that bed of sots, lurched forward, leaned against the walls, fell down, got back up, and went out of the smoking parlor, wailing as if in a dream, "The *Carnatic*! The *Carnatic*!"

The ocean liner had steam up nearby, all set to leave. Passepartout had only a few steps to go. He dashed down the slip, climbed the gangway, and fell unconscious in the bow just as the *Carnatic* loosed its moorings.

A couple of sailors, fellows used to such goings-on, took the poor lad down to a second-class cabin, and when Passepartout awoke the next morning, the shores of China were 150 miles behind him.

Which is how Passepartout wound up that morning on the *Carnatic*'s deck, where he'd come to inhale lungfuls of the fresh sea breeze. The clean air brought him around. He tried to gather his wits about him and was having a hard time of it. But finally he remembered what had gone on the day before, Fix's confiding in him, the smoking parlor, etc.

"Obviously I got stinking drunk!" he said to himself. "What'll Mr. Fogg say? Anyhow I didn't miss the boat, and that's the main thing."

Then, thinking about Fix:

"After what that man proposed to me," he said to himself, "I hope he's out of our lives for good and won't dare follow us on the *Carnatic*. A police inspector—a detective on my master's heels—blaming him for that robbery committed at the Bank of England! Come off it! Mr. Fogg's no more a robber than I'm a paid political assassin!"

Should Passepartout reveal these things to his master? Would it be appropriate to tell him the role Fix was playing in the business? Before informing him that a Scotland Yard investigator had been tailing him around the world, wouldn't it be best to wait till they'd arrived in London where they could laugh about it? Yes, surely. In any event it was food for thought. His more immediate need was to rejoin Mr. Fogg and beg forgiveness for his unspeakable conduct.

So Passepartout stood up. The sea was rough and the ocean liner rolling a great deal. The good fellow was still unsteady on his feet, but somehow he made it to the ship's stern.

He didn't see anybody on deck resembling his master or Lady Aouda.

"Fine," he put in. "At this hour Lady Aouda's still in bed. As for Mr. Fogg, it's his standard procedure to find somebody up for a game of whist . . ."

With that Passepartout went below to the lounge. Mr. Fogg wasn't there. Passepartout had only one option: ask the purser which cabin belonged to Mr. Fogg. The purser answered him that he didn't know of any passenger with that name.

"Excuse me," Passepartout said, not giving up. "The gentleman I'm talking about is tall, calm, not very sociable, and there's a young lady with him—"

"We haven't a single young lady on this ship," the purser replied. "Anyhow here's the passenger list. You can check it yourself."

Passepartout checked the list . . . it didn't include his master's name.

He stood in a daze. Then a thought crossed his mind.

"Oh drat!" he exclaimed. "This *is* the *Carnatic*, isn't it?"

"It is," the purser replied.

"On the way to Yokohama?"

"Positively."

For a second Passepartout was afraid he'd gotten on the wrong ship! However, though he himself had boarded the *Carnatic*, his master very definitely hadn't.

Passepartout collapsed into an easy chair. This was a lightning bolt from the blue. And suddenly the truth dawned on him. He remembered that the *Carnatic*'s departure time had been moved forward, that he was supposed to warn his master, and that he hadn't done so! Consequently it was his own fault that Mr. Fogg and Lady Aouda had missed the ship's departure!

Yes, it was his own fault, but even more the fault of that villain who had gotten him drunk—to keep him away from his master so the latter could be detained in Hong Kong! He finally saw through the police inspector's scheme. And now Mr. Fogg faced unavoidable financial ruin, had lost his bet, had been arrested, had maybe been clapped in jail . . . ! Passepartout tore his hair at the thought. Oh, if he ever got his hands on Fix, he would settle that man's account in full!

After this initial moment of desperation, Passepartout finally regained his composure and examined his circumstances. They weren't exactly enviable. He was a Frenchman on his way to Japan. He would arrive there for sure, but how would he depart? His pockets were empty. Not one shilling, not one penny! Even so, his transportation and his meals on board were already paid for. Therefore he had five or six days ahead of him and during that time he could come to a decision. As for what he ate and drank during this crossing, words fail us. He ate enough for himself, his master, and Lady Aouda put together. His destination was Japan, but he ate as if it was a barren wasteland without a single edible commodity.

On the 13th the *Carnatic* entered the harbor of Yokohama on the morning tide.

This stop is a major anchorage in the Pacific, a port of call for all steamers doing mail and passenger runs between North America, China, Japan, and the islands of Malaysia. Yokohama is located right on Tokyo Bay and a short distance from this immense town, which is the Japanese empire's second capital, the former home of the shōgun back when that civil ruler existed, and the competitor of Kyoto—that great city where the mikado lives, the ecclesiastic ruler descended from the gods.

Amid a large number of ships hailing from all nations, the *Carnatic* drew up alongside a Yokohama pier near the port jetties and customhouses.

This land belonging to the Children of the Rising Sun is quite an unusual place, but Passepartout set foot on it without any enthusiasm. Having nothing better to do, he let fortune be his guide and wandered at random through the city streets.

It was a thoroughly European town that Passepartout stood in at first—the low fronts of its houses were adorned with porches spreading above stylish colonnades, and its streets, squares, docks, and warehouses covered the whole area in between Treaty Point and the river. Here, just as in Hong Kong and Calcutta, people of all races were milling around helter-skelter, American, English,

Chinese, and Dutch, traders ready to buy or sell anything—and the Frenchman felt as out of place in their midst as if he'd been dropped off in the land of the Hottentots.

Passepartout did have one option: to pay his respects at the French or English consulates that had been set up in Yokohama; but his tale was so intimately bound up with his master's that he hated having to tell it, so he didn't want to take this step till he'd exhausted every other alternative.

Therefore, after going through the European side of town and not having any luck, he headed for the Japanese side, determined, if need be, to push on to Tokyo.

Named after a sea goddess revered on the neighboring isles, this native sector of Yokohama is called Benten. There you can view marvelous walkways lined with firs and cedars, the sacred portals of an alien school of architecture, bridges hidden among bamboos and reeds, temples taking shelter beneath the mournful cover of immense century-old cedars, monasteries housing the static existences of Buddhist monks and followers of Confucius, endless streets where you could harvest crops of rosy-cheeked, pink-skinned children, little folks straight out of the pictures on the folding screens hereabouts; they were playing in the midst of short-legged poodles and yellowish, bobtailed cats that looked very lazy and cuddly.

The streets were full of commotion, people continually going to and fro: processions of Buddhist monks went by, monotonously tapping their tambourines, then customs officials or police officers known as *yakounines* who sported lacquer-coated pointy hats and two sabers in their belts, soldiers packing percussion firearms and dressed in blue cotton cloth with white stripes, the mikado's men at arms encased in their silk doublets and their metal tunics and coats of mail, plus a number of other military men of every rank—because the soldier's profession is as honored in Japan as it's sneered at in China. Then came holy men begging alms, pilgrims in long robes, and regular citizens with glossy hair as black as ebony, heads squat, upper torsos long, legs slender, stature on the small side, coloring from dark copper hues to

plain white—but never yellow like the Chinese, from whom they fundamentally differ. The area was full of buggies, covered litters, horses, carriers, wind-powered wheelbarrows, litters with lacquered sides known as *norimons*, plush sedan chairs called *kagos*, and honest-to-goodness stretchers made of bamboo; among these you could see, finally, a few women walking around, taking tiny steps on tiny feet that were shod in canvas slippers, straw sandals, or delicately carved wooden pumps; with their slanted eyes, flat chests, and teeth blackened in the fashion of the time, they weren't exactly pretty, but they wore their national costume with style: the kimono, a sort of dressing gown with a silk sash across it and a wide belt expanding at the rear into a flamboyant knot—which, these days, the females of Japan seem to have lent to the females of Paris.

Passepartout strolled for a few hours in the midst of this motley crowd, looking all the while at the interesting and richly filled shops, the bazaars crammed with every kind of showy Japanese metalwork, the made-over restaurants that were decked with streamers and flags and were now out of bounds for him, and the teahouses where you drink cupfuls of that fragrant hot water along with a liquor brewed from fermenting rice that's called *sake*, and those cozy smoking parlors where folks smoke a really choice tobacco instead of opium, whose use is almost unheard-of in Japan.

Then Passepartout ended up out in the country in the midst of immense rice paddies. There, among the flowers giving off their final colors and scents, brilliant camellias were in bloom, no longer growing on bushes but on trees, and inside bamboo pens were cherry, plum, and apple trees that the locals nurture for their blossoms rather than their fruits, which were protected from the beaks of sparrows, pigeons, ravens, and other voracious winged creatures by scowling scarecrows that squealed on their revolving bases. Every majestic cedar harbored a huge eagle in its branches; every weeping willow spread its foliage over a heron perched gloomily on one leg; on all sides, finally, there were rooks, ducks, hawks, wild geese, and a large number of those cranes that the Japanese treat like royalty and regard as symbols of long life and happiness.

Wandering around in this way, Passepartout spotted some violets among the weeds:

"Good," he said, "there's my supper!"[12]

But when he sniffed them, he found they no longer had any scent.

Just my luck, he thought.

To be sure, he'd had the foresight to eat the heartiest breakfast he could before leaving the *Carnatic;* but the good fellow had been strolling around all day and his belly felt pretty hollow. He did notice that lamb, goat, and pork all were absent from the local butcher shops, and since he knew it was a sacrilege to slay cattle, which are reserved exclusively for plowing purposes, he had to conclude that butcher's meat was scarce in Japan. He wasn't mistaken; but in place of such meat, his belly was quite amenable to a haunch of deer or wild boar, some partridge or quail, poultry or fish—which, along with the output from their rice paddies, are about the only things Japanese people eat. But he had to shrug off his bad luck and postpone his foraging for food till the following day.

Night fell. Passepartout went back into the Japanese side of town and he roamed the streets in the midst of their multicolored lanterns, watching companies of street performers do their acclaimed acrobatics and open-air stargazers draw crowds around their spyglasses. Then he saw the docks again, spangled with flickering lights from fishermen who were luring fish with resin torches.

At last the streets emptied out. Once the crowds were gone, the *yakounines* started their rounds. In their magnificent costumes and surrounded by their retinues, these officials looked like government emissaries on parade, and every time Passepartout bumped into one of these splendiferous patrols, he cracked the same joke:

"Would you look at that! The whole Japanese diplomatic corps is heading back to Europe!"

---

[12] *Translator's note.* Violets are a garnish or foodstuff in many cultures.

23

In which Passepartout's nose gets outlandishly long

RAVENOUS, DONE IN, Passepartout told himself the next morning that he had to get some food at any cost, and the sooner the better. He did have the option of selling his watch, but he would have starved to death first. It was now or never—nature had given the gallant fellow a voice that was loud if not mellifluous, so it was time to put it to use.

He knew a few French and English ditties and decided to give them a try. No doubt about it, the Japanese had to be music lovers, since they did everything to the sound of cymbals, tom-toms, and drums, so they couldn't fail to appreciate the virtuoso artistry of a European performer.

But maybe it was a bit early for putting on a concert, and if a singer wakes his fans up at an ungodly hour, his payment might not come in the form of money bearing the mikado's likeness.

So Passepartout decided to wait a little while; but as he moseyed along, it occurred to him that he looked too well dressed for a wandering minstrel, and he came up with the idea of exchanging his clothes for some cast-off things more in keeping with his vocation. Besides, such an exchange was bound to leave him with money left over, which he could immediately put to work in appeasing his hunger pangs.

This decision made, all he had to do was carry it out. It was only after a long search that Passepartout discovered a local second-hand dealer and made his desires known. The dealer was delighted with Passepartout's European getup, and the Frenchman soon left outfitted in some old Japanese robes and topped by a sort of ribbed turban that had faded from exposure to the elements. But to make up the difference, a few small silver coins were jingling in his pocket.

Fine, he thought, I'll just imagine it's carnival season!

After "going Japanese" in this manner, Passepartout's first priority was to enter a teahouse of humble appearance; there his breakfast consisted of some leftover poultry scraps and a few handfuls of rice, which he ate like a man for whom dinner was a problem he would worry about later.

"Now," he said to himself after he'd eaten heartily, "I've got to keep my wits about me. I no longer have the option of selling these cast-off clothes for something even more Japanese. So I need to find the quickest possible way of leaving this Land of the Rising Sun and putting these painful memories behind me!"

Then it dawned on Passepartout to inspect the ocean liners ready to leave for America. He figured he could get hired in the capacity of a cook or waiter, asking only for his transportation and meals as pay. Once he was in San Francisco, he would look into sorting things out. The main thing was to cross those 4,700 miles of Pacific Ocean lying between Japan and the New World.

Passepartout wasn't the type to sit on a good idea, so he headed toward the port of Yokohama. However, though his plan had seemed quite simple when he first came up with it, his idea struck him as more and more impractical the closer he came to the docks. Wouldn't an American ocean liner already have the cooks and waiters it needed? And how could he inspire any confidence the way he was dressed? What references could he furnish? What letters of recommendation could he whip out?

As he was brooding along these lines, his eyes fell on an immense signboard that a clownlike person was carrying through Yokohama's streets. The signboard was in English and this is how it read:

THE HONORABLE WILLIAM BATULCAR'S

COMPANY OF JAPANESE ACROBATS

———

FINAL PERFORMANCES

before they go off to the United States of America

OF THE

LONG NOSES — LONG NOSES

WITH THE PERSONAL BLESSING OF THE GOD TENGU

Major Attraction!

"The United States of America!" Passepartout exclaimed. "Just what the doctor ordered . . . !"

He followed the signboard carrier and on his heels soon reentered the Japanese side of town. Fifteen minutes later he halted in front of a huge hut crowned by several bouquets of streamers; in garish colors and without any attempt at perspective drawing, its outside walls portrayed a whole team of jugglers.

This was the honorable Mr. Batulcar's place of business—he was an American promoter in the style of P. T. Barnum, the director of a company of tumblers, jugglers, clowns, acrobats, gymnasts, and balancing acts who, according to the signboard, were giving their final performances before leaving the Empire of the Rising Sun for the states of the Union.

Passepartout went under the colonnade in front of the hut and asked for Mr. Batulcar. Mr. Batulcar appeared in person.

"What is it?" he said to Passepartout, whom he mistook at first for a local.

"Would you be in need of a servant?" Passepartout asked.

"A servant!" exclaimed this second Barnum, stroking the heavy gray beard that flourished under his chin. "I've already got two who are obedient and loyal, who have never quit on me, who work for nothing so long as I feed them . . . and here they are," he added, holding up his two beefy arms, furrowed with veins as thick as the strings on a bass fiddle.

"So there isn't a thing I can do for you?"

"Not a thing."

"Blast, it would have suited me just fine to go overseas with you!"

"Drat the fellow!" said the honorable Mr. Batulcar. "If you're Japanese, I'm a monkey's uncle! Why are you wearing that getup?"

"Folks wear what they can afford."

"That's true. You're French, right?"

"Yes, a thoroughgoing Parisian."

"So you must be good at sneering and smirking?"

"Oh ye gods," Passepartout replied, aggravated at seeing his nationality inspire this question. "It's true, we Frenchmen are good at sneering and smirking—but no more than you Americans!"

"Granted. All right, if I don't take you on as a servant, I *can* take you on as a clown. Here's how it is, my hearty. In France they headline funny men from other countries, and in other countries funny men from France."

"Aha!"

"Are you strong as well?"

"Especially after I get up from the table."

"And you can sing?"

"Yes," answered Passepartout, who had participated in a couple of street concerts in the old days.

"But could you sing standing on your head, with a top spinning on the sole of your left foot, and a saber balanced on the sole of your right foot?"

"Of course!" Passepartout replied, remembering his youthful stints as a gymnast.

"That's all we ask, you understand?" responded the honorable Mr. Batulcar.

They completed the hiring process *hic et nunc*.[13]

Passepartout had finally landed a job. He'd been hired as an all-purpose performer in this famous company of Japanese acrobats. It wasn't anything to brag about, but before the week was up, he would be on his way to San Francisco.

Announced with much fanfare by the honorable Mr. Batulcar, the performance was to start at three o'clock, and soon the fearsome instruments of a Japanese orchestra—drums and tom-toms—were thundering away by the entrance. As you can appreciate, Passepartout wasn't able to rehearse any solo turns but had to be ready to contribute his sturdy shoulders to the main gymnastic feat, a "human edifice" executed by the Long Noses of the god Tengu.[14] After a whole series of gymnastic stunts, this "major attraction" was to close the performance.

Even before three o'clock spectators were overrunning the huge hut. Europeans and locals, Chinese and Japanese, men, women, and children all were rushing to get seats on the cramped benches and in the boxes facing the stage. The musicians came back inside and the full orchestra of gongs, tom-toms, ratchets, flutes, tambourines, and bass drums went furiously to work.

The performance was a typical display of acrobatics. But it does need to be acknowledged that the Japanese are the world's best when it comes to feats of balance. In one stunt the performer used a fan and little pieces of paper to create a dainty vista of butterflies and flowers. In another, the performer paid a verbal compliment to the audience by swiftly scribbling a sequence of bluish words in the air—with the fragrant smoke from his pipe. A different performer juggled some lighted candles, consecutively blowing them out as they passed in front of his lips and then relighting them one from the other, all without interrupting his world-class juggling for a single second. Still another performer did the most mind-boggling tricks with spinning tops; in his hands these droning gadgets whirled so constantly, they seemed to have lives of their own; they ran along the stems of pipes, along the edges of sabers, along steel wires—virtual strands of hair stretched from one side of the stage to the other; they went around the rims of big crystal vases, they scaled bamboo ladders, and as they scattered off in all directions, they droned in different keys, which in combination created the oddest kinds of harmonic effects. Then jugglers used them to juggle with, and the tops would spin around in midair; the performers batted the tops with wooden rackets as if they were shuttlecocks, yet they kept on spinning; the jugglers stuffed the tops in their pockets and pulled them back out, still spinning away—till the moment when the performers released springs inside the tops and made them burst into sprays of fireworks!

There's no need for these pages to describe the prodigious stunts performed by the acrobats and gymnasts in the company. They performed their feats on ladders, poles, balls, barrels, etc., executing them with noteworthy precision. But the Long Noses were the performance's main draw—a wondrous balancing act that's still unknown in Europe.

---

[13] *Translator's note*. Latin: "then and there."

[14] *Translator's note*. Mischievous spirit in Japanese folklore.

These Long Noses make up a unique guild that enjoys the personal blessing of the god Tengu. Dressed like medieval heralds, they sported glittering sets of wings on their shoulders. But their most individual characteristic was the long nose adorning each of their faces, and especially the uses these organs were put to. These noses were nothing less than pieces of bamboo five, six, and ten feet in length, some straight, others curved, these smooth, those warty. Now then, it was on these securely attached appendages that their whole balancing act took place. About a dozen of these followers of the god Tengu lay on their backs, then their comrades came and romped on their noses, bouncing and flitting from this one to that one, executing the most unbelievable shenanigans on these protuberances, which were as erect as lightning rods.

As a climax, they'd specifically promised the public they would do a human pyramid, during which some fifty Long Noses were to depict the "Car of Juggernaut," the wagon that carries Krishna's statue during Hindu ceremonies. But instead of forming this pyramid by using their shoulders as points of purchase, the honorable Mr. Batulcar had his showmen make do with their noses. Now then, one of the gymnasts who formed the base of the wagon had left the company, and since this task needed nothing more than muscles and good reflexes, Passepartout had been picked to replace him.

To be sure, the fine lad was consumed with self-pity when (dismal reminder of his youth) he put on his medieval costume adorned with its multicolored wings, then had a six-foot nose fastened to his face. But still and all, this nose was his meal ticket and he accepted his lot.

Passepartout went onstage and fell into line next to those of his colleagues who were to make up the base of the Car of Juggernaut. They all lay down on the ground, erect noses reaching skyward. A second layer of acrobats took up positions on these long appendages, a third tier above these, then a fourth; and on these noses that made contact only with their tips, a human monument soon rose nearly to the playhouse cornice.

Now then, just as the applause was increasing and the instruments of the orchestra were cutting loose even more thunderously, the pyramid gave a shudder, tipped off balance, one of the noses forming its base took French leave, and the whole monument collapsed like a house of cards . . .

The fault lay with Passepartout, who had abandoned his post, cleared the footlights without the help of his wings, clambered up the right side of the gallery, and fallen at the feet of a spectator, hollering:

"Oh master, master!"

"It's you?"

"It's me."

"Very well, my lad, in that case we have an ocean liner to catch . . . !"

Lady Aouda had come along, and she rushed with Mr. Fogg and Passepartout down the corridors leading out of the hut. But once outside, they found the honorable Mr. Batulcar, who was furious, claimed he'd been injured, and demanded restitution for "the damage done." Phileas Fogg tossed a handful of banknotes at him and quelled his fury. And at 6:30, just as it was about to leave, Mr. Fogg and Lady Aouda set foot on the American ocean liner; Passepartout followed them, on his back a set of wings, on his front that six-foot nose he still hadn't managed to snatch from his face!

24

During which they cross the whole Pacific Ocean

YOU CAN GATHER what had taken place within view of Shanghai. The ocean liner to Yokohama had picked up the signals sent by the *Tankadère.* Seeing its flag at half mast, the steamship's captain headed over to the little schooner. A few seconds later, settling his transportation expenses with John Bunsby as agreed, Phileas Fogg put £550 ($2,750) into the skipper's pocket. Then the distinguished gentleman, Lady Aouda, and Fix climbed aboard the steamer, which set out at once for Nagasaki and Yokohama.

Arriving on the morning of November 14, right at the scheduled time, Phileas Fogg left

Fix to his own devices and made his way aboard the *Carnatic;* there he learned, much to Lady Aouda's delight (and maybe his own, though he didn't let anything show), that the Frenchman Passepartout had indeed arrived in Yokohama the day before.

Since he was to leave again for San Francisco that same evening, Phileas Fogg immediately set about looking for his manservant. He inquired without success at the French and English consulates, and after scouring Yokohama's streets to no avail, he despaired of finding Passepartout again; then chance—or maybe some sort of hunch—led him inside the honorable Mr. Batulcar's hut. To be sure, he never would have recognized his employee in that freakish herald's costume; but as the latter was lying supine, he spotted his master in the gallery. He couldn't help twitching his nose. Ergo the loss of balance and all that followed.

This is what Passepartout learned right from the lips of Lady Aouda, who then described to him how they'd made the crossing from Hong Kong to Shanghai, along with a certain Mr. Fix, on the schooner *Tankadère.*

Passepartout didn't bat an eye when Fix's name came up. He felt it still wasn't time to tell his master what had taken place between himself and the police inspector. Accordingly, in the tale Passepartout told of his adventures, he took all the blame and simply begged forgiveness for getting drugged on opium in a Hong Kong smoking parlor.

Mr. Fogg listened coolly to this account without replying; then he gave his manservant enough of a salary advance that the latter could obtain more presentable clothing aboard ship. And an hour hadn't gone by, in fact, before the good fellow had cut off his nose, clipped his wings, and left nothing on his person to identify him as a follower of the god Tengu.

Christened the *General Grant,* the ocean liner making the crossing from Yokohama to San Francisco belonged to the Pacific Mail Steam Co. A huge paddle-wheel steamer with a burden of 2,750 tons, it was well fitted out and gifted with great speed. An enormous beam consecutively rose and fell above the deck; at one end a piston rod went back and forth, at the other end a tie rod converted the rectilinear motion into a circular motion and transmitted it right to the axle of the paddle wheels. The *General Grant* was rigged like a three-masted schooner and had a huge expanse of canvas that could lend forceful assistance to its steam power. If it did its usual twelve miles per hour, the ocean liner would be able to cross the Pacific in twenty-one days or less. So Phileas Fogg had grounds for thinking he would make it to San Francisco by December 2, New York by the 11th, and London by the 20th—thus getting a few hours' jump on that drop-dead date of December 21.

There were a fair number of passengers aboard the steamer: Englishmen, lots of Americans, enough coolies heading to America to make up an honest-to-goodness migration, and some East Indian army officers who were spending their leave going around the world.

Nautically speaking, the crossing was uneventful. Braced by its wide paddle wheels and buttressed by its mighty sails, the ocean liner rolled very little. The Pacific Ocean largely lived up to its peace-loving name. Mr. Fogg was as calm and unsociable as ever. His young companion felt more and more attached to this man by ties other than those of gratitude. His reserved and yet deeply generous personality affected her more than she knew, and almost without realizing it, she gave in to the types of feelings that apparently hadn't any influence on the mystifying Mr. Fogg.

What's more, Lady Aouda took a prodigious interest in the gentleman's plans. She worried about the various difficulties that could jeopardize his journey's success. Often she chatted with Passepartout, who could read between the lines of Lady Aouda's heart. These days the gallant fellow's attitude toward his master was close to blind faith; he never ran out of praise for Phileas Fogg's integrity, generosity, and dedication; then he reassured Lady Aouda about the journey's outcome, saying again and again that the hardest part was over, that the fantastic countries of China and Japan were behind them, that they were on their way back to civilization, and finally that a train from San Francisco to New York and a transatlantic liner from New York to London would surely be all they needed to finish this impossible world tour within the time frame agreed upon.

Nine days after leaving Yokohama, Phileas Fogg had traveled exactly halfway around the planet earth.

In essence, on November 23 the *General Grant* crossed the 180th meridian, the spot in the southern hemisphere that lies directly opposite London. True, Mr. Fogg had used up fifty-two of the eighty days at his disposal, so there were only twenty-eight left to work with. But it should be noted that though the gentleman had reached his halfway point "meridian-wise," he'd actually completed over two-thirds of his total trip. What detours he'd been forced to make in reality—London to Aden, Aden to Bombay, Calcutta to Hong Kong, Hong Kong to Yokohama! If he'd stayed on the 50th parallel (that of London) and traveled around it, the distance would only have been about 12,000 miles; but since he lay at the mercy of his means of transportation, Phileas Fogg would be forced to travel 26,000 miles, out of which he'd done about 17,500 by this date of November 23. But now he had a straight run ahead of him, and Fix was no longer around to pile on the obstacles!

On November 23 something else happened that filled Passepartout with much glee. You'll recall that the pigheaded fellow had stubbornly kept his notorious family watch on London time, insisting that the clocks were wrong in all the countries he'd gone through. Now then, though he hadn't moved his watch either forward or backward, that day he found it agreeing with the ship's chronometers.

Passepartout's triumph was unalloyed. He dearly wished he knew what Fix would have said if the detective had been there!

"That rascal told me a bunch of tales about the sun, the moon, and the meridians!" Passepartout said over and over. "Hah! If we listened to folks like him, timekeeping would be in a fine state! I was pretty sure the sun would decide to go by my watch sooner or later . . . !"

Passepartout was unaware of one thing: if his watch dial had been divided into twenty-four hours like Italian clocks, he wouldn't have felt so triumphant, because when it was nine o'clock in the morning on board, the hands on his instrument would have said nine o'clock in the evening, in other words, twenty-one hours past midnight—exactly equal to the time difference between London and the 180th meridian.

Fix may have been able to explain this effect as a simple matter of physics, but it's doubtful that Passepartout would have been able to understand him, let alone agree with him. And in any case, if, by all that's fantastic, the police inspector had suddenly showed up on board right then, the justly aggrieved Passepartout very likely would have tackled him on quite a different topic and in quite another fashion.

Now then, where *was* Fix at this juncture . . . ?

Sure enough, Fix was aboard the *General Grant.*

In essence, once he'd arrived in Yokohama, the investigator left Mr. Fogg, figuring to rejoin him later in the day, and immediately proceeded to the English consulate. There he finally found the warrant that had been in hot pursuit since Bombay and was already forty days old—a warrant that had been forwarded to him from Hong Kong aboard the same *Carnatic* he was thought to be traveling on. The reader can imagine how disappointed the detective felt! His warrant was now useless! This Fogg fellow had gone outside English territory! To arrest him now, a writ of extradition would be required!

"So be it!" Fix told himself, getting over his initial fury. "Here my warrant's no good anymore, but back in England it'll be fine. It definitely looks like the rogue thinks he has outfoxed the police and is returning to his own country. Good. I'll follow him home. As for the money, I hope to God there's something left over! The fellow has already gone through more than £5,000 in fares, bonuses, fines, bail, an elephant, and all kinds of expenses along the way. Oh well, the bank has plenty!"

His mind made up, he boarded the *General Grant* at once. He was on deck when Mr. Fogg and Lady Aouda arrived. To his tremendous surprise, he recognized Passepartout in his herald garb. Fix instantly hid in his cabin to keep from having to do any explaining, which would have jeopardized everything—and due to the number of passengers, he figured the Frenchman would never notice him; then, that very day, he came face to face with his enemy in the bow of the ship.

Without a word of explanation, Passepartout was at Fix's throat in a single bound, and much to the delight of some nearby Americans (who instantly put their money on him), he gave the unfortunate inspector a superb drubbing that demonstrated the towering superiority of French boxing to English boxing.

When Passepartout was done, he felt calmer as if a load was off his chest. Fix was in pretty poor condition when he got to his feet; he faced his opponent and coolly said to him:

"Are you through?"

"For right now, yes."

"Then let's go talk."

"I have nothing to—"

"It's in your master's best interests."

As if Fix's composure had some sort of power over him, Passepartout followed the police inspector and they sat down together in the steamer's bow.

"You've given me a walloping," Fix said. "Fine. Now hear me out. Till this point I've been Mr. Fogg's opponent, but starting today I'm on his side."

"So," Passepartout exclaimed, "you finally think he's a respectable man?"

"No," Fix replied coolly, "I still think he's a rascal . . . hush, be quiet and let me speak! As long as Mr. Fogg was in English territory, it was in my best interests to detain him till I'd received a warrant for his arrest. I did everything I could to make that happen. I sent those priests after him from Bombay, I got you drunk in Hong Kong, I separated you from your master, I made him

miss the ocean liner to Yokohama . . ."

Passepartout listened, fists clenched.

"Now," Fix went on, "it seems Mr. Fogg is heading back to England? So be it, I'll keep following him. But from this day forward, I'll work as carefully and zealously to clear obstacles out of his way as I've worked till now to pile 'em on. As you can see, I've changed sides, and I've changed because it's in my best interests to do so. I would add that your interests are the same as mine, because only in England will you find out whether you're in the employ of a criminal or a respectable man!"

Passepartout had listened very intently to Fix and felt convinced Fix was speaking in complete good faith.

"Are we friends?" Fix asked.

"Friends, no," Passepartout answered. "Allies, yes—but subject to reappraisal, because if I see the tiniest sign of villainy, I'll wring your neck."

"Agreed," the police inspector said calmly.

Eleven days later, on December 3, the *General Grant* entered the bay beyond Golden Gate Strait and arrived in San Francisco.

Mr. Fogg still hadn't gained or lost a single day.

25

*Which gives a brief glimpse
of San Francisco at election time*

IT WAS SEVEN O'CLOCK in the morning when Phileas Fogg, Lady Aouda, and Passepartout set foot on the American continent—assuming you can give this name to the floating wharf that was their landing place. Rising and falling with the tide, these wharves make it easier to load and unload vessels. The slips were arrayed with clippers of all dimensions, steamers of all nations, and those triple-decker steamboats that run up and down the Sacramento River and its tributaries. In addition the slips were piled high with the output of an international trade that reaches as far as Mexico, Peru, Chile, Brazil, Europe, Asia, and every island in the Pacific Ocean.

In his glee at finally stepping onto American soil, Passepartout felt he just had to go ashore by executing an aerial somersault in his best manner. But when he landed on the wharf's worm-eaten planks, he nearly went right through them. Thoroughly flustered by this way of "setting foot" on a new continent, the good fellow let out a fearsome yell that flushed endless flocks of cormorants and pelicans, the regular residents of these moving wharves.

The instant he was ashore, Mr. Fogg inquired about the next train for New York. It left at six o'clock that evening. Consequently Mr. Fogg had a full workday to spend in this California metropolis. He hailed a buggy for Lady Aouda and himself. Passepartout climbed up by the coachman, and for a fare of three dollars, the vehicle headed toward the International Hotel.

Looking down from on high, Passepartout examined this great American town with much interest: wide streets, neat lines of low houses, churches and chapels in Anglo-Saxon Gothic, immense docks, palatial warehouses made of wood or brick; in the streets were countless buggies, horse buses, and "cable cars," and on the packed sidewalks not only Americans and Europeans but also Chinese and Indians—adding up, all in all, to a population of over 200,000 people.

Passepartout felt some surprise at what he saw. He thought this was still the legendary city of 1849, a town of bandits, pyromaniacs, and murderers who had hurried there in quest of nuggets, an immense Capernaum full of outcasts who gambled with gold dust, revolver in one hand, knife in the other. But that "golden age" was gone. San Francisco was the very image of a big business town. Watchmen were on duty in the lofty tower of its city hall, which looked down on that whole picture of streets and avenues intersecting at right angles, on the greenery-covered squares flourishing among them, and finally on Chinatown, looking as if it had been imported from the Celestial Empire in a toy chest. No more sombreros, no more red shirts from the days of placer mining, no more feathered Indian headdresses, just silk

top hats and black frock coats worn by a large number of gentlemen consumed with hyperactivity. Certain streets, among others Montgomery St. (the equivalent of Regent St. in London, the Boulevard des Italiens in Paris, and Broadway in New York), were lined with splendid stores whose display windows featured items from all over the world.

When Passepartout arrived at the International Hotel, it didn't seem to him that he'd ever left England.

An immense barroom took up the hotel's ground floor, a sort of free-of-charge cafeteria that was open to all passersby. Beef jerky, oyster soup, crackers, and Cheshire cheese were on offer without the consumer needing to undo his purse strings. All he had to pay for were his drinks (ale, port, or sherry), should his inclinations run to liquid refreshment. This struck Passepartout as "so American."

The hotel had a cozy restaurant. Mr. Fogg and Lady Aouda took up residence at a table where they were served large portions on Lilliputian plates by the handsomest ebony Negroes.

Lady Aouda at his side, Phileas Fogg left the hotel after breakfast and made his way to the English consul's office so as to get a visa stamp on his passport. Out on the sidewalk he found his manservant, who asked him if it wouldn't be wise to buy a couple dozen Enfield rifles or Colt revolvers before riding on the Pacific Railroad. Passepartout had heard about Sioux and Pawnee Indians holding up trains like regular Spanish bandits. Mr. Fogg replied that this was an unnecessary precaution but left him at liberty to do as he saw fit. Then he headed off to the offices of the consulate.

Phileas Fogg hadn't gone 200 steps, when, by "an amazing coincidence," he met up with Fix. The inspector acted tremendously surprised. Excuse me? He and Mr. Fogg had crossed the Pacific together and hadn't bumped into each other on board? In any event Fix could only feel honored to reconnect with this gentleman whom he owed so much, and since business concerns were calling him back to Europe, he would be overjoyed to continue his journey in such pleasant company.

Mr. Fogg replied that the honor was all his, and Fix—who didn't want to let the man out of his sight—requested that they tour this unusual town of San Francisco together. His wish was granted.

So Lady Aouda, Phileas Fogg, and Fix sauntered through the streets. Soon they were on Montgomery St., where the masses were milling around in enormous numbers. There were endless crowds on the sidewalks, in the middle of the road, on the cable car tracks, in the way of the carriages and horse buses forever going by, on the doorsteps of shops, in the windows of all the houses, and even up on the roofs. Signboard carriers were moving around in the midst of the throngs. Flags and streamers fluttered in the wind. Shouts were erupting on every side.

"Hooray for Kamerfield!"

"Hooray for Mandiboy!"

It was a political rally. At least that's what Fix thought, and he conveyed this belief to Mr. Fogg, adding:

"Sir, maybe it would be best to not get mixed up with this mob. We might be on the receiving end of a nasty punch or two."

"True," Phileas Fogg replied. "And a smack of the fist, even in politics, is still a smack of the fist!"

Fix smiled dutifully when he heard this comment, and in order to see without getting caught up in the ruckus, he, Lady Aouda, and Phileas Fogg stood on the top landing of some stairs leading to a terrace located above Montgomery St. Straight across the way from them, between a coal merchant's loading dock and the warehouse of an oil broker, a big open-air office had been set up, and the various streams of people seemed to be converging on it.

And now what was behind this rally? What was the occasion for it? Phileas Fogg had absolutely no idea. Was it for the purpose of nominating some high-ranking military or civil functionary, some state governor or congressional member? Given the extraordinary excitement you saw gripping the town, this was a reasonable guess.

Just then a mass movement took place in the crowd. Every hand was in the air. Some were tightly closed, seeming to shoot swiftly up and down to the accompaniment of shouts—an energetic way, no doubt, of casting a vote. The horde surged, eddied, and ebbed. Flags waved, disappeared for a second, and reappeared in shreds. The undulations of this human tide spread as far as the stairs, while all those bare heads formed whitecaps on the surface, like a sea suddenly churned up by a squall. The black hats had visibly decreased in number, most of the remainder having a squashed look about them.

"It's obviously a rally," Fix said, "and there must be an overpowering reason for it. I wouldn't be amazed if it was still about the *Alabama* Claims, even though they've been settled."

"Maybe," Mr. Fogg merely replied.

"In any event," Fix continued, "we've got two challengers squaring off here, the honorable Mr. Kamerfield and the honorable Mr. Mandiboy."

Lady Aouda, on Phileas Fogg's arm, was looking in surprise at this tumultuous drama, and Fix was about to ask one of his neighbors the reason for this widespread exuberance, when the crowd movements grew more emphatic. The hoorays were increasingly embellished with boos. Flagpoles turned into aggressive weapons. Every hand had become a fist. Fierce blows were exchanged from the tops of stalled buggies and horse buses stopped in their tracks. All sorts of things served as projectiles. Boots and shoes swept through the air along quite extended flight paths, and a couple of revolvers actually seemed to be adding their all-American punctuation to the crowd's shouting.

The mob drew nearer to the stairs, ebbing over the bottom steps. Clearly one of the parties was being driven back, but the average spectator couldn't tell whether it was Mandiboy or Kamerfield who had the upper hand.

"I think we would be wise to beat a retreat," Fix said, intent on "his man" not getting any hard knocks or being given a hard time. "If all this has to do with England and they recognize us and start a ruckus, we'll be in real jeopardy!"

"An English citizen . . . " Phileas Fogg responded.

But the gentleman couldn't finish his sentence. Fearful outcries came from behind him on that terrace at the head of the stairs. Voices yelled, "Hooray! Three cheers for Mandiboy!" It was a brigade of voters coming to the rescue, carrying out a flank attack against Kamerfield's supporters.

Mr. Fogg, Lady Aouda, and Fix were caught in the crossfire. It was too late to escape. Armed with lead-weighted sticks and blackjacks, this torrent of humanity was an irresistible force. While protecting the young woman, Phileas Fogg and Fix were horribly butted around. As stoic as ever, Mr. Fogg tried to defend himself with those innate weapons nature has put at the end of every Englishman's arms, but it was no use. A huge strapping fellow with a red beard and broad shoulders, apparently the ringleader, swung his fearsome fist at Mr. Fogg, and he would have done that gentleman major damage if the self-sacrificing Fix hadn't taken the punch instead. Instantly an enormous lump started spreading under the detective's silk top hat, now transformed into a lowly pillbox.

"Yankee!" Mr. Fogg said, casting a look of deep scorn at his opponent.

"Englishman!" the other replied.

"We'll meet again!"

"Whenever you like. What's your name?"

"Phileas Fogg. Yours?"

"Colonel Stamp W. Proctor."

With that the tide went back out. Toppled off his feet, Fix got up again with his clothing torn but without any traumatic contusions. His traveler's overcoat had been divided into two unequal parts, and his pants looked like those britches it's the custom for some Indians to wear only after they've first removed the seat. But Lady Aouda had come though unscathed, so only Fix, due to that smack of the fist, had been hard hit.

"Thank you," Mr. Fogg told the inspector, once they were out of the crowd.

"It was nothing," Fix replied. "But come on!"

"Where to?"

"To a shop selling ready-made clothes."

Such a visit was timely indeed. Fix's and Phileas Fogg's garments were in tatters, as if these two gentlemen had personally battled on behalf of the honorable Messrs. Kamerfield and Mandiboy.

An hour later they sported socially acceptable suits and top hats. Then they went back to the International Hotel.

There Passepartout was waiting for his master, equipped with half a dozen central-fire, six-shot knife pistols. When he noticed Fix in Mr. Fogg's company, his brow darkened. But Lady Aouda gave him a brief account of what had happened, and Passepartout calmed down again. Obviously Fix wasn't their enemy anymore, he was an ally. He'd kept his word.

Dinner over, they summoned a carriage, which was to take the travelers and their luggage to the railroad terminal. Just as he was climbing into the buggy, Mr. Fogg said to Fix:

"Have you seen anything further of that Colonel Proctor?"

"No," Fix replied.

"I'll come back to America and find him," Phileas Fogg said coolly. "It wouldn't be proper for an English citizen to overlook that kind of treatment."

The inspector smiled and didn't reply. But as you can see, Mr. Fogg belonged to that race of Englishmen who don't tolerate dueling in their homeland but are willing to uphold their honor by fighting in foreign parts.

At 5:45 the travelers reached the terminal and found the train ready to leave.

Just as Mr. Fogg was about to board it, he caught sight of an attendant and went up to him:

"My friend," he said to the man, "wasn't there some civil unrest in San Francisco today?"

"We had a rally, sir," the attendant replied.

"But I believe I noted a certain agitation in the streets."

"It was simply a political rally having to do with an election."

"The election, no doubt, of a top government official?" Mr. Fogg asked.

"No, sir. Justice of the peace."

With that Phileas Fogg climbed into a passenger car and the train took off full steam ahead.

26

In which we ride an express train on the Pacific Railroad

"OCEAN TO OCEAN," as Americans say, and these three words will do as an overall description of the "great trunk line" that crosses the United States of America at its widest point. But in reality the "Pacific Railroad" is divided into two different parts: the "Central Pacific" between San Francisco and Ogden, and the "Union Pacific" between Ogden and Omaha. There you can make connections with five different railroad lines that put Omaha in frequent contact with New York.

So New York and San Francisco are currently joined together by an unbroken metal ribbon that measures no less than 3,786 miles long. Between Omaha and the Pacific Ocean, the railroad goes through a region still frequented by Indians and wild animals—a huge stretch of territory that Mormons started colonizing around 1845, after they'd been driven out of Illinois.

Formerly it required six months to go from New York to San Francisco, even under optimum conditions. Now it takes seven days.

Despite the opposition of delegations from the South, who wanted a more southerly route, it was decreed in 1862 that the roadbed for the tracks would run between the 41st and 42nd parallels. President Lincoln, of such sorrowful memory, personally decided that the town of Omaha in the state of Nebraska would be the point of departure for the new rail system. Work got under way at once, proceeding with that American energy that has no room for red tape and pencil pushers. The crew's speed didn't detract in any way from the project's expert execution. They moved forward across the prairie at the rate of 1½ miles of track per day. Rolling down the rails laid the day before, a locomotive brought the next day's rails, then rode over them as soon as they were in place.

As the Pacific Railroad goes along, it shoots out several branch lines into the states of Iowa, Kansas, Colorado, and Oregon. Leaving Omaha, it skirts the left bank of the Platte River as far as the mouth of its northern arm, follows its southern arm, crosses the territories of Laramie and the Wasatch Mountains, winds around Great Salt Lake, reaches the Mormon metropolis of Salt Lake City, plunges into Tooele Valley, skirts the American desert regions, Cedar and Humboldt peaks, the Humboldt River, and the Sierra Nevadas, then goes back down to the Pacific by way of Sacramento—without the slope of its roadbed exceeding 112 feet to the mile, not even while crossing the Rocky Mountains.

This was the long thoroughfare that trains took seven days to travel, which would allow the honorable Phileas Fogg—or so he hoped—to catch the ocean liner from New York to Liverpool on the 11th.

The passenger car housing Phileas Fogg was a sort of long bus that rested on two sets of four-wheeled trucks, their turning radius able to handle sharp curves. Its interior didn't have any compartments: just rows of double seats on each side and at a right angle to the center aisle, which led to the powder rooms and other amenities available in each car. From front to back the cars were connected to each other by crossovers, so passengers could move all the way through the train and avail themselves of its lounge car, observation car, dining car, and club car. The only thing missing was a theater car. But they'll get around to it one of these days.

By means of these crossovers, newspaper and book peddlers continually moved back and forth hawking their wares, nor was there any shortage of business for vendors of food, drink, and cigars.

The travelers had left Oakland Station at six o'clock in the evening. It was already nighttime—a chilly, gloomy nighttime with an overcast sky whose clouds were threatening to opt for snow. The train didn't go very fast. Including stops, it didn't travel over twenty miles per hour, a speed that should, however, allow it to cross the United States on schedule.

There wasn't much chitchat in the car. Besides, its passengers were on the verge of falling asleep. Passepartout took a seat next to the police inspector but didn't talk to him. After recent developments their relationship had significantly cooled. No more closeness, no more chumminess. Fix's behavior hadn't changed in any way, but Passepartout by contrast stayed strictly on his guard, all set to strangle his former friend at the slightest suspicion.

An hour after the train left, it started snowing—luckily it was a lightweight snow that wouldn't slow the train down. All you could see through the windows was an immense blanket of white, smoke from the locomotive spreading over it in curls that had a grayish cast.

At eight o'clock a "porter" came into the car and announced to the travelers that it was bedtime. Their car was a "sleeper" and in a couple minutes it had been transformed into a dormitory. Seat backs reclined, neatly tucked berths unfolded in the cleverest fashion, makeshift cabins appeared in a few seconds, and soon there was a cozy bed at every traveler's disposal, plus heavy curtains that offered protection from peeping toms. The sheets were white, the pillows soft. All that remained was to lie down and fall asleep— which everybody did, their cabins as cozy as if they were on an ocean liner—while the train charged full steam ahead across the state of California.

In the stretch of countryside that extends from San Francisco to Sacramento, the terrain isn't very rugged. Going by the name "Central Pacific," this section of the railroad originally took Sacramento as its starting point, then headed eastward to meet up with the tracks coming from Omaha. From San Francisco to California's capital, the line ran directly northeast while skirting the American River, which empties into San Pablo Bay. It took six hours to cover the 120 miles that lay between these two major cities, and toward midnight, while they were enjoying their first hours of sleep, the travelers went through Sacramento. So they didn't see any

part of this good-sized town, the lawmaking headquarters for the state of California—not its handsome loading docks, wide streets, splendid hotels, squares, or houses of worship.

Leaving Sacramento behind and exiting the stations in Junction, Rocklin, Auburn, and Colfax, the train tackled the Sierra Nevada range. By seven o'clock in the morning, it had pulled out of the station in Cisco. An hour later the dormitory became an ordinary passenger car again, and through its windows the travelers could get a glimpse of the picturesque panoramas in this mountain region. The roadbed under their train humored the Sierra's eccentricities, here clinging to the mountainside, there hanging over a precipice, dodging sharp corners by taking daredevil curves, shooting into narrow ravines you would have sworn had no way out. Gleaming like a church vessel, sporting a silver-plated bell, its big headlight giving off a lurid glow, its "cowcatcher" sticking out like a ship's ram, the locomotive blended its whistling and roaring with the sounds of mountain torrents and waterfalls, its smoke writhing through the dark branches of the fir trees.

There were no bridges on this route, and tunnels were few to none. The railroad tracks worked their way around each mountainside, never looking for straight lines or shortcuts from one point to another, never violating nature.

Near nine o'clock the train entered the state of Nevada by way of Carson Valley, its direction still to the northeast. At noon it left Reno, where its passengers had twenty minutes for lunch.

From this point forward the iron rails hugged the Humboldt River, following its bed and heading northward for a few miles. Then they adjusted their bearings eastward and weren't to leave this stream till they'd gone past its headwaters in the East Humboldt Mountains, almost at the far edge of the state of Nevada.

After lunch Mr. Fogg, Lady Aouda, and their companions got situated in the passenger car again. From their comfortable seats Phileas Fogg, the young woman, Fix, and Passepartout watched the varied countryside

going by under their eyes—wide prairies, mountains outlined on the horizon, "creeks" of foamy water tumbling along. Sometimes huddling in the distance, big herds of bison looked like moving embankments. These endless armies of ruminants often throw an invincible roadblock in the way of trains. Travelers have seen thousands of these beasts take several hours to march in close formation across the railroad tracks. So a locomotive has no choice but to stop and wait till the line is clear again.

Which is exactly what happened on this occasion. Around three o'clock in the afternoon, a bison herd 10,000 to 12,000 strong blocked the railroad tracks. After slowing down, the engine tried using its "ram" to carry out a flank attack against this immense column of animals, but it had to halt in the face of this impregnable mass.

As the travelers watched, these ruminants—which Americans wrongly call buffaloes—ambled serenely along, occasionally bellowing in a fearsome manner. They grew to bigger sizes than bulls in Europe, they had stubby legs and tails, their withers bulged into a muscular hump, their horns were set well apart at the base, their heads, necks, and shoulders were covered with a long furry mane. Trying to halt such a migration was unthinkable. When bison have made up their minds to go a particular way, nothing can stop them or change their direction. They're a torrent of living flesh that no embankment could hold back.

Out on the crossovers sprinklings of passengers looked at this unusual sight. But Phileas Fogg, surely the passenger in the biggest hurry of all, stayed in his seat and waited philosophically till it suited the buffaloes to get out of his way. Passepartout was furious over the delay caused by these clusters of animals. He wished he could fire his whole arsenal of revolvers at them.

"What a country!" he exclaimed. "Ordinary steers stop trains, parade on by, hold up traffic, and take their own sweet time! By God, I would sure like to know if Mr. Fogg expected *this* setback in his schedule! And our engineer hasn't the nerve to drive his train through this beastly blockade!"

The engine driver had no inclination to remove the obstacle, and this was a sensible policy. No doubt he could crush the first buffaloes he attacked with the ram on his locomotive; but as powerful as it was, his engine would soon grind to a halt, inevitably jump the tracks, and leave the whole train in distress.

So it was best to wait patiently, then make up for lost time afterward by increasing the train's speed. It took a good three hours for the bison to troop by, and it was nightfall before the line was clear again. By then the last ranks of the herd were crossing over the tracks, while the first were vanishing below the southern horizon.

So it was 8:00 when the train cleared the gorges of the East Humboldt Mountains, and 9:30 when it entered Utah territory, the district around Great Salt Lake, that unusual country where Mormons live.

27

During which Passepartout takes a course in Mormon history at a speed of twenty miles per hour

DURING THE NIGHT of December 5–6, the train ran in a southeasterly direction for about fifty miles; then it headed just as far back toward the northeast, drawing nearer to Great Salt Lake.

Around nine o'clock in the morning, Passepartout went for a breath of fresh air on the crossovers. It was cold out, the skies were gray, but it had stopped snowing. Magnified by the haze, the sun's disk looked like an enormous gold coin, and Passepartout was busy working out its value in pounds sterling, when he was distracted from this educational task by the appearance of a rather strange individual.

This individual, who had boarded the train at the station in Elko, was a man of great height with a very dark complexion, black mustache, black socks, black silk top hat, black vest, black pants, white tie, and dogskin gloves. You could tell he was a preacher. Going from one end of the train to the other, he used sealing wax to stick a handwritten notice on the door of each car.

Passepartout walked up to one of these notices and read that from eleven to twelve o'clock, a distinguished "elder," the Mormon missionary William Hitch, would make good use of his presence aboard train no. 48 by delivering a lecture on Mormonism in car no. 117—and he invited all gentlemen to hear him who desired instruction in the religious mysteries of the "Latter-day Saints."

"I'll definitely go," Passepartout said to himself. He didn't know a thing about Mormonism except that the practice of polygamy is the basis of Mormon society.

The news spread swiftly through the train, which was carrying about a hundred passengers. Out of this number no more than thirty took the bait and came to the lecture, grabbing seats in car no. 117 at eleven o'clock. Passepartout was visible in the front row of the faithful. Neither his master nor Fix felt moved to attend.

At the appointed time Elder William Hitch stood up, and as if somebody had been arguing with him beforehand, he exclaimed in a rather angry voice:

"I'm telling you—Joe Smith is a martyr, his brother Hyrum is a martyr, and now that the Union government is persecuting the prophets, they'll make Brigham Young a martyr too! Who would dare dispute this?"

Nobody felt like arguing with the missionary, whose emotionalism contrasted with his normally placid features. But no doubt his bad temper was explained by the fact that Mormonism was currently facing hard times. And it was true that the United States government had recently gone to some trouble to quell these unregulated fanatics. The Union put Brigham Young in jail on charges of sedition and polygamy, then took over Utah and made it subject to U.S. laws. Since that time the prophet's disciples had stepped up their efforts, and while waiting till they could take action, they were offering verbal resistance to congress's demands.

Even on the railroad, as you can see, Elder William Hitch was trying to make converts to their cause.

And livening up his account with explosive inflections and vehement gestures, he then described the history of Mormonism from biblical times . . . how a Mormon prophet from the tribe of Joseph in Israel made the annals of the new religion public and left them to his son Moroni; how this precious text, written in the Egyptian alphabet, came out many centuries later in a translation by Joseph Smith Jr. from the state of Vermont, a farmer who revealed in 1825 that he was a mystical prophet; how, in sum, a heavenly messenger appeared to him in a forest of light and delivered the annals to him from the Lord. . . .

Not much interested in the missionary's backward-looking account, a few listeners left the car just then; but William Hitch went on to describe . . . how Smith Jr. joined up with his father, two brothers, and a few disciples to found the religion of the Latter-day Saints—a religion practiced not only in America but in England, Scandinavia, and Germany, numbering among the faithful both manual laborers and many educated professionals; how a colony took form in Ohio; how they built a temple at a cost of $200,000, and a town sprang up in Kirkland; how Smith became a daring banker and got from a humble exhibitor of mummies a sheet of papyrus that contained an account in the handwriting of Abraham and other famous Egyptians. . . .

The narrative was getting a bit long-winded, the ranks of listeners kept thinning, and no more than twenty people were left in the audience.

But these defections didn't trouble the elder, who described in detail . . . the way in which Joe Smith went broke in 1837; the way in which his bankrupt stockholders coated him with tar and rolled him in feathers; the way in which he turned up a few years later, more honorable and honored than ever—he headed a flourishing community of at least 3,000 disciples in Independence, Missouri, then was hounded by the hatred of gentiles and had to flee into the American wild west. . . .

Ten listeners yet remained, among them our good Passepartout, still all ears. In this fashion he learned . . . how, after being persecuted for quite a while, Smith reappeared in Illinois and in 1839 on the banks of the Mississippi founded a town called Nauvoo, meaning "beautiful place," whose population grew to 25,000 souls; how Smith became mayor, chief justice, and top governing official; how in 1843 he announced his candidacy for president of the United States, and finally how he was lured into a trap in Carthage, was thrown in jail, and was assassinated by a gang of masked men. . . .

By this point Passepartout was totally alone in the car; the elder looked him in the eye, mesmerized him with his words, and reminded him that two years after Smith's assassination, his successor, the exalted prophet Brigham Young, left Nauvoo and went to take up residence on the shores of Great Salt Lake—and there in that wonderful territory, in the midst of that fertile country, in the path of people migrating across Utah on their way to California, the new colony enjoyed an enormous growth spurt due to the Mormon belief in polygamy. . . .

"And that's why congress is taking out its envy on us!" William Hitch added. "That's why Union soldiers are setting foot in Utah! And thanks to a total miscarriage of justice, that's why our leader, the prophet Brigham Young, has been put in jail! Will they take us by force? Never! Driven out of Vermont, driven out of Illinois, driven out of Ohio, driven out of Missouri, driven out of Utah, we'll still find some independent territory where we'll pitch our tents. . . . And you, my faithful one," the elder added, looking at his sole listener with wrathful eyes, "will you pitch yours in the shade of our flag?"

"No way," Passepartout replied staunchly, then fled in his turn and left the maniac all by himself, a voice crying in the wilderness.

But during that lecture the train had made rapid headway and at about 12:30 it reached the northwest tip of Great Salt Lake. From there you can take in the vista of this inland sea over a wide perimeter, a body of water that's also known as "America's Dead Sea" and has its own Jordan River emptying into it. This wonderful lake is framed by handsome, rugged boulders on broad foundations that are caked with white salt; it's a superb sheet of water that used to cover a more con-siderable expanse—but as time went by, its banks rose little by little, shrinking its surface area while increasing its depth.

Located 3,800 feet above sea level, Great Salt Lake is about seventy miles in length and thirty-five in width. Quite different from the asphalt-filled Dead Sea (which lies in a depression 1,200 feet *below* sea level), its salt content is considerable, and the solid matter that its water holds in solution makes up a quarter of its weight. Its specific gravity is 1.170, as against 1.000 for distilled water. Accordingly fish can't survive in this lake. Those carried in by the Jordan, Weber, and other creeks soon perish; but it's not true that the water's density is so great that people can't swim in it.

The countryside around the lake was marvelously cultivated, because Mormons know how to work the land: six months later you would see a region of ranches and corrals for farm animals, fields of wheat, corn, and sorghum, fruited plains, hedges of wild rose, sprays of acacia and spurge on every side; but just then the ground was hidden by a thin layer of light, powdery snow.

Around two o'clock our travelers stepped down at the station in Ogden. The train wasn't due to leave again till six o'clock, so Mr. Fogg, Lady Aouda, and their two companions had time to visit the City of the Saints[15] by way of the short branch line peeling off from the station in Ogden. Two hours were all they needed for touring this thoroughly American town, which, as such, was cut from the same bolt as every Union town: it had the long chilly lines of a huge chessboard, with "glum, dreary right angles," to borrow Victor Hugo's phrase. When he designed the City of the Saints, its founder couldn't get away from that need for symmetry characteristic of Anglo-Saxons. In this unusual country whose citizens are definitely not as lofty as their institutions, people do everything "fair and square," towns, houses, and even bad decisions.

By three o'clock, then, the travelers were strolling down the streets of this city, which had sprung up between the banks of the Jor-

---

[15] *Translator's note.* Salt Lake City.

dan River and the rolling foothills of the Wasatch Mountains. They noted few or no churches, but tourist attractions included the prophet's home, the courthouse, and the armory; then they saw houses of bluish brick that boasted porches and balconies, had gardens surrounding them, and were flanked by acacia, palm, and carob trees. Built in 1853, a wall of clay and pebbles girdled the town. On its main street, where folks go to market, there stood a few hotels adorned with awnings, Salt Lake House among others.

The city didn't seem very populous to Mr. Fogg and his companions. Its streets were almost empty—except, however, on the side of town by the Mormon Temple, which they reached only after going through several neighborhoods surrounded by stockades. Women were pretty plentiful, which is explained by the unusual composition of Mormon households. Nevertheless you mustn't assume that all Mormons are polygamous. They're free to choose, but it's worth noting that Utah's female citizens are the ones especially intent on getting married—because, according to the religion of the land, the Heaven promised to Mormons doesn't allow single persons of the feminine gender to share in its blessings. These poor creatures didn't seem either comfortable or content. A few of them—the wealthiest, no doubt—had on a black silk jacket open at the waist, then over it an ultra demure hood or shawl. The others wore only calico print dresses.

As for Passepartout, in his capacity as confirmed bachelor, he looked with definite trepidation at these Mormon women who had to be jointly responsible for the happiness of just one Mormon male. In his commonsense way he especially pitied the husband. It struck him as dreadful to have to guide so many ladies at one time through life's complications, leading them in a body to their Mormon paradise—and all with the prospect of their spending eternity in the company of the glorious Smith, who had to be the high spot of that delectable locale. No doubt about it, the Frenchman didn't feel called to any such thing, and he found—though maybe he was kidding himself—that the female citi-

zens of Salt Lake City were shooting some slightly disturbing looks at his person.

Luckily he didn't have to stay long in the City of the Saints. A few minutes shy of four o'clock, the travelers were back at the terminal and getting seated in their passenger cars again.

They heard a whistle blow; but just as the locomotive's driving wheels gained traction on the rails and started to put the train in speedy motion, shouts of "Wait! Wait!" rang out.

Moving trains don't wait for anybody. The gentleman doing the shouting was obviously some tardy Mormon. He was out of breath from running. Luckily for him the terminal didn't have any gates or barriers. So he dashed down the tracks, leaped onto the boarding steps at the end of the train, and fell exhausted into one of the seats in the car.

Passepartout had been watching these athletic goings-on with some interest, went to take a look at the latecomer, and was deeply intrigued to learn that this Utah citizen had run away as the result of a marital squabble.

When the Mormon got his wind back, Passepartout politely ventured to ask him how many wives he had to take care of—from the way he'd just skedaddled, presumably there were at least twenty.

"One, sir," the Mormon answered, raising his arms to high heaven. "One, and she's enough!"

28

In which Passepartout can't get anybody to use his head

LEAVING GREAT SALT LAKE and the station in Ogden, the train headed northward for an hour up to Weber River, having covered around 900 miles since San Francisco. From this point on it went east again through the rugged rocks of the Wasatch Mountains. It was in this section of territory—which lies between those mountains and the Rocky Mountains proper—that the American engineers came up against the severest difficulties. For this stretch of track, accordingly, the Union government increased its subsidy to

$48,000 per mile, whereas it had paid only $16,000 on the plains; but as we've stated, the engineers didn't violate nature but made shrewd compromises with her, going around difficulties instead of through them—and in order to reach the Great Basin east of the Sierra Nevadas, they cut only a single tunnel, just 1,400 feet long, over this whole stretch of railroad.

Right at Great Salt Lake, the roadbed reaches its highest elevation to that point. From then on its outline sweeps in a very protracted curve, gravitating toward Bitter Creek Valley so as to head back up to the Continental Divide, which separates the waters flowing to the Atlantic from those heading to the Pacific. Streams were plentiful in this mountainous district. You had to ride over little bridges to reach the far sides of Muddy Creek, the Green River, and others. The closer they got to their destination, the more impatient Passepartout became. But Fix also wanted to put this trying region behind him. He was afraid of delays, in dread of accidents, and in a bigger hurry than Phileas Fogg himself to set foot on English soil!

At ten o'clock that night, the train stopped at the station by Fort Bridger, pulled out almost immediately, ten miles farther on entered the state of Wyoming—once part of Dakota territory—and went along the entire length of Bitter Creek Valley, a trough for some of the waters that form Colorado's hydrographic network.

The next day, December 7, they stopped for fifteen minutes at the station in Green River. They'd had a pretty heavy snowfall during the night, but a rainfall got into the mix and the half-melted snow couldn't hinder the train's progress. Even so, the foul weather didn't give Passepartout a moment's peace, because the wheels on the cars might well get bogged down in some snowdrift, which would definitely put their journey in jeopardy.

"Honestly, what was he thinking!" the lad said to himself. "My master just *had* to travel in the wintertime! Couldn't he have waited for warm weather and improved his odds?"

But right then, while the good fellow was worrying about the state of the sky and the drop in temperature, Lady Aouda was feeling deeper fears for an entirely different reason.

In essence, while waiting for the train to leave again, a few passengers had stepped down from their car and were strolling along the boarding platform outside the terminal in Green River. Now then, as the young woman was looking out the window, she recognized one of them as Colonel Stamp W. Proctor, that American who had behaved so abusively toward Phileas Fogg during the rally in San Francisco. Lady Aouda shrank back, to keep from being seen.

This state of affairs concerned the young woman deeply. She'd grown attached to the gentleman, who, as icy as he seemed, revealed every day how totally dedicated he was to her. No doubt she didn't fully grasp the depth of feeling that her rescuer had inspired in her, so she still identified this feeling as gratitude—but without her realizing, it had become more than that. Accordingly she felt her heart constrict when she recognized that abusive individual, because sooner or later Mr. Fogg would demand satisfaction from him for his actions. Obviously it was sheer chance that had put Colonel Proctor on this train, but there he was nevertheless, and at any cost they had to keep Phileas Fogg from catching sight of his opponent.

Once the train was back under way, Mr. Fogg dozed off, and Lady Aouda took advantage of this fact to bring Fix and Passepartout up to date on the situation.

"That Proctor's on the train?" Fix snapped. "Well, ma'am, you can rest assured—before he deals with this Fogg fel . . . uh, with Mr. Fogg . . . he'll have *me* to deal with! I believe I'm still the injured party who has suffered the most in this whole business!"

"And furthermore," Passepartout added, "I'll show him who's boss, colonel or no colonel."

"Mr. Fix," Lady Aouda went on, "Mr. Fogg would never let anybody else avenge him. He's the sort who would come back to America and track down his offender, just as he said. If he caught sight of Colonel Proctor, we wouldn't be able to prevent a confrontation, which could have grievous consequences. So he mustn't ever see this man."

"You're right, ma'am," Fix replied. "A confrontation could spoil everything. Win or lose, Mr. Fogg would be delayed, and—"

"—and that would play into the hands of the gentlemen at the Reform Club," Passepartout added. "We'll reach New York in four days! All right, if my master doesn't leave his passenger car during these next four days, then there's a chance he won't come face to face with that blasted American, may God strike him dead! Now then, we've got to keep him from . . ."

Their conversation hung fire. Mr. Fogg was awake again and watching the scenery through the snow-specked window. But later on, without his master or Lady Aouda overhearing, Passepartout said to the police inspector:

"Would you really strike a blow for him?"

"I would do anything to bring him back to Europe alive!" Fix merely replied, his tone indicating that his will was implacable.

Passepartout felt a shiver run over his body, but his belief in his master didn't weaken.

And now, was there some way or other that they could tie Mr. Fogg down to this location and keep him from ever running into the colonel? Normally the gentleman wasn't very restless or inquisitive, so it shouldn't be too hard. In any event the police inspector felt he'd hit on a way, because a few seconds later he said to Phileas Fogg:

"The time certainly goes by slowly on these long train trips."

"True," the gentleman replied, "but it does go by."

"Aboard all those ocean liners," the inspector continued, "weren't you in the habit of playing whist?"

"Yes," Phileas Fogg replied, "but here that would be hard to do. I don't have any cards or partners."

"Oh, we'll easily find a pack of cards to buy. They sell everything on American passenger cars. As for partners, if the lady by any chance . . ."

"Of course, sir," the young woman was quick to reply. "I know how to play whist. It was part of my English upbringing."

"And I too," Fix went on, "have some claim to playing a decent game. Now then, with the three of us and a dummy . . ."

"As you wish, sir," Phileas Fogg replied, delighted to resume his favorite pastime—even aboard a railroad train.

They sent Passepartout to look for the porter, and he soon came back with two full decks, scorecards, chips, and a felt-topped card table. They weren't missing a thing. The game got under way. Lady Aouda was more than adequate as a whist player and even earned a few compliments from the stringent Phileas Fogg. As for the inspector, he was nothing less than world class and quite worthy of going toe to toe with the gentleman.

"Now we've got him," Passepartout said to himself. "He won't budge from here!"

By eleven o'clock that morning, the train had made it to the Continental Divide, which parcels out the water going to the two oceans. They were on Bridger Peak at an elevation of 7,524 English feet above sea level, one of the highest points reached by the roadbed's layout on its route through the Rocky Mountains. About 200 miles later our travelers finally arrived on those long plains that stretch as far as the Atlantic and that nature has made so handy for the purpose of putting down railroad tracks.

The first streams—branches or subbranches of the North Platte River—were already taking shape on the slopes that led to the Atlantic basin. The whole horizon to the north and east was covered by the immense semicircular curtain that makes up the northerly portion of the Rocky Mountains, Laramie Peak towering above. Between this curving line and the train tracks stretched wide, well-irrigated plains. To the railroad's right the lower gradients of that mountainous mass rose in stages, sweeping south to the headwaters of the Arkansas River, one of the Missouri's major tributaries.

At 12:30 the travelers caught a momentary glimpse of Fort Halleck, which is in charge of this region. A few more hours and their trip across the Rocky Mountains would be over with. So they had grounds for hoping no accidents would distinguish their train ride through this trying territory. It had stopped snowing. The weather turned cold and dry. Frightened away by the locomotive, large birds flew off into the distance. No wildcats, bears, or wolves were visible on the plain. It was a vast barren wilderness.

After a nice cozy lunch served right in their car, Mr. Fogg and his partners had just resumed their endless whist playing, when they heard a loud shriek of the whistle. The train came to a stop.

Passepartout poked his head out the door but didn't see anything to account for their stopping. No station was in sight.

For a second Lady Aouda and Fix were afraid Mr. Fogg would take a notion to step down beside the tracks. But the gentleman was content to tell his manservant:

"Go see what the trouble is."

Passepartout dashed out of the car. Some forty passengers had already left their seats, among them Colonel Stamp W. Proctor.

Their train had halted in front of a signal light that had turned red, barring the way. The engineer and conductor had stepped down and were arguing pretty noisily with a trackwalker who had been sent to head off the train by the stationmaster in Medicine Bow, their next stop. Passengers were coming up and taking part in the argument—among others the aforementioned Colonel Proctor with his loud voice and bossy manner.

Passepartout joined the group and listened to the trackwalker, who was saying:

"No, there isn't any way you can get across! The bridge to Medicine Bow is in shaky condition and it can't handle the weight of a train!"

The bridge in question was a suspension bridge built across some rapids a mile from the locality where the train had come to a halt. According to the trackwalker, several of its cables had snapped, it was on the verge of collapse, and it was impossibly dangerous to travel over. In claiming they couldn't get across, the trackwalker wasn't exaggerating one iota. And don't forget that Americans are usually happy-go-lucky—anytime they're in-clined to turn cautious, you would be insane not to do likewise.

Not daring to go alert his master, Passepartout listened with clenched teeth, as still as a statue.

"Oh drat!" Colonel Proctor exclaimed. "Are we supposed to just stand here and grow roots in the snow?"

"Colonel," the conductor replied, "we've wired the station in Omaha and asked for a train, but it isn't likely to reach Medicine Bow for another six hours."

"Six hours!" Passepartout blurted out.

"That's right," the conductor replied. "Besides, it'll take us that long to get to the station on foot."

"On foot?" exclaimed all the passengers.

"So how far is this station?" one of them asked the conductor.

"It's twelve miles to get to the other side of the river."

"Twelve miles in this snow?" Stamp W. Proctor howled.

The colonel cut loose with a barrage of cusswords, castigating both the company and the conductor, and Passepartout was almost furious enough to echo his sentiments. This time they were up against a tangible obstacle that his master's entire supply of banknotes couldn't clear away.

Otherwise there was universal dismay among the passengers, who, on top of the delay, saw that they would need to trek through some fifteen miles of snow-covered plain. Accordingly there was such a hullabaloo, such shouting and yelling, it definitely would have attracted Phileas Fogg's attention if the gentleman hadn't been so wrapped up in his card playing.

Meanwhile Passepartout realized it was essential to alert him and was disconsolately heading back to their passenger car, when the engineer—a certified Yankee named Forster—raised his voice and said:

"Gentlemen, maybe there is a way of getting across."

"Over the bridge?" a passenger responded.

"Over the bridge."

"With our train?" the colonel asked.

"With our train."

Passepartout came to a stop and hungrily took in the engine driver's words.

"But the bridge is on the verge of collapse!" the conductor reminded them.

"Makes no difference," Forster replied. "If I drive the train at top speed, I think we'll have a chance or two of getting across."

"Holy blazes!" Passepartout put in.

But a number of passengers immediately felt this was an alluring proposition. Colonel Proctor was especially tickled with it. That hothead found the idea quite feasible. He even recalled some design engineers who thought they could cross "bridgeless" rivers by inventing rigid trains, propelling them at full speed, etc. And ultimately everybody in the discussion sided with the engine driver.

"We've got fifty chances out of a hundred of getting across," one of them said.

"Sixty," said another.

"Eighty . . . ninety out of a hundred!"

Passepartout was dumbfounded; though he was open to anything that might get them across the Medicine Bow River, this suggestion struck him as "a little too American."

Besides, he thought, there's a much simpler way, and it hasn't even occurred to these people . . . !

"Sir," he told one of the passengers, "this method the driver is proposing seems a bit risky to me, but—"

"We've got eighty chances out of a hundred!" the passenger replied, turning his back on him.

"Yes, I know," Passepartout responded, facing another gentleman, "but if you simply think about it—"

"We don't need to do any thinking!" the American interrupted, shrugging his shoulders. "The driver says we'll get across!"

"Certainly we'll get across," Passepartout went on, "but maybe it would be wiser—"

"What! Wiser?" Colonel Proctor hollered, giving a jump when he chanced to hear this word. "We'll be going at high speed, I tell you! Don't you get it? At high speed!"

"I know . . . I get it," Passepartout echoed, nobody letting him finish a sentence. "But if it wouldn't be wiser, since that word offends you, at least it would be more realistic—"

"Huh . . . who . . . why? What's all this

hooey about realistic?" exclaimed everybody around him.

The poor fellow didn't know where to turn anymore.

"Does this mean you're scared?" Colonel Proctor asked him.

"Scared? Me?" Passepartout snorted. "Fine, so be it! I'll show these people that a Frenchman can be just as American as they are!"

"All aboard! All aboard!" the conductor called.

"Yes, all aboard!" Passepartout echoed. "All aboard! And right this instant! But I still think it would be more realistic to have us passengers *walk* over the bridge first, then drive the train across afterward . . . !"

But nobody heard this sage remark, and nobody would have agreed with it anyway.

The passengers got reinstated in their respective cars. Passepartout took his seat again, not saying a word about what had gone on. The whist players were all caught up in their game.

The locomotive whistled energetically. The engine driver reversed steam and backed the train up for nearly a mile—like a long jumper who wants to get a good running start.

Then, with a second shriek of the whistle, he started to move forward again: he let out the throttle; soon they were going frightfully fast; all you could hear was one long wail coming from the locomotive; the pistons were chugging away at twenty strokes per second; the axles of the wheels were giving off smoke from their grease boxes. They were speeding along at a hundred miles per hour, and it felt like the whole train was lifting off the rails, so to speak. They were going so fast, they were almost weightless.

And they got across! It took place like lightning. Nobody even saw the bridge. The train vaulted, you might say, from one bank to the other, and the driver couldn't bring his out-of-control engine to a stop till it had gone five miles past the station.

But the train had barely cleared the stream when the bridge collapsed for good, plunging with a crash into the rapids of the Medicine Bow River.

29

Which will describe assorted incidents that are met with only on Union railroads

THAT SAME EVENING the train proceeded on its way unhindered, going beyond Fort Saunders, clearing Cheyenne Pass, and arriving at Evans Pass. At this locality the railroad reached the highest point on its run, namely 8,091 feet above sea level. Nothing remained except for the travelers to head down to the Atlantic over the endless plains nature had leveled off for them.

There the "great trunk line" sprouted a branch line to Denver, the chief town in Colorado. This area is rich in gold and silver mines, and more than 50,000 people have already made it their home.

By this point they'd come 1,382 miles from San Francisco over a period of three days and three nights. According to official forecasts, four more days and nights were all it would take to reach New York. So Phileas Fogg was keeping within his prescribed time frame.

During the night they passed Camp Walbach on their left. Lodgepole Creek ran parallel to the tracks along the straightedge boundary line shared by the states of Wyoming and Colorado. At eleven o'clock they entered Nebraska, after passing close to Sedgwick and right by Julesburg, which sits on the southern arm of the Platte River.

This was the place where the grand opening took place on October 23, 1867, of the Union Pacific Railroad, General G. M. Dodge, chief engineer. There two powerful locomotives had pulled up, and coupled to them were nine passenger cars carrying guests, including Mr. Thomas C. Durant, the company's vice president; there cheers rang out; there Sioux and Pawnee warriors staged a miniature Indian battle; there fireworks exploded in the sky; there, finally, a portable printing press published the first issue of the trade journal *Railway Pioneer*. That's how they celebrated the grand opening of this great railroad, the instrument of progress and civilization, built across the wilderness and destined to link together towns and cities that

didn't even exist yet. More potent than Amphion's magic lyre in Greek myth, the whistle of a locomotive would soon bid them rise up on American soil.

They left Fort McPherson to the rear at eight o'clock in the morning. 357 miles separated this spot from Omaha. Staying on the left bank, the iron rails went along the unpredictable windings of the Platte River's southern arm. At nine o'clock they arrived in the major town of North Platte, built between the great watercourse's two branches—which come together around it to form a single thoroughfare, a substantial tributary whose waters merge with those of the Missouri a little above Omaha.

They cleared the 101st meridian.

Mr. Fogg and his partners were back at their card playing. None of them had any complaints about the length of the trip, not even the dummy. Fix had started off by winning a few guineas, which he was now in the process of losing, but his passion for the game seemed as great as Mr. Fogg's. That morning luck was distinctly on the latter's side. Trumps and honors just poured from his hands. At one point he'd planned a daring move and was about to play spades, when a voice came from behind his seat, saying:

"If it was up to me, I would play diamonds."

Mr. Fogg, Lady Aouda, and Fix raised their heads. Colonel Proctor was standing beside them.

Stamp W. Proctor and Phileas Fogg recognized each other at once.

"Oh, so it's you, Mr. Englishman!" the colonel snarled. "You're the one who wants to play spades!"

"And who does so," Phileas Fogg coolly replied, throwing down a ten of that suit.

"Well, I feel it should be diamonds," Colonel Proctor countered in an angry voice.

And he made a move to grab the card just played, adding:

"You don't know the first thing about this game."

"Maybe there's another I'll be more skillful at," Phileas Fogg said, getting to his feet.

"Just go ahead and try, son of John Bull," the abusive fellow remarked.

Lady Aouda turned pale. All the blood drained from her heart. She clutched Phileas Fogg by the arm, but he gently shook her off. Passepartout was ready to tear into the American, who was looking at his opponent with the most offensive expression. But Fix got up, went over to Colonel Proctor, and told him:

"You forget, sir, that you have *me* to deal with—you not only insulted me, you struck me!"

"I beg your pardon, Mr. Fix," Phileas Fogg said, "but this is strictly my affair. By claiming I was wrong to play spades, the colonel has insulted me yet again and he'll give me satisfaction."

"Anytime you like, anywhere you like, and with any weapon you like!" the American said.

Lady Aouda tried in vain to hold Mr. Fogg back. The inspector attempted without success to revive his own quarrel with the fellow. Passepartout wanted to heave the colonel out the door, but a signal from his master stopped him. Phileas Fogg left the car, and the American followed him onto the crossover.

"Sir," Mr. Fogg told his opponent, "I'm in a great hurry to get back to Europe, and any delay whatever will be highly detrimental to my best interests."

"Well now, and what's that got to do with me?" Colonel Proctor responded.

"Sir," Mr. Fogg went on with great courtesy, "after our meeting in San Francisco, I'd planned to come back to America and find you, as soon as I'd finished the business calling me to the Old World."

"Really."

"Will you give me an appointment for six months from now?"

"Why not six years?"

"I'm asking for six months," Mr. Fogg replied, "and I'll keep our appointment to the second."

"All you're trying to do is wriggle out of it!" Stamp W. Proctor exclaimed. "It's now or never!"

"So be it," Mr. Fogg replied. "Are you going to New York?"

"No."

"To Chicago?"

"No."

"To Omaha?"

"Why would you care. Have you heard of Plum Creek?"

"No," Mr. Fogg answered.

"It's the next station. The train will be there in an hour. It'll stop over for ten minutes. In ten minutes we can trade a few revolver shots."

"Done," Mr. Fogg replied. "I'll get off at Plum Creek."

"And I have a feeling you'll stay off," the American added with consummate cheek.

"We'll see," Mr. Fogg replied. And he went back into his car, as cool as ever.

There the gentleman set about reassuring Lady Aouda, telling her that braggarts were never to be feared. Then he asked Fix to act as his second in the duel about to take place. Fix couldn't refuse, and Phileas Fogg serenely resumed his interrupted card game, playing spades without a worry in the world.

At eleven o'clock the locomotive's whistle announced they were nearing the station in Plum Creek. With Fix right behind, Mr. Fogg stood up and proceeded out onto the crossover. Passepartout went with him, carrying a pair of revolvers. Lady Aouda stayed in the car, as pale as death.

Just then the door of the other passenger car opened, and Colonel Proctor likewise appeared on the crossover; behind him was his own second, a Yankee of the same stripe. But the instant that the two opponents were about to step down beside the tracks, the conductor ran over and called to them:

"You mustn't step down, gentlemen!"

"And why not?" the colonel demanded.

"We're twenty minutes late and the train's going right on."

"But I need to fight a duel with this gentleman."

"Sorry," the official replied, "but we're leaving again immediately. There's the bell ringing now!"

The bell was indeed ringing, and the train got back under way.

"My sincerest regrets, gentlemen," the conductor said. "Under any other circumstances I could have cooperated with you.

631

But after all, since you don't have time to fight your duel here, what's to keep you from fighting as we go?"

"Maybe that wouldn't suit the gentleman's fancy," the colonel said with a taunting expression.

"It suits me perfectly," Phileas Fogg replied.

Well, Passepartout thought, were definitely in America. And our train conductor's a gentleman of the old school!

And with that he fell in behind his master.

Led by the conductor, the two opponents and their seconds went from one car to another till they reached the rear of the train. Only a dozen or so passengers occupied the last car. The conductor inquired if they would be kind enough to momentarily free up the area for two gentlemen who had an affair of honor to settle.

No need to ask! Why, the passengers were more than happy to be helpful to the two gentlemen and they withdrew onto the crossovers.

This car was some fifty feet long and lent itself quite nicely to the business at hand. The two opponents could go after each other in the aisle between the seats and blast away at their leisure. No duel had ever been more easily arranged. Mr. Fogg and Colonel Proctor went into the car, each armed with a pair of six-guns. Their seconds stayed outside and closed the door on them. At the first shriek of the locomotive's whistle, they were to open fire. . . . Then, after two minutes had gone by, all that remained of the two gentlemen would be removed from the car.

Honestly, nothing could be simpler. It was so very simple, Fix and Passepartout felt their hearts pounding fit to burst.

So they were waiting for the agreed-upon shriek of the whistle, when wild yells suddenly rang out. There were gunshots along with them, but not from the passenger car earmarked for the duelists. On the contrary, these gunshots came from up and down the whole train. You could hear terrified screams from the passengers inside.

Gripping their revolvers, Colonel Proctor and Mr. Fogg instantly left their car and rushed toward the front, where the shots and shouts were ringing out with greater intensity.

They discovered that the train was under attack by a band of Sioux warriors.

This wasn't the first attempt by these bold Indians, who already had more than one train holdup to their credit. As usual with them, they didn't wait till the train had come to a halt; to the tune of a hundred or so, they'd dashed onto the boarding steps and clambered into the cars the way a circus clown leaps on a galloping horse.

These Sioux carried rifles. Ergo those shots—which the travelers, armed nearly to a man, were answering with revolver fire. Right off the Indians had scrambled aboard the engine. A couple cracks of the cudgel left the driver and stoker half stunned. A Sioux chieftain tried to stop the train but didn't know how to operate the throttle lever; instead of shutting off the steam, he opened the valve all the way, and the out-of-control locomotive raced ahead with appalling speed.

Meanwhile other Sioux warriors were overrunning the cars, racing like angry monkeys along the roofs, staving in doors, and fighting the travelers at close quarters. They broke into the baggage car and looted it, throwing luggage alongside the tracks. The yells and gunshots didn't let up.

But the passengers defended themselves courageously. They barricaded some of the cars and took on all comers in these virtual traveling fortresses, which were flying along at a speed of a hundred miles per hour.

From the onset of the attack, Lady Aouda was the picture of courage. Revolver in hand, she defended herself heroically, firing through the shattered windows at any savage who got close to her. Some twenty Sioux, mortally wounded, had fallen alongside the tracks, and when some of them slid off the crossovers onto the rails, they were crushed like worms by the wheels of the passenger cars.

Grievously injured by bullets or cudgels, several travelers lay across the seats.

But this couldn't go on. The battle had already been raging for ten minutes—it was sure to end with the Sioux having the upper hand if the train didn't come to a stop. In essence the station by Fort Kearney was barely two miles away. It was an American army outpost, but once they went beyond this outpost, the Sioux would take over the train between Fort Kearney and the next station.

The conductor was fighting at Mr. Fogg's side when a bullet toppled him. As he fell, the man exclaimed:

"If we don't stop the train within the next five minutes, we're done for!"

"We'll stop it!" Phileas Fogg said, all set to dash out of the car.

"Wait, sir," Passepartout called to him. "That's my department!"

Phileas Fogg had no time to stop the courageous fellow, who opened a door without the Indians spotting him and managed to slide beneath the car. And then, while the battle continued, as bullets crisscrossed above his head, he tapped into his jester's suppleness and agility, squirming along underneath the passenger cars, clinging to chains, helping himself to brake levers and sections of framework, crawling from one car to another with marvelous skill, and in this fashion reaching the front of the train. Nobody spotted him, nobody *could* spot him.

There, between the baggage car and the tender, he hung on with one hand and unhooked the safety chains with the other; but the couplers were tugging against each other, and he would never have succeeded in pulling the pin from the link if the engine hadn't given a lurch, made the pin pop out, and unhitched the train from its locomotive, which took off with a fresh burst of speed while the cars fell farther and farther behind.

Carried along by its own momentum, the train kept rolling for another few minutes, but they threw on the brakes inside the cars, and the whole procession finally came to a halt less than a hundred steps from the station in Kearney.

There, drawn by the gunfire, soldiers from the fort promptly rushed over; the Sioux weren't expecting them and the whole band skedaddled before the train had come to a full stop.

But when the travelers took a head count on the boarding platform at the station, they realized that several people were missing from roll call, among others the courageous Frenchman whose dedication had just saved their lives.

30

*In which Phileas Fogg
simply does what's right*

THREE PASSENGERS had vanished, Passepartout included. Had they been slain during the struggle? Had the Sioux warriors taken them prisoner? Nobody could say as yet.

It emerged that a fair number of people had been injured, though none fatally. Among the more grievously wounded was Colonel Proctor, who had fought bravely but had been toppled by a bullet to the groin. They transferred him to the terminal along with other travelers whose condition called for immediate attention.

Lady Aouda was safe. Though Phileas Fogg hadn't spared himself, he didn't have a scratch. Fix had been injured in the arm, an injury of no consequence. But Passepartout was missing, and tears streamed from the young woman's eyes.

Meanwhile all the travelers had gotten off the train. The wheels on the passenger cars were smeared with blood. Shapeless scraps of flesh hung from their hubs and spokes. Long red trails stood out over the white plains as far as the eye could see. By then the last of those Indians had vanished into the south, in the direction of the Republican River.

Mr. Fogg stood motionless, arms folded. He had a serious decision to make. Lady Aouda waited at his side and looked at him without saying a word. . . . He knew what that look meant. If his servant had been taken prisoner, should he risk everything in order to snatch him from the clutches of those Indians . . . ?

He merely said to Lady Aouda, "I'll find him whether he's dead or alive."

"Oh, sir . . . Oh, Mr. Fogg!" the young woman exclaimed, grasping her companion's hands and covering them with tears.

"Alive," Mr. Fogg added, "if we don't waste another minute."

With this decision Phileas Fogg made a sweeping self-sacrifice. He'd just decreed his financial ruin. A single day's delay would cause him to miss the ocean liner from New York. He would inevitably lose his bet. But foremost in his mind was the thought "I must do what's right," and he didn't hesitate.

The captain in charge of Fort Kearney was at hand. His soldiers—about a hundred strong—stayed on the defensive in case the Sioux should launch a direct attack against the terminal.

"Sir," Mr. Fogg told the captain, "three passengers have vanished."

"Dead?" the captain asked.

"Dead or taken prisoner," Phileas Fogg replied. "That's the uncertainty we need to clear up. Is it your intention to hunt down those Sioux?"

"That's a serious matter, sir," the captain said. "Those Indians could escape to the other side of the Arkansas River! This fort is under my command, and I can't just leave it."

"Sir," Phileas Fogg went on, "the lives of three men are at stake."

"No doubt . . . but to rescue three men, can I risk the lives of fifty?"

"I don't know if you can, sir, but it's the right thing to do."

"Sir," the captain replied, "I don't need anybody here to lecture me on what's right."

"So be it," Phileas Fogg said icily. "I'll go alone!"

"You, sir?" Fix exclaimed, coming up. "You want to go out there alone and hunt down those Indians?"

"How can I let that poor fellow perish when all the rest of us owe him our lives? I'm going after him."

"Fine, but you aren't going alone!" the captain exclaimed, affected in spite of himself. "Not a gallant fellow like you . . . ! I need thirty volunteers!" he added, turning to his soldiers.

The entire company stepped forward in unison. The captain had only to pick and choose among these gallant men. He singled out thirty soldiers and an old sergeant to head them up.

"Thank you, captain!" Mr. Fogg said.

"Will you allow me to come with you?" Fix asked the gentleman.

"Sir, you may do what you like," Phileas Fogg answered him. "But if you want to be of benefit to me, you'll stay here with Lady Aouda. In case some misfortune should befall me . . ."

Suddenly the police inspector's face turned white. Part company with the man he'd followed step by step with such persistence? Let him venture out into the wilderness like this? Fix looked closely at the gentleman, and for whatever reason, regardless of his qualms, despite the struggle raging inside him, he lowered his eyes in the face of that calm, candid look.

"I'll stay behind," he said.

A few seconds later Mr. Fogg squeezed the young woman's hand; then, after giving her his precious overnight bag, he left with the sergeant and his little band.

But before setting out, he told the soldiers:

"My friends, if we rescue the prisoners, there's £1,000 in it for you!"

By then it was a few minutes past noon.

Lady Aouda withdrew into a room at the terminal and waited there alone, thinking about Phileas Fogg, his across-the-board generosity, his serene courage. Mr. Fogg had sacrificed his fortune and now he was gambling his life—without any hesitation at all, without any grandstanding, and because it was the right thing to do. In her eyes Phileas Fogg was a hero.

As for Inspector Fix, his thoughts were running along different lines and he couldn't control his agitation. He strolled feverishly around the boarding platform outside the terminal. Momentarily subdued, his old self reemerged. Once Fogg had left, Fix realized how foolish it was to let him go off. What! He'd just followed the man around the world, then agreed to part company with him? His true nature took over again, and he covered himself with reproaches, accusations, and reprimands, as if he were the police commissioner at Scotland Yard dressing down one of his investigators for being a flagrant simpleton.

I've been a dunce, he thought. That

Frenchman will have told him who I am! He's gone and he's not coming back! Where will I be able to recapture him now? And how could I let him pull the wool over my eyes like that—I, Fix, with a warrant for his arrest right in my pocket! No doubt about it, I'm a total idiot!"

Which is how the police inspector reasoned it out, while the hours went by too slowly for his liking. He wasn't sure what to do. Sometimes he had an urge to tell Lady Aouda everything. But he knew how the young woman would react. What options did he have? He was tempted to stride across those long white plains and hunt that Fogg fellow down! It shouldn't be impossible to find the man again. Footprints still stood out against the snow . . . ! But a fresh layer soon wiped out every trace.

Then Fix grew despondent. He had an overwhelming urge to throw in the towel. Then, sure enough, a chance came up for him to leave the station in Kearney and continue this journey, which had been so full of disappointment.

In essence, around two o'clock in the afternoon and while huge snowflakes were falling, you could hear a whistle blowing at great length to the east. An enormous shadow was slowly coming on, preceded by a lurid glow and considerably magnified by the fog, which gave it a phantasmagoric appearance.

Even so, no train coming from the east was expected as yet. They'd sent a wire asking for help, but it couldn't have arrived as quickly as this, and the train from Omaha to San Francisco wasn't due till the next day. But soon they understood.

Traveling at half steam, emitting loud shrieks of the whistle, this was the locomotive that had come uncoupled from its train and continued on its way with such terrifying speed, carrying off the unconscious stoker and engineer. It had raced along the rails for several miles; then, running short of fuel, its fires burned low; its steam pressure slackened, it gradually slowed down, and an hour later the engine finally ground to a halt twenty miles beyond the station in Kearney.

Neither the engineer nor the stoker had been fatally injured; after fairly protracted blackouts, they came to again.

By then the engine was stationary. Seeing the wilderness around him, the locomotive on its own, the passenger cars no longer to the rear, the engineer realized what had happened. He couldn't imagine how the locomotive had come uncoupled from its train, but there was no question in his mind that the train they'd left behind was in distress.

The engineer didn't hesitate to do what was necessary. To continue on his way toward Omaha would be sensible; to go back to the train, which the Indians were maybe still looting, would be dangerous . . . but it didn't matter! He fed the boiler's furnace with shovelfuls of coal and wood, the fire sprang to life again, the pressure rose once more, and the engine backed into the station in Kearney around two o'clock in the afternoon. Folks had heard it whistling in the fog as it came closer.

The travelers were extremely pleased to see the locomotive at the head of the train. They would be able to resume this journey that had been so unfortunately interrupted.

When the engine arrived, Lady Aouda went outside the terminal and spoke to the conductor:

"You're leaving right away?" she asked him.

"This second, ma'am."

"But what about those people taken prisoner . . . our unfortunate companions . . ."

"I can't change our schedule," the conductor replied. "We're three hours late already."

"And when will another train come through from San Francisco?"

"Tomorrow evening, ma'am."

"Tomorrow evening! But that will be too late! You need to wait—"

"It isn't possible," the conductor answered. "If you're coming with us, climb aboard."

"I'm not coming," the young woman responded.

Fix overheard this conversation. A few seconds earlier, when he'd had no means of travel whatever, he was determined to leave Kearney; now that the train was here and ready to get going, all he had to do was take his seat in the car—but an irresistible force glued him to the ground. His feet were itching to leave the boarding platform, yet they couldn't tear themselves away. Once again he was at war with himself. The thought of failure left him choking with anger. He would struggle on to the very end.

Meanwhile the travelers and a few injured parties in serious condition—Colonel Procter among others—were seated again in the passenger cars. You could hear the supercharged boiler throbbing away and the steam escaping from its valves. The engineer blew the whistle, then the train moved out and soon vanished, its white smoke mingling with the snow flurries.

Inspector Fix stayed behind.

A couple hours went by. The weather was thoroughly foul, the cold quite brisk. Fix sat on a bench in the terminal and didn't move. You would have sworn he'd fallen asleep. Every other second Lady Aouda left the room that had been put at her disposal. Despite the gusts outside, she would go to the end of the boarding platform, hoping to see through the snowstorm, trying to pierce the fog that shrank the horizon around her, listening for any sound she could hear. There wasn't a thing. Then, chilled to the bone, she went back inside, only to go out again a few moments later—always to no avail.

Evening drew on. The little detachment of soldiers hadn't returned. Where were they just then? Did they manage to catch up with the Indians? Had they engaged the enemy, or were they lost in the fog and aimlessly wandering around? The captain in command of Fort Kearney felt very anxious, though he tried not to let any of his anxiety show.

Night fell, the snow let up a little, but the cold grew increasingly bitter. Even the bravest eyes wouldn't have peered into that dark vastness without some trepidation. Utter silence reigned over those plains. No soaring birds or stalking beasts troubled the deathless calm.

That whole night Lady Aouda wandered around the edge of the prairie, her mind full of grim forebodings, her heart bursting with anguish. Her imagination ran away with her and she envisioned a thousand dangers. She suffered indescribably during those long hours.

Fix wasn't asleep either, though he hadn't moved and was still in the same place. At one point some fellow came up and actually spoke to him, but the investigator put him off, answering his words with a gesture that meant no.

And that's how their night went. At dawn the sun's half-faded disk rose above the fogbound horizon. But you could see as far as two miles away. Phileas Fogg and the detachment of soldiers had headed southward. . . . The south looked utterly deserted. By then it was seven o'clock in the morning.

Tremendously concerned, the captain wasn't sure how to proceed. Should he send a second detachment to rescue the first? Should he sacrifice additional men with such a slim chance of saving the ones he'd previously sacrificed? But he didn't hesitate for long; motioning one of his lieutenants over, he directed the man to lead a scouting expedition to the south—and then gunshots rang out. Was it a signal? His soldiers dashed outside the fort and spotted a little band of men half a mile away, coming back in good order.

Mr. Fogg was walking out in front, and near him were Passepartout and the other two passengers, snatched from the clutches of those Sioux warriors.

The battle had taken place ten miles south of Kearney. A few seconds before the detachment had arrived, Passepartout and his two companions were already fighting with their captors, and the Frenchman had decked three of them with his bare fists, when his master and the soldiers rushed to their assistance.

All of them, rescuers and rescued, were greeted with shouts of glee. While Phileas Fogg doled out the bonus he'd promised the soldiers, Passepartout kept telling himself, and with good reason:

"No getting around it, I'm certainly costing my master a bundle!"

Fix looked at Mr. Fogg without saying a word, and it would have been hard to analyze the conflicting emotions he felt at this point.

As for Lady Aouda, she took the gentleman's hand and squeezed it between hers, also unable to say a word!

But as soon as Passepartout had arrived, he looked for the train outside the terminal. He figured it would be waiting there, all set to take off for Omaha, and he hoped they could still make up the time they'd lost.

"What happened to the train?" he exclaimed.

"It left," Fix replied.

"And when does the next train come through?" Phileas Fogg asked.

"Not till this evening."

"Oh," the unemotional gentleman merely replied.

31

*Where Inspector Fix behaves
in Phileas Fogg's best interests*

PHILEAS FOGG WAS RUNNING twenty hours behind schedule. As the unintentional reason for his being so behindhand, Passepartout was in despair. No doubt about it, he'd financially ruined his master!

Just then the inspector went up to Mr. Fogg and looked him right in the eye:

"Really and truly, sir," he asked the gentleman, "are you pressed for time?"

"Really and truly," Phileas Fogg answered.

"I want to be clear on this," Fix went on. "Isn't it in your best interests to reach New York by the 11th, before nine o'clock in the evening, the departure time of the ocean liner to Liverpool?"

"It's in my very best interests."

"And if your journey hadn't been interrupted by that Indian attack, you would be arriving in New York on the morning of the 11th?"

"Yes, with a jump of twelve hours on the liner's departure."

"Fine. So you're twenty hours behind. Twenty minus twelve leaves eight. You need to make up eight hours. Would you like to give it a try?"

"On foot?" Mr. Fogg asked.

"No, by sled," Fix replied. "A sled with sails. A fellow here tells me he has this form of transportation for hire."

It was the fellow who had spoken to the police inspector during the night, whose offer Fix had turned down.

Phileas Fogg didn't answer Fix; but Fix pointed out the fellow in question, who was strolling around in front of the terminal, and the gentleman walked up to him. A second later Mr. Fogg and this American, whose name was Mudge, went inside a shack built at the foot of Fort Kearney.

There Mr. Fogg ran his eyes over a pretty unusual vehicle, a sort of framework on which five or six people could take a seat; it was mounted on two long beams, which, in front, curved slightly upward like the runners on a sled. On the forward third of the framework stood a very tall mast with an immense spanker sail fastened to it. Securely supported by metal shrouds, this mast held an iron stay that was used for upping a jib of huge dimensions. To the rear a sort of oarlike rudder let you steer the contraption.

As you can see, this sled had been rigged like a sloop. During the winter, when the trains are snowbound, these vehicles can travel at tremendous speed over the frozen plains between stations. What's more, they carry a prodigious spread of sail, even more sail than is feasible for racing cutters, which are vulnerable to tipping over; when these sleds run ahead of the wind, they glide across the surface of the prairies at a speed equal, if not superior, to an express train's.

In a few seconds Mr. Fogg had made a deal with the skipper of this dry-land boat. There was a good wind. A stiff breeze blew out of the west. The snow had hardened, and Mudge promised that within a few hours he would have Mr. Fogg at the station in Omaha. At that location there were frequent trains and many railroad lines going to Chicago and New York. It would be possible for them to get back on schedule. So they had nothing to lose by taking the risk.

Mr. Fogg didn't want to expose Lady Aouda to the torments of traveling in the open air, because their speed would make the cold even more unbearable, so he proposed to leave her in Passepartout's care at the station in Kearney. The good fellow would be responsible for taking the young woman back to Europe by a better route and under more reasonable conditions.

Lady Aouda refused to part company with Mr. Fogg, and Passepartout was overjoyed at her decision. In essence he wasn't about to leave his master for anything in the world, not with Fix coming along.

As for what the police inspector was thinking at this juncture, it would be hard to say. Did he still consider Phileas Fogg a highly accomplished villain, a rascal who believed that by going all around the world, he was sure to be perfectly safe in England? Or had his return shaken the investigator's convictions? It was indeed possible that Fix had changed his views with respect to Phileas Fogg. But the detective wasn't any less determined to do his job; he was the most impatient of all, working to get them back to England as quickly as he could.

By eight o'clock the sled was set to go. The travelers—or passengers, we're tempted to say—took their seats on it and wrapped themselves tightly in their travel blankets. The skipper hoisted his vehicle's two immense sails, and it shot across the hardened snow at a speed of forty miles per hour, driven by the wind.

Staying on a straight course (or going in a beeline, as Americans put it), the distance between Fort Kearney and Omaha is 200 miles at the most. If the wind held up, they could cover this distance in five hours. If their journey was uneventful, the sled should reach Omaha by one o'clock in the afternoon.

What a trip! The travelers huddled against each other and couldn't say a thing. Intensified by their speed, the cold would have cut them off midword. The sled glided as lightly over the surface of the plains as a longboat over the surface of the waters—but without any swell. Whenever the breeze skimmed the earth, their sails seemed to lift the sled off the ground as if they were immense, widespreading wings. Mudge was at the tiller, keeping them on a straight course, twitching his oarlike rudder to correct any swerve the contraption felt inclined to make. They were running under full canvas. The jib was in

place and no longer covered by the spanker sail. Their skipper upped a topmast and spread his gaff topsail to the wind, adding its propulsive force to that of the other sails. Though you couldn't estimate the sled's speed with mathematical certainty, it had to be going at least forty miles per hour.

"If we don't bust anything," Mudge said, "we'll make it!"

And it was in Mudge's best interests to make it within the time frame agreed upon, because Mr. Fogg had followed his standard procedure and enticed the man with a hefty bonus.

Their sled was cutting straight across a prairie as flat as the sea. You would have sworn it was an immense frozen pond. The railroad service for this stretch of country went from the southwest up to the northwest by way of Grand Island, the major Nebraska town of Columbus, Schuyler, Fremont, then Omaha. For the entire run it went along the right bank of the Platte River. The iron rails swept in a longbow-shaped curve, but the sled took a shortcut down the bowstring. The Platte River makes a little jog before Fremont, but its surface was frozen over and Mudge had no fear of being stopped by it. The route, then, was completely clear of obstacles, and Phileas Fogg was in dread of just two things happening: a vehicular breakdown or shifts and lulls in the wind.

But the breeze didn't let up. On the contrary. It blew hard enough to bend the mast, which still stayed firmly in place thanks to its iron shrouds. Like the strings on a musical instrument, those strands of metal kept making sounds, as if a violin bow were setting them in vibration. The sled raced along in the midst of plaintive, strangely intense chords.

"Those strings are playing fifths and octaves," Mr. Fogg said.

And these were the only words he spoke during this trip. Carefully bundled up in protective furs and travel blankets, Lady Aouda stayed as far out of the cold's reach as she could.

As for Passepartout, he inhaled that biting air, his face as red as the sun's disk when it sets in a fog. Thanks to that core of unflappa-

ble optimism inside him, he had his hopes up again. Instead of reaching New York in the morning, they would reach it in the evening, but there was still a chance they would arrive before the ocean liner left for Liverpool.

Passepartout even had a strong urge to shake hands with his ally Fix. He remembered that it was the inspector himself who had gotten them this sail-powered sled, thereby supplying their only way of making it to Omaha in a timely manner. But some sort of hunch, Lord knows what, still made him keep his guard up.

In any event there was one thing Passepartout would always remember: the sacrifice Mr. Fogg had unhesitatingly made in order to snatch him from the clutches of those Sioux warriors. In doing so Mr. Fogg had risked both his life and his fortune . . . no, his servant would never forget this!

While all the travelers were deep in their different thoughts, the sled flew over that immense carpet of snow. If it went across a couple creeks, branches or subbranches of the Little Blue River, nobody even noticed. Fields and streams were invisible beneath that uniform whiteness. The plains were completely empty. Lying between the Union Pacific Railroad and the branch line designed to connect Kearney with St. Joseph, Missouri, this prairie looked like a big desert island. No villages, stations, or even forts. Now and then you saw some scowling tree go past like lightning, its white skeleton writhing in the breeze. Sometimes flocks of wild birds took off in unison. Sometimes, too, large numbers of prairie wolves ran races with the sled, lean and ravenous, driven by fierce cravings. On those occasions Passepartout would watch with revolver in hand, all set to fire away at the closest ones. If some accident had brought the sled to a halt, our travelers would have been attacked by those ferocious predators and in the gravest danger. But the sled held its own, promptly took the lead, and soon left the whole howling pack of them to the rear.

At noon Mudge recognized from certain signs that he'd gone over the frozen bed of the Platte River. He didn't say anything, but he already felt sure he would reach the sta-

tion in Omaha before he'd traveled another twenty miles.

And as a matter of fact, it was barely one o'clock when their skillful guide left the tiller and rushed to the ropes that hoisted his sails; he hauled them in at one go while the sled shot along under its own irresistible momentum, covering an additional half a mile with sails stowed. Finally it came to a stop, and Mudge pointed to a clump of snow-white roofs, saying:

"We've arrived!"

Arrived! Truly arrived at that station, which, thanks to its many trains, is in daily contact with the eastern United States!

Passepartout and Fix jumped to the ground and shook their limbs awake. They helped Mr. Fogg and the young woman down from the sled. Phileas Fogg generously squared accounts with Mudge, Passepartout shook the man's hand as if he were an old friend, then they all rushed off to the Omaha terminal.

This major Nebraska city marks the end of the line for the Pacific Railroad proper, which puts the Mississippi basin in contact with the earth's biggest ocean. Going from Omaha to Chicago, a line named the "Chicago & Rock Island Railroad" runs straight east and has fifty stations along its route.

An express train was all set to leave. Phileas Fogg and his companions had just enough time to hurry aboard a passenger car. They saw nothing of Omaha, but Passepartout admitted to himself that he hadn't any grounds for complaint, because this wasn't about sightseeing.

Their train headed into the state of Iowa at tremendous speed, going through Council Bluffs, Des Moines, and Iowa City. During the night it crossed the Mississippi by way of Davenport and entered Illinois by way of Rock Island. The next day, the 10th, it reached Chicago at four o'clock in the afternoon; the city had already risen from its ashes and stood more proudly than ever on the lovely shores of Lake Michigan.[16]

Nine hundred miles separated Chicago

---

[16] *Translator's note.* The Great Chicago Fire took place just fourteen months earlier.

from New York. There was no shortage of trains out of Chicago. Mr. Fogg went straight from one to another. A peppy locomotive on the "Pittsburgh, Fort Wayne & Chicago Railroad" left at top speed, as if appreciating that the honorable gentleman hadn't a moment to lose. It shot like lightning through Indiana, Ohio, Pennsylvania, and New Jersey, going past new towns with old-sounding names, a few of which had streets and trolley cars but no houses as yet. Finally the Hudson River came in sight, and on December 11 at 11:15 in the evening, the train drew to a halt in the terminal on the right bank of the river, in front of the very pier reserved for steamers on the Cunard line, also known as the "British & North American Royal Mail Steam Packet Co."

The *China*, bound for Liverpool, had left forty-five minutes earlier.

32

*In which Phileas Fogg
grapples with misfortune*

WHEN THE *CHINA* LEFT, it apparently took Phileas Fogg's last hopes along with it.

In essence none of the other ocean liners doing direct runs from America to Europe were a help to the gentleman's plans, not the ships in the French transatlantic fleet, the vessels on the White Star Line, the steamers of the Inman Co., the ones belonging to the Hamburg Line, nor any others.

In point of fact the *Pereire* of the French transatlantic firm—whose marvelous boats match the speed and surpass the comfort of those on every other line bar none—wasn't to leave till the day after next on December 14. And what's more, like the vessels on the Hamburg Line, it didn't do a direct run to Liverpool or London but to Le Havre, so all of Phileas Fogg's last-minute efforts would be canceled out by the additional time it would take to cross from Le Havre to Southampton.

As for the Inman Co.'s liners (one of which, the *City of Paris*, would put to sea the following day), they were unthinkable. These vessels are specifically geared to migrant

travel, their engines are underpowered, they navigate as much by sail as by steam, and their speed is nothing to write home about. The time they would take to cross from New York to England was more than Mr. Fogg had left for winning his bet.

All this became perfectly clear to the gentleman when he checked his Bradshaw, which gave him the transatlantic navigational schedules for every day of the year.

Passepartout was devastated. Missing their ocean liner by forty-five minutes had totally done him in. It was entirely his own fault—instead of helping Mr. Fogg, he'd continually thrown obstacles in his master's path! And when he reviewed all the incidents of their journey in his mind, when he tallied up the amounts the gentleman had spent solely on his behalf and would have to write off, when he thought about that enormous bet, adding it to the considerable expenses of this now-futile journey and seeing Mr. Fogg in absolute financial ruin, he called himself every name in the book.

But Mr. Fogg didn't criticize him in any way and as he left that pier reserved for transatlantic ocean liners, these were the only words he said:

"We'll look into this tomorrow. Come along."

Mr. Fogg, Lady Aouda, Fix, and Passepartout took the Jersey City ferryboat across the Hudson River, then climbed into a cab that drove them to the St. Nicholas Hotel on Broadway. It had rooms available, they booked them, and the night went by—quickly for Phileas Fogg, who dozed off and slept perfectly, but very slowly for Lady Aouda and her companions, whose worries kept them awake.

The next day was December 12. From 7:00 in the morning on the 12th to 8:45 in the evening on the 21st, there were nine days, thirteen hours, and forty-five minutes to go. Consequently, if Phileas Fogg had departed the evening before on the *China*, one of the Cunard line's fastest racers, he would have reached Liverpool, then London, within the desired time frame!

Mr. Fogg left the hotel on his own—after instructing his manservant to wait for him and alert Lady Aouda to be ready at a second's notice.

Mr. Fogg proceeded to the banks of the Hudson, where he carefully searched for outbound ships among those tied up along the pier or anchored in midriver. Several vessels flew their departure pennants and were getting ready to put to sea on the morning tide, because, in this immense and marvelous port of New York, there isn't a day when a hundred ships aren't making their way to every corner of the world; but most of them were sailboats and wouldn't suit Phileas Fogg's purposes.

It seemed like the gentleman's latest endeavor was doomed to failure, when he spotted a smartly designed, propeller-driven merchantman in front of the Battery; it rode at anchor no more than 600 feet out, releasing huge swirls of smoke from its funnel, which meant it was getting ready to set sail.

Phileas Fogg hailed a dinghy, got into it, and after a few strokes of the oar reached the boarding ladder of the *Henrietta*, an iron-hulled steamer whose topside was made entirely of wood.

The *Henrietta*'s captain was on board. Phileas Fogg climbed on deck and asked for him. The captain showed up at once.

He was a fellow of fifty, a species of old sea wolf, a sourpuss who wasn't going to be easy. Bulging eyes, skin like oxidized copper, red hair, powerful neck—nothing in his appearance suggested an individual with good manners.

"Captain?" Mr. Fogg asked.

"That's me."

"I'm Phileas Fogg from London."

"And I'm Andrew Speedy from Cardiff."

"You're setting out . . . ?"

"In one hour."

"You're laden for . . . ?"

"Bordeaux."

"And what's your cargo?"

"Gizzard stones. No freight. I'm sailing in ballast."

"Have you any passengers?"

"No passengers. Never take passengers. Just goods that get underfoot and argue with you."

"Your ship makes good time?"

"Eleven to twelve knots. The *Henrietta*'s well known."

"Will you take me to Liverpool, myself and three others?"

"Liverpool? Why not China?"

"I'm asking about Liverpool."

"No!"

"No?"

"No. I'm bound for Bordeaux and I'm going to Bordeaux."

"Regardless of how much I'll pay?"

"Regardless of how much you'll pay."

The captain said this in a tone that shut down the discussion.

"But what about the *Henrietta*'s owners . . . " Phileas Fogg resumed.

"I'm its owner," the captain replied. "This ship belongs to me."

"I'll charter it from you."

"No."

"I'll buy it from you."

"No."

Phileas Fogg didn't bat an eye. But the situation was serious. New York wasn't working out the way Hong Kong had, and the captain of the *Henrietta* wasn't like the skipper of the *Tankadère*. Till now the gentleman's money had gotten the best of every obstacle. This time money didn't do the trick.

Even so, he had to find some way of crossing the Atlantic by boat . . . unless he crossed it by balloon, which would have been terrifically risky, not to mention impossible.

It seemed, however, that Phileas Fogg had come up with an idea, because he said to the captain:

"All right, may I sail with you to Bordeaux?"

"No, not even if you paid me $200!"

"I'll give you $2,000."

"Per person?"

"Per person."

"And you're four in all?"

"Four."

Captain Speedy started to scratch his forehead, like a man bent on scraping the skin off. $8,000 in his pocket without changing course! He had a clear-cut hostility to passengers of every kind, but if he set his feelings aside, he would be richly rewarded for his trouble. Besides, passengers at $2,000 a pop aren't just passengers, they're valuable merchandise.

"I'm sailing at nine o'clock," Captain Speedy merely said. "And if you and your party are here . . . "

"We'll be on board by nine o'clock," Mr. Fogg merely said back to him.

It was 8:30. With the calmness that never left him under any circumstances, the gentleman went ashore from the *Henrietta*, climbed into a buggy, proceeded to the St. Nicholas Hotel, then brought back Lady Aouda, Passepartout, and even the inseparable Fix, whose way he graciously offered to pay.

All four were on board by the time the *Henrietta* set sail.

When Passepartout learned what this latest crossing was going to cost, he let out a sort of drawn-out "Oh!" that ran all the way down the chromatic scale.

As for Inspector Fix, he told himself that the Bank of England definitely wasn't going to get through this business unscathed. In essence, assuming this Fogg fellow didn't toss a few extra handfuls overboard, more than £7,000 ($35,000) would be missing from that bag of banknotes when they got back home!

33

In which Phileas Fogg rises to the occasion

AN HOUR LATER the steamer *Henrietta* went past the lightship marking the entrance to the Hudson River, doubled the spit of Sandy Hook, and put to sea. During the day it skirted Long Island, gave a wide berth to the lighthouse on Fire Island, and ran swiftly eastward.

At noon the next day, December 13, a man climbed onto the bridge to get a position fix. Naturally you would think this man was Captain Speedy, yes? Not even close. It was Phileas Fogg, Esq.

As for Captain Speedy, he was safely under lock and key in his cabin where he was letting out loud howls, which suggested that his anger, though perfectly excusable, was at the point of a conniption fit.

What had happened was quite simple. Phileas Fogg wanted to go to Liverpool, the captain wouldn't take him there. So Phileas Fogg had agreed to travel to Bordeaux; then, during the thirty hours he'd been on board, he'd put his banknotes to such productive use, the whole crew of sailors and stokers—a rather shifty-eyed crew on baddish terms with the captain—were now in his back pocket. And that's why Phileas Fogg was in command instead of Captain Speedy, why the captain was locked up in his cabin, and in short why the *Henrietta* was heading for Liverpool. Only it was quite clear, after seeing Mr. Fogg in operation, that Mr. Fogg had been a seaman.

Still, it remained to be seen how the venture would play out. Nevertheless Lady Aouda couldn't stop worrying, though she said nothing. Fix, for his part, was appalled at first. As for Passepartout, he found the whole thing simply enchanting.

"Eleven to twelve knots," Captain Speedy had said. And this actually was the average speed the *Henrietta* kept up.

If, then—and plenty of "ifs" still remained—if, then, the sea didn't get too rough, if the wind didn't shift to the east, if the craft didn't experience any mechanical breakdowns or its engine any accidents, the *Henrietta* could cover those 3,000 miles from New York to Liverpool in the nine days left between December 12 and December 21. It's true, however, that once the gentleman had arrived, this *Henrietta* business tacked onto the Bank of England business could land him in deeper waters than he might like.

During their first days out, they navigated under first-rate conditions. The sea wasn't too taxing; the wind seemed to be holding steady from the northeast; the *Henrietta* spread its canvas and tooled along under its trysails like a real transatlantic liner.

Passepartout was delighted. His master's latest exploit—whose consequences he didn't want to think about—filled him with enthusiasm. Never had the crew seen a cheerier, sprightlier fellow. He formed a thousand friendships with the sailors and amazed them with his acrobatic feats. He showered them with the highest compliments and the tastiest drinks. In his eyes they operated like true gentlemen and the stokers stoked like real heroes. He was so sociable, his good mood rubbed off on everybody. He'd forgotten the past, its hazards and hardships. The ultimate objective was close within reach and he thought of nothing else, sometimes bubbling over with impatience as if he'd been heated up in the *Henrietta*'s boilers. Often, too, the fine fellow hung around Fix; he watched the man with eyes that "spoke volumes," but he didn't talk to him, because there was no friendliness left between the two old chums.

But Fix, we should mention, didn't know what to make of it all. The *Henrietta* taken over, its crew bought off, this Fogg fellow operating like an accomplished seaman—the whole combination of events left him in a daze. He wasn't sure what to think anymore! But after all, a gentleman who started out stealing £55,000 could easily end up stealing a steamboat. And with Fogg at the helm, Fix was naturally inclined to think that the *Henrietta* wouldn't head for Liverpool at all but to some corner of the world where the robber—now turned pirate—could serenely take refuge! This was a supremely plausible theory, you have to admit, and the detective was very seriously starting to regret that he'd ever gotten involved in the business.

As for Captain Speedy, he kept howling away in his cabin; Passepartout was responsible for bringing the fellow his food, but as strong as the Frenchman was, he did so with only the greatest caution. Mr. Fogg, for his part, didn't look as if he even suspected there was a captain on board.

On the 13th they went past the tail end of the Grand Banks of Newfoundland. These are rough waterways. They feature frequent fogs and alarming squalls, especially during the winter. The ship's barometer, which had abruptly fallen the night before, forecast an atmospheric change on the way. The temperature did indeed alter during the night, the cold becoming more brisk, the wind simultaneously shifting to the southeast.

This was a setback. To keep from veering off course, Mr. Fogg had to furl his sails and clap on more steam. Nevertheless the ship slowed down owing to the state of the sea, whose long billows were dashing against the stempost. The vessel made vicious pitching movements at the expense of its speed. Little by little the breeze turned into a hurricane, and already they could foresee a situation where the *Henrietta* wouldn't be able to face into the waves anymore. Now then, if they were forced to turn tail, that meant coping with the unknown and all its nasty risks.

As the skies grew darker, so did Passepartout's face, and for two days the good fellow lived in mortal agony. But Phileas Fogg was a bold seaman, knew how to sail head-on into the billows, and kept to his course without even resorting to half steam. When the *Henrietta* couldn't rise to the waves, it cut across them—the sea swept over its whole deck, but the craft got through. Sometimes, when mountains of water raised its stern above the waves, its propeller came into view and churned the air with flailing blades, yet the ship still made steady headway.

Even so, the wind didn't pick up as much as they might have feared. It wasn't one of those hurricanes that go past at a speed of ninety miles per hour. It stayed in the category of a stiff breeze, but unfortunately it insisted on blowing out of the southeast quadrant and wouldn't let them spread sail. And yet, as you'll see, giving the steam some assistance would have been quite beneficial!

December 16 was the seventy-fifth day that had gone by since they'd left London. All in all the *Henrietta* still hadn't been alarmingly delayed. Its crossing was almost half over, and the roughest waterways were behind them. During the summer their success would have been assured. During the winter they were at the mercy of foul weather. Passepartout didn't say anything. Deep down he was hopeful, and if the wind gave out, at least they had steam to depend on.

Now then, that day the head mechanic climbed on deck, met with Mr. Fogg, and had a pretty animated conversation with him.

Without knowing why—some hunch, no doubt—Passepartout felt a vague anxiety. He would have given his right ear to learn with his left one what the two men were saying. However he managed to catch a few words, among others these spoken by his master:

"You're positive that's the case?"

"Positive, sir," the mechanic answered. "Don't forget, we've kept all our furnaces fired up since we left. We have enough coal to get from New York to Bordeaux at half steam, but we don't have enough to get from New York to Liverpool at full steam!"

"I'll think on it," Mr. Fogg replied.

Passepartout understood. He was gripped with mortal anxiety.

Their coal was about to run out!

"Well, if my master squeaks through this time," he said to himself, "he's a superman for sure!"

And when he bumped into Fix, he couldn't resist bringing him up to date on things.

"So," the investigator answered him through clenched teeth, "you actually think we're going to Liverpool?"

"Certainly."

"Nitwit," the inspector replied, shrugging his shoulders and walking away.

Passepartout was about to raise a sharp objection to this label, yet he couldn't figure out what was really on the man's mind; but he told himself that the unlucky Fix must feel very disappointed, very down on himself, after ineptly following a false scent all around the world—so he withheld judgment.

And what would Phileas Fogg's decision be at this point? It was hard to imagine. Even so, the stoic gentleman did seem to have made one, because that same evening he summoned the head mechanic and told him:

"Keep stoking your fires and stay on course till we've used up all our fuel."

A few seconds later the *Henrietta* spewed torrents of smoke out of its funnel.

So the ship forged ahead under full steam; but two days later on the 18th, the mechanic reported that their coal would run out during the day, just as he'd predicted.

"Don't let your fires die down," Mr. Fogg responded. "On the contrary. Keep your valves charged."

Toward noon that day, after Phileas Fogg took his sights and plotted the ship's position, he summoned Passepartout and directed him to go get Captain Speedy. He might as well have ordered him to let a tiger out of its cage, and as the gallant lad went below the afterdeck, he said to himself:

"He'll be positively raving!"

True enough, amid much yelling and cussing, a bomb arrived on the afterdeck a few minutes later. This bomb was Captain Speedy. Clearly he was about to explode.

"Where are we?" was the first sentence out of his mouth. The good man was choking with rage and if he'd been even slightly apoplectic, he would have been a goner for sure.

"Where are we?" he said again, his face purple.

"Seven hundred and seventy miles, or 300 geographic leagues, from Liverpool," Mr. Fogg replied with unruffled calm.

"Pirate!" Andrew Speedy shouted.

"Sir, I've summoned you to—"

"Corsair!"

"—to ask you," Mr. Fogg went on, "to sell me your ship."

"Not only no, but hell no!"

"It's just that I'm going to have to burn it."

"Burn my ship?"

"Yes, the topside at least, because we're running out of fuel."

"Burn my ship? Captain Speedy shrieked, barely able to get the syllables out. "A ship worth $50,000?"

"Here's $60,000," Phileas Fogg replied, offering the captain a stack of banknotes.

This had a prodigious effect on Andrew Speedy. No true American can remain unmoved at the sight of $60,000.[17] The captain forgot his anger, his incarceration, and all his grievances against his passenger in one second. His ship was twenty years old. This could be a golden opportunity . . . ! The bomb had already lost its ability to explode. Mr. Fogg had removed the fuse.

"And the iron hull stays with me?" the captain said in a significantly sweeter tone.

---

[17] *Translator's note.* This is roughly comparable to $1,200,000 in today's dollars.

"The iron hull and the engine, sir. Have we a deal?"

"Deal!"

And Andrew Speedy grabbed the stack of banknotes, counted it, and stowed it deep in his pocket.

Passepartout had turned white during this episode. As for Fix, he was on the verge of a stroke. After already spending nearly £20,000, this Fogg fellow was leaving the hull and engine with the seller, in other words, the bulk of what the ship was worth! True, the amount taken during the bank robbery came to £55,000, but still . . . !

After Andrew Speedy had pocketed his money:

"Sir," Mr. Fogg told him, "don't let any of this surprise you. You see, I'll lose £20,000 if I'm not back in London by 8:45 in the evening on December 21. Now then, I missed the ocean liner from New York, and since you refused to take me to Liverpool . . ."

"And by all the fiends in hell, I did right," Andrew Speedy exclaimed, "because I ended up at least $40,000 richer!"

Then he added more sedately:

"You know something, Captain, uh—"

"Fogg."

"Captain Fogg, fine. You know something, you've got a bit of Yankee blood in you."

And after he'd paid Phileas Fogg his idea of a high compliment, he was heading off when his passenger said to him:

"This ship now belongs to me?"

"That's right, from the keel to the mastheads—but just the timber, mind you."

"Fine. Have them demolish the inside furnishings and use every piece to stoke the fires."

You can imagine how much dry wood they had to feed the furnaces in order to keep the steam pressure high enough. That day the afterdeck, cabins, deckhouses, accommodations, and bottom deck all had to go.

The next day, December 19, they burned the masting along with the spare poles and yards. They cut the masts down, chopping them into logs with swipes of the ax. The crew went at it with unbelievable zeal. Passepartout hacked, hewed, sawed, and did

the work of ten men. It was a demolition orgy.

The next day, the 20th, the railings, bulwarks, topside, and most of the deck slid down the ship's gullet. The *Henrietta* had been scraped so flat, it was practically a pontoon boat.

That day, however, they raised the coast of Ireland and the lighthouse on Fastnet Rock.

Even so, by ten o'clock that night, the ship was still only abreast of Queenstown. Phileas Fogg had barely twenty-four hours left in which to reach London! Now then, even going full steam ahead, the *Henrietta* would need that much time just to get to Liverpool. And the daring gentleman was finally about to run out of steam!

"I really feel sorry for you, sir," Captain Speedy told him, now interested in his plans. "Everything's against you! We're still only level with Queenstown."

"Ah," Mr. Fogg put in. "That's Queenstown, that city where we see those lights?"

"Right."

"Can we enter the harbor?"

"Not for another three hours. Only at high tide."

"We'll wait," Phileas Fogg replied serenely. Though his expression was unreadable, he was going to try, with one crowning brainwave, to overcome his bad luck yet again!

In essence Queenstown is a port on the coast of Ireland where transatlantic liners from the United States drop off their mailbags as they go by. Express trains are always ready and waiting to carry the mail to Dublin. It goes from Dublin to Liverpool by highspeed steamers—thus gaining twelve hours on the fastest liners in the overseas travel firms.

If the postal service from America could pick up twelve hours, Phileas Fogg presumed he could pick them up as well. Instead of arriving in Liverpool the next evening aboard the *Henrietta*, he would be there by noon and consequently would have time to reach London before 8:45 in the evening.

Near one o'clock in the morning, the *Henrietta* entered the port of Queenstown at peak tide; after getting a hearty handshake from Captain Speedy, Phileas Fogg left him on the skinned carcass of his ship, still worth half of its selling price!

The passengers went ashore at once. Just then Fix had a fierce impulse to arrest this Fogg fellow. Yet he didn't do so. Why not? What inner conflict was he coping with? Had he come to his senses with regard to Mr. Fogg? Had he finally realized he was mistaken? Nevertheless the detective didn't let his man go. Along with Mr. Fogg, Lady Aouda, and Passepartout (who no longer took the time to breathe), Fix boarded the train from Queenstown at 1:30 in the morning, arrived in Dublin at daybreak, and instantly set out on one of those steamers that are authentic steel rockets, nothing but engines—they sneer at the very idea of rising to the waves and always cut right through them.

At 11:40 on December 21, Phileas Fogg finally stepped down onto a Liverpool pier. He was no more than six hours from London.

But just then Fix came up, put his hand on the gentleman's shoulder, and held out his warrant:

"Would you be Mr. Phileas Fogg?" he said.

"Yes, sir."

"Then I arrest you in the name of the Queen!"

34

Which gives Passepartout the chance to crack an outrageous but possibly original joke

PHILEAS FOGG WAS in jail. They'd locked him up at the customhouse station in Liverpool, where he was to spend the night while waiting to be transferred to London.

At the moment of his arrest, Passepartout had made a lunge at the detective. Some policemen restrained him. Horrified at this shocking event, Lady Aouda didn't know or understand a thing about it. Passepartout explained the situation to her. Mr. Fogg, that decent and courageous gentleman to whom she owed her life, was under arrest as a rob-

ber. The young woman indignantly objected to this allegation, and tears streamed from her eyes when she saw that she couldn't do anything—or even attempt anything—to rescue her rescuer.

As for Fix, he'd arrested the gentleman because his job required him to, whether the fellow was guilty or not. That was for the courts to decide.

But then a thought occurred to Passepartout, the dreadful thought that he was the definite cause of all this misfortune! Honestly, why had he hidden this danger from Mr. Fogg? When Fix revealed the assignment that he'd been given, that he was there in his capacity as police inspector, why had Passepartout chosen to not warn his master? If the latter had been alerted, he undoubtedly would have given Fix proofs of his innocence; he would have shown the detective his mistake; in any event his master wouldn't have incurred the burden and expense of taking Fix along, that ill-omened investigator whose top priority was to arrest him as soon as they set foot on United Kingdom soil. When the poor lad thought about his mistakes and misjudgments, he was gripped with overpowering remorse. He wept, he was a sight to behold. He wanted to dash his brains out!

Despite the cold, he and Lady Aouda waited under the customhouse colonnade. Neither of them wanted to leave the place. They wanted to see Mr. Fogg one more time.

As for that gentleman, he was financially ruined, ruined good and proper just as he was about to achieve his goal. This arrest doomed him beyond recall. Reaching Liverpool at 11:40 in the morning on December 21, he had till 8:45 that night to show up at the Reform Club, hence he had nine hours and fifteen minutes left—and he needed only six to reach London.

Just then anybody entering the customhouse station would have found Mr. Fogg seated on a wooden bench, motionless, unruffled, not at all angry. You couldn't tell whether he'd accepted his fate, but this final blow hadn't managed to arouse him, at least outwardly. Was a fit of rage secretly building inside him, rage all the more dreadful because it was pent up, because it would explode with irresistible power at the last minute? Who knows. But Phileas Fogg sat there, calm, waiting . . . for what? Did he have a vestige of hope left? Though his jail door was closed and locked, did he still dream of succeeding?

Be that as it may, Mr. Fogg carefully placed his watch on the table and eyed its moving hands. Not a word escaped from his lips, but there was an odd intensity in his look.

In any case he was in a dreadful position, and for anybody who couldn't read his thoughts, it might be summed up like this:

If innocent, Phileas Fogg was financially ruined.

If guilty, he was laid by the heels.

So did he have any notions of saving himself? Did he consider looking over this station to see if it offered any feasible way out? Did he hope to escape? You might be tempted to think so, because at one point he walked around the room. But the door was securely locked and the window adorned with iron bars. He sat down again and out of his wallet took the itinerary for his journey. One line of it held these words:

Liverpool, Saturday, December 21.

He added to it:

11:40 in the morning, 80th day. Then he waited.

The hour of one chimed on the customhouse clock. Mr. Fogg noted that his watch was running two minutes faster than the clock.

Then it chimed the hour of two! If he climbed aboard an express train right then, he could still reach London and the Reform Club before 8:45 that evening. His forehead wrinkled slightly . . .

At 2:33 there was a racket outside, the hubbub of opening doors. You could hear Passepartout's voice, then Fix's voice.

Phileas Fogg's eyes lit up for a second.

The station door opened and he saw Lady Aouda, Passepartout, and Fix, who rushed over to him.

Fix was out of breath, his hair in disarray . . . he couldn't talk!

"Sir," he stammered, "sir . . . just found out . . . forgive me . . . the real robber was arrested three days ago . . . by an unfortunate irony you resembled him . . . you're . . . free to go . . . !"

Phileas Fogg was free! He went to the detective. He looked him straight in the eye, and with the only swift movement he'd ever made or ever would make in his life, he drew in both his arms, then with robotlike precision he slugged the unlucky inspector with both fists.

"Good punch!" Passepartout exclaimed, then like a true Frenchman he couldn't help cracking an outrageous joke. "By God," he added, "that's what I call striking while the irony is hot!"

Down on the floor, Fix didn't say a word. He had it coming. But Mr. Fogg, Lady Aouda, and Passepartout instantly left the customhouse. They hurried into a cab and a few minutes later arrived at the Liverpool railway terminal.

Phileas Fogg asked if there was an express train ready to leave for London . . .

It was 2:40. . . . The express train had left thirty-five minutes earlier.

Phileas Fogg then chartered a special train.

There were several high-speed locomotives with steam up; but the timetables wouldn't let a special train leave the terminal before three o'clock.

At three o'clock, along with the young woman and his loyal servant, Phileas Fogg took off in the direction of London, after saying a few words to the engineer about a certain bonus to be earned

They needed to cover the distance between Liverpool and London in 5½ hours— something that's perfectly feasible when the line is clear all the way. But there were unavoidable delays, and when the gentleman arrived at the terminal in London, every clock in town said 8:50.

After journeying completely around the world, Phileas Fogg had arrived five minutes late . . . !

He'd lost.

35

*In which Passepartout doesn't need to be
told twice to do what his master says*

THE NEXT DAY the residents of Savile Row
would have been quite startled if you'd informed them that Mr. Fogg was reinstated in
his living quarters. From the outside nothing
looked any different.

In fact, after he'd left the terminal, Phileas
Fogg gave Passepartout instructions to buy a
few supplies, then he reentered his home.

The gentleman had reacted to a crushing
blow with his usual lack of emotion. Financially ruined! And thanks to the mistakes of
that inept police inspector! After making that
long trip without setting a foot wrong, after
toppling a thousand obstacles, braving a
thousand perils, and still finding time to do
some good as he went, he'd sunk in sight of
shore due to a shocking event he couldn't
have foreseen and was helpless to avert: it
was dreadful! Out of the considerable sum
he'd taken along on his departure, only a piddling residue was left. All that remained of
his fortune was the £20,000 in his account at
Baring Brothers & Co., and he owed this
£20,000 to his colleagues at the Reform Club.
Even if he'd won the bet, he surely wouldn't
have come out ahead after incurring so many
expenses, and in all likelihood he wasn't trying to come out ahead (being one of those
men who make bets as a point of honor), but
losing the bet meant his total financial ruin.
Given this fact, the gentleman reached a decision. He knew there was only one thing left
for him to do.

Lady Aouda had been assigned a bedroom
in the house on Savile Row. The young
woman was in despair. From certain words
Mr. Fogg let drop, she realized he was planning a fatal move.

In essence, as you know, these English
monomaniacs will sometimes go to the most
deplorable lengths in the throes of their fixations. Accordingly, and without seeming
to, Passepartout kept a close watch on his
master.

But first the good fellow had gone up to
his bedroom and turned off the gas jet he'd
left burning for eighty days. After finding a
bill from the gas company in the mailbox, he
felt it was high time he put a stop to the
charges he was running up.

The night went by. Mr. Fogg had gone to
bed, but was he asleep? As for Lady Aouda,
she couldn't rest for one second. Passepartout, for his part, waited like a watchdog outside his master's door.

The next day Mr. Fogg summoned him
and instructed him in a few crisp words to see
about Lady Aouda's breakfast. As for himself, he would be content with a cup of tea
and a slice of toast. He hoped that Lady
Aouda would kindly excuse him from joining
her for breakfast and dinner, because he
would be devoting all his time to putting his
affairs in order. He wouldn't be coming
downstairs. Only in the evening would he ask
Lady Aouda's permission to converse with
her for a few seconds.

Being in receipt of his schedule for the
day, all Passepartout had to do was adhere to
it. He looked at his master, who still showed
no signs of emotion, and couldn't bring himself to leave the room. His heart was heavy
and his conscience stricken with remorse, because he blamed himself more than ever for
this irreparable disaster. Yes, if he'd warned
Mr. Fogg, if he'd revealed Inspector Fix's
plans to him, Mr. Fogg definitely wouldn't
have dragged Inspector Fix as far as Liverpool, and then . . .

Passepartout couldn't hold back any
longer.

"Master!" he exclaimed. "Mr. Fogg! Why
aren't you cursing me? It's all my fault
that—"

"I blame nobody," Phileas Fogg replied in
the calmest tone. "You may go."

Passepartout left the room, went to find
the young woman, and made his master's
wishes known to her.

"Ma'am," he added, "I can't do a thing
with him on my own, not a thing! I have no
influence over the way my master thinks. But
maybe you . . ."

"What influence would I have?" Lady
Aouda responded. "Nothing sways Mr. Fogg.
Has he ever grasped that my gratitude to him
is at flood point? Has he ever read the depths

of my heart . . . ? My friend, we mustn't leave him by himself, not for a single second. You say he has expressed a wish to speak with me this evening?"

"Yes, ma'am. No doubt it's about safeguarding your status in England."

"We'll see," the young woman replied, still deeply thoughtful.

Thus, during that whole Sunday the dwelling on Savile Row seemed vacant, and for the first time since he'd made it his home, Phileas Fogg didn't go to his club when the clock tower at the Houses of Parliament struck 11:30.

And why would the gentleman show up at the Reform Club? His colleagues weren't waiting there anymore. At 8:45 the night before, on that drop-dead date of Saturday, December 21, Phileas Fogg hadn't appeared in the Reform Club's lounge, so he'd lost the bet. It wasn't necessary for him to even go to his bankers and fetch that sum of £20,000. His opponents had his signed check in their hands; all it took was a simple ledger entry at Baring Brothers & Co. and the £20,000 would be posted to their credit.

Consequently Mr. Fogg had no need to go out and didn't. He stayed in his bedroom and put his affairs in order. Passepartout never stopped going up and down the stairs of that house on Savile Row. The hours inched by for the poor fellow. He listened at his master's bedroom door and did so without feeling he was the least bit out of line. He peeped through the keyhole and believed he had a right to! Passepartout was afraid of a catastrophe any second. Sometimes he thought about Fix, but a shift had taken place in his thinking. He no longer bore the police inspector any ill will. Like everybody Fix had been mistaken about Phileas Fogg, had only been doing his job in tailing and arresting the gentleman, whereas he himself. . . . This thought overwhelmed him, and he called himself the lowliest wretch on earth.

When Passepartout finally felt too unhappy to stay alone, he knocked on Lady Aouda's door, went into her room, sat in a corner without saying a word, and studied the young woman, who still looked thoughtful.

At about 7:30 that evening, Mr. Fogg asked Lady Aouda if he could visit with her; a few seconds later he and the young woman were alone in her room.

Phileas Fogg sat down, taking a chair near the fireplace in front of Lady Aouda. His features gave no clue to his feelings. The Fogg who had come back was identical to the Fogg who had gone away. Same calmness, same lack of emotion.

He kept silent for five minutes. Then, looking up at Lady Aouda:

"My lady," he said, "will you forgive me for bringing you to England?"

"Forgive *you*, Mr. Fogg?" Lady Aouda responded, trying to slow the pounding of her heart.

"Please let me finish," Mr. Fogg went on. "When your country had become so perilous for you and I decided to take you far away from it, I was a wealthy man and expected to put part of my fortune at your disposal. You would have enjoyed a life of freedom and happiness. Today my finances are in ruins."

"I know, Mr. Fogg," the young woman answered, "and I ask this of you in my turn: will you forgive me for coming with you and—who knows—maybe contributing to your financial ruin by delaying you?"

"My lady, you couldn't stay in India, and your safety wasn't guaranteed till you were so far away, those fanatics couldn't recapture you."

"Therefore, Mr. Fogg," Lady Aouda continued, "you weren't content with snatching me from the jaws of a horrible death, you felt obliged to guarantee my status elsewhere?"

"Yes, my lady," Fogg replied, "but developments have turned against me. Even so, I ask your leave to put the little I still have at your disposal."

"But what about you, Mr. Fogg? What will happen to you?" Lady Aouda asked.

"Me, my lady?" the gentleman replied calmly. "I won't be needing a thing."

"But what kind of future, sir, do you see ahead of you?"

"One that befits me," Mr. Fogg answered.

"In any case," Lady Aouda went on, "a man like you will never live in poverty. Your friends—"

"I have no friends, my lady."

"Your relatives—"

"I no longer have relatives."

"Then I feel sorry for you, Mr. Fogg, because it's a sad thing to be all alone. What! Not one heart to whom you can pour out your troubles? Yet even poverty, they say, is bearable for two."

"So they say, my lady."

"Mr. Fogg," Lady Aouda said, standing and holding her hand out to the gentleman, "would you like both a relative and a friend? Would you like me to be your wife?"

At this Mr. Fogg stood in his turn. His eyes seemed to have a new glint, his lips seemed to quiver. Lady Aouda gazed at him. The sincerity, honesty, fortitude, and affection in the lovely gaze of this noble woman— daring everything to rescue the one to whom she owed everything—amazed him at first, then touched him to the core. He closed his eyes for a second, as if to keep that gaze from reaching still deeper. . . . When he opened them again:

"I love you!" he merely said. "Yes, by all that's most sacred in this world, I truly love you, and I'm yours completely!"

"Oh!" Lady Aouda exclaimed, putting a hand to her heart.

They rang for Passepartout. He arrived at once. Mr. Fogg still had his hand in Lady Aouda's hand. Passepartout got the picture, and his broad face shone like the noonday sun in the tropics.

Mr. Fogg asked him if it was too late to go notify Reverend Samuel Wilson at St. Marylebone Parish Church.

Passepartout smiled his finest smile.

"Never too late," he said.

It was just 8:05.

"You're looking at Monday tomorrow?" he said.

"Monday tomorrow?" Mr. Fogg asked, turning to the young woman.

"Monday tomorrow!" Lady Aouda replied.

Passepartout took off at top speed.

36

Where shares in Phileas Fogg are back at a premium on the stock market

IT'S TIME TO SPEAK HERE of how public opinion shifted in the United Kingdom when folks learned that the real bank robber—one James Strand—had been arrested in Edinburgh on December 17.

Three days earlier Phileas Fogg was a criminal with the police in hot pursuit, now he was the most respectable of gentlemen, mathematically carrying out his eccentric journey around the world.

What an impact it had, what a noise it made in the newspapers! Everybody who had bet on him to win or lose in this business —which they'd already forgotten about— magically reemerged from the woodwork. Every transaction became valid again. Every commitment was reconfirmed, and we should mention that new bets were being placed with vigor. The name Phileas Fogg was back at a premium on the stock market.

The gentleman's five colleagues at the Reform Club spent these three days in some agitation. This Phileas Fogg they'd forgotten about was back in view! Where was he just then? On December 17, the day James Strand was arrested, Phileas Fogg had been gone seventy-six days—and not a word of news from him! Had he lost his life? Had he given up the struggle, or was he still following his agreed-upon itinerary? And at 8:45 on Saturday evening, December 21, would he appear, like the patron saint of punctuality, in the doorway of the Reform Club's lounge?

We won't attempt to portray the anxiety in which the whole English social world lived during these three days. They fired off telegrams to America and Asia, trying to get news of Phileas Fogg! From morning till evening they kept the house on Savile Row under surveillance . . . nothing. The police didn't even know what had happened to the ill-fated Inspector Fix, who had hared off on such a false scent. Which didn't keep people from laying new bets on a grander scale. Phileas Fogg was like a racehorse reaching the final turn. They didn't quote him at a hundred to one anymore, but at twenty, then ten, then five, and paralyzed old Lord Albemarle, who had bet on him to win, got even odds.

That Saturday evening, accordingly, throngs of people were on Pall Mall and in the nearby streets. You would have sworn an immense mob of stockbrokers had taken up permanent residence on the steps of the Reform Club. There were traffic jams. People were discussing, arguing, and calling out quotes on "Phileas Foggs" as if they were treasury bonds. Crowd control turned into a major police issue, and the closer it got to the time Phileas Fogg was to arrive, the more unbelievably excited everybody became.

That evening the gentleman's five colleagues had been gathered in the main lounge of the Reform Club since eight o'clock. All of them waited anxiously—the two bankers John Sullivan and Samuel Fallentin, Andrew Stuart the engineer, Walter Ralph, one of the Bank of England's directors, and Thomas Flanagan the brewer.

Just as the clock in the main lounge pointed to 8:25, Andrew Stuart stood up and said:

"Gentlemen, in twenty minutes Mr. Fogg will have gone beyond the time frame we've agreed upon."

"When did the last train arrive from Liverpool?" Thomas Flanagan asked.

"At 7:23," Walter Ralph replied, "and the next train won't arrive till ten minutes past midnight."

"Very well, gentlemen," Andrew Stuart resumed, "if Phileas Fogg had arrived on that 7:23 train, he would already be here. So we can consider this bet as good as won."

"Hold on, let's not jump to conclusions," Samuel Fallentin replied. "As you're aware, our colleague is a world-class eccentric. He's well known for being punctual in everything he does. He never arrives too early or too late, and I wouldn't be entirely surprised if he showed up here at the last minute."

"Speaking for myself," Andrew Stuart said, as high-strung as ever, "I wouldn't believe it if I *did* see him."

"Exactly," Thomas Flanagan went on. "Mr. Fogg's whole plan was loony. As punc-

tual as he is, he can't keep inevitable delays from happening, and a delay of just two or three days would be enough to jeopardize his journey."

"You'll note, too," John Sullivan added, "that we haven't gotten any news from our colleague, even though there are plenty of telegraph lines on his itinerary."

"He has lost, gentleman," Andrew Stuart continued, "he has lost a hundred times over! As you're also aware, the *China* was the only ocean liner from New York he could have taken to reach Liverpool in a timely manner—and it arrived yesterday. Now then, here's the passenger list published by the *Shipping Gazette*, and it doesn't include the name Phileas Fogg. Even if we assume he's had the greatest possible luck, our colleague can barely have reached America! I estimate he'll turn up at least twenty days later than the date we've agreed upon, and old Lord Albemarle will be out £5,000 to boot!"

"That's obvious," Walter Ralph replied, "and tomorrow all we'll have to do is take Mr. Fogg's check to Baring Brothers & Co."

At this point the clock in the lounge said 8:40.

"Five minutes to go," Andrew Stuart said.

The five colleagues looked at each other. You would have sworn their heartbeats were suddenly going a little faster—after all, these were high stakes even for serious gamblers! But they weren't letting their feelings show, because, at Samuel Fallentin's suggestion, they sat down to play cards.

"My share in this bet is £4,000," Andrew Stuart said, taking his seat at the table, "and I wouldn't part with it for a pound less!"

The clock hands pointed to 8:42 at this juncture.

The players picked up the cards, but every instant their eyes squinted at the clock. As safe as they felt, you could tell that they found these minutes the longest they'd ever lived through!

"It's 8:43," Thomas Flanagan said, cutting the deck Walter Ralph handed him.

Then there was a moment of silence. The club's huge lounge fell still. But outside you could hear the hullabaloo the crowd was making, the occasional high-pitched yells rising above it. The clock's pendulum beat the seconds with mathematical steadiness. They reached the ear every sixtieth of a minute, and each cardplayer counted them.

"It's 8:44!" John Sullivan said, his voice unintentionally giving his feelings away.

Just one more minute and they would win the bet. Andrew Stuart and his colleagues didn't play any longer. They ignored the cards! They counted the seconds!

At the 40th second, nothing. At the 50th, still nothing!

At the 55th you heard something like a rumbling sound outside, applause, hoorays, and even cusswords, swelling into one continuous roll of thunder.

The cardplayers stood up.

At the 57th second the lounge door opened, and the pendulum hadn't beat the 60th second when Phileas Fogg appeared, followed by a delirious crowd that had forced its way into the club, and in his calm voice:

"Here I am, gentlemen," he said.

37

Which demonstrates that Phileas Fogg didn't gain a thing by going around the world—other than happiness

THAT'S RIGHT. None other than Phileas Fogg.

You'll recall that at 8:05 in the evening—about twenty-three hours after our travelers had arrived in London—Passepartout's master had ordered him to notify Reverend Samuel Wilson about a certain marriage that was to be finalized the very next day.

Passepartout left in high delight. He made his way at a quick pace to Reverend Samuel Wilson's residence and learned that the clergyman hadn't returned home yet. Naturally Passepartout waited—waited, in fact, a good twenty minutes at least.

To make a long story short, it was 8:35 when he left the preacher's home. But what a state he was in! Hair in disarray, hatless, running as folks had never seen anybody run in human memory, toppling passersby, rushing like a whirlwind down the sidewalk!

In three minutes he was back at the house on Savile Row, where he collapsed breathlessly in Mr. Fogg's bedroom.

He couldn't talk.

"What is it?" Mr. Fogg asked.

"Master . . . !" Passepartout stammered. "Marriage . . . impossible . . . !"

"Impossible?"

"Impossible . . . tomorrow anyway."

"Why?"

"Because tomorrow . . . is Sunday!"

"Monday," Mr. Fogg replied.

"No . . . today's . . . Saturday."

"Saturday? Impossible!"

"It is! It is! It is!" Passepartout shrieked. "You're off by one day! We arrived twenty-four hours ahead of time . . . but you've got only ten minutes left . . . !"

Passepartout grabbed his master by the collar and dragged him away with irresistible power!

Abducted in this fashion, given no time to think things over, Phileas Fogg left his room, left his house, leaped into a cab, promised the cabbie £100, and reached the Reform Club after running over two dogs and sideswiping five buggies.

The clock pointed to 8:45 when he appeared in the main lounge . . .

Phileas Fogg had gone around the world in eighty days . . . !

Phileas Fogg had won his £20,000 bet!

And now, how could a man so stringent, so meticulous, have made this mistake of one day? How could he have believed he'd gotten back to London on Saturday evening, December 21, when it was only Friday, December 20, just seventy-nine days after he'd left?

Here's the reason for this mistake. It's quite simple.

Phileas Fogg had, "unbeknownst to him," gained a day on his itinerary—which happened solely because he'd gone around the world by traveling *eastward;* whereas he would have lost a day if he'd gone the opposite way, hence *westward.*

In essence, as he was traveling eastward Phileas Fogg faced the sun—and as a result the days grew shorter for him at the rate of four minutes for each degree he crossed in this direction. Now then, there are 360 degrees on the earth's circumference, and when these 360 degrees are multiplied by four minutes, the total is exactly twenty-four hours—in other words, that day he'd unconsciously gained. Putting it a different way, as Phileas Fogg traveled eastward, he saw the noonday sun *eighty times*, while his colleagues staying in London saw it just *seventy-nine times*. This is why the latter were waiting for him in the Reform Club's lounge that very day, since it wasn't Sunday as Mr. Fogg believed, but Saturday.

And because Passepartout's notorious watch always kept London time, it would have verified this fact—if it had indicated the days along with the hours and minutes!

Therefore Phileas Fogg had won £20,000. But since he'd spent about £19,000 on the road, the pecuniary outcome was only so-so. All the same, as we've said, the eccentric gentleman hadn't made this bet to increase his income but to prove a point. And what's more, he split up the leftover £1,000 between the good Passepartout and the hapless Fix, against whom he was incapable of bearing any ill will. Only in the former case, to keep things even-steven, he deducted the cost of those 1,920 hours of gas that his servant had mistakenly run up.

As stoic and unemotional as ever, Mr. Fogg said to Lady Aouda that same evening:

"Is our marriage still suitable to you, my lady?"

"Mr. Fogg," Lady Aouda replied, "I'm the one who should ask *you* that question. You were financially ruined, but now you're wealthy . . ."

"Excuse me, my lady, this fortune belongs to you. If you hadn't conceived the idea of our marrying, my manservant wouldn't have gone to Reverend Samuel Wilson's home, I wouldn't have learned about my mistake, and . . ."

"Darling Mr. Fogg . . ." the young woman said.

"Darling Aouda . . ." Phileas Fogg responded.

It scarcely needs mentioning that they were married forty-eight hours later; proud, radiant, dazzling, Passepartout gave the bride away. Hadn't he rescued her and didn't he deserve this honor?

But the next day at the crack of dawn, Passepartout knocked noisily on his master's door.

The door opened and the unemotional gentleman appeared.

"What's wrong, Passepartout?"

"Wrong, sir? Just that I've found out this very second . . ."

"Found out what?"

"That we could have gone around the world in only seventy-eight days."

"By not traveling through India, no doubt," Mr. Fogg replied. "But if I hadn't traveled through India, I wouldn't have rescued Lady Aouda, she wouldn't have become my wife, and . . ."

Mr. Fogg quietly shut the door.

Hence Phileas Fogg had won his bet. He'd journeyed completely around the world in eighty days! To do so he'd used every form of transportation—ocean liners, railways, buggies, yachts, merchantmen, sleds, and elephants. In the course of things, the eccentric gentleman had displayed his wondrous virtues of composure and punctuality. But what now? What had he gained from this gadding about? What had he brought back from this journey?

Not a thing, you say? So be it, not a thing—other than a delightful woman, who, as inconceivable as it might seem, made him the happiest man alive!

In all honesty isn't this more than enough reason to go around the world?

TEXTUAL NOTES

RECOMMENDED READING

TEXTUAL NOTES

These English renderings adhere to the paragraphing in the original French texts and are complete down to the smallest substantive detail. I've used the Livre de Poche red-cover reissues as working editions, but since no editions seem entirely free of typos and production slips, I've double-checked the LdP reprints against the many available online texts as well as early Hetzel and Hachette editions.

My translations are intended for the U.S. public. Consequently I've worked to create English texts that are both faithful and communicative—faithful in mirroring the effect and apparent intent of the original French, communicative in their overall wording, in their efforts to suggest Verne's comic and narrative styles, and in their presentation of period, cultural, and specialized detail. Where the original French texts refer to people, places, things, or concepts that may be obscure to a 21st century American, I've sometimes attached a footnote or incorporated a quick gloss in the text proper. My footnotes are labeled *Translator's note*. All others are from the French editions.

As for rendering proper names, the translations favor spellings in regular use today; modern usages are likewise favored for geographical designations except where this could create an obtrusive anachronism. Where helpful equivalents aren't certain, I've kept the versions in the original French. For American readers my translations also convert metric figures to feet, miles, pounds, and other U.S. equivalents: in the process I've attempted to approximate the effect of the French—where Verne works with round numbers, I have too; where Verne's numbers are specific, I've sought their close equivalents. Metric tons in the French are converted to short tons in the English, Celsius readings to Fahrenheit. To insure accuracy I've used two conversion instruments: http://www.convertit.com/Go/ConvertIt/Measurement/Converter.ASP, double-checked against http://www.sciencemadesimple.com/conversions.html.

Among other figures found in the French, there are many references to the *league*, a unit of measurement that seems surprisingly dicey, its sense fluctuating from place to place and period to period. The most frequent allusions are to the "geographic league," which equals 4 kilometers, or 2.484 statute miles, and which my translations often round up to 2½ miles. Sometimes, too, the original texts favor slightly lower equivalences for no stated reason: Chapter 7 of *From the Earth to the Moon*, for instance, features an aerial league that works out to about 2⅓ miles; in chapters 11 and 12 of *Journey to the Center of the Earth*, Lidenbrock's league seems to equal about 1⅓ miles. Otherwise Verne's best-known league citations are in the title and text of *20,000 Leagues Under the Seas:* his "nautical league" also rounds up to 2½ statute miles but remains unconverted in my rendering of this novel.

As for currency, I generally convert francs into U.S. money using a rough rate of 5 francs = $1.00, a rate consistent through most of the 19th century according to *Gold and Silver Standards* at http://www.cyberussr.com/hcunn/gold-std.html. I generally convert pounds sterling at a rough rate of £1 = $5.00. The purchasing power of one 19th century dollar seems to have been equal to around twenty modern dollars.

A final point. As mentioned on p. 10, "the USA itself is crucial to these novels," so American mores and folkways often figure prominently. At times, then, the French texts add footnotes for the purpose of explaining Anglo-American usages and customs to Gallic readers. Even where an American doesn't require such explanations, I've kept them for the sake of completeness but have shifted them to these endnotes. And I've made additional shifts of this sort in instances where foreign moneys are converted to French currency in the original texts but to U.S. currency in my translations.

Of course scholars and specialists will need to concentrate on the French originals, which, fortunately, are available these days at many websites. Even so, I hope these endnotes will interest both the educator and the general reader. *Translator*.

JOURNEY TO THE CENTER OF THE EARTH

First published as *Voyage au centre de la Terre* by P.-J. Hetzel in November 1864; Hetzel issued a revised and expanded edition in May 1867 with additional prehistoric material inserted in Chapters 37–39.

The translation makes the following adjustments where the French editions appear to contain production errors or other problematic details.

Page:	*Item:*	*Note:*
18	Grauben	French texts give "Graüben" throughout. The name may be a humorous fabrication since no such diphthong as *aü* exists in the German language. Some prior translations (into Dutch, English, and German itself) shift the umlaut, substitute the actual dipthong *äu*, and revise the spelling to "Gräuben."
25	in its second and third lines	Some French editions give just "in the third line."
29	back in 1219	Given as 1229 in some French editions, but 1219 is historically correct.
30	360,000° Fahrenheit	Some French texts inflate this to an equivalent of 3,600,000° Fahrenheit.
32	Harburg railway line	Some French editions give "Hamburg."
36	four marks (about 55¢)	In French texts a footnote from the author gives the currency conversion for Gallic readers: "About 2 francs, 75 centimes."
38	southeast quadrant	Southwest in the French.
	Baron Trampe	Count Trampe in the French, apparently a a slip since he's consistently called baron later on.
39	the westernmost of this group	Easternmost in the French.
45	three riksdalers	In French texts a footnote gives the currency conversion for Gallic readers: "16 francs, 98 centimes."
	Eigel thermometer	Specified in the French as a centigrade thermometer.
47	40,000 square miles	14,000 in the French.
53	four-hour trek	24-hour trek in some French editions.
54	sixty marks	French texts give a footnote for Gallic readers: "Hamburg currency, equivalent to about 90 francs."
54, 63	1219	1229 in French editions, but 1219 is historically correct.
69	over three days	Five days in the French.
	July 7	Some French texts give July 8.
71	"*Mester*," he put in.	Spelled "*Master*" in the French.
75	July 11 and 12	July 6 and 7 in some French texts.

77	on the 13th	Some French texts give the 8th.
78	we've gone 40	French texts give the equivalent of 30.
85	three long days	Four in the French.
88	in Venezuela	French texts say Colombia.
93	blowing from the northwest	Northeast in the French.
106	during three days of the storm	In the French: during those three days of storm.
127	*Dove siamo?*	In the French: *Dove noi siamo?*

FROM THE EARTH TO THE MOON

First published as *De la Terre à la Lune* in the *Journal des débats*, September–October 1865. Verne's first "American novel," it has an unusually large number of footnotes explaining U.S. customs, slang, weights, and measures to Gallic readers. Even where an American doesn't require such explanations, this volume keeps them for the sake of completeness but shifts them to these endnotes. In addition the French texts convert dollars to francs at a slightly higher rate: 5.4 francs = $1.00.

The translation makes the following adjustments where the French editions appear to contain production errors or other problematic details.

Page:	*Item:*	*Note:*
Title page	97 Hours and 13 Minutes	French editions give 20 Minutes. But in both moon novels, the texts proper consistently give 13.
134	nincompoop	For Gallic readers French texts attach a footnote: "*badaud* [rubbernecker]."
135	half-ton shell	To clarify Anglo-American measures for Gallic readers, French texts add a footnote with the rough metric equivalent: "500 kilograms."
	seven miles	French texts attach another footnote for Gallic readers: "One mile is equal to 1,609 meters and 31 centimeters. So this would be almost three geographic leagues."
	Kesselsdorf in 1745	1742 in French texts.
139	moon's physical features	French texts call maps of such features "Selenographic," again adding a footnote: "Derived from σελήνη [Selene], the Greek word meaning 'moon.'" French editions employ this adjective in both moon novels, but it has fallen out of use in the United States.
140	eighty yards	For the benefit of Gallic readers, French texts furnish another footnote: "A yard is equal to slightly less than a meter—hence .91 m."
	moonpeople	Called "Selenites" in French texts, which attach a footnote: "Residents of the moon." French editions use "Selenite" throughout both moon novels, but in the United States it has quite a different meaning—it's a crystallized form of gypsum.
141	12,000 yards	A footnote in French texts gives the equivalent for Gallic readers: "About 11,000 meters."

142	Footnote 12	For Gallic readers French texts conclude this note with an added sentence: "Barrooms are a variety of café."
143	*Much Ado About Nothing, As You Like It*	French texts add footnotes translating these Shakespearean titles: *Beaucoup de bruit pour rien* and *Comme il vous plaira*.
	deemed it expedient	French editions add a sly footnote for Gallic readers: "The letter's text uses the word 'expedient,' which absolutely can't be translated into French." Verne's rendering substitutes *à propos* [pertinent].
148	Cleomedes	Cleomenes in French texts, apparently a slip.
	1,095	1,905 in French texts. Ch. 16 of *Circling the Moon* gives the more conservative 1,095.
150	75 miles	70 in French texts.
	354½ hours	354⅓ in French texts. But see Ch. 14 of *Circling the Moon*.
153	1/640,000 as fast as light	Per the MS at the Bibliothèque municipale de Nantes; many French editions give 1/640.
	8,614 aerial leagues	French texts give 8,640.
155	a weight of 20,000 pounds	5,000 pounds in French texts, apparently a slip since later references in both moon novels consistently give 20,000, or the exact figure 19,250.
	$260 to $280 . . . $27 . . . $9	For Gallic readers French texts give the currency conversions in parentheses: about 1,500 francs . . . 150 francs . . . 48 francs, 75 centimes.
	12 inches thick	French texts add a footnote for Gallic readers: "30 centimeters; the American inch equals 25 millimeters."
	don't forget that at $9 per pound	French texts have an apparent slip, giving $18.
156	$173,250	French texts give the currency conversion in parentheses: 928,437 francs, 50 centimes.
	fifteen feet the first second	A footnote in French texts gives equivalents for Gallic readers: "Or 4 meters, 90 centimeters in the first second; at the moon's distance, the object would drop just 1⅓ millimeters or one 590,000th of a line."
	247,552 miles up	257,142 in French texts.
157	4,800,000 pounds	7,200,000 in French texts.
158	75,001.26 tons	French texts cite metric equivalents: 64,040 metric tons (64,040,000 kilograms).
	two cents per pound	French texts give the currency conversion in parentheses: 10 centimes.
	$3,000,050.40	French texts give $2,510,701, with the currency conversion in parentheses: 13,608,000 francs. However these figures don't jibe with "two cents per pound."

159	close to two pounds	French texts add a parenthetical detail for Gallic readers (900 grams), then explain it with a footnote: "The American pound is 453 g."
	666 pounds	333 pounds in French texts.
160	22,000 cubic feet . . . 54,000 cubic feet	French texts add footnotes giving the metric equivalents: "A little less than 800 cubic meters," and "2,000 cubic meters."
164	$15,000	A footnote in French texts gives the currency conversion for Gallic readers: "81,300 francs."
168	$16,000,000	French texts give another footnote for Gallic readers: "82,000,000 francs."
169	$4,000,000	French texts give yet another conversion in a footnote: "Twenty-one million francs (21,680,000)."
170	368,733 rubles	A footnote in French texts reads: "1,475,000 francs."
	216,000 florins	A footnote in French texts reads: "520,000 francs."
	52,000 riksdalers	A footnote in French texts reads: "294,320 francs."
	250,000 talers	A footnote in French texts reads: "937,500 francs."
	1,372,640 piasters	A footnote in French texts reads: "343,160 francs."
	110,000 florins	A footnote in French texts reads: "235,400 francs."
	9,000 ducats	A footnote in French texts reads: "117,414 francs."
	34,285 florins	A footnote in French texts reads: "72,000 francs."
	7,040 Roman scudi	A footnote in French texts reads: "38,016 francs."
	30,000 crusados	A footnote in French texts reads: "113,200 francs."
	eighty-six sure piasters	A footnote in French texts reads: "1,727 francs."
	110 reals	A footnote in French texts reads: "59 francs, 48 centimes."
171	$300,000	A footnote in French texts reads: "1,626,000 francs."
	$5,446,675	For Gallic readers a footnote in French texts gives: "29,520,983 francs, 40 centimes."
	$100 per day	For Gallic readers a footnote in French texts gives: "542 francs."
	Cleland on the Cultivating of Sugarcane in East Florida	Given in French texts as *Cleland on the culture of the Sugar-Cane in East Florida.*

172	84° Fahrenheit	For Gallic readers French texts add a footnote: "This would be 28° centigrade."
	38,033,267 acres	For Gallic readers French texts give the metric figure in a footnote: "15,365,440 hectares."
173	in 1513	1512 in French texts.
	$658,100	A footnote in French texts gives a currency conversion for Gallic readers: "3,566,902 francs."
174	Stony Hill	French texts add a footnote translating this: "*Colline de pierres*."
176	a 99° heat	For Gallic readers French texts add a footnote: "40° centigrade."
177	two miles long	A footnote in French texts gives a conversion for Gallic readers: "About 3,600 meters."
178	68,000 tons	French texts give the metric equivalent of 66,000.
182	*Shipping Gazette*	French texts add a footnote translating this: "*Gazette maritime*."
	"Moon City"	French texts add a footnote translating this: "*Cité de la Lune*."
183	$500,000	A footnote in French texts converts this for Gallic readers: "2,710,000 francs."
187	"ruling passion"	French texts add a footnote translating this: "*Sa maîtresse passion*."
202	*E pluribus unum*	*Ex pluribus* in French texts.
204	32-inch mortar	French texts give the metric conversion in parentheses: 0.75 cm.
208	fifteen inches across	French texts give the metric conversion in parentheses: 38 centimeters.
	nineteen inches across	French texts give the metric conversion in parenthesis: 48 cm.
209	6 feet wide	French texts give the metric conversion in parentheses: 1.93 m.
210	10,000-foot	French texts give the metric conversion in parentheses: 3½ kilometers.
	over $400,000	A footnote in French texts converts this for Gallic readers: "1,600,000 francs."
214	fifty gallons' worth	A footnote in French texts gives a conversion for Gallic readers: "About 200 liters."
215	"fish chowder"	French texts add a footnote for Gallic readers: "Soup made with various types of fish."
216	red and black	In French texts *rouge et noir*, presumably the game attributed to Charles Jewell.
221	1,100 geographic leagues	Given as 4,500 leagues in French texts (here and in the Preliminary Chapter of *Circling the Moon*); apparently Verne meant kilometers.

CIRCLING THE MOON

First published as *Autour de la Lune* in the *Journal des débats*, November–December 1869.

The translation makes the following adjustments where the French editions appear to contain production errors or other problematic details.

Page:	Item:	Note:
227	1,100 geographic leagues	4,500 leagues in French texts (here and in *From the Earth to the Moon*, Ch. 28); apparently Verne meant kilometers.
244	*v* to the second power	French texts give *v* zero to the second power.
252	Meanwhile tell me this, Barbicane—do you think the moon was once a comet?"	Ardan's line, per the MS at the Bibliothèque municipale de Nantes; in French editions it's a separate line from an unidentified speaker.
253	December 5	November 5 in French texts.
260	fifteen feet per hour	French texts add an equivalent per second: one 590,000th of a line.
261	75 on the surface of the moon	French texts give the equivalent of 66.
264	410 miles per hour	French texts give the equivalent of 425.
265, 277	Earl of Rosse	John Ross in French texts.
266	27,000 feet	The French equivalent is closer to 29,000 feet, which conflicts with p. 291 and Ch. 5 of *From the Earth to the Moon*.
278	six o'clock in the morning	five o'clock in French texts.
283	below -38° Fahrenheit	French texts give the equivalent of -43.6°.
284, 292	thirty miles up	It's nearer forty miles in the French—which disagrees with pp. 278 and 280.
303	audible outside	audible inside, according to French texts.
305	coast of Mexico	New Mexico in French texts.
308	10,000 feet	French texts give the equivalent of 12,000.
309	latitude 27° 7′ north	French texts give 20° 7′.
309, 311, 312	cousin Blomsberry	Brother Blomsberry in the French, though the Blomsberrys are called first cousins in Ch. 20.
313	Captain Blomsberry	French texts call him commander twice here.
316	New Hampshire	French texts give New Brunswick.

20,000 LEAGUES UNDER THE SEAS

First published as *Vingt mille lieues sous les mers* in the *Magasin d'éducation et de récréation*, March 1869–June 1870. This English text is a comprehensive paragraph-by-paragraph overhaul of an unpublished rendering drafted in 1991.

The translation makes the following adjustments where the French editions appear to contain production errors or other problematic details.

Page:	Item:	Note:
322	chapter numbering	In French editions PART TWO starts over with Ch. 1.

323	500 miles	French texts give 5 miles. William Butcher reports that the MS of this chapter in the Bibliothèque Nationale gives 500.
	350 English feet	To clarify Anglo-American measurements for Gallic readers, French texts attach a footnote: "About 106 meters. An English foot is only 30.4 centimeters."
	those rorqual whales	Called "the Kulammak" and "the Umgullick" in French texts.
325	high tea	French texts give "lunch."
328	June 2	In the French July 2; July 3 in some editions.
	the *Tampico*	Omitted from some French editions.
333	June 25	In French texts July 30.
350	*Mobilis in Mobili*	This recurs in French editions (starting with the early Hetzel reprints) as *Mobilis in Mobile*, possibly an editor's emendation. Given the stated sense and context, it seems an overcorrection. In the ablative singular, when adjectives serve as substantives they normally keep their adjective declension. So the correct Latin would appear to be *Mobilis in Mobili*.
359	fitted out before then	French texts read "since then."
361	Victor Massé	Omitted from some French editions.
365	120 revolutions per minute	French texts give "per second."
366	1,661.4 tons	French texts give the equivalent of 1,653.6.
368	32 feet of water	30 feet in French texts.
370	two-billion-dollar French national debt	Some French texts give the equivalent of 2.4 billion.
	94 billion acres	French texts give the equivalent of 94 million.
	24 billion acres	French texts give the equivalent of 32 billion.
371	137° 15′	Repeated in French texts as "37° 15′."
375	east-northeast	"North-northeast" in French texts.
383	red, green, yellow	Red is omitted from some French editions.
392	per biennium	French texts give "per century."
	the cooling of basaltic rocks	Omitted from some French editions.
393	Captain Cook in 1774	1714 in French texts.
396	sweepers	French texts give *pomphérides*, apparently a misspelling of *pemphérides*—the family Pempheridae, featuring many species of sweeper.
398	Gueboroa Island	Spelled "Gueboroar" in French texts.
414	the western tip of the	French texts give "eastern tip."
416	stern of the platform	French texts say "bow of the platform."
419	My chief officer was standing . . . everybody aboard the *Nautilus*.	These four sentences are omitted from some French editions.

424	slender sea moths	*Pigeons spatulés* in the French—apparently a slip for *pégases spatulés*, a junior synonym for the longtail sea moths cited just before.
427	January 28	February 28 in French texts.
453	low latitudes	French texts say "high latitudes."
455	ten geographic leagues	Twelve in French texts.
468	8,000 years	In French texts 800 years.
	ninety centuries	In French texts 900 centuries.
471	mineral kingdom	French texts give "animal kingdom."
475	1,800 feet	800 feet in French texts.
483	those rorqual whales	In French texts called "the Hullamock" and "the Umgallick." Ch. 1 gives different spellings for these Inuit names; compare the note for p. 323.
484	a million pounds	100,000 pounds in French texts.
486	bowhead whale	Oddly, French texts read "beluga whale" (*baleine blanche*) rather than "bowhead whale" (*baleine franche*).
489	March 17	March 18 in French texts.
492	March 18	March 19 in French texts.
	1,500 feet	In French texts 1,000 feet.
	500 feet	In French texts again 1,000 feet.
	1,000 feet	French texts give the equivalent of 650 feet.
	height had tripled	French texts say "doubled."
493	coral belonging to the species *Procellaria pelagica*	An odd slip in the French: this is a species of bird, the stormy petrel; it may have been intended for the paragraph immediately following.
499	the American Wilkes	French texts make Wilkes an Englishman.
	latitude 70° 56′	In French texts 76° 56′.
510	a variety of kelp	French texts give "velp."
524	May 13	May 18 in French texts.
	a third that of the wind	French texts say "half."
	December 23, 1854	1864 in French texts.
526	average haul of 4,400	In French texts 40,000.
	making 22,000,000	In French texts 25,000,000.
532	At seven o'clock	Five o'clock in French texts.

AROUND THE WORLD IN 80 DAYS

First published as *Le Tour du monde en quatre-vingts jours* in the *Temps*, November–December 1872. The English text converts Victorian pounds sterling to dollars at the rate of £1 = about $4.80, or rounding up, $5.00. The purchasing power of that $5.00 would be about $100.00 in today's marketplace.

The translation makes the following adjustments where the French editions appear to contain production errors or other problematic details.

Page:	Item:	Note:
543	7 Savile Row	Consistently spelled "Saville" in the French.
	died in 1816	1814 in the French.
547	Walter Ralph	For Gallic readers French texts give a variant form of his first name: Gauthier.
	£55,000	For Gallic readers French texts give the currency conversion in parentheses: 1,375,000 francs.
550	£4,000	For Gallic readers French texts give the currency conversion in parentheses: 100,000 francs.
	his fellow cardplayer	French texts give "his partner." But Fogg is Fallentin's partner, not Stuart's.
	£20,000	For Gallic readers French texts give the currency conversion in parentheses: 500,000 francs.
554	£5,000 ($25,000)	French texts give the equivalent of $20,000.
578	late spouse	Widower in French texts.
	Lady Aouda	Consistently "Mrs. Aouda" in French texts. But in English usage this honorific isn't attached to a stand-alone first name.
582	Mr. Oysterpuff	Spelled "Oysterpuf" in French texts.
583	a fine of £300	For Gallic readers French texts give the currency conversion in parentheses: 7,500 francs.
589	November 5 for Yokohama	French texts give November 6, conflicting with the departure date repeatedly given in Ch. 18.
595	£500 of that	For Gallic readers French texts give the currency conversion in parentheses: 12,500 francs.
596	on September 29	French texts give September 28, conflicting with the robbery date repeatedly given in Ch. 3.
598	£100 per day	For Gallic readers French texts give the currency conversion in parentheses: 2,500 francs.
607	kimono	Oddly, French texts give "kirimon," one of the Japanese imperial crests.
613	Hong Kong to Shanghai	French texts give "Hong Kong to Yokohama."
	Hong Kong smoking parlor	French texts give "Yokohama smoking parlor."
614	Calcutta to Hong Kong, Hong Kong to Yokohama	French texts give "Calcutta to Singapore, Singapore to Yokohama."
620	church vessel	Reliquary in the French.
624	asphalt-filled Dead Sea	French texts give "Lake Asphaltite."

626	1,400 feet long	14,000 feet in French texts, clearly a slip. (In 1870, according to *Van Nostrand's Eclectic Engineering Magazine*, the total length of tunneling over both the Union and Central Pacific was 8,005 feet.)
	ten miles farther on	French texts give twenty miles, though today's Fort Bridger is already in Wyoming, not far from this Oregon Trail outpost. The MS at the Bibliothèque municipale de Nantes gives ten, closer to the truth.
630	General G. M. Dodge	Misspelled J. M. Dodge in French texts.
642	I'll give you $2,000	For Gallic readers French texts provide the currency conversion in parentheses: 10,000 francs.
645	$50,000 . . . $60,000	For Gallic readers French texts provide the respective currency conversions in parentheses: 250,000 francs and 300,000 francs.
648	striking while the irony is hot	In French texts the joke takes the form of a pun, unfortunately not translatable: *poings d'Angleterre* (English fisticuffs) versus its soundalike *point d'Angleterre* (English needlepoint).
652	since eight o'clock	French texts give nine o'clock.
653	about twenty-three hours	Twenty-five in the French.

RECOMMENDED READING

OTHER BOOKS BY VERNE IN MODERN TRANSLATIONS

Adventures of Captain Hatteras, The. 2005. Translated by William Butcher. New York: Oxford.
> Conquest of the North Pole four decades before Peary.

Backwards to Britain. 1992. Translated by Janice Valls-Russell. Edinburgh: Chambers.
> Chatty but hard-hitting UK travelogue that took 130 years to reach print.

Begum's millions, The. 2005. Translated by Stanford L. Luce. Middletown, CT: Wesleyan.
> Grimly prophetic tale of German armament building and military aggression.

Fantasy of Dr. Ox, A. 2003. Translated by Andrew Brown. London: Hesperus.
> Comic SF novella featuring behavior modification of an entire town.

Fur country, The. 1987. Translated by Edward Baxter. Toronto: NC Press.
> Scientific thriller where a polar expedition goes badly astray.

Golden volcano, The. 2008. Translated by Edward Baxter. Lincoln: University of Nebraska.
> Adventure tale set in the Yukon during the gold rush era.

Green ray, The. 2009. Translated by Karen Loukes. Edinburgh: Luath.
> Highland romance inspired by Verne's own travels in the Hebrides.

Invasion of the sea. 2001. Translated by Edward Baxter. Middletown, CT: Wesleyan.
> Techno thriller about creating an inland sea in the Sahara desert.

Journey through the impossible. 2003. Translated by Edward Baxter. Amherst, NY: Prometheus.
> Three-act play on SF and fantasy themes drawn from Verne's bestsellers.

Kip brothers, The. 2007. Translated by Stanford L. Luce. Middletown, CT: Wesleyan.
> Scientific crime thriller about murder in the South Seas.

Lighthouse at the end of the world. 2007. Translated by William Butcher. Lincoln: University of Nebraska.
> Duel to the death on the lowermost crags of South America.

Meteor hunt, The. 2006. Translated by Frederick Paul Walter and Walter James Miller. Lincoln: University of Nebraska.
> Comic SF tale in which U.S. astronomers feud over a mind-boggling meteor.

Mighty Orinoco, The. 2002. Translated by Stanford L. Luce. Middletown, CT: Wesleyan.
> Jungle adventure thriller about searching for the Orinoco's headwaters.

Mysterious island, The. 2001. Translated by Jordan Stump. New York: Modern Library.
> Masterful desert-island yarn complete with do-it-yourself science.

Paris in the twentieth century. 1996. Translated by Richard Howard. New York: Random.
> "Long lost" character novel featuring future developments in the City of Light.

Underground city, The. 2005. Translated by Sarah Crozier. Edinburgh: Luath.
> Spooky, mystical thriller set in a Scottish coal mine; aka *The Black Indies*.

NOTABLE MODERN BOOKS ABOUT VERNE

Butcher, William. 2006. *Jules Verne: The definitive biography*. New York: Thunder's Mouth.
> Gorgeously written and full of valuable new detail, though no Verne biography can be literally "definitive" till more is known about his love life.

Chesneaux, Jean. 1972. *The political and social ideas of Jules Verne*. Translated by Thomas Wikely. London: Thames and Hudson.
> Near-classic investigation of an important side of Verne little known to Americans.

Evans, Arthur B. 1988. *Jules Verne rediscovered: Didacticism and the scientific novel*. New York: Greenwood.
> Lively exploration of educational strategies and gimmicks in Verne's fiction.

Jules-Verne, Jean. 1976. *Jules Verne: A biography*. Translated and adapted by Roger Greaves. New York: Taplinger.
> Indispensable biography by Verne's grandson.

Lottman, Herbert R. 1996. *Jules Verne: An exploratory biography*. New York: St. Martins.
> Controversial modern biography, but tightly researched and highly readable.

Martin, Andrew. 1990. *The mask of the prophet: The extraordinary fictions of Jules Verne*. New York: Oxford.
> Examines mythic archetypes and symbols in Verne's fiction.

Saint-Bris, Gonzague. 2006. *The world of Jules Verne*. Translated by Helen Marx. New York: Mars.
> Colorfully illustrated celebration of Verne for the general reader.

Taves, Brian, and Stephen Michaluk, Jr. 1996. *The Jules Verne encyclopedia*. Lanham, MD: Scarecrow.
> Miscellany that's fun to browse; invaluable for its listings and descriptions of early English editions.

JULES VERNE

Verne was born in 1828 into a French lawyering family in the Atlantic coastal city of Nantes. Though his father sent him off to a Paris law school, young Jules had been writing on the side since his early teens, and his pet topics were the theater, travel, and science. Predictably enough, his legal studies led nowhere, so Verne took a day job with a stock brokerage, in his off hours penning scripts for farces and musical comedies while also publishing short stories and novelettes of scientific exploration and adventure.

His big breakthrough came when he combined his theatrical knack with his scientific bent and in 1863 published an African adventure yarn, *Five Weeks in a Balloon*. After that and till his death in 1905, Jules Verne was one of the planet's best-loved and best-selling novelists, publishing over sixty books. In addition to the five visionary classics in this volume, other imaginative favorites by him include *The Mysterious Island*, *Hector Servadac*, *The Begum's Millions*, *Master of the World*, and *The Meteor Hunt*. Verne ranks among the five most translated authors in history, along with Mark Twain and the Bible.

FREDERICK PAUL WALTER

Scriptwriter, broadcaster, librarian, and amateur paleontologist, Walter is a long-standing member of the North American Jules Verne Society and served as its Vice President from 2000 to 2008. He has produced many media programs, articles, reviews, and papers on aspects of Jules Verne and has collaborated on translations and scholarly editions of three Verne novels: *The Meteor Hunt*, *The Mighty Orinoco*, and a special edition of *20,000 Leagues Under the Sea* for the U.S. Naval Institute in Annapolis. Known to friends as Rick Walter, he lives in Albuquerque, New Mexico.

Frontispiece: Verne photographed in 1856. Drawings from hardcover editions published by P.-J. Hetzel: pp. 14, 37, 52, 76, 89, 98, 118 by Édouard Riou from *Voyage au centre de la Terre*, 1867; pp. 130, 144, 192, 222 by Henri de Montaut from *De la Terre à la Lune*, 1868; pp. 166, 180, 211, 218 by George Roux from an 1897 ed. of the same novel; p. 233 by Alphonse de Neuville and pp. 273, 282, 289, 304, 314 by Émile-Antoine Bayard from *Autour de la Lune*, 1870; p. 318 by Jules Férat from *L'Isle mystérieuse*, 1875; p. 337 by Édouard Riou and pp. 367, 376, 399, 409, 436, 469, 481, 498, 518 by Alphonse de Neuville from *Vingt mille lieues sous les mers*, 1871; pp. 538, 567, 587, 603, 611, 621, 639 by Léon Benett from *Le Tour du monde en quatre-vingts jours*, 1873.